MONA WILSHER

THE
OLD CURIOSITY SHOP

Editor's Note

The Old Curiosity Shop *at first centres upon the misfortunes of the keepers of the shop—little Nell and her gambling grandfather—and their wanderings. It then widens, in the characteristically Dickensian way, to make room for—among other interests—the comedy of Dick Swiveller in his relation to the lawyer Sampson Brass, Miss Sally Brass, and the "Marchioness"; also, the almost diabolic interferences of the dwarf, Daniel Quilp, in the affairs of the missing wanderers. Dickens became unusually enthralled in this tale as it developed. Once he wrote to his friend Forster (who was responsible for urging the death of Little Nell): "All night I have been pursued by the child . . . . I think the close of the story will be great." And later: "The difficulty has been tremendous—the anguish unspeakable." When published (1840–1841), the story was an extraordinary success. Of its characters, the "Marchioness" is a portrait of the maid-of-all-work who waited upon Dickens's father and mother when they were in the debtors' prison of Marshalsea. The Garlands were his own genial landlord and landlady when he was a boy, aged ten, working in George Lamert's Blacking warehouse. And Mr. Slum was one of the poets who wrote Lamert's advertisements in rivalry with Robert Warren—famous for his blacking and for his poets. The present edition is printed from the one carefully corrected by the Author in 1867–1868.*

'In the midst of all this slumber and decay, and ugly age,
the beautiful child in her gentle slumber.'

THE OLD CURIOSITY SHOP

BY

CHARLES DICKENS

ILLUSTRATED BY
PHIZ

LONDON:
HAZELL, WATSON & VINEY, LTD.

PREFACE

[TO THE FIRST CHEAP EDITION]

IN April, 1840, I issued the first number of a new weekly publication, price threepence, called MASTER HUMPHREY'S CLOCK. It was intended to consist, for the most part, of detached papers, but was to include one continuous story, to be resumed from time to time, with such indefinite intervals between each period of resumption as might best accord with the exigencies and capabilities of the proposed Miscellany.

The first chapter of this tale appeared in the fourth number of MASTER HUMPHREY'S CLOCK, when I had already been made uneasy by the desultory character of that work, and when, I believe, my readers had thoroughly participated in the feeling. The commencement of a story was a great satisfaction to me, and I had reason to believe that my readers participated in this feeling too. Hence, being pledged to some interruptions and some pursuit of the original design, I cheerfully set about disentangling myself from those impediments as fast as I could; and, that done, from that time until its completion THE OLD CURIOSITY SHOP was written and published from week to week, in weekly parts.

When the story was finished, that it might be freed from the incumbrance of associations and interruptions with which it had no kind of concern, I caused the few sheets of MASTER HUMPHREY'S CLOCK, which had been printed in connexion with it, to be cancelled; and, like the unfinished tale of the windy night and the notary in The Sentimental Journey, they became the property of the trunk-maker and butterman. I was especially unwilling, I confess, to enrich those respectable trades with the paper of the abandoned design, in which MASTER HUMPHREY described himself and his manner of life. Though I now affect to make the confession philosophically, as referring to a byegone emotion, I am conscious that my pen winces a little even while I write these words. But it was done, and wisely done, and MASTER HUMPHREY'S CLOCK, as originally constructed, became one of the lost books of the earth—which, we all know, are far more precious than any that can be read for love or money.

In reference to the tale itself, I desire to say very little here. The many friends it has won me, and the many hearts it has turned to me when they were full of private sorrow, invest it with an interest, in my mind, which is not a public one, and the rightful place of which appears to be "a more removed ground."

I will merely observe, therefore, that, in writing the book, I had it

8   Preface

always in my fancy to surround the lonely figure of the child with
grotesque and wild, but not impossible companions, and to gather
about her innocent face and pure intentions, associates as strange
and uncongenial as the grim objects that are about her bed when her
history is first fore-shadowed.

MASTER HUMPHREY (before his devotion to the trunk and butter
business) was originally supposed to be the narrator of the story. As
it was constructed from the beginning, however, with a view to
separate publication when completed, his demise has not involved
the necessity of any alteration.

I have a mournful pride in one recollection associated with "little
Nell." While she was yet upon her wanderings, not then concluded,
there appeared in a literary journal, an essay of which she was the
principal theme, so earnestly, so eloquently, and tenderly appreci-
ative of her, and of all her shadowy kith and kin, that it would have
been insensibility in me, if I could have read it without an unusual
glow of pleasure and encouragement. Long afterwards, and when I
had come to know him well, and to see him, stout of heart, going
slowly down into his grave, I knew the writer of that essay to be
THOMAS HOOD.

LONDON, *September*, 1848.

THE OLD CURIOSITY SHOP

CHAPTER I

NIGHT is generally my time for walking. In the summer I often leave home early in the morning, and roam about fields and lanes all day, or even escape for days or weeks together, but saving in the country I seldom go out until after dark, though, Heaven be thanked, I love its light and feel the cheerfulness it sheds upon the earth, as much as any creature living.

I have fallen insensibly into this habit, both because it favours my infirmity and because it affords me greater opportunity of speculating on the characters and occupations of those who fill the streets. The glare and hurry of broad noon are not adapted to idle pursuits like mine; a glimpse of passing faces caught by the light of a street lamp or a shop window is often better for my purpose than their full revelation in the daylight, and, if I must add the truth, night is kinder in this respect than day, which too often destroys an air-built castle at the moment of its completion, without the smallest ceremony or remorse.

That constant pacing to and fro, that never-ending restlessness, that incessant tread of feet wearing the rough stones smooth and glossy—is it not a wonder how the dwellers in narrow ways can bear to hear it! Think of a sick man in such a place as Saint Martin's Court, listening to the footsteps, and in the midst of pain and weariness obliged, despite himself (as though it were a task he must perform) to detect the child's step from the man's, the slipshod beggar from the booted exquisite, the lounging from the busy, the dull heel of the sauntering outcast from the quick tread of an expectant pleasure-seeker—think of the hum and noise being always present to his senses, and of the stream of life that will not stop, pouring on, on, on, through all his restless dreams, as if he were condemned to lie dead but conscious, in a noisy churchyard, and had no hope of rest for centuries to come.

Then the crowds for ever passing and repassing on the bridges (on those which are free of toll at least) where many stop on fine evenings looking listlessly down upon the water with some vague idea that by-and-by it runs between green banks which grow wider and wider until at last it joins the broad vast sea—where some halt to rest from heavy loads and think as they look over the parapet that to smoke and lounge away one's life, and lie sleeping in the sun upon a hot

tarpaulin, in a dull slow sluggish barge, must be happiness unalloyed
—and where some, and a very different class, pause with heavier
loads than they, remembering to have heard or read in some old time
that drowning was not a hard death, but of all means of suicide the
easiest and best.

Covent Garden Market at sunrise too, in the spring or summer
when the fragrance of sweet flowers is in the air, overpowering even
the unwholesome streams of last night's debauchery, and driving the
dusky thrush, whose cage has hung outside a garret window all night
long, half mad with joy! Poor bird! the only neighbouring thing at all
akin to the other little captives, some of whom, shrinking from the
hot hands of drunken purchasers, lie drooping on the path already,
while others, soddened by close contact, await the time when they
shall be watered and freshened up to please more sober company,
and make old clerks who pass them on their road to business,
wonder what has filled their breasts with visions of the country.

But my present purpose is not to expatiate upon my walks. An
adventure which I am about to relate, and to which I shall recur at
intervals, arose out of one of these rambles, and thus I have been led
to speak of them by way of preface.

One night I had roamed into the City, and was walking slowly on
in my usual way, musing upon a great many things, when I was
arrested by an inquiry, the purport of which did not reach me, but
which seemed to be addressed to myself, and was preferred in a soft
sweet voice that struck me very pleasantly. I turned hastily round
and found at my elbow a pretty little girl, who begged to be directed
to a certain street at a considerable distance, and indeed in quite
another quarter of the town.

"It is a very long way from here," said I, "my child."

"I know that, sir," she replied timidly. "I am afraid it is a very
long way, for I came from there to-night."

"Alone?" said I, in some surprise.

"Oh yes, I don't mind that, but I am a little frightened now, for
I have lost my road."

"And what made you ask it of me? Suppose I should tell you
wrong."

"I am sure you will not do that," said the little creature, "you are
such a very old gentleman, and walk so slow yourself."

I cannot describe how much I was impressed by this appeal and
the energy with which it was made, which brought a tear into the
child's clear eye, and made her slight figure tremble as she looked up
into my face.

"Come," said I, "I'll take you there."

She put her hand in mine as confidingly as if she had known me
from her cradle, and we trudged away together: the little creature
accommodating her pace to mine, and rather seeming to lead and
take care of me than I to be protecting her. I observed that every
now and then she stole a curious look at my face as if to make quite
sure that I was not deceiving her, and that these glances (very sharp

and keen they were too) seemed to increase her confidence at every repetition.

For my part, my curiosity and interest were at least equal to the child's, for child she certainly was, although I thought it probable from what I could make out, that her very small and delicate frame imparted a peculiar youthfulness to her appearance. Though more scantily attired than she might have been she was dressed with perfect neatness, and betrayed no marks of poverty or neglect.

"Who has sent you so far by yourself?" said I.

"Somebody who is very kind to me, sir."

"And what have you been doing?"

"That, I must not tell," said the child firmly.

There was something in the manner of this reply which caused me to look at the little creature with an involuntary expression of surprise; for I wondered what kind of errand it might be that occasioned her to be prepared for questioning. Her quick eye seemed to read my thoughts, for as it met mine she added that there was no harm in what she had been doing, but it was a great secret—a secret which she did not even know herself.

This was said with no appearance of cunning or deceit, but with an unsuspicious frankness that bore the impress of truth. She walked on as before, growing more familiar with me as we proceeded and talking cheerfully by the way, but she said no more about her home, beyond remarking that we were going quite a new road and asking if it were a short one.

While we were thus engaged, I revolved in my mind a hundred different explanations of the riddle and rejected them every one. I really felt ashamed to take advantage of the ingenuousness or grateful feeling of the child for the purpose of gratifying my curiosity. I love these little people; and it is not a slight thing when they, who are so fresh from God, love us. As I had felt pleased at first by her confidence I determined to deserve it, and to do credit to the nature which had prompted her to repose it in me.

There was no reason, however, why I should refrain from seeing the person who had inconsiderately sent her to so great a distance by night and alone, and as it was not improbable that if she found herself near home she might take farewell of me and deprive me of the opportunity, I avoided the most frequented ways and took the most intricate, and thus it was not until we arrived in the street itself that she knew where we were. Clapping her hands with pleasure and running on before me for a short distance, my little acquaintance stopped at a door and remaining on the step till I came up knocked at it when I joined her.

A part of this door was of glass unprotected by any shutter, which I did not observe at first, for all was very dark and silent within, and I was anxious (as indeed the child was also) for an answer to our summons. When she had knocked twice or thrice there was a noise as if some person were moving inside, and at length a faint light appeared through the glass which, as it approached very slowly, the bearer having to make his way through a great many scattered articles, enabled me to see both what kind of person it was who advanced and what kind of place it was through which he came.

It was a little old man with long grey hair, whose face and figure as he held the light above his head and looked before him as he approached, I could plainly see. Though much altered by age, I fancied I could recognise in his spare and slender form something of that delicate mould which I had noticed in the child. Their bright blue eyes were certainly alike, but his face was so deeply furrowed and so very full of care, that here all resemblance ceased.

The place through which he made his way at leisure was one of those receptacles for old and curious things which seem to crouch in odd corners of this town and to hide their musty treasures from the public eye in jealousy and distrust. There were suits of mail standing like ghosts in armour here and there, fantastic carvings brought from monkish cloisters, rusty weapons of various kinds, distorted figures in china and wood and iron and ivory: tapestry and strange furniture that might have been designed in dreams. The haggard aspect of the little old man was wonderfully suited to the place; he might have groped among old churches and tombs and deserted houses and gathered all the spoils with his own hands. There was nothing in the whole collection but was in keeping with himself; nothing that looked older or more worn than he.

As he turned the key in the lock, he surveyed me with some astonishment which was not diminished when he looked from me to my companion. The door being opened, the child addressed him as grandfather, and told him the little story of our companionship.

"Why bless thee, child," said the old man patting her on the head, "how couldst thou miss thy way? What if I had lost thee, Nell!"

"I would have found my way back to *you*, grandfather," said the child boldly; "never fear."

The old man kissed her, then turning to me and begging me to walk in, I did so. The door was closed and locked. Preceding me with the light, he led me through the place I had already seen from without, into a small sitting-room behind, in which was another door opening into a kind of closet, where I saw a little bed that a fairy might have slept in, it looked so very small and was so prettily arranged. The child took a candle and tripped into this little room, leaving the old man and me together.

"You must be tired, sir," said he as he placed a chair near the fire, "how can I thank you?"

"By taking more care of your grandchild another time, my good friend," I replied.

"More care!" said the old man in a shrill voice, "more care of Nelly! Why, who ever loved a child as I love Nell?"

He said this with such evident surprise that I was perplexed what answer to make, and the more so because coupled with something feeble and wandering in his manner, there were in his face marks of deep and anxious thought which convinced me that he could not be, as I had been at first inclined to suppose, in a state of dotage or imbecility.

"I don't think you consider——" I began.

"I don't consider!" cried the old man interrupting me, "I don't consider her! Ah, how little you know of the truth! Little Nelly, little Nelly!"

It would be impossible for any man, I care not what his form of speech might be, to express more affection than the dealer in curiosities did, in these four words. I waited for him to speak again, but he rested his chin upon his hand and shaking his head twice or thrice fixed his eyes upon the fire.

While we were sitting thus in silence, the door of the closet opened, and the child returned, her light brown hair hanging loose about her neck, and her face flushed with the haste she had made to rejoin us. She busied herself immediately in preparing supper, and while she was thus engaged I remarked that the old man took an opportunity of observing me more closely than he had done yet. I was surprised to see that all this time everything was done by the child, and that there appeared to be no other persons but ourselves in the house. I took advantage of a moment when she was absent to venture a hint on this point, to which the old man replied that there were few grown persons as trustworthy or as careful as she.

"It always grieves me," I observed, roused by what I took to be his selfishness, "it always grieves me to contemplate the initiation of children into the ways of life, when they are scarcely more than infants. It checks their confidence and simplicity—two of the best qualities that Heaven gives them—and demands that they share our sorrows before they are capable of entering into our enjoyments."

"It will never check hers," said the old man, looking steadily at me, "the springs are too deep. Besides, the children of the poor know but few pleasures. Even the cheap delights of childhood must be bought and paid for."

"But—forgive me for saying this—you are surely not so very poor" —said I.

"She is not my child, sir," returned the old man. "Her mother was, and she was poor. I save nothing—not a penny—though I live as you see, but"—he laid his hand upon my arm and leant forward to whisper—"she shall be rich one of these days, and a fine lady. Don't you think ill of me, because I use her help. She gives it cheerfully as you see, and it would break her heart if she knew that I suffered anybody else to do for me what her little hands could undertake. I don't consider!"—he cried with sudden querulousness, "why, God knows that this one child is the thought and object of my life, and yet he never prospers me—no, never!"

At this juncture, the subject of our conversation again returned, and the old man motioning to me to approach the table, broke off, and said no more.

We had scarcely begun our repast when there was a knock at the door by which I had entered and Nell bursting into a hearty laugh, which I was rejoiced to hear, for it was childlike and full of hilarity, said it was no doubt dear old Kit come back at last.

"Foolish Nell!" said the old man fondling with her hair. "She always laughs at poor Kit."

The child laughed again more heartily than before, and I could not help smiling from pure sympathy. The little old man took up a candle and went to open the door. When he came back, Kit was at his heels.

Kit was a shock-headed shambling awkward lad with an uncommonly wide mouth, very red cheeks, a turned-up nose, and certainly the most comical expression of face I ever saw. He stopped short at the door on seeing a stranger, twirled in his hand a perfectly round old hat without any vestige of a brim, and resting himself now on one leg and now on the other and changing them constantly, stood in the doorway, looking into the parlour with the most extraordinary leer I ever beheld. I entertained a grateful feeling towards the boy from that minute, for I felt that he was the comedy of the child's life.

"A long way, wasn't it, Kit?" said the little old man.

"Why then, it was a goodish stretch, master," returned Kit.

"Did you find the house easily?"

"Why then, not over and above easy, master," said Kit.

"Of course you have come back hungry?"

"Why then, I do consider myself rather so, master," was the answer.

The lad had a remarkable manner of standing sideways as he spoke, and thrusting his head forward over his shoulder, as if he could not get at his voice without that accompanying action. I think he would have amused one anywhere, but the child's exquisite enjoyment of his oddity, and the relief it was to find that there was something she associated with merriment in a place that appeared so unsuited to her, were quite irresistible. It was a great point too that Kit himself was flattered by the sensation he created, and after several efforts to preserve his gravity, burst into a loud roar, and so stood with his mouth wide open and his eyes nearly shut, laughing violently.

The old man had again relapsed into his former abstraction and took no notice of what passed, but I remarked that when her laugh was over, the child's bright eyes were dimmed with tears, called forth by the fulness of heart with which she welcomed her uncouth favourite after the little anxiety of the night. As for Kit himself (whose laugh had been all the time one of that sort which very little would change into a cry) he carried a large slice of bread and meat and and a mug of beer into a corner, and applied himself to disposing of them with great voracity.

"Ah!" said the old man turning to me with a sigh as if I had spoken to him but that moment, "you don't know what you say when you tell me that I don't consider her."

"You must not attach too great weight to a remark founded on first appearances, my friend," said I.

"No," returned the old man thoughtfully, "no. Come hither, Nell."

The little girl hastened from her seat, and put her arm about his neck.

"Do I love thee, Nell?" said he. "Say—do I love thee, Nell, or no?"

The child only answered by her caresses, and laid her head upon his breast.

"Why dost thou sob ?" said the grandfather pressing her closer to him and glancing towards me. "Is it because thou know'st I love thee, and dost not like that I should seem to doubt it by my question? Well, well—then let us say I love thee dearly."

"Indeed, indeed you do," replied the child with great earnestness, "Kit knows you do."

Kit, who in despatching his bread and meat had been swallowing two thirds of his knife at every mouthful with the coolness of a juggler, stopped short in his operations on being thus appealed to, and bawled "Nobody isn't such a fool as to say he doosn't," after which he incapacitated himself for further conversation by taking a most prodigious sandwich at one bite.

"She is poor now"—said the old man patting the child's cheek, "but I say again that the time is coming when she shall be rich. It has been a long time coming, but it must come at last; a very long time, but it surely must come. It has come to other men who do nothing but waste and riot. When *will* it come to me!"

"I am very happy as I am, grandfather," said the child.

"Tush, tush!" returned the old man, "thou dost not know—how should'st thou!" Then he muttered again between his teeth, "The time must come, I am very sure it must. It will be all the better for coming late;" and then he sighed and fell into his former musing state, and still holding the child between his knees appeared to be insensible to everything around him. By this time it wanted but a few minutes of midnight and I rose to go, which recalled him to himself.

"One moment, sir," he said. "Now, Kit—near midnight, boy, and you still here! Get home, get home, and be true to your time in the morning, for there's work to do. Good night! There, bid him good night, Nell, and let him be gone!"

"Good night, Kit," said the child, her eyes lighting up with merriment and kindness.

"Good night, Miss Nell," returned the boy.

"And thank this gentleman," interposed the old man, "but for whose care I might have lost my little girl to-night."

"No, no, master," said Kit, "that won't do, that won't."

"What do you mean?" cried the old man.

"I'd have found her, master," said Kit, "I'd have found her. I'd bet that I'd find her if she was above ground, I would, as quick as anybody, master. Ha, ha ha!"

Once more opening his mouth and shutting his eyes, and laughing like a stentor, Kit gradually backed to the door, and roared himself out.

Free of the room, the boy was not slow in taking his departure; when he had gone, and the child was occupied in clearing the table, the old man said:

"I haven't seemed to thank you, sir, enough for what you have done to-night, but I do thank you humbly and heartily, and so does she, and her thanks are better worth than mine. I should be sorry that you went away and thought I was unmindful of your goodness, or careless of her—I am not indeed."

I was sure of that, I said, from what I had seen. "But," I added, "may I ask you a question?"

"Ay, sir," replied the old man, "what is it?"

"This delicate child," said I, "with so much beauty and intelligence—has she nobody to care for her but you? Has she no other companion or adviser?"

"No," he returned looking anxiously in my face, "no, and she wants no other."

"But are you not fearful," said I, "that you may misunderstand a charge so tender? I am sure you mean well, but are you quite certain that you know how to execute such a trust as this? I am an old man, like you, and I am actuated by an old man's concern in all that is young and promising. Do you not think that what I have seen of you and this little creature to-night must have an interest not wholly free from pain?"

"Sir," rejoined the old man after a moment's silence, "I have no right to feel hurt at what you say. It is true that in many respects I am the child, and she the grown person—that you have seen already. But waking or sleeping, by night or day, in sickness or health, she is the one object of my care, and if you knew of how much care, you would look on me with different eyes, you would indeed. Ah! it's a weary life for an old man—a weary, weary life—but there is a great end to gain and that I keep before me."

Seeing that he was in a state of excitement and impatience, I turned to put on an outer coat which I had thrown off on entering the room, purposing to say no more. I was surprised to see the child standing patiently by with a cloak upon her arm, and in her hand a hat and stick.

"Those are not mine, my dear," said I.

"No," returned the child quietly, "they are grandfather's."

"But he is not going out to-night."

"Oh yes he is," said the child, with a smile.

"And what becomes of you, my pretty one?"

"Me! I stay here of course. I always do."

I looked in astonishment towards the old man, but he was, or feigned to be, busied in the arrangement of his dress. From him I looked back to the slight gentle figure of the child. Alone! In that gloomy place all the long, dreary night.

She evinced no consciousness of my surprise, but cheerfully helped the old man with his cloak, and when he was ready took a candle to light us out. Finding that we did not follow as she expected, she looked back with a smile and waited for us. The old man showed by his face that he plainly understood the cause of my hesitation, but he merely signed to me with an inclination of the head to pass out of the room before him, and remained silent. I had no resource but to comply.

When we reached the door, the child setting down the candle, turned to say good night and raised her face to kiss me. Then she ran to the old man, who folded her in his arms and bade God bless her.

"Sleep soundly, Nell," he said in a low voice, "and angels guard thy bed! Do not forget thy prayers, my sweet."

"No indeed," answered the child fervently, "they make me feel so happy!"

"That's well; I know they do; they should," said the old man. "Bless thee a hundred times! Early in the morning I shall be home."

"You'll not ring twice," returned the child. "The bell wakes me, even in the middle of a dream."

With this, they separated. The child opened the door (now guarded by a shutter which I had heard the boy put up before he left the house) and with another farewell whose clear and tender note I have recalled a thousand times, held it until we had passed out. The old man paused a moment while it was gently closed and fastened on the inside, and, satisfied that this was done, walked on at a slow pace. At the street-corner he stopped, and regarding me with a troubled countenance said that our ways were widely different and that he must take his leave. I would have spoken, but summoning up more alacrity than might have been expected in one of his appearance, he hurried away. I could see that twice or thrice he looked back as if to ascertain if I were still watching him, or perhaps to assure himself that I was not following at a distance. The obscurity of the night favoured his disappearance, and his figure was soon beyond my sight.

I remained standing on the spot where he had left me, unwilling to depart, and yet unknowing why I should loiter there. I looked wistfully into the street we had lately quitted, and after a time directed my steps that way. I passed and repassed the house, and stopped and listened at the door; all was dark, and silent as the grave.

Yet I lingered about, and could not tear myself away, thinking of all possible harm that might happen to the child—of fires and robberies and even murder—and feeling as if some evil must ensue if I turned my back upon the place. The closing of a door or window in the street brought me before the curiosity-dealer's once more; I crossed the road and looked up at the house to assure myself that the noise had not come from there. No, it was black, cold, and lifeless as before.

There were few passengers astir; the street was sad and dismal, and pretty well my own. A few stragglers from the theatres hurried by, and now and then I turned aside to avoid some noisy drunkard as he reeled homewards, but these interruptions were not frequent and soon ceased. The clocks struck one. Still I paced up and down, promising myself that every time should be the last, and breaking faith with myself on some new plea as often as I did so.

The more I thought of what the old man had said, and of his looks and bearing, the less I could account for what I had seen and heard. I had a strong misgiving that his nightly absence was for no good purpose. I had only come to know the fact through the innocence of the child, and though the old man was by at the time, and saw my undisguised surprise, he had preserved a strange mystery upon the subject and offered no word of explanation. These reflections naturally recalled again more strongly than before his haggard face, his wandering manner, his restless anxious looks. His affection for the child might not be inconsistent with villany of the worst kind; even that very affection was in itself an extraordinary contradiction, or how could he leave her thus? Disposed as I was to think badly of him, I never doubted that his love for her was real. I could not admit the thought, remembering what had passed between us, and the tone of voice in which he had called her by her name.

"Stay here of course," the child had said in answer to my question, "I always do!" What could take him from home by night, and every night! I called up all the strange tales I had ever heard of dark and secret deeds committed in great towns and escaping detection for a long series of years; wild as many of these stories were, I could not find one adapted to this mystery, which only became the more impenetrable, in proportion as I sought to solve it.

Occupied with such thoughts as these, and a crowd of others all tending to the same point, I continued to pace the street for two long hours; at length the rain began to descend heavily, and then overpowered by fatigue though no less interested than I had been at first, I engaged the nearest coach and so got home. A cheerful fire was blazing on the hearth, my lamp burnt brightly, my clock received me with its old familiar welcome; everything was quiet, warm and cheering, and in happy contrast to the gloom and darkness I had quitted.

But all that night, waking or in my sleep, the same thoughts recurred and the same images retained possession of my brain. I had ever before me the old dark murky rooms—the gaunt suits of mail with their ghostly silent air—the faces all awry, grinning from wood and stone—the dust and rust and worm that lives in wood—and alone in the midst of all this lumber and decay and ugly age, the beautiful child in her gentle slumber, smiling through her light and sunny dreams.

CHAPTER II

AFTER combating, for nearly a week, the feeling which impelled me to revisit the place I had quitted under the circumstances already detailed, I yielded to it at length; and determining that this time I would present myself by the light of day, bent my steps thither early in the afternoon.

I walked past the house, and took several turns in the street, with that kind of hesitation which is natural to a man who is conscious that the visit he is about to pay is unexpected, and may not be very acceptable. However, as the door of the shop was shut, and it did not appear likely that I should be recognised by those within, if I continued merely to pass up and down before it, I soon conquered this irresolution, and found myself in the Curiosity Dealer's warehouse.

The old man and another person were together in the back part, and there seemed to have been high words between them, for their voices which were raised to a very loud pitch suddenly stopped on my entering, and the old man advancing hastily towards me, said in a tremulous tone that he was very glad I had come.

"You interrupted us at a critical moment," he said, pointing to the man whom I had found in company with him; "this fellow will murder me one of these days. He would have done so, long ago, if he had dared."

"Bah! You would swear away my life if you could," returned the other, after bestowing a stare and a frown on me; "we all know that!"

"I almost think I could," cried the old man, turning feebly upon him. "If oaths, or prayers, or words, could rid me of you, they should. I would be quit of you, and would be relieved if you were dead."

"I know it," returned the other. "I said so, didn't I? But neither oaths nor prayers, nor words, *will* kill me, and therefore I live, and mean to live."

"And his mother died!" cried the old man, passionately clasping his hands and looking upward; "and this is Heaven's justice!"

The other stood lounging with his foot upon a chair, and regarded him with a contemptuous sneer. He was a young man of one-and-twenty or thereabouts; well made, and certainly handsome, though the expression of his face was far from prepossessing, having in common with his manner and even his dress, a dissipated, insolent air which repelled one.

"Justice or no justice," said the young fellow, "here I am and here I shall stop till such time as I think fit to go, unless you send for assistance to put me out—which you won't do, I know. I tell you again that I want to see my sister."

"*Your* sister!" said the old man bitterly.

"Ah! You can't change the relationship," returned the other. "If you could, you'd have done it long ago. I want to see my sister, that you keep cooped up here, poisoning her mind with your sly secrets and pretending an affection for her that you may work her to death, and add a few scraped shillings every week to the money you can hardly count. I want to see her; and I will."

"Here's a moralist to talk of poisoned minds! Here's a generous spirit to scorn scraped-up shillings!" cried the old man, turning from him to me. "A profligate, sir, who has forfeited every claim not only upon those who have the misfortune to be of his blood, but upon society which knows nothing of him but his misdeeds. A liar too," he added, in a lower voice as he drew closer to me, "who knows how dear she is to me, and seeks to wound me even there, because there is a stranger by."

"Strangers are nothing to me, grandfather," said the young fellow catching at the word, "nor I to them, I hope. The best they can do, is to keep an eye to their business and leave me to mine. There's a friend of mine waiting outside, and as it seems that I may have to wait some time, I'll call him in, with your leave."

Saying this, he stepped to the door, and looking down the street beckoned several times to some unseen person, who, to judge from the air of impatience with which these signals were accompanied, required a great quantity of persuasion to induce him to advance. At length there sauntered up, on the opposite side of the way—with a bad pretence of passing by accident—a figure conspicuous for its dirty smartness, which after a great many frowns and jerks of the head, in resistance of the invitation, ultimately crossed the road and was brought into the shop.

"There. It's Dick Swiveller," said the young fellow, pushing him in. "Sit down, Swiveller."

"But is the old min agreeable?" said Mr. Swiveller in an under tone.

"Sit down," repeated his companion.

Mr. Swiveller complied, and looking about him with a propitiatory smile, observed that last week was a fine week for the ducks, and this week was a fine week for the dust; he also observed that whilst standing by the post at the street-corner, he had observed a pig with a straw in his mouth issuing out of the tobacco-shop, from which appearance he augured that another fine week for the ducks was approaching, and that rain would certainly ensue. He furthermore took occasion to apologise for any negligence that might be perceptible in his dress, on the ground that last night he had had "the sun very strong in his eyes;" by which expression he was understood to convey to his hearers in the most delicate manner possible, the information that he had been extremely drunk.

"But what," said Mr. Swiveller with a sigh, "what is the odds so long as the fire of soul is kindled at the taper of conwiviality, and the wing of friendship never moults a feather! What is the odds so long as the spirit is expanded by means of rosy wine, and the present moment is the least happiest of our existence!"

"You needn't act the chairman here," said his friend, half aside.

"Fred!" cried Mr. Swiveller, tapping his nose, "a word to the wise is sufficient for them—we may be good and happy without riches, Fred. Say not another syllable. I know my cue; smart is the word. Only one little whisper, Fred—is the old min friendly?"

"Never you mind," replied his friend.

"Right again, quite right," said Mr. Swiveller, "caution is the word, and caution is the act." With that, he winked as if in preservation of some deep secret, and folding his arms and leaning back in his chair, looked up at the ceiling with profound gravity.

It was perhaps not very unreasonable to suspect from what had already passed, that Mr. Swiveller was not quite recovered from the effects of the powerful sunlight to which he had made allusion; but if no such suspicion had been awakened by his speech, his wiry hair, dull eyes, and sallow face, would still have been strong witnesses against him. His attire was not, as he had himself hinted, remarkable for the nicest arrangement, but was in a state of disorder which strongly induced the idea that he had gone to bed in it. It consisted of a brown body-coat with a great many brass buttons up the front and only one behind, a bright check neckerchief, a plaid waistcoat, soiled white trousers, and a very limp hat, worn with the wrong side foremost, to hide a hole in the brim. The breast of his coat was ornamented with an outside pocket from which there peeped forth the cleanest end of a very large and very ill-favoured handkerchief; his dirty wristbands were pulled down as far as possible and ostentatiously folded back over his cuffs; he displayed no gloves, and carried a yellow cane having at the top a bone hand with the semblance of a ring on its little finger and a black ball in its grasp. With all these personal advantages (to which may be added a strong savour of tobacco-smoke, and a prevailing greasiness of appearance) Mr. Swiveller leant back in his chair with his eyes fixed on the ceiling, and occasionally pitching his voice to the needful key, obliged the company with a few bars of an intensely dismal air, and then, in the middle of a note, relapsed into his former silence.

The old man sat himself down in a chair, and, with folded hands, looked sometimes at his grandson and sometimes at his strange companion, as if he were utterly powerless and had no resource but to leave them to do as they pleased. The young man reclined against a table at no great distance from his friend, in apparent indifference to everything that had passed; and I—who felt the difficulty of any interference, notwithstanding that the old man had appealed to me, both by words and looks—made the best feint I could of being occupied in examining some of the goods that were disposed for sale, and paying very little attention to the persons before me.

The silence was not of long duration, for Mr. Swiveller, after favouring us with several melodious assurances that his heart was in the Highlands, and that he wanted but his Arab steed as a preliminary to the achievement of great feats of valour and loyalty, removed his eyes from the ceiling and subsided into prose again.

"Fred," said Mr. Swiveller, stopping short as if the idea had suddenly occurred to him, and speaking in the same audible whisper as before, "*is* the old min friendly?"

"What does it matter?" returned his friend peevishly.

"No, but *is* he?" said Dick.

"Yes, of course. What do I care whether he is or not."

Emboldened as it seemed by this reply to enter into a more general conversation, Mr. Swiveller plainly laid himself out to captivate our attention.

He began by remarking that soda-water, though a good thing in the abstract, was apt to lie cold upon the stomach unless qualified with ginger, or a small infusion of brandy, which latter article he held to be preferable in all cases, saving for the one consideration of expense. Nobody venturing to dispute these positions, he proceeded to observe that the human hair was a great retainer of tobacco-smoke, and that the young gentlemen of Westminster and Eton, after eating vast quantities of apples to conceal any scent of cigars from their anxious friends, were usually detected in consequence of their heads possessing this remarkable property; whence he concluded that if the Royal Society would turn their attention to the circumstance, and endeavour to find in the resources of science a means of preventing such untoward revelations, they might indeed be looked upon as benefactors to mankind. These opinions being equally incontrovertible with those he had already pronounced, he went on to inform us that Jamaica rum, though unquestionably an agreeable spirit of great richness and flavour, had the drawback of remaining constantly present to the taste next day; and nobody being venturous enough to argue this point either, he increased in confidence and became yet more companionable and communicative.

"It's a devil of a thing, gentlemen," said Mr. Swiveller, "when relations fall out and disagree. If the wing of friendship should never moult a feather, the wing of relationship should never be clipped, but be always expanded and serene. Why should a grandson and grandfather peg away at each other with mutual wiolence when all might be bliss and concord? Why not jine hands and forgit it?"

"Hold your tongue," said his friend.

"Sir," replied Mr. Swiveller, "don't you interrupt the chair. Gentlemen, how does the case stand, upon the present occasion? Here is a jolly old grandfather—I say it with the utmost respect—and here is a wild young grandson. The jolly old grandfather says to the wild young grandson, 'I have brought you up and educated you, Fred; I have put you in the way of getting on in life; you have bolted a little out of the course, as young fellows often do; and you shall never have another chance, nor the ghost of half a one.' The wild young grandson makes answer to this and says, 'You're as rich as rich can be; you have been at no uncommon expense on my account, you're saving up piles of money for my little sister that lives with you in a secret, stealthy, hugger-muggering kind of way and with no manner of enjoyment—why can't you stand a trifle for your grown-up relation?' The jolly old grandfather unto this, retorts, not only that he declines to fork out with that cheerful readiness which is always so agreeable and pleasant in a gentleman of his time of life, but that he will blow up, and call names, and make reflections whenever they meet. Then the plain question is, an't it a pity that this state of things should continue, and how much better would it be for the old gentleman to hand over a reasonable amount of tin, and make it all right and comfortable?"

Having delivered this oration with a great many waves and flourishes of the hand, Mr. Swiveller abruptly thrust the head of his cane into his mouth as if to prevent himself from impairing the effect of his speech by adding one other word.

"Why do you hunt and persecute me, God help me!" said the old man turning to his grandson. "Why do you bring your profligate companions here? How often am I to tell you that my life is one of care and self-denial, and that I am poor?"

"How often am I to tell you," returned the other, looking coldly at him, "that I know better?"

"You have chosen your own path," said the old man. "Follow it. Leave Nell and me to toil and work."

"Nell will be a woman soon," returned the other, "and, bred in your faith, she'll forget her brother unless he shows himself sometimes."

"Take care," said the old man with sparkling eyes, "that she does not forget you when you would have her memory keenest. Take care that the day don't come when you walk barefoot in the streets, and she rides by in a gay carriage of her own."

"You mean when she has your money?" retorted the other. "How like a poor man he talks!"

"And yet," said the old man dropping his voice and speaking like one who thinks aloud, "how poor we are, and what a life it is! The cause is a young child's, guiltless of all harm or wrong, but nothing goes well with it! Hope and patience, hope and patience!"

These words were uttered in too low a tone to reach the ears of the young men. Mr. Swiveller appeared to think that they implied some mental struggle consequent upon the powerful effect of his address, for he poked his friend with his cane and whispered his conviction that he had administered "a clincher," and that he expected a commission on the profits. Discovering his mistake after a while, he appeared to grow rather sleepy and discontented, and more than once suggested the propriety of an immediate departure, when the door opened, and the child herself appeared.

CHAPTER III

THE child was closely followed by an elderly man of remarkably hard features and forbidding aspect, and so low in stature as to be quite a dwarf, though his head and face were large enough for the body of a giant. His black eyes were restless, sly, and cunning; his mouth and chin, bristly with the stubble of a coarse hard beard; and his complexion was one of that kind which never looks clean or wholesome. But what added most to the grotesque expression of his face, was a ghastly smile, which, appearing to be the mere result of habit and to have no connexion with any mirthful or complacent feeling, constantly revealed the few discoloured fangs that were yet scattered in his mouth, and gave him the aspect of a panting dog. His dress consisted of a large high-crowned hat, a worn dark suit, a pair of capacious shoes, and a dirty white neckerchief sufficiently limp and crumpled to disclose the greater portion of his wiry throat. Such hair as he had, was of a grizzled black, cut short and straight upon his temples, and hanging in a frowsy fringe about his ears. His hands, which were of a rough coarse grain, were very dirty; his finger-nails were crooked, long, and yellow.

There was ample time to note these particulars, for besides that they were sufficiently obvious without very close observation, some moments elapsed before any one broke silence. The child advanced timidly towards her brother and put her hand in his, the dwarf (if we may call him so) glanced keenly at all present, and the curiosity-dealer, who plainly had not expected his uncouth visitor, seemed disconcerted and embarrassed.

"Ah!" said the dwarf, who with his hand stretched out above his eyes had been surveying the young man attentively, "that should be your grandson, neighbour!"

"Say rather that he should not be," replied the old man. "But he is."

"And that?" said the dwarf, pointing to Dick Swiveller.

"Some friend of his, as welcome here as he," said the old man.

"And that?" inquired the dwarf wheeling round and pointing straight at me.

"A gentleman who was so good as to bring Nell home the other night when she lost her way, coming from your house."

The little man turned to the child as if to chide her or express his wonder, but as she was talking to the young man, held his peace, and bent his head to listen.

"Well, Nelly," said the young fellow aloud. "Do they teach you to hate me, eh?"

"No, no. For shame. Oh, no!" cried the child.

"To love me, perhaps?" pursued her brother with a sneer.

"To do neither," she returned. "They never speak to me about you. Indeed they never do."

"I dare be bound for that," he said, darting a bitter look at the grandfather. "I dare be bound for that, Nell. Oh! I believe you there!"

"But I love you dearly, Fred," said the child.

"No doubt!"

"I do indeed, and always will," the child repeated with great emotion, "but oh! if you would leave off vexing him and making him unhappy, then I could love you more."

"I see!" said the young man, as he stooped carelessly over the child, and having kissed her, pushed her from him: "There—get you away now you have said your lesson. You needn't whimper. We part good friends enough, if that's the matter."

He remained silent, following her with his eyes, until she had gained her little room and closed the door; and then turning to the dwarf, said abruptly,

"Harkee, Mr.——"

"Meaning me?" returned the dwarf. "Quilp is my name. You might remember. It's not a long one—Daniel Quilp."

"Harkee, Mr. Quilp, then," pursued the other. "You have some influence with my grandfather there."

"Some," said Mr. Quilp emphatically.

"And are in a few of his mysteries and secrets."

"A few," replied Quilp, with equal dryness.

"Then let me tell him once for all, through you, that I will come into and go out of this place as often as I like, so long as he keeps Nell here; and that if he wants to be quit of me, he must first be quit of her. What have I done to be made a bugbear of, and to be shunned and dreaded as if I brought the plague? He'll tell you that I have no natural affection; and that I care no more for Nell, for her own sake, than I do for him. Let him say so. I care for the whim, then, of coming to and fro and reminding her of my existence. I *will* see her when I please. That's my point. I came here to-day to maintain it, and I'll come here again fifty times with the same object and always with the same success. I said I would stop till I had gained it. I have done so, and now my visit's ended. Come, Dick."

"Stop!" cried Mr. Swiveller, as his companion turned towards the door. "Sir!"

"Sir, I am your humble servant," said Mr. Quilp, to whom the monosyllable was addressed.

"Before I leave the gay and festive scene, and halls of dazzling light, sir," said Mr. Swiveller, "I will, with your permission, attempt a slight remark. I came here, sir, this day, under the impression that the old min was friendly."

"Proceed, sir," said Daniel Quilp; for the orator had made a sudden stop.

"Inspired by this idea and the sentiments it awakened, sir, and feeling as a mutual friend that badgering, baiting, and bullying, was not the sort of thing calculated to expand the souls and promote the social harmony of the contending parties, I took upon myself to suggest a course which is *the* course to be adopted on the present occasion. Will you allow me to whisper half a syllable, sir?"

Without waiting for the permission he sought, Mr. Swiveller stepped up to the dwarf, and leaning on his shoulder and stooping down to get at his ear, said in a voice which was perfectly audible to all present,

"The watch-word to the old min is—fork."

"Is what?" demanded Quilp.

"Is fork, sir, fork," replied Mr. Swiveller slapping his pocket. "You are awake, sir?"

The dwarf nodded. Mr. Swiveller drew back and nodded likewise, then drew a little further back and nodded again, and so on. By these means he in time reached the door, where he gave a great cough to attract the dwarf's attention and gain an opportunity of expressing in dumb show, the closest confidence and most inviolable secrecy. Having performed the serious pantomime that was necessary for the due conveyance of these ideas, he cast himself upon his friend's track, and vanished.

"Humph!" said the dwarf with a sour look and a shrug of his shoulders, "so much for dear relations. Thank God I acknowledge none! Nor need you either," he added, turning to the old man, "if you were not as weak as a reed, and nearly as senseless."

"What would you have me do?" he retorted in a kind of helpless desperation. "It is easy to talk and sneer. What would you have me do?"

"What would *I* do if I was in your case?" said the dwarf.

"Something violent, no doubt."

"You're right there," returned the little man, highly gratified by the compliment, for such he evidently considered it; and grinning like a devil as he rubbed his dirty hands together. "Ask Mrs. Quilp, pretty Mrs. Quilp, obedient, timid, loving Mrs. Quilp. But that reminds me—I have left her all alone, and she will be anxious and know not a moment's peace till I return. I know she's always in that condition when I'm away, though she doesn't dare to say so, unless I lead her on and tell her she may speak freely and I won't be angry with her. Oh! well-trained Mrs. Quilp!"

The creature appeared quite horrible with his monstrous head and little body, as he rubbed his hands slowly round, and round, and round again—with something fantastic even in his manner of performing this slight action—and, dropping his shaggy brows and cocking his chin in the air, glanced upward with a stealthy look of exultation that an imp might have copied and appropriated to himself.

"Here," he said, putting his hand into his breast and sidling up to the old man as he spoke; "I brought it myself for fear of accidents, as, being in gold, it was something large and heavy for Nell to carry in her bag. She need be accustomed to such loads betimes though, neighbour; for she will carry weight when you are dead."

"Heaven send she may! I hope so," said the old man with something like a groan.

"Hope so!" echoed the dwarf, approaching close to his ear; "neighbour, I would I knew in what good investment all these supplies are sunk. But you are a deep man, and keep your secret close."

"My secret!" said the other with a haggard look. "Yes, you're right —I—I—keep it close—very close."

He said no more, but taking the money turned away with a slow uncertain step, and pressed his hand upon his head like a weary and dejected man. The dwarf watched him sharply, while he passed into the little sitting-room and locked it in an iron safe above the chimney-piece; and after musing for a short space, prepared to take his leave, observing that unless he made good haste, Mrs. Quilp would certainly be in fits on his return.

"And so, neighbour," he added, "I'll turn my face homewards, leaving my love for Nelly and hoping she may never lose her way again, though her doing so *has* procured me an honour I didn't expect." With that he bowed and leered at me, and with a keen glance around which seemed to comprehend every object within his range of vision, however small or trivial, went his way.

I had several times essayed to go myself, but the old man had always opposed it and entreated me to remain. As he renewed his entreaties on our being left alone, and adverted with many thanks to the former occasion of our being together, I willingly yielded to his persuasions, and sat down, pretending to examine some curious miniatures and a few old medals which he had placed before me. It needed no great pressing to induce me to stay, for if my curiosity had been excited on the occasion of my first visit, it certainly was not diminished now.

Nell joined us before long, and bringing some needlework to the table, sat by the old man's side. It was pleasant to observe the fresh flowers in the room, the pet bird with a green bough shading his little cage, the breath of freshness and youth which seemed to rustle through the dull old house and hover round the child. It was curious, but not so pleasant, to turn from the beauty and grace of the girl, to the stooping figure, care-worn face, and jaded aspect of the old man. As he grew weaker and more feeble, what would become of this lonely little creature; poor protector as he was, say that he died—what would her fate be, then?

The old man almost answered my thoughts, as he laid his hand on hers, and spoke aloud.

"I'll be of better cheer, Nell," he said; "there must be good fortune in store for thee—I do not ask it for myself, but thee. Such miseries must fall on thy innocent head without it, that I cannot believe but that, being tempted, it will come at last!"

She looked cheerfully into his face, but made no answer.

"When I think," said he, "of the many years—many in thy short life—that thou hast lived alone with me; of thy monotonous existence, knowing no companions of thy own age nor any childish pleasures; of the solitude in which thou hast grown to be what thou art, and in which thou hast lived apart from nearly all thy kind but one old man; I sometimes fear I have dealt hardly by thee, Nell."

"Grandfather!" cried the child in unfeigned surprise.

"Not in intention—no no," said he. "I have ever looked forward to the time that should enable thee to mix among the gayest and prettiest, and take thy station with the best. But I still look forward, Nell, I still look forward, and if I should be forced to leave thee, meanwhile, how have I fitted thee for struggles with the world? The poor bird yonder is as well qualified to encounter it, and be turned adrift upon its mercies—Hark! I hear Kit outside. Go to him, Nell, go to him."

She rose, and hurrying away, stopped, turned back, and put her arms about the old man's neck, then left him and hurried away again —but faster this time, to hide her falling tears.

"A word in your ear, sir," said the old man in a hurried whisper. "I have been rendered uneasy by what you said the other night, and can only plead that I have done all for the best—that it is too late to retract, if I could (though I cannot)—and that I hope to triumph yet. All is for her sake. I have borne great poverty myself, and would spare her the sufferings that poverty carries with it. I would spare her the miseries that brought her mother, my own dear child, to an early grave. I would leave her—not with resources which could be easily spent or squandered away, but with what would place her beyond the reach of want for ever. You mark me, sir? She shall have no pittance, but a fortune—Hush! I can say no more than that, now or at any other time, and she is here again!"

The eagerness with which all this was poured into my ear, the trembling of the hand with which he clasped my arm, the strained and starting eyes he fixed upon me, the wild vehemence and agitation of his manner, filled me with amazement. All that I had heard and seen, and a great part of what he had said himself, led me to suppose that he was a wealthy man. I could form no comprehension of his character, unless he were one of those miserable wretches who, having made gain the sole end and object of their lives and having succeeded in amassing great riches, are constantly tortured by the dread of poverty, and beset by fears of loss and ruin. Many things he had said which I had been at a loss to understand, were quite reconcileable with the idea thus presented to me, and at length I concluded that beyond all doubt he was one of this unhappy race.

The opinion was not the result of hasty consideration, for which indeed there was no opportunity at that time, as the child came back directly, and soon occupied herself in preparations for giving Kit a writing lesson, of which it seemed he had a couple every week, and one regularly on that evening, to the great mirth and enjoyment both of himself and his instructress. To relate how it was a long time before his modesty could be so far prevailed upon as to admit of his sitting down in the parlour, in the presence of an unknown gentleman—how, when he did sit down, he tucked up his sleeves and squared his elbows and put his face close to the copy-book and squinted horribly at the lines—how, from the very first moment of having the pen in his hand, he began to wallow in blots, and to daub himself with ink up to the very roots of his hair—how, if he did by accident form a letter properly, he immediately smeared it out again with his arm in his preparations to make another—how, at every fresh mistake, there was a fresh burst of merriment from the child and a louder and not less hearty laugh from poor Kit himself—and how there was all the way through, notwithstanding, a gentle wish on her part to teach, and an anxious desire on his to learn—to relate all these particulars would no doubt occupy more space and time than they deserve. It will be sufficient to say that the lesson was given—that evening passed and night came on—that the old man again grew restless and impatient—that he quitted the house secretly at the same hour as before—and that the child was once more left alone within its gloomy walls.

And now, that I have carried this history so far in my own

character and introduced these personages to the reader, I shall for the convenience of the narrative detach myself from its further course, and leave those who have prominent and necessary parts in it to speak and act for themselves.

CHAPTER IV

MR. and Mrs. Quilp resided on Tower Hill; and in her bower on Tower Hill Mrs. Quilp was left to pine the absence of her lord, when he quitted her on the business which he has been already seen to transact.

Mr. Quilp could scarcely be said to be of any particular trade or calling, though his pursuits were diversified and his occupations numerous. He collected the rents of whole colonies of filthy streets and alleys by the waterside, advanced money to the seamen and petty officers of merchant vessels, had a share in the ventures of divers mates of East Indiamen, smoked his smuggled cigars under the very nose of the Custom House, and made appointments on 'Change with men in glazed hats and round jackets pretty well every day. On the Surrey side of the river was a small rat-infested dreary yard called "Quilp's Wharf," in which were a little wooden counting-house burrowing all awry in the dust as if it had fallen from the clouds and ploughed into the ground; a few fragments of rusty anchors; several large iron rings; some piles of rotten wood; and two or three heaps of old sheet copper, crumpled, cracked, and battered. On Quilp's Wharf, Daniel Quilp was a ship-breaker, yet to judge from these appearances he must either have been a ship-breaker on a very small scale, or have broken his ships up very small indeed. Neither did the place present any extraordinary aspect of life or activity, as its only human occupant was an amphibious boy in a canvas suit, whose sole change of occupation was from sitting on the head of a pile and throwing stones into the mud when the tide was out, to standing with his hands in his pockets gazing listlessly on the motion and on the bustle of the river at high-water.

The dwarf's lodging on Tower Hill comprised, besides the needful accommodation for himself and Mrs. Quilp, a small sleeping-closet for that lady's mother, who resided with the couple and waged perpetual war with Daniel; of whom, notwithstanding, she stood in no slight dread. Indeed, the ugly creature contrived by some means or other—whether by his ugliness or his ferocity or his natural cunning is no great matter—to impress with a wholesome fear of his anger, most of those with whom he was brought into daily contact and communication. Over nobody had he such complete ascendancy as Mrs. Quilp herself—a pretty little, mild-spoken, blue-eyed woman, who having allied herself in wedlock to the dwarf in one of those strange infatuations of which examples are by no means scarce, performed a sound practical penance for her folly, every day of her life.

It has been said that Mrs. Quilp was pining in her bower. In her bower she was, but not alone, for besides the old lady her mother of whom mention has recently been made, there were present some half-dozen ladies of the neighbourhood who had happened by a strange accident (and also by a little understanding among themselves) to drop in one after another, just about tea-time. This being a season favourable to conversation, and the room being a cool, shady, lazy kind of place, with some plants at the open window shutting out the dust, and interposing pleasantly enough between the tea table within and the old Tower without, it is no wonder that the ladies felt an inclination to talk and linger, especially when there are taken into account the additional inducements of fresh butter, new bread, shrimps, and water-cresses.

Now, the ladies being together under these circumstances, it was extremely natural that the discourse should turn upon the propensity of mankind to tyrannise over the weaker sex, and the duty that devolved upon the weaker sex to resist that tyranny and assert their rights and dignity. It was natural for four reasons: firstly, because Mrs. Quilp being a young woman and notoriously under the dominion of her husband ought to be excited to rebel; secondly, because Mrs. Quilp's parent was known to be laudably shrewish in her disposition and inclined to resist male authority; thirdly, because each visitor wished to show for herself how superior she was in this respect to the generality of her sex; and fourthly, because the company being accustomed to scandalise each other in pairs, were deprived of their usual subject of conversation now that they were all assembled in close friendship, and had consequently no better employment than to attack the common enemy.

Moved by these considerations, a stout lady opened the proceedings by inquiring, with an air of great concern and sympathy, how Mr. Quilp was; whereunto Mr. Quilp's wife's mother replied sharply, "Oh! he was well enough—nothing much was ever the matter with him—and ill weeds were sure to thrive." All the ladies then sighed in concert, shook their heads gravely, and looked at Mrs. Quilp as at a martyr.

"Ah!" said the spokeswoman, "I wish you'd give her a little of your advice, Mrs. Jiniwin "—Mrs. Quilp had been a Miss Jiniwin it should be observed—"nobody knows better than you, ma'am, what us women owe to ourselves."

"Owe indeed, ma'am!" replied Mrs. Jiniwin. "When my poor husband, her dear father, was alive, if he had ever ventur'd a cross word to *me*, I'd have——" the good old lady did not finish the sentence, but she twisted off the head of a shrimp with a vindictiveness which seemed to imply that the action was in some degree a substitute for words. In this light it was clearly understood by the other party, who immediately replied with great approbation, "You quite enter into my feelings, ma'am, and it's jist what I'd do myself."

"But you have no call to do it," said Mrs. Jiniwin. "Luckily for you, you have no more occasion to do it than I had."

"No woman need have, if she was true to herself," rejoined the stout lady.

"Do you hear that, Betsy?" said Mrs. Jiniwin, in a warning voice. "How often have I said the very same words to you, and almost gone down on my knees when I spoke 'em!"

Poor Mrs. Quilp, who had looked in a state of helplessness from one face of condolence to another, coloured, smiled, and shook her head doubtfully. This was the signal for a general clamour, which beginning in a low murmur gradually swelled into a great noise in which everybody spoke at once, and all said that she being a young woman had no right to set up her opinions against the experiences of those who knew so much better; that it was very wrong of her not to take the advice of people who had nothing at heart but her good; that it was next door to being downright ungrateful to conduct herself in that manner; that if she had no respect for herself she ought to have some for other women, all of whom she compromised by her meekness; and that if she had no respect for other women, the time would come when other women would have no respect for her; and she would be very sorry for that, they could tell her. Having dealt out these admonitions, the ladies fell to a more powerful assault than they had yet made upon the mixed tea, new bread, fresh butter, shrimps, and water-cresses, and said that their vexation was so great to see her going on like that, that they could hardly bring themselves to eat a single morsel.

"It's all very fine to talk," said Mrs. Quilp with much simplicity, "but I know that if I was to die to-morrow, Quilp could marry anybody he pleased—now that he could, I know!"

There was quite a scream of indignation at this idea. Marry whom he pleased! They would like to see him dare to think of marrying any of them; they would like to see the faintest approach to such a thing. One lady (a widow) was quite certain she should stab him if he hinted at it.

"Very well," said Mrs. Quilp, nodding her head, "as I said just now, it's very easy to talk, but I say again that I know—that I'm sure—Quilp has such a way with him when he likes, that the best-looking woman here couldn't refuse him if I was dead, and she was free, and he chose to make love to her. Come!"

Everybody bridled up at this remark, as much as to say "I know you mean me. Let him try—that's all." And yet for some hidden reason they were all angry with the widow, and each lady whispered in her neighbour's ear that it was very plain the said widow thought herself the person referred to, and what a puss she was!

"Mother knows," said Mrs. Quilp, " that what I say is quite correct, for she often said so before we were married. Didn't you say so, mother?"

This inquiry involved the respected lady in rather a delicate position, for she certainly had been an active party in making her daughter Mrs. Quilp, and, besides, it was not supporting the family credit to encourage the idea that she had married a man whom nobody else would have. On the other hand, to exaggerate the captivating qualities of her son-in-law would be to weaken the cause of revolt, in which all her energies were deeply engaged. Beset by these opposing considerations, Mrs. Jiniwin admitted the powers of insinuation, but denied the right to govern, and with a timely compliment to the stout lady brought back the discussion to the point from which it had strayed.

"Oh! It's a sensible and proper thing indeed, what Mrs. George has said!" exclaimed the old lady. "If women are only true to themselves!—But Betsy isn't, and more's the shame and pity."

"Before I'd let a man order me about as Quilp orders her," said Mrs. George; "before I'd consent to stand in awe of a man as she does of him, I'd—I'd kill myself, and write a letter first to say he did it!"

This remark being loudly commended and approved of, another lady (from the Minories) put in her word:

"Mr. Quilp may be a very nice man," said this lady, "and I suppose there's no doubt he is, because Mrs. Quilp says he is, and Mrs. Jiniwin says he is, and they ought to know, or nobody does. But still he is not quite a—what one calls a handsome man, nor quite a young man neither, which might be a little excuse for him if anything could be; whereas his wife is young, and is good-looking, and is a woman—which is the great thing after all."

This last clause being delivered with extraordinary pathos, elicited a corresponding murmur from the hearers, stimulated by which the lady went on to remark that if such a husband was cross and unreasonable with such a wife, then—

"If he is!" interposed the mother, putting down her tea-cup and brushing the crumbs out of her lap, preparatory to making a solemn declaration. "If he is! He is the greatest tyrant that ever lived, she daren't call her soul her own, he makes her tremble with a word and even with a look, he frightens her to death, and she hasn't the spirit to give him a word back, no, not a single word."

Notwithstanding that the fact had been notorious beforehand to all the tea-drinkers, and had been discussed and expatiated on at every tea-drinking in the neighbourhood for the last twelve months, this official communication was no sooner made than they all began to talk at once and to vie with each other in vehemence and volubility. Mrs. George remarked that people would talk, that people had often said this to her before, that Mrs. Simmons then and there present had told her so twenty times, that she had always said, "No, Henrietta Simmons, unless I see it with my own eyes and hear it with my own ears, I never will believe it." Mrs. Simmons corroborated this testimony and added strong evidence of her own. The lady from the Minories recounted a successful course of treatment under which she had placed her own husband, who, from manifesting one month after marriage unequivocal symptoms of the tiger, had by this means become subdued into a perfect lamb. Another lady recounted her own personal struggle and final triumph, in the course whereof she had found it necessary to call in her mother and two aunts, and to weep incessantly night and day for six weeks. A third, who in the general confusion could secure no other listener, fastened herself upon a young woman still unmarried who happened to be amongst them, and conjured her as she valued her own peace of mind and happiness to profit by this solemn occasion, to take example from the weakness of Mrs. Quilp, and from that time forth to direct her whole thoughts to taming and subduing the rebellious spirit of man. The noise was at its height, and half the company had elevated their voices into a perfect shriek in order to drown the voices of the other half, when Mrs. Jiniwin was seen to change colour and shake her forefinger stealthily, as if exhorting them to silence. Then, and not until then, Daniel Quilp himself, the cause and occasion of all this clamour, was observed to be in the room, looking on and listening with profound attention.

"Go on, ladies, go on," said Daniel. "Mrs. Quilp, pray ask the ladies to stop to supper, and have a couple of lobsters and something light and palatable."

"I—I—didn't ask them to tea, Quilp," stammered his wife. "It's quite an accident."

"So much the better, Mrs. Quilp; these accidental parties are always the pleasantest," said the dwarf, rubbing his hands so hard that he seemed to be engaged in manufacturing, of the dirt with which they were encrusted, little charges for popguns. "What! Not going, ladies, you are not going, surely!"

His fair enemies tossed their heads slightly as they sought their respective bonnets and shawls, but left all verbal contention to Mrs. Jiniwin, who finding herself in the position of champion, made a faint struggle to sustain the character.

"And why *not* stop to supper, Quilp," said the old lady, "if my daughter had a mind?"

"To be sure," rejoined Daniel. "Why not?"

"There's nothing dishonest or wrong in a supper, I hope?" said Mrs. Jiniwin.

"Surely not," returned the dwarf. "Why should there be? Nor anything unwholesome either, unless there's lobster-salad or prawns, which I'm told are not good for digestion."

"And you wouldn't like *your* wife to be attacked with that, or anything else that would make her uneasy, would you?" said Mrs. Jiniwin.

"Not for a score of worlds," replied the dwarf with a grin. "Not even to have a score of mothers-in-law at the same time—and what a blessing that would be!"

"My daughter's your wife, Mr. Quilp, certainly," said the old lady with a giggle, meant for satirical and to imply that he needed to be reminded of the fact; "your wedded wife."

"So she is, certainly. So she is," observed the dwarf.

"And she has a right to do as she likes, I hope, Quilp," said the old lady trembling, partly with anger and partly with a secret fear of her impish son-in-law.

"Hope she has!" he replied. "Oh! Don't you know she has? Don't you know she has, Mrs. Jiniwin?"

"I know she ought to have, Quilp, and would have, if she was of my way of thinking."

"Why an't you of your mother's way of thinking, my dear?" said the dwarf, turning round and addressing his wife, "why don't you always imitate your mother, my dear? She's the ornament of her sex—your father said so every day of his life. I am sure he did."

"Her father was a blessed creetur, Quilp, and worth twenty thousand of some people," said Mrs. Jiniwin; "twenty hundred million thousand."

"I should like to have known him," remarked the dwarf. "I dare say he was a blessed creature then; but I'm sure he is now. It was a happy release. I believe he had suffered a long time?"

The old lady gave a gasp, but nothing came of it; Quilp resumed, with the same malice in his eye and the same sarcastic politeness on his tongue.

"You look ill, Mrs. Jiniwin; I know you have been exciting yourself too much—talking perhaps, for it is your weakness. Go to bed. Do go to bed."

"I shall go when I please, Quilp, and not before."

"But please to go now. Do please to go now," said the dwarf.

The old woman looked angrily at him, but retreated as he advanced, and falling back before him, suffered him to shut the door upon her and bolt her out among the guests, who were by this time crowding down stairs. Being left alone with his wife, who sat trembling in a corner with her eyes fixed upon the ground, the little man planted himself before her, and folding his arms looked steadily at her for a long time without speaking.

"Mrs. Quilp," he said at last.

"Yes, Quilp," she replied meekly.

Instead of pursuing the theme he had in his mind, Quilp folded his arms again, and looked at her more sternly than before, while she averted her eyes and kept them on the ground.

"Mrs. Quilp."

"Yes, Quilp."

"If ever you listen to these beldames again, I'll bite you."

With this laconic threat, which he accompanied with a snarl that gave him the appearance of being particularly in earnest, Mr. Quilp bade her clear the teaboard away, and bring the rum. The spirit being set before him in a huge case-bottle, which had originally come out of some ship's locker, he ordered cold water and the box of cigars; and these being supplied, he settled himself in an arm-chair with his large head and face squeezed up against the back, and his little legs planted on the table.

"Now, Mrs. Quilp," he said; "I feel in a smoking humour, and shall probably blaze away all night. But sit where you are, if you please, in case I want you."

His wife returned no other reply than the customary "Yes, Quilp," and the small lord of the creation took his first cigar and mixed his first glass of grog. The sun went down and the stars peeped out, the Tower turned from its own proper colours to grey and from grey to black, the room became perfectly dark and the end of the cigar a deep fiery red, but still Mr. Quilp went on smoking and drinking in the same position, and staring listlessly out of the window with the dog-like smile always on his face, save when Mrs. Quilp made some involuntary movement of restlessness or fatigue; and then it expanded into a grin of delight.

CHAPTER V

WHETHER Mr. Quilp took any sleep by snatches of a few winks at a time, or whether he sat with his eyes wide open all night long, certain it is that he kept his cigar alight, and kindled every fresh one from the ashes of that which was nearly consumed, without requiring the assistance of a candle. Nor did the striking of the clocks, hour after hour, appear to inspire him with any sense of drowsiness or any natural desire to go to rest, but rather to increase his wakefulness, which he showed, at every such indication of the progress of the night, by a suppressed cackling in his throat, and a motion of his shoulders, like one who laughs heartily but at the same time slyly and by stealth.

At length the day broke, and poor Mrs. Quilp, shivering with the cold of early morning and harassed by fatigue and want of sleep, was discovered sitting patiently on her chair, raising her eyes at intervals in mute appeal to the compassion and clemency of her lord, and gently reminding him by an occasional cough that she was still unpardoned and that her penance had been of long duration. But her dwarfish spouse still smoked his cigar and drank his rum without heeding her; and it was not until the sun had some time risen, and the activity and noise of city day were rife in the street, that he deigned to recognise her presence by any word or sign. He might not have done so even then, but for certain impatient tappings at the door which seemed to denote that some pretty hard knuckles were actively engaged upon the other side.

"Why dear me!" he said looking round with a malicious grin, "it's day! Open the door, sweet Mrs. Quilp!"

His obedient wife withdrew the bolt, and her lady mother entered.

Now, Mrs. Jiniwin bounced into the room with great impetuosity; for, supposing her son-in-law to be still a-bed, she had come to relieve her feelings by pronouncing a strong opinion upon his general conduct and character. Seeing that he was up and dressed, and that the room appeared to have been occupied ever since she quitted it on the previous evening, she stopped short, in some embarrassment.

Nothing escaped the hawk's eye of the ugly little man, who, perfectly understanding what passed in the old lady's mind, turned uglier still in the fulness of his satisfaction, and bade her good morning, with a leer of triumph.

"Why, Betsy," said the old woman, "you haven't been a—you don't mean to say you've been a——"

"Sitting up all night?" said Quilp, supplying the conclusion of the sentence. "Yes she has!"

"All night!" cried Mrs. Jiniwin.

"Ay, all night. Is the dear old lady deaf?" said Quilp, with a smile of which a frown was part. "Who says man and wife are bad company? Ha ha! The time has flown."

"You're a brute!" exclaimed Mrs. Jiniwin.

"Come come," said Quilp, wilfully misunderstanding her, of course, "you mustn't call her names. She's married now, you know. And though she *did* beguile the time and keep me from my bed, you must not be so tenderly careful of me as to be out of humour with her. Bless you for a dear old lady. Here's your health!"

"I am *much* obliged to you," returned the old woman, testifying by a certain restlessness in her hands a vehement desire to shake her matronly fist at her son-in-law. "Oh! I'm very much obliged to you!"

"Grateful soul!" cried the dwarf. "Mrs. Quilp."

"Yes, Quilp," said the timid sufferer.

"Help your mother to get breakfast, Mrs. Quilp. I am going to the wharf this morning—the earlier, the better, so be quick."

Mrs. Jiniwin made a faint demonstration of rebellion by sitting down in a chair near the door and folding her arms as if in a resolute determination to do nothing. But a few whispered words from her daughter, and a kind inquiry from her son-in-law whether she felt faint, with a hint that there was abundance of cold water in the next apartment, routed these symptoms effectually, and she applied herself to the prescribed preparations with sullen diligence.

While they were in progress, Mr. Quilp withdrew to the adjoining room, and, turning back his coat-collar, proceeded to smear his countenance with a damp towel of very unwholesome appearance, which made his complexion rather more cloudy than it was before. But, while he was thus engaged, his caution and inquisitiveness did not forsake him, for with a face as sharp and cunning as ever, he often stopped, even in this short process, and stood listening for any conversation in the next room, of which he might be the theme.

"Ah!" he said after a short effort of attention, "it was not the towel over my ears, I thought it wasn't. I'm a little hunchy villain and a monster, am I, Mrs. Jiniwin? Oh!"

The pleasure of this discovery called up the old doglike smile in full force. When he had quite done with it, he shook himself in a very doglike manner, and rejoined the ladies.

Mr. Quilp now walked up to the front of a looking-glass, and was standing there putting on his neckerchief, when Mrs. Jiniwin, happening to be behind him, could not resist the inclination she felt to shake her fist at her tyrant son-in-law. It was the gesture of an instant, but as she did so and accompanied the action with a menacing look, she met his eye in the glass, catching her in the very act. The same glance at the mirror conveyed to her the reflection of a horribly grotesque and distorted face with the tongue lolling out; and the next instant the dwarf, turning about with a perfectly bland and placid look, inquired in a tone of great affection,

"How are you now, my dear old darling?"

Slight and ridiculous as the incident was, it made him appear such a little fiend, and withal such a keen and knowing one, that the old woman felt too much afraid of him to utter a single word, and suffered herself to be led with extraordinary politeness to the breakfast-table. Here he by no means diminished the impression he had just produced, for he ate hard eggs, shell and all, devoured gigantic prawns with the heads and tails on, chewed tobacco and water-cresses at the same time and with extraordinary greediness, drank boiling tea without winking, bit his fork and spoon till they bent again, and in short performed so many horrifying and uncommon acts that the women were nearly frightened out of their wits, and began to doubt if he were really a human creature. At last, having gone through these proceedings and many others which were equally a part of his system, Mr. Quilp left them, reduced to a very obedient and humbled state, and betook himself to the river-side, where he took boat for the wharf on which he had bestowed his name.

It was flood tide when Daniel Quilp sat himself down in the wherry to cross to the opposite shore. A fleet of barges were coming lazily on, some sideways, some head first, some stern first; all in a wrong-headed, dogged, obstinate way, bumping up against the larger craft, running under the bows of steamboats, getting into every kind of nook and corner where they had no business, and being crunched on all sides like so many walnut shells; while each with its pair of long sweeps struggling and splashing in the water looked like some lumbering fish in pain. In some of the vessels at anchor all hands were busily engaged in coiling ropes, spreading out sails to dry, taking in or discharging their cargoes; in others no life was visible but two or three tarry boys, and perhaps a barking dog running to and fro upon the deck or scrambling up to look over the side and bark the louder for the view. Coming slowly on through the forests of masts was a great steam ship, beating the water in short impatient strokes with her heavy paddles as though she wanted room to breathe, and advancing in her huge bulk like a sea monster among the minnows of the Thames. On either hand were long black tiers of colliers; between them vessels slowly working out of harbour with sails glistening in the sun, and creaking noise on board, re-echoed from a hundred quarters. The water and all upon it was in active motion, dancing and buoyant and bubbling up; while the old grey Tower and piles of building on the shore, with many a church-spire shooting up between, looked coldly on, and seemed to disdain their chafing, restless neighbour.

Daniel Quilp, who was not much affected by a bright morning save in so far as it spared him the trouble of carrying an umbrella, caused himself to be put ashore hard by the wharf, and proceeded thither through a narrow lane which, partaking of the amphibious character of its frequenters, had as much water as mud in its composition, and a very liberal supply of both. Arrived at his destination, the first object that presented itself to his view was a pair of very imperfectly shod feet elevated in the air with the soles upwards, which remarkable appearance was referable to the boy, who being of an eccentric spirit and having a natural taste for tumbling, was now standing on his head and contemplating the aspect of the river under these uncommon circumstances. He was speedily brought on his heels by the sound of his master's voice, and as soon as his head was in its right position, Mr. Quilp, to speak expressively in the absence of a better verb, "punched it" for him.

"Come, you let me alone," said the boy, parrying Quilp's hand with both his elbows alternately. "You'll get something you won't like if you don't, and so I tell you."

"You dog," snarled Quilp, "I'll beat you with an iron rod, I'll scratch you with a rusty nail, I'll pinch your eyes, if you talk to me— I will."

With these threats he clenched his hand again, and dexterously diving in between the elbows and catching the boy's head as it dodged from side to side, gave it three or four good hard knocks. Having now carried his point and insisted on it, he left off.

"You won't do it again," said the boy, nodding his head and drawing back, with the elbows ready in case of the worst; "now——"

"Stand still, you dog," said Quilp. "I won't do it again, because I've done it as often as I want. Here. Take the key."

"Why don't you hit one of your size?" said the boy approaching very slowly.

"Where is there one of my size, you dog?" returned Quilp. "Take the key, or I'll brain you with it"—indeed he gave him a smart tap with the handle as he spoke. "Now, open the counting-house."

The boy sulkily complied, muttering at first, but desisting when he looked round and saw that Quilp was following him with a steady look. And here it may be remarked, that between this boy and the dwarf there existed a strange kind of mutual liking. How born or bred, or how nourished upon blows and threats on one side, and retorts and defiances on the other, is not to the purpose. Quilp would certainly suffer nobody to contradict him but the boy, and the boy would assuredly not have submitted to be so knocked about by anybody but Quilp, when he had the power to run away at any time he chose.

"Now," said Quilp, passing into the wooden counting-house, "you mind the wharf. Stand upon your head again, and I'll cut one of your feet off."

The boy made no answer, but directly Quilp shut himself in, stood on his head before the door, then walked on his hands to the back and stood on his head there, and then to the opposite side and repeated the performance. There were indeed four sides to the counting-house, but he avoided that one where the window was, deeming it probable that Quilp would be looking out of it. This was prudent, for in point of fact the dwarf, knowing his disposition, was lying in wait at a little distance from the sash armed with a large piece of wood, which, being rough and jagged and studded in many parts with broken nails, might possibly have hurt him.

It was a dirty little box, this counting-house, with nothing in it but an old ricketty desk and two stools, a hat-peg, an ancient almanack, an inkstand with no ink and the stump of one pen, and an eight-day clock which hadn't gone for eighteen years at least, and of which the minute-hand had been twisted off for a tooth-pick. Daniel Quilp pulled his hat over his brows, climbed on to the desk (which had a flat top), and stretching his short length upon it went to sleep with the ease of an old practitioner; intending, no doubt, to compensate himself for the deprivation of last night's rest, by a long and sound nap.

Sound it might have been, but long it was not, for he had not been asleep a quarter of an hour when the boy opened the door and thrust in his head, which was like a bundle of badly-picked oakum. Quilp was a light sleeper and started up directly.

"Here's somebody for you," said the boy.

"Who?"

"I don't know."

"Ask!" said Quilp, seizing the trifle of wood before mentioned and throwing it at him with such dexterity that it was well the boy disappeared before it reached the spot on which he had stood. "Ask, you dog."

Not caring to venture within range of such missiles again, the boy discreetly sent in his stead the first cause of the interruption, who now presented herself at the door.

"What, Nelly!" cried Quilp.

"Yes,"—said the child, hesitating whether to enter or retreat, for the dwarf just roused, with his dishevelled hair hanging all about him and a yellow handkerchief over his head, was something fearful to behold; "it's only me, sir."

"Come in," said Quilp, without getting off the desk. "Come in. Stay. Just look out into the yard, and see whether there's a boy standing on his head."

"No, sir," replied Nell. "He's on his feet."

"You're sure he is?" said Quilp. "Well. Now, come in and shut the door. What's your message, Nelly?"

The child handed him a letter; Mr. Quilp, without changing his position further than to turn over a little more on his side and rest his chin on his hand, proceeded to make himself acquainted with its contents.

CHAPTER VI

LITTLE NELL stood timidly by, with her eyes raised to the countenance of Mr. Quilp as he read the letter, plainly showing by her looks that while she entertained some fear and distrust of the little man, she was much inclined to laugh at his uncouth appearance and grotesque attitude. And yet there was visible on the part of the child a painful anxiety for his reply, and a consciousness of his power to render it disagreeable or distressing, which was strongly at variance with this impulse and restrained it more effectually than she could possibly have done by any efforts of her own.

That Mr. Quilp was himself perplexed, and that in no small degree, by the contents of the letter, was sufficiently obvious. Before he had got through the first two or three lines he began to open his eyes very wide and to frown most horribly, the next two or three caused him to scratch his head in an uncommonly vicious manner, and when he came to the conclusion he gave a long dismal whistle indicative of surprise and dismay. After folding and laying it down beside him, he bit the nails of all his ten fingers with extreme voracity; and taking it up sharply, read it again. The second perusal was to all appearance as unsatisfactory as the first, and plunged him into a profound reverie from which he awakened to another assault upon his nails and a long stare at the child, who with her eyes turned towards the ground awaited his further pleasure.

"Halloa here!" he said at length, in a voice, and with a suddenness, which made the child start as though a gun had been fired off at her ear. "Nelly!"

"Yes, sir."

"Do you know what's inside this letter, Nell?"

"No, sir!"

"Are you sure, quite sure, quite certain, upon your soul?"

"Quite sure, sir."

"Do you wish you may die if you do know, hey?" said the dwarf.

"Indeed I don't know," returned the child.

"Well!" muttered Quilp as he marked her earnest look. "I believe you. Humph! Gone already? Gone in four-and-twenty hours! What the devil has he done with it, that's the mystery!"

This reflection set him scratching his head and biting his nails once more. While he was thus employed his features gradually relaxed into what was with him a cheerful smile, but which in any other man would have been a ghastly grin of pain, and when the child looked up again she found that he was regarding her with extraordinary favour and complacency.

"You look very pretty to-day, Nelly, charmingly pretty. Are you tired, Nelly?"

"No, sir. I'm in a hurry to get back, for he will be anxious while I am away."

"There's no hurry, little Nell, no hurry at all," said Quilp. "How should you like to be my number two, Nelly?"

"To be what, sir?"

"My number two, Nelly, my second, my Mrs. Quilp," said the dwarf.

The child looked frightened, but seemed not to understand him, which Mr. Quilp observing, hastened to explain his meaning more distinctly.

"To be Mrs. Quilp the second, when Mrs. Quilp the first is dead, sweet Nell," said Quilp, wrinkling up his eyes and luring her towards him with his bent forefinger, "to be my wife, my little cherry-cheeked, red-lipped wife. Say that Mrs. Quilp lives five years, or only four, you'll be just the proper age for me. Ha ha! Be a good girl, Nelly, a very good girl, and see if one of these days you don't come to be Mrs. Quilp of Tower Hill."

So far from being sustained and stimulated by this delightful prospect, the child shrank from him in great agitation, and trembled violently. Mr. Quilp, either because frightening anybody afforded him a constitutional delight, or because it was pleasant to contemplate the death of Mrs. Quilp number one, and the elevation of Mrs. Quilp number two to her post and title, or because he was determined for purposes of his own to be agreeable and good-humoured at that particular time, only laughed and feigned to take no heed of her alarm.

"You shall come with me to Tower Hill, and see Mrs. Quilp that is, directly," said the dwarf. "She's very fond of you, Nell, though not so fond as I am. You shall come home with me."

"I must go back indeed," said the child. "He told me to return directly I had the answer."

"But you haven't it, Nelly," retorted the dwarf, "and won't have it, and can't have it, until I have been home, so you see that to do your errand you must go with me. Reach me yonder hat, my dear, and we'll go directly." With that, Mr. Quilp suffered himself to roll gradually off the desk until his short legs touched the ground, when he got upon them and led the way from the counting-house to the wharf outside, when the first objects that presented themselves were the boy who had stood on his head and another young gentleman of about his own stature, rolling in the mud together, locked in a tight embrace, and cuffing each other with mutual heartiness.

"It's Kit!" cried Nelly, clasping her hands, "poor Kit who came with me! oh pray stop them, Mr. Quilp!"

"I'll stop 'em," cried Quilp, diving into the little counting-house and returning with a thick stick, "I'll stop 'em. Now, my boys, fight away. I'll fight you both. I'll take both of you, both together, both together!"

With which defiances the dwarf flourished his cudgel, and dancing round the combatants and treading upon them and skipping over them, in a kind of frenzy, laid about him, now on one and now on the other, in a most desperate manner, always aiming at their heads and

dealing such blows as none but the veriest little savage would have
inflicted. This being warmer work than they had calculated upon,
speedily cooled the courage of the belligerents, who scrambled to
their feet and called for quarter.

"I'll beat you to a pulp, you dogs," said Quilp, vainly endeavouring to get near either of them for a parting blow. "I'll bruise you till
you're copper-coloured, I'll break your faces till you haven't a profile between you, I will."

"Come, you drop that stick or it'll be worse for you," said his boy,
dodging round him and watching an opportunity to rush in; "you
drop that stick."

"Come a little nearer, and I'll drop it on your skull, you dog,"
said Quilp with gleaming eyes; "a little nearer—nearer yet."

But the boy declined the invitation until his master was apparently a little off his guard, when he darted in and seizing the weapon
tried to wrest it from his grasp. Quilp, who was as strong as a lion,
easily kept his hold until the boy was tugging at it with his utmost
power, when he suddenly let it go and sent him reeling backwards,
so that he fell violently upon his head. The success of this manœuvre
tickled Mr. Quilp beyond description, and he laughed and stamped
upon the ground as at a most irresistible jest.

"Never mind," said the boy, nodding his head and rubbing it at
the same time; "you see if ever I offer to strike anybody again
because they say you're a uglier dwarf than can be seen anywheres
for a penny, that's all."

"Do you mean to say, I'm not, you dog?" returned Quilp.

"No!" retorted the boy.

"Then what do you fight on my wharf for, you villain?" said
Quilp.

"Because he said so," replied the boy, pointing to Kit, "not because you an't."

"Then why did he say," bawled Kit, "that Miss Nelly was ugly,
and that she and my master was obliged to do whatever his master
liked? Why did he say that?"

"He said what he did because he's a fool, and you said what you
did because you're very wise and clever—almost too clever to live,
unless you're very careful of yourself, Kit," said Quilp, with great
suavity in his manner, but still more of quiet malice about his eyes
and mouth. "Here's sixpence for you, Kit. Always speak the truth.
At all times, Kit, speak the truth. Lock the counting-house, you dog,
and bring me the key."

The other boy, to whom this order was addressed, did as he was
told, and was rewarded for his partisanship in behalf of his master,
by a dexterous rap on the nose with the key, which brought the
water into his eyes. Then Mr. Quilp departed with the child and Kit
in a boat, and the boy revenged himself by dancing on his head at
intervals on the extreme verge of the wharf, during the whole time
they crossed the river.

There was only Mrs. Quilp at home, and she, little expecting the return of her lord, was just composing herself for a refreshing slumber when the sound of his footsteps roused her. She had barely time to seem to be occupied in some needle-work, when he entered, accompanied by the child; having left Kit down stairs.

"Here's Nelly Trent, dear Mrs. Quilp," said her husband. "A glass of wine, my dear, and a biscuit, for she has had a long walk. She'll sit with you, my soul, while I write a letter."

Mrs. Quilp looked tremblingly in her spouse's face to know what this unusual courtesy might portend, and obedient to the summons she saw in his gesture, followed him into the next room.

"Mind what I say to you," whispered Quilp. "See if you can get out of her anything about her grandfather, or what they do, or how they live, or what he tells her. I've my reasons for knowing, if I can. You women talk more freely to one another than you do to us, and you have a soft, mild way with you that'll win upon her. Do you hear?"

"Yes, Quilp."

"Go, then. What's the matter now?"

"Dear Quilp," faltered his wife, "I love the child—if you *could* do without making me deceive her——"

The dwarf muttering a terrible oath looked round as if for some weapon with which to inflict condign punishment upon his disobedient wife. The submissive little woman hurriedly entreated him not to be angry, and promised to do as he bade her.

"Do you hear me," whispered Quilp, nipping and pinching her arm; "worm yourself into her secrets; I know you can. I'm listening, recollect. If you're not sharp enough I'll creak the door, and woe betide you if I have to creak it much. Go!"

Mrs. Quilp departed according to order, and her amiable husband, ensconcing himself behind the partly opened door, and applying his ear close to it, began to listen with a face of great craftiness and attention.

Poor Mrs. Quilp was thinking, however, in what manner to begin or what kind of inquiries she could make; and it was not until the door, creaking in a very urgent manner, warned her to proceed without further consideration, that the sound of her voice was heard.

"How very often you have come backwards and forwards lately to Mr. Quilp, my dear."

"I have said so to grandfather, a hundred times," returned Nell innocently.

"And what has he said to that?"

"Only sighed, and dropped his head, and seemed so sad and wretched that if you could have seen him I am sure you must have cried; you could not have helped it more than I, I know. How that door creaks!"

"It often does," returned Mrs. Quilp, with an uneasy glance towards it. "But your grandfather—he used not to be so wretched?"

"Oh no!" said the child eagerly, "so different! we were once so happy and he so cheerful and contented! You cannot think what a sad change has fallen on us since."

"I am very, very sorry, to hear you speak like this, my dear!" said Mrs. Quilp. And she spoke the truth.

"Thank you," returned the child, kissing her cheek, "you are always kind to me, and it is a pleasure to talk to you. I can speak to no one else about him, but poor Kit. I am very happy still, I ought to feel happier perhaps than I do, but you cannot think how it grieves me sometimes to see him alter so."

"He'll alter again, Nelly," said Mrs. Quilp, "and be what he was before."

"Oh, if God would only let that come about!" said the child with streaming eyes; "but it is a long time now, since he first began to—I thought I saw that door moving!"

"It's the wind," said Mrs. Quilp faintly. "Began to——?"

"To be so thoughtful and dejected, and to forget our old way of spending the time in the long evenings," said the child. "I used to read to him by the fireside, and he sat listening, and when I stopped and we began to talk, he told me about my mother, and how she once looked and spoke just like me when she was a little child. Then, he used to take me on his knee, and try to make me understand that she was not lying in her grave, but had flown to a beautiful country beyond the sky, where nothing died or ever grew old—we were very happy once!"

"Nelly, Nelly!"—said the poor woman, "I can't bear to see one as young as you, so sorrowful. Pray don't cry."

"I do so very seldom," said Nell, "but I have kept this to myself a long time, and I am not quite well, I think, for the tears come into my eyes and I cannot keep them back. I don't mind telling you my grief, for I know you will not tell it to any one again."

Mrs. Quilp turned away her head and made no answer.

"Then," said the child, "we often walked in the fields and among the green trees, and when we came home at night, we liked it better for being tired, and said what a happy place it was. And if it was dark and rather dull, we used to say, what did it matter to us, for it only made us remember our last walk with greater pleasure, and look forward to our next one. But now we never have these walks, and though it is the same house it is darker and much more gloomy than it used to be, indeed!"

She paused here, but though the door creaked more than once, Mrs. Quilp said nothing.

"Mind you don't suppose," said the child earnestly, "that grandfather is less kind to me than he was. I think he loves me better every day, and is kinder and more affectionate than he was the day before. You do not know how fond he is of me!"

"I am sure he loves you dearly," said Mrs. Quilp.

"Indeed, indeed he does!" cried Nell, "as dearly as I love him. But I have not told you the greatest change of all, and this you must never breathe again to any one. He has no sleep or rest, but that which he takes by day in his easy chair; for every night and nearly all night long he is away from home."

"Nelly!"

"Hush!" said the child, laying her finger on her lip and looking round. "When he comes home in the morning, which is generally just before day, I let him in. Last night he was very late, and it was quite light. I saw that his face was deadly pale, that his eyes were bloodshot, and that his legs trembled as he walked. When I had gone to bed again, I heard him groan. I got up and ran back to him, and heard him say, before he knew that I was there, that he could not bear his life much longer, and if it was not for the child, would wish to die. What shall I do! Oh! what shall I do!"

The fountains of her heart were opened; the child, overpowered by the weight of her sorrows and anxieties, by the first confidence she had ever shown, and the sympathy with which her little tale had been received, hid her face in the arms of her helpless friend, and burst into a passion of tears.

In a few moments Mr. Quilp returned, and expressed the utmost surprise to find her in this condition, which he did very naturally and with admirable effect, for that kind of acting had been rendered familiar to him by long practice, and he was quite at home in it.

"She's tired, you see, Mrs. Quilp," said the dwarf, squinting in a hideous manner to imply that his wife was to follow his lead. "It's a long way from her home to the wharf, and then she was alarmed to see a couple of young scoundrels fighting, and was timorous on the water besides. All this together has been too much for her. Poor Nell!"

Mr. Quilp unintentionally adopted the very best means he could have devised for the recovery of his young visitor, by patting her on the head. Such an application from any other hand might not have produced a remarkable effect, but the child shrank so quickly from his touch and felt such an instinctive desire to get out of his reach, that she rose directly and declared herself ready to return.

"But you'd better wait, and dine with Mrs. Quilp and me," said the dwarf.

"I have been away too long, sir, already," returned Nell, drying her eyes.

"Well," said Mr. Quilp, "if you will go, you will, Nelly. Here's the note. It's only to say that I shall see him to-morrow or maybe next day, and that I couldn't do that little business for him this morning. Good-bye, Nelly. Here, you sir; take care of her, d'ye hear?"

Kit, who appeared at the summons, deigned to make no reply to so needless an injunction, and after staring at Quilp in a threatening manner as if he doubted whether he might not have been the cause of Nelly shedding tears, and felt more than half-disposed to revenge the fact upon him on the mere suspicion, turned about and followed his young mistress, who had by this time taken her leave of Mrs. Quilp and departed.

"You're a keen questioner, an't you, Mrs. Quilp?" said the dwarf, turning upon her as soon as they were left alone.

"What more could I do?" returned his wife mildly.

"What more could you do?" sneered Quilp, "couldn't you have done something less? couldn't you have done what you had to do, without appearing in your favourite part of the crocodile, you minx?"

"I am very sorry for the child, Quilp," said his wife. "Surely I've done enough. I've led her on to tell her secret when she supposed we were alone; and you were by, God forgive me."

"You led her on! You did a great deal truly!" said Quilp. "What did I tell you about making me creak the door? It's lucky for you that from what she let fall, I've got the clue I want, for if I hadn't, I'd have visited the failure upon you, I can tell you."

Mrs. Quilp being fully persuaded of this, made no reply. Her husband added with some exultation,

"But you may thank your fortunate stars—the same stars that made you Mrs. Quilp—you may thank them that I'm upon the old gentleman's track, and have got a new light. So let me hear no more about this matter now or at any other time, and don't get anything too nice for dinner, for I shan't be home to it."

So saying, Mr. Quilp put his hat on and took himself off, and Mrs. Quilp, who was afflicted beyond measure by the recollection of the part she had just acted, shut herself up in her chamber, and smothering her head in the bed-clothes bemoaned her fault more bitterly than many less tender-hearted persons would have mourned a much greater offence; for, in the majority of cases, conscience is an elastic and very flexible article, which will bear a deal of stretching and adapt itself to a great variety of circumstances. Some people by prudent management and leaving it off piece by piece like a flannel waistcoat in warm weather, even contrive, in time, to dispense with it altogether; but there be others who can assume the garment and throw it off at pleasure; and this, being the greatest and most convenient improvement, is the one most in vogue.

CHAPTER VII

"Fred," said Mr. Swiveller, "remember the once popular melody of 'Begone dull care;' fan the sinking flame of hilarity with the wing of friendship; and pass the rosy wine."

Mr. Richard Swiveller's apartments were in the neighbourhood of Drury Lane, and in addition to this conveniency of situation had the advantage of being over a tobacconist's shop, so that he was enabled to procure a refreshing sneeze at any time by merely stepping out upon the staircase, and was saved the trouble and expense of maintaining a snuff-box. It was in these apartments that Mr.

Swiveller made use of the expressions above recorded for the consolation and encouragement of his desponding friend; and it may not be uninteresting or improper to remark that even these brief observations partook in a double sense of the figurative and poetical character of Mr. Swiveller's mind, as the rosy wine was in fact represented by one glass of cold gin-and-water, which was replenished as occasion required from a bottle and jug upon the table, and was passed from one to another, in a scarcity of tumblers which, as Mr. Swiveller's was a bachelor's establishment, may be acknowledged without a blush. By a like pleasant fiction his single chamber was always mentioned in the plural number. In its disengaged times, the tobacconist had announced it in his window as "apartments" for a single gentleman, and Mr. Swiveller, following up the hint, never failed to speak of it as his rooms, his lodgings, or his chambers, conveying to his hearers a notion of indefinite space, and leaving their imaginations to wander through long suites of lofty halls, at pleasure.

In this flight of fancy, Mr. Swiveller was assisted by a deceptive piece of furniture, in reality a bedstead, but in semblance a bookcase, which occupied a prominent situation in his chamber and seemed to defy suspicion and challenge inquiry. There is no doubt that by day Mr. Swiveller firmly believed this secret convenience to be a bookcase and nothing more; that he closed his eyes to the bed, resolutely denied the existence of the blankets, and spurned the bolster from his thoughts. No word of its real use, no hint of its mighty service, no allusion to its peculiar properties, had ever passed between him and his most intimate friends. Implicit faith in the deception was the first article of his creed. To be the friend of Swiveller you must reject all circumstantial evidence, all reason, observation, and experience, and repose a blind relief in the bookcase. It was his pet weakness, and he cherished it.

"Fred!" said Mr. Swiveller, finding that his former adjuration had been productive of no effect. "Pass the rosy."

Young Trent with an impatient gesture pushed the glass towards him, and fell again into the moody attitude from which he had been unwillingly roused.

"I'll give you, Fred," said his friend, stirring the mixture, "a little sentiment appropriate to the occasion. Here's May the——"

"Pshaw!" interposed the other. "You worry me to death with your chattering. You can be merry under any circumstances."

"Why, Mr. Trent," returned Dick, "there is a proverb which talks about being merry and wise. There are some people who can be merry and can't be wise, and some who can be wise (or think they can) and can't be merry. I'm one of the first sort. If the proverb's a good 'un, I suppose it's better to keep to half of it than none; at all events I'd rather be merry and not wise, than like you, neither one nor t'other."

"Bah!" muttered his friend, peevishly.

"With all my heart," said Mr. Swiveller. "In the polite circles I believe this sort of thing isn't usually said to a gentleman in his own apartments, but never mind that. Make yourself at home." Adding to this retort an observation to the effect that his friend appeared to be rather "cranky" in point of temper, Richard Swiveller finished the rosy and applied himself to the composition of another glassful, in which, after tasting it with great relish, he proposed a toast to an imaginary company.

"Gentlemen, I'll give you, if you please, Success to the ancient family of the Swivellers, and good luck to Mr. Richard in particular— Mr. Richard, gentlemen," said Dick with great emphasis, "who spends all his money on his friends, and is *Bah!'d* for his pains. Hear, hear!"

"Dick!" said the other, returning to his seat after having paced the rooms twice or thrice, "will you talk seriously for two minutes, if I show you a way to make your fortune with very little trouble?"

"You've shown me so many," returned Dick; "and nothing has come of any one of 'em but empty pockets——"

"You'll tell a different story of this one, before a very long time is over," said his companion drawing his chair to the table. "You saw my sister Nell?"

"What about her?" returned Dick.

"She has a pretty face, has she not?"

"Why, certainly," replied Dick, "I must say for her that there's not any very strong family likeness between her and you."

"Has she a pretty face?" repeated his friend impatiently.

"Yes," said Dick, "she has a pretty face, a very pretty face. What of that?"

"I'll tell you," returned his friend. "It's very plain that the old man and I will remain at daggers-drawn to the end of our lives, and that I have nothing to expect from him. You see that, I suppose?"

"A bat might see that, with the sun shining," said Dick.

"It's equally plain that the money which the old flint—rot him— first taught me to expect that I should share with her at his death, will all be hers, is it not?"

"I should say it was," replied Dick; "unless the way in which I put the case to him, made an impression. It may have done so. It was powerful, Fred. 'Here is a jolly old grandfather'—that was strong, I thought—very friendly and natural. Did it strike you in that way?"

"It didn't strike *him*," returned the other, "so we needn't discuss it. Now look here. Nell is nearly fourteen."

"Fine girl of her age, but small," observed Richard Swiveller parenthetically.

"If I am to go on, be quiet for one minute," returned Trent, fretting at the very slight interest the other appeared to take in the conversation. "Now I'm coming to the point."

"That's right," said Dick.

"The girl has strong affections, and brought up as she has been, may, at her age, be easily influenced and persuaded. If I take her in hand, I will be bound by a very little coaxing and threatening to bend her to my will. Not to beat about the bush (for the advantages of the scheme would take a week to tell) what's to prevent your marrying her?"

Richard Swiveller, who had been looking over the rim of the tumbler while his companion addressed the foregoing remarks to him with great energy and earnestness of manner, no sooner heard these words than he evinced the utmost consternation, and with difficulty ejaculated the monosyllable,

"What!"

"I say, what's to prevent," repeated the other with a steadiness of manner, of the effect of which upon his companion he was well assured by long experience, "what's to prevent your marrying her?"

"And she's 'nearly fourteen'!" cried Dick.

"I don't mean marrying her now"—returned the brother angrily; "say in two years' time, in three, in four. Does the old man look like a long-liver?"

"He don't look like it," said Dick shaking his head, "but these old people—there's no trusting 'em, Fred. There's an aunt of mine down in Dorsetshire that was going to die when I was eight years old, and hasn't kept her word yet. They're so aggravating, so unprincipled, so spiteful—unless there's apoplexy in the family, Fred, you can't calculate upon 'em, and even then they deceive you just as often as not."

"Look at the worst side of the question then," said Trent as steadily as before, and keeping his eyes upon his friend. "Suppose he lives."

"To be sure," said Dick. "There's the rub."

"I say," resumed his friend, "suppose he lives, and I persuaded, or if the word sounds more feasible, forced Nell to a secret marriage with you. What do you think would come of that?"

"A family and an annual income of nothing, to keep 'em on," said Richard Swiveller after some reflection.

"I tell you," returned the other with an increased earnestness, which, whether it were real or assumed, had the same effect on his companion, "that he lives for her, that his whole energies and thoughts are bound up in her, that he would no more disinherit her for an act of disobedience than he would take me into his favour again for any act of obedience or virtue that I could possibly be guilty of. He could not do it. You or any other man with eyes in his head may see that, if he chooses."

"It seems improbable certainly," said Dick, musing.

"It seems improbable because it is improbable," his friend returned. "If you would furnish him with an additional inducement to forgive you, let there be an irreconcileable breach, a most deadly quarrel, between you and me—let there be a pretence of such a thing, I mean, of course—and he'll do so fast enough. As to Nell, constant dropping will wear away a stone; you know you may trust to me as far as she is concerned. So, whether he lives or dies, what does it come to? That you become the sole inheritor of the wealth of this rich old hunks, that you and I spend it together, and that you get into the bargain a beautiful young wife."

"I suppose there's no doubt about his being rich"—said Dick.

"Doubt! Did you hear what he let fall the other day when we were there? Doubt! What will you doubt next, Dick?"

It would be tedious to pursue the conversation through all its artful windings, or to develop the gradual approaches by which the heart of Richard Swiveller was gained. It is sufficient to know that vanity, interest, poverty, and every spendthrift consideration urged him to look upon the proposal with favour, and that where all other inducements were wanting, the habitual carelessness of his disposition stepped in and still weighed down the scale on the same side. To these impulses must be added the complete ascendancy which his friend had long been accustomed to exercise over him—an ascendancy exerted in the beginning sorely at the expense of the unfortunate Dick's purse and prospects, but still maintained without the slightest relaxation, notwithstanding that Dick suffered for all his friend's vices, and was in nine cases out of ten looked upon as his designing tempter when he was indeed nothing but his thoughtless light-headed tool.

The motives on the other side were something deeper than any which Richard Swiveller entertained or understood, but these being left to their own development, require no present elucidation. The negotiation was concluded very pleasantly, and Mr. Swiveller was in the act of stating in flowery terms that he had no insurmountable objection to marrying anybody plentifully endowed with money or moveables, who could be induced to take him, when he was interrupted in his observations by a knock at the door, and the consequent necessity of crying "Come in."

The door was opened, but nothing came in except a soapy arm and a strong gush of tobacco. The gush of tobacco came from the shop down stairs, and the soapy arm proceeded from the body of a servant girl, who being then and there engaged in cleaning the stairs had just drawn it out of a warm pail to take in a letter, which letter she now held in her hand, proclaiming aloud with that quick perception of surnames peculiar to her class that it was for Mister Snivelling.

Dick looked rather pale and foolish when he glanced at the direction, and still more so when he came to look at the inside, observing that this was one of the inconveniences of being a lady's man, and that it was very easy to talk as they had been talking, but he had quite forgotten her.

"*Her*. Who?" demanded Trent.

"Sophy Wackles," said Dick.

"Who's she?"

"She's all my fancy painted her, sir, that's what she is," said Mr. Swiveller, taking a long pull at "the rosy" and looking gravely at his friend. "She is lovely, she's divine. You know her."

"I remember," said his companion carelessly. "What of her?"

"Why, sir," returned Dick, "between Miss Sophia Wackles and

the humble individual who has now the honour to address you, warm and tender sentiments have been engendered, sentiments of the most honourable and inspiring kind. The Goddess Diana, sir, that calls aloud for the chace, is not more particular in her behaviour than Sophia Wackles; I can tell you that."

"Am I to believe there's anything real in what you say?" demanded his friend; "you don't mean to say that any love-making has been going on?"

"Love-making, yes. Promising, no," said Dick. "There can be no action for breach, that's one comfort. I've never committed myself in writing, Fred."

"And what's in the letter, pray?"

"A reminder, Fred, for to-night—a small party of twenty, making two hundred light fantastic toes in all, supposing every lady and gentleman to have the proper complement. I must go, if it's only to begin breaking off the affair—I'll do it, don't you be afraid. I should like to know whether she left this herself. If she did, unconscious of any bar to her happiness, it's affecting, Fred."

To solve this question, Mr. Swiveller summoned the handmaid and ascertained that Miss Sophy Wackles had indeed left the letter with her own hands; and that she had come accompanied, for decorum's sake no doubt, by a younger Miss Wackles; and that on learning that Mr. Swiveller was at home and being requested to walk up stairs, she was extremely shocked and professed that she would rather die. Mr. Swiveller heard this account with a degree of admiration not altogether consistent with the project in which he had just concurred, but his friend attached very little importance to his behaviour in this respect, probably because he knew that he had influence sufficient to control Richard Swiveller's proceedings in this or any other matter, whenever he deemed it necessary, for the advancement of his own purpose, to exert it.

CHAPTER VIII

BUSINESS disposed of, Mr. Swiveller was inwardly reminded of its being near dinner-time, and to the intent that his health might not be endangered by longer abstinence, despatched a messenger to the nearest eating-house requiring an immediate supply of boiled beef and greens for two. With this demand, however, the eating-house (having experience of its customer) declined to comply, churlishly sending back for answer that if Mr. Swiveller stood in need of beef perhaps he would be so obliging as to come there and eat it, bringing with him, as grace before meat, the amount of a certain small account which had been long outstanding. Not at all intimidated by this rebuff, but rather sharpened in wits and appetite, Mr. Swiveller forwarded the same message to another and more distant eating-

house, adding to it by way of rider that the gentleman was induced
to send so far, not only by the great fame and popularity its beef
had acquired, but in consequence of the extreme toughness of the
beef retailed at the obdurate cook's shop, which rendered it quite
unfit not merely for gentlemanly food but for any human consump-
tion. The good effect of this politic course was demonstrated by the
speedy arrival of a small pewter pyramid, curiously constructed of
platters and covers, whereof the boiled-beef-plates formed the base,
and a foaming quart-pot the apex; the structure being resolved into
its component parts afforded all things requisite and necessary for a
hearty meal, to which Mr. Swiveller and his friend applied themselves
with great keenness and enjoyment.

"May the present moment," said Dick, sticking his fork into a
large carbuncular potato, "be the worst of our lives! I like this plan
of sending 'em with the peel on; there's a charm in drawing a potato
from its native element (if I may so express it) to which the rich and
powerful are strangers. Ah! 'Man wants but little here below, nor
wants that little long!' How true that is!—after dinner."

"I hope the eating-house keeper will want but little and that *he*
may not want that little long," returned his companion; "but I
suspect you've no means of paying for this!"

"I shall be passing presently, and I'll call," said Dick, winking
his eye significantly. "The waiter's quite helpless. The goods are
gone, Fred, and there's an end of it."

In point of fact, it would seem that the waiter felt this wholesome
truth, for when he returned for the empty plates and dishes and was
informed by Mr. Swiveller with dignified carelessness that he would
call and settle when he should be passing presently, he displayed
some perturbation of spirit, and muttered a few remarks about
"payment on delivery," and "no trust," and other unpleasant subjects, but was fain to content himself with inquiring at what hour
it was likely the gentleman would call, in order that being personally
responsible for the beef, greens, and sundries, he might take care to
be in the way at the time. Mr. Swiveller, after mentally calculating his
engagements to a nicety, replied that he should look in at from two
minutes before six to seven minutes past; and the man disappearing
with this feeble consolation, Richard Swiveller took a greasy memor-
andum-book from his pocket and made an entry therein.

"Is that a reminder, in case you should forget to call?" said Trent,
with a sneer.

"Not exactly, Fred," replied the imperturbable Richard, continuing to write with a business-like air, "I enter in this little book the
names of the streets that I can't go down while the shops are open.
This dinner to-day closes Long Acre. I bought a pair of boots in
Great Queen Street last week, and made that no thoroughfare too.
There's only one avenue to the Strand left open now, and I shall
have to stop up that to-night with a pair of gloves. The roads are
closing so fast in every direction, that in about a month's time, unless
my aunt sends me a remittance, I shall have to go three or four

miles out of town to get over the way."

"There's no fear of her failing, in the end?" said Trent.

"Why, I hope not," returned Mr. Swiveller, "but the average number of letters it takes to soften her is six, and this time we have got as far as eight without any effect at all. I'll write another to-morrow morning. I mean to blot it a good deal and shake some water over it out of the pepper-castor, to make it look penitent. 'I'm in such a state of mind that I hardly know what I write'—blot—'if you could see me at this minute shedding tears for my past misconduct' —pepper-castor—'my hand trembles when I think'—blot again—if that don't produce the effect, it's all over."

By this time Mr. Swiveller had finished his entry, and he now replaced his pencil in its little sheath and closed the book, in a perfectly grave and serious frame of mind. His friend discovered that it was time for him to fulfil some other engagement, and Richard Swiveller was accordingly left alone, in company with the rosy wine and his own meditations touching Miss Sophy Wackles.

"It's rather sudden," said Dick shaking his head with a look of infinite wisdom, and running on (as he was accustomed to do) with scraps of verse as if they were only prose in a hurry; "when the heart of a man is depressed with fears, the mist is dispelled when Miss Wackles appears: she's a very nice girl. She's like the red red rose that's newly sprung in June—there's no denying that—she's also like a melody that's sweetly played in tune. It's really very sudden. Not that there's any need, on account of Fred's little sister, to turn cool directly, but it's better not to go too far. If I begin to cool at all I must begin at once, I see that. There's the chance of an action for breach, that's one reason. There's a chance of Sophy's getting another husband, that's another. There's the chance of—no, there's no chance of that, but it's as well to be on the safe side."

This undeveloped consideration was the possibility, which Richard Swiveller sought to conceal even from himself, of his not being proof against the charms of Miss Wackles, and in some unguarded moment, by linking his fortunes to hers for ever, of putting it out of his own power to further the notable scheme to which he had so readily become a party. For all these reasons, he decided to pick a quarrel with Miss Wackles without delay, and casting about for a pretext determined in favour of groundless jealousy. Having made up his mind on this important point, he circulated the glass (from his right hand to his left, and back again) pretty freely, to enable him to act his part with the greater discretion, and then, after making some slight improvements in his toilet, bent his steps towards the spot hallowed by the fair object of his meditations.

This spot was Chelsea, for there Miss Sophia Wackles resided with her widowed mother and two sisters, in conjunction with whom she maintained a very small day-school for young ladies of proportionate dimensions; a circumstance which was made known to the neighbourhood by an oval board over the front first-floor window, whereon appeared in circumambient flourishes the words "Ladies'

Seminary;" and which was further published and proclaimed at intervals between the hours of half-past nine and ten in the morning, by a straggling and solitary young lady of tender years standing on the scraper on the tips of her toes and making futile attempts to reach the knocker with a spelling-book. The several duties of instruction in this establishment were thus discharged. English grammar, composition, geography, and the use of the dumb-bells, by Miss Melissa Wackles; writing, arithmetic, dancing, music, and general fascination, by Miss Sophy Wackles; the art of needle-work, marking, and samplery, by Miss Jane Wackles; corporal punishment, fasting, and other tortures and terrors, by Mrs. Wackles. Miss Melissa Wackles was the eldest daughter, Miss Sophy the next, and Miss Jane the youngest. Miss Melissa might have seen five-and-thirty summers or thereabouts, and verged on the autumnal; Miss Sophy was a fresh, good-humoured, buxom girl of twenty; and Miss Jane numbered scarcely sixteen years. Mrs. Wackles was an excellent but rather venomous old lady of three-score.

To this Ladies' Seminary, then, Richard Swiveller hied, with designs obnoxious to the peace of the fair Sophia, who, arrayed in virgin white, embellished by no ornament but one blushing rose, received him on his arrival, in the midst of very elegant, not to say brilliant preparations; such as the embellishment of the room with the little flower-pots which always stood on the window-sill outside, save in windy weather when they blew into the area; the choice attire of the day-scholars who were allowed to grace the festival; the un-wonted curls of Miss Jane Wackles who had kept her head during the whole of the preceding day screwed up tight in a yellow play-bill; and the solemn gentility and stately bearing of the old lady and her eldest daughter, which struck Mr. Swiveller as being uncommon but made no further impression upon him.

The truth is—and, as there is no accounting for tastes, even a taste so strange as this may be recorded without being looked upon as a wilful and malicious invention—the truth is that neither Mrs. Wackles nor her eldest daughter had at any time greatly favoured the pre-tensions of Mr. Swiveller, being accustomed to make slight mention of him as "a gay young man" and to sigh and shake their heads ominously whenever his name was mentioned. Mr. Swiveller's conduct in respect to Miss Sophy having been of that vague and dilatory kind which is usually looked upon as betokening no fixed matri-monial intentions, the young lady herself began in course of time to deem it highly desirable, that it should be brought to an issue one way or other. Hence she had at last consented to play off against Richard Swiveller a stricken market-gardener known to be ready with his offer on the smallest encouragement, and hence—as this occasion has been specially assigned for the purpose—that great anxiety on her part for Richard Swiveller's presence which had occasioned her to leave the note he has been seen to receive. "If he has any expectations at all or any means of keeping a wife well," said Mrs. Wackles to her eldest daughter, "he'll state 'em to us now or never."—"If he really cares about me," thought Miss Sophy, "he must tell me so, to-night."

But all these sayings and doings and thinkings being unknown to Mr. Swiveller, affected him not in the least; he was debating in his mind how he could best turn jealous, and wishing that Sophy were for that occasion only far less pretty than she was, or that she were her own sister, which would have served his turn as well, when the company came, and among them the market-gardener, whose name was Cheggs. But Mr. Cheggs came not alone or unsupported, for he prudently brought along with him his sister, Miss Cheggs, who making straight to Miss Sophy and taking her by both hands, and kissing her on both cheeks, hoped in an audible whisper that they had not come too early.

"Too early, no!" replied Miss Sophy.

"Oh my dear," rejoined Miss Cheggs in the same whisper as before, "I've been so tormented, so worried, that it's a mercy we were not here at four o'clock in the afternoon. Alick has been in *such* a state of impatience to come! You'd hardly believe that he was dressed before dinner-time and has been looking at the clock and teasing me ever since. It's all your fault, you naughty thing."

Hereupon Miss Sophy blushed, and Mr. Cheggs (who was bashful before ladies) blushed too, and Miss Sophy's mother and sisters, to prevent Mr. Cheggs from blushing more, lavished civilities and attentions upon him, and left Richard Swiveller to take care of himself. Here was the very thing he wanted, here was good cause reason and foundation for pretending to be angry; but having this cause reason and foundation which he had come expressly to see, not expecting to find, Richard Swiveller was angry in sound earnest, and wondered what the devil Cheggs meant by his impudence.

However, Mr. Swiveller had Miss Sophy's hand for the first quadrille (country-dances being low, were utterly proscribed)and so gained an advantage over his rival, who sat despondingly in a corner and contemplated the glorious figure of the young lady as she moved through the mazy dance. Nor was this the only start Mr. Swiveller had of the market-gardener, for determining to show the family what quality of man they trifled with, and influenced perhaps by his late libations, he performed such feats of agility and such spins and twirls as filled the company with astonishment, and in particular caused a very long gentleman who was dancing with a very short scholar, to stand quite transfixed by wonder and admiration. Even Mrs. Wackles forgot for the moment to snub three small young ladies who were inclined to be happy, and could not repress a rising thought that to have such a dancer as that in the family would be a pride indeed.

At this momentous crisis, Miss Cheggs proved herself a vigorous and useful ally, for not confining herself to expressing by scornful smiles a contempt for Mr. Swiveller's accomplishments, she took every opportunity of whispering into Miss Sophy's ear expressions of condolence and sympathy on her being worried by such a ridiculous creature, declaring that she was frightened to death lest Alick should fall upon, and beat him, in the fulness of his wrath, and entreating Miss Sophy to observe how the eyes of the said Alick gleamed with love and fury; passions, it may be observed, which being too much for his eyes rushed into his nose also, and suffused it with a crimson glow.

"You must dance with Miss Cheggs," said Miss Sophy to Dick Swiveller, after she had herself danced twice with Mr. Cheggs and made great show of encouraging his advances. "She's such a nice girl—and her brother's quite delightful."

"Quite delightful is he?" muttered Dick. "Quite delighted too, I should say, from the manner in which he's looking this way."

Here Miss Jane (previously instructed for the purpose) interposed her many curls and whispered her sister to observe how jealous Mr. Cheggs was.

"Jealous! Like his impudence!" said Richard Swiveller.

"His impudence, Mr. Swiveller!" said Miss Jane, tossing her head. "Take care he don't hear you, sir, or you may be sorry for it."

"Oh pray, Jane——" said Miss Sophy.

"Nonsense!" replied her sister. "Why shouldn't Mr. Cheggs be jealous if he likes? I like that, certainly. Mr. Cheggs has as good a right to be jealous as anybody else has, and perhaps he may have a better right soon if he hasn't already. You know best about that, Sophy!"

Though this was a concerted plot between Miss Sophy and her sister, originating in humane intentions and having for its object the inducing Mr. Swiveller to declare himself in time, it failed in its effect; for Miss Jane being one of those young ladies who are prematurely shrill and shrewish, gave such undue importance to her part that Mr. Swiveller retired in dudgeon, resigning his mistress to Mr. Cheggs and conveying a defiance into his looks which that gentleman indignantly returned.

"Did you speak to me, sir?" said Mr. Cheggs, following him into a corner. "Have the kindness to smile, sir, in order that we may not be suspected. Did you speak to me, sir?"

Mr. Swiveller looked with a supercilious smile at Mr. Cheggs's toes, then raised his eyes from them to his ankle, from that to his shin, from that to his knee, and so on very gradually, keeping up his right leg, until he reached his waistcoat, when he raised his eyes from button to button until he reached his chin, and travelling straight up the middle of his nose came at last to his eyes, when he said abruptly,

"No, sir, I didn't."

"Hem!" said Mr. Cheggs, glancing over his shoulder, "have the goodness to smile again, sir. Perhaps you wished to speak to me, sir."

"No, sir, I didn't do that, either."

"Perhaps you may have nothing to say to me *now*, sir," said Mr. Cheggs fiercely.

At these words Richard Swiveller withdrew his eyes from Mr. Cheggs's face, and travelling down the middle of his nose and down his waistcoat and down his right leg, reaching his toes again, and carefully surveyed them; this done, he crossed over, and coming up the other leg and thence approaching by the waistcoat as before, said when he had got to his eyes, "No, sir, I haven't."

"Oh indeed, sir!" said Mr. Cheggs. "I'm glad to hear it. You know where I'm to be found, I suppose, sir, in case you *should* have anything to say to me?"

"I can easily inquire, sir, when I want to know."

"There's nothing more we need say, I believe, sir?"

"Nothing more, sir."—With that they closed the tremendous dialogue by frowning mutually. Mr. Cheggs hastened to tender his hand to Miss Sophy, and Mr. Swiveller sat himself down in a corner in a very moody state.

Hard by this corner, Mrs. Wackles and Miss Wackles were seated, looking on at the dance; and unto Mrs. and Miss Wackles, Miss Cheggs occasionally darted when her partner was occupied with his share of the figure, and made some remark or other which was gall and wormwood to Richard Swiveller's soul. Looking into the eyes of Mrs. and Miss Wackles for encouragement, and sitting very upright and uncomfortable on a couple of hard stools, were two of the day-scholars; and when Miss Wackles smiled, and Mrs. Wackles smiled, the two little girls on the stools sought to curry favour by smiling likewise, in gracious acknowledgment of which attention the old lady frowned them down instantly, and said that if they dared to be guilty of such an impertinence again, they should be sent under convoy to their respective homes. This threat caused one of the young ladies, she being of a weak and trembling temperament, to shed tears, and for this offence they were both filed off immediately, with a dreadful promptitude that struck terror into the souls of all the pupils.

"I've got such news for you," said Miss Cheggs approaching once more, "Alick has been saying such things to Sophy. Upon my word, you know, it's quite serious and in earnest, that's clear."

"What's he been saying, my dear?" demanded Mrs. Wackles.

"All manner of things," replied Miss Cheggs, "you can't think how out he has been speaking!"

Richard Swiveller considered it advisable to hear no more, but taking advantage of a pause in the dancing, and the approach of Mr. Cheggs to pay his court to the old lady, swaggered with an extremely careful assumption of extreme carelessness towards the door, passing on the way Miss Jane Wackles, who in all the glory of her curls was holding a flirtation (as good practice when no better was to be had) with a feeble old gentleman who lodged in the parlour. Near the door sat Miss Sophy, still fluttered and confused by the attentions of Mr. Cheggs, and by her side Richard Swiveller lingered for a moment to exchange a few parting words.

"My boat is on the shore and my bark is on the sea, but before I pass this door I will say farewell to thee," murmured Dick, looking gloomily upon her.

"Are you going?" said Miss Sophy, whose heart sank within her at the result of her stratagem, but who affected a light indifference notwithstanding.

"Am I going!" echoed Dick bitterly. "Yes, I am. What then?"

"Nothing, except that it's very early," said Miss Sophy; "but you are your own master, of course."

"I would that I had been my own mistress too," said Dick, "before I had ever entertained a thought of you. Miss Wackles, I believed you true, and I was blest in so believing, but now I mourn that e'er I knew, a girl so fair yet so deceiving."

Miss Sophy bit her lip and affected to look with great interest after Mr. Cheggs, who was quaffing lemonade in the distance.

"I came here," said Dick, rather oblivious of the purpose with which he had really come, "with my bosom expanded, my heart dilated, and my sentiments of a corresponding description. I go away with feelings that may be conceived but cannot be described, feeling within myself the desolating truth that my best affections have experienced this night a stifler!"

"I am sure I don't know what you mean, Mr. Swiveller," said Miss Sophy with downcast eyes. "I'm very sorry if——"

"Sorry, ma'am!" said Dick, "sorry in the possession of a Cheggs! But I wish you a very good night, concluding with this slight remark, that there is a young lady growing up at this present moment for me, who has not only great personal attractions but great wealth, and who has requested her next of kin to propose for my hand, which, having a regard for some members of her family, I have consented to promise. It's a gratifying circumstance which you'll be glad to hear, that a young and lovely girl is growing into a woman expressly on my account, and is now saving up for me. I thought I'd mention it. I have now merely to apologise for trespassing so long upon your attention. Good night."

"There's one good thing springs out of all this," said Richard Swiveller to himself when he had reached home and was hanging over the candle with the extinguisher in his hand, "which is, that I now go heart and soul, neck and heels, with Fred in all his scheme about little Nelly, and right glad he'll be to find me so strong upon it. He shall know all about that to-morrow, and in the meantime, as it's rather late, I'll try and get a wink or two of the balmy."

"The balmy" came almost as soon as it was courted. In a very few minutes Mr. Swiveller was fast asleep, dreaming that he had married Nelly Trent and come into her property, and that his first act of power was to lay waste the market-garden of Mr. Cheggs and turn it into a brick-field.

CHAPTER IX

THE child, in her confidence with Mrs. Quilp, had but feebly described the sadness and sorrow of her thoughts, or the heaviness of the cloud which overhung her home, and cast dark shadows on its hearth. Besides that it was very difficult to impart to any person not intimately acquainted with the life she led, an adequate sense of its gloom and loneliness, a constant fear of in some way committing or injuring the old man to whom she was so tenderly attached, had restrained her even in the midst of her heart's overflowing, and made her timid of allusion to the main cause of her anxiety and distress.

For, it was not the monotonous day unchequered by variety and uncheered by pleasant companionship, it was not the dark dreary evenings or the long solitary nights, it was not the absence of every slight and easy pleasure for which young hearts beat high, or the knowing nothing of childhood but its weakness and its easily wounded spirit, that had wrung such tears from Nell. To see the old man struck down beneath the pressure of some hidden grief, to mark his wavering and unsettled state, to be agitated at times with a dreadful fear that his mind was wandering, and to trace in his words and looks the dawning of despondent madness; to watch and wait and listen for confirmation of these things day after day, and to feel and know that, come what might, they were alone in the world with no one to help or advise or care about them—these were causes of depression and anxiety that might have sat heavily on an older breast with many influences at work to cheer and gladden it, but how heavily on the mind of a young child to whom they were ever present, and who was constantly surrounded by all that could keep such thoughts in restless action!

And yet, to the old man's vision, Nell was still the same. When he could for a moment disengage his mind from the phantom that haunted and brooded on it always, there was his young companion with the same smile for him, the same earnest words, the same merry laugh, the same love and care that sinking deep into his soul seemed to have been present to him through his whole life. And so he went on, content to read the book of her heart from the page first presented to him, little dreaming of the story that lay hidden in its other leaves, and murmuring within himself that at least the child was happy.

She had been once. She had gone singing through the dim rooms, and moving with gay and lightsome step among their dusty treasures, making them older by her young life, and sterner and more grim by her gay and cheerful presence. But now the chambers were cold and gloomy, and when she left her own little room to while away the tedious hours, and sat in one of them, she was still and motionless as their inanimate occupants, and had no heart to startle the echoes—hoarse from their long silence—with her voice.

In one of these rooms was a window looking into the street, where the child sat, many and many a long evening, and often far into the night, alone and thoughtful. None are so anxious as those who watch and wait, and at these times, mournful fancies came flocking on her mind, in crowds.

She would take her station here at dusk, and watch the people as they passed up and down the street, or appeared at the windows of the opposite houses, wondering whether those rooms were as lonesome as that in which she sat, and whether those people felt it company to see her sitting there, as she did only to see them look out and draw in their heads again. There was a crooked stack of chimneys on one of the roofs, in which by often looking at them she had fancied ugly faces that were frowning over at her and trying to peer into the room, and she felt glad when it grew too dark to make them out, though she was sorry too, when the man came to light the lamps in the street, for it made it late, and very dull inside. Then she would draw in her head to look round the room and see that everything was in its place and hadn't moved; and looking out into the street again, would perhaps see a man passing with a coffin on his back, and two or three others silently following him to a house where somebody lay dead, which made her shudder and think of such things until they suggested afresh the old man's altered face and manner, and a new train of fears and speculations. If he were to die—if sudden illness had happened to him, and he were never to come home again, alive—if, one night, he should come home, and kiss and bless her as usual, and after she had gone to bed and had fallen asleep and was perhaps dreaming pleasantly, and smiling in her sleep, he should kill himself and his blood come creeping, creeping, on the ground to her own bedroom door! These thoughts were too terrible to dwell upon, and again she would have recourse to the street, now trodden by fewer feet and darker and more silent than before. The shops were closing fast, and lights began to shine from the upper windows, as the neighbours went to bed. By degrees these dwindled away and disappeared, or were replaced here and there by a feeble rush-candle which was to burn all night. Still there was one late shop at no great distance which sent forth a ruddy glare upon the pavement even yet, and looked bright and companionable. But in a little time this closed, the light was extinguished, and all was gloomy and quiet, except when some stray footsteps sounded on the pavement, or a neighbour, out later than his wont, knocked lustily at his house-door to rouse the sleeping inmates.

When the night had worn away thus far (and seldom now until it had) the child would close the window, and steal softly down stairs, thinking as she went that if one of those hideous faces below, which often mingled with her dreams, were to meet her by the way, rendering itself visible by some strange light of its own, how terrified she would be. But these fears vanished before a well-trimmed lamp and the familiar aspect of her own room. After praying fervently and with many bursting tears for the old man, and the restoration of his peace of mind and the happiness they had once enjoyed, she would lay her head upon the pillow and sob herself to sleep, often starting up again, before the daylight came, to listen for the bell, and respond to the imaginary summons which had roused her from her slumber.

One night, the third after Nelly's interview with Mrs. Quilp, the old man, who had been weak and ill all day, said he should not leave home. The child's eyes sparkled at the intelligence, but her joy subsided when they reverted to his worn and sickly face.

"Two days," he said, "two whole, clear, days have passed, and there is no reply. What *did* he tell thee, Nell?"

"Exactly what I told you, dear grandfather, indeed."

"True," said the old man, faintly. "Yes. But tell me again, Nell. My head fails me. What was it that he told thee? Nothing more than that he would see me to-morrow or next day? That was in the note."

"Nothing more," said the child. "Shall I go to him again to-morrow, dear grandfather? Very early? I will be there and back, before breakfast."

The old man shook his head, and sighing mournfully, drew her towards him.

" 'Twould be of no use, my dear, no earthly use. But if he deserts me, Nell, at this moment—if he deserts me now, when I should, with his assistance, be recompensed for all the time and money I have lost, and all the agony of mind I have undergone, which makes me what you see, I am ruined, and—worse, far worse than that—have ruined thee, for whom I ventured all. If we are beggars——!"

"What if we are?" said the child boldly. "Let us be beggars, and be happy."

"Beggars—and happy!" said the old man. "Poor child!"

"Dear grandfather," cried the girl with an energy which shone in her flushed face, trembling voice, and impassioned gesture, "I am not a child in that I think, but even if I am, oh hear me pray that we may beg, or work in open roads or fields, to earn a scanty living, rather than live as we do now."

"Nelly!" said the old man.

"Yes, yes, rather than live as we do now," the child repeated, more earnestly than before. "If you are sorrowful, let me know why and be sorrowful too; if you waste away and are paler and weaker every day, let me be your nurse and try to comfort you. If you are poor, let us be poor together, but let me be with you, do not let me see such change and not know why, or I shall break my heart and die. Dear grandfather, let us leave this sad place to-morrow, and beg our way from door to door."

The old man covered his face with his hands, and hid it in the pillow of the couch on which he lay.

"Let us be beggars," said the child passing an arm round his neck, "I have no fear but we shall have enough, I am sure we shall. Let us walk through country places, and sleep in fields and under trees, and never think of money again, or anything that can make you sad, but rest at nights, and have the sun and wind upon our faces in the day, and thank God together. Let us never set foot in dark rooms or melancholy houses any more, but wander up and down wherever we like to go, and when you are tired, you shall stop to rest in the pleasantest place that we can find, and I will go and beg for both."

The child's voice was lost in sobs as she dropped upon the old man's neck; nor did she weep alone.

These were not words for other ears, nor was it a scene for other eyes. And yet other ears and eyes were there and greedily taking in all that passed, and moreover they were the ears and eyes of no less a person than Mr. Daniel Quilp, who, having entered unseen when the child first placed herself at the old man's side, refrained—actuated, no doubt, by motives of the purest delicacy—from interrupting the conversation, and stood looking on with his accustomed grin. Standing, however, being a tiresome attitude to a gentleman already fatigued with walking, and the dwarf being one of that kind of persons who usually make themselves at home, he soon cast his eyes upon a chair into which he skipped with uncommon agility, and perching himself on the back with his feet upon the seat, was thus enabled to look on and listen with greater comfort to himself, besides gratifying at the same time that taste for doing something fantastic and monkey-like, which on all occasions had strong possession of him. Here, then, he sat, one leg cocked carelessly over the other, his chin resting on the palm of his hand, his head turned a little on one side, and his ugly features twisted into a complacent grimace. And in this position the old man, happening in course of time to look that way, at length chanced to see him, to his unbounded astonishment.

The child uttered a suppressed shriek on beholding this agreeable figure; in their first surprise both she and the old man, not knowing what to say, and half doubting its reality, looked shrinkingly at it. Not at all disconcerted by this reception, Daniel Quilp preserved the same attitude, merely nodding twice or thrice with great condescension. At length the old man pronounced his name, and inquired how he came there.

"Through the door," said Quilp pointing over his shoulder with his thumb. "I'm not quite small enough to get through key-holes. I wish I was. I want to have some talk with you, particularly, and in private—with nobody present, neighbour. Good-bye, little Nelly."

Nell looked at the old man, who nodded to her to retire, and kissed her cheek.

"Ah!" said the dwarf, smacking his lips, "what a nice kiss that was —just upon the rosy part. What a capital kiss!"

Nell was none the slower in going away, for this remark. Quilp looked after her with an admiring leer, and when she had closed the door, fell to complimenting the old man upon her charms.

"Such a fresh, blooming, modest little bud, neighbour," said Quilp, nursing his short leg, and making his eyes twinkle very much; "such a chubby, rosy, cosy, little Nell!"

The old man answered by a forced smile, and was plainly struggling with a feeling of the keenest and most exquisite impatience. It was not lost upon Quilp, who delighted in torturing him, or indeed anybody else when he could.

"She's so," said Quilp, speaking very slowly, and feigning to be quite absorbed in the subject, "so small, so compact, so beautifully modelled, so fair, with such blue veins and such a transparent skin, and such little feet, and such winning ways—but bless me, you're nervous! Why neighbour, what's the matter? I swear to you," continued the dwarf dismounting from the chair and sitting down in it, with a careful slowness of gesture very different from the rapidity with which he had sprung up unheard, "I swear to you that I had no idea old blood ran so fast or kept so warm. I thought it was sluggish in its course, and cool, quite cool. I am pretty sure it ought to be. Yours must be out of order, neighbour."

"I believe it is," groaned the old man, clasping his head with both hands. "There's burning fever here, and something now and then to which I fear to give a name."

The dwarf said never a word, but watched his companion as he paced restlessly up and down the room, and presently returned to his seat. Here he remained, with his head bowed upon his breast for some time, and then suddenly raising it, said,

"Once, and once for all, have you brought me any money?"

"No!" returned Quilp.

"Then," said the old man, clenching his hands desperately, and looking upward, "the child and I are lost!"

"Neighbour," said Quilp, glancing sternly at him, and beating his hand twice or thrice upon the table to attract his wandering attention, "let me be plain with you, and play a fairer game than when you held all the cards, and I saw but the backs and nothing more. You have no secret from me now."

The old man looked up, trembling.

"You are surprised," said Quilp. "Well, perhaps that's natural. You have no secret from me now, I say; no, not one. For now I know that all those sums of money, that all those loans, advances, and supplies that you have had from me, have found their way to—shall I say the word?"

"Ay!" replied the old man, "say it, if you will."

"To the gaming-table," rejoined Quilp, "your nightly haunt. This was the precious scheme to make your fortune, was it; this was the secret certain source of wealth in which I was to have sunk my money (if I had been the fool you took me for); this was your inexhaustible mine of gold, your El Dorado, eh?"

"Yes," cried the old man, turning upon him with gleaming eyes, "it was. It is. It will be till I die."

"That I should have been blinded," said Quilp looking contemptuously at him, "by a mere shallow gambler!"

"I am no gambler," cried the old man fiercely. "I call Heaven to witness that I never played for gain of mine, or love of play; that at every piece I staked, I whispered to myself that orphan's name and called on Heaven to bless the venture, which it never did. Whom did it prosper? Who were those with whom I played? Men who lived by plunder, profligacy, and riot, squandering their gold in doing ill and propagating vice and evil. My winnings would have been from them, my winnings would have been bestowed to the last farthing on a young sinless child whose life they would have sweetened and made happy. What would they have contracted? The means of corruption, wretchedness, and misery. Who would not have hoped in such a cause —tell me that; now who would not have hoped as I did?''

"When did you first begin this mad career?'' asked Quilp, his taunting inclination subdued for a moment by the old man's grief and wildness.

"When did I first begin?'' he rejoined, passing his hand across his brow. "When *was* it, that I first began? When should it be, but when I began to think how little I had saved, how long a time it took to save at all, how short a time I might have at my age to live, and how she would be left to the rough mercies of the world, with barely enough to keep her from the sorrows that wait on poverty; then it was that I began to think about it.''

"After you first came to me to get your precious grandson packed off to sea?'' said Quilp.

"Shortly after that,'' replied the old man. "I thought of it a long time, and had it in my sleep for months. Then I began. I found no pleasure in it, I expected none. What has it ever brought to me but anxious days and sleepless nights, but loss of health and peace of mind, and gain of feebleness and sorrow!''

"You lost what money you had laid by, first, and then came to me. While I thought you were making your fortune (as you said you were) you were making yourself a beggar, eh? Dear me! And so it comes to pass that I hold every security you could scrape together, and a bill of sale upon the—upon the stock and property,'' said Quilp standing up and looking about him, as if to assure himself that none of it had been taken away. "But did you never win?''

"Never!'' groaned the old man. "Never won back my loss!''

"I thought,'' sneered the dwarf, "that if a man played long enough he was sure to win at last, or at the worst not to come off a loser.''

"And so he is,'' cried the old man, suddenly rousing himself from his state of despondency, and lashed into the most violent excitement, "so he is; I have felt that from the first, I have always known it, I've seen it, I never felt it half so strongly as I feel it now. Quilp, I have dreamed three nights of winning the same large sum, I never could dream that dream before, though I have often tried. Do not desert me now I have this chance. I have no resource but you, give me some help, let me try this one last hope.''

The dwarf shrugged his shoulders and shook his head.

"See, Quilp, good tender-hearted Quilp,'' said the old man, drawing some scraps of paper from his pocket with a trembling hand, and clasping the dwarf's arm, "only see here. Look at these figures, the result of long calculation, and painful and hard experience. I *must* win. I only want a little help once more, a few pounds, but two score pounds, dear Quilp."

"The last advance was seventy," said the dwarf; "and it went in one night."

"I know it did," answered the old man, "but that was the very worst fortune of all, and the time had not come then. Quilp, consider, consider," the old man cried, trembling so much the while that the papers in his hand fluttered as if they were shaken by the wind, "that orphan child. If I were alone, I could die with gladness—perhaps even anticipate that doom which is dealt out so unequally, coming as it does on the proud and happy in their strength, and shunning the needy and afflicted and all who court it in their despair —but what I have done, has been for her. Help me for her sake I implore you—not for mine, for hers!"

"I'm sorry I've got an appointment in the City," said Quilp, looking at his watch with perfect self-possession, "or I should have been very glad to have spent half an hour with you while you composed yourself—very glad."

"Nay, Quilp, good Quilp," gasped the old man, catching at his skirts—"you and I have talked together more than once of her poor mother's story. The fear of her coming to poverty has perhaps been bred in me by that. Do not be hard upon me, but take that into account. You are a great gainer by me. Oh spare me the money for this one last hope!"

"I couldn't do it really," said Quilp with unusual politeness, "though I tell you what—and this is a circumstance worth bearing in mind as showing how the sharpest among us may be taken in sometimes—I was so deceived by the penurious way in which you lived, alone with Nelly——"

"All done to save money for tempting fortune, and make her triumph greater," cried the old man.

"Yes yes, I understand that now," said Quilp; "but I was going to say, I was so deceived by that, your miserly way, the reputation you had among those who knew you of being rich, and your repeated assurances that you would make of my advances treble and quadruple the interest you paid me, that I'd have advanced you even now what you want, on your simple note of hand, though I had been led to suspect something wrong, if I hadn't unexpectedly become acquainted with your secret way of life."

"Who is it," retorted the old man desperately, "that notwithstanding all my caution, told you that? Come. Let me know the name —the person."

The crafty dwarf, bethinking himself that his giving up the child would lead to the disclosure of the artifice he had employed, which, as nothing was to be gained by it, it was as well to conceal, stopped short in his answer and said, "Now, who do you think?"

"It was Kit, it must have been the boy; he played the spy and you tampered with him?" said the old man.

"How came you to think of him?" said the dwarf in a tone of great commiseration. "Yes, it was Kit. Poor Kit!"

So saying, he nodded in a friendly manner, and took his leave, stopping when he had passed the outer door a little distance, and grinning with extraordinary delight.

"Poor Kit!" muttered Quilp. "I think it was Kit who said I was an uglier dwarf than could be seen anywhere for a penny, wasn't it. Ha ha ha! Poor Kit!"

And with that he went his way, still chuckling as he went.

CHAPTER X

DANIEL QUILP neither entered nor left the old man's house, unobserved. In the shadow of an archway nearly opposite, leading to one of the many passages which diverged from the main street, there lingered one who having taken up his position when the twilight first came on, still maintained it with undiminished patience, and leaning against the wall with the manner of one who had a long time to wait, and being well used to it was quite resigned, scarcely changed his attitude for the hour together.

This patient lounger attracted little attention from any of those who passed, and bestowed as little upon them. His eyes were constantly directed towards one object, the window at which the child was accustomed to sit. If he withdrew them for a moment, it was only to glance at a clock in some neighbouring shop, and then to strain his sight once more in the old quarter with increased earnestness and attention.

It has been remarked that this personage evinced no weariness in his place of concealment, nor did he, long as his waiting was. But as the time went on, he manifested some anxiety and surprise, glancing at the clock more frequently and at the window less hopefully than before. At length the clock was hidden from his sight by some envious shutters, then the church steeples proclaimed eleven at night, then the quarter past, and then the conviction seemed to obtrude itself upon his mind that it was of no use tarrying there any longer.

That the conviction was an unwelcome one, and that he was by no means willing to yield to it, was apparent from his reluctance to quit the spot; from the tardy steps with which he often left it, still looking over his shoulder at the same window; and from the precipitation with which he as often returned, when a fancied noise or the changing and imperfect light induced him to suppose it had been softly raised. At length he gave the matter up as hopeless for that night, and suddenly breaking into a run as though to force himself away, scampered off at his utmost speed, nor once ventured to look behind him lest he should be tempted back again.

Without relaxing his pace or stopping to take breath, this mysterious individual dashed on through a great many alleys and narrow ways until he at length arrived in a square paved court, when he subsided into a walk, and making for a small house from the window of which a light was shining, lifted the latch of the door and passed in.

"Bless us!" cried a woman turning sharply round, "who's that? Oh! It's you, Kit!"

"Yes, mother, it's me."

"Why, how tired you look, my dear!"

"Old master an't gone out to-night," said Kit; "and so she hasn't been at the window at all." With which words, he sat down by the fire and looked very mournful and discontented.

The room in which Kit sat himself down in this condition was an extremely poor and homely place, but with that air of comfort about it, nevertheless, which—or the spot must be a wretched one indeed—cleanliness and order can always impart in some degree. Late as the Dutch clock showed it to be, the poor woman was still hard at work at an ironing-table; a young child lay sleeping in a cradle near the fire; and another, a sturdy boy of two or three years old, very wide awake, with a very tight night-cap on his head, and a night-gown very much too small for him on his body, was sitting bolt upright in a clothes-basket, staring over the rim with his great round eyes, and looking as if he had thoroughly made up his mind never to go to sleep any more; which, as he had already declined to take his natural rest and had been brought out of bed in consequence, opened a cheerful prospect for his relations and friends. It was rather a queer-looking family; Kit, his mother, and the children, being all strongly alike.

Kit was disposed to be out of temper, as the best of us are too often —but he looked at the youngest child who was sleeping soundly, and from him to his other brother in the clothes-basket, and from him to their mother, who had been at work without complaint since morning, and thought it would be a better and kinder thing to be good-humoured. So he rocked the cradle with his foot, made a face at the rebel in the clothes-basket, which put him in high good-humour directly, and stoutly determined to be talkative and make himself agreeable.

"Ah mother!" said Kit, taking out his clasp-knife and falling upon a great piece of bread and meat which she had had ready for him, hours before, "what a one you are! There an't many such as you, *I* know."

"I hope there are many a great deal better, Kit," said Mrs. Nubbles; "and that there are, or ought to be, accordin' to what the parson at chapel says."

"Much *he* knows about it," returned Kit contemptuously. "Wait till he's a widder and works like you do, and gets as little, and does as much, and keeps his spirits up the same, and then I'll ask him what's o'clock and trust him for being right to half a second."

"Well," said Mrs. Nubbles, evading the point, "your beer's down there by the fender, Kit."

"I see," replied her son, taking up the porter pot, "my love to you, mother. And the parson's health too if you like. I don't bear him any malice, not I!"

"Did you tell me just now that your master hadn't gone out to-night?" inquired Mrs. Nubbles.

"Yes," said Kit, "worse luck."

"You should say better luck, I think," returned his mother, "because Miss Nelly won't have been left alone."

"Ah!" said Kit, "I forgot that. I said worse luck, because I've been watching ever since eight o'clock, and seen nothing of her."

"I wonder what she'd say," cried his mother, stopping in her work and looking round, "if she knew that every night, when she—poor thing—is sitting alone at that window, you are watching in the open street for fear any harm should come to her, and that you never leave the place or come home to your bed though you're ever so tired, till such time as you think she's safe in hers."

"Never mind what she'd say," replied Kit, with something like a blush on his uncouth face; "she'll never know nothing, and consequently, she'll never say nothing."

Mrs. Nubbles ironed away in silence for a minute or two, and coming to the fireplace for another iron, glanced stealthily at Kit while she rubbed it on a board and dusted it with a duster, but said nothing until she had returned to her table again, when holding the iron at an alarmingly short distance from her cheek, to test its temperature, and looking round with a smile, she observed:

"I know what some people would say, Kit——"

"Nonsense," interposed Kit with a perfect apprehension of what was to follow.

"No, but they would indeed. Some people would say that you'd fallen in love with her, I know they would."

To this Kit only replied by bashfully bidding his mother "get out," and forming sundry strange figures with his legs and arms, accompanied by sympathetic contortions of his face. Not deriving from these means the relief which he sought, he bit off an immense mouthful from the bread and meat, and took a quick drink of the porter, by which artificial aids he choked himself and effected a diversion of the subject.

"Speaking seriously though, Kit," said his mother taking up the theme afresh, after a time, "for of course I was only in joke just now, it's very good and thoughtful, and like you, to do this, and never let anybody know it, though some day I hope she may come to know it, for I'm sure she would be very grateful to you, and feel it very much. It's a cruel thing to keep the dear child shut up there. I don't wonder that the old gentleman wants to keep it from you."

"He don't think it's cruel, bless you," said Kit, "and don't mean it to be so, or he wouldn't do it—I do consider, mother, that he wouldn't do it for all the gold and silver in the world. No, no, that he wouldn't. I know him better than that."

"Then what does he do it for, and why does he keep it so close from you?" said Mrs. Nubbles.

"I know what some people would say, Kit."

"That I don't know," returned her son. "If he hadn't tried to keep it so close though, I should never have found it out, for it was his betting me away at night and sending me off so much earlier than he used to, that first made me curious to know what was going on. Hark! what's that?"

"It's only somebody outside."

"It's somebody crossing over here"—said Kit, standing up to listen, "and coming very fast too. He can't have gone out after I left, and the house caught fire, mother!"

The boy stood for a moment, really bereft, by the apprehension he had conjured up, of the power to move. The footsteps drew nearer, the door was opened with a hasty hand, and the child herself, pale and breathless, and hastily wrapped in a few disordered garments, hurried into the room.

"Miss Nelly! What is the matter!" cried mother and son together.

"I must not stay a moment," she returned, "grandfather has been taken very ill, I found him in a fit upon the floor——"

"I'll run for a doctor"—said Kit, seizing his brimless hat. "I'll be there directly, I'll——"

"No, no," cried Nell, "there is one there, you're not wanted, you—you—must never come near us any more!"

"What!" roared Kit.

"Never again," said the child. "Don't ask me why, for I don't know. Pray don't ask me why, pray don't be sorry, pray don't be vexed with me, I have nothing to do with it indeed!"

Kit looked at her with his eyes stretched wide, and opened and shut his mouth a great many times, but couldn't get out one word.

"He complains and raves of you," said the child, "I don't know what you have done, but I hope it's nothing very bad."

"*I* done!" roared Kit.

"He cries that you're the cause of all his misery," returned the child with tearful eyes; "he screamed and called for you, they say you must not come near him or he will die. You must not return to us any more. I came to tell you. I thought it would be better that I should come than somebody quite strange. Oh, Kit, what *have* you done? You, in whom I trusted so much, and who were almost the only friend I had!"

The unfortunate Kit looked at his young mistress harder and harder, and with eyes growing wider and wider, but was perfectly motionless and silent.

"I have brought his money for the week," said the child, looking to the woman and laying it on the table—"and—and—a little more, for he was always good and kind to me. I hope he will be sorry and do well somewhere else and not take this to heart too much. It grieves me very much to part with him like this, but there is no help. It must be done. Good night!"

With the tears streaming down her face, and her slight figure trembling with the agitation of the scene she had left, the shock she had received, the errand she had just discharged, and a thousand painful and affectionate feelings, the child hastened to the door, and disappeared as rapidly as she had come.

The poor woman, who had no cause to doubt her son, but every reason for relying on his honesty and truth, was staggered, notwithstanding, by his not having advanced one word in his defence. Visions of gallantry, knavery, robbery; and of the nightly absences from home for which he had accounted so strangely, having been occasioned by some unlawful pursuit; flocked into her brain and rendered her afraid to question him. She rocked herself upon a chair, wringing her hands and weeping bitterly, but Kit made no attempt to comfort her and remained quite bewildered. The baby in the cradle woke up and cried, the boy in the clothes-basket fell over on his back with the basket upon him and was seen no more, the mother wept louder yet and rocked faster, but Kit, insensible to all the din and tumult, remained in a state of utter stupefaction.

CHAPTER XI

QUIET and solitude were destined to hold uninterrupted rule no longer, beneath the roof that sheltered the child. Next morning the old man was in a raging fever accompanied with delirium, and sinking under the influence of this disorder he lay for many weeks in imminent peril of his life. There was watching enough now, but it was the watching of strangers who made of it a greedy trade, and who, in the intervals of their attendance upon the sick man, huddled together with a ghastly good-fellowship, and ate and drank and made merry; for disease and death were their ordinary household gods.

Yet in all the hurry and crowding of such a time, the child was more alone than she had ever been before; alone in spirit, alone in her devotion to him who was wasting away upon his burning bed; alone in her unfeigned sorrow, and her unpurchased sympathy. Day after day, and night after night, found her still by the pillow of the unconscious sufferer, still anticipating his every want, and still listening to those repetitions of her name and those anxieties and cares for her, which were ever uppermost among his feverish wanderings.

The house was no longer theirs. Even the sick chamber seemed to be retained on the uncertain tenure of Mr. Quilp's favour. The old man's illness had not lasted many days when he took formal possession of the premises and all upon them, in virtue of certain legal powers to that effect, which few understood and none presumed to call in question. This important step secured, with the assistance of a man of law whom he brought with him for the purpose, the dwarf proceeded to establish himself and his coadjutor in the house, as an assertion of his claim against all comers; and then set about making his quarters comfortable after his own fashion.

To this end, Mr. Quilp encamped in the back parlour, having first put an effectual stop to any further business by shutting up the shop. Having looked out from among the old furniture the handsomest and most commodious chair he could possibly find, which he reserved for his own use, and an especially hideous and uncomfortable one, which he considerately appropriated to the accommodation of his friend, he caused them to be carried into this room and took up his position in great state. The apartment was very far removed from the old man's chamber, but Mr. Quilp deemed it prudent, as a precaution against infection from fever, and a means of wholesome fumigation, not only to smoke himself without cessation, but to insist upon it that his legal friend did the like. Moreover, he sent an express to the wharf for the tumbling boy, who arriving with all despatch was enjoined to sit himself down in another chair just inside the door, continually to smoke a great pipe which the dwarf had provided for the purpose, and to take it from his lips under any pretence whatever, were it only for one minute at a time, if he dared. These arrangements completed, Mr. Quilp looked around him with chuckling satisfaction, and remarked that he called that comfort.

The legal gentleman, whose melodious name was Brass, might have called it comfort also but for two drawbacks, one was that he could by no exertion sit easily in his chair, the seat of which was very hard, angular, slippery, and sloping; the other that tobacco-smoke always caused him great internal discomposure and annoyance. But as he was quite a creature of Mr. Quilp's and had a thousand reasons for conciliating his good opinion, he tried to smile, and nodded his acquiescence with the best grace he could assume.

This Brass was an attorney of no very good repute from Bevis Marks in the City of London; he was a tall, meagre man, with a nose like a wen, a protruding forehead, retreating eyes, and hair of a deep red. He wore a long black surtout reaching nearly to his ankles, short black trousers, high shoes, and cotton stockings of a bluish grey. He had a cringing manner but a very harsh voice, and his blandest smiles were so extremely forbidding, that to have had his company under the least repulsive circumstances, one would have wished him to be out of temper that he might only scowl.

Quilp looked at his legal adviser, and seeing that he was winking very much in the anguish of his pipe, that he sometimes shuddered when he happened to inhale its full flavour, and that he constantly fanned the smoke from him, was quite overjoyed and rubbed his hands with glee.

"Smoke away, you dog," said Quilp turning to the boy; "fill your pipe again and smoke it fast, down to the last whiff, or I'll put the sealing-waxed end of it in the fire and rub it red hot upon your tongue."

Luckily the boy was case-hardened, and would have smoked a small lime-kiln if anybody had treated him with it. Wherefore he only muttered a brief defiance of his master, and did as he was ordered.

"Is it good, Brass, is it nice, is it fragrant, do you feel like the Grand Turk?" said Quilp.

Mr. Brass thought that if he did, the Grand Turk's feelings were by no means to be envied, but he said it was famous, and he had no doubt he felt very like that Potentate.

"This is the way to keep off fever," said Quilp, "this is the way to keep off every calamity of life. We'll never leave off all the time we stop here—smoke away, you dog, or you shall swallow the pipe."

"Shall we stop here long, Mr. Quilp?" inquired his legal friend, when the dwarf had given his boy this last gentle admonition.

"We must stop, I suppose, till the old gentleman up stairs is dead," returned Quilp.

"He he he!" laughed Mr. Brass, "oh! very good!"

"Smoke away!" cried Quilp. "Never stop! you can talk as you smoke. Don't lose time."

"He he he!" cried Brass faintly, as he again applied himself to the odious pipe. "But if he should get better, Mr. Quilp?"

"Then we shall stop till he does, and no longer," returned the dwarf.

"How kind it is of you, sir, to wait till then!" said Brass. "Some people, sir, would have sold or removed the goods—oh dear, the very instant the law allowed 'em. Some people, sir, would have been all flintiness and granite. Some people, sir, would have——"

"Some people would have spared themselves the jabbering of such a parrot as you," interposed the dwarf.

"He he he!" cried Brass. "You have *such* spirits!"

The smoking sentinel at the door interposed in this place, and without taking his pipe from his lips, growled,

"Here's the gal a comin' down."

"The what, you dog?" said Quilp.

"The gal," returned the boy. "Are you deaf?"

"Oh!" said Quilp, drawing in his breath with great relish as if he were taking soup, "you and I will have such a settling presently; there's such a scratching and bruising in store for you, my dear young friend. Aha! Nelly! How is he now, my duck of diamonds?"

"He's very bad," replied the weeping child.

"What a pretty little Nell!" cried Quilp.

"Oh beautiful, sir, beautiful indeed," said Brass. "Quite charming!"

"Has she come to sit upon Quilp's knee," said the dwarf, in what he meant to be a soothing tone, "or is she going to bed in her own little room inside here—which is poor Nelly going to do?"

"What a remarkable pleasant way he has with children!" muttered Brass, as if in confidence between himself and the ceiling; "upon my word it's quite a treat to hear him."

"I'm not going to stay at all," faltered Nell. "I want a few things out of that room, and then I—I—won't come down here any more."

"And a very nice little room it is!" said the dwarf looking into it as the child entered. "Quite a bower. You're sure you're not going to use it, you're sure you're not coming back, Nelly?"

"No," replied the child, hurrying away, with the few articles of dress she had come to remove; "never again, never again."

"She's very sensitive," said Quilp, looking after her. "Very sensitive; that's a pity. The bedstead is much about my size. I think I shall make it *my* little room."

Mr. Brass encouraging this idea, as he would have encouraged any other emanating from the same source, the dwarf walked in to try the effect, which he did by throwing himself on his back upon the bed with his pipe in his mouth, and then kicking up his legs and smoking violently. Mr. Brass applauding this picture very much, and the bed being soft and comfortable, Mr. Quilp determined to use it, both as a sleeping place by night and as a kind of divan by day, and in order that it might be converted to the latter purpose at once, remained where he was and smoked his pipe out. The legal gentleman being by this time rather giddy and perplexed in his ideas (for this was one of the operations of the tobacco upon his nervous system), took the opportunity of slinking away into the open air where in course of time he recovered sufficiently to return with a countenance of tolerable composure. He was soon led on by the malicious dwarf to smoke himself into a relapse, and in that state stumbled upon a settee where he slept till morning.

Such were Mr. Quilp's first proceedings on entering upon his new property. He was for some days restrained by business from performing any particular pranks, as his time was pretty well occupied between taking, with the assistance of Mr. Brass, a minute inventory of all the goods in the place, and going abroad upon his other concerns which happily engaged him for several hours at a time. His avarice and caution being now thoroughly awakened, however, he was never absent from the house one night, and his eagerness for some termination, good or bad, to the old man's disorder, increasing rapidly as the time passed by, soon began to vent itself in open murmurs and exclamations of impatience.

Nell shrank timidly from all the dwarf's advances towards conversation and fled from the very sound of his voice, nor were the lawyer's smiles less terrible to her than Quilp's grimaces. She lived in such continual dread and apprehension of meeting one or other of them upon the stairs or in the passages if she stirred from her grandfather's chamber, that she seldom left it for a moment until late at night, when the silence encouraged her to venture forth and breathe the purer air of some empty room.

One night she had stolen to her usual window and was sitting there very sorrowfully, for the old man had been worse that day, when she thought that she heard her name pronounced by a voice in the street, and looking down, recognised Kit, whose endeavours to attract her attention had roused her from her sad reflections.

"Miss Nell!" said the boy in a low voice.

"Yes," replied the child, doubtful whether she ought to hold any communication with the supposed culprit, but inclining to her old favourite still, "what do you want?"

"I have wanted to say a word to you for a long time," the boy replied, "but the people below have driven me away and wouldn't let me see you. You don't believe—I hope you don't really believe—

that I deserve to be cast off as I have been; do you, miss?"

"I must believe it," returned the child. "Or why would grandfather have been so angry with you?"

"I don't know," replied Kit. "I'm sure I've never deserved it from him, no, nor from you. I can say that with a true and honest heart any way. And then to be driven from the door, when I only came to ask how old master was——!"

"They never told me that," said the child. "I didn't know it indeed. I wouldn't have had them do it for the world."

"Thank'ee, miss," returned Kit, "it's comfortable to hear you say that. I said I never would believe that it was your doing."

"That was right!" said the child eagerly.

"Miss Nell," cried the boy, coming under the window and speaking in a lower tone, "there are new masters down stairs. It's a change for you."

"It is indeed," replied the child.

"And so it will be for him when he gets better," said the boy, pointing towards the sick room.

"—If he ever does," added the child, unable to restrain her tears.

"Oh, he'll do that, he'll do that," said Kit, "I'm sure he will. You mustn't be cast down, Miss Nell. Now don't be, pray."

These words of encouragement and consolation were few and roughly said, but they affected the child and made her for the moment weep the more.

"He'll be sure to get better now," said the boy anxiously, "if you don't give way to low spirits and turn ill yourself, which would make him worse and throw him back just as he was recovering. When he does, say a good word—say a kind word for me, Miss Nell."

"They tell me I must not even mention your name to him for a long, long time," rejoined the child. "I dare not; and even if I might, what good would a kind word do you, Kit? We shall be very poor. We shall scarcely have bread to eat."

"It's not that I may be taken back," said the boy, "that I ask the favour of you. It isn't for the sake of food and wages that I've been waiting about so long in hopes to see you. Don't think that I'd come in a time of trouble to talk of such things as them."

The child looked gratefully and kindly at him, but waited that he might speak again.

"No, it's not that," said Kit hesitating, "it's something very different from that. I haven't got much sense I know, but if he could be brought to believe that I'd been a faithful servant to him, doing the best I could, and never meaning harm, perhaps he mightn't——"

Here Kit faltered so long that the child entreated him to speak out, and quickly, for it was very late, and time to shut the window.

"Perhaps he mightn't think it over venturesome of me to say— well then, to say this,"—cried Kit with sudden boldness. "This home is gone from you and him. Mother and I have got a poor one, but that's better than this with all these people here; and why not come there, till he's had time to look about and find a better!"

The child did not speak. Kit, in the relief of having made his proposition, found his tongue loosened, and spoke out in its favour with his utmost eloquence.

"You think," said the boy, "that it's very small and inconvenient. So it is, but it's very clean. Perhaps you think it would be noisy, but there's not a quieter court than ours in all the town. Don't be afraid of the children; the baby hardly ever cries, and the other one is very good—besides, *I*'d mind 'em. They wouldn't vex you much, I'm sure. Do try, Miss Nell, do try. The little front room up stairs is very pleasant. You can see a piece of the church-clock through the chimneys and almost tell the time; mother says it would be just the thing for you, and so it would, and you'd have her to wait upon you both, and me to run of errands. We don't want money, bless you; you're not to think of that. Will you try him, Miss Nell? Only say you'll try him. Do try to make old master come, and ask him first what I have done—will you only promise that, Miss Nell?"

Before the child could reply to this earnest solicitation, the street-door opened, and Mr. Brass thrusting out his night-capped head called in a surly voice, "Who's there!" Kit immediately glided away, and Nell, closing the window softly, drew back into the room.

Before Mr. Brass had repeated his inquiry many times, Mr. Quilp, also embellished with a night-cap, emerged from the same door and looked carefully up and down the street, and up at all the windows of the house from the opposite side. Finding that there was nobody in sight he presently returned into the house with his legal friend, protesting (as the child heard from the staircase) that there was a league and plot against him, that he was in danger of being robbed and plundered by a band of conspirators who prowled about the house at all seasons, and that he would delay no longer but take immediate steps for disposing of the property and returning to his own peaceful roof. Having growled forth these and a great many other threats of the same nature, he coiled himself once more in the child's little bed, and Nell crept softly up the stairs.

It was natural enough that her short and unfinished dialogue with Kit should leave a strong impression on her mind, and influence her dreams that night, and her recollections for a long, long time. Surrounded by unfeeling creditors, and mercenary attendants upon the sick, and meeting in the height of her anxiety and sorrow with little regard or sympathy even from the women about her, it is not surprising that the affectionate heart of the child should have been touched to the quick by one kind and generous spirit, however uncouth the temple in which it dwelt. Thank Heaven that the temples of such spirits are not made with hands, and that they may be more worthily hung with poor patchwork than with purple and fine linen!

CHAPTER XII

AT length, the crisis of the old man's disorder was past, and he began
to mend. By very slow and feeble degrees his consciousness came
back, but the mind was weakened and its functions were impaired.
He was patient, and quiet; often sat brooding, but not despondently,
for a long space; was easily amused, even by a sunbeam on the wall
or ceiling; made no complaint that the days were long or the nights
tedious; and appeared indeed to have lost all count of time and every
sense of care or weariness. He would sit for hours together with Nell's
small hand in his, playing with the fingers and stopping sometimes
to smooth her hair or kiss her brow; and when he saw that tears
were glistening in her eyes would look, amazed, about him for the
cause, and forget his wonder even while he looked.

The child and he rode out: the old man propped up with pillows,
and the child beside him. They were hand in hand as usual. The noise
and motion in the streets fatigued his brain at first, but he was not
surprised, or curious, or pleased, or irritated. He was asked if he
remembered this, or that. "Oh yes," he said, "quite well—why not?"
Sometimes he turned his head and looked with earnest gaze and
outstretched neck, after some stranger in the crowd, until he disappeared from sight; but, to the question why he did this, he
answered not a word.

He was sitting in his easy chair one day, and Nell upon a stool
beside him, when a man outside the door inquired if he might enter.
"Yes," he said without emotion, "it was Quilp, he knew. Quilp was
master there. Of course he might come in." And so he did.

"I'm glad to see you well again at last, neighbour," said the dwarf,
sitting down opposite to him. "You're quite strong now?"

"Yes," said the old man feebly, "yes."

"I don't want to hurry you, you know, neighbour," said the
dwarf, raising his voice, for the old man's senses were duller than
they had been; "but, as soon as you *can* arrange your future proceedings, the better."

"Surely," said the old man. "The better for all parties."

"You see," pursued Quilp after a short pause, "the goods being
once removed, this house would be uncomfortable; uninhabitable
in fact."

"You say true," returned the old man. "Poor Nell, too, what
would *she* do?"

"Exactly," bawled the dwarf nodding his head; "that's very well
observed. Then will you consider about it, neighbour?"

"I will, certainly," replied the old man. "We shall not stop here."

"So I supposed," said the dwarf. "I have sold the things. They
have not yielded quite as much as they might have done, but pretty
well—pretty well. To-day's Tuesday. When shall they be moved?

There's no hurry—shall we say this afternoon?"

"Say Friday morning," returned the old man.

"Very good," said the dwarf. "So be it,—with the understanding that I can't go beyond that day, neighbour, on any account."

"Good," returned the old man. "I shall remember it."

Mr. Quilp seemed rather puzzled by the strange, even spiritless way in which all this was said; but as the old man nodded his head and repeated "on Friday morning. I shall remember it," he had no excuse for dwelling upon the subject any further, and so took a friendly leave with many expressions of good-will and many compliments to his friend on his looking so remarkably well; and went below stairs to report progress to Mr. Brass.

All that day, and all the next, the old man remained in this state. He wandered up and down the house and into and out of the various rooms, as if with some vague intent of bidding them adieu, but he referred neither by direct allusion nor in any other manner to the interview of the morning or the necessity of finding some other shelter. An indistinct idea he had, that the child was desolate and in want of help, for he often drew her to his bosom and bade her be of good cheer, saying that they would not desert each other; but he seemed unable to contemplate their real position more distinctly, and was still the listless, passionless creature, that suffering of mind and body had left him.

We call this a state of childishness, but it is the same poor hollow mockery of it, that death is of sleep. Where, in the dull eyes of doating men, are the laughing light and life of childhood, the gaiety that has known no check, the frankness that has felt no chill, the hope that has never withered, the joys that fade in blossoming? Where, in the sharp lineaments of rigid and unsightly death, is the calm beauty of slumber, telling of rest for the waking hours that are past, and the gentle hopes and loves for those which are to come? Lay death and sleep down, side by side, and say who shall find the two akin. Send forth the child and childish man together, and blush for the pride that libels our own old happy state, and gives its title to an ugly and distorted image.

Thursday arrived, and there was no alteration in the old man. But, a change came upon him that evening, as he and the child sat silently together.

In a small dull yard below his window, there was a tree—green and flourishing enough, for such a place—and as the air stirred among its leaves, it threw a rippling shadow on the white wall. The old man sat watching the shadows as they trembled in this patch of light until the sun went down, and when it was night and the moon was slowly rising he still sat in the same spot.

To one who had been tossing on a restless bed so long, even these few green leaves and this tranquil light, although it languished among chimneys and house-tops, were pleasant things. They suggested quiet places afar off, and rest, and peace.

The child thought more than once that he was moved, and had

forborne to speak. But now he shed tears—tears that it lightened her aching heart to see—and making as though he would fall upon his knees, besought her to forgive him.

"Forgive you—what?" said Nell, interposing to prevent his purpose. "Oh grandfather, what should I forgive?"

"All that is past, all that has come upon thee, Nell, all that was done in that uneasy dream," returned the old man.

"Do not talk so," said the child. "Pray do not. Let us speak of something else."

"Yes, yes, we will," he rejoined. "And it shall be of what we talked of long ago—many months—months is it, or weeks, or days? which is it, Nell?"

"I do not understand you," said the child.

"It has come back upon me to-day, it has all come back since we have been sitting here. I bless thee for it, Nell!"

"For what, dear grandfather?"

"For what you said when we were first made beggars, Nell. Let us speak softly. Hush! for if they knew our purpose down stairs, they would cry that I was mad and take thee from me. We will not stop here another day. We will go far away from here."

"Yes, let us go," said the child earnestly. "Let us begone from this place, and never turn back or think of it again. Let us wander barefoot through the world, rather than linger here."

"We will," answered the old man, "we will travel afoot through fields and woods, and by the side of rivers, and trust ourselves to God in the places where He dwells. It is far better to lie down at night beneath an open sky like that yonder—see how bright it is—than to rest in close rooms which are always full of care and weary dreams. Thou and I together, Nell, may be cheerful and happy yet, and learn to forget this time, as if it had never been."

"We will be happy," cried the child. "We never can be here."

"No, we never can again—never again—that's truly said," rejoined the old man. "Let us steal away to-morrow morning—early and softly, that we may not be seen or heard—and leave no trace or track for them to follow by. Poor Nell, thy cheek is pale and thy eyes are heavy with watching and weeping—with watching and weeping for me—I know—for me; but thou wilt be well again, and merry too, when we are far away. To-morrow morning, dear, we'll turn our faces from this scene of sorrows, and be as free and happy as the birds."

And then the old man clasped his hands above her head, and said in a few broken words that from that time forth they would wander up and down together, and never part more until Death took one or other of the twain.

The child's heart beat high with hope and confidence. She had no thought of hunger or cold, or thirst, or suffering. She saw in this, but a return of the simple pleasures they had once enjoyed, a relief from the gloomy solitude in which she had lived, an escape from the heartless people by whom she had been surrounded in her late time of trial, the restoration of the old man's health and peace, and a life of tranquil happiness. Sun, and stream, and meadow, and summer days, shone brightly in her view, and there was no dark tint in all the sparkling picture.

The old man had slept for some hours soundly in his bed, and she was yet busily engaged in preparing for their flight. There were a few articles of clothing for herself to carry, and a few for him; old garments, such as became their fallen fortunes, laid out to wear; and a staff to support his feeble steps, put ready for his use. But this was not all her task, for now she must visit the old rooms for the last time.

And how different the parting with them was from any she had expected, and most of all from that which she had oftenest pictured to herself. How could she ever have thought of bidding them farewell in triumph, when the recollections of the many hours she had passed among them rose to her swelling heart, and made her feel the wish a cruelty, lonely and sad though many of those hours had been! She sat down at the window where she had spent so many evenings— darker far than this—and every thought of hope or cheerfulness that had occurred to her in that place came vividly upon her mind, and blotted out all its dull and mournful associations in an instant.

Her own little room, too, where she had so often knelt down and prayed at night—prayed for the time which she hoped was dawning now—the little room where she had slept so peacefully, and dreamed such pleasant dreams—it was hard not to be able to glance round it once more, and to be forced to leave it without one kind look or grateful tear. There were some trifles there—poor useless things—that she would have liked to take away; but that was impossible.

This brought to mind her bird, her poor bird, who hung there yet. She wept bitterly for the loss of this little creature—until the idea occurred to her—she did not know how or why it came into her head —that it might by some means fall into the hands of Kit who would keep it for her sake, and think perhaps that she had left it behind in the hope that he might have it, and as an assurance that she was grateful to him. She was calm and comforted by the thought, and went to rest with a lighter heart.

From many dreams of rambling through light and sunny places, but with some vague object unattained which ran indistinctly through them all, she awoke to find that it was yet night, and that the stars were shining brightly in the sky. At length the day began to glimmer, and the stars to grow pale and dim. As soon as she was sure of this, she arose, and dressed herself for the journey.

The old man was yet asleep, and as she was unwilling to disturb him, she left him to slumber on until the sun rose. He was anxious that they should leave the house without a minute's loss of time, and was soon ready.

The child then took him by the hand, and they trod lightly and cautiously down the stairs, trembling whenever a board creaked, and often stopping to listen. The old man had forgotten a kind of wallet which contained the light burden he had to carry, and the going back a few steps to fetch it seemed an interminable delay.

At last they reached the passage on the ground floor, where the snoring of Mr. Quilp and his legal friend sounded more terrible in their ears than the roars of lions. The bolts of the door were rusty, and difficult to unfasten without noise. When they were all drawn back it was found to be locked, and, worst of all, the key was gone. Then the child remembered for the first time one of the nurses having told her that Quilp always locked both the house-doors at night, and kept the keys on the table in his bedroom.

It was not without great fear and trepidation that little Nell slipped off her shoes and gliding through the store-room of old curiosities, where Mr. Brass—the ugliest piece of goods in all the stock—lay sleeping on a mattress, passed into her own little chamber.

Here she stood for a few moments quite transfixed with terror at the sight of Mr. Quilp, who was hanging so far out of bed that he almost seemed to be standing on his head, and who, either from the uneasiness of this posture or in one of his agreeable habits, was gasping and growling with his mouth wide open, and the whites (or rather the dirty yellows) of his eyes distinctly visible. It was no time, however, to ask whether anything ailed him, so possessing herself of the key after one hasty glance about the room, and repassing the prostrate Mr. Brass, she rejoined the old man in safety. They got the door open without noise, and passing into the street, stood still.

"Which way?" said the child.

The old man looked, irresolutely and helplessly, first at her, then to the right and left, then at her again, and shook his head. It was plain that she was thenceforth his guide and leader. The child felt it, but had no doubts or misgiving, and putting her hand in his, led him gently away.

It was the beginning of a day in June; the deep blue sky unsullied by a cloud, and teeming with brilliant light. The streets were as yet nearly free from passengers, the houses and shops were closed, and the healthful air of morning fell like breath from angels, on the sleeping town.

The old man and the child passed on through the glad silence, elate with hope and pleasure. They were alone together once again; every object was bright and fresh; nothing reminded them, otherwise than by contrast, of the monotony and constraint they had left behind; church towers and steeples, frowning and dark at other times, now shone and dazzled in the sun; each humble nook and corner rejoiced in light; and the sky, dimmed by excessive distance, shed its placid smile on everything beneath.

Forth from the city, while it yet slumbered, went the two poor adventurers, wandering they knew not whither.

CHAPTER XIII

DANIEL QUILP of Tower Hill, and Sampson Brass of Bevis Marks in the city of London, Gentleman, one of her Majesty's attornies of the Courts of King's Bench and Common Pleas at Westminster and a solicitor of the High Court of Chancery, slumbered on unconscious and unsuspicious of any mischance, until a knocking at the street-door, often repeated and gradually mounting up from a modest single rap into a perfect battery of knocks, fired in long discharges with a very short interval between, caused the said Daniel Quilp to struggle into a horizontal position, and to stare at the ceiling with a drowsy indifference, betokening that he heard the noise and rather wondered at the same, but couldn't be at the trouble of bestowing any further thought upon the subject.

As the knocking, however, instead of accommodating itself to his lazy state, increased in vigour and became more importunate, as if in earnest remonstrance against his falling asleep again now that he had once opened his eyes, Daniel Quilp began by degrees to comprehend the possibility of there being somebody at the door, and thus he gradually came to recollect that it was Friday morning, and he had ordered Mrs. Quilp to be in waiting upon him at an early hour.

Mr. Brass, after writhing about in a great many strange attitudes, and often twisting his face and eyes into an expression like that which is usually produced by eating gooseberries very early in the season, was by this time awake also, and seeing that Mr. Quilp invested himself in his every-day garments, hastened to do the like, putting on his shoes before his stockings, and thrusting his legs into his coat sleeves, and making such other small mistakes in his toilet as are not uncommon to those who dress in a hurry, and labour under the agitation of having been suddenly roused.

While the attorney was thus engaged, the dwarf was groping under the table, muttering desperate imprecations upon himself and mankind in general and all inanimate objects to boot, which suggested to Mr. Brass the question "what's the matter?"

"The key," said the dwarf, looking viciously at him, "the door-key,—that's the matter. D'ye know anything of it?"

"How should I know anything of it, sir?" returned Mr. Brass.

"How should you?" repeated Quilp with a sneer. "You're a nice lawyer, an't you. Ugh, you idiot!"

Not caring to represent to the dwarf in his present humour, that the loss of a key by another person could scarcely be said to affect his (Brass's) legal knowledge in any material degree, Mr. Brass humbly suggested that it must have been forgotten over night, and was doubtless at that moment in its native key-hole. Notwithstanding that Mr. Quilp had a strong conviction to the contrary, founded on his recollection of having carefully taken it out, he was fain to admit that this was possible, and therefore went grumbling to the door where, sure enough, he found it.

Now, just as Mr. Quilp laid his hand upon the lock and saw with great astonishment that the fastenings were undone, the knocking came again with most irritating violence, and the daylight which had been shining through the key-hole was intercepted on the outside by a human eye. The dwarf was very much exasperated, and wanting somebody to wreak his ill-humour upon, determined to dart out suddenly and favour Mrs. Quilp with a gentle acknowledgment of her attention in making that hideous uproar.

With this view he drew back the lock very silently and softly, and opening the door all at once, pounced out upon the person on the other side, who had at that moment raised the knocker for another application, and at whom the dwarf ran head first, throwing out his hands and feet together, and biting the air in the fulness of his malice.

So far, however, from rushing upon somebody who offered no resistance and implored his mercy, Mr. Quilp was no sooner in the arms of the individual whom he had taken for his wife than he found himself complimented with two staggering blows on the head, and two more, of the same quality, in the chest, and closing with his assailant, such a shower of buffets rained down upon his person as sufficed to convince him that he was in skilful and experienced hands. Nothing daunted by this reception, he clung tight to his opponent, and bit and hammered away with such good-will and heartiness, that it was at least a couple of minutes before he was dislodged. Then, and not until then, Daniel Quilp found himself, all flushed and dishevelled in the middle of the street, with Mr. Richard Swiveller performing a kind of dance round him and requiring to know "whether he wanted any more?"

"There's plenty more of it at the same shop," said Mr. Swiveller, by turns advancing and retreating in a threatening attitude, "a large and extensive assortment always on hand—country orders executed with promptitude and despatch—will you have a little more, sir—don't say no, if you'd rather not."

"I thought it was somebody else," said Quilp rubbing his shoulders, "why didn't you say who you were?"

"Why didn't you say who *you* were?" returned Dick, "instead of flying out of the house like a Bedlamite?"

"It was you that—that knocked," said the dwarf, getting up with a short groan, "was it?"

"Yes, I am the man," replied Dick. "That lady had begun when I came, but she knocked too soft, so I relieved her." As he said this, he pointed towards Mrs. Quilp, who stood trembling at a little distance.

"Humph!" muttered the dwarf, darting an angry look at his wife, "I thought it was your fault! And you, sir—don't you know there has been somebody ill here, that you knock as if you'd beat the door down?"

"Damme!" answered Dick, "that's why I did it. I thought there was somebody dead here."

"You came for some purpose, I suppose," said Quilp. "What is it you want?"

"I want to know how the old gentleman is," rejoined Mr. Swiveller, "and to hear from Nell herself, with whom I should like to have a little talk. I'm a friend of the family, sir,—at least I'm the friend of one of the family, and that's the same thing."

"You'd better walk in then," said the dwarf. "Go on, sir, go on. Now, Mrs. Quilp—after you, ma'am."

Mrs. Quilp hesitated, but Mr. Quilp insisted. And it was not a contest of politeness, or by any means a matter of form, for she knew very well that her husband wished to enter the house in this order, that he might have a favourable opportunity of inflicting a few pinches on her arms, which were seldom free from impressions of his fingers in black and blue colours. Mr. Swiveller, who was not in the secret, was a little surprised to hear a suppressed scream, and, looking round, to see Mrs. Quilp following him with a sudden jerk; but he did not remark on these appearances, and soon forgot them.

"Now, Mrs. Quilp," said the dwarf when they had entered the shop, "go you up stairs, if you please, to Nelly's room, and tell her that she's wanted."

"You seem to make yourself at home here," said Dick, who was unacquainted with Mr. Quilp's authority.

"I *am* at home, young gentleman," returned the dwarf.

Dick was pondering what these words might mean, and still more what the presence of Mr. Brass might mean, when Mrs. Quilp came hurrying down stairs, declaring that the rooms above were empty.

"Empty, you fool!" said the dwarf.

"I give you my word, Quilp," answered his trembling wife, "that I have been into every room and there's not a soul in any of them."

"And that," said Mr. Brass, clapping his hands once, with an emphasis, "explains the mystery of the key!"

Quilp looked frowningly at him, and frowningly at his wife, and frowningly at Richard Swiveller; but, receiving no enlightenment from any of them, hurried up stairs, whence he soon hurried down again, confirming the report which had been already made.

"It's a strange way of going," he said, glancing at Swiveller, "very strange not to communicate with me who am such a close and intimate friend of his! Ah! he'll write to me no doubt, or he'll bid Nelly write—yes, yes, that's what he'll do. Nelly's very fond of me. Pretty Nell!"

Mr. Swiveller looked, as he was, all open-mouthed astonishment. Still glancing furtively at him, Quilp turned to Mr. Brass and observed with assumed carelessness, that this need not interfere with the removal of the goods.

"For indeed," he added, "we knew that they'd go away to-day, but not that they'd go so early or so quietly. But they have their reasons, they have their reasons."

"Where in the devil's name are they gone?" said the wondering Dick.

Quilp shook his head and pursed up his lips, in a manner which implied that he knew very well, but was not at liberty to say.

"And what," said Dick, looking at the confusion about him, "what do you mean by moving the goods?"

"That I have bought 'em, sir," rejoined Quilp. "Eh? What then?"

"Has the sly old fox made his fortune then, and gone to live in a tranquil cot in a pleasant spot with a distant view of the changing sea?" said Dick, in great bewilderment.

"Keeping his place of retirement very close, that he may not be visited too often by affectionate grandsons and their devoted friends, eh?" added the dwarf, rubbing his hands hard; "*I* say nothing, but is that your meaning, sir?"

Richard Swiveller was utterly aghast at this unexpected alteration of circumstances, which threatened the complete overthrow of the project in which he bore so conspicuous a part, and seemed to nip his prospects in the bud. Having only received from Frederick Trent, late on the previous night, information of the old man's illness, he had come upon a visit of condolence and inquiry to Nell, prepared with the first instalment of that long train of fascinations which was to fire her heart at last. And here, when he had been thinking of all kinds of graceful and insinuating approaches, and meditating on the fearful retaliation which was slowly working against Sophy Wackles —here were Nell, the old man, and all the money gone, melted away, decamped he knew not whither, as if with a fore-knowledge of the scheme and a resolution to defeat it in the very outset, before a step was taken.

In his secret heart, Daniel Quilp was both surprised and troubled by the flight which had been made. It had not escaped his keen eye that some indispensable articles of clothing were gone with the fugitives, and knowing the old man's weak state of mind, he marvelled what that course of proceeding might be in which he had so readily procured the concurrence of the child. It must not be supposed (or it would be a gross injustice to Mr. Quilp) that he was tortured by any disinterested anxiety on behalf of either. His uneasiness arose from a misgiving that the old man had some secret store of money which he had not suspected, and the bare idea of its escaping his clutches, overwhelmed him with mortification and self-reproach.

In this frame of mind, it was some consolation to him to find that Richard Swiveller was, for different reasons, evidently irritated and disappointed by the same cause. It was plain, thought the dwarf, that he had come there on behalf of his friend to cajole or frighten the old man out of some small fraction of that wealth of which they supposed him to have an abundance. Therefore it was a relief to vex his heart with a picture of the riches the old man hoarded, and to expatiate on his cunning in removing himself even beyond the reach of importunity.

"Well," said Dick, with a blank look, "I suppose it's of no use my staying here."

"Not the least in the world," rejoined the dwarf.

"You'll mention that I called, perhaps?" said Dick.

Mr. Quilp nodded, and said he certainly would, the very first time he saw them.

"And say," added Mr. Swiveller, "say, sir, that I was wafted here upon the pinions of concord; that I came to remove, with the rake of friendship, the seeds of mutual wiolence and heart-burning, and to sow in their place, the germs of social harmony. Will you have the goodness to charge yourself with that commission, sir?"

"Certainly!" rejoined Quilp.

"Will you be kind enough to add to it, sir," said Dick, producing a very small limp card, "that *that* is my address, and that I am to be found at home every morning. Two distinct knocks, sir, will produce the slavey at any time. My particular friends, sir, are accustomed to sneeze when the door is opened, to give her to understand that they *are* my friends and have no interested motives in asking if I'm at home. I beg your pardon; will you allow me to look at that card again?"

"Oh! by all means," rejoined Quilp.

"By a slight and not unnatural mistake, sir," said Dick, substituting another in its stead, "I had handed you the pass-ticket of a select convivial circle called the Glorious Apollers, of which I have the honour to be Perpetual Grand. That is the proper document, sir. Good morning."

Quilp bade him good day; the Perpetual Grand Master of the Glorious Apollers, elevating his hat in honour of Mrs. Quilp, dropped it carelessly on the side of his head again, and disappeared with a flourish.

By this time certain vans had arrived for the conveyance of the goods, and divers strong men in carpet caps were balancing chests of drawers and other trifles of that nature upon their heads, and performing muscular feats which heightened their complexions considerably. Not to be behind-hand in the bustle, Mr. Quilp went to work with surprising vigour; hustling and driving the people about, like an evil spirit; setting Mrs. Quilp upon all kinds of arduous and impracticable tasks; carrying great weights up and down with no apparent effort; kicking the boy from the wharf whenever he could get near him; and inflicting with his loads a great many sly bumps and blows upon the shoulders of Mr. Brass, as he stood upon the door-steps to answer all the inquiries of curious neighbours, which was his department. His presence and example diffused such alacrity among the persons employed, that in a few hours the house was emptied of everything, but pieces of matting, empty porter-pots, and scattered fragments of straw.

Seated, like an African chief, on one of these pieces of matting, the dwarf was regaling himself in the parlour with bread and cheese and beer, when he observed, without appearing to do so, that a boy was prying in at the outer door. Assured that it was Kit, though he saw little more than his nose, Mr. Quilp hailed him by his name; whereupon Kit came in and demanded what he wanted.

"Come here, you sir," said the dwarf. "Well, so your old master and young mistress have gone?"

"Where?" rejoined Kit, looking round.

"Do you mean to say you don't know where?" answered Quilp sharply. "Where have they gone, eh?"

"I don't know," said Kit.

"Come," retorted Quilp, "let's have no more of this! Do you mean to say that you don't know they went away by stealth, as soon as it was light this morning?"

"No," said the boy, in evident surprise.

"You don't know that?" cried Quilp. "Don't I know that you were hanging about the house the other night, like a thief, eh? Weren't you told then?"

"No," replied the boy.

"You were not?" said Quilp. "What were you told then; what were you talking about?"

Kit, who knew no particular reason why he should keep the matter secret now, related the purpose for which he had come on that occasion, and the proposal he had made.

"Oh!" said the dwarf after a little consideration. "Then, I think they'll come to you yet."

"Do you think they will?" cried Kit eagerly.

"Ay, I think they will," returned the dwarf. "Now, when they do, let me know; d'ye hear? Let me know, and I'll give you something. I want to do 'em a kindness, and I can't do 'em a kindness unless I know where they are. You hear what I say?"

Kit might have returned some answer which would not have been agreeable to his irascible questioner, if the boy from the wharf, who had been skulking about the room in search of anything that might have been left about by accident, had not happened to cry, "Here's a bird! What's to be done with this?"

"Wring its neck," rejoined Quilp.

"Oh no, don't do that," said Kit, stepping forward. "Give it to me."

"Oh yes, I dare say," cried the other boy. "Come! You let the cage alone, and let me wring its neck, will you? He said I was to do it. You let the cage alone, will you?"

"Give it here, give it to me, you dogs," roared Quilp. "Fight for it, you dogs, or I'll wring its neck myself!"

Without further persuasion, the two boys fell upon each other tooth and nail, while Quilp, holding up the cage in one hand, and chopping the ground with his knife in an ecstasy, urged them on by his taunts and cries to fight more fiercely. They were a pretty equal match, and rolled about together, exchanging blows which were by no means child's play, until at length, Kit, planting a well-directed hit in his adversary's chest, disengaged himself, sprang nimbly up, and snatching the cage from Quilp's hands made off with his prize.

He did not stop once until he reached home, where his bleeding face occasioned great consternation, and caused the elder child to howl dreadfully.

"Goodness gracious, Kit, what is the matter, what have you been doing?" cried Mrs. Nubbles.

"Never you mind, mother," answered her son, wiping his face on the jack-towel behind the door. "I'm not hurt, don't you be afraid for me. I've been a fightin' for a bird and won him, that's all. Hold your noise, little Jacob. I never see such a naughty boy in all my days!"

"You have been fighting for a bird!" exclaimed his mother.

"Ah! Fightin' for a bird!" replied Kit, "and here he is—Miss Nelly's bird, mother, that they was a goin' to wring the neck of! I stopped that though—ha ha ha! They wouldn't wring his neck and me by, no no. It wouldn't do, mother, it wouldn't do at all. Ha ha ha!"

Kit laughed so heartily, with his swoln and bruised face looking out of the towel, made little Jacob laugh, and then his mother laughed, and then the baby crowed and kicked with great glee, and then they all laughed in concert, partly because of Kit's triumph, and partly because they were very fond of each other. When this fit was over, Kit exhibited the bird to both children, as a great and precious rarity—it was only a poor linnet—and looking about the wall for an old nail, made a scaffolding of a chair and table and twisted it out with great exultation.

"Let me see," said the boy, "I think I'll hang him in the winder, because it's more light and cheerful, and he can see the sky there, if he looks up very much. He's such a one to sing, I can tell you!"

So, the scaffolding was made again, and Kit, climbing up with the poker for a hammer, knocked in the nail and hung up the cage, to the immeasurable delight of the whole family. When it had been adjusted and straightened a good many times, and he had walked backwards into the fireplace in his admiration of it, the arrangement was pronounced to be perfect.

"And now, mother," said the boy, "before I rest any more, I'll go out and see if I can find a horse to hold, and then I can buy some birdseed, and a bit of something nice for you, into the bargain."

CHAPTER XIV

As it was very easy for Kit to persuade himself that the old house was in his way, his way being anywhere, he tried to look upon his passing it once more as a matter of imperative and disagreeable necessity, quite apart from any desire of his own, to which he could not choose but yield. It is not uncommon for people who are much better fed and taught than Christopher Nubbles had ever been, to make duties of their inclinations in matters of more doubtful propriety, and to take great credit for the self-denial with which they gratify themselves.

There was no need of any caution this time and no fear of being detained by having to play out a return match with Daniel Quilp's boy. The place was entirely deserted, and looked as dusty and dingy as if it had been so for months. A rusty padlock was fastened on the door, ends of discoloured blinds and curtains flapped drearily against the half-opened upper windows, and the crooked holes cut in the closed shutters below, were black with the darkness of the inside. Some of the glass in the window he had so often watched, had been broken in the rough hurry of the morning, and that room looked more deserted and dull than any. A group of idle urchins had taken possession of the door-steps; some were plying the knocker and listening with delighted dread to the hollow sounds it spread through the dismantled house; others were clustered about the keyhole, watching half in jest and half in earnest for "the ghost," which an hour's gloom, added to the mystery that hung about the late inhabitants, had already raised. Standing all alone in the midst of the business and bustle of the street, the house looked a picture of cold desolation; and Kit, who remembered the cheerful fire that used to burn there on a winter's night and the no less cheerful laugh that made the small room ring, turned quite mournfully away.

It must be specially observed in justice to poor Kit that he was by no means of a sentimental turn, and perhaps had never heard that adjective in all his life. He was only a soft-hearted grateful fellow, and had nothing genteel or polite about him; consequently instead of going home again in his grief to kick the children and abuse his mother (for when your finely strung people are out of sorts they must have everybody else unhappy likewise), he turned his thoughts to the vulgar expedient of making them more comfortable if he could.

Bless us, what a number of gentlemen on horseback there were riding up and down, and how few of them wanted their horses held! A good city speculator or a parliamentary commissioner could have told to a fraction, from the crowds that were cantering about, what sum of money was realised in London in the course of a year, by holding horses alone. And undoubtedly it would have been a very large one, if only a twentieth part of the gentlemen without grooms had had occasion to alight; but they hadn't; and it is often an ill-natured circumstance like this, which spoils the most ingenious estimate in the world.

Kit walked about, now with quick step and now with slow; now lingering as some rider slackened his horse's pace and looked about him; and now darting at full speed up a bye-street as he caught a glimpse of some distant horseman going lazily up the shady side of the road, and promising to stop, at every door. But on they all went, one after another, and there was not a penny stirring. "I wonder," thought the boy, "if one of these gentlemen knew there was nothing in the cupboard at home, whether he'd stop on purpose, and make believe that he wanted to call somewhere, that I might earn a trifle?"

He was quite tired out with pacing the streets, to say nothing of
repeated disappointments, and was sitting down upon a step to rest,
when there approached towards him a little clattering jingling four-
wheeled chaise, drawn by a little obstinate-looking rough-coated
pony, and driven by a little fat placid-faced old gentleman. Beside
the little old gentleman sat a little old lady, plump and placid like
himself, and the pony was coming along at his own pace and doing
exactly as he pleased with the whole concern. If the old gentleman
remonstrated by shaking the reins, the pony replied by shaking his
head. It was plain that the utmost the pony would consent to do,
was to go in his own way up any street that the old gentleman particularly wished to traverse, but that it was an understanding between
them that he must do this after his own fashion or not at all.

As they passed where he sat, Kit looked so wistfully at the little
turn-out that the old gentleman looked at him, and Kit rising and
putting his hand to his hat, the old gentleman intimated to the pony
that he wished to stop, to which proposal the pony (who seldom
objected to that part of his duty) graciously acceded.

"I beg your pardon, sir," said Kit. "I'm sorry you stopped, sir.
I only meant did you want your horse minded."

"I'm going to get down in the next street," returned the old gentleman. "If you like to come on after us, you may have the job."

Kit thanked him, and joyfully obeyed. The pony ran off at a sharp
angle to inspect a lamp-post on the opposite side of the way, and then
went off at a tangent to another lamp-post on the other side. Having
satisfied himself that they were of the same pattern and materials, he
came to a stop, apparently absorbed in meditation.

"Will you go on, sir?" said the old gentleman, gravely, "or are we
to wait here for you till it's too late for our appointment?"

The pony remained immoveable.

"Oh you naughty Whisker," said the old lady. "Fie upon you!
I'm ashamed of such conduct."

The pony appeared to be touched by this appeal to his feelings,
for he trotted on directly, though in a sulky manner, and stopped no
more until he came to a door whereon was a brass plate with the
words "Witherden—Notary." Here the old gentleman got out and
helped out the old lady, and then took from under the seat a nosegay
resembling in shape and dimensions a full-sized warming-pan with
the handle cut short off. This, the old lady carried into the house
with a staid and stately air, and the old gentleman (who had a club-
foot) followed close upon her.

They went, as it was easy to tell from the sound of their voices,
into the front parlour, which seemed to be a kind of office. The day
being very warm and the street a quiet one, the windows were wide
open, and it was easy to hear through the Venetian blinds all that
passed inside.

At first there was a great shaking of hands and shuffling of feet,
succeeded by the presentation of the nosegay, for a voice, supposed
by the listener to be that of Mr. Witherden the Notary, was heard

to exclaim a great many times, "oh, delicious!" "oh, fragrant, indeed!" and a nose, also supposed to be the property of that gentleman, was heard to inhale the scent with a snuffle of exceeding pleasure.

"I brought it in honour of the occasion, sir," said the old lady.

"Ah! an occasion indeed, ma'am; an occasion which does honour to me, ma'am, honour to me," rejoined Mr. Witherden the Notary. "I have had many a gentleman articled to me, ma'am, many a one. Some of them are now rolling in riches, unmindful of their old companion and friend, ma'am, others are in the habit of calling upon me to this day and saying, 'Mr. Witherden, some of the pleasantest hours I ever spent in my life were spent in this office—were spent, sir, upon this very stool;' but there was never one among the number, ma'am, attached as I have been to many of them, of whom I augured such bright things as I do of your only son."

"Oh dear!" said the old lady. "How happy you do make us when you tell us that, to be sure!"

"I tell you, ma'am," said Mr. Witherden, "what I think as an honest man, which, as the poet observes, is the noblest work of God. I agree with the poet in every particular, ma'am. The mountainous Alps on the one hand, or a humming-bird on the other, is nothing, in point of workmanship, to an honest man—or woman—or woman."

"Anything that Mr. Witherden can say of me," observed a small quiet voice, "I can say with interest of him, I am sure."

"It's a happy circumstance, a truly happy circumstance," said the Notary, "to happen too upon his eight-and-twentieth birthday, and I hope I know how to appreciate it. I trust, Mr. Garland, my dear sir, that we may mutually congratulate each other upon this auspicious occasion."

To this the old gentleman replied that he felt assured they might. There appeared to be another shaking of hands in consequence, and when it was over, the old gentleman said that, though he said it who should not, he believed no son had ever been a greater comfort to his parents than Abel Garland had been to his.

"Marrying as his mother and I did, late in life, sir, after waiting for a great many years, until we were well enough off—coming together when we were no longer young, and then being blessed with one child who has always been dutiful and affectionate—why, it's a source of great happiness to us both, sir."

"Of course it is, I have no doubt of it," returned the Notary in a sympathising voice. "It's the contemplation of this sort of thing, that makes me deplore my fate in being a bachelor. There was a young lady once, sir, the daughter of an outfitting warehouse of the first respectability—but that's a weakness. Chuckster, bring in Mr. Abel's articles."

"You see, Mr. Witherden," said the old lady, "that Abel has not been brought up like the run of young men. He has always had a pleasure in our society, and always been with us. Abel has never been absent from us, for a day; has he, my dear?"

"Never, my dear," returned the old gentleman, "except when he went to Margate one Saturday with Mr. Tomkinley that had been a teacher at that school he went to, and came back upon the Monday; but he was very ill after that, you remember, my dear; it was quite a dissipation."

"He was not used to it, you know," said the old lady, "and he couldn't bear it, that's the truth. Besides he had no comfort in being there without us, and had nobody to talk to or enjoy himself with."

"That was it, you know," interposed the same small quiet voice that had spoken once before. "I was quite abroad, mother, quite desolate, and to think that the sea was between us—oh, I never shall forget what I felt when I first thought that the sea was between us!"

"Very natural under the circumstances," observed the Notary. "Mr. Abel's feelings did credit to his nature, and credit to your nature, ma'am, and his father's nature, and human nature. I trace the same current now, flowing through all his quiet and unobtrusive proceedings.—I am about to sign my name, you observe, at the foot of the articles which Mr. Chuckster will witness; and, placing my finger upon this blue wafer with the vandyked corners, I am constrained to remark in a distinct tone of voice—don't be alarmed, ma'am, it is merely a form of law—that I deliver this, as my act and deed. Mr. Abel will place his name against the other wafer, repeating the same cabalistic words, and the business is over. Ha ha ha! You see how easily these things are done!"

There was a short silence, apparently, while Mr. Abel went through the prescribed form, and then the shaking of hands and shuffling of feet were renewed, and shortly afterwards there was a clinking of wine-glasses and a great talkativeness on the part of everybody. In about a quarter of an hour Mr. Chuckster (with a pen behind his ear and his face inflamed with wine) appeared at the door, and condescending to address Kit by the jocose appellation of "Young Snob," informed him that the visitors were coming out.

Out they came forthwith; Mr. Witherden, who was short, chubby, fresh-coloured, brisk, and pompous, leading the old lady with extreme politeness, and the father and son following them, arm in arm. Mr. Abel, who had a quaint old-fashioned air about him, looked nearly of the same age as his father, and bore a wonderful resemblance to him in face and figure, though wanting something of his full, round cheerfulness, and substituting in its place, a timid reserve. In all other respects, in the neatness of the dress, and even in the club-foot, he and the old gentleman were precisely alike.

Having seen the old lady safely in her seat, and assisted in the arrangement of her cloak and a small basket which formed an indispensable portion of her equipage, Mr. Abel got into a little box behind which had evidently been made for his express accommodation, and smiled at everybody present by turns, beginning with his mother and ending with the pony. There was then a great to-do to make the pony hold up his head that the bearing-rein might be fastened; at last even this was effected; and the old gentleman, taking his seat and the reins, put his hand in his pocket to find a sixpence for Kit.

He had no sixpences, neither had the old lady, nor Mr. Abel, nor the Notary, nor Mr. Chuckster. The old gentleman thought a shilling too much, but there was no shop in the street to get change at, so he gave it to the boy.

"There," he said jokingly, "I'm coming here again next Monday at the same time, and mind you're here, my lad, to work it out."

"Thank you, sir," said Kit. "I'll be sure to be here."

He was quite serious, but they all laughed heartily at his saying so, especially Mr. Chuckster, who roared outright and appeared to relish the joke amazingly. As the pony, with a presentiment that he was going home, or a determination that he would not go anywhere else (which was the same thing), trotted away pretty nimbly, Kit had no time to justify himself, and went his way also. Having expended his treasure in such purchases as he knew would be most acceptable at home, not forgetting some seed for the wonderful bird, he hastened back as fast as he could, so elated with his success and great good fortune, that he more than half expected Nell and the old man would have arrived before him.

CHAPTER XV

OFTEN, while they were yet pacing the silent streets of the town on the morning of their departure, the child trembled with a mingled sensation of hope and fear as in some far-off figure imperfectly seen in the clear distance, her fancy traced a likeness to honest Kit. But although she would gladly have given him her hand and thanked him for what he had said at their last meeting, it was always a relief to find, when they came nearer to each other, that the person who approached was not he, but a stranger; for even if she had not dreaded the effect which the sight of him might have wrought upon her fellow-traveller, she felt that to bid farewell to anybody now, and most of all to him who had been so faithful and so true, was more than she could bear. It was enough to leave dumb things behind, and objects that were insensible both to her love and sorrow. To have parted from her only other friend upon the threshold of that wild journey, would have wrung her heart indeed.

Why is it that we can better bear to part in spirit than in body, and while we have the fortitude to act farewell have not the nerve to say it? On the eve of long voyages or an absence of many years, friends who are tenderly attached will separate with the usual look, the usual pressure of the hand, planning one final interview for the morrow, while each well knows that it is but a poor feint to save the pain of uttering that one word, and that the meeting will never be. Should possibilities be worse to bear than certainties? We do not shun our dying friends; the not having distinctly taken leave of one among them, whom we left in all kindness and affection, will often embitter the whole remainder of a life.

The town was glad with morning light: places that had shown ugly and distrustful all night long, now wore a smile; and sparkling sunbeams dancing on chamber windows, and twinkling through blind and curtain before sleepers' eyes, shed light even into dreams, and chased away the shadows of the night. Birds in hot rooms, covered up close and dark, felt it was morning, and chafed and grew restless in their little cells; bright-eyed mice crept back to their tiny homes and nestled timidly together; the sleek house-cat, forgetful of her prey, sat winking at the rays of sun starting through key-hole and cranny in the door, and longed for her stealthy run and warm sleek bask outside. The nobler beasts confined in dens stood motionless behind their bars, and gazed on fluttering boughs and sunshine peeping through some little window, with eyes in which old forests gleamed— then trod impatiently the track their prisoned feet had worn— —and stopped and gazed again. Men in their dungeons stretched their cramp cold limbs and cursed the stone that no bright sky could warm. The flowers that sleep by night, opened their gentle eyes and turned them to the day. The light, creation's mind, was everywhere, and all things owned its power.

The two pilgrims, often pressing each other's hands, or exchanging a smile or cheerful look, pursued their way in silence. Bright and happy as it was, there was something solemn in the long deserted streets, from which like bodies without souls all habitual character and expression had departed, leaving but one dead uniform repose, that made them all alike. All was so still at that early hour, that the few pale people whom they met seemed as much unsuited to the scene as the sickly lamp which had been here and there left burning was powerless and faint in the full glory of the sun.

Before they had penetrated very far into the labyrinth of man's abodes which yet lay between them and the outskirts, this aspect began to melt away, and noise and bustle to usurp its place. Some straggling carts and coaches rumbling by, first broke the charm, then others came, then others yet more active, then a crowd. The wonder was at first to see a tradesman's window open, but it was a rare thing soon to see one closed; then smoke rose slowly from the chimneys, and sashes were thrown up to let in air, and doors were opened, and servant-girls, looking lazily in all directions but their brooms, scattered brown clouds of dust into the eyes of shrinking passengers, or listened disconsolately to milkmen who spoke of country fairs, and told of waggons in the mews, with awnings and all things complete and gallant swains to boot, which another hour would see upon their journey.,

This quarter passed, they came upon the haunts of commerce and great traffic, where many people were resorting, and business was already rife. The old man looked about him with a startled and bewildered gaze, for these were places that he hoped to shun. He pressed his finger on his lip, and drew the child along by narrow courts and winding ways, nor did he seem at ease until they had left it far behind, often casting a backward look towards it, murmuring that ruin and self-murder were crouching in every street, and would follow if they scented them; and that they could not fly too fast.

Again this quarter passed, they came upon a straggling neighbourhood, where the mean houses parcelled off in rooms, and windows patched with rags and paper, told of the populous poverty that sheltered there. The shops sold goods that only poverty could buy, and sellers and buyers were pinched and gripped alike. Here were poor streets where faded gentility essayed with scanty space and shipwrecked means to make its last feeble stand, but tax-gatherer and creditor came there as elsewhere, and the poverty that yet faintly struggled was hardly less squalid and manifest than that which had long ago submitted and given up the game.

This was a wide, wide track—for the humble followers of the camp of wealth pitch their tents round about it for many a mile—but its character was still the same. Damp rotten houses, many to let, many yet building, many half-built and mouldering away—lodgings, where it would be hard to tell which needed pity most, those who let or those who came to take—children, scantily fed and clothed, spread over every street, and sprawling in the dust—scolding mothers, stamping their slipshod feet with noisy threats upon the pavement—shabby fathers, hurrying with dispirited looks to the occupation which brought them "daily bread" and little more—mangling-women, washerwomen, cobblers, tailors, chandlers, driving their trades in parlours and kitchens and back rooms and garrets, and sometimes all of them under the same roof—brick-fields, skirting gardens paled with staves of old casks, or timber pillaged from houses burnt down and blackened and blistered by the flames—mounds of dockweed, nettles, coarse grass and oyster-shells, heaped in rank confusion—small Dissenting chapels to teach, with no lack of illustration the miseries of Earth, and plenty of new churches, erected with a little superfluous wealth, to show the way to Heaven.

At length these streets, becoming more straggling yet, dwindled and dwindled away, until there were only small garden patches bordering the road, with many a summer-house innocent of paint and built of old timber or some fragments of a boat, green as the tough cabbage-stalks that grew about it, and grottoed at the seams with toadstools and tight-sticking snails. To these succeeded pert cottages, two and two with plots of ground in front, laid out in angular beds with stiff box borders and narrow paths between, where footsteps never strayed to make the gravel rough. Then came the public-house, freshly painted in green and white, with tea-gardens and a bowling-green, spurning its old neighbour with the horse-trough where the waggons stopped; then fields; and then some houses, one by one, of goodly size with lawns, some even with a lodge where dwelt a porter and his wife. Then came a turnpike; then fields again with trees and haystacks; then a hill; and on the top of that the traveller might stop, and—looking back at old Saint Paul's looming through the smoke, its cross peeping above the cloud (if the day were clear), and glittering in the sun; and casting his eyes upon the Babel out of which it grew until he traced it down to the furthest outposts of the invading army of bricks and mortar whose station lay for the present nearly at his feet—might feel at last that he was clear of London.

Near such a spot as this, and in a pleasant field, the old man and his little guide (if guide she were, who knew not whither they were bound) sat down to rest. She had had the precaution to furnish her basket with some slices of bread and meat, and here they made their frugal breakfast.

The freshness of the day, the singing of the birds, the beauty of the waving grass, the deep green leaves, the wild flowers, and the thousand exquisite scents and sounds that floated in the air,—deep joys to most of us, but most of all to those whose life is in a crowd or who live solitarily in great cities as in the bucket of a human well,—sank into their breasts and made them very glad. The child had repeated her artless prayers once that morning, more earnestly perhaps than she had ever done in all her life, but as she felt all this, they rose to her lips again. The old man took off his hat—he had no memory for the words—but he said amen, and that they were very good.

There had been an old copy of the Pilgrim's Progress, with strange plates, upon a shelf at home, over which she had often pored whole evenings, wondering whether it was true in every word, and where those distant countries with the curious names might be. As she looked back upon the place they had left, one part of it came strongly on her mind.

"Dear grandfather," she said, "only that this place is prettier and a great deal better than the real one, if that in the book is like it, I feel as if we were both Christian, and laid down on this grass all the cares and troubles we brought with us; never to take them up again."

"No—never to return—never to return"—replied the old man, waving his hand towards the city. "Thou and I are free of it now, Nell. They shall never lure us back."

"Are you tired?" said the child, "are you sure you don't feel ill from this long walk?"

"I shall never feel ill again, now that we are once away," was his reply. "Let us be stirring, Nell. We must be further away—a long, long way further. We are too near to stop, and be at rest. Come!"

There was a pool of clear water in the field, in which the child laved her hands and face, and cooled her feet before setting forth to walk again. She would have the old man refresh himself in this way too, and making him sit down upon the grass, cast the water on him with her hands, and dried it with her simple dress.

"I can do nothing for myself, my darling," said the grandfather, "I don't know how it is, I could once, but the time's gone. Don't leave me, Nell; say that thou'lt not leave me. I loved thee all the while, indeed I did. If I lose thee too, my dear, I must die!"

He laid his head upon her shoulder and moaned piteously. The time had been, and a very few days before, when the child could not have restrained her tears and must have wept with him. But now she soothed him with gentle and tender words, smiled at his thinking they could ever part, and rallied him cheerfully upon the jest. He was soon calmed and fell asleep, singing to himself in a low voice, like a little child.

He awoke refreshed, and they continued their journey. The road was pleasant, lying between beautiful pastures and fields of corn, above which, poised high in the clear blue sky, the lark trilled out her happy song. The air came laden with the fragrance it caught upon its way, and the bees, upborne upon its scented breath, hummed forth their drowsy satisfaction as they floated by.

They were now in the open country; the houses were very few and scattered at long intervals, often miles apart. Occasionally they came upon a cluster of poor cottages, some with a chair or low board put across the open door to keep the scrambling children from the road, others shut up close while all the family were working in the fields. These were often the commencement of a little village: and after an interval came a wheelwright's shed or perhaps a blacksmith's forge; then a thriving farm with sleepy cows lying about the yard, and horses peering over the low wall and scampering away when harnessed horses passed upon the road, as though in triumph at their freedom. There were dull pigs too, turning up the ground in search of dainty food, and grunting their monotonous grumblings as they prowled about, or crossed each other in their quest; plump pigeons skimming round the roof or strutting on the eaves; and ducks and geese, far more graceful in their own conceit, waddling awkwardly about the edges of the pond or sailing glibly on its surface. The farm-yard passed, then came the little inn; the humbler beer-shop; and the village tradesman's; then the lawyer's and the parson's, at whose dread names the beer-shop trembled; the church then peeped out modestly from a clump of trees; then there were a few more cottages; then the cage, and pound, and not unfrequently, on a bank by the way-side, a deep old dusty well. Then came the trim-hedged fields on either hand, and the open road again.

They walked all day, and slept that night at a small cottage where beds were let to travellers. Next morning they were afoot again, and though jaded at first, and very tired, recovered before long and proceeded briskly forward.

They often stopped to rest, but only for a short space at a time, and still kept on, having had but slight refreshment since the morning. It was nearly five o'clock in the afternoon, when, drawing near another cluster of labourers' huts, the child looked wistfully in each, doubtful at which to ask for permission to rest awhile, and buy a draught of milk.

It was not easy to determine, for she was timid and fearful of being repulsed. Here was a crying child, and there a noisy wife. In this, the people seemed too poor; in that, too many. At length she stopped at one where the family were seated round the table—

chiefly because there was an old man sitting in a cushioned chair beside the hearth, and she thought he was a grandfather and would feel for hers.

There were besides, the cottager and his wife, and three young sturdy children, brown as berries. The request was no sooner preferred, than granted. The eldest boy ran out to fetch some milk, the second dragged two stools towards the door, and the youngest crept to his mother's gown, and looked at the strangers from beneath his sunburnt hand.

"God save you, master," said the old cottager in a thin piping voice; "are you travelling far?"

"Yes, sir, a long way"—replied the child; for her grandfather appealed to her.

"From London?" inquired the old man.

The child said yes.

Ah! He had been in London many a time—used to go there often once, with waggons. It was nigh two-and-thirty year since he had been there last, and he did hear say there were great changes. Like enough! He had changed, himself, since then. Two-and-thirty year was a long time and eighty-four a great age, though there was some he had known that had lived to very hard upon a hundred—and not so hearty as he, neither—no, nothing like it.

"Sit thee down, master, in the elbow chair," said the old man, knocking his stick upon the brick floor, and trying to do so sharply. "Take a pinch out o' that box; I don't take much myself, for it comes dear, but I find it wakes me up sometimes, and ye're but a boy to me. I should have a son pretty nigh as old as you if he'd lived, but they listed him for a so'ger—he come back home though, for all he had but one poor leg. He always said he'd be buried near the sun-dial he used to climb upon when he was a baby, did my poor boy, and his words come true—you can see the place with your own eyes; we've kept the turf up, ever since."

He shook his head, and looking at his daughter with watery eyes, said she needn't be afraid that he was going to talk about that any more. He didn't wish to trouble nobody, and if he had troubled anybody by what he said, he asked pardon, that was all.

The milk arrived, and the child producing her little basket and selecting its best fragments for her grandfather, they made a hearty meal. The furniture of the room was very homely of course—a few rough chairs and a table, a corner cupboard with their little stock of crockery and delf, a gaudy tea-tray, representing a lady in bright red, walking out with a very blue parasol, a few common, coloured Scripture subjects in frames upon the wall and chimney, an old dwarf clothes-press and an eight-day clock, with a few bright saucepans and a kettle, comprised the whole. But everything was clean and neat, and as the child glanced round, she felt a tranquil air of comfort and content to which she had long been unaccustomed.

"How far is it to any town or village?" she asked of the husband.

"A matter of good five mile, my dear," was the reply, "but

you're not going on to-night?"

"Yes yes, Nell," said the old man hastily, urging her too by signs. "Further on, further on, darling, further away if we walk till midnight."

"There's a good barn hard by, master," said the man, "or there's travellers' lodgings, I know, at the Plow an' Harrer. Excuse me, but you do seem a little tired, and unless you're very anxious to get on——"

"Yes yes, we are," returned the old man fretfully. "Further away, dear Nell, pray further away."

"We must go on, indeed," said the child, yielding to his restless wish. "We thank you very much, but we cannot stop so soon. I'm quite ready, grandfather."

But the woman had observed, from the young wanderer's gait, that one of her little feet was blistered and sore, and being a woman and a mother too, she would not suffer her to go until she had washed the place and applied some simple remedy, which she did so carefully and with such a gentle hand—rough-grained and hard though it was, with work—that the child's heart was too full to admit of her saying more than a fervent "God bless you!" nor could she look back nor trust herself to speak, until they had left the cottage some distance behind. When she turned her head, she saw that the whole family, even the old grandfather, were standing in the road watching them as they went, and so, with many waves of the hand, and cheering nods, and on one side at least not without tears, they parted company.

They trudged forward, more slowly and painfully than they had done yet, for another mile or thereabouts, when they heard the sound of wheels behind them, and looking round observed an empty cart approaching pretty briskly. The driver on coming up to them stopped his horse and looked earnestly at Nell.

"Didn't you stop to rest at a cottage yonder?" he said.

"Yes, sir," replied the child.

"Ah! They asked me to look out for you," said the man. "I'm going your way. Give me your hand—jump up, master."

This was a great relief, for they were very much fatigued and could scarcely crawl along. To them the jolting cart was a luxurious carriage, and the ride the most delicious in the world. Nell had scarcely settled herself on a little heap of straw in one corner, when she fell asleep, for the first time that day.

She was awakened by the stopping of the cart, which was about to turn up a bye-lane. The driver kindly got down to help her out, and pointing to some trees at a very short distance before them, said that the town lay there, and that they had better take the path which they would see, leading through the churchyard. Accordingly, towards this spot they directed their weary steps.

Exhibitors of the freaks of Punch.

CHAPTER XVI

THE sun was setting when they reached the wicket-gate at which the path began, and, as the rain falls upon the just and unjust alike, it shed its warm tint even upon the resting-places of the dead, and bade them be of good hope for its rising on the morrow. The church was old and grey, with ivy clinging to the walls, and round the porch. Shunning the tombs, it crept about the mounds, beneath which slept poor humble men, twining for them the first wreaths they had ever won, but wreaths less liable to wither and far more lasting in their kind, than some which were graven deep in stone and marble, and told in pompous terms of virtues meekly hidden for many a year, and only revealed at last to executors and mourning legatees.

The clergyman's horse, stumbling with a dull blunt sound among the graves, was cropping the grass; at once deriving orthodox consolation from the dead parishioners, and enforcing last Sunday's text that this was what all flesh came to; a lean ass who had sought to expound it also, without being qualified and ordained, was pricking his ears in an empty pound hard by, and looking with hungry eyes upon his priestly neighbour.

The old man and the child quitted the gravel path, and strayed among the tombs; for there the ground was soft, and easy to their tired feet. As they passed behind the church, they heard voices near at hand, and presently came on those who had spoken.

They were two men who were seated in easy attitudes upon the grass, and so busily engaged as to be at first unconscious of intruders. It was not difficult to divine that they were of a class of itinerant showmen—exhibitors of the freaks of Punch—for, perched cross-legged upon a tombstone behind them, was a figure of that hero himself, his nose and chin as hooked and his face as beaming as usual. Perhaps his imperturbable character was never more strikingly developed, for he preserved his usual equable smile notwithstanding that his body was dangling in a most uncomfortable position, all loose and limp and shapeless, while his long peaked cap, unequally balanced against his exceedingly slight legs, threatened every instant to bring him toppling down.

In part scattered upon the ground at the feet of the two men, and in part jumbled together in a long flat box, were the other persons of the Drama. The hero's wife and one child, the hobby-horse, the doctor, the foreign gentleman who not being familiar with the language is unable in the representation to express his ideas otherwise than by the utterance of the word "Shallabalah" three distinct times, the Radical neighbour who will by no means admit that a tin bell is an organ, the executioner, and the Devil, were all here. Their owners had evidently come to that spot to make some needful repairs in the stage arrangements, for one of them was engaged in binding together a small gallows with thread, while the other was intent upon fixing a new black wig, with the aid of a small hammer and some tacks, upon the head of the Radical neighbour, who had been beaten bald.

They raised their eyes when the old man and his young companion were close upon them, and pausing in their work, returned their looks of curiosity. One of them, the actual exhibitor no doubt, was a little merry-faced man with a twinkling eye and a red nose, who seemed to have unconsciously imbibed something of his hero's character. The other—that was he who took the money—had rather a careful and cautious look, which was perhaps inseparable from his occupation also.

The merry man was the first to greet the strangers with a nod; and following the old man's eyes, he observed that perhaps that was the first time he had ever seen a Punch off the stage. (Punch, it may be remarked, seemed to be pointing with the tip of his cap to a most flourishing epitaph, and to be chuckling over it with all his heart.)

"Why do you come here to do this?" said the old man, sitting down beside them, and looking at the figures with extreme delight.

"Why you see," rejoined the little man, "we're putting up for to-night at the public-house yonder, and it wouldn't do to let 'em see the present company undergoing repair."

"No!" cried the old man, making signs to Nell to listen, "why not, eh? why not?"

"Because it would destroy all the delusion, and take away all the interest, wouldn't it?" replied the little man. "Would you care a ha'penny for the Lord Chancellor if you know'd him in private and without his wig—certainly not."

"Good!" said the old man, venturing to touch one of the puppets, and drawing away his hand with a shrill laugh. "Are you going to show 'em to-night? are you?"

"That is the intention, governor," replied the other, "and unless I'm much mistaken, Tommy Codlin is a calculating at this minute what we've lost through your coming upon us. Cheer up, Tommy, it can't be much."

The little man accompanied these latter words with a wink, expressive of the estimate he had formed of the travellers' finances.

To this Mr. Codlin, who had a surly, grumbling manner, replied, as he twitched Punch off the tombstone and flung him into the box,

"I don't care if we haven't lost a farden, but you're too free. If you stood in front of the curtain and see the public's faces as I do, you'd know human natur' better."

"Ah! it's been the spoiling of you, Tommy, your taking to that branch," rejoined his companion. "When you played the ghost in the reg'lar drama in the fairs, you believed in everything—except ghosts. But now you're a universal mistruster. _I_ never see a man so changed."

"Never mind," said Mr. Codlin, with the air of a discontented philosopher. "I know better now, and p'raps I'm sorry for it."

Turning over the figures in the box like one who knew and despised them, Mr. Codlin drew one forth and held it up for the inspection of his friend:

"Look here; here's all this Judy's clothes falling to pieces again. You haven't got a needle and thread I suppose?"

The little man shook his head, and scratched it ruefully as he contemplated this severe indisposition of a principal performer. Seeing that they were at a loss, the child said timidly:

"I have a needle, sir, in my basket, and thread too. Will you let me try to mend it for you? I think I can do it neater than you could."

Even Mr. Codlin had nothing to urge against a proposal so seasonable. Nelly, kneeling down beside the box, was soon busily engaged in her task, and accomplishing it to a miracle.

While she was thus engaged, the merry little man looked at her with an interest which did not appear to be diminished when he glanced at her helpless companion. When she had finished her work he thanked her, and inquired whither they were travelling.

"N—no further to-night, I think," said the child, looking towards her grandfather.

"If you're wanting a place to stop at," the man remarked, "I should advise you to take up at the same house with us. That's it— the long, low, white house there. It's very cheap."

The old man, notwithstanding his fatigue, would have remained in the churchyard all night if his new acquaintance had stayed there too. As he yielded to this suggestion a ready and rapturous assent, they all rose and walked away together; he keeping close to the box of puppets in which he was quite absorbed, the merry little man carrying it slung over his arm by a strap attached to it for the purpose, Nelly having hold of her grandfather's hand, and Mr. Codlin sauntering slowly behind, casting up at the church tower and neighbouring trees such looks as he was accustomed in town-practice to direct to drawing-room and nursery windows, when seeking for a profitable spot on which to plant the show.

The public-house was kept by a fat old landlord and landlady who made no objection to receiving their new guests, but praised Nelly's beauty and were at once prepossessed in her behalf. There was no other company in the kitchen but the two showmen, and the child felt very thankful that they had fallen upon such good quarters. The landlady was very much astonished to learn that they had come all the way from London, and appeared to have no little curiosity touching their farther destination. The child parried her enquiries as well as she could, and with no great trouble, for finding that they appeared to give her pain, the old lady desisted.

"These two gentlemen have ordered supper in an hour's time," she said, taking her into the bar; "and your best plan will be to sup with them. Meantime you shall have a little taste of something that'll do you good, for I'm sure you must want it after all you've gone through to-day. Now, don't look after the old gentleman, because when you've drunk that, he shall have some too."

As nothing could induce the child to leave him alone, however, or to touch anything in which he was not the first and greatest sharer, the old lady was obliged to help him first. When they had been thus refreshed, the whole house hurried away into an empty stable where the show stood, and where, by the light of a few flaring candles stuck round a hoop which hung by a line from the ceiling, it was to be forthwith exhibited.

And now Mr. Thomas Codlin, the misanthrope, after blowing away at the Pan's pipes until he was intensely wretched, took his station on one side of the checked drapery which concealed the mover of the figures, and putting his hands in his pockets prepared to reply to all questions and remarks of Punch, and to make a dismal feint of being his most intimate private friend, of believing in him to the fullest and most unlimited extent, of knowing that he enjoyed day and night a merry and glorious existence in that temple, and that he was at all times and under every circumstance the same intelligent and joyful person that the spectators then beheld him. All this Mr. Codlin did with the air of a man who had made up his mind for the worst and was quite resigned; his eye slowly wandering about during the briskest repartee to observe the effect upon the audience, and particularly the impression made upon the landlord and land-lady, which might be productive of very important results in con-nexion with the supper.

Upon this head, however, he had no cause for any anxiety, for the whole performance was applauded to the echo, and voluntary con-tributions were showered in with a liberality which testified yet more strongly to the general delight. Among the laughter none was more loud and frequent than the old man's. Nell's was unheard, for she, poor child, with her head drooping on his shoulder, had fallen asleep, and slept too soundly to be roused by any of his efforts to awaken her to a participation in his glee.

The supper was very good, but she was too tired to eat, and yet would not leave the old man until she had kissed him in his bed. He, happily insensible to every care and anxiety, sat listening with a vacant smile and admiring face to all that his new friends said; and it was not until they retired yawning to their room, that he followed the child up stairs.

It was but a loft partitioned into two compartments, where they were to rest, but they were well pleased with their lodging and had hoped for none so good. The old man was uneasy when he had lain down, and begged Nell would come and sit at his bedside as she had done for so many nights. She hastened to him, and sat there till he slept.

There was a little window, hardly more than a chink in the wall, in her room, and when she left him, she opened it, quite wondering at the silence. The sight of the old church and the graves about it in the moonlight, and the dark trees whispering among themselves, made her more thoughtful than before. She closed the window again, and sitting down upon the bed, thought of the life that was before them.

She had a little money, but it was very little, and when that was gone, they must begin to beg. There was one piece of gold among it, and an emergency might come when its worth to them would be increased a hundred fold. It would be best to hide this coin, and never produce it unless their case was absolutely desperate, and no other resource was left them.

Her resolution taken, she sewed the piece of gold into her dress, and going to bed with a lighter heart sank into a deep slumber.

CHAPTER XVII

ANOTHER bright day shining in through the small casement, and claiming fellowship with the kindred eyes of the child, awoke her. At sight of the strange room and its unaccustomed objects she started up in alarm, wondering how she had been moved from the familiar chamber in which she seemed to have fallen asleep last night, and whither she had been conveyed. But another glance around called to her mind all that had lately passed, and she sprang from her bed, hoping and trustful.

It was yet early, and the old man being still asleep, she walked out into the churchyard, brushing the dew from the long grass with her feet, and often turning aside into places where it grew longer than in others, that she might not tread upon the graves. She felt a curious kind of pleasure in lingering among these houses of the dead, and read the inscriptions on the tombs of the good people (a great number of good people were buried there), passing on from one to another with increasing interest.

It was a very quiet place, as such a place should be, save for the cawing of the rooks who had built their nests among the branches of some tall old trees, and were calling to one another, high up in the air. First one sleek bird, hovering near his ragged house as it swung and dangled in the wind, uttered his hoarse cry, quite by chance as it would seem, and in a sober tone as though he were but talking to himself. Another answered, and he called again, but louder than before; then another spoke and then another; and each time the first, aggravated by contradiction, insisted on his case more strongly. Other voices, silent till now, struck in from boughs lower down and higher up and midway, and to the right and left, and from the tree-tops; and others, arriving hastily from the grey church turrets and old belfry window, joined the clamour which rose and fell, and swelled and dropped again, and still went on; and all this noisy contention amidst a skimming to and fro, and lighting on fresh branches, and frequent change of place, which satirised the old restlessness of those who lay so still beneath the moss and turf below, and the use-less strife in which they had worn away their lives.

Frequently raising her eyes to the trees whence these sounds came down, and feeling as though they made the place more quiet than perfect silence would have done, the child loitered from grave to grave, now stopping to replace with careful hands the bramble which had started from some green mound it helped to keep in shape, and now peeping through one of the low latticed windows into the church, with its worm-eaten books upon the desks, and baize of whitened-green mouldering from the pew sides and leaving the naked wood to view. There were the seats where the poor old people sat, worn spare, and yellow like themselves; the rugged font where children had their names, the homely altar where they knelt in after life, the plain black tressels that bore their weight on their last visit to the cool old shady church. Everything told of long use and quiet slow decay; the very bell-rope in the porch was frayed into a fringe, and hoary with old age.

She was looking at a humble stone which told of a young man who had died at twenty-three years old, fifty-five years ago, when she heard a faltering step approaching, and looking round saw a feeble woman bent with the weight of years, who tottered to the foot of that same grave and asked her to read the writing on the stone. The old woman thanked her when she had done, saying that she had had the words by heart for many a long, long year, but could not see them now.

"Were you his mother?" said the child.

"I was his wife, my dear."

She the wife of a young man of three-and-twenty! Ah, true! It was fifty-five years ago.

"You wonder to hear me say that," remarked the old woman, shaking her head. "You're not the first. Older folk than you have wondered at the same thing before now. Yes, I was his wife. Death doesn't change us more than life, my dear."

"Do you come here often?" asked the child.

"I sit here very often in the summer time," she answered; "I used to come here once to cry and mourn, but that was a weary while ago, bless God!"

"I pluck the daisies as they grow, and take them home," said the old woman after a short silence. "I like no flowers so well as these, and haven't for five-and-fifty year. It's a long time, and I'm getting very old!"

Then growing garrulous upon a theme which was new to one listener though it were but a child, she told her how she had wept and moaned and prayed to die herself, when this happened; and how when she first came to that place, a young creature strong in love and grief, she had hoped that her heart was breaking as it seemed to be. But that time passed by, and although she continued to be sad when she came there, still she could bear to come, and so went on until it was pain no longer, but a solemn pleasure, and a duty she had learned to like. And now that five-and-fifty years were gone, she spoke of the

dead man as if he had been her son or grandson, with a kind of pity
for his youth, growing out of her own old age, and an exalting of his
strength and manly beauty as compared with her own weakness and
decay; and yet she spoke about him as her husband too, and thinking
of herself in connexion with him, as she used to be and not as she was
now, talked of their meeting in another world as if he were dead but
yesterday, and she, separated from her former self, were thinking of
the happiness of that comely girl who seemed to have died with him.

The child left her gathering the flowers that grew upon the grave,
and thoughtfully retraced her steps.

The old man was by this time up and dressed. Mr. Codlin, still
doomed to contemplate the harsh realities of existence, was packing
among his linen the candle-ends which had been saved from the
previous night's performance; while his companion received the
compliments of all the loungers in the stable-yard, who, unable to
separate him from the master-mind of Punch, set him down as next
in importance to that merry outlaw, and loved him scarcely less.
When he had sufficiently acknowledged his popularity he came in to
breakfast, at which meal they all sat down together.

"And where are you going to-day?" said the little man, addressing
himself to Nell.

"Indeed I hardly know,—we have not determined yet," replied
the child.

"We're going on to the races," said the little man. "If that's your
way and you like to have us for company, let us travel together. If
you prefer going alone, only say the word and you'll find that we
shan't trouble you."

"We'll go with you," said the old man, "Nell,—with them, with
them."

The child considered for a moment, and reflecting that she must
shortly beg, and could scarcely hope to do so at a better place than
where crowds of rich ladies and gentlemen were assembled together
for purposes of enjoyment and festivity, determined to accompany
these men so far. She therefore thanked the little man for his offer,
and said, glancing timidly towards his friend, that if there was no
objection to their accompanying them as far as the race town—

"Objection!" said the little man. "Now be gracious for once,
Tommy, and say that you'd rather they went with us. I know you
would. Be gracious, Tommy."

"Trotters," said Mr. Codlin, who talked very slowly and eat very
greedily, as is not uncommon with philosophers and misanthropes;
"you're too free."

"Why, what harm can it do?" urged the other.

"No harm at all in this particular case, perhaps," replied Mr.
Codlin; "but the principle's a dangerous one, and you're too free I
tell you."

"Well, are they to go with us or not?"

"Yes, they are," said Mr. Codlin; "but you might have made a
favour of it, mightn't you?"

The real name of the little man was Harris, but it had gradually merged into the less euphonious one of Trotters, which, with the prefatory adjective, Short, had been conferred upon him by reason of the small size of his legs. Short Trotters, however, being a compound name, inconvenient of use in friendly dialogue, the gentleman on whom it had been bestowed was known among his intimates either as "Short," or "Trotters," and was seldom accosted at full length as Short Trotters, except in formal conversations and on occasions of ceremony.

Short, then, or Trotters, as the reader pleases, returned unto the remonstrance of his friend Mr. Thomas Codlin a jocose answer calculated to turn aside his discontent; and applying himself with great relish to the cold boiled beef, the tea, and bread and butter, strongly impressed upon his companions that they should do the like. Mr. Codlin indeed required no such persuasion, as he had already eat as much as he could possibly carry and was now moistening his clay with strong ale, whereof he took deep draughts with a silent relish and invited nobody to partake,—thus again strongly indicating his misanthropical turn of mind.

Breakfast being at length over, Mr. Codlin called the bill, and charging the ale to the company generally (a practice also savouring of misanthropy) divided the sum-total into two fair and equal parts, assigning one moiety to himself and friend, and the other to Nelly and her grandfather. These being duly discharged and all things ready for their departure, they took farewell of the landlord and landlady and resumed their journey.

And here Mr. Codlin's false position in society and the effect it wrought upon his wounded spirit, were strongly illustrated; for whereas he had been last night accosted by Mr. Punch as " master," and had by inference left the audience to understand that he maintained that individual for his own luxurious entertainment and delight, here he was, now, painfully walking beneath the burden of that same Punch's temple, and bearing it bodily upon his shoulders on a sultry day and along a dusty road. In place of enlivening his patron with a constant fire of wit or the cheerful rattle of his quarter-staff on the heads of his relations and acquaintance, here was that beaming Punch utterly devoid of spine, all slack and drooping in a dark box, with his legs doubled up round his neck, and not one of his social qualities remaining.

Mr. Codlin trudged heavily on, exchanging a word or two at intervals with Short, and stopping to rest and growl occasionally. Short led the way; with the flat box, the private luggage (which was not extensive) tied up in a bundle, and a brazen trumpet slung from his shoulder-blade. Nell and her grandfather walked next him on either hand, and Thomas Codlin brought up the rear.

When they came to any town or village, or even to a detached house of good appearance, Short blew a blast upon the brazen trumpet and carolled a fragment of a song in that hilarious tone common to Punches and their consorts. If people hurried to the windows,

Mr. Codlin pitched the temple, and hastily unfurling the drapery and concealing Short therewith, flourished hysterically on the pipes and performed an air. Then the entertainment began as soon as might be; Mr. Codlin having the responsibility of deciding on its length and of protracting or expediting the time for the hero's final triumph over the Enemy of mankind, according as he judged that the after-crop of halfpence would be plentiful or scant. When it had been gathered in to the last farthing, he resumed his load and on they went again.

Sometimes they played out the toll across a bridge or ferry, and once exhibited by particular desire at a turnpike, where the collector, being drunk in his solitude, paid down a shilling to have it to himself. There was one small place of rich promise in which their hopes were blighted, for a favourite character in the play having gold-lace upon his coat and being a meddling wooden-headed fellow was held to be a libel on the beadle, for which reason the authorities enforced a quick retreat; but they were generally well received, and seldom left a town without a troop of ragged children shouting at their heels.

They made a long day's journey, despite these interruptions, and were yet upon the road when the moon was shining in the sky. Short beguiled the time with songs and jests, and made the best of everything that happened. Mr. Codlin, on the other hand, cursed his fate, and all the hollow things of earth (but Punch especially), and limped along with the theatre on his back, a prey to the bitterest chagrin.

They had stopped to rest beneath a finger-post where four roads met, and Mr. Codlin in his deep misanthropy had let down the draper and seated himself in the bottom of the show, invisible to mortal eyes and disdainful of the company of his fellow-creatures, when two monstrous shadows were seen stalking towards them from a turning in the road by which they had come. The child was at first quite terrified by the sight of these gaunt giants—for such they looked as they advanced with lofty strides beneath the shadow of the trees—but Short, telling her there was nothing to fear, blew a blast upon the trumpet, which was answered by a cheerful shout.

"It's Grinder's lot, an't it?" cried Mr. Short in a loud key.

"Yes," replied a couple of shrill voices.

"Come on then," said Short. "Let's have a look at you. I thought it was you."

Thus invited, "Grinder's lot" approached with redoubled speed and soon came up with the little party. Mr. Grinder's company, familiarly termed a lot, consisted of a young gentleman and a young lady on stilts, and Mr. Grinder himself, who used his natural legs for pedestrian purposes and carried at his back a drum. The public costume of the young people was of the Highland kind, but the night being damp and cold, the young gentleman wore over his kilt a man's pea jacket reaching to his ankles, and a glazed hat; the young lady too was muffled in an old cloth pelisse and had a handkerchief tied about her head. Their Scotch bonnets, ornamented with plumes of jet black feathers, Mr. Grinder carried on his instrument.

"Bound for the races, I see," said Mr. Grinder coming up out of breath. "So are we. How are you, Short?" With that they shook hands in a very friendly manner. The young people being too high up for the ordinary salutations, saluted Short after their own fashion. The young gentleman twisted up his right stilt and patted him on the shoulder, and the young lady rattled her tambourine.

"Practice?" said Short, pointing to the stilts.

"No," returned Grinder. "It comes either to walkin' in 'em or carryin' of 'em, and they like walkin' in 'em best. It's wery pleasant for the prospects. Which road are you takin'? We go the nighest."

"Why, the fact is," said Short, "that we were going the longest way, because then we could stop for the night, a mile and a half on. But three or four mile gained to-night is so many saved to-morrow, and if you keep on, I think our best way is to do the same."

"Where's your partner?" inquired Grinder.

"Here he is," cried Mr. Thomas Codlin, presenting his head and face in the proscenium of the stage, and exhibiting an expression of countenance not often seen there; "and he'll see *his* partner boiled alive before he'll go on to-night. That's what *he* says."

"Well, don't say such things as them, in a spear which is dewoted to something pleasanter," urged Short. "Respect associations, Tommy, even if you do cut up rough."

"Rough or smooth," said Mr. Codlin, beating his hand on the little footboard where Punch, when suddenly struck with the symmetry of his legs and their capacity for silk stockings, is accustomed to exhibit them to popular admiration, "rough or smooth, I won't go further than the mile and a half to-night. I put up at the Jolly Sandboys and nowhere else. If you like to come there, come there. If you like to go on by yourself, go on by yourself, and do without me if you can."

So saying, Mr. Codlin disappeared from the scene and immediately presented himself outside the theatre, took it on his shoulders at a jerk, and made off with most remarkable agility.

Any further controversy being now out of the question, Short was fain to part with Mr. Grinder and his pupils and to follow his morose companion. After lingering at the finger-post for a few minutes to see the stilts frisking away in the moonlight and the bearer of the drum toiling slowly after them, he blew a few notes upon the trumpet as a parting salute, and hastened with all speed to follow Mr. Codlin. With this view he gave his unoccupied hand to Nell, and bidding her be of good cheer as they would soon be at the end of their journey for that night, and stimulating the old man with a similar assurance, led them at a pretty swift pace towards their destination, which he was the less unwilling to make for, as the moon was now overcast and the clouds were threatening rain.

CHAPTER XVIII

THE Jolly Sandboys was a small road-side inn of pretty ancient date, with a sign representing three Sandboys increasing their jollity with as many jugs of ale and bags of gold, creaking and swinging on its post on the opposite side of the road. As the travellers had observed that day many indications of their drawing nearer and nearer to the race town, such as gipsy camps, carts laden with gambling booths and their appurtenances, itinerant showmen of various kinds, and beggars and trampers of every degree, all wending their way in the same direction, Mr. Codlin was fearful of finding the accommodations forestalled; this fear increasing as he diminished the distance between himself and the hostelry, he quickened his pace, and notwithstanding the burden he had to carry, maintained a round trot until he reached the threshold. Here he had the gratification of finding that his fears were without foundation, for the landlord was leaning against the door-post looking lazily at the rain, which had by this time begun to descend heavily, and no tinkling of cracked bell, nor boisterous shout, nor noisy chorus, gave note of company within.

"All alone?" said Mr. Codlin, putting down his burden and wiping his forehead.

"All alone as yet," rejoined the landlord, glancing at the sky, "but we shall have more company to-night I expect. Here one of you boys, carry that show into the barn. Make haste in out of the wet, Tom; when it came on to rain I told 'em to make the fire up, and there's a glorious blaze in the kitchen, I can tell you."

Mr. Codlin followed with a willing mind, and soon found that the landlord had not commended his preparations without good reason. A mighty fire was blazing on the hearth and roaring up the wide chimney with a cheerful sound, which a large iron cauldron, bubbling and simmering in the heat, lent its pleasant aid to swell. There was a deep red ruddy blush upon the room, and when the landlord stirred the fire, sending the flames skipping and leaping up—when he took off the lid of the iron pot and there rushed out a savoury smell, while the bubbling sound grew deeper and more rich, and an unctuous steam came floating out, hanging in a delicious mist above their heads—when he did this, Mr. Codlin's heart was touched. He sat down in the chimney-corner and smiled.

Mr. Codlin sat smiling in the chimney-corner, eyeing the landlord as with a roguish look he held the cover in his hand, and, feigning that his doing so was needful to the welfare of the cookery, suffered the delightful steam to tickle the nostrils of his guest. The glow of the fire was upon the landlord's bald head, and upon his twinkling eye, and upon his watering mouth, and upon his pimpled face, and upon his round fat figure. Mr. Codlin drew his sleeve across his lips, and said in a murmuring voice, "What is it?"

"It's a stew of tripe," said the landlord smacking his lips, "and cow-heel," smacking them again, "and bacon," smacking them once more, "and steak," smacking them for the fourth time, "and peas, cauliflowers, new pototoes, and sparrow-grass, all working up together in one delicious gravy." Having come to the climax, he smacked his lips a great many times, and taking a long hearty sniff of the fragrance that was hovering about, put on the cover again with the air of one whose toils on earth were over.

"At what time will it be ready?" asked Mr. Codlin faintly.

"It'll be done to a turn," said the landlord looking up at the clock —and the very clock had a colour in its fat white face, and looked a clock for Jolly Sandboys to consult—"it'll be done to a turn at twenty-two minutes before eleven."

"Then," said Mr. Codlin, "fetch me a pint of warm ale, and don't let anybody bring into the room even so much as a biscuit till the time arrives."

Nodding his approval of this decisive and manly course of procedure, the landlord retired to draw the beer, and presently returning with it, applied himself to warm the same in a small tin vessel shaped funnel-wise, for the convenience of sticking it far down in the fire and getting at the bright places. This was soon done, and he handed it over to Mr. Codlin with that creamy froth upon the surface which is one of the happy circumstances attendant upon mulled malt.

Greatly softened by this soothing beverage, Mr. Codlin now bethought him of his companions, and acquainted mine host of the Sandboys that their arrival might be shortly looked for. The rain was rattling against the windows and pouring down in torrents, and such was Mr. Codlin's extreme amiability of mind, that he more than once expressed his earnest hope that they would not be so foolish as to get wet.

At length they arrived, drenched with the rain and presenting a most miserable appearance, notwithstanding that Short had sheltered the child as well as he could under the skirts of his own coat, and they were nearly breathless from the haste they had made. But their steps were no sooner heard upon the road than the landlord, who had been at the outer door anxiously watching for their coming, rushed into the kitchen and took the cover off. The effect was electrical. They all came in with smiling faces, though the wet was dripping from their clothes upon the floor, and Short's first remark was, "What a delicious smell!"

It is not very difficult to forget rain and mud by the side of a cheerful fire, and in a bright room. They were furnished with slippers and such dry garments as the house or their own bundles afforded, and ensconcing themselves, as Mr. Codlin had already done, in the warm chimney-corner, soon forgot their late troubles or only remembered them as enhancing the delights of the present time. Overpowered by the warmth and comfort and the fatigue they had undergone, Nelly and the old man had not long taken their seats here, when they fell asleep.

"Who are they?" whispered the landlord.

Short shook his head, and wished he knew himself.

"Don't *you* know?" asked the host, turning to Mr. Codlin.

"Not I," he replied. "They're no good, I suppose."

"They're no harm," said Short. "Depend upon that. I tell you what—it's plain that the old man an't in his right mind——"

"If you haven't got anything newer than that to say," growled Mr. Codlin, glancing at the clock, "you'd better let us fix our minds upon the supper, and not disturb us."

"Hear me out, won't you?" retorted his friend. "It's very plain to me, besides, that they're not used to this way of life. Don't tell me that that handsome child has been in the habit of prowling about as she's done these last two or three days. I know better."

"Well, who *does* tell you she has?" growled Mr. Codlin, again glancing at the clock and from it to the cauldron, "can't you think of anything more suitable to present circumstances than saying things and then contradicting 'em?"

"I wish somebody would give you your supper," returned Short, "for there'll be no peace till you've got it. Have you seen how anxious the old man is to get on—always wanting to be furder away—furder away. Have you seen that?"

"Ah! what then?" muttered Thomas Codlin.

"This, then," said Short. "He has given his friends the slip. Mind what I say,—he has given his friends the slip, and persuaded this delicate young creetur all along of her fondness for him to be his guide and travelling companion—where to, he knows no more than the Man in the Moon. Now, I'm not a going to stand that."

"*You're* not a going to stand that!" cried Mr. Codlin, glancing at the clock again and pulling his hair with both hands in a kind of frenzy, but whether occasioned by his companion's observation or the tardy pace of Time, it was difficult to determine. "Here's a world to live in!"

"I," repeated Short emphatically and slowly, "am not a going to stand it. I am not a going to see this fair young child a falling into bad hands, and getting among people that she's no more fit for, than they are to get among angels as their ordinary chums. Therefore when they dewelope an intention of parting company from us, I shall take measures for detaining of 'em, and restoring 'em to their friends, who I dare say have had their disconsolation pasted up on every wall in London by this time."

"Short," said Mr. Codlin, who with his head upon his hands, and his elbows on his knees, had been shaking himself impatiently from side to side up to this point and occasionally stamping on the ground, but who now looked up with eager eyes; "it's possible that there may be uncommon good sense in what you've said. If there is, and there should be a reward, Short, remember that we're partners in everything!"

His companion had only time to nod a brief assent to this position, for the child awoke at the instant. They had drawn close together during the previous whispering, and now hastily separated and were rather awkwardly endeavouring to exchange some casual remarks in their usual tone, when strange footsteps were heard without, and fresh company entered.

These were no other than four very dismal dogs, who came pattering in one after the other, headed by an old bandy dog of particularly mournful aspect, who, stopping when the last of his followers had got as far as the door, erected himself upon his hind legs and looked round at his companions, who immediately stood upon their hind legs, in a grave and melancholy row. Nor was this the only remarkable circumstance about these dogs, for each of them wore a kind of little coat of some gaudy colour trimmed with tarnished spangles, and one of them had a cap upon his head, tied very carefully under his chin, which had fallen down upon his nose and completely obscured one eye; add to this, that the gaudy coats were all wet through and discoloured with rain, and that the wearers were splashed and dirty, and some idea may be formed of the unusual appearance of these new visitors to the Jolly Sandboys.

Neither Short nor the landlord nor Thomas Codlin, however, were the least surprised, merely remarking that these were Jerry's dogs and that Jerry could not be far behind. So there the dogs stood, patiently winking and gaping and looking extremely hard at the boiling pot, until Jerry himself appeared, when they all dropped down at once and walked about the room in their natural manner. This posture it must be confessed did not much improve their appearance, as their own personal tails and their coat tails—both capital things in their way—did not agree together.

Jerry, the manager of these dancing dogs, was a tall black-whiskered man in a velveteen coat, who seemed well known to the landlord and his guests and accosted them with great cordiality. Disencumbering himself of a barrel organ which he placed upon a chair, and retaining in his hand a small whip wherewith to awe his company of comedians, he came up to the fire to dry himself, and entered into conversation.

"Your people don't usually travel in character, do they?" said Short, pointing to the dresses of the dogs. "It must come expensive if they do?"

"No," replied Jerry, "no, it's not the custom with us. But we've been playing a little on the road to-day, and we come out with a new wardrobe at the races, so I didn't think it worth while to stop to undress. Down, Pedro!"

This was addressed to the dog with the cap on, who being a new member of the company and not quite certain of his duty, kept his unobscured eye anxiously on his master, and was perpetually starting upon his hind legs when there was no occasion, and falling down again.

"I've got a animal here," said Jerry, putting his hand into the capacious pocket of his coat, and diving into one corner as if he were feeling for a small orange or an apple or some such article, "a animal here, wot I think you know something of, Short."

"Ah!" cried Short, "let's have a look at him."

"Here he is," said Jerry, producing a little terrier from his pocket. "He was once a Toby of yours, warn't he!"

In some versions of the great drama of Punch there is a small dog—a modern innovation—supposed to be the private property of that gentleman, whose name is always Toby. This Toby has been stolen in youth from another gentleman, and fraudulently sold to the confiding hero, who having no guile himself has no suspicion that it lurks in others; but Toby, entertaining a grateful recollection of his old master, and scorning to attach himself to any new patrons, not only refuses to smoke a pipe at the bidding of Punch, but to mark his old fidelity more strongly, seizes him by the nose and wrings the same with violence, at which instance of canine attachment the spectators are deeply affected. This was the character which the little terrier in question had once sustained; if there had been any doubt upon the subject he would speedily have resolved it by his conduct; for not only did he, on seeing Short, give the strongest tokens of recognition, but catching sight of the flat box he barked so furiously at the pasteboard nose which he knew was inside, that his master was obliged to gather him up and put him into his pocket again, to the great relief of the whole company. ,

The landlord now busied himself in laying the cloth, in which process Mr. Codlin obligingly assisted by setting forth his own knife and fork in the most convenient place and establishing himself behind them. When everything was ready, the landlord took off the cover for the last time, and then indeed there burst forth such a goodly promise of supper, that if he had offered to put it on again or had hinted at postponement, he would certainly have been sacrificed on his own hearth.

However, he did nothing of the kind, but instead thereof assisted a stout servant girl in turning the contents of the cauldron into a large tureen; a proceeding which the dogs, proof against various hot splashes which fell upon their noses, watched with terrible eagerness. At length the dish was lifted on the table, and mugs of ale having been previously set round, little Nell ventured to say grace, and supper began.

At this juncture the poor dogs were standing on their hind legs quite surprisingly; the child, having pity on them, was about to cast some morsels of food to them before she tasted it herself, hungry though she was, when their master interposed.

"No, my dear, no, not an atom from anybody's hand but mine if you please. That dog," said Jerry, pointing out the old leader of the troop, and speaking in a terrible voice, "lost a halfpenny to-day. *He* goes without his supper."

The unfortunate creature dropped upon his fore-legs directly, wagged his tail, and looked imploringly at his master.

"You must be more careful, sir," said Jerry, walking coolly to the chair where he had placed the organ, and setting the stop. "Come here. Now, sir, you play away at that, while we have supper, and leave off if you dare."

The dog immediately began to grind most mournful music. His master having shown him the whip resumed his seat and called up the others, who, at his directions, formed in a row, standing upright as a file of soldiers.

"Now, gentlemen," said Jerry, looking at them attentively. "The dog whose name's called, eats. The dogs whose names an't called, keep quiet. Carlo!"

The lucky individual whose name was called, snapped up the morsel thrown towards him, but none of the others moved a muscle. In this manner they were fed at the discretion of their master. Meanwhile the dog in disgrace ground hard at the organ, sometimes in quick time, sometimes in slow, but never leaving off for an instant. When the knives and forks rattled very much, or any of his fellows got an unusually large piece of fat, he accompanied the music with a short howl, but he immediately checked it on his master looking round and applied himself with increasing diligence to the Old Hundredth.

CHAPTER XIX

SUPPER was not yet over, when there arrived at the Jolly Sandboys two more travellers bound for the same haven as the rest, who had been walking in the rain for some hours, and came in shining and heavy with water. One of these was the proprietor of a giant, and a little lady without legs or arms, who had jogged forward in a van; the other, a silent gentleman who earned his living by showing tricks upon the cards, and who had rather deranged the natural expression of his countenance by putting small leaden lozenges into his eyes and bringing them out at his mouth, which was one of his professional accomplishments. The name of the first of these new-comers was Vuffin; the other, probably as a pleasant satire upon his ugliness, was called Sweet William. To render them as comfortable as he could, the landlord bestirred himself nimbly, and in a very short time both gentlemen were perfectly at their ease.

"How's the Giant?" said Short, when they all sat smoking round the fire.

"Rather weak upon his legs," returned Mr. Vuffin. "I begin to be afraid he's going at the knees."

"That's a bad look-out," said Short.

"Ay! Bad indeed," replied Mr. Vuffin, contemplating the fire with a sigh. "Once get a giant shaky on his legs, and the public care no more about him than they do for a dead cabbage-stalk."

"What becomes of the old giants?" said Short, turning to him again after a little reflection.

"They're usually kept in carawans to wait upon the dwarfs," said Mr. Vuffin.

"The maintaining of 'em must come expensive when they can't be shown, eh?" remarked Short, eyeing him doubtfully.

"It's better that, than letting 'em go upon the parish or about the streets," said Mr. Vuffin. "Once make a giant common and giants will never draw again. Look at wooden legs. If there was only one man with a wooden leg what a property *he*'d be!"

"So he would!" observed the landlord and Short both together. "That's very true."

"Instead of which," pursued Mr. Vuffin, "if you was to advertise Shakspeare played entirely by wooden legs, it's my belief you wouldn't draw a sixpence."

"I don't suppose you would," said Short. And the landlord said so too.

"This shows, you see," said Mr. Vuffin, waving his pipe with an argumentative air, "this shows the policy of keeping the used-up giants still in the carawans, where they get food and lodging for nothing, all their lives, and in general very glad they are to stop there. There was one giant—a black 'un—as left his carawan some year ago and took to carrying coach-bills about London, making himself as cheap as crossing-sweepers. He died. I make no insinuation against anybody in particular," said Mr. Vuffin, looking solemnly round, "but he was ruining the trade;—and he died."

The landlord drew his breath hard, and looked at the owner of the dogs, who nodded and said gruffly that *he* remembered.

"I know you do, Jerry," said Mr. Vuffin with profound meaning. "I know you remember it, Jerry, and the universal opinion was, that it served him right. Why, I remember the time when old Maunders as had three-and-twenty wans—I remember the time when old Maunders had in his cottage in Spa Fields in the winter time when the season was over, eight male and female dwarfs setting down to dinner every day, who was waited on by eight old giants in green coats, red smalls, blue cotton stockings, and high-lows: and there was one dwarf as had grown elderly and wicious who whenever his giant wasn't quick enough to please him, used to stick pins in his legs, not being able to reach up any higher. I know that's a fact, for Maunders told it me himself."

"What about the dwarfs, when *they* get old?" inquired the landlord.

"The older a dwarf is, the better worth he is," returned Mr. Vuffin; "a grey-headed dwarf, well wrinkled, is beyond all suspicion. But a giant weak in the legs and not standing upright!—keep him in the carawan, but never show him, never show him, for any persuasion that can be offered."

While Mr. Vuffin and his two friends smoked their pipes and beguiled the time with such conversation as this, the silent gentleman sat in a warm corner, swallowing, or seeming to swallow, sixpennyworth of halfpence for practice, balancing a feather upon his nose, and rehearsing other feats of dexterity of that kind, without paying any regard whatever to the company, who in their turn left him utterly unnoticed. At length the weary child prevailed upon her grandfather to retire, and they withdrew, leaving the company yet seated round the fire, and the dogs fast asleep at a humble distance.

After bidding the old man good night, Nell retired to her poor garret, but had scarcely closed the door, when it was gently tapped at. She opened it directly, and was a little startled by the sight of Mr. Thomas Codlin, whom she had left, to all appearance, fast asleep down stairs.

"What is the matter?" said the child.

"Nothing's the matter, my dear," returned her visitor. "I'm your friend. Perhaps you haven't thought so, but it's me that's your friend —not him."

"Not who?" the child inquired.

"Short, my dear. I tell you what," said Codlin, "for all his having a kind of way with him that you'd be very apt to like, I'm the real, open-hearted man. I mayn't look it, but I am indeed."

The child began to be alarmed, considering that the ale had taken effect upon Mr. Codlin, and that this commendation of himself was the consequence.

"Short's very well, and seems kind," resumed the misanthrope, "but he overdoes it. Now I don't."

Certainly if there were any fault in Mr. Codlin's usual deportment, it was that he rather underdid his kindness to those about him, than overdid it. But the child was puzzled, and could not tell what to say.

"Take my advice," said Codlin; "don't ask me why, but take it. As long as you travel with us, keep as near me as you can. Don't offer to leave us—not on any account—but always stick to me and say that I'm your friend. Will you bear that in mind, my dear, and always say that it was me that was your friend?"

"Say so where,—and when?" inquired the child innocently.

"Oh, nowhere in particular," replied Codlin, a little put out as it seemed by the question; "I'm only anxious that you should think me so, and do me justice. You can't think what an interest I have in you. Why didn't you tell me your little history—that about you and the poor old gentleman? I'm the best adviser that ever was, and *so* interested in you—so much more interested in you than Short. I think they're breaking up down stairs; you needn't tell Short, you know, that we've had this little talk together. God bless you. Recollect the friend. Codlin's the friend, not Short. Short's very well as far as he goes, but the real friend is Codlin—not Short."

Eking out these professions with a number of benevolent and protecting looks and great fervour of manner, Thomas Codlin stole away on tiptoe, leaving the child in a state of extreme surprise. She was still ruminating upon his curious behaviour, when the floor of the crazy stairs and landing cracked beneath the tread of the other travellers who were passing to their beds. When they had all passed, and the sound of their footsteps had died away, one of them returned, and after a little hesitation and rustling in the passage, as if he were doubtful what door to knock at, knocked at hers.

"Yes?" said the child from within.

"It's me—Short"—a voice called through the key-hole. "I only wanted to say that we must be off early to-morrow morning, my dear, because unless we get the start of the dogs and the conjuror, the villages won't be worth a penny. You'll be sure to be stirring early and go with us? I'll call you."

The child answered in the affirmative, and returning his "good night" heard him creep away. She felt some uneasiness at the anxiety of these men, increased by the recollection of their whispering together down stairs and their slight confusion when she awoke, nor was she quite free from a misgiving that they were not the fittest companions she could have stumbled on. Her uneasiness, however, was nothing, weighed against her fatigue; and she soon forgot it in sleep.

Very early next morning Short fulfilled his promise, and knocking softly at her door, entreated that she would get up directly, as the proprietor of the dogs was still snoring, and if they lost no time they might get a good deal in advance both of him and the conjuror, who was talking in his sleep, and from what he could be heard to say, appeared to be balancing a donkey in his dreams. She started from her bed without delay, and roused the old man with so much expedition that they were both ready as soon as Short himself, to that gentleman's unspeakable gratification and relief.

After a very unceremonious and scrambling breakfast, of which the staple commodities were bacon and bread, and beer, they took leave of the landlord and issued from the door of the Jolly Sandboys. The morning was fine and warm, the ground cool to the feet after the late rain, the hedges gayer and more green, the air clear, and everything fresh and healthful. Surrounded by these influences, they walked on pleasantly enough.

They had not gone very far, when the child was again struck by the altered behaviour of Mr. Thomas Codlin, who instead of plodding on sulkily by himself as he had theretofore done, kept close to her, and when he had an opportunity of looking at her unseen by his companion, warned her by certain wry faces and jerks of the head not to put any trust in Short, but to reserve all confidences for Codlin. Neither did he confine himself to looks and gestures, for when she and her grandfather were walking on beside the aforesaid Short, and that little man was talking with his accustomed cheerfulness on a variety of indifferent subjects, Thomas Codlin testified his jealousy and distrust by following close at her heels, and occasionally admonishing her ankles with the legs of the theatre in a very abrupt and painful manner.

All these proceedings naturally made the child more watchful and suspicious, and she soon observed that whenever they halted to perform outside a village alehouse or other place, Mr. Codlin while he went through his share of the entertainments kept his eye steadily upon her and the old man, or with a show of great friendship and consideration invited the latter to lean upon his arm, and so held him tight till the representation was over and they again went forward. Even Short seemed to change in this respect, and to mingle with his good nature something of a desire to keep them in safe custody. This increased the child's misgivings, and made her yet more anxious and uneasy.

Meanwhile, they were drawing near the town where the races were to begin next day; for, from passing numerous groups of gipsies and trampers on the road, wending their way towards it, and straggling out from every by-way and cross-country lane, they gradually fell into a stream of people, some walking by the side of covered carts, others with horses, others with donkeys, others toiling on with heavy loads upon their backs, but all tending to the same point. The public-houses by the wayside, from being empty and noiseless as those in the remoter parts had been, now sent out boisterous shouts and clouds of smoke; and, from the misty windows, clusters of broad red faces looked down upon the road. On every piece of waste or common ground, some small gambler drove his noisy trade, and bellowed to the idle passers-by to stop and try their chance; the crowd grew thicker and more noisy; gilt gingerbread in blanket-stalls exposed its glories to the dust; and often a four-horse carriage, dashing by, obscured all objects in the gritty cloud it raised, and left them, stunned and blinded, far behind.

It was dark before they reached the town itself, and long indeed the few last miles had been. Here all was tumult and confusion; the streets were filled with throngs of people—many strangers were there, it seemed, by the looks they cast about—the church-bells rang out their noisy peals, and flags streamed from windows and house-tops. In the large inn-yards waiters flitted to and fro and ran against each other, horses clattered on the uneven stones, carriage steps fell rattling down, and sickening smells from many dinners came in a heavy lukewarm breath upon the sense. In the smaller public-houses, fiddles with all their might and main were squeaking out the tune to staggering feet; drunken men, oblivious of the burden of their song, joined in a senseless howl, which drowned the tinkling of the feeble bell and made them savage for their drink; vagabond groups assembled round the doors to see the stroller woman dance, and add their uproar to the shrill flageolet and deafening drum.

Through this delirious scene the child, frightened and repelled by all she saw, led on her bewildered charge, clinging close to her conductor, and trembling lest in the press she should be separated from him and left to find her way alone. Quickening their steps to get clear of all the roar and riot, they at length passed through the town and made for the race-course, which was upon an open heath, situated on an eminence, a full mile distant from its furthest bounds.

Although there were many people here, none of the best favoured or best clad, busily erecting tents and driving stakes into the ground, and hurrying to and fro with dusty feet and many a grumbled oath—

although there were tired children cradled on heaps of straw between the wheels of carts, crying themselves to sleep—and poor lean horses and donkeys just turned loose, grazing among the men and women, and pots and kettles, and half-lighted fires, and ends of candles flaring and wasting in the air—for all this, the child felt it an escape from the town and drew her breath more freely. After a scanty supper, the purchase of which reduced her little stock so low, that she had only a few halfpence with which to buy a breakfast on the morrow, she and the old man lay down to rest in a corner of a tent, and slept, despite the busy preparations that were going on around them all night long.

And now they had come to the time when they must beg their bread. Soon after sunrise in the morning she stole out from the tent, and rambling into some fields at a short distance, plucked a few wild roses and such humble flowers, purposing to make them into little nosegays and offer them to the ladies in the carriages when the company arrived. Her thoughts were not idle while she was thus employed; when she returned and was seated beside the old man in one corner of the tent, tying her flowers together, while the two men lay dozing in another corner, she plucked him by the sleeve, and slightly glancing towards them, said in a low voice—

"Grandfather, don't look at those I talk of, and don't seem as if I spoke of anything but what I am about. What was that you told me before we left the old house? That if they knew what we were going to do, they would say that you were mad, and part us?"

The old man turned to her with an aspect of wild terror; but she checked him by a look, and bidding him hold her flowers while she tied them up, and so bringing her lips closer to his ear, said—

"I know that was what you told me. You needn't speak, dear. I recollect it very well. It was not likely that I should forget it. Grandfather, these men suspect that we have secretly left our friends, and mean to carry us before some gentleman and have us taken care of and sent back. If you let your hand tremble so, we can never get away from them, but if you're only quiet now, we shall do so, easily."

"How?" muttered the old man. "Dear Nelly, how? They will shut me up in a stone room, dark and cold, and chain me up to the wall, Nell—flog me with whips, and never let me see thee more!"

"You're trembling again," said the child. "Keep close to me all day. Never mind them, don't look at them, but me. I shall find a time when we can steal away. When I do, mind you come with me, and do not stop or speak a word. Hush! That's all."

"Halloa! what are you up to, my dear?" said Mr. Codlin, raising his head, and yawning. Then observing that his companion was fast asleep, he added in an earnest whisper, "Codlin's the friend, remember—not Short."

"Making some nosegays," the child replied; "I am going to try and sell some, these three days of the races. Will you have one—as a present I mean?"

Mr. Codlin would have risen to receive it, but the child hurried towards him and placed it in his hand. He stuck it in his buttonhole with an air of ineffable complacency for a misanthrope, and leering exultingly at the unconscious Short, muttered, as he laid himself down again, "Tom Codlin's the friend, by G—!"

As the morning wore on, the tents assumed a gayer and more brilliant appearance, and long lines of carriages came rolling softly on the turf. Men who had lounged about all night in smock-frocks and leather leggings, came out in silken vests and hats and plumes, as jugglers or mountebanks; or in gorgeous liveries as soft-spoken servants at gambling booths; or in sturdy yeoman dress as decoys at unlawful games. Black-eyed gipsy girls, hooded in showy handkerchiefs, sallied forth to tell fortunes, and pale slender women with consumptive faces lingered upon the footsteps of ventriloquists and conjurors, and counted the sixpences with anxious eyes long before they were gained. As many of the children as could be kept within bounds, were stowed away, with all the other signs of dirt and poverty, among the donkeys, carts, and horses; and as many as could not be thus disposed of ran in and out in all intricate spots, crept between people's legs and carriage wheels, and came forth unharmed from under horses' hoofs. The dancing-dogs, the stilts, the little lady and the tall man, and all the other attractions, with organs out of number and bands innumerable, emerged from the holes and corners in which they had passed the night, and flourished boldly in the sun.

Along the uncleared course, Short led his party, sounding the brazen trumpet and revelling in the voice of Punch; and at his heels went Thomas Codlin, bearing the show as usual, and keeping his eye on Nelly and her grandfather, as they rather lingered in the rear. The child bore upon her arm the little basket with her flowers, and sometimes stopped, with timid and modest looks, to offer them at some gay carriage; but alas! there were many bolder beggars there, gipsies who promised husbands, and other adepts in their trade, and although some ladies smiled gently as they shook their heads, and others cried to the gentlemen beside them "See what a pretty face!" they let the pretty face pass on, and never thought that it looked tired or hungry.

There was but one lady who seemed to understand the child, and she was one who sat alone in a handsome carriage, while two young men in dashing clothes, who had just dismounted from it, talked and laughed loudly at a little distance, appearing to forget her, quite. There were many ladies all around, but they turned their backs, or looked another way, or at the two young men (not unfavourably at *them*), and left her to herself. She motioned away a gipsy-woman urgent to tell her fortune, saying that it was told already and had been for some years, but called the child towards her, and taking her flowers put money into her trembling hand, and bade her go home and keep at home for God's sake.

Many a time they went up and down those long, long lines, seeing everything but the horses and the race; when the bell rang to clear the course, going back to rest among the carts and donkeys, and not coming out again until the heat was over. Many a time, too, Punch displayed in the full zenith of his humour, but all this while the eye of Thomas Codlin was upon them, and to escape without notice was impracticable.

At length, late in the day, Mr. Codlin pitched the show in a convenient spot, and the spectators were soon in the very triumph of the scene. The child, sitting down with the old man close behind it, had been thinking how strange it was that horses who were such fine honest creatures should seem to make vagabonds of all the men that drew about them, when a loud laugh at some extemporaneous witticism of Mr. Short's, having allusion to the circumstances of the day, roused her from her meditation and caused her to look around.

If they were ever to get away unseen, that was the very moment. Short was plying the quarter-staves vigorously and knocking the characters in the fury of the combat against the sides of the show, the people were looking on with laughing faces, and Mr. Codlin relaxed into a grim smile as his roving eye detected hands going into waistcoat pockets and groping secretly for sixpences. If they were ever to get away unseen, that was the very moment. They seized it and fled.

They made a path through booths and carriages and throngs of people, and never once stopped to look behind. The bell was ringing and the course was cleared by the time they reached the ropes, but they dashed across it insensible to the shouts and screeching that assailed them for breaking in upon its sanctity, and creeping under the brow of the hill at a quick pace, made for the open fields.

CHAPTER XX

DAY after day as he bent his steps homeward, returning from some new effort to procure employment, Kit raised his eyes to the window of the little room he had so much commended to the child, and hoped to see some indication of her presence. His own earnest wish, coupled with the assurance he had received from Quilp, filled him with the belief that she would yet arrive to claim the humble shelter he had offered, and from the death of each day's hope, another hope sprang up to live to-morrow.

"I think they must certainly come to-morrow, eh mother?" said Kit, laying aside his hat with a weary air and sighing as he spoke. "They have been gone a week. They surely couldn't stop away more than a week, could they now?"

The mother shook her head, and reminded him how often he had been disappointed already.

"For the matter of that," said Kit, "you speak true and sensible enough, as you always do, mother. Still, I do consider that a week is quite long enough for 'em to be rambling about; don't you say so?"

"Quite long enough, Kit, longer than enough, but they may not come back for all that."

Kit was for a moment disposed to be vexed by this contradiction, and not the less so from having anticipated it in his own mind and knowing how just it was. But the impulse was only momentary, and the vexed look became a kind one before it had crossed the room.

"Then what do you think, mother, has become of 'em? You don't think they've gone to sea, anyhow?"

"Not gone for sailors, certainly," returned the mother with a smile. "But I can't help thinking that they have gone to some foreign country."

"I say," cried Kit with a rueful face, "don't talk like that, mother."

"I am afraid they have, and that's the truth," she said. "It's the talk of all the neighbours, and there are some even that know of their having been seen on board ship, and can tell you the name of the place they've gone to, which is more than I can, my dear, for it's a very hard one."

"I don't believe it," said Kit. "Not a word of it. A set of idle chatterboxes, how should they know!"

"They may be wrong of course," returned the mother, "I can't tell about that, though I don't think it's at all unlikely that they're in the right, for the talk is that the old gentleman had put by a little money that nobody knew of, not even that ugly little man you talk to me about—what's his name—Quilp; and that he and Miss Nell have gone to live abroad where it can't be taken from them, and they will never be disturbed. That don't seem very far out of the way now, do it?"

Kit scratched his head mournfully, in reluctant admission that it did not, and clambering up to the old nail took down the cage and set himself to clean it and to feed the bird. His thoughts reverting from his occupation to the little old gentleman who had given him the shilling, he suddenly recollected that that was the very day—nay nearly the very hour—at which the little old gentleman had said he should be at the notary's house again. He no sooner remembered this than he hung up the cage with great precipitation, and hastily explaining the nature of his errand, went off at full speed to the appointed place.

It was some two minutes after the time when he reached the spot, which was a considerable distance from his home, but by great good luck the little old gentleman had not yet arrived; at least there was no pony-chaise to be seen, and it was not likely that he had come and gone again in so short a space. Greatly relieved to find that he was not too late, Kit leant against a lamp-post to take breath, and waited the advent of the pony and his charge.

Sure enough, before long the pony came trotting round the corner of the street, looking as obstinate as a pony might, and picking his steps as if he were spying about for the cleanest places, and would by no means dirty his feet or hurry himself inconveniently. Behind the pony sat the little old gentleman, and by the old gentleman's side sat the little old lady, carrying just such a nosegay as she had brought before.

The old gentleman, the old lady, the pony, and the chaise, came up the street in perfect unanimity, until they arrived within some half a dozen doors of the notary's house, when the pony, deceived by a brass-plate beneath a tailor's knocker, came to a halt, and maintained by a sturdy silence, that that was the house they wanted.

"Now, sir, will you have the goodness to go on; this is *not* the place," said the old gentleman.

The pony looked with great attention into a fire-plug which was near him, and appeared to be quite absorbed in contemplating it.

"Oh dear, such a naughty Whisker!" cried the old lady. "After being so good too, and coming along so well! I am quite ashamed of him. I don't know what we are to do with him, I really don't."

The pony having thoroughly satisfied himself as to the nature and properties of the fire-plug, looked into the air after his old enemies the flies, and as there happened to be one of them tickling his ear at that moment he shook his head and whisked his tail, after which he appeared full of thought but quite comfortable and collected. The old gentleman having exhausted his powers of persuasion, alighted to lead him; whereupon the pony, perhaps because he held this to be a sufficient concession, perhaps because he happened to catch sight of the other brass-plate, or perhaps because he was in a spiteful humour, darted off with the old lady and stopped at the right house, leaving the old gentleman to come panting on behind.

It was then that Kit presented himself at the pony's head, and touched his hat with a smile.

"Why, bless me," cried the old gentleman, "the lad *is* here! My dear, do you see?"

"I said I'd be here, sir," said Kit, patting Whisker's neck. "I hope you've had a pleasant ride, sir. He's a very nice little pony."

"My dear," said the old gentleman. "This is an uncommon lad; a good lad, I'm sure."

"I'm sure he is," rejoined the old lady. "A very good lad, and I'm sure he is a good son."

Kit acknowledged these expressions of confidence by touching his hat again and blushing very much. The old gentleman then handed the old lady out, and after looking at him with an approving smile, they went into the house—talking about him as they went, Kit could not help feeling. Presently Mr. Witherden, smelling very hard at the nosegay, came to the window and looked at him, and after that Mr. Abel came and looked at him, and after that the old gentleman and lady came and looked at him again, and after that they all came and looked at him together, which Kit, feeling very much embarrassed by, made a pretence of not observing. Therefore he patted the pony more and more; and this liberty the pony most handsomely permitted.

The faces had not disappeared from the window many moments, when Mr. Chuckster in his official coat, and with his hat hanging on his head just as it happened to fall from its peg, appeared upon the pavement, and telling him he was wanted inside, bade him go in and he would mind the chaise the while. In giving him this direction Mr. Chuckster remarked that he wished he might be blessed if he could make out whether he (Kit) was "precious raw" or "precious deep," but intimated by a distrustful shake of the head, that he inclined to the latter opinion.

Kit entered the office in a great tremor, for he was not used to going among strange ladies and gentlemen, and the tin boxes and bundles of dusty papers had in his eyes an awful and venerable air. Mr. Witherden too was a bustling gentleman who talked loud and fast, and all eyes were upon him, and he was very shabby.

"Well, boy," said Mr. Witherden, "you came to work out that shilling;—not to get another, hey?"

"No indeed, sir," replied Kit, taking courage to look up. "I never thought of such a thing."

"Father alive?" said the notary.

"Dead, sir."

"Mother?"

"Yes, sir."

"Married again—eh?"

Kit made answer, not without some indignation, that she was a widow with three children, and that as to her marrying again, if the gentleman knew her he wouldn't think of such a thing. At this reply Mr. Witherden buried his nose in the flowers again, and whispered behind the nosegay to the old gentleman that he believed the lad was as honest a lad as need be.

"Now," said Mr. Garland when they had made some further inquiries of him, "I am not going to give you anything——"

"Thank you, sir," Kit replied; and quite seriously too, for this announcement seemed to free him from the suspicion which the notary had hinted.

"—But," resumed the old gentleman, "perhaps I may want to know something more about you, so tell me where you live, and I'll put it down in my pocket-book."

Kit told him, and the old gentleman wrote down the address with his pencil. He had scarcely done so, when there was a great uproar in the street, and the old lady hurrying to the window cried that Whisker had run away, upon which Kit darted out to the rescue, and the others followed.

It seemed that Mr. Chuckster had been standing with his hands in his pockets looking carelessly at the pony, and occasionally insulting him with such admonitions as "Stand still,"—"Be quiet,"—"Woa-a-a," and the like, which by a pony of spirit cannot be borne. Consequently, the pony being deterred by no considerations of duty or obedience, and not having before him the slightest fear of the human eye, had at length started off, and was at that moment rattling down the street,—Mr. Chuckster, with his hat off and a pen behind his ear, hanging on in the rear of the chaise and making futile attempts to draw it the other way, to the unspeakable admiration of all beholders. Even in running away, however, Whisker was perverse, for he had not gone very far when he suddenly stopped, and before assistance could be rendered, commenced backing at nearly as quick a pace as he had gone forward. By these means Mr. Chuckster was pushed and hustled to the office again, in a most inglorious manner, and arrived in a state of great exhaustion and discomfiture.

The old lady then stepped into her seat, and Mr. Abel (whom they had come to fetch) into his. The old gentleman, after reasoning with the pony on the extreme impropriety of his conduct, and making the best amends in his power to Mr. Chuckster, took his place also, and they drove away, waving a farewell to the notary and his clerk, and more than once turning to nod kindly to Kit as he watched them from the road.

CHAPTER XXI

Kit turned away and very soon forgot the pony, and the chaise, and the little old lady, and the little old gentleman, and the little young gentleman to boot, in thinking what could have become of his late master and his lovely grandchild, who were the fountain-head of all his meditations. Still casting about for some plausible means of accounting for their non-appearance, and of persuading himself that they must soon return, he bent his steps towards home, intending to finish the task which the sudden recollection of his contract had interrupted, and then to sally forth once more to seek his fortune for the day.

When he came to the corner of the court in which he lived, lo and behold there was the pony again! Yes, there he was, looking more obstinate than ever; and alone in the chaise, keeping a steady watch upon his every wink, sat Mr. Abel, who, lifting up his eyes by chance and seeing Kit pass by, nodded to him as though he would have nodded his head off.

Kit wondered to see the pony again, so near his own home too, but it never occurred to him for what purpose the pony might have come there, or where the old lady and the old gentleman had gone, until he lifted the latch of the door, and walking in, found them seated in the room in conversation with his mother, at which unexpected sight he pulled off his hat and made his best bow in some confusion.

"We are here before you, you see, Christopher," said Mr. Garland smiling.

"Yes, sir," said Kit; and as he said it he looked towards his mother for an explanation of the visit.

"The gentleman's been kind enough, my dear," said she, in reply to this mute interrogation, "to ask me whether you were in a good place, or in any place at all, and when I told him no, you were not in any, he was so good as to say that——"

"That we wanted a good lad in our house," said the old gentleman and the old lady both together, "and that perhaps we might think of it, if we found everything as we would wish it to be."

As this thinking of it, plainly meant the thinking of engaging Kit, he immediately partook of his mother's anxiety and fell into a great flutter; for the little old couple were very methodical and cautious, and asked so many questions that he began to be afraid there was no chance of his success.

"You see, my good woman," said Mrs. Garland to Kit's mother, "that it's necessary to be very careful and particular in such a matter as this, for we're only three in family, and are very quiet, regular folks, and it would be a sad thing if we made any kind of mistake, and found things different from what we hoped and expected."

To this, Kit's mother replied, that certainly it was quite true, and quite right, and quite proper, and Heaven forbid that she should shrink, or have cause to shrink, from any inquiry into her character or that of her son, who was a very good son though she was his mother, in which respect, she was bold to say, he took after his father, who was not only a good son to *his* mother, but the best of husbands and the best of fathers besides, which Kit could and would corroborate she knew, and so would little Jacob and the baby likewise if they were old enough, which unfortunately they were not, though as they didn't know what a loss they had had, perhaps it was a great deal better that they should be as young as they were; and so Kit's mother wound up a long story by wiping her eyes with her apron, and patting little Jacob's head, who was rocking the cradle and staring with all his might at the strange lady and gentleman.

When Kit's mother had done speaking, the old lady struck in again, and said that she was quite sure she was a very honest and very respectable person or she never would have expressed herself in that manner, and that certainly the appearance of the children and the cleanliness of the house deserved great praise and did her the utmost credit, whereat Kit's mother dropped a curtsey and became consoled. Then the good woman entered into a long and minute account of Kit's life and history from the earliest period down to that time, not omitting to make mention of his miraculous fall out of a back-parlour window when an infant of tender years, or his uncommon sufferings in a state of measles, which were illustrated by correct imitations of the plaintive manner in which he called for toast and water, day and night, and said "don't cry, mother, I shall soon be better;" for proof of which statements reference was made to Mrs. Green, lodger, at the cheesemonger's round the corner, and divers other ladies and gentlemen in various parts of England and Wales (and one Mr. Brown who was supposed to be then a corporal in the East Indies, and who could of course be found with very little trouble), within whose personal knowledge the circumstances had occurred. This narration ended, Mr. Garland put some questions to Kit respecting his qualifications and general acquirements, while Mrs. Garland noticed the children, and hearing from Kit's mother certain remarkable circumstances which had attended the birth of each, related certain other remarkable circumstances which had attended the birth of her own son, Mr. Abel, from which it appeared that both Kit's mother and herself had been, above and beyond all other women of what condition or age soever, peculiarly hemmed in with perils and dangers. Lastly, inquiry was made into the nature and extent of Kit's wardrobe, and a small advance being made to improve the same, he was formally hired at an annual income of Six Pounds, over and above his board and lodgings, by Mr. and Mrs. Garland, of Abel Cottage, Finchley.

It would be difficult to say which party appeared most pleased with this arrangement, the conclusion of which was hailed with nothing but pleasant looks and cheerful smiles on both sides. It was settled that Kit should repair to his new abode on the next day but one, in the morning; and finally, the little old couple, after bestowing a bright half-crown on little Jacob and another on the baby, took their leaves; being escorted as far as the street by their new attendant, who held the obdurate pony by the bridle while they took their seats, and saw them drive away with a lightened heart.

"Well, mother," said Kit, hurrying back into the house, "I think my fortune's about made now."

"I should think it was indeed, Kit," rejoined his mother. "Six pound a year! Only think!"

"Ah!" said Kit, trying to maintain the gravity which the consideration of such a sum demanded, but grinning with delight in spite of himself. "There's a property!"

Kit drew a long breath when he had said this, and putting his hands deep into his pockets as if there were one year's wages at least in each, looked at his mother, as though he saw through her, and down an immense perspective of sovereigns beyond.

"Please God we'll make such a lady of you for Sundays, mother! such a scholar of Jacob, such a child of the baby, such a room of the one up stairs! Six pound a year!"

"Hem!" croaked a strange voice. "What's that about six pound a year? What about six pound a year?" And as the voice made this inquiry, Daniel Quilp walked in with Richard Swiveller at his heels.

"Who said he was to have six pound a year?" said Quilp, looking sharply round. "Did the old man say it, or did little Nell say it? And what's he to have it for, and where are they, eh?"

The good woman was so much alarmed by the sudden apparition of this unknown piece of ugliness, that she hastily caught the baby from its cradle and retreated into the furthest corner of the room; while little Jacob, sitting upon his stool with his hands on his knees, looked full at him in a species of fascination, roaring lustily all the time. Richard Swiveller took an easy observation of the family over Mr. Quilp's head, and Quilp himself, with his hands in his pockets, smiled in an exquisite enjoyment of the commotion he occasioned.

"Don't be frightened, mistress," said Quilp, after a pause. "Your son knows me: I don't eat babies; I don't like 'em. It will be as well to stop that young screamer though, in case I should be tempted to do him a mischief. Holloa, sir! Will you be quiet?"

Little Jacob stemmed the course of two tears which he was squeezing out of his eyes, and instantly subsided into a silent horror.

"Mind you don't break out again, you villain," said Quilp, looking sternly at him, "or I'll make faces at you and throw you into fits, I will. Now you sir, why haven't you been to me as you promised?"

"What should I come for?" retorted Kit. "I hadn't any business with you, no more than you had with me."

"Here, mistress," said Quilp, turning quickly away, and appealing from Kit to his mother. "When did his old master come or send here last? Is he here now? If not, where's he gone?"

"He has not been here at all," she replied. "I wish we knew where they have gone, for it would make my son a good deal easier in his mind, and me too. If you're the gentleman named Mr. Quilp, I should have thought you'd have known, and so I told him only this very day."

"Humph!" muttered Quilp, evidently disappointed to believe that this was true. "That's what you tell this gentleman too, is it?"

"If the gentleman comes to ask the same question, I can't tell him anything else, sir; and I only wish I could, for our own sakes," was the reply.

Quilp glanced at Richard Swiveller, and observed that having met him on the threshold, he assumed that he had come in search of some intelligence of the fugitives. He supposed he was right?

"Yes," said Dick, "that was the object of the present expedition. I fancied it possible—but let us go ring fancy's knell. *I'll* begin it."

"You seem disappointed," observed Quilp.

"A baffler, sir, a baffler, that's all," returned Dick. "I have entered upon a speculation which has proved a baffler; and a Being of brightness and beauty will be offered up a sacrifice at Cheggs's altar. That's all, sir."

The dwarf eyed Richard with a sarcastic smile, but Richard, who had been taking a rather strong lunch with a friend, observed him not, and continued to deplore his fate with mournful and despondent looks. Quilp plainly discerned that there was some secret reason for this visit and his uncommon disappointment, and, in the hope that there might be means of mischief lurking beneath it, resolved to worm it out. He had no sooner adopted this resolution, than he conveyed as much honesty into his face as it was capable of expressing, and sympathised with Mr. Swiveller exceedingly.

"I am disappointed myself," said Quilp, "out of mere friendly feeling for them; but you have real reasons, private reasons I have no doubt, for your disappointment, and therefore it comes heavier than mine."

"Why, of course it does," Dick observed, testily.

"Upon my word, I'm very sorry, very sorry. I'm rather cast down myself. As we are companions in adversity, shall we be companions in the surest way of forgetting it? If you had no particular business, now, to lead you in another direction," urged Quilp, plucking him by the sleeve and looking slyly up into his face out of the corners of his eyes, "there is a house by the waterside where they have some of the noblest Schiedam—reputed to be smuggled, but that's between ourselves—that can be got in all the world. The landlord knows me. There's a little summer-house, overlooking the river, where we might take a glass of this delicious liquor with a whiff of the best tobacco—it's in this case, and of the rarest quality, to my certain knowledge—and be perfectly snug and happy, could we possibly contrive it; or is there any very particular engagement that peremptorily takes you another way, Mr. Swiveller, eh?"

As the dwarf spoke, Dick's face relaxed into a compliant smile, and his brows slowly unbent. By the time he had finished, Dick was looking down at Quilp in the same sly manner as Quilp was looking up at him, and there remained nothing more to be done but to set out for the house in question. This they did, straightway. The moment their backs were turned, little Jacob thawed, and resumed his crying from the point where Quilp had frozen him.

The summer-house of which Mr. Quilp had spoken was a rugged wooden box, rotten and bare to see, which overhung the river's mud, and threatened to slide down into it. The tavern to which it belonged was a crazy building, sapped and undermined by the rats, and only upheld by great bars of wood which were reared against its walls, and had propped it up so long that even they were decaying and yielding with their load, and of a windy night might be heard to creak and crack as if the whole fabric were about to come toppling down. The house stood—if anything so old and feeble could be said to stand—on a piece of waste ground, blighted with the unwholesome smoke of factory chimneys, and echoing the clank of iron wheels and rush of troubled water. Its internal accommodations amply fulfilled the promise of the outside. The rooms were low and damp, the clammy walls were pierced with chinks and holes, the rotten floors had sunk from their level, the very beams started from their places and warned the timid stranger from their neighbourhood.

To this inviting spot, entreating him to observe its beauties as they passed along, Mr. Quilp led Richard Swiveller, and on the table of the summer-house, scored deep with many a gallows and initial letter, there soon appeared a wooden keg, full of the vaunted liquor. Drawing it off into the glasses with the skill of a practised hand, and mixing it with about a third part of water, Mr. Quilp assigned to Richard Swiveller his portion, and lighting his pipe from an end of a candle in a very old and battered lantern, drew himself together upon a seat and puffed away.

"Is it good?" said Quilp, as Richard Swiveller smacked his lips, "is it strong and fiery? Does it make you wink, and choke, and your eyes water, and your breath come short—does it?"

"Does it?" cried Dick, throwing away part of the contents of his glass, and filling it up with water, "why, man, you don't mean to tell me that you drink such fire as this?"

"No!" rejoined Quilp. "Not drink it! Look here. And here. And here again. Not drink it!"

As he spoke, Daniel Quilp drew off and drank three small glassfuls of the raw spirit, and then with a horrible grimace took a great many pulls at his pipe, and swallowing the smoke, discharged it in a heavy cloud from his nose. This feat accomplished, he drew himself together in his former position, and laughed excessively.

"Give us a toast!" cried Quilp, rattling on the table in a dexterous manner with his fist and elbow alternately, in a kind of tune, "a woman, a beauty. Let's have a beauty for our toast and empty our glasses to the last drop. Her name, come!"

"If you want a name," said Dick, "here's Sophy Wackles."

"Sophy Wackles," screamed the dwarf, "Miss Sophy Wackles that is—Mrs. Richard Swiveller that shall be—that shall be—ha ha ha!"

"Ah!" said Dick, "you might have said that a few weeks ago, but it won't do now, my buck. Immolating herself upon the shrine of Cheggs——"

"Poison Cheggs, cut Cheggs's ears off," rejoined Quilp. "I won't hear of Cheggs. Her name is Swiveller or nothing. I'll drink her health again, and her father's, and her mother's ; and to all her sisters and brothers—the glorious family of the Wackleses—all the Wackleses in one glass—down with it to the dregs!"

"Well," said Richard Swiveller, stopping short in the act of raising the glass to his lips and looking at the dwarf in a species of stupor as he flourished his arms and legs about: "you're a jolly fellow, but of all the jolly fellows I ever saw or heard of, you have the queerest and most extraordinary way with you, upon my life you have."

This candid declaration tended rather to increase than restrain Mr. Quilp's eccentricities, and Richard Swiveller, astonished to see him in such a roystering vein, and drinking not a little himself, for company,—began imperceptibly to become more companionable and confiding, so that, being judiciously led on by Mr. Quilp, he grew at last very confiding indeed. Having once got him into this mood, and knowing now the key-note to strike whenever he was at a loss, Daniel Quilp's task was comparatively an easy one, and he was soon in possession of the whole details of the scheme contrived between the easy Dick and his more designing friend.

"Stop!" said Quilp. "That's the thing, that's the thing. It can be brought about, it shall be brought about. There's my hand upon it; I am your friend from this minute."

"What! do you think there's still a chance?" inquired Dick, in surprise at this encouragement.

"A chance!" echoed the dwarf, "a certainty! Sophy Wackles may become a Cheggs or anything else she likes, but not a Swiveller. Oh you lucky dog! He's richer than any Jew alive; you're a made man. I see in you now nothing but Nelly's husband, rolling in gold and silver. I'll help you. It shall be done. Mind my words, it shall be done."

"But how?" said Dick.

"There's plenty of time," rejoined the dwarf, "and it shall be done. We'll sit down and talk it over again all the way through. Fill your glass while I'm gone. I shall be back directly—directly."

With these hasty words, Daniel Quilp withdrew into a dismantled skittle-ground behind the public-house, and, throwing himself upon the ground, actually screamed and rolled about in the most uncontrollable delight.

"Here's sport!" he cried, "sport ready to my hand, all invented and arranged, and only to be enjoyed. It was this shallow-pated fellow who made my bones ache t'other day, was it? It was his friend and fellow-plotter, Mr. Trent, that once made eyes at Mrs. Quilp, and leered and looked, was it? After labouring for two or three years in their precious scheme, to find that they've got a beggar at last, and one of them tied for life. Ha ha ha! He shall marry Nell. He shall have her, and I'll be the first man, when the knot's tied hard and fast, to tell 'em what they've gained and what I've helped 'em to. Here will be a clearing of old scores, here will be a time to remind 'em what a capital friend I was, and how I helped 'em to the heiress. Ha ha ha!"

In the height of his ecstasy, Mr. Quilp had like to have met with a disagreeable check, for, rolling very near a broken dog-kennel, there leapt forth a large fierce dog, who, but that his chain was of the shortest, would have given him a disagreeable salute. As it was, the dwarf remained upon his back in perfect safety, taunting the dog with hideous faces, and triumphing over him in his inability to advance another inch, though there were not a couple of feet between them.

"Why don't you come and bite me, why don't you come and tear me to pieces, you coward?" said Quilp, hissing and worrying the animal till he was nearly mad. "You're afraid, you bully, you're afraid, you know you are."

The dog tore and strained at his chain with starting eyes and furious bark, but there the dwarf lay, snapping his fingers with gestures of defiance and contempt. When he had sufficiently recovered from his delight, he rose, and with his arms a-kimbo, achieved a kind of demon-dance round the kennel, just without the limits of the chain, driving the dog quite wild. Having by this means composed his spirits and put himself in a pleasant train, he returned to his unsuspicious companion, whom he found looking at the tide with exceeding gravity, and thinking of that same gold and silver which Mr. Quilp had mentioned.

CHAPTER XXII

THE remainder of that day and the whole of the next were a busy time for the Nubbles family, to whom everything connected with Kit's outfit and departure was a matter of as great moment as if he had been about to penetrate into the interior of Africa, or to take a cruise round the world. It would be difficult to suppose that there ever was a box which was opened and shut so many times within four-and-twenty hours, as that which contained his wardrobe and necessaries; and certainly there never was one which to two small eyes presented such a mine of clothing, as this mighty chest with its three shirts and proportionate allowance of stockings and pocket-handkerchiefs, disclosed to the astonished vision of little Jacob. At last it was conveyed to the carrier's, at whose house at Finchley Kit was to find it next day; and the box being gone, there remained but two questions for consideration: firstly, whether the carrier would lose, or dishonestly feign to lose, the box upon the road; and secondly, whether Kit's mother perfectly understood how to take care of herself in the absence of her son.

"I don't think there's hardly a chance of his really losing it, but carriers are under great temptation to pretend they lose things, no doubt," said Mrs. Nubbles apprehensively, in reference to the first point.

"No doubt about it," returned Kit, with a serious look; "upon my word, mother, I don't think it was right to trust it to itself. Somebody ought to have gone with it, I'm afraid."

"We can't help it now," said his mother; "but it was foolish and wrong. People oughtn't to be tempted."

Kit inwardly resolved that he would never tempt a carrier any more, save with an empty box; and having formed this Christian determination, he turned his thoughts to the second question.

"You know you must keep up your spirits, mother, and not be lonesome because I'm not at home. I shall very often be able to look in when I come into town I dare say, and I shall send you a letter sometimes, and when the quarter comes round, I can get a holiday of course; and then see if we don't take little Jacob to the play, and let him know what oysters means."

"I hope plays mayn't be sinful, Kit, but I'm a'most afraid," said Mrs. Nubbles.

"I know who has been putting that in your head," rejoined her son disconsolately; "that's Little Bethel again. Now I say, mother, pray don't take to going there regularly, for if I was to see your good-humoured face that has always made home cheerful, turned into a grievous one, and the baby trained to look grievous too, and to call itself a young sinner (bless its heart) and a child of the devil (which is calling its dead father names); if I was to see this, and see little Jacob looking grievous likewise, I should so take it to heart that I'm sure I should go and list for a soldier, and run my head on purpose against the first cannon-ball I saw coming my way."

"Oh, Kit, don't talk like that."

"I would, indeed, mother, and unless you want to make me feel very wretched and uncomfortable, you'll keep that bow on your bonnet, which you'd more than half a mind to pull off last week. Can you suppose there's any harm in looking as cheerful and being as cheerful as our poor circumstances will permit? Do I see anything in the way I'm made, which calls upon me to be a snivelling, solemn, whispering chap, sneaking about as if I couldn't help it, and expressing myself in a most unpleasant snuffle? on the contrairy, don't I see every reason why I shouldn't? Just hear this! Ha ha ha! An't that as nat'ral as walking, and as good for the health? Ha ha ha! An't that as nat'ral as a sheep's bleating, or a pig's grunting, or a horse's neighing, or a bird's singing? Ha ha ha! Isn't it, mother?"

There was something contagious in Kit's laugh, for his mother, who had looked grave before, first subsided into a smile, and then fell to joining in it heartily, which occasioned Kit to say that he knew it was natural, and to laugh the more. Kit and his mother, laughing together in a pretty loud key, woke the baby, who, finding that there was something very jovial and agreeable in progress, was no sooner in its mother's arms than it began to kick and laugh, most vigorously. This new illustration of his argument so tickled Kit, that he fell backward in his chair in a state of exhaustion, pointing at the baby and shaking his sides till he rocked again. After recovering twice or thrice, and as often relapsing, he wiped his eyes and said grace; and a very cheerful meal their scanty supper was.

With more kisses, and hugs, and tears, than many young gentlemen who start upon their travels, and leave well-stocked homes behind them would deem within the bounds of probability (if matter so low could be herein set down), Kit left the house at an early hour next morning, and set out to walk to Finchley; feeling a sufficient pride in his appearance to have warranted his excommunication from Little Bethel from that time forth, if he had ever been one of that mournful congregation.

Lest anybody should feel a curiosity to know how Kit was clad, it may be briefly remarked that he wore no livery, but was dressed in a coat of pepper-and-salt with waistcoat of canary colour, and nether garments of iron-grey; besides these glories, he shone in the lustre of a new pair of boots and an extremely stiff and shiny hat, which on being struck anywhere with the knuckles, sounded like a drum. And in this attire, rather wondering that he attracted so little attention, and attributing the circumstances to the insensibility of those who got up early, he made his way towards Abel Cottage.

Without encountering any more remarkable adventure on the road, than meeting a lad in a brimless hat, the exact counterpart of his old one, on whom he bestowed half the sixpence he possessed, Kit arrived in course of time at the carrier's house, where, to the lasting honour of human nature, he found the box in safety. Receiving from the wife of this immaculate man, a direction to Mr. Garland's, he took the box upon his shoulder and repaired thither directly.

To be sure, it was a beautiful little cottage with a thatched roof and little spires at the gable-ends, and pieces of stained glass in some of the windows, almost as large as pocket-books. On one side of the house was a little stable, just the size for the pony, with a little room over it, just the size for Kit. White curtains were fluttering, and birds, in cages that looked as bright as if they were made of gold, were singing at the windows; plants were arranged on either side of the path, and clustered about the door; and the garden was bright with flowers in full bloom, which shed a sweet odour all round, and had a charming and elegant appearance. Everything, within the house and without, seemed to be the perfection of neatness and order. In the garden there was not a weed to be seen, and to judge from some dapper gardening-tools, a basket, and a pair of gloves which were lying in one of the walks, old Mr. Garland had been at work in it that very morning.

Kit looked about him, and admired, and looked again, and this a great many times before he could make up his mind to turn his head another way and ring the bell. There was abundance of time to look about him again though, when he had rung it, for nobody came, so after ringing twice or thrice he sat down upon his box and waited.

He rang the bell a great many times, and yet nobody came. But at last, as he was sitting upon the box thinking about giants' castles, and princesses tied up to pegs by the hair of their heads, and dragons bursting out from behind gates, and other incidents of the like nature, common in story-books to youths of low degree on their first visit to strange houses, the door was gently opened, and a little servant-girl, very tidy, modest, and demure, but very pretty too, appeared.

"I suppose you're Christopher, sir," said the servant-girl.

Kit got off the box, and said yes, he was.

"I'm afraid you've rung a good many times perhaps," she rejoined, "but we couldn't hear you, because we've been catching the pony."

Kit rather wondered what this meant, but as he couldn't stop there, asking questions, he shouldered the box again and followed the girl into the hall, where through a back-door he descried Mr. Garland leading Whisker in triumph up the garden, after that self-willed pony had (as he afterwards learned) dodged the family round a small paddock in the rear, for one hour and three quarters.

The old gentleman received him very kindly and so did the old lady, whose previous good opinion of him was greatly enhanced by his wiping his boots on the mat until the soles of his feet burnt again. He was then taken into the parlour to be inspected in his new clothes; and when he had been surveyed several times, and had afforded by his appearance unlimited satisfaction, he was taken into the stable (where the pony received him with uncommon complaisance); and thence into the little chamber he had already observed, which was very clean and comfortable; and thence into the garden, in which the old gentleman told him he would be taught to employ himself, and where he told him, besides, what great things he meant to do to make him comfortable, and happy, if he found he deserved it. All these kindnesses, Kit acknowledged with various expressions of gratitude, and so many touches of the new hat, that the brim suffered considerably. When the old gentleman had said all he had to say in the way of promise and advice, and Kit had said all he had to say in the way of assurance and thankfulness, he was handed over again to the old lady, who, summoning the little servant-girl (whose name was Barbara) instructed her to take him down stairs and give him something to eat and drink, after his walk.

Down stairs, therefore, Kit went; and at the bottom of the stairs there was such a kitchen as was never before seen or heard of out of a toy-shop window, with everything in it as bright and glowing, and as precisely ordered too, as Barbara herself. And in this kitchen, Kit sat himself down at a table as white as a tablecloth, to eat cold meat, and drink small ale, and use his knife and fork the more awkwardly, because there was an unknown Barbara looking on and observing him.

It did not appear, however, that there was anything remarkably tremendous about this strange Barbara, who having lived a very quiet life, blushed very much and was quite as embarrassed and uncertain what she ought to say or do, as Kit could possibly be. When he had sat for some little time, attentive to the ticking of the sober clock, he ventured to glance curiously at the dresser, and there, among the plates and dishes, were Barbara's little workbox with a sliding lid to shut in the balls of cotton, and Barbara's prayer-book, and Barbara's hymn-book, and Barbara's Bible. Barbara's little looking-glass hung in a good light near the window, and Barbara's bonnet was on a nail behind the door. From all these mute signs and tokens of her presence, he naturally glanced at Barbara herself, who sat as mute as they, shelling peas into a dish; and just when Kit was looking at her eyelashes and wondering—quite in the simplicity of his heart—what colour her eyes might be, it perversely happened that Barbara raised her head a little to look at him, when both pair of eyes were hastily withdrawn, and Kit leant over his plate, and Barbara over her pea-shells, each in extreme confusion at having been detected by the other.

CHAPTER XXIII

MR. RICHARD SWIVELLER wending homewards from the Wilderness (for such was the appropriate name of Quilp's choice retreat), after a sinuous and corkscrew fashion, with many checks and stumbles; after stopping suddenly and staring about him, then as suddenly running forward for a few paces, and as suddenly halting again and shaking his head; doing everything with a jerk and nothing by premeditation; —Mr. Richard Swiveller wending his way homewards after this fashion, which is considered by evil-minded men to be symbolical of intoxication, and is not held by such persons to denote that state of deep wisdom and reflection in which the actor knows himself to be, began to think that possibly he had misplaced his confidence and that the dwarf might not be precisely the sort of person to whom to entrust a secret of such delicacy and importance. And being led and tempted on by this remorseful thought into a condition which the evil-minded class before referred to would term the maudlin state or stage of drunkenness, it occurred to Mr. Swiveller to cast his hat upon the ground, and moan, crying aloud that he was an unhappy orphan, and that if he had not been an unhappy orphan things had never come to this.

"Left an infant by my parents, at an early age," said Mr. Swiveller, bewailing his hard lot, "cast upon the world in my tenderest period, and thrown upon the mercies of a deluding dwarf, who can wonder at my weakness! Here's a miserable orphan for you. Here," said Mr. Swiveller raising his voice to a high pitch, and looking sleepily round, "is a miserable orphan!"

"Then," said somebody hard by, "let me be a father to you."

Mr. Swiveller swayed himself to and fro to preserve his balance, and, looking into a kind of haze which seemed to surround him, at last perceived two eyes dimly twinkling through the mist, which he observed after a short time were in the neighbourhood of a nose and mouth. Casting his eyes down towards that quarter in which, with reference to a man's face, his legs are usually to be found, he observed that the face had a body attached; and when he looked more intently he was satisfied that the person was Mr. Quilp, who indeed had been in his company all the time, but whom he had some vague idea of having left a mile or two behind.

"You have deceived an orphan, sir," said Mr. Swiveller solemnly.

"I! I'm a second father to you," replied Quilp.

"You my father, sir!" retorted Dick. "Being all right myself, sir, I request to be left alone—instantly, sir."

"What a funny fellow you are!" cried Quilp.

"Go, sir," returned Dick, leaning against a post and waving his hand. "Go, deceiver, go, some day, sir, p'r'aps you'll waken, from pleasure's dream to know, the grief of orphans forsaken. Will you go, sir?"

The dwarf taking no heed of this adjuration, Mr. Swiveller advanced with the view of inflicting upon him condign chastisement. But forgetting his purpose or changing his mind before he came close to him, he seized his hand and vowed eternal friendship, declaring with an agreeable frankness that from that time forth they were brothers in everything but personal appearance. Then he told his secret all over again, with the addition of being pathetic on the subject of Miss Wackles, who, he gave Mr. Quilp to understand, was the occasion of any slight incoherency he might observe in his speech at that moment, which was attributable solely to the strength of his affection and not to rosy wine or other fermented liquor. And then they went on arm in arm, very lovingly together.

"I'm as sharp," said Quilp to him, at parting, "as sharp as a ferret, and as cunning as a weasel. You bring Trent to me; assure him that I'm his friend though I fear he a little distrusts me (I don't know why, I have not deserved it); and you've both of you made your fortunes—in perspective."

"That's the worst of it," returned Dick. "These fortunes in perspective look such a long way off."

"But they look smaller than they really are, on that account," said Quilp pressing his arm. "You'll have no conception of the value of your prize until you draw close to it. Mark that."

"D'ye think not?" said Dick.

"Ay, I do; and I am certain of what I say, that's better," returned the dwarf. "You bring Trent to me. Tell him I am his friend and yours—why shouldn't I be?"

"There's no reason why you shouldn't, certainly," replied Dick, "and perhaps there are a great many why you should—at least there would be nothing strange in your wanting to be my friend, if you were a choice spirit, but then you know you're *not* a choice spirit."

"I not a choice spirit!" cried Quilp.

"Devil a bit, sir," returned Dick. "A man of your appearance couldn't be. If you're any spirit at all, sir, you're an evil spirit. Choice spirits," added Dick, smiting himself on the breast, "are quite a different looking sort of people, you may take your oath of that, sir."

Quilp glanced at his free-spoken friend with a mingled expression of cunning and dislike, and wringing his hand almost at the same moment, declared that he was an uncommon character and had his warmest esteem. With that they parted; Mr. Swiveller to make the best of his way home and sleep himself sober; and Quilp to cogitate upon the discovery he had made, and exult in the prospect of the rich field of enjoyment and reprisal it opened to him.

It was not without great reluctance and misgiving that Mr. Swiveller, next morning, his head racked by the fumes of the renowned Schiedam, repaired to the lodging of his friend Trent (which was in the roof of an old house in an old ghostly inn), and recounted by very slow degrees what had yesterday taken place between him and Quilp. Nor was it without great surprise and much speculation on Quilp's probable motives, nor without many bitter comments on Dick Swiveller's folly, that his friend received the tale.

"I don't defend myself, Fred," said the penitent Richard; "but the fellow has such a queer way with him and is such an artful dog, that first of all he set me upon thinking whether there was any harm in telling him, and while I was thinking, screwed it out of me. If you had seen him drink and smoke, as I did, you couldn't have kept anything from him. He's a salamander you know, that's what *he* is."

Without inquiring whether salamanders were of necessity good confidential agents, or whether a fire-proof man was as a matter of course trustworthy, Frederick Trent threw himself into a chair, and, burying his head in his hands, endeavoured to fathom the motives which had led Quilp to insinuate himself into Richard Swiveller's confidence;—for that the disclosure was of his seeking, and had not been spontaneously revealed by Dick, was sufficiently plain from Quilp's seeking his company and enticing him away.

The dwarf had twice encountered him when he was endeavouring to obtain intelligence of the fugitives. This, perhaps, as he had not shown any previous anxiety about them, was enough to awaken suspicion in the breast of a creature so jealous and distrustful by nature, setting aside any additional impulse to curiosity that he might have derived from Dick's incautious manner. But knowing the scheme they had planned, why should he offer to assist it? This was a question more difficult of solution; but as knaves generally overreach themselves by imputing their own designs to others, the idea immediately presented itself that some circumstances of irritation between Quilp and the old man, arising out of their secret transactions and not unconnected perhaps with his sudden disappearance, now rendered the former desirous of revenging himself upon him by seeking to entrap the sole object of his love and anxiety into a connexion of which he knew he had a dread and hatred. As Frederick Trent himself, utterly regardless of his sister, had this object at heart, only second to the hope of gain, it seemed to him the more likely to be Quilp's main principle of action. Once investing the dwarf with a design of his own in abetting them, which the attainment of their purpose would serve, it was easy to believe him sincere and hearty in the cause; and as there could be no doubt of his proving a powerful and useful auxiliary, Trent determined to accept his invitation and go to his house that night, and if what he said and did confirmed him in the impression he had formed, to let him share the labour of their plan, but not the profit.

Having revolved these things in his mind and arrived at this conclusion, he communicated to Mr. Swiveller as much of his meditations as he thought proper (Dick would have been perfectly satisfied with less), and giving him the day to recover himself from his late salamandering, accompanied him at evening to Mr. Quilp's house.

Mightily glad Mr. Quilp was to see them, or mightily glad he seemed to be; and fearfully polite Mr. Quilp was to Mrs. Quilp and Mrs. Jiniwin; and very sharp was the look he cast on his wife to observe how she was affected by the recognition of young Trent. Mrs. Quilp was as innocent as her own mother of any emotion, painful or pleasant, which the sight of him awakened, but as her husband's glance made her timid and confused, and uncertain what to do or what was required of her, Mr. Quilp did not fail to assign her embarrassment to the cause he had in his mind, and while he chuckled at his penetration was secretly exasperated by his jealousy.

Nothing of this appeared, however. On the contrary, Mr. Quilp was all blandness and suavity, and presided over the case-bottle of rum with extraordinary open-heartedness.

"Why, let me see," said Quilp. "It must be a matter of nearly two years since we were first acquainted."

"Nearer three, I think," said Trent.

"Nearer three!" cried Quilp. "How fast time flies. Does it seem as long as that to you, Mrs. Quilp?"

"Yes, I think it seems full three years, Quilp," was the unfortunate reply.

"Oh indeed, ma'am," thought Quilp, "you have been pining, have you? Very good, ma'am."

"It seems to me but yesterday that you went out to Demerara in the Mary Anne," said Quilp; "but yesterday, I declare. Well, I like a little wildness. I was wild myself once."

Mr. Quilp accompanied this admission with such an awful wink, indicative of old rovings and backslidings, that Mrs. Jiniwin was indignant, and could not forbear from remarking under her breath that he might at least put off his confessions until his wife was absent; for which act of boldness and insubordination Mr. Quilp first stared her out of countenance and then drank her health ceremoniously.

"I thought you'd come back directly, Fred. I always thought that," said Quilp setting down his glass. "And when the Mary Anne returned with you on board, instead of a letter to say what a contrite heart you had, and how happy you were in the situation that had been provided for you, I was amused—exceedingly amused. Ha ha ha!"

The young man smiled, but not as though the theme were the most agreeable one that could have been selected for his entertainment; and for that reason Quilp pursued it.

"I always will say," he resumed, "that when a rich relation having two young people—sisters or brothers, or brother and sister— dependent on him, attaches himself exclusively to one, and casts off the other, he does wrong."

The young man made a movement of impatience, but Quilp went on as calmly as if he were discussing some abstract question in which nobody present had the slightest personal interest.

"It's very true," said Quilp, "that your grandfather urged repeated forgiveness, ingratitude, riot, and extravagance, and all that; but as I told him 'these are common faults.' 'But he's a scoundrel,' said he. 'Granting that,' said I (for the sake of argument of course), 'a great many young noblemen and gentlemen are scoundrels too!' But he wouldn't be convinced."

"I wonder at that, Mr. Quilp," said the young man sarcastically.

"Well, so did I at the time," returned Quilp, "but he was always obstinate. He was in a manner a friend of mine, but he was always obstinate and wrong-headed. Little Nell is a nice girl, a charming girl, but you're her brother, Frederick. You're her brother after all; as you told him the last time you met, he can't alter that."

"He would if he could, confound him for that and all other kindnesses," said the young man impatiently. "But nothing can come of this subject now, and let us have done with it in the Devil's name."

"Agreed," returned Quilp, "agreed on my part, readily. Why have I alluded to it? Just to show you, Frederick, that I have always stood your friend. You little knew who was your friend, and who your foe; now did you? You thought I was against you, and so there has been a coolness between us; but it was all on your side, entirely on your side. Let's shake hands again, Fred."

With his head sunk down between his shoulders, and a hideous grin overspreading his face, the dwarf stood up and stretched his short arm across the table. After a moment's hesitation, the young man stretched out his to meet it; Quilp clutched his fingers in a grip that for the moment stopped the current of the blood within them, and pressing his other hand upon his lip and frowning towards the unsuspicious Richard, released them and sat down.

This action was not lost upon Trent, who, knowing that Richard Swiveller was a mere tool in his hands and knew no more of his designs than he thought proper to communicate, saw that the dwarf perfectly understood their relative position, and fully entered into the character of his friend. It is something to be appreciated, even in knavery. This silent homage to his superior abilities, no less than a sense of the power with which the dwarf's quick perception had already invested him, inclined the young man towards that ugly worthy, and determined him to profit by his aid.

It being now Mr. Quilp's cue to change the subject with all convenient expedition, lest Richard Swiveller in his heedlessness should reveal anything which it was inexpedient for the women to know, he proposed a game at four-handed cribbage; and partners being cut for, Mrs. Quilp fell to Frederick Trent, and Dick himself to Quilp. Mrs. Jiniwin being very fond of cards was carefully excluded by her son-in-law from any participation in the game, and had assigned to her the duty of occasionally replenishing the glasses from the casebottle; Mr. Quilp from that moment keeping one eye constantly upon her, lest she should by any means procure a taste of the same, and thereby tantalising the wretched old lady (who was as much attached to the case-bottle as the cards) in a double degree and most ingenious manner.

But it was not to Mrs. Jiniwin alone that Mr. Quilp's attention was restricted, as several other matters required his constant vigilance. Among his various eccentric habits he had a humorous one of always cheating at cards, which rendered necessary on his part, not only a close observance of the game, and a sleight-of-hand in counting and scoring, but also involved the constant correction, by looks, and frowns, and kicks under the table, of Richard Swiveller, who being bewildered by the rapidity with which his cards were told, and the rate at which the pegs travelled down the board, could not be prevented from sometimes expressing his surprise and incredulity. Mrs. Quilp too was the partner of young Trent, and for every look that passed between them, and every word they spoke, and every card they played, the dwarf had eyes and ears; not occupied alone with what was passing above the table, but with signals that might be exchanging beneath it, which he laid all kinds of traps to detect; besides often treading on his wife's toes to see whether she cried out or remained silent under the infliction, in which latter case it would have been quite clear that Trent had been treading on her toes before. Yet, in the midst of all these distractions, the one eye was upon the old lady always, and if she so much as stealthily advanced a tea-spoon towards a neighbouring glass (which she often did), for the purpose of abstracting but one sup of its contents, Quilp's hand would overset it in the very moment of her triumph, and Quilp's mocking voice implore her to regard her precious health. And in any one of these his many cares, from first to last, Quilp never flagged nor faltered.

At length, when they had played a great many rubbers and drawn pretty freely upon the case-bottle, Mr. Quilp warned his lady to retire to rest, and that submissive wife complying, and being followed by her indignant mother, Mr. Swiveller fell asleep. The dwarf beckoning his remaining companion to the other end of the room, held a short conference with him in whispers.

"It's as well not to say more than one can help before our worthy friend," said Quilp, making a grimace towards the slumbering Dick. "Is it a bargain between us, Fred? Shall he marry little rosy Nell by-and-by?"

"You have some end of your own to answer, of course," returned the other.

"Of course I have, dear Fred," said Quilp, grinning to think how little he suspected what the real end was. "It's retaliation perhaps; perhaps whim. I have influence, Fred, to help or oppose. Which way shall I use it? There are a pair of scales, and it goes into one."

"Throw it into mine then," said Trent.

"It's done, Fred," rejoined Quilp, stretching out his clenched hand and opening it as if he had let some weight fall out. "It's in the scale from this time, and turns it, Fred. Mind that."

"Where have they gone?" asked Trent.

Quilp shook his head, and said that point remained to be discovered, which it might be, easily. When it was, they would begin their preliminary advances. He would visit the old man, or even Richard Swiveller might visit him, and by affecting a deep concern in his behalf, and imploring him to settle in some worthy home, lead to the child's remembering him with gratitude and favour. Once impressed to this extent, it would be easy, he said, to win her in a year or two, for she supposed the old man to be poor, as it was a part of his jealous policy (in common with many other misers) to feign to be so, to those about him.

"He has feigned it often enough to me, of late," said Trent.

"Oh! and to me too!" replied the dwarf. "Which is more extra-ordinary, as I know how rich he really is."

"I suppose you should," said Trent.

"I think I should indeed," rejoined the dwarf; and in that, at least, he spoke the truth.

After a few more whispered words, they returned to the table, and the young man rousing Richard Swiveller informed him that he was waiting to depart. This was welcome news to Dick, who started up directly. After a few words of confidence in the result of their project had been exchanged, they bade the grinning Quilp good night.

Quilp crept to the window as they passed in the street below, and listened. Trent was pronouncing an encomium upon his wife, and they were both wondering by what enchantment she had been brought to marry such a mis-shapen wretch as he. The dwarf after watching their retreating shadows with a wider grin than his face had yet displayed, stole softly in the dark to bed.

In this hatching of their scheme, neither Trent nor Quilp had had one thought about the happiness or misery of poor innocent Nell. It would have been strange if the careless profligate, who was the butt of both, had been harassed by any such consideration; for his high opinion of his own merits and deserts rendered the project rather a laudable one than otherwise; and if he had been visited by so unwonted a guest as reflection, he would—being a brute only in the gratification of his appetites—have soothed his conscience with the plea that he did not mean to beat or kill his wife, and would therefore, after all said and done, be a very tolerable, average husband.

CHAPTER XXIV

IT was not until they were quite exhausted and could no longer maintain the pace at which they had fled from the race-ground, that the old man and the child ventured to stop, and sit down to rest upon the borders of a little wood. Here, though the course was hidden from their view, they could yet faintly distinguish the noise of distant shouts, the hum of voices, and the beating of drums. Climbing the eminence which lay between them and the spot they had left, the child could even discern the fluttering flags and white tops of booths; but no person was approaching towards them, and their resting-place was solitary and still.

Some time elapsed before she could reassure her trembling companion, or restore him to a state of moderate tranquillity. His disordered imagination represented to him a crowd of persons stealing towards them beneath the cover of the bushes, lurking in every ditch, and peeping from the boughs of every rustling tree. He was haunted by apprehensions of being led captive to some gloomy place where he would be chained and scourged, and worse than all, where Nell would never come to see him, save through iron bars and gratings in the wall. His terrors affected the child. Separation from her grandfather was the greatest evil she could dread; and feeling for the time as though, go where they would, they were to be hunted down, and could never be safe but in hiding, her heart failed her, and her courage drooped.

In one so young, and so unused to the scenes in which she had lately moved, this sinking of the spirit was not surprising. But, Nature often enshrines gallant and noble hearts in weak bosoms—oftenest, God bless her, in female breasts—and when the child, casting her tearful eyes upon the old man, remembered how weak he was, and how destitute and helpless he would be if she failed him, her heart swelled within her, and animated her with new strength and fortitude.

"We are quite safe now, and have nothing to fear indeed, dear grandfather," she said.

"Nothing to fear!" returned the old man. "Nothing to fear if they took me from thee! Nothing to fear if they parted us! Nobody is true to me. No, not one. Not even Nell!"

"Oh! do not say that," replied the child, "for if ever anybody was true at heart, and earnest, I am. I am sure you know I am."

"Then how," said the old man, looking fearfully round, "how can you bear to think that we are safe, when they are searching for me everywhere, and may come here, and steal upon us, even while we're talking?"

"Because I'm sure we have not been followed," said the child. "Judge for yourself, dear grandfather; look round, and see how quiet and still it is. We are alone together, and may ramble where we like. Not safe! Could I feel easy—did I feel at ease—when any danger threatened you?"

"True, true," he answered, pressing her hand, but still looking anxiously about. "What noise was that?"

"A bird," said the child, "flying into the wood, and leading the way for us to follow. You remember that we said we would walk in woods and fields, and by the side of rivers, and how happy we would be—you remember that? But here, while the sun shines above our heads, and everything is bright and happy, we are sitting sadly down, and losing time. See what a pleasant path; and there's the bird —the same bird—now he flies to another tree, and stays to sing. Come!"

When they rose up from the ground, and took the shady track which led them through the wood, she bounded on before, printing her tiny footsteps in the moss, which rose elastic from so light a pressure and gave it back as mirrors throw off breath; and thus she lured the old man on, with many a backward look and merry beck, now pointing stealthily to some lone bird as it perched and twittered on a branch that strayed across their path, now stopping to listen to the songs that broke the happy silence, or watch the sun as it trembled through the leaves, and stealing in among the ivied trunks of stout old trees, opening long paths of light. As they passed onward, parting the boughs that clustered in their way, the serenity which the child had first assumed, stole into her breast in earnest; the old man cast no longer fearful looks behind, but felt at ease and cheerful, for the further they passed into the deep green shade, the more they felt that the tranquil mind of God was there, and shed its peace on them.

At length, the path becoming clearer and less intricate, brought them to the end of the wood, and into a public road. Taking their way along it for a short distance, they came to a lane, so shaded by the trees on either hand that they met together overhead, and arched the narrow way. A broken finger-post announced that this led to a village three miles off; and thither they resolved to bend their steps.

The miles appeared so long that they sometimes thought they must have missed their road. But at last, to their great joy, it led downward in a steep descent, with overhanging banks over which the footpaths led; and the clustered houses of the village peeped out from the woody hollow below.

It was a very small place. The men and boys were playing at cricket on the green; and as the other folk were looking on, they wandered up and down, uncertain where to seek a humble lodging. There was but one old man in the little garden before his cottage, and him they were timid of approaching, for he was the schoolmaster, and had "School" written up over his window in black letters on a white board. He was a pale, simple-looking man, of a spare and meagre habit, and sat among his flowers and beehives, smoking his pipe, in the little porch before his door.

"Speak to him, dear," the old man whispered.

"I am almost afraid to disturb him," said the child timidly. "He does not seem to see us. Perhaps if we wait a little, he may look this way."

They waited, but the schoolmaster cast no look towards them, and still sat, thoughtful and silent, in the little porch. He had a kind face. In his plain old suit of black, he looked pale and meagre. They fancied, too, a lonely air about him and his house, but perhaps that was because the other people formed a merry company upon the green, and he seemed the only solitary man in all the place.

They were very tired, and the child would have been bold enough to address even a schoolmaster, but for something in his manner which seemed to denote that he was uneasy or distressed. As they stood hesitating at a little distance, they saw that he sat for a few minutes at a time like one in a brown study, then laid aside his pipe and took a few turns in his garden, then approached the gate and looked towards the green, then took up his pipe again with a sigh, and sat down thoughtfully as before.

As nobody else appeared and it would soon be dark, Nell at length took courage, and when he had resumed his pipe and seat, ventured to draw near, leading her grandfather by the hand. The slight noise they made in raising the latch of the wicket-gate, caught his attention. He looked at them kindly but seemed disappointed too, and slightly shook his head.

Nell dropped a curtsey, and told him they were poor travellers who sought a shelter for the night which they would gladly pay for, so far as their means allowed. The schoolmaster looked earnestly at her as she spoke, laid aside his pipe, and rose up directly.

"If you could direct us anywhere, sir," said the child, "we should take it very kindly."

"You have been walking a long way," said the schoolmaster.

"A long way, sir," the child replied.

"You're a young traveller, my child," he said, laying his hand gently on her head. "Your grandchild, friend?"

"Ay, sir," cried the old man, "and the stay and comfort of my life."

"Come in," said the schoolmaster.

Without further preface he conducted them into his little school-room, which was parlour and kitchen likewise, and told them they were welcome to remain under his roof till morning. Before they had done thanking him, he spread a coarse white cloth upon the table, with knives and platters; and bringing out some bread and cold meat and a jug of beer, besought them to eat and drink.

The child looked round the room as she took her seat. There were a couple of forms, notched and cut and inked all over; a small deal desk perched on four legs, at which no doubt the master sat; a few dog's-eared books upon a high shelf; and beside them a motley collection of peg-tops, balls, kites, fishing-lines, marbles half-eaten apples, and other confiscated property of idle urchins. Displayed on hooks upon the wall in all their terrors, were the cane and ruler; and near them, on a small shelf of its own, the dunce's cap, made of old newspapers and decorated with glaring wafers of the largest size. But, the great ornaments of the walls were certain moral sentences fairly copied in good round text, and well-worked sums in simple addition and multiplication, evidently achieved by the same hand, which were plentifully pasted all round the room: for the double purpose, as it seemed, of bearing testimony to the excellence of the school, and kindling a worthy emulation in the bosoms of the scholars.

"Yes," said the old schoolmaster, observing that her attention was caught by these latter specimens. "That's beautiful writing, my dear."

"Very, sir," replied the child modestly, "is it yours?"

"Mine!" he returned, taking out his spectacles and putting them on, to have a better view of the triumphs so dear to his heart. "*I* couldn't write like that, now-a-days. No. They're all done by one hand; a little hand it is, not so old as yours, but a very clever one."

As the schoolmaster said this, he saw that a small blot of ink had been thrown on one of the copies, so he took a penknife from his pocket, and going up to the wall, carefully scraped it out. When he had finished, he walked slowly backward from the writing, admiring it as one might contemplate a beautiful picture, but with something of sadness in his voice and manner which quite touched the child, though she was unacquainted with its cause.

"A little hand indeed," said the poor schoolmaster. "Far beyond all his companions, in his learning and his sports too, how did he ever come to be so fond of me! That I should love him is no wonder, but that he should love me—" and there the schoolmaster stopped, and took off his spectacles to wipe them, as though they had grown dim.

"I hope there is nothing the matter, sir," said Nell anxiously.

"Not much, my dear," returned the schoolmaster. "I hoped to have seen him on the green to-night. He was always foremost among them. But he'll be there to-morrow."

"Has he been ill?" asked the child, with a child's quick sympathy.

"Not very. They said he was wandering in his head yesterday, dear boy, and so they said the day before. But that's a part of that kind of disorder; it's not a bad sign—not at all a bad sign."

The child was silent. He walked to the door, and looked wistfully out. The shadows of night were gathering, and all was still.

"If he could lean upon anybody's arm, he would come to me, I know," he said, returning into the room. "He always came into the garden to say good night. But perhaps his illness has only just taken a favourable turn, and it's too late for him to come out, for it's very damp and there's a heavy dew. It's much better he shouldn't come to-night."

The schoolmaster lighted a candle, fastened the window-shutter, and closed the door. But after he had done this, and sat silent a little time, he took down his hat, and said he would go and satisfy himself, if Nell would sit up till he returned. The child readily complied, and he went out.

She sat there half an hour or more, feeling the place very strange and lonely, for she had prevailed upon the old man to go to bed, and there was nothing to be heard but the ticking of an old clock, and the whistling of the wind among the trees. When he returned, he took his seat in the chimney-corner, but remained silent for a long time. At length he turned to her, and speaking very gently, hoped she would say a prayer that night for a sick child.

"My favourite scholar!" said the poor schoolmaster, smoking a pipe he had forgotten to light, and looking mournfully round about the walls. "It is a little hand to have done all that, and waste away with sickness. It is a very, very little hand!"

CHAPTER XXV

AFTER a sound night's rest in a chamber in the thatched roof, in which it seemed the sexton had for some years been a lodger, but which he had lately deserted for a wife and a cottage of his own, the child rose early in the morning and descended to the room where she had supped last night. As the schoolmaster had already left his bed and gone out, she bestirred herself to make it neat and comfortable, and had just finished its arrangement when the kind host returned.

He thanked her many times, and said that the old dame who usually did such offices for him had gone to nurse the little scholar whom he had told her of. The child asked how he was, and hoped he was better.

"No," rejoined the schoolmaster shaking his head sorrowfully, "No better. They even say he is worse."

"I am very sorry for that, sir," said the child.

The poor schoolmaster appeared to be gratified by her earnest manner, but yet rendered more uneasy by it, for he added hastily that anxious people often magnified an evil and thought it greater than it was; "for my part," he said, in his quiet, patient way, "I hope it's not so. I don't think he can be worse."

The child asked his leave to prepare breakfast, and her grandfather coming down stairs, they all three partook of it together. While the meal was in progress, their host remarked that the old man seemed much fatigued, and evidently stood in need of rest.

"If the journey you have before you is a long one," he said, "and don't press you for one day, you're very welcome to pass another night here. I should really be glad if you would, friend."

He saw that the old man looked at Nell, uncertain whether to accept or decline his offer; and added,

"I shall be glad to have your young companion with me for one day. If you can do a charity to a lone man, and rest yourself at the same time, do so. If you must proceed upon your journey, I wish you well through it, and will walk a little way with you before school begins."

"What are we to do, Nell?" said the old man irresolutely, "say what we're to do, dear."

It required no great persuasion to induce the child to answer that they had better accept the invitation and remain. She was happy to show her gratitude to the kind schoolmaster by busying herself in the performance of such household duties as his little cottage stood in need of. When these were done, she took some needle-work from her basket, and sat herself down upon a stool beside the lattice, where the honeysuckle and woodbine entwined their tender stems, and stealing into the room filled it with their delicious breath. Her grandfather was basking in the sun outside, breathing the perfume of the flowers, and idly watching the clouds as they floated on before the light summer wind.

As the schoolmaster, after arranging the two forms in due order, took his seat behind his desk and made other preparations for school, the child was apprehensive that she might be in the way, and offered to withdraw to her little bedroom. But this he would not allow, and as he seemed pleased to have her there, she remained, busying herself with her work.

"Have you many scholars, sir?" she asked.

The poor schoolmaster shook his head, and said that they barely filled the two forms.

"And are the others clever, sir?" asked the child, glancing at the trophies on the wall.

"Good boys," returned the schoolmaster, "good boys enough, my dear, but they'll never do like that."

A small white-headed boy with a sunburnt face appeared at the door while he was speaking, and stopping there to make a rustic bow, came in and took his seat upon one of the forms. The white-headed boy then put an open book astonishingly dog's-eared, upon his knees, and thrusting his hands into his pockets began counting the marbles with which they were filled; displaying in the expression of his face a remarkable capacity of totally abstracting his mind from the spelling on which his eyes were fixed. Soon afterwards another white-headed little boy came straggling in, and after him a red-headed lad, and after him two more with white heads, and then one with a flaxen poll, and so on until the forms were occupied by a dozen boys or thereabouts, with heads of every colour but grey, and ranging in their ages from four years old to fourteen years or more; for the legs of the youngest were a long way from the floor when he sat upon the form, and the eldest was a heavy good-tempered foolish fellow, about half a head taller than the schoolmaster.

At the top of the first form—the post of honour in the school—was the vacant place of the little sick scholar, and at the head of the rows of pegs on which those who came in hats or caps were wont to hang them up, one was left empty. No boy attempted to violate the sanctity of seat or peg, but many a one looked from the empty spaces to the schoolmaster, and whispered his idle neighbour behind his hand.

Then began the hum of conning over lessons and getting them by heart, the whispered jest and stealthy game, and all the noise and drawl of school; and in the midst of the din sat the poor schoolmaster, the very image of meekness and simplicity, vainly attempting to fix his mind upon the duties of the day, and to forget his little friend. But the tedium of his office reminded him more strongly of the willing scholar, and his thoughts were rambling from his pupils—it was plain.

None knew this better than the idlest boys, who, growing bolder with impunity, waxed louder and more daring; playing odd-or-even under the master's eye, eating apples openly and without rebuke, pinching each other in sport or malice without the least reserve, and cutting their autographs in the very legs of his desk. The puzzled dunce, who stood beside it to say his lesson out of book, looked no longer at the ceiling for forgotten words, but drew closer to the master's elbow and boldly cast his eye upon the page; the wag of the little troop squinted and made grimaces (at the smallest boy of course), holding no book before his face, and his approving audience knew no constraint in their delight. If the master did chance to rouse himself and seem alive to what was going on, the noise subsided for a

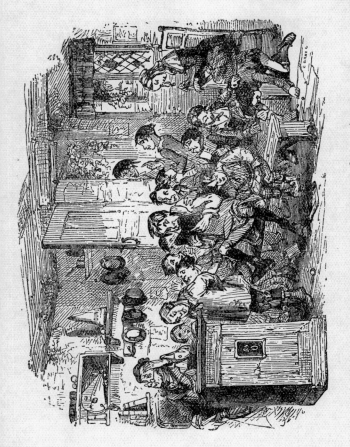

'His thoughts were rambling from his pupils.'

moment and no eyes met his but wore a studious and a deeply humble look; but the instant he relapsed again, it broke out afresh, and ten times louder than before.

Oh! how some of those idle fellows longed to be outside, and how they looked at the open door and window, as if they half meditated rushing violently out, plunging into the wood, and being wild boys and savages from that time forth. What rebellious thoughts of the cool river, and some shady bathing-place beneath willow trees with branches dipping in the water, kept tempting and urging that sturdy boy, who, with his shirt-collar unbuttoned and flung back as far as it could go, sat fanning his flushed face with a spelling-book, wishing himself a whale, or a tittlebat, or a fly, or anything but a boy at school on that hot, broiling day! Heat! ask that other boy, whose seat being nearest to the door gave him opportunities of gliding out into the garden and driving his companions to madness by dipping his face into the bucket of the well and then rolling on the grass—ask him if there were ever such a day as that, when even the bees were diving deep down into the cups of flowers and stopping there, as if they had made up their minds to retire from business and be manufacturers of honey no more. The day was made for laziness, and lying on one's back in green places, and staring at the sky till its brightness forced one to shut one's eyes and go to sleep; and was this a time to be poring over musty books in a dark room, slighted by the very sun itself? Monstrous!

Nell sat by the window occupied with her work, but attentive still to all that passed, though sometimes rather timid of the boisterous boys. The lessons over, writing-time began; and there being but one desk and that the master's, each boy sat at it in turn and laboured at his crooked copy, while the master walked about. This was a quieter time; for he would come and look over the writer's shoulder, and tell him mildly to observe how such a letter was turned in such a copy on the wall, praise such an up-stroke here and such a down-stroke there, and bid him take it for his model. Then he would stop and tell them what the sick child had said last night, and how he had longed to be among them once again; and such was the poor schoolmaster's gentle and affectionate manner, that the boys seemed quite remorseful that they had worried him so much, and were absolutely quiet; eating no apples, cutting no names, inflicting no pinches, and making no grimaces, for full two minutes afterwards.

"I think, boys," said the schoolmaster when the clock struck twelve, "that I shall give an extra half-holiday this afternoon."

At this intelligence, the boys, led on and headed by the tall boy, raised a great shout, in the midst of which the master was seen to speak, but could not be heard. As he held up his hand, however, in token of his wish that they should be silent, they were considerate enough to leave off, as soon as the longest-winded among them were quite out of breath.

"You must promise me first," said the schoolmaster, "that you'll not be noisy, or at least, if you are, that you'll go away and be so—

away out of the village I mean. I'm sure you wouldn't disturb your old playmate and companion."

There was a general murmur (and perhaps a very sincere one, for they were but boys) in the negative; and the tall boy, perhaps as sincerely as any of them, called those about him to witness that he had only shouted in a whisper.

"Then pray don't forget, there's my dear scholars," said the schoolmaster, "what I have asked you, and do it as a favour to me. Be as happy as you can, and don't be unmindful that you are blessed with health. Good-bye all!"

"Thank'ee, sir," and "good-bye, sir," were said a great many times in a variety of voices, and the boys went out very slowly and softly. But there was the sun shining and there were the birds singing, as the sun only shines and the birds only sing on holidays and half-holidays; there were the trees waving to all free boys to climb and nestle among their leafy branches; the hay, entreating them to come and scatter it to the pure air; the green corn, gently beckoning towards wood and stream; the smooth ground, rendered smoother still by blending lights and shadows, inviting to runs and leaps, and long walks God knows whither. It was more than boy could bear, and with a joyous whoop the whole cluster took to their heels and spread themselves about, shouting and laughing as they went.

"It's natural, thank Heaven!" said the poor schoolmaster looking after them. "I'm very glad they didn't mind me!"

It is difficult, however, to please everybody, as most of us would have discovered, even without the fable which bears that moral; and in the course of the afternoon several mothers and aunts of pupils looked in to express their entire disapproval of the schoolmaster's proceeding. A few confined themselves to hints, such as politely inquiring what red-letter day or saint's day the almanack said it was; a few (these were the profound village politicians) argued that it was a slight to the Throne and an affront to Church and State, and savoured of revolutionary principles, to grant a half-holiday upon any lighter occasion than the birthday of the Monarch; but the majority expressed their displeasure on private grounds and in plain terms, arguing that to put the pupils on this short allowance of learning was nothing but an act of downright robbery and fraud: and one old lady, finding that she could not inflame or irritate the peaceable schoolmaster by talking to him, bounced out of his house and talked at him for half an hour outside his own window, to another old lady, saying that of course he would deduct this half-holiday from his weekly charge, or of course he would naturally expect to have an opposition started against him; there was no want of idle chaps in that neighbourhood (here the old lady raised her voice), and some chaps who were too idle even to be schoolmasters, might soon find that there were other chaps put over their heads, and so she would have them take care, and look pretty sharp about them. But all these taunts and vexations failed to elicit one word from the meek schoolmaster, who sat with the child by his side,—a little more dejected perhaps, but quite silent and uncomplaining.

Towards night an old woman came tottering up the garden as speedily as she could, and meeting the schoolmaster at the door, said he was to go to Dame West's directly, and had best run on before her. He and the child were on the point of going out together for a walk, and without relinquishing her hand, the schoolmaster hurried away, leaving the messenger to follow as she might.

They stopped at a cottage-door, and the schoolmaster knocked softly at it with his hand. It was opened without loss of time. They entered a room where a little group of women were gathered about one, older than the rest, who was crying very bitterly, and sat wringing her hands and rocking herself to and fro.

"Oh dame!" said the schoolmaster, drawing near her chair, "is it so bad as this?"

"He's going fast," cried the old woman; "my grandson's dying. It's all along of you. You shouldn't see him now, but for his being so earnest on it. This is what his learning has brought him to. Oh dear, dear, dear, what can I do!"

"Do not say that I am in any fault," urged the gentle schoolmaster. "I am not hurt, dame. No, no. You are in great distress of mind, and don't mean what you say. I am sure you don't."

"I do," returned the old woman. "I mean it all. If he hadn't been poring over his books out of fear of you, he would have been well and merry now, I know he would."

The schoolmaster looked round upon the other women as if to entreat some one among them to say a kind word for him, but they shook their heads, and murmured to each other that they never thought there was much good in learning, and that this convinced them. Without saying a word in reply, or giving them a look of reproach, he followed the old woman who had summoned him (and who had now rejoined them) into another room, where his infant friend, half-dressed, lay stretched upon a bed.

He was a very young boy; quite a little child. His hair still hung in curls about his face, and his eyes were very bright; but their light was of Heaven, not earth. The schoolmaster took a seat beside him, and stooping over the pillow, whispered his name. The boy sprang up, stroked his face with his hand, and threw his wasted arms around his neck, crying out that he was his dear kind friend.

"I hope I always was. I meant to be, God knows," said the poor schoolmaster.

"Who is that?" said the boy, seeing Nell. "I am afraid to kiss her, lest I should make her ill. Ask her to shake hands with me."

The sobbing child came closer up, and took the little languid hand in hers. Releasing his again after a time, the sick boy laid him gently down.

"You remember the garden, Harry," whispered the schoolmaster, anxious to rouse him, for a dulness seemed gathering upon the child, "and how pleasant it used to be in the evening time? You must make haste to visit it again, for I think the very flowers have missed you, and are less gay than they used to be. You will come soon, my dear, very soon now,—won't you?"

The boy smiled faintly—so very, very faintly—and put his hand upon his friend's grey head. He moved his lips too, but no voice came from them; no, not a sound.

In the silence that ensued, the hum of distant voices borne upon the evening air came floating through the open window. "What's that?" said the sick child, opening his eyes.

"The boys at play upon the green."

He took a handkerchief from his pillow, and tried to wave it above his head. But the feeble arm dropped powerless down.

"Shall I do it?" said the schoolmaster.

"Please wave it at the window," was the faint reply. "Tie it to the lattice. Some of them may see it there. Perhaps they'll think of me, and look this way."

He raised his head, and glanced from the fluttering signal to his idle bat, that lay with slate and book and other boyish property upon a table in the room. And then he laid him softly down once more, and asked if the little girl were there, for he could not see her.

She stepped forward, and pressed the passive hand that lay upon the coverlet. The two old friends and companions—for such they were, though they were man and child—held each other in a long embrace, and then the little scholar turned his face towards the wall, and fell asleep.

The poor schoolmaster sat in the same place, holding the small cold hand in his, and chafing it. It was but the hand of a dead child. He felt that; and yet he chafed it still, and could not lay it down.

CHAPTER XXVI

ALMOST broken-hearted, Nell withdrew with the schoolmaster from the bedside and returned to his cottage. In the midst of her grief and tears she was yet careful to conceal their real cause from the old man, for the dead boy had been a grandchild, and left but one aged relative to mourn his premature decay.

She stole away to bed as quickly as she could, and when she was alone, gave free vent to the sorrow with which her breast was overcharged. But the sad scene she had witnessed, was not without its lesson of content and gratitude; of content with the lot which left her health and freedom; and gratitude that she was spared to the one relative and friend she loved, and to live and move in a beautiful world, when so many young creatures—as young and full of hope as she—were stricken down and gathered to their graves. How many of the mounds in that old churchyard where she had lately strayed, grew green above the graves of children! And though she thought as a child herself, and did not perhaps sufficiently consider to what a bright and happy existence those who die young are borne, and how in death they lose the pain of seeing others die around them, bearing to the tomb some strong affection of their hearts (which makes the old die many times in one long life), still she thought, wisely enough, to draw a plain and easy moral from what she had seen that night, and to store it, deep in her mind.

Her dreams were of the little scholar: not coffined and covered up, but mingling with angels, and smiling happily. The sun darting his cheerful rays into the room, awoke her; and now there remained but to take leave of the poor schoolmaster and wander forth once more.

By the time they were ready to depart, school had begun. In the darkened room, the din of yesterday was going on again: a little sobered and softened down, perhaps, but only a very little, if at all. The schoolmaster rose from his desk and walked with them to the gate.

It was with a trembling and reluctant hand, that the child held out to him the money which the lady had given her at the races for her flowers: faltering in her thanks as she thought how small the sum was, and blushing as she offered it. But he bade her put it up, and stooping to kiss her cheek, turned back into his house.

They had not gone half a dozen paces when he was at the door again; the old man retraced his steps to shake hands, and the child did the same.

"Good fortune and happiness go with you!" said the poor schoolmaster. "I am quite a solitary man now. If ever you pass this way again, you'll not forget the little village-school."

"We shall never forget it, sir," rejoined Nell; "nor ever forget to be grateful to you for your kindness to us."

"I have heard such words from the lips of children very often," said the schoolmaster, shaking his head and smiling thoughtfully, "but they were soon forgotten. I had attached one young friend to me, the better friend for being young—but that's over—God bless you!"

They bade him farewell very many times, and turned away, walking slowly and often looking back, until they could see him no more. At length they had left the village far behind, and even lost sight of the smoke among the trees. They trudged onward now, at a quicker pace, resolving to keep the main road, and go wherever it might lead them.

But main roads stretch a long, long way. With the exception of two or three inconsiderable clusters of cottages which they passed, without stopping, and one lonely roadside public-house where they had some bread and cheese, this highway had led them to nothing—late in the afternoon—and still lengthened out, far in the distance, the same dull, tedious, winding course, that they had been pursuing all day. As they had no resource, however, but to go forward, they still kept on, though at a much slower pace, being very weary and fatigued.

The afternoon had worn away into a beautiful evening, when they arrived at a point where the road made a sharp turn and struck across a common. On the border of this common, and close to the hedge which divided it from the cultivated fields, a caravan was drawn up to rest; upon which, by reason of its situation, they came so suddenly that they could not have avoided it if they would.

It was not a shabby, dingy, dusty cart, but a smart little house upon wheels, with white dimity curtains festooning the windows, and window-shutters of green picked out with panels of a staring red, in which happily-contrasted colours the whole concern shone brilliant. Neither was it a poor caravan drawn by a single donkey or emaciated horse, for a pair of horses in pretty good condition were released from the shafts and grazing on the frowzy grass. Neither was it a gipsy caravan, for at the open door (graced with a bright brass knocker) sat a Christian lady, stout and comfortable to look upon, who wore a large bonnet trembling with bows. And that it was not an unprovided or destitute caravan was clear from this lady's occupation, which was the very pleasant and refreshing one of taking tea. The tea-things, including a bottle of rather suspicious character and a cold knuckle of ham, were set forth upon a drum, covered with a white napkin; and there, as if at the most convenient round-table in all the world, sat this roving lady, taking her tea and enjoying the prospect.

It happened that at that moment the lady of the caravan had her cup (which, that everything about her might be of a stout and comfortable kind, was a breakfast cup) to her lips, and that having her eyes lifted to the sky in her enjoyment of the full flavour of the tea, not unmingled possibly with just the slightest dash or gleam of something out of the suspicious bottle—but this is mere speculation and not distinct matter of history—it happened that being thus agreeably engaged, she did not see the travellers when they first came up. It was not until she was in the act of setting down the cup, and drawing a long breath after the exertion of causing its contents to disappear, that the lady of the caravan beheld an old man and a young child walking slowly by, and glancing at her proceedings with eyes of modest but hungry admiration.

"Hey!" cried the lady of the caravan, scooping the crumbs out of her lap and swallowing the same before wiping her lips. "Yes, to be sure—Who won the Helter-Skelter Plate, child?"

"Won what, ma'am?" asked Nell.

"The Helter-Skelter Plate at the races, child—the plate that was run for on the second day."

"On the second day, ma'am?"

"Second day! Yes, second day," repeated the lady with an air of impatience. "Can't you say who won the Helter-Skelter Plate when you're asked the question civilly?"

"I don't know, ma'am."

"Don't know!" repeated the lady of the caravan; "why, you were there. I saw you with my own eyes."

Nell was not a little alarmed to hear this, supposing that the lady might be intimately acquainted with the firm of Short and Codlin; but what followed tended to reassure her.

"And very sorry I was," said the lady of the caravan, "to see you in company with a Punch; a low, practical, wulgar wretch, that people should scorn to look at."

"I was not there by choice," returned the child; "we didn't know our way, and the two men were very kind to us, and let us travel with them. Do you—do you know them, ma'am?"

"Know 'em, child!" cried the lady of the caravan in a sort of shriek. "Know *them!* But you're young and inexperienced, and that's your excuse for asking sich a question. Do I look as if I know'd 'em, does the caravan look as if *it* know'd 'em?"

"No, ma'am, no," said the child, fearing she had committed some grievous fault. "I beg your pardon."

It was granted immediately, though the lady still appeared much ruffled and discomposed by the degrading supposition. The child then explained that they had left the races on the first day, and were travelling to the next town on that road, where they purposed to spend the night. As the countenance of the stout lady began to clear up, she ventured to inquire how far it was. The reply—which the stout lady did not come to, until she had thoroughly explained that she went to the races on the first day in a gig, and as an expedition of pleasure, and that her presence there had no connexion with any matters of business or profit—was, that the town was eight miles off.

This discouraging information a little dashed the child, who could scarcely repress a tear as she glanced along the darkening road. Her grandfather made no complaint, but he sighed heavily as he leaned upon his staff, and vainly tried to pierce the dusty distance.

The lady of the caravan was in the act of gathering her tea equipage together preparatory to clearing the table, but noting the child's anxious manner she hesitated and stopped. The child curtseyed, thanked her for her information, and giving her hand to the old man had already got some fifty yards or so away, when the lady of the caravan called to her to return.

"Come nearer, nearer still"—said she, beckoning to her to ascend the steps. "Are you hungry, child?"

"Not very, but we are tired, and it's—it *is* a long way——"

"Well, hungry or not, you had better have some tea," rejoined her new acquaintance. "I suppose you are agreeable to that, old gentleman?"

The grandfather humbly pulled off his hat and thanked her. The lady of the caravan then bade him come up the steps likewise, but the drum proving an inconvenient table for two, they descended again, and sat upon the grass, where she handed down to them the tea-tray, the bread and butter, the knuckle of ham, and in short everything of which she had partaken herself, except the bottle which she had already embraced an opportunity of slipping into her pocket.

"Set 'em out near the hind wheels, child, that's the best place"—

said their friend, superintending the arrangements from above. "Now hand up the teapot for a little more hot water, and a pinch of fresh tea, and then both of you eat and drink as much as you can, and don't spare anything; that's all I ask of you."

They might perhaps have carried out the lady's wish, if it had been less freely expressed, or even if it had not been expressed at all. But as this direction relieved them from any shadow of delicacy or uneasiness, they made a hearty meal and enjoyed it to the utmost.

While they were thus engaged, the lady of the caravan alighted on the earth, and with her hands clasped behind her, and her large bonnet trembling excessively, walked up and down in a measured tread and very stately manner, surveying the caravan from time to time with an air of calm delight, and deriving particular gratification from the red panels and the brass knocker. When she had taken this gentle exercise for some time, she sat down upon the steps and called "George;" whereupon a man in a carter's frock, who had been so shrouded in a hedge up to this time as to see everything that passed without being seen himself, parted the twigs that concealed him, and appeared in a sitting attitude, supporting on his legs a baking-dish and a half-gallon stone bottle, and bearing in his right hand a knife, and in his left a fork.

"Yes, missus"—said George.

"How did you find the cold pie, George?"

"It warn't amiss, mum."

"And the beer," said the lady of the caravan, with an appearance of being more interested in this question than the last; "is it passable, George?"

"It's more flatterer than it might be," George returned, "but it an't so bad for all that."

To set the mind of his mistress at rest, he took a sip (amounting in quantity to a pint or thereabouts) from the stone bottle, and then smacked his lips, winked his eye, and nodded his head. No doubt with the same amiable desire, he immediately resumed his knife and fork, as a practical assurance that the beer had wrought no bad effect upon his appetite.

The lady of the caravan looked on approvingly for some time, and then said.

"Have you nearly finished?"

"Wery nigh, mum." And indeed, after scraping the dish all round with his knife and carrying the choice brown morsels to his mouth, and after taking such a scientific pull at the stone bottle that, by degrees almost imperceptible to the sight, his head went further and further back until he lay nearly at his full length upon the ground, this gentleman declared himself quite disengaged, and came forth from his retreat.

"I hope I haven't hurried you, George," said his mistress, who appeared to have a great sympathy with his late pursuit.

"If you have," returned the follower, wisely reserving himself for any favourable contingency that might occur, "we must make up for it next time, that's all."

"We are not a heavy load, George?"

"That's always what the ladies say," replied the man, looking a long way round, as if he were appealing to Nature in general against such monstrous propositions. "If you see a woman a driving, you'll always perceive that she never will keep her whip still; the horse can't go fast enough for her. If cattle have got their proper load, you never can persuade a woman that they'll not bear something more. What is the cause of this here?"

"Would these two travellers make much difference to the horses, if we took them with us?" asked his mistress, offering no reply to the philosophical inquiry, and pointing to Nell and the old man, who were painfully preparing to resume their journey on foot.

"They'd make a difference in course," said George doggedly.

"Would they make much difference?" repeated his mistress. "They can't be very heavy."

"The weight o' the pair, mum," said George, eyeing them with the look of a man who was calculating within half an ounce or so, "would be a trifle under that of Oliver Cromwell."

Nell was very much surprised that the man should be so accurately acquainted with the weight of one whom she had read of in books as having lived considerably before their time, but speedily forgot the subject in the joy of hearing that they were to go forward in the caravan, for which she thanked its lady with unaffected earnestness. She helped with great readiness and alacrity to put away the tea-things and other matters that were lying about, and, the horses being by that time harnessed, mounted into the vehicle, followed by her delighted grandfather. Their patroness then shut the door and sat herself down by her drum at an open window; and, the steps being struck by George and stowed under the carriage, away they went, with a great noise of flapping and creaking and straining, and the bright brass knocker, which nobody ever knocked at, knocking one perpetual double knock of its own accord as they jolted heavily along.

CHAPTER XXVII

WHEN they had travelled slowly forward for some short distance, Nell ventured to steal a look round the caravan and observe it more closely. One half of it—that moiety in which the comfortable proprietress was then seated—was carpeted, and so partitioned off at the further end as to accommodate a sleeping place, constructed after the fashion of a berth on board ship, which was shaded, like the little windows, with fair white curtains, and looked comfortable enough, though by what kind of gymnastic exercise the lady of the caravan ever contrived to get into it, was an unfathomable mystery. The other half served for a kitchen, and was fitted up with a stove whose small chimney passed through the roof. It held also a closet or larder, several chests, a great pitcher of water, and a few cooking-utensils and articles of crockery. These latter necessaries hung upon the walls, which, in that portion of the establishment devoted to the lady of the caravan, were ornamented with such gayer and lighter decorations as a triangle and a couple of well-thumbed tambourines.

The lady of the caravan sat at one window in all the pride and poetry of the musical instruments, and little Nell and her grandfather sat at the other in all the humility of the kettle and saucepans, while the machine jogged on and shifted the darkening prospect very slowly. At first the two travellers spoke little, and only in whispers, but as they grew more familiar with the place they ventured to converse with greater freedom, and talked about the country through which they were passing, and the different objects that presented themselves, until the old man fell asleep; when the lady of the caravan observing, invited Nell to come and sit beside her.

"Well, child," she said, "how do you like this way of travelling?"

Nell replied that she thought it was very pleasant indeed, to which the lady assented in the case of people who had their spirits. For herself, she said, she was troubled with a lowness in that respect which required a constant stimulant; though whether the aforesaid stimulant was derived from the suspicious bottle of which mention has been already made, or from other sources, she did not say.

"That's the happiness of you young people," she continued. "You don't know what it is to be low in your feelings. You always have your appetites too, and what a comfort that is."

Nell thought that she could sometimes dispense with her own appetite very conveniently; and thought, moreover, that there was nothing either in the lady's personal appearance or in her manner of taking tea, to lead to the conclusion that her natural relish for meat and drink had at all failed her. She silently assented, however, as in duty bound, to what the lady had said, and waited until she should speak again.

Instead of speaking, however, she sat looking at the child for a long time in silence, and then getting up, brought out from a corner a large roll of canvas about a yard in width, which she laid upon the floor and spread open with her foot until it nearly reached from one end of the caravan to the other.

"There, child," she said, "read that."

Nell walked down it, and read aloud, in enormous black letters, the inscription, "JARLEY's WAX-WORK."

"Read it again," said the lady, complacently.

"Jarley's Wax-Work," repeated Nell.

"That's me," said the lady. "I am Mrs. Jarley."

Giving the child an encouraging look, intended to reassure her and let her know, that, although she stood in the presence of the original Jarley, she must not allow herself to be utterly overwhelmed and borne down, the lady of the caravan unfolded another scroll, whereon was the inscription, "One hundred figures the full size of life," and then another scroll, on which was written, "The only stupendous collection of real wax-work in the world," and then several smaller scrolls with such inscriptions as "Now exhibiting within"—"The genuine and only Jarley"—"Jarley's unrivalled collection"—"Jarley is the delight of the Nobility and Gentry"—"The Royal Family are the Patrons of Jarley." When she had exhibited these leviathans of public announcement to the astonished child, she brought forth specimens of the lesser fry in the shape of hand-bills, some of which were couched in the form of parodies on popular melodies, as "Believe me if all Jarley's wax-work so rare"—"I saw thy show in youthful prime"—"Over the water to Jarley;" while, to consult all tastes, others were composed with a view to the lighter and more facetious spirits, as a parody on the favourite air of "If I had a donkey," beginning

> If I know'd a donkey wot wouldn't go
> To see Mrs. JARLEY'S wax-work show,
> Do you think I'd acknowledge him?
> Oh no no!
> > Then run to Jarley's—

—besides several compositions in prose, purporting to be dialogues between the Emperor of China and an oyster, or the Archbishop of Canterbury and a Dissenter on the subject of church-rates, but all having the same moral, namely, that the reader must make haste to Jarley's, and that children and servants were admitted at half-price. When she had brought all these testimonials of her important position in society to bear upon her young companion, Mrs. Jarley rolled them up, and having put them carefully away, sat down again, and looked at the child in triumph.

"Never go into the company of a filthy Punch any more," said Mrs. Jarley, "after this."

"I never saw any wax-work, ma'am," said Nell. "Is it funnier than Punch?"

"Funnier!" said Mrs. Jarley in a shrill voice. "It is not funny at all."

"Oh!" said Nell, with all possible humility.

"It isn't funny at all," repeated Mrs. Jarley. "It's calm and—what's that word again—critical?—no—classical, that's it—it's calm and classical. No low beatings and knockings about, no jokings and squeakings like your precious Punches, but always the same, with a constantly unchanging air of coldness and gentility; and so like life, that if wax-work only spoke and walked about, you'd hardly know the difference. I won't go so far as to say, that, as it is, I've seen wax-work quite like life, but I've certainly seen some life that was exactly like wax-work."

"Is it here, ma'am?" asked Nell, whose curiosity was awakened by this description.

"Is what here, child?"

"The wax-work, ma'am?"

"Why, bless you, child, what are you thinking of? How could such a collection be here, where you see everything except the inside of one little cupboard and a few boxes? It's gone on in the other wans to the assembly-rooms, and there it'll be exhibited the day after to-morrow. You are going to the same town, and you'll see it I dare say. It's natural to expect that you'll see it, and I've no doubt you will. I suppose you couldn't stop away if you was to try ever so much."

"I shall not be in the town, I think, ma'am," said the child.

"Not there!" cried Mrs. Jarley. "Then where will you be?"

"I—I—don't quite know. I am not certain."

"You don't mean to say that you're travelling about the country without knowing where you're going to?" said the lady of the caravan. "What curious people you are! What line are you in? You looked to me at the races, child, as if you were quite out of your element, and got there by accident."

"We were there quite by accident," returned Nell, confused by this abrupt questioning. "We are poor people, ma'am, and are only wandering about. We have nothing to do;—I wish we had."

"You amaze me more and more," said Mrs. Jarley, after remaining for some time as mute as one of her own figures. "Why, what do you call yourselves? Not beggars?"

"Indeed, ma'am, I don't know what else we are," returned the child.

"Lord bless me," said the lady of the caravan. "I never heard of such a thing. Who'd have thought it!"

She remained so long silent after this exclamation, that Nell feared she felt her having been induced to bestow her protection and conversation upon one so poor, to be an outrage upon her dignity that nothing could repair. This persuasion was rather confirmed than otherwise by the tone in which she at length broke silence and said,

"And yet you can read. And write too, I shouldn't wonder?"

"Yes, ma'am," said the child, fearful of giving new offence by the confession.

"Well, and what a thing that is," returned Mrs. Jarley. "*I* can't!"

Nell said "indeed " in a tone which might imply, either that she was reasonably surprised to find the genuine and only Jarley, who was the delight of the Nobility and Gentry and the peculiar pet of the Royal Family, destitute of these familiar arts; or that she presumed so great a lady could scarcely stand in need of such ordinary accomplishments. In whatever way Mrs. Jarley received the response, it did not provoke her to further questioning, or tempt her into any more remarks at the time, for she relapsed into a thoughtful silence, and remained in that state so long that Nell withdrew to the other window and rejoined her grandfather, who was now awake.

At length the lady of the caravan shook off her fit of meditation, and, summoning the driver to come under the window at which she was seated, held a long conversation with him in a low tone of voice, as if she were asking his advice on an important point, and discussing the pros and cons of some very weighty matter. This conference at length concluded, she drew in her head again, and beckoned Nell to approach.

"And the old gentleman too," said Mrs. Jarley; "for I want to have a word with him. Do you want a good situation for your grand-daughter, master? If you do, I can put her in the way of getting one. What do you say?"

"I can't leave her," answered the old man. "We can't separate. What would become of me without her?"

"I should have thought you were old enough to take care of your-self, if you ever will be," retorted Mrs. Jarley sharply.

"But he never will be," said the child in an earnest whisper. "I fear he never will be again. Pray do not speak harshly to him. We are very thankful to you," she added aloud; "but neither of us could part from the other if all the wealth of the world were halved between us."

Mrs. Jarley was a little disconcerted by this reception of her pro-posal, and looked at the old man, who tenderly took Nell's hand and detained it in his own, as if he could have very well dispensed with his company or even his earthly existence. After an awkward pause, she thrust her head out of the window again, and had another con-ference with the driver upon a point on which they did not seem to agree quite so readily as on their former topic of discussion; but they concluded at last, and she addressed the grandfather again.

"If you're really disposed to employ yourself," said Mrs. Jarley, "there would be plenty for you to do in the way of helping to dust the figures, and take the checks, and so forth. What I want your grand-daughter for, is to point 'em out to the company; they would be soon learnt, and she has a way with her that people wouldn't think unpleasant, though she does come after me; for I've been always accustomed to go round with visitors myself, which I should keep on doing now, only that my spirits make a little ease absolutely neces-sary. It's not a common offer, bear in mind," said the lady, rising into the tone and manner in which she was accustomed to address her audiences; "it's Jarley's wax-work, remember. The duty's very light and genteel, the company particular select, the exhibition takes place in assembly rooms, town-halls, large rooms at inns, or auction galleries. There is none of your open-air wagrancy at Jarley's, recol-lect; there is no tarpaulin and sawdust at Jarley's, remember. Every expectation held out in the handbills is realised to the utmost, and the whole forms an effect of imposing brilliancy hitherto unrivalled in this kingdom. Remember that the price of admission is only six-pence, and that this is an opportunity which may never occur again!"

Descending from the sublime when she had reached this point, to the details of common life, Mrs. Jarley remarked that with reference to salary she could pledge herself to no specific sum until she had sufficiently tested Nell's abilities, and narrowly watched her in the performance of her duties. But board and lodging, both for her and her grandfather, she bound herself to provide, and she furthermore passed her word that the board should always be good in quality, and in quantity plentiful.

Nell and her grandfather consulted together, and while they were so engaged, Mrs. Jarley with her hands behind her walked up and down the caravan, as she had walked after tea on the dull earth, with uncommon dignity and self-esteem. Nor will this appear so slight a circumstance as to be unworthy of mention, when it is remembered that the caravan was in uneasy motion all the time, and that none but a person of great and natural stateliness and acquired grace could have forborne to stagger.

"Now, child?" cried Mrs. Jarley, coming to a halt as Nell turned towards her.

"We are very much obliged to you, ma'am," said Nell, "and thankfully accept your offer."

"And you'll never be sorry for it," returned Mrs. Jarley. "I'm pretty sure of that. So as that's all settled, let us have a bit of supper."

In the meanwhile, the caravan blundered on as if it too had been drinking strong beer and was drowsy, and came at last upon the paved streets of a town which were clear of passengers, and quiet, for it was by this time near midnight, and the townspeople were all abed. As it was too late an hour to repair to the exhibition room, they turned aside into a piece of waste ground that lay just within the old towngate, and drew up there for the night, near to another caravan, which, notwithstanding that it bore on the lawful panel the great name of Jarley, and was employed besides in conveying from place to place the wax-work which was its country's pride, was designated by a grovelling stamp-office as a " Common Stage Waggon," and numbered too—seven thousand odd hundred—as though its precious freight were mere flour or coals!

This ill-used machine being empty (for it had deposited its burden at the place of exhibition, and lingered here until its services were again required) was assigned to the old man as his sleeping-place for the night; and within its wooden walls, Nell made him up the best bed she could, from the materials at hand. For herself, she was to sleep in Mrs. Jarley's own travelling carriage, as a signal mark of that lady's favour and confidence.

She had taken leave of her grandfather and was returning to the other waggon, when she was tempted by the pleasant coolness of the night to linger for a little while in the air. The moon was shining down upon the old gateway of the town, leaving the low archway very black and dark; and with a mingled sensation of curiosity and fear, she slowly approached the gate, and stood still to look up at it, wondering to see how dark, and grim, and old, and cold, it looked.

There was an empty niche from which some old statue had fallen or been carried away hundreds of years ago, and she was thinking what strange people it must have looked down upon when it stood there, and how many hard struggles might have taken place, and how many murders might have been done, upon that silent spot, when there suddenly emerged from the black shade of the arch, a man,

The instant he appeared, she recognised him—Who could have failed to recognise, in that instant, the ugly mis-shapen Quilp!

The street beyond was so narrow, and the shadow of the houses on one side of the way so deep, that he seemed to have risen out of the earth. But there he was. The child withdrew into a dark corner, and saw him pass close to her. He had a stick in his hand, and, when he had got clear of the shadow of the gateway, he leant upon it, looked back—directly, as it seemed, towards where she stood—and beckoned.

To her? oh no, thank God, not to her; for as she stood, in an extremity of fear, hesitating whether to scream for help, or come from her hiding-place and fly, before he should draw nearer, there issued slowly forth from the arch another figure—that of a boy—who carried on his back a trunk.

"Faster, sirrah!" said Quilp, looking up at the old gateway, and showing in the moonlight like some monstrous image that had come down from its niche and was casting a backward glance at its old house, "faster!"

"It's a dreadful heavy load, sir," the boy pleaded. "I've come on very fast, considering."

"*You* have come fast, considering!" retorted Quilp; "you creep, you dog, you crawl, you measure distance like a worm. There are the chimes now, half-past twelve."

He stopped to listen, and then turning upon the boy with a suddenness and ferocity that made him start, asked at what hour that London coach passed the corner of the road. The boy replied, at one.

"Come on then," said Quilp, "or I shall be too late. Faster—do you hear me? Faster."

The boy made all the speed he could, and Quilp led onward, constantly turning back to threaten him, and urge him to greater haste. Nell did not dare to move until they were out of sight and hearing, and then hurried to where she had left her grandfather, feeling as if the very passing of the dwarf so near him must have filled him with alarm and terror. But he was sleeping soundly, and she softly withdrew.

As she was making her way to her own bed, she determined to say nothing of this adventure, as upon whatever errand the dwarf had come (and she feared it must have been in search of them) it was clear by his inquiry about the London coach that he was on his way homeward, and as he had passed through that place, it was but reasonable to suppose that they were safer from his inquiries there, than they could be elsewhere. These reflections did not remove her own alarm, for she had been too much terrified to be easily composed, and felt as if she were hemmed in by a legion of Quilps, and the very air itself were filled with them.

The delight of the Nobility and Gentry and the patronised of Royalty had, by some process of self-abridgment known only to herself, got into her travelling bed, where she was snoring peacefully, while the large bonnet, carefully disposed upon the drum, was revealing its glories by the light of a dim lamp that swung from the roof. The child's bed was already made upon the floor, and it was a great comfort to her to hear the steps removed as soon as she had entered, and to know that all easy communication between persons outside and the brass knocker was by this means effectually prevented. Certain guttural sounds, too, which from time to time ascended through the floor of the caravan, and a rustling of straw in the same direction, apprised her that the driver was couched upon the ground beneath, and gave her an additional feeling of security.

Notwithstanding these protections, she could get none but broken sleep by fits and starts all night, for fear of Quilp, who throughout her uneasy dreams was somehow connected with the wax-work, or was wax-work himself, or was Mrs. Jarley and wax-work too, or was himself, Mrs. Jarley, wax-work, and a barrel organ all in one, and yet not exactly any of them either. At length, towards break of day, that deep sleep came upon her which succeeds to weariness and over-watching, and which has no consciousness but one of overpowering and irresistible enjoyment.

CHAPTER XXVIII

SLEEP hung upon the eyelids of the child so long, that, when she awoke, Mrs. Jarley was already decorated with her large bonnet, and actively engaged in preparing breakfast. She received Nell's apology for being so late with perfect good humour, and said that she should not have roused her if she had slept on until noon.

"Because it does you good," said the lady of the caravan, "when you're tired, to sleep as long as ever you can, and get the fatigue quite off; and that's another blessing of your time of life—you can sleep so very sound."

"Have you had a bad night, ma'am?" asked Nell.

"I seldom have anything else, child," replied Mrs. Jarley, with the air of a martyr. "I sometimes wonder how I bear it."

Remembering the snores which had proceeded from that cleft in the caravan in which the proprietress of the wax-work passed the night, Nell rather thought she must have been dreaming of lying awake. However, she expressed herself very sorry to hear such a dismal account of her state of health, and shortly afterwards sat down with her grandfather and Mrs. Jarley to breakfast. The meal finished, Nell assisted to wash the cups and saucers, and put them in their proper places, and these household duties performed, Mrs. Jarley arrayed herself in an exceedingly bright shawl for the purpose of making a progress through the streets of the town.

"The wan will come on to bring the boxes," said Mrs. Jarley, "and you had better come in it, child. I am obliged to walk, very much against my will; but the people expect it of me, and public characters can't be their own masters and mistresses in such matters as these. How do I look, child?''

Nell returned a satisfactory reply, and Mrs. Jarley, after sticking a great many pins into various parts of her figure, and making several abortive attempts to obtain a full view of her own back, was at last satisfied with her appearance, and went forth majestically.

The caravan followed at no great distance. As it went jolting through the streets, Nell peeped from the window, curious to see in what kind of place they were, and yet fearful of encountering at every turn the dreaded face of Quilp. It was a pretty large town, with an open square which they were crawling slowly across, and in the middle of which was the Town-Hall, with a clock-tower and a weathercock. There were houses of stone, houses of red brick, houses of yellow brick, houses of lath and plaster; and houses of wood, many of them very old, with withered faces carved upon the beams, and staring down into the street. These had very little winking windows, and low-arched doors, and, in some of the narrower ways, quite overhung the pavement. The streets were very clean, very sunny, very empty, and very dull. A few idle men lounged about the two inns, and the empty market-place, and the tradesmen's doors, and some old people were dozing in chairs outside an almshouse wall; but scarcely any passengers who seemed bent on going anywhere, or to have any object in view, went by; and if perchance some straggler did, his footsteps echoed on the hot bright pavement for minutes afterwards. Nothing seemed to be going on but the clocks, and they had such drowsy faces, such heavy lazy hands, and such cracked voices, that they surely must have been too slow. The very dogs were all asleep, and the flies, drunk with moist sugar in the grocer's shop, forgot their wings and briskness, and baked to death in dusty corners of the window.

Rumbling along with most unwonted noise, the caravan stopped at last at the place of exhibition, where Nell dismounted amidst an admiring group of children, who evidently supposed her to be an important item of the curiosities, and were fully impressed with the belief that her grandfather was a cunning device in wax. The chests were taken out with all convenient despatch, and taken in to be unlocked by Mrs. Jarley, who, attended by George and another man in velveteen shorts and a drab hat ornamented with turnpike tickets, were waiting to dispose their contents (consisting of red festoons and other ornamental devices in upholstery work) to the best advantage in the decoration of the room.

They all got to work without loss of time, and very busy they were. As the stupendous collection were yet concealed by cloths, lest the envious dust should injure their complexions, Nell bestirred herself to assist in the embellishment of the room, in which her grandfather also was of great service. The two men being well used to it, did a great deal in a short time; and Mrs. Jarley served out the tin tacks from a linen pocket like a toll-collector's which she wore for the purpose, and encouraged her assistants to renewed exertion.

While they were thus employed, a tallish gentleman with a hook nose and black hair, dressed in a military surtout very short and tight in the sleeves, and which had once been frogged and braided all over, but was now sadly shorn of its garniture and quite threadbare—dressed too in ancient grey pantaloons fitting tight to the leg, and a pair of pumps in the winter of their existence—looked in at the door, and smiled affably. Mrs. Jarley's back being then towards him, the military gentleman shook his forefinger as a sign that her myrmidons were not to apprise her of his presence, and stealing up close behind her, tapped her on the neck, and cried playfully, " Boh!"

" What, Mr. Slum!" cried the lady of the wax-work. "Lor! who'd have thought of seeing you here!"

" 'Pon my soul and honour," said Mr. Slum, "that's a good remark. 'Pon my soul and honour, that's a wise remark. Who *would* have thought it! George, my faithful feller, how are you?"

George received this advance with a surly indifference, observing that he was well enough for the matter of that, and hammering lustily all the time.

"I came here," said the military gentleman turning to Mrs. Jarley, —"'pon my soul and honour, I hardly know what I came here for. It would puzzle me to tell you, it would by Gad. I wanted a little inspiration, a little freshening up, a little change of ideas, and—— 'Pon my soul and honour," said the military gentleman, checking himself and looking round the room, "what a devilish classical thing this is! By Gad, it's quite Minervian!"

"It'll look well enough when it comes to be finished," observed Mrs. Jarley.

"Well enough!" said Mr. Slum. "Will you believe me when I say it's the delight of my life to have dabbled in poetry, when I think I've exercised my pen upon this charming theme? By the way—any orders? Is there any little thing I can do for you?"

"It comes so very expensive, sir," replied Mrs. Jarley, "and I really don't think it does much good."

"Hush! No, no!" returned Mr. Slum, elevating his hand. "No fibs. I'll not hear it. Don't say it don't do good. Don't say it. I know better!"

"I don't think it does," said Mrs. Jarley.

"Ha, ha!" cried Mr. Slum, "you're giving way, you're coming down. Ask the perfumers, ask the blacking-makers, ask the hatters, ask the old lottery-office-keepers—ask any man among 'em what my poetry has done for him, and mark my words, he blesses the name of Slum. If he's an honest man, he raises his eyes to heaven, and blesses the name of Slum—mark that! You are acquainted with Westminster Abbey, Mrs. Jarley?"

"Yes, surely."

"Then upon my soul and honour, ma'am, you'll find in a certain angle of that dreary pile, called Poets' Corner, a few smaller names than Slum," retorted that gentleman, tapping himself expressively on the forehead to imply that there was some slight quantity of brains behind it. "I've got a little trifle here, now," said Mr. Slum, taking off his hat which was full of scraps of paper, "a little trifle here, thrown off in the heat of the moment, which I should say was exactly the thing you wanted to set this place on fire with. It's an acrostic—the name at this moment is Warren, but the idea's a convertible one, and a positive inspiration for Jarley. Have the acrostic."

"I suppose it's very dear," said Mrs. Jarley.

"Five shillings," returned Mr. Slum, using his pencil as a toothpick. "Cheaper than any prose."

"I couldn't give more than three," said Mrs. Jarley.

"—And six," retorted Slum. "Come. Three-and-six."

Mrs. Jarley was not proof against the poet's insinuating manner, and Mr. Slum entered the order in a small note-book as a three-and-sixpenny one. Mr. Slum then withdrew to alter the acrostic, after taking a most affectionate leave of his patroness, and promising to return, as soon as he possibly could, with a fair copy for the printer.

As his presence had not interfered with or interrupted the preparations, they were now far advanced, and were completed shortly after his departure. When the festoons were all put up as tastily as they might be, the stupendous collection was uncovered, and there were displayed, on a raised platform some two feet from the floor, running round the room and parted from the rude public by a crimson rope breast high, divers sprightly effigies of celebrated characters, singly and in groups, clad in glittering dresses of various climes and times, and standing more or less unsteadily upon their legs, with their eyes very wide open, and their nostrils very much inflated, and the muscles of their legs and arms very strongly developed, and all their countenances expressing great surprise. All the gentlemen were very pigeon-breasted and very blue about the beards; and all the ladies were miraculous figures; and all the ladies and all the gentlemen were looking intensely nowhere, and staring with extraordinary earnestness at nothing.

When Nell had exhausted her first raptures at this glorious sight, Mrs. Jarley ordered the room to be cleared of all but herself and the child, and, sitting herself down in an arm-chair in the centre, formally invested her with a willow wand, long used by herself for pointing out the characters, and was at great pains to instruct her in her duty.

"That," said Mrs. Jarley in her exhibition tone, as Nell touched a figure at the beginning of the platform, "is an unfortunate Maid of Honour in the Time of Queen Elizabeth, who died from pricking her finger in consequence of working upon a Sunday. Observe the blood which is trickling from her finger; also the gold-eyed needle of the period, with which she is at work."

All this Nell repeated twice or thrice, pointing to the finger and the needle at the right times, and then passed on to the next.

"That, ladies and gentlemen," said Mrs. Jarley, "is Jasper Packlemerton of atrocious memory, who courted and married fourteen wives, and destroyed them all by tickling the soles of their feet when they was sleeping in the consciousness of innocence and virtue. On being brought to the scaffold and asked if he was sorry for what he had done, he replied yes, he was sorry for having let 'em off so easy, and hoped all Christian husbands would pardon him the offence. Let this be a warning to all young ladies to be particular in the character of the gentlemen of their choice. Observe that his fingers is curled as if in the act of tickling, and that his face is represented with a wink, as he appeared when committing his barbarous murders."

When Nell knew all about Mr. Packlemerton, and could say it without faltering, Mrs. Jarley passed on to the fat man, and then to the thin man, the tall man, the short man, the old lady who died of dancing at a hundred and thirty-two, the wild boy of the woods, the woman who poisoned fourteen families with pickled walnuts, and other historical characters and interesting but misguided individuals. And so well did Nell profit by her instructions, and so apt was she to remember them, that by the time they had been shut up together for a couple of hours, she was in full possession of the history of the whole establishment, and perfectly competent to the enlightenment of visitors.

Mrs. Jarley was not slow to express her admiration at this happy result, and carried her young friend and pupil to inspect the remaining arrangements within doors, by virtue of which the passage had been already converted into a grove of green-baize hung with the inscriptions she had already seen (Mr. Slum's productions), and a highly ornamented table placed at the upper end for Mrs. Jarley herself, at which she was to preside and take the money, in company with his Majesty King George the Third, Mr. Grimaldi as clown, Mary Queen of Scots, an anonymous gentleman of the Quaker persuasion, and Mr. Pitt holding in his hand a correct model of the bill for the imposition of the window duty. The preparations without doors had not been neglected either; for a nun of great personal attractions was telling her beads on the little portico over the door; and a brigand with the blackest possible head of hair, and the clearest possible complexion, was at that moment going round the town in a cart, consulting the miniature of a lady.

It now only remained that Mr. Slum's compositions should be judiciously distributed; that the pathetic effusions should find their way to all private houses and tradespeople; and that the parody commencing "If I know'd a donkey," should be confined to the taverns, and circulated only among the lawyers' clerks and choice spirits of the place. When this had been done, and Mrs. Jarley had waited upon the boarding-schools in person, with a handbill composed expressly for them, in which it was distinctly proved that wax-work refined the mind, cultivated the taste, and enlarged the sphere of the human understanding, that indefatigable lady sat down to dinner, and drank out of the suspicious bottle to a flourishing campaign.

CHAPTER XXIX

UNQUESTIONABLY Mrs. Jarley had an inventive genius. In the midst of the various devices for attracting visitors to the exhibition, little Nell was not forgotten. The light cart in which the Brigand usually made his perambulations being gaily dressed with flags and streamers, and the Brigand placed therein, contemplating the miniature of his beloved as usual, Nell was accompanied with a seat beside him, decorated with artificial flowers, and in this state and ceremony rode slowly through the town every morning, dispersing hand-bills from a basket, to the sound of drum and trumpet. The beauty of the child, coupled with her gentle and timid bearing, produced quite a sensation in the little country place. The Brigand, heretofore a source of exclusive interest in the street, became a mere secondary consideration, and to be important only as a part of the show of which she was the chief attraction. Grown-up folks began to be interested in the bright-eyed girl, and some score of little boys fell desperately in love, and constantly left inclosures of nuts and apples, directed in small text, at the wax-work door.

This desirable impression was not lost upon Mrs. Jarley, who, lest Nell should become too cheap, soon sent the Brigand out alone again, and kept her in the exhibition room, where she described the figures every half-hour to the great satisfaction of admiring audiences. And these audiences were of a very superior description, including a great many young ladies' boarding-schools, whose favour Mrs. Jarley had been at great pains to conciliate, by altering the face and costume of Mr. Grimaldi as clown to represent Mr. Lindley Murray as he appeared when engaged in the composition of his English Grammar, and turning a murderess of great renown into Mrs. Hannah More— both of which likenesses were admitted by Miss Monflathers, who was at the head of the head Boarding and Day Establishment in the town, and who condescended to take a Private View with eight chosen young ladies, to be quite startling from their extreme correctness. Mr. Pitt in a night-cap and bedgown, and without his boots, represented the poet Cowper with perfect exactness; and Mary Queen of Scots in a dark wig, white shirt-collar, and male attire, was such a complete image of Lord Byron that the young ladies quite screamed when they saw it. Miss Monflathers, however, rebuked this enthusiasm, and took occasion to reprove Mrs. Jarley for not keeping her collection more select, observing that His Lordship had held certain free opinions quite incompatible with wax-work honours, and adding something about a Dean and Chapter, which Mrs. Jarley did not understand.

Although her duties were sufficiently laborious, Nell found in the lady of the caravan a very kind and considerate person, who had not only a peculiar relish for being comfortable herself, but for making everybody about her comfortable also; which latter taste, it may be remarked, is, even in persons who live in much finer places than caravans, a far more rare and uncommon one than the first, and is not by any means its necessary consequence. As her popularity procured her various little fees from the visitors on which her patroness never demanded any toll, and as her grandfather too was well-treated and useful, she had no cause of anxiety in connexion with the wax-work, beyond that which sprang from her recollection of Quilp, and her fears that he might return and one day suddenly encounter them.

Quilp indeed was a perpetual nightmare to the child, who was constantly haunted by a vision of his ugly face and stunted figure. She slept, for their better security, in the room where the wax-work figures were, and she never retired to this place at night but she tortured herself—she could not help it—with imagining a resemblance, in some one or other of their death-like faces, to the dwarf, and this fancy would sometimes so gain upon her that she would almost believe he had removed the figure and stood within the clothes. Then there were so many of them with their great glassy eyes—and, as they stood one behind the other all about her bed, they looked so like living creatures, and yet so unlike in their grim stillness and silence, that she had a kind of terror of them for their own sakes, and would often lie watching their dusky figures until she was obliged to rise and light a candle, or go and sit at the open window and feel a companionship in the bright stars. At these times, she would recall the old house and the window at which she used to sit alone; and then she would think of poor Kit and all his kindness, until the tears came into her eyes, and she would weep and smile together.

Often and anxiously at this silent hour, her thoughts reverted to her grandfather, and she would wonder how much he remembered of their former life, and whether he was ever really mindful of the change in their condition and of their late helplessness and destitution. When they were wandering about, she seldom thought of this, but now she could not help considering what would become of them if he fell sick, or her own strength were to fail her. He was very patient and willing, happy to execute any little task, and glad to be of use; but he was in the same listless state, with no prospect of improvement —a mere child—a poor, thoughtless, vacant creature—a harmless fond old man, susceptible of tender love and regard for her, and of pleasant and painful impressions, but alive to nothing more. It made her very sad to know that this was so—so sad to see it that sometimes when he sat idly by, smiling and nodding to her when she looked round, or when he caressed some little child and carried it to and fro, as he was fond of doing by the hour together, perplexed by its simple questions, yet patient under his own infirmity, and seeming almost conscious of it too, and humbled even before the mind of an infant— so sad it made her to see him thus, that she would burst into tears, and, withdrawing into some secret place, fall down upon her knees and pray that he might be restored.

But the bitterness of her grief was not in beholding him in this condition, when he was at least content and tranquil, nor in her solitary meditations on his altered state, though these were trials for a young heart. Cause for deeper and heavier sorrow was yet to come.

One evening, a holiday night with them, Nell and her grandfather went out to walk. They had been rather closely confined for some days, and the weather being warm, they strolled a long distance. Clear of the town, they took a footpath which struck through some pleasant fields, judging that it would terminate in the road they quitted and enable them to return that way. It made, however, a much wider circuit than they had supposed, and thus they were tempted onward until sunset, when they reached the track of which they were in search, and stopped to rest.

It had been gradually getting overcast, and now the sky was dark and lowering, save where the glory of the departing sun piled up masses of gold and burning fire, decaying embers of which gleamed here and there through the black veil, and shone redly down upon the earth. The wind began to moan in hollow murmurs, as the sun went down carrying glad day elsewhere; and a train of dull clouds coming up against it, menaced thunder and lightning. Large drops of rain soon began to fall, and, as the storm clouds came sailing onward, others supplied the void they left behind and spread over all the sky. Then was heard the low rumbling of distant thunder, then the lightning quivered, and then the darkness of an hour seemed to have gathered in an instant.

Fearful of taking shelter beneath a tree or hedge, the old man and the child hurried along the high road, hoping to find some house in which they could seek a refuge from the storm, which had now burst forth in earnest, and every moment increased in violence. Drenched with the pelting rain, confused by the deafening thunder, and bewildered by the glare of the forked lightning, they would have passed a solitary house without being aware of its vicinity, had not a man, who was standing at the door, called lustily to them to enter.

"Your ears ought to be better than other folks' at any rate, if you make so little of the chance of being struck blind," he said, retreating from the door and shading his eyes with his hands as the jagged lightning came again. "What were you going past for, eh?" he added, as he closed the door and led the way along a passage to a room behind.

"We didn't see the house, sir, till we heard you calling," Nell replied.

"No wonder," said the man, "with this lightning in one's eyes, by the bye. You had better stand by the fire here, and dry yourselves a bit. You can call for what you like if you want anything. If you don't want anything, you are not obliged to give an order, don't be afraid of that. This is a public-house, that's all. The Valiant Soldier is pretty well known hereabouts."

"Is this house called the Valiant Soldier, sir?" asked Nell.

"I thought everybody knew that," replied the landlord. "Where have you come from, if you don't know the Valiant Soldier as well as the Church catechism? This is the Valiant Soldier, by James Groves,—Jem Groves—honest Jem Groves, as is a man of unblemished moral character, and has a good dry skittle-ground. If any man has got anything to say again Jem Groves, let him say it *to* Jem Groves, and Jem Groves can accommodate him with a customer on any terms from four pound a side to forty."

With these words, the speaker tapped himself on the waistcoat to intimate that he was the Jem Groves so highly eulogised; sparred scientifically at a counterfeit Jem Groves, who was sparring at society in general from a black frame over the chimney-piece; and, applying a half-emptied glass of spirits and water to his lips, drank Jem Groves's health.

The night being warm, there was a large screen drawn across the room, for a barrier against the heat of the fire. It seemed as if somebody on the other side of this screen had been insinuating doubts of Mr. Groves's prowess, and had thereby given rise to these egotistical expressions, for Mr. Groves wound up his defiance by giving a loud knock upon it with his knuckles and pausing for a reply from the other side.

"There an't many men," said Mr. Groves, no answer being returned, "who would ventur' to cross Jem Groves under his own roof. There's only one man, I know, that has nerve enough for that, and that man's not a hundred mile from here neither. But he's worth a dozen men, and I let him say of me whatever he likes in consequence,—he knows that."

In return for this complimentary address, a very gruff hoarse voice bade Mr. Groves "hold his noise and light a candle." And the same voice remarked that the same gentleman "needn't waste his breath in brag, for most people knew pretty well what sort of stuff he was made of."

"Nell, they're—they're playing cards," whispered the old man, suddenly interested. "Don't you hear them?"

"Look sharp with that candle," said the voice; "it's as much as I can do to see the pips on the cards as it is; and get this shutter closed as quick as you can, will you? Your beer will be the worse for to-night's thunder I expect.—Game! Seven-and-sixpence to me, old Isaac. Hand over."

"Do you hear, Nell, do you hear them?" whispered the old man again, with increased earnestness, as the money chinked upon the table.

"I haven't seen such a storm as this," said a sharp cracked voice of most disagreeable quality, when a tremendous peal of thunder had died away, "since the night when old Luke Withers won thirteen times running, upon the red. We all said he had the Devil's luck and his own, and as it was the kind of night for the Devil to be out and busy, I suppose he *was* looking over his shoulder, if anybody could have seen him."

"Ah!" returned the gruff voice; "for all old Luke's winning through thick and thin of late years, I remember the time when he was the unluckiest and unfortunatest of men. He never took a dice-box in his hand, or held a card, but he was plucked, pigeoned, and cleaned out completely."

"Do you hear what he says?" whispered the old man. "Do you hear that, Nell?"

The child saw with astonishment and alarm that his whole appearance had undergone a complete change. His face was flushed and eager, his eyes were strained, his teeth set, his breath came short and thick, and the hand he laid upon her arm trembled so violently that she shook beneath its grasp.

"Bear witness," he muttered, looking upward, "that I always said it; that I knew it, dreamed of it, felt it was the truth, and that it must be so! What money have we, Nell? Come! I saw you with money yesterday. What money have we? Give it to me."

"No, no, let me keep it, grandfather," said the frightened child. "Let us go away from here. Do not mind the rain. Pray let us go."

"Give it to me, I say," returned the old man fiercely. "Hush, hush, don't cry, Nell. If I spoke sharply, dear, I didn't mean it. It's for thy good. I have wronged thee, Nell, but I will right thee yet, I will indeed. Where is the money?"

"Do not take it," said the child. "Pray do not take it, dear. For both our sakes let me keep it, or let me throw it away—better let me throw it away, than you take it now. Let us go; do let us go."

"Give me the money," returned the old man, "I must have it. There—there—that's my dear Nell. I'll right thee one day, child, I'll right thee, never fear!"

She took from her pocket a little purse. He seized it with the same rapid impatience which had characterised his speech, and hastily made his way to the other side of the screen. It was impossible to restrain him, and the trembling child followed close behind.

The landlord had placed a light upon the table, and was engaged in drawing the curtain of the window. The speakers whom they had heard were two men, who had a pack of cards and some silver money between them, while upon the screen itself the games they had played were scored in chalk. The man with the rough voice was a burly fellow of middle age, with large black whiskers, broad cheeks, a coarse wide mouth, and bull neck, which was pretty freely displayed as his shirt-collar was only confined by a loose red neckerchief. He wore his hat, which was of a brownish-white, and had beside him a thick knotted stick. The other man, whom his companion had called Isaac, was of a more slender figure—stooping, and high in the shoulders—with a very ill-favoured face, and a most sinister and villainous squint.

"Now, old gentleman," said Isaac, looking round. "Do you know either of us? This side of the screen is private, sir."

"No offence, I hope," returned the old man.

"But by G——, sir, there is offence," said the other, interrupting him, "when you intrude yourself upon a couple of gentlemen who are particularly engaged."

"I had no intention to offend," said the old man, looking anxiously at the cards, "I thought that——"

"But you had no right to think, sir," retorted the other. "What the devil has a man at your time of life to do with thinking?"

"Now, bully boy," said the stout man, raising his eyes from his cards for the first time, "can't you let him speak?"

The landlord, who had apparently resolved to remain neutral until he knew which side of the question the stout man would espouse, chimed in at this place with "Ah, to be sure, can't you let him speak, Isaac List?"

"Can't I let him speak," sneered Isaac in reply, mimicking as nearly as he could, in his shrill voice, the tones of the landlord. "Yes, I can let him speak, Jemmy Groves."

"Well then, do it, will you?" said the landlord.

Mr. List's squint assumed a portentous character, which seemed to threaten a prolongation of this controversy, when his companion, who had been looking sharply at the old man, put a timely stop to it.

"Who knows," said he, with a cunning look, "but the gentleman may have civilly meant to ask if he might have the honour to take a hand with us!"

"I did mean it," cried the old man. "That is what I mean. That is what I want now!"

"I thought so," returned the same man. "Then who knows but the gentleman, anticipating our objection to play for love, civilly desired to play for money?"

The old man replied by shaking the little purse in his eager hand, and then throwing it down upon the table, and gathering up the cards as a miser would clutch at gold.

"Oh! That indeed—" said Isaac; "if that's what the gentleman meant, I beg the gentleman's pardon. Is this the gentleman's little purse? A very pretty little purse. Rather a light purse," added Isaac, throwing it into the air and catching it dexterously, "but enough to amuse a gentleman for half an hour or so."

"We'll make a four-handed game of it, and take in Groves," said the stout man. "Come, Jemmy."

The landlord, who conducted himself like one who was well used to such little parties, approached the table and took his seat. The child, in a perfect agony, drew her grandfather aside, and implored him, even then, to come away.

"Come; and we may be so happy," said the child.

"We *will* be happy," replied the old man hastily. "Let me go, Nell. The means of happiness are on the cards and in the dice. We must rise from little winnings to great. There's little to be won here; but great will come in time. I shall but win back my own, and it's all for thee, my darling.

"God help us!" cried the child. "Oh! what hard fortune brought us here?"

"Hush!" rejoined the old man, laying his hand upon her mouth, "Fortune will not bear chiding. We must not reproach her, or she shuns us; I have found that out."

"Now, mister," said the stout man. "If you're not coming yourself, give us the cards, will you?"

"I am coming," cried the old man. "Sit thee down, Nell, sit thee down and look on. Be of good heart, it's all for thee—all—every penny. I don't tell them, no, no, or else they wouldn't play, dreading the chance that such a cause must give me. Look at them. See what they are and what thou art. Who doubts that we must win!"

"The gentleman has thought better of it, and isn't coming," said Isaac, making as though he would rise from the table. "I'm sorry the gentleman's daunted—nothing venture, nothing have—but the gentleman knows best."

"Why, I am ready. You have all been slow but me," said the old man. "I wonder who's more anxious to begin than I."

As he spoke he drew a chair to the table; and the other three closing round it at the same time, the game commenced.

The child sat by, and watched its progress with a troubled mind. Regardless of the run of luck, and mindful only of the desperate passion which had its hold upon her grandfather, losses and gain were to her alike. Exulting in some brief triumph, or cast down by a defeat, there he sat so wild and restless, so feverishly and intensely anxious, so terribly eager, so ravenous for the paltry stakes, that she could have almost better borne to see him dead. And yet she was the innocent cause of all this torture, and he, gambling with such a savage thirst for gain as the most insatiable gambler never felt, had not one selfish thought!

On the contrary, the other three—knaves and gamesters by their trade—while intent upon their game, were yet as cool and quiet as if every virtue had been centred in their breast. Sometimes one would look up to smile to another, or to snuff the feeble candle, or to glance at the lightning as it shot through the open window and fluttering curtain, or to listen to some louder peal of thunder than the rest, with a kind of momentary impatience, as if it put him out; but there they sat, with a calm indifference to everything but their cards, perfect philosophers in appearance, and with no greater show of passion or excitement than if they had been made of stone.

The storm had raged for full three hours; the lightning had grown fainter and less frequent; the thunder, from seeming to roll and break above their heads, had gradually died away into a deep hoarse distance; and still the game went on, and still the anxious child was quite forgotten.

CHAPTER XXX

AT length the play came to an end, and Mr. Isaac List rose the only winner. Mat and the landlord bore their losses with professional fortitude. Isaac pocketed his gains with the air of a man who had quite made up his mind to win, all along, and was neither surprised nor pleased.

Nell's little purse was exhausted; but, although it lay empty by his side, and the other players had now risen from the table, the old man sat poring over the cards, dealing them as they had been dealt before, and turning up the different hands to see what each man would have held if they had still been playing. He was quite absorbed in this occupation, when the child drew near and laid her hand upon his shoulder, telling him it was near midnight.

"See the curse of poverty, Nell," he said, pointing to the packs he had spread out upon the table. "If I could have gone on a little longer, only a little longer, the luck would have turned on my side. Yes, it's as plain as the marks upon the cards. See here—and there—and here again."

"Put them away," urged the child. "Try to forget them."

"Try to forget them!" he rejoined, raising his haggard face to hers, and regarding her with an incredulous stare. "To forget them! How are we ever to grow rich if I forget them?"

The child could only shake her head.

"No, no, Nell," said the old man, patting her cheek; "they must not be forgotten. We must make amends for this as soon as we can. Patience—patience, and we'll right thee yet, I promise thee. Lose to-day, win to-morrow. And nothing can be won without anxiety and care—nothing.   Come, I am ready."

"Do you know what the time is?" said Mr. Groves, who was smoking with his friends. "Past twelve o'clock——"

—"And a rainy night," added the stout man.

" The Valiant Soldier, by James Groves. Good beds. Cheap entertainment for man and beast," said Mr. Groves, quoting his signboard. "Half-past twelve o'clock."

"It's very late," said the uneasy child. "I wish we had gone before. What will they think of us! It will be two o'clock by the time we get back. What would it cost, sir, if we stopped here?"

"Two good beds, one-and-sixpence; supper and beer, one shilling; total, two shillings and sixpence," replied the Valiant Soldier.

Now, Nell had still the piece of gold sewn in her dress; and when she came to consider the lateness of the hour, and the somnolent habits of Mrs. Jarley, and to imagine the state of consternation in which they would certainly throw that good lady by knocking her up in the middle of the night—and when she reflected, on the other hand, that if they remained where they were, and rose early in the morning, they might get back before she awoke, and could plead the violence of the storm by which they had been overtaken, as a good apology for their absence—she decided, after a great deal of hesitation, to remain. She therefore took her grandfather aside, and telling him that she had still enough left to defray the cost of their lodging, proposed that they should stay there for the night.

"If I had had but that money before—if I had only known of it a few minutes ago!" muttered the old man.

"We will decide to stop here if you please," said Nell, turning hastily to the landlord.

"I think that's prudent," returned Mr. Groves. "You shall have your suppers directly."

Accordingly, when Mr. Groves had smoked his pipe out, knocked out the ashes, and placed it carefully in a corner of the fireplace, with the bowl downwards, he brought in the bread and cheese, and beer, with many high encomiums upon their excellence, and bade his guests to fall to and make themselves at home. Nell and her grandfather ate sparingly, for both were occupied with their own reflections; the other gentlemen, for whose constitutions beer was too weak and tame a liquid, consoled themselves with spirits and tobacco.

As they would leave the house very early in the morning, the child was anxious to pay for their entertainment before they retired to bed. But as she felt the necessity of concealing her little hoard from her grandfather, and had to change the piece of gold, she took it secretly from its place of concealment, and embraced an opportunity of following the landlord when he went out of the room, and tendered it to him in the little bar.

"Will you give me the change here, if you please?" said the child.

Mr. James Groves was evidently surprised, and looked at the money, and rang it, and looked at the child, and at the money again, as though he had a mind to inquire how she came by it. The coin being genuine, however, and changed at his house, he probably felt, like a wise landlord, that it was no business of his. At any rate, he counted out the change, and gave it to her. The child was returning to the room where they had passed the evening, when she fancied she saw a figure just gliding in at the door. There was nothing but a long dark passage between this door and the place where she had changed the money, and, being very certain that no person had passed in or out while she stood there, the thought struck her that she had been watched.

But by whom? When she re-entered the room, she found its inmates exactly as she had left them. The stout fellow lay upon two chairs, resting his head on his hand, and the squinting man reposed in a similar attitude on the opposite side of the table. Between them sat her grandfather, looking intently at the winner with a kind of hungry admiration, and hanging upon his words as if he were some superior being. She was puzzled for a moment, and looked round to see if any one else were there. No. Then she asked her grandfather in a whisper whether anybody had left the room while she was absent. "No," he said, "nobody."

It must have been her fancy then; and yet it was strange, that, without anything in her previous thoughts to lead to it, she should have imagined this figure so very distinctly. She was still wondering and thinking of it, when a girl came to light her to bed.

The old man took leave of the company at the same time, and they went up stairs together. It was a great, rambling house, with dull corridors and wide staircases which the flaring candles seemed to make more gloomy. She left her grandfather in his chamber, and followed her guide to another, which was at the end of a passage, and approached by some half-dozen crazy steps. This was prepared for her. The girl lingered a little while to talk, and tell her grievances. She had not a good place, she said; the wages were low, and the work was hard. She was going to leave it in a fortnight; the child couldn't recommend her to another, she supposed? Indeed she was afraid another would be difficult to get after living there, for the house had a very indifferent character; there was far too much card-playing, and such like. She was very much mistaken if some of the people who came there oftenest were quite as honest as they might be, but she wouldn't have it known that she had said so, for the world. Then there were some rambling allusions to a rejected sweetheart, who had threatened to go a soldiering—a final promise of knocking at the door early in the morning—and "Good night."

The child did not feel comfortable when she was left alone. She could not help thinking of the figure stealing through the passage down stairs; and what the girl had said did not tend to reassure her. The men were very ill-looking. They might get their living by robbing and murdering travellers. Who could tell?

Reasoning herself out of these fears, or losing sight of them for a little while, there came the anxiety to which the adventures of the night gave rise. Here was the old passion awakened again in her grandfather's breast, and to what further distraction it might tempt him Heaven only knew. What fears their absence might have occasioned already! Persons might be seeking for them even then. Would they be forgiven in the morning, or turned adrift again? Oh! why had they stopped in that strange place? It would have been better, under any circumstances, to have gone on!

At last, sleep gradually stole upon her—a broken, fitful sleep, troubled by dreams of falling from high towers, and waking with a start and in great terror. A deeper slumber followed this—and then ——What! That figure in the room.

A figure was there. Yes, she had drawn up the blind to admit the light when it should dawn, and there, between the foot of the bed and the dark casement, it crouched and slunk along, groping its way with noiseless hands, and stealing round the bed. She had no voice to cry for help, no power to move, but lay still watching it.

On it came—on, silently and stealthily, to the bed's head. The breath so near her pillow, that she shrank back into it, lest those wandering hands should light upon her face. Back again it stole to the window—then turned its head towards her.

The dark form was a mere blot upon the lighter darkness of the room, but she saw the turning of the head, and felt and knew how the eyes looked and the ears listened. There it remained, motionless as she. At length, still keeping the face towards her, it busied its hands in something, and she heard the chink of money.

Then, on it came again, silent and stealthy as before, and, replacing the garments it had taken from the bedside, dropped upon its hands and knees, and crawled away. How slowly it seemed to move, now that she could hear but not see it, creeping along the floor! It reached the door at last, and stood upon its feet. The steps creaked beneath its noiseless tread, and it was gone.

The first impulse of the child was to fly from the terror of being by herself in that room—to have somebody by—not to be alone—and then her power of speech would be restored. With no consciousness of having moved, she gained the door.

There was the dreadful shadow, pausing at the bottom of the steps.

She could not pass it; she might have done so, perhaps, in the darkness, without being seized, but her blood curdled at the thought. The figure stood quite still, and so did she; not boldly, but of necessity; for going back into the room was hardly less terrible than going on.

The rain beat fast and furiously without, and ran down in plashing streams from the thatched roof. Some summer insect, with no escape into the air, flew blindly to and fro, beating its body against the walls and ceiling, and filling the silent place with his murmurs. The figure moved again. The child involuntarily did the same. Once in her grandfather's room, she would be safe.

It crept along the passage until it came to the very door she longed so ardently to reach. The child, in the agony of being so near, had almost darted forward with the design of bursting into the room and closing it behind her, when the figure stopped again.

The idea flashed suddenly upon her—what if it entered there, and had a design upon the old man's life! She turned faint and sick. It did. It went in. There was a light inside. The figure was now within the chamber, and she, still dumb—quite dumb, and almost senseless—stood looking on.

The door was partly open. Not knowing what she meant to do, but meaning to preserve him or be killed herself, she staggered forward and looked in. What sight was that which met her view!

The bed had not been lain on, but was smooth and empty. And at a table sat the old man himself, the only living creature there, his white face pinched and sharpened by the greediness which made his eyes unnaturally bright, counting the money of which his hands had robbed her.

CHAPTER XXXI

WITH steps more faltering and unsteady than those with which she had approached the room, the child withdrew from the door, and groped her way back to her own chamber. The terror she had lately felt was nothing compared with that which now oppressed her. No strange robber, no treacherous host conniving at the plunder of his guests, or stealing to their beds to kill them in their sleep, no nightly prowler, however terrible and cruel, could have awakened in her bosom half the dread which the recognition of her silent visitor inspired. The grey-headed old man gliding like a ghost into her room and acting the thief while he supposed her fast asleep, then bearing off his prize and hanging over it with the ghastly exultation she had witnessed, was worse—immeasurably worse, and far more dreadful, for the moment, to reflect upon—than anything her wildest fancy could have suggested. If he should return—there was no lock or bolt upon the door, and if, distrustful of having left some money yet behind, he should come back to seek for more—a vague awe and horror surrounded the idea of his slinking in again with stealthy tread, and turning his face toward the empty bed, while she shrank down close at his feet to avoid his touch, which was almost insupportable. She sat and listened. Hark! A footstep on the stairs, and now the door was slowly opening. It was but imagination, yet imagination had all the terrors of reality; nay, it was worse, for the reality would have come and gone, and there an end, but in imagination it was always coming, and never went away.

The feeling which beset the child was one of dim uncertain horror. She had no fear of the dear old grandfather, in whose love for her this disease of the brain had been engendered; but the man she had seen that night, wrapt in the game of chance, lurking in her room, and counting the money by the glimmering light, seemed like another creature in his shape, a monstrous distortion of his image, a something to recoil from, and be the more afraid of, because it bore a likeness to him, and kept close about her, as he did. She could scarcely connect her own affectionate companion, save by his loss, with this old man, so like yet so unlike him. She had wept to see him dull and quiet. How much greater cause she had for weeping now!

The child sat watching and thinking of these things, until the phantom in her mind so increased in gloom and terror, that she felt it would be a relief to hear the old man's voice, or, if he were asleep, even to see him, and banish some of the fears that clustered round his image. She stole down the stairs and passage again. The door was still ajar as she had left it, and the candle burning as before.

She had her own candle in her hand, prepared to say, if he were waking, that she was uneasy and could not rest, and had come to see if his were still alight. Looking into the room, she saw him lying calmly on his bed, and so took courage to enter.

Fast asleep—no passion in the face, no avarice, no anxiety, no wild desire; all gentle, tranquil, and at peace. This was not the gambler, or the shadow in her room; this was not even the worn and jaded man whose face had so often met her own in the grey morning light; this was her dear old friend, her harmless fellow-traveller, her good, kind grandfather.

She had no fear as she looked upon his slumbering features, but she had a deep and weighty sorrow, and it found its relief in tears.

"God bless him!" said the child, stooping softly to kiss his placid cheek. "I see too well now, that they would indeed part us if they found us out, and shut him up from the light of the sun and sky. He has only me to help him. God bless us both!"

Lighting her candle, she retreated as silently as she had come, and, gaining her own room once more, sat up during the remainder of that long, long, miserable night.

At last the day turned her waning candle pale, and she fell asleep. She was quickly roused by the girl who had shown her up to bed; and, as soon as she was dressed, prepared to go down to her grandfather. But first she searched her pocket and found that her money was all gone—not a sixpence remained.

The old man was ready, and in a few seconds they were on their road. The child thought he rather avoided her eye, and appeared to expect that she would tell him of her loss. She felt she must do that, or he might suspect the truth.

"Grandfather," she said in a tremulous voice, after they had walked about a mile in silence, "do you think they are honest people at the house yonder?"

"Why?" returned the old man trembling. "Do I think them honest—yes, they played honestly."

"I'll tell you why I ask," rejoined Nell. "I lost some money last night—out of my bedroom I am sure. Unless it was taken by somebody in jest—only in jest, dear grandfather, which would make me laugh heartily if I could but know it—"

"Who would take money in jest?" returned the old man in a hurried manner. "Those who take money, take it to keep. Don't talk of jest."

"Then it was stolen out of my room, dear," said the child, whose last hope was destroyed by the manner of this reply.

"But is there no more, Nell?" said the old man; "no more anywhere? Was it all taken—every farthing of it—was there nothing left?"

"Nothing," replied the child.

"We must get more," said the old man, "we must earn it, Nell, hoard it up, scrape it together, come by it somehow. Never mind this loss. Tell nobody of it and perhaps we may regain it. Don't ask how;—we may regain it, and a great deal more;—but tell nobody, or trouble may come of it. And so they took it out of thy room, when thou wert asleep!" he added in a compassionate tone, very different from the secret, cunning way in which he had spoken until now.

"Poor Nell, poor little Nell!"

The child hung down her head and wept. The sympathising tone in which he spoke, was quite sincere; she was sure of that. It was not the lightest part of her sorrow to know that this was done for her.

"Not a word about it to any one but me," said the old man, "no, not even to me," he added hastily, "for it can do no good. All the losses that ever were, are not worth tears from thy eyes, darling. Why should they be, when we will win them back?"

"Let them go," said the child looking up. "Let them go, once and for ever, and I would never shed another tear if every penny had been a thousand pounds."

"Well, well," returned the old man, checking himself as some impetuous answer rose to his lips, "she knows no better. I ought to be thankful for it."

"But listen to me," said the child earnestly, "will you listen to me?"

"Ay, ay, I'll listen," returned the old man, still without looking at her; "a pretty voice. It has always a sweet sound to me. It always had when it was her mother's, poor child."

"Let me persuade you, then—oh, do let me persuade you," said the child, "to think no more of gains or losses, and to try no fortune but the fortune we pursue together."

"We pursue this aim together," retorted her grandfather, still looking away and seeming to confer with himself. "Whose image sanctifies the game?"

"Have we been worse off," resumed the child, "since you forgot these cares, and we have been travelling on together? Have we not been much better and happier without a home to shelter us, than ever we were in that unhappy house, when they were on your mind?"

"She speaks the truth," murmured the old man in the same tone as before. "It must not turn me, but it is the truth—no doubt it is."

"Only remember what we have been since that bright morning when we turned our backs upon it for the last time," said Nell, "only remember what we have been since we have been free of all those miseries—what peaceful days and quiet nights we have had—what pleasant times we have known—what happiness we have enjoyed. If we have been tired or hungry, we have been soon refreshed, and slept the sounder for it. Think what beautiful things we have seen, and how contented we have felt. And why was this blessed change?"

He stopped her with a motion of his hand, and bade her talk to him no more just then, for he was busy. After a time he kissed her cheek, still motioning her to silence, and walked on, looking far before him, and sometimes stopping and gazing with a puckered brow upon the ground, as if he were painfully trying to collect his disordered thoughts. Once she saw tears in his eyes. When he had gone on thus for some time, he took her hand in his as he was accustomed to do, with nothing of the violence or animation of his late manner; and so, by degrees so fine that the child could not trace them, settled down into his usual quiet way, and suffered her to lead him where she would.

When they presented themselves in the midst of the stupendous collection, they found, as Nell had anticipated, that Mrs. Jarley was not yet out of bed, and that, although she had suffered some uneasiness on their account overnight, and had indeed sat up for them until past eleven o'clock, she had retired in the persuasion, that, being overtaken by storm at some distance from home, they had sought the nearest shelter, and would not return before morning. Nell immediately applied herself with great assiduity to the decoration and preparation of the room, and had the satisfaction of completing her task, and dressing herself neatly, before the beloved of the Royal Family came down to breakfast.

"We haven't had," said Mrs. Jarley when the meal was over, "more than eight of Miss Monflathers's young ladies all the time we've been here, and there's twenty-six of 'em, as I was told by the cook when I asked her a question or two and put her on the free-list. We must try 'em with a parcel of new bills, and you shall take it, my dear, and see what effect that has upon 'em."

The proposed expedition being one of paramount importance, Mrs. Jarley adjusted Nell's bonnet with her own hands, and declaring that she certainly did look very pretty, and reflected credit on the establishment, dismissed her with many commendations, and certain needful directions as to the turnings on the right which she was to take, and the turnings on the left which she was to avoid. Thus instructed, Nell had no difficulty in finding out Miss Monflathers's Boarding and Day Establishment, which was a large house, with a high wall, and a large garden-gate with a large brass plate, and a small grating through which Miss Monflathers's parlour-maid inspected all visitors before admitting them; for nothing in the shape of a man—no, not even a milkman—was suffered, without special licence, to pass that gate. Even the tax-gatherer, who was stout, and wore spectacles and a broad-brimmed hat, had the taxes handed through the grating. More obdurate than gate of adamant or brass, this gate of Miss Monflathers's frowned on all mankind. The very butcher respected it as a gate of mystery, and left off whistling when he rang the bell.

As Nell approached the awful door, it turned slowly upon its hinges with a creaking noise, and, forth from the solemn grove beyond, came a long file of young ladies, two and two, all with open books in their hands, and some with parasols likewise. And last of the goodly procession came Miss Monflathers, bearing herself a parasol of lilac silk, and supported by two smiling teachers, each mortally envious of the other, and devoted unto Miss Monflathers.

Confused by the looks and whispers of the girls, Nell stood with downcast eyes and suffered the procession to pass on, until Miss Monflathers, bringing up the rear, approached her, when she curtseyed and presented her little packet; on receipt whereof Miss Monflathers commanded that the line should halt.

"You're the wax-work child, are you not?" said Miss Monflathers.

"Yes, ma'am," replied Nell, colouring deeply, for the young ladies had collected about her, and she was the centre on which all eyes were fixed.

"And don't you think you must be a very wicked little child," said Miss Monflathers, who was of rather uncertain temper, and lost no opportunity of impressing moral truths upon the tender minds of the young ladies, "to be a wax-work child at all?"

Poor Nell had never viewed her position in this light, and not knowing what to say, remained silent, blushing more deeply than before.

"Don't you know," said Miss Monflathers, "that it's very naughty and unfeminine, and a perversion of the properties wisely and benignantly transmitted to us, with expansive powers to be roused from their dormant state through the medium of cultivation?"

The two teachers murmured their respectful approval of this home-thrust, and looked at Nell as though they would have said that there indeed Miss Monflathers had hit her very hard. Then they smiled and glanced at Miss Monflathers, and then, their eyes meeting, they exchanged looks which plainly said that each considered herself smiler in ordinary to Miss Monflathers, and regarded the other as having no right to smile, and that her so doing was an act of presumption and impertinence.

"Don't you feel how naughty it is of you," resumed Miss Monflathers, "to be a wax-work child, when you might have the proud consciousness of assisting, to the extent of your infant powers, the manufactures of your country; of improving your mind by the constant contemplation of the steam-engine; and of earning a comfortable and independent subsistence of from two-and-ninepence to three shillings per week? Don't you know that the harder you are at work, the happier you are?"

"'How doth the little—'" murmured one of the teachers, in quotation from Doctor Watts.

"Eh?" said Miss Monflathers, turning smartly round. "Who said that?"

Of course the teacher who had not said it, indicated the rival who had, whom Miss Monflathers frowningly requested to hold her peace; by that means throwing the informing teacher into raptures of joy.

"The little busy bee," said Miss Monflathers, drawing herself up, "is applicable only to genteel children.

> 'In books, or work, or healthful play'

is quite right as far as they are concerned; and the work means painting on velvet, fancy needle-work, or embroidery. In such cases as these," pointing to Nell, with her parasol, "and in the case of all poor people's children, we should read it thus:

> 'In work, work, work. In work alway
> Let my first years be past,
> That I may give for ev'ry day
> Some good account at last.' "

A deep hum of applause rose not only from the two teachers, but from all the pupils, who were equally astonished to hear Miss Monflathers improvising after this brilliant style; for although she had been long known as a politician, she had never appeared before as an original poet. Just then somebody happened to discover that Nell was crying, and all eyes were again turned towards her.

There were indeed tears in her eyes, and drawing out her handkerchief to brush them away, she happened to let it fall. Before she could stoop to pick it up, one young lady of about fifteen or sixteen, who had been standing a little apart from the others, as though she had no recognised place among them, sprang forward and put it in her hand. She was gliding timidly away again, when she was arrested by the governess.

"It was Miss Edwards who did that, I *know*," said Miss Monflathers predictively. "Now I am sure that was Miss Edwards."

It was Miss Edwards, and everybody said it was Miss Edwards, and Miss Edwards herself admitted that it was.

"Is it not," said Miss Monflathers, putting down her parasol to take a severer view of the offender, "a most remarkable thing, Miss Edwards, that you have an attachment to the lower classes which always draws you to their sides; or, rather, is it not a most extraordinary thing that all I say and do will not wean you from propensities which your original station in life have unhappily rendered habitual to you, you extremely vulgar-minded girl?"

"I really intended no harm, ma'am," said a sweet voice. "It was a momentary impulse, indeed."

"An impulse!" repeated Miss Monflathers scornfully. "I wonder that you presume to speak of impulses to me"—both the teachers assented—"I am astonished"—both the teachers were astonished—"I suppose it is an impulse which induces you to take the part of every grovelling and debased person that comes in your way"—both the teachers supposed so too.

"But I would have you know, Miss Edwards," resumed the governess in a tone of increased severity, "that you cannot be permitted—if it be only for the sake of preserving a proper example and decorum in this establishment—that you cannot be permitted, and that you shall not be permitted, to fly in the face of your superiors in this exceedingly gross manner. If *you* have no reason to feel a becoming pride before wax-work children, there are young ladies here who have, and you must either defer to those young ladies or leave the establishment, Miss Edwards."

This young lady, being motherless and poor, was apprenticed at the school—taught for nothing—teaching others what she learnt, for nothing—boarded for nothing—lodged for nothing—and set down and rated as something immeasurably less than nothing, by all the dwellers in the house. The servant-maids felt her inferiority, for they were better treated; free to come and go, and regarded in their stations with much more respect. The teachers were infinitely superior, for they had paid to go to school in their time, and were paid now. The pupils cared little for a companion who had no grand stories to tell about home; no friends to come with post-horses, and be received in all humility, with cake and wine, by the governess; no deferential servant to attend and bear her home for the holidays; nothing genteel to talk about, and nothing to display. But why was Miss Monflathers always vexed and irritated with the poor apprentice —how did that come to pass?

Why, the gayest feather in Miss Monflathers's cap, and the brightest glory of Miss Monflathers's school, was a baronet's daughter —the real live daughter of a real live baronet—who, by some extraordinary reversal of the Laws of Nature, was not only plain in features but dull in intellect, while the poor apprentice had both a ready wit, and a handsome face and figure. It seems incredible. Here was Miss Edwards, who only paid a small premium which had been spent long ago, every day outshining and excelling the baronet's daughter, who learned all the extras (or was taught them all) and whose half-yearly bill came to double that of any other young lady's in the school, making no account of the honour and reputation of her pupilage. Therefore, and because she was a dependant, Miss Monflathers had a great dislike to Miss Edwards, and was spiteful to her, and aggravated by her, and when she had compassion on little Nell, verbally fell upon and maltreated her as we have already seen.

"You will not take the air to-day, Miss Edwards," said Miss Monflathers. "Have the goodness to retire to your own room, and not to leave it without permission."

The poor girl was moving hastily away, when she was suddenly, in nautical phrase, "brought to" by a subdued shriek from Miss Monflathers.

"She has passed me without any salute!" cried the governess, raising her eyes to the sky. "She has actually passed me without the slightest acknowledgment of my presence!"

The young lady turned and curtsied. Nell could see that she raised her dark eyes to the face of her superior, and that their expression, and that of her whole attitude for the instant, was one of mute but most touching appeal against this ungenerous usage. Miss Monflathers only tossed her head in reply, and the great gate closed upon a bursting heart.

"As for you, you wicked child," said Miss Monflathers, turning to Nell, "tell your mistress that if she presumes to take the liberty of sending to me any more, I will write to the legislative authorities and have her put in the stocks, or compelled to do penance in a white sheet; and you may depend upon it that you shall certainly experience the treadmill if you dare to come here again. Now ladies, on."

The procession filed off, two and two, with the books and parasols, and Miss Monflathers, calling the Baronet's daughter to walk with her and smooth her ruffled feelings, discarded the two teachers— who by this time had exchanged their smiles for looks of sympathy— and left them to bring up the rear, and hate each other a little more for being obliged to walk together.

CHAPTER XXXII

MRS. JARLEY'S wrath on first learning that she had been threatened with the indignity of Stocks and Penance, passed all description. The genuine and only Jarley exposed to public scorn, jeered by children, and flouted by beadles! The delight of the Nobility and Gentry shorn of a bonnet which a Lady Mayoress might have sighed to wear, and arrayed in a white sheet as a spectacle of mortification and humility! And Miss Monflathers, the audacious creature who presumed, even in the dimmest and remotest distance of her imagination, to conjure up the degrading picture, "I am a'most inclined," said Mrs. Jarley, bursting with the fulness of her anger and the weakness of her means of revenge, "to turn atheist when I think of it!"

But instead of adopting this course of retaliation, Mrs. Jarley, on second thoughts, brought out the suspicious bottle, and ordering glasses to be set forth upon her favourite drum, and sinking into a chair behind it, called her satellites about her, and to them several times recounted, word for word, the affronts she had received. This done, she begged them in a kind of deep despair to drink; then laughed, then cried, then took a little sip herself, then laughed and cried again, and took a little more; and so by degrees the worthy lady went on, increasing in smiles and decreasing in tears, until at last she could not laugh enough at Miss Monflathers, who, from being an object of dire vexation, became one of sheer ridicule and absurdity.

"For which of us is best off, I wonder," quoth Mrs. Jarley, "she or me! It's only talking, when all is said and done, and if she talks of me in the stocks, why I can talk of her in the stocks, which is a good deal funnier if we come to that. Lord, what *does* it matter, after all!"

Having arrived at this comfortable frame of mind (to which she had been greatly assisted by certain short interjectional remarks of the philosophic George), Mrs. Jarley consoled Nell with many kind words, and requested as a personal favour that whenever she thought of Miss Monflathers she would do nothing else but laugh at her, all the days of her life.

So ended Mrs. Jarley's wrath, which subsided long before the going down of the sun. Nell's anxieties, however, were of a deeper kind, and the checks they imposed upon her cheerfulness were not so easily removed.

That evening, as she had dreaded, her grandfather stole away, and did not come back until the night was far spent. Worn out as she was, and fatigued in mind and body, she sat up alone, counting the minutes, until he returned—penniless, broken-spirited, and wretched, but still hotly bent upon his infatuation.

"Get me money," he said wildly, as they parted for the night. "I must have money, Nell. It shall be paid thee back with gallant interest one day, but all the money that comes unto thy hands, must be mine—not for myself, but to use for thee. Remember, Nell, to use for thee!''

What could the child do, with the knowledge she had, but give him every penny that came into her hands, lest he should be tempted on to rob their benefactress? If she told the truth (so thought the child) he would be treated as a madman; if she did not supply him with money, he would supply himself; supplying him, she fed the fire that burnt him up, and put him perhaps beyond recovery. Distracted by these thoughts, borne down by the weight of the sorrow which she dared not tell, tortured by a crowd of apprehensions whenever the old man was absent, and dreading alike his stay and his return, the colour forsook her cheek, her eye grew dim, and her heart was oppressed and heavy. All her old sorrows had come back upon her, augmented by new fears and doubts; by day they were ever present to her mind; by night they hovered round her pillow, and haunted her in dreams.

It was natural that, in the midst of her affliction, she should often revert to that sweet young lady of whom she had only caught a hasty glance, but whose sympathy, expressed in one slight brief action, dwelt in her memory like the kindnesses of years. She would often think, if she had such a friend as that to whom to tell her griefs, how much lighter her heart would be—that if she were but free to hear that voice, she would be happier. Then she would wish that she were something better, that she were not quite so poor and humble, that she dared address her without fearing a repulse; and then feel that there was an immeasurable distance between them, and have no hope that the young lady thought of her any more.

It was now holiday-time at the schools, and the young ladies had gone home, and Miss Monflathers was reported to be flourishing in London and damaging the hearts of middle-aged gentlemen, but nobody said anything about Miss Edwards, whether she had gone home, or whether she had any home to go to, whether she was still at the school, or anything about her. But one evening, as Nell was returning from a lonely walk, she happened to pass the inn where the stage-coaches stopped, just as one drove up, and there was the beautiful girl she so well remembered, pressing forward to embrace a young child whom they were helping down from the roof.

Well, this was her sister, her little sister, much younger than Nell, whom she had not seen (so the story went afterwards) for five years, and to bring home to that place on a short visit, she had been saving her poor means all that time. Nell felt as if her heart would break when she saw them meet. They went a little apart from the knot of people who had congregated about the coach, and fell upon each other's neck, and sobbed, and wept with joy. Their plain and simple dress, the distance which the child had come alone, their agitation and delight, and the tears they shed, would have told their history by themselves.

They became a little more composed in a short time, and went away, not so much hand in hand as clinging to each other. "Are you sure you're happy, sister?" said the child as they passed where Nell was standing. "Quite happy now," she answered. "But always?" said the child. "Ah, sister, why do you turn away your face?"

Nell could not help following at a little distance. They went to the house of an old nurse, where the elder sister had engaged a bedroom for the child. "I shall come to you early every morning," she said, "and we can be together all the day."—"Why not at night-time too? Dear sister, would they be angry with you for *that?*"

Why were the eyes of little Nell wet, that night, with tears like those of the two sisters? Why did she bear a grateful heart because they had met, and feel it pain to think that they would shortly part? Let us not believe that any selfish reference—unconscious though it might have been—to her own trials awoke this sympathy, but thank God that the innocent joys of others can strongly move us, and that we, even in our fallen nature, have one source of pure emotion which must be prized in Heaven!

By morning's cheerful glow, but oftener still by evening's gentle light, the child, with a respect for the short and happy intercourse of these two sisters which forbade her to approach and say a thankful word, although she yearned to do so, followed them at a distance in their walks and rambles, stopping when they stopped, sitting on the grass when they sat down, rising when they went on, and feeling it a companionship and delight to be so near them. Their evening walk was by the river's side. Here, every night, the child was too, unseen by them, unthought of, unregarded; but feeling as if they were her friends, as if they had confidences and trusts together, as if her load were lightened and less hard to bear; as if they mingled their sorrows, and found mutual consolation. It was a weak fancy, perhaps, the childish fancy of a young and lonely creature; but night after night, and still the sisters loitered in the same place, and still the child followed with a mild and softened heart.

She was much startled, on returning home one night, to find that Mrs. Jarley had commanded an announcement to be prepared, to the effect that the stupendous collection would only remain in its present quarters one day longer; in fulfilment of which threat (for all announcements connected with public amusements are well known to be irrevocable and most exact), the stupendous collection shut up next day.

"Are we going from this place directly, ma'am?" said Nell.

"Look here, child," returned Mrs. Jarley. "That'll inform you." And so saying, Mrs. Jarley produced another announcement, wherein it was stated, that, in consequence of numerous inquiries at the wax-work door, and in consequence of crowds having been disappointed in obtaining admission, the Exhibition would be continued for one week longer, and would re-open next day.

"For now that the schools are gone, and the regular sightseers exhausted," said Mrs. Jarley, "we come to the General Public, and they want stimulating."

Upon the following day at noon, Mrs. Jarley established herself behind the highly-ornamented table, attended by the distinguished effigies before mentioned, and ordered the doors to be thrown open for the re-admission of a discerning and enlightened public. But the first day's operations were by no means of a successful character, inasmuch as the general public, though they manifested a lively interest in Mrs. Jarley personally, and such of her waxen satellites as were to be seen for nothing, were not affected by any impulses moving them to the payment of sixpence a head. Thus, notwithstanding that a great many people continued to stare at the entry and the figures therein displayed; and remained there with great perseverance, by the hour at a time, to hear the barrel organ played and to read the bills; and notwithstanding that they were kind enough to recommend their friends to patronise the exhibition in the like manner, until the doorway was regularly blockaded by half the population of the town, who, when they went off duty, were relieved by the other half; it was not found that the treasury was any the richer, or that the prospects of the establishment were at all encouraging.

In this depressed state of the classical market, Mrs. Jarley made extraordinary efforts to stimulate the popular taste, and whet the popular curiosity. Certain machinery in the body of the nun on the leads over the door was cleaned up and put in motion, so that the figure shook its head paralytically all day long, to the great admiration of a drunken, but very Protestant barber over the way, who looked upon the said paralytic motion as typical of the degrading effect wrought upon the human mind by the ceremonies of the Romish Church, and discoursed upon that theme with great eloquence and morality. The two carters constantly passed in and out of the exhibition-room, under various disguises, protesting aloud that the sight was better worth the money than anything they had beheld in all their lives, and urging the bystanders, with tears in their eyes, not to neglect such a brilliant gratification. Mrs. Jarley sat in the pay-place, chinking silver moneys from noon till night, and solemnly calling upon the crowd to take notice that the price of admission was only sixpence, and that the departure of the whole collection, on a short tour among the Crowned Heads of Europe, was positively fixed for that day week.

"So be in time, be in time, be in time," said Mrs. Jarley, at the close of every such address. "Remember that this is Jarley's stupendous collection of upwards of One Hundred Figures, and that it is the only collection in the world; all others being impostors and deceptions. Be in time, be in time, be in time!"

CHAPTER XXXIII

As the course of this tale requires that we should become acquainted, somewhere hereabouts, with a few particulars connected with the domestic economy of Mr. Sampson Brass, and as a more convenient place than the present is not likely to occur for that purpose, the historian takes the friendly reader by the hand, and springing with him into the air, and cleaving the same at a greater rate than ever Don Cleophas Leandro Perez Zambullo and his familiar travelled through that pleasant region in company, alights with him upon the pavement of Bevis Marks.

The intrepid aeronauts alight before a small dark house, once the residence of Mr. Sampson Brass.

In the parlour window of this little habitation, which is so close upon the footway that the passenger who takes the wall brushes the dim glass with his coat sleeve—much to its improvement, for it is very dirty—in this parlour window in the days of its occupation by Sampson Brass, there hung, all awry and slack, and discoloured by the sun, a curtain of faded green, so threadbare from long service as by no means to intercept the view of the little dark room, but rather to afford a favourable medium through which to observe it accurately. There was not much to look at. A rickety table, with spare bundles of papers, yellow and ragged from long carriage in the pocket, ostentatiously displayed upon its top; a couple of stools set face to face on opposite sides of this crazy piece of furniture; a treacherous old chair by the fireplace, whose withered arms had hugged full many a client and helped to squeeze him dry; a second-hand wig box, used as a depository for blank writs and declarations and other small forms of law, once the sole contents of the head which belonged to the wig which belonged to the box, as they were now of the box itself; two or three common books of practice; a jar of ink, a pounce box, a stunted hearth-broom, a carpet trodden to shreds but still clinging with the tightness of desperation to its tacks—these, with the yellow wainscot of the walls, the smoke-discoloured ceiling, the dust and cobwebs, were among the most prominent decorations of the office of Mr. Sampson Brass.

But this was mere still-life, of no greater importance than the plate, "Brass, Solicitor," upon the door, and the bill, "First floor to let to a single gentleman," which was tied to the knocker. The office commonly held two examples of animated nature, more to the purpose of this history, and in whom it has a stronger interest and more particular concern.

Of these, one was Mr. Brass himself, who has already appeared in these pages. The other was his clerk, assistant, housekeeper, secretary, confidential plotter, adviser, intriguer, and bill of cost increaser, Miss Brass—a kind of amazon at common law, of whom it may be desirable to offer a brief description.

Miss Sally Brass, then, was a lady of thirty-five or thereabouts, of a gaunt and bony figure, and a resolute bearing, which if it repressed the softer emotions of love, and kept admirers at a distance, certainly inspired a feeling akin to awe in the breasts of those male strangers who had the happiness to approach her. In face she bore a striking resemblance to her brother, Sampson—so exact, indeed, was the likeness between them, that had it consorted with Miss Brass's maiden modesty and gentle womanhood to have assumed her brother's clothes in a frolic and sat down beside him, it would have been difficult for the oldest friend of the family to determine which was Sampson and which Sally, especially as the lady carried upon her upper lip certain reddish demonstrations, which, if the imagination had been assisted by her attire, might have been mistaken for a beard. These were, however, in all probability, nothing more than eyelashes in a wrong place, as the eyes of Miss Brass were quite free from any such natural impertinences. In complexion Miss Brass was sallow—rather a dirty sallow, so to speak—but this hue was agreeably relieved by the healthy glow which mantled in the extreme tip of her laughing nose. Her voice was exceedingly impressive—deep and rich in quality, and, once heard, not easily forgotten. Her usual dress was a green gown, in colour not unlike the curtain of the office window, made tight to the figure, and terminating at the throat, where it was fastened behind by a peculiarly large and massive button. Feeling, no doubt, that simplicity and plainness are the soul of elegance, Miss Brass wore no collar or kerchief except upon her head, which was invariably ornamented with a brown gauze scarf, like the wing of the fabled vampire, and which, twisted into any form that happened to suggest itself, formed an easy and graceful head-dress.

Such was Miss Brass in person. In mind, she was of a strong and vigorous turn, having from her earliest youth devoted herself with uncommon ardour to the study of the law; not wasting her speculation upon its eagle flights, which are rare, but tracing it attentively through all the slippery and eel-like crawlings in which it commonly pursues its way. Nor had she, like many persons of great intellect, confined herself to theory, or stopped short where practical usefulness begins; inasmuch as she could ingross, fair-copy, fill up printed forms with perfect accuracy, and in short transact any ordinary duty of the office down to pouncing a skin of parchment or mending a pen. It is difficult to understand how, possessed of these combined attractions, she should remain Miss Brass; but whether she had steeled her heart against mankind, or whether those who might have wooed and won her, were deterred by fears that, being learned in the law, she might have too near her fingers' ends those particular statutes which regulate what are familiarly termed actions for breach, certain it is that she was still in a state of celibacy, and still in daily occupation of her old stool opposite to that of her brother Sampson. And equally certain it is, by the way, that between these two stools a great many people had come to the ground.

One morning Mr. Sampson Brass sat upon his stool copying some legal process, and viciously digging his pen deep into the paper, as if he were writing upon the very heart of the party against whom it was directed; and Miss Sally Brass sat upon her stool making a new pen preparatory to drawing out a little bill, which was her favourite occupation; and so they sat in silence for a long time, until Miss Brass broke silence.

"Have you nearly done, Sammy?" said Miss Brass; for in her mild and feminine lips, Sampson became Sammy, and all things were softened down.

"No," returned her brother. "It would have been all done though, if you had helped at the right time."

"Oh yes, indeed," cried Miss Sally; "you want my help, don't you —*you*, too, that are going to keep a clerk!"

"Am I going to keep a clerk for my own pleasure, or because of my own wish, you provoking rascal?" said Mr. Brass, putting his pen in his mouth, and grinning spitefully at his sister. "What do you taunt me about going to keep a clerk for?"

It may be observed in this place, lest the fact of Mr. Brass calling a lady a rascal, should occasion any wonderment or surprise, that he was so habituated to having her near him in a man's capacity, that he had gradually accustomed himself to talk to her as though she were really a man. And this feeling was so perfectly reciprocal, that not only did Mr. Brass often call Miss Brass a rascal, or even put an adjective before the rascal, but Miss Brass looked upon it as quite a matter of course, and was as little moved as any other lady would be by being called an angel.

"What do you taunt me, after three hours' talk last night, with going to keep a clerk for?" repeated Mr. Brass, grinning again with the pen in his mouth, like some nobleman's or gentleman's crest. "Is it my fault?"

"All I know is," said Miss Sally, smiling dryly, for she delighted in nothing so much as irritating her brother, "that if every one of your clients is to force us to keep a clerk, whether we want to or not, you had better leave off business, strike yourself off the roll, and get taken in execution as soon as you can."

"Have we got any other client like him?" said Brass. "Have we got another client like him, now—will you answer me that?"

"Do you mean in the face?" said his sister.

"Do I mean in the face!" sneered Sampson Brass, reaching over to take up the bill-book, and fluttering its leaves rapidly. "Look here— Daniel Quilp, Esquire—Daniel Quilp, Esquire—Daniel Quilp, Esquire —all through. Whether should I take a clerk that he recommends, and says 'this is the man for you,' or lose all this—eh?"

Miss Sally deigned to make no reply, but smiled again, and went on with her work.

"But I know what it is," resumed Brass after a short silence. "You're afraid you won't have as long a finger in the business as you've been used to have. Do you think I don't see through that?"

"The business wouldn't go on very long, I expect, without me,"
returned his sister composedly. "Don't you be a fool and provoke me,
Sammy, but mind what you're doing, and do it."

Sampson Brass, who was at heart in great fear of his sister, sulkily
bent over his writing again, and listened as she said:

"If I determined that the clerk ought not to come, of course he
wouldn't be allowed to come. You know that well enough; so don't
talk nonsense."

Mr. Brass received this observation with increased meekness,
merely remarking, under his breath, that he didn't like that kind of
joking, and that Miss Sally would be "a much better fellow" if she
forbore to aggravate him. To this compliment Miss Sally replied that
she had a relish for the amusement, and had no intention to forego
its gratification. Mr. Brass not caring, as it seemed, to pursue the
subject any further, they both plied their pens at a great pace, and
there the discussion ended.

While they were thus employed, the window was suddenly darkened, as by some person standing close against it. As Mr. Brass and
Miss Sally looked up to ascertain the cause, the top sash was nimbly
lowered from without, and Quilp thrust in his head.

"Hallo!" he said, standing on tiptoe on the window-sill, and looking
down into the room. "Is there anybody at home? Is there any of the
Devil's ware here? Is Brass at a premium, eh?"

"Ha, ha, ha!" laughed the lawyer in an affected ecstasy. "Oh, very
good, sir! Oh, very good indeed! Quite eccentric! Dear me, what
humour he has!"

"Is that my Sally?" croaked the dwarf, ogling the fair Miss Brass.
"Is it Justice with the bandage off her eyes, and without the sword
and scales? Is it the Strong Arm of the Law? Is it the Virgin of
Bevis?"

"What an amazing flow of spirits!" cried Brass. "Upon my word,
it's quite extraordinary!"

"Open the door," said Quilp, "I've got him here. Such a clerk for
you, Brass, such a prize, such an ace of trumps. Be quick and open
the door, or, if there's another lawyer near and he should happen
to look out of window, he'll snap him up before your eyes, he
will."

It is probable that the loss of the phœnix of clerks, even to a rival
practitioner, would not have broken Mr. Brass's heart; but, pretending great alacrity, he rose from his seat, and going to the door,
returned, introducing his client, who led by the hand no less a person
than Mr. Richard Swiveller.

"There she is," said Quilp, stopping short at the door, and wrinkling
up his eyebrows as he looked towards Miss Sally; "there is the woman
I ought to have married—there is the beautiful Sarah—there is the
female who has all the charms of her sex and none of their weaknesses.
Oh Sally, Sally!"

To this amorous address Miss Brass briefly responded "Bother!"

"Hard-hearted as the metal from which she takes her name," said

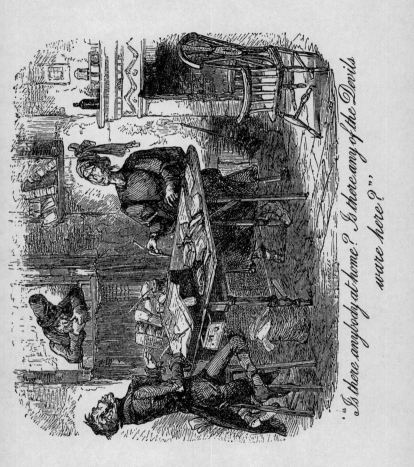

"Is there anybody at home? Is there any of the Devils were here?"

Quilp. "Why don't she change it—melt down the brass, and take another name?"

"Hold your nonsense, Mr. Quilp, do," returned Miss Sally, with a grim smile. "I wonder you're not ashamed of yourself before a strange young man."

"The strange young man," said Mr. Quilp, handing Dick Swiveller forward, "is too susceptible himself not to understand me well. This is Mr. Swiveller, my intimate friend—a gentleman of good family and great expectations, but who, having rather involved himself by youthful indiscretion, is content for a time to fill the humble station of a clerk—humble, but here most enviable. What a delicious atmosphere!"

If Mr. Quilp spoke figuratively, and meant to imply that the air breathed by Miss Sally Brass was sweetened and rarefied by that dainty creature, he had doubtless good reason for what he said. But if he spoke of the delights of the atmosphere of Mr. Brass's office in a literal sense, he had certainly a peculiar taste, as it was of a close and earthy kind, and, besides being frequently impregnated with strong whiffs of the second-hand wearing apparel exposed for sale in Duke's Place and Houndsditch, had a decided flavour of rats and mice, and a taint of mouldiness. Perhaps some doubts of its pure delight presented themselves to Mr. Swiveller, as he gave vent to one or two short abrupt sniffs, and looked incredulously at the grinning dwarf.

"Mr. Swiveller," said Quilp, "being pretty well accustomed to the agricultural pursuits of sowing wild oats, Miss Sally, prudently considers that half a loaf is better than no bread. To be out of harm's way he prudently thinks is something too, and therefore he accepts your brother's offer. Brass, Mr. Swiveller is yours."

"I am very glad, sir," said Mr. Brass, "very glad indeed. Mr. Swiveller, sir, is fortunate to have your friendship. You may be very proud, sir, to have the friendship of Mr. Quilp."

Dick murmured something about never wanting a friend or a bottle to give him, and also gasped forth his favourite allusion to the wing of friendship and its never moulting a feather; but his faculties appeared to be absorbed in the contemplation of Miss Sally Brass, at whom he stared with blank and rueful looks, which delighted the watchful dwarf beyond measure. As to the divine Miss Sally herself, she rubbed her hands as men of business do, and took a few turns up and down the office with her pen behind her ear.

"I suppose," said the dwarf, turning briskly to his legal friend, "that Mr. Swiveller enters upon his duties at once? It's Monday morning."

"At once, if you please, sir, by all means," returned Brass.

"Miss Sally will teach him law, the delightful study of the law," said Quilp; "she'll be his guide, his friend, his companion, his Blackstone, his Coke upon Littleton, his Young Lawyer's Best Companion."

"He is exceedingly eloquent," said Brass, like a man abstracted, and looking at the roofs of the opposite houses, with his hands in his pockets; "he has an extraordinary flow of language. Beautiful, really."

"With Miss Sally," Quilp went on, "and the beautiful fictions of the law, his days will pass like minutes. Those charming creations of the poet, John Doe and Richard Roe, when they first dawn upon him, will open a new world for the enlargement of his mind and the improvement of his heart."

"Oh, beautiful, beautiful! Beau-ti-ful indeed!" cried Brass. "It's a treat to hear him."

"Where will Mr. Swiveller sit?" said Quilp, looking round.

"Why, we'll buy another stool, sir," returned Brass. "We hadn't any thoughts of having a gentleman with us, sir, until you were kind enough to suggest it, and our accommodation's not extensive. We'll look about for a second-hand stool, sir. In the meantime, if Mr. Swiveller will take my seat, and try his hand at a fair copy of this ejectment, as I shall be out pretty well all the morning——"

"Walk with me," said Quilp. "I have a word or two to say to you on points of business. Can you spare the time?"

"Can I spare the time to walk with *you*, sir? You're joking, sir, you're joking with me," replied the lawyer, putting on his hat. "I'm ready, sir, quite ready. My time must be fully occupied indeed, sir, not to leave me time to walk with you. It's not everybody, sir, who has an opportunity of improving himself by the conversation of Mr. Quilp."

The dwarf glanced sarcastically at his brazen friend, and, with a short dry cough, turned upon his heel to bid adieu to Miss Sally. After a very gallant parting on his side, and a very cool and gentlemanly sort of one on hers, he nodded to Dick Swiveller, and withdrew with the attorney.

Dick stood at the desk in a state of utter stupefaction, staring with all his might at the beauteous Sally, as if she had been some curious animal whose like had never lived. When the dwarf got into the street, he mounted again upon the window-sill, and looked into the office for a moment with a grinning face, as a man might peep into a cage. Dick glanced upward at him, but without any token of recognition; and long after he had disappeared, still stood gazing upon Miss Sally Brass, seeing or thinking of nothing else, and rooted to the spot.

Miss Brass being by this time deep in the bill of costs, took no notice whatever of Dick, but went scratching on, with a noisy pen, scoring down the figures with evident delight, and working like a steam-engine. There stood Dick, gazing now at the green gown, now at the brown head-dress, now at the face, and now at the rapid pen, in a state of stupid perplexity, wondering how he got into the company of that strange monster, and whether it was a dream and he would ever wake. At last he heaved a deep sigh, and began slowly pulling off his coat.

Mr. Swiveller pulled off his coat and folded it up with great elaboration, staring at Miss Sally all the time; then put on a blue jacket with a double row of gilt buttons, which he had originally ordered for aquatic expeditions, but had brought with him that morning for office purposes; and, still keeping his eye upon her, suffered himself to drop down silently upon Mr. Brass's stool. Then he underwent a relapse, and becoming powerless again, rested his chin upon his hand, and opened his eyes so wide, that it appeared quite out of the question that he could ever close them any more.

When he had looked so long that he could see nothing, Dick took his eyes off the fair object of his amazement, turned over the leaves of the draft he was to copy, dipped his pen into the inkstand, and at last, and by slow approaches, began to write. But he had not written half a dozen words when, reaching over to the inkstand to take a fresh dip, he happened to raise his eyes, and there was the intolerable brown head-dress—there was the green gown—there, in short, was Miss Sally Brass, arrayed in all her charms, and more tremendous than ever.

This happened so often, that Mr. Swiveller by degrees began to feel strange influences creeping over him—horrible desires to annihilate this Sally Brass—mysterious promptings to knock her head-dress off and try how she looked without it. There was a very large ruler on the table—a large, black, shining ruler. Mr. Swiveller took it up and began to rub his nose with it.

From rubbing his nose with the ruler, to poising it in his hand and giving it an occasional flourish after the tomahawk manner, the transition was easy and natural. In some of these flourishes it went close to Miss Sally's head; the ragged edges of the head-dress fluttered with the wind it raised; advance it but an inch, and that great brown knot was on the ground: yet still the unconscious maiden worked away, and never raised her eyes.

Well, this was a great relief. It was a good thing to write doggedly and obstinately until he was desperate, and then snatch up the ruler and whirl it about the brown head-dress with the consciousness that he could have it off if he liked. It was a good thing to draw it back, and rub his nose very hard with it, if he thought Miss Sally was going to look up, and to recompense himself with more hardy flourishes when he found she was still absorbed. By these means Mr. Swiveller calmed the agitation of his feelings, until his applications to the ruler became less fierce and frequent, and he could even write as many as half a dozen consecutive lines without having recourse to it,—which was a great victory.

CHAPTER XXXIV

IN course of time, that is to say, after a couple of hours or so, of diligent application, Miss Brass arrived at the conclusion of her task, and recorded the fact by wiping her pen upon the green gown, and taking a pinch of snuff from a little round tin box which she carried in her pocket. Having disposed of this temperate refreshment, she arose from her stool, tied her papers into a formal packet with red tape, and taking them under her arm, marched out of the office.

Mr. Swiveller had scarcely sprung off his seat and commenced the performance of a maniac hornpipe, when he was interrupted, in the fulness of his joy at being again alone, by the opening of the door, and the reappearance of Miss Sally's head.

"I am going out," said Miss Brass.

"Very good, ma'am," returned Dick. "And don't hurry yourself on my account to come back, ma'am," he added inwardly.

"If anybody comes on office business, take their messages, and say that the gentleman who attends to that matter isn't in at present, will you?" said Miss Brass.

"I will, ma'am," replied Dick.

"I shan't be very long," said Miss Brass, retiring.

"I'm sorry to hear it, ma'am," rejoined Dick when she had shut the door. "I hope you may be unexpectedly detained, ma'am. If you could manage to be run over, ma'am, but not seriously, so much the better."

Uttering these expressions of good-will with extreme gravity, Mr. Swiveller sat down in the client's chair and pondered; then took a few turns up and down the room and fell into the chair again.

"So I'm Brass's clerk, am I?" said Dick. "Brass's clerk, eh? And the clerk of Brass's sister—clerk to a female Dragon. Very good, very good! What shall I be next? Shall I be a convict in a felt hat and a grey suit, trotting about a dockyard with my number neatly embroidered on my uniform, and the order of the garter on my leg, restrained from chafing my ankle by a twisted Belcher handkerchief? Shall I be that? Will that do, or is it too genteel? Whatever you please, have it your own way of course."

As he was entirely alone, it may be presumed that, in these remarks, Mr. Swiveller addressed himself to his fate or destiny, whom, as we learn by the precedents, it is the custom of heroes to taunt in a very bitter and ironical manner when they find themselves in situations of an unpleasant nature. This is the more probable from the circumstance of Mr. Swiveller directing his observations to the ceiling, which these bodily personages are usually supposed to inhabit—except in theatrical cases, when they live in the heart of the great chandelier.

"Quilp offers me this place, which he says he can insure me," resumed Dick after a thoughtful silence, and telling off the circumstances of his position, one by one, upon his fingers; "Fred, who, I could have taken my affidavit, would not have heard of such a thing, backs Quilp to my astonishment, and urges me to take it also—staggerer, number one. My aunt in the country stops the supplies, and writes an affectionate note to say that she has made a new will, and left me out of it—staggerer, number two. No money; no credit; no support from Fred, who seems to turn steady all at once; notice to quit the old lodgings—staggerers three, four, five, and six. Under an accumulation of staggerers, no man can be considered a free agent. No man knocks himself down; if his destiny knocks him down, his destiny must pick him up again. Then I'm very glad that mine has brought all this upon itself, and I shall be as careless as I can, and make myself quite at home to spite it. So go on, my buck," said Mr. Swiveller, taking his leave of the ceiling with a significant nod, "and let us see which of us will be tired first!"

Dismissing the subject of his downfall with these reflections, which were no doubt very profound, and are indeed not altogether unknown in certain systems of moral philosophy, Mr. Swiveller shook off his despondency and assumed the cheerful ease of an irresponsible clerk.

As a means towards his composure and self-possession, he entered into a more minute examination of the office than he had yet had time to make ; looked into the wig-box, the books, and ink-bottle; untied and inspected all the papers; carved a few devices on the table with the sharp blade of Mr. Brass's penknife; and wrote his name on the inside of the wooden coal-scuttle. Having, as it were, taken formal possession of his clerkship in virtue of these proceedings, he opened the window and leaned negligently out of it until a beer-boy happened to pass, whom he commanded to set down his tray and to serve him with a pint of mild porter, which he drank upon the spot and promptly paid for, with the view of breaking ground for a system of future credit and opening a correspondence tending thereto, without loss of time. Then three or four little boys dropped in, on legal errands from three or four attorneys of the Brass grade: whom Mr. Swiveller received and dismissed with about as professional a manner, and as correct and comprehensive an understanding of their business, as would have been shown by a clown in a pantomime under similar circumstances. These things done and over, he got upon his stool again and tried his hand at drawing caricatures of Miss Brass with a pen and ink, whistling very cheerfully all the time.

He was occupied in this diversion when a coach stopped near the door, and presently afterwards there was a loud double knock. As this was no business of Mr. Swiveller's, the person not ringing the office bell, he pursued his diversions with perfect composure, not-withstanding that he rather thought there was nobody else in the house.

In this, however, he was mistaken; for, after the knock had been repeated with increased impatience, the door was opened, and some-body with a very heavy tread went up the stairs and into the room above. Mr. Swiveller was wondering whether this might be another Miss Brass, twin sister to the Dragon, when there came a rapping of knuckles at the office door.

"Come in!" said Dick. "Don't stand upon ceremony. The business will get rather complicated if I've many more customers. Come in!"

"Oh, please," said a little voice very low down in the doorway, "will you come and show the lodgings?"

Dick leant over the table, and descried a small slipshod girl in a dirty coarse apron and bib, which left nothing of her visible but her face and feet. She might as well have been dressed in a violin-case.

"Why, who are you?" said Dick.

To which the only reply was, "Oh, please will you come and show the lodgings?"

There never was such an old-fashioned child in her looks and manner. She must have been at work from her cradle. She seemed as much afraid of Dick as Dick was amazed at her.

"I hav'n't got anything to do with the lodgings," said Dick. "Tell 'em to call again."

"Oh, but please will you come and show the lodgings," returned the girl; "it's eighteen shillings a week and us finding plate and linen. Boots and clothes is extra, and fires in winter time is eightpence a day."

"Why don't you show 'em yourself? You seem to know all about 'em," said Dick.

"Miss Sally said I wasn't to, because people wouldn't believe the attendance was good if they saw how small I was first."

"Well, but they'll see how small you are afterwards, won't they?" said Dick.

"Ah! But then they'll have taken 'em for a fortnight certain," replied the child with a shrewd look; "and people don't like moving when they're once settled."

"This is a queer sort of thing," muttered Dick, rising. "What do you mean to say you are—the cook?"

"Yes, I do plain cooking," replied the child. "I'm housemaid too; I do all the work of the house."

"I suppose Brass and the Dragon and I, do the dirtiest part of it," thought Dick. And he might have thought much more, being in a doubtful and hesitating mood, but that the girl again urged her request, and certain mysterious bumping sounds on the passage and staircase seemed to give note of the applicant's impatience. Richard Swiveller, therefore, sticking a pen behind each ear, and carrying another in his mouth as a token of his great importance and devotion to business, hurried out to meet and treat with the single gentleman.

He was a little surprised to perceive that the bumping sounds were occasioned by the progress up stairs of the single gentleman's trunk, which, being nearly twice as wide as the staircase, and exceedingly heavy withal, it was no easy matter for the united exertions of the single gentleman and the coachman to convey up the steep ascent. But there they were, crushing each other, and pushing and pulling with all their might, and getting the trunk tight and fast in all kinds of impossible angles, and to pass them was out of the question; for which sufficient reason, Mr. Swiveller followed slowly behind, entering a new protest on every stair against the house of Mr. Sampson Brass being thus taken by storm.

To these remonstrances, the single gentleman answered not a word, but when the trunk was at last got into the bedroom, sat down upon it and wiped his bald head and face with his handkerchief. He was very warm, and well he might be; for, not to mention the exertion of getting the trunk up stairs, he was closely muffled up in winter garments, though the thermometer had stood all day at eighty-one in the shade.

"I believe, sir," said Richard Swiveller, taking his pen out of his mouth, "that you desire to look at these apartments. They are very charming apartments, sir. They command an uninterrupted view of —of over the way, and they are within one minute's walk of—of the corner of the street. There is exceedingly mild porter, sir, in the immediate vicinity, and the contingent advantages are extraordinary."

"What's the rent?" said the single gentleman.

"One pound per week," replied Dick, improving on the terms.

"I'll take 'em."

"The boots and clothes are extras," said Dick; "and the fires in winter time are——"

"Are all agreed to," answered the single gentleman.

"Two weeks certain," said Dick, "are the——"

"Two weeks!" cried the single gentleman gruffly, eyeing him from top to toe. "Two years. I shall live here for two years. Here. Ten pounds down. The bargain's made."

"Why, you see," said Dick, "my name is not Brass, and——"

"Who said it was? *My* name's not Brass. What then?"

"The name of the master of the house is," said Dick.

"I'm glad of it," returned the single gentleman; "it's a good name for a lawyer. Coachman, you may go. So may you, sir."

Mr. Swiveller was so much confounded by the single gentleman riding rough-shod over him at this rate, that he stood looking at him almost as hard as he had looked at Miss Sally. The single gentleman, however, was not in the slightest degree affected by this circumstance, but proceeded with perfect composure to unwind the shawl which was tied round his neck, and then to pull off his boots. Freed of these encumbrances, he went on to divest himself of his other clothing, which he folded up piece by piece, and ranged in order upon the trunk. Then he pulled down the window-blinds, drew the curtains, wound up his watch, and, quite leisurely and methodically, got into bed.

"Take down the bill," were his parting words, as he looked out from between the curtains; "and let nobody call me till I ring the bell."

With that the curtains closed, and he seemed to snore immediately.

"This is a most remarkable and supernatural sort of house!" said Mr. Swiveller, as he walked into the office with the bill in his hand. "She-dragons in the business, conducting themselves like professional gentlemen; plain cooks of three feet high appearing mysteriously from under ground; strangers walking in and going to bed without leave or licence in the middle of the day! If he should be one of the miraculous fellows that turn up now and then, and has gone to sleep for two years, I shall be in a pleasant situation. It's my destiny, however, and I hope Brass may like it. I shall be sorry if he don't. But it's no business of mine—I have nothing whatever to do with it!"

CHAPTER XXXV

MR. BRASS on returning home received the report of his clerk with much complacency and satisfaction, and was particular in inquiring after the ten-pound note, which, proving on examination to be a good and lawful note of the Governor and Company of the Bank of England, increased his good-humour considerably. Indeed he so overflowed with liberality and condescension, that in the fulness of his heart he invited Mr. Swiveller to partake of a bowl of punch with him at that remote and indefinite period which is currently denominated "one of these days," and paid him many handsome compliments on the uncommon aptitude for business which his conduct on the first day of his devotion to it had so plainly evinced.

It was a maxim with Mr. Brass that the habit of paying compliments kept a man's tongue oiled without any expense; and, as that useful member ought never to grow rusty or creak in turning on its hinges in the case of a practitioner of the law, in whom it should be always glib and easy, he lost few opportunities of improving himself by the utterance of handsome speeches and eulogistic expressions. And this had passed into such a habit with him, that, if he could not be correctly said to have his tongue at his fingers' ends, he might certainly be said to have it anywhere but in his face : which being, as we have already seen, of a harsh and repulsive character, was not oiled so easily, but frowned above all the smooth speeches— one of nature's beacons, warning off those who navigated the shoals and breakers of the World, or of that dangerous strait the Law, and admonishing them to seek less treacherous harbours and try their fortune elsewhere.

While Mr. Brass by turns overwhelmed his clerk with compliments and inspected the ten-pound note, Miss Sally showed little emotion and that of no pleasurable kind, for as the tendency of her legal practice had been to fix her thoughts on small gains and gripings, and to whet and sharpen her natural wisdom, she was not a little disappointed that the single gentleman had obtained the lodgings at such an easy rate, arguing that when he was seen to have set his mind upon them, he should have been at the least charged double or treble the usual terms, and that, in exact proportion as he pressed forward, Mr. Swiveller should have hung back. But neither the good opinion of Mr. Brass, nor the dissatisfaction of Miss Sally, wrought any impression upon that young gentleman, who, throwing the responsibility of this and all other acts and deeds thereafter to be done by him, upon his unlucky destiny, was quite resigned and comfortable : fully prepared for the worst, and philosophically indifferent to the best.

"Good morning, Mr. Richard," said Brass, on the second day of Mr. Swiveller's clerkship. "Sally found you a second-hand stool, sir, yesterday evening in Whitechapel. She's a rare fellow at a bargain, I can tell you, Mr. Richard. You'll find that a first-rate stool, sir, take my word for it."

"It's rather a crazy one to look at," said Dick.

"You'll find it a most amazing stool to sit down upon, you may depend," returned Mr. Brass. "It was bought in the open street just opposite the hospital, and as it has been standing there a month or two, it has got rather dusty and a little brown from being in the sun, that's all."

"I hope it hasn't got any fevers or anything of that sort in it," said Dick, sitting himself down discontentedly, between Mr. Sampson and the chaste Sally. "One of the legs is longer than the other."

"Then we get a bit of timber in, sir," retorted Brass. "Ha, ha, ha! We get a bit of timber in, sir, and that's another advantage of my sister's going to market for us. Miss Brass, Mr. Richard, is the——"

"Will you keep quiet?" interrupted the fair subject of these remarks, looking up from her papers. "How am I to work if you keep on chattering?"

"What an uncertain chap you are!" returned the lawyer. "Sometimes you're all for a chat. At another time you're all for work. A man never knows what humour he'll find you in."

"I'm in a working humour now," said Miss Sally, "so don't disturb me, if you please. And don't take him," Miss Sally pointed with the feather of her pen to Richard, "off his business. He won't do more than he can help, I dare say."

Mr. Brass had evidently a strong inclination to make an angry reply, but was deterred by prudent or timid considerations, as he only muttered something about aggravation and a vagabond; not associating the terms with any individual, but mentioning them as connected with some abstract ideas which happened to occur to him. They went on writing for a long time in silence after this—in such a dull silence that Mr. Swiveller (who required excitement) had several times fallen asleep, and written divers strange words in an unknown character with his eyes shut, when Miss Sally at length broke in upon the monotony of the office by pulling out the little tin box, taking a noisy pinch of snuff, and then expressing her opinion that Mr. Richard Swiveller had "done it."

"Done what, ma'am?" said Richard.

"Do you know," returned Miss Brass, "that the lodger isn't up yet —that nothing has been seen or heard of him since he went to bed yesterday afternoon?"

"Well, ma'am," said Dick, "I suppose he may sleep his ten pound out, in peace and quietness, if he likes."

"Ah! I begin to think he'll never wake," observed Miss Sally.

"It's a very remarkable circumstance," said Brass, laying down his pen; "really, very remarkable. Mr. Richard, you'll remember, if this gentleman should be found to have hung himself to the bed-post, or any unpleasant accident of that kind should happen—you'll remember, Mr. Richard, that this ten-pound note was given to you in part payment of two years' rent? You'll bear that in mind, Mr. Richard; you had better make a note of it, sir, in case you should ever be called upon to give evidence."

Mr. Swiveller took a large sheet of foolscap, and with a countenance of profound gravity, began to make a very small note in one corner.

"We can never be too cautious," said Mr. Brass. "There is a deal of wickedness going about the world, a deal of wickedness. Did the gentleman happen to say, sir——but never mind that at present, sir; finish that little memorandum first."

Dick did so, and handed it to Mr. Brass, who had dismounted from his stool and was walking up and down the office.

"Oh, this is the memorandum, is it?" said Brass, running his eye over the document. "Very good. Now, Mr. Richard, did the gentleman say anything else?"

"No."

"Are you sure, Mr. Richard," said Brass, solemnly, "that the gentleman said nothing else?"

"Devil a word, sir," replied Dick.

"Think again, sir," said Brass; "it's my duty, sir, in the position in which I stand, and as an honourable member of the legal profession—the first profession in this country, sir, or in any other country, or in any of the planets that shine above us at night and are supposed to be inhabited—it's my duty, sir, as an honourable member of that profession, not to put to you a leading question in a matter of this delicacy and importance. Did the gentleman, sir, who took the first floor of you yesterday afternoon, and who brought with him a box of property—a box of property—say anything more than is set down in this memorandum?"

"Come, don't be a fool," said Miss Sally.

Dick looked at her, and then at Brass, and then at Miss Sally again, and still said "No."

"Pooh, pooh! Deuce take it, Mr. Richard, how dull you are!" cried Brass, relaxing into a smile. "Did he say anything about his property?—there!"

"That's the way to put it," said Miss Sally, nodding to her brother.

"Did he say, for instance," added Brass, in a kind of comfortable, cozy tone—"I don't assert that he did say so, mind; I only ask you, to refresh your memory—did he say, for instance, that he was a stranger in London—that it was not his humour or within his ability to give any references—that he felt we had a right to require them—and that, in case anything should happen to him at any time, he particularly desired that whatever property he had upon the premises should be considered mine, as some slight recompense for the trouble and annoyance I should sustain—and were you, in short," added Brass, still more comfortably and cozily than before, "were you induced to accept him on my behalf, as a tenant, upon those conditions?"

"Certainly not," replied Dick.

"Why, then, Mr. Richard," said Brass, darting at him a supercilious and reproachful look, "it's my opinion that you've mistaken your calling, and will never make a lawyer."

"Not if you live a thousand years," added Miss Sally. Whereupon the brother and sister took each a noisy pinch of snuff from the little tin box, and fell into gloomy thoughtfulness.

Nothing further passed up to Mr. Swiveller's dinner-time, which was at three o'clock, and seemed about three weeks in coming. At the first stroke of the hour, the new clerk disappeared. At the last stroke of five, he reappeared, and the office, as if by magic, became fragrant with the smell of gin and water and lemon-peel.

"Mr. Richard," said Brass, "this man's not up yet. Nothing will wake him, sir. What's to be done?"

"I should let him have his sleep out," returned Dick.

"Sleep out!" cried Brass; "why he has been asleep now, six-and-twenty hours. We have been moving chests of drawers over his head, we have knocked double-knocks at the street-door, we have made the servant-girl fall down stairs several times (she's a light weight, and it don't hurt her much), but nothing wakes him."

"Perhaps a ladder," suggested Dick, "and getting in at the first-floor window——"

"But then there's a door between; besides, the neighbourhood would be up in arms," said Brass.

"What do you say to getting on the roof of the house through the trap-door, and dropping down the chimney?" suggested Dick.

"That would be an excellent plan," said Brass, "if anybody would be——" and here he looked very hard at Mr. Swiveller—"would be kind, and friendly, and generous enough, to undertake it. I dare say it would not be anything like as disagreeable as one supposes."

Dick had made the suggestion, thinking that the duty might possibly fall on Miss Sally's department. As he said nothing further, and declined taking the hint, Mr. Brass was fain to propose that they should go up stairs together, and make a last effort to awaken the sleeper by some less violent means, which, if they failed on this last trial, must positively be succeeded by stronger measures. Mr. Swiveller, assenting, armed himself with his stool and the large ruler, and repaired with his employer to the scene of action, where Miss Brass was already ringing a handbell with all her might, and yet without producing the smallest effect upon their mysterious lodger.

"There are his boots, Mr. Richard," said Brass.

"Very obstinate-looking articles they are too," quoth Richard Swiveller. And truly they were as sturdy and bluff a pair of boots as one would wish to see; as firmly planted on the ground as if their owner's legs and feet had been in them, and seeming, with their broad soles and blunt toes, to hold possession of their place by main force.

"I can't see anything but the curtain of the bed," said Brass, applying his eye to the key-hole of the door. "Is he a strong man, Mr. Richard?"

"Very," answered Dick.

"It would be an extremely unpleasant circumstance if he was to bounce out suddenly," said Brass. "Keep the stairs clear. I should be more than a match for him, of course, but I'm the master of the house, and the laws of hospitality must be respected.—Hallo there! Hallo, hallo!"

While Mr. Brass, with his eye curiously twisted into the key-hole, uttered these sounds as a means of attracting the lodger's attention, and while Miss Brass plied the hand-bell, Mr. Swiveller put his stool close against the wall by the side of the door, and mounting on the top and standing bolt upright, so that if the lodger did make a rush, he would most probably pass him in its onward fury, began a violent battery with the ruler upon the upper panels of the door. Captivated with his own ingenuity, and confident in the strength of his position, which he had taken up after the method of those hardy individuals who open the pit and gallery doors of theatres on crowded nights, Mr. Swiveller rained down such a shower of blows that the noise of the bell was drowned; and the small servant, who lingered on the stairs below, ready to fly at a moment's notice, was obliged to hold her ears lest she should be rendered deaf for life.

Suddenly the door was unlocked on the inside and flung violently open. The small servant fled to the coal-cellar; Miss Sally dived into her own bedroom; Mr. Brass, who was not remarkable for personal courage, ran into the next street, and finding that nobody followed him, armed with a poker or other offensive weapon, put his hands in his pockets, walked very slowly all at once, and whistled.

Meanwhile Mr. Swiveller, on the top of the stool, drew himself into as flat a shape as possible against the wall and looked, not unconcernedly, down upon the single gentleman, who appeared at the door growling and cursing in a very awful manner, and, with the boots in his hand, seemed to have an intention of hurling them down stairs on speculation. This idea, however, he abandoned, and he was turning into his room again, still growling vengefully, when his eyes met those of the watchful Richard.

"Have *you* been making that horrible noise?" said the single gentleman.

"I have been helping, sir," returned Dick, keeping his eye upon him, and waving the ruler gently in his right hand, as an indication of what the single gentleman had to expect if he attempted any violence.

"How dare you then," said the lodger, "Eh?"

To this, Dick made no other reply than by inquiring whether the lodger held it to be consistent with the conduct and character of a gentleman to go to sleep for six-and-twenty hours at a stretch, and whether the peace of an amiable and virtuous family was to weigh as nothing in the balance.

"Is my peace nothing, sir?" said the single gentleman.

"Is their peace nothing, sir?" returned Dick. "I don't wish to hold out any threats, sir—indeed the law does not allow of threats, for to threaten is an indictable offence—but if ever you do that again, take care you're not sat upon by the coroner and buried in a cross road before you wake. We have been distracted with fears that you were dead, sir," said Dick, gently sliding to the ground, "and the short and the long of it is, that we cannot allow single gentlemen to come into this establishment and sleep like double gentlemen without paying extra for it."

"Indeed!" cried the lodger.

"Yes, sir, indeed," returned Dick, yielding to his destiny and saying whatever came uppermost; "an equal quantity of slumber was never got out of one bed and bedstead, and if you're going to sleep in that way, you must pay for a double-bedded room."

Instead of being thrown into a greater passion by these remarks, the lodger lapsed into a broad grin and looked at Mr. Swiveller, with twinkling eyes. He was a brown-faced sun-burnt man, and appeared browner and more sun-burnt from having a white night-cap on. As it was clear that he was a choleric fellow in some respects, Mr. Swiveller was relieved to find him in such good humour, and, to encourage him in it, smiled himself.

The lodger, in the testiness of being so rudely roused, had pushed his night-cap very much on one side of his bald head. This gave him a rakish eccentric air which, now that he had leisure to observe it, charmed Mr. Swiveller exceedingly; therefore, by way of propitiation, he expressed his hope that the gentleman was going to get up, and further that he would never do so any more.

"Come here, you impudent rascal!" was the lodger's answer as he re-entered his room.

Mr. Swiveller followed him in, leaving the stool outside, but reserving the ruler in case of a surprise. He rather congratulated himself upon his prudence when the single gentleman, without notice or explanation of any kind, double-locked the door.

"Can you drink anything?" was his next inquiry.

Mr. Swiveller replied that he had very recently been assuaging the pangs of thirst, but that he was still open to "a modest quencher," if the materials were at hand. Without another word spoken on either side, the lodger took from his great trunk a kind of temple, shining as of polished silver, and placed it carefully on the table.

Greatly interested in his proceedings, Mr. Swiveller observed him closely. Into one little chamber of this temple he dropped an egg, into another some coffee, into a third a compact piece of raw steak from a neat tin case, into a fourth he poured some water. Then, with the aid of a phosphorus-box and some matches, he procured a light and applied it to a spirit-lamp which had a place of its own below the temple; then he shut down the lids of all the little chambers; then he opened them; and then, by some wonderful and unseen agency, the steak was done, the egg was boiled, the coffee was accurately prepared, and his breakfast was ready.

"Hot water—" said the lodger, handing it to Mr. Swiveller with as much coolness as if he had a kitchen fire before him—"extraordinary rum—sugar—and a travelling glass. Mix for yourself. And make haste."

Dick complied, his eyes wandering all the time from the temple on the table which seemed to do everything, to the great trunk which seemed to hold everything. The lodger took his breakfast like a man who was used to work these miracles, and thought nothing of them.

"The man of the house is a lawyer, is he not?" said the lodger.

Dick nodded. The rum was amazing.

"The woman of the house—what's she?"

"A dragon," said Dick.

The single gentleman, perhaps because he had met with such things in his travels, or perhaps because he *was* a single gentleman, evinced no surprise, but merely inquired "Wife or sister?" "Sister," said Dick.—"So much the better," said the single gentleman, "he can get rid of her when he likes."

"I want to do as I like, young man," he added after a short silence; "to go to bed when I like, get up when I like, come in when I like, go out when I like,—to be asked no questions and be surrounded by no spies. In this last respect, servants are the devil. There's only one here."

"And a very little one," said Dick.

"And a very little one," repeated the lodger. "Well, the place will suit me, will it?"

"Yes," said Dick.

"Sharks, I suppose?" said the lodger.

Dick nodded his assent, and drained his glass.

"Let them know my humour," said the single gentleman, rising. "If they disturb me, they lose a good tenant. If they know me to be that, they know enough. If they try to know more, it's a notice to quit. It's better to understand these things at once. Good day."

"I beg your pardon," said Dick, halting in his passage to the door, which the lodger prepared to open. "When he who adores thee has left but the name——"

"What do you mean?"

"—But the name," said Dick—"has left but the name—in case of letters or parcels——"

"I never have any," returned the lodger.

"Or in case anybody should call."

"Nobody ever calls on me."

"If any mistake should arise from not having the name, don't say it was my fault, sir," added Dick, still lingering. "Oh blame not the bard——"

"I'll blame nobody," said the lodger, with such irascibility that in a moment Dick found himself on the staircase, and the locked door between them.

Mr. Brass and Miss Sally were lurking hard by, having been, indeed, only routed from the key-hole by Mr. Swiveller's abrupt exit. As their utmost exertions had not enabled them to overhear a word of the interview, however, in consequence of a quarrel for precedence, which, though limited of necessity to pushes and pinches and such quiet pantomime, had lasted the whole time, they hurried him down to the office to hear his account of the conversation.

This Mr. Swiveller gave them—faithfully as regarded the wishes and character of the single gentleman, and poetically as concerned the great trunk, of which he gave a description more remarkable for brilliancy of imagination than a strict adherence to truth; declaring, with many strong asseverations, that it contained a specimen of every kind of rich food and wine known in these times, and in particular that it was of a self-acting kind and served up whatever was required, as he supposed by clockwork. He also gave them to understand that the cooking apparatus roasted a fine piece of sirloin of beef, weighing about six pounds avoirdupois, in two minutes and a quarter, as he had himself witnessed, and proved by his sense of taste; and further that, however the effect was produced, he had distinctly seen water boil and bubble up when the single gentleman winked; from which facts he (Mr. Swiveller) was led to infer that the lodger was some great conjuror or chemist, or both, whose residence under that roof could not fail at some future date to shed a great credit and distinction upon the name of Brass, and add a new interest to the history of Bevis Marks.

There was one point which Mr. Swiveller deemed it unnecessary to enlarge upon, and that was the fact of the modest quencher, which, by reason of its intrinsic strength and its coming close upon the heels of the temperate beverage he had discussed at dinner, awakened a slight degree of fever, and rendered necessary two or three other modest quenchers at the public-house in the course of the evening.

CHAPTER XXXVI

As the single gentleman, after some weeks' occupation of his lodgings, still declined to correspond by word or gesture either with Mr. Brass or his sister Sally, but invariably chose Richard Swiveller as his channel of communication; and as he proved himself in all respects a highly desirable inmate, paying for everything beforehand, giving very little trouble, making no noise, and keeping early hours; Mr. Richard imperceptibly rose to an important position in the family, as one who had influence over this mysterious lodger, and could negotiate with him, for good or evil, when nobody else durst approach his person.

If the truth must be told, even Mr. Swiveller's approaches to the single gentleman were of a very distant kind, and met with small encouragement; but, as he never returned from a monosyllabic conference with the unknown, without quoting such expressions as

"Swiveller, I know I can rely upon you,"—"I have no hesitation in saying, Swiveller, that I entertain a regard for you,"—"Swiveller, you are my friend, and will stand by me I am sure," with many other short speeches of the same familiar and confiding kind, purporting to have been addressed by the single gentleman to himself, and to form the staple of their ordinary discourse, neither Mr. Brass nor Miss Sally for a moment questioned the extent of his influence, but accorded to him their fullest and most unqualified belief.

But quite apart from and independent of this source of popularity, Mr. Swiveller had another, which promised to be equally enduring, and to lighten his position considerably.

He found favour in the eyes of Miss Sally Brass. Let not the light scorners of female fascination erect their ears to listen to a new tale of love which shall serve them for a jest; for Miss Brass, however accurately formed to be beloved, was not of the loving kind. That amiable virgin, having clung to the skirts of the Law from her earliest youth—having sustained herself by their aid, as it were, in her first running alone, and maintained a firm grasp upon them ever since—had passed her life in a kind of legal childhood. She had been remarkable, when a tender prattler, for an uncommon talent in counterfeiting the walk and manner of a bailiff: in which character she had learned to tap her little playfellows on the shoulder, and to carry them off to imaginary sponging-houses, with a correctness of imitation which was the surprise and delight of all who witnessed her performances, and which was only to be exceeded by her exquisite manner of putting an execution into her doll's house, and taking an exact inventory of the chairs and tables. These artless sports had naturally soothed and cheered the decline of her widowed father: a most exemplary gentleman (called "old Foxey" by his friends from his extreme sagacity), who encouraged them to the utmost, and whose chief regret on finding that he drew near to Houndsditch Churchyard was, that his daughter could not take out an attorney's certificate and hold a place upon the roll. Filled with this affectionate and touching sorrow, he had solemnly confided her to his son Sampson as an invaluable auxiliary; and from the old gentleman's decease to the period of which we treat, Miss Sally Brass had been the prop and pillar of his business.

It is obvious that, having devoted herself from infancy to this one pursuit and study, Miss Brass could know but little of the world, otherwise than in connexion with the law; and that from a lady gifted with such high tastes, proficiency in those gentler and softer arts in which women usually excel, was scarcely to be looked for. Miss Sally's accomplishments were all of a masculine and strictly legal kind. They began with the practice of an attorney and they ended with it. She was in a state of lawful innocence, so to speak. The law had been her nurse, and, as bandy-legs or such physical deformities in children are held to be the consequence of bad nursing, so, if in a mind so beautiful any moral twist or bandiness could be found, Miss Sally Brass's nurse was alone to blame.

It was upon this lady, then, that Mr. Swiveller burst in full freshness as something new and hitherto undreamed of, lighting up the office with scraps of song and merriment, conjuring with inkstands and boxes of wafers, catching three oranges in one hand, balancing stools upon his chin and penknives on his nose, and constantly performing a hundred other feats of equal ingenuity; for with such unbendings did Richard, in Mr. Brass's absence, relieve the tedium of his confinement. These social qualities, which Miss Sally first discovered by accident, gradually made such an impression upon her, that she would entreat Mr. Swiveller to relax as though she were not by, which Mr. Swiveller, nothing loth, would readily consent to do. By these means a friendship sprang up between them. Mr. Swiveller gradually came to look upon her as her brother Sampson did, and as he would have looked upon any other clerk. He imparted to her the mystery of going the odd man or plain Newmarket for fruit, ginger-beer, baked potatoes, or even a modest quencher, of which Miss Brass did not scruple to partake. He would often persuade her to undertake his share of writing in addition to her own; nay, he would sometimes reward her with a hearty slap on the back, and protest that she was a devilish good fellow, a jolly dog, and so forth; all of which compliments Miss Sally would receive in entire good part and with perfect satisfaction.

One circumstance troubled Mr. Swiveller's mind very much, and that was that the small servant always remained somewhere in the bowels of the earth under Bevis Marks, and never came to the surface unless the single gentleman rang his bell, when she would answer it and immediately disappear again. She never went out, or came into the office, or had a clean face, or took off the coarse apron, or looked out of any one of the windows, or stood at the street-door for a breath of air, or had any rest or enjoyment whatever. Nobody ever came to see her, nobody spoke of her, nobody cared about her. Mr. Brass had said once, that he believed she was a "love-child " (which means anything but a child of love), and that was all the information Richard Swiveller could obtain.

"It's of no use asking the dragon," thought Dick one day, as he sat contemplating the features of Miss Sally Brass. "I suspect if I asked any questions on that head, our alliance would be at an end. I wonder whether she *is* a dragon by the bye, or something in the mermaid way. She has rather a scaly appearance. But mermaids are fond of looking at themselves in the glass, which she can't be. And they have a habit of combing their hair, which she hasn't. No, she's a dragon."

"Where are you going, old fellow?" said Dick aloud, as Miss Sally wiped her pen as usual on the green dress, and uprose from her seat.

"To dinner," answered the dragon.

"To dinner!" thought Dick, "that's another circumstance. I don't believe that small servant ever has anything to eat."

"Sammy won't be home," said Miss Brass. "Stop till I come back. I shan't be long."

Dick nodded, and followed Miss Brass—with his eyes to the door and with his ears to a little back parlour, where she and her brother took their meals.

"Now," said Dick, walking up and down with his hands in his pockets, "I'd give something—if I had it—to know how they use that child, and where they keep her. My mother must have been a very inquisitive woman; I have no doubt I'm marked with a note of interrogation somewhere. My feelings I smother, but thou hast been the cause of this anguish, my—upon my word," said Mr. Swiveller, checking himself and falling thoughtfully into the client's chair, "I should like to know how they use her!"

After running on in this way for some time, Mr. Swiveller softly opened the office door, with the intention of darting across the street for a glass of the mild porter. At that moment he caught a parting glimpse of the brown head-dress of Miss Brass flitting down the kitchen stairs. "And by Jove!" thought Dick, "she's going to feed the servant. Now or never!"

First peeping over the handrail and allowing the head-dress to disappear in the darkness below, he groped his way down, and arrived at the door of a back kitchen immediately after Miss Brass had entered the same, bearing in her hand a cold leg of mutton. It was a very dark miserable place, very low and very damp: the walls disfigured by a thousand rents and blotches. The water was trickling out of a leaky butt, and a most wretched cat was lapping up the drops with the sickly eagerness of starvation. The grate, which was a wide one, was wound and screwed up tight, so as to hold no more than a little thin sandwich of fire. Everything was locked up; the coal-cellar, the candle-box, the salt-box, the meat-safe, were all padlocked. There was nothing that a beetle could have lunched upon. The pinched and meagre aspect of the place would have killed a chameleon. He would have known at the first mouthful that the air was not eatable, and must have given up the ghost in despair.—The small servant stood with humility in presence of Miss Sally, and hung her head.

"Are you there?" said Miss Sally.

"Yes, ma'am," was the answer in a weak voice.

"Go further away from the leg of mutton, or you'll be picking it, I know," said Miss Sally.

The girl withdrew into a corner, while Miss Brass took a key from her pocket, and opening the safe, brought from it a dreary waste of cold potatoes, looking as eatable as Stonehenge. This she placed before the small servant, ordering her to sit down before it, and then, taking up a great carving-knife, made a mighty show of sharpening it upon the carving-fork.

"Do you see this?" said Miss Brass, slicing off about two square inches of cold mutton, after all this preparation, and holding it out on the point of the fork.

The small servant looked hard enough at it with her hungry eyes to see every shred of it, small as it was, and answered, "yes."

"Then don't you ever go and say," retorted Miss Sally, "that you hadn't meat here. There, eat it up."

This was soon done. "Now, do you want any more?" said Miss Sally.

The hungry creature answered with a faint "No." They were evidently going through an established form.

"You've been helped once to meat," said Miss Brass, summing up the facts; "you have had as much as you can eat, you're asked if you want any more, and you answer, 'No!' Then don't you ever go and say you were allowanced, mind that."

With those words, Miss Sally put the meat away and locked the safe, and then drawing near to the small servant, overlooked her while she finished the potatoes.

It was plain that some extraordinary grudge was working in Miss Brass's gentle breast, and that it was this which impelled her, without the smallest present cause, to rap the child with the blade of the knife, now on her hand, now on her head, and now on her back, as if she found it quite impossible to stand so close to her without administering a few slight knocks. But Mr. Swiveller was not a little surprised to see his fellow-clerk, after walking slowly backwards towards the door, as if she were trying to withdraw herself from the room but could not accomplish it, dart suddenly forward, and falling on the small servant give her some hard blows with her clenched hand. The victim cried, but in a subdued manner as if she feared to raise her voice, and Miss Sally, comforting herself with a pinch of snuff, ascended the stairs, just as Richard had safely reached the office.

CHAPTER XXXVII

THE single gentleman among his other peculiarities—and he had a very plentiful stock, of which he every day furnished some new specimen—took a most extraordinary and remarkable interest in the exhibition of Punch. If the sound of a Punch's voice, at ever so remote a distance, reached Bevis Marks, the single gentleman, though in bed and asleep, would start up, and, hurrying on his clothes, make for the spot with all speed, and presently return at the head of a long procession of idlers, having in the midst the theatre and its proprietors. Straightway, the stage would be set up in front of Mr. Brass's house; the single gentleman would establish himself at the first-floor window; and the entertainment would proceed with all its exciting accompaniments of fife and drum and shout, to the excessive consternation of all sober votaries of business in that silent thoroughfare. It might have been expected that when the play was done, both players and audience would have dispersed; but the epilogue was as bad as the play, for no sooner was the Devil dead, than the manager of the puppets and his partner were summoned by the single gentleman to his chamber, where they were regaled with strong waters from his private store, and where they held with him long conversations, the purport of which no human being could fathom. But the secret of these discussions was of little importance. It was sufficient to know that while they were proceeding, the concourse without still lingered round the house; that boys beat upon the drum with their fists, and imitated Punch with their tender voices; that the office-window was rendered opaque by flattened noses, and the key-hole of the street-door luminous with eyes; that every time the single gentleman or either of his guests was seen at the upper window, or so much as the end of one of their noses was visible, there was a great shout of execration from the excluded mob, who remained howling and yelling, and refusing consolation, until the exhibitors were delivered up to them to be attended elsewhere. It was sufficient, in short, to know that Bevis Marks was revolutionised by these popular movements, and that peace and quietness fled from its precincts.

Nobody was rendered more indignant by these proceedings than Mr. Sampson Brass, who, as he could by no means afford to lose so profitable an inmate, deemed it prudent to pocket his lodger's affront along with his cash, and to annoy the audiences who clustered round his door by such imperfect means of retaliation as were open to him, and which were confined to the trickling down of foul water on their heads from unseen watering-pots, pelting them with fragments of tile and mortar from the roof of the house, and bribing the drivers of hackney cabriolets to come suddenly round the corner and dash in among them precipitately. It may at first sight be matter of surprise to the thoughtless few that Mr. Brass, being a professional gentleman, should not have legally indicted some party or parties, active in the promotion of the nuisance; but they will be good enough to remember that as Doctors seldom take their own prescriptions, and Divines do not always practise what they preach, so Lawyers are shy of meddling with the Law on their own account, knowing it to be an edged tool of uncertain application, very expensive in the working, and rather remarkable for its properties of close shaving, than for its always shaving the right person.

"Come," said Mr. Brass one afternoon, "this is two days without a Punch. I'm in hopes he has run through 'em all, at last."

"Why are you in hopes?" returned Miss Sally. "What harm do they do?"

"Here's a pretty sort of fellow!" cried Brass, laying down his pen in despair. "Now here's an aggravating animal!"

"Well, what harm do they do?" retorted Sally.

"What harm!" cried Brass. "Is it no harm to have a constant hallooing and hooting under one's very nose, distracting one from business, and making one grind one's teeth with vexation? Is it no harm to be blinded and choked up, and have the King's highway stopped with a set of screamers and roarers whose throats must be made of—of——"

"Brass," suggested Mr. Swiveller.

"Ah! of brass," said the lawyer, glancing at his clerk, to assure himself that he had suggested the word in good faith and without any sinister intention. "Is that no harm?"

The lawyer stopped short in his invective, and listening for a moment, and recognising the well-known voice, rested his head upon his hand, raised his eyes to the ceiling and muttered faintly, "There's another!"

Up went the single gentleman's window directly.

"There's another," repeated Brass; "and if I could get a break and four blood horses to cut into the Marks when the crowd is at its thickest, I'd give eighteen-pence and never grudge it!"

The distant squeak was heard again. The single gentleman's door burst open. He ran violently down the stairs, out into the street, and so past the window, without any hat, towards the quarter whence the sound proceeded—bent, no doubt, upon securing the strangers' services directly.

"I wish I only knew who his friends were," muttered Sampson, filling his pockets with papers; "if they'd just get up a pretty little Commission de lunatico at the Gray's Inn Coffee House and give me the job, I'd be content to have the lodgings empty for one while, at all events."

With which words, and knocking his hat over his eyes as if for the purpose of shutting out even a glimpse of the dreadful visitation, Mr. Brass rushed from the house and hurried away.

As Mr. Swiveller was decidedly favourable to these performances upon the ground that looking at a Punch, or indeed looking at anything out of window, was better than working; and as he had been for this reason at some pains to awaken in his fellow-clerk a sense of their beauties and manifold deserts; both he and Miss Sally rose as with one accord and took up their positions at the window: upon the sill whereof, as in a post of honour, sundry young ladies and gentlemen who were employed in the dry nurture of babies, and who made a point of being present, with their young charges, on such occasions, had already established themselves as comfortably as the circumstances would allow.

The glass being dim, Mr. Swiveller, agreeably to a friendly custom which he had established between them, hitched off the brown head-dress from Miss Sally's head, and dusted it carefully therewith. By the time he had handed it back, and its beautiful wearer had put it on again (which she did with perfect composure and indifference), the lodger returned with the show and showmen at his heels, and a strong addition to the body of spectators. The exhibitor disappeared with all speed behind the drapery, and his partner, stationing himself by the side of the Theatre, surveyed the audience with a remarkable expression of melancholy, which became more remarkable still when he breathed a hornpipe tune into that sweet musical instrument which is popularly termed a mouth-organ, without at all changing the mournful expression of the upper part of his face, though his mouth and chin were, of necessity, in lively spasms.

The drama proceeded to its close, and held the spectators enchained in the customary manner. The sensation which kindles in large assemblies, when they are relieved from a state of breathless suspense and are again free to speak and move, was yet rife, when the lodger, as usual, summoned the men up stairs.

"Both of you," he called from the window; for only the actual exhibitor—a little fat man—prepared to obey the summons "I want to talk to you. Come, both of you."

"Come, Tommy," said the little man.

"I an't a talker," replied the other. "Tell him so. What should I go and talk for?"

"Don't you see the gentleman's got a bottle and glass up here?" returned the little man.

"And couldn't you have said so, at first?" retorted the other with sudden alacrity. "Now, what are you waiting for? Are you going to keep the gentleman expecting us all day? haven't you *no* manners?"

With this remonstance, the melancholy man, who was no other than Mr. Thomas Codlin, pushed past his friend and brother in the craft, Mr. Harris, otherwise Short or Trotters, and hurried before him to the single gentleman's apartment.

"Now, my men," said the single gentleman; "you have done very well. What will you take? Tell that little man behind, to shut the door."

"Shut the door, can't you?" said Mr. Codlin, turning gruffly to his friend. "You might have knowed that the gentleman wanted the door shut, without being told, I think."

Mr. Short obeyed, observing under his breath that his friend seemed unusually "cranky," and expressing a hope that there was no dairy in the neighbourhood, or his temper would certainly spoil its contents.

The gentleman pointed to a couple of chairs, and intimated by an emphatic nod of his head that he expected them to be seated. Messrs. Codlin and Short, after looking at each other with considerable doubt and indecision, at length sat down—each on the extreme edge of the chair pointed out to him—and held their hats very tight, while the single gentleman filled a couple of glasses from a bottle on the table beside him, and presented them in due form.

"You're pretty well browned by the sun, both of you," said their entertainer. "Have you been travelling?"

Mr. Short replied in the affirmative with a nod and a smile. Mr. Codlin added a corroborative nod and a short groan, as if he still felt the weight of the Temple upon his shoulders.

"To fairs, markets, races, and so forth, I suppose?" pursued the single gentleman.

"Yes, sir," returned Short, "pretty nigh all over the West of England."

"I have talked to men of your craft from North, East, and South," returned their host, in rather a hasty manner; "but I never lighted on any from the West before."

"It's our reg'lar summer circuit is the West, master," said Short; "that's where it is. We take the East of London in the spring and winter, and the West of England in the summer time. Many's the hard day's walking in rain and mud, and with never a penny earned, we've had down in the West."

"Let me fill your glass again."

"Much obleeged to you, sir, I think I will," said Mr. Codlin, suddenly thrusting in his own and turning Short's aside. "I'm the sufferer, sir, in all the travelling, and in all the staying at home. In town or country, wet or dry, hot or cold, Tom Codlin suffers. But Tom Codlin isn't to complain for all that. Oh, no! Short may complain, but if Codlin grumbles by so much as a word—oh dear, down with him, down with *him* directly. It isn't *his* place to grumble. That's quite out of the question."

"Codlin an't without his usefulness," observed Short with an arch look, "but he don't always keep his eyes open. He falls asleep sometimes, you know. Remember them last races, Tommy."

"Will you never leave off aggravating a man?" said Codlin. "It's very likely I was asleep when five-and-tenpence was collected, in one round, isn't it? I was attending to my business, and couldn't have my eyes in twenty places at once, like a peacock, no more than you could. If I an't a match for an old man and a young child, you an't neither, so don't throw that out against me, for the cap fits your head quite as correct as it fits mine."

"You may as well drop the subject, Tom," said Short. "It isn't particularly agreeable to the gentleman, I dare say."

"Then you shouldn't have brought it up," returned Mr. Codlin; "and I ask the gentleman's pardon on your account, as a giddy chap that likes to hear himself talk, and don't much care what he talks about, so that he does talk."

Their entertainer had sat perfectly quiet in the beginning of this dispute, looking first at one man and then at the other, as if he were lying in wait for an opportunity of putting some further question, or reverting to that from which the discourse had strayed. But, from the point where Mr. Codlin was charged with sleepiness, he had shown an increasing interest in the discussion: which now attained a very high pitch.

"You are the two men I want," he said, "the two men I have been looking for, and searching after. Where are that old man and that child you speak of?"

"Sir?" said Short, hesitating, and looking towards his friend.

"The old man and his grandchild who travelled with you—where are they? It will be worth your while to speak out, I assure you; much better worth your while than you believe. They left you, you say,— at those races, as I understand. They have been traced to that place, and there lost sight of. Have you no clue, can you suggest no clue, to their recovery?"

"Did I always say, Thomas," cried Short, turning with a look of amazement to his friend, "that there was sure to be an inquiry after them two travellers?"

"*You* said!" returned Mr. Codlin. "Did I always say that that 'ere blessed child was the most interesting I ever see? Did I always say I loved her, and doted on her? Pretty creetur, I think I hear her now. 'Codlin's my friend,' she says, with a tear of gratitude a trickling down her little eye; 'Codlin's my friend,' she says—'not Short. Short's very well,' she says; 'I've no quarrel with Short; he means to be kind, I dare say; but Codlin,' she says, 'has the feelings for my money, though he mayn't look it.' "

Repeating these words with great emotion, Mr. Codlin rubbed the bridge of his nose with his coat-sleeve, and shaking his head mournfully from side to side, left the single gentleman to infer that, from the moment when he lost sight of his dear young charge, his peace of mind and happiness had fled.

"Good God!" said the single gentleman, pacing up and down the room, "have I found these men at last, only to discover that they can give me no information or assistance! It would have been better to have lived on in hope from day to day, and never to have lighted on them, than to have my expectations scattered."

"Stay a minute," said Short. "A man of the name of Jerry—you know Jerry, Thomas?"

"Oh, don't talk to me of Jerrys," replied Mr. Codlin. "How can I care a pinch of snuff for Jerrys, when I think of that 'ere darling child? 'Codlin's my friend,' she says, 'dear, good, kind Codlin, as is always a devising pleasures for me! I don't object to Short,' she says, 'but I cotton to Codlin.' Once," said that gentleman reflectively, "she called me Father Codlin. I thought I should have bust!"

"A man of the name of Jerry, sir," said Short, turning from his selfish colleague to their new acquaintance, "wot keeps a company of dancing dogs, told me in a accidental sort of way, that he had seen the old gentleman in connexion with a travelling wax-work, unbeknown to him. As they'd given us the slip, and nothing had come of it, and this was down in the country that he'd been seen, I took no measures about it, and asked no questions. But I can, if you like."

"Is this man in town?" said the impatient single gentleman. "Speak faster."

"No he isn't, but he will be to-morrow, for he lodges in our house," replied Mr. Short rapidly.

"Then bring him here," said the single gentleman. "Here's a sovereign a-piece. If I can find these people through your means, it is but a prelude to twenty more. Return to me to-morrow, and keep your own counsel upon this subject—though I need hardly tell you that, for you'll do so for your own sakes. Now, give me your address, and leave me."

The address was given, the two men departed, the crowd went with them, and the single gentleman for two mortal hours walked in uncommon agitation up and down his room, over the wondering heads of Mr. Swiveller and Miss Sally Brass.

CHAPTER XXXVIII

Kit—for it happens at this juncture, not only that we have breathing time to follow his fortunes, but that the necessities of these adventures so adapt themselves to our ease and inclination as to call upon us imperatively to pursue the track we most desire to take—Kit, while the matters treated of in the last fifteen chapters were yet in progress, was, as the reader may suppose, gradually familiarising himself more and more with Mr. and Mrs. Garland, Mr. Abel, the pony, and Barbara, and gradually coming to consider them one and all as his particular private friends, and Abel Cottage, Finchley, as his own proper home.

Stay—the words are written, and may go, but if they convey any notion that Kit, in the plentiful board and comfortable lodging of his new abode, began to think slightingly of the poor fare and furniture of his old dwelling, they do their office badly and commit injustice. Who so mindful of those he left at home—albeit they were but a mother and two young babies—as Kit? What boastful father in the fulness of his heart ever related such wonders of his infant prodigy, as Kit never wearied of telling Barbara in the evening time, concerning little Jacob? Was there ever such a mother as Kit's mother, on her son's showing; or was there ever such comfort in poverty as in the poverty of Kit's family, if any correct judgment might be arrived at, from his own glowing account!

And let us linger in this place for an instant to remark that if ever household affections and loves are graceful things, they are graceful in the poor. The ties that bind the wealthy and the proud to home may be forged on earth, but those which link the poor man to his humble hearth are of the true metal and bear the stamp of Heaven. The man of high descent may love the halls and lands of his inheritance as a part of himself, as trophies of his birth and power; his associations with them are associations of pride and wealth and triumph; the poor man's attachment to the tenements he holds, which strangers have held before, and may to-morrow occupy again, has a worthier root, struck deep into a purer soil. His household gods are of flesh and blood, with no alloy of silver, gold, or precious stone; he has no property but in the affections of his own heart; and when they endear bare floors and walls, despite of rags and toil and scanty meals, that man has his love of home from God, and his rude hut becomes a solemn place.

Oh! if those who rule the destinies of nations would but remember this—if they would but think how hard it is for the very poor to have engendered in their hearts that love of home from which all domestic virtues spring, when they live in dense and squalid masses where social decency is lost, or rather never found,—if they would but turn aside from the wide thoroughfares and great houses, and strive to improve the wretched dwellings in bye-ways where only Poverty may walk,—many low roofs would point more truly to the sky, than the loftiest steeple that now rears proudly up from the midst of guilt, and crime, and horrible disease, to mock them by its contrast. In hollow voices from Workhouse, Hospital, and Jail, this truth is preached from day to day, and has been proclaimed for years. It is no light matter—no outcry from the working vulgar— no mere question of the people's health and comforts that may be whistled down on Wednesday nights. In love of home, the love of country has its rise; and who are the truer patriots or the best in time of need—those who venerate the land, owning its wood, and stream, and earth, and all that they produce? or those who love their country, boasting not a foot of ground in all its wide domain?

Kit knew nothing about such questions, but he knew that his old home was a very poor place and that his new one was very unlike it, and yet he was constantly looking back with grateful satisfaction and affectionate anxiety, and often indited square-folded letters to his mother, inclosing a shilling or eighteen-pence or such other small remittance, which Mr. Abel's liberality enabled him to make. Sometimes, being in the neighbourhood, he had leisure to call upon her, and then great was the joy and pride of Kit's mother, and extremely noisy the satisfaction of little Jacob and the baby, and cordial the congratulations of the whole court, who listened with admiring ears to the accounts of Abel Cottage, and could never be told too much of its wonders and magnificence.

Although Kit was in the very highest favour with the old lady and gentleman, and Mr. Abel, and Barbara, it is certain that no member of the family evinced such a remarkable partiality for him as the self-willed pony, who, from being the most obstinate and opinionated pony on the face of the earth, was in his hands the meekest and most tractable of animals. It is true that in exact proportion as he became manageable by Kit he became utterly ungovernable by anybody else (as if he had determined to keep him in the family at all risks and hazards), and that, even under the guidance of his favourite, he would sometimes perform a great variety of strange freaks and capers, to the extreme discomposure of the old lady's nerves; but as Kit always represented that this was only his fun, or a way he had of showing his attachment to his employers, Mrs. Garland gradually suffered herself to be persuaded into the belief, in which she at last became so strongly confirmed that if in one of these ebullitions he had overturned the chaise, she would have been quite satisfied that he did it with the very best intentions.

Besides becoming in a short time a perfect marvel in all stable matters, Kit soon made himself a very tolerable gardener, a handy fellow within doors, and an indispensable attendant on Mr. Abel, who every day gave him some new proof of his confidence and approbation. Mr. Witherden the notary, too, regarded him with a friendly eye; and even Mr. Chuckster would sometimes condescend to give him a slight nod, or to honour him with that peculiar form of recognition which is called "taking a sight," or to favour him with some other salute combining pleasantry with patronage.

One morning Kit drove Mr. Abel to the Notary's office, as he sometimes did, and having set him down at the house, was about to drive off to a livery stable hard by, when this same Mr. Chuckster emerged from the office door, and cried "Whoa-a-a-a-a!"—dwelling upon the note a long time, for the purpose of striking terror into the pony's heart, and asserting the supremacy of man over the inferior animals.

"Pull up, Snobby," cried Mr. Chuckster, addressing himself to Kit. "You're wanted inside here."

"Has Mr. Abel forgotten anything, I wonder?" said Kit as he dismounted.

"Ask no questions, Snobby," returned Mr. Chuckster, "but go and see. Woa-a-a then, will you? If that pony was mine, *I*'d break him."

"You must be very gentle with him, if you please," said Kit, "or you'll find him troublesome. You'd better not keep on pulling his ears, please. I know he won't like it."

To this remonstrance Mr. Chuckster deigned no other answer, than addressing Kit with a lofty and distant air as "young feller," and requesting him to cut and come again with all speed. The "young feller" complying, Mr. Chuckster put his hands in his pockets, and tried to look as if he were not minding the pony, but happened to be lounging there by accident.

Kit scraped his shoes very carefully (for he had not yet lost his reverence for the bundles of papers and the tin boxes), and tapped at the office door, which was quickly opened by the Notary himself.

"Oh! come in, Christopher," said Mr. Witherden.

"Is that the lad?" asked an elderly gentleman, but of a stout, bluff figure—who was in the room.

"That's the lad," said Mr. Witherden. "He fell in with my client, Mr. Garland, sir, at this very door. I have reason to think he is a good lad, sir, and that you may believe what he says. Let me introduce Mr. Abel Garland, sir—his young master; my articled pupil, sir, and most particular friend. My most particular friend, sir," repeated the Notary, drawing out his silk handkerchief and flourishing it about his face.

"Your servant, sir," said the stranger gentleman.

"Yours, sir, I'm sure," replied Mr. Abel mildly. "You were wishing to speak to Christopher, sir?"

"Yes, I was. Have I your permission?"

"By all means."

"My business is no secret; or I should rather say it need be no secret *here*," said the stranger, observing that Mr. Abel and the Notary were preparing to retire. "It relates to a dealer in curiosities with whom he lived, and in whom I am earnestly and warmly interested. I have been a stranger to this country, gentlemen, for very many years, and if I am deficient in form and ceremony, I hope you will forgive me."

"No forgiveness is necessary, sir;—none whatever," replied the Notary, and so said Mr. Abel.

"I have been making inquiries in the neighbourhood in which his old master lived," said the stranger, "and I learnt that he had been served by this lad. I found out his mother's house, and was directed by her to this place as the nearest in which I should be likely to find him. That's the cause of my presenting myself here this morning."

"I am very glad of any cause, sir," said the Notary, "which procures me the honour of this visit."

"Sir," retorted the stranger, "you speak like a mere man of the world, and I think you something better. Therefore, pray do not sink your real character in paying unmeaning compliments to me."

"Hem!" coughed the Notary. "You're a plain speaker, sir."

"And a plain dealer," returned the stranger. "It may be my long absence and inexperience that lead me to the conclusion, but if plain speakers are scarce in this part of the world, I fancy that plain dealers are still scarcer. If my speaking should offend you, sir, my dealing, I hope, will make amends."

Mr. Witherden seemed a little disconcerted by the elderly gentleman's mode of conducting the dialogue; and as for Kit, he looked at him in open-mouthed astonishment, wondering what kind of language he would address to him, if he talked in that free and easy way to a Notary. It was with no harshness, however, though with something of constitutional irritability and haste, that he turned to Kit and said:

"If you think, my lad, that I am pursuing these inquiries with any other view than that of serving and reclaiming those I am in search of, you do me a very great wrong, and deceive yourself. Don't be deceived, I beg of you, but rely upon my assurance. The fact is, gentlemen," he added, turning again to the Notary and his pupil, "that I am in a very painful and wholly unexpected position. I came to this city with a darling object at my heart, expecting to find no obstacle or difficulty in the way of its attainment. I find myself suddenly checked and stopped short in the execution of my design, by a mystery which I cannot penetrate. Every effort I have made to penetrate it, has only served to render it darker and more obscure; and I am afraid to stir openly in the matter, lest those whom I anxiously pursue should fly still farther from me. I assure you that if you could give me any assistance, you would not be sorry to do so, if you knew how greatly I stand in need of it, and what a load it would relieve me from."

There was a simplicity in this confidence which occasioned it to find a quick response in the breast of the good-natured Notary, who replied, in the same spirit, that the stranger had not mistaken his desire, and that if he could be of service to him, he would most readily.

Kit was then put under examination and closely questioned by the unknown gentleman touching his old master and the child, their lonely way of life, their retired habits, and strict seclusion. The nightly absence of the old man, the solitary existence of the child at those times, his illness and recovery, Quilp's possession of the house, and their sudden disappearance, were all the subjects of much questioning and answer. Finally, Kit informed the gentleman that the premises were now to let, and that a board upon the door referred all inquirers to Mr. Sampson Brass, Solicitor, of Bevis Marks, from whom he might perhaps learn some further particulars.

"Not by inquiry," said the gentleman shaking his head. "I live there."

"Live at Brass's the attorney's!" cried Mr. Witherden in some surprise, having professional knowledge of the gentleman in question.

"Ay," was the reply. "I entered upon his lodgings t'other day, chiefly because I had seen this very board. It matters little to me where I live, and I had a desperate hope that some intelligence might be cast in my way there, which would not reach me elsewhere. Yes, I live at Brass's—more shame for me, I suppose?"

"That's a mere matter of opinion," said the Notary, shrugging his shoulders. "He is looked upon as rather a doubtful character."

"Doubtful?" echoed the other. "I am glad to hear there's any doubt about it. I supposed that had been thoroughly settled, long ago. But will you let me speak a word or two with you in private?"

Mr. Witherden consenting, they walked into that gentleman's private closet, and remained there in close conversation for some quarter of an hour, when they returned into the outer office. The stranger had left his hat in Mr. Witherden's room, and seemed to have established himself in this short interval on quite a friendly footing.

"I'll not detain you any longer now," he said, putting a crown into Kit's hand, and looking towards the Notary. "You shall hear from me again. Not a word of this, you know, except to your master and mistress."

"Mother, sir, would be glad to know—" said Kit, faltering.

"Glad to know what?"

"Anything—so that it was no harm—about Miss Nell."

"Would she? Well then, you may tell her if she can keep a secret. But mind, not a word of this to anybody else. Don't forget that. Be particular."

"I'll take care, sir," said Kit. "Thankee, sir, and good morning."

Now, it happened that the gentleman, in his anxiety to impress upon Kit that he was not to tell anybody what had passed between them, followed him out to the door to repeat his caution, and it further happened that at that moment the eyes of Mr. Richard Swiveller were turned in that direction, and beheld his mysterious friend and Kit together.

It was quite an accident, and the way in which it came about was this. Mr. Chuckster, being a gentleman of a cultivated taste and refined spirit, was one of that Lodge of Glorious Apollos whereof Mr. Swiveller was Perpetual Grand. Mr. Swiveller, passing through the street in the execution of some Brazen errand, and beholding one of his Glorious Brotherhood intently gazing on a pony, crossed over to give him that fraternal greeting with which Perpetual Grands are, by the very constitution of their office, bound to cheer and encourage their disciples. He had scarcely bestowed upon him his blessing, and followed it with a general remark touching the present state and prospects of the weather, when lifting up his eyes he beheld the single gentleman of Bevis Marks in earnest conversation with Christopher Nubbles.

"Hallo!" said Dick, "who *is* that?"

"He called to see my Governor this morning," replied Mr. Chuckster; "and beyond that I don't know him from Adam."

"At least you know his name?" said Dick.

To which Mr. Chuckster replied, with an elevation of speech becoming a Glorious Apollo, that he was "everlastingly blessed" if he did.

"All I know, my dear feller," said Mr. Chuckster, running his fingers through his hair, "is, that he is the cause of my having stood here twenty minutes, for which I hate him with a mortal and undying hatred, and would pursue him to the confines of eternity, if I could afford the time."

While they were thus discoursing, the subject of their conversation (who had not appeared to recognise Mr. Richard Swiveller) re-entered the house, and Kit came down the steps and joined them: to whom Mr. Swiveller again propounded his inquiry with no better success.

"He is a very nice gentleman, sir," said Kit, "and that's all *I* know about him."

Mr. Chuckster waxed wroth at this answer, and without applying the remark to any particular case, mentioned as a general truth that it was expedient to break the heads of Snobs, and to tweak their noses. Without expressing his concurrence in this sentiment, Mr. Swiveller after a few moments of abstraction inquired which way Kit was driving, and, being informed, declared it was his way, and that he would trespass on him for a lift. Kit would gladly have declined the proffered honour, but as Mr. Swiveller was already established in the seat beside him, he had no means of doing so otherwise than by a forcible ejectment, and therefore drove briskly off—so briskly indeed as to cut short the leave-taking between Mr. Chuckster and his Grand Master, and to occasion the former gentleman some inconvenience from having his corns squeezed by the impatient pony.

As Whisker was tired of standing, and Mr. Swiveller was kind enough to stimulate him still further by shrill whistles, and various sporting cries, they rattled off at too sharp a pace to admit of much conversation, especially as the pony, incensed by Mr. Swiveller's admonitions, took a particular fancy for the lamp-posts and cart-wheels, and evinced a strong desire to run on the pavement and rasp himself against brick walls. It was not, therefore, until they had arrived at the stable, and the chaise had been extricated from a very small doorway, into which the pony dragged it under the impression that he would take it along with him into his usual stall, that Mr.

Swiveller found time to talk.

"It's hard work," said Richard. "What do you say to some beer?"

Kit at first declined, but presently consented, and they adjourned to the neighbouring bar together.

"We'll drink our friend what's-his-name," said Dick, holding up the bright frothy pot; "—that was talking to you this morning, you know—I know him—a good fellow, but eccentric—very—here's what's-his-name!"

Kit pledged him.

"He lives in my house," said Dick; "at least in the house occupied by the firm in which I'm a sort of a—of a managing partner—a difficult fellow to get anything out of, but we like him—we like him."

"I must be going, sir, if you please," said Kit, moving away.

"Don't be in a hurry, Christopher," replied his patron, "we'll drink your mother."

"Thank you, sir."

"An excellent woman, that mother of yours, Christopher," said Mr. Swiveller. "Who ran to catch me when I fell, and kissed the place to make it well? My mother. A charming woman. He's a liberal sort of fellow. We must get him to do something for your mother. Does he know her, Christopher?"

Kit shook his head, and glancing slyly at his questioner, thanked him, and made off before he could say another word.

"Humph!" said Mr. Swiveller pondering, "this is queer. Nothing but mysteries in connexion with Brass's house. I'll keep my own counsel, however. Everybody and anybody has been in my confidence as yet, but now I think I'll set up in business for myself. Queer—very queer!"

After pondering deeply and with a face of exceeding wisdom for some time, Mr. Swiveller drank some more of the beer, and summoning a small boy who had been watching his proceedings, poured forth the few remaining drops as a libation upon the gravel, and bade him carry the empty vessel to the bar with his compliments, and above all things to lead a sober and temperate life, and abstain from all intoxicating and exciting liquors. Having given him this piece of moral advice for his trouble (which, as he wisely observed, was far better than half-pence) the Perpetual Grand Master of the Glorious Apollos thrust his hands into his pockets and sauntered away; still pondering as he went.

CHAPTER XXXIX

ALL that day, though he waited for Mr. Abel until the evening, Kit kept clear of his mother's house, determined not to anticipate by the slightest approach the pleasures of the morrow, but to let them come in their full rush of delight; for to-morrow was the great and long-looked-for epoch in his life—to-morrow was the end of his first quarter—the day of receiving for the first time one fourth part of his annual income of Six Pounds in one vast sum of Thirty Shillings—to-morrow was to be a half-holiday devoted to a whirl of entertainments, and little Jacob was to know what oysters meant, and to see a play.

All manner of incidents combined in favour of the occasion: not only had Mr. and Mrs. Garland forewarned him that they intended to make no deduction for his outfit from the great amount, but to pay it him unbroken in all its gigantic grandeur; not only had the unknown gentleman increased the stock by the sum of five shillings, which was a perfect godsend and in itself a fortune; not only had these things come to pass which nobody could have calculated upon, or in their wildest dreams have hoped; but it was Barbara's quarter too—Barbara's quarter, that very day—and Barbara had a half-holiday as well as Kit, and Barbara's mother was going to make one of the party, and to take tea with Kit's mother, and cultivate her acquaintance.

To be sure Kit looked out of his window very early that morning to see which way the clouds were flying, and to be sure Barbara would have been at hers too if she had not sat up so late over-night, starching and ironing small pieces of muslin, and crimping them into frills, and sewing them on to other pieces to form magnificent wholes for next day's wear. But they were both up very early for all that, and had small appetites for breakfast and less for dinner, and were in a state of great excitement when Barbara's mother came in with astonishing accounts of the fineness of the weather out of doors (but with a very large umbrella notwithstanding, for people like Barbara's mother seldom make holiday without one), and when the bell rang for them to go up stairs and receive their quarter's money in gold and silver.

Well, wasn't Mr. Garland kind when he said "Christopher, here's your money, and you have earned it well;" and wasn't Mrs. Garland kind when she said "Barbara, here's yours, and I'm much pleased with you;" and didn't Kit sign his name bold to his receipt, and didn't Barbara sign her name all a trembling to hers; and wasn't it beautiful to see how Mrs. Garland poured out Barbara's mother a glass of wine; and didn't Barbara's mother speak up when she said "Here's blessing you, ma'am, as a good lady, and you, sir, as a good gentleman, and Barbara, my love to you, and here's towards you, Mr. Christopher;" and wasn't she as long drinking it as if it had been a tumblerful; and didn't she look genteel standing there with her gloves on; and wasn't there plenty of laughing and talking among them as they reviewed all these matters upon the top of the coach; and didn't they pity the people who hadn't got a holiday!

But Kit's mother, again—wouldn't anybody have supposed she had come of a good stock and been a lady all her life? There she was, quite ready to receive them, with a display of tea-things that might have warmed the heart of a china-shop; and little Jacob and the baby in such a state of perfection that their clothes looked as good as new, though Heaven knows they were old enough! Didn't she say before they had sat down five minutes that Barbara's mother was exactly the sort of lady she expected, and didn't Barbara's mother say that Kit's mother was the very picture of what *she* had expected, and didn't Kit's mother compliment Barbara's mother on Barbara, and didn't Barbara's mother compliment Kit's mother on Kit, and wasn't Barbara herself quite fascinated with little Jacob, and did ever a child show off when he was wanted, as that child did, or make such friends as he made?

"And we are both widows too!" said Barbara's mother. "We must have been made to know each other."

"I haven't a doubt about it," returned Mrs. Nubbles. "And what a pity it is we didn't know each other sooner."

"But then you know it's such a pleasure," said Barbara's mother, "to have it brought about by one's son and daughter, that it's fully made up for, now, an't it?"

To this, Kit's mother yielded her full assent, and tracing things back from effects to causes, they naturally reverted to their deceased husbands, respecting whose lives, deaths, and burials, they compared notes, and discovered sundry circumstances that tallied with wonderful exactness; such as Barbara's father having been exactly four years and ten months older than Kit's father, and one of them having died on a Wednesday and the other on a Thursday, and both of them having been of a very fine make and remarkably good-looking, with other extraordinary coincidences. These recollections being of a kind calculated to cast a shadow on the brightness of the holiday, Kit diverted the conversation to general topics, and they were soon in great force again, and as merry as before. Among other things, Kit told them about his old place, and the extraordinary beauty of Nell (of whom he had talked to Barbara a thousand times already); but the last-named circumstance failed to interest his hearers to anything like the extent he had supposed, and even his mother said (looking accidentally at Barbara at the same time) that there was no doubt Miss Nell was very pretty, but she was but a child after all, and there were many young women quite as pretty as she; and Barbara mildly observed that she should think so, and that she never could help believing Mr. Christopher must be under a mistake—which Kit wondered at very much, not being able to conceive what reason she had for doubting him. Barbara's mother too observed that it was very common for young folks to change at about fourteen or fifteen, and whereas they had been pretty before, to grow up quite plain; which truth she illustrated by many forcible examples, especially one of a young man who, being a builder with great prospects, had been particular in his attentions to Barbara, but whom Barbara would have nothing to say to; which (though everything happened for the best) she almost thought was a pity. Kit said he thought so too, and so he did honestly, and he wondered what made Barbara so silent all at once, and why his mother looked at him as if he shouldn't have said it.

However, it was high time now to be thinking of the play; for which great preparation was required in the way of shawls and bonnets, not to mention one handkerchief full of oranges and another of apples, which took some time tying up, in consequence of the fruit having a tendency to roll out at the corners. At length everything was ready, and they went off very fast; Kit's mother carrying the baby, who was dreadfully wide awake, and Kit holding little Jacob in one hand, and escorting Barbara with the other—a state of things which occasioned the two mothers, who walked behind, to declare that they looked quite family folks, and caused Barbara to blush and say, "Now don't, mother!" But Kit said she had no call to mind what they said; and indeed she need not have had, if she had known how very far from Kit's thoughts any love-making was. Poor Barbara!

At last they got to the theatre, which was Astley's: and in some two minutes after they had reached the yet unopened door, little Jacob was squeezed flat, and the baby had received divers concussions, and Barbara's mother's umbrella had been carried several yards off and passed back to her over the shoulders of the people, and Kit had hit a man on the head with the handkerchief of apples for "scrowdging" his parent with unnecessary violence, and there was a great uproar. But when they were once past the pay-place and tearing away for very life with their checks in their hands; and above all, when they were fairly in the theatre, and seated in such places that they couldn't have had better if they had picked them out and taken them beforehand; all this was looked upon as quite a capital joke, and an essential part of the entertainment.

Dear, dear, what a place it looked, that Astley's! with all the paint, gilding, and looking-glass; the vague smell of horses suggestive of coming wonders; the curtain that hid such gorgeous mysteries; the clean white sawdust down in the circus; the company coming in and taking their places; the fiddlers looking carelessly up at them while they tuned their instruments, as if they didn't want the play to begin, and knew it all beforehand! What a glow was that which burst upon them all, when that long, clear, brilliant row of lights came slowly up; and what the feverish excitement when the little bell rang and the music began in good earnest, with strong parts for the drums, and sweet effects for the triangles! Well might Barbara's mother say to Kit's mother that the gallery was the place to see from, and wonder it wasn't much dearer than the boxes; and well might Barbara feel doubtful whether to laugh or cry, in her flutter of delight.

Then the play itself! the horses which little Jacob believed from the first to be alive, and the ladies and gentlemen of whose reality he could be by no means persuaded, having never seen or heard anything at all like them—the firing, which made Barbara wink—the forlorn lady, who made her cry—the tyrant, who made her tremble—the man who sang the song with the lady's-maid and danced the

'Astley's.'

chorus, who made her laugh—the pony who reared up on his hind legs when he saw the murderer, and wouldn't hear of walking on all fours again until he was taken into custody—the clown who ventured on such familiarities with the military man in boots—the lady who jumped over the nine-and-twenty ribbons and came down safe upon the horse's back—everything was delightful, splendid, and surprising. Little Jacob applauded till his hands were sore; Kit cried "ankor" at the end of everything, the three-act piece included; and Barbara's mother beat her umbrella on the floor, in her ecstasies, until it was nearly worn down to the gingham.

In the midst of all these fascinations, Barbara's thoughts seemed to have been still running upon what Kit had said at tea-time; for when they were coming out of the play, she asked him, with an hysterical simper, if Miss Nell was as handsome as the lady who jumped over the ribbons.

"As handsome as *her*?" said Kit. "Double as handsome."

"Oh, Christopher! I'm sure she was the beautifullest creature ever was," said Barbara.

"Nonsense!" returned Kit. "She was well enough, I don't deny that; but think how she was dressed and painted, and what a difference that made. Why *you* are a good deal better-looking than her, Barbara."

"Oh, Christopher!" said Barbara, looking down.

"You are, any day," said Kit,—"and so's your mother."

Poor Barbara!

What was all this though—even all this—to the extraordinary dissipation that ensued, when Kit, walking into an oyster-shop as bold as if he lived there, and not so much as looking at the counter or the man behind it, led his party into a box—a private box, fitted up with red curtains, white table-cloth, and cruet-stand complete—and ordered a fierce gentleman with whiskers, who acted as waiter and called him, him Christopher Nubbles, "sir," to bring three dozen of his largest-sized oysters, and to look sharp about it! Yes, Kit told this gentleman to look sharp, and he not only said he would look sharp, but he actually did, and presently came running back with the newest loaves, and the freshest butter, and the largest oysters, ever seen. Then said Kit to this gentleman, "a pot of beer," —just so—and the gentleman, instead of replying, "Sir, did you address that language to me?" only said, "Pot o' beer, sir? Yes, sir," and went off and fetched it, and put it on the table in a small de-canter-stand, like those which blind men's dogs carry about the streets in their mouths to catch the half-pence in; and both Kit's mother and Barbara's mother declared as he turned away that he was one of the slimmest and gracefullest young men she had ever looked upon.

Then they fell to work upon the supper in earnest; and there was Barbara, that foolish Barbara, declaring that she couldn't eat more than two, and wanting more pressing than you would believe before she would eat four; though her mother and Kit's mother made up for it pretty well, and ate and laughed and enjoyed themselves so thoroughly that it did Kit good to see them, and made him laugh and eat likewise from strong sympathy. But the greatest miracle of the night was little Jacob, who ate oysters as if he had been born and bred to the business, sprinkled the pepper and the vinegar with a discretion beyond his years, and afterwards built a grotto on the table with the shells. There was the baby too, who had never closed an eye all night, but had sat as good as gold, trying to force a large orange into his mouth, and gazing intently at the lights in the chandelier—there he was, sitting up in his mother's lap, staring at the gas without winking, and making indentations in his soft visage with an oyster-shell, to that degree that a heart of iron must have loved him! In short, there never was a more successful supper; and when Kit ordered in a glass of something hot to finish with, and proposed Mr. and Mrs. Garland before sending it round, there were not six happier people in all the world.

But all happiness has an end—hence the chief pleasure of its next beginning—and as it was now growing late, they agreed it was time to turn their faces homewards. So, after going a little out of their way to see Barbara and Barbara's mother safe to a friend's house where they were to pass the night, Kit and his mother left them at the door, with an early appointment for returning to Finchley next morning, and a great many plans for next quarter's enjoyment. Then Kit took little Jacob on his back, and giving his arm to his mother, and a kiss to the baby, they all trudged merrily home together.

CHAPTER XL

FULL of that vague kind of penitence which holidays awaken next morning, Kit turned out at sunrise, and, with his faith in last night's enjoyments a little shaken by cool daylight and the return to everyday duties and occupations, went to meet Barbara and her mother at the appointed place. And being careful not to awaken any of the little household, who were yet resting from their unusual fatigues, Kit left his money on the chimney-piece, with an inscription in chalk calling his mother's attention to the circumstance, and informing her that it came from her dutiful son; and went his way, with a heart something heavier than his pockets, but free from any very great oppression notwithstanding.

Oh these holidays! why will they leave us some regret! why cannot we push them back only a week or two in our memories, so as to put them at once at that convenient distance whence they may be regarded either with a calm indifference or a pleasant effort of recollection! why will they hang about us like the flavour of yesterday's wine, suggestive of headaches and lassitude, and those good intentions for the future, which under the earth form the everlasting pavement of a large estate, and upon it usually endure until dinner-time or thereabouts!

Who will wonder that Barbara had a headache, or that Barbara's mother was disposed to be cross, or that she slightly underrated Astley's, and thought the clown was older than they had taken him to be last night? Kit was not surprised to hear her say so—not he. He had already had a misgiving that the inconstant actors in that dazzling vision had been doing the same thing the night before last, and would do it again that night, and the next, and for weeks and months to come, though he would not be there. Such is the difference between yesterday and to-day. We are all going to the play, or coming home from it.

However, the Sun himself is weak when he first rises, and gathers strength and courage as the day gets on. By degrees, they began to recall circumstances more and more pleasant in their nature, until, what between talking, walking, and laughing, they reached Finchley in such good heart, that Barbara's mother declared she never felt less tired or in better spirits, and so said Kit. Barbara had been silent all the way, but she said so too. Poor little Barbara! she was very quiet.

They were at home in such good time that Kit had rubbed down the pony and made him as spruce as a racehorse, before Mr. Garland came down to breakfast; which punctual and industrious conduct the old lady, and the old gentleman, and Mr. Abel, highly extolled. At his usual hour (or rather at his usual minute and second, for he was the soul of punctuality) Mr. Abel walked out, to be overtaken by the London coach, and Kit and the old gentleman went to work in the garden.

This was not the least pleasant of Kit's employments, for on a fine day they were quite a family party; the old lady sitting hard by with her work-basket on a little table; the old gentleman digging, or pruning, or clipping about with a large pair of shears, or helping Kit in some way or other with great assiduity; and Whisker looking on from his paddock in placid contemplation of them all. To-day they were to trim the grape-vine, so Kit mounted half-way up a short ladder, and began to snip and hammer away, while the old gentleman, with a great interest in his proceedings, handed up the nails and shreds of cloth as he wanted them. The old lady and Whisker looked on as usual.

"Well, Christopher," said Mr. Garland, "and so you have made a new friend, eh?"

"I beg your pardon, sir?" returned Kit, looking down from the ladder.

"You have made a new friend, I hear from Mr. Abel," said the old gentleman, "at the office?"

"Oh—yes, sir, yes. He behaved very handsome, sir."

"I'm glad to hear it," returned the old gentleman with a smile. "He is disposed to behave more handsomely still, though, Christopher."

"Indeed, sir! It's very kind in him, but I don't want him to, I'm sure," said Kit, hammering stoutly at an obdurate nail.

"He is rather anxious," pursued the old gentleman, "to have you in his own service—take care what you're doing, or you will fall down and hurt yourself."

"To have me in his service, sir!" cried Kit, who had stopped short in his work and faced about upon the ladder like some dexterous tumbler. "Why, sir, I don't think he can be in earnest when he says that."

"Oh! But he is indeed," said Mr. Garland. "And he has told Mr. Abel so."

"I never heard of such a thing!" muttered Kit, looking ruefully at his master and mistress. "I wonder at him; that I do."

"You see, Christopher," said Mr. Garland, "this is a point of much importance to you, and you should understand and consider it in that light. This gentleman is able to give you more money than I—not, I hope, to carry through the various relations of master and servant, more kindness and confidence, but certainly, Christopher, to give you more money."

"Well," said Kit, "after that, sir——"

"Wait a moment," interposed Mr. Garland. "That is not all. You were a very faithful servant to your old employers, as I understand, and should this gentleman recover them, as it is his purpose to attempt doing by every means in his power, I have no doubt that you, being in his service, would meet with your reward. Besides," added the old gentleman with stronger emphasis, "besides having the pleasure of being again brought into communication with those to whom you seem to be so very strongly and disinterestedly attached. You must think of all this, Christopher, and not be rash or hasty in your choice."

Kit did suffer one twinge, one momentary pang in keeping the resolution he had already formed, when this last argument passed swiftly into his thoughts, and conjured up the realisation of all his hopes and fancies. But it was gone in a minute, and he sturdily rejoined that the gentleman must look out for somebody else, as he did think he might have done at first.

"He has no right to think that I'd be led away to go to him, sir," said Kit, turning round again after half a minute's hammering. "Does he think I'm a fool?"

"He may, perhaps, Christopher, if you refuse his offer," said Mr. Garland gravely.

"Then let him, sir," retorted Kit; "what do I care, sir, what he thinks? why should I care for his thinking, sir, when I know that I should be a fool, and worse than a fool, sir, to leave the kindest master and mistress that ever was or can be, who took me out of the streets a very poor and hungry lad indeed—poorer and hungrier perhaps than ever you think for, sir—to go to him or anybody? If Miss Nell was to come back, ma'am," added Kit, turning suddenly to his mistress, "why that would be another thing, and perhaps if *she* wanted me, I might ask you now and then to let me work for her when all was done at home. But when she comes back, I see now that she'll be rich as old master always said she would, and being a rich young lady, what could she want of me? No, no," added Kit, shaking his head sorrowfully, "she'll never want me any more, and bless her, I hope she never may, though I *should* like to see her too!"

Here Kit drove a nail into the wall, very hard—much harder than was necessary—and having done so, faced about again.

"There's the pony, sir," said Kit—"Whisker, ma'am (and he knows so well I'm talking about him that he begins to neigh directly, sir),—would he let anybody come near him but me, ma'am? Here's the garden, sir, and Mr. Abel, ma'am. Would Mr. Abel part with me, sir, or is there anybody that could be fonder of the garden, ma'am? It would break mother's heart, sir, and even little Jacob would have sense enough to cry his eyes out, ma'am, if he thought Mr. Abel could wish to part with me so soon, after having told me only the other day, that he hoped we might be together for years to come——"

There is no telling how long Kit might have stood upon the ladder, addressing his master and mistress by turns, and generally turning towards the wrong person, if Barbara had not at that moment come running up to say that a messenger from the office had brought a note, which, with an expression of some surprise at Kit's oratorical appearance, she put into her master's hand.

"Oh!" said the old gentleman after reading it, "ask the messenger to walk this way." Barbara tripping off to do as she was bid, he turned to Kit and said that they would not pursue the subject any further, and that Kit could not be more unwilling to part with them, than they would be to part with Kit; a sentiment which the old lady very generously echoed.

"At the same time, Christopher," added Mr. Garland, glancing at the note in his hand, "if the gentleman should want to borrow you now and then for an hour or so, or even a day or so, at a time, we must consent to lend you, and you must consent to be lent.—Oh! here is the young gentleman. How do you do, sir?"

This salutation was addressed to Mr. Chuckster, who, with his hat extremely on one side, and his hair a long way beyond it, came swaggering up the walk.

"Hope I see you well, sir," returned that gentleman. "Hope I see *you* well, ma'am. Charming box this, sir. Delicious country, to be sure."

"You want to take Kit back with you, I find?" observed Mr. Garland.

"I have got a chariot-cab waiting on purpose," replied the clerk. "A very spanking grey in that cab, sir, if you're a judge of horse-flesh."

Declining to inspect the spanking grey, on the plea that he was but poorly acquainted with such matters, and would but imperfectly appreciate his beauties, Mr. Garland invited Mr. Chuckster to partake of a slight repast in the way of lunch, and that gentleman readily consenting, certain cold viands, flanked with ale and wine, were speedily prepared for his refreshment.

At this repast, Mr. Chuckster exerted his utmost abilities to enchant his entertainers, and impress them with a conviction of the mental superiority of those who dwelt in town; with which view he led the discourse to the small scandal of the day, in which he was justly considered by his friends to shine prodigiously. Thus, he was in a condition to relate the exact circumstances of the difference between the Marquis of Mizzler and Lord Bobby, which it appeared originated in a disputed bottle of champagne, and not in a pigeon-pie, as erroneously reported in the newspapers; neither had Lord Bobby said to the Marquis of Mizzler, "Mizzler, one of us two tells a lie, and I'm not the man," as incorrectly stated by the same authorities; but "Mizzler, you know where I'm to be found, and damme, sir, find me if you want me"—which, of course, entirely changed the aspect of this interesting question, and placed it in a very different light. He also acquainted them with the precise amount of the income guaranteed by the Duke of Thigsberry to Violetta Stetta of the Italian Opera, which it appeared was payable quarterly, and not half-yearly, as the public had been given to understand, and which was *ex*clusive, and not *in*clusive (as had been monstrously stated), of jewellery, perfumery, hair-powder for five footmen, and two daily changes of kid-gloves for a page. Having entreated the old lady and gentleman to set their minds at rest upon these absorbing points, for they might rely on his statement being the correct one, Mr. Chuckster entertained them with theatrical chit-chat and the court circular; and so wound up a brilliant and fascinating conversation which he had maintained alone, and without any assistance whatever, for upwards of three-quarters of an hour.

"And now that the nag has got his wind again," said Mr. Chuckster, rising in a graceful manner, "I'm afraid I must cut my stick."

Neither Mr. nor Mrs. Garland offered any opposition to his tearing himself away (feeling, no doubt, that such a man could ill be spared from his proper sphere of action), and therefore Mr. Chuckster and Kit were shortly afterwards upon their way to town; Kit being perched upon the box of the cabriolet beside the driver, and Mr. Chuckster seated in solitary state inside, with one of his boots sticking out at each of the front windows.

When they reached the Notary's house, Kit followed into the office, and was desired by Mr. Abel to sit down and wait, for the gentleman who wanted him had gone out, and perhaps might not return for some time. This anticipation was strictly verified, for Kit had had his dinner, and his tea, and had read all the light matter in the Law-List, and the Post-Office Directory, and had fallen asleep a great many times, before the gentleman whom he had seen before, came in; which he did at last in a very great hurry.

He was closeted with Mr. Witherden for some little time, and Mr. Abel had been called in to assist at the conference, before Kit, wondering very much what he was wanted for, was summoned to attend them.

"Christopher," said the gentleman, turning to him directly he entered the room, "I have found your old master and young mistress."

"No, sir! Have you, though?" returned Kit, his eyes sparkling with delight. "Where are they, sir? How are they, sir? Are they—are they near here?"

"A long way from here," returned the gentleman, shaking his head. "But I am going away to-night to bring them back, and I want you to go with me."

"Me, sir," cried Kit, full of joy and surprise.

"The place," said the strange gentleman, turning thoughtfully to the Notary, "indicated by this man of the dogs, is—how far from here—sixty miles?"

"From sixty to seventy."

"Humph! If we travel post all night, we shall reach there in good time to-morrow morning. Now, the only question is, as they will not know me, and the child, God bless her, would think that any stranger pursuing them had a design upon her grandfather's liberty,—can I do better than take this lad, whom they both know and will readily remember, as an assurance to them of my friendly intentions?"

"Certainly not," replied the Notary. "Take Christopher by all means."

"I beg your pardon, sir," said Kit, who had listened to this discourse with a lengthening countenance, "but if that's the reason, I'm afraid I should do more harm than good—Miss Nell, sir, *she* knows me, and would trust in me, I am sure; but old master—I don't know why, gentlemen; nobody does—would not bear me in his sight after he had been ill, and Miss Nell herself told me that I must not go near him or let him see me any more. I should spoil all that you were doing if I went, I'm afraid. I'd give the world to go, but you had better not take me, sir."

"Another difficulty!" cried the impetuous gentleman. "Was ever man so beset as I? Is there nobody else that knew them, nobody else in whom they had any confidence? Solitary as their lives were, is there no one person who would serve my purpose?"

"*Is* there, Christopher?" said the Notary.

"Not one, sir," replied Kit.—"Yes, though—there's my mother."

"Did they know her?" said the single gentleman.

"Know her, sir! why, she was always coming backwards and forwards. They were as kind to her as they were to me. Bless you, sir, she expected they'd come back to her house."

"Then where the devil is the woman?" said the impatient gentleman, catching up his hat. "Why isn't she here? Why is that woman always out of the way when she is most wanted?"

In a word, the single gentleman was bursting out of the office, bent upon laying violent hands on Kit's mother, forcing her into a post-chaise, and carrying her off, when this novel kind of abduction was with some difficulty prevented by the joint efforts of Mr. Abel and the Notary, who restrained him by dint of their remonstrances, and persuaded him to sound Kit upon the probability of her being able and willing to undertake such a journey on so short a notice.

This occasioned some doubts on the part of Kit, and some violent demonstrations on that of the single gentleman, and a great many soothing speeches on that of the Notary and Mr. Abel. The upshot of the business was, that Kit, after weighing the matter in his mind and considering it carefully, promised, on behalf of his mother, that she should be ready within two hours from that time to undertake the expedition, and engaged to produce her in that place, in all respects equipped and prepared for the journey, before the specified period had expired.

Having given this pledge, which was rather a bold one, and not particularly easy of redemption, Kit lost no time in sallying forth, and taking measures for its immediate fulfilment.

CHAPTER XLI

KIT made his way through the crowded streets, dividing the stream of people, dashing across the busy roadways, diving into lanes and alleys, and stopping or turning aside for nothing, until he came in front of the Old Curiosity Shop, when he came to a stand; partly from habit and partly from being out of breath.

It was a gloomy autumn evening, and he thought the old place had never looked so dismal as in its dreary twilight. The windows broken, the rusty sashes rattling in their frames, the deserted house a dull barrier dividing the glaring lights and bustle of the street into two long lines, and standing in the midst, cold, dark, and empty,— presented a cheerless spectacle which mingled harshly with the bright prospects the boy had been building up for its late inmates, and came like a disappointment or misfortune. Kit would have had a good fire roaring up the empty chimneys, lights sparkling and shining through the windows, people moving briskly to and fro, voices in cheerful conversation, something in unison with the new hopes that were astir. He had not expected that the house would wear any different aspect—had known indeed that it could not— but coming upon it in the midst of eager thoughts and expectations, it checked the current in its flow, and darkened it with a mournful shadow.

Kit, however, fortunately for himself, was not learned enough or contemplative enough to be troubled with presages of evil afar off, and, having no mental spectacles to assist his vision in this respect, saw nothing but the dull house, which jarred uncomfortably upon his previous thoughts. So, almost wishing that he had not passed it, though hardly knowing why, he hurried on again, making up by his increased speed for the few moments he had lost.

"Now, if she should be out," thought Kit, as he approached the poor dwelling of his mother, "and I not able to find her, this impatient gentleman would be in a pretty taking. And sure enough there's no light, and the door's fast. Now, God forgive me for saying so, but if this is Little Bethel's doing, I wish Little Bethel was—was farther off," said Kit checking himself, and knocking at the door.

A second knock brought no reply from within the house; but caused a woman over the way to look out and inquire who that was, awanting Mrs. Nubbles.

"Me," said Kit. "She's at—at Little Bethel, I suppose?"—getting out the name of the obnoxious conventicle with some reluctance, and laying a spiteful emphasis upon the words.

The neighbour nodded assent.

"Then pray tell me where it is," said Kit, "for I have come on a pressing matter, and must fetch her out, even if she was in the pulpit."

It was not very easy to procure a direction to the fold in question, as none of the neighbours were of the flock that resorted thither, and few knew anything more of it than the name. At last a gossip of Mrs. Nubbles's, who had accompanied her to chapel on one or two occasions when a comfortable cup of tea had preceded her devotions, furnished the needful information, which Kit had no sooner obtained than he started off again.

Little Bethel might have been nearer, and might have been in a straighter road, though in that case the reverend gentleman who presided over its congregation would have lost his favourite allusion to the crooked ways by which it was approached, and which enabled him to liken it to Paradise itself, in contradistinction to the parish church and the broad thoroughfare leading thereunto. Kit found it at last after some trouble, and pausing at the door to take breath that he might enter with becoming decency, passed into the chapel.

It was not badly named in one respect, being in truth a particularly little Bethel—a Bethel of the smallest dimensions—with a small number of small pews, and a small pulpit, in which a small gentleman (by trade a Shoemaker, and by calling a Divine) was delivering in a by no means small voice, a by no means small sermon, judging of its dimensions by the condition of his audience, which, if their gross amount were but small, comprised a still smaller number of hearers, as the majority were slumbering.

Among these was Kit's mother, who, finding it matter of extreme difficulty to keep her eyes open after the fatigues of last night, and feeling their inclination to close strongly backed and seconded by the arguments of the preacher, had yielded to the drowsiness that overpowered her, and fallen asleep; though not so soundly but that she could from time to time utter a slight and almost inaudible groan, as if in recognition of the orator's doctrines. The baby in her arms was as fast asleep as she; and little Jacob, whose youth prevented him from recognising in this prolonged spiritual nourishment anything half as interesting as oysters, was alternately very fast asleep and very wide awake, as his inclination to slumber, or his terror of being personally alluded to in the discourse, gained the mastery over him.

"And now I'm here," thought Kit, gliding into the nearest empty pew which was opposite his mother's, and on the other side of the little aisle, "how am I ever to get at her, or persuade her to come out! I might as well be twenty miles off. She'll never wake till it's all over, and there goes the clock again! If he would but leave off for a minute, or if they'd only sing!"—

But there was little encouragement to believe that either event would happen for a couple of hours to come. The preacher went on telling them what he meant to convince them of before he had done, and it was clear that if he only kept to one-half of his promises and forgot the other, he was good for that time at least.

In his desperation and restlessness Kit cast his eyes about the chapel, and happening to let them fall upon a little seat in front of the clerk's desk, could scarcely believe them when they showed him —Quilp!

He rubbed them twice or thrice, but still they insisted that Quilp was there, and there indeed he was, sitting with his hands upon his knees, and his hat between them on a little wooden bracket, with the accustomed grin upon his dirty face, and his eyes fixed upon the ceiling. He certainly did not glance at Kit or at his mother, and appeared utterly unconscious of their presence; still Kit could not help feeling directly that the attention of the sly little fiend was fastened upon them, and upon nothing else.

But astounded as he was by the apparition of the dwarf among the Little Bethelites, and not free from a misgiving that it was the forerunner of some trouble or annoyance, he was compelled to subdue his wonder and to take active measures for the withdrawal of his parent, as the evening was now creeping on, and the matter grew serious. Therefore the next time little Jacob woke, Kit set himself to attract his wandering attention, and this not being a very difficult task (one sneeze effected it), he signed to him to rouse his mother.

Ill luck would have it, however, that just then the preacher, in a forcible exposition of one head of his discourse, leaned over upon the pulpit desk so that very little more of him than his legs remained inside; and, while he made vehement gestures with his right hand, and held on with his left, stared, or seemed to stare, straight into little Jacob's eyes, threatening him by his strained look and attitude —so it appeared to the child—that if he so much as moved a muscle, he, the preacher, would be literally, and not figuratively, "down upon him," that instant. In this fearful state of things, distracted by the sudden appearance of Kit, and fascinated by the eyes of the preacher, the miserable Jacob sat bolt upright, wholly incapable of motion, strongly disposed to cry but afraid to do so, and returning his pastor's gaze until his infant eyes seemed starting from their sockets.

"If I must do it openly, I must," thought Kit. With that, he walked softly out of his pew and into his mother's, and as Mr. Swiveller would have observed if he had been present, "collared" the baby without speaking a word.

"Hush, mother!" whispered Kit. "Come along with me, I've got something to tell you."

"Where am I?" said Mrs. Nubbles.

"In this blessed Little Bethel," returned her son, peevishly.

"Blessed indeed!" cried Mrs. Nubbles, catching at the word. "Oh, Christopher, how have I been edified this night!"

"Yes, yes, I know," said Kit hastily; "but come along, mother, everybody's looking at us. Don't make a noise—bring Jacob— that's right."

"Stay, Satan, stay!" cried the preacher, as Kit was moving off.

"The gentleman says you're to stay, Christopher," whispered his mother.

"Stay, Satan, stay!" roared the preacher again. "Tempt not the woman that doth incline her ear to thee, but hearken to the voice of him that calleth. He hath a lamb from the fold!" cried the preacher, raising his voice still higher and pointing to the baby. "He beareth off a lamb, a precious lamb! He goeth about like a wolf in the night season, and inveigleth the tender lambs!"

Kit was the best-tempered fellow in the world, but considering this strong language, and being somewhat excited by the circumstances in which he was placed, he faced round to the pulpit with the baby in his arms, and replied aloud,

"No, I don't. He's my brother."

"He's *my* brother!" cried the preacher.

"He isn't," said Kit indignantly. "How can you say such a thing? —And don't call me names, if you please; what harm have I done? I shouldn't have come to take 'em away unless I was obliged, you may depend upon that; and I wanted to do it very quiet, but you wouldn't let me. Now, you have the goodness to abuse Satan and them as much as you like, sir, and to let me alone if you please."

So saying, Kit marched out of the chapel, followed by his mother and little Jacob, and found himself in the open air, with an indistinct recollection of having seen the people wake up and look surprised, and of Quilp having remained throughout the interruption in his old attitude, without moving his eyes from the ceiling, or appearing to take the smallest notice of anything that passed.

"Oh Kit!" said his mother, with her handkerchief to her eyes, "what have you done! I never can go there again—never!"

"I'm glad of it, mother. What was there in the little bit of pleasure you took last night that made it necessary for you to be low-spirited and sorrowful to-night? That's the way you do. If you're happy or merry ever, you come here to say, along with that chap, that you're sorry for it. More shame for you, mother, I was going to say."

"Hush, dear!" said Mrs. Nubbles; "you don't mean what you say, I know, but you're talking sinfulness."

"Don't mean it? But I do mean it!" retorted Kit. "I don't believe, mother, that harmless cheerfulness and good-humour are thought greater sins in Heaven than shirt-collars are, and that those chaps are just about as right and sensible in putting down the one as in leaving off the other—that's my belief. But I won't say anything more about it, if you'll promise not to cry, that's all; and you take the baby that's a lighter weight, and give me little Jacob; and as we go along (which we must do pretty quick) I'll tell you the news I bring, which will surprise you a little, I can tell you. There—that's right. Now you look as if you'd never seen Little Bethel in all your life, as I hope you never will again; and here's the baby; and little Jacob, you get atop of my back and catch hold of me tight round the neck, and whenever a Little Bethel parson calls you a precious lamb or says your brother's one, you tell him it's the truest things he's said for a twelvemonth, and that if he'd got a little more of the lamb himself, and less of the mint-sauce—not being quite so sharp and sour over it—I should like him all the better. That's what you've got to say to *him*, Jacob."

Talking on in this way, half in jest and half in earnest, and cheering up his mother, the children, and himself, by the one simple process of determining to be in a good humour, Kit led them briskly forward; and on the road home he related what had passed at the Notary's house, and the purpose with which he had intruded on the solemnities of Little Bethel.

His mother was not a little startled on learning what service was required of her, and presently fell into a confusion of ideas, of which the most prominent were that it was a great honour and dignity to ride in a post-chaise, and that it was a moral impossibility to leave the children behind. But this objection, and a great many others, founded upon certain articles of dress being at the wash, and certain other articles having no existence in the wardrobe of Mrs. Nubbles, were overcome by Kit, who opposed to each and every of them, the pleasure of recovering Nell, and the delight it would be to bring her back in triumph.

"There's only ten minutes now, mother"—said Kit when they reached home. "There's a bandbox. Throw in what you want, and we'll be off directly."

To tell how Kit then hustled into the box all sorts of things which could by no remote contingency be wanted, and how he left out everything likely to be of the smallest use; how a neighbour was persuaded to come and stop with the children, and how the children at first cried dismally, and then laughed heartily on being promised all kinds of impossible and unheard-of toys; how Kit's mother wouldn't leave off kissing them, and how Kit couldn't make up his mind to be vexed with her for doing it; would take more time and room than we can spare. So, passing over all such matters, it is sufficient to say that within a few minutes after the two hours had expired, Kit and his mother arrived at the Notary's door, where a post-chaise was already waiting.

"With four horses I declare!" said Kit, quite aghast at the preparations. "Well you *are* going to do it, mother! Here she is, sir. Here's my mother. She's quite ready, sir."

"That's well"—returned the gentleman. "Now, don't be in a flutter, ma'am; you'll be taken great care of. Where's the box with the new clothing and necessaries for them?"

"Here it is," said the Notary. "In with it, Christopher."

"All right, sir," replied Kit. "Quite ready now, sir."

"Then come along," said the single gentleman. And thereupon he gave his arm to Kit's mother, handed her into the carriage as politely as you please, and took his seat beside her.

Up went the steps, bang went the door, round whirled the wheels, and off they rattled, with Kit's mother hanging out at one window waving a damp pocket-handkerchief and screaming out a great many messages to little Jacob and the baby, of which nobody heard a word.

Kit stood in the middle of the road, and looked after them with tears in his eyes—not brought there by the departure he witnessed, but by the return to which he looked forward. "They went away," he thought, "on foot with nobody to speak to them or say a kind word at parting, and they'll come back, drawn by four horses, with this rich gentleman for their friend, and all their troubles over! She'll forget that she taught me to write—"

Whatever Kit thought about after this, took some time to think of, for he stood gazing up at the lines of shining lamps, long after the chaise had disappeared, and did not return into the house until the Notary and Mr. Abel, who had themselves lingered outside till the sound of the wheels was no longer distinguishable, had several times wondered what could possibly detain him.

CHAPTER XLII

It behoves us to leave Kit for a while, thoughtful and expectant, and to follow the fortunes of little Nell; resuming the thread of the narrative at the point where it was left, some chapters back.

In one of those wanderings in the evening time, when, following the two sisters at a humble distance, she felt, in her sympathy with them and her recognition in the trials of something akin to her own loneliness of spirit, a comfort and consolation which made such moments a time of deep delight, though the softened pleasure they yielded was of that kind which lives and dies in tears—in one of those wanderings at the quiet hour of twilight, when sky, and earth, and air, and rippling water, and sound of distant bells, claimed kindred with the emotions of the solitary child, and inspired her with soothing thoughts, but not of a child's world or its easy joys—in one of those rambles which had now become her only pleasure or relief from care, light had faded into darkness and evening deepened into night, and still the young creature lingered in the gloom; feeling a companionship in Nature so serene and still, when noise of tongues and glare of garish lights would have been solitude indeed.

The sisters had gone home, and she was alone. She raised her eyes to the bright stars, looking down so mildly from the wide worlds of air, and, gazing on them, found new stars burst upon her view, and more beyond, and more beyond again, until the whole great expanse sparkled with shining spheres, rising higher and higher in immeasurable space, eternal in their numbers as in their changeless and incorruptible existence. She bent over the calm river, and saw them shining in the same majestic order as when the dove beheld them gleaming through the swollen waters, upon the mountain tops down far below, and dead mankind, a million fathoms deep.

The child sat silently beneath a tree, hushed in her very breath by the stillness of the night, and all its attendant wonders. The time and place awoke reflection, and she thought with a quiet hope—less hope, perhaps, than resignation—on the past, and present, and what was yet before her. Between the old man and herself there had come a gradual separation, harder to bear than any former sorrow. Every evening, and often in the day-time too, he was absent, alone; and although she well knew where he went, and why—too well from the constant drain upon her scanty purse and from his haggard looks—he evaded all inquiry, maintained a strict reserve, and even shunned her presence.

She sat meditating sorrowfully upon this change, and mingling it, as it were, with everything about her, when the distant church-clock bell struck nine. Rising at the sound, she retraced her steps, and turned thoughtfully towards the town.

She had gained a little wooden bridge, which, thrown across the stream, led into a meadow in her way, when she came suddenly upon a ruddy light, and looking forward more attentively, discerned that it proceeded from what appeared to be an encampment of gipsies, who had made a fire in one corner at no great distance from the path, and were sitting or lying round it. As she was too poor to have any fear of them, she did not alter her course (which, indeed, she could not have done without going a long way round), but quickened her pace a little, and kept straight on.

A movement of timid curiosity impelled her, when she approached the spot, to glance towards the fire. There was a form between it and her, the outline strongly developed against the light, which caused her to stop abruptly. Then, as if she had reasoned with herself and were assured that it could not be, or had satisfied herself that it was not that of the person she had supposed, she went on again.

But at that instant the conversation, whatever it was, which had been carrying on near this fire was resumed, and the tones of the voice that spoke—she could not distinguish words—sounded as familiar to her as her own.

She turned, and looked back. The person had been seated before, but was now in a standing posture, and leaning forward upon a stick on which he rested both hands. The attitude was no less familiar to her than the tone of voice had been. It *was* her grandfather.

Her first impulse was to call to him; her next to wonder who his associates could be, and for what purpose they were together. Some vague apprehension succeeded, and, yielding to the strong inclination it awakened, she drew nearer to the place; not advancing across the open field, however, but creeping towards it by the hedge.

In this way she advanced within a few feet of the fire, and standing among a few young trees, could both see and hear, without much danger of being observed.

There were no women or children, as she had seen in other gipsy camps they had passed in their wayfaring, and but one gipsy—a tall, athletic man, who stood with his arms folded, leaning against a tree at a little distance off, looking now at the fire, and now, under his black eyelashes, at three other men who were there, with a watchful but half-concealed interest in their conversation. Of these her grandfather was one; the others she recognised as the first card-players at the public-house on the eventful night of the storm—the man whom they had called Isaac List, and his gruff companion. One of the low, arched gipsy-tents, common to that people, was pitched hard by, but it either was, or appeared to be, empty.

"Well, are you going?" said the stout man, looking up from the ground where he was lying at his ease, into her grandfather's face. "You were in a mighty hurry a minute ago. Go, if you like. You're your own master, I hope?"

"Don't vex him," returned Isaac List, who was squatting like a frog on the other side of the fire, and had so screwed himself up that he seemed to be squinting all over; "he didn't mean any offence."

"You keep me poor, and plunder me, and make a sport and jest of me besides," said the old man, turning from one to the other. "Ye'll drive me mad among ye."

The utter irresolution and feebleness of the grey-haired child, contrasted with the keen and cunning looks of those in whose hands he was, smote upon the little listener's heart. But she constrained herself to attend to all that passed, and to note each look and word.

"Confound you, what do you mean?" said the stout man rising a little, and supporting himself upon his elbow. "Keep you poor! You'd keep us poor if you could, wouldn't you? That's the way with you whining, puny, pitiful players. When you lose, you're martyrs; but I don't find that when you win, you look upon the other losers in that light. As to plunder!" cried the fellow, raising his voice— "Damme, what do you mean by such ungentlemanly language as plunder, eh?"

The speaker laid himself down again at full length, and gave one or two short, angry kicks, as if in further expression of his unbounded indignation. It was quite plain that he acted the bully, and his friend the peacemaker, for some particular purpose; or rather, it would have been to any one but the weak old man; for they exchanged glances quite openly, both with each other and with the gipsy, who grinned his approval of the jest until his white teeth shone again.

The old man stood helplessly among them for a little time, and then said, turning to his assailant:

"You yourself were speaking of plunder just now, you know. Don't be so violent with me. You were, were you not?"

"Not of plundering among present company! Honour among—among gentlemen, sir," returned the other, who seemed to have been very near giving an awkward termination to the sentence.

"Don't be hard upon him, Jowl," said Isaac List. "He's very sorry for giving offence. There—go on with what you were saying—go on."

"I'm a jolly old tender-hearted lamb, I am," cried Mr. Jowl, "to be sitting here at my time of life giving advice when I know it won't be taken, and that I shall get nothing but abuse for my pains. But that's the way I've gone through life. Experience has never put a chill upon my warm-heartedness."

"I tell you he's very sorry, don't I?" remonstrated Isaac List, "and that he wishes you'd go on."

"*Does* he wish it?" said the other.

"Ay," groaned the old man sitting down, and rocking himself to and fro. "Go on, go on. It's in vain to fight with it; I can't do it; go on."

"I go on then," said Jowl, "where I left off, when you got up so quick. If you're persuaded that it's time for luck to turn, as it certainly is, and find that you haven't means enough to try it (and that's where it is, for you know yourself that you never have the funds to keep on long enough at a sitting), help yourself to what seems put in your way on purpose. Borrow it, I say, and, when you're able, pay it back again."

"Certainly," Isaac List struck in, "if this good lady as keeps the wax-works has money, and does keep it in a tin box when she goes to bed, and doesn't lock her door for fear of fire, it seems a easy thing; quite a Providence, *I* should call it—but then I've been religiously brought up."

"You see, Isaac," said his friend, growing more eager, and drawing himself closer to the old man, while he signed to the gipsy not to come between them; "you see, Isaac, strangers are going in and out every hour of the day; nothing would be more likely than for one of these strangers to get under the good lady's bed, or lock himself in the cupboard; suspicion would be very wide, and would fall a long way from the mark, no doubt. I'd give him his revenge to the last farthing he brought, whatever the amount was."

"But could you?" urged Isaac List. "Is your bank strong enough?"

"Strong enough!" answered the other, with assumed disdain. "Here, you sir, give me that box out of the straw!"

This was addressed to the gipsy, who crawled into the low tent on all fours, and after some rummaging and rustling returned with a cash-box, which the man who had spoken opened with a key he wore about his person.

"Do you see this?" he said, gathering up the money in his hand and letting it drop back into the box, between his fingers, like water. "Do you hear it? Do you know the sound of gold? There, put it back—and don't talk about banks again, Isaac, till you've got one of your own."

Isaac List, with great apparent humility, protested that he had never doubted the credit of a gentleman so notorious for his honourable dealing as Mr. Jowl, and that he had hinted at the production of the box, not for the satisfaction of his doubts, for he could have none, but with a view to being regaled with a sight of so much wealth, which, though it might be deemed by some but an unsubstantial and visionary pleasure, was to one in his circumstances a source of extreme delight, only to be surpassed by its safe depository in his own personal pockets. Although Mr. List and Mr. Jowl addressed themselves to each other, it was remarkable that they both looked narrowly at the old man, who, with his eyes fixed upon the fire, sat brooding over it, yet listening eagerly—as it seemed from a certain involuntary motion of the head, or twitching of the face from time to time—to all they said.

"My advice," said Jowl, lying down again with a careless air, "is plain—I have given it, in fact. I act as a friend. Why should I help a man to the means perhaps of winning all I have, unless I considered him my friend? It's foolish, I dare say, to be so thoughtful of the welfare of other people, but that's my constitution, and I can't help it; so don't blame me, Isaac List."

"*I* blame you!" returned the person addressed; "not for the world, Mr. Jowl. I wish I could afford to be as liberal as you; and, as you say, he might pay it back if he won—and if he lost——"

"You're not to take that into consideration at all," said Jowl. "But suppose he did (and nothing's less likely, from all I know of chances), why, it's better to lose other people's money than one's own, I hope?"

"Ah!" cried Isaac List rapturously, "the pleasures of winning! The delight of picking up the money—the bright, shining yellow-boys—and sweeping 'em into one's pocket! The deliciousness of having a triumph at last, and thinking that one didn't stop short and turn back, but went half-way to meet it! The—but you're not going, old gentleman?"

"I'll do it," said the old man, who had risen and taken two or three hurried steps away, and now returned as hurriedly. "I'll have it, every penny."

"Why, that's brave," cried Isaac, jumping up and slapping him on the shoulder; "and I respect you for having so much young blood left. Ha, ha, ha! Joe Jowl's half sorry he advised you now. We've got the laugh against him. Ha, ha, ha!"

"He gives me my revenge, mind," said the old man, pointing to him eagerly with his shrivelled hand: "mind—he stakes coin against coin, down to the last one in the box, be there many or few. Remember that!"

"I'm witness," returned Isaac. "I'll see fair between you."

"I have passed my word," said Jowl with feigned reluctance, "and I'll keep it. When does this match come off? I wish it was over —To-night?"

"I must have the money first," said the old man; "and that I'll have to-morrow——"

"Why not to-night?" urged Jowl.

"It's late now, and I should be flushed and flurried," said the old man. "It must be softly done. No, to-morrow night."

"Then to-morrow be it," said Jowl. "A drop of comfort here. Luck to the best man! Fill!"

The gipsy produced three tin cups, and filled them to the brim with brandy. The old man turned aside and muttered to himself before he drank. Her own name struck upon the listener's ear, coupled with some wish so fervent, that he seemed to breathe it in an agony of supplication.

"God be merciful to us!" cried the child within herself, "and help us in this trying hour? What shall I do to save him!"

The remainder of their conversation was carried on in a lower tone of voice, and was sufficiently concise; relating merely to the execution of the project, and the best precautions for diverting suspicion. The old man then shook hands with his tempters, and withdrew.

They watched his bowed and stooping figure as it retreated slowly, and when he turned his head to look back, which he often did, waved their hands, or shouted some brief encouragement. It was not until they had seen him gradually diminish into a mere speck upon the distant road, that they turned to each other, and ventured to laugh aloud.

"So," said Jowl, warming his hands at the fire, "it's done at last. He wanted more persuading than I expected. It's three weeks ago since we first put this in his head. What'll he bring, do you think?"

"Whatever he brings, it's halved between us," returned Isaac List.

The other man nodded. "We must make quick work of it," he said, "and then cut his acquaintance, or we may be suspected. Sharp's the word."

List and the gipsy acquiesced. When they had all three amused themselves a little with their victim's infatuation, they dismissed the subject as one which had been sufficiently discussed, and began to talk in a jargon which the child did not understand. As their discourse appeared to relate to matters in which they were warmly interested, however, she deemed it the best time for escaping unobserved; and crept away with slow and cautious steps, keeping in the shadow of the hedges, or forcing a path through them or the dry ditches, until she could emerge upon the road at a point beyond their range of vision. Then she fled homewards as quickly as she could, torn and bleeding from the wounds of thorns and briars, but more lacerated in mind, and threw herself upon her bed, distracted.

The first idea that flashed upon her mind was flight, instant flight; dragging him from that place, and rather dying of want upon the roadside, than ever exposing him again to such terrible temptations. Then she remembered that the crime was not to be committed until next night, and there was the intermediate time for thinking, and resolving what to do. Then she was distracted with a horrible fear that he might be committing it at that moment; with a dread of hearing shrieks and cries piercing the silence of the night; with fearful thoughts of what he might be tempted and led on to do, if he were detected in the act, and had but a woman to struggle with. It was impossible to bear such torture. She stole to the room where the money was, opened the door, and looked in. God be praised! He was not there, and she was sleeping soundly.

She went back to her own room, and tried to prepare herself for bed. But who could sleep—sleep! who could lie passively down, distracted by such terrors? They came upon her more and more strongly yet. Half undressed, and with her hair in wild disorder, she flew to the old man's bedside, clasped him by the wrist, and roused him from his sleep.

"What's this!" he cried, starting up in bed, and fixing his eyes upon her spectral face.

"I have had a dreadful dream," said the child, with an energy that nothing but such terrors could have inspired. "A dreadful, horrible dream. I have had it once before. It is a dream of grey-haired men like you, in darkened rooms by night, robbing the sleepers of their gold. Up, up!" The old man shook in every joint, and folded his hands like one who prays.

"Not to me," said the child, "not to me—to Heaven, to save us from such deeds! This dream is too real. I cannot sleep, I cannot stay here, I cannot leave you alone under the roof where such dreams come. Up! We must fly."

He looked at her as if she were a spirit—she might have been, for all the look of earth she had—and trembled more and more.

"There is no time to lose; I will not lose one minute," said the child. "Up! and away with me!"

"To-night!" murmured the old man.

"Yes, to-night," replied the child. "To-morrow night will be too late. The dream will have come again. Nothing but flight can save us. Up!"

The old man rose from his bed, his forehead bedewed with the cold sweat of fear, and, bending before the child as if she had been an angel messenger sent to lead him where she would, made ready to follow her. She took him by the hand and led him on. As they passed the door of the room he had proposed to rob, she shuddered and looked up into his face. What a white face was that, and with what a look did he meet hers!

She took him to her own chamber, and, still holding him by the hand as if she feared to lose him for an instant, gathered together the little stock she had, and hung her basket on her arm. The old man took his wallet from her hands and strapped it on his shoulders—his staff, too, she had brought away—and then she led him forth.

Through the strait streets, and narrow crooked outskirts, their trembling feet passed quickly. Up the steep hill too, crowned by the old grey castle, they toiled with rapid steps, and had not once looked behind.

But as they drew nearer the ruined walls, the moon rose in all her gentle glory, and, from their venerable age, garlanded with ivy, moss, and waving grass, the child looked back upon the sleeping town, deep in the valley's shade, and on the far-off river with its winding track of light, and on the distant hills; and as she did so, she clasped the hand she held, less firmly, and bursting into tears, fell upon the old man's neck.

CHAPTER XLIII

HER momentary weakness past, the child again summoned the resolution which had until now sustained her, and, endeavouring to keep steadily in her view the one idea that they were flying from disgrace and crime, and that her grandfather's preservation must depend solely upon her firmness, unaided by one word of advice or any helping hand, urged him onward and looked back no more.

While he, subdued and abashed, seemed to crouch before her, and to shrink and cower down as if in the presence of some superior creature, the child herself was sensible of a new feeling within her, which elevated her nature, and inspired her with an energy and confidence she had never known. There was no divided responsibility now; the whole burden of their two lives had fallen upon her, and henceforth she must think and act for both. "I have saved him," she thought. "In all dangers and distress, I will remember that."

At any other time the recollection of having deserted the friend who had shown them so much homely kindness, without a word of justification—the thought that they were guilty, in appearance, of treachery and ingratitude—even the having parted from the two sisters—would have filled her with sorrow and regret. But now, all other considerations were lost in the new uncertainties and anxieties of their wild and wandering life; and the very desperation of their condition roused and stimulated her.

In the pale moonlight, which lent a wanness of its own to the delicate face where thoughtful care already mingled with the winning grace and loveliness of youth, the too bright eye, the spiritual head, the lips that pressed each other with such high resolve and courage of the heart, the slight figure firm in its bearing and yet so very weak, told their silent tale; but told it only to the wind that rustled by, which, taking up its burden, carried, perhaps to some mother's pillow, faint dreams of childhood fading in its bloom, and resting in the sleep that knows no waking.

The night crept on apace, the moon went down, the stars grew pale and dim, and morning, cold as they, slowly approached. Then, from behind a distant hill, the noble sun rose up, driving the mists in phantom shapes before it, and clearing the earth of their ghostly forms till darkness came again. When it had climbed higher into the sky, and there was warmth in its cheerful beams, they laid them down to sleep, upon a bank, hard by some water.

But Nell retained her grasp upon the old man's arm, and long after he was slumbering soundly, watched him with untiring eyes. Fatigue stole over her at last; her grasp relaxed, tightened, relaxed again, and they slept side by side.

A confused sound of voices, mingled with her dreams, awoke her. A man of very uncouth and rough appearance was standing over them, and two of his companions were looking on from a long heavy boat which had come close to the bank while they were sleeping. The boat had neither oar nor sail, but was towed by a couple of horses who, with the rope to which they were harnessed slack and dripping in the water, were resting on the path.

"Holloa!" said the man roughly. "What's the matter here, eh?"

"We were only asleep, sir," said Nell. "We have been walking all night."

"A pair of queer travellers to be walking all night," observed the man who had first accosted them. "One of you is a trifle too old for that sort of work, and the other a trifle too young. Where are you going?"

Nell faltered, and pointed at hazard towards the West, upon which the man inquired if she meant a certain town which he named. Nell, to avoid further questioning, said "Yes, that was the place."

"Where have you come from?" was the next question; and this being an easier one to answer, Nell mentioned the name of the village in which their friend the schoolmaster dwelt, as being less likely to be known to the men or to provoke further inquiry.

"I thought somebody had been robbing and ill-using you, might be," said the man. "That's all. Good day."

Returning his salute and feeling greatly relieved by his departure, Nell looked after him as he mounted one of the horses, and the boat went on. It had not gone very far, when it stopped again, and she saw the men beckoning to her.

"Did you call to me?" said Nell, running up to them.

"You may go with us if you like," replied one of those in the boat. "We're going to the same place."

The child hesitated for a moment, and thinking, as she had thought with great trepidation more than once before, that the men whom she had seen with her grandfather might perhaps, in their eagerness for the booty, follow them, and, regaining their influence over him, set hers at nought; and that if they went with these men, all traces of them must surely be lost at that spot; determined to accept the offer. The boat came close to the bank again, and before she had had any time for further consideration, she and her grandfather were on board, and gliding smoothly down the canal.

The sun shone pleasantly upon the bright water, which was sometimes shaded by trees, and sometimes open to a wide extent of country, intersected by running streams, and rich with wooded hills, cultivated land, and sheltered farms. Now and then a village with its modest spire, thatched roofs, and gable-ends, would peep out from among the trees; and more than once a distant town, with great church towers looming through its smoke, and high factories or workshops rising above the mass of houses, would come in view, and, by the length of time it lingered in the distance, show them how slowly they travelled. Their way lay for the most part through the low grounds, and open plains; and except these distant places, and occasionally some men working in the fields, or lounging on the bridges under which they passed, to see them creep along, nothing encroached on their monotonous and secluded track.

Nell was rather disheartened, when they stopped at a kind of wharf late in the afternoon, to learn from one of the men that they would not reach their place of destination until next day, and that if she had no provision with her she had better buy it there. She had but a few pence, having already bargained with them for some bread, but even of these it was necessary to be very careful, as they were on their way to an utterly strange place, with no resource whatever. A small loaf and a morsel of cheese, therefore, were all she could afford, and with these she took her place in the boat again, and, after half an hour's delay during which the men were drinking at the public-house, proceeded on the journey.

They brought some beer and spirits into the boat with them, and what with drinking freely before, and again now, were soon in a fair way of being quarrelsome and intoxicated. Avoiding the small cabin, therefore, which was very dark and filthy, and to which they often invited both her and her grandfather, Nell sat in the open air with the old man by her side, listening to their boisterous hosts with a palpitating heart, and almost wishing herself safe on shore again though she should have to walk all night.

They were in truth very rugged, noisy fellows, and quite brutal among themselves, though civil enough to their two passengers. Thus, when a quarrel arose between the man who was steering and his friend in the cabin, upon the question who had first suggested the propriety of offering Nell some beer, and when the quarrel led to a scuffle in which they beat each other fearfully, to her inexpressible terror, neither visited his displeasure upon her, but each contented himself with venting it on his adversary, on whom, in addition to blows, he bestowed a variety of compliments, which, happily for the child, were conveyed in terms, to her quite unintelligible. The difference was finally adjusted, by the man who had come out of the cabin knocking the other into it head first, and taking the helm into his own hands, without evincing the least discomposure himself, or causing any in his friend, who, being of a tolerably strong constitution and perfectly inured to such trifles, went to sleep as he was, with his heels upwards, and in a couple of minutes or so was snoring comfortably.

By this time it was night again, and though the child felt cold, being but poorly clad, her anxious thoughts were far removed from her own sufferings or uneasiness, and busily engaged in endeavouring to devise some scheme for their joint subsistence. The same spirit which had supported her on the previous night, upheld and sustained her now. Her grandfather lay sleeping safely at her side, and the crime to which his madness urged him, was not committed. That was her comfort.

How every circumstance of her short, eventful life, came thronging into her mind as they travelled on! Slight incidents, never thought of or remembered until now; faces seen once and ever since forgotten; words spoken and scarcely heeded at the time; scenes of a year ago and those of yesterday mixing up and linking themselves together; familiar places shaping themselves out in the darkness from things which, when approached, were of all others the most remote and most unlike them; sometimes a strange confusion in her mind relative to the occasion of her being there, and the place to which she was going, and the people she was with; and imagination suggesting remarks and questions which sounded so plainly in her ears, that she would start, and turn, and be almost tempted to reply; —all the fancies and contradictions common in watching and excitement and restless change of place, beset the child.

She happened, while she was thus engaged, to encounter the face of the man on deck, in whom the sentimental stage of drunkenness had now succeeded to the boisterous, and who, taking from his mouth a short pipe, quilted over with string for its longer preservation, requested that she would oblige him with a song.

"You've got a very pretty voice, a very soft eye, and a very strong memory," said this gentleman; "the voice and eye I've got evidence for, and the memory's an opinion of my own. And I'm never wrong. Let me hear a song this minute."

"I don't think I know one, sir," returned Nell.

"You know forty-seven songs," said the man, with a gravity which admitted of no altercation on the subject. "Forty-seven's your number. Let me hear one of 'em—the best. Give me a song this minute."

Not knowing what might be the consequences of irritating her friend, and trembling with the fear of doing so, poor Nell sang him some little ditty which she had learned in happier times, and which was so agreeable to his ear, that on its conclusion he in the same peremptory manner requested to be favoured with another, to which he was so obliging as to roar a chorus to no particular tune, and with no words at all, but which amply made up in its amazing energy for its deficiency in other respects. The noise of this vocal performance awakened the other man, who, staggering upon deck and shaking his late opponent by the hand, swore that singing was his pride and joy and chief delight, and that he desired no better entertainment. With a third call, more imperative than either of the two former, Nell felt obliged to comply, and this time, a chorus was maintained not only by the two men together, but also by the third man on horseback, who, being by his position debarred from a nearer participation in the revels of the night, roared when his companions roared, and rent the very air. In this way, with little cessation, and singing the same songs again and again, the tired and exhausted child kept them in good humour all that night: and many a cottager, who was roused from his soundest sleep by the discordant chorus as it floated away upon the wind, hid his head beneath the bed-clothes, and trembled at the sounds.

At length the morning dawned. It was no sooner light than it began to rain heavily. As the child could not endure the intolerable vapours of the cabin, they covered her, in return for her exertions, with some pieces of sail-cloth and ends of tarpaulin, which sufficed to keep her tolerably dry and to shelter her grandfather besides. As the day advanced the rain increased. At noon it poured down more hopelessly and heavily than ever, without the faintest promise of abatement.

They had for some time been gradually approaching the place for which they were bound. The water had become thicker and dirtier; other barges coming from it passed them frequently; the paths of coal-ash and huts of staring brick, marked the vicinity of some great manufacturing town; while scattered streets and houses, and smoke from distant furnaces, indicated that they were already in the out-skirts. Now, the clustered roofs, and piles of buildings trembling with the working of engines, and dimly resounding with their shrieks and throbbings; the tall chimneys vomiting forth a black vapour, which hung in a dense ill-favoured cloud above the housetops and filled the air with gloom; the clank of hammers beating upon iron, the roar of busy streets and noisy crowds, gradually augmenting until all the various sounds blended into one and none was distin-guishable for itself, announced the termination of their journey.

The boat floated into the wharf to which it belonged. The men were occupied directly. The child and her grandfather, after waiting in vain to thank them, or ask them whither they should go, passed through a dirty lane into a crowded street, and stood amid its din and tumult, and in the pouring rain, as strange, bewildered, and confused, as if they had lived a thousand years before, and were raised from the dead and placed there by a miracle.

CHAPTER XLIV

THE throng of people hurried by, in two opposite streams, with no symptom of cessation or exhaustion; intent upon their own affairs; and undisturbed in their business speculations, by the roar of carts and waggons laden with clashing wares, the slipping of horses' feet upon the wet and greasy pavement, the rattling of the rain on windows and umbrella-tops, the jostling of the more impatient passengers, and all the noise and tumult of a crowded street in the high tide of its occupation; while the two poor strangers, stunned and bewildered by the hurry they beheld but had no part in, looked mournfully on; feeling amidst the crowd a solitude which has no parallel but in the thirst of the ship-wrecked mariner, who, tossed to and fro upon the billows of a mighty ocean, his red eyes blinded by looking on the water which hems him in on every side, has not one drop to cool his burning tongue.

They withdrew into a low archway for shelter from the rain, and watched the faces of those who passed, to find in one among them a ray of encouragement or hope. Some frowned, some smiled, some muttered to themselves, some made slight gestures, as if anticipating the conversation in which they would shortly be engaged, some wore the cunning look of bargaining and plotting, some were anxious and eager, some slow and dull; in some countenances were written gain; in others loss. It was like being in the confidence of all these people to stand quietly there, looking into their faces as they flitted past. In busy places, where each man has an object of his own, and feels assured that every other man has his, his character and purpose are written broadly in his face. In the public walks and lounges of a town, people go to see and to be seen, and there the same expression, with little variety, is repeated a hundred times. The working-day faces come nearer to the truth, and let it out more plainly.

Falling into that kind of abstraction which such a solitude awakens, the child continued to gaze upon the passing crowd with a wondering interest, amounting almost to a temporary forgetfulness of her own condition. But cold, wet, hunger, want of rest, and lack of any place in which to lay her aching head, soon brought her thoughts back to the point whence they had strayed. No one passed who seemed to notice them, or to whom she durst appeal. After some time, they left their place of refuge from the weather, and mingled with the concourse.

Evening came on. They were still wandering up and down, with fewer people about them, but with the same sense of solitude in their own breasts, and the same indifference from all around. The lights in the streets and shops made them feel yet more desolate, for with their help, night and darkness seemed to come on faster. Shivering with the cold and damp, ill in body, and sick to death at heart, the child needed her utmost firmness and resolution even to creep along.

Why had they ever come to this noisy town, when there were peaceful country places, in which, at least, they might have hungered and thirsted, with less suffering than in its squalid strife! They were but an atom, here, in a mountain heap of misery, the very sight of which increased their hopelessness and suffering.

The child had not only to endure the accumulated hardships of their destitute condition, but to bear the reproaches of her grandfather, who began to murmur at having been led away from their late abode, and demand that they should return to it. Being now penniless, and no relief or prospect of relief appearing, they retraced their steps through the deserted streets, and went back to the wharf, hoping to find the boat in which they had come, and to be allowed to sleep on board that night. But here again they were disappointed, for the gate was closed, and some fierce dogs, barking at their approach, obliged them to retreat.

"We must sleep in the open air to-night, dear," said the child in a weak voice, as they turned away from this last repulse; "and to-morrow we will beg our way to some quiet part of the country, and try to earn our bread in very humble work."

"Why did you bring me here?" returned the old man fiercely. "I cannot bear these close eternal streets. We came from a quiet part. Why did you force me to leave it?"

"Because I must have that dream I told you of, no more," said the child, with a momentary firmness that lost itself in tears; "and we must live among poor people, or it will come again. Dear grandfather, you are old and weak, I know; but look at me. I never will complain if you will not, but I have some suffering indeed."

"Ah! poor, houseless, wandering motherless child!" cried the old man, clasping his hands and gazing as if for the first time upon her anxious face, her travel-stained dress, and bruised and swollen feet; "has all my agony of care brought her to this at last! Was I a happy man once, and have I lost happiness and all I had, for this!'"

"If we were in the country now," said the child, with assumed cheerfulness, as they walked on looking about them for a shelter, "we should find some good old tree, stretching out his green arms as if he loved us, and nodding and rustling as if he would have us fall asleep, thinking of him while he watched. Please God, we shall be there soon—to-morrow or next day at the farthest—and in the meantime let us think, dear, that it was a good thing we came here; for we are lost in the crowd and hurry of this place, and if any cruel people should pursue us, they could surely never trace us further. There's comfort in that. And here's a deep old doorway—very dark, but quite dry, and warm too, for the wind don't blow in here—What's that!"

Uttering a half shriek, she recoiled from a black figure which came suddenly out of the dark recess in which they were about to take refuge, and stood still looking at them.

"Speak again," it said; "do I know the voice?"

"No," replied the child timidly; "we are strangers, and having no money for a night's lodging, were going to rest here."

There was a feeble lamp at no great distance; the only one in the place, which was a kind of square yard, but sufficient to show how poor and mean it was. To this, the figure beckoned them; at the same time drawing within its rays, as if to show that it had no desire to conceal itself or take them at an advantage.

The form was that of a man, miserably clad and begrimed with smoke, which, perhaps by its contrast with the natural colour of his skin, made him look paler than he really was. That he was naturally of a very wan and pallid aspect, however, his hollow cheeks, sharp features, and sunken eyes, no less than a certain look of patient endurance, sufficiently testified. His voice was harsh by nature, but not brutal; and though his face, besides possessing the characteristics already mentioned, was overshadowed by a quantity of long dark hair, its expression was neither ferocious nor cruel.

"How came you to think of resting there?" he said. "Or how," he added, looking more attentively at the child, "do you come to want a place of rest at this time of night?"

"Our misfortunes," the grandfather answered, "are the cause."

"Do you know," said the man, looking still more earnestly at Nell, "how wet she is, and that the damp streets are not a place for her?"

"I know it well, God help me," he replied. "What can I do!"

The man looked at Nell again, and gently touched her garments, from which the rain was running off in little streams. "I can give you warmth," he said, after a pause; "nothing else. Such lodging as I have is in that house," pointing to the doorway from which he had emerged, "but she is safer and better there than here. The fire is in a rough place, but you can pass the night beside it safely, if you'll trust yourselves to me. You see that red light yonder?"

They raised their eyes, and saw a lurid glare hanging in the dark sky; the dull reflection of some distant fire.

"It's not far," said the man. "Shall I take you there? You were going to sleep upon cold bricks; I can give you a bed of warm ashes—nothing better."

Without waiting for any further reply than he saw in their looks, he took Nell in his arms, and bade the old man follow.

Carrying her as tenderly, and as easily too, as if she had been an infant, and showing himself both swift and sure of foot, he led the way through what appeared to be the poorest and most wretched quarter of the town; not turning aside to avoid the overflowing kennels or running waterspouts, but holding his course, regardless of such obstructions, and making his way straight through them. They had proceeded thus in silence for some quarter of an hour, and had lost sight of the glare to which he had pointed, in the dark and narrow ways by which they had come, when it suddenly burst upon them, again, streaming up from the high chimney of a building close before them.

"This is the place," he said, pausing at a door to put Nell down and take her hand. "Don't be afraid. There's nobody here will harm you."

It needed a strong confidence in this assurance to induce them to enter, and what they saw inside did not diminish their apprehension and alarm. In a large and lofty building, supported by pillars of iron, with great black apertures in the upper walls, open to the external air; echoing to the roof with the beating of hammers and roar of furnaces, mingled with the hissing of red-hot metal plunged in water, and a hundred strange unearthly noises never heard elsewhere; in this gloomy place, moving like demons among the flame and smoke, dimly and fitfully seen, flushed and tormented by the burning fires, and wielding great weapons, a faulty blow from any one of which must have crushed some workman's skull, a number of men laboured like giants. Others, reposing upon heaps of coals or ashes with their faces turned to the black vault above, slept or rested from their toil. Others again, opening the white-hot furnace-doors, cast fuel on the flames, which came rushing and roaring forth to meet it, and licked it up like oil. Others drew forth, with clashing noise upon the ground, great sheets of glowing steel, emitting an insupportable heat, and a dull deep light like that which reddens in the eyes of savage beasts.

Through these bewildering sights and deafening sounds, their conductor led them to where, in a dark portion of the building, one furnace burnt by night and day—so at least they gathered from the motion of his lips, for as yet they could only see him speak: not hear him. The man who had been watching this fire, and whose task was ended for the present, gladly withdrew, and left them with their friend, who, spreading Nell's little cloak upon a heap of ashes, and showing her where she could hang her outer clothes to dry, signed to her and the old man to lie down and sleep. For himself, he took his station on a rugged mat before the furnace-door, and resting his chin upon his hands, watched the flame as it shone through the iron chinks, and the white ashes as they fell into their bright hot grave below.

The warmth of her bed, hard and humble as it was, combined with the great fatigue she had undergone, soon caused the tumult of the place to fall with a gentler sound upon the child's tired ears, and was not long in lulling her to sleep. The old man was stretched beside her, and with her hand upon his neck she lay and dreamed.

It was yet night when she awoke, nor did she know how long, or for how short a time, she had slept. But she found herself protected, both from any cold air that might find its way into the building, and from the scorching heat, by some of the workmen's clothes; and glancing at their friend saw that he sat in exactly the same attitude, looking with a fixed earnestness of attention towards the fire, and keeping so very still that he did not even seem to breathe. She lay in the state between sleeping and waking, looking so long at his motionless figure that at length she almost feared he had died as he sat there; and, softly rising and drawing close to him, ventured to whisper in his ear.

He moved, and glancing from her to the place she had lately occupied, as if to assure himself that it was really the child so near

"The fire nursed me – the same fire It has never gone out."

him, looked inquiringly into her face.

"I feared you were ill," she said. "The other men are all in motion, and you are so very quiet."

"They leave me to myself," he replied. "They know my humour. They laugh at me, but don't harm me in it. See yonder there—that's *my* friend."

"The fire?" said the child.

"It has been alive as long as I have," the man made answer. "We talk and think together all night long."

The child glanced quickly at him in her surprise, but he had turned his eyes in their former direction, and was musing as before.

"It's like a book to me," he said—"the only book I ever learned to read; and many an old story it tells me. It's music, for I should know its voice among a thousand, and there are other voices in its roar. It has its pictures too. You don't know how many strange faces and different scenes I trace in the red-hot coals. It's my memory, that fire, and shows me all my life."

The child, bending down to listen to his words, could not help remarking with what brightened eyes he continued to speak and muse.

"Yes," he said, with a faint smile, "it was the same when I was quite a baby, and crawled about it, till I fell asleep. My father watched it then."

"Had you no mother?" asked the child.

"No, she was dead. Women work hard in these parts. She worked herself to death they told me, and, as they said so then, the fire has gone on saying the same thing ever since. I suppose it was true. I have always believed it."

"Were you brought up here, then?" said the child.

"Summer and winter," he replied. "Secretly at first, but when they found it out, they let him keep me here. So the fire nursed me— the same fire. It has never gone out."

"You are fond of it?" said the child.

"Of course I am. He died before it. I saw him fall down—just there, where those ashes are burning now—and wondered, I remember, why it didn't help him."

"Have you been here ever since?" asked the child.

"Ever since I came to watch it; but there was a while between, and a very cold dreary while it was. It burned all the time though, and roared and leaped when I came back, as it used to do in our play days. You may guess from looking at me what kind of child I was, but for all the difference between us I was a child, and when I saw you in the street to-night, you put me in mind of myself as I was after he died, and made me wish to bring you to the old fire. I thought of those old times again when I saw you sleeping by it. You should be sleeping now. Lie down again, poor child, lie down again."

With that he led her to her rude couch, and covering her with the clothes with which she had found herself enveloped when she woke, returned to his seat, whence he moved no more unless to feed the furnace, but remained motionless as a statue. The child continued to watch him for a little time, but soon yielded to the drowsiness that came upon her, and, in the dark strange place and on the heap of ashes, slept as peacefully as if the room had been a palace chamber, and the bed a bed of down.

When she awoke again, broad day was shining through the lofty openings in the walls, and, stealing in slanting rays but midway down, seemed to make the building darker than it had been at night. The clang and tumult were still going on, and the remorseless fires were burning fiercely as before; for few changes of night and day brought rest or quiet there.

Her friend parted his breakfast—a scanty mess of coffee and some coarse bread—with the child and her grandfather, and inquired whither they were going. She told him that they sought some distant country place remote from towns or even other villages, and with a faltering tongue inquired what road they would do best to take.

"I know little of the country," he said, shaking his head, "for such as I, pass all our lives before our furnace doors, and seldom go forth to breathe. But there *are* such places yonder."

"And far from here?" said Nell.

"Ay surely. How could they be near us, and be green and fresh? The road lies too, through miles and miles, all lighted up by fires like ours—a strange black road, and one that would frighten you by night."

"We are here and must go on," said the child boldly; for she saw that the old man listened with anxious ears to this account.

"Rough people—paths never made for little feet like yours—a dismal, blighted way—is there no turning back, my child?"

"There is none," cried Nell, pressing forward. "If you can direct us, do. If not, pray do not seek to turn us from our purpose. Indeed you do not know the danger that we shun, and how right and true we are in flying from it, or you would not try to stop us, I am sure you would not."

"God forbid, if it is so!" said their uncouth protector, glancing from the eager child to her grandfather, who hung his head and bent his eyes upon the ground. "I'll direct you from the door, the best I can. I wish I could do more."

He showed them, then, by which road they must leave the town, and what course they should hold when they had gained it. He lingered so long on these instructions, that the child, with a fervent blessing, tore herself away, and stayed to hear no more.

But before they had reached the corner of the lane, the man came running after them, and, pressing her hand, left something in it— two old, battered, smoke-encrusted penny pieces. Who knows but they shone as brightly in the eyes of angels as golden gifts that have been chronicled on tombs?

And thus they separated; the child to lead her sacred charge farther from guilt and shame; and the labourer to attach a fresh interest to the spot where his guests had slept, and read new histories in his furnace fire.

CHAPTER XLV

IN all their journeying, they had never longed so ardently, they had never so pined and wearied, for the freedom of pure air and open country, as now. No, not even on that memorable morning, when, deserting their old home, they abandoned themselves to the mercies of a strange world, and left all the dumb and senseless things they had known and loved, behind—not even then, had they so yearned for the fresh solitudes of wood, hillside, and field, as now; when the noise and dirt and vapour of the great manufacturing town, reeking with lean misery and hungry wretchedness, hemmed them in on every side, and seemed to shut out hope, and render escape impossible.

"Two days and nights!" thought the child. "He said two days and nights we should have to spend among such scenes as these. Oh! if we live to reach the country once again, if we get clear of these dreadful places, though it is only to lie down and die, with what a grateful heart I shall thank God for so much mercy!"

With thoughts like this, and with some vague design of travelling to a great distance among streams and mountains, where only very poor and simple people lived, and where they might maintain themselves by very humble helping work in farms, free from such terrors as that from which they fled—the child, with no resource but the poor man's gift, and no encouragement but that which flowed from her own heart, and its sense of the truth and right of what she did, nerved herself to this last journey and boldly pursued her task.

"We shall be very slow to-day, dear," she said, as they toiled painfully through the streets; "my feet are sore, and I have pains in all my limbs from the wet of yesterday. I saw that he looked at us and thought of that, when he said how long we should be upon the road."

"It was a dreary way he told us of," returned her grandfather, piteously. "Is there no other road? Will you not let me go some other way than this?"

"Places lie beyond these," said the child, firmly, "where we may live in peace, and be tempted to do no harm. We will take the road that promises to have that end, and we would not turn out of it, if it were a hundred times worse than our fears lead us to expect. We would not, dear, would we?"

"No," replied the old man, wavering in his voice, no less than in his manner. "No. Let us go on. I am ready. I am quite ready, Nell."

The child walked with more difficulty than she had led her companion to expect, for the pains that racked her joints were of no common severity, and every exertion increased them. But they wrung from her no complaint, or look of suffering; and, though the two travellers proceeded very slowly, they did proceed; and clearing the town in course of time, began to feel that they were fairly on their way.

A long suburb of red brick houses,—some with patches of garden ground, where coal-dust and factory smoke darkened the shrinking leaves, and coarse rank flowers; and where the struggling vegetation sickened and sank under the hot breath of kiln and furnace, making them by its presence seem yet more blighting and unwholesome than in the town itself,—a long, flat, straggling suburb passed, they came by slow degrees upon a cheerless region, where not a blade of grass was seen to grow; where not a bud put forth its promise in the spring; where nothing green could live but on the surface of the stagnant pools, which here and there lay idly sweltering by the black roadside.

Advancing more and more into the shadow of this mournful place, its dark depressing influence stole upon their spirits, and filled them with a dismal gloom. On every side, and as far as the eye could see into the heavy distance, tall chimneys, crowding on each other, and presenting that endless repetition of the same dull, ugly form, which is the horror of oppressive dreams, poured out their plague of smoke, obscured the light, and made foul the melancholy air. On mounds of ashes by the wayside, sheltered only by a few rough boards, or rotten pent-house roofs, strange engines spun and writhed like tortured creatures; clanking their iron chains, shrieking in their rapid whirl from time to time as though in torment unendurable, and making the ground tremble with their agonies. Dismantled houses here and there appeared, tottering to the earth, propped up by fragments of others that had fallen down, unroofed, windowless, blackened, desolate, but yet inhabited. Men, women, children, wan in their looks and ragged in attire, tended the engines, fed their tributary fires, begged upon the road, or scowled half-naked from the doorless houses. Then came more of the wrathful monsters, whose like they almost seemed to be in their wildness and their untamed air, screeching and turning round and round again; and still, before, behind, and to the right and left, was the same interminable perspective of brick towers, never ceasing in their black vomit, blasting all things living or inanimate, shutting out the face of day, and closing in on all these horrors with a dense dark cloud.

But night-time in this dreadful spot!—night, when the smoke was changed to fire; when every chimney spirited up its flame; and places, that had been dark vaults all day, now shone red-hot, with figures moving to and fro within their blazing jaws, and calling to one another with hoarse cries—night, when the noise of every strange machine was aggravated by the darkness; when the people near them looked wilder and more savage; when bands of unemployed labourers paraded in the roads, or clustered by torchlight round their leaders, who told them in stern language of their wrongs, and urged them on to frightful cries and threats; when maddened men, armed with sword and firebrand, spurning the tears and prayers of women who would restrain them, rushed forth on errands of terror and destruction, to work no ruin half so surely as their own—night, when carts came rumbling by, filled with rude coffins (for contagious disease and death had been busy with the living crops); when orphans cried, and distracted women shrieked and followed in their wake—night, when some called for bread, and some for drink to drown their cares; and some with tears, and some with staggering feet, and some with blood-shot eyes, went brooding home—night, which, unlike the night that Heaven sends on earth, brought with it no peace, nor quiet, nor signs of blessed sleep—who shall tell the terrors of the night to that young wandering child!

And yet she lay down, with nothing between her and the sky; and, with no fear for herself, for she was past it now, put up a prayer for the poor old man. So very weak and spent she felt, so very calm and unresisting, that she had no thought of any wants of her own, but prayed that God would raise up some friend for *him*. She tried to recall the way they had come, and to look in the direction where the fire by which they had slept last night was burning. She had forgotten to ask the name of the poor man, their friend, and when she had remembered him in her prayers, it seemed ungrateful not to turn one look towards the spot where he was watching.

A penny loaf was all they had had that day. It was very little, but even hunger was forgotten in the strange tranquillity that crept over her senses. She lay down very gently, and, with a quiet smile upon her face, fell into a slumber. It was not like sleep—and yet it must have been, or why those pleasant dreams of the little scholar all night long!

Morning came. Much weaker, diminished powers even of sight and hearing, and yet the child made no complaint—perhaps would have made none, even if she had not that inducement to be silent, travelling by her side. She felt a hopelessness of their ever being extricated together from that forlorn place, a dull conviction that she was very ill, perhaps dying; but no fear or anxiety.

A loathing of food, that she was not conscious of until they expended their last penny in the purchase of another loaf, prevented her partaking even of this poor repast. Her grandfather ate greedily, which she was glad to see.

Their way lay through the same scenes as yesterday, with no variety or improvement. There was the same thick air, difficult to breathe; the same blighted ground, the same hopeless prospect, the same misery and distress. Objects appeared more dim, the noise less, the path more rugged and uneven, for sometimes she stumbled, and became roused, as it were, in the effort to prevent herself from falling. Poor child! the cause was in her tottering feet.

Towards the afternoon, her grandfather complained bitterly of hunger. She approached one of the wretched hovels by the wayside, and knocked with her hand upon the door.

"What would you have here?" said a gaunt miserable man, opening it.

"Charity. A morsel of bread."

"Do you see that?" returned the man hoarsely, pointing to a kind of bundle on the ground. "That's a dead child. I and five hundred other men were thrown out of work three months ago. That is my third dead child, and last. Do you think I have charity to bestow, or a morsel of bread to spare?"

The child recoiled from the door, and it closed upon her. Impelled by strong necessity, she knocked at another: a neighbouring one, which, yielding to the slight pressure of her hand, flew open.

It seemed that a couple of poor families lived in this hovel, for two women, each among children of her own, occupied different portions of the room. In the centre stood a grave gentleman in black who appeared to have just entered, and who held by the arm a boy.

"Here, woman," he said, "here's your deaf and dumb son. You may thank me for restoring him to you. He was brought before me this morning, charged with theft; and with any other boy it would have gone hard, I assure you. But as I had compassion on his infirmities, and thought he might have learnt no better, I have managed to bring him back to you. Take more care of him for the future."

"And won't you give me back *my* son!" said the other woman, hastily rising and confronting him. "Won't you give me back *my* son, sir, who was transported for the same offence!"

"Was *he* deaf and dumb, woman?" asked the gentleman sternly.

"Was he not, sir?"

"You know he was not."

"He was," cried the woman. "He was deaf, dumb, and blind, to all that was good and right, from his cradle. Her boy may have learnt no better! where did mine learn better? where could he? who was there to teach him better, or where was it to be learnt?"

"Peace, woman," said the gentleman, "your boy was in possession of all his senses."

"He was," cried the mother; "and he was the more easy to be led astray because he had them. If you save this boy because he may not know right from wrong, why did you not save mine who was never taught the difference? You gentlemen have as good a right to punish her boy, that God has kept in ignorance of sound and speech, as you have to punish mine, that you kept in ignorance yourselves. How many of the girls and boys—ah, men and women too—that are brought before you and you don't pity, are deaf and dumb in their minds, and go wrong in that state, and are punished in that state, body and soul, while you gentlemen are quarrelling among yourselves whether they ought to learn this or that?—Be a just man, sir, and give me back my son."

"You are desperate," said the gentleman, taking out his snuff-box, "and I am sorry for you."

"I *am* desperate," returned the woman, "and you have made me so. Give me back my son, to work for these helpless children. Be a just man, sir, and for God's sake, as you have had mercy upon this boy, give me back my son!''

The child had seen and heard enough to know that this was not a place at which to ask for alms. She led the old man softly from the door, and they pursued their journey.

With less and less of hope or strength, as they went on, but with an undiminished resolution not to betray by any word or sign her sinking state, so long as she had energy to move, the child through-out the remainder of that hard day compelled herself to proceed: not even stopping to rest as frequently as usual, to compensate in some measure for the tardy pace at which she was obliged to walk. Evening was drawing on, but had not closed in, when—still travelling among the same dismal objects—they came to a busy town.

Faint and spiritless as they were, its streets were insupportable. After humbly asking for relief at some few doors and being repulsed, they agreed to make their way out of it as speedily as they could, and try if the inmates of any lone house beyond, would have more pity on their exhausted state.

They were dragging themselves along through the last street, and the child felt that the time was close at hand when her enfeebled powers would bear no more. There appeared before them, at this juncture, going in the same direction as themselves, a traveller on foot, who, with a portmanteau strapped to his back, leant upon a stout stick as he walked, and read from a book which he held in his other hand.

It was not an easy matter to come up with him, and beseech his aid, for he walked fast, and was a little distance in advance. At length he stopped to look more attentively at some passage in his book. Animated with a ray of hope, the child shot on before her grandfather, and, going close to the stranger without rousing him by sound of her footsteps, began in a few faint words to implore his help.

He turned his head, the child clapped her hands together, uttered a wild shriek, and fell senseless at his feet.

CHAPTER XLVI

IT was the poor schoolmaster. No other than the poor schoolmaster. Scarcely less moved and surprised by the sight of the child than she had been on recognising him, he stood for a moment silent and con-founded by this unexpected apparition, without even the presence of mind to raise her from the ground.

But, quickly recovering his self-possession, he threw down his stick and book, and dropping on one knee beside her, endeavoured by such simple means as occurred to him, to restore her to herself; while her grandfather, standing idly by, wrung his hands, and implored her with many endearing expressions to speak to him, were it only a word.

"She is quite exhausted," said the schoolmaster, glancing upward into his face. "You have taxed her powers too far, friend."

"She is perishing of want," rejoined the old man. "I never thought how weak and ill she was, till now."

Casting a look upon him, half-reproachful and half-compassionate, the schoolmaster took the child in his arms, and, bidding the old man gather up her little basket and follow him directly, bore her away at his utmost speed.

There was a small inn within sight, to which it would seem he had been directing his steps when so unexpectedly overtaken. Towards this place he hurried with his unconscious burden, and rushing into the kitchen, and calling upon the company there assembled to make way for God's sake, deposited it on a chair before the fire.

The company, who rose in confusion upon the schoolmaster's entrance, did as people usually do under such circumstances. Everybody called for his or her favourite remedy, which nobody brought; each cried for more air, at the same time carefully excluding what air there was, by closing round the object of sympathy; and all wondered why somebody else didn't do what it never appeared to occur to them might be done by themselves.

The landlady, however, who possessed more readiness and activity than any of them, and who had withal a quicker perception of the merits of the case, soon came running in, with a little hot brandy and water, followed by her servant-girl, carrying vinegar, hartshorn, smelling-salts, and such other restoratives; which, being duly administered, recovered the child so far as to enable her to thank them in a faint voice, and to extend her hand to the poor schoolmaster, who stood with an anxious face, hard by. Without suffering her to speak another word, or so much as to stir a finger any more, the women straightway carried her off to bed; and having covered her up warm, bathed her cold feet, and wrapped them in flannel, they despatched a messenger for the doctor.

The doctor, who was a red-nosed gentleman with a great bunch of seals dangling below a waistcoat of ribbed black satin, arrived with all speed, and taking his seat by the bedside of poor Nell, drew out his watch, and felt her pulse. Then he looked at her tongue, then he felt her pulse again, and while he did so, he eyed the half-emptied wine-glass as if in profound abstraction.

"I should give her——" said the doctor at length, "a teaspoonful, every now and then, of hot brandy and water."

"Why, that's exactly what we've done, sir!" said the delighted landlady.

"I should also," observed the doctor, who had passed the foot-bath on the stairs, "I should also," said the doctor, in the voice of an oracle, "put her feet in hot water, and wrap them up in flannel. I should likewise," said the doctor with increased solemnity, "give her something light for supper—the wing of a roasted fowl now——"

"Why, goodness gracious me, sir, it's cooking at the kitchen fire this instant!" cried the landlady. And so indeed it was, for the schoolmaster had ordered it to be put down, and it was getting on so well that the doctor might have smelt it if he had tried—perhaps he did.

"You may then," said the doctor, rising gravely, "give her a glass of hot mulled port wine, if she likes wine——"

"And a toast, sir?" suggested the landlady.

"Ay," said the doctor, in the tone of a man who makes a dignified concession. "And a toast—of bread. But be very particular to make it of bread, if you please, ma'am."

With which parting injunction, slowly and portentously delivered, the doctor departed, leaving the whole house in admiration of that wisdom which tallied so closely with their own. Everybody said he was a very shrewd doctor indeed, and knew perfectly what people's constitutions were; which there appears some reason to suppose he did.

While her supper was preparing, the child fell into a refreshing sleep, from which they were obliged to rouse her when it was ready. As she evinced extraordinary uneasiness on learning that her grandfather was below stairs, and as she was greatly troubled at the thought of their being apart, he took his supper with her. Finding her still very restless on this head, they made him up a bed in an inner room, to which he presently retired. The key of this chamber happened by good fortune to be on that side of the door which was in Nell's room; she turned it on him when the landlady had withdrawn, and crept to bed again with a thankful heart.

The schoolmaster sat for a long time smoking his pipe by the kitchen fire, which was now deserted, thinking, with a very happy face, on the fortunate chance which had brought him so opportunely to the child's assistance, and parrying, as well as in his simple way he could, the inquisitive cross-examination of the landlady, who had a great curiosity to be made acquainted with every particular of Nell's life and history. The poor schoolmaster was so open-hearted, and so little versed in the most ordinary cunning or deceit, that she could not have failed to succeed in the first five minutes, but that he happened to be unacquainted with what she wished to know; and so he told her. The landlady, by no means satisfied with this assurance, which she considered an ingenious evasion of the question, rejoined that he had his reasons of course. Heaven forbid that she should wish to pry into the affairs of her customers, which indeed were no business of hers, who had so many of her own. She had merely asked a civil question, and to be sure she knew it would meet with a civil answer. She was quite satisfied—quite. She had rather perhaps that he would have said at once that he didn't choose to be communicative, because that would have been plain and intelligible. However, she had no right to be offended of course. He was the best judge, and had a perfect right to say what he pleased; nobody could dispute that, for a moment. Oh dear, no!

"I assure you, my good lady," said the mild schoolmaster, "that I have told you the plain truth—as I hope to be saved, I have told you the truth."

"Why then, I do believe you are in earnest," rejoined the land-lady, with ready good-humour, "and I'm very sorry I have teased you. But curiosity you know is the curse of our sex, and that's the fact."

The landlord scratched his head, as if he thought the curse some-times involved the other sex likewise; but he was prevented from making any remark to that effect, if he had it in contemplation to do so, by the schoolmaster's rejoinder.

"You should question me for half a dozen hours at a sitting, and welcome, and I would answer you patiently for the kindness of heart you have shown to-night, if I could," he said. "As it is, please to take care of her in the morning, and let me know early how she is; and to understand that I am paymaster for the three."

So, parting with them on most friendly terms, not the less cordial perhaps for this last direction, the schoolmaster went to his bed, and the host and hostess to theirs.

The report in the morning was, that the child was better, but was extremely weak, and would at least require a day's rest, and careful nursing, before she could proceed upon her journey. The schoolmaster received this communication with perfect cheerfulness, observing that he had a day to spare—two days for that matter—and could very well afford to wait. As the patient was to sit up in the evening, he appointed to visit her in her room at a certain hour, and rambling out with his book, did not return until the hour arrived.

Nell could not help weeping when they were left alone; whereat, and at sight of her pale face and wasted figure, the simple school-master shed a few tears himself, at the same time showing in very energetic language how foolish it was to do so, and how very easily it could be avoided, if one tried.

"It makes me unhappy even in the midst of all this kindness," said the child, "to think that we should be a burden upon you. How can I ever thank you? If I had not met you so far from home, I must have died, and he would have been left alone."

"We'll not talk about dying," said the schoolmaster; "and as to burdens, I have made my fortune since you slept at my cottage."

"Indeed!" cried the child joyfully.

"Oh yes," returned her friend. "I have been appointed clerk and schoolmaster to a village a long way from here—and a long way from the old one as you may suppose—at five-and-thirty pounds a year. Five-and-thirty pounds!"

"I am very glad," said the child—"so very, very glad."

"I am on my way there now," resumed the schoolmaster. "They allowed me the stage-coach hire—outside stage-coach hire all the way. Bless you, they grudge me nothing. But as the time at which I am expected there, left me ample leisure, I determined to walk instead. How glad I am, to think I did so!"

"How glad should we be!"

"Yes, yes," said the schoolmaster, moving restlessly in his chair, "certainly, that's very true. But you—where are you going, where are you coming from, what have you been doing since you left me, what had you been doing before? Now, tell me—do tell me. I know very little of the world, and perhaps you are better fitted to advise me in its affairs than I am qualified to give advice to you; but I am very sincere, and I have a reason (you have not forgotten it) for loving you. I have felt since that time as if my love for him who died, had been transferred to you who stood beside his bed. If this," he added, looking upwards, "is the beautiful creation that springs from ashes, let its peace prosper with me, as I deal tenderly and compassionately by this young child!"

The plain, frank kindness of the honest schoolmaster, the affectionate earnestness of his speech and manner, the truth which was stamped upon his every word and look, gave the child a confidence in him, which the utmost arts of treachery and dissimulation could never have awakened in her breast. She told him all—that they had no friend or relative—that she had fled with the old man, to save him from a madhouse and all the miseries he dreaded—that she was flying now, to save him from himself—and that she sought an asylum in some remote and primitive place, where the temptation before which he fell would never enter, and her late sorrows and distresses could have no place.

The schoolmaster heard her with astonishment. "This child!"—he thought—"has this child heroically persevered under all doubts and dangers, struggled with poverty and suffering, upheld and sustained by strong affection and the consciousness of rectitude alone! And yet the world is full of such heroism. Have I yet to learn that the hardest and best-borne trials are those which are never chronicled in any earthly record, and are suffered every day! And should I be surprised to hear the story of this child!"

What more he thought or said, matters not. It was concluded that Nell and her grandfather should accompany him to the village whither he was bound, and that he should endeavour to find them some humble occupation by which they could subsist. "We shall be sure to succeed," said the schoolmaster, heartily. "The cause is too good a one to fail."

They arranged to proceed upon their journey next evening, as a stage-waggon, which travelled for some distance on the same road as they must take, would stop at the inn to change horses, and the driver for a small gratuity would give Nell a place inside. A bargain was soon struck when the waggon came; and in due time it rolled away; with the child comfortably bestowed among the softer packages, her grandfather and the schoolmaster walking on beside the driver, and the landlady and all the good folks of the inn screaming out their good wishes and farewells.

What a soothing, luxurious, drowsy way of travelling, to lie inside that slowly-moving mountain, listening to the tinkling of the horses' bells, the occasional smacking of the carter's whip, the smooth rolling of the great broad wheels, the rattle of the harness, the cheery good nights of passing travellers jogging past on little short-stepped horses—all made pleasantly indistinct by the thick awning, which seemed made for lazy listening under, till one fell asleep! The very going to sleep, still with an indistinct idea, as the head jogged to and fro upon the pillow, of moving onward with no trouble or fatigue, and hearing all these sounds like dreamy music, lulling to the senses—and the slow waking up, and finding one's self staring out through the breezy curtain half-opened in the front, far up into the cold bright sky with its countless stars, and downward at the driver's lantern dancing on like its namesake Jack of the swamps and marshes, and sideways at the dark grim trees, and forward at the long bare road rising up, up, up, until it stopped abruptly at a sharp high ridge as if there were no more road, and all beyond was sky—and the stopping at the inn to bait, and being helped out, and going into a room with fire and candles, and winking very much, and being agreeably reminded that the night was cold, and anxious for very comfort's sake to think it colder than it was!—What a delicious journey was that journey in the waggon!

Then the going on again—so fresh at first, and shortly afterwards so sleepy. The waking from a sound nap as the mail came dashing past like a highway comet, with gleaming lamps and rattling hoofs, and visions of a guard behind, standing up to keep his feet warm, and of a gentleman in a fur cap opening his eyes and looking wild and stupefied—the stopping at the turnpike where the man was gone to bed, and knocking at the door until he answered with a smothered shout from under the bedclothes in the little room above, where the faint light was burning, and presently came down, night-capped and shivering, to throw the gate wide open, and wish all waggons off the road except by day. The cold sharp interval between night and morning—the distant streak of light widening and spreading, and turning from grey to white, and from white to yellow, and from yellow to burning red—the presence of day, with all its cheerfulness and life—men and horses at the plough—birds in the trees and hedges, and boys in solitary fields, frightening them away with rattles. The coming to a town—people busy in the markets; light carts and chaises round the tavern yard; tradesmen standing at their doors; men running horses up and down the street for sale; pigs plunging and grunting in the dirty distance, getting off with long strings at their legs, running into clean chemists' shops and being dislodged with brooms by 'prentices; the night coach changing horses—the passengers cheerless, cold, ugly, and discontented, with three months' growth of hair in one night—the coachman fresh as from a bandbox, and exquisitely beautiful by contrast:—so much bustle, so many things in motion, such a variety of incidents—when was there a journey with so many delights as that journey in the waggon!

Sometimes walking for a mile or two while her grandfather rode inside, and sometimes even prevailing upon the schoolmaster to take her place and lie down to rest, Nell travelled on very happily until they came to a large town, where the waggon stopped, and where they spent a night. They passed a large church; and in the streets were a number of old houses, built of a kind of earth or plaster, crossed and re-crossed in a great many directions with black beams, which gave them a remarkable and very ancient look. The doors, too, were arched and low, some with oaken portals and quaint benches, where the former inhabitants had sat on summer evenings. The windows were latticed in little diamond panes, that seemed to wink and blink upon the passengers as if they were dim of sight. They had long since got clear of the smoke and furnaces, except in one or two solitary instances, where a factory planted among fields withered the space about it, like a burning mountain. When they had passed through this town, they entered again upon the country, and began to draw near their place of destination.

It was not so near, however, but that they spent another night upon the road; not that their doing so was quite an act of necessity, but that the schoolmaster, when they approached within a few miles of his village, had a fidgety sense of his dignity as the new clerk, and was unwilling to make his entry in dusty shoes, and travel-disordered dress. It was a fine, clear, autumn morning, when they came upon the scene of his promotion, and stopped to contemplate its beauties.

"See—here's the church!" cried the delighted schoolmaster, in a low voice; "and that old building close beside it, is the school-house, I'll be sworn. Five-and-thirty pounds a year in this beautiful place!"

They admired everything—the old grey porch, the mullioned windows, the venerable gravestones dotting the green churchyard, the ancient tower, the very weathercock; the brown thatched roofs of cottage, barn, and homestead, peeping from among the trees; the stream that rippled by the distant watermill; the blue Welsh mountains far away. It was for such a spot the child had wearied in the dense, dark, miserable haunts of labour. Upon her bed of ashes, and amidst the squalid horrors through which they had forced their way, visions of such scenes—beautiful indeed, but not more beautiful than this sweet reality—had been always present to her mind. They had seemed to melt into a dim and airy distance, as the prospect of ever beholding them again grew fainter; but, as they receded. she had loved and panted for them more.

"I must leave you somewhere for a few minutes," said the schoolmaster, at length breaking the silence into which they had fallen in their gladness. "I have a letter to present, and inquiries to make, you know. Where shall I take you? To the little inn yonder?"

"Let us wait here," rejoined Nell. "The gate is open. We will sit in the church porch till you come back."

"A good place too," said the schoolmaster, leading the way towards it, disencumbering himself of his portmanteau, and placing it on the stone seat. "Be sure that I come back with good news, and am not long gone."

So, the happy schoolmaster put on a bran-new pair of gloves which he had carried in a little parcel in his pocket all the way, and hurried off, full of ardour and excitement.

The child watched him from the porch until the intervening foliage hid him from her view, and then stepped softly out into the old churchyard—so solemn and quiet, that every rustle of her dress upon the fallen leaves, which strewed the path and made her footsteps noiseless, seemed an invasion of its silence. It was a very aged, ghostly place; the church had been built many hundreds of years ago, and had once had a convent or monastery attached; for arches in ruins, remains of oriel windows, and fragments of blackened walls, were yet standing; while other portions of the old building, which had crumbled away and fallen down, were mingled with the church-yard earth and overgrown with grass, as if they too claimed a bury-ing-place and sought to mix their ashes with the dust of men. Hard by these gravestones of dead years, and forming a part of the ruin which some pains had been taken to render habitable in modern times, were two small dwellings with sunken windows and oaken doors, fast hastening to decay, empty and desolate.

Upon these tenements, the attention of the child became ex-clusively riveted. She knew not why. The church, the ruin, the anti-quated graves, had equal claims at least upon a stranger's thoughts, but from the moment when her eyes first rested on these two dwell-ings, she could turn to nothing else. Even when she had made the circuit of the inclosure and, returning to the porch, sat pensively waiting for their friend, she took her station where she could still look upon them, and felt as if fascinated towards that spot.

CHAPTER XLVII

Kit's mother and the single gentleman—upon whose track it is expedient to follow with hurried steps, lest this history should be chargeable with inconstancy, and the offence of leaving its characters in situations of uncertainty and doubt—Kit's mother and the single gentleman, speeding onward in the post-chaise-and-four whose de-parture from the Notary's door we have already witnessed, soon left the town behind them, and struck fire from the flints of the broad highway.

The good woman, being not a little embarrassed by the novelty of her situation, and certain maternal apprehensions that perhaps by this time little Jacob, or the baby, or both, had fallen into the fire, or tumbled down stairs, or had been squeezed behind doors, or had scalded their windpipes in endeavouring to allay their thirst at the spouts of tea-kettles, preserved an uneasy silence; and meeting from the window the eyes of turnpike-men, omnibus-drivers, and others, felt in the new dignity of her position like a mourner at a funeral, who, not being greatly afflicted by the loss of the departed, recog-nises his every-day acquaintance from the window of the mourning-coach, but is constrained to preserve a decent solemnity, and the appearance of being indifferent to all external objects.

To have been indifferent to the companionship of the single gentleman would have been tantamount to being gifted with nerves of steel. Never did chaise inclose, or horses draw, such a restless gentleman as he. He never sat in the same position for two minutes together, but was perpetually tossing his arms and legs about, pulling up the sashes and letting them violently down, or thrusting his head out of one window to draw it in again and thrust it out of another. He carried in his pocket, too, a fire-box of mysterious and unknown construction; and as sure as ever Kit's mother closed her eyes, so surely—whisk, rattle, fizz—there was the single gentleman consulting his watch by a flame of fire, and letting the sparks fall down among the straw as if there were no such thing as a possibility of himself and Kit's mother being roasted alive before the boys could stop their horses. Whenever they halted to change, there he was— out of the carriage without letting down the steps, bursting about the inn-yard like a lighted cracker, pulling out his watch by lamp-light and forgetting to look at it before he put it up again, and in short committing so many extravagances that Kit's mother was quite afraid of him. Then, when the horses were to, in he came like a harlequin, and before they had gone a mile, out came the watch and the fire-box together, and Kit's mother was wide awake again, with no hope of a wink of sleep for that stage.

"Are you comfortable?" the single gentleman would say after one of these exploits, turning sharply round.

"Quite, sir, thank you."

"Are you sure? An't you cold?"

"It is a little chilly, sir," Kit's mother would reply.

"I knew it!" cried the single gentleman, letting down one of the front glasses. "She wants some brandy and water! Of course she does. How could I forget it? Hallo! Stop at the next inn, and call out for a glass of hot brandy and water."

It was in vain for Kit's mother to protest that she stood in need of nothing of the kind. The single gentleman was inexorable; and whenever he had exhausted all other modes and fashions of restlessness, it invariably occurred to him that Kit's mother wanted brandy and water.

In this way they travelled on until near midnight, when they stopped to supper, for which meal the single gentleman ordered everything eatable that the house contained; and because Kit's mother didn't eat everything at once, and eat it all, he took it into his head that she must be ill.

"You're faint," said the single gentleman, who did nothing himself but walk about the room. "I see what's the matter with you, ma'am. You're faint."

"Thank you, sir, I'm not indeed."

"I know you are. I'm sure of it. I drag this poor woman from the bosom of her family at a minute's notice, and she goes on getting fainter and fainter before my eyes. I'm a pretty fellow! How many children have you got, ma'am?"

"Two, sir, besides Kit."

"Boys, ma'am?"

"Yes, sir."

"Are they christened?"

"Only half baptised, as yet, sir."

"I'm godfather to both of 'em. Remember that, if you please, ma'am, You had better have some mulled wine."

"I couldn't touch a drop indeed, sir."

"You must," said the single gentleman. "I see you want it. I ought to have thought of it before."

Immediately flying to the bell, and calling for mulled wine as impetuously as if it had been wanted for instant use in the recovery of some person apparently drowned, the single gentleman made Kit's mother swallow a bumper of it at such a high temperature that the tears ran down her face, and then hustled her off to the chaise again, where—not impossibly from the effects of this agreeable sedative— she soon became insensible to his restlessness, and fell fast asleep. Nor were the happy effects of this prescription of a transitory nature, as, notwithstanding that the distance was greater, and the journey longer, than the single gentleman had anticipated, she did not awake until it was broad day, and they were clattering over the pavement of a town.

"This is the place!" cried her companion, letting down all the glasses. "Drive to the wax-work!"

The boy on the wheeler touched his hat, and setting spurs to his horse, to the end that they might go in brilliantly, all four broke into a smart canter, and dashed through the streets with a noise that brought the good folks wondering to their doors and windows, and drowned the sober voices of the town-clocks as they chimed out half-past eight. They drove up to a door round which a crowd of persons were collected, and there stopped.

"What's this?" said the single gentleman thrusting out his head. "Is anything the matter here?"

"A wedding, sir, a wedding!" cried several voices. "Hurrah!"

The single gentleman, rather bewildered by finding himself the centre of this noisy throng, alighted with the assistance of one of the postilions, and handed out Kit's mother, at sight of whom the populace cried out, "Here's another wedding!" and roared and leaped for joy.

"The world has gone mad, I think," said the single gentleman, pressing through the concourse with his supposed bride. "Stand back here, will you, and let me knock."

Anything that makes a noise is satisfactory to a crowd. A score of dirty hands were raised directly to knock for him, and seldom has a knocker of equal powers been made to produce more deafening sounds than this particular engine on the occasion in question. Having rendered these voluntary services, the throng modestly retired a little, preferring that the single gentleman should bear their consequences alone.

"Now, sir, what do you want?" said a man with a large white bow at his button-hole, opening the door, and confronting him with a very stoical aspect.

"Who has been married here, my friend?" said the single gentleman.

"I have."

"You! and to whom in the devil's name?"

"What right have you to ask?" returned the bridegroom, eyeing him from top to toe.

"What right!" cried the single gentleman, drawing the arm of Kit's mother more tightly through his own, for that good woman evidently had it in contemplation to run away. "A right you little dream of. Mind, good people, if this fellow has been marrying a minor—tut, tut, that can't be. Where is the child you have here, my good fellow? You call her Nell. Where is she?"

As he propounded this question, which Kit's mother echoed, somebody in a room near at hand uttered a great shriek, and a stout lady in a white dress came running to the door, and supported herself upon the bridegroom's arm.

"Where is she!" cried this lady. "What news have you brought me? What has become of her?"

The single gentleman started back, and gazed upon the face of the late Mrs. Jarley (that morning wedded to the philosophic George, to the eternal wrath and despair of Mr. Slum the poet), with looks of conflicting apprehension, disappointment, and incredulity. At length he stammered out.

"I ask *you* where she is? What do you mean?"

"Oh sir!" cried the bride, "If you have come here to do her any good, why weren't you here a week ago?"

"She is not—not dead?" said the person to whom she addressed herself, turning very pale.

"No, not so bad as that."

"I thank God!" cried the single gentleman feebly. "Let me come in."

They drew back to admit him, and when he had entered, closed the door.

"You see in me, good people," he said, turning to the newly-married couple, "one to whom life itself is not dearer than the two persons whom I seek. They would not know me. My features are strange to them, but if they or either of them are here, take this good woman with you, and let them see her first, for her they both know. If you deny them from any mistaken regard or fear for them, judge of my intentions by their recognition of this person as their old humble friend."

"I always said it!" cried the bride, "I knew she was not a common child! Alas, sir! we have no power to help you, for all that we could do has been tried in vain."

With that, they related to him, without disguise or concealment, all that they knew of Nell and her grandfather, from their first meeting with them, down to the time of their sudden disappearance; adding (which was quite true) that they had made every possible effort to trace them, but without success; having been at first in great alarm for their safety, as well as on account of the suspicions to which they themselves might one day be exposed in consequence of their abrupt departure. They dwelt upon the old man's imbecility of mind, upon the uneasiness the child had always testified when he was absent, upon the company he had been supposed to keep, and upon the increased depression which had gradually crept over her and changed her both in health and spirits. Whether she had missed the old man in the night, and, knowing or conjecturing whither he had bent his steps, had gone in pursuit, or whether they had left the house together, they had no means of determining. Certain they considered it, that there was but slender prospect left of hearing of them again, and that whether their flight originated with the old man, or with the child, there was now no hope of their return.

To all this, the single gentleman listened with the air of a man quite borne down by grief and disappointment. He shed tears when he spoke of the grandfather, and appeared in deep affliction.

Not to protract this portion of our narrative, and to make short work of a long story, let it be briefly written that before the interview came to a close, the single gentleman deemed he had sufficient evidence of having been told the truth, and that he endeavoured to force upon the bride and bridegroom an acknowledgment of their kindness to the unfriendly child, which, however, they steadily declined accepting. In the end, the happy couple jolted away in the caravan to spend their honeymoon in a country excursion; and the single gentleman and Kit's mother stood ruefully before their carriage-door.

"Where shall we drive you, sir?" said the post-boy.

"You may drive me," said the single gentleman, "to the——" He was not going to add "inn," but he added it for the sake of Kit's mother; and to the inn they went.

Rumours had already got abroad that the little girl who used to show the wax-work, was the child of great people who had been stolen from her parents in infancy, and had only just been traced. Opinion was divided whether she was the daughter of a prince, a duke, an earl, a viscount, or a baron, but all agreed upon the main fact, and that the single gentleman was her father; and all bent forward to catch a glimpse, though it were only of the tip of his noble nose, as he rode away, desponding, in his four-horse chaise.

What would he have given to know, and what sorrow would have been saved if he had only known, that at that moment both child and grandfather were seated in the old church porch, patiently awaiting the schoolmaster's return!

CHAPTER XLVIII

POPULAR rumour concerning the single gentleman and his errand, travelling from mouth to mouth, and waxing stronger in the marvellous as it was bandied about—for your popular rumour, unlike the rolling stone of the proverb, is one which gathers a deal of moss in its wanderings up and down,—occasioned his dismounting at the inn-door to be looked upon as an exciting and attractive spectacle, which could scarcely be enough admired; and drew together a large concourse of idlers, who having recently been, as it were, thrown out of employment by the closing of the wax-work and the completion of the nuptial ceremonies, considered his arrival as little else than a special providence, and hailed it with demonstrations of the liveliest joy.

Not at all participating in the general sensation, but wearing the depressed and wearied look of one who sought to meditate on his disappointment in silence and privacy, the single gentleman alighted, and handed out Kit's mother with a gloomy politeness which impressed the lookers-on extremely. That done, he gave her his arm and escorted her into the house, while several active waiters ran on before as a skirmishing party, to clear the way and to show the room which was ready for their reception.

"Any room will do," said the single gentleman. "Let it be near at hand, that's all."

"Close here, sir, if you please to walk this way."

"Would the gentleman like this room?" said a voice, as a little out-of-the-way door at the foot of the well-staircase flew briskly open and a head popped out. "He's quite welcome to it. He's as welcome as flowers in May, or coals at Christmas. *Would* you like this room, sir? Honour me by walking in. Do me the favour, pray."

"Goodness gracious me!" cried Kit's mother, falling back in extreme surprise, "only think of this!"

She had some reason to be astonished, for the person who had proffered the gracious invitation was no other than Daniel Quilp. The little door out of which he had thrust his head was close to the inn larder; and there he stood, bowing with grotesque politeness; as much at his ease as if the door were that of his own house; blighting all the legs of mutton and cold roast fowls by his close companionship, and looking like the evil genius of the cellars come from under ground upon some work of mischief.

"Would you do me the honour?" said Quilp.

"I prefer being alone," replied the single gentleman.

"Oh!" said Quilp. And with that, he darted in again with one jerk and clapped the little door to, like a figure in a Dutch clock when the hour strikes.

"Why it was only last night, sir," whispered Kit's mother, "that I left him in Little Bethel."

"Indeed!" said her fellow-passenger. "When did that person come here, waiter?"

"Come down by the night-coach this morning, sir."

"Humph! And when is he going?"

"Can't say, sir, really. When the chambermaid asked him just now if he should want a bed, sir, he first made faces at her, and then wanted to kiss her."

"Beg him to walk this way," said the single gentleman. "I should be glad to exchange a word with him, tell him. Beg him to come at once, do you hear?"

The man stared on receiving these instructions, for the single gentleman had not only displayed as much astonishment as Kit's mother at sight of the dwarf, but, standing in no fear of him, had been at less pains to conceal his dislike and repugnance. He departed on his errand, however, and immediately returned, ushering in its object.

"Your servant, sir," said the dwarf. "I encountered your messenger half-way. I thought you'd allow me to pay my compliments to you. I hope you're well. I hope you're very well."

There was a short pause, while the dwarf, with half-shut eyes and puckered face, stood waiting for an answer. Receiving none, he turned towards his more familiar acquaintance.

"Christopher's mother!" he cried. "Such a dear lady, such a worthy woman, so blest in her honest son! How is Christopher's mother? Have change of air and scene improved her? Her little family too, and Christopher? Do they thrive? Do they flourish? Are they growing into worthy citizens, eh?"

Making his voice ascend in the scale with every succeeding question, Mr. Quilp finished in a shrill squeak, and subsided into the panting look which was customary with him, and which, whether it were assumed or natural, had equally the effect of banishing all expression from his face, and rendering it, as far as it afforded any index to his mood or meaning, a perfect blank.

"Mr. Quilp," said the single gentleman.

The dwarf put his hand to his great flapped ear, and counterfeited the closest attention.

"We two have met before——"

"Surely," cried Quilp, nodding his head. "Oh surely, sir. Such an honour and pleasure—it's both, Christopher's mother, it's both—is not to be forgotten so soon. By no means!"

"You may remember that the day I arrived in London, and found the house to which I drove empty and deserted, I was directed by some of the neighbours to you, and waited upon you without stopping for rest or refreshment?"

"How precipitate that was, and yet what an earnest and vigorous measure!" said Quilp, conferring with himself, in imitation of his friend Mr. Sampson Brass.

"I found," said the single gentleman, "you, most unaccountably, in possession of everything that had so recently belonged to another man, and that other man, who up to the time of your entering upon his property had been looked upon as affluent, reduced to sudden beggary, and driven from house and home."

"We had warrant for what we did, my good sir," rejoined Quilp, "we had our warrant. Don't say driven either. He went of his own accord—vanished in the night, sir."

"No matter," said the single gentleman angrily. "He was gone."

"Yes, he was gone," said Quilp, with the same exasperating composure. "No doubt he was gone. The only question was, where. And it's a question still."

"Now, what am I to think," said the single gentleman, sternly regarding him, "of you, who, plainly indisposed to give me any information then—nay, obviously holding back, and sheltering yourself with all kinds of cunning, trickery, and evasion,—are dogging my footsteps now?"

"I dogging!" cried Quilp.

"Why, are you not?" returned his questioner, fretted into a state of the utmost irritation. "Were you not a few hours since, sixty miles off, and in the chapel to which this good woman goes to say her prayers?"

"She was there too, I think?" said Quilp, still perfectly unmoved. "I might say, if I was inclined to be rude, how do I know but you are dogging *my* footsteps. Yes, I was at chapel. What then? I've read in books that pilgrims were used to go to chapel before they went on journeys, to put up petitions for their safe return. Wise men! journeys are very perilous—especially outside the coach. Wheels come off, horses take fright, coachmen drive too fast, coaches overturn. I always go to chapel before I start on journeys. It's the last thing I do on such occasions, indeed."

That Quilp lied most heartily in this speech, it needed no very great penetration to discover, although for anything that he suffered to appear in his face, voice, or manner, he might have been clinging to the truth with the quiet constancy of a martyr.

"In the name of all that's calculated to drive one crazy, man," said the unfortunate single gentleman, "have you not, for some reason of your own, taken upon yourself my errand? don't you know with what object I have come here, and if you do know, can you throw no light upon it?"

"You think I'm a conjuror, sir," replied Quilp, shrugging up his shoulders. "If I was, I should tell my own fortune—and make it."

"Ah! we have said all we need say, I see," returned the other, throwing himself impatiently upon a sofa. "Pray leave us, if you please."

"Willingly," returned Quilp. "Most willingly. Christopher's mother, my good soul, farewell. A pleasant journey—*back*, sir. Ahem!"

With these parting words, and with a grin upon his features altogether indescribable, but which seemed to be compounded of every monstrous grimace of which men or monkeys are capable, the dwarf slowly retreated and closed the door behind him.

"Oho!" he said when he had regained his own room, and sat himself down in a chair with his arms akimbo. "Oho! Are you there, my friend? In-deed!"

Chuckling as though in very great glee, and recompensing himself for the restraint he had lately put upon his countenance by twisting it into all imaginable varieties of ugliness, Mr. Quilp, rocking himself to and fro in his chair and nursing his left leg at the same time, fell into certain meditations, of which it may be necessary to relate the substance.

First, he reviewed the circumstances which had led to his repairing to that spot, which were briefly these. Dropping in at Mr. Sampson Brass's office on the previous evening, in the absence of that gentleman and his learned sister, he had lighted upon Mr. Swiveller, who chanced at the moment to be sprinkling a glass of warm gin and water on the dust of the law, and to be moistening his clay, as the phrase goes, rather copiously. But as clay in the abstract, when too much moistened, becomes of a weak and uncertain consistency, breaking down in unexpected places, retaining impressions but faintly, and preserving no strength or steadiness of character, so Mr. Swiveller's clay, having imbibed a considerable quantity of moisture, was in a very loose and slippery state, insomuch that the various ideas impressed upon it were fast losing their distinctive character, and running unto each other. It is not uncommon for human clay in this condition to value itself above all things upon its great prudence and sagacity; and Mr. Swiveller, especially prizing himself upon these qualities, took occasion to remark that he had made strange discoveries in connexion with the single gentleman who lodged above, which he had determined to keep within his own bosom, and which neither tortures nor cajolery should ever induce him to reveal. Of this determination Mr. Quilp expressed his high approval, and setting himself in the same breath to goad Mr. Swiveller on to further hints, soon made out that the single gentleman had been seen in communication with Kit, and that this was the secret which was never to be disclosed.

Possessed of this piece of information, Mr. Quilp directly supposed that the single gentleman above stairs must be the same individual who had waited on him, and having assured himself by further inquiries that this surmise was correct, had no difficulty in arriving at the conclusion that the intent and object of his correspondence with Kit was the recovery of his old client and the child. Burning with curiosity to know what proceedings were afoot, he resolved to pounce upon Kit's mother as the person least likely to resist his arts, and consequently the most likely to be entrapped into such revelations as he sought; so taking an abrupt leave of Mr. Swiveller, he hurried to her house. The good woman being from home, he made inquiries of a neighbour, as Kit himself did soon afterwards, and being directed to the chapel betook himself there, in order to waylay her, at the conclusion of the service.

He had not sat in the chapel more than a quarter of an hour, and with his eyes piously fixed upon the ceiling was chuckling inwardly over the joke of his being there at all, when Kit himself appeared. Watchful as a lynx, one glance showed the dwarf that he had come on business. Absorbed in appearance, as we have seen, and feigning a profound abstraction, he noted every circumstance of his behaviour, and when he withdrew with his family, shot out after him. In fine, he traced them to the Notary's house; learnt the destination of the carriage from one of the postilions; and knowing that a fast night-coach started for the same place, at the very hour which was on the point of striking, from a street hard by, darted round to the coach-office without more ado, and took his seat upon the roof. After passing and repassing the carriage on the road, and being passed and repassed by it sundry times in the course of the night, according as their stoppages were longer or shorter, or their rate of travelling varied, they reached the town almost together. Quilp kept the chaise in sight, mingled with the crowd, learnt the single gentleman's errand, and its failure, and having possessed himself of all that it was material to know, hurried off, reached the inn before him, had the interview just now detailed, and shut himself up in the little room in which he hastily reviewed all these occurrences.

"You are there, are you, my friend?" he repeated, greedily biting his nails, "I am suspected and thrown aside, and Kit's the confidential agent, is he? I shall have to dispose of him, I fear. If we had come up with them this morning," he continued, after a thoughtful pause, "I was ready to prove a pretty good claim. I could have made my profit. But for these canting hypocrites, the lad and his mother, I could get this fiery gentleman as comfortably into my net as our old friend—our mutual friend, ha! ha!—and chubby, rosy Nell. At the worst, it's a golden opportunity, not to be lost. Let us find them first, and I'll find means of draining you of some of your superfluous cash, sir, while there are prison bars, and bolts, and locks, to keep your friend or kinsman safely. I hate your virtuous people!" said the dwarf, throwing off a bumper of brandy, and smacking his lips, "ah! I hate 'em every one!"

This was not a mere empty vaunt, but a deliberate avowal, of his real sentiments; for Mr. Quilp, who loved nobody, had by little and little come to hate everybody nearly or remotely connected with his ruined client:—the old man himself, because he had been able to deceive him and elude his vigilance—the child, because she was the object of Mrs. Quilp's commiseration and constant self-reproach—the single gentleman, because of his unconcealed aversion to himself —Kit and his mother, most mortally, for the reasons already shown. Above and beyond that general feeling of opposition to them, which would have been inseparable from his ravenous desire to enrich himself by these altered circumstances, Daniel Quilp hated them every one.

In this amiable mood, Mr. Quilp enlivened himself and his hatreds with more brandy, and then, changing his quarters, withdrew to an obscure alehouse, under cover of which seclusion he instituted all possible inquiries that might lead to the discovery of the old man and his grandchild. But all was in vain. Not the slightest trace or clue could be obtained. They had left the town by night; no one had seen them go; no one had met them on the road; the driver of no coach, cart, or waggon, had seen any travellers answering their description; nobody had fallen in with them, or heard of them. Convinced at last that for the present all such attempts were hopeless, he appointed two or three scouts, with promises of large rewards in case of their forwarding him any intelligence, and returned to London by next day's coach.

It was some gratification to Mr. Quilp to find, as he took his place upon the roof, that Kit's mother was alone inside; from which circumstance he derived in the course of the journey much cheerfulness of spirit, inasmuch as her solitary condition enabled him to terrify her with many extraordinary annoyances; such as hanging over the side of the coach at the risk of his life, and staring in with his great goggle eyes, which seemed in hers the more horrible from his face being upside down; dodging her in this way from one window to another; getting nimbly down whenever they changed horses and thrusting his head in at the window with a dismal squint: which ingenious tortures had such an effect upon Mrs. Nubbles, that she was quite unable for the time to resist the belief that Mr. Quilp did in his own person represent and embody that Evil Power, who was so vigorously attacked at Little Bethel, and who, by reason of her backslidings in respect of Astley's and oysters, was now frolicsome and rampant.

Kit, having been apprised by letter of his mother's intended return, was waiting for her at the coach-office; and great was his surprise when he saw, leering over the coachman's shoulder like some familiar demon invisible to all eyes but his, the well-known face of Quilp.

"How are you, Christopher?" croaked the dwarf from the coach-top. "All right, Christopher. Mother's inside."

"Why, how did he come here, mother?" whispered Kit.

"I don't know how he came or why, my dear," rejoined Mrs. Nubbles, dismounting with her son's assistance, "but he has been a terrifying of me out of my seven senses all this blessed day."

"He has?" cried Kit.

"You wouldn't believe it, that you wouldn't," replied his mother; "but don't say a word to him, for I really don't believe he's human. Hush! Don't turn round as if I was talking of him, but he's a squinting at me now in the full blaze of the coach-lamp, quite awful!"

In spite of his mother's injunction, Kit turned sharply round to look. Mr. Quilp was serenely gazing at the stars, quite absorbed in celestial contemplation.

"Oh, he's the artfullest creetur!" cried Mrs. Nubbles. "But come away. Don't speak to him for the world."

"Yes I will, mother. What nonsense. I say, sir——"

Mr. Quilp affected to start, and looked smilingly round.

"You let my mother alone, will you?" said Kit. "How dare you tease a poor lone woman like her, making her miserable and melancholy as if she hadn't got enough to make her so, without you. An't you ashamed of yourself, you little monster?"

"Monster!" said Quilp inwardly, with a smile. "Ugliest dwarf that could be seen anywhere for a penny—monster—ah!"

"You show her any of your impudence again," resumed Kit, shouldering the bandbox, "and I tell you what, Mr. Quilp, I won't bear with you any more. You have no right to do it; I'm sure we never interfered with you. This isn't the first time; and if ever you worry or frighten her again, you'll oblige me (though I should be very sorry to do it, on account of your size) to beat you."

Quilp said not a word in reply, but walking up so close to Kit as to bring his eyes within two or three inches of his face, looked fixedly at him, retreated a little distance without averting his gaze, approached again, again withdrew, and so on for half a dozen times, like a head in a phantasmagoria. Kit stood his ground as if in expectation of an immediate assault, but finding that nothing came of these gestures, snapped his fingers and walked away; his mother dragging him off as fast as she could, and, even in the midst of his news of little Jacob and the baby, looking anxiously over her shoulder to see if Quilp were following.

CHAPTER XLIX

KIT's mother might have spared herself the trouble of looking back so often, for nothing was further from Mr. Quilp's thoughts than any intention of pursuing her and her son, or renewing the quarrel with which they had parted. He went his way, whistling from time to time some fragments of a tune; and with a face quite tranquil and composed, jogged pleasantly towards home; entertaining himself as he went with visions of the fears and terrors of Mrs. Quilp, who, having received no intelligence of him for three whole days and two nights, and having had no previous notice of his absence, was doubtless by that time in a state of distraction, and constantly fainting away with anxiety and grief.

This facetious probability was so congenial to the dwarf's humour, and so exquisitely amusing to him, that he laughed as he went along until the tears ran down his cheeks; and more than once, when he found himself in a bye-street, vented his delight in a shrill scream, which greatly terrifying any lonely passenger, who happened to be walking on before him expecting nothing so little, increased his mirth, and made him remarkably cheerful and light-hearted.

In this happy flow of spirits Mr. Quilp reached Tower Hill, when, gazing up at the window of his own sitting-room, he thought he descried more light than is usual in a house of mourning. Drawing nearer, and listening attentively, he could hear several voices in earnest conversation, among which he could distinguish, not only those of his wife and mother-in-law, but the tongues of men.

"Ha!" cried the jealous dwarf. "What's this! Do they entertain such visitors while I'm away!"

A smothered cough from above, was the reply. He felt in his pockets for his latch-key, but had forgotten it. There was no resource but to knock at the door.

"A light in the passage," said Quilp, peeping through the key-hole. "A very soft knock; and, by your leave, my lady, I may yet steal upon you unawares. Soho!"

A very low and gentle rap received no answer from within. But after a second application to the knocker, no louder than the first, the door was softly opened by the boy from the wharf, whom Quilp instantly gagged with one hand, and dragged into the street with the other.

"You'll throttle me, master," whispered the boy. "Let go, will you."

"Who's up stairs, you dog?" retorted Quilp in the same tone. "Tell me. And don't speak above your breath, or I'll choke you in good earnest."

The boy could only point to the window, and reply with a stifled giggle, expressive of such intense enjoyment, that Quilp clutched him by the throat again and might have carried his threat into execution, or at least have made very good progress towards that end, but for the boy's nimbly extricating himself from his grasp, and fortifying himself behind the nearest post, at which, after some fruit-less attempts to catch him by the hair of his head, his master was obliged to come to a parley.

"Will you answer me?" said Quilp. "What's going on, above?"

"You won't let one speak," replied the boy. "They—ha ha ha!—they think you're—you're dead. Ha ha ha!"

"Dead!" cried Quilp, relaxing into a grim laugh himself. "No. Do they? Do they really, you dog?"

"They think you're—you're drowned," replied the boy, who in his malicious nature had a strong infusion of his master. "You was last seen on the brink of the wharf, and they think you tumbled over. Ha ha!"

The prospect of playing the spy under such delicious circum-stances, and of disappointing them all by walking in alive, gave more delight to Quilp than the greatest stroke of good fortune could possibly have inspired him with. He was no less tickled than his hopeful assistant, and they both stood for some seconds, grinning and gasping, and wagging their heads at each other, on either side of the post, like an unmatchable pair of Chinese idols.

"Not a word," said Quilp, making towards the door on tiptoe. "Not a sound, not so much as a creaking board, or a stumble against a cobweb. Drowned, eh, Mrs. Quilp? Drowned!"

So saying, he blew out the candle, kicked off his shoes, and groped his way up stairs; leaving his delighted young friend in an ecstasy of

"Who knows but he may be looking down upon us now!"

summersets on the pavement.

The bedroom-door on the staircase being unlocked, Mr. Quilp slipped in, and planted himself behind the door of communication between that chamber and the sitting-room, which standing ajar to render both more airy, and having a very convenient chink (of which he had often availed himself for purposes of espial, and had indeed enlarged with his pocket-knife), enabled him not only to hear, but to see distinctly, what was passing.

Applying his eye to this convenient place, he descried Mr. Brass seated at the table with pen, ink, and paper, and the case-bottle of rum—his own case-bottle, and his own particular Jamaica—convenient to his hand; with hot water, fragrant lemons, white lump sugar, and all things fitting; from which choice materials, Sampson, by no means insensible to their claims upon his attention, had compounded a mighty glass of punch reeking hot; which he was at that very moment stirring up with a teaspoon, and contemplating with looks in which a faint assumption of sentimental regret struggled but weakly with a bland and comfortable joy. At the same table, with both her elbows upon it, was Mrs. Jiniwin; no longer sipping other people's punch feloniously with teaspoons, but taking deep draughts from a jorum of her own; while her daughter—not exactly with ashes on her head, or sackcloth on her back, but preserving a very decent and becoming appearance of sorrow nevertheless—was reclining in an easy chair, and soothing her grief with a smaller allowance of the same glib liquid. There were also present a couple of water-side men, bearing between them certain machines called drags; even these fellows were accommodated with a stiff glass apiece; and as they drank with a great relish, and were naturally of a red-nosed, pimple-faced, convivial look, their presence rather increased than detracted from that decided appearance of comfort, which was the great characteristic of the party.

"If I could poison that dear old lady's rum and water," murmured Quilp, "I'd die happy."

"Ah!" said Mr. Brass, breaking the silence, and raising his eyes to the ceiling with a sigh, "Who knows but he may be looking down upon us now! Who knows but he may be surveying of us from—from somewheres or another, and contemplating us with a watchful eye! Oh Lor!"

Here Mr. Brass stopped to drink half his punch, and then resumed; looking at the other half, as he spoke, with a dejected smile.

"I can almost fancy," said the lawyer shaking his head, "that I see his eye glistening down at the very bottom of my liquor. When shall we look upon his like again? Never, never! One minute we are here"—holding his tumbler before his eyes—"the next we are there"—gulping down its contents, and striking himself emphatically a little below the chest—"in the silent tomb. To think that I should be drinking his very rum! It seems like a dream."

With the view, no doubt, of testing the reality of his position, Mr. Brass pushed his tumbler as he spoke towards Mrs. Jiniwin for the purpose of being replenished; and turned towards the attendant mariners.

"The search has been quite unsuccessful then?"

"Quite, master. But I should say that if he turns up anywhere, he'll come ashore somewhere about Grinidge to-morrow, at ebb tide, eh, mate?"

The other gentleman assented, observing that he was expected at the Hospital, and that several pensioners would be ready to receive him whenever he arrived.

"Then we have nothing for it but resignation," said Mr. Brass; "nothing but resignation, and expectation. It would be a comfort to have his body; it would be a dreary comfort."

"Oh, beyond a doubt," assented Mrs. Jiniwin hastily; "if we once had that, we should be quite sure."

"With regard to the descriptive advertisement," said Sampson Brass, taking up his pen. "It is a melancholy pleasure to recall his traits. Respecting his legs now——?"

"Crooked, certainly," said Mrs. Jiniwin.

"Do you think they *were* crooked?" said Brass, in an insinuating tone. "I think I see them now coming up the street very wide apart, in nankeen pantaloons a little shrunk and without straps. Ah! what a vale of tears we live in. Do we say crooked?"

"I think they were a little so," observed Mrs. Quilp with a sob.

"Legs crooked," said Brass, writing as he spoke. "Large head, short body, legs crooked——"

"Very crooked," suggested Mrs. Jiniwin.

"We'll not say very crooked, ma'am," said Brass piously. "Let us not bear hard upon the weaknesses of the deceased. He is gone, ma'am, to where his legs will never come in question.—We will content ourselves with crooked, Mrs. Jiniwin."

"I thought you wanted the truth," said the old lady. "That's all."

"Bless your eyes, how I love you," muttered Quilp. "There she goes again. Nothing but punch!"

"This is an occupation," said the lawyer, laying down his pen and emptying his glass, "which seems to bring him before my eyes like the Ghost of Hamlet's father, in the very clothes that he wore on work-a-days. His coat, his waistcoat, his shoes and stockings, his trousers, his hat, his wit and humour, his pathos and his umbrella, all come before me like visions of my youth. His linen!" said Mr. Brass smiling fondly at the wall, "his linen which was always of a particular colour, for such was his whim and fancy—how plain I see his linen now!"

"You had better go on, sir," said Mrs. Jiniwin impatiently.

"True, ma'am, true," cried Mr. Brass. "Our faculties must not freeze with grief. I'll trouble you for a little more of that, ma'am. A question now arises, with relation to his nose."

"Flat," said Mrs. Jiniwin.

"Aquiline!" cried Quilp, thrusting in his head, and striking the feature with his fist. "Aquiline, you hag. Do you see it? Do you call this flat? Do you? Eh?"

"Oh capital, capital!" shouted Brass, from the mere force of habit. "Excellent! How very good he is! He's a most remarkable man —so extremely whimsical! Such an amazing power of taking people by surprise!"

Quilp paid no regard whatever to these compliments, nor to the dubious and frightened look into which the lawyer gradually subsided, nor to the shrieks of his wife and mother-in-law, nor to the latter's running from the room, nor to the former's fainting away. Keeping his eye fixed on Sampson Brass, he walked up to the table, and beginning with his glass, drank off the contents, and went regularly round until he had emptied the other two, when he seized the case-bottle, and hugging it under his arm, surveyed him with a most extraordinary leer.

"Not yet, Sampson," said Quilp. "Not just yet!"

"Oh, very good indeed!" cried Brass, recovering his spirits a little. "Ha ha ha! Oh exceedingly good! There's not another man alive who could carry it off like that. A most difficult position to carry off. But he has such a flow of good-humour, such an amazing flow!"

"Good night," said the dwarf, nodding expressively.

"Good night, sir, good night," cried the lawyer, retreating back wards towards the door. "This is a joyful occasion indeed, extremely joyful. Ha ha ha! oh very rich, very rich indeed, re-markably so!"

Waiting until Mr. Brass's ejaculations died away in the distance (for he continued to pour them out, all the way down stairs), Quilp advanced towards the two men, who yet lingered in a kind of stupid amazement.

"Have you been dragging the river all day, gentlemen?" said the dwarf, holding the door open with great politeness.

"And yesterday too, master."

"Dear me, you've had a deal of trouble. Pray consider everything yours that you find upon the—upon the body. Good night!"

The men looked at each other, but had evidently no inclination to argue the point just then, and shuffled out of the room. This speedy clearance effected, Quilp locked the doors; and, still embracing the case-bottle with shrugged-up shoulders and folded arms, stood looking at his insensible wife like a dismounted nightmare.

CHAPTER L

MATRIMONIAL differences are usually discussed by the parties concerned in the form of dialogue, in which the lady bears at least her full half share. Those of Mr. and Mrs. Quilp, however, were an exception to the general rule; the remarks which they occasioned being limited to a long soliloquy on the part of the gentleman, with perhaps a few deprecatory observations from the lady, not extending beyond a trembling monosyllable uttered at long intervals, and in a very submissive and humble tone. On the present occasion, Mrs. Quilp did not for a long time venture even upon this gentle defence, but when she had recovered from her fainting-fit sat in a tearful silence, meekly listening to the reproaches of her lord and master.

Of these Mr. Quilp delivered himself with the utmost animation and rapidity, and with so many distortions of limb and feature, that even his wife, although tolerably well accustomed to his proficiency in these respects, was well-nigh beside herself with alarm. But the Jamaica rum, and the joy of having occasioned a heavy disappointment, by degrees cooled Mr. Quilp's wrath; which, from being at savage heat, dropped slowly to the bantering or chuckling point, at which it steadily remained.

"So you thought I was dead and gone, did you?" said Quilp. "You thought you were a widow, eh? Ha, ha, ha, you jade!"

"Indeed, Quilp," returned his wife. "I'm very sorry——"

"Who doubts it!" cried the dwarf. "You very sorry! to be sure you are. Who doubts that you're *very* sorry!"

"I don't mean sorry that you have come home again alive and well," said his wife, "but sorry that I should have been led into such a belief. I am glad to see you, Quilp; indeed I am."

In truth Mrs. Quilp did seem a great deal more glad to behold her lord than might have been expected, and did evince a degree of interest in his safety which, all things considered, was rather unaccountable. Upon Quilp, however, this circumstance made no impression, further than as it moved him to snap his fingers close to his wife's eyes, with divers grins of triumph and derision.

"How could you go away so long without saying a word to me or letting me hear of you or know anything about you?" asked the poor little woman, sobbing. "How could you be so cruel, Quilp?"

"How could I be so cruel! cruel" cried the dwarf. "Because I was in the humour. I'm in the humour now. I shall be cruel when I like. I'm going away again."

"Not again!"

"Yes again. I'm going away now. I'm off directly. I mean to go and live wherever the fancy seizes me, at the wharf—at the counting-house—and be a jolly bachelor. You were a widow in anticipation. Damme," screamed the dwarf, "I'll be a bachelor in earnest."

"You can't be serious, Quilp," sobbed his wife.

"I tell you," said the dwarf, exulting in his project, "that I'll be a bachelor, a devil-may-care bachelor; and I'll have my bachelor's hall at the counting-house, and at such times come near it if you dare. And mind too that I don't pounce in upon you at unseasonable hours again, for I'll be a spy upon you, and come and go like a mole or a weazel. Tom Scott—where's Tom Scott?"

"Here I am, master," cried the voice of the boy, as Quilp threw up the window.

"Wait there, you dog," returned the dwarf, "to carry a bachelor's portmanteau. Pack it up, Mrs. Quilp. Knock up the dear old lady to help; knock her up. Hallo there! Hallo!"

With these exclamations, Mr. Quilp caught up the poker, and hurrying to the door of the good lady's sleeping-closet beat upon it therewith until she awoke in inexpressible terror, thinking that her amiable son-in-law surely intended to murder her in justification of the legs she had slandered. Impressed with this idea, she was no sooner fairly awake than she screamed violently, and would have quickly precipitated herself out of the window and through a neighbouring skylight, if her daughter had not hastened in to undeceive her, and implore her assistance. Somewhat reassured by her account of the service she was required to render, Mrs. Jiniwin made her appearance in a flannel dressing-gown; and both mother and daughter, trembling with terror and cold—for the night was now far advanced —obeyed Mr. Quilp's directions in submissive silence. Prolonging his preparations as much as possible, for their greater comfort, that eccentric gentleman superintended the packing of his wardrobe, and having added to it with his own hands, a plate, knife and fork, spoon, tea-cup and saucer, and other small household matters of that nature, strapped up the portmanteau, took it on his shoulders, and actually marched off without another word, and with the case-bottle (which he had never once put down) still tightly clasped under his arm. Consigning his heavier burden to the care of Tom Scott when he reached the street, taking a dram from the bottle for his own encouragement, and giving the boy a rap on the head with it as a small taste for himself, Quilp very deliberately led the way to the wharf, and reached it at between three and four o'clock in the morning.

"Snug!" said Quilp, when he had groped his way to the wooden counting-house, and opened the door with a key he carried about with him. "Beautifully snug! Call me at eight, you dog."

With no more formal leave-taking or explanation, he clutched the portmanteau, shut the door upon his attendant, and climbing on the desk, and rolling himself up as round as a hedgehog, in an old boat-cloak, fell fast asleep.

Being roused in the morning at the appointed time, and roused with difficulty, after his late fatigues, Quilp instructed Tom Scott to make a fire in the yard of sundry pieces of old timber, and to prepare some coffee for breakfast; for the better furnishing of which repast he entrusted him with certain small moneys, to be expended in the purchase of hot rolls, butter, sugar, Yarmouth bloaters, and other articles of housekeeping; so that in a few minutes a savoury meal was smoking on the board. With this substantial comfort, the dwarf regaled himself to his heart's content; and being highly satisfied with this free and gipsy mode of life (which he had often meditated, as offering, whenever he chose to avail himself of it, an agreeable freedom from the restraints of matrimony, and a choice means of keeping Mrs. Quilp and her mother in a state of incessant agitation and suspense), bestirred himself to improve his retreat, and render it more commodious and comfortable.

With this view, he issued forth to a place hard by, where such stores were sold; purchased a second-hand hammock, and had it slung in seamanlike fashion from the ceiling of the counting-house. He also caused to be erected, in the same mouldy cabin, an old ship's stove with a rusty funnel to carry the smoke through the roof; and these arrangements completed, surveyed them with ineffable delight.

"I've got a country-house like Robinson Crusoe—" said the dwarf, ogling the accommodations; "a solitary, sequestered, desolate-island sort of spot, where I can be quite alone when I have business on hand, and be secure from all spies and listeners. Nobody near me here, but rats, and they are fine stealthy secret fellows. I shall be as merry as a grig among these gentry. I'll look out for one like Christopher, and poison him—ha, ha, ha! Business though—business—we must be mindful of business in the midst of pleasure, and the time has flown this morning, I declare."

Enjoining Tom Scott to await his return, and not to stand upon his head, or throw a summerset, or so much as walk upon his hands meanwhile, on pain of lingering torments, the dwarf threw himself into a boat, and crossing to the other side of the river, and then speeding away on foot, reached Mr. Swiveller's usual house of entertainment in Bevis Marks, just as that gentleman sat down alone to dinner in its dusky parlour.

"Dick"—said the dwarf, thrusting his head in at the door, "my pet, my pupil, the apple of my eye, hey, hey!"

"Oh you're there, are you?" returned Mr. Swiveller; "*how* are you?"

"How's Dick?" retorted Quilp. "How's the cream of clerkship, eh?"

"Why, rather sour, sir," replied Mr. Swiveller. "Beginning to border upon cheesiness, in fact."

"What's the matter?" said the dwarf, advancing. "Has Sally proved unkind? 'Of all the girls that are so smart, there's none like—' eh, Dick!"

"Certainly not," replied Mr. Swiveller, eating his dinner with great gravity, "none like her. She's the sphynx of private life is Sally B."

"You're out of spirits," said Quilp, drawing up a chair. "What's the matter?"

"The law don't agree with me," returned Dick. "It isn't moist enough, and there's too much confinement. I have been thinking of running away."

"Bah!" said the dwarf. "Where would you run to, Dick?"

"I don't know," returned Mr. Swiveller. "Towards Highgate, I suppose. Perhaps the bells might strike up 'Turn again Swiveller, Lord Mayor of London.' Whittington's name was Dick. I wish cats were scarcer."

Quilp looked at his companion with his eyes screwed up into a comical expression of curiosity, and patiently awaited his further explanation; upon which, however, Mr. Swiveller appeared in no hurry to enter, as he ate a very long dinner in profound silence, and finally pushed away his plate, threw himself back into his chair, folded his arms, and stared ruefully at the fire, in which some ends of cigars were smoking on their own account, and sending up a fragrant odour.

"Perhaps you'd like a bit of cake"—said Dick, at last turning to the dwarf. "You're quite welcome to it. You ought to be, for it's of your making."

"What do you mean?" said Quilp.

Mr. Swiveller replied by taking from his pocket a small and very greasy parcel, slowly unfolding it, and displaying a little slab of plum cake extremely indigestible in appearance, and bordered with a paste of white sugar an inch and a half deep.

"What should you say this was?" demanded Mr. Swiveller.

"It looks like bride-cake," replied the dwarf, grinning.

"And whose should you say it was?" inquired Mr. Swiveller, rubbing the pastry against his nose with a dreadful calmness. "Whose?"

"Not——"

"Yes," said Dick, "the same. You needn't mention her name. There's no such name now. Her name is Cheggs now, Sophy Cheggs. Yet loved I as man never loved that hadn't wooden legs, and my heart, my heart is breaking for the love of Sophy Cheggs."

With this extemporary adaptation of a popular ballad to the distressing circumstances of his own case, Mr. Swiveller folded up the parcel again, beat it very flat between the palms of his hands, thrust it into his breast, buttoned his coat over it, and folded his arms upon the whole.

"Now I hope you're satisfied, sir," said Dick; "and I hope Fred's satisfied. You went partners in the mischief, and I hope you like it. This is the triumph I was to have, is it? It's like the old country-dance of that name, where there are two gentlemen to one lady, and one has her, and the other hasn't, but comes limping up behind to make out the figure. But it's Destiny, and mine's a crusher!"

Disguising his secret joy in Mr. Swiveller's defeat, Daniel Quilp adopted the surest means of soothing him, by ringing the bell, and ordering in a supply of rosy wine (that is to say, of its usual representative), which he put about with great alacrity, calling upon Mr. Swiveller to pledge him in various toasts derisive of Cheggs, and eulogistic of the happiness of single men. Such was their impression on Mr. Swiveller, coupled with the reflection that no man could oppose his destiny, that in a very short space of time his spirits rose surprisingly, and he was enabled to give the dwarf an account of the receipt of the cake, which, it appeared, had been brought to Bevis Marks by the two surviving Miss Wackleses in person, and delivered at the office door with much giggling and joyfulness.

"Ha!" said Quilp. "It will be our turn to giggle soon. And that reminds me—you spoke of young Trent—where is he?"

Mr. Swiveller explained that his respectable friend had recently accepted a responsible situation in a locomotive gaming-house, and was at that time absent on a professional tour among the adventurous spirits of Great Britain.

"That's unfortunate," said the dwarf, "for I came, in fact, to ask you about him. A thought has occurred to me, Dick; your friend over the way——"

"Which friend?"

"In the first floor."

"Yes?"

"Your friend in the first floor, Dick, may know him."

"No, he don't," said Mr. Swiveller, shaking his head.

"Don't! No, because he has never seen him," rejoined Quilp; "but if we were to bring them together, who knows, Dick, but Fred, properly introduced, would serve his turn almost as well as little Nell or her grandfather—who knows but it might make the young fellow's fortune, and through him, yours, eh?"

"Why, the fact is, you see," said Mr. Swiveller, "that they *have been* brought together."

"Have been!" cried the dwarf, looking suspiciously at his companion. "Through whose means?"

"Through mine," said Dick, slightly confused. "Didn't I mention it to you the last time you called over yonder?"

"You know you didn't," returned the dwarf.

"I believe you're right," said Dick. "No. I didn't, I recollect. Oh yes, I brought 'em together that very day. It was Fred's suggestion."

"And what came of it?"

"Why, instead of my friend's bursting into tears when he knew who Fred was, embracing him kindly, and telling him that he was his grandfather, or his grandmother in disguise (which we fully expected), he flew into a tremendous passion; called him all manner of names; said it was in a great measure his fault that little Nell and the old gentleman had ever been brought to poverty; didn't hint at our taking anything to drink; and—and in short rather turned us out of the room than otherwise."

"That's strange," said the dwarf, musing.

"So we remarked to each other at the time," returned Dick coolly, "but quite true."

Quilp was plainly staggered by this intelligence, over which he brooded for some time in moody silence, often raising his eyes to Mr. Swiveller's face, and sharply scanning its expression. As he could read in it, however, no additional information or anything to lead him to believe he had spoken falsely; and as Mr. Swiveller, left to his own meditations, sighed deeply, and was evidently growing maudlin on the subject of Mrs. Cheggs; the dwarf soon broke up the conference and took his departure, leaving the bereaved one to his melancholy ruminations.

"Have been brought together, eh?" said the dwarf as he walked the streets alone. "My friend has stolen a march upon me. It led him to nothing, and therefore is no great matter, save in the intention.

I'm glad he has lost his mistress. Ha ha! The blockhead mustn't leave the law at present. I'm sure of him where he is, whenever I want him for my own purposes, and, besides, he's a good unconscious spy on Brass, and tells, in his cups, all that he sees and hears. You're useful to me, Dick, and cost nothing but a little treating now and then. I am not sure that it may not be worth while, before long, to take credit with the stranger, Dick, by discovering your designs upon the child; but for the present, we'll remain the best friends in the world, with your good leave."

Pursuing these thoughts, and gasping as he went along, after his own peculiar fashion, Mr. Quilp once more crossed the Thames and shut himself up in his Bachelor's Hall, which, by reason of its newly-erected chimney depositing the smoke inside the room and carrying none of it off, was not quite so agreeable as more fastidious people might have desired. Such inconveniences, however, instead of disgusting the dwarf with his new abode, rather suited his humour; so, after dining luxuriously from the public-house, he lighted his pipe, and smoked against the chimney until nothing of him was visible through the mist but a pair of red and highly inflamed eyes, with sometimes a dim vision of his head and face, as, in a violent fit of coughing, he slightly stirred the smoke and scattered the heavy wreaths by which they were obscured. In the midst of this atmosphere, which must infallibly have smothered any other man, Mr. Quilp passed the evening with great cheerfulness; solacing himself all the time with the pipe and the case-bottle; and occasionally entertaining himself with a melodious howl, intended for a song, but bearing not the faintest resemblance to any scrap of any piece of music, vocal or instrumental, ever invented by man. Thus he amused himself until nearly midnight, when he turned into his hammock with the utmost satisfaction.

The first sound that met his ears in the morning—as he half opened his eyes, and, finding himself unusually near the ceiling, entertained a drowsy idea that he must have been transformed into a fly or blue-bottle in the course of the night,—was that of a stifled sobbing and weeping in the room. Peeping cautiously over the side of his hammock, he descried Mrs. Quilp, to whom, after contemplating her for some time in silence, he communicated a violent start by suddenly yelling out,

"Halloa!"

"Oh, Quilp!" cried his poor little wife, looking up. "How you frightened me!"

"I meant to, you jade," returned the dwarf. "What do you want here? I'm dead, an't I?"

"Oh, please come home, do come home," said Mrs. Quilp, sobbing; "we'll never do so any more, Quilp, and after all it was only a mistake that grew out of our anxiety."

"Out of your anxiety," grinned the dwarf. "Yes, I know that—out of your anxiety for my death. I shall come home when I please, I tell you. I shall come home when I please, and go when I please.

I'll be a Will o' the Wisp, now here, now there, dancing about you always, starting up when you least expect me, and keeping you in a constant state of restlessness and irritation. Will you begone?"

Mrs. Quilp durst only make a gesture of entreaty.

"I tell you no," cried the dwarf. "No. If you dare to come here again unless you're sent for, I'll keep watch-dogs in the yard that'll growl and bite—I'll have man-traps, cunningly altered and improved for catching women—I'll have spring guns, that shall explode when you tread upon the wires, and blow you into little pieces. Will you begone?"

"Do forgive me. Do come back," said his wife, earnestly.

"No-o-o-o-o!" roared Quilp. "Not till my own good time, and then I'll return again as often as I choose, and be accountable to nobody for my goings or comings. You see the door there. Will you go?"

Mr. Quilp delivered this last command in such a very energetic voice, and moreover accompanied it with such a sudden gesture, indicative of an intention to spring out of his hammock, and, night-capped as he was, bear his wife home again through the public streets, that she sped away like an arrow. Her worthy lord stretched his neck and eyes until she had crossed the yard, and then, not at all sorry to have had this opportunity of carrying his point, and asserting the sanctity of his castle, fell into an immoderate fit of laughter, and laid himself down to sleep again.

CHAPTER LI

THE bland and open-hearted proprietor of Bachelor's Hall slept on amidst the congenial accompaniments of rain, mud, dirt, damp, fog, and rats, until late in the day; when, summoning his valet Tom Scott to assist him to rise, and to prepare breakfast, he quitted his couch and made his toilet. This duty performed, and his repast ended, he again betook himself to Bevis Marks.

This visit was not intended for Mr. Swiveller, but for his friend and employer Mr. Sampson Brass. Both gentlemen, however, were from home, nor was the life and light of law, Miss Sally, at her post either. The fact of their joint desertion of the office was made known to all comers by a scrap of paper in the handwriting of Mr. Swiveller, which was attached to the bell-handle, and which, giving the reader no clue to the time of day when it was first posted, furnished him with the rather vague and unsatisfactory information that that gentleman would "return in an hour."

"There's a servant, I suppose," said the dwarf, knocking at the house-door. "She'll do."

After a sufficiently long interval, the door was opened, and a small voice immediately accosted him with, "Oh please will you leave a card or message?"

" Eh?" said the dwarf, looking down (it was something quite new to him) upon the small servant.

To this, the child, conducting her conversation as upon the occasion of her first interview with Mr. Swiveller, again replied, "Oh please will you leave a card or message?"

"I'll write a note," said the dwarf, pushing past her into the office; "and mind your master has it directly he comes home." So Mr. Quilp climbed up to the top of a tall stool to write the note, and the small servant, carefully tutored for such emergencies, looked on with her eyes wide open, ready, if he so much as abstracted a wafer, to rush into the street and give the alarm to the police.

As Mr. Quilp folded his note (which was soon written: being a very short one) he encountered the gaze of the small servant. He looked at her long and earnestly.

"How are you?" said the dwarf, moistening a wafer with horrible grimaces.

The small servant, perhaps frightened by his looks, returned no audible reply; but it appeared from the motion of her lips that she was inwardly repeating the same form of expression concerning the note or message.

"Do they use you ill here? is your mistress a Tartar?" said Quilp with a chuckle.

In reply to the last interrogation, the small servant, with a look of infinite cunning mingled with fear, screwed up her mouth very tight and round, and nodded violently.

Whether there was anything in the peculiar slyness of her action which fascinated Mr. Quilp, or anything in the expression of her features at the moment which attracted his attention for some other reason; or whether it merely occurred to him as a pleasant whim to stare the small servant out of countenance; certain it is, that he planted his elbows square and firmly on the desk, and squeezing up his cheeks with his hands, looked at her fixedly.

"Where do you come from?" he said after a long pause, stroking his chin.

"I don't know."

"What's your name?"

"Nothing."

"Nonsense!" retorted Quilp. "What does your mistress call you when she wants you?"

"A little devil," said the child.

She added in the same breath, as if fearful of any further questioning, "But please will you leave a card or message?"

These unusual answers might naturally have provoked some more inquiries. Quilp, however, without uttering another word, withdrew his eyes from the small servant, stroked his chin more thoughtfully than before, and then, bending over the note as if to direct it with scrupulous and hairbreadth nicety, looked at her, covertly but very narrowly, from under his bushy eyebrows. The result of this secret survey was, that he shaded his face with his hands, and laughed slyly and noiselessly, until every vein in it was swollen almost to bursting. Pulling his hat over his brow to conceal his mirth and its effects, he tossed the letter to the child, and hastily withdrew.

Once in the street, moved by some secret impulse, he laughed, and held his sides, and laughed again, and tried to peer through the dusty area railings as if to catch another glimpse of the child, until he was quite tired out. At last, he travelled back to the Wilderness, which was within rifle-shot of his bachelor retreat, and ordered tea in the wooden summer-house that afternoon for three persons; an invitation to Miss Sally Brass and her brother to partake of that entertainment at that place, having been the object both of his journey and his note.

It was not precisely the kind of weather in which people usually take tea in summer-houses, far less in summer-houses in an advanced state of decay, and overlooking the slimy banks of a great river at low water. Nevertheless, it was in this choice retreat that Mr. Quilp ordered a cold collation to be prepared, and it was beneath its cracked and leaky roof that he in due course of time received Mr. Sampson and his sister Sally.

"You're fond of the beauties of nature," said Quilp with a grin. "Is this charming, Brass? Is it unusual, unsophisticated, primitive?"

"It's delightful indeed, sir," replied the lawyer.

"Cool?" said Quilp.

"N-not particularly so, I think, sir," rejoined Brass, with his teeth chattering in his head.

"Perhaps a little damp and ague-ish?" said Quilp.

"Just damp enough to be cheerful, sir," rejoined Brass. "Nothing more, sir, nothing more."

"And Sally?" said the delighted dwarf. "Does *she* like it?"

"She'll like it better," returned that strong-minded lady, "when she has tea; so let us have it, and don't bother."

"Sweet Sally?" cried Quilp, extending his arms as if about to embrace her. "Gentle, charming, overwhelming Sally."

"He's a very remarkable man indeed!" soliloquised Mr. Brass. "He's quite a Troubadour, you know; quite a Troubadour!"

These complimentary expressions were uttered in a somewhat absent and distracted manner; for the unfortunate lawyer, besides having a bad cold in his head, had got wet in coming, and would have willingly borne some pecuniary sacrifice if he could have shifted his present raw quarters to a warm room, and have dried himself at a fire. Quilp, however,—who, beyond the gratification of his demon whims, owed Sampson some acknowledgment of the part he had played in the mourning scene of which he had been a hidden witness, marked these symptoms of uneasiness with a delight past all expression, and derived from them a secret joy which the costliest banquet could never have afforded him.

It is worthy of remark, too, as illustrating a little feature in the character of Miss Sally Brass, that, although on her own account she would have borne the discomforts of the Wilderness with a very ill

"Mr. Quilp......seated himself upon an empty beer-barrel."

grace, and would probably, indeed, have walked off before the tea appeared, she no sooner beheld the latent uneasiness and misery of her brother than she developed a grim satisfaction, and began to enjoy herself after her own manner. Though the wet came stealing through the roof and trickling down upon their heads, Miss Brass uttered no complaint, but presided over the tea equipage with imperturbable composure. While Mr. Quilp, in his uproarious hospitality, seated himself upon an empty beer-barrel, vaunted the place as the most beautiful and comfortable in the three kingdoms, and elevating his glass, drank to their next merry-meeting in that jovial spot; and Mr. Brass, with the rain plashing down into his tea-cup, made a dismal attempt to pluck up his spirits and appear at his ease; and Tom Scott, who was in waiting at the door under an old umbrella, exulted in his agonies and bade fair to split his sides with laughing; while all this was passing, Miss Sally Brass, unmindful of the wet which dripped down upon her own feminine person and fair apparel, sat placidly behind the tea-board, erect and grizzly, contemplating the unhappiness of her brother with a mind at ease, and content, in her amiable disregard of self, to sit there all night, witnessing the torments which his avaricious and grovelling nature compelled him to endure and forbade him to resent. And this, it must be observed, or the illustration would be incomplete, although in a business point of view she had the strongest sympathy with Mr. Sampson, and would have been beyond measure indignant if he had thwarted their client in any one respect.

In the height of his boisterous merriment, Mr. Quilp, having on some pretence dismissed his attendant sprite for the moment, resumed his usual manner all at once, dismounted from his cask, and laid his hand upon the lawyer's sleeve.

"A word," said the dwarf, "before we go further. Sally, hark'ee for a minute."

Miss Sally drew closer, as if accustomed to business conferences with their host which were the better for not having air.

"Business," said the dwarf, glancing from brother to sister. "Very private business. Lay your heads together when you're by yourselves."

"Certainly, sir," returned Brass, taking out his pocket-book and pencil. "I'll take down the heads if you please, sir. Remarkable documents," added the lawyer, raising his eyes to the ceiling, "most remarkable documents. He states his points so clearly that it's a treat to have 'em! I don't know any Act of Parliament that's equal to him in clearness."

"I shall deprive you of a treat," said Quilp. "Put up your book. We don't want any documents. So. There's a lad named Kit——"

Miss Sally nodded, implying that she knew of him.

"Kit!" said Mr. Sampson.—"Kit! Ha! I've heard the name before, but I don't exactly call to mind—I don't exactly——"

"You're as slow as a tortoise, and more thick-headed than a rhinoceros," returned his obliging client with an impatient gesture.

"He's extremely pleasant!" cried the obsequious Sampson. "His acquaintance with Natural History too is surprising. Quite a Buffoon, quite!"

There is no doubt that Mr. Brass intended some compliment or other; and it has been argued with show of reason that he would have said Buffon, but made use of a superfluous vowel. Be this as it may, Quilp gave him no time for correction, as he performed that office himself by more than tapping him on the head with the handle of his umbrella.

"Don't let's have any wrangling," said Miss Sally, staying his hand. "I've showed you that I know him, and that's enough."

"She's always foremost!" said the dwarf, patting her on the back and looking contemptuously at Sampson. "I don't like Kit, Sally."

"Nor I," rejoined Miss Brass.

"Nor I," said Sampson.

"Why, that's right!" cried Quilp. "Half our work is done already. This Kit is one of your honest people; one of your fair characters; a prowling prying hound; a hypocrite; a double-faced, white-livered, sneaking spy; a crouching cur to those that feed and coax him, and a barking yelping dog to all besides."

"Fearfully eloquent!" cried Brass with a sneeze. "Quite appalling!"

"Come to the point," said Miss Sally, "and don't talk so much."

"Right again!" exclaimed Quilp, with another contemptuous look at Sampson, "always foremost! I say, Sally, he is a yelping, insolent dog to all besides, and most of all, to me. In short, I owe him a grudge."

"That's enough, sir," said Sampson.

"No, it's not enough, sir," sneered Quilp; "will you hear me out? Besides that I owe him a grudge on that account, he thwarts me at this minute, and stands between me and an end which might otherwise prove a golden one to us all. Apart from that, I repeat that he crosses my humour, and I hate him. Now, you know the lad, and can guess the rest. Devise your own means of putting him out of my way, and execute them. Shall it be done?"

"It shall, sir," said Sampson.

"Then give me your hand," retorted Quilp. "Sally, girl, yours. I rely as much or more, on you than him. Tom Scott comes back. Lantern, pipes, more grog, and a jolly night of it!"

No other word was spoken, no other look exchanged, which had the slightest reference to this, the real occasion of their meeting. The trio were well accustomed to act together, and were linked to each other by ties of mutual interest and advantage, and nothing more was needed. Resuming his boisterous manner with the same ease with which he had thrown it off, Quilp was in an instant the same uproarious, reckless little savage he had been a few seconds before. It was ten o'clock at night before the amiable Sally supported her beloved and loving brother from the Wilderness, by which time he needed the utmost support her tender frame could render; his walk being for some unknown reason anything but steady, and his legs constantly doubling up in unexpected places.

Overpowered, notwithstanding his late prolonged slumbers, by the fatigues of the last few days, the dwarf lost no time in creeping to his dainty house, and was soon dreaming in his hammock. Leaving him to visions, in which perhaps the quiet figures we quitted in the old church porch were not without their share, be it our task to rejoin them as they sat and watched.

CHAPTER LII

AFTER a long time, the schoolmaster appeared at the wicket-gate of the churchyard, and hurried towards them, jingling in his hand, as he came along, a bundle of rusty keys. He was quite breathless with pleasure and haste when he reached the porch, and at first could only point towards the old building which the child had been contemplating so earnestly.

"You see those two old houses," he said at last.

"Yes surely," replied Nell. "I have been looking at them nearly all the time you have been away."

"And you would have looked at them more curiously yet, if you could have guessed what I have to tell you," said the friend. "One of those houses is mine."

Without saying any more, or giving the child time to reply, the schoolmaster took her hand, and, his honest face quite radiant with exultation, led her to the place of which he spoke.

They stopped before its low arched door. After trying several of the keys in vain, the schoolmaster found one to fit the huge lock, which turned back, creaking, and admitted them into the house.

The room into which they entered was a vaulted chamber once nobly ornamented by cunning architects, and still retaining, in its beautiful groined roof and rich stone tracery, choice remnants of its ancient splendour. Foliage carved in the stone, and emulating the mastery of Nature's hand, yet remained to tell how many times the leaves outside had come and gone, while it lived on unchanged. The broken figures supporting the burden of the chimney-piece, though mutilated, were still distinguishable for what they had been—far different from the dust without—and showed sadly by the empty hearth, like creatures who had outlived their kind, and mourned their own too slow decay.

In some old time—for even change was old in that old place—a wooden partition had been constructed in one part of the chamber to form a sleeping closet, into which the light was admitted at the same period by a rude window, or rather niche, cut in the solid wall. This screen, together with two seats in the broad chimney, had at some forgotten date been part of the church or convent; for the oak, hastily appropriated to its present purpose, had been little altered from its former shape, and presented to the eye a pile of fragments of rich carving from old monkish stalls.

An open door leading to a small room or cell, dim with the light that came through leaves of ivy, completed the interior of this portion of the ruin. It was not quite destitute of furniture. A few strange chairs, whose arms and legs looked as though they had dwindled away with age: a table, the very spectre of its race: a great old chest that had once held records in the church, with other quaintly-fashioned domestic necessaries, and store of firewood for the winter, were scattered around, and gave evident tokens of its occupation as a dwelling-place at no very distant time.

The child looked around her, with that solemn feeling with which we contemplate the work of ages that have become but drops of water in the great ocean of eternity. The old man had followed them, but they were all three hushed for a space, and drew their breath softly, as if they feared to break the silence even by so slight a sound.

"It is a very beautiful place!" said the child, in a low voice.

"I almost feared you thought otherwise," returned the schoolmaster. "You shivered when we first came in, as if you felt it cold or gloomy."

"It was not that," said Nell, glancing round with a slight shudder. "Indeed I cannot tell you what it was, but when I saw the outside, from the church porch, the same feeling came over me. It is its being so old and grey perhaps."

"A peaceful place to live in, don't you think so?" said her friend.

"Oh yes," rejoined the child, clasping her hands earnestly. "A quiet, happy place—a place to live and learn to die in!" She would have said more, but that the energy of her thoughts caused her voice to falter, and come in trembling whispers from her lips.

"A place to live, and learn to live, and gather health of mind and body in," said the schoolmaster; "for this old house is yours."

"Ours!" cried the child.

"Ay," returned the schoolmaster gaily, "for many a merry year to come, I hope. I shall be a close neighbour—only next door—but this house is yours."

Having now disburdened himself of his great surprise, the schoolmaster sat down, and drawing Nell to his side, told her how he had learnt that that ancient tenement had been occupied for a very long time by an old person, nearly a hundred years of age, who kept the keys of the church, opened and closed it for the services, and showed it to strangers; how she had died not many weeks ago, and nobody had yet been found to fill the office; how, learning all this in an interview with the sexton, who was confined to his bed by rheumatism, he had been bold to make mention of his fellow-traveller, which had been so favourably received by that high authority, that he had taken courage, acting on his advice, to propound the matter to the clergyman. In a word, the result of his exertions was, that Nell and her grandfather were to be carried before the last-named gentleman next day; and, his approval of their conduct and appearance reserved as a matter of form, that they were already appointed to the vacant post.

"There's a small allowance of money," said the schoolmaster. "It is not much, but still enough to live upon in this retired spot. By clubbing our funds together, we shall do bravely; no fear of that."

"Heaven bless and prosper you!" sobbed the child.

"Amen, my dear," returned her friend cheerfully; "and all of us, as it will, and has, in leading us through sorrow and trouble to this tranquil life. But we must look at *my* house now. Come!"

They repaired to the other tenement; tried the rusty keys as before; at length found the right one; and opened the worm-eaten door. It led into a chamber, vaulted and old, like that from which they had come, but not so spacious, and having only one other little room attached. It was not difficult to divine that the other house was of right the schoolmaster's, and that he had chosen for himself the least commodious, in his care and regard for them. Like the adjoining habitation, it held such old articles of furniture as were absolutely necessary, and had its stack of firewood.

To make these dwellings as habitable and full of comfort as they could, was now their pleasant care. In a short time, each had its cheerful fire glowing and crackling on the hearth, and reddening the pale old wall with a hale and healthy blush. Nell, busily plying her needle, repaired the tattered window-hangings, drew together the rents that time had worn in the threadbare scraps of carpet, and made them whole and decent. The schoolmaster swept and smoothed the ground before the door, trimmed the long grass, trained the ivy and creeping plants which hung their drooping heads in melancholy neglect; and gave to the outer walls a cheery air of home. The old man, sometimes by his side and sometimes with the child, lent his aid to both, went here and there on little patient services, and was happy. Neighbours too, as they came from work, proffered their help; or sent their children with such small presents or loans as the strangers needed most. It was a busy day; and night came on, and found them wondering that there was yet so much to do, and that it should be dark so soon.

They took their supper together, in the house which may be henceforth called the child's; and when they had finished their meal drew round the fire, and almost in whispers—their hearts were too quiet and glad for loud expression—discussed their future plans. Before they separated, the schoolmaster read some prayers aloud; and then, full of gratitude and happiness, they parted for the night.

At that silent hour, when her grandfather was sleeping peacefully in his bed, and every sound was hushed, the child lingered before the dying embers, and thought of her past fortunes as if they had been a dream and she only now awoke. The glare of the sinking flame, reflected in the oaken panels whose carved tops were dimly seen in the gloom of the dusky roof—the aged walls, where strange shadows came and went with every flickering of the fire—the solemn presence, within, of that decay which falls on senseless things the most enduring in their nature: and, without, and round about on every side, of Death—filled her with deep and thoughtful feelings, but with none of terror or alarm. A change had been gradually stealing over her, in the time of her loneliness and sorrow. With failing strength and heightening resolution, there had sprung up a purified and altered mind; there had grown in her bosom blessed thoughts and hopes, which are the portion of few but the weak and drooping. There were none to see the frail, perishable figure, as it glided from the fire and leaned pensively at the open casement; none but the stars, to look into the upturned face and read its history. The old church bell rang out the hour with a mournful sound, as if it had grown sad from so much communing with the dead and unheeded warning to the living; the fallen leaves rustled; the grass stirred upon the graves; all else was still and sleeping.

Some of those dreamless sleepers lay close within the shadow of the church—touching the wall, as if they clung to it for comfort and protection. Others had chosen to lie beneath the changing shade of trees; others by the path, that footsteps might come near them; others among the graves of little children. Some had desired to rest beneath the very ground they had trodden in their daily walks; some where the setting sun might shine upon their beds; some where its light would fall upon them when it rose. Perhaps not one of the imprisoned souls had been able quite to separate itself in living thought from its old companion. If any had, it had still felt for it a love like that which captives have been known to bear towards the cell in which they have been long confined, and even at parting hung upon its narrow bounds affectionately.

It was long before the child closed the window, and approached her bed. Again something of the same sensation as before—an involuntary chill—a momentary feeling akin to fear—but vanishing directly, and leaving no alarm behind. Again, too, dreams of the little scholar; of the roof opening, and a column of bright faces, rising far away into the sky, as she had seen in some old Scriptural picture once, and looking down on her, asleep. It was a sweet and happy dream. The quiet spot, outside, seemed to remain the same, saving that there was music in the air, and a sound of angels' wings. After a time the sisters came there hand in hand, and stood among the graves. And then the dream grew dim, and faded.

With the brightness and joy of morning, came the renewal of yesterday's labours, the revival of its pleasant thoughts, the restoration of its energies, cheerfulness, and hope. They worked gaily in ordering and arranging their houses until noon, and then went to visit the clergyman.

He was a simple-hearted old gentleman, of a shrinking, subdued spirit, accustomed to retirement, and very little acquainted with the world, which he had left many years before to come and settle in that place. His wife had died in the house in which he still lived, and he had long since lost sight of any earthly cares or hopes beyond it.

He received them very kindly, and at once showed an interest in Nell; asking her name, and age, her birthplace, the circumstances which had led her there, and so forth. The schoolmaster had already told her story. They had no other friends or home to leave, he said, and had come to share his fortunes. He loved the child as though she were his own.

"Well, well," said the clergyman. "Let it be as you desire. She is very young."

"Old in adversity and trial, sir," replied the schoolmaster.

"God help me! Let her rest, and forget them," said the old gentleman. "But an old church is a dull and gloomy place for one so young as you, my child."

"Oh no, sir," returned Nell. "I have no such thoughts, indeed."

"I would rather see her dancing on the green at nights," said the old gentleman, laying his hand upon her head, and smiling sadly, "than have her sitting in the shadow of our mouldering arches. You must look to this, and see that her heart does not grow heavy among these solemn ruins. Your request is granted, friend."

After more kind words, they withdrew, and repaired to the child's house; where they were yet in conversation on their happy fortune, when another friend appeared.

This was a little old gentleman, who lived in the parsonage-house, and had resided there (so they learnt soon afterwards) ever since the death of the clergyman's wife, which had happened fifteen years before. He had been his college friend and always his close companion; in the first shock of his grief had come to console and comfort him; and from that time they had never parted company. The little old gentleman was the active spirit of the place; the adjuster of all differences, the promoter of all merry-makings, the dispenser of his friend's bounty, and of no small charity of his own besides; the universal mediator, comforter, and friend. None of the simple villagers had cared to ask his name, or, when they knew it, to store it in their memory. Perhaps from some vague rumour of his college honours which had been whispered abroad on his first arrival, perhaps because he was an unmarried, unencumbered gentleman, he had been called the Bachelor. The name pleased him, or suited him as well as any other, and the Bachelor he had ever since remained. And the bachelor it was, it may be added, who with his own hands had laid in the stock of fuel which the wanderers had found in their new habitation.

The bachelor, then—to call him by his usual appellation—lifted the latch, showed his little round mild face for a moment at the door, and stepped into the room like one who was no stranger to it.

"You are Mr. Marton, the new schoolmaster?" he said, greeting Nell's kind friend.

"I am, sir."

"You come well recommended, and I am glad to see you. I should have been in the way yesterday, expecting you, but I rode across the country to carry a message from a sick mother to her daughter in service some miles off, and have but just now returned. This is our young church-keeper? You are not the less welcome, friend, for her sake, or for this old man's; nor the worst teacher for having learnt humanity."

"She has been ill, sir, very lately," said the schoolmaster, in answer to the look with which their visitor regarded Nell when he had kissed her cheek.

"Yes, yes. I know she has," he rejoined. "There have been suffering and heartache here."

"Indeed there have, sir."

The little old gentleman glanced at the grandfather, and back again at the child, whose hand he took tenderly in his, and held.

"You will be happier here," he said; "we will try, at least, to make you so. You have made great improvements here already. Are they the work of your hands?"

"Yes, sir."

"We may make some others—not better in themselves, but with better means perhaps," said the bachelor. "Let us see now, let us see."

Nell accompanied him into the other little rooms, and over both the houses, in which he found various small comforts wanting, which he engaged to supply from a certain collection of odds and ends he had at home, and which must have been a very miscellaneous and extensive one, as it comprehended the most opposite articles imaginable. They all came, however, and came without loss of time; for the little old gentleman, disappearing for some five or ten minutes, presently returned, laden with old shelves, rugs, blankets, and other household gear, and followed by a boy bearing a similar load. These being cast on the floor in a promiscuous heap, yielded a quantity of occupation in arranging, erecting, and putting away; the superintendence of which task evidently afforded the old gentleman extreme delight, and engaged him for some time with great briskness and activity. When nothing more was left to be done, he charged the boy to run off and bring his schoolmates to be marshalled before their new master, and solemnly reviewed.

"As good a set of fellows, Marton, as you'd wish to see," he said, turning to the schoolmaster when the boy was gone; "but I don't let 'em know I think so. That wouldn't do, at all."

The messenger soon returned at the head of a long row of urchins, great and small, who, being confronted by the bachelor at the house door, fell into various convulsions of politeness; clutching their hats and caps, squeezing them into the smallest possible dimensions, and making all manner of bows and scrapes, which the little old gentleman contemplated with excessive satisfaction, and expressed his approval of by a great many nods and smiles. Indeed, his approbation of the boys was by no means so scrupulously disguised as he had led the schoolmaster to suppose, inasmuch as it broke out in sundry loud whispers and confidential remarks which were perfectly audible to them every one.

"This first boy, schoolmaster," said the bachelor, "is John Owen, a lad of good parts, sir, and frank, honest temper; but too thoughtless, too playful, too light-headed by far. That boy, my good sir, would break his neck with pleasure, and deprive his parents of their chief comfort—and between ourselves, when you come to see him at hare and hounds, taking the fence and ditch by the finger-post, and sliding down the face of the little quarry, you'll never forget it. It's beautiful!"

John Owen having been thus rebuked, and being in perfect possession of the speech aside, the bachelor singled out another boy.

"Now, look at that lad, sir," said the bachelor. "You see that fellow? Richard Evans his name is, sir. An amazing boy to learn, blessed with a good memory, and a ready understanding, and more-over with a good voice and ear for psalm-singing, in which he is the best among us. Yet, sir, that boy will come to a bad end; he'll never die in his bed; he's always falling asleep in church in sermon-time—and to tell you the truth, Mr. Marton, I always did the same at his age, and feel quite certain that it was natural to my constitution and I couldn't help it."

This hopeful pupil edified by the above terrible reproval, the bachelor turned to another.

"But if we talk of examples to be shunned," said he, "if we come to boys that should be a warning and a beacon to all their fellows, here's the one, and I hope you won't spare him. This is the lad, sir; this one with the blue eyes and light hair. This is a swimmer, sir, this fellow—a diver, Lord save us! This is a boy, sir, who had a fancy for plunging into eighteen feet of water, with his clothes on, and bringing up a blind man's dog, who was being drowned by the weight of his chain and collar, while his master stood wringing his hands upon the bank, bewailing the loss of his guide and friend. I sent the boy two guineas anonymously, sir," added the bachelor, in his peculiar whisper, "directly I heard of it; but never mention it on any account, for he hasn't the least idea that it came from me."

Having disposed of this culprit, the bachelor turned to another, and from him to another, and so on through the whole array, laying, for their wholesome restriction within due bounds, the same cutting emphasis on such of their propensities as were dearest to his heart and were unquestionably referable to his own precept and example. Thoroughly persuaded, in the end, that he had made them miserable by his severity, he dismissed them with a small present, and an admonition to walk quietly home, without any leapings, scufflings, or turnings out of the way; which injunction (he informed the school-master in the same audible confidence) he did not think he could have obeyed when he was a boy, had his life depended on it.

Hailing these little tokens of the bachelor's disposition as so many assurances of his own welcome course from that time, the school-master parted from him with a light heart and joyous spirits, and deemed himself one of the happiest men on earth. The windows of the two old houses were ruddy again that night with the reflection of the cheerful fires that burnt within; and the bachelor and his friend, pausing to look upon them as they returned from their evening walk, spoke softly together of the beautiful child, and looked round upon the churchyard with a sigh.

CHAPTER LIII

NELL was stirring early in the morning; and having discharged her household tasks, and put everything in order for the good schoolmaster (though sorely against his will, for he would have spared her the pains), took down, from its nail by the fireside, a little bundle of keys with which the bachelor had formally invested her on the previous day, and went out alone to visit the old church.

The sky was serene and bright, the air clear, perfumed with the fresh scent of newly-fallen leaves, and grateful to every sense. The neighbouring stream sparkled, and rolled onward with a tuneful sound; the dew glistened on the green mounds, like tears shed by Good Spirits over the dead.

Some young children sported among the tombs, and hid from each other, with laughing faces. They had an infant with them, and had laid it down asleep upon a child's grave, in a little bed of leaves. It was a new grave—the resting-place, perhaps, of some little creature, who, meek and patient in its illness, had often sat and watched them ; and now seemed to their minds scarcely changed.

She drew near and asked one of them whose grave it was. The child answered that that was not its name; it was a garden—his brother's. It was greener, he said, than all the other gardens, and the birds loved it better because he had been used to feed them. When he had done speaking, he looked at her with a smile, and kneeling down and nestling for a moment with his cheek against the turf, bounded merrily away.

She passed the church, gazing upward at its old tower, went through the wicket-gate, and so into the village. The old sexton, leaning on a crutch, was taking the air at his cottage door, and gave her good morrow.

"You are better?" said the child, stopping to speak with him.

"Ay surely," returned the old man. "I'm thankful to say, much better."

"You will be quite well soon."

"With Heaven's leave, and a little patience. But come in, come in."

The old man limped on before, and warning her of the downward step, which he achieved himself with no small difficulty, led the way into his little cottage.

"It is but one room you see. There is another up above, but the stair has got harder to climb o' late years, and I never use it. I'm thinking of taking to it again next summer, though."

The child wondered how a grey-headed man like him—one of his trade too—could talk of time so easily. He saw her eyes wandering to the tools that hung upon the wall, and smiled.

"I warrant now," he said, "that you think all those are used in making graves."

"Indeed, I wondered that you wanted so many."

"And well you might. I am a gardener. I dig the ground, and plant things that are to live and grow. My works don't all moulder away and rot in the earth. You see that spade in the centre?"

"The very old one—so notched and worn? Yes."

"That's the sexton's spade, and it's a well-used one, as you see. We're healthy people here, but it has done a power of work. If it could speak now, that spade, it would tell you of many an unexpected job that it and I have done together; but I forget 'em, for my memory's a poor one. That's nothing new," he added hastily. "It always was."

"There are flowers and shrubs to speak to your other work," said the child.

"Oh yes. And tall trees. But they are not so separated from the sexton's labours as you think."

"No!"

"Not in my mind, and recollection—such as it is," said the old man. "Indeed they often help it. For say that I planted such a tree for such a man. There it stands to remind me that he died. When I look at its broad shadow, and remember what it was in his time, it helps me to the age of my other work, and I can tell you pretty nearly when I made his grave."

"But it may remind you of one who is still alive," said the child.

"Of twenty that are dead, in connexion with that one who lives, then," rejoined the old man; "wife, husband, parents, brothers, sisters, children, friends—a score at least. So it happens that the sexton's spade gets worn and battered. I shall need a new one—next summer."

The child looked quickly towards him, thinking that he jested with his age and infirmity; but the unconscious sexton was quite in earnest.

"Ah!" he said, after a brief silence. "People never learn. They never learn. It's only we who turn up the ground, where nothing grows and everything decays, who think of such things as these—who think of them properly, I mean. You have been into the church?"

"I am going there now," the child replied.

"There's an old well there," said the sexton, "right underneath the belfry; a deep, dark, echoing well. Forty year ago, you had only to let down the bucket till the first knot in the rope was free of the windlass, and you heard it splashing in the cold dull water. By little and little the water fell away, so that in ten year after that, a second knot was made, and you must unwind so much rope, or the bucket swung tight and empty at the end. In ten years' time, the water fell again, and a third knot was made. In ten years more the well dried

up; and now, if you lower the bucket till your arms are tired and let
out nearly all the cord, you'll hear it of a sudden clanking and
rattling on the ground below, with a sound of being so deep and so far
down, that your heart leaps into your mouth, and you start away as
if you were falling in."

"A dreadful place to come on in the dark!" exclaimed the child,
who had followed the old man's looks and words until she seemed to
stand upon its brink.

"What is it but a grave!" said the sexton. "What else! And which
of our old folks, knowing all this, thought, as the spring subsided, of
their own failing strength, and lessening life? Not one!"

"Are you very old yourself?" asked the child, involuntarily.

"I shall be seventy-nine—next summer."

"You still work when you are well?"

"Work! To be sure. You shall see my gardens hereabout. Look at
the window there. I made, and have kept, that plot of ground
entirely with my own hands. By this time next year I shall hardly
see the sky, the boughs will have grown so thick. I have my winter
work at night besides."

He opened, as he spoke, a cupboard close to where he sat, and
produced some miniature boxes, carved in a homely manner and made
of old wood.

"Some gentlefolks who are fond of ancient days, and what belongs
to them," he said, "like to buy these keepsakes from our church and
ruins. Sometimes, I make them of scraps of oak, that turn up here
and there; sometimes of bits of coffins which the vaults have long
preserved. See here—this is a little chest of the last kind, clasped at
the edges with fragments of brass plates that had writing on 'em
once, though it would be hard to read it now. I haven't many by me
at this time of year, but these shelves will be full—next summer."

The child admired and praised his work, and shortly afterwards
departed; thinking as she went, how strange it was, that this old
man, drawing from his pursuits, and everything around him, one
stern moral, never contemplated its application to himself; and,
while he dwelt upon the uncertainty of human life, seemed both in
word and deed to deem himself immortal. But her musings did not
stop here, for she was wise enough to think that by a good and
merciful adjustment this must be human nature, and that the old
sexton, with his plans for next summer, was but a type of all mankind.

Full of these meditations, she reached the church. It was easy to
find the key belonging to the outer door, for each was labelled on a
scrap of yellow parchment. Its very turning in the lock awoke a
hollow sound, and when she entered with a faltering step, the echoes
that it raised in closing made her start.

Everything in our lives, whether of good or evil, affects us most by
contrast. If the peace of the simple village had moved the child more
strongly, because of the dark and troubled ways that lay beyond
and through which she had journeyed with such failing feet, what

was the deep impression of finding herself alone in that solemn building; where the very light, coming through sunken windows, seemed old and grey, and the air, redolent of earth and mould, seemed laden with decay, purified by time of all its grosser particles, and sighing through arch and aisle, and clustered pillars, like the breath of ages gone! Here was the broken pavement, worn so long ago by pious feet, that Time, stealing on the pilgrims' steps, had trodden out their track, and left but crumbling stones. Here were the rotten beam, the sinking arch, the sapped and mouldering wall, the lowly trench of earth, the stately tomb on which no epitaph remained,—all,—marble, stone, iron, wood, and dust, one common monument of ruin. The best work and the worst, the plainest and the richest, the stateliest and the least imposing—both of Heaven's work and Man's—all found one common level here, and told one common tale.

Some part of the edifice had been a baronial chapel, and here were effigies of warriors stretched upon their beds of stone with folded hands, cross-legged—those who had fought in the Holy Wars—girded with their swords, and cased in armour as they had lived. Some of these knights had their own weapons, helmets, coats of mail, hanging upon the walls hard by, and dangling from rusty hooks. Broken and dilapidated as they were, they yet retained their ancient form, and something of their ancient aspect. Thus violent deeds live after men upon the earth, and traces of war and bloodshed will survive in mournful shapes, long after those who worked the desolation are but atoms of earth themselves.

The child sat down in this old, silent place, among the stark figures on the tombs—they made it more quiet there, than elsewhere, to her fancy—and gazing round with a feeling of awe, tempered with a calm delight, felt that now she was happy, and at rest. She took a Bible from the shelf, and read; then, laying it down, thought of the summer days and the bright spring-time that would come—of the rays of sun that would fall in aslant upon the sleeping forms—of the leaves that would flutter at the window, and play in glistening shadows on the pavement—of the songs of birds, and growth of buds and blossoms out of doors—of the sweet air, that would steal in and gently wave the tattered banners overhead. What if the spot awakened thoughts of death! Die who would, it would still remain the same; these sights and sounds would still go on as happily as ever. It would be no pain to sleep amidst them.

She left the chapel—very slowly and often turning back to gaze again—and coming to a low door, which plainly led into the tower, opened it, and climbed the winding stair in darkness; save where she looked down through narrow loopholes on the place she had left, or caught a glimmering vision of the dusty bells. At length she gained the end of the ascent and stood upon the turret top.

Oh! the glory of the sudden burst of light; the freshness of the fields and woods, stretching away on every side and meeting the bright blue sky; the cattle grazing in the pasturage; the smoke, that, coming from among the trees, seemed to rise upward from the green earth; the children yet at their gambols down below—all, everything, so beautiful and happy! It was like passing from death to life; it was drawing nearer Heaven.

The children were gone by the time she emerged into the porch, and locked the door. As she passed the school-house she could hear the busy hum of voices. Her friend had begun his labours only that day. The noise grew louder, and, looking back, she saw the boys come trooping out and disperse themselves with merry shouts and play. "It's a good thing," thought the child, "I am very glad they pass the church." And then she stopped, to fancy how the noise would sound inside, and how gently it would seem to die away upon the ear.

Again that day, yes, twice again, she stole back to the old chapel, and in her former seat read from the same book, or indulged the same quiet train of thought. Even when it had grown dusk, and the shadows of coming night made it more solemn still, the child remained like one rooted to the spot, and had no fear, or thought of stirring.

They found her there at last, and took her home. She looked pale but very happy, until they separated for the night; and then, as the poor schoolmaster stooped down to kiss her cheek, he thought he felt a tear upon his face.

CHAPTER LIV

THE bachelor, among his various occupations, found in the old church a constant source of interest and amusement. Taking that pride in it which men conceive for the wonders of their own little world, he had made its history his study ; and many a summer day within its walls, and many a winter's night beside the parsonage fire, had found the bachelor still poring over and adding to his goodly store of tale and legend.

As he was not one of those rough spirits who would strip fair Truth of every little shadowy vestment in which time and teeming fancies love to array her—and some of which become her pleasantly enough, serving, like the waters of her well, to add new graces to the charms they half conceal and half suggest, and to awaken interest and pursuit rather than languor and indifference—as, unlike this stern and obdurate class, he loved to see the goddess crowned with those garlands of wild flowers which tradition wreathes for her gentle wearing, and which are often freshest in their homeliest shapes,—he trod with a light step and bore with a light hand upon the dust of centuries, unwilling to demolish any of the airy shrines that had been raised above it, if one good feeling or affection of the human heart were hiding thereabouts. Thus, in the case of an ancient coffin of rough stone, supposed for many generations to contain the bones of a certain baron, who, after ravaging, with cut, and thrust, and plunder, in foreign lands, came back with a penitent and sorrowing heart to die at home, but which had been lately shown by learned antiquaries to be no such thing, as the baron in question (so they contended) had died hard in battle, gnashing his teeth and cursing with his latest breath,—the bachelor stoutly maintained that the old tale was the true one; that the baron, repenting him of the evil, had done great charities and meekly given up the ghost; and that, if ever baron went to heaven, that baron was then at peace. In like manner, when the aforesaid antiquaries did argue and contend that a certain secret vault was not the tomb of a grey-haired lady who had been hanged and drawn and quartered by glorious Queen Bess for succouring a wretched priest who fainted of thirst and hunger at her door, the bachelor did solemnly maintain against all comers that the church was hallowed by the said poor lady's ashes; that her remains had been collected in the night from four of the city's gates, and thither in secret brought, and there deposited; and the bachelor did further (being highly excited at such times) deny the glory of Queen Bess, and assert the immeasurably greater glory of the meanest woman in her realm who had a merciful and tender heart. As to the assertion that the flat stone near the door was not the grave of the miser who had disowned his only child and left a sum of money to the church to buy a peal of bells, the bachelor did readily admit the same, and that the place had given birth to no such man. In a word, he would have had every stone, and plate of brass, the monument only of deeds whose memory should survive. All others he was willing to forget. They might be buried in consecrated ground, but he would have had them buried deep, and never brought to light again.

It was from the lips of such a tutor, that the child learnt her easy task. Already impressed, beyond all telling, by the silent building and the peaceful beauty of the spot in which it stood—majestic age surrounded by perpetual youth—it seemed to her, when she heard these things, sacred to all goodness and virtue. It was another world, where sin and sorrow never came ; a tranquil place of rest, where nothing evil entered.

When the bachelor had given her in connexion with almost every tomb and flat grave-stone some history of its own, he took her down into the old crypt, now a mere dull vault, and showed her how it had been lighted up in the time of the monks, and how, amid lamps depending from the roof, and swinging censers exhaling scented odours, and habits glittering with gold and silver, and pictures, and precious stuffs, and jewels all flashing and glistening through the low arches, the chant of aged voices had been many a time heard there at midnight in old days, while hooded figures knelt and prayed around, and told their rosaries of beads. Thence, he took her above ground again, and showed her, high up in the old walls, small galleries, where the nuns had been wont to glide along—dimly seen in their dark dresses so far off—or to pause like gloomy shadows, listening to the prayers. He showed her too, how the warriors, whose figures rested on the tombs, had worn those rotting scraps of armour up above—how this had been a helmet, and that a shield, and that a gauntlet—and how they had wielded the great two-handed swords, and beaten men down with yonder iron mace. All that he told the child she treasured in her mind; and sometimes, when she woke at night from dreams of those old times, and rising from her bed looked out at the dark church, she almost hoped to see the windows lighted up, and hear the organ's swell, and sound of voices, on the rushing wind.

The old sexton soon got better, and was about again. From him the child learnt many other things, though of a different kind. He was not able to work, but one day there was a grave to be made, and he came to overlook the man who dug it. He was in a talkative mood; and the child, at first standing by his side, and afterwards sitting on the grass at his feet, with her thoughtful face raised towards his, began to converse with him.

Now the man who did the sexton's duty was a little older than he, though much more active. But he was deaf; and when the sexton (who peradventure, on a pinch, might have walked a mile with great difficulty in half a dozen hours) exchanged a remark with him about his work, the child could not help noticing that he did so with an impatient kind of pity for his infirmity, as if he were himself the strongest and heartiest man alive.

"I'm sorry to see there is this to do," said the child, when she approached. "I heard of no one having died."

"She lived in another hamlet, my dear," returned the sexton. "Three mile away."

"Was she young?"

"Ye—yes," said the sexton; "not more than sixty-four, I think. David, was she more than sixty-four?"

David, who was digging hard, heard nothing of the question. Ths sexton, as he could not reach to touch him with his crutch, and wae too infirm to rise without assistance, called his attention by throwing a little mould upon his red night-cap.

"What's the matter now?" said David, looking up.

"How old was Becky Morgan?" asked the sexton.

"Becky Morgan?" repeated David.

"Yes," replied the sexton; adding in a half compassionate, half irritable tone, which the old man couldn't hear, "you're getting very deaf, Davy, very deaf to be sure!"

The old man stopped in his work, and cleansing his spade with a piece of slate he had by him for the purpose—and scraping off, in the process, the essence of Heaven knows how many Becky Morgans— set himself to consider the subject.

"Let me think," quoth he. "I saw last night what they had put upon the coffin—was it seventy-nine?"

"No, no," said the sexton.

"Ah yes, it was though," returned the old man with a sigh. "For I remember thinking she was very near our age. Yes, it was seventy-nine."

"Are you sure you didn't mistake a figure, Davy?" asked the sexton, with signs of some emotion.

"What?" said the old man. "Say that again."

"He's very deaf. He's very deaf indeed," cried the sexton petulantly; "are you sure you're right about the figures?"

"Oh quite," replied the old man. "Why not?"

"He's exceedingly deaf," muttered the sexton to himself. "I think he's getting foolish."

The child rather wondered what had led him to this belief, as, to say the truth, the old man seemed quite as sharp as he, and was infinitely more robust. As the sexton said nothing more just then, however, she forgot it for the time, and spoke again.

"You were telling me," she said, "about your gardening. Do you ever plant things here?"

"In the churchyard?" returned the sexton. "Not I."

"I have seen some flowers and little shrubs about," the child rejoined; "there are some over there, you see. I thought they were of your rearing, though indeed they grow but poorly."

"They grow as Heaven wills," said the old man; "and it kindly ordains that they shall never flourish here."

"I do not understand you."

"Why, this it is," said the sexton. "They mark the graves of those who had very tender, loving friends."

"I was sure they did!" the child exclaimed. "I am very glad to know they do!"

"Ay," returned the old man, "but stay. Look at them. See how they hang their heads, and droop, and wither. Do you guess the reason?"

"No," the child replied.

"Because the memory of those who lie below, passes away so soon. At first they tend them, morning, noon, and night; they soon begin to come less frequently; from once a day, to once a week; from once a week to once a month; then, at long and uncertain intervals; then, not at all. Such tokens seldom flourish long. I have known the briefest summer flowers outlive them."

"I grieve to hear it," said the child.

"Ah! so say the gentlefolks who come down here to look about them," returned the old man, shaking his head, "but I say otherwise. 'It's a pretty custom you have in this part of the country,' they say to me sometimes, 'to plant the graves, but it's melancholy to see these things all withering or dead.' I crave their pardon and tell them that, as I take it, 'tis a good sign for the happiness of the living. And so it is. It's nature."

"Perhaps the mourners learn to look to the blue sky by day, and to the stars by night, and to think that the dead are there, and not in graves," said the child in an earnest voice.

"Perhaps so," replied the old man doubtfully. "It may be."

"Whether it be as I believe it is, or no," thought the child within herself, "I'll make this place my garden. It will be no harm at least to work here day by day, and pleasant thoughts will come of it, I am sure."

Her glowing cheek and moistened eye passed unnoticed by the sexton, who turned towards old David, and called him by his name. It was plain that Becky Morgan's age still troubled him; though why, the child could scarcely understand.

The second or third repetition of his name attracted the old man's attention. Pausing from his work, he leant upon his spade, and put his hand to his dull ear.

"Did you call?" he said.

"I have been thinking, Davy," replied the sexton, "that she," he pointed to the grave, "must have been a deal older than you or me."

"Seventy-nine," answered the old man with a sorrowful shake of the head, "I tell you that I saw it."

"Saw it?" replied the sexton; "ay, but, Davy, women don't always tell the truth about their age."

"That's true indeed," said the other old man, with a sudden sparkle in his eye. "She might have been older."

"I'm sure she must have been. Why, only think how old she looked. You and I seemed but boys to her."

"She did look old," rejoined David. "You're right. She did look old."

"Call to mind how old she looked for many a long, long year, and say if she could be but seventy-nine at last—only our age," said the sexton.

"Five year older at the very least!" cried the other.

"Five!" retorted the sexton. "Ten. Good eighty-nine. I call to mind the time her daughter died. She was eighty-nine if she was a day, and tries to pass upon us now, for ten year younger. Oh! human vanity!"

The other old man was not behindhand with some moral reflections on this fruitful theme, and both adduced a mass of evidence, of such weight as to render it doubtful—not whether the deceased was of the age suggested, but whether she had not almost reached the patriarchal term of a hundred. When they had settled this question to their mutual satisfaction, the sexton, with his friend's assistance, rose to go.

"It's chilly, sitting here, and I must be careful—till the summer," he said, as he prepared to limp away.

"What?" asked old David.

"He's very deaf, poor fellow!" cried the sexton. "Good-bye."

"Ah!" said old David, looking after him. "He's failing very fast. He ages every day."

And so they parted: each persuaded that the other had less life in him than himself; and both greatly consoled and comforted by the little fiction they had agreed upon, respecting Becky Morgan, whose decease was no longer a precedent of uncomfortable application, and would be no business of theirs for half a score of years to come.

The child remained for some minutes, watching the deaf old man as he threw out the earth with his shovel, and, often stopping to cough and fetch his breath, still muttered to himself, with a kind of sober chuckle, that the sexton was wearing fast. At length she turned away, and walking thoughtfully through the churchyard, came unexpectedly upon the schoolmaster, who was sitting on a green grave in the sun, reading.

"Nell here?" he said cheerfully, as he closed his book. "It does me good to see you in the air and light. I feared you were again in the church, where you so often are."

"Feared!" replied the child, sitting down beside him. "Is it not a good place?"

"Yes, yes," said the schoolmaster. "But you must be gay sometimes—nay, don't shake your head and smile so very sadly."

"Not sadly, if you knew my heart. Do not look at me as if you thought me sorrowful. There is not a happier creature on the earth than I am now."

Full of grateful tenderness, the child took his hand, and folded it between her own. "It's God's will!" she said, when they had been silent for some time.

"What?"

"All this," she rejoined; "all this about us. But which of us is sad now? You see that *I* am smiling."

"And so am I," said the schoolmaster; "smiling to think how often we shall laugh in this same place. Were you not talking yonder?"

"Yes," the child rejoined.

"Of something that has made you sorrowful?"

There was a long pause.

"What was it?" said the schoolmaster, tenderly. "Come. Tell me what it was."

"I rather grieve—I *do* rather grieve to think," said the child, bursting into tears, "that those who die about us, are so soon forgotten."

"And do you think," said the schoolmaster, marking the glance she had thrown around, "that an unvisited grave, a withered tree, a faded flower or two, are tokens of forgetfulness or cold neglect? Do you think there are no deeds far away from here, in which these dead may be best remembered? Nell, Nell, there may be people busy in the world at this instant, in whose good actions and good thoughts these very graves—neglected as they look to us—are the chief instruments."

"Tell me no more," said the child quickly. "Tell me no more. I feel, I know it. How could *I* be unmindful of it, when I thought of you?"

"There is nothing," cried her friend, "no, nothing innocent or good, that dies, and is forgotten. Let us hold to that faith, or none. An infant, a prattling child, dying in its cradle, will live again in the better thoughts of those who loved it, and play its part, through them, in the redeeming actions of the world, though its body be burnt to ashes or drowned in the deepest sea. There is not an angel added to the Host of Heaven but does its blessed work on earth in those that loved it here. Forgotten! oh, if the good deeds of human creatures could be traced to their source, how beautifully would even death appear; for how much charity, mercy, and purified affection, would be seen to have their growth in dusty graves!"

"Yes," said the child, "it is the truth; I know it is. Who should feel its force so much as I, in whom your little scholar lives again! Dear, dear, good friend, if you knew the comfort you have given me!"

The poor schoolmaster made her no answer, but bent over her in silence; for his heart was full.

They were yet seated in the same place, when the grandfather approached. Before they had spoken many words together, the church clock struck the hour of school, and their friend withdrew.

"A good man," said the grandfather, looking after him; "a kind man. Surely *he* will never harm us, Nell. We are safe here, at last—eh? We will never go away from here."

The child shook her head and smiled.

"She needs rest," said the old man, patting her cheek; "too pale—too pale. She is not like what she was."

"When?" asked the child.

"Ha!" said the old man, "to be sure—when? How many weeks ago? Could I count them on my fingers? Let them rest though; they're better gone."

"Much better, dear," replied the child. "We will forget them; or, if we ever call them to mind, it shall be only as some uneasy dream that has passed away."

"Hush!" said the old man, motioning hastily to her with his hand and looking over his shoulder; "no more talk of the dream, and all the miseries it brought. There are no dreams here. 'Tis a quiet place, and they keep away. Let us never think about them, lest they should pursue us again. Sunken eyes and hollow cheeks—wet, cold, and famine—and horrors before them all, that were even worse—we must forget such things if we would be tranquil here."

"Thank Heaven!" inwardly exclaimed the child, "for this most happy change!"

"I will be patient," said the old man, "humble, very thankful and obedient, if you will let me stay. But do not hide from me; do not steal away alone; let me keep beside you. Indeed, I will be very true and faithful, Nell."

"I steal away alone! why that," replied the child, with assumed gaiety, "would be a pleasant jest indeed. See here, dear grandfather, we'll make this place our garden—why not? It is a very good one—and to-morrow we'll begin, and work together, side by side."

"It is a brave thought!" cried her grandfather. "Mind, darling—we begin to-morrow!"

Who so delighted as the old man, when they next day began their labour! Who so unconscious of all associations connected with the spot, as he! They plucked the long grass and nettles from the tombs, thinned the poor shrubs and roots, made the turf smooth, and cleared it of the leaves and weeds. They were yet in the ardour of their work, when the child, raising her head from the ground over which she bent, observed that the bachelor was sitting on the stile close by, watching them in silence.

"A kind office," said the little gentleman, nodding to Nell as she curtseyed to him. "Have you done all that, this morning?"

"It is very little, sir," returned the child, with downcast eyes, "to what we mean to do."

"Good work, good work," said the bachelor. "But do you only labour at the graves of children, and young people?"

"We shall come to the others in good time, sir," replied Nell, turning her head aside, and speaking softly.

It was a slight incident, and might have been design or accident, or the child's unconscious sympathy with youth. But it seemed to strike upon her grandfather, though he had not noticed it before. He looked in a hurried manner at the graves, then anxiously at the child, then pressed her to his side, and bade her stop to rest. Something he had long forgotten appeared to struggle faintly in his mind. It did not pass away, as weightier things had done; but came uppermost again, and yet again, and many times that day, and often afterwards. Once, while they were yet at work, the child, seeing that he often turned and looked uneasily at her, as though he were trying to resolve some painful doubts or collect some scattered thoughts, urged him to tell the reason. But he said it was nothing—nothing —and, laying her head upon his arm, patted her fair cheek with his hand, and muttered that she grew stronger every day, and would be a woman, soon.

CHAPTER LV

FROM that time, there sprang up in the old man's mind, a solicitude about the child which never slept or left him. There are chords in the human heart—strange, varying strings—which are only struck by accident; which will remain mute and senseless to appeals the most passionate and earnest, and respond at last to the slightest casual touch. In the most insensible or childish minds, there is some train of reflection which art can seldom lead, or skill assist, but which will reveal itself, as great truths have done, by chance, and when the discoverer has the plainest and simplest end in view. From that time, the old man never for a moment forgot the weakness and devotion of the child: from the time of that slight incident, he, who had seen her toiling by his side through so much difficulty and suffering, and had scarcely thought of her otherwise than as the partner of miseries which he felt severely in his own person, and deplored for his own sake at least as much as hers, awoke to a sense of what he owed her, and what those miseries had made her. Never, no, never once, in one unguarded moment from that time to the end, did any care for himself, any thought of his own comfort, any selfish consideration or regard distract his thoughts from the gentle object of his love.

He would follow her up and down, waiting till she should tire and lean upon his arm—he would sit opposite to her in the chimney-corner, content to watch, and look, until she raised her head and smiled upon him as of old—he would discharge, by stealth, those household duties which tasked her powers too heavily—he would rise, in the cold dark nights, to listen to her breathing in her sleep, and sometimes crouch for hours by her bedside only to touch her hand. He Who knows all, can only know what hopes, and fears, and thoughts of deep affection, were in that one disordered brain, and what a change had fallen on the poor old man.

Sometimes—weeks had crept on, then—the child, exhausted, though with little fatigue, would pass whole evenings on a couch beside the fire. At such times, the schoolmaster would bring in books, and read to her aloud; and seldom an evening passed, but the bachelor came in, and took his turn of reading. The old man sat and listened,—with little understanding for the words, but with his eyes fixed upon the child,—and if she smiled or brightened with the story, he would say it was a good one, and conceive a fondness for the very book. When, in their evening talk, the bachelor told some tale that pleased her (as his tales were sure to do), the old man would painfully try to store it in his mind; nay, when the bachelor left them, he would sometimes slip out after him, and humbly beg that he would tell him such a part again, that he might learn to win a smile from Nell.

But these were rare occasions, happily; for the child yearned to be out of doors, and walking in her solemn garden. Parties, too, would come to see the church; and those who came, speaking to others of the child, sent more; so that even at that season of the year they had visitors almost daily. The old man would follow them at a little distance through the building, listening to the voice he loved so well; and when the strangers left, and parted from Nell, he would mingle with them to catch up fragments of their conversation; or he would stand for the same purpose, with his grey head uncovered, at the gate, as they passed through. They always praised the child, her sense and beauty, and he was proud to hear them! But what was that, so often added, which wrung his heart, and made him sob and weep alone, in some dull corner! Alas! even careless strangers—they who had no feeling for her, but the interest of the moment—they who would go away and forget next week that such a being lived—even they saw it—even they pitied her—even they bade him good day compassionately, and whispered as they passed.

The people of the village, too, of whom there was not one but grew to have a fondness for poor Nell; even among them, there was the same feeling; a tenderness towards her—a compassionate regard for her, increasing every day. The very schoolboys, light-hearted and thoughtless as they were, even they cared for her. The roughest among them was sorry if he missed her in the usual place upon his way to school, and would turn out of the path to ask for her at the latticed window. If she were sitting in the church, they perhaps might peep in softly at the open door; but they never spoke to her, unless she rose and went to speak to them. Some feeling was abroad which raised the child above them all.

So, when Sunday came. They were all poor country people in the church, for the castle in which the old family had lived, was an empty ruin, and there were none but humble folks for seven miles around. There, as elsewhere, they had an interest in Nell. They would gather round her in the porch, before and after service; young children would cluster at her skirts; and aged men and women forsake their gossips, to give her kindly greeting. None of them, young or old, thought of passing the child without a friendly word. Many who came from three or four miles distant, brought her little presents; the humblest and rudest had good wishes to bestow.

She had sought out the young children whom she first saw playing in the churchyard. One of these—he who had spoken of his brother —was her little favourite and friend, and often sat by her side in the church, or climbed with her to the tower-top. It was his delight to help her, or to fancy that he did so, and they soon became close companions.

It happened, that, as she was reading in the old spot by herself one day, this child came running in with his eyes full of tears, and after holding her from him and looking at her eagerly for a moment, clasped his little arms passionately about her neck.

"What now?" said Nell, soothing him. "What is the matter?"

"She is not one yet!" cried the boy, embracing her still more closely. "No, no. Not yet!"

She looked at him wonderingly, and putting his hair back from his face, and kissing him, asked what he meant.

"You must not be one, dear Nell," cried the boy. "We can't see them. They never come to play with us, or talk to us. Be what you are. You are better so."

"I do not understand you," said the child. "Tell me what you mean."

"Why, they say," replied the boy, looking up into her face, "that you will be an Angel, before the birds sing again. But you won't be, will you? Don't leave us, Nell, though the sky *is* bright. Do not leave us!"

The child drooped her head, and put her hands before her face.

"She cannot bear the thought!" cried the boy, exulting through his tears. "You will not go. You know how sorry we should be. Dear Nell, tell me that you'll stay amongst us. Oh! Pray, pray, tell me that you will."

The little creature folded his hands, and knelt down at her feet.

"Only look at me, Nell," said the boy, "and tell me that you'll stop, and then I shall know that they are wrong, and will cry no more. Won't you say yes, Nell?"

Still the drooping head and hidden face, and the child quite silent —save for her sobs.

"After a time," pursued the boy, trying to draw away her hand, "the kind angels will be glad to think that you are not among them, and that you stayed here to be with us. Willy went away, to join them; but if he had known how I should miss him in our little bed at night, he never would have left me, I am sure."

Yet the child could make him no answer, and sobbed as though her heart were bursting.

"Why would you go, dear Nell? I know you would not be happy when you heard that we were crying for your loss. They say that Willy is in Heaven now, and that it's always summer there, and yet I'm sure he grieves when I lie down upon his garden bed, and he cannot turn to kiss me. But if you do go, Nell," said the boy, caressing her, and pressing his face to hers, "be fond of him, for my sake. Tell him how I love him still, and how much I loved you; and when I think that you two are together, and are happy, I'll try to bear it, and never give you pain by doing wrong—indeed I never will!"

The child suffered him to move her hands, and put them round his neck. There was a tearful silence, but it was not long before she looked upon him with a smile, and promised him, in a very gentle, quiet voice, that she would stay, and be his friend, as long as Heaven would let her. He clapped his hands for joy, and thanked her many times; and being charged to tell no person what had passed between them, gave her an earnest promise that he never would.

Nor did he, so far as the child could learn; but was her quiet companion in all her walks and musings, and never again adverted to the theme, which he felt had given her pain, although he was unconscious of its cause. Something of distrust lingered about him still; for he would often come, even in the dark evenings, and call in a timid voice outside the door to know if she were safe within; and being answered yes, and bidden to enter, would take his station on a low stool at her feet, and sit there patiently until they came to seek, and take him home. Sure as the morning came, it found him lingering near the house to ask if she were well; and, morning, noon, or night, go where she would, he would forsake his playmates and his sports to bear her company.

"And a good little friend he is, too," said the old sexton to her once. "When his elder brother died—elder seems a strange word, for he was only seven year old—I remember this one took it sorely to heart."

The child thought of what the schoolmaster had told her, and felt how its truth was shadowed out even in this infant.

"It has given him something of a quiet way, I think," said the old man, "though for that he is merry enough at times. I'd wager now that you and he have been listening by the old well."

"Indeed we have not," the child replied. "I have been afraid to go near it; for I am not often down in that part of the church, and do not know the ground."

compliance with a solemn custom of the ancient Brotherhood to which they belonged, joined in a fragment of the popular duet of "All's Well," with a long shake at the end.

"And what's the news?" said Richard.

"The town's as flat, my dear feller," replied Mr. Chuckster, "as the surface of a Dutch oven. There's no news. By the bye, that lodger of yours is a most extraordinary person. He quite eludes the most vigorous comprehension, you know. Never was such a feller!"

"What has he been doing now?" said Dick.

"By Jove, sir," returned Mr. Chuckster, taking out an oblong snuff-box, the lid whereof was ornamented with a fox's head curiously carved in brass, "that man is an unfathomable. Sir, that man has made friends with our articled clerk. There's no harm in him, but he is so amazingly slow and soft. Now, if he wanted a friend, why couldn't he have one that knew a thing or two, and could do him some good by his manners and conversation. I have my faults, sir," said Mr. Chuckster.

"No, no," interposed Mr. Swiveller.

"Oh yes I have, I have my faults, no man knows his faults better than I know mine. But," said Mr. Chuckster, "I'm not meek. My worst enemies—every man has his enemies, sir, and I have mine—never accused me of being meek. And I tell you what, sir, if I hadn't more of these qualities that commonly endear man to man, than our articled clerk has, I'd steal a Cheshire cheese, tie it round my neck, and drown myself. I'd die degraded, as I had lived. I would upon my honour."

Mr. Chuckster paused, rapped the fox's head exactly on the nose with the knuckle of the forefinger, took a pinch of snuff, and looked steadily at Mr. Swiveller, as much as to say that if he thought he was going to sneeze, he would find himself mistaken.

"Not contented, sir," said Mr. Chuckster, "with making friends with Abel, he has cultivated the acquaintance of his father and mother. Since he came home from that wild-goose chase, he has been there—actually been there. He patronises young Snobby besides; you'll find, sir, that he'll be constantly coming backwards and forwards to this place: yet I don't suppose that beyond the common forms of civility, he has ever exchanged half a dozen words with *me*. Now, upon my soul, you know," said Mr. Chuckster, shaking his head gravely, as men are wont to do when they consider things are going a little too far, "this is altogether such a low-minded affair, that if I didn't feel for the governor, and know that he could never get on without me, I should be obliged to cut the connexion. I should have no alternative."

Mr. Swiveller, who sat on another stool opposite to his friend, stirred the fire in an excess of sympathy, but said nothing.

"As to young Snob, sir," pursued Mr. Chuckster with a prophetic look, "you'll find he'll turn out bad. In our profession we know something of human nature, and take my word for it, that the feller that came back to work out that shilling, will show himself one of these days in his true colours. He's a low thief, sir. He must be."

Mr. Chuckster being roused, would probably have pursued this subject further, and in more emphatic language, but for a tap at the door, which seeming to announce the arrival of somebody on business, caused him to assume a greater appearance of meekness than was perhaps quite consistent with his late declaration. Mr. Swiveller, hearing the same sound, caused his stool to revolve rapidly on one leg until it brought him to his desk, into which, having forgotten in the sudden flurry of his spirits to part with the poker, he thrust it as he cried "Come in!"

Who should present himself but that very Kit who had been the theme of Mr. Chuckster's wrath! Never did man pluck up his courage so quickly, or look so fierce, as Mr. Chuckster when he found it was he. Mr. Swiveller stared at him for a moment, and then leaping from his stool, and drawing out the poker from its place of concealment, performed the broad-sword exercise with all the cuts and guards complete, in a species of frenzy.

"Is the gentleman at home?" said Kit, rather astonished by this uncommon reception.

Before Mr. Swiveller could make any reply, Mr. Chuckster took occasion to enter his indignant protest against this form of inquiry; which he held to be of a disrespectful and snobbish tendency, inasmuch as the inquirer, seeing two gentlemen then and there present, should have spoken of the other gentleman; or rather (for it was not impossible that the object of his search might be of inferior quality) should have mentioned his name, leaving it to his hearers to determine his degree as they thought proper. Mr. Chuckster further remarked, that he had some reason to believe this form of address was personal to himself, and that he was not a man to be trifled with, as certain snobs (whom he did not more particularly mention or describe) might find, to their cost.

"I mean the gentleman up stairs," said Kit, turning to Richard Swiveller. "Is he at home?"

"Why?" rejoined Dick.

"Because if he is, I have a letter for him."

"From whom?" said Dick.

"From Mr. Garland."

"Oh!" said Dick, with extreme politeness. "Then you may hand it over, sir. And if you're to wait for an answer, sir, you may wait in the passage, sir, which is an airy and well-ventilated apartment, sir."

"Thank you," returned Kit. "But I am to give it to himself, if you please."

The excessive audacity of this retort so overpowered Mr. Chuckster, and so moved his tender regard for his friend's honour, that he declared, if he were not restrained by official considerations, he must certainly have annihilated Kit upon the spot; a resentment of the affront which he did consider, under the extraordinary circumstances of aggravation attending it, could but have met with the proper sanction and approval of a jury of Englishmen, who, he had no doubt, would have returned a verdict of Justifiable Homicide, coupled with a high testimony to the morals and character of the Avenger. Mr. Swiveller, without being quite so hot upon the matter, was rather shamed by his friend's excitement, and not a little puzzled how to act (Kit being quite cool and good-humoured), when the single gentleman was heard to call violently down the stairs.

"Didn't I see somebody for me, come in?" cried the lodger.

"Yes, sir," replied Dick. "Certainly, sir."

"Then where is he!" roared the single gentleman.

"He's here, sir," rejoined Mr. Swiveller. "Now young man, don't you hear you're to go up stairs? Are you deaf?"

Kit did not appear to think it worth his while to enter into any further altercation, but hurried off and left the Glorious Apollos gazing at each other in silence.

"Didn't I tell you so?" said Mr. Chuckster. "What do you think of that?"

Mr. Swiveller being in the main a good-natured fellow, and not perceiving in the conduct of Kit any villany of enormous magnitude, scarcely knew what answer to return. He was relieved from his perplexity, however, by the entrance of Mr. Sampson and his sister, Sally, at sight of whom Mr. Chuckster precipitately retired.

Mr. Brass and his lovely companion appeared to have been holding a consultation over their temperate breakfast, upon some matter of great interest and importance. On the occasion of such conferences, they generally appeared in the office some half an hour after their usual time, and in a very smiling state, as though their late plots and designs had tranquillised their minds and shed a light upon their toilsome way. In the present instance, they seemed particularly gay; Miss Sally's aspect being of a most oily kind, and Mr. Brass rubbing his hands in an exceedingly jocose and light-hearted manner.

"Well, Mr. Richard," said Brass. "How are we this morning? Are we pretty fresh and cheerful, sir—eh, Mr. Richard?"

"Pretty well, sir," replied Dick.

"That's well," said Brass. "Ha ha! We should be gay as larks, Mr. Richard—why not? It's a pleasant world we live in, sir, a very pleasant world. There are bad people in it, Mr. Richard, but if there were no bad people, there would be no good lawyers. Ha ha! Any letters by the post this morning, Mr. Richard?"

Mr. Swiveller answered in the negative.

"Ha!" said Brass, "no matter. If there's little business to-day, there'll be more to-morrow. A contented spirit, Mr. Richard, is the sweetness of existence. Anybody been here, sir?"

"Only my friend"—replied Dick. "'May we ne'er want a——'"

"'Friend,'" Brass chimed in quickly, "'or a bottle to give him.'" Ha ha! That's the way the song runs, isn't it? A very good song, Mr. Richard, very good. I like the sentiment of it. Ha ha! Your friend's the young man from Witherden's office, I think—yes—'May we ne'er want a——.' Nobody else at all, been, Mr. Richard?"

"Only somebody to the lodger," replied Mr. Swiveller.

"Oh indeed!" cried Brass. "Somebody to the lodger, eh? Ha ha! 'May we ne'er want a friend, or a—' Somebody to the lodger, eh, Mr. Richard?"

"Yes," said Dick, a little disconcerted by the excessive buoyancy of spirits which his employer displayed. "With him now."

"With him now!" cried Brass; "Ha ha! There let 'em be, merry and free, toor rul rol le. Eh, Mr. Richard? Ha ha!"

"Oh certainly," replied Dick.

"And who," said Brass, shuffling among his papers, "who is the lodger's visitor—not a lady visitor, I hope, eh, Mr. Richard? The morals of the Marks you know, sir—'when lovely woman stoops to folly'—and all that—eh, Mr. Richard?"

"Another young man, who belongs to Witherden's too, or half belongs there," returned Richard. "Kit, they call him."

"Kit, eh!" said Brass. "Strange name—name of a dancing-master's fiddle, eh, Mr. Richard? Ha ha! Kit's there, is he? Oh!"

Dick looked at Miss Sally, wondering that she didn't check this uncommon exuberance on the part of Mr. Sampson; but as she made no attempt to do so, and rather appeared to exhibit a tacit acquiescence in it, he concluded that they had just been cheating somebody, and receiving the bill.

"Will you have the goodness, Mr. Richard," said Brass, taking a letter from his desk, "just to step over to Peckham Rye with that? There's no answer, but it's rather particular and should go by hand. Charge the office with your coach-hire back, you know; don't spare the office; get as much out of it as you can—clerk's motto—Eh, Mr. Richard? Ha ha!"

Mr. Swiveller solemnly doffed the aquatic jacket, put on his coat, took down his hat from its peg, pocketed the letter, and departed. Directly he was gone, up rose Miss Sally Brass, and smiling sweetly at her brother (who nodded and smote his nose in return) withdrew also.

Sampson Brass was no sooner left alone, than he set the office-door wide open, and establishing himself at his desk directly opposite, so that he could not fail to see anybody who came down stairs and passed out at the street-door, began to write with extreme cheerfulness and assiduity; humming as he did so, in a voice that was anything but musical, certain vocal snatches which appeared to have reference to the union between Church and State, inasmuch as they were compounded of the Evening Hymn and God save the King.

Thus, the attorney of Bevis Marks sat, and wrote, and hummed, for a long time, except when he stopped to listen with a very cunning face, and hearing nothing, went on humming louder, and writing slower than ever. At length, in one of these pauses, he heard his lodger's door opened and shut, and footsteps coming down the stairs. Then Mr. Brass left off writing entirely, and with his pen in his hand hummed his very loudest; shaking his head meanwhile from side to side like a man whose whole soul was in the music, and smiling in a manner quite seraphic.

It was towards this moving spectacle that the staircase and the sweet sounds guided Kit, on whose arrival before his door, Mr. Brass stopped his singing, but not his smiling, and nodded affably, at the same time beckoning to him with his pen.

"Kit," said Mr. Brass, in the pleasantest way imaginable, "how do you do?"

Kit, being rather shy of his friend, made a suitable reply, and had his hand upon the lock of the street-door when Mr. Brass called him softly back.

"You are not to go, if you please, Kit," said the attorney in a mysterious and yet business-like way. "You are to step in here, if you please. Dear me, dear me! When I look at you," said the lawyer, quitting his stool, and standing before the fire with his back towards it, "I am reminded of the sweetest little face that ever my eyes beheld. I remember your coming there twice or thrice when we were in possession. Ah, Kit, my dear fellow, gentlemen in my profession have such painful duties to perform sometimes, that you needn't envy us—you needn't indeed!"

"I don't, sir," said Kit, "though it isn't for the like of me to judge."

"Our only consolation, Kit," pursued the lawyer, looking at him in a sort of pensive abstraction, "is, that although we cannot turn away the wind, we can soften it; we can temper it, if I may say so, to the shorn lambs."

"Shorn indeed!" thought Kit. "Pretty close!" But he didn't say so.

"On that occasion, Kit," said Mr. Brass, "on that occasion that I have just alluded to, I had a hard battle with Mr. Quilp (for Mr. Quilp is a very hard man) to obtain them the indulgence they had. It might have cost me a client. But suffering virtue inspired me, and I prevailed."

"He's not so bad after all," thought honest Kit, as the attorney pursed up his lips and looked like a man who was struggling with his better feelings.

"I respect *you*, Kit," said Brass with emotion. "I saw enough of your conduct at that time to respect you, though your station is humble, and your fortune lowly. It isn't the waistcoat that I look at. It is the heart. The checks in the waistcoat are but the wires of the cage. But the heart is the bird. Ah! How many sich birds are perpetually moulting, and putting their beaks through the wires to peck at all mankind!"

This poetic figure, which Kit took to be in special allusion to his own checked waistcoat, quite overcame him; Mr. Brass's voice and manner added not a little to its effect, for he discoursed with all the mild austerity of a hermit, and wanted but a cord round the waist of his rusty surtout, and a skull on the chimney-piece, to be completely set up in that line of business.

"Well, well," said Sampson, smiling as good men smile when they compassionate their own weakness or that of their fellow-creatures, "this is wide of the bull's-eye. You're to take that, if you please." As he spoke, he pointed to a couple of half-crowns upon the desk.

Kit looked at the coins, and then at Sampson, and hesitated.

"For yourself," said Brass.

"From——"

"No matter about the person they came from," replied the lawyer. "Say me, if you like. We have eccentric friends overhead, Kit, and we mustn't ask questions or talk too much—you understand. You're to take them, that's all; and between you and me, I don't think they'll be the last you'll have to take from the same place. I hope not. Good-bye, Kit. Good-bye!"

With many thanks, and many more self-reproaches for having on such slight grounds suspected one who in their very first conversation turned out such a different man from what he had supposed, Kit took the money and made the best of his way home. Mr. Brass remained airing himself at the fire, and resumed his vocal exercise, and his seraphic smile, simultaneously.

"May I come in?" said Miss Sally, peeping.

"Oh yes, you may come in," returned her brother.

"Ahem?" coughed Miss Brass interrogatively.

"Yes," returned Sampson, "I should say as good as done."

CHAPTER LVII

MR. CHUCKSTER'S indignant apprehensions were not without foundation. Certainly the friendship between the single gentleman and Mr. Garland was not suffered to cool, but had a rapid growth and flourished exceedingly. They were soon in habits of constant intercourse and communication; and the single gentleman labouring at this time under a slight attack of illness—the consequence most probably of his late excited feelings and subsequent disappointment —furnished a reason for their holding yet more frequent correspondence; so that some one of the inmates of Abel Cottage, Finchley, came backwards and forwards between that place and Bevis Marks, almost every day.

As the pony had now thrown off all disguise, and without any mincing of the matter or beating about the bush, sturdily refused to be driven by anybody but Kit, it generally happened that whether old Mr. Garland came, or Mr. Abel, Kit was of the party. Of all messages and inquiries, Kit was in right of his position the bearer; thus it came about that, while the single gentleman remained indisposed, Kit turned into Bevis Marks every morning with nearly as much regularity as the General Postman.

Mr. Sampson Brass, who no doubt had his reasons for looking sharply about him, soon learnt to distinguish the pony's trot and the clatter of the little chaise at the corner of the street. Whenever this sound reached his ears, he would immediately lay down his pen and fall to rubbing his hands and exhibiting the greatest glee.

"Ha ha!" he would cry. "Here's the pony again. Most remarkable pony, extremely docile, eh, Mr. Richard, eh, sir?"

Dick would return some matter-of-course reply, and Mr. Brass, standing on the bottom rail of his stool, so as to get a view of the street over the top of the window-blind, would take an observation of the visitors.

"The old gentleman again!" he would exclaim, "a very prepossessing old gentleman, Mr. Richard—charming countenance, sir—extremely calm—benevolence in every feature, sir. He quite realises my idea of King Lear, as he appeared when in possession of his kingdom, Mr. Richard—the same good humour, the same white hair and partial baldness, the same liability to be imposed upon. Ah! A sweet subject for contemplation, sir, very sweet!"

Then, Mr. Garland having alighted and gone up stairs, Sampson would nod and smile to Kit from the window, and presently walk out into the street to greet him, when some such conversation as the following would ensue.

"Admirably groomed, Kit"—Mr. Brass is patting the pony—"does you great credit—amazingly sleek and bright to be sure. He literally looks as if he had been varnished all over."

Kit touches his hat, smiles, pats the pony himself, and expresses his conviction, "that Mr. Brass will not find many like him."

"A beautiful animal indeed!" cries Brass. "Sagacious too!"

"Bless you!" replies Kit, "he knows what you say to him as well as a Christian does."

"Does he indeed!" cries Brass, who has heard the same thing in the same place from the same person in the same words a dozen times, but is paralysed with astonishment notwithstanding. "Dear me!"

"I little thought the first time I saw him, sir," says Kit, pleased with the attorney's strong interest in his favourite, "that I should come to be as intimate with him as I am now."

"Ah!" rejoins Mr. Brass, brim-full of moral precepts and love of virtue. "A charming subject of reflection for you, very charming. A subject of proper pride and congratulation, Christopher. Honesty is the best policy.—I always find it so myself. I lost forty-seven pound ten by being honest this morning. But it's all gain, it's gain!"

Mr. Brass slyly tickles his nose with his pen, and looks at Kit with the water standing in his eyes. Kit thinks that if ever there was a good man who belied his appearance, that man is Sampson Brass.

"A man," says Sampson, "who loses forty-seven pound ten in one morning by his honesty, is a man to be envied. If it had been eighty pound, the luxuriousness of feeling would have been increased. Every pound lost, would have been a hundredweight of happiness gained. The still, small voice, Christopher," cries Brass smiling, and tapping himself on the bosom, "is a singing comic songs within me, and all is happiness and joy!"

Kit is so improved by the conversation, and finds it go so completely home to his feelings, that he is considering what he shall say, when Mr. Garland appears. The old gentleman is helped into the chaise with great obsequiousness by Mr. Sampson Brass; and the pony, after shaking his head several times, and standing for three or four minutes with all his four legs planted firmly on the ground as if he had made up his mind never to stir from that spot, but there to live and die, suddenly darts off without the smallest notice, at the rate of twelve English miles an hour. Then Mr. Brass and his sister (who has joined him at the door) exchange an odd kind of smile—not at all a pleasant one in its expression—and return to the society of Mr. Richard Swiveller, who during their absence has been regaling himself with various feats of pantomime, and is discovered at his desk, in a very flushed and heated condition, violently scratching out nothing with half a penknife.

Whenever Kit came alone, and without the chaise, it always happened that Sampson Brass was reminded of some mission, calling Mr. Swiveller, if not to Peckham Rye again, at all events to some pretty distant place from which he could not be expected to return for two or three hours, or in all probability a much longer period, as that gentleman was not, to say the truth, renowned for using great expedition on such occasions, but rather for protracting and spinning out the time to the very utmost limit of possibility. Mr. Swiveller out of sight, Miss Sally immediately withdrew. Mr. Brass would then set the office-door wide open, hum his old tune with great gaiety of heart, and smile seraphically as before. Kit coming down stairs would be called in; entertained with some moral and agreeable conversation; perhaps entreated to mind the office for an instant while Mr. Brass stepped over the way; and afterwards presented with one or two half-crowns as the case might be. This occurred so often, that Kit, nothing doubting but that they came from the single gentleman, who had already rewarded his mother with great liberality, could not enough admire his generosity; and bought so many cheap presents for her, and for little Jacob, and for the baby, and for Barbara to boot, that one or other of them was having some new trifle every day of their lives.

While these acts and deeds were in progress in and out of the office of Sampson Brass, Richard Swiveller, being often left alone therein, began to find the time hang heavy on his hands. For the better preservation of his cheerfulness therefore, and to prevent his faculties from rusting, he provided himself with a cribbage-board and pack of cards, and accustomed himself to play at cribbage with a dummy, for twenty, thirty, or sometimes even fifty thousand pounds a side, besides many hazardous bets to a considerable amount.

As these games were very silently conducted, notwithstanding the magnitude of the interests involved, Mr. Swiveller began to think that on those evenings when Mr. and Miss Brass were out (and they often went out now) he heard a kind of snorting or hard-breathing sound in the direction of the door, which it occurred to him, after some reflection, must proceed from the small servant, who always had a cold from damp living. Looking intently that way one night, he plainly distinguished an eye gleaming and glistening at the key-hole; and having now no doubt that his suspicions were correct, he stole softly to the door, and pounced upon her before she was aware of his approach.

"Oh! I didn't mean any harm indeed. Upon my word I didn't," cried the small servant, struggling like a much larger one. "It's so very dull, down stairs. Please don't you tell upon me; please don't."

"Tell upon you!" said Dick. "Do you mean to say you were looking through the key-hole for company?"

"Yes, upon my word I was," replied the small servant.

"How long have you been cooling your eye there?" said Dick.

"Oh ever since you first began to play them cards, and long before."

Vague recollections of several fantastic exercises with which he had refreshed himself after the fatigues of business, and to all of which, no doubt, the small servant was a party, rather disconcerted Mr. Swiveller; but he was not very sensitive on such points, and recovered himself speedily.

"Well,—come in"—he said, after a little consideration. "Here—sit down, and I'll teach you how to play."

"Oh! I durstn't do it," rejoined the small servant; "Miss Sally 'ud kill me, if she know'd I came up here."

"Have you got a fire down stairs?" said Dick.

"A very little one," replied the small servant.

"Miss Sally couldn't kill me if she know'd I went down there, so I'll come," said Richard, putting the cards into his pocket. "Why, how thin you are! What do you mean by it?"

"It an't my fault."

"Could you eat any bread and meat?" said Dick, taking down his hat. "Yes? Ah! I thought so. Did you ever taste beer?"

"I had a sip of it once," said the small servant.

"Here's a state of things!" cried Mr. Swiveller, raising his eyes to the ceiling. "She *never* tasted it—it can't be tasted in a sip! Why, how old are you?"

"I don't know."

Mr. Swiveller opened his eyes very wide, and appeared thoughtful for a moment; then, bidding the child mind the door until he came back, vanished straightway.

Presently he returned, followed by the boy from the public-house, who bore in one hand a plate of bread and beef, and in the other a great pot, filled with some very fragrant compound, which sent forth a grateful steam, and was indeed choice purl, made after a particular recipe which Mr Swiveller had imparted to the landlord at a period when he was deep in his books and desirous to conciliate his friendship. Relieving the boy of his burden at the door, and charging his little companion to fasten it to prevent surprise, Mr. Swiveller followed her into the kitchen.

"There!" said Richard, putting the plate before her. "First of all, clear that off, and then you'll see what's next."

The small servant needed no second bidding, and the plate was soon empty.

"Next," said Dick, handing the purl, "take a pull at that; but moderate your transports, you know, for you're not used to it. Well, is it good?"

"Oh! isn't it?" said the small servant.

Mr. Swiveller appeared gratified beyond all expression by this reply, and took a long draught himself, steadfastly regarding his companion while he did so. These preliminaries disposed of, he applied himself to teaching her the game, which she soon learnt tolerably well, being both sharp-witted and cunning.

"Now," said Mr. Swiveller, putting two sixpences into a saucer, and trimming the wretched candle, when the cards had been cut and dealt, "those are the stakes. If you win, you get 'em all. If I win, I get 'em. To make it seem more real and pleasant, I shall call you the Marchioness, do you hear?"

The small servant nodded.

"Then, Marchioness," said Mr. Swiveller, "fire away!"

The Marchioness, holding her cards very tight in both hands, considered which to play, and Mr. Swiveller, assuming the gay and fashionable air which such society required, took another pull at the tankard, and waited for her lead.

CHAPTER LVIII

MR. SWIVELLER and his partner played several rubbers with varying success, until the loss of three sixpences, the gradual sinking of the purl, and the striking of ten o'clock, combined to render that gentleman mindful of the flight of Time, and the expediency of withdrawing before Mr. Sampson and Miss Sally Brass returned.

"With which object in view, Marchioness," said Mr. Swiveller gravely, "I shall ask your ladyship's permission to put the board in my pocket, and to retire from the presence when I have finished this tankard; merely observing, Marchioness, that since life like a river is flowing, I care not how fast it rolls on, ma'am, on, while such purl on the bank still is growing, and such eyes light the waves as they run. Marchioness, your health. You will excuse my wearing my hat, but the palace is damp, and the marble floor is—if I may be allowed the expression—sloppy."

As a precaution against this latter inconvenience, Mr. Swiveller had been sitting for some time with his feet on the hob, in which attitude he now gave utterance to these apologetic observations, and slowly sipped the last choice drops of nectar.

"The Baron Sampsono Brasso and his fair sister are (you tell me) at the Play?" said Mr. Swiveller, leaning his left arm heavily upon the table, and raising his voice and his right leg after the manner of a theatrical bandit.

The Marchioness nodded.

"Ha!" said Mr. Swiveller, with a portentous frown. "'Tis well. Marchioness!—but no matter. Some wine there. Ho!" He illustrated these melodramatic morsels by handing the tankard to himself with great humility, receiving it haughtily, drinking from it thirstily, and smacking his lips fiercely.

The small servant, who was not so well acquainted with theatrical conventionalities as Mr. Swiveller (having indeed never seen a play, or heard one spoken of, except by chance through chinks of doors and in other forbidden places), was rather alarmed by demonstrations so novel in their nature, and showed her concern so plainly in her looks, that Mr. Swiveller felt it necessary to discharge his brigand manner for one more suitable to private life, as he asked,

"Do they often go where glory waits 'em, and leave you here?"

"Oh, yes; I believe you they do," returned the small servant. "Miss Sally's such a one-er for that, she is."

"Such a what?" said Dick.

"Such a one-er," returned the Marchioness.

After a moment's reflection, Mr. Swiveller determined to forego his responsible duty of setting her right, and to suffer her to talk on; as it was evident that her tongue was loosened by the purl, and her opportunities for conversation were not so frequent as to render a momentary check of little consequence.

"They sometimes go to see Mr. Quilp," said the small servant with a shrewd look; "they go to a many places, bless you."

"Is Mr. Brass a wunner?" said Dick.

"Not half what Miss Sally is, he isn't," replied the small servant, shaking her head. "Bless you, he'd never do anything without her."

"Oh! He wouldn't, wouldn't he?" said Dick.

"Miss Sally keeps him in such order," said the small servant; "he always asks her advice, he does; and he catches it sometimes. Bless you, you wouldn't believe how much he catches it."

"I suppose," said Dick, "that they consult together a good deal, and talk about a great many people—about me for instance, sometimes, eh, Marchioness?"

The Marchioness nodded amazingly.

"Complimentary?" said Mr. Swiveller.

The Marchioness changed the motion of her head, which had not yet left off nodding, and suddenly began to shake it from side to side with a vehemence which threatened to dislocate her neck.

"Humph!" Dick muttered. "Would it be any breach of confidence, Marchioness, to relate what they say of the humble individual who has now the honour to——?"

"Miss Sally says you're a funny chap," replied his friend.

"Well, Marchioness," said Mr. Swiveller, "that's not uncomplimentary. Merriment, Marchioness, is not a bad or degrading quality. Old King Cole was himself a merry old soul, if we may put any faith in the pages of history."

"But she says," pursued his companion, "that you an't to be trusted."

"Why, really, Marchioness," said Mr. Swiveller, thoughtfully; "several ladies and gentlemen—not exactly professional persons, but tradespeople, ma'am, tradespeople—have made the same remark. The obscure citizen who keeps the hotel over the way, inclined strongly to that opinion to-night when I ordered him to prepare the banquet. It's a popular prejudice, Marchioness; and yet I am sure I don't know why, for I have been trusted in my time to a considerable amount, and I can safely say that I never forsook my trust until it deserted me—never. Mr. Brass is of the same opinion, I suppose?"

His friend nodded again, with a cunning look which seemed to hint that Mr. Brass held stronger opinions on the subject than his sister; and seeming to recollect herself, added imploringly, "But don't you ever tell upon me, or I shall be beat to death."

"Marchioness," said Mr. Swiveller, rising, "the word of a gentleman is as good as his bond—sometimes better; as in the present case, where his bond might prove but a doubtful sort of security. I am your friend, and I hope we shall play many more rubbers together in this same saloon. But, Marchioness," added Richard, stopping in his way to the door, and wheeling slowly round upon the small servant, who was following with the candle; "it occurs to me that you must be in the constant habit of airing your eye at key-holes, to know all this."

"I only wanted," replied the trembling Marchioness, "to know where the key of the safe was hid; that was all; and I wouldn't have taken much, if I had found it—only enough to squench my hunger."

"You didn't find it then?" said Dick. "But of course you didn't or you'd be plumper. Good night, Marchioness. Fare thee well, and if for ever, then for ever fare thee well—and put up the chain, Marchioness, in case of accidents."

With this parting injunction, Mr. Swiveller emerged from the house; and feeling that he had by this time taken quite as much to drink as promised to be good for his constitution (purl being a rather strong and heady compound), wisely resolved to betake himself to his lodgings, and to bed at once. Homeward he went therefore; and his apartments (for he still retained the plural fiction) being at no great distance from the office, he was soon seated in his own bed-chamber, where, having pulled off one boot and forgotten the other, he fell into deep cogitation.

"This Marchioness," said Mr. Swiveller, folding his arms, "is a very extraordinary person—surrounded by mysteries, ignorant of the taste of beer, unacquainted with her own name (which is less remarkable), and taking a limited view of society through the key-holes of doors—can these things be her destiny, or has some unknown person started an opposition to the decrees of fate? It is a most inscrutable and unmitigated staggerer!"

When his meditations had attained this satisfactory point, he became aware of his remaining boot, of which, with unimpaired solemnity, he proceeded to divest himself; shaking his head with exceeding gravity all the time, and sighing deeply.

"Away with meelancholy"

"These rubbers," said Mr. Swiveller, putting on his night-cap in exactly the same style as he wore his hat, "remind me of the matrimonial fireside. Cheggs's wife plays cribbage; all-fours likewise. She sings the changes on 'em now. From sport to sport they hurry her, to banish her regrets, and when they win a smile from her, they think that she forgets—but she don't. By this time, I should say," added Richard, getting his left cheek into profile, and looking complacently at the reflection of a very little scrap of whisker in the looking-glass; "by this time, I should say, the iron has entered into her soul. It serves her right!"

Melting from this stern and obdurate, into the tender and pathetic mood, Mr. Swiveller groaned a little, walked wildly up and down, and even made a show of tearing his hair, which however he thought better of, and wrenched the tassel from his night-cap instead. At last, undressing himself with a gloomy resolution, he got into bed.

Some men in his blighted position would have taken to drinking; but as Mr. Swiveller had taken to that before, he only took, on receiving the news that Sophy Wackles was lost to him for ever, to playing the flute; thinking after mature consideration that it was a good, sound, dismal occupation, not only in unison with his own sad thoughts, but calculated to awaken a fellow-feeling in the bosoms of his neighbours. In pursuance of this resolution, he now drew a little table to his bedside, and arranging the light and a small oblong music-book to the best advantage, took his flute from its box, and began to play most mournfully.

The air was "Away with melancholy"—a composition, which, when it is played very slowly on the flute in bed, with the further disadvantage of being performed by a gentleman but imperfectly acquainted with the instrument, who repeats one note a great many times before he can find the next, has not a lively effect. Yet for half the night, or more, Mr. Swiveller, lying sometimes on his back with his eyes upon the ceiling, and sometimes half out of bed to correct himself by the book, played this unhappy tune over and over again; never leaving off, save for a minute or two at a time to take breath and soliloquise about the Marchioness, and then beginning again with renewed vigour. It was not until he had quite exhausted his several subjects of meditation, and had breathed into the flute the whole sentiment of the purl down to its very dregs, and had nearly maddened the people of the house, and at both the next doors, and over the way,—that he shut up the music-book, extinguished the candle, and finding himself greatly lightened and relieved in his mind, turned round and fell asleep.

He awoke in the morning, much refreshed; and having taken half an hour's exercise at the flute, and graciously received a notice to quit from his landlady, who had been in waiting on the stairs for that purpose since the dawn of day, repaired to Bevis Marks; where the beautiful Sally was already at her post, bearing in her looks a radiance, mild as that which beameth from the virgin moon.

Mr. Swiveller acknowledged her presence by a nod, and exchanged his coat for the aquatic jacket; which usually took some time fitting on, for in consequence of a tightness in the sleeves, it was only to be got into by a series of struggles. This difficulty overcome, he took his seat at the desk.

"I say"—quoth Miss Brass, abruptly breaking the silence, "you haven't seen a silver pencil-case this morning, have you?"

"I didn't meet many in the street," rejoined Mr. Swiveller. "I saw one—a stout pencil-case of respectable appearance—but as he was in company with an elderly pen-knife and a young toothpick, with whom he was in earnest conversation, I felt a delicacy in speaking to him."

"No, but have you?" returned Miss Brass. "Seriously, you know."

"What a dull dog you must be to ask me such a question seriously," said Mr. Swiveller. "Haven't I this moment come?"

"Well, all I know is," replied Miss Sally, "that it's not to be found, and that it disappeared one day this week, when I left it on the desk."

"Halloa!" thought Richard, "I hope the Marchioness hasn't been at work here."

"There was a knife too," said Miss Sally, "of the same pattern. They were given to me by my father, years ago, and are both gone. You haven't missed anything yourself, have you?"

Mr. Swiveller involuntarily clapped his hands to the jacket to be quite sure that it *was* a jacket and not a skirted coat; and having satisfied himself of the safety of this, his only moveable in Bevis Marks, made answer in the negative.

"It's a very unpleasant thing, Dick—" said Miss Brass, pulling out the tin box and refreshing herself with a pinch of snuff; "but between you and me—between friends you know, for if Sammy knew it, I should never hear the last of it—some of the office money, too, that has been left about, has gone in the same way. In particular, I have missed three half-crowns at three different times."

"You don't mean that?" cried Dick. "Be careful what you say, old boy, for this is a serious matter. Are you quite sure? Is there no mistake?"

"It is so, and there can't be any mistake at all," rejoined Miss Brass emphatically.

"Then, by Jove," thought Richard, laying down his pen, "I'm afraid the Marchioness is done for!"

The more he discussed the subject in his thoughts, the more probable it appeared to Dick that the miserable little servant was the culprit. When he considered on what a spare allowance of food she lived, how neglected and untaught she was, and how her natural cunning had been sharpened by necessity and privation, he scarcely doubted it. And yet he pitied her so much, and felt so unwilling to have a matter of such gravity disturbing the oddity of their acquaintance, that he thought, and thought truly, that rather than receive fifty pounds down, he would have the Marchioness proved innocent.

While he was plunged in very profound and serious meditation upon this theme, Miss Sally sat shaking her head with an air of great mystery and doubt; when the voice of her brother Sampson, carolling a cheerful strain, was heard in the passage, and that gentleman himself, beaming with virtuous smiles, appeared.

"Mr. Richard, sir, good morning! Here we are again, sir, entering upon another day, with our bodies strengthened by slumber and breakfast, and our spirits fresh and flowing. Here we are, Mr. Richard, rising with the sun to run our little course—our course of duty, sir—and, like him, get through our day's work with credit to ourselves and advantage to our fellow-creatures. A charming reflection, sir, very charming!"

While he addressed his clerk in these words, Mr. Brass was somewhat ostentatiously engaged in minutely examining and holding up against the light a five-pound bank-note, which he had brought in, in his hand.

Mr. Richard not receiving his remarks with anything like enthusiasm, his employer turned his eyes to his face, and observed that it wore a troubled expression.

"You're out of spirits, sir," said Brass. "Mr. Richard, sir, we should fall to work cheerfully, and not in a despondent state. It becomes us, Mr. Richard, sir, to——"

Here the chaste Sarah heaved a loud sigh.

"Dear me!" said Mr. Sampson, "you too! Is anything the matter? Mr. Richard, sir——"

Dick, glancing at Miss Sally, saw that she was making signals to him, to acquaint her brother with the subject of their recent conversation. As his own position was not a very pleasant one until the matter was set at rest one way or other, he did so; and Miss Brass, plying her snuff-box at a most wasteful rate, corroborated his account.

The countenance of Sampson fell, and anxiety overspread his features. Instead of passionately bewailing the loss of his money, as Miss Sally had expected, he walked on tip-toe to the door, opened it, looked outside, shut it softly, returned on tiptoe, and said in a whisper.

"This is a most extraordinary and painful circumstance—Mr. Richard, sir, a most painful circumstance. The fact is, that I myself have missed several small sums from the desk of late, and have refrained from mentioning it, hoping that accident would discover the offender; but it has not done so—it has not done so. Sally—Mr. Richard, sir—this is a particularly distressing affair!"

As Sampson spoke, he laid the bank-note upon the desk among some papers, in an absent manner, and thrust his hands into his pockets. Richard Swiveller pointed to it, and admonished him to take it up.

"No, Mr. Richard, sir," rejoined Brass with emotion. "I will not take it up. I will let it lie there, sir. To take it up, Mr. Richard, sir, would imply a doubt of you; and in you, sir, I have unlimited confidence. We will let it lie there, sir, if you please, and we will not take it up by any means." With that, Mr. Brass patted him twice or thrice upon the shoulder, in a most friendly manner, and entreated him to believe that he had as much faith in his honesty as he had in his own.

Although at another time Mr. Swiveller might have looked upon this as a doubtful compliment, he felt it, under the then-existing circumstances, a great relief to be assured that he was not wrongfully suspected. When he had made a suitable reply, Mr. Brass wrung him by the hand, and fell into a brown study, as did Miss Sally likewise. Richard too remained in a thoughtful state; fearing every moment to hear the Marchioness impeached, and unable to resist the conviction that she must be guilty.

When they had severally remained in this condition for some minutes, Miss Sally all at once gave a loud rap upon the desk with her clenched fist, and cried, "I've hit it!"—as indeed she had, and chipped a piece out of it too; but that was not her meaning.

"Well!" cried Brass anxiously. "Go on, will you?"

"Why," replied his sister with an air of triumph, "hasn't there been somebody always coming in and out of this office for the last three or four weeks; hasn't that somebody been left alone in it sometimes—thanks to you; and do you mean to tell me that that somebody isn't the thief!"

"What somebody?" blustered Brass.

"Why, what do you call him—Kit?"

"Mr. Garland's young man?"

"To be sure."

"Never!" cried Brass. "Never. I'll not hear of it. Don't tell me—" said Sampson, shaking his head, and working with both his hands as if he were clearing away ten thousand cobwebs. "I'll never believe it of him. Never!"

"I say," repeated Miss Brass, taking another pinch of snuff, "that he's the thief."

"I say," returned Sampson violently, "that he is *not*. What do you mean? How dare you? Are characters to be whispered away like this? Do you know that he's the honestest and faithfullest fellow that ever lived, and that he has an irreproachable good name? Come in, come in!"

These last words were not addressed to Miss Sally, though they partook of the tone in which the indignant remonstrances that preceded them had been uttered. They were addressed to some person who had knocked at the office-door; and they had hardly passed the lips of Mr. Brass, when this very Kit himself looked in.

"Is the gentleman up stairs, sir, if you please?"

"Yes, Kit," said Brass, still fired with an honest indignation, and frowning with knotted brows upon his sister; "Yes, Kit, he is. I am glad to see you, Kit, I am rejoiced to see you. Look in again, as you come down stairs, Kit. *That* lad a robber!" cried Brass when he had withdrawn, "with that frank and open countenance! I'd trust him with untold gold. Mr. Richard, sir, have the goodness to step directly to Wrasp and Co.'s in Broad Street, and inquire if they have had instructions to appear in Carkem and Painter. *That* lad a robber," sneered Sampson, flushed and heated with his wrath. "Am I blind, deaf, silly; do I know nothing of human nature when I see it before me? Kit a robber! Bah!"

Flinging this final interjection at Miss Sally with immeasurable scorn and contempt, Sampson Brass thrust his head into his desk as if to shut the base world from his view, and breathed defiance from under its half-closed lid.

CHAPTER LIX

WHEN Kit, having discharged his errand, came down stairs from the single gentleman's apartment after the lapse of a quarter of an hour or so, Mr. Sampson Brass was alone in the office. He was not singing as usual, nor was he seated at his desk. The open door showed him standing before the fire with his back towards it, and looking so very strange that Kit supposed he must have been suddenly taken ill.

"Is anything the matter, sir?" said Kit.

"Matter!" cried Brass. "No. Why anything the matter?"

"You are so very pale," said Kit, "that I should hardly have known you."

"Pooh pooh! mere fancy," cried Brass, stooping to throw up the cinders. "Never better, Kit, never better in all my life. Merry too. Ha ha! How's our friend above-stairs, eh?"

"A great deal better," said Kit.

"I'm glad to hear it," rejoined Brass; "thankful, I may say. An excellent gentleman—worthy, liberal, generous, gives very little trouble—an admirable lodger. Ha ha! Mr. Garland—he's well, I hope, Kit—and the pony—my friend, my particular friend, you know. Ha ha!"

Kit gave a satisfactory account of all the little household at Abel Cottage. Mr. Brass, who seemed remarkably inattentive and impatient, mounted on his stool, and beckoning him to come nearer, took him by the button-hole.

"I have been thinking, Kit," said the lawyer, that I could throw some little emoluments into your mother's way—You have a mother, I think? If I recollect right, you told me——"

"Oh yes, sir, yes certainly."

"A widow, I think? an industrious widow?"

"A harder-working woman or a better mother never lived, sir."

"Ah!" cried Brass. "That's affecting, truly affecting. A poor widow struggling to maintain her orphans in decency and comfort, is a delicious picture of human goodness.—Put down your hat, Kit."

"Thank you, sir, I must be going directly."

"Put it down while you stay, at any rate," said Brass, taking it from him and making some confusion among the papers, in finding a place for it on the desk. "I was thinking, Kit, that we have often houses to let for people we are concerned for, and matters of that sort. Now you know we're obliged to put people into those houses to take care of 'em—very often undeserving people that we can't depend upon. What's to prevent our having a person that we *can* depend upon, and enjoying the delight of doing a good action at the same time? I say, what's to prevent our employing this worthy woman, your mother? What with one job and another, there's lodging—and good lodging too—pretty well all the year round, rent free, and a weekly allowance besides, Kit, that would provide them with a great many comforts they don't at present enjoy. Now what do you think of that? Do you see any objection? My only desire is to serve you, Kit; therefore if you do, say so freely."

As Brass spoke, he moved the hat twice or thrice, and shuffled among the papers again, as if in search of something.

"How can I see any objection to such a kind offer, sir?" replied Kit with his whole heart. "I don't know how to thank you, sir, I don't indeed."

"Why then," said Brass, suddenly turning upon him and thrusting his face close to Kit's with such a repulsive smile that the latter, even in the very height of his gratitude, drew back quite startled. "Why then, *it's done.*"

Kit looked at him in some confusion.

"Done, I say—" added Sampson, rubbing his hands and veiling himself again in his usual oily manner. "Ha ha! and so you shall find, Kit, so you shall find. But dear me," said Brass, "what a time Mr. Richard is gone! A sad loiterer to be sure! Will you mind the office one minute, while I run up stairs? Only one minute. I'll not detain you an instant longer, on any account, Kit."

Talking as he went, Mr. Brass bustled out of the office, and in a very short time returned. Mr. Swiveller came back almost at the same instant; and as Kit was leaving the room hastily to make up for lost time, Miss Brass herself encountered him in the doorway.

"Oh!" sneered Sally, looking after him as she entered. "There goes your pet, Sammy, eh?"

"Ah! There he goes," replied Brass. "My pet, if you please. An honest fellow, Mr. Richard, sir—a worthy fellow indeed!"

"Hem!" coughed Miss Brass.

"I tell you, you aggravating vagabond," said the angry Sampson, "that I'd stake my life upon his honesty. Am I never to hear the last of this? Am I always to be baited, and beset, by your mean suspicions? Have you no regard for true merit, you malignant fellow? If you come to that, I'd sooner suspect your honesty than his."

Miss Sally pulled out the tin snuff-box, and took a long, slow pinch: regarding her brother with a steady gaze all the time.

"She drives me wild, Mr. Richard, sir," said Brass, "she exasperates me beyond all bearing. I am heated and excited, sir, I know I am. These are not business manners, sir, nor business looks, but she carries me out of myself."

"Why don't you leave him alone?" said Dick.

"Because she can't, sir," retorted Brass; "because to chafe and vex me is a part of her nature, sir, and she will and must do it, or I don't believe she'd have her health. But never mind," said Brass, "never mind. I've carried my point. I've shown my confidence in the lad. He has minded the office again. Ha ha! Ugh, you viper!"

The beautiful virgin took another pinch, and put the snuff-box in her pocket; still looking at her brother with perfect composure.

"He has minded the office again," said Brass triumphantly; "he has had my confidence, and he shall continue to have it; he—why, where's the—"

"What have you lost?" inquired Mr. Swiveller.

"Dear me!" said Brass, slapping all his pockets one after another, and looking into his desk, and under it, and upon it, and wildly tossing the papers about, "the note, Mr. Richard, sir, the five-pound note—what can have become of it? I laid it down here—God bless me!"

"What!" cried Miss Sally, starting up, clapping her hands, and scattering the papers on the floor. "Gone! Now, who's right? Now, who's got it? Never mind five pounds—what's five pounds? He's honest you know, quite honest. It would be mean to suspect him. Don't run after him. No, no, not for the world!"

"Is it really gone though?" said Dick, looking at Brass with a face as pale as his own.

"Upon my word, Mr. Richard, sir," replied the lawyer, feeling in all his pockets with looks of the greatest agitation, "I fear this is a black business. It's certainly gone, sir. What's to be done?"

"Don't run after him," said Miss Sally, taking more snuff. "Don't run after him on any account. Give him time to get rid of it, you know. It would be cruel to find him out!"

Mr. Swiveller and Sampson Brass looked from Miss Sally to each other in a state of utter bewilderment, and then, as by one impulse, caught up their hats and rushed out into the street—darting along in the middle of the road, and dashing aside all obstructions as though they were running for their lives.

It happened that Kit had been running too, though not so fast, and having the start of them by some few minutes, was a good distance ahead. As they were pretty certain of the road he must have taken, however, and kept on at a great pace, they came up with him, at the very moment when he had taken breath, and was breaking into a run again.

"Stop!" cried Sampson, laying his hand on one shoulder, while Mr. Swiveller pounced upon the other. "Not so fast, sir. You're in a hurry?"

"Yes, I am," said Kit, looking from one to the other in great surprise.

"I—I—can hardly believe it," panted Sampson, "but something of value is missing from the office. I hope you don't know what."

"Know what! good Heaven, Mr. Brass!" cried Kit, trembling from head to foot; "you don't suppose——"

"No, no," rejoined Brass quickly, "I don't suppose anything. Don't say *I* said you did. You'll come back quietly, I hope?"

"Of course I will," returned Kit. "Why not?"

"To be sure!" said Brass. "Why not? I hope there may turn out to be no why not. If you knew the trouble I've been in this morning through taking your part, Christopher, you'd be sorry for it."

"And I am sure you'll be sorry for having suspected me, sir," replied Kit. "Come. Let us make haste back."

"Certainly!" cried Brass, "the quicker, the better. Mr. Richard—have the goodness, sir, to take that arm. I'll take this one. It's not easy walking three abreast, but under these circumstances it must be done, sir; there's no help for it."

Kit did turn from white to red, and from red to white again, when they secured him thus, and for a moment seemed disposed to resist. But quickly recollecting himself, and remembering that if he made any struggle, he would perhaps be dragged by the collar through the public streets, he only repeated, with great earnestness and with tears standing in his eyes, that he would be sorry for this—and suffered them to lead him off. While they were on the way back, Mr. Swiveller, upon whom his present functions sat very irksomely, took an opportunity of whispering in his ear that if he would confess his guilt, even by so much as a nod, and promise not to do so any more, he would connive at his kicking Sampson Brass on the shins and escaping up a court; but Kit indignantly rejecting this proposal, Mr. Richard had nothing for it, but to hold him tight until they reached Bevis Marks, and ushered him into the presence of the charming Sarah, who immediately took the precaution of locking the door.

"Now, you know," said Brass, "if this is a case of innocence, it is a case of that description, Christopher, where the fullest disclosure is the best satisfaction for everybody. Therefore if you'll consent to an examination," he demonstrated what kind of examination he meant by turning back the cuffs of his coat, "it will be a comfortable and pleasant thing for all parties."

"Search me," said Kit, proudly, holding up his arms. "But mind, sir—I know you'll be sorry for this, to the last day of your life."

"It is certainly a very painful occurrence," said Brass with a sigh, as he dived into one of Kit's pockets, and fished up a miscellaneous collection of small articles; "very painful. Nothing here, Mr. Richard, sir, all perfectly satisfactory. Not here, sir. Nor in the waistcoat, Mr. Richard, nor in the coat tails. So far, I am rejoiced, I am sure."

Richard Swiveller, holding Kit's hat in his hand, was watching the proceedings with great interest, and bore upon his face the slightest possible indication of a smile, as Brass, shutting one of his eyes, looked with the other up the inside of one of the poor fellow's sleeves as if it were a telescope, when Sampson turning hastily to him, bade him search the hat.

"Here's a handkerchief," said Dick.

"No harm in that, sir," rejoined Brass, applying his eye to the other sleeve, and speaking in the voice of one who was contemplating an immense extent of prospect. "No harm in a handkerchief, sir, whatever. The faculty don't consider it a healthy custom, I believe, Mr. Richard, to carry one's handkerchief in one's hat—I have heard that it keeps the head too warm—but in every other point of view, its being there, is extremely satisfactory—ex-tremely so."

An exclamation, at once from Richard Swiveller, Miss Sally, and Kit himself, cut the lawyer short. He turned his head, and saw Dick standing with the bank-note in his hand.

"In the hat?" cried Brass, in a sort of shriek.

"Under the handkerchief, and tucked beneath the lining," said Dick, aghast at the discovery.

Mr. Brass looked at him, at his sister, at the walls, at the ceiling, at the floor—everywhere but at Kit, who stood quite stupefied and motionless.

"And this," cried Sampson, clasping his hands, "is the world that turns upon its own axis, and has Lunar influences, and revolutions round Heavenly Bodies, and various games of that sort! This is human natur, is it! Oh natur, natur! This is the miscreant that I was going to benefit with all my little arts, and that even now I feel so much for, as to wish to let him go! But," added Mr. Brass with great fortitude, "I am myself a lawyer, and bound to set an example in carrying the laws of my happy country into effect. Sally my dear, forgive me, and catch hold of him on the other side. Mr. Richard, sir, have the goodness to run and fetch a constable. The weakness is past and over, sir, and moral strength returns. A constable, sir, if *you* please!"

CHAPTER LX

KIT stood as one entranced, with his eyes opened wide and fixed upon the ground, regardless alike of the tremulous hold which Mr. Brass maintained on one side of his cravat, and of the firmer grasp of Miss Sally upon the other; although this latter detention was in itself no small inconvenience, as that fascinating woman, besides screwing her knuckles rather inconveniently into his throat from time to time, had fastened upon him in the first instance with so tight a grip that even in the disorder and distraction of his thoughts he could not divest himself of an uneasy sense of choking. Between the brother and sister he remained in this posture, quite unresisting and passive, until Mr. Swiveller returned with a police constable at his heels.

This functionary, being of course well used to such scenes, looking upon all kinds of robbery from petty larceny up to house-breaking or ventures on the highway as matters in the regular course of business, and regarding the perpetrators in the light of so many customers coming to be served at the wholesale and retail shop of criminal law where he stood behind the counter, received Mr. Brass's statement of facts with about as much interest and surprise, as an undertaker might evince if required to listen to a circumstantial account of the last illness of a person whom he was called in to wait upon professionally; and took Kit into custody with a decent indifference.

"We had better," said this subordinate minister of justice, "get to the office while there's a magistrate sitting. I shall want you to come along with us, Mr. Brass, and the——" he looked at Miss Sally as if in some doubt whether she might not be a griffin or other fabulous monster.

"The lady, eh?" said Sampson.

"Ah!" replied the constable. "Yes—the lady. Likewise the young man that found the property."

"Mr. Richard, sir," said Brass in a mournful voice. "A sad necessity. But the altar of our country, sir——"

"You'll have a hackney-coach, I suppose?" interrupted the constable, holding Kit (whom his other captors had released) carelessly by the arm, a little above the elbow. "Be so good as send for one, will you?"

"But hear me speak a word," cried Kit, raising his eyes and looking imploringly about him. "Hear me speak a word. I am no more guilty than any one of you. Upon my soul I am not. I a thief! Oh, Mr. Brass, you know me better. I am sure you know me better. This is not right of you, indeed."

"I give you my word, constable——" said Brass. But here the constable interposed with the constitutional principle "words be blowed;" observing that words were but spoonmeat for babes and sucklings, and that oaths were the food for strong men.

"Quite true, constable," assented Brass in the same mournful tone. "Strictly correct. I give you my oath, constable, that down to a few minutes ago, when this fatal discovery was made, I had such confidence in that lad, that I'd have trusted him with—a hackney-coach, Mr. Richard, sir; you're very slow, sir."

"Who is there that knows me," cried Kit, "that would not trust me—that does not? ask anybody whether they have ever doubted me; whether I have ever wronged them of a farthing. Was I ever once dishonest when I was poor and hungry, and is it likely I would begin now! Oh consider what you do. How can I meet the kindest friends that ever human creature had, with this dreadful charge upon me!"

Mr. Brass rejoined that it would have been well for the prisoner if he had thought of that before, and was about to make some other gloomy observations, when the voice of the single gentleman was heard demanding from above-stairs what was the matter, and what was the cause of all that noise and hurry. Kit made an involuntary start towards the door in his anxiety to answer for himself, but being speedily detained by the constable, had the agony of seeing

Sampson Brass run out alone to tell the story in his own way.

"And he can hardly believe it either," said Sampson, when he returned, "nor nobody will. I wish I could doubt the evidence of my senses, but their depositions are unimpeachable. It's of no use cross-examining my eyes," cried Sampson, winking and rubbing them, "they stick to their first account, and will. Now, Sarah, I hear the coach in the Marks; get on your bonnet, and we'll be off. A sad errand! a moral funeral, quite!"

"Mr. Brass," said Kit, "do me one favour. Take me to Mr. Witherden's first."

Sampson shook his head irresolutely.

"Do," said Kit. "My master's there. For Heaven's sake, take me there first."

"Well, I don't know," stammered Brass, who perhaps had his reasons for wishing to show as fair as possible in the eyes of the notary. "How do we stand in point of time, constable, eh?"

The constable, who had been chewing a straw all this while with great philosophy, replied that if they went away at once they would have time enough, but that if they stood shilly-shallying there any longer they must go straight to the Mansion House; and finally expressed his opinion that that was where it was, and that was all about it.

Mr. Richard Swiveller having arrived inside the coach, and still remaining immoveable in the most commodious corner with his face to the horses, Mr. Brass instructed the officer to remove his prisoner, and declared himself quite ready. Therefore the constable, still holding Kit in the same manner, and pushing him on a little before him, so as to keep him at about three-quarters of an arm's length in advance (which is the professional mode), thrust him into the vehicle and followed himself. Miss Sally entered next; and there being now four inside, Sampson Brass got upon the box, and made the coachman drive on.

Still completely stunned by the sudden and terrible change which had taken place in his affairs, Kit sat gazing out of the coach window, almost hoping to see some monstrous phenomenon in the streets which might give him reason to believe he was in a dream. Alas! Everything was too real and familiar: the same succession of turnings, the same houses, the same streams of people running side by side in different directions upon the pavement, the same bustle of carts and carriages in the road, the same well-remembered objects in the shop windows: a regularity in the very noise and hurry which no dream ever mirrored. Dreamlike as the story was, it was true. He stood charged with robbery; the note had been found upon him, though he was innocent in thought and deed; and they were carrying him back, a prisoner.

Absorbed in these painful ruminations, thinking with a drooping heart of his mother and little Jacob, feeling as though even the consciousness of innocence would be insufficient to support him in the presence of his friends if they believed him guilty, and sinking in hope and courage more and more as they drew nearer to the notary's, poor Kit was looking earnestly out of the window, observant of nothing,—when all at once, as though it had been conjured up by magic, he became aware of the face of Quilp.

And what a leer there was upon the face! It was from the open window of a tavern that it looked out; and the dwarf had so spread himself over it, with his elbows on the window-sill and his head resting on both his hands, that what between this attitude and his being swoln with suppressed laughter, he looked puffed and bloated into twice his usual breadth. Mr. Brass on recognising him immediately stopped the coach. As it came to a halt directly opposite to where he stood, the dwarf pulled off his hat, and saluted the party with a hideous and grotesque politeness.

"Aha!" he cried. "Where now, Brass? where now? Sally with you too? Sweet Sally! And Dick? Pleasant Dick! and Kit? Honest Kit!"

"He's extremely cheerful!" said Brass to the coachman. "Very much so! Ah, sir—a sad business! Never believe in honesty any more, sir."

"Why not?" returned the dwarf. "Why not, you rogue of a lawyer, why not?"

"Bank-note lost in our office, sir," said Brass, shaking his head. "Found in his hat, sir—he previously left alone there—no mistake at all, sir—chain of evidence complete—not a link wanting."

"What!" cried the dwarf, leaning half his body out of window. "Kit a thief! Kit a thief! Ha ha ha! Why, he's an uglier-looking thief than can be seen anywhere for a penny. Eh, Kit—eh? Ha ha ha! Have you taken Kit into custody before he had time and opportunity to beat me! Eh, Kit—eh?" And with that, he burst into a yell of laughter, manifestly to the great terror of the coachman, and pointed to a dyer's pole hard by, where a dangling suit of clothes bore some resemblance to a man upon a gibbet.

"It is coming to that, Kit!" cried the dwarf, rubbing his hands violently. "Ha ha ha ha! What a disappointment for little Jacob, and for his darling mother! Let him have the Bethel minister to comfort and console him, Brass. Eh, Kit—eh? Drive on, coachey, drive on. Bye bye, Kit; all good go with you; keep up your spirits; my love to the Garlands—the dear old lady and gentleman. Say I inquired after 'em, will you? Blessings on 'em, on you, and on everybody, Kit. Blessings on all the world!"

With such good wishes and farewells, poured out in a rapid torrent until they were out of hearing, Quilp suffered them to depart; and when he could see the coach no longer, drew in his head, and rolled upon the ground in an ecstasy of enjoyment.

When they reached the notary's, which they were not long in doing, for they had encountered the dwarf in a bye-street at a very little distance from the house, Mr. Brass dismounted; and opening the coach-door with a melancholy visage, requested his sister to accompany him into the office, with a view of preparing the good people within for the mournful intelligence that awaited them. Miss

Sally complying, he desired Mr. Swiveller to accompany them. So, into the office they went; Mr. Sampson and his sister arm in arm; and Mr. Swiveller following, alone.

The notary was standing before the fire in the outer office, talking to Mr. Abel and the elder Mr. Garland, while Mr. Chuckster sat writing at the desk, picking up such crumbs of their conversation as happened to fall in his way. This posture of affairs Mr. Brass observed through the glass-door as he was turning the handle, and seeing that the notary recognised him, he began to shake his head and sigh deeply while that partition yet divided them.

"Sir," said Sampson, taking off his hat, and kissing the two fore-fingers of his right-hand beaver glove, "my name is Brass—Brass of Bevis Marks, sir. I have had the honour and pleasure, sir, of being concerned against you in some little testamentary matters. How do you do, sir?"

"My clerk will attend to any business you may have come upon, Mr. Brass," said the notary, turning away.

"Thank you, sir," said Brass, "thank you, I am sure. Allow me, sir, to introduce my sister—quite one of us, sir, although of the weaker sex—of great use in my business, sir, I assure you. Mr. Richard, sir, have the goodness to come forward if you please—No really," said Brass, stepping between the notary and his private office (towards which he had begun to retreat), and speaking in the tone of an injured man, "really, sir, I must, under favour, request a word or two with you, indeed."

"Mr. Brass," said the other, in a decided tone, "I am engaged. You see that I am occupied with these gentlemen. If you will communicate your business to Mr. Chuckster yonder, you will receive every attention."

"Gentlemen," said Brass, laying his right hand on his waistcoat, and looking towards the father and son with a smooth smile—"Gentlemen, I appeal to you—really, gentlemen—consider, I beg of you. I am of the law. I am styled 'gentleman' by Act of Parliament. I maintain the title by the annual payment of twelve pound sterling for a certificate. I am not one of your players of music, stage actors, writers of books, or painters of pictures, who assume a station that the laws of their country don't recognise. I am none of your strollers or vagabonds. If any man brings his action against me, he must describe me as a gentleman, or his action is null and void. I appeal to you—is this quite respectful? Really, gentlemen—"

"Well, will you have the goodness to state your business then, Mr. Brass?" said the notary.

"Sir," rejoined Brass, "I will. Ah, Mr. Witherden! you little know the—but I will not be tempted to travel from the point, sir. I believe the name of one of these gentlemen is Garland."

"Of both," said the notary.

"In-deed!" rejoined Brass, cringing excessively. "But I might have known that, from the uncommon likeness. Extremely happy, I am sure, to have the honour of an introduction to two such gentlemen, although the occasion is a most painful one. One of you gentlemen has a servant called Kit?"

"Both," replied the notary.

"Two Kits?" said Brass, smiling. "Dear me!"

"One Kit, sir," returned Mr. Witherden angrily, "who is employed by both gentlemen. What of him?"

"This of him, sir," rejoined Brass, dropping his voice impressively. "That young man, sir, that I have felt unbounded and unlimited confidence in, and always behaved to as if he was my equal—that young man has this morning committed a robbery in my office, and been taken almost in the fact."

"This must be some falsehood!" cried the notary.

"It is not possible," said Mr. Abel.

"I'll not believe one word of it," exclaimed the old gentleman.

Mr. Brass looked mildly round upon them, and rejoined,

"Mr. Witherden, sir, *your* words are actionable, and if I was a man of low and mean standing, who couldn't afford to be slandered, I should proceed for damages. Hows'ever, sir, being what I am, I merely scorn such expressions. The honest warmth of the other gentleman I respect, and I'm truly sorry to be the messenger of such unpleasant news. I shouldn't have put myself in this painful position, I assure you, but that the lad himself desired to be brought here in the first instance, and I yielded to his prayers. Mr. Chuckster, sir, will you have the goodness to tap at the window for the constable that's waiting in the coach?"

The three gentlemen looked at each other with blank faces when these words were uttered, and Mr. Chuckster, doing as he was desired, and leaping off his stool with something of the excitement of an inspired prophet whose foretellings had in the fulness of time been realised, held the door open for the entrance of the wretched captive.

Such a scene as there was, when Kit came in, and bursting into the rude eloquence with which Truth at length inspired him, called Heaven to witness that he was innocent, and that how the property came to found upon him he knew not! Such a confusion of tongues, before the circumstances were related, and the proofs disclosed! Such a dead silence when all was told, and his three friends exchanged looks of doubt and amazement!

"Is it not possible," said Mr. Witherden, after a long pause, "that this note may have found its way into the hat by some accident,—such as the removal of papers on the desk, for instance?"

But this was clearly shown to be quite impossible. Mr. Swiveller, though an unwilling witness, could not help proving to demonstration, from the position in which it was found, that it must have been designedly secreted.

"It's very distressing," said Brass, "immensely distressing, I am sure. When he comes to be tried, I shall be very happy to recommend him to mercy on account of his previous good character. I did lose money before, certainly, but it doesn't quite follow that he took it.

The presumption's against him—strongly against him—but we're Christians, I hope?"

"I suppose," said the constable, looking round, "that no gentleman here can give evidence as to whether he's been flush of money of late. Do you happen to know, sir?"

"He has had money from time to time, certainly," returned Mr. Garland, to whom the man had put the question. "But that, as he always told me, was given him by Mr. Brass himself."

"Yes to be sure," said Kit eagerly. "You can bear me out in that, sir?"

"Eh?" cried Brass, looking from face to face with an expression of stupid amazement.

"The money you know, the half-crowns, that you gave me—from the lodger," said Kit.

"Oh dear me!" cried Brass, shaking his head and frowning heavily. "This is a bad case, I find; a very bad case indeed."

"What! Did you give him no money on account of anybody, sir?" asked Mr. Garland, with great anxiety.

"*I* give him money, sir!" returned Sampson. "Oh, come you know, this is too barefaced. Constable, my good fellow, we had better be going."

"What!" shrieked Kit. "Does he deny that he did? ask him, somebody, pray. Ask him to tell you whether he did or not!"

"Did you, sir?" asked the notary.

"I tell you what, gentlemen," replied Brass, in a very grave manner, "he'll not serve his case this way, and really, if you feel any interest in him, you had better advise him to go upon some other tack. Did I, sir? Of course I never did."

"Gentlemen," cried Kit, on whom a light broke suddenly, "Master, Mr. Abel, Mr. Witherden, every one of you—he did it! What I have done to offend him I don't know, but this is a plot to ruin me. Mind, gentlemen, it's a plot, and whatever comes of it, I will say with my dying breath that he put that note in my hat himself! Look at him, gentlemen! see how he changes colour. Which of us looks the guilty person—he, or I?"

"You hear him, gentlemen?" said Brass, smiling, "you hear him. Now, does this case strike you as assuming rather a black complexion, or does it not? Is it at all a treacherous case, do you think, or is it one of mere ordinary guilt? Perhaps, gentlemen, if he had not said this in your presence and I had reported it, you'd have held this to be impossible likewise, eh?"

With such pacific and bantering remarks did Mr. Brass refute the foul aspersion on his character; but the virtuous Sarah, moved by stronger feelings, and having at heart, perhaps, a more jealous regard for the honour of her family, flew from her brother's side, without any previous intimation of her design, and darted at the prisoner with the utmost fury. It would undoubtedly have gone hard with Kit's face, but that the wary constable, foreseeing her design, drew him aside at the critical moment, and thus placed Mr.

Chuckster in circumstances of some jeopardy; for that gentleman happening to be next the object of Miss Brass's wrath; and rage being, like Love and Fortune, blind; was pounced upon by the fair enslaver, and had a false collar plucked up by the roots, and his hair very much dishevelled, before the exertions of the company could make her sensible of her mistake.

The constable, taking warning by this desperate attack, and thinking perhaps that it would be more satisfactory to the ends of justice if the prisoner was taken before a magistrate, whole, rather than in small pieces, led him back to the hackney-coach without more ado, and further insisted on Miss Brass becoming an outside passenger; to which proposal the charming creature, after a little angry discussion, yielded her consent; and so took her brother Sampson's place upon the box: Mr. Brass with some reluctance agreeing to occupy her seat inside. These arrangements perfected, they drove to the justice-room with all speed, followed by the notary and his two friends in another coach. Mr. Chuckster alone was left behind—greatly to his indignation; for he held the evidence he could have given, relative to Kit's returning to work out the shilling, to be so very material as bearing upon his hypocritical and designing character, that he considered its suppression little better than a compromise of felony.

At the justice-room, they found the single gentleman, who had gone straight there, and was expecting them with desperate impatience. But not fifty single gentlemen rolled into one could have helped poor Kit, who in half an hour afterwards was committed for trial, and was assured by a friendly officer on his way to prison that there was no occasion to be cast down, for the sessions would soon be on, and he would in all likelihood get his little affair disposed of, and be comfortably transported, in less than a fortnight.

CHAPTER LXI

LET moralists and philosophers say what they may, it is very questionable whether a guilty man would have felt half as much misery that night, as Kit did, being innocent. The world, being in the constant commission of vast quantities of injustice, is a little too apt to comfort itself with the idea that if the victim of its falsehood and malice have a clear conscience, he cannot fail to be sustained under his trials, and somehow or other to come right at last; "in which case," say they who have hunted him down, "—though we certainly don't expect it—nobody will be better pleased than we." Whereas, the world would do well to reflect, that injustice is in itself, to every generous and properly constituted mind, an injury, of all others the most insufferable, the most torturing, and the most hard to bear; and that many clear consciences have gone to their account elsewhere, and many sound hearts have broken, because of this very reason; the knowledge of their own deserts only aggravating their sufferings, and rendering them the less endurable.

The world, however, was not in fault in Kit's case. But Kit was innocent; and knowing this, and feeling that his best friends deemed him guilty—that Mr. and Mrs. Garland would look upon him as a monster of ingratitude—that Barbara would associate him with all that was bad and criminal—that the pony would consider himself forsaken—and that even his own mother might perhaps yield to the strong appearances against him, and believe him to be the wretch he seemed—knowing and feeling all this, he experienced at first an agony of mind which no words can describe, and walked up and down the little cell in which he was locked up for the night, almost beside himself with grief.

Even when the violence of these emotions had in some degree subsided, and he was beginning to grow more calm, there came into his mind a new thought, the anguish of which was scarcely less. The child—the bright star of the simple fellow's life—she, who always came back upon him like a beautiful dream,—who had made the poorest part of his existence, the happiest and best—who had ever been so gentle, and considerate, and good—if she were ever to hear of this, what would she think! As this idea occurred to him, the walls of the prison seemed to melt away, and the old place to reveal itself in their stead, as it was wont to be on winter nights—the fireside, the little supper-table, the old man's hat and coat, and stick —the half-opened door, leading to her little room—they were all there. And Nell herself was there, and he—both laughing heartily as they had often done—and when he had got as far as this, Kit could go no farther, but flung himself upon his poor bedstead and wept.

It was a long night, which seemed as though it would have no end; but he slept too, and dreamed—always of being at liberty, and roving about, now with one person and now with another, but ever with a vague dread of being recalled to prison; not that prison, but one which was in itself a dim idea, not of a place, but of a care and sorrow: of something oppressive and always present, and yet impossible to define. At last the morning dawned, and there was the jail itself—cold, black, and dreary, and very real indeed.

He was left to himself, however, and there was comfort in that. He had liberty to walk in a small paved yard at a certain hour, and learnt from the turnkey, who came to unlock his cell and show him where to wash, that there was a regular time for visiting, every day, and that if any of his friends came to see him, he would be fetched down to the grate. When he had given him this information, and a tin porringer containing his breakfast, the man locked him up again; and went clattering along the stone passage, opening and shutting a great many other doors, and raising numberless loud echoes which resounded through the building for a long time, as if they were in prison too, and unable to get out.

This turnkey had given him to understand that he was lodged, like some few others in the jail, apart from the mass of prisoners; because he was not supposed to be utterly depraved and irreclaimable, and had never occupied apartments in that mansion before. Kit was thankful for this indulgence, and sat reading the Church Catechism very attentively (though he had known it by heart from a little child), until he heard the key in the lock, and the man entered again.

"Now then," he said, "come on!"

"Where to, sir?" asked Kit.

The man contented himself by briefly replying "Wisitors;" and taking him by the arm in exactly the same manner as the constable had done the day before, led him through several winding ways and strong gates into a passage, where he placed him at a grating, and turned upon his heel. Beyond this grating, at the distance of about four or five feet, was another exactly like it. In the space between, sat a turnkey reading a newspaper; and outside the further railing, Kit saw, with a palpitating heart, his mother with the baby in her arms; Barbara's mother with her never-failing umbrella; and poor little Jacob, staring in with all his might, as though he were looking for the bird, or the wild beast, and thought the men were mere accidents with whom the bars could have no possible concern.

But directly little Jacob saw his brother, and thrusting his arms between the rails to hug him, found that he came no nearer, but still stood afar off with his head resting on the arm by which he held to one of the bars, he began to cry most piteously; whereupon, Kit's mother and Barbara's mother, who had restrained themselves as much as possible, burst out sobbing and weeping afresh. Poor Kit could not help joining them, and not one of them could speak a word.

During this melancholy pause, the turnkey read his newspaper with a waggish look (he had evidently got among the facetious paragraphs), until, happening to take his eyes off it for an instant, as if to get by dint of contemplation at the very marrow of some joke of a deeper sort than the rest, it appeared to occur to him for the first time that somebody was crying.

"Now, ladies, ladies," he said, looking round with surprise, "I'd advise you not to waste time like this. It's allowanced here, you know. You mustn't let that child make that noise either. It's against all rules."

"I'm his poor mother, sir," sobbed Mrs. Nubbles, curtseying humbly, "and this is his brother, sir. Oh dear me, dear me!"

"Well!" replied the turnkey, folding his paper on his knee, so as to get with greater convenience at the top of the next column. "It can't be helped, you know. He an't the only one in the same fix. You mustn't make a noise about it!"

With that, he went on reading. The man was not unnaturally cruel or hard-hearted. He had come to look upon felony as a kind of disorder, like the scarlet fever or erysipelas: some people had it—some hadn't—just as it might be.

"Oh! my darling Kit—" said his mother, whom Barbara's mother had charitably relieved of the baby—"that I should see my poor boy here!"

"You don't believe that I did what they accuse me of, mother dear?" cried Kit, in a choking voice.

"*I* believe it!" exclaimed the poor woman, "*I* that never knew you tell a lie, or do a bad action from your cradle—that have never had a moment's sorrow on your account, except it was for the poor meals that you have taken with such good-humour and content, that I forgot how little there was when I thought how kind and thoughtful you were, though you were but a child!—*I* believe it of the son that's been a comfort to me from the hour of his birth to this time, and that I never laid down one night in anger with! *I* believe it of you, Kit!——"

"Why then, thank God!" said Kit, clutching the bars with an earnestness that shook them, "and I can bear it, mother. Come what may, I shall always have one drop of happiness in my heart when I think that you said that."

At this the poor woman fell a-crying again, and Barbara's mother too. And little Jacob, whose disjointed thoughts had by this time resolved themselves into a pretty distinct impression that Kit couldn't go out for a walk if he wanted, and that there were no birds, lions, tigers, or other natural curiosities behind those bars—nothing indeed, but a caged brother—added his tears to theirs with as little noise as possible.

Kit's mother, drying her eyes (and moistening them, poor soul, more than she dried them), now took from the ground a small basket, and submissively addressed herself to the turnkey, saying, would he please to listen to her for a minute? The turnkey, being in the very crisis and passion of a joke, motioned to her with his hand to keep silent one minute longer, for her life. Nor did he remove his hand into its former posture, but kept it in the same warning attitude until he had finished the paragraph, when he paused for a few seconds, with a smile upon his face, as who should say "this editor is a comical blade—a funny dog," and then asked her what she wanted.

"I have brought him a little something to eat," said the good woman. "If you please, sir, might he have it?"

"Yes,—he may have it. There's no rule against that. Give it to me when you go, and I'll take care he has it."

"No, but if you please, sir—don't be angry with me, sir—I am his mother, and you had a mother once—if I might only see him eat a little bit, I should go away so much more satisfied that he was all comfortable."

And again the tears of Kit's mother burst forth, and of Barbara's mother, and of little Jacob. As to the baby, it was crowing and laughing with all its might—under the idea, apparently, that the whole scene had been invented and got up for its particular satisfaction.

The turnkey looked as if he thought the request a strange one and rather out of the common way, but nevertheless he laid down his paper, and coming round to where Kit's mother stood, took the basket from her, and after inspecting its contents, handed it to Kit, and went back to his place. It may be easily conceived that the prisoner had no great appetite, but he sat down upon the ground, and ate as hard as he could, while, at every morsel he put into his mouth, his mother sobbed and wept afresh, though with a softened grief that bespoke the satisfaction the sight afforded her.

While he was thus engaged, Kit made some anxious inquiries about his employers, and whether they had expressed any opinion about him; but all he could learn was that Mr. Abel had himself broken the intelligence to his mother with great kindness and delicacy late on the previous night, but had himself expressed no opinion of his innocence or guilt. Kit was on the point of mustering courage to ask Barbara's mother about Barbara, when the turnkey who had conducted him re-appeared, a second turnkey appeared behind his visitors, and the third turnkey with the newspaper cried "Time's up!"—adding in the same breath "Now for the next party!" and then plunging deep into his newspaper again. Kit was taken off in an instant, with a blessing from his mother, and a scream from little Jacob, ringing in his ears. As he was crossing the next yard with the basket in his hand, under the guidance of his former conductor, another officer called to them to stop, and came up with a pint-pot of porter in his hand.

"This is Christopher Nubbles, isn't it, that come in last night for felony?" said the man.

His comrade replied that this was the chicken in question.

"Then here's your beer," said the other man to Christopher. "What are you looking at? There an't a discharge in it.

"I beg your pardon," said Kit. "Who sent it me?"

"Why, your friend," replied the man. "You're to have it every day, he says. And so you will, if he pays for it."

"My friend!" repeated Kit.

"You're all abroad, seemingly," returned the other man. "There's his letter. Take hold!"

Kit took it, and when he was locked up again, read as follows.

"Drink of this cup. You'll find there's a spell in its every drop 'gainst the ills of mortality. Talk of the cordial that sparkled for Helen! *Her* cup was a fiction, but this is reality (Barclay & Co.'s). If they ever send it in a flat state, complain to the Governor. Yours, R.S."

"R.S.!" said Kit, after some consideration. "It must be Mr. Richard Swiveller. Well, it's very kind of him, and I thank him heartily."

CHAPTER LXII

A FAINT light, twinkling from the window of the counting-house on Quilp's wharf, and looking inflamed and red through the night-fog, as though it suffered from it like an eye, forewarned Mr. Sampson Brass, as he approached the wooden cabin with a cautious step, that the excellent proprietor, his esteemed client, was inside, and probably waiting with his accustomed patience and sweetness of temper the fulfilment of the appointment which now brought Mr. Brass within his fair domain.

"A treacherous place to pick one's steps in of a dark night," muttered Sampson, as he stumbled for the twentieth time over some stray lumber, and limped in pain. "I believe that boy strews the ground differently every day, on purpose to bruise and maim one; unless his master does it with his own hands, which is more than likely. I hate to come to this place without Sally. She's more protection than a dozen men."

As he paid this compliment to the merit of the absent charmer, Mr. Brass came to a halt; looking doubtfully towards the light, and over his shoulder.

"What's he about, I wonder?" murmured the lawyer, standing on tiptoe and endeavouring to obtain a glimpse of what was passing inside, which at that distance was impossible—"drinking, I suppose, —making himself more fiery and furious, and heating his malice and mischievousness till they boil. I'm always afraid to come here by myself, when his account's a pretty large one. I don't believe he'd mind throttling me, and dropping me softly into the river when the tide was at its strongest, any more than he'd mind killing a rat— indeed I don't know whether he wouldn't consider it a pleasant joke. Hark! Now he's singing!"

Mr. Quilp was certainly entertaining himself with vocal exercise, but it was rather a kind of chant than a song; being a monotonous repetition of one sentence in a very rapid manner, with a long stress upon the last word, which he swelled into a dismal roar. Nor did the burden of this performance bear any reference to love, or war, or wine, or loyalty, or any other, the standard topics of song, but to a subject not often set to music or generally known in ballads; the words being these:—"The worthy magistrate, after remarking that the prisoner would find some difficulty in persuading a jury to believe his tale, committed him to take his trial at the approaching sessions; and directed the customary recognisances to be entered into for the pros-e-cu-tion."

Every time he came to this concluding word, and had exhausted all possible stress upon it, Quilp burst into a shriek of laughter, and began again.

"He's dreadfully imprudent," muttered Brass, after he had listened to two or three repetitions of the chant. "Horribly imprudent. I wish he was dumb. I wish he was deaf. I wish he was blind. Hang him," cried Brass, as the chant began again, "I wish he was dead!"

Giving utterance to these friendly aspirations in behalf of his client, Mr. Sampson composed his face into its usual state of smoothness, and waiting until the shriek came again and was dying away, went up to the wooden house, and knocked at the door.

"Come in!" cried the dwarf.

"How do you do to-night, sir?" said Sampson, peeping in. "Ha ha ha! How do you do, sir? Oh dear me, how very whimsical! Amazingly whimsical to be sure!"

"Come in, you fool!" returned the dwarf, "and don't stand there shaking your head and showing your teeth. Come in, you false witness, you perjurer, you suborner of evidence, come in!"

"He has the richest humour!" cried Brass, shutting the door behind him; "the most amazing vein of comicality! But isn't it *rather* injudicious, sir——?"

"What?" demanded Quilp, "What, Judas?"

"Judas!" cried Brass. "He has such extraordinary spirits! His humour is so extremely playful! Judas! Oh yes—dear me, how very good! Ha ha ha!"

All this time, Sampson was rubbing his hands, and staring, with ludicrous surprise and dismay, at a great, goggle-eyed, blunt-nosed figure-head of some old ship, which was reared up against the wall in a corner near the stove, looking like a goblin or hideous idol whom the dwarf worshipped. A mass of timber on its head, carved into the dim and distant semblance of a cocked hat, together with a representation of a star on the left breast and epaulettes on the shoulders, denoted that it was intended for the effigy of some famous admiral; but, without those helps, any observer might have supposed it the authentic portrait of a distinguished merman, or great sea-monster. Being originally much too large for the apartment which it was now employed to decorate, it had been sawn short off at the waist. Even in this state it reached from floor to ceiling; and thrusting itself forward with that excessively wide-awake aspect, and air of somewhat obtrusive politeness, by which figure-heads are usually characterised, seemed to reduce everything else to mere pigmy proportions.

"Do you know it?" said the dwarf, watching Sampson's eyes. "Do you see the likeness?"

"Eh?" said Brass, holding his head on one side, and throwing it a little back, as connoisseurs do. "Now I look at it again, I fancy I see a—yes, there certainly is something in the smile that reminds me of—and yet upon my word I——"

Now, the fact was, that Sampson, having never seen anything in the smallest degree resembling this substantial phantom, was much perplexed; being uncertain whether Mr. Quilp considered it like himself, and had therefore bought it for a family portrait; or whether he was pleased to consider it as the likeness of some enemy. He was not very long in doubt; for, while he was surveying it with that knowing

"Do you know it? ... Do you see the likeness?"

look which people assume when they are contemplating for the first time portraits which they ought to recognise but don't, the dwarf threw down the newspaper from which he had been chanting the words already quoted, and seizing a rusty iron bar, which he used in lieu of poker, dealt the figure such a stroke on the nose that it rocked again.

"Is it like Kit—is it his picture, his image, his very self?" cried the dwarf, aiming a shower of blows at the insensible countenance, and covering it with deep dimples. "Is it the exact model and counterpart of the dog—is it—is it—is it?" And with every repetition of the question, he battered the great image until the perspiration streamed down his face with the violence of the exercise.

Although this might have been a very comical thing to look at from a secure gallery, as a bull-fight is found to be a comfortable spectacle by those who are not in the arena, and a house on fire is better than a play to people who don't live near it, there was something in the earnestness of Mr. Quilp's manner which made his legal adviser feel that the counting-house was a little too small, and a great deal too lonely, for the due enjoyment of these humours. Therefore he stood as far off as he could while the dwarf was thus engaged; whimpering out but feeble applause; and when he left off and sat down again from pure exhaustion, approached with more obsequiousness than ever.

"Excellent indeed!" cried Brass. "He he! Oh, very good, sir. You know," said Sampson, looking round as if in appeal to the bruised admiral, "he's quite a remarkable man—quite!"

"Sit down," said the dwarf. "I bought the dog yesterday. I've been screwing gimlets into him, and sticking forks in his eyes, and cutting my name on him. I mean to burn him at last."

"Ha ha!" cried Brass. "Extremely entertaining, indeed!"

"Come here!" said Quilp, beckoning him to draw near. "What's injudicious, hey?"

"Nothing, sir—nothing. Scarcely worth mentioning, sir; but I thought that song—admirably humorous in itself you know—was perhaps rather——"

"Yes," said Quilp, "rather what?"

"Just bordering, or as one may say remotely verging upon the confines of injudiciousness perhaps, sir," returned Brass, looking timidly at the dwarf's cunning eyes, which were turned towards the fire and reflected its red light.

"Why?" inquired Quilp, without looking up.

"Why, you know, sir," returned Brass, venturing to be more familiar: "—the fact is, sir, that any allusion to these little combinings together of friends for objects in themselves extremely laudable, but which the law terms conspiracies, are—you take me, sir?—best kept snug and among friends, you know."

"Eh!" said Quilp, looking up with a perfectly vacant countenance. "What do you mean?"

"Cautious, exceedingly cautious, very right and proper!" cried

Brass, nodding his head. "Mum, sir, even here—my meaning, sir, exactly."

"*Your* meaning exactly, you brazen scarecrow,—what's your meaning?" retorted Quilp. "Why do you talk to me of combining together? Do *I* combine? Do I know anything about your combinings?"

"No no, sir—certainly not; not by any means," returned Brass.

"If you so wink and nod at me," said the dwarf, looking about him as if for his poker, "I'll spoil the expression of your monkey's face, I will."

"Don't put yourself out of the way I beg, sir," rejoined Brass, checking himself with great alacrity. "You're quite right, sir, quite right. I shouldn't have mentioned the subject, sir. It's much better not to. You're quite right, sir. Let us change it, if you please. You were asking, sir, Sally told me, about our lodger. He has not returned, sir."

"No?" said Quilp, heating some rum in a little saucepan, and watching it to prevent its boiling over. "Why not?"

"Why, sir," returned Brass, "he—dear me, Mr. Quilp, sir—"

"What's the matter?" said the dwarf, stopping his hand in the act of carrying the saucepan to his mouth.

"You have forgotten the water, sir," said Brass. "And—excuse me, sir—but it's burning hot."

Deigning no other than a practical answer to this remonstrance, Mr. Quilp raised the hot saucepan to his lips, and deliberately drank off all the spirit it contained, which might have been in quantity about half a pint, and had been but a moment before, when he took it off the fire, bubbling and hissing fiercely. Having swallowed this gentle stimulant, and shaken his fist at the admiral, he bade Mr. Brass proceed.

"But first," said Quilp, with his accustomed grin, "have a drop yourself—a nice drop—a good, warm, fiery drop."

"Why, sir," replied Brass, "if there was such a thing as a mouthful of water that could be got without trouble——"

"There's no such thing to be had here," cried the dwarf. "Water for lawyers! Melted lead and brimstone, you mean, nice hot blistering pitch and tar—that's the thing for them—eh, Brass, eh?"

"Ha ha ha!" laughed Mr. Brass. "Oh very biting! and yet it's like being tickled—there's a pleasure in it too, sir!"

"Drink that," said the dwarf, who had by this time heated some more. "Toss it off, don't leave any heeltap, scorch your throat and be happy."

The wretched Sampson took a few short sips of the liquor, which immediately distilled itself into burning tears, and in that form came rolling down his cheeks into the pipkin again, turning the colour of his face and eyelids to a deep red, and giving rise to a violent fit of coughing, in the midst of which he was still heard to declare, with the constancy of a martyr, that it was "beautiful indeed!" While he was yet in unspeakable agonies, the dwarf renewed their conversation.

"The lodger," said Quilp,—"what about him?"

"He is still, sir," returned Brass, with intervals of coughing, "stopping with the Garland family. He has only been home once, sir, since the day of the examination of that culprit. He informed Mr. Richard, sir, that he couldn't bear the house after what had taken place; that he was wretched in it; and that he looked upon himself as being in a certain kind of way the cause of the occurrence.—A very excellent lodger, sir. I hope we may not lose him."

"Yah!" cried the dwarf. "Never thinking of anybody but yourself—why don't you retrench then—scrape up, hoard, economise, eh?"

"Why, sir," replied Brass, "upon my word I think Sarah's as good an economiser as any going. I do indeed, Mr. Quilp."

"Moisten your clay, wet the other eye, drink, man!" cried the dwarf. "You took a clerk to oblige me."

"Delighted, sir, I am sure, at any time," replied Sampson. "Yes, sir, I did."

"Then, now you may discharge him," said Quilp. "There's a means of retrenchment for you at once."

"Discharge Mr. Richard, sir?" cried Brass.

"Have you more than one clerk, you parrot, that you ask the question? Yes."

"Upon my word, sir," said Brass, "I wasn't prepared for this—"

"How could you be?" sneered the dwarf, "when *I* wasn't! How often am I to tell you that I brought him to you that I might always have my eye on him and know where he was—and that I had a plot, a scheme, a little quiet piece of enjoyment afoot, of which the very cream and essence was, that this old man and grandchild (who have sunk underground I think) should be, while he and his precious friend believed them rich, in reality as poor as frozen rats?"

"I quite understood that, sir," rejoined Brass. "Thoroughly."

"Well, sir," retorted Quilp, "and do you understand now, that they're *not* poor—that they can't be, if they have such men as your lodger searching for them and scouring the country far and wide?"

"Of course I do, sir," said Sampson.

"Of course you do," retorted the dwarf, viciously snapping at his words. "Of course do you understand then, that it's no matter what comes of this fellow? of course do you understand that for any other purpose he's no man for me, nor for you?"

"I have frequently said to Sarah, sir," returned Brass, "that he was of no use at all in the business. You can't put any confidence in him, sir. If you'll believe me I've found that fellow, in the commonest little matters of the office that have been trusted to him, blurting out the truth, though expressly cautioned. The aggravation of that chap, sir, has exceeded anything you can imagine, it has indeed. Nothing but the respect and obligation I owe to you, sir—"

As it was plain that Sampson was bent on a complimentary harangue, unless he received a timely interruption, Mr. Quilp politely tapped him on the crown of his head with the little saucepan, and requested that he would be so obliging as to hold his peace.

"Practical, sir, practical," said Brass, rubbing the place and smiling; "but still extremely pleasant—immensely so!"

"Hearken to me, will you?" returned Quilp, "or I'll be a little more pleasant, presently. There's no chance of his comrade and friend returning. The scamp has been obliged to fly, as I learn, for some knavery, and has found his way abroad. Let him rot there."

"Certainly, sir. Quite proper.—Forcible!" cried Brass, glancing at the admiral again, as if he made a third in company. "Extremely forcible!"

"I hate him," said Quilp between his teeth, "and have always hated him, for family reasons. Besides, he was an intractable ruffian; otherwise *he* would have been of use. This fellow is pigeon-hearted, and light-headed. I don't want him any longer. Let him hang or drown—starve—go to the devil."

"By all means, sir," returned Brass. "When would you wish him, sir, to—ha, ha!—to make that little excursion?"

"When this trial's over," said Quilp. "As soon as that's ended, send him about his business."

"It shall be done, sir," returned Brass; "by all means. It will be rather a blow to Sarah, sir, but she has all her feelings under control. Ah, Mr. Quilp, I often think, sir, if it had only pleased Providence to bring you and Sarah together in earlier life, what blessed results would have flowed from such a union! You never saw our dear father, sir?—A charming gentleman. Sarah was his pride and joy, sir. He would have closed his eyes in bliss, would Foxey, Mr. Quilp, if he could have found her such a partner. You esteem her, sir?"

"I love her," croaked the dwarf.

"You're very good, sir," returned Brass, "I am sure. Is there any other order, sir, that I can take a note of, besides this little matter of Mr. Richard?"

"None," replied the dwarf, seizing the saucepan. "Let us drink the lovely Sarah."

"If we could do it in something, sir, that wasn't quite boiling," suggested Brass humbly, "perhaps it would be better. I think it will be more agreeable to her feelings, when she comes to hear from me of the honour you have done her, if she learns it was in liquor rather cooler than the last, sir."

But to these remonstrances Mr. Quilp turned a deaf ear. Sampson Brass, who was by this time anything but sober, being compelled to take further draughts of the same strong bowl, found that, instead of at all contributing to his recovery, they had the novel effect of making the counting-house spin round and round with extreme velocity, and causing the floor and ceiling to heave in a very distressing manner. After a brief stupor, he awoke to a consciousness of being partly under the table and partly under the grate. This position not being the most comfortable one he could have chosen for himself, he managed to stagger to his feet, and, holding on by the admiral, looked round for his host.

Mr. Brass's first impression was, that his host was gone and had left him there alone—perhaps locked him in for the night. A strong smell of tobacco, however, suggested a new train of ideas, he looked upwards, and saw that the dwarf was smoking in his hammock.

"Good-bye, sir," cried Brass faintly. "Good-bye, sir."

"Won't you stop all night?" said the dwarf, peeping out. "Do stop all night."

"I couldn't indeed, sir," replied Brass, who was almost dead from nausea and the closeness of the room. "If you'd have the goodness to show me a light, so that I may see my way across the yard, sir—"

Quilp was out in an instant; not with his legs first, or his head first, or his arms first, but bodily—altogether.

"To be sure," he said, taking up a lantern, which was now the only light in the place. "Be careful how you go, my dear friend. Be sure to pick your way among the timber, for all the rusty nails are upwards. There's a dog in the lane. He bit a man last night, and a woman the night before, and last Tuesday he killed a child—but that was in play. Don't go too near him."

"Which side of the road is he, sir?" asked Brass, in great dismay.

"He lives on the right hand," said Quilp, "but sometimes he hides on the left, ready for a spring. He's uncertain in that respect. Mind you take care of yourself. I'll never forgive you if you don't. There's the light out—never mind—you know the way—straight on!"

Quilp had slightly shaded the light by holding it against his breast, and now stood chuckling and shaking from head to foot in a rapture of delight, as he heard the lawyer stumbling up the yard, and now and then falling heavily down. At length, however, he got quit of the place, and was out of hearing.

The dwarf shut himself up again, and sprang once more into his hammock.

CHAPTER LXIII

THE professional gentleman who had given Kit that consolatory piece of information relative to the settlement of his trifle of business at the Old Bailey, and the probability of its being very soon disposed of, turned out to be quite correct in his prognostications. In eight days' time, the sessions commenced. In one day afterwards, the Grand Jury found a True Bill against Christopher Nubbles for felony; and in two days from that finding, the aforesaid Christopher Nubbles was called upon to plead Guilty or Not Guilty to an Indictment for that he the said Christopher did feloniously abstract and steal from the dwelling-house and office of one Sampson Brass, gentleman, one Bank Note for Five Pounds issued by the Governor and Company of the Bank of England; in contravention of the Statutes in that case made and provided, and against the peace of our Sovereign Lord the King, his crown, and dignity.

To this indictment, Christopher Nubbles, in a low and trembling voice, pleaded Not Guilty. and here let those who are in the habit of forming hasty judgments from appearances, and who would have had Christopher, if innocent, speak out very strong and loud, observe, that confinement and anxiety will subdue the stoutest hearts; and that to one who has been close shut up, though it be only for ten or eleven days, seeing but stone walls and a very few stony faces, the sudden entrance into a great hall filled with life is a rather disconcerting and startling circumstance. To this it must be added, that life in a wig is to a large class of people much more terrifying and impressive than life with its own head of hair; and if, in addition to these considerations, there be further taken ino account Kit's natural emotion on seeing the two Mr. Garlands and the little Notary looking on with pale and anxious faces, it will perhaps seem matter of no very great wonder that he should have been rather out of sorts, and unable to make himself exactly at home.

Although he had never seen either of the Mr. Garlands, or Mr. Witherden, since the time of his arrest, he had been given to understand that they had employed counsel for him. Therefore, when one of the gentlemen in wigs got up and said "I am for the prisoner, my Lord," Kit made him a bow; and when another gentleman in a wig got up and said "And I'm against him, my Lord," Kit trembled very much, and bowed to him too. And didn't he hope in his own heart that his gentleman was a match for the other gentleman, and would make him ashamed of himself in no time!

The gentleman who was against him had to speak first, and being in dreadfully good spirits (for he had, in the last trial, very nearly procured the acquittal of a young gentleman who had had the misfortune to murder his father) he spoke up you may be sure; telling the Jury that if they acquitted this prisoner they must expect to suffer no less pangs and agonies than he had told the other Jury they would certainly undergo if they convicted that prisoner. And when he had told them all about the case, and that he had never known a worse case, he stopped a little while, like a man who had something terrible to tell them, and then said that he understood an attempt would be made by his learned friend (and here he looked sideways at Kit's gentleman) to impeach the testimony of those immaculate witnesses whom he should call before them; but he did hope and trust that his learned friend would have a greater respect and veneration for the character of the prosecutor; than whom, as he well knew, there did not exist, and never had existed, a more honourable member of that most honourable profession to which he was attached. And then he said, did the Jury know Bevis Marks? And if they did know Bevis Marks (as he trusted, for their own characters, they did) did they know the historical and elevating associations connected with that most remarkable spot? Did they believe that a man like Brass could reside in a place like Bevis Marks, and not be a virtuous and most upright character? And when he had said a great deal to them on this point, he remembered that it was an insult to their understandings to make any remarks on what they must have felt so strongly without him, and therefore called Sampson Brass into the witness-box, straightway.

Then up comes Mr. Brass, very brisk and fresh; and, having bowed to the judge, like a man who has had the pleasure of seeing him before and who hopes he has been pretty well since their last meeting, folds his arms, and looks at his gentleman as much as to say "Here I am— full of evidence—Tap me!" And the gentleman does tap him presently, and with great discretion too; drawing off the evidence by little and little, and making it run quite clear and bright in the eyes of all present. Then Kit's gentleman takes him in hand, but can make nothing of him; and after a great many very long questions and very short answers, Mr. Sampson Brass goes down in glory.

To him succeeds Sarah, who in like manner is easy to be managed by Mr. Brass's gentleman, but very obdurate to Kit's. In short, Kit's gentleman can get nothing out of her but a repetition of what she has said before (only a little stronger this time, as against his client), and therefore lets her go, in some confusion. Then Mr. Brass's gentleman calls Richard Swiveller, and Richard Swiveller appears accordingly.

Now, Mr. Brass's gentleman has it whispered in his ear that this witness is disposed to be friendly to the prisoner—which, to say the truth, he is rather glad to hear, as his strength is considered to lie in what is familiarly termed badgering. Wherefore, he begins by requesting the officer to be quite sure that this witness kisses the book, and then goes to work at him, tooth and nail.

"Mr. Swiveller," says this gentleman to Dick, when he has told his tale with evident reluctance and a desire to make the best of it: "Pray, sir, where did you dine yesterday?"—"Where did I dine yesterday?"—"Aye, sir, where did you dine yesterday—was it near here, sir?"—"Oh to be sure—yes—just over the way."—"To be sure. Yes. Just over the way," repeats Mr. Brass's gentleman, with a glance at the Court—"Alone, sir?"—"I beg your pardon," says Mr. Swiveller, who has not caught the question—"*Alone*, sir?" repeats Mr. Brass's gentleman in a voice of thunder, "did you dine alone? Did you treat anybody, sir? Come!"—"Oh yes, to be sure—yes, I did," says Mr. Swiveller with a smile. "Have the goodness to banish a levity, sir, which is very ill-suited to the place in which you stand (though perhaps you have reason to be thankful that it's only that place)," says Mr. Brass's gentleman, with a nod of the head insinuating that the dock is Mr. Swiveller's legitimate sphere of action; "and attend to me. You were waiting about here yesterday in expectation that this trial was coming on. You dined over the way. You treated somebody. Now, was that somebody brother to the prisoner at the bar?"—Mr. Swiveller is proceeding to explain—"Yes or No, sir," cries Mr. Brass's gentleman—"But will you allow me—"—"Yes or No, sir"—"Yes it was, but—"—"Yes it was," cried the gentleman, taking him up short—"And a very pretty witness *you* are!"

Down sits Mr. Brass's gentleman. Kit's gentleman, not knowing how the matter really stands, is afraid to pursue the subject. Richard

Swiveller retires abashed. Judge, jury, and spectators have visions of his lounging about with an ill-looking, large-whiskered, dissolute young fellow of six feet high. The reality is, little Jacob, with the calves of his legs exposed to the open air, and himself tied up in a shawl. Nobody knows the truth, everybody believes a falsehood— and all because of the ingenuity of Mr. Brass's gentleman!

Then came the witness to character, and here Mr. Brass's gentleman shines again. It turns out that Mr. Garland has had no character with Kit, no recommendation of him but from his own mother, and that he was suddenly dismissed by his former master for unknown reasons. "Really, Mr. Garland," says Mr. Brass's gentleman, "for a person who has arrived at your time of life, you are, to say the least of it, singularly indiscreet, I think." The Jury think so too, and find Kit guilty. He is taken off, humbly protesting his innocence. The spectators settle themselves in their places with renewed attention, for there are several female witnesses to be examined in the next case, and it has been rumoured that Mr. Brass's gentleman will make great fun in cross-examining them for the prisoner.

Kit's mother, poor woman, is waiting at the grate below stairs, accompanied by Barbara's mother (who, honest soul! never does anything but cry, and hold the baby) and a sad interview ensues. The newspaper-reading turnkey has told them all. He don't think it will be transportation for life, because there's time to prove the good character yet, and that is sure to serve him. He wonders what he did it for. "He never did it!" cries Kit's mother. "Well," says the turnkey, "I won't contradict you. It's all one now, whether he did or not."

Kit's mother can reach his hand through the bars, and clasps it— God, and those to whom he has given such tenderness, only know in how much agony. Kit bids her keep a good heart, and, under pretence of having the children lifted up to kiss him, prays Barbara's mother in a whisper to take her home.

"Some friend will rise up for us, mother," cries Kit, "I am sure. If not now, before long. My innocence will come out, mother, and I shall be brought back again; I feel confidence in that. You must teach little Jacob and the baby how all this was, for if they thought I had ever been dishonest, when they grow old enough to understand, it would break my heart to know it, if I was thousands of miles away.— Oh! is there no good gentleman here, who will take care of her!"

The hand slips out of his, for the poor creature sinks down upon the earth, insensible. Richard Swiveller comes hastily up, elbows the bystanders out of the way, takes her (after some trouble) in one arm after the manner of theatrical ravishers, and nodding to Kit, and commanding Barbara's mother to follow, for he has a coach waiting, bears her swiftly off.

Well; Richard took her home. And what astonishing absurdities in the way of quotation from song and poem he perpetrated on the road, no man knows. He took her home, and stayed till she was recovered; and, having no money to pay the coach, went back in state to Bevis Marks, bidding the driver (for it was Sunday night) wait at the door while he went in for "change."

"Mr. Richard, sir," said Brass cheerfully, "good evening."

Monstrous as Kit's tale had appeared at first, Mr. Richard did, that night, half suspect his affable employer of some deep villany. Perhaps it was but the misery he had just witnessed which gave his careless nature this impulse; but, be that as it may, it was very strong upon him, and he said in as few words as possible, what he wanted.

"Money!" cried Brass, taking out his purse. "Ha ha! To be sure, Mr. Richard, to be sure, sir. All men must live. You haven't change for a five-pound note, have you, sir?"

"No," returned Dick, shortly.

"Oh!" said Brass, "here's the very sum. That saves trouble. You're very welcome I'm sure.—Mr. Richard, sir—"

Dick, who had by this time reached the door, turned round.

"You needn't," said Brass, "trouble yourself to come back any more, sir."

"Eh?"

"You see, Mr. Richard," said Brass, thrusting his hands in his pockets and rocking himself to and fro upon his stool, "the fact is, that a man of your abilities is lost, sir, quite lost, in our dry and mouldy line. It's terrible drudgery—shocking. I should say now that the stage, or the—or the army, Mr. Richard—or something very superior in the licensed victualling way—was the kind of thing that would call out the genius of such a man as you. I hope you'll look in to see us now and then. Sally, sir, will be delighted I'm sure. She's extremely sorry to lose you, Mr. Richard, but a sense of her duty to society reconciles her.—An amazing creature that, sir! You'll find the money quite correct, I think. There's a cracked window, sir, but I've not made any deduction on that account. Whenever we part with friends, Mr. Richard, let us part liberally. A delightful sentiment, sir!"

To all these rambling observations, Mr. Swiveller answered not one word, but, returning for the aquatic jacket, rolled it into a tight round ball, looking steadily at Brass meanwhile as if he had some intention of bowling him down with it. He only took it under his arm, however, and marched out of the office in profound silence. Directly he had closed the door, he opened it, stared in again for a few moments with the same portentous gravity; and nodding his head once, in a slow and ghost-like manner, vanished.

He paid the coachman and turned his back on Bevis Marks, big with great designs for the comforting of Kit's mother and the aid of Kit himself.

But the lives of gentlemen devoted to such pleasures as Richard Swiveller, are extremely precarious. The spiritual excitement of the last fortnight, working upon a system affected in no slight degree by the spirituous excitement of some years, proved a little too much for him. That very night, Mr. Richard was seized with an alarming illness, and in twenty-four hours was stricken with a raging fever.

CHAPTER LXIV

TOSSING to and fro upon his hot, uneasy bed; tormented by a fierce thirst which nothing could appease; unable to find, in any change of posture, a moment's peace or ease; and rambling ever through deserts of thought where there was no resting-place, no sight or sound suggestive of refreshment or repose, nothing but a dull eternal weariness, with no change but the restless shiftings of his miserable body, and the weary wanderings of his mind, constant still to one ever-present anxiety—to a sense of something left undone, of some fearful obstacle to be surmounted, of some carking care that would not be driven away, and haunted the distempered brain, now in this form, now in that—always shadowy and dim, but recognisable for the same phantom in every shape it took, darkening every vision like an evil conscience, and making slumber horrible; in these slow tortures of his dread disease, the unfortunate Richard lay wasting and consuming inch by inch, until at last, when he seemed to fight and struggle to rise up, and to be held down by devils, he sank into a deep sleep, and dreamed no more.

He awoke; and, with a sensation of most blissful rest, better than sleep itself, began gradually to remember something of these sufferings, and to think what a long night it had been, and whether he had not been delirious twice or thrice. Happening in the midst of these cogitations to raise his hand, he was astonished to find how heavy it seemed, and yet how thin and light it really was. Still he felt indifferent and happy; and having no curiosity to pursue the subject, remained in the same waking slumber until his attention was attracted by a cough. This made him doubt whether he had locked his door last night, and feel a little surprised at having a companion in the room. Still, he lacked energy to follow up this train of thought; and unconsciously fell, in a luxury of repose, to staring at some green stripes upon the bed-furniture, and associating them strangely with patches of fresh turf, while the yellow ground between made gravel-walks, and so helped out a long perspective of trim gardens.

He was rambling in imagination upon these terraces, and had quite lost himself among them indeed, when he heard the cough once more. The walks shrank into stripes again at the sound; and raising himself a little in the bed, and holding the curtain open with one hand, he looked out.

The same room certainly, and still by candle-light; but with what unbounded astonishment did he see all those bottles, and basins, and articles of linen airing by the fire, and such-like furniture of a sick chamber—all very clean and neat, but all quite different from anything he had left there, when he went to bed! The atmosphere, too, filled with a cool smell of herbs and vinegar; the floor newly sprinkled; the—the what? The Marchioness? Yes; playing cribbage with herself

"The Marchioness? Yes: playing cribbage with herself."

at the table. There she sat, intent upon her game, coughing now and then in a subdued manner as if she feared to disturb him—shuffling the cards, cutting, dealing, playing, counting, pegging—going through all the mysteries of cribbage as though she had been in full practice from her cradle!

Mr. Swiveller contemplated these things for a short time, and suffering the curtain to fall into its former position, laid his head upon the pillow again.

"I'm dreaming," thought Richard, "that's clear. When I went to bed, my hands were not made of eggshells; and now I can almost see through 'em. If this is not a dream, I have woke up by mistake in an Arabian Night, instead of a London one. But I have no doubt I'm asleep. Not the least."

Here the small servant had another cough.

"Very remarkable!" thought Mr. Swiveller. "I never dreamt such a real cough as that before. I don't know, indeed, that I ever dreamt either a cough or a sneeze. Perhaps it's part of the philosophy of dreams that one never does. There's another—and another—I say,— I'm dreaming rather fast!"

For the purpose of testing his real condition, Mr. Swiveller, after some reflection, pinched himself in the arm.

"Queerer still!" he thought. "I came to bed rather plump than otherwise, and now there's nothing to lay hold of. I'll take another survey."

The result of this further inspection was, to convince Mr. Swiveller that the objects by which he was surrounded were real, and that he saw them, beyond all question, with his waking eyes.

"It's an Arabian Night, that's what it is," said Richard. "I'm in Damascus or Grand Cairo. The Marchioness is a Genie, and having had a wager with another Genie about who is the handsomest young man alive, and the worthiest to be the husband of the Princess of China, has brought me away, room and all, to compare us together. Perhaps," said Mr. Swiveller, turning languidly round upon his pillow, and looking on that side of his bed which was next the wall, "the Princess may be still—No, she's gone."

Not feeling quite satisfied with this explanation, as, even taking it to be the correct one, it still involved a little mystery and doubt, Mr. Swiveller raised the curtain again, determined to take the first favourable opportunity of addressing his companion. An occasion soon presented itself. The Marchioness dealt, turned up a knave, and omitted to take the usual advantage; upon which Mr. Swiveller called out as loud as he could—"Two for his heels!"

The Marchioness jumped up quickly, and clapped her hands. "Arabian Night, certainly," thought Mr. Swiveller; "they always clap their hands instead of ringing the bell. Now for the two thousand black slaves, with jars of jewels on their heads!"

It appeared, however, that she had only clapped her hands in joy; for directly afterwards she began to laugh, and then to cry; declaring, not in choice Arabic but in familiar English, that she was "so glad, she didn't know what to do."

"Marchioness," said Mr. Swiveller, thoughtfully, "be pleased to draw nearer. First of all, will you have the goodness to inform me where I shall find my voice; and secondly, what has become of my flesh?"

The Marchioness only shook her head mournfully, and cried again; whereupon Mr. Swiveller (being very weak) felt his own eyes affected likewise.

"I begin to infer, from your manner and these appearances, Marchioness,"—said Richard after a pause, and smiling with a trembling lip, "that I have been ill."

"You just have!" replied the small servant, wiping her eyes. "And haven't you been a talking nonsense!"

"Oh!" said Dick. "Very ill, Marchioness, have I been?"

"Dead, all but," replied the small servant. "I never thought you'd get better. Thank Heaven you have!"

Mr. Swiveller was silent for a long while. By-and-by, he began to talk again—inquiring how long he had been there.

"Three weeks to-morrow," replied the small servant.

"Three what?" said Dick.

"Weeks," returned the Marchioness emphatically; "three long, slow weeks."

The bare thought of having been in such extremity caused Richard to fall into another silence, and to lie flat down again at his full length. The Marchioness, having arranged the bed-clothes more comfortably, and felt that his hands and forehead were quite cool—a discovery that filled her with delight—cried a little more, and then applied herself to getting tea ready, and making some thin dry toast.

While she was thus engaged, Mr. Swiveller looked on with a grateful heart, very much astonished to see how thoroughly at home she made herself, and attributing this attention, in its origin, to Sally Brass, whom, in his own mind, he could not thank enough. When the Marchioness had finished her toasting, she spread a clean cloth on a tray, and brought him some crisp slices and a great basin of weak tea, with which (she said) the doctor had left word he might refresh himself when he awoke. She propped him up with pillows, if not as skilfully as if she had been a professional nurse all her life, at least as tenderly; and looked on with unutterable satisfaction while the patient —stopping every now and then to shake her by the hand—took his poor meal with an appetite and relish, which the greatest dainties of the earth, under any other circumstances, would have failed to provoke. Having cleared away, and disposed everything comfortably about him again, she sat down at the table to take her own tea.

"Marchioness," said Mr. Swiveller, "how's Sally?"

The small servant screwed her face into an expression of the very uttermost entanglement of slyness, and shook her head.

"What, haven't you seen her lately?" said Dick.

"Seen her!" cried the small servant. "Bless you, I've run away!"

Mr. Swiveller immediately laid himself down again quite flat, and so remained for about five minutes. By slow degrees he resumed his sitting posture after that lapse of time, and inquired:

"And where do you live, Marchioness?"

"Live!" cried the small servant. "Here!"

"Oh!" said Mr. Swiveller.

And with that he fell down flat again, as suddenly as if he had been shot. Thus he remained, motionless and bereft of speech, until she had finished her meal, put everything in its place, and swept the hearth; when he motioned her to bring a chair to the bedside, and, being propped up again, opened a farther conversation.

"And so," said Dick, "you have run away?"

"Yes," said the Marchioness, "and they've been a tizing of me."

"Been—I beg your pardon," said Dick—"what have they been doing?"

"Been a tizing of me—tizing you know—in the newspapers," rejoined the Marchioness.

"Ay, ay," said Dick, "advertising?"

The small servant nodded, and winked. Her eyes were so red with waking and crying, that the Tragic Muse might have winked with greater consistency. And so Dick felt.

"Tell me," said he, "how it was that you thought of coming here."

"Why, you see," returned the Marchioness, "when you was gone, I hadn't any friend at all, because the lodger he never come back, and I didn't know where either him or you was to be found, you know. But one morning, when I was——"

"Was near a key-hole?" suggested Mr. Swiveller, observing that she faltered.

"Well, then" said the small servant, nodding; "when I was near the office key-hole—as you see me through, you know—I heard somebody saying that she lived here, and was the lady whose house you lodged at, and that you was took very bad, and wouldn't nobody come and take care of you. Mr. Brass, he says, 'It's no business of mine;' and Miss Sally, she says, 'He's a funny chap, but it's no business of mine;' and the lady went away, and slammed the door to, when she went out, I can tell you. So I run away that night, and come here, and told 'em you was my brother, and they believed me, and I've been here ever since."

"This poor little Marchioness has been wearing herself to death!" cried Dick.

"No I haven't," she returned, "not a bit of it. Don't you mind about me. I like sitting up, and I've often had a sleep, bless you, in one of them chairs. But if you could have seen how you tried to jump out o' winder, and if you could have heard how you used to keep on singing and making speeches, you wouldn't have believed it—I'm so glad you're better, Mr. Liverer."

"Liverer indeed!" said Dick thoughtfully. "It's well I *am* a liverer. I strongly suspect I should have died, Marchioness, but for you."

At this point, Mr. Swiveller took the small servant's hand in his again, and being, as we have seen, but poorly, might in struggling to express his thanks have made his eyes as red as hers, but that she quickly changed the theme by making him lie down, and urging him to keep very quiet.

"The doctor," she told him, "said you was to be kept quite still, and there was to be no noise nor nothing. Now, take a rest, and then we'll talk again. I'll sit by you, you know. If you shut your eyes, perhaps you'll go to sleep. You'll be all the better for it, if you do."

The Marchioness, in saying these words, brought a little table to the bedside, took her seat at it, and began to work away at the concoction of some cooling drink, with the address of a score of chemists. Richard Swiveller, being indeed fatigued, fell into a deep slumber, and waking in about half an hour, inquired what time it was.

"Just gone half after six," replied his small friend, helping him to sit up again.

"Marchioness," said Richard, passing his hand over his forehead and turning suddenly round, as though the subject but that moment flashed upon him, "what has become of Kit?"

He had been sentenced to transportation for a great many years, she said.

"Has he gone?" asked Dick—"his mother—how is she,—what has become of her?"

His nurse shook her head, and answered that she knew nothing about them.

"But, if I thought," said she, very slowly, "that you'd keep quiet, and not put yourself into another fever, I could tell you—but I won't now."

"Yes, do," said Dick. "It will amuse me."

"Oh! would it though!" rejoined the small servant, with a horrified look. "I know better than that. Wait till you're better and then I'll tell you."

Dick looked very earnestly at his little friend: and his eyes, being large and hollow from illness, assisted the expression so much, that she was quite frightened, and besought him not to think any more about it. What had already fallen from her, however, had not only piqued his curiosity, but seriously alarmed him, wherefore he urged her to tell him the worst at once.

"Oh! there's no worst in it," said the small servant. "It hasn't anything to do with you."

"Has it anything to do with—is it anything you heard through chinks or key-holes—and that you were not intended to hear?" asked Dick, in a breathless state.

"Yes," replied the small servant.

"In—in Bevis Marks?" pursued Dick hastily. "Conversations between Brass and Sally?"

"Yes," cried the small servant again.

Richard Swiveller thrust his lank arm out of bed, and, gripping her by the wrist and drawing her close to him, bade her out with it, and freely too, or he would not answer for the consequences; being wholly unable to endure that state of excitement and expectation. She, seeing that he was greatly agitated, and that the effects of postponing her revelation might be much more injurious than any that were likely to ensue from its being made at once, promised compliance, on condition that the patient kept himself perfectly quiet, and abstained from starting up or tossing about.

"But if you begin to do that," said the small servant, "I'll leave off. And so I tell you."

"You can't leave off till you have gone on," said Dick. "And do go on, there's a darling. Speak, sister, speak. Pretty Polly say—Oh tell me when, and tell me where, pray Marchioness, I beseech you!"

Unable to resist these fervent adjurations, which Richard Swiveller poured out as passionately as if they had been of the most solemn and tremendous nature, his companion spoke thus:

"Well! Before I run away, I used to sleep in the kitchen—where we played cards, you know. Miss Sally used to keep the key of the kitchen door in her pocket, and she always come down at night to take away the candle and rake out the fire. When she had done that, she left me to go to bed in the dark, locked the door on the outside, put the key in her pocket again, and kept me locked up till she come down in the morning—very early I can tell you—and let me out. I was terrible afraid of being kept like this, because if there was a fire, I thought they might forget me and only take care of themselves, you know. So whenever I see an old rusty key anywhere, I picked it up and tried if it would fit the door, and at last I found in the dust cellar a key that *did* fit it."

Here Mr. Swiveller made a violent demonstration with his legs. But the small servant immediately pausing in her talk, he subsided again, and, pleading a momentary forgetfulness of their compact, entreated her to proceed.

"They kept me very short," said the small servant. "Oh! you can't think how short they kept me! So I used to come out at night after they'd gone to bed, and feel about in the dark for bits of biscuits, or sangwitches that you'd left in the office, or even pieces of orange peel to put into cold water and make believe it was wine. Did you ever taste orange peel and water?"

Mr. Swiveller replied that he had never tasted that ardent liquor; and once more urged his friend to resume the thread of her narrative.

"If you make believe very much, it's quite nice," said the small servant; "but if you don't, you know, it seems as if it would bear a little more seasoning, certainly. Well, sometimes I used to come out after they'd gone to bed, and sometimes before, you know; and one or two nights before there was all that precious noise in the office—when the young man was took, I mean—I come up stairs while Mr. Brass and Miss Sally was a sittin' at the office fire; and I'll tell you the truth, that I come to listen again about the key of the safe."

Mr. Swiveller gathered up his knees so as to make a great cone of the bed-clothes, and conveyed into his countenance an expression of the utmost concern. But the small servant pausing, and holding up her finger, the cone gently disappeared, though the look of concern did not.

"There was him and her," said the small servant, "a sittin' by the fire, and talking softly together. Mr. Brass says to Miss Sally, 'Upon my word,' he says, 'it's a dangerous thing, and it might get us into a world of trouble, and I don't half like it.' She says—you know her way—she says, 'You're the chickenest-hearted, feeblest, faintest man I ever see, and I think,' she says, 'that I ought to have been the brother, and you the sister. Isn't Quilp,' she says, 'our principal support?' 'He certainly is,' says Mr. Brass. 'And an't we,' she says, 'constantly ruining somebody or other in the way of business?' 'We certainly are,' says Mr. Brass. 'Then does it signify,' she says, 'about ruining this Kit when Quilp desires it?' 'It certainly does not signify,' says Brass. Then, they whispered and laughed for a long time about there being no danger if it was well done, and then Mr. Brass pulls out his pocket-book, and says, 'Well,' he says, 'here it is—Quilp's own five-pound note. We'll agree that way, then,' he says. 'Kit's coming to-morrow morning, I know. While he's up stairs, you'll get out of the way, and I'll clear off Mr. Richard. Having Kit alone, I'll hold him in conversation, and put this property in his hat. I'll manage so, besides,' he says, 'that Mr. Richard shall find it there, and be the evidence. And if that don't get Christopher out of Mr. Quilp's way, and satisfy Mr. Quilp's grudges,' he says, 'the Devil's in it.' Miss Sally laughed, and said that was the plan, and as they seemed to be moving away, and I was afraid to stop any longer, I went down stairs again.—There!"

The small servant had gradually worked herself into as much agitation as Mr. Swiveller, and therefore made no effort to restrain him when he sat up in bed and hastily demanded whether this story had been told to anybody.

"How could it be?" replied his nurse. "I was almost afraid to think about it, and hoped the young man would be let off. When I heard 'em say they had found him guilty of what he didn't do, you was gone, and so was the lodger—though I think I should have been frightened to tell him, even if he'd been there. Ever since I come here, you've been out of your senses, and what would have been the good of telling you then?"

"Marchioness," said Mr. Swiveller, plucking off his night-cap and flinging it to the other end of the room; "if you'll do me the favour to retire for a few minutes and see what sort of a night it is, I'll get up."

"You mustn't think of such a thing," cried his nurse.

"I must indeed," said the patient, looking round the room. "Whereabouts are my clothes?"

"Oh, I'm so glad—you haven't got any," replied the Marchioness.

"Ma'am!" said Mr. Swiveller, in great astonishment.

"I've been obliged to sell them, every one, to get the things that was ordered for you. But don't take on about that," urged the Marchioness, as Dick fell back upon his pillow. "You're too weak to stand, indeed."

"I am afraid," said Richard dolefully, "that you're right! What ought I to do ! What is to be done!"

It naturally occurred to him on very little reflection, that the first step to take would be to communicate with one of the Mr. Garlands instantly. It was very possible that Mr. Abel had not yet left the office. In as little time as it takes to tell it, the small servant had the address in pencil on a piece of paper; a verbal description of father and son, which would enable her to recognise either without difficulty; and a special caution to be shy of Mr. Chuckster, in consequence of that gentleman's known antipathy to Kit. Armed with these slender powers, she hurried away, commissioned to bring either old Mr. Garland or Mr. Abel, bodily, to that apartment.

"I suppose," said Dick, as she closed the door slowly, and peeped into the room again to make sure that he was comfortable, "I suppose there's nothing left—not so much as a waistcoat even?"

"No, nothing."

"It's embarrassing," said Mr. Swiveller, "in case of fire—even an umbrella would be something—but you did quite right, dear Marchioness. I should have died without you!"

CHAPTER LXV

It was well for the small servant that she was of a sharp, quick nature, or the consequence of sending her out alone, from the very neighbourhood in which it was most dangerous for her to appear, would probably have been the restoration of Miss Sally Brass to the supreme authority over her person. Not unmindful of the risk she ran, however, the Marchioness no sooner left the house than she dived into the first dark by-way that presented itself, and, without any present reference to the point to which her journey tended, made it her first business to put two good miles of brick and mortar between herself and Bevis Marks.

When she had accomplished this object, she began to shape her course for the notary's office, to which—shrewdly inquiring of apple-women and oyster-sellers at street-corners, rather than in lighted shops or of well-dressed people, at the hazard of attracting notice—she easily procured a direction. As carrier-pigeons, on being first let loose in a strange place beat the air at random for a short time, before darting off towards the spot for which they are designed, so did the Marchioness flutter round and round until she believed herself in safety, and then bear swiftly down upon the port for which she was bound.

She had no bonnet—nothing on her head but a great cap which in some old time had been worn by Sally Brass, whose taste in head-dresses was, as we have seen, peculiar—and her speed was rather retarded than assisted by her shoes, which, being extremely large and slipshod, flew off every now and then, and were difficult to find again, among the crowd of passengers. Indeed, the poor little creature experienced so much trouble and delay from having to grope for these articles of dress in mud and kennel, and suffered in these researches so much jostling, pushing, squeezing, and bandying from hand to hand, that by the time she reached the street in which the notary lived, she was fairly worn out and exhausted, and could not refrain from tears.

But to have got there at last was a great comfort, especially as there were lights still burning in the office window, and therefore some hope that she was not too late. So, the Marchioness dried her eyes with the backs of her hands, and, stealing softly up the steps, peeped in through the glass door.

Mr. Chuckster was standing behind the lid of his desk, making such preparations towards finishing off for the night as pulling down his wristbands and pulling up his shirt-collar, settling his neck more gracefully in his stock, and secretly arranging his whiskers by the aid of a little triangular bit of looking-glass. Before the ashes of the fire stood two gentlemen, one of whom she rightly judged to be the notary, and the other (who was buttoning his great-coat) and was evidently about to depart immediately) Mr. Abel Garland.

Having made these observations, the small spy took counsel with herself, and resolved to wait in the street until Mr. Abel came out, as there would be then no fear of having to speak before Mr. Chuckster, and less difficulty in delivering her message. With this purpose she slipped out again, and crossing the road, sat down upon a doorstep just opposite.

She had hardly taken this position, when there came dancing up the street, with his legs all wrong, and his head everywhere by turns, a pony. This pony had a little phaeton behind him, and a man in it; but neither man nor phaeton seemed to embarrass him in the least, as he reared up on his hind legs, or stopped, or went on, or stood still again, or backed, or went sideways, without the smallest reference to them,—just as the fancy seized him, and as if he were the freest animal in creation. When they came to the notary's door, the man called out in a very respectful manner, "Woa then,"—intimating that if he might venture to express a wish, it would be that they stopped there. The pony made a moment's pause; but as if it occurred to him that to stop when he was required might be to establish an inconvenient and dangerous precedent, he immediately started off again, rattled at a fast trot to the street-corner, wheeled round, came back, and then stopped of his own accord.

"Oh! you're a precious creatur!" said the man—who didn't venture by the bye to come out in his true colours until he was safe on the pavement. "I wish I had the rewarding of you,—I do."

"What has he been doing?" said Mr. Abel, tying a shawl round his neck as he came down the steps.

"He's enough to fret a man's heart out," replied the hostler. "He is the most wicious rascal—Woa then, will you?"

"He'll never stand still, if you call him names," said Mr. Abel, getting in, and taking the reins. "He's a very good fellow if you know how to manage him. This is the first time he has been out, this long while, for he has lost his old driver and wouldn't stir for anybody else, till this morning. The lamps are right, are they? That's well. Be here to take him to-morrow, if you please. Good night!"

And after one or two strange plunges, quite of his own invention, the pony yielded to Mr. Abel's mildness, and trotted gently off.

All this time Mr. Chuckster had been standing at the door, and the small servant had been afraid to approach. She had nothing for it now, therefore, but to run after the chaise, and to call to Mr. Abel to stop. Being out of breath when she came up with it, she was unable to make him hear. The case was desperate; for the pony was quickening his pace. The Marchioness hung on behind for a few moments, and, feeling that she could go no farther, and must soon yield, clambered by a vigorous effort into the hinder seat, and in so doing lost one of the shoes for ever.

Mr. Abel being in a thoughtful frame of mind, and having quite enough to do to keep the pony going, went jogging on without looking round: little dreaming of the strange figure that was close behind him, until the Marchioness, having in some degree recovered her breath, and the loss of her shoe, and the novelty of her position, uttered close into his ear, the words—

"I say, sir—"

He turned his head quickly enough then, and stopping the pony, cried, with some trepidation, "God bless me, what is this!"

"Don't be frightened, sir," replied the still panting messenger. "Oh, I've run such a way after you!"

"What do you want with me?" said Mr. Abel. "How did you come here?"

"I got in behind," replied the Marchioness. "Oh please drive on, sir—don't stop—and go towards the City, will you? And oh do please make haste, because it's of consequence. There's somebody wants to see you there. He sent me to say would you come directly, and that he knowed all about Kit, and could save him yet, and prove his innocence."

"What do you tell me, child?"

"The truth, upon my word and honour I do. But please to drive on —quick, please! I've been such a time gone, he'll think I'm lost."

Mr. Abel involuntarily urged the pony forward. The pony, impelled by some secret sympathy or some caprice, burst into a great pace, and neither slackened it, nor indulged in any eccentric perform-ances, until they arrived at the door of Mr. Swiveller's lodging, where, marvellous to relate, he consented to stop when Mr. Abel checked him.

"See! It's that room up there," said the Marchioness, pointing to one where there was a faint light. "Come!"

Mr. Abel, who was one of the simplest and most retiring creatures in existence, and naturally timid withal, hesitated; for he had heard of people being decoyed into strange places to be robbed and murdered, under circumstances very like the present, and, for anything he knew to the contrary, by guides very like the Marchioness. His regard for Kit, however, overcame every other consideration. So, entrusting Whisker to the charge of a man who was lingering hard by in expectation of the job, he suffered his companion to take his hand, and to lead him up the dark and narrow stairs.

He was not a little surprised to find himself conducted into a dimly-lighted sick chamber, where a man was sleeping tranquilly in bed.

"An't it nice to see him lying there so quiet?" said his guide, in an earnest whisper. "Oh! you'd say it was, if you had only seen him two or three days ago."

Mr. Abel made no answer, and, to say the truth, kept a long way from the bed and very near the door. His guide, who appeared to understand his reluctance, trimmed the candle, and taking it in her hand, approached the bed. As she did so, the sleeper started up, and he recognised in the wasted face the features of Richard Swiveller.

"Why, how is this?" said Mr. Abel kindly, as he hurried towards him. "You have been ill?"

"Very," replied Dick. "Nearly dead. You might have chanced to hear of your Richard on his bier, but for the friend I sent to fetch you. Another shake of the hand, Marchioness, if you please. Sit down, sir."

Mr. Abel seemed rather astonished to hear of the quality of his guide, and took a chair by the bedside.

"I have sent for you, sir," said Dick—"but she told you on what account?"

"She did. I am quite bewildered by all this. I really don't know what to say or think," replied Mr. Abel.

"You'll say that presently," retorted Dick. "Marchioness, take a seat on the bed, will you? Now, tell this gentleman all that you told me; and be particular. Don't you speak another word, sir."

The story was repeated; it was, in effect, exactly the same as before, without any deviation or omission. Richard Swiveller kept his eyes fixed on his visitor during its narration, and directly it was concluded, took the word again.

"You have heard it all, and you'll not forget it. I'm too giddy and too queer to suggest anything; but you and your friends will know what to do. After this long delay, every minute is an age. If ever you went home fast in your life, go home fast to-night. Don't stop to say one word to me, but go. She will be found here, whenever she's wanted; and as to me, you're pretty sure to find me at home, for a week or two. There are more reasons than one for that. Marchioness, a light! If you lose another minute in looking at me, sir, I'll never forgive you!"

Mr. Abel needed no more remonstrance or persuasion. He was gone in an instant; and the Marchioness, returning from lighting him down stairs, reported that the pony, without any preliminary objection whatever, had dashed away at full gallop.

"That's right," said Dick; "and hearty of him; and I honour him from this time. But get some supper and a mug of beer, for I am sure you must be tired. Do have a mug of beer. It will do me as much good to see you take it as if I might drink it myself."

Nothing but this assurance could have prevailed upon the small nurse to indulge in such a luxury. Having eaten and drunk to Mr. Swiveller's extreme contentment, given him his drink, and put everything in neat order, she wrapped herself in an old coverlet and lay down upon the rug before the fire.

Mr. Swiveller was by that time murmuring in his sleep, "Strew then, oh strew, a bed of rushes. Here will we stay, till morning blushes. Good night, Marchioness!"

CHAPTER LXVI

ON awaking in the morning, Richard Swiveller became conscious by slow degrees of whispering voices in his room. Looking out between the curtains, he espied Mr. Garland, Mr. Abel, the Notary, and the single gentleman, gathered round the Marchioness, and talking to her with great earnestness but in very subdued tones—fearing, no doubt, to disturb him. He lost no time in letting them know that this precaution was unnecessary, and all four gentlemen directly approached his bedside. Old Mr. Garland was the first to stretch out his hand, and inquire how he felt.

Dick was about to answer that he felt much better, though still as weak as need be, when his little nurse, pushing the visitors aside and pressing up to his pillow as if in jealousy of their interference, set his breakfast before him, and insisted on his taking it before he underwent the fatigue of speaking or of being spoken to. Mr. Swiveller, who was perfectly ravenous, and had had, all night, amazingly distinct and consistent dreams of mutton chops, double stout, and similar delicacies, felt even the weak tea and dry toast such irresistible temptations, that he consented to eat and drink upon one condition.

"And that is," said Dick, returning the pressure of Mr. Garland's hand, "that you answer me this question truly, before I take a bit or drop. Is it too late?"

"For completing the work you began so well last night?" returned the old gentleman. "No. Set your mind at rest upon that point. It is not, I assure you."

Comforted by this intelligence, the patient applied himself to his food with a keen appetite, though evidently not with a greater zest in the eating than his nurse appeared to have in seeing him eat. The manner of his meal was this:—Mr. Swiveller, holding the slice of toast or cup of tea in his left hand, and taking a bite or drink as the case might be, constantly kept, in his right, one palm of the Marchioness tight locked; and to shake, or even to kiss this imprisoned hand, he would stop every now and then, in the very act of swallowing, with perfect seriousness of intention, and the utmost gravity. As often as he put anything into his mouth, whether for eating or drinking, the face of the Marchioness lighted up beyond all description; but whenever he gave her one or other of these tokens of recognition, her countenance became over-shadowed, and she began to sob. Now, whether she was in her laughing joy, or in her crying one, the Marchioness could not help turning to the visitors with an appealing look, which seemed to say, "You see this fellow—can I help this?"— and they being thus made, as it were, parties to the scene, as regularly answered by another look, "No. Certainly not." This dumb-show taking place during the whole time of the invalid's breakfast, and the invalid himself, pale and emaciated, performing no small part in the same, it may be fairly questioned whether at any meal, where no word, good or bad, was spoken from beginning to end, so much was expressed by gestures in themselves so slight and unimportant.

At length—and to say the truth before very long—Mr. Swiveller had despatched as much toast and tea as in that stage of his recovery it was discreet to let him have. But the cares of the Marchioness did not stop here; for, disappearing for an instant and presently returning with a basin of fair water, she laved his face and hands, brushed his hair, and in short made him as spruce and smart as anybody under such circumstances could be made; and all this in as brisk and business-like a manner, as if he were a very little boy, and she his grown-up nurse. To these various attentions, Mr. Swiveller submitted in a kind of grateful astonishment beyond the reach of language. When they were at last brought to an end, and the Marchioness had withdrawn into a distant corner to take her own poor breakfast (cold enough by that time), he turned his face away for some few moments, and shook hands heartily with the air.

"Gentlemen," said Dick, rousing himself from this pause, and turning round again, "you'll excuse me. Men who have been brought so low as I have been, are easily fatigued. I am fresh again now, and fit for talking. We're short of chairs here, among other trifles, but if you'll do me the favour to sit upon the bed—"

"What can we do for you?" said Mr. Garland, kindly.

"If you could make the Marchioness yonder, a Marchioness in real, sober earnest," returned Dick, "I'd thank you to get it done off-hand. But as you can't, and as the question is not what you will do for me, but what you will do for somebody else who has a better claim upon you, pray, sir, let me know what you intend doing."

"It's chiefly on that account that we have come just now," said the single gentleman, "for you will have another visitor presently. We feared you would be anxious unless you knew from ourselves what steps we intended to take, and therefore came to you before we stirred in the matter."

"Gentlemen," returned Dick, "I thank you. Anybody in the helpless state that you see me in, is naturally anxious. Don't let me interrupt you, sir."

"Then, you see, my good fellow," said the single gentleman, "that while we have no doubt whatever of the truth of this disclosure, which has so providentially come to light—"

"Meaning hers?" said Dick, pointing towards the Marchioness.

"—Meaning hers, of course. While we have no doubt of that, or that a proper use of it would procure the poor lad's immediate pardon and liberation, we have a great doubt whether it would, by itself, enable us to reach Quilp, the chief agent in this villany. I should tell you that this doubt has been confirmed into something very nearly approaching certainty by the best opinions we have been enabled, in this short space of time, to take upon the subject. You'll agree with us, that to give him even the most distant chance of escape, if we could help it, would be monstrous. You say with us, no doubt, if somebody must escape, let it be any one but he."

"Yes," returned Dick, "certainly. That is if somebody *must*—but upon my word, I'm unwilling that anybody should. Since laws were made for every degree, to curb vice in others as well as in me—and so forth you know—doesn't it strike you in that light?"

The single gentleman smiled as if the light in which Mr. Swiveller had put the question were not the clearest in the world, and proceeded to explain that they contemplated proceeding by stratagem in the first instance; and that their design was to endeavour to extort a confession from the gentle Sarah.

"When she finds how much we know, and how we know it," he said, "and that she is clearly compromised already, we are not without strong hopes that we may be enabled through her means to punish the other two effectually. If we could do that, she might go scot-free for aught I cared."

Dick received this project in anything but a gracious manner, representing with as much warmth as he was then capable of showing, that they would find the old buck (meaning Sarah) more difficult to manage than Quilp himself—that for any tampering, terrifying, or cajolery, she was a very unpromising and unyielding subject—that she was of a kind of brass not easily melted or moulded into shape—in short, that they were no match for her, and would be signally defeated. But, it was in vain to urge them to adopt some other course. The single gentleman has been described as explaining their joint intentions, but it should have been written that they all spoke together; that if any one of them by chance held his peace for a moment, he stood gasping and panting for an opportunity to strike in again: in a word, that they had reached that pitch of impatience and anxiety where men can neither be persuaded nor reasoned with; and that it would have been easier to turn the most impetuous wind that ever blew, than to prevail on them to reconsider their determination. So, after telling Mr. Swiveller how they had not lost sight of Kit's mother and the children; how they had never once even lost sight of Kit himself, but had been unremitting in their endeavours to procure a mitigation of his sentence; how they had been perfectly distracted between the strong proofs of his guilt, and their own fading hopes of his innocence; and how he, Richard Swiveller, might keep his mind at rest, for everything should be happily adjusted between that time and night;—after telling him all this, and adding a great many kind and cordial expressions, personal to himself, which it is unnecessary to recite, Mr. Garland, the notary, and the single gentleman, took their leaves at a very critical time, or Richard Swiveller must assuredly have been driven into another fever, whereof the results might have been fatal.

Mr. Abel remained behind, very often looking at his watch and at the room-door, until Mr. Swiveller was roused from a short nap, by the setting-down on the landing-place outside, as from the shoulders of a porter, of some giant load, which seemed to shake the house, and made the little physic bottles on the mantel-shelf ring again. Directly this sound reached his ears, Mr. Abel started up, and hobbled to the door, and opened it; and behold! there stood a strong man, with a mighty hamper, which, being hauled into the room and presently unpacked, disgorged such treasures of tea, and coffee, and wine, and rusks, and oranges, and grapes, and fowls ready trussed for boiling, and calves'-foot jelly, and arrow-root, and sago, and other delicate restoratives, that the small servant, who had never thought it possible that such things could be, except in shops, stood rooted to the spot in her one shoe, with her mouth and eyes watering in unison, and her power of speech quite gone. But not so Mr. Abel; or the strong man who emptied the hamper, big as it was, in a twinkling; and not so the nice old lady, who appeared so suddenly that she might have come out of the hamper too (it was quite large enough), and who, bustling about on tiptoe and without noise—now here, now there, now everywhere at once—began to fill out the jelly in tea-cups, and to make chicken broth in small saucepans, and to peel oranges for the sick man and to cut them up in little pieces, and to ply the small servant with glasses of wine and choice bits of everything until more substantial meat could be prepared for her refreshment. The whole of which appearances were so unexpected and bewildering, that Mr. Swiveller, when he had taken two oranges and a little jelly, and had seen the strong man walk off with the empty basket, plainly leaving all that abundance for his use and benefit, was fain to lie down and fall asleep again, from sheer inability to entertain such wonders in his mind.

Meanwhile the single gentleman, the notary, and Mr. Garland, repaired to a certain coffee-house, and from that place indited and sent a letter to Miss Sally Brass, requesting her, in terms mysterious and brief, to favour an unknown friend who wished to consult her, with her company there, as speedily as possible. The communication performed its errand so well, that within ten minutes of the messenger's return and report of its delivery, Miss Brass herself was announced.

"Pray, ma'am," said the single gentleman, whom she found alone in the room, "take a chair."

Miss Brass sat herself down in a very stiff and frigid state, and seemed—as indeed she was—not a little astonished to find that the lodger and her mysterious correspondent were one and the same person.

"You did not expect to see me?" said the single gentleman.

"I didn't think much about it," returned the beauty. "I supposed it was business of some kind or other. If it's about the apartments, of course you'll give my brother regular notice, you know—or money. That's very easily settled. You're a responsible party, and in such a case lawful money and lawful notice are pretty much the same."

"I am obliged to you for your good opinion," retorted the single gentleman, "and quite concur in those sentiments. But that is not the subject on which I wish to speak with you."

"Oh!" said Sally. "Then just state the particulars, will you? I suppose it's professional business?"

"Why, it *is* connected with the law, certainly."

"Very well," returned Miss Brass. "My brother and I are just the same. I can take any instructions, or give you any advice."

"As there are other parties interested besides myself," said the single gentleman, rising and opening the door of an inner room, "we had better confer together. Miss Brass is here, gentlemen!"

Mr. Garland and the notary walked in, looking very grave; and drawing up two chairs, one on each side of the single gentleman, formed a kind of fence round the gentle Sarah, and penned her into a corner. Her brother Sampson under such circumstances would certainly have evinced some confusion or anxiety, but she—all composure—pulled out the tin box and calmly took a pinch of snuff.

"Miss Brass," said the notary, taking the word at this crisis, "we professional people understand each other, and, when we choose, can say what we have to say, in very few words. You advertised a runaway servant, the other day?"

"Well," returned Miss Sally, with a sudden flush over-spreading her features, "what of that?"

"She is found, ma'am," said the notary, pulling out his pocket-handkerchief with a flourish. "She is found."

"Who found her?" demanded Sarah hastily.

"We did, ma'am—we three. Only last night, or you would have heard from us before."

"And now I *have* heard from you," said Miss Brass, folding her arms resolutely, as though she were about to deny something to the death, "what have you got to say? Something you have got into your heads about her, of course. Prove it, will you—that's all. Prove it. You have found her, you say. I can tell you (if you don't know it) that you have found the most artful, lying, pilfering, and devilish little minx that was ever born.—Have you got her here?" she added, looking sharply round.

"No, she is not here at present," returned the notary. "But she is quite safe."

"Ha!" cried Sally, twitching a pinch of snuff out of her box, as spitefully as if she were in the very act of wrenching off the small servant's nose; "she shall be safe enough from this time, I warrant you."

"I hope so," replied the notary.—"Did it occur to you for the first time when you found she had run away, that there were two keys to your kitchen door?"

Miss Sally took another pinch, and putting her head on one side, looked at her questioner with a curious kind of spasm about her mouth, but with a cunning aspect of immense expression.

"Two keys," repeated the notary; "one of which gave her the opportunities of roaming through the house at nights when you supposed her fast locked up, and of overhearing confidential consultations—among others, that particular conference to be described to-day before a justice, which you will have an opportunity of hearing her relate; that conference which you and Mr. Brass held together on the night before that most unfortunate and innocent young man was accused of robbery, by a horrible device of which I will only say that it may be characterised by the epithets you have applied to this wretched little witness, and by a few stronger ones besides."

Sally took another pinch. Although her face was wonderfully composed, it was apparent that she was wholly taken by surprise, and that what she had expected to be taxed with, in connexion with her small servant, was something very different from this.

"Come, come, Miss Brass," said the notary, "you have great command of feature, but you feel, I see, that by a chance which never entered your imagination, this base design is revealed, and two of its plotters must be brought to justice. Now, you know the pains and penalties you are liable to, and so I need not dilate upon them, but I have a proposal to make to you. You have the honour of being sister to one of the greatest scoundrels unhung; and, if I may venture to say so to a lady, you are in every respect quite worthy of him. But, connected with you two is a third party, a villain of the name of Quilp, the prime mover of the whole diabolical device, who I believe to be worse than either. For his sake, Miss Brass, do us the favour to reveal the whole history of this affair. Let me remind you that your doing so at our instance will place you in a safe and comfortable position—your present one is not desirable—and cannot injure your brother, for against him and you we have quite sufficient evidence (as you hear) already. I will not say to you that we suggest this course in mercy (for, to tell you the truth, we do not entertain any regard for you), but it is a necessity to which we are reduced, and I recommend it to you as a matter of the very best policy. Time," said Mr. Witherden, pulling out his watch, "in a business like this, is exceedingly precious. Favour us with your decision as speedily as possible, ma'am."

With a smile upon her face, and looking at each of the three by turns, Miss Brass took two or three more pinches of snuff, and having by this time very little left, travelled round and round the box with her forefinger and thumb, scraping up another. Having disposed of this likewise and put the box carefully in her pocket, she said,—

"I am to accept or reject at once, am I?"

"Yes," said Mr. Witherden.

The charming creature was opening her lips to speak in reply, when the door was hastily opened too, and the head of Sampson Brass was thrust into the room.

"Excuse me," said that gentleman hastily. "Wait a bit!"

So saying, and quite indifferent to the astonishment his presence occasioned, he crept in, shut the door, kissed his greasy glove as servilely as if it were the dust, and made a most abject bow.

"Sarah," said Brass, "hold your tongue if you please, and let me speak. Gentlemen, if I could express the pleasure it gives me to see three such men in a happy unity of feeling and concord of sentiment, I think you would hardly believe me. But though I am unfortunate—nay, gentlemen, criminal, if we are to use harsh expressions in a company like this—still I have my feelings like other men. I have heard of a poet, who remarked that feelings were the common lot of all. If he could have been a pig, gentlemen, and have uttered that sentiment, he would still have been immortal."

"If you're not an idiot," said Miss Brass harshly, "hold your peace."

"Sarah, my dear," returned her brother, "thank you. But I know what I am about, my love, and will take the liberty of expressing myself accordingly. Mr. Witherden, sir, your handkerchief is hanging out of your pocket—would you allow me to—"

As Mr. Brass advanced to remedy this accident, the notary shrank from him with an air of great disgust. Brass, who over and above his usual prepossessing qualities, had a scratched face, a green shade over one eye, and a hat grievously crushed, stopped short, and looked round with a pitiful smile.

"He shuns me," said Sampson, "even when I would, as I may say, heap coals of fire upon his head. Well! Ah! But I am a falling house, and the rays (if I may be allowed the expression in reference to a gentleman that I respect and love beyond everything) fly from me! Gentlemen—regarding your conversation just now, I happened to see my sister on her way here, and, wondering where she could be going to, and being—may I venture to say—naturally of a suspicious turn, followed her. Since then, I have been listening."

"If you're not mad," interposed Miss Sally, "stop there, and say no more."

"Sarah, my dear," rejoined Brass with undiminished politeness, "I thank you kindly, but will still proceed. Mr. Witherden, sir, as we have the honour to be members of the same profession—to say nothing of that other gentleman having been my lodger, and having partaken, as one may say, of the hospitality of my roof—I think you might have given me the refusal of this offer in the first instance. I do indeed. Now, my dear sir," cried Brass, seeing that the notary was about to interrupt him, "suffer me to speak, I beg."

Mr. Witherden was silent, and Brass went on.

"If you will do me the favour," he said, holding up the green shade, and revealing an eye most horribly discoloured, "to look at this, you will naturally inquire in your own minds how did I get it. If you look from that, to my face, you will wonder what could have been the cause of all these scratches. And if from them to my hat, how it came into the state in which you see it. Gentlemen," said Brass, striking the hat fiercely with his clenched hand, "to all these questions I answer—Quilp!"

The three gentlemen looked at each other, but said nothing.

"I say," pursued Brass, glancing aside at his sister, as though he were talking for her information, and speaking with a snarling malignity, in violent contrast to his usual smoothness, "that I answer to all these questions,—Quilp—Quilp, who deludes me into his infernal den, and takes a delight in looking on and chuckling while I scorch, and burn, and bruise, and maim myself—Quilp, who never once, no never once, in all our communications together, has treated me otherwise than as a dog—Quilp, whom I have always hated with my whole heart, but never so much as lately. He gives me the cold shoulder on this very matter as if he had had nothing to do with it, instead of being the first to propose it. I can't trust him. In one of his howling, raving, blazing humours, I believe he'd let it out if it was murder, and never think of himself so long as he could terrify me. Now," said Brass, picking up his hat again, replacing the shade over his eye, and actually crouching down, in the excess of his servility, "What does all this lead me to?—what should you say it led me to, gentlemen?—could you guess at all near the mark?"

Nobody spoke. Brass stood smirking for a little while as if he had propounded some choice conundrum; and then said:

"To be short with you, then, it leads me to this. If the truth has come out, as it plainly has in a manner that there's no standing up against—and a very sublime and grand thing is Truth, gentlemen, in its way, though like other sublime and grand things, such as thunder-storms and that, we're not always over and above glad to see it—I had better turn upon this man than let this man turn upon me. It's clear to me that I am done for. Therefore, if anybody is to split, I had better be the person and have the advantage of it. Sarah, my dear, comparatively speaking you're safe. I relate these circumstances for my own profit."

With that, Mr. Brass, in a great hurry, revealed the whole story; bearing as heavily as possible on his amiable employer, and making himself out to be rather a saint-like and holy character, though subject—he acknowledged—to human weaknesses. He concluded thus:

"Now, gentlemen, I am not a man who does things by halves. Being in for a penny, I am ready, as the saying is, to be in for a pound. You must do with me what you please, and take me where you please. If you wish to have this in writing, we'll reduce it into manuscript immediately. You will be tender with me, I am sure. I am quite confident you will be tender with me. You are men of honour, and have feeling hearts. I yielded from necessity to Quilp, for though necessity has no law, she has her lawyers. I yield to you from necessity too; from policy besides; and because of feelings that have been a pretty long time working within me. Punish Quilp, gentlemen. Weigh heavily upon him. Grind him down. Tread him under foot. He has done as much by me, for many and many a day."

Having now arrived at the conclusion of his discourse, Sampson checked the current of his wrath, kissed his glove again, and smiled as only parasites and cowards can.

"And this," said Miss Brass, raising her head, with which she had hitherto sat resting on her hands, and surveying him from head to foot with a bitter sneer, "this is my brother, is it! This is my brother, that I have worked and toiled for, and believed to have had something of the man in him!"

"Sarah, my dear," returned Sampson, rubbing his hands feebly; "you disturb our friends. Besides you—you're disappointed, Sarah, and, not knowing what you say, expose yourself."

"Yes, you pitiful dastard," retorted the lovely damsel, "I understand you. You feared that I should be beforehand with you. But do you think that I would have been enticed to say a word! I'd have scorned it, if they had tried and tempted me for twenty years."

"He he!" simpered Brass, who in his deep debasement really seemed to have changed sexes with his sister, and to have made over to her any spark of manliness he might have possessed. "You think so, Sarah, you think so perhaps; but you would have acted quite different, my good fellow. You will not have forgotten that it was a maxim with Foxey—our reverend father, gentlemen—'Always suspect everybody.' That's the maxim to go through life with! If you were not actually about to purchase your own safety when I showed myself, I suspect you'd have done it by this time. And therefore I've done it myself, and spared you the trouble as well as the shame. The shame, gentlemen," added Brass, allowing himself to be slightly overcome, "if there is any, is mine. It's better that a female should be spared it."

With deference to the better opinion of Mr. Brass, and more particularly to the authority of his Great Ancestor, it may be doubted with humility whether the elevating principle laid down by the latter gentleman, and acted upon by his descendant, is always a prudent one, or attended in practice with the desired results. This is beyond question a bold and presumptuous doubt, inasmuch as many distinguished characters, called men of the world, long-headed customers knowing dogs, shrewd fellows, capital hands at business, and the like, have made, and do daily make, this axiom their polar star and compass. Still the doubt may be gently insinuated. And in illustration it may be observed that if Mr. Brass, not being over-suspicious, had, without prying and listening, left his sister to manage the conference on their joint behalf, or prying and listening, had not been in such a mighty hurry to anticipate her (which he would not have been, but for his distrust and jealousy), he would probably have found himself much better off in the end. Thus it will always happen that these men of the world, who go through it in armour, defend themselves from quite as much good as evil; to say nothing of the inconvenience and absurdity of mounting guard with a microscope at all times, and of wearing a coat of mail on the most innocent occasions.

The three gentlemen spoke together apart for a few moments. At the end of their consultation, which was very brief, the notary pointed to the writing-materials on the table, and informed Mr. Brass that if he wished to make any statement in writing, he had the opportunity of doing so. At the same time he felt bound to tell him that they would require his attendance presently before a Justice of the Peace, and that in what he did or said, he was guided entirely by his own discretion.

"Gentlemen," said Brass, drawing off his gloves, and crawling in spirit upon the ground before them, "I will justify the tenderness with which I know I shall be treated; and as, without tenderness, I should, now that this discovery has been made, stand in the worst position of the three, you may depend upon it I will make a clean breast. Mr. Witherden, sir, a kind of faintness is upon my spirits—if you would do me the favour to ring the bell and order up a glass of something warm and spicy, I shall, notwithstanding what has passed, have a melancholy pleasure in drinking your good health. I had hoped," said Brass, looking round with a mournful smile, "to have seen you three gentlemen one day or another with your legs under the mahogany in my humble parlour in the Marks. But hopes are fleeting. Dear me!"

Mr. Brass found himself so exceedingly affected at this point that he could say or do nothing more until some refreshment arrived. Having partaken of it, pretty freely for one in his agitated state, he sat down to write.

The lovely Sarah, now with her arms folded, and now with her hands clasped behind her, paced the room with manly strides while her brother was thus employed, and sometimes stopped to pull out her snuff-box and bite the lid. She continued to pace up and down until she was quite tired, and then fell asleep on a chair near the door.

It has been since supposed with some reason that this slumber was a sham or feint, as she contrived to slip away unobserved in the dusk of the afternoon. Whether this was an intentional and waking departure, or a somnambulistic leave-taking and walking in her sleep, may remain a subject of contention; but on one point (and indeed the main one) all parties are agreed. In whatever state she walked away, she certainly did not walk back again.

Mention having been made of the dusk of the afternoon, it will be inferred that Mr. Brass's task occupied some time in the completion. It was not finished until evening; but being done at last, that worthy person and the three friends adjourned in a hackney-coach to the private office of a Justice, who, giving Mr. Brass a warm reception and detaining him in a secure place that he might insure to himself the pleasure of seeing him on the morrow, dismissed the others with the cheering assurance that a warrant could not fail to be granted next day for the apprehension of Mr. Quilp, and that a proper application and statement of all the circumstances to the Secretary of State (who was fortunately in town), would no doubt procure Kit's free pardon and liberation without delay.

And now indeed it seemed that Quilp's malignant career was drawing to a close, and that retribution, which often travels slowly—especially when heaviest, had tracked his footsteps with a sure and certain scent and was gaining on him fast. Unmindful of her stealthy tread, her victim holds his course in fancied triumph. Still at his heels she comes, and once afoot, is never turned aside.

Their business ended, the three gentlemen hastened back to the lodgings of Mr. Swiveller, whom they found progressing so favourably in his recovery as to have been able to sit up for half an hour, and to have conversed with cheerfulness. Mrs. Garland had gone home some time since, but Mr. Abel was still sitting with him. After telling him all they had done, the two Mr. Garlands and the single gentleman, as if by some previous understanding, took their leaves for the night, leaving the invalid alone with the notary and the small servant.

"As you are so much better," said Mr. Witherden, sitting down at the bedside, "I may venture to communicate to you a piece of news which has come to me professionally."

The idea of any professional intelligence from a gentleman connected with legal matters appeared to afford Richard anything but a pleasing anticipation. Perhaps he connected it in his own mind with one or two outstanding accounts, in reference to which he had already received divers threatening letters. His countenance fell as he replied,

"Certainly, sir. I hope it's not anything of a very disagreeable nature, though?"

"If I thought it so, I should choose some better time for communicating it," replied the notary. "Let me tell you, first, that my friends who have been here to-day, know nothing of it, and that their kindness to you has been quite spontaneous, and with no hope of return. It may do a thoughtless, careless man good to know that."

Dick thanked him, and said he hoped it would.

"I have been making some inquiries about you," said Mr. Witherden, "little thinking that I should find you under such circumstances as those which have brought us together. You are the nephew of Rebecca Swiveller, spinster, deceased, of Cheselbourne in Dorsetshire."

"Deceased!" cried Dick.

"Deceased. If you had been another sort of nephew, you would have come into possession (so says the will, and I see no reason to doubt it) of five-and-twenty thousand pounds. As it is, you have fallen into an annuity of one hundred and fifty pounds a year; but I think I may congratulate you even upon that."

"Sir," said Dick, sobbing and laughing together, "you may. For, please God, we'll make a scholar of the poor Marchioness yet. And she shall walk in silk attire, and siller have to spare, or may I never rise from this bed again!"

CHAPTER LXVII

UNCONSCIOUS of the proceedings faithfully narrated in the last chapter, and little dreaming of the mine which had been sprung beneath him (for, to the end that he should have no warning of the business afoot, the profoundest secrecy was observed in the whole transaction), Mr. Quilp remained shut up in his hermitage, undisturbed by any suspicion, and extremely well satisfied with the result of his machinations. Being engaged in the adjustment of some accounts—an occupation to which the silence and solitude of his retreat were very favourable—he had not strayed from his den for two whole days. The third day of his devotion to this pursuit found him still hard at work, and little disposed to stir abroad.

It was the day next after Mr. Brass's confession, and consequently that which threatened the restriction of Mr. Quilp's liberty, and the abrupt communication to him of some very unpleasant and unwelcome facts. Having no intuitive perception of the cloud which lowered upon his house, the dwarf was in his ordinary state of cheerfulness; and, when he found he was becoming too much engrossed by business with a due regard to his health and spirits, he varied its monotonous routine with a little screeching, or howling, or some other innocent relaxation of that nature.

He was attended, as usual, by Tom Scott, who sat crouching over the fire after the manner of a toad, and from time to time, when his master's back was turned, imitated his grimaces with a fearful exactness. The figure-head had not yet disappeared, but remained in its old place. The face, horribly seared by the frequent application of the red-hot poker, and further ornamented by the insertion in the tip of the nose of a tenpenny nail, yet smiled blandly in its less lacerated parts, and seemed, like a sturdy martyr, to provoke its tormentor to the commission of new outrages and insults.

The day, in the highest and brightest quarters of the town, was damp, dark, cold, and gloomy. In that low and marshy spot, the fog filled every nook and corner with a thick dense cloud. Every object was obscure at one or two yards' distance. The warning lights and fires upon the river were powerless beneath this pall, and, but for a raw and piercing chillness in the air, and now and then the cry of some bewildered boatman as he rested on his oars and tried to make out where he was, the river itself might have been miles away.

The mist, though sluggish and slow to move, was of a keenly

searching kind. No muffling up in furs and broadcloth kept it out. It seemed to penetrate into the very bones of the shrinking wayfarers, and to rack them with cold and pains. Everything was wet, and clammy to the touch. The warm blaze alone defied it, and leaped and sparkled merrily. It was a day to be at home, crowding about the fire, telling stories of travellers who had lost their way in such weather on heaths and moors; and to love a warm hearth more than ever.

The dwarf's humour, as we know, was to have a fireside to himself; and when he was disposed to be convivial, to enjoy himself alone. By no means insensible to the comfort of being within doors, he ordered Tom Scott to pile the little stove with coals, and, dismissing his work for that day, determined to be jovial.

To this end, he lighted up fresh candles and heaped more fuel on the fire; and having dined off a beefsteak, which he cooked himself in somewhat of a savage and cannibal-like manner, brewed a great bowl of hot punch, lighted his pipe, and sat down to spend the evening.

At this moment, a low knocking at the cabin door arrested his attention. When it had been twice or thrice repeated, he softly opened the little window, and thrusting his head out, demanded who was there.

"Only me, Quilp," replied a woman's voice.

"Only you!" cried the dwarf, stretching his neck to obtain a better view of his visitor. "And what brings you here, you jade? How dare you approach the ogre's castle, eh?"

"I have come with some news," rejoined his spouse. "Don't be angry with me."

"Is it good news, pleasant news, news to make a man skip and snap his fingers?" said the dwarf. "Is the dear old lady dead?"

"I don't know what news it is, or whether it's good or bad," rejoined his wife.

"Then she's alive," said Quilp, "and there's nothing the matter with her. Go home again, you bird of evil note, go home!"

"I have brought a letter—" cried the meek little woman.

"Toss it in at the window here, and go your ways," said Quilp, interrupting her, "or I'll come out and scratch you."

"No, but please, Quilp—do hear me speak," urged his submissive wife, in tears. "Please do!"

"Speak then," growled the dwarf, with a malicious grin. "Be quick and short about it. Speak, will you?"

"It was left at our house this afternoon," said Mrs. Quilp, trembling, "by a boy who said he didn't know from whom it came, but that it was given to him to leave, and that he was told to say it must be brought on to you directly, for it was of the very greatest consequence.—But please," she added, as her husband stretched out his hand for it, "please let me in. You don't know how wet and cold I am, or how many times I have lost my way in coming here through this thick fog. Let me dry myself at the fire for five minutes. I'll go away directly you tell me to, Quilp. Upon my word I will."

Her amiable husband hesitated for a few moments; but bethinking himself that the letter might require some answer, of which she could be the bearer, closed the window, opened the door, and bade her enter. Mrs. Quilp obeyed right willingly, and, kneeling down before the fire to warm her hands, delivered into his a little packet.

"I'm glad you're wet," said Quilp, snatching it, and squinting at her. "I'm glad you're cold. I'm glad you've lost your way. I'm glad your eyes are red with crying. It does my heart good to see your little nose so pinched and frosty."

"Oh, Quilp!" sobbed his wife. "How cruel it is of you!"

"Did she think I was dead!" said Quilp, wrinkling his face into a most extraordinary series of grimaces. "Did she think she was going to have all the money, and to marry somebody she liked! Ha ha ha! Did she!"

These taunts elicited no reply from the poor little woman, who remaining on her knees, warming her hands, and sobbing, to Mr. Quilp's great delight. But as he was contemplating her, and chuckling excessively, he happened to observe that Tom Scott was delighted too; wherefore, that he might have no presumptuous partner in his glee, the dwarf instantly collared him, dragged him to the door, and after a short scuffle, kicked him into the yard. In return for this mark of attention, Tom immediately walked upon his hands to the window, and—if the expression be allowable—looked in with his shoes: besides rattling his feet upon the glass like a Banshee upside down. As a matter of course, Mr. Quilp lost not time in resorting to the infallible poker, with which, after some dodging and lying in ambush, he paid his young friend one or two such unequivocal compliments that he vanished precipitately, and left him in quiet possession of the field.

"So! That little job being disposed of," said the dwarf, coolly, "I'll read my letter. Humph!" he muttered, looking at the direction. "I ought to know this writing. Beautiful Sally!"

Opening it, he read, in a fair, round, legal hand, as follows:

"Sammy has been practised upon, and has broken confidence. It has all come out. You had better not be in the way, for strangers are going to call upon you. They have been very quiet as yet, because they mean to surprise you. Don't lose time. I didn't. I am not to be found anywhere. If I was you, I wouldn't be, either. S. B., late of B. M."

To describe the changes that passed over Quilp's face as he read this letter half a dozen times, would require some new language; such, for power of expression, as was never written, read, or spoken. For a long time he did not utter one word; but after a considerable interval, during which Mrs. Quilp was almost paralysed with the alarm his looks engendered, he contrived to gasp out,

"—If I had him here. If I only had him here——"

"Oh, Quilp!" said his wife, "what's the matter? Who are you angry with?"

"—I should drown him," said the dwarf, not heeding her. "Too easy a death, too short, too quick—but the river runs close at hand. Oh! if I had him here! Just to take him to the brink, coaxingly and pleasantly,—holding him by the buttonhole—joking with him,—and, with a sudden push, to send him splashing down! Drowning men come to the surface three times, they say. Ah! To see him those three times, and mock him as his face came bobbing up,—oh, what a rich treat that would be!"

"Quilp!" stammered his wife, venturing at the same time to touch him on the shoulder: "what has gone wrong?"

She was so terrified by the relish with which he pictured this pleasure to himself, that she could scarcely make herself intelligible.

"Such a bloodless cur!" said Quilp, rubbing his hands very slowly, and pressing them tight together. "I thought his cowardice and servility were the best guarantee for his keeping silence. Oh Brass, Brass—my dear, good, affectionate, faithful, complimentary, charming friend—if I only had you here!"

His wife, who had retreated lest she should seem to listen to these mutterings, ventured to approach him again, and was about to speak, when he hurried to the door and called Tom Scott, who, remembering his late gentle admonition, deemed it prudent to appear immediately.

"There!" said the dwarf, pulling him in. "Take her home. Don't come here to-morrow, for this place will be shut up. Come back no more till you hear from me or see me. Do you mind?"

Tom nodded sulkily, and beckoned Mrs. Quilp to lead the way.

"As for you," said the dwarf, addressing himself to her, "ask no questions about me, make no search for me, say nothing concerning me. I shall not be dead, mistress, and that'll comfort you. He'll take care of you."

"But, Quilp? What is the matter? Where are you going? Do say something more."

"I'll say that," said the dwarf, seizing her by the arm, "and do that too, which undone and unsaid would be best for you unless you go directly."

"Has anything happened?" cried his wife. "Oh! Do tell me that."

"Yes," snarled the dwarf. "No. What matter which? I have told you what to do. Woe betide you if you fail to do it, or disobey me by a hair's breadth. Will you go!"

"I am going, I'll go directly; but," faltered his wife, "answer me one question first. Has this letter any connexion with dear little Nell? I must ask you that—I must indeed, Quilp. You cannot think what days and nights of sorrow I have had through having once deceived that child. I don't know what harm I may have brought about, but, great or little, I did it for you, Quilp. My conscience misgave me when I did it. Do answer me this qustion, if you please."

The exasperated dwarf returned no answer, but turned round and caught up his usual weapon with such vehemence, that Tom Scott dragged his charge away by main force, and as swiftly as he could.

It was well he did so, for Quilp, who was nearly mad with rage,
pursued them to the neighbouring land, and might have prolonged
the chase, but for the dense mist which obscured them from his view,
and appeared to thicken every moment.

"It will be a good night for travelling anonymously," he said, as he
returned slowly, being pretty well breathed with his run. "Stay. We
may look better here. This is too hospitable and free."

By a great exertion of strength, he closed the two old gates which
were deeply sunken in the mud, and barred them with a heavy beam.
That done, he shook his matted hair from about his eyes, and tried
them.—Strong and fast.

"The fence between this wharf and the next is easily climbed," said
the dwarf, when he had taken these precautions. "There's a back
lane too from there. That shall be my way out. A man need know his
road well, to find it in this lovely place to-night. I need fear no unwelcome visitors while this lasts, I think."

Almost reduced to the necessity of groping his way with his
hands (it had grown so dark and the fog had so much increased), he
returned to his lair; and, after musing for some time over the fire,
busied himself in preparations for a speedy departure.

While he was collecting a few necessaries and cramming them into
his pockets, he never once ceased communing with himself in a low
voice, or unclenched his teeth, which he had ground together on
finishing Miss Brass's note.

"Oh Sampson!" he muttered, "good, worthy creature—if I could
but hug you! If I could only fold you in my arms, and squeeze your
ribs, as I *could* squeeze them if I once had you tight, what a meeting
there would be between us! If we ever do cross each other again,
Sampson, we'll have a greeting not easily to be forgotten, trust me.
This time, Sampson, this moment when all had gone on so well, was
so nicely chosen! It was so thoughtful of you, so penitent, so good.
Oh, if we were face to face in this room again, my white-livered man
of law, how well contented one of us would be!"

Then he stopped; and raising the bowl of punch to his lips, drank
a long deep draught, as if it were fair water and cooling to his parched
mouth. Setting it down abruptly, and resuming his preparations,
he went on with his soliloquy.

"There's Sally," he said with flashing eyes; "the woman has spirit,
determination, purpose—was she asleep, or petrified? She could have
stabbed him—poisoned him safely. She might have seen this coming
on. Why does she give me notice when it's too late? When he sat
there,—yonder there, over there,—with his white face, and red head,
and sickly smile, why didn't I know what was passing in his heart?
It should have stopped beating that night, if I had been in his secret;
or there are no drugs to lull a man to sleep, and fire to burn him!"

Another draught from the bowl; and, cowering over the fire with a
ferocious aspect, he muttered to himself again.

"And this, like every other trouble and anxiety I have had of
late times, springs from that old dotard and his darling child—two

wretched feeble wanderers! I'll be their evil genius yet. And you, sweet Kit, honest Kit, virtuous, innocent Kit, look to yourself. When I hate, I bite. I hate you, my darling fellow, with good cause, and proud as you are to-night, I'll have my turn.—What's that?"

A knocking at the gate he had closed. A loud and violent knocking. Then a pause; as if those who knocked had stopped to listen. Then the noise again, more clamorous and importunate than before.

"So soon!" said the dwarf. "And so eager! I am afraid I shall disappoint you. It's well I'm quite prepared. Sally, I thank you!"

As he spoke, he extinguished the candle. In his impetuous attempts to subdue the brightness of the fire, he overset the stove, which came tumbling forward, and fell with a crash upon the burning embers it had shot forth in its descent, leaving the room in pitchy darkness. The noise at the gate still continuing, he felt his way to the door, and stepped into the open air.

At that moment the knocking ceased. It was about eight o'clock; but the dead of the darkest night would have been as noon-day, in comparison with the thick cloud which then rested upon the earth, and shrouded everything from view. He darted forward for a few paces, as if into the mouth of some dim, yawning cavern; then, thinking he had gone wrong, changed the direction of his steps; then stood still, not knowing where to turn.

"If they would knock again," said Quilp, trying to peer into the gloom by which he was surrounded, "the sound might guide me. Come. Batter the gate once more!"

He stood listening intently, but the noise was not renewed. Nothing was to be heard in that deserted place, but at intervals the distant barking of dogs. The sound was far away—now in one quarter, now answered in another—nor was it any guide, for it often came from shipboard, as he knew.

"If I could find a wall or fence," said the dwarf, stretching out his arms, and walking slowly on, "I should know which way to turn. A good, black, devil's night this, to have my dear friend here! If I had but that wish, it might, for anything I cared, never be day again."

As the word passed his lips, he staggered and fell; and next moment was fighting with the cold dark water.

For all its bubbling up and rushing in his ears, he could hear the knocking at the gate again—could hear a shout that followed it—could recognise the voice. For all his struggling and plashing, he could understand that they had lost their way, and had wandered back to the point from which they started; that they were all but looking on while he was drowned; that they were close at hand, but could not make an effort to save him; and he himself had shut and barred them out. He answered the shout—with a yell, which seemed to make the hundred fires that danced before his eyes tremble and flicker as if a gust of wind had stirred them. It was of no avail. The strong tide filled his throat, and bore him on, upon its rapid current.

Another mortal struggle, and he was up again, beating the water with his hands, and looking out with wild and glaring eyes that showed him some black object he was drifting close upon. The hull of a ship! He could touch its smooth and slippery surface with his hand. One loud cry now—but the resistless water bore him down before he could give it utterance, and, driving him under it, carried away a corpse.

It toyed and sported with its ghastly freight, now bruising it against the slimy piles, now hiding it in mud or long rank grass, now dragging it heavily over rough stones and gravel, now feigning to yield it to its own element, and in the same action luring it away, until, tired of the ugly plaything, it flung it on a swamp—a dismal place where pirates had swung in chains, through many a wintry night—and left it there to bleach.

And there it lay, alone. The sky was red with flame, and the water that bore it there had been tinged with the sullen light as it flowed along. The place the deserted carcase had left so recently, a living man, was now a blazing ruin. There was something of the glare upon its face. The hair, stirred by the damp breeze, played in a kind of mockery of death—such a mockery as the dead man himself would have revelled in when alive—about its head, and its dress fluttered idly in the night wind.

CHAPTER LXVIII

LIGHTED rooms, bright fires, cheerful faces, the music of glad voices, words of love and welcome, warm hearts, and tears of happiness—what a change is this! But it is to such delights that Kit is hastening. They are awaiting him, he knows. He fears he will die of joy before he gets among them.

They have prepared him for this, all day. He is not to be carried off to-morrow with the rest, they tell him first. By degrees they let him know that doubts have arisen, that inquiries are to be made, and perhaps he may be pardoned after all. At last, the evening being come, they bring him to a room where some gentlemen are assembled. Foremost among them is his good old master, who comes and takes him by the hand. He hears that his innocence is established, and that he is pardoned. He cannot see the speaker, but he turns towards the voice, and in trying to answer, falls down insensible.

They recover him again, and tell him he must be composed, and bear this like a man. Somebody says he must think of his poor mother. It is because he does think of her so much, that the happy news has overpowered him. They crowd about him, and tell him that the truth has gone abroad, and that all the town and country ring with sympathy for his misfortunes. He has no ears for this. His thoughts as yet have no wider range than home. Does *she* know it? what did she say? who told her? He can speak of nothing else.

They make him drink a little wine, and talk kindly to him for a while, until he is more collected, and can listen, and thank them. He is free to go. Mr. Garland thinks, if he feels better, it is time they went away. The gentlemen cluster round him, and shake hands with him. He feels very grateful to them for the interest they have in him, and for the kind promises they make ; but the power of speech is gone again, and he has much ado to keep his feet, even though leaning on his master's arm.

As they pass through the dismal passages, some officers of the jail who are in waiting there, congratulate him in their rough way on his release. The newsmonger is of the number, but his manner is not quite hearty—there is something of surliness in his compliments. He looks upon Kit as an intruder, as one who has obtained admission to that place on false pretences, who has enjoyed a privilege without being duly qualified. He may be a very good sort of young man, he thinks, but he has no business there, and the sooner he is gone, the better.

The last door shuts behind them. They have passed the outer wall, and stand in the open air—in the street he has so often pictured to himself when hemmed in by those gloomy stones, and which has been in all his dreams. It seems wider and more busy than it used to be. The night is bad, and yet how cheerful and gay in his eyes! One of the gentlemen, in taking leave of him, pressed some money into his hand. He has not counted it; but when they have gone a few paces beyond the box for poor Prisoners, he hastily returns and drops it in.

Mr. Garland has a coach waiting in a neighbouring street, and, taking Kit inside with him, bids the man drive home. At first they can only travel at a foot pace, and then with torches going on before, because of the heavy fog. But as they get farther from the river, and leave the closer portions of the town behind, they are able to dispense with this precaution and to proceed at a brisker rate. On the road, hard galloping would be too slow for Kit; but when they are drawing near their journey's end, he begs they may go more slowly, and when the house appears in sight, that they may stop—only for a minute or two, to give him time to breathe.

But there is no stopping then, for the old gentleman speaks stoutly to him, the horses mend their pace, and they are already at the garden-gate. Next minute they are at the door. There is a noise of tongues, and tread of feet inside. It opens. Kit rushes in, and finds his mother clinging round his neck.

And there, too, is the ever faithful Barbara's mother, still holding the baby as if she had never put it down since that sad day when they little hoped to have such joy as this—there she is, Heaven bless her, crying her eyes out, and sobbing as never woman sobbed before; and there is little Barbara—poor little Barbara, so much thinner and so much paler, and yet so very pretty—trembling like a leaf and supporting herself against the wall; and there is Mrs. Garland, neater and nicer than ever, fainting away stone dead with nobody to help her; and there is Mr. Abel, violently blowing his nose, and wanting to embrace everybody; and there is the single gentleman hovering round them all, and constant to nothing for an instant; and there is that good, dear, thoughtful little Jacob, sitting all alone by himself on the bottom stair, with his hands on his knees like an old man, roaring fearfully without giving any trouble to anybody; and each and all of them are for the time clean out of their wits, and do jointly and severally commit all manner of follies.

And even when the rest have in some measure come to themselves again, and can find words and smiles, Barbara—that soft-hearted, gentle, foolish little Barbara—is suddenly missed, and found to be in a swoon by herself in the back parlour, from which swoon she falls into hysterics, and from which hysterics into a swoon again, and is, indeed, so bad, that despite a mortal quantity of vinegar and cold water she is hardly a bit better at last than she was at first. Then Kit's mother comes in and says, will he come and speak to her; and Kit says "Yes," and goes; and he says in a kind voice "Barbara!" and Barbara's mother tells her that "it's only Kit;" and Barbara says (with her eyes closed all the time) "Oh! but is it him indeed?" and Barbara's mother says "To be sure it is, my dear; there's nothing the matter now." And in further assurance that he's safe and sound, Kit speaks to her again; and then Barbara goes off into another fit of laughter, and then into another fit of crying; and then Barbara's mother and Kit's mother nod to each other and pretend to scold her —but only to bring her to herself the faster, bless you—and being experienced matrons, and acute at perceiving the first dawning symptoms of recovery, they comfort Kit with the assurance that "she'll do now," and so dismiss him to the place from whence he came.

Well! In that place (which is the next room) there are decanters of wine, and all that sort of thing, set out as grand as if Kit and his friends were first-rate company; and there is little Jacob, walking, as the popular phrase is, into a home-made plum-cake at a most surprising pace, and keeping his eye on the figs and oranges which are to follow, and making the best use of his time, you may believe. Kit no sooner comes in, than that single gentleman (never was such a busy gentleman) charges all the glasses—bumpers —and drinks his health, and tells him he shall never want a friend while he lives; and so does Mr. Garland, and so does Mrs. Garland, and so does Mr. Abel. But even this honour and distinction is not all, for the single gentleman forthwith pulls out of his pocket a massive silver watch—going hard, and right to half a second—and upon the back of this watch is engraved Kit's name, with flourishes all over; and in short it is Kit's watch, bought expressly for him, and presented to him on the spot. You may rest assured that Mr. and Mrs. Garland can't help hinting about their present, in store, and that Mr. Abel tells outright that he has his; and that Kit is the happiest of the happy.

There is one friend he has not seen yet, and as he cannot be conveniently introduced into the family circle, by reason of his being an iron-shod quadruped. Kit takes the first opportunity of slipping away and hurrying to the stable. The moment he lays his hand upon the latch, the pony neighs the loudest pony's greeting; before he has crossed the threshold, the pony is capering about his loose box (for he brooks not the indignity of a halter), mad to give him welcome; and when Kit goes up to caress and pat him, the pony rubs his nose against his coat, and fondles him more lovingly than ever pony fondled man. It is the crowning circumstance of his earnest, heart-felt reception; and Kit fairly puts his arm round Whisker's neck and hugs him.

But how comes Barbara to trip in there? and how smart she is again! she has been at her glass since she recovered. How comes Barbara in the stable, of all places in the world? Why, since Kit has been away, the pony would take his food from nobody but her, and Barbara, you see, not dreaming Christopher was there, and just looking in to see that everything was right, has come upon him unawares. Blushing little Barbara!

It may be that Kit has caressed the pony enough; it may be that there are even better things to caress than ponies. He leaves him for Barbara at any rate, and hopes she is better. Yes. Barbara is a great deal better. She is afraid—and here Barbara looks down and blushes more—that he must have thought her very foolish. "Not at all," says Kit. Barbara is glad of that, and coughs—Hem!—just the slightest cough possible—not more than that.

What a discreet pony, when he chooses! He is as quiet now, as if he were of marble. He has a very knowing look, but that he always has. "We have hardly had time to shake hands, Barbara," says Kit. Barbara gives him hers. Why, she is trembling now! Foolish, fluttering Barbara!

Arm's length! The length of an arm is not much. Barbara's was not a long arm by any means, and besides, she didn't hold it out straight, but bent a little. Kit was so near her when they shook hands, that he could see a small tiny tear, yet trembling on an eyelash. It was natural that he should look at it, unknown to Barbara. It was natural that Barbara should raise her eyes unconsciously, and find him out. Was it natural that at that instant, without any previous impulse or design, Kit should kiss Barbara? He did it, whether or no. Barbara said "for shame," but let him do it too—twice. He might have done it thrice, but the pony kicked up his heels and shook his head, as if he were suddenly taken with convulsions of delight, and Barbara being frightened, ran away—not straight to where her mother and Kit's mother were, though, lest they should see how red her cheeks were, and should ask her why. Sly little Barbara!

When the first transports of the whole party had subsided, and Kit and his mother, and Barbara and her mother, with little Jacob and the baby to boot, had had their suppers together—which there was no hurrying over, for they were going to stop there all night—Mr. Garland called Kit to him, and taking him into a room where they could be alone, told him that he had something yet to say, which would surprise him greatly. Kit looked so anxious and turned so pale on hearing this, that the old gentleman hastened to add, he would be agreeably surprised; and asked him if he would be ready next morning for a journey.

"For a journey, sir!" cried Kit.

"In company with me and my friend in the next room. Can you guess its purpose?"

Kit turned paler yet, and shook his head.

"Oh yes. I think you do already," said his master. "Try."

Kit murmured something rather rambling and unintelligible, but he plainly pronounced the words "Miss Nell," three or four times—shaking his head while he did so, as if he would add there was no hope of that.

But Mr. Garland, instead of saying "Try again," as Kit had made sure he would, told him very seriously that he had guessed right.

"The place of their retreat is indeed discovered," he said, "at last. And that is our journey's end."

Kit faltered out such questions as, where was it, and how had it been found, and how long since, and was she well, and happy?

"Happy she is, beyond all doubt," said Mr. Garland. "And well, I—I trust she will be soon. She has been weak and ailing, as I learn, but she was better when I heard this morning, and they were full of hope. Sit you down, and you shall hear the rest."

Scarcely venturing to draw his breath, Kit did as he was told. Mr. Garland then related to him, how he had a brother (of whom he would remember to have heard him speak, and whose picture, taken when he was a young man, hung in the best room), and how this brother lived a long way off in a country-place, with an old clergyman who had been his early friend. How, although they loved each other as brothers should, they had not met for many years, but had communicated by letter from time to time, always looking forward to some period when they would take each other by the hand once more, and still letting the Present time steal on, as it was the habit of men to do, and suffering the Future to melt into the Past. How this brother, whose temper was very mild and quiet and retiring—such as Mr. Abel's—was greatly beloved by the simple people among whom he dwelt, who quite revered the Bachelor (for so they called him), and had every one experienced his charity and benevolence. How even those slight circumstances had come to his knowledge, very slowly and in course of years, for the Bachelor was one of those whose goodness shuns the light, and who have more pleasure in discovering and extolling the good deeds of others, than in trumpeting their own, be they never so commendable. How, for that reason, he seldom told them of his village friends; but how, for all that, his mind had become so full of two among them—a child and an old man, to whom he had been very kind—that, in a letter received a few days before, he had dwelt upon them from first to last, and had told there such a tale of their wanderings, and mutual love, that few could read it without being moved to tears. How he, the recipient of that letter, was directly led to the belief that these must be the very wanderers for whom so much search had been made, and whom Heaven had directed to his brother's care. How he had written for such further information as would put the fact beyond all doubt; how it had that morning arrived; had confirmed his first impression into a certainty; and was the immediate cause of that journey being planned, which they were to take to-morrow.

"In the meantime," said the old gentleman rising, and laying his hand on Kit's shoulder, "you have great need of rest, for such a day as this would wear out the strongest man. Good night, and Heaven send our journey may have a prosperous ending!"

CHAPTER LXIX

KIT was no sluggard next morning, but, springing from his bed some time before day, began to prepare for his welcome expedition. The hurry of spirits consequent upon the events of yesterday, and the unexpected intelligence he had heard at night, had troubled his sleep through the long dark hours, and summoned such uneasy dreams about his pillow that it was rest to rise.

But had it been the beginning of some great labour with the same end in view—had it been the commencement of a long journey, to be performed on foot in that inclement season of the year; to be pursued under every privation and difficulty; and to be achieved only with great distress, fatigue, and suffering—had it been the dawn of some painful enterprise, certain to task his utmost powers of resolution and endurance, and to need his utmost fortitude, but only likely to end, if happily achieved, in good fortune and delight to Nell—Kit's cheerful zeal would have been as highly roused, Kit's ardour and impatience would have been at least the same.

Nor was he alone excited and eager. Before he had been up a quarter of an hour the whole house were astir and busy. Everybody hurried to do something towards facilitating the preparations. The single gentleman, it is true, could do nothing himself, but he overlooked everybody else and was more locomotive than anybody. The work of packing and making ready went briskly on, and by daybreak every preparation for the journey was completed. Then Kit began to wish they had not been quite so nimble; for the travelling-carriage which had been hired for the occasion was not to arrive until nine o'clock, and there was nothing but breakfast to fill up the intervening blank of one hour and a half.

Yes there was, though. There was Barbara. Barbara was busy, to be sure, but so much the better—Kit could help her, and that would pass away the time better than any means that could be devised. Barbara had no objection to this arrangement, and Kit, tracking out the idea which had come upon him so suddenly overnight, began to think that surely Barbara was fond of him, and surely he was fond of Barbara.

Now, Barbara, if the truth must be told—as it must and ought to

be—Barbara seemed, of all the little household, to take least pleasure
in the bustle of the occasion; and when Kit, in the openness of his
heart, told her how glad and overjoyed it made him, Barbara became
more downcast still, and seemed to have even less pleasure in it than
before!

"You have not been home so long, Christopher," said Barbara—
and it is impossible to tell how carelessly she said it—"You have not
been home so long, that you need be glad to go away again, I should
think."

"But for such a purpose," returned Kit. "To bring back Miss Nell!
To see her again! Only think of that! I am so pleased too, to think
that *you* will see her, Barbara, at last."

Barbara did not absolutely say that she felt no great gratification
on this point, but she expressed the sentiment so plainly by one little
toss of her head, that Kit was quite disconcerted, and wondered in
his simplicity why she was so cool about it.

"You'll say she has the sweetest and beautifullest face you ever
saw, I know," said Kit, rubbing his hands. "I'm sure you'll say that!"

Barbara tossed her head again.

"What's the matter, Barbara?" said Kit.

"Nothing," cried Barbara. And Barbara pouted—not sulkily, or
in an ugly manner, but just enough to make her look more cherry-
lipped than ever.

There is no school in which a pupil gets on so fast, as that in which
Kit became a scholar when he gave Barbara the kiss. He saw what
Barbara meant now—he had his lesson by heart all at once—she was
the book—there it was before him as plain as print.

"Barbara," said Kit, "you're not cross with me?"

Oh dear no! Why should Barbara be cross? And what right had
she to be cross? And what did it matter whether she was cross or no?
Who minded *her!*

"Why, *I* do," said Kit. "Of course I do."

Barbara didn't see why it was of course, at all.

Kit was sure she must. Would she think again?

Certainly, Barbara would think again. No, she didn't see why it was
of course. She didn't understand what Christopher meant. And besides she was sure they wanted her up stairs by this time, and she
must go, indeed——

"No, but Barbara," said Kit, detaining her gently, "let us part
friends. I was always thinking of you, in my troubles. I should have
been a great deal more miserable than I was, if it hadn't been for
you."

Goodness gracious, how pretty Barbara was when she coloured—
and when she trembled, like a little shrinking bird!

"I am telling you the truth, Barbara, upon my word, but not half
so strong as I could wish," said Kit, earnestly. "When I want you to
be pleased to see Miss Nell, it's only because I like you to be pleased
with what pleases me—that's all. As to her, Barbara, I think I could
almost die to do her service, but you would think so too if you knew

her as I do. I am sure you would."

Barbara was touched, and sorry to have appeared indifferent.

"I have been used, you see," said Kit, "to talk and think of her, almost as if she was an angel. When I look forward to meeting her again, I think of her smiling as she used to do, and being glad to see me, and putting out her hand and saying, 'It's my own old Kit,' or some such words as those—like what she used to say. I think of seeing her happy, and with friends about her, and brought up as she deserves, and as she ought to be. When I think of myself, it's as her old servant, and one that loved her dearly, as his kind, good, gentle mistress; and who would have gone—yes, and still would go—through any harm to serve her. Once I couldn't help being afraid that if she came back with friends about her she might forget, or be ashamed of having known, a humble lad like me, and so speak coldly, which would have cut me, Barbara, deeper than I can tell. But when I came to think again, I felt sure that I was doing her wrong in this; and so I went on as I did at first, hoping to see her once more, just as she used to be. Hoping this, and remembering what she was, has made me feel as if I would always try to please her, and always be what I should like to seem to her if I was still her servant. If I'm the better for that—and I don't think I'm the worse—I am grateful to her for it, and love and honour her the more. That's the plain honest truth, dear Barbara, upon my word it is!"

Little Barbara was not of a wayward or capricious nature, and, being full of remorse, melted into tears. To what further conversation this might have led, we need not stop to inquire; for the wheels of the carriage were heard at that moment, and, being followed by a smart ring at the garden-gate, caused the bustle in the house, which had lain dormant for a short time, to burst again into tenfold life and vigour.

Simultaneously with the travelling equipage, arrived Mr. Chuckster in a hackney-cab, with certain papers and supplies of money for the single gentleman, into whose hands he delivered them. This duty discharged, he subsided into the bosom of the family; and entertaining himself with a strolling or peripatetic breakfast, watched with a genteel indifference the process of loading the carriage.

"Snobby's in this, I see, sir?" he said to Mr. Abel Garland. "I thought he wasn't in the last trip because it was expected that his presence wouldn't be very acceptable to the ancient buffalo."

"To whom, sir?" demanded Mr. Abel.

"To the old gentleman," returned Mr. Chuckster, slightly abashed.

"Our client prefers to take him now," said Mr. Abel, dryly. "There is no longer any need for that precaution, as my father's relationship to a gentleman in whom the objects of his search have full confidence, will be a sufficient guarantee for the friendly nature of their errand."

"Ah!" thought Mr. Chuckster, looking out of window, "anybody but me! Snobby before me, of course. He didn't happen to take that particular five-pound note, but I have not the smallest doubt that he's always up to something of that sort. I always said it, long before this came out. Devilish pretty girl that! 'Pon my soul, an amazing little creature!"

Barbara was the subject of Mr. Chuckster's commendations; and as she was lingering near the carriage (all being now ready for its departure), that gentleman was suddenly seized with a strong interest in the proceedings, which impelled him to swagger down the garden, and take up his position at a convenient ogling distance. Having had great experience of the sex, and being perfectly acquainted with all those little artifices which find the readiest road to their hearts, Mr. Chuckster, on taking his ground, planted one hand on his hip, and with the other adjusted his flowing hair. This is a favourite attitude in the polite circles, and accompanied with a graceful whistling has been known to do immense execution.

Such, however, is the difference between town and country, that nobody took the smallest notice of this insinuating figure; the wretches being wholly engaged in bidding the travellers farewell, in kissing hands to each other, waving handkerchiefs, and the like tame and vulgar practices. For now the single gentleman and Mr. Garland were in the carriage, and the postboy was in the saddle, and Kit, well wrapped and muffled up, was in the rumble behind; and Mrs. Garland was there, and Mr. Abel was there, and Kit's mother was there, and little Jacob was there, and Barbara's mother was visible in remote perspective, nursing the ever-wakeful baby; and all were nodding, beckoning, curtseying, or crying out "Good-bye!" with all the energy they could express. In another minute, the carriage was out of sight; and Mr. Chuckster remained alone upon the spot where it had lately been, with a vision of Kit standing up in the rumble waving his hand to Barbara, and of Barbara in the full light and lustre of his eyes—*his* eyes—Chuckster's—Chuckster the successful —on whom ladies of quality had looked with favour from phaetons in the parks on Sundays—waving hers to Kit!

How Mr. Chuckster, entranced by this monstrous fact, stood for some time rooted to the earth, protesting within himself that Kit was the Prince of felonious characters, and very Emperor or Great Mogul of Snobs, and how he clearly traced this revolting circumstance back to that old villany of the shilling, are matters foreign to our purpose; which is to track the rolling wheels, and bear the travellers company on their cold, bleak journey.

It was a bitter day. A keen wind was blowing, and rushed against them fiercely: bleaching the hard ground, shaking the white frost from the trees and hedges, and whirling it away like dust. But little cared Kit for weather. There was a freedom and freshness in the wind, as it came howling by, which, let it cut never so sharp, was welcome. As it swept on with its cloud of frost, bearing down the dry twigs and boughs and withered leaves, and carrying them away pell-mell, it seemed as though some general sympathy had got abroad, and everything was in a hurry like themselves. The harder the gusts, the better progress they appeared to make. It was a good thing to go struggling and fighting forward, vanquishing them one by one; to watch them driving up, gathering strength and fury as they came along; to bend for a moment, as they whistled past; and then to look back and see them speed away, their hoarse noise dying in the distance, and the stout trees cowering down before them.

All day long it blew without cessation. The night was clear and starlight, but the wind had not fallen, and the cold was piercing. Sometimes—towards the end of a long stage—Kit could not help wishing it were a little warmer; but when they stopped to change horses, and he had had a good run; and what with that, and the bustle of paying the old postilion, and rousing the new one, and running to and fro again until the horses were put to, he was so warm that the blood tingled and smarted in his fingers' ends; then he felt as if to have it one degree less cold would be to lose half the delight and glory of the journey: and up he jumped again right cheerily, singing to the merry music of the wheels as they rolled away, and, leaving the townspeople in their warm beds, pursued their course along the lonely road.

Meantime the two gentlemen inside, who were little disposed to sleep, beguiled the time with conversation. As both were anxious and expectant, it naturally turned upon the subject of their expedition, on the manner in which it had been brought about, and on the hopes and fears they entertained respecting it. Of the former they had many, of the latter few—none perhaps beyond that indefinable uneasiness which is inseparable from suddenly awakened hope, and protracted expectation.

In one of the pauses of their discourse, and when half the night had worn away, the single gentleman, who had gradually become more and more silent and thoughtful, turned to his companion and said abruptly:

"Are you a good listener?"

"Like most other men, I suppose," returned Mr. Garland, smiling. "I can be, if I am interested; and if not interested I should still try to appear so. Why do you ask?"

"I have a short narrative on my lips," rejoined his friend, "and will try you with it. It is very brief."

Pausing for no reply, he laid his hand on the old gentleman's sleeve, and proceeded thus:

"There were once two brothers, who loved each other dearly. There was a disparity in their ages—some twelve years. I am not sure but they may insensibly have loved each other the better for that reason. Wide as the interval between them was, however, they became rivals too soon. The deepest and strongest affection of both their hearts settled upon one object.

"The youngest—there were reasons for *his* being sensitive and watchful—was the first to find this out. I will not tell you what misery he underwent, what agony of soul he knew, how great his mental struggle was. He had been a sickly child. His brother, patient and considerate in the midst of his own high health and strength, had many and many a day denied himself the sports he loved, to sit beside his couch, telling him old stories till his pale face lighted up with an unwonted glow; to carry him in his arms to some green spot, where he could tend the poor pensive boy as he looked upon the bright summer day, and saw all nature healthy but himself; to be in any way his fond and faithful nurse. I may not dwell on all he did, to make the poor, weak creature love him, or my tale would have no end. But when the time of trial came, the younger brother's heart was full of those old days. Heaven strengthened it to repay the sacrifices of inconsiderate youth by one of thoughtful manhood. He left his brother to be happy. The truth never passed his lips, and he quitted the country, hoping to die abroad.

"The elder brother married her. She was in Heaven before long, and left him with an infant daughter.

"If you have seen the picture-gallery of any one old family, you will remember how the same face and figure—often the fairest and slightest of them all—come upon you in different generations; and how you trace the same sweet girl through a long line of portraits—never growing old or changing—the Good Angel of the race—abiding by them in all reverses—redeeming all their sins——

"In this daughter the mother lived again. You may judge with what devotion he who lost that mother almost in the winning, clung to this girl, her breathing image. She grew to womanhood, and gave her heart to one who could not know its worth. Well! Her fond father could not see her pine and droop. He might be more deserving than he thought him. He surely might become so with a wife like her. He joined their hands, and they were married.

"Through all the misery which followed this union; through all the cold neglect and undeserved reproach; through all the poverty he brought upon her; through all the struggles of their daily life, too mean and pitiful to tell, but dreadful to endure; she toiled on, in the deep devotion of her spirit, and in her better nature, as only women can. Her means and substance wasted; her father nearly beggared by her husband's hand, and the hourly witness (for they lived now under one roof) of her ill-usage and unhappiness,—she never, but for him, bewailed her fate. Patient, and upheld by strong affection to the last, she died a widow of some three weeks' date, leaving to her father's care two orphans; one a son of ten or twelve years old; the other a girl—such another infant child—the same in helplessness, in age, in form, in feature—as she had been herself when her young mother died.

"The elder brother, grandfather of these two children, was now a broken man; crushed and borne down, less by the weight of years than by the heavy hand of sorrow. With the wreck of his possessions he began to trade—in pictures first, and then in curious ancient things. He had entertained a fondness for such matters from a boy, and the tastes he had cultivated were now to yield him an anxious and precarious subsistence.

"The boy grew like his father in mind and person; the girl so like her mother, that when the old man had her on his knee, and looked into her mild blue eyes, he felt as if awakening from a wretched dream, and his daughter were a little child again. The wayward boy soon spurned the shelter of his roof, and sought associates more congenial to his taste. The old man and the child dwelt alone together.

"It was then, when the love of two dead people who had been nearest and dearest to his heart, was all transferred to this slight creature; when her face, constantly before him, reminded him from hour to hour of the too early change he had seen in such another—of all the suffering he had watched and known, and all his child had undergone; when the young man's profligate and hardened course drained him of money as his father's had, and even sometimes occasioned them temporary privation and distress; it was then that there began to beset him, and to be ever in his mind, a gloomy dread of poverty and want. He had no thought for himself in this. His fear was for the child. It was a spectre in his house, and haunted him night and day.

"The younger brother had been a traveller in many countries, and had made his pilgrimage through life alone. His voluntary banishment had been misconstrued, and he had borne (not without pain) reproach and slight for doing that which had wrung his heart, and cast a mournful shadow on his path. Apart from this, communication between him and the elder was difficult, and uncertain, and often failed; still it was not so wholly broken off but that he learnt—with long blanks and gaps between each interval of information—all that I have told you now.

"Then, dreams of their young, happy life—happy to him though laden with pain and early care—visited his pillow yet oftener than before; and every night, a boy again, he was at his brother's side. With the utmost speed he could exert, he settled his affairs; converted into money all the goods he had; and, with honourable wealth enough for both, with open heart and hand, with limbs that trembled as they bore him on, with emotion such as men can hardly bear and live, arrived one evening at his brother's door!"

The narrator, whose voice had faltered lately, stopped. "The rest," said Mr. Garland, pressing his hand, "I know."

"Yes," rejoined his friend after a pause, "we may spare ourselves the sequel. You know the poor result of all my search. Even when, by dint of such inquiries as the utmost vigilance and sagacity could set on foot, we found they had been seen with two poor travelling showmen; and in time discovered the men themselves—and in time, the actual place of their retreat; even then, we were too late. Pray God we are not too late again!"

"We cannot be," said Mr. Garland. "This time we must succeed."

"I have believed and hoped so," returned the other. "I try to believe and hope so still. But a heavy weight has fallen on my spirits, my good friend, and the sadness that gathers over me, will yield to neither hope nor reason."

"That does not surprise me," said Mr. Garland; "it is a natural consequence of the events you have recalled; of this dreary time and place; and above all, of this wild and dismal night. A dismal night, indeed! Hark! how the wind is howling!"

CHAPTER LXX

DAY broke, and found them still upon their way. Since leaving home, they had halted here and there for necessary refreshment, and had frequently been delayed, especially in the night time, by waiting for fresh horses. They had made no other stoppages; but the weather continued rough, and the roads were often steep and heavy. It would be night again before they reached their place of destination.

Kit, all bluff and hardened with the cold, went on manfully; and having enough to do to keep his blood circulating, to picture to himself the happy end of this adventurous journey, and to look about him and be amazed at everything, had little spare time for thinking of discomforts. Though his impatience, and that of his fellow-travellers, rapidly increased as the day waned, the hours did not stand still. The short daylight of winter soon faded away, and it was dark again when they had yet many miles to travel.

As it grew dusk, the wind fell; its distant moanings were more low and mournful; and as it came creeping up the road, and rattling covertly among the dry brambles on either hand, it seemed like some great phantom for whom the way was narrow, whose garments rustled as it stalked along. By degrees it lulled and died away; and then it came on to snow.

The flakes fell fast and thick, soon covering the ground some inches deep, and spreading abroad a solemn stillness. The rolling wheels were noiseless; and the sharp ring and clatter of the horses' hoofs, became a dull, muffled tramp. The life of their progress seemed to be slowly hushed, and something death-like to usurp its place.

Shading his eyes from the falling snow, which froze upon their lashes and obscured his sight, Kit often tried to catch the earliest glimpse of twinkling lights denoting their approach to some not distant town. He could descry objects enough at such times, but none correctly. Now a tall church-spire appeared in view, which presently became a tree, a barn, a shadow on the ground, thrown on it by their own bright lamps. Now there were horsemen, foot-passengers, carriages, going on before, or meeting them in narrow ways; which, when they were close upon them, turned to shadows too. A wall, a ruin, a sturdy gable-end, would rise up in the road; and when they were plunging headlong at it, would be the road itself. Strange turnings too, bridges, and sheets of water, appeared to start up here and there, making the way doubtful and uncertain; and yet they were on the same bare road, and these things, like the others, as they were passed, turned into dim illusions.

He descended slowly from his seat—for his limbs were numbed—when they arrived at a lone posting-house, and inquired how far they had to go to reach their journey's end. It was a late hour in such by-places, and the people were abed; but a voice answered from an upper window, Ten miles. The ten minutes that ensued appeared an hour; but at the end of that time, a shivering figure led out the horses they required, and after another brief delay they were again in motion.

It was a cross-country road, full, after the first three or four miles, of holes and cart-ruts, which, being covered by the snow, were so many pitfalls to the trembling horses, and obliged them to keep a footpace. As it was next to impossible for men so much agitated as they were by this time, to sit still and move so slowly, all three got out and plodded on behind the carriage. The distance seemed interminable, and the walk was most laborious. As each was thinking within himself that the driver must have lost his way, a church bell, close at hand, struck the hour of midnight, and the carriage stopped. It had moved softly enough, but when it ceased to crunch the snow, the silence was as startling as if some great noise had been replaced by perfect stillness.

"This is the place, gentlemen," said the driver, dismounting from his horse, and knocking at the door of a little inn. "Halloa! Past twelve o'clock is the dead of night here."

The knocking was loud and long, but it failed to rouse the drowsy inmates. All continued dark and silent as before. They fell back a little and looked up at the windows, which were mere black patches, in the whitened house front. No light appeared. The house might have been deserted, or the sleepers dead, for any air of life it had about it.

They spoke together, with a strange inconsistency, in whispers; unwilling to disturb again the dreary echoes they had just now raised.

"Let us go on," said the younger brother, "and leave this good fellow to wake them, if he can. I cannot rest until I know that we are not too late. Let us go on, in the name of Heaven!"

They did so, leaving the postilion to order such accommodation as the house afforded, and to renew his knocking. Kit accompanied them with a little bundle, which he had hung in the carriage when they left home, and had not forgotten since—the bird in his old cage —just as she had left him. She would be glad to see her bird, he knew.

The road wound gently downward. As they proceeded, they lost sight of the church whose clock they had heard, and of the small village clustering round it. The knocking, which was now renewed, and which in that stillness they could plainly hear, troubled them. They wished the man would forbear, or that they had told him not to break the silence until they returned.

The old church-tower, clad in a ghostly garb of pure cold white, again rose up before them, and a few moments brought them close beside it. A venerable building—grey, even in the midst of the hoary landscape. An ancient sundial on the belfry wall was nearly hidden by the snow-drift, and scarcely to be known for what it was. Time itself seemed to have grown dull and old, as if no day were ever to displace the melancholy night.

A wicket-gate was close at hand, but there was more than one path across the churchyard to which it led, and, uncertain which to take, they came to a stand again.

The village street—if street that could be called which was an irregular cluster of poor cottages of many heights and ages, some with their fronts, some with their backs, and some with gable-ends towards the road, with here and there a sign-post, or a shed encroaching on the path—was close at hand. There was a faint light in a chamber window not far off, and Kit ran towards that house to ask their way.

His first shout was answered by an old man within, who presently appeared at the casement, wrapping some garment round his throat as a protection from the cold, and demanded who was abroad at that unseasonable hour, wanting him.

"'Tis hard weather this," he grumbled, "and not a night to call me up in. My trade is not of that kind that I need be roused from bed. The business on which folks want me, will keep cold, especially at this season. What do you want?"

"I would not have roused you, if I had known you were old and ill," said Kit.

"Old!" repeated the other peevishly. "How do you know I am old? Not so old as you think, friend, perhaps. As to being ill, you will find many young people in worse case than I am. More's the pity that it should be so—not that I should be strong and hearty for my years, I mean, but that they should be weak and tender. I ask your pardon though," said the old man, "if I spoke rather rough at first. My eyes are not good at night—that's neither age nor illness; they never were—and I didn't see you were a stranger."

"I am sorry to call you from your bed," said Kit, "but those gentlemen you may see by the churchyard gate, are strangers too, who have just arrived from a long journey, and seek the parsonage-house. You can direct us?"

"I should be able to," answered the old man, in a trembling voice, "for come next summer I have been sexton here good fifty years. The right-hand path, friend, is the road.—There is no ill news for our good gentleman, I hope?"

Kit thanked him, and made him a hasty answer in the negative; he was turning back, when his attention was caught by the voice of a child. Looking up, he saw a very little creature at a neighbouring window.

"What is that?" cried the child, earnestly. "Has my dream come true? Pray speak to me, whoever that is, awake and up."

"Poor boy!" said the sexton, before Kit could answer, "how goes it, darling?"

"Has my dream come true?" exclaimed the child again, in a voice so fervent that it might have thrilled to the heart of any listener. "But no, that can never be. How could it be—Oh! how could it!"

"I guess his meaning," said the sexton. "To thy bed again, dear boy!"

"Ay!" cried the child, in a burst of despair, "I knew it could never be, I felt too sure of that, before I asked. But, all to-night and last night too, it was the same. I never fall asleep, but that cruel dream comes back."

"Try to sleep again," said the old man, soothingly. "It will go, in time."

"No no, I would rather that it staid—cruel as it is, I would rather that it staid," rejoined the child. "I am not afraid to have it in my sleep, but I am so sad—so very, very sad."

The old man blessed him, the child in tears replied Good night, and Kit was again alone.

He hurried back, moved by what he had heard, though more by the child's manner than by anything he had said, as his meaning was hidden from him. They took the path indicated by the sexton, and soon arrived before the parsonage wall. Turning round to look about them when they had got thus far, they saw, among some ruined buildings at a distance, one single solitary light.

It shone from what appeared to be an old oriel window, and being surrounded by the deep shadows of overhanging walls, sparkled like a star. Bright and glimmering as the stars above their heads, lonely and motionless as they, it seemed to claim some kindred with the eternal lamps of Heaven, and to burn in fellowship with them.

"What light is that!" exclaimed the younger brother.

"It is surely," said Mr. Garland, "in the ruin where they live. I see no other ruin hereabouts."

"They cannot," returned the brother hastily, "be waking at this late hour—"

Kit interposed directly, and begged that, while they rang and waited at the gate, they would let him make his way to where this light was shining and try to ascertain if any people were about. Obtaining the permission he desired, he darted off with breathless eagerness, and, still carrying the birdcage in his hand, made straight towards the spot.

It was not easy to hold that pace among the graves, and at another time he might have gone more slowly, or round by the path. Unmindful of all obstacles, however, he pressed forward without slackening his speed, and soon arrived within a few yards of the window.

He approached as softly as he could, and advancing so near the wall as to brush the whitened ivy with his dress, listened. There was no sound inside. The church itself was not more quiet. Touching the glass with his cheek, he listened again. No. And yet there was such a silence all around, that he felt sure he could have heard even the breathing of a sleeper, if there had been one there.

A strange circumstance, a light in such a place at that time of night, with no one near it.

A curtain was drawn across the lower portion of the window, and he could not see into the room. But there was no shadow thrown upon it from within. To have gained a footing on the wall and tried to look in from above, would have been attended with some danger —certainly with some noise, and the chance of terrifying the child, if that really were her habitation. Again and again he listened; again and again the same wearisome blank.

Leaving the spot with slow and cautious steps, and skirting the ruin for a few paces, he came at length to a door. He knocked. No answer. But there was a curious noise inside. It was difficult to determine what it was. It bore a resemblance to the low moaning of one in pain, but it was not that, being far too regular and constant. Now it seemed a kind of song, now a wail—seemed, that is, to his changing fancy, for the sound itself was never changed or checked. It was unlike anything he had ever heard, and in its tone there was something fearful, chilling, and unearthly.

The listener's blood ran colder now than ever it had done in frost and snow, but he knocked again. There was no answer, and the sound went on without any interruption. He laid his hand softly upon the latch, and put his knee against the door. It was not secured on the inside, but yielded to the pressure, and turned upon its hinges. He saw the glimmering of a fire upon the old walls, and entered.

CHAPTER LXXI

THE dull, red glow of a wood fire—for no lamp or candle burnt within the room—showed him a figure, seated on the hearth with its back towards him, bending over the fitful light. The attitude was that of one who sought the heat. It was, and yet was not. The stooping posture and the cowering form were there, but no hands were stretched out to meet the grateful warmth, no shrug or shiver compared its luxury with the piercing cold outside. With limbs huddled together, head bowed down, arms crossed upon the breast, and fingers tightly clenched, it rocked to and fro upon its seat without a moment's pause, accompanying the action with the mournful sound he had heard.

The heavy door had closed behind him on his entrance, with a crash that made him start. The figure neither spoke nor turned to look, nor gave in any other way the faintest sign of having heard the noise. The form was that of an old man, his white head akin in colour to the mouldering embers upon which he gazed. He, and the failing light and dying fire, the time-worn room, the solitude, the wasted life, and gloom, were all in fellowship. Ashes, and dust, and ruin!

Kit tried to speak, and did pronounce some words, though what they were he scarcely knew. Still the same terrible low cry went on —still the same rocking in the chair—the same stricken figure was there, unchanged and heedless of his presence.

He had his hand upon the latch, when something in the form—distinctly seen as one log broke and fell, and, as it fell, blazed up—arrested it. He returned to where he had stood before—advanced a pace—another—another still. Another, and he saw the face. Yes! Changed as it was, he knew it well.

"Master!" he cried, stooping on one knee and catching at his hand. "Dear master. Speak to me!"

The old man turned slowly towards him; and muttered, in a hollow voice,

"This is another!—How many of these spirits there have been to-night!"

"No spirit, master. No one but your old servant. You know me now, I am sure? Miss Nell—where is she—where is she?"

"They all say that!" cried the old man. "They all ask the same question. A spirit!"

"Where is she?" demanded Kit. "Oh tell me but that—but that, dear master!"

"She is asleep—yonder—in there."

"Thank God!"

"Ay! Thank God!" returned the old man. "I have prayed to Him, many, and many, and many a livelong night, when she has been asleep, He knows. Hark! Did she call?"

"I heard no voice."

"You did. You hear her now. Do you tell me that you don't hear *that?*"

He started up, and listened again.

"Nor that?" he cried, with a triumphant smile. "Can anybody know that voice so well as I! Hush! hush!"

Motioning to him to be silent, he stole away into another chamber. After a short absence (during which he could be heard to speak in a softened soothing tone) he returned, bearing in his hand a lamp.

"She is still asleep," he whispered. "You were right. She did not call—unless she did so in her slumber. She has called to me in her sleep before now, sir; as I sat by, watching, I have seen her lips move, and have known, though no sound came from them, that she spoke of me. I feared the light might dazzle her eyes and wake her, so I brought it here."

He spoke rather to himself than to the visitor, but when he had put the lamp upon the table, he took it up, as if impelled by some momentary recollection or curiosity, and held it near his face. Then, as if forgetting his motive in the very action, he turned away and put it down again.

"She is sleeping soundly," he said; "but no wonder. Angel hands have strewn the ground deep with snow, that the lightest footstep may be lighter yet; and the very birds are dead, that they may not wake her. She used to feed them, sir. Though never so cold and hungry, the timid things would fly from us. They never flew from her!"

Again he stopped to listen, and scarcely drawing breath, listened for a long, long time. That fancy past, he opened an old chest, took out some clothes as fondly as if they had been living things, and began to smooth and brush them with his hand.

"Why dost thou lie so idle there, dear Nell," he murmured, "when there are bright red berries out of doors waiting for thee to pluck them! Why dost thou lie so idle there, when thy little friends come creeping to the door, crying 'where is Nell—sweet Nell?'—and sob, and weep, because they do not see thee. She was always gentle with children. The wildest would do her bidding—she had a tender way with them, indeed she had!"

Kit had no power to speak. His eyes were filled with tears.

"Her little homely dress,—her favourite!" cried the old man, pressing it to his breast, and patting it with his shrivelled hand. "She will miss it when she wakes. They have hid it here in sport, but she shall have it—she shall have it. I would not vex my darling, for the wide world's riches. See here—these shoes—how worn they are—she kept them to remind her of our last long journey. You see where the little feet were bare upon the ground. They told me, afterwards, that the stones had cut and bruised them. *She* never told me that. No, no, God bless her! and, I have remembered since, she walked behind me, sir, that I might not see how lame she was—but yet she had my hand in hers, and seemed to lead me still."

He pressed them to his lips, and having carefully put them back again, went on communing with himself—looking wistfully from time to time towards the chamber he had lately visited.

"She was not wont to be a lie-abed; but she was well then. We must have patience. When she is well again, she will rise early, as she used to do, and ramble abroad in the healthy morning time. I often tried to track the way she had gone, but her small fairy footstep left no print upon the dewy ground, to guide me. Who is that? Shut the door. Quick!—Have we not enough to do to drive away that marble cold, and keep her warm!"

The door was indeed opened, for the entrance of Mr. Garland and his friend, accompanied by two other persons. These were the schoolmaster, and the bachelor. The former held a light in his hand. He had, it seemed, but gone to his own cottage to replenish the exhausted lamp, at the moment when Kit came up and found the old man alone.

He softened again at sight of these two friends, and, laying aside the angry manner—if to anything so feeble and so sad the term can be applied—in which he had spoken when the door opened, resumed his former seat, and subsided, by little and little, into the old action, and the old, dull, wandering sound.

Of the strangers he took no heed whatever. He had seen them, but appeared quite incapable of interest or curiosity. The younger brother stood apart. The bachelor drew a chair towards the old man, and sat down close beside him. After a long silence, he ventured to speak.

"Another night, and not in bed!" he said softly; "I hoped you would be more mindful of your promise to me. Why do you not take some rest?"

"Sleep has left me," returned the old man. "It is all with her!"

"It would pain her very much to know that you were watching thus," said the bachelor. "You would not give her pain?"

"I am not so sure of that, if it would only rouse her. She has slept so very long. And yet I am rash to say so. It is a good and happy sleep—eh?"

"Indeed it is," returned the bachelor. "Indeed, indeed, it is!"

"That's well!—and the waking,"—faltered the old man.

"Happy too. Happier than tongue can tell, or heart of man conceive."

They watched him as he rose and stole on tiptoe to the other chamber where the lamp had been replaced. They listened as he spoke again within its silent walls. They looked into the faces of each other, and no man's cheek was free from tears. He came back, whispering that she was still asleep, but that he thought she had moved. It was her hand, he said—a little—a very, very little—but he was pretty sure she had moved it—perhaps in seeking his. He had known her do that before now, though in the deepest sleep the while. And when he had said this, he dropped into his chair again, and clasping his hands above his head, uttered a cry never to be forgotten.

The poor schoolmaster motioned to the bachelor that he would come upon the other side, and speak to him. They gently unlocked his fingers, which he had twisted in his grey hair, and pressed them in their own.

"He will hear me," said the schoolmaster, "I am sure. He will hear either me or you if we beseech him. She would, at all times."

"I will hear any voice she liked to hear," cried the old man. "I love all she loved!"

"I know you do," returned the schoolmaster. "I am certain of it. Think of her; think of all the sorrows and afflictions you have shared together; of all the trials, and all the peaceful pleasures, you have jointly known."

"I do. I do. I think of nothing else."

"I would have you think of nothing else to-night—of nothing but those things which will soften your heart, dear friend, and open it to old affections and old times. It is so that she would speak to you herself, and in her name it is that I speak now."

"You do well to speak softly," said the old man. "We will not wake her. I should be glad to see her eyes again, and to see her smile. There is a smile upon her young face now, but it is fixed and changeless. I would have it come and go. That shall be in Heaven's good time. We will not wake her."

"Let us not talk of her in her sleep, but as she used to be when you were journeying together, far away—as she was at home, in the old house from which you fled together—as she was in the old cheerful time," said the schoolmaster.

"She was always cheerful—very cheerful," cried the old man,

looking steadfastly at him. "There was ever something mild and quiet about her, I remember, from the first; but she was of a happy nature."

"We have heard you say," pursued the schoolmaster, "that in this, and in all goodness, she was like her mother. You can think of, and remember her?"

He maintained his steadfast look, but gave no answer.

"Or even one before her," said the bachelor. "It is many years ago, and affliction makes the time longer, but you have not forgotten her whose death contributed to make this child so dear to you, even before you knew her worth or could read her heart? Say, that you could carry back your thoughts to very distant days—to the time of your early life—when, unlike this fair flower, you did not pass your youth alone. Say, that you could remember, long ago, another child who loved you dearly, you being but a child yourself. Say, that you had a brother, long forgotten, long unseen, long separated from you, who now, at last, in your utmost need came back to comfort and console you—"

"To be to you what you were once to him," cried the younger, falling on his knee before him; "to repay your old affection, brother dear, by constant care, solicitude, and love; to be, at your right hand, what he never ceased to be when oceans rolled between us; to call to witness his unchanging truth and mindfulness of bygone days, whole years of desolation. Give me but one word of recognition, brother—and never—no never, in the brightest moment of our youngest days, when, poor silly boys, we thought to pass our lives together—have we been half as dear and precious to each other as we shall be from this time hence!"

The old man looked from face to face, and his lips moved; but no sound came from them in reply.

"If we were knit together then," pursued the younger brother, "what will be the bond between us now! Our love and fellowship began in childhood, when life was all before us, and will be resumed when we have proved it, and are but children at the last. As many restless spirits, who have hunted fortune, fame, or pleasure through the world, retire in their decline to where they first drew breath, vainly seeking to be children once again before they die, so we, less fortunate than they in early life, but happier in its closing scenes, will set up our rest again among our boyish haunts; and going home with no hope realised, that had its growth in manhood—carrying back nothing that we brought away, but our old yearnings to each other—saving no fragment from the wreck of life, but that which first endeared it—may be indeed but children as at first. And even," he added in an altered voice, "even if what I dread to name has come to pass—even if that be so, or is to be (which Heaven forbid and spare us!)—still, dear brother, we are not apart, and have that comfort in our great affliction."

By little and little, the old man had drawn back towards the inner chamber, while these words were spoken. He pointed there, as he replied, with trembling lips.

"You plot among you to wean my heart from her. You never will do that—never while I have life. I have no relative or friend but her —I never had—I never will have. She is all in all to me. It is too late to part us now."

Waving them off with his hand, and calling softly to her as he went, he stole into the room. They who were left behind, drew close together, and after a few whispered words—not unbroken by emotion, or easily uttered—followed him. They moved so gently, that their footsteps made no noise; but there were sobs from among the group, and sounds of grief and mourning.

For she was dead. There, upon her little bed, she lay at rest. The solemn stillness was no marvel now.

She was dead. No sleep so beautiful and calm, so free from trace of pain, so fair to look upon. She seemed a creature fresh from the hand of God, and waiting for the breath of life; not one who had lived and suffered death.

Her couch was dressed with here and there some winter berries and green leaves, gathered in a spot she had been used to favour. "When I die, put near me something that has loved the light, and had the sky above it always." Those were her words.

She was dead. Dear, gentle, patient, noble Nell was dead. Her little bird—a poor slight thing the pressure of a finger would have crushed—was stirring nimbly in its cage; and the strong heart of its child-mistress was mute and motionless for ever.

Where were the traces of her early cares, her sufferings, and fatigues? All gone. Sorrow was dead indeed in her, but peace and perfect happiness were born; imaged in her tranquil beauty and profound repose.

And still her former self lay there, unaltered in this change. Yes. The old fireside had smiled upon that same sweet face; it had passed like a dream through haunts of misery and care; at the door of the poor schoolmaster on the summer evening, before the furnace fire upon the cold wet night, at the still bedside of the dying boy, there had been the same mild lovely look. So shall we know the angels in their majesty, after death.

The old man held one languid arm in his, and had the small hand tight folded to his breast, for warmth. It was the hand she had stretched out to him with her last smile—the hand that had led him on through all their wanderings. Ever and anon he pressed it to his lips; then hugged it to his breast again, murmuring that it was warmer now; and as he said it he looked, in agony, to those who stood around, as if imploring them to help her.

She was dead, and past all help, or need of it. The ancient rooms she had seemed to fill with life, even while her own was waning fast— the garden she had tended—the eyes she had gladdened—the noise-less haunts of many a thoughtful hour—the paths she had trodden as it were but yesterday—could know her no more.

"It is not," said the schoolmaster, as he bent down to kiss her on the cheek, and gave his tears free vent, "it is not on earth that Heaven's justice ends. Think what it is, compared with the World to which her young spirit has winged its early flight, and say, if one deliberate wish expressed in solemn terms above this bed could call her back to life, which of us would utter it!"

CHAPTER LXXII

WHEN morning came, and they could speak more calmly on the subject of their grief, they heard how her life had closed.

She had been dead two days. They were all about her at the time, knowing that the end was drawing on. She died soon after daybreak. They had read and talked to her in the earlier portion of the night, but as the hours crept on, she sank to sleep. They could tell, by what she faintly uttered in her dreams, that they were of her journeyings with the old man; they were of no painful scenes, but of those who had helped and used them kindly, for she often said "God bless you!" with great fervour. Waking, she never wandered in her mind but once, and that was of beautiful music which she said was in the air. God knows. It may have been.

Opening her eyes at last, from a very quiet sleep, she begged that they would kiss her once again. That done, she turned to the old man with a lovely smile upon her face—such, they said, as they had never seen, and never could forget—and clung with both her arms about his neck. They did not know that she was dead, at first.

She had spoken very often of the two sisters, who, she said, were like dear friends to her. She wished they could be told how much she thought about them, and how she had watched them as they walked together, by the river side at night. She would like to see poor Kit, she had often said of late. She wished there was somebody to take her love to Kit. And even then, she never thought or spoke about him, but with something of her old, clear, merry laugh.

For the rest, she had never murmured or complained; but, with a quiet mind, and manner quite unaltered—save that she every day became more earnest and more grateful to them—faded like the light upon a summer's evening.

The child who had been her little friend came there almost as soon as it was day, with an offering of dried flowers which he begged them to lay upon her breast. It was he who had come to the window overnight and spoken to the sexton, and they saw in the snow traces of small feet, where he had been lingering near the room in which she lay before he went to bed. He had a fancy, it seemed, that they had left her there alone; and could not bear the thought.

He told them of his dream again, and that it was of her being restored to them, just as she used to be. He begged hard to see her, saying that he would be very quiet, and that they need not fear his being alarmed, for he had sat alone by his young brother all day long, when *he* was dead, and had felt glad to be so near him. They let him have his wish; and indeed he kept his word, and was in his childish way a lesson to them all.

Up to that time, the old man had not spoken once—except to her —or stirred from the bedside. But when he saw her little favourite, he was moved as they had not seen him yet, and made as though he would have him come nearer. Then pointing to the bed, he burst into tears for the first time, and they who stood by, knowing that the sight of this child had done him good, left them alone altogether.

Soothing him with his artless talk of her, the child persuaded him to take some rest, to walk abroad, to do almost as he desired him. And when the day came on, which must remove her in her earthly shape from earthly eyes for ever, he led him away, that he might not know when she was taken from him.

They were to gather fresh leaves and berries for her bed. It was Sunday—a bright, clear, wintry afternoon—and as they traversed the village street, those who were walking in their path drew back to make way for them, and gave them a softened greeting. Some shook the old man kindly by the hand, some stood uncovered while he tottered by, and many cried, "God help him!" as he passed along.

"Neighbour!" said the old man, stopping at the cottage where his young guide's mother dwelt, "how is it that the folks are nearly all in black to-day? I have seen a mourning ribbon or a piece of crape on almost every one."

She could not tell, the woman said.

"Why, you yourself—you wear the colour too!" he cried. "Windows are closed that never used to be by day. What does this mean?"

Again the woman said she could not tell.

"We must go back," said the old man, hurriedly. "We must see what this is."

"No, no," cried the child, detaining him. "Remember what you promised. Our way is to the old green lane, where she and I so often were, and where you found us more than once making those garlands for her garden. Do not turn back!"

"Where is she now?" said the old man. "Tell me that."

"Do you not know?" returned the child. "Did we not leave her, but just now?"

"True. True. It *was* her we left—was it!"

He pressed his hand upon his brow, looked vacantly round, and as if impelled by a sudden thought, crossed the road, and entered the sexton's house. He and his deaf assistant were sitting before the fire. Both rose up, on seeing who it was.

The child made a hasty sign to them with his hand. It was the action of an instant, but that, and the old man's look, were quite enough.

"Do you—do you bury any one to-day?" he said, eagerly.

"No, no! Who should we bury, sir!" returned the sexton.

"Ay, who indeed! I say with you, who indeed!"

"It is a holiday with us, good sir," returned the sexton mildly. "We have no work to do to-day."

"Why then, I'll go where you will," said the old man, turning to the child. "You're sure of what you tell me? You would not deceive me? I am changed even in the little time since you last saw me."

"Go thy ways with him, sir," cried the sexton, "and Heaven be with ye both!"

"I am quite ready," said the old man, meekly. "Come, boy, come—" and so submitted to be led away.

And now the bell—the bell she had so often heard by night and day, and listened to with solemn pleasure almost as a living voice—rang its remorseless toll for her, so young, so beautiful, so good. Decrepit age, and vigorous life, and blooming youth, and helpless infancy, poured forth—on crutches, in the pride of strength and health, in the full blush of promise, in the mere dawn of life—to gather round her tomb. Old men were there, whose eyes were dim and senses failing—grandmothers, who might have died ten years ago, and still been old—the deaf, the blind, the lame, the palsied, the living dead in many shapes and forms, to see the closing of that early grave. What was the death it would shut in, to that which still could crawl and creep above it!

Along the crowded path they bore her now; pure as the newly-fallen snow that covered it; whose day on earth had been as fleeting. Under that porch, where she had sat when Heaven in its mercy brought her to that peaceful spot, she passed again, and the old church received her in its quiet shade.

They carried her to one old nook, where she had many and many a time sat musing, and laid their burden softly on the pavement. The light streamed on it through the coloured window—a window, where the boughs of trees were ever rustling in the summer, and where the birds sang sweetly all day long. With every breath of air that stirred among those branches in the sunshine, some trembling, changing light would fall upon her grave.

Earth to earth, ashes to ashes, dust to dust. Many a young hand dropped in its little wreath, many a stifled sob was heard. Some—and they were not a few—knelt down. All were sincere and truthful in their sorrow.

The service done, the mourners stood apart, and the villagers closed round to look into the grave before the pavement-stone should be replaced. One called to mind how he had seen her sitting on that very spot, and how her book had fallen on her lap, and she was gazing with a pensive face upon the sky. Another told how he had wondered much that one so delicate as she, should be so bold; how she had never feared to enter the church alone at night, but had loved to linger there when all was quiet, and even to climb the tower stair, with no more light than that of the moon rays stealing through the loopholes in the thick old wall. A whisper went about among the oldest there, that she had seen and talked with angels; and when they called to mind how she had looked, and spoken, and her early death, some thought it might be so, indeed. Thus, coming to the grave in little knots, and glancing down, and giving place to others, and falling off in whispering groups of three or four, the church was cleared in time of all but the sexton and the mourning friends.

They saw the vault covered and the stone fixed down. Then, when the dusk of evening had come on, and not a sound disturbed the sacred stillness of the place—when the bright moon poured in her light on tomb and monument, on pillar, wall, and arch, and most of all (it seemed to them) upon her quiet grave—in that calm time, when all outward things and inward thoughts teem with assurances of immortality, and worldly hopes and fears are humbled in the dust before them—then, with tranquil and submissive hearts they turned away, and left the child with God.

Oh! it is hard to take to heart the lesson that such deaths will teach, but let no man reject it, for it is one that all must learn, and is a mighty, universal Truth. When Death strikes down the innocent and young, for every fragile form from which he lets the panting spirit free, a hundred virtues rise, in shapes of mercy, charity, and love, to walk the world, and bless it. Of every tear that sorrowing mortals shed on such green graves, some good is born, some gentler nature comes. In the Destroyer's steps there spring up bright creations that defy his power, and his dark path becomes a way of light to Heaven.

It was late when the old man came home. The boy had led him to his own dwelling, under some pretence, on their way back; and, rendered drowsy by his long ramble and late want of rest, he had sunk into a deep sleep by the fireside. He was perfectly exhausted, and they were careful not to rouse him. The slumber held him a long time, and when he at length awoke the moon was shining.

The younger brother, uneasy at his protracted absence, was watching at the door for his coming, when he appeared in the pathway with his little guide. He advanced to meet them, and tenderly obliging the old man to lean upon his arm, conducted him with slow and trembling steps towards the house.

He repaired to her chamber, straight. Not finding what he had left there, he returned with distracted looks to the room in which they were assembled. From that, he rushed into the schoolmaster's cottage, calling her name. They followed close upon him, and when he had vainly searched it, brought him home.

With such persuasive words as pity and affection could suggest, they prevailed upon him to sit among them and hear what they should tell him. Then, endeavouring by every little artifice to prepare his mind for what must come, and dwelling with many fervent words upon the happy lot to which she had been removed, they told him, at last, the truth. The moment it had passed their lips, he fell down among them like a murdered man.

For many hours, they had little hope of his surviving; but grief is strong, and he recovered.

If there be any who have never known the blank that follows

death—the weary void—the sense of desolation that will come upon the strongest minds, when something familiar and beloved is missed at every turn—the connexion between inanimate and senseless things, and the object of recollection, when every household god becomes a monument and every room a grave—if there be any who have not known this, and proved it by their own experience, they can never faintly guess how, for many days, the old man pined and moped away the time, and wandered here and there as seeking something, and had no comfort.

Whatever power of thought or memory he retained, was all bound up in her. He never understood, or seemed to care to understand, about his brother. To every endearment and attention he continued listless. If they spoke to him on this, or any other theme—save one —he would hear them patiently for awhile, then turn away, and go on seeking as before.

On that one theme, which was in his and all their minds, it was impossible to touch. Dead! He could not hear or bear the word. The slightest hint of it would throw him into a paroxysm, like that he had had when it was first spoken. In what hope he lived, no man could tell; but that he had some hope of finding her again—some faint and shadowy hope, deferred from day to day, and making him from day to day more sick and sore at heart—was plain to all.

They bethought them of a removal from the scene of this last sorrow; of trying whether change of place would rouse or cheer him. His brother sought the advice of those who were accounted skilful in such matters, and they came and saw him. Some of the number staid upon the spot, conversed with him when he would converse, and watched him as he wandered up and down, alone and silent. Move him where they might, they said, he would ever seek to get back there. His mind would run upon that spot. If they confined him closely, and kept a strict guard upon him, they might hold him prisoner, but if he could by any means escape, he would surely wander back to that place, or die upon the road.

The boy, to whom he had submitted at first, had no longer any influence with him. At times he would suffer the child to walk by his side, or would even take such notice of his presence as giving him his hand, or would stop to kiss his cheek, or pat him on the head. At other times, he would entreat him—not unkindly—to be gone, and would not brook him near. But whether alone; or with this pliant friend; or with those who would have given him, at any cost or sacrifice, some consolation or some peace of mind, if happily the means could have been devised; he was at all times the same—with no love or care for anything in life—a broken-hearted man.

At length they found one day that he had risen early, and, with his knapsack on his back, his staff in hand, her own straw hat, and little basket full of such things as she had been used to carry, was gone. As they were making ready to pursue him far and wide, a frightened schoolboy came who had seen him, but a moment before, sitting in the church—upon her grave, he said.

They hastened there, and going softly to the door, espied him in the attitude of one who waited patiently. They did not disturb him then, but kept a watch upon him all that day. When it grew quite dark, he rose and returned home, and went to bed, murmuring to himself, "She will come to-morrow!"

Upon the morrow he was there again from sunrise until night; and still at night he laid him down to rest, and muttered, "She will come to-morrow!"

And thenceforth, every day, and all day long, he waited at her grave for her. How many pictures of new journeys over pleasant country, of resting-places under the free broad sky, of rambles in the fields and woods, and paths not often trodden—how many tones of that one well-remembered voice—how many glimpses of the form, the fluttering dress, the hair that waved so gaily in the wind—how many visions of what had been, and what he hoped was yet to be— rose up before him, in the old, dull, silent church! He never told them what he thought, or where he went. He would sit with them at night, pondering with a secret satisfaction, they could see, upon the flight that he and she would take before night came again; and still they would hear him whisper in his prayers, "Oh! Let her come to-morrow!"

The last time was on a genial day in spring. He did not return at the usual hour, and they went to seek him. He was lying dead upon the stone.

They laid him by the side of her whom he had loved so well; and, in the church where they had often prayed, and mused, and lingered hand in hand, the child and the old man slept together.

CHAPTER THE LAST

THE magic reel, which, rolling on before, has led the chronicler thus far, now slackens in its pace, and stops. It lies before the goal; the pursuit is at an end.

It remains but to dismiss the leaders of the little crowd who have borne us company upon the road, and so to close the journey.

Foremost among them, smooth Sampson Brass and Sally, arm in arm, claim our polite attention.

Mr. Sampson, then, being detained, as already has been shown, by the Justice upon whom he called, and being so strongly pressed to protract his stay that he could by no means refuse, remained under his protection for a considerable time, during which the great attention of his entertainer kept him so extremely close, that he was quite lost to society, and never even went abroad for exercise saving into a small paved yard. So well, indeed, was his modest and retiring temper understood by those with whom he had to deal, and so jealous were they of his absence, that they required a kind of friendly bond to be entered into by two substantial housekeepers, in the sum of fifteen hundred pounds a-piece, before they would suffer him to quit their hospitable roof—doubting, it appeared, that he would return, if once let loose, on any other terms. Mr. Brass, struck with the humour of this jest, and carrying out its spirit to the utmost, sought from his wide connexion a pair of friends whose joint possessions fell some halfpence short of fifteen pence, and proffered them as bail—for that was the merry word agreed upon on both sides. These gentlemen being rejected after twenty-four hours' pleasantry, Mr. Brass consented to remain, and did remain, until a club of choice spirits called a Grand Jury (who were in the joke) summoned him to a trial before twelve other wags for perjury and fraud, who in their turn found him guilty with a most facetious joy,—nay, the very populace entered into the whim, and when Mr. Brass was moving in a hackney-coach towards the building where these wags assembled, saluted him with rotten eggs and carcases of kittens, and feigned to wish to tear him into shreds, which greatly increased the comicality of the thing, and made him relish it the more, no doubt.

To work this sportive vein still further, Mr. Brass, by his counsel, moved in arrest of judgment that he had been led to criminate himself, by assurances of safety and promises of pardon, and claimed the leniency which the law extends to such confiding natures as are thus deluded. After solemn argument, this point (with others of a technical nature, whose humorous extravagance it would be difficult to exaggerate) was referred to the judges for their decision, Sampson being meantime removed to his former quarters. Finally, some of the points were given in Sampson's favour, and some against him; and the upshot was that, instead of being desired to travel for a time in foreign parts, he was permitted to grace the mother country under certain insignificant restrictions.

These were that he should, for a term of years, reside in a spacious mansion where several other gentlemen were lodged and boarded at the public charge, who went clad in a sober uniform of grey turned up with yellow, had their hair cut extremely short, and chiefly lived on gruel and light soup. It was also required of him that he should partake their exercise of constantly ascending an endless flight of stairs; and lest his legs, unused to such exertion, should be weakened by it, that he should wear upon one ankle an amulet or charm of iron. These conditions being arranged, he was removed one evening to his new abode, and enjoyed, in common with nine other gentlemen and two ladies, the privilege of being taken to his place of retirement in one of Royalty's own carriages.

Over and above these trifling penalties, his name was erased and blotted out from the roll of attorneys; which erasure has been always held in these latter times to be a great degradation and reproach, and to imply the commission of some amazing villany—as indeed would seem to be the case, when so many worthless names remain among its better records, unmolested.

Of Sally Brass, conflicting rumours went abroad. Some said with confidence that she had gone down to the docks in male attire, and had become a female sailor; others darkly whispered that she had enlisted as a private in the second regiment of Foot Guards, and had been seen in uniform and on duty, to wit, leaning on her musket and looking out of a sentry-box in St. James's Park, one evening. There were many such whispers as these in circulation; but the truth appears to be that, after a lapse of some five years (during which there is no direct evidence of her having been seen at all), two wretched people were more than once observed to crawl at dusk from the inmost recesses of St. Giles's, and to take their way along the streets, with shuffling steps and cowering shivering forms, looking into the roads and kennels as they went in search of refuse food or disregarded offal. These forms were never beheld but in those nights of cold and gloom, when the terrible spectres, who lie at all other times in the obscene hiding-places of London, in archways, dark vaults and cellars, venture to creep into the streets; the embodied spirits of Disease, and Vice, and Famine. It was whispered by those who should have known, that these were Sampson and his sister Sally; and to this day, it is said, they sometimes pass, on bad nights, in the same loathsome guise, close at the elbow of the shrinking passenger.

The body of Quilp being found—though not until some days had elapsed—an inquest was held on it near the spot where it had been washed ashore. The general supposition was that he had committed suicide, and, this appearing to be favoured by all the circumstances of his death, the verdict was to that effect. He was left to be buried with a stake through his heart in the centre of four lonely roads.

It was rumoured afterwards that this horrible and barbarous ceremony had been dispensed with, and that the remains had been secretly given up to Tom Scott. But even here, opinion was divided; for some said Tom had dug them up at midnight, and carried them to a place indicated to him by the widow. It is probable that both these stories may have had their origin in the simple fact of Tom's shedding tears upon the inquest—which he certainly did, extraordinary as it may appear. He manifested, besides, a strong desire to assault the jury; and being restrained and conducted out of court, darkened its only window by standing on his head upon the sill, until he was dexterously tilted upon his feet again by a cautious beadle.

Being cast upon the world by his master's death, he determined to go through it upon his head and hands, and accordingly began to tumble for his bread. Finding, however, his English birth an insurmountable obstacle to his advancement in this pursuit (notwithstanding that his art was in high repute and favour), he assumed the name of an Italian image lad, with whom he had become acquainted; and afterwards tumbled with extraordinary success, and to overflowing audiences.

Little Mrs. Quilp never quite forgave herself the one deceit that lay so heavy on her conscience, and never spoke or thought of it but with bitter tears. Her husband had no relations, and she was rich. He had made no will, or she would probably have been poor. Having married the first time at her mother's instigation, she consulted in her second choice nobody but herself. It fell upon a smart young fellow enough; and as he made it a preliminary condition that Mrs. Jiniwin should be thenceforth an out-pensioner, they lived together after marriage with no more than the average amount of quarrelling, and led a merry life upon the dead dwarf's money.

Mr. and Mrs. Garland, and Mr. Abel, went on as usual (except that there was a change in their household, as will be seen presently), and in due time the latter went into partnership with his friend the notary, on which occasion there was a dinner, and a ball, and great extent of dissipation. Unto this ball there happened to be invited the most bashful young lady that was ever seen, with whom Mr. Abel happened to fall in love. *How* it happened, or how they found it out, or which of them first communicated the discovery to the other, nobody knows. But certain it is that in course of time they were married; and equally certain it is that they were the happiest of the happy; and no less certain it is that they deserved to be so. And it is pleasant to write down that they reared a family; because any propagation of goodness and benevolence is no small addition to the aristocracy of nature, and no small subject of rejoicing for mankind at large.

The pony preserved his character for independence and principle down to the last moment of his life; which was an unusually long one, and caused him to be looked upon, indeed, as the very Old Parr of ponies. He often went to and fro with the little phaeton between Mr. Garland's and his son's, and, as the old people and the young were frequently together, had a stable of his own at the new establishment, into which he would walk of himself with surprising dignity. He condescended to play with the children, as they grew old enough to cultivate his friendship, and would run up and down the little paddock with them like a dog; but though he relaxed so far, and allowed them such small freedoms as caresses, or even to look at his shoes or hang on by his tail, he never permitted any one among them to mount his back or drive him; thus showing that even their familiarity must have its limits, and that there were points between them far too serious for trifling.

He was not unsusceptible of warm attachments in his later life, for when the good bachelor came to live with Mr. Garland upon the clergyman's decease, he conceived a great friendship for him, and amiably submitted to be driven by his hands without the least resistance. He did no work for two or three years before he died, but lived in clover; and his last act (like a choleric old gentleman) was to kick his doctor.

Mr. Swiveller, recovering very slowly from his illness, and entering into the receipt of his annuity, bought for the Marchioness a handsome stock of clothes, and put her to school forthwith, in redemption of the vow he had made upon his fevered bed. After casting about for some time for a name which should be worthy of her, he decided in favour of Sophronia Sphynx, as being euphonious and genteel, and furthermore indicative of mystery. Under this title

the Marchioness repaired, in tears, to the school of his selection'
from which, as she soon distanced all competitors, she was removed
before the lapse of many quarters to one of a higher grade. It is but
bare justice to Mr. Swiveller to say, that, although the expenses of
her education kept him in straitened circumstances for half-a-dozen
years, he never slackened in his zeal, and always held himself sufficiently repaid by the accounts he heard (with great gravity) of her
advancement, on his monthly visits to the governess, who looked
upon him as a literary gentleman of eccentric habits, and of a most
prodigious talent in quotation.

In a word, Mr. Swiveller kept the Marchioness at this establishment until she was, at a moderate guess, full nineteen years of age—
good-looking, clever, and good-humoured; when he began to consider
seriously what was to be done next. On one of his periodical visits,
while he was revolving this question in his mind, the Marchioness
came down to him, alone, looking more smiling and more fresh than
ever. Then it occurred to him, but not for the first time, that if she
would marry him, how comfortable they might be! So Richard asked
her; whatever she said, it wasn't No; and they were married in good
earnest that day week, which gave Mr. Swiveller frequent occasion
to remark at divers subsequent periods that there had been a young
lady saving up for him after all.

A little cottage at Hampstead being to let, which had in its garden
a smoking-box, the envy of the civilised world, they agreed to become
its tenants; and when the honey-moon was over, entered upon its
occupation. To this retreat Mr. Chuckster repaired regularly every
Sunday to spend the day—usually beginning with breakfast; and
here he was the great purveyor of general news and fashionable
intelligence. For some years he continued a deadly foe to Kit, protesting that he had a better opinion of him when he was supposed
to have stolen the five-pound note, than when he was shown to be
perfectly free of the crime; inasmuch as his guilt would have had in it
something daring and bold, whereas his innocence was but another
proof of a sneaking and crafty disposition. By slow degrees, however,
he was reconciled to him in the end; and even went so far as to honour
him with his patronage, as one who had in some measure reformed,
and was therefore to be forgiven. But he never forgot or pardoned
that circumstance of the shilling; holding that if he had come back
to get another he would have done well enough, but that his returning to work out the former gift was a stain upon his moral character
which no penitence or contrition could ever wash away.

Mr. Swiveller, having always been in some measure of a philosophic
and reflective turn, grew immensely contemplative, at times, in the
smoking-box, and was accustomed at such periods to debate in his
own mind the mysterious question of Sophronia's parentage.
Sophronia herself supposed she was an orphan; but Mr. Swiveller,
putting various slight circumstances together, often thought Miss
Brass must know better than that; and, having heard from his wife
of her strange interview with Quilp, entertained sundry misgivings

whether that person, in his lifetime, might not also have been able to solve the riddle, had he chosen. These speculations, however, gave him no uneasiness; for Sophronia was ever a most cheerful, affectionate, and provident wife to him; and Dick (excepting for an occasional outbreak with Mr. Chuckster, which she had the good sense rather to encourage than oppose) was to her an attached and domesticated husband. And they played many hundred thousand games of cribbage together. And let it be added, to Dick's honour, that, though we have called her Sophronia, he called her the Marchioness from first to last; and that upon every anniversary of the day on which he found her in his sick room Mr. Chuckster came to dinner, and there was great glorification.

The gamblers, Isaac List and Jowl, with their trusty confederate Mr. James Groves of unimpeachable memory, pursued their course with varying success, until the failure of a spirited enterprise in the way of their profession, dispersed them in various directions, and caused their career to receive a sudden check from the long and strong arm of the law. This defeat had its origin in the untoward detection of a new associate—young Frederick Trent—who thus became the unconscious instrument of their punishment and his own.

For the young man himself, he rioted abroad for a brief term, living by his wits—which means by the abuse of every faculty that worthily employed raises man above the beasts, and so degraded, sinks him far below them. It was not long before his body was recognised by a stranger, who chanced to visit that hospital in Paris where the drowned are laid out to be owned; despite the bruises and disfigurements which were said to have been occasioned by some previous scuffle. But the stranger kept his own counsel until he returned home, and it was never claimed or cared for.

The younger brother, or the single gentleman, for that designation is more familiar, would have drawn the poor schoolmaster from his lone retreat, and made him his companion and friend. But the humble village-teacher was timid of venturing into the noisy world, and had become fond of his dwelling in the old churchyard. Calmly happy in his school, and in the spot, and in the attachment of Her little mourner, he pursued his quiet course in peace; and was, through the righteous gratitude of his friend—let this brief mention suffice for that—a *poor* schoolmaster no more.

That friend—single gentleman, or younger brother, which you will—had at his heart a heavy sorrow; but it bred in him no misanthropy or monastic gloom. He went forth into the world, a lover of his kind. For a long, long time, it was his chief delight to travel in the steps of the old man and the child (so far as he could trace them from her last narrative), to halt where they had halted, sympathise where they had suffered, and rejoice where they had been made glad. Those who had been kind to them, did not escape his search. The sisters at the school—they who were her friends, because themselves so friendless—Mrs. Jarley of the wax-work, Codlin, Short—he found them all; and trust me, that the man who fed the furnace fire was not forgotten.

Kit's story having got abroad, raised him up a host of friends, and many offers of provision for his future life. He had no idea at first of ever quitting Mr. Garland's service; but, after serious remonstrance and advice from that gentleman, began to contemplate the possibility of such a change being brought about in time. A good post was procured for him, with a rapidity which took away his breath, by some of the gentlemen who had believed him guilty of the offence laid to his charge, and who had acted upon that belief. Through the same kind agency, his mother was secured from want, and made quite happy. Thus, as Kit often said, his great misfortune turned out to be the source of all his subsequent prosperity.

Did Kit live a single man all his days, or did he marry? Of course he married, and who should be his wife but Barbara? And the best of it was, he married so soon that little Jacob was an uncle, before the calves of his legs, already mentioned in this history, had ever been encased in broadcloth pantaloons,—though that was not quite the best either, for of necessity the baby was an uncle too. The delight of Kit's mother and of Barbara's mother upon the great occasion is past all telling; finding they agreed so well on that, and on all other subjects, they took up their abode together, and were a most harmonious pair of friends from that time forth. And hadn't Astley's cause to bless itself for their all going together once a quarter—to the pit—and didn't Kit's mother always say, when they painted the outside, that Kit's last treat had helped to that, and wonder what the manager would feel if he but knew it as they passed his house!

When Kit had children six and seven years old, there was a Barbara among them, and a pretty Barbara she was. Nor was there wanting an exact facsimile and copy of little Jacob as he appeared in those remote times when they taught him what oysters meant. Of course there was an Abel, own godson to the Mr. Garland of that name; and there was a Dick, whom Mr. Swiveller did especially favour. The little group would often gather round him of a night and beg him to tell again that story of good Miss Nell who died. This Kit would do; and when they cried to hear it, wishing it longer too, he would teach them how she had gone to Heaven, as all good people did; and how, if they were good like her, they might hope to be there too one day, and to see and know her as he had done when he was quite a boy. Then he would relate to them how needy he used to be, and how she had taught him what he was otherwise too poor to learn, and how the old man had been used to say "she always laughs at Kit;" at which they would brush away their tears, and laugh themselves to think that she had done so, and be again quite merry.

He sometimes took them to the street where she had lived; but new improvements had altered it so much, it was not like the same. The old house had been long ago pulled down, and a fine broad road was in its place. At first he would draw with his stick a square upon the ground to show them where it used to stand. But he soon became uncertain of the spot, and could only say it was thereabouts, he thought, and that these alterations were confusing.

Such are the changes which a few years bring about, and so do things pass away, like a tale that is told!

THE END

A CHILD'S
HISTORY OF ENGLAND

Editor's Note

There are a number of points of similarity in the careers and methods of Sir Walter Scott and Charles Dickens. A remarkable one has been mentioned in the Editorial Note to Oliver Twist; *and the present book supplies another. Scott wrote history for his sick grandson, and called it* Tales of a Grandfather. *Dickens wrote* A Child's History of England, *and dedicated it to his children. Both works are history told by fond parents having the magic gift of word-picturing, rather than historical studies carefully weighed and documented. One other point about* A Child's History, *it is said to be the only book dictated by Charles Dickens. It first appeared in his* "Household Words" *(January, 1851, to December, 1853). This edition is printed from the one carefully corrected by the Author in 1867–1868.*

A CHILD'S
HISTORY OF
ENGLAND

BY

CHARLES DICKENS

LONDON:
HAZELL, WATSON & VINEY, LTD.

TABLE OF THE REIGNS

BEGINNING WITH KING ALFRED THE GREAT
THE SAXONS.

	BEGAN	ENDED	LASTED
The Reign of Alfred the Great	871	901	30 years.
The Reign of Edward the Elder . . .	901	925	24 years.
The Reign of Athelstan	925	941	16 years.
The Reigns of the Six Boy-Kings . .	941	1016	75 years.

THE DANES, AND THE RESTORED SAXONS.

The Reign of Canute	1016	1035	19 years.
The Reign of Harold Harefoot . . .	1035	1040	5 years.
The Reign of Hardicanute . . .	1040	1042	2 years.
The Reign of Edward the Confessor . .	1042	1066	24 years.

The Reign of Harold the Second, and the Norman Conquest, were also within the year 1066.

THE NORMANS.

The Reign of William the First, called the Conqueror	1066	1087	21 years.
The Reign of William the Second, called Rufus .	1087	1100	13 years.
The Reign of Henry the First, called Fine-Scholar	1100	1135	35 years.
The Reigns of Matilda and Stephen . . .	1135	1154	19 years.

THE PLANTAGENETS.

The Reign of Henry the Second . . .	1154	1189	35 years.
The Reign of Richard the First, called the Lion-Heart	1189	1199	10 years.
The Reign of John, called Lackland . . .	1199	1216	17 years.
The Reign of Henry the Third . . .	1216	1272	56 years.
The Reign of Edward the First, called Longshanks	1272	1307	35 years.
The Reign of Edward the Second . . .	1307	1327	20 years.
The Reign of Edward the Third . . .	1327	1377	50 years.
The Reign of Richard the Second . . .	1377	1399	22 years.
The Reign of Henry the Fourth, called Bolingbroke	1399	1413	14 years.
The Reign of Henry the Fifth . . .	1413	1422	9 years.
The Reign of Henry the Sixth . . .	1422	1461	39 years.
The Reign of Edward the Fourth . . .	1461	1483	22 years.
The Reign of Edward the Fifth . . .	1483	1483	a few weeks.
The Reign of Richard the Third . . .	1483	1485	2 years.

THE TUDORS.

The Reign of Henry the Seventh . .	1485	1509	24 years.
The Reign of Henry the Eighth . .	1509	1547	38 years.
The Reign of Edward the Sixth . .	1547	1553	6 years.
The Reign of Mary	1553	1558	5 years.
The Reign of Elizabeth	1558	1603	45 years.

THE STUARTS.

	BEGAN	ENDED	LASTED
The Reign of James the First	1603	1625	22 years.
The Reign of Charles the First	1625	1649	24 years.

THE COMMONWEALTH.

	BEGAN	ENDED	LASTED
The Council of State and Government by Parliament	1649	1653	4 years.
The Protectorate of Oliver Cromwell . . .	1653	1658	5 years.
The Protectorate of Richard Cromwell . .	1658	1659	7 months.
The Council of State and Government by Parliament, resumed in	1659	1660	13 months.

THE STUARTS RESTORED.

	BEGAN	ENDED	LASTED
The Reign of Charles the Second . . .	1660	1685	25 years.
The Reign of James the Second. . . .	1685	1688	3 years.

THE REVOLUTION.—1688. (Comprised in the concluding chapter.)

	BEGAN	ENDED	LASTED
The Reign of William III. and Mary II. . .	1689	1695	6 years.
The Reign of William the Third . . .		1702	13 years.
The Reign of Anne	1702	1714	12 years.
The Reign of George the First . . .	1714	1727	13 years.
The Reign of George the Second . . .	1727	1760	33 years.
The Reign of George the Third . . .	1760	1820	60 years.
The Reign of George the Fourth . . .	1820	1830	10 years.
The Reign of William the Fourth . . .	1830	1837	7 years.
The Reign of Victoria	1837		

CHRONOLOGICAL TABLE, AND TABLE OF CONTENTS

180*

A CHILD'S
HISTORY OF ENGLAND

CHAPTER I

ANCIENT ENGLAND AND THE ROMANS

IF you look at a Map of the World, you will see, in the left-hand upper corner of the Eastern Hemisphere, two Islands lying in the sea. They are England and Scotland, and Ireland. England and Scotland form the greater part of these Islands. Ireland is the next in size. The little neighbouring islands, which are so small upon the Map as to be mere dots, are chiefly little bits of Scotland,—broken off, I dare say, in the course of a great length of time, by the power of the restless water.

In the old days, a long, long while ago, before Our Saviour was born on earth and lay asleep in a manger, these Islands were in the same place, and the stormy sea roared round them, just as it roars now. But the sea was not alive, then, with great ships and brave sailors, sailing to and from all parts of the world. It was very lonely. The Islands lay solitary, in the great expanse of water. The foaming waves dashed against their cliffs, and the bleak winds blew over their forests; but the winds and waves brought no adventurers to land upon the Islands, and the savage Islanders knew nothing of the rest of the world, and the rest of the world knew nothing of them.

It is supposed that the Phœnicians, who were an ancient people, famous for carrying on trade, came in ships to these Islands, and found that they produced tin and lead; both very useful things, as you know, and both produced to this very hour upon the sea-coast. The most celebrated tin mines in Cornwall are, still, close to the sea. One of them, which I have seen, is so close to it that it is hollowed out underneath the ocean; and the miners say, that in stormy weather, when they are at work down in that deep place, they can hear the noise of the waves thundering above their heads. So, the Phœnicians, coasting about the Islands, would come, without much difficulty, to where the tin and lead were.

The Phœnicians traded with the Islanders for these metals, and gave the Islanders some other useful things in exchange. The Islanders were, at first, poor savages, going almost naked, or only dressed in the rough skins of beasts, and staining their bodies, as other savages do, with coloured earths and the juices of plants. But the Phœnicians, sailing over to the opposite coasts of France and Belgium, and saying to the people there, "We have been to those white cliffs across the water, which you can see in fine weather, and from that country, which is called BRITAIN, we bring this tin and lead," tempted some of the French and Belgians to come over also. These people settled themselves on the south coast of England, which is now called Kent; and, although they were a rough people too, they taught the savage Britons some useful arts, and improved that part of the Islands. It is probable that other people came over from Spain to Ireland, and settled there.

Thus, by little and little, strangers became mixed with the Islanders, and the savage Britons grew into a wild bold people; almost savage, still, especially in the interior of the country away from the sea where the foreign settlers seldom went; but hardy, brave, and strong.

The whole country was covered with forests, and swamps. The greater part of it was very misty and cold. There were no roads, no bridges, no streets, no houses that you would think deserving of the name. A town was nothing but a collection of straw-covered huts, hidden in a thick wood, with a ditch all round, and a low wall, made of mud, or the trunks of trees placed one upon another. The people planted little or no corn, but lived upon the flesh of their flocks and cattle. They made no coins, but used metal rings for money. They were clever in basket-work, as savage people often are; and they could make a coarse kind of cloth, and some very bad earthenware. But in building fortresses they were much more clever.

They made boats of basket-work, covered with the skins of animals, but seldom, if ever, ventured far from the shore. They made swords, of copper mixed with tin; but, these swords were of an awkward shape, and so soft that a heavy blow would bend one. They made light shields, short pointed daggers, and spears—which they jerked back after they had thrown them at an enemy, by a long strip of leather fastened to the stem. The butt-end was a rattle, to frighten an enemy's horse. The ancient Britons, being divided into as many as thirty or forty tribes, each commanded by its own little king, were constantly fighting with one another, as savage people usually do; and they always fought with these weapons.

They were very fond of horses. The standard of Kent was the picture of a white horse. They could break them in and manage them wonderfully well. Indeed, the horses (of which they had an abundance, though they were rather small) were so well taught in those days, that they can scarcely be said to have improved since; though the men are so much wiser. They understood, and obeyed, every word of command; and would stand still by themselves, in all the din and noise of battle, while their masters went to fight on foot. The Britons could not have succeeded in their most remarkable art, without the aid of these sensible and trusty animals. The art I mean, is the construction and management of war-chariots or cars for which they have ever been celebrated in history. Each of the best sort of these chariots, not quite breast high in front, and open at the back, contained one man to drive, and two or three others to fight— all standing up. The horses who drew them were so well trained, that they would tear, at full gallop, over the most stony ways, and even through the woods; dashing down their masters' enemies beneath their hoofs, and cutting them to pieces with the blades of swords, or scythes, which were fastened to the wheels, and stretched out beyond the car on each side, for that cruel purpose. In a moment, while at full speed, the horses would stop, at the driver's command. The men within would leap out, deal blows about them with their swords like hail, leap on the horses, on the pole, spring back into the chariots anyhow; and, as soon as they were safe, the horses tore away again.

The Britons had a strange and terrible religion, called the Religion of the Druids. It seems to have been brought over, in very early times indeed, from the opposite country of France, anciently called Gaul, and to have mixed up the worship of the Serpent, and of the Sun and Moon, with the worship of some of the Heathen Gods and Goddesses. Most of its ceremonies were kept secret by the priests, the Druids, who pretended to be enchanters, and who carried magicians' wands, and wore, each of them, about his neck, what he told the ignorant people was a Serpent's egg in a golden case. But it is certain that the Druidical ceremonies included the sacrifice of human victims, the torture of some suspected criminals, and, on particular occasions, even the burning alive, in immense wicker cages, of a number of men and animals together. The Druid Priests had some kind of veneration for the Oak, and for the mistletoe—the same plant that we hang up in houses at Christmas Time now—when its white berries grew upon the Oak. They met together in dark woods, which they called Sacred Groves; and there they instructed, in their mysterious arts, young men who came to them as pupils, and who sometimes stayed with them as long as twenty years.

These Druids built great Temples and altars, open to the sky, fragments of some of which are yet remaining. Stonehenge, on Salisbury Plain, in Wiltshire, is the most extraordinary of these. Three curious stones, called Kits Coty House, on Bluebell Hill, near Maidstone, in Kent, form another. We know, from examination of the great blocks of which such buildings are made, that they could not have been raised without the aid of some ingenious machines, which are common now, but which the ancient Britons certainly did not use in making their own uncomfortable houses. I should not wonder if the Druids, and their pupils who stayed with them twenty years, knowing more than the rest of the Britons, kept the people out of sight while they made these buildings, and then pretended that they built them by magic. Perhaps they had a hand in the fortresses too; at all events, as they were very powerful, and very much believed in, and as they made and executed the laws, and paid no taxes, I don't wonder that they liked their trade. And, as they persuaded the people the more Druids there were, the better off the people would be, I don't wonder that there were a good many of them. But it is pleasant to think that there are no Druids, *now*, who go on in that way, and pretend to carry Enchanters' Wands and Serpents' Eggs—and of course there is nothing of the kind, anywhere.

Such was the improved condition of the ancient Britons, fifty-five years before the birth of Our Saviour, when the Romans, under their great General, Julius Cæsar, were masters of all the rest of the known world. Julius Cæsar had then just conquered Gaul; and hearing, in Gaul, a good deal about the opposite Island with the white cliffs, and about the bravery of the Britons who inhabited it—some of whom had been fetched over to help the Gauls in the war against him—he resolved, as he was so near, to come and conquer Britain next.

So, Julius Cæsar came sailing over to this Island of ours, with eighty vessels and twelve thousand men. And he came from the French coast between Calais and Boulogne, "because thence was the shortest passage into Britain;" just for the same reason as our steam-boats now take the same track, every day. He expected to conquer Britain easily: but it was not such easy work as he supposed —for the bold Britons fought most bravely; and, what with not having his horse-soldiers with him (for they had been driven back by a storm), and what with having some of his vessels dashed to pieces by a high tide after they were drawn ashore, he ran great risk of being totally defeated. However, for once that the bold Britons beat him, he beat them twice; though not so soundly but that he was very glad to accept their proposals of peace, and go away.

But, in the spring of the next year, he came back; this time, with eight hundred vessels and thirty thousand men. The British tribes chose, as their general-in-chief, a Briton, whom the Romans in their Latin language called CASSIVELLAUNUS, but whose British name is supposed to have been CASWALLON. A brave general he was, and well he and his soldiers fought the Roman army! So well, that whenever in that war the Roman soldiers saw a great cloud of dust, and heard the rattle of the rapid British chariots, they trembled in their hearts. Besides a number of smaller battles, there was a battle fought near Canterbury, in Kent; there was a battle fought near Chertsey, in Surrey; there was a battle fought near a marshy little town in a wood, the capital of that part of Britain which belonged to CASSIVEL-LAUNUS, and which was probably near what is now Saint Albans, in Hertfordshire. However, brave CASSIVELLAUNUS had the worst of it, on the whole; though he and his men always fought like lions. As the other British chiefs were jealous of him, and were always quarrelling with him, and with one another, he gave up, and proposed peace. Julius Cæsar was very glad to grant peace easily, and to go away again with all his remaining ships and men. He had expected to find pearls in Britain, and he may have found a few for anything I know; but, at all events, he found delicious oysters, and I am sure he found tough Britons—of whom, I dare say, he made the same complaint as Napoleon Bonaparte the great French General did, eighteen hundred years afterwards, when he said they were such unreasonable fellows that they never knew when they were beaten. They never *did* know, I believe, and never will.

Nearly a hundred years passed on, and all that time, there was peace in Britain. The Britons improved their towns and mode of life: became more civilised, travelled, and learnt a great deal from the Gauls and Romans. At last, the Roman Emperor, Claudius, sent AULUS PLAUTIUS, a skilful general, with a mighty force, to subdue the Island, and shortly afterwards arrived himself. They did little; and OSTORIUS SCAPULA, another general, came. Some of the British Chiefs of Tribes submitted. Others resolved to fight to the death. Of these brave men, the bravest was CARACTACUS, or CARADOC, who gave battle to the Romans, with his army, among the mountains of North Wales. "This day," said he to his soldiers, "decides the fate of Britain! Your liberty, or your eternal slavery, dates from this hour. Remember your brave ancestors, who drove the great Cæsar himself across the sea!" On hearing these words, his men, with a great shout, rushed upon the Romans. But the strong Roman swords and armour were too much for the weaker British weapons in close conflict. The Britons lost the day. The wife and daughter of the brave CARACTACUS were taken prisoners; his brothers delivered themselves up; he himself was betrayed into the hands of the Romans by his false and base step-mother: and they carried him, and all his family, in triumph to Rome.

But a great man will be great in misfortune, great in prison, great in chains. His noble air, and dignified endurance of distress, so touched the Roman people who thronged the streets to see him, that he and his family were restored to freedom. No one knows whether his great heart broke, and he died in Rome, or whether he ever returned to his own dear country. English oaks have grown up from acorns, and withered away, when they were hundreds of years old— and other oaks have sprung up in their places, and died too, very aged—since the rest of the history of the brave CARACTACUS was forgotten.

Still, the Britons *would not* yield. They rose again and again, and died by thousands, sword in hand. They rose, on every possible occasion. SUETONIUS, another Roman general, came, and stormed the Island of Anglesey (then called MONA), which was supposed to be sacred, and he burnt the Druids in their own wicker cages, by their own fires. But, even while he was in Britain, with his victorious troops, the BRITONS rose. Because BOADICEA, a British queen, the widow of the King of the Norfolk and Suffolk people, resisted the plundering of her property by the Romans who were settled in England, she was scourged, by order of CATUS, a Roman officer; and her two daughters were shamefully insulted in her presence, and her husband's relations were made slaves. To avenge this injury, the Britons rose, with all their might and rage. They drove CATUS into Gaul; they laid the Roman possessions waste; they forced the

Romans out of London, then a poor little town, but a trading place; they hanged, burnt, crucified, and slew by the sword, seventy thousand Romans in a few days. SUETONIUS strengthened his army, and advanced to give them battle. They strengthened their army, and desperately attacked his, on the field where it was strongly posted. Before the first charge of the Britons was made, BOADICEA, in a war-chariot, with her fair hair streaming in the wind, and her injured daughters lying at her feet, drove among the troops, and cried to them for vengeance on their oppressors, the licentious Romans. The Britons fought to the last; but they were vanquished with great slaughter, and the unhappy queen took poison.

Still, the spirit of the Britons was not broken. When SUETONIUS left the country, they fell upon his troops, and retook the Island of Anglesey. AGRICOLA came, fifteen or twenty years afterwards, and retook it once more and devoted seven years to subduing the country, especially that part of it which is now called SCOTLAND; but, its people, the Caledonians, resisted him at every inch of ground. They fought the bloodiest battles with him; they killed their very wives and children, to prevent his making prisoners of them; they fell, fighting, in such great numbers that certain hills in Scotland are yet supposed to be vast heaps of stones piled up above their graves. HADRIAN came, thirty years afterwards, and still they resisted him. SEVERUS came, nearly a hundred years afterwards, and they worried his great army like dogs, and rejoiced to see them die, by thousands, in the bogs and swamps. CARACALLA, the son and successor of SEVERUS, did the most to conquer them, for a time; but not by force of arms. He knew how little that would do. He yielded up a quantity of land to the Caledonians, and gave the Britons the same privileges as the Romans possessed. There was peace, after this, for seventy years.

Then new enemies arose. They were the SAXONS, a fierce, seafaring people from the countries to the North of the Rhine, the great river of Germany on the banks of which the best grapes grow to make the German wine. They began to come, in pirate ships, to the sea-coast of Gaul and Britain, and to plunder them. They were repulsed by CARAUSIUS, a native either of Belgium or of Britain, who was appointed by the Romans to the command, and under whom the Britons first began to fight upon the sea. But, after this time, they renewed their ravages. A few years more, and the Scots (which was then the name for the people of Ireland), and the Picts, a northern people, began to make frequent plundering incursions into the South of Britain. All these attacks were repeated, at intervals, during two hundred years, and through a long succession of Roman Emperors and chiefs; during all which length of time, the Britons rose against the Romans, over and over again. At last, in the days of the Roman HONORIUS, when the Roman power all over the world was fast declining, and when Rome wanted all her soldiers at home, the Romans abandoned all hope of conquering Britain, and went away. And still, at last, as at first, the Britons rose against them, in their old brave manner; for, a very little while before, they had turned away the Roman magistrates, and declared themselves an independent people.

Five hundred years had passed, since Julius Cæsar's first invasion of the Island, when the Romans departed from it for ever. In the course of that time, although they had been the cause of terrible fighting and bloodshed, they had done much to improve the condition of the Britons. They had made great military roads; they had built forts; they had taught them how to dress, and arm themselves, much better than they had ever known how to do before; they had refined the whole British way of living. AGRICOLA had built a great wall of earth, more than seventy miles long, extending from Newcastle to beyond Carlisle, for the purpose of keeping out the Picts and Scots; HADRIAN had strengthened it; SEVERUS, finding it much in want of repair, had built it afresh of stone. Above all, it was in the Roman time, and by means of Roman ships, that the Christian Religion was first brought into Britain, and its people first taught the great lesson that, to be good in the sight of GOD, they must love their neighbours as themselves, and do unto others as they would be done by. The Druids declared that it was very wicked to believe in any such thing, and cursed all the people who did believe it, very heartily. But, when the people found that they were none the better for the blessings of the Druids, and none the worse for the curses of the Druids, but, that the sun shone and the rain fell without consulting the Druids at all, they just began to think that the Druids were mere men, and that it signified very little whether they cursed or blessed. After which, the pupils of the Druids fell off greatly in numbers, and the Druids took to other trades.

Thus I have come to the end of the Roman time in England. It is but little that is known of those five hundred years; but some remains of them are still found. Often, when labourers are digging up the ground, to make foundations for houses or churches, they light on rusty money that once belonged to the Romans. Fragments of plates from which they ate, of goblets from which they drank, and of pavement on which they trod, are discovered among the earth that is broken by the plough, or the dust that is crumbled by the gardener's spade. Wells that the Romans sunk, still yield water; roads that the Romans made, form part of our highways. In some old battle-fields, British spear-heads and Roman armour have been found, mingled together in decay, as they fell in the thick pressure of the fight. Traces of Roman camps overgrown with grass, and of mounds that are the burial-places of heaps of Britons, are to be seen in almost all parts of the country. Across the bleak moors of Northumberland, the wall of SEVERUS, overrun with moss and weeds, still stretches, a strong ruin; and the shepherds and their dogs lie sleeping on it in the summer weather. On Salisbury Plain, Stonehenge yet stands: a monument of the earlier time when the Roman name was unknown in Britain, and when the Druids, with their best magic wands, could not have written it in the sands of the wild sea-shore.

CHAPTER II

ANCIENT ENGLAND UNDER THE EARLY SAXONS

THE Romans had scarcely gone away from Britain, when the Britons began to wish they had never left it. For, the Romans being gone, and the Britons being much reduced in numbers by their long wars, the Picts and Scots came pouring in, over the broken and unguarded wall of SEVERUS, in swarms. They plundered the richest towns, and killed the people; and came back so often for more booty and more slaughter, that the unfortunate Britons lived a life of terror. As if the Picts and Scots were not bad enough on land, the Saxons attacked the islanders by sea; and, as if something more were still wanting to make them miserable, they quarrelled bitterly among themselves as to what prayers they ought to say, and how they ought to say them. The priests, being very angry with one another on these questions, cursed one another in the heartiest manner; and (uncommonly like the old Druids) cursed all the people whom they could not persuade. So, altogether, the Britons were very badly off, you may believe.

They were in such distress, in short, that they sent a letter to Rome entreating help—which they called the Groans of the Britons; and in which they said, "The barbarians chase us into the sea, the sea throws us back upon the barbarians, and we have only the hard choice left us of perishing by the sword, or perishing by the waves." But, the Romans could not help them, even if they were so inclined; for they had enough to do to defend themselves against their own enemies, who were then very fierce and strong. At last, the Britons, unable to bear their hard condition any longer, resolved to make peace with the Saxons, and to invite the Saxons to come into their country, and help them to keep out the Picts and Scots.

It was a British Prince named VORTIGERN who took this resolution, and who made a treaty of friendship with HENGIST and HORSA, two Saxon chiefs. Both of these names, in the old Saxon language, signify Horse; for the Saxons, like many other nations in a rough state, were fond of giving men the names of animals, as Horse, Wolf, Bear, Hound. The Indians of North America,—a very inferior people to the Saxons, though—do the same to this day.

HENGIST and HORSA drove out the Picts and Scots; and VORTIGERN, being grateful to them for that service, made no opposition to their settling themselves in that part of England which is called the Isle of Thanet, or to their inviting over more of their countrymen to join them. But HENGIST had a beautiful daughter named ROWENA; and when, at a feast, she filled a golden goblet to the brim with wine, and gave it to VORTIGERN, saying in a sweet voice, "Dear King, thy health!" the King fell in love with her. My opinion is, that the cunning HENGIST meant him to do so, in order that the Saxons might have greater influence with him; and that the fair ROWENA came to that feast, golden goblet and all, on purpose.

At any rate, they were married; and, long afterwards, whenever the King was angry with the Saxons, or jealous of their encroachments, ROWENA would put her beautiful arms round his neck, and softly say, "Dear King, they are my people! Be favourable to them, as you loved that Saxon girl who gave you the golden goblet of wine at the feast!" And, really, I don't see how the King could help himself.

Ah! We must all die! In the course of years, VORTIGERN died—he was dethroned, and put in prison, first, I am afraid; and ROWENA died; and generations of Saxons and Britons died; and events that happened during a long, long time, would have been quite forgotten but for the tales and songs of the old Bards, who used to go about from feast to feast, with their white beards, recounting the deeds of their forefathers. Among the histories of which they sang and talked, there was a famous one, concerning the bravery and virtues of KING ARTHUR, supposed to have been a British Prince in those old times. But, whether such a person really lived, or whether there were several persons whose histories came to be confused together under that one name, or whether all about him was invention, no one knows.

I will tell you, shortly, what is most interesting in the early Saxon times, as they are described in these songs and stories of the Bards.

In, and long after, the days of VORTIGERN, fresh bodies of Saxons, under various chiefs, came pouring into Britain. One body, conquering the Britons in the East, and settling there, called their kingdom Essex; another body settled in the West, and called their kingdom Wessex; the Northfolk, or Norfolk people, established themselves in one place; the Southfolk, or Suffolk people, established themselves in another; and gradually seven kingdoms or states arose in England, which were called the Saxon Heptarchy. The poor Britons, falling back before these crowds of fighting men whom they had innocently invited over as friends, retired into Wales and the adjacent country; into Devonshire, and into Cornwall. Those parts of England long remained unconquered. And in Cornwall now—where the sea-coast is very gloomy, steep, and rugged—where, in the dark winter-time, ships have often been wrecked close to the land, and every soul on board has perished—where the winds and waves howl drearily, and split the solid rocks into arches and caverns—there are very ancient ruins, which the people call the ruins of KING ARTHUR'S Castle.

Kent is the most famous of the seven Saxon kingdoms, because the Christian religion was preached to the Saxons there (who domineered over the Britons too much, to care for what *they* said about their religion, or anything else) by AUGUSTINE, a monk from Rome. KING ETHELBERT, of Kent, was soon converted; and the moment he said he was a Christian, his courtiers all said *they* were Christians; after which, ten thousand of his subjects said they were Christians too. AUGUSTINE built a little church, close to this King's palace, on the ground now occupied by the beautiful cathedral of

Canterbury. SEBERT, the King's nephew, built on a muddy marshy place near London, where there had been a temple to Apollo, a church dedicated to Saint Peter, which is now Westminster Abbey. And, in London itself, on the foundation of a temple to Diana, he built another little church which has risen up, since that old time, to be Saint Paul's.

After the death of ETHELBERT, EDWIN, King of Northumbria, who was such a good king that it was said a woman or child might openly carry a purse of gold, in his reign, without fear, allowed his child to be baptised, and held a great council to consider whether he and his people should all be Christians or not. It was decided that they should be. COIFI, the chief priest of the old religion, made a great speech on the occasion. In this discourse, he told the people that he had found out the old gods to be impostors. "I am quite satisfied of it," he said. "Look at me! I have been serving them all my life, and they have done nothing for me; whereas, if they had been really powerful, they could not have decently done less, in return for all I have done for them, than make my fortune. As they have never made my fortune, I am quite convinced they are impostors!" When this singular priest had finished speaking, he hastily armed himself with sword and lance, mounted a war-horse, rode at a furious gallop in sight of all the people to the temple, and flung his lance against it as an insult. From that time, the Christian religion spread itself among the Saxons, and became their faith.

The next very famous prince was EGBERT. He lived about a hundred and fifty years afterwards, and claimed to have a better right to the throne of Wessex than BEORTRIC, another Saxon prince who was at the head of that kingdom, and who married EDBURGA, the daughter of OFFA, king of another of the seven kingdoms. This QUEEN EDBURGA was a handsome murderess, who poisoned people when they offended her. One day, she mixed a cup of poison for a certain noble belonging to the court; but her husband drank of it too, by mistake, and died. Upon this, the people revolted, in great crowds; and running to the palace, and thundering at the gates, cried, "Down with the wicked queen, who poisons men!" They drove her out of the country, and abolished the title she had disgraced. When years had passed away, some travellers came home from Italy, and said that in the town of Pavia they had seen a ragged beggar-woman, who had once been handsome, but was then shrivelled, bent, and yellow, wandering about the streets, crying for bread; and that this beggar-woman was the poisoning English queen. It was, indeed, EDBURGA; and so she died without a shelter for her wretched head.

EGBERT, not considering himself safe in England, in consequence of his having claimed the crown of Wessex (for he thought his rival might take him prisoner and put him to death), sought refuge at the court of CHARLEMAGNE, King of France. On the death of BEORTRIC, so unhappily poisoned by mistake, EGBERT came back to Britain; succeeded to the throne of Wessex; conquered some of the other monarchs of the seven kingdoms; added their territories to his own;

and, for the first time, called the country over which he ruled,
ENGLAND.

And now, new enemies arose, who, for a long time, troubled
England sorely. These were the Northmen, the people of Denmark
and Norway, whom the English called the Danes. They were a warlike people, quite at home upon the sea; not Christians; very daring
and cruel. They came over in ships, and plundered and burned
wheresoever they landed. Once, they beat EGBERT in battle. Once,
EGBERT beat them. But, they cared no more for being beaten than
the English themselves. In the four following short reigns, of ETHEL-
WULF, and his sons, ETHELBALD, ETHELBERT, and ETHELRED, they
came back, over and over again, burning and plundering, and laying
England waste. In the last-mentioned reign, they seized EDMUND,
King of East England, and bound him to a tree. Then, they proposed
to him that he should change his religion; but he, being a good
Christian, steadily refused. Upon that, they beat him, made cowardly
jests upon him, all defenceless as he was, shot arrows at him, and,
finally, struck off his head. It is impossible to say whose head they
might have struck off next, but for the death of KING ETHELRED
from a wound he had received in fighting against them, and the
succession to his throne of the best and wisest king that ever lived
in England.

CHAPTER III

ENGLAND UNDER THE GOOD SAXON, ALFRED

ALFRED THE GREAT was a young man, three-and-twenty years of
age, when he became king. Twice in his childhood, he had been taken
to Rome, where the Saxon nobles were in the habit of going on
journeys which they supposed to be religious; and, once, he had
stayed for some time in Paris. Learning, however, was so little cared
for, then, that at twelve years old he had not been taught to read;
although, of the sons of KING ETHELWULF, he, the youngest, was the
favourite. But he had—as most men who grow up to be great and
good are generally found to have had—an excellent mother; and,
one day, this lady, whose name was OSBURGA, happened, as she was
sitting among her sons, to read a book of Saxon poetry. The art of
printing was not known until long and long after that period, and
the book, which was written, was what is called "illuminated," with
beautiful bright letters, richly painted. The brothers admiring it
very much, their mother said, "I will give it to that one of you four
princes who first learns to read." ALFRED sought out a tutor that
very day, applied himself to learn with great diligence, and soon won
the book. He was proud of it, all his life.

This great king, in the first year of his reign, fought nine battles
with the Danes. He made some treaties with them too, by which

the false Danes swore they would quit the country. They pretended to consider that they had taken a very solemn oath, in swearing this upon the holy bracelets that they wore, and which were always buried with them when they died; but they cared little for it, for they thought nothing of breaking oaths and treaties too, as soon as it suited their purpose, and coming back again to fight, plunder, and burn, as usual. One fatal winter, in the fourth year of KING ALFRED'S reign, they spread themselves in great numbers over the whole of England; and so dispersed and routed the King's soldiers that the King was left alone, and was obliged to disguise himself as a common peasant, and to take refuge in the cottage of one of his cowherds who did not know his face.

Here, KING ALFRED, while the Danes sought him far and near, was left alone one day, by the cowherd's wife, to watch some cakes which she put to bake upon the hearth. But, being at work upon his bow and arrows, with which he hoped to punish the false Danes when a brighter time should come, and thinking deeply of his poor unhappy subjects whom the Danes chased through the land, his noble mind forgot the cakes, and they were burnt. "What!" said the cowherd's wife, who scolded him well when she came back, and little thought she was scolding the King, "you will be ready enough to eat them by-and-by, and yet you cannot watch them, idle dog?"

At length, the Devonshire men made head against a new host of Danes who landed on their coast; killed their chief, and captured their flag; on which was represented the likeness of a Raven—a very fit bird for a thievish army like that, I think. The loss of their standard troubled the Danes greatly, for they believed it to be enchanted—woven by the three daughters of one father in a single afternoon—and they had a story among themselves that when they were victorious in battle, the Raven stretched his wings and seemed to fly; and that when they were defeated, he would droop. He had good reason to droop, now, if he could have done anything half so sensible; for, KING ALFRED joined the Devonshire men; made a camp with them on a piece of firm ground in the midst of a bog in Somersetshire; and prepared for a great attempt for vengeance on the Danes, and the deliverance of his oppressed people.

But, first, as it was important to know how numerous those pestilent Danes were, and how they were fortified, KING ALFRED, being a good musician, disguised himself as a glee-man or minstrel, and went, with his harp, to the Danish camp. He played and sang in the very tent of GUTHRUM the Danish leader, and entertained the Danes as they caroused. While he seemed to think of nothing but his music, he was watchful of their tents, their arms, their discipline, everything that he desired to know. And right soon did this great king entertain them to a different tune; for, summoning all his true followers to meet him at an appointed place, where they received him with joyful shouts and tears, as the monarch whom many of them had given up for lost or dead, he put himself at their head, marched on the Danish camp, defeated the Danes with great slaughter, and besieged them for fourteen days to prevent their escape. But, being as merciful as he was good and brave, he then, instead of killing them, proposed peace: on condition that they should altogether depart from that Western part of England, and settle in the East; and that GUTHRUM should become a Christian, in remembrance of the Divine religion which now taught his conqueror, the noble ALFRED, to forgive the enemy who had so often injured him. This, GUTHRUM did. At his baptism, KING ALFRED was his god-father. And GUTHRUM was an honourable chief who well deserved that clemency; for, ever afterwards he was loyal and faithful to the King. The Danes under him were faithful too. They plundered and burned no more, but worked like honest men. They ploughed, and sowed, and reaped, and led good honest English lives. And I hope the children of those Danes played, many a time, with Saxon children in the sunny fields; and that Danish young men fell in love with Saxon girls, and married them; and that English travellers, benighted at the doors of Danish cottages, often went in for shelter until morning; and that Danes and Saxons sat by the red fire, friends, talking of KING ALFRED THE GREAT.

All the Danes were not like these under GUTHRUM; for, after some years, more of them came over, in the old plundering and burning way—among them a fierce pirate of the name of HASTINGS, who had the boldness to sail up the Thames to Gravesend, with eighty ships. For three years, there was a war with these Danes; and there was a famine in the country, too, and a plague, both upon human creatures and beasts. But KING ALFRED, whose mighty heart never failed him, built large ships nevertheless, with which to pursue the pirates on the sea; and he encouraged his soldiers, by his brave example, to fight valiantly against them on the shore. At last, he drove them all away; and then there was repose in England.

As great and good in peace, as he was great and good in war, KING ALFRED never rested from his labours to improve his people. He loved to talk with clever men, and with travellers from foreign countries, and to write down what they told him, for his people to read. He had studied Latin after learning to read English, and now another of his labours was, to translate Latin books into the English-Saxon tongue, that his people might be interested, and improved by their contents. He made just laws, that they might live more happily and freely; he turned away all partial judges, that no wrong might be done them; he was so careful of their property, and punished robbers so severely, that it was a common thing to say that under the great KING ALFRED, garlands of golden chains and jewels might have hung across the streets, and no man would have touched one. He founded schools; he patiently heard causes himself in his Court of Justice; the great desires of his heart were, to do right to all his subjects, and to leave England better, wiser, happier in all ways, than he found it. His industry in these efforts was quite astonishing. Every day he divided into certain portions, and in each portion devoted himself to a certain pursuit. That he might divide his time exactly, he had wax torches or candles made, which were all of the same size, were notched across at regular distances, and were always kept burning. Thus, as the candles burnt down, he divided the day into notches, almost as accurately as we now divide it into hours upon the clock. But when the candles were first invented, it was found that the wind and draughts of air, blowing into the palace through the doors and windows, and through the chinks in the walls, caused them to gutter and burn unequally. To prevent this, the King had them put into cases formed of wood and white horn. And these were the first lanthorns ever made in England.

All this time, he was afflicted with a terrible unknown disease, which caused him violent and frequent pain that nothing could relieve. He bore it, as he had borne all the troubles of his life, like a brave good man, until he was fifty-three years old; and then, having reigned thirty years, he died. He died in the year nine hundred and one; but, long ago as that is, his fame, and the love and gratitude with which his subjects regarded him, are freshly remembered to the present hour.

In the next reign, which was the reign of EDWARD, surnamed THE ELDER, who was chosen in council to succeed, a nephew of KING ALFRED troubled the country by trying to obtain the throne. The Danes in the East of England took part with this usurper (perhaps because they had honoured his uncle so much, and honoured him for his uncle's sake), and there was hard fighting; but, the King, with the assistance of his sister, gained the day, and reigned in peace for four and twenty years. He gradually extended his power over the whole of England, and so the Seven Kingdoms were united into one.

When England thus became one kingdom, ruled over by one Saxon king, the Saxons had been settled in the country more than four hundred and fifty years. Great changes had taken place in its customs during that time. The Saxons were still greedy eaters and great drinkers, and their feasts were often of a noisy and drunken kind; but many new comforts and even elegances had become known, and were fast increasing. Hangings for the walls of rooms, where, in these modern days, we paste up paper, are known to have been sometimes made of silk, ornamented with birds and flowers in needlework. Tables and chairs were curiously carved in different woods; were sometimes decorated with gold or silver; sometimes even made of those precious metals. Knives and spoons were used at table ; golden ornaments were worn—with silk and cloth, and golden tissues and embroideries; dishes were made of gold and silver, brass and bone. There were varieties of drinking-horns, bedsteads, musical instruments. A harp was passed round, at a feast, like the drinking-bowl, from guest to guest; and each one usually sang or played when his turn came. The weapons of the Saxons were stoutly made, and among them was a terrible iron hammer that gave deadly blows, and was long remembered. The Saxons themselves were a handsome people. The men were proud of their long fair hair, parted on the forehead; their ample beards, their fresh complexions, and clear eyes. The beauty of the Saxon women filled all England with a new delight and grace.

I have more to tell of the Saxons yet, but I stop to say this now, because under the GREAT ALFRED, all the best points of the English-Saxon character were first encouraged, and in him first shown. It has been the greatest character among the nations of the earth. Wherever the descendants of the Saxon race have gone, have sailed, or otherwise made their way, even to the remotest regions of the world, they have been patient, persevering, never to be broken in spirit, never to be turned aside from enterprises on which they have resolved. In Europe, Asia, Africa, America, the whole world over; in the desert, in the forest, on the sea; scorched by a burning sun, or frozen by ice that never melts; the Saxon blood remains unchanged. Wheresoever that race goes, there, law, and industry, and safety for life and property, and all the great results of steady perseverance, are certain to arise.

I pause to think with admiration, of the noble king who, in his single person, possessed all the Saxon virtues. Whom misfortune could not subdue, whom prosperity could not spoil, whose perseverance nothing could shake. Who was hopeful in defeat, and generous in success. Who loved justice, freedom, truth, and knowledge. Who, in his care to instruct his people, probably did more to preserve the beautiful old Saxon language, than I can imagine. Without whom, the English tongue in which I tell this story might have wanted half its meaning. As it is said that his spirit still inspires some of our best English laws, so, let you and I pray that it may animate our English hearts, at least to this—to resolve, when we see any of our fellow-creatures left in ignorance, that we will do our best, while life is in us, to have them taught; and to tell those rulers whose duty it is to teach them, and who neglect their duty, that they have profited very little by all the years that have rolled away since the year nine hundred and one, and that they are far behind the bright example of KING ALFRED THE GREAT.

CHAPTER IV

ENGLAND UNDER ATHELSTAN AND THE SIX BOY-KINGS

ATHELSTAN, the son of Edward the Elder, succeeded that king. He reigned only fifteen years; but he remembered the glory of his grandfather, the great Alfred, and governed England well. He reduced the turbulent people of Wales, and obliged them to pay him a tribute in money, and in cattle, and to send him their best hawks and hounds. He was victorious over the Cornish men, who were not yet quite under the Saxon government. He restored such of the old laws as were good, and had fallen into disuse; made some wise new laws, and took care of the poor and weak. A strong alliance, made against him by ANLAF a Danish prince, CONSTANTINE King of the Scots, and the people of North Wales, he broke and defeated in one great battle, long famous for the vast numbers slain in it. After that, he had a quiet reign; the lords and ladies about him had leisure to become polite and agreeable; and foreign princes were glad (as they have sometimes been since) to come to England on visits to the English court.

When Athelstan died, at forty-seven years old, his brother EDMUND, who was only eighteen, became king. He was the first of six boy-kings, as you will presently know.

They called him the Magnificent, because he showed a taste for improvement and refinement. But he was beset by the Danes, and had a short and troubled reign, which came to a troubled end. One night, when he was feasting in his hall, and had eaten much and drunk deep, he saw, among the company, a noted robber named LEOF, who had been banished from England. Made very angry by the boldness of this man, the King turned to his cup-bearer, and said, "There is a robber sitting at the table yonder, who, for his crimes, is an outlaw in the land—a hunted wolf, whose life any man may take, at any time. Command that robber to depart!" "I will not depart!" said Leof. "No?" cried the King. "No, by the Lord!" said Leof. Upon that the King rose from his seat, and, making passionately at the robber, and seizing him by his long hair, tried to throw him down. But the robber had a dagger underneath his cloak, and, in the scuffle, stabbed the King to death. That done, he set his back against the wall, and fought so desperately, that although he was soon cut to pieces by the King's armed men, and the wall and pavement were splashed with his blood, yet it was not before he had killed and wounded many of them. You may imagine what rough lives the kings of those times led, when one of them could struggle, half drunk, with a public robber in his own dining-hall, and be stabbed in presence of the company who ate and drank with him.

Then succeeded the boy-king EDRED, who was weak and sickly in body, but of a strong mind. And his armies fought the Northmen, the Danes, the Norwegians, or the Sea-Kings, as they were called, and beat them for the time. And, in nine years, Edred died, and passed away.

Then came the boy-king EDWY, fifteen years of age; but the real king, who had the real power, was a monk named DUNSTAN—a clever priest, a little mad, and not a little proud and cruel.

Dunstan was then Abbot of Glastonbury Abbey, whither the body of King Edmund the Magnificent was carried, to be buried. While yet a boy, he had got out of his bed one night (being then in a fever), and walked about Glastonbury Church when it was under repair; and, because he did not tumble off some scaffolds that were there, and break his neck, it was reported that he had been shown over the building by an angel. He had also made a harp that was said to play of itself—which it very likely did, as Æolian Harps, which are played by the wind, and are understood now, always do. For these wonders he had been once denounced by his enemies, who were jealous of his favour with the late King Athelstan, as a magician; and he had been waylaid, bound hand and foot, and thrown into a marsh. But he got out again, somehow, to cause a great deal of trouble yet.

The priests of those days were, generally, the only scholars. They were learned in many things. Having to make their own convents and monasteries on uncultivated grounds that were granted to them by the Crown, it was necessary that they should be good farmers and good gardeners, or their lands would have been too poor to support them. For the decoration of the chapels where they prayed, and for the comfort of the refectories where they ate and drank, it was necessary that there should be good carpenters, good smiths, good painters, among them. For their greater safety in sickness and accident, living alone by themselves in solitary places, it was necessary that they should study the virtues of plants and herbs, and should know how to dress cuts, burns, scalds, and bruises, and how to set broken limbs. Accordingly, they taught themselves, and one another, a great variety of useful arts; and became skilful in agriculture, medicine, surgery, and handicraft. And when they wanted the aid of any little piece of machinery, which would be simple enough now, but was marvellous then, to impose a trick upon the poor peasants, they knew very well how to make it; and *did* make it many a time and often, I have no doubt.

Dunstan, Abbot of Glastonbury Abbey, was one of the most sagacious of these monks. He was an ingenious smith, and worked at a forge in a little cell. This cell was made too short to admit of his lying at full length, when he went to sleep—as if *that* did any good to anybody!—and he used to tell the most extraordinary lies about demons and spirits, who, he said, came there to persecute him. For instance, he related that one day when he was at work, the devil looked in at the little window, and tried to tempt him to lead a life of idle pleasure; whereupon, having his pincers in the fire, red hot, he seized the devil by the nose, and put him to such pain, that his bellowings were heard for miles and miles. Some people are inclined to think this nonsense a part of Dunstan's madness (for his head never quite recovered the fever), but I think not. I observe that it induced the ignorant people to consider him a holy man, and that it made him very powerful. Which was exactly what he always wanted.

On the day of the coronation of the handsome boy-king Edwy, it was remarked by ODO, Archbishop of Canterbury (who was a Dane by birth), that the King quietly left the coronation feast, while all the company were there. Odo, much displeased, sent his friend Dunstan to seek him. Dunstan finding him in the company of his beautiful young wife ELGIVA, and her mother ETHELGIVA, a good and virtuous lady, not only grossly abused them, but dragged the young King back into the feasting-hall by force. Some, again, think Dunstan did this because the young King's fair wife was his own cousin, and the monks objected to people marrying their own cousins; but I believe he did it, because he was an imperious, audacious, ill-conditioned priest, who, having loved a young lady himself before he became a sour monk, hated all love now, and everything belonging to it.

The young King was quite old enough to feel this insult. Dunstan had been Treasurer in the last reign, and he soon charged Dunstan with having taken some of the last king's money. The Glastonbury Abbot fled to Belgium (very narrowly escaping some pursuers who were sent to put out his eyes, as you will wish they had, when you read what follows), and his abbey was given to priests who were married; whom he always, both before and afterwards, opposed. But he quickly conspired with his friend, Odo the Dane, to set up the King's young brother, EDGAR, as his rival for the throne; and, not content with this revenge, he caused the beautiful queen Elgiva, though a lovely girl of only seventeen or eighteen, to be stolen from one of the Royal Palaces, branded in the cheek with a red-hot iron, and sold into slavery in Ireland. But the Irish people pitied and befriended her; and they said, "Let us restore the girl-queen to the boy-king, and make the young lovers happy!" and they cured her of her cruel wound, and sent her home as beautiful as before. But the villain Dunstan, and that other villain, Odo, caused her to be waylaid at Gloucester as she was joyfully hurrying to join her husband, and to be hacked and hewn with swords, and to be barbarously maimed and lamed, and left to die. When Edwy the Fair (his people called him so, because he was so young and handsome) heard of her dreadful fate, he died of a broken heart; and so the pitiful story of the poor young wife and husband ends! Ah! Better to be two cottagers in these better times, than king and queen of England in those bad days, though never so fair!

Then came the boy-king, EDGAR, called the Peaceful, fifteen years old. Dunstan, being still the real king, drove all married priests out of the monasteries and abbeys, and replaced them by solitary monks like himself, of the rigid order called the Benedictines. He made himself Archbishop of Canterbury, for his greater glory; and exercised such power over the neighbouring British princes, and so collected them about the King, that once, when the King held his court at Chester, and went on the river Dee to visit the monastery of St. John, the eight oars of his boat were pulled (as the people used to delight in relating in stories and songs) by eight crowned kings, and steered by the King of England. As Edgar was very obedient to Dunstan and the monks, they took great pains to represent him as the best of kings. But he was really profligate, debauched, and vicious. He once forcibly carried off a young lady from the convent at Wilton; and Dunstan, pretending to be very much shocked, condemned him not to wear his crown upon his head for seven years— no great punishment, I dare say, as it can hardly have been a more comfortable ornament to wear, than a stewpan without a handle. His marriage with his second wife, ELFRIDA, is one of the worst events of his reign. Hearing of the beauty of this lady, he despatched his favourite courtier, ATHELWOLD, to her father's castle in Devonshire, to see if she were really as charming as fame reported. Now, she was so exceedingly beautiful that Athelwold fell in love with her himself, and married her; but he told the King that she was only rich —not handsome. The King, suspecting the truth when they came home, resolved to pay the newly-married couple a visit; and, suddenly, told Athelwold to prepare for his immediate coming. Athelwold, terrified, confessed to his young wife what he had said and done, and implored her to disguise her beauty by some ugly dress or silly manner, that he might be safe from the King's anger. She promised that she would; but she was a proud woman, who would far rather have been a queen than the wife of a courtier. She dressed herself in her best dress, and adorned herself with her richest jewels; and when the King came, presently, he discovered the cheat. So, he caused his false friend, Athelwold, to be murdered in a wood, and married his widow, this bad Elfrida. Six or seven years afterwards, he died; and was buried, as if he had been all that the monks said he was, in the abbey of Glastonbury, which he—or Dunstan for him—had much enriched.

England, in one part of this reign, was so troubled by wolves, which, driven out of the open country, hid themselves in the mountains of Wales when they were not attacking travellers and animals, that the tribute payable by the Welsh people was forgiven them, on condition of their producing, every year, three hundred wolves' heads. And the Welshmen were so sharp upon the wolves, to save their money, that in four years there was not a wolf left.

Then came the boy-king, EDWARD, called the Martyr, from the manner of his death. Elfrida had a son, named ETHELRED, for whom she claimed the throne; but Dunstan did not choose to favour him, and he made Edward king. The boy was hunting, one day, down in Dorsetshire, when he rode near to Corfe Castle, where Elfrida and Ethelred lived. Wishing to see them kindly, he rode away from his attendants and galloped to the castle gate, where he arrived at twilight, and blew his hunting-horn. "You are welcome, dear King," said Elfrida, coming out, with her brightest smiles. "Pray you dismount and enter." "Not so, dear madam," said the King. "My company will miss me, and fear that I have met with some harm. Please you to give me a cup of wine, that I may drink here, in the saddle, to you and to my little brother, and so ride away with the good speed I have made in riding here." Elfrida, going in to bring the wine, whispered to an armed servant, one of her attendants, who stole out of the darkening gateway, and crept round behind the King's horse. As the King raised the cup to his lips, saying, "Health!" to the wicked woman who was smiling on him, and to his innocent brother whose hand she held in hers, and who was only ten years old, this armed man made a spring and stabbed him in the back. He dropped the cup and spurred his horse away; but, soon fainting with loss of blood, drooped from the saddle, and, in his fall, entangled one of his feet in the stirrup. The frightened horse dashed on; trailing his rider's curls upon the ground; dragging his smooth young face through ruts, and stones, and briers, and fallen leaves, and mud; until the hunters, tracking the animal's course by the King's blood, caught his bridle, and released the disfigured body.

Then came the sixth and last of the boy-kings, ETHELRED, whom Elfrida, when he cried out at the sight of his murdered brother riding away from the castle gate, unmercifully beat with a torch which she snatched from one of the attendants. The people so disliked this boy, on account of his cruel mother and the murder she had done to promote him, that Dunstan would not have had him for king, but would have made EDGITHA, the daughter of the dead King Edgar, and of the lady whom he stole out of the convent at Wilton, Queen of England, if she would have consented. But she knew the stories of the youthful kings too well, and would not be persuaded from the convent where she lived in peace; so, Dunstan put Ethelred on the throne, having no one else to put there and gave him the nick-name of THE UNREADY—knowing that he wanted resolution and firmness.

At first, Elfrida possessed great influence over the young King, but, as he grew older and came of age, her influence declined. The infamous woman, not having it in her power to do any more evil, then retired from court, and, according to the fashion of the time, built churches and monasteries, to expiate her guilt. As if a church, with a steeple reaching to the very stars, would have been any sign of true repentance for the blood of the poor boy, whose murdered form was trailed at his horse's heels! As if she could have buried her wickedness beneath the senseless stones of the whole world, piled up one upon another, for the monks to live in!

About the ninth or tenth year of this reign, Dunstan died. He was growing old then, but was as stern and artful as ever. Two circumstances that happened in connexion with him, in this reign of Ethelred, made a great noise. Once, he was present at a meeting of the Church, when the question was discussed whether priests should have permission to marry; and, as he sat with his head hung down, apparently thinking about it, a voice seemed to come out of a crucifix in the room, and warn the meeting to be of his opinion. This was some juggling of Dunstan's, and was probably his own voice disguised. But he played off a worse juggle than that, soon afterwards; for, another meeting being held on the same subject, and he and his supporters being seated on one side of a great room, and their opponents on the other, he rose and said, "To Christ himself, as Judge, do I commit this cause!" Immediately on these words being spoken, the floor where the opposite party sat gave way, and some were killed and many wounded. You may be pretty sure that it had been weakened under Dunstan's direction, and that it fell at Dunstan's signal. *His* part of the floor did not go down. No, no. He was too good a workman for that.

When he died, the monks settled that he was a Saint, and called him Saint Dunstan ever afterwards. They might just as well have settled that he was a coach-horse, and could just as easily have called him one.

Ethelred the Unready was glad enough, I dare say, to be rid of this holy saint; but, left to himself, he was a poor weak king, and his reign was a reign of defeat and shame. The restless Danes, led by SWEYN, a son of the King of Denmark who had quarrelled with his father and had been banished from home, again came into England, and, year after year, attacked and despoiled large towns. To coax these sea-kings away, the weak Ethelred paid them money; but, the more money he paid, the more money the Danes wanted. At first, he gave them ten thousand pounds; on their next invasion, sixteen thousand pounds; on their next invasion, four and twenty thousand pounds: to pay which large sums, the unfortunate English people were heavily taxed. But, as the Danes still came back and wanted more, he thought it would be a good plan to marry into some powerful foreign family that would help him with soldiers. So, in the year one thousand and two, he courted and married Emma, the sister of Richard Duke of Normandy; a lady who was called the Flower of Normandy.

And now, a terrible deed was done in England, the like of which was never done on English ground before or since. On the thirteenth of November, in pursuance of secret instructions sent by the King over the whole country, the inhabitants of every town and city armed, and murdered all the Danes who were their neighbours. Young and old, babies and soldiers, men and women, every Dane was killed. No doubt there were among them many ferocious men who had done the English great wrong, and whose pride and insolence, in swaggering in the houses of the English and insulting their wives and daughters, had become unbearable; but no doubt there were also among them many peaceful Christian Danes who had married English women and become like English men. They were all slain, even to GUNHILDA, the sister of the King of Denmark, married to an English lord; who was first obliged to see the murder of her husband and her child, and then was killed herself.

When the King of the sea-kings heard of this deed of blood, he swore that he would have a great revenge. He raised an army, and a mightier fleet of ships than ever yet had sailed to England; and in all his army there was not a slave or an old man, but every soldier was a free man, and the son of a free man, and in the prime of life, and sworn to be revenged upon the English nation, for the massacre of that dread thirteenth of November, when his countrymen and countrywomen, and the little children whom they loved, were killed with fire and sword. And so, the sea-kings came to England in many great ships, each bearing the flag of its own commander. Golden eagles, ravens, dragons, dolphins, beasts of prey, threatened England from the prows of those ships, as they came onward through the water; and were reflected in the shining shields that hung upon their sides. The ship that bore the standard of the King of the sea-kings was carved and painted like a mighty serpent; and the King in his anger prayed that the Gods in whom he trusted might all desert him, if his serpent did not strike its fangs into England's heart.

And indeed it did. For, the great army landing from the great fleet, near Exeter, went forward, laying England waste, and striking their lances in the earth as they advanced, or throwing them into rivers, in token of their making all the island theirs. In remembrance of the black November night when the Danes were murdered, wheresoever the invaders came, they made the Saxons prepare and spread for them great feasts; and when they had eaten those feasts, and had drunk a curse to England with wild rejoicings, they drew their swords, and killed their Saxon entertainers, and marched on. For six long years they carried on this war: burning the crops, farmhouses, barns, mills, granaries; killing the labourers in the fields; preventing the seed from being sown in the ground; causing famine and starvation; leaving only heaps of ruin and smoking ashes, where they had found rich towns. To crown this misery, English officers and men deserted, and even the favourites of Ethelred the Unready, becoming traitors, seized many of the English ships, turned pirates against their own country, and aided by a storm occasioned the loss of nearly the whole English navy.

There was but one man of note, at this miserable pass, who was true to his country and the feeble King. He was a priest, and a brave one. For twenty days, the Archbishop of Canterbury defended that city against its Danish besiegers; and when a traitor in the town threw the gates open and admitted them, he said, in chains, "I will not buy my life with money that must be extorted from the suffering people. Do with me what you please!" Again and again, he steadily refused to purchase his release with gold wrung from the poor.

At last, the Danes, being tired of this, and being assembled at a drunken merry-making, had him brought into the feasting-hall.

"Now, bishop," they said, "we want gold!"

He looked round on the crowd of angry faces; from the shaggy beards close to him, to the shaggy beards against the walls, where men were mounted on tables and forms to see him over the heads of others: and he knew that his time was come.

"I have no gold," he said.

"Get it, bishop!" they all thundered.

"That, I have often told you I will not," said he.

They gathered closer round him, threatening, but he stood unmoved. Then, one man struck him; then, another; then a cursing soldier picked up from a heap in a corner of the hall, where fragments had been rudely thrown at dinner, a great ox-bone, and cast it at his face, from which the blood came spurting forth; then, others ran to the same heap, and knocked him down with other bones, and bruised and battered him; until one soldier whom he had baptised (willing, as I hope for the sake of that soldier's soul, to shorten the sufferings of the good man) struck him dead with his battle-axe.

If Ethelred had had the heart to emulate the courage of this noble

archbishop, he might have done something yet. But he paid the
Danes forty-eight thousand pounds, instead, and gained so little by
the cowardly act, that Sweyn soon afterwards came over to subdue
all England. So broken was the attachment of the English people, by
this time, to their incapable King and their forlorn country which
could not protect them, that they welcomed Sweyn on all sides, as
a deliverer.   London faithfully stood out, as long as the King was
within its walls; but, when he sneaked away, it also welcomed the
Dane. Then, all was over; and the King took refuge abroad with
the Duke of Normandy, who had already given shelter to the
King's wife, once the Flower of that country, and to her children.

Still, the English people, in spite of their sad sufferings, could not
quite forget the great King Alfred and the Saxon race. When Sweyn
died suddenly, in little more than a month after he had been proclaimed King of England, they generously sent to Ethelred, to say
that they would have him for their King again, "if he would only
govern them better than he had governed them before." The Unready
instead of coming himself, sent Edward, one of his sons, to make
promises for him. At last, he followed, and the English declared him
King. The Danes declared CANUTE, the son of Sweyn, King. Thus,
direful war began again, and lasted for three years, when the
Unready died. And I know of nothing better that he did, in all his
reign of eight and thirty years.

Was Canute to be King now? Not over the Saxons, they said; they
must have EDMUND, one of the sons of the Unready, who was surnamed IRONSIDE, because of his strength and stature. Edmund and
Canute thereupon fell to, and fought five battles—O unhappy
England, what a fighting-ground it was!—and then Ironside, who was
a big man, proposed to Canute, who was a little man, that they two
should fight it out in single combat. If Canute had been the big man,
he would probably have said yes, but, being the little man, he decidedly
said no. However, he declared that he was willing to divide the kingdom—to take all that lay north of Watling Street, as the old Roman
military road from Dover to Chester was called, and to give Ironside
all that lay south of it. Most men being weary of so much bloodshed,
this was done. But Canute soon became sole King of England; for
Ironside died suddenly within two months. Some think that he was
killed, and killed by Canute's orders. No one knows.

CHAPTER V

ENGLAND UNDER CANUTE THE DANE

CANUTE reigned eighteen years. He was a merciless King at first.
After he had clasped the hands of the Saxon chiefs, in token of the
sincerity with which he swore to be just and good to them in return
for their acknowledging him, he denounced and slew many of them,

as well as many relations of the late King. "He who brings me the head of one of my enemies," he used to say, "shall be dearer to me than a brother." And he was so severe in hunting down his enemies that he must have got together a pretty large family of these dear brothers. He was strongly inclined to kill EDMUND and EDWARD, two children, sons of poor Ironside; but, being afraid to do so in England, he sent them over to the King of Sweden, with a request that the King would be so good as "dispose of them." If the King of Sweden had been like many, many other men of that day, he would have had their innocent throats cut; but he was a kind man, and brought them up tenderly.

Normandy ran much in Canute's mind. In Normandy were the two children of the late king—EDWARD and ALFRED by name; and their uncle the Duke might one day claim the crown for them. But the Duke showed so little inclination to do so now, that he proposed to Canute to marry his sister, the widow of The Unready; who, being but a showy flower, and caring for nothing so much as becoming a queen again, left her children and was wedded to him.

Successful and triumphant, assisted by the valour of the English in his foreign wars, and with little strife to trouble him at home, Canute had a prosperous reign, and made many improvements. He was a poet and a musician. He grew sorry, as he grew older, for the blood he had shed at first; and went to Rome in a Pilgrim's dress, by way of washing it out. He gave a great deal of money to foreigners on his journey; but he took it from the English before he started. On the whole, however, he certainly became a far better man when he had no opposition to contend with, and was as great a King as England had known for some time.

The old writers of history relate how that Canute was one day disgusted with his courtiers for their flattery, and how he caused his chair to be set on the sea-shore, and feigned to command the tide as it came up not to wet the edge of his robe, for the land was his; how the tide came up, of course, without regarding him; and how he then turned to his flatterers, and rebuked them, saying, what was the might of any earthly king, to the might of the Creator, who could say unto the sea, "Thus far shalt thou go, and no farther!" We may learn from this, I think, that a little sense will go a long way in a king; and that courtiers are not easily cured of flattery, nor kings of a liking for it. If the courtiers of Canute had not known, long before, that the King was fond of flattery, they would have known better than to offer it in such large doses. And if they had not known that he was vain of this speech (anything but a wonderful speech it seems to me, if a good child had made it), they would not have been at such great pains to repeat it. I fancy I see them all on the sea-shore together; the King's chair sinking in the sand; the King in a mighty good humour with his own wisdom; and the courtiers pretending to be quite stunned by it!

It is not the sea alone that is bidden to go "thus far, and no farther." The great command goes forth to all the kings upon the earth, and went to Canute in the year one thousand and thirty-five, and stretched him dead upon his bed. Beside it, stood his Norman wife. Perhaps, as the King looked his last upon her, he, who had so often thought distrustfully of Normandy, long ago, thought once more of the two exiled Princes in their uncle's court, and of the little favour they could feel for either Danes or Saxons, and of a rising cloud in Normandy that slowly moved towards England.

CHAPTER VI

ENGLAND UNDER HAROLD HAREFOOT, HARDICANUTE, AND EDWARD THE CONFESSOR

CANUTE left three sons, by name SWEYN, HAROLD, and HARDI-CANUTE; but his Queen, Emma, once the Flower of Normandy, was the mother of only Hardicanute. Canute had wished his dominions to be divided between the three, and had wished Harold to have England; but the Saxon people in the South of England, headed by a nobleman with great possessions, called the powerful EARL GODWIN (who is said to have been originally a poor cow-boy), opposed this, and desired to have, instead, either Hardicanute, or one of the two exiled Princes who were over in Normandy. It seemed so certain that there would be more bloodshed to settle this dispute, that many people left their homes, and took refuge in the woods and swamps. Happily, however, it was agreed to refer the whole question to a great meeting at Oxford, which decided that Harold should have all the country north of the Thames, with London for his capital city, and that Hardicanute should have all the south. The quarrel was so arranged; and, as Hardicanute was in Denmark troubling himself very little about anything but eating and getting drunk, his mother and Earl Godwin governed the south for him.

They had hardly begun to do so, and the trembling people who had hidden themselves were scarcely at home again, when Edward, the elder of the two exiled Princes, came over from Normandy with a few followers, to claim the English Crown. His mother Emma, however, who only cared for her last son Hardicanute, instead of assisting him, as he expected, opposed him so strongly with all her influence that he was very soon glad to get safely back. His brother Alfred was not so fortunate. Believing in an affectionate letter, written some time afterwards to him and his brother, in his mother's name (but whether really with or without his mother's knowledge is now uncertain), he allowed himself to be tempted over to England, with a good force of soldiers, and landing on the Kentish coast, and being met and welcomed by Earl Godwin, proceeded into Surrey, as far as the town of Guildford. Here, he and his men halted in the evening to rest, having still the Earl in their company; who had ordered lodgings and good cheer for them. But, in the dead of the night, when they were off their guard, being divided into small parties sleeping soundly after a long march and a plentiful supper in different houses, they were set upon by the King's troops, and taken prisoners. Next morning they were drawn out in a line, to the number of six hundred men, and were barbarously tortured and killed; with the exception of every tenth man, who was sold into slavery. As to the wretched Prince Alfred, he was stripped naked, tied to a horse and sent away into the Isle of Ely, where his eyes were torn out of his head, and where in a few days he miserably died. I am not sure that the Earl had wilfully entrapped him, but I suspect it strongly.

Harold was now King all over England, though it is doubtful whether the Archbishop of Canterbury (the greater part of the priests were Saxons, and not friendly to the Danes) ever consented to crown him. Crowned or uncrowned, with the Archbishop's leave or without it, he was King for four years: after which short reign he died, and was buried; having never done much in life but go a hunting. He was such a fast runner at this, his favourite sport, that the people called him Harold Harefoot.

Hardicanute was then at Bruges, in Flanders, plotting, with his mother (who had gone over there after the cruel murder of Prince Alfred), for the invasion of England. The Danes and Saxons, finding themselves without a King, and dreading new disputes, made common cause, and joined in inviting him to occupy the Throne. He consented, and soon troubled them enough; for he brought over numbers of Danes, and taxed the people so insupportably to enrich those greedy favourites that there were many insurrections, especially one at Worcester, where the citizens rose and killed his tax-collectors; in revenge for which he burned their city. He was a brutal King, whose first public act was to order the dead body of poor Harold Harefoot to be dug up, beheaded, and thrown into the river. His end was worthy of such a beginning. He fell down drunk, with a goblet of wine in his hand, at a wedding-feast at Lambeth, given in honour of the marriage of his standard-bearer, a Dane named Towed the Proud. And he never spoke again.

Edward, afterwards called by the monks The Confessor, succeeded; and his first act was to oblige his mother Emma, who had favoured him so little, to retire into the country; where she died some ten years afterwards. He was the exiled prince whose brother Alfred had been so foully killed. He had been invited over from Normandy by Hardicanute, in the course of his short reign of two years, and had been handsomely treated at Court. His cause was now favoured by the powerful Earl Godwin, and he was soon made King. This Earl had been suspected by the people, ever since Prince Alfred's cruel death; he had even been tried in the last reign for the Prince's murder, but had been pronounced not guilty; chiefly, as it was supposed, because of a present he had made to the swinish King, of a gilded ship with a figure-head of solid gold, and a crew of eighty splendidly armed men. It was his interest to help the new King with his power, if the new King would help him against the popular distrust and hatred.

So they made a bargain. Edward the Confessor got the Throne. The Earl got more power and more land, and his daughter Editha was made queen; for it was a part of their compact that the King should take her for his wife.

But, although she was a gentle lady, in all things worthy to be beloved—good, beautiful, sensible, and kind—the King from the first neglected her. Her father and her six proud brothers, resenting this cold treatment, harassed the King greatly by exerting all their power to make him unpopular. Having lived so long in Normandy, he preferred the Normans to the English. He made a Norman Archbishop, and Norman Bishops; his great officers and favourites were all Normans; he introduced the Norman fashions and the Norman language; in imitation of the state custom of Normandy, he attached a great seal to his state documents, instead of merely marking them, as the Saxon Kings had done, with the sign of the cross—just as poor people who have never been taught to write, now make the same mark for their names. All this, the powerful Earl Godwin and his six proud sons represented to the people as disfavour shown towards the English; and thus they daily increased their own power, and daily diminished the power of the King.

They were greatly helped by an event that occurred when he had reigned eight years. Eustace, Earl of Bologne, who had married the King's sister, came to England on a visit. After staying at the court some time, he set forth, with his numerous train of attendants, to return home. They were to embark at Dover. Entering that peaceful town in armour, they took possession of the best houses, and noisily demanded to be lodged and entertained without payment. One of the bold men of Dover, who would not endure to have these domineering strangers jingling their heavy swords and iron corselets up and down his house, eating his meat and drinking his strong liquor, stood in his doorway and refused admission to the first armed man who came there. The armed man drew, and wounded him. The man of Dover struck the armed man dead. Intelligence of what he had done, spreading through the streets to where the Count Eustace and his men were standing by their horses, bridle in hand, they passionately mounted, galloped to the house, surrounded it, forced their way in (the doors and windows being closed when they came up), and killed the man of Dover at his own fireside. They then clattered through the streets, cutting down and riding over men, women, and children. This did not last long, you may believe. The men of Dover set upon them with great fury, killed nineteen of the foreigners, wounded many more, and, blockading the road to the port so that they should not embark, beat them out of the town by the way they had come. Hereupon, Count Eustace rides as hard as man can ride to Gloucester, where Edward is, surrounded by Norman monks and Norman lords. "Justice!" cries the Count, "upon the men of Dover, who have set upon and slain my people!" The King sends immediately for the powerful Earl Godwin, who happens to be near; reminds him that Dover is under his government; and orders him to repair to Dover and do military execution on the inhabitants. "It does not become you," says the proud Earl in reply, "to condemn without a hearing those whom you have sworn to protect. I will not do it."

The King, therefore, summoned the Earl, on pain of banishment and loss of his titles and property, to appear before the court to answer this disobedience. The Earl refused to appear. He, his eldest son Harold, and his second son Sweyn, hastily raised as many fighting men as their utmost power could collect, and demanded to have Count Eustace and his followers surrendered to the justice of the country. The King, in his turn, refused to give them up, and raised a strong force. After some treaty and delay, the troops of the great Earl and his sons began to fall off. The Earl, with a part of his family and abundance of treasure, sailed to Flanders; Harold escaped to Ireland; and the power of the great family was for that time gone in England. But, the people did not forget them.

Then, Edward the Confessor, with the true meanness of a mean spirit, visited his dislike of the once powerful father and sons upon the helpless daughter and sister, his unoffending wife, whom all who saw her (her husband and his monks excepted) loved. He seized rapaciously upon her fortune and her jewels, and allowing her only one attendant, confined her in a gloomy convent, of which a sister of his—no doubt an unpleasant lady after his own heart—was abbess or jailor.

Having got Earl Godwin and his six sons well out of his way, the King favoured the Normans more than ever. He invited over WILLIAM, DUKE OF NORMANDY, the son of that Duke who had received him and his murdered brother long ago, and of a peasant girl, a tanner's daughter, with whom that Duke had fallen in love for her beauty as he saw her washing clothes in a brook. William, who was a great warrior, with a passion for fine horses, dogs, and arms, accepted the invitation; and the Normans in England, finding themselves more numerous than ever when he arrived with his retinue, and held in still greater honour at court than before, became more and more haughty towards the people, and were more and more disliked by them.

The old Earl Godwin, though he was abroad, knew well how the people felt; for, with part of the treasure he had carried away with him, he kept spies and agents in his pay all over England. Accordingly, he thought the time was come for fitting out a great expedition against the Norman-loving King. With it, he sailed to the Isle of Wight, where he was joined by his son Harold, the most gallant and brave of all his family. And so the father and son came sailing up the Thames to Southwark; great numbers of the people declaring for them, and shouting for the English Earl and the English Harold, against the Norman favourites!

The King was at first as blind and stubborn as kings usually have been whensoever they have been in the hands of monks. But the people rallied so thickly round the old Earl and his son, and the old Earl was so steady in demanding without bloodshed the restoration of himself and his family to their rights, that at last the court took the alarm. The Norman Archbishop of Canterbury, and the Norman Bishop of London, surrounded by their retainers, fought their way out of London, and escaped from Essex to France in a fishing-boat. The other Norman favourites dispersed in all directions. The old Earl and his sons (except Sweyn, who had committed crimes against the law) were restored to their possessions and dignities. Editha, the virtuous and lovely Queen of the insensible King, was triumphantly released from her prison, the convent, and once more sat in her chair of state, arrayed in the jewels of which, when she had no champion to support her rights, her cold-blooded husband had deprived her.

The old Earl Godwin did not long enjoy his restored fortune. He fell down in a fit at the King's table, and died upon the third day afterwards. Harold succeeded to his power, and to a far higher place in the attachment of the people than his father had ever held. By his valour he subdued the King's enemies in many bloody fights. He was vigorous against rebels in Scotland—this was the time when Macbeth slew Duncan, upon which event our English Shakespeare, hundreds of years afterwards, wrote his great tragedy; and he killed the restless Welsh King GRIFFITH, and brought his head to England.

What Harold was doing at sea, when he was driven on the French coast by a tempest, is not at all certain; nor does it at all matter. That his ship was forced by a storm on that shore, and that he was taken prisoner, there is no doubt. In those barbarous days, all ship-wrecked strangers were taken prisoners, and obliged to pay ransom. So, a certain Count Guy, who was the Lord of Ponthieu where Harold's disaster happened, seized him, instead of relieving him like a hospitable and Christian lord as he ought to have done, and expected to make a very good thing of it.

But Harold sent off immediately to Duke William of Normandy, complaining of this treatment; and the Duke no sooner heard of it than he ordered Harold to be escorted to the ancient town of Rouen, where he then was, and where he received him as an honoured guest. Now, some writers tell us that Edward the Confessor, who was by this time old and had no children, had made a will, appointing Duke William of Normandy his successor, and had informed the Duke of his having done so. There is no doubt that he was anxious about his successor; because he had even invited over, from abroad, EDWARD THE OUTLAW, a son of Ironside, who had come to England with his wife and three children, but whom the King had strangely refused to see when he did come, and who had died in London suddenly (princes were terribly liable to sudden death in those days), and had been buried in St. Paul's Cathedral. The King might possibly have made such a will; or, having always been fond of the Normans, he might have encouraged Norman William to aspire to the English crown, by something that he said to him when he was staying at the English court. But, certainly William did now aspire to it; and knowing that Harold would be a powerful rival, he called together a great assembly of his nobles, offered Harold his daughter ADELE in marriage, informed him that he meant on King Edward's death to claim the English crown as his own inheritance, and required Harold then and there to swear to aid him. Harold, being in the Duke's power, took this oath upon the Missal, or Prayer-book. It is a good example of the superstitions of the monks, that this Missal, instead of being placed upon a table, was placed upon a tub; which, when Harold had sworn, was uncovered, and shown to be full of dead men's bones—bones, as the monks pretended, of saints. This was supposed to make Harold's oath a great deal more impressive and binding. As if the great name of the Creator of Heaven and earth could be made more solemn by a knuckle-bone, or a double-tooth, or a finger-nail, of Dunstan!

Within a week or two after Harold's return to England, the dreary old Confessor was found to be dying. After wandering in his mind like a very weak old man, he died. As he had put himself entirely in the hands of the monks when he was alive, they praised him lustily when he was dead. They had gone so far, already, as to persuade him that he could work miracles; and had brought people afflicted with a bad disorder of the skin, to him, to be touched and cured. This was called "touching for the King's Evil," which afterwards became a royal custom. You know, however, Who really touched the sick, and healed them; and you know His sacred name is not among the dusty line of human kings.

CHAPTER VII

ENGLAND UNDER HAROLD THE SECOND, AND CONQUERED BY THE NORMANS

HAROLD was crowned King of England on the very day of the maudlin Confessor's funeral. He had good need to be quick about it. When the news reached Norman William, hunting in his park at Rouen, he dropped his bow, returned to his palace, called his nobles to council, and presently sent ambassadors to Harold, calling on him to keep his oath and resign the Crown. Harold would do no such thing. The barons of France leagued together round Duke William for the invasion of England. Duke William promised freely to distribute English wealth and English lands among them. The Pope sent to Normandy a consecrated banner, and a ring containing a hair which he warranted to have grown on the head of Saint Peter. He blessed the enterprise; and cursed Harold; and requested that the Normans would pay "Peter's Pence"—or a tax to himself of a penny a year on every house—a little more regularly in future, if they could make it convenient.

King Harold had a rebel brother in Flanders, who was a vassal of HAROLD HARDRADA, King of Norway. This brother, and this Norwegian King, joining their forces against England, with Duke

William's help, won a fight in which the English were commanded by two nobles; and then besieged York. Harold, who was waiting for the Normans on the coast at Hastings, with his army, marched to Stamford Bridge upon the river Derwent to give them instant battle.

He found them drawn up in a hollow circle, marked out by their shining spears. Riding round this circle at a distance, to survey it, he saw a brave figure on horseback, in a blue mantle and a bright helmet, whose horse suddenly stumbled and threw him.

"Who is that man who has fallen?" Harold asked of one of his captains.

"The King of Norway," he replied.

"He is a tall and stately king," said Harold, "but his end is near." He added, in a little while, "Go yonder to my brother, and tell him, if he withdraw his troops, he shall be Earl of Northumberland, and rich and powerful in England."

The captain rode away and gave the message.

"What will he give to my friend, the King of Norway?" asked the brother.

"Seven feet of earth for a grave," replied the captain.

"No more?" returned the brother, with a smile.

"The King of Norway, being a tall man, perhaps a little more," replied the captain.

"Ride back!" said the brother, "and tell King Harold to make ready for the fight!"

He did so, very soon. And such a fight King Harold led against that force, that his brother, and the Norwegian King, and every chief of note in all their host, except the Norwegian King's son, Olave, to whom he gave honourable dismissal, were left dead upon the field. The victorious army marched to York. As King Harold sat there at the feast, in the midst of all his company, a stir was heard at the doors; and messengers all covered with mire from riding far and fast through broken ground came hurrying in, to report that the Normans had landed in England.

The intelligence was true. They had been tossed about by contrary winds, and some of their ships had been wrecked. A part of their own shore, to which they had been driven back, was strewn with Norman bodies. But they had once more made sail, led by the Duke's own galley, a present from his wife, upon the prow whereof the figure of a golden boy stood pointing towards England. By day, the banner of the three Lions of Normandy, the diverse coloured sails, the gilded vanes, the many decorations of this gorgeous ship, had glittered in the sun and sunny water; by night, a light had sparkled like a star at her mast-head. And now, encamped near Hastings, with their leader lying in the old Roman castle of Pevensey, the English retiring in all directions, the land for miles around scorched and smoking, fired and pillaged, was the whole Norman power, hopeful and strong on English ground.

Harold broke up the feast and hurried to London. Within a week, his army was ready. He sent out spies to ascertain the Norman strength. William took them, caused them to be led through his whole camp, and then dismissed. "The Normans," said these spies to Harold, "are not bearded on the upper lip, as we English are, but are shorn. They are priests." "My men," replied Harold, with a laugh, "will find those priests good soldiers!"

"The Saxons," reported Duke William's outposts of Norman soldiers, who were instructed to retire as King Harold's army advanced, "rush on us through their pillaged country with the fury of madmen."

"Let them come, and come soon!" said Duke William.

Some proposals for a reconciliation were made, but were soon abandoned. In the middle of the month of October, in the year one thousand and sixty-six, the Normans and the English came front to front. All night the armies lay encamped before each other, in a part of the country then called Senlac, now called (in remembrance of them) Battle. With the first dawn of day, they arose. There, in the faint light, were the English on a hill; a wood behind them; in their midst, the Royal banner, representing a fighting warrior, woven in gold thread, adorned with precious stones; beneath the banner, as it rustled in the wind, stood King Harold on foot, with two of his remaining brothers by his side; around them, still and silent as the dead, clustered the whole English army—every soldier covered by his shield, and bearing in his hand his dreaded English battle-axe.

On an opposite hill, in three lines, archers, foot-soldiers, horsemen, was the Norman force. Of a sudden, a great battle-cry, "God help us!" burst from the Norman lines. The English answered with their own battle-cry, "God's Rood! Holy Rood!" The Normans then came sweeping down the hill to attack the English.

There was one tall Norman Knight who rode before the Norman army on a prancing horse, throwing up his heavy sword and catching it, and singing of the bravery of his countrymen. An English Knight who rode out from the English force to meet him, fell by this Knight's hand. Another English Knight rode out, and he fell too. But then a third rode out, and killed the Norman. This was in the first beginning of the fight. It soon raged everywhere.

The English, keeping side by side in a great mass, cared no more for the showers of Norman arrows than if they had been showers of Norman rain. When the Norman horsemen rode against them, with their battle-axes they cut men and horses down. The Normans gave way. The English pressed forward. A cry went forth among the Norman troops that Duke William was killed. Duke William took off his helmet, in order that his face might be distinctly seen, and rode along the line before his men. This gave them courage. As they turned again to face the English, some of their Norman horse divided the pursuing body of the English from the rest, and thus all that foremost portion of the English army fell, fighting bravely. The main body still remaining firm, heedless of the Norman arrows, and with their battle-axes cutting down the crowds of horsemen when they rode up, like forests of young trees, Duke William pretended to retreat. The eager English followed. The Norman army closed again, and fell upon them with great slaughter.

"Still," said Duke William, "there are thousands of the English, firm as rocks around their King. Shoot upward, Norman archers, that your arrows may fall down upon their faces!"

The sun rose high, and sank, and the battle still raged. Through all the wild October day, the clash and din resounded in the air. In the red sunset, and in the white moonlight, heaps upon heaps of dead men law strewn, a dreadful spectacle, all over the ground. King Harold, wounded with an arrow in the eye, was nearly blind. His brothers were already killed. Twenty Norman Knights, whose battered armour had flashed fiery and golden in the sunshine all day long, and now looked silvery in the moonlight, dashed forward to seize the Royal banner from the English Knights and soldiers, still faithfully collected round their blinded King. The King received a mortal wound, and dropped. The English broke and fled. The Normans rallied, and the day was lost.

O what a sight beneath the moon and stars, when lights were shining in the tent of the victorious Duke William, which was pitched near the spot where Harold fell—and he and his knights were carousing, within—and soldiers with torches, going slowly to and fro, without, sought for the corpse of Harold among piles of dead—and the Warrior, worked in golden thread and precious stones, lay low, all torn and soiled with blood—and the three Norman Lions kept watch over the field!

CHAPTER VIII

ENGLAND UNDER WILLIAM THE FIRST, THE NORMAN CONQUEROR

UPON the ground where the brave Harold fell, William the Norman afterwards founded an abbey, which, under the name of Battle Abbey, was a rich and splendid place through many a troubled year, though now it is a grey ruin overgrown with ivy. But the first work he had to do, was to conquer the English thoroughly; and that, as you know by this time, was hard work for any man.

He ravaged several counties; he burned and plundered many towns; he laid waste scores upon scores of miles of pleasant country; he destroyed innumerable lives. At length STIGAND, Archbishop of Canterbury, with other representatives of the clergy and the people, went to his camp and submitted to him. EDGAR, the insignificant son of Edmund Ironside, was proclaimed King by others, but nothing came of it. He fled to Scotland afterwards, where his sister, who was young and beautiful, married the Scottish King. Edgar himself was not important enough for anybody to care much about him.

On Christmas Day, William was crowned in Westminster Abbey,

under the title of WILLIAM THE FIRST; but he is best known as WILLIAM THE CONQUEROR. It was a strange coronation. One of the bishops who performed the ceremony asked the Normans in French, if they would have Duke William for their king? They answered Yes. Another of the bishops put the same question to the Saxons, in English. They too answered Yes, with a loud shout. The noise being heard by a guard of Norman horse-soldiers outside, was mistaken for resistance on the part of the English. The guard instantly set fire to the neighbouring houses, and a tumult ensued; in the midst of which the King, being left alone in the Abbey, with a few priests (and they all being in a terrible fright together), was hurriedly crowned. When the crown was placed upon his head, he swore to govern the English as well as the best of their own monarchs. I dare say you think, as I do, that if we except the Great Alfred, he might pretty easily have done that.

Numbers of the English nobles had been killed in the last disastrous battle. Their estates, and the estates of all the nobles who had fought against him there, King William seized upon, and gave to his own Norman knights and nobles. Many great English families of the present time acquired their English lands in this way, and are very proud of it.

But what is got by force must be maintained by force. These nobles were obliged to build castles all over England, to defend their new property; and, do what he would, the King could neither soothe nor quell the nation as he wished. He gradually introduced the Norman language and the Norman customs; yet, for a long time the great body of the English remained sullen and revengeful. On his going over to Normandy, to visit his subjects there, the oppressions of his half-brother ODO, whom he left in charge of his English kingdom, drove the people mad. The men of Kent even invited over, to take possession of Dover, their old enemy Count Eustace of Boulogne, who had led the fray when the Dover man was slain at his own fireside. The men of Hereford, aided by the Welsh, and commanded by a chief named EDRIC THE WILD, drive the Normans out of their country. Some of those who had been dispossessed of their lands, banded together in the North of England; some, in Scotland; some, in the thick woods and marshes; and whensoever they could fall upon the Normans, or upon the English who had submitted to the Normans, they fought, despoiled, and murdered, like the desperate outlaws that they were. Conspiracies were set on foot for a general massacre of the Normans, like the old massacre of the Danes. In short, the English were in a murderous mood all through the kingdom.

King William, fearing he might lose his conquest, came back, and tried to pacify the London people by soft words. He then set forth to repress the country people by stern deeds. Among the towns which he besieged, and where he killed and maimed the inhabitants without any distinction, sparing none, young or old, armed or unarmed, were Oxford, Warwick, Leicester, Nottingham, Derby, Lincoln, York.

In all these places, and in many others, fire and sword worked their utmost horrors, and made the land dreadful to behold. The streams and rivers were discoloured with blood; the sky was blackened with smoke; the fields were wastes of ashes; the waysides were heaped up with dead. Such are the fatal results of conquest and ambition! Although William was a harsh and angry man, I do not suppose that he deliberately meant to work this shocking ruin, when he invaded England. But what he had got by the strong hand, he could only keep by the strong hand, and in so doing he made England a great grave.

Two sons of Harold, by name EDMUND and GODWIN, came over from Ireland, with some ships, against the Normans, but were defeated. This was scarcely done, when the outlaws in the woods so harassed York, that the Governor sent to the King for help. The King despatched a general and a large force to occupy the town of Durham. The Bishop of that place met the general outside the town, and warned him not to enter, as he would be in danger there. The general cared nothing for the warning, and went in with all his men. That night, on every hill within sight of Durham, signal fires were seen to blaze. When the morning dawned, the English, who had assembled in great strength, forced the gates, rushed into the town, and slew the Normans every one. The English afterwards besought the Danes to come and help them. The Danes came, with two hundred and forty ships. The outlawed nobles joined them; they captured York, and drove the Normans out of that city. Then, William bribed the Danes to go away; and took such vengeance on the English, that all the former fire and sword, smoke and ashes, death and ruin, were nothing compared with it. In melancholy songs, and doleful stories, it was still sung and told by cottage fires on winter evenings, a hundred years afterwards, how, in those dreadful days of the Normans, there was not, from the River Humber to the River Tyne, one inhabited village left, nor one cultivated field—how there was nothing but a dismal ruin, where the human creatures and the beasts lay dead together.

The outlaws had, at this time, what they called a Camp of Refuge, in the midst of the fens of Cambridgeshire. Protected by those marshy grounds which were difficult of approach, they lay among the reeds and rushes, and were hidden by the mists that rose up from the watery earth. Now, there also was, at that time, over the sea in Flanders, an Englishman named HEREWARD, whose father had died in his absence, and whose property had been given to a Norman. When he heard of this wrong that had been done him (from such of the exiled English as chanced to wander into that country), he longed for revenge; and joining the outlaws in their camp of refuge, became their commander. He was so good a soldier, that the Normans supposed him to be aided by enchantment. William, even after he had made a road three miles in length across the Cambridgeshire marshes, on purpose to attack this supposed enchanter, thought it necessary to engage an old lady, who pretended to be a sorceress, to come and do a little enchantment in the royal cause. For this purpose she was pushed on before the troops in a wooden tower; but Hereward very soon disposed of this unfortunate sorceress, by burning her, tower and all. The monks of the convent of Ely near at hand, however, who were fond of good living, and who found it very uncomfortable to have the country blockaded and their supplies of meat and drink cut off, showed the King a secret way of surprising the camp. So Hereward was soon defeated. Whether he afterwards died quietly, or whether he was killed after killing sixteen of the men who attacked him (as some old rhymes relate that he did), I cannot say. His defeat put an end to the Camp of Refuge; and, very soon afterwards, the King, victorious both in Scotland and in England, quelled the last rebellious English noble. He then surrounded himself with Norman lords, enriched by the property of English nobles; had a great survey made of all the land in England, which was entered as the property of its new owners, on a roll called Doomsday Book; obliged the people to put out their fires and candles at a certain hour every night, on the ringing of a bell which was called The Curfew; introduced the Norman dresses and manners; made the Normans masters everywhere, and the English, servants; turned out the English bishops, and put Normans in their places; and showed himself to be the Conqueror indeed.

But, even with his own Normans, he had a restless life. They were always hungering and thirsting for the riches of the English; and the more he gave, the more they wanted. His priests were as greedy as his soldiers. We know of only one Norman who plainly told his master, the King, that he had come with him to England to do his duty as a faithful servant, and that property taken by force from other men had no charms for him. His name was GUILBERT. We should not forget his name, for it is good to remember and to honour honest men.

Besides all these troubles, William the Conqueror was troubled by quarrels among his sons. He had three living. ROBERT, called CURTHOSE, because of his short legs; WILLIAM, called RUFUS or the Red, from the colour of his hair; and HENRY, fond of learning, and called, in the Norman language, BEAUCLERC, or Fine-Scholar. When Robert grew up, he asked of his father the government of Normandy, which he had nominally possessed, as a child, under his mother, MATILDA. The King refusing to grant it, Robert became jealous and discontented; and happening one day, while in this temper, to be ridiculed by his brothers, who threw water on him from a balcony as he was walking before the door, he drew his sword, rushed upstairs, and was only prevented by the King himself from putting them to death. That same night, he hotly departed with some followers from his father's court, and endeavoured to take the Castle of Rouen by surprise. Failing in this, he shut himself up in another Castle in Normandy, which the King besieged, and where Robert one day unhorsed and nearly killed him without knowing who he was. His submission when he discovered his father, and the intercession of the queen and others, reconciled them; but not soundly; for Robert soon strayed abroad, and went from court to court with his complaints. He was a gay, careless, thoughtless fellow, spending all he got on musicians and dancers; but his mother loved him, and often, against the King's command, supplied him with money through a messenger named SAMSON. At length the incensed King swore he would tear out Samson's eyes; and Samson, thinking that his only hope of safety was in becoming a monk, became one, went on such errands no more, and kept his eyes in his head.

All this time, from the turbulent day of his strange coronation, the Conqueror had been struggling, you see, at any cost of cruelty and bloodshed, to maintain what he had seized. All his reign, he struggled still, with the same object ever before him. He was a stern bold man, and he succeeded in it.

He loved money, and was particular in his eating, but he had only leisure to indulge one other passion, and that was his love of hunting. He carried it to such a height that he ordered whole villages and towns to be swept away to make forests for the deer. Not satisfied with sixty-eight Royal Forests, he laid waste an immense district, to form another in Hampshire, called the New Forest. The many thousands of miserable peasants who saw their little houses pulled down, and themselves and children turned into the open country without a shelter, detested him for his merciless addition to their many sufferings; and when, in the twenty-first year of his reign (which proved to be the last), he went over to Rouen, England was as full of hatred against him, as if every leaf on every tree in all his Royal Forests had been a curse upon his head. In the New Forest, his son Richard (for he had four sons) had been gored to death by a Stag; and the people said that this so cruelly-made Forest would yet be fatal to others of the Conqueror's race.

He was engaged in a dispute with the King of France about some territory. While he stayed at Rouen, negotiating with that King, he kept his bed and took medicines: being advised by his physicians to do so, on account of having grown to an unwieldy size. Word being brought to him that the King of France made light of this, and joked about it, he swore in a great rage that he should rue his jests. He assembled his army, marched into the disputed territory, burnt— his old way!—the vines, the crops, and fruit, and set the town of Mantes on fire. But, in an evil hour; for, as he rode over the hot ruins, his horse, setting his hoofs upon some burning embers, started, threw him forward against the pommel of the saddle, and gave him a mortal hurt. For six weeks he lay dying in a monastery near Rouen, and then made his will, giving England to William, Normandy to Robert, and five thousand pounds to Henry. And now, his violent deeds lay heavy on his mind. He ordered money to be given to many English churches and monasteries, and—which was much better repentance—released his prisoners of state, some of whom had been confined in his dungeons twenty years.

It was a September morning, and the sun was rising, when the

King was awakened from slumber by the sound of a church bell. "What bell is that?" he faintly asked. They told him it was the bell of the chapel of Saint Mary. "I commend my soul," said he, "to Mary!" and died.

Think of his name, The Conqueror, and then consider how he lay in death! The moment he was dead, his physicians, priest, and nobles, not knowing what contest for the throne might now take place, or what might happen in it, hastened away, each man for himself and his own property; the mercenary servants of the court began to rob and plunder; the body of the King, in the indecent strife, was rolled from the bed, and lay alone, for hours, upon the ground. O Conqueror, of whom so many great names are proud now, of whom so many great names thought nothing then, it were better to have conquered one true heart, than England!

By-and-by, the priests came creeping in with prayers and candles; and a good knight, named HERLUIN, undertook (which no one else would do) to convey the body to Caen, in Normandy, in order that it might be buried in St. Stephen's church there, which the Conqueror had founded. But fire, of which he had made such bad use in his life, seemed to follow him of itself in death. A great conflagration broke out in the town when the body was placed in the church; and those present running out to extinguish the flames, it was once again left alone.

It was not even buried in peace. It was about to be let down, in its Royal robes, into a tomb near the high altar, in presence of a great concourse of people, when a loud voice in the crowd cried out, "This ground is mine! Upon it, stood my father's house. This King despoiled me of both ground and house to build this church. In the great name of GOD, I here forbid his body to be covered with the earth that is my right!" The priests and bishops present, knowing the speaker's right, and knowing that the King had often denied him justice, paid him down sixty shillings for the grave. Even then, the corpse was not at rest. The tomb was too small, and they tried to force it in. It broke, a dreadful smell arose, the people hurried out into the air, and, for the third time, it was left alone.

Where were the Conqueror's three sons, that they were not at their father's burial? Robert was lounging among minstrels, dancers, and gamesters, in France or Germany. Henry was carrying his five thousand pounds safely away in a convenient chest he had got made. William the Red was hurrying to England, to lay hands upon the Royal treasure and the crown.

CHAPTER IX

ENGLAND UNDER WILLIAM THE SECOND, CALLED RUFUS

WILLIAM THE RED, in breathless haste, secured the three great forts of Dover, Pevensey, and Hastings, and made with hot speed for Winchester, where the Royal treasure was kept. The treasurer delivering him the keys, he found that it amounted to sixty thousand pounds in silver, besides gold and jewels. Possessed of this wealth, he soon persuaded the Archbishop of Canterbury to crown him, and became William the Second, King of England.

Rufus was no sooner on the throne, than he ordered into prison again the unhappy state captives whom his father had set free, and directed a goldsmith to ornament his father's tomb profusely with gold and silver. It would have been more dutiful in him to have attended the sick Conqueror when he was dying; but England, itself, like this Red King, who once governed it, has sometimes made expensive tombs for dead men whom it treated shabbily when they were alive.

The King's brother, Robert of Normandy, seeming quite content to be only Duke of that country; and the King's other brother, Fine-Scholar, being quite enough with his five thousand pounds in a chest; the King flattered himself, we may suppose, with the hope of an easy reign. But easy reigns were difficult to have in those days. The turbulent Bishop ODO (who had blessed the Norman army at the Battle of Hastings, and who, I dare say, took all the credit of the victory to himself) soon began, in concert with some powerful Norman nobles, to trouble the Red King.

The truth seems to be that this bishop and his friends, who had lands in England and lands in Normandy, wished to hold both under one Sovereign; and greatly preferred a thoughtless good-natured person, such as Robert was, to Rufus; who, though far from being an amiable man in any respect, was keen, and not to be imposed upon. They declared in Robert's favour, and retired to their castles (those castles were very troublesome to kings) in a sullen humour. The Red King, seeing the Normans thus falling from him, revenged himself upon them by appealing to the English; to whom he made a variety of promises, which he never meant to perform—in particular, promises to soften the cruelty of the Forest Laws; and who, in return, so aided him with their valour, that ODO was besieged in the Castle of Rochester, and forced to abandon it, and to depart from England for ever: whereupon the other rebellious Norman nobles were soon reduced and scattered.

Then, the Red King went over to Normandy, where the people suffered greatly under the loose rule of Duke Robert. The King's object was to seize upon the Duke's dominions. This, the Duke, of course, prepared to resist: and miserable war between the two brothers seemed inevitable, when the powerful nobles on both sides, who had seen so much of war, interfered to prevent it. A treaty was made. Each of the two brothers agreed to give up something of his claims, and that the longer-liver of the two should inherit all the dominions of the other. When they had come to this loving understanding, they embraced and joined their forces against Fine-Scholar; who had bought some territory of Robert with a part of his five thousand pounds, and was considered a dangerous individual in consequence.

St. Michael's Mount, in Normandy (there is another St. Michael's Mount, in Cornwall, wonderfully like it), was then, as it is now, a strong place perched upon the top of a high rock, around which, when the tide is in, the sea flows, leaving no road to the mainland. In this place, Fine-Scholar shut himself up with his soldiers, and here he was closely besieged by his two brothers. At one time, when he was reduced to great distress for want of water, the generous Robert not only permitted his men to get water, but sent Fine-Scholar wine from his own table; and, on being remonstrated with by the Red King, said "What! shall we let our own brother die of thirst? Where shall we get another, when he is gone?" At another time, the Red King riding alone on the shore of the bay, looking up at the Castle, was taken by two of Fine-Scholar's men, one of whom was about to kill him, when he cried out, "Hold, knave! I am the King of England!" The story says that the soldier raised him from the ground respectfully and humbly, and that the King took him into his service. The story may or may not be true; but at any rate it is true that Fine-Scholar could not hold out against his united brothers, and that he abandoned Mount St. Michael, and wandered about—as poor and forlorn as other scholars have been sometimes known to be.

The Scotch became unquiet in the Red King's time, and were twice defeated—the second time, with the loss of their King, Malcolm, and his son. The Welsh became unquiet too. Against them, Rufus was less successful; for they fought among their native mountains, and did great execution on the King's troops. Robert of Normandy became unquiet too; and, complaining that his brother the King did not faithfully perform his part of their agreement, took up arms, and obtained assistance from the King of France, whom Rufus, in the end, bought off with vast sums of money. England became unquiet too. Lord Mowbray, the powerful Earl of Northumberland, headed a great conspiracy to depose the King, and to place upon the throne, STEPHEN, the Conqueror's near relative. The plot was discovered; all the chief conspirators were seized; some were fined, some were put in prison, some were put to death. The Earl of Northumberland himself was shut up in a dungeon beneath Windsor Castle, where he died, an old man, thirty long years afterwards. The Priests in England were more unquiet than any other class, or power; for the Red King treated them with such small ceremony that he refused to appoint new bishops or archbishops when the old ones died, but kept all the wealth belonging to those offices in his own hands. In return for this, the Priests wrote his life when he was dead, and abused him well. I am inclined to think, myself, that there was little to choose between the Priests and the Red King; that both sides were greedy and designing; and that they were fairly matched.

The Red King was false of heart, selfish, covetous, and mean. He had a worthy minister in his favourite, Ralph, nicknamed—for almost every famous person had a nickname in those rough days— Flambard, or the Firebrand. Once, the King being ill, became penitent, and made ANSELM, a foreign priest and a good man, Archbishop of Canterbury. But he no sooner got well again than he repented of his repentance, and persisted in wrongfully keeping to himself some of the wealth belonging to the archbishopric. This led to violent disputes, which were aggravated by there being in Rome at that time two rival Popes; each of whom declared he was the only real original infallible Pope, who couldn't make a mistake. At last, Anselm, knowing the Red King's character, and not feeling himself safe in England, asked leave to return abroad. The Red King gladly gave it; for he knew that as soon as Anselm was gone, he could begin to store up all the Canterbury money again, for his own use.

By such means, and by taxing and oppressing the English people in every possible way, the Red King became very rich. When he wanted money for any purpose, he raised it by some means or other, and cared nothing for the injustice he did, or the misery he caused. Having the opportunity of buying from Robert the whole duchy of Normandy for five years, he taxed the English people more than ever, and made the very convents sell their plate and valuables to supply him with the means to make the purchase. But he was as quick and eager in putting down revolt as he was in raising money; for, a part of the Norman people objecting—very naturally, I think— to being sold in this way, he headed an army against them with all the speed and energy of his father. He was so impatient, that he embarked for Normandy in a great gale of wind. And when the sailors told him it was dangerous to go to sea in such angry weather, he replied, "Hoist sail and away! Did you ever hear of a king who was drowned?"

You will wonder how it was that even the careless Robert came to sell his dominions. It happened thus. It had long been the custom for many English people to make journeys to Jerusalem, which were called pilgrimages, in order that they might pray beside the tomb of Our Saviour there. Jerusalem belonging to the Turks, and the Turks hating Christianity, these Christian travellers were often insulted and ill-used. The Pilgrims bore it patiently for some time, but at length a remarkable man, of great earnestness and eloquence, called PETER THE HERMIT, began to preach in various places against the Turks, and to declare that it was the duty of good Christians to drive away those unbelievers from the tomb of Our Saviour, and to take possession of it, and protect it. An excitement such as the world had never known before was created. Thousands and thousands of men of all ranks and conditions departed for Jerusalem to make war against the Turks. The war is called in history the first Crusade; and every Crusader wore a cross marked on his right shoulder.

All the Crusaders were not zealous Christians. Among them were vast numbers of the restless, idle, profligate, and adventurous spirits of the time. Some became Crusaders for the love of change; some, in the hope of plunder; some, because they had nothing to do at home; some, because they did what the priests told them; some, because they liked to see foreign countries; some, because they were fond of knocking men about, and would as soon knock a Turk about as a Christian. Robert of Normandy may have been influenced by all these motives; and by a kind desire, besides, to save the Christian Pilgrims from bad treatment in future. He wanted to raise a number of armed men, and to go to the Crusade. He could not do so without money. He had no money; and he sold his dominions to his brother, the Red King, for five years. With the large sum he thus obtained, he fitted out his Crusaders gallantly, and went away to Jerusalem in martial state. The Red King, who made money out of everything, stayed at home, busily squeezing more money out of Normans and English.

After three years of great hardship and suffering—from shipwreck at sea; from travel in strange lands; from hunger, thirst, and fever, upon the burning sands of the desert; and from the fury of the Turks —the valiant Crusaders got possession of Our Saviour's tomb. The Turks were still resisting and fighting bravely, but this success increased the general desire in Europe to join the Crusade. Another great French Duke was proposing to sell his dominions for a term to the rich Red King, when the Red King's reign came to a sudden and violent end.

You have not forgotten the New Forest which the Conqueror made, and which the miserable people whose homes he had laid waste, so hated. The cruelty of the Forest Laws, and the torture and death they brought upon the peasantry, increased this hatred. The poor persecuted country people believed that the New Forest was enchanted. They said that in thunder-storms, and on dark nights, demons appeared, moving beneath the branches of the gloomy trees. They said that a terrible spectre had foretold to Norman hunters that the Red King should be punished there. And now, in the pleasant season of May, when the Red King had reigned almost thirteen years; and a second Prince of the Conqueror's blood—another Richard, the son of Duke Robert—was killed by an arrow in this dreaded Forest; the people said that the second time was not the last, and that there was another death to come.

It was a lonely forest, accursed in the people's hearts for the wicked deeds that had been done to make it; and no man save the King and his Courtiers and Huntsmen, liked to stray there. But, in reality, it was like any other forest. In the spring, the green leaves broke out of the buds; in the summer, flourished heartily, and made deep shades; in the winter, shrivelled and blew down, and lay in brown heaps on the moss. Some trees were stately, and grew high

and strong; some had fallen of themselves; some were felled by the
forester's axe; some were hollow, and the rabbits burrowed at their
roots; some few were struck by lightning, and stood white and bare.
There were hill-sides covered with rich fern, on which the morning
dew so beautifully sparkled; there were brooks, where the deer went
down to drink, or over which the whole herd bounded, flying from
the arrows of the huntsmen; there were sunny glades, and solemn
places where but little light came through the rustling leaves. The
songs of the birds in the New Forest were pleasanter to hear than the
shouts of fighting men outside; and even when the Red King and his
Court came hunting through its solitudes, cursing loud and riding
hard, with a jingling of stirrups and bridles and knives and daggers,
they did much less harm there than among the English or Normans,
and the stags died (as they lived) far easier than the people.

Upon a day in August, the Red King, now reconciled to his
brother, Fine-Scholar, came with a great train to hunt in the New
Forest. Fine-Scholar was of the party. They were a merry party, and
had lain all night at Malwood-Keep, a hunting-lodge in the forest,
where they had made good cheer, both at supper and breakfast, and
had drunk a deal of wine. The party dispersed in various directions,
as the custom of hunters then was. The King took with him only SIR
WALTER TYRREL, who was a famous sportsman, and to whom he had
given, before they mounted that morning, two fine arrows.

The last time the King was ever seen alive, he was riding with Sir
Walter Tyrrel, and their dogs were hunting together.

It was almost night, when a poor charcoal-burner, passing through
the forest with his cart, came upon the solitary body of a dead man,
shot with an arrow in the breast, and still bleeding. He got it into
his cart. It was the body of the King. Shaken and tumbled, with its
red beard all whitened with lime and clotted with blood, it was
driven in the cart by the charcoal-burner next day to Winchester
Cathedral, where it was received and buried.

Sir Walter Tyrrel, who escaped to Normandy, and claimed the
protection of the King of France, swore in France that the Red King
was suddenly shot dead by an arrow from an unseen hand, while
they were hunting together; that he was fearful of being suspected
as the King's murderer; and that he instantly set spurs to his horse,
and fled to the sea-shore. Others declared that the King and Sir
Walter Tyrrel were hunting in company, a little before sunset,
standing in bushes opposite one another, when a stag came between
them. That the King drew his bow and took aim, but the string broke.
That the King then cried, "Shoot, Walter, in the Devil's name!"
That Sir Walter shot. That the arrow glanced against a tree, was
turned aside from the stag, and struck the King from his horse, dead.

By whose hand the Red King really fell, and whether that hand
despatched the arrow to his breast by accident or by design, is only
known to GOD. Some think his brother may have caused him to be
killed; but the Red King had made so many enemies, both among
priests and people, that suspicion may reasonably rest upon a less

unnatural murderer. Men know no more than that he was found dead in the New Forest, which the suffering people had regarded as a doomed ground for his race.

CHAPTER X

ENGLAND UNDER HENRY THE FIRST, CALLED FINE-SCHOLAR

FINE-SCHOLAR, on hearing of the Red King's death, hurried to Winchester with as much speed as Rufus himself had made, to seize the Royal treasure. But the keeper of the treasure, who had been one of the hunting-party in the Forest, made haste to Winchester too, and, arriving there at about the same time, refused to yield it up. Upon this, Fine-Scholar drew his sword, and threatened to kill the treasurer; who might have paid for his fidelity with his life, but that he knew longer resistance to be useless when he found the Prince supported by a company of powerful barons, who declared they were determined to make him King. The treasurer, therefore, gave up the money and jewels of the Crown; and on the third day after the death of the Red King, being a Sunday, Fine-Scholar stood before the high altar in Westminster Abbey, and made a solemn declaration that he would resign the Church property which his brother had seized; that he would do no wrong to the nobles; and that he would restore to the people the laws of Edward the Confessor, with all the improvements of William the Conqueror. So began the reign of KING HENRY THE FIRST.

The people were attached to their new King, both because he had known distresses, and because he was an Englishman by birth and not a Norman. To strengthen this last hold upon them, the King wished to marry an English lady; and could think of no other wife than MAUD THE GOOD, the daughter of the King of Scotland. Although this good Princess did not love the King, she was so affected by the representations the nobles made to her of the great charity it would be in her to unite the Norman and Saxon races, and prevent hatred and bloodshed between them for the future, that she consented to become his wife. After some disputing among the priests, who said that as she had been in a convent in her youth, and had worn the veil of a nun, she could not lawfully be married—against which the Princess stated that her aunt, with whom she had lived in her youth, had indeed sometimes thrown a piece of black stuff over her, but for no other reason than because the nun's veil was the only dress the conquering Normans respected in girl or woman, and not because she had taken the vows of a nun, which she never had—she was declared free to marry, and was made King Henry's Queen. A good Queen she was; beautiful, kind-hearted, and worthy of a better husband than the King.

For he was a cunning and unscrupulous man, though firm and

clever. He cared very little for his word, and took any means to gain his ends. All this is shown in his treatment of his brother Robert— Robert, who had suffered him to be refreshed with water, and who had sent him the wine from his own table, when he was shut up, with the crows flying below him, parched with thirst, in the castle on the top of St. Michael's Mount, where his Red brother would have let him die.

Before the King began to deal with Robert, he removed and disgraced all the favourites of the late King; who were for the most part base characters, much detested by the people. Flambard, or Firebrand, whom the late King had made Bishop of Durham, of all things in the world, Henry imprisoned in the Tower; but Firebrand was a great joker and a jolly companion, and made himself so popular with his guards that they pretended to know nothing about a long rope that was sent into his prison at the bottom of a deep flagon of wine. The guards took the wine, and Firebrand took the rope; with which, when they were fast asleep, he let himself down from a window in the night, and so got cleverly aboard ship and away to Normandy.

Now Robert, when his brother Fine-Scholar came to the throne, was still absent in the Holy Land. Henry pretended that Robert had been made Sovereign of that country; and he had been away so long, that the ignorant people believed it. But, behold, when Henry had been some time King of England, Robert came home to Normandy; having leisurely returned from Jerusalem through Italy, in which beautiful country he had enjoyed himself very much, and had married a lady as beautiful as itself! In Normandy, he found Fire-brand waiting to urge him to assert his claim to the English crown, and declare war against King Henry. This, after great loss of time in feasting and dancing with his beautiful Italian wife among his Nor-man friends, he at last did.

The English in general were on King Henry's side, though many of the Normans were on Robert's. But the English sailors deserted the King, and took a great part of the English fleet over to Normandy; so that Robert came to invade this country in no foreign vessels, but in English ships. The virtuous Anselm, however, whom Henry had invited back from abroad, and made Archbishop of Canterbury, was steadfast in the King's cause; and it was so well supported that the two armies, instead of fighting, made a peace. Poor Robert, who trusted anybody and everybody, readily trusted his brother, the King; and agreed to go home and receive a pension from England, on condition that all his followers were fully pardoned. This the King very faithfully promised, but Robert was no sooner gone than he began to punish them.

Among them was the Earl of Shrewsbury, who, on being sum-moned by the King to answer to five-and-forty accusations, rode away to one of his strong castles, shut himself up therein, called around him his tenants and vassals, and fought for his liberty, but was defeated and banished. Robert, with all his faults, was so true to his word, that when he first heard of this nobleman having risen against his brother, he laid waste the Earl of Shrewsbury's estates in Normandy, to show the King that he would favour no breach of their treaty. Finding, on better information, afterwards, that the Earl's only crime was having been his friend, he came over to England, in his old thoughtless, warm-hearted way, to intercede with the King, and remind him of the solemn promise to pardon all his followers.

This confidence might have put the false King to the blush, but it did not. Pretending to be very friendly, he so surrounded his brother with spies and traps, that Robert, who was quite in his power, had nothing for it but to renounce his pension and escape while he could. Getting home to Normandy, and understanding the King better now, he naturally allied himself with his old friend the Earl of Shrewsbury, who had still thirty castles in that country. This was exactly what Henry wanted. He immediately declared that Robert had broken the treaty, and next year invaded Normandy.

He pretended that he came to deliver the Normans, at their own request, from his brother's misrule. There is reason to fear that his misrule was bad enough; for his beautiful wife had died, leaving him with an infant son, and his court was again so careless, dissipated, and ill-regulated, that it was said he sometimes lay in bed of a day for want of clothes to put on—his attendants having stolen all his dresses.   But he headed his army like a brave prince and a gallant soldier, though he had the misfortune to be taken prisoner by King Henry, with four hundred of his Knights. Among them was poor harmless Edgar Atheling, who loved Robert well. Edgar was not important enough to be severe with. The King afterwards gave him a small pension, which he lived upon and died upon, in peace, among the quiet woods and fields of England.

And Robert—poor, kind, generous, wasteful, heedless Robert, with so many faults, and yet with virtues that might have made a better and a happier man—what was the end of him? If the King had had the magnanimity to say with a kind air, "Brother, tell me, before these noblemen, that from this time you will be my faithful follower and friend, and never raise your hand against me or my forces more!" he might have trusted Robert to the death. But the King was not a magnanimous man. He sentenced his brother to be confined for life in one of the Royal Castles. In the beginning of his imprisonment, he was allowed to ride out, guarded; but he one day broke away from his guard and galloped off. He had the evil fortune to ride into a swamp, where his horse stuck fast and he was taken. When the King heard of it he ordered him to be blinded, which was done by putting a red-hot metal basin on his eyes.

And so, in darkness and in prison, many years, he thought of all his past life, of the time he had wasted, of the treasure he had squandered, of the opportunities he had lost, of the youth he had thrown away, of the talents he had neglected. Sometimes, on fine autumn mornings, he would sit and think of the old hunting parties in the free Forest, where he had been the foremost and the gayest.

Sometimes, in the still nights, he would wake, and mourn for the many nights that had stolen past him at the gaming-table; sometimes, would seem to hear, upon the melancholy wind, the old songs of the minstrels; sometimes, would dream, in his blindness, of the light and glitter of the Norman Court. Many and many a time, he groped back, in his fancy, to Jerusalem, where he had fought so well; or, at the head of his brave companions, bowed his feathered helmet to the shouts of welcome greeting him in Italy, and seemed again to walk among the sunny vineyards, or on the shore of the blue sea, with his lovely wife. And then, thinking of her grave, and of his fatherless boy, he would stretch out his solitary arms and weep.

At length, one day, there lay in prison, dead, with cruel and disfiguring scars upon his eyelids, bandaged from his jailer's sight, but on which the eternal Heavens looked down, a worn old man of eighty. He had once been Robert of Normandy. Pity him!

At the time when Robert of Normandy was taken prisoner by his brother, Robert's little son was only five years old. This child was taken, too, and carried before the King, sobbing and crying; for, young as he was, he knew he had good reason to be afraid of his Royal uncle. The King was not much accustomed to pity those who were in his power, but his cold heart seemed for the moment to soften towards the boy. He was observed to make a great effort, as if to prevent himself from being cruel, and ordered the child to be taken away; whereupon a certain Baron, who had married a daughter of Duke Robert's (by name, Helie of Saint Saen), took charge of him, tenderly. The King's gentleness did not last long. Before two years were over, he sent messengers to this lord's Castle to seize the child and bring him away. The Baron was not there at the time, but his servants were faithful, and carried the boy off in his sleep and hid him. When the Baron came home, and was told what the King had done, he took the child abroad, and, leading him by the hand, went from King to King and from Court to Court, relating how the child had a claim to the throne of England, and how his uncle the King, knowing that he had that claim, would have murdered him, perhaps, but for his escape.

The youth and innocence of the pretty little WILLIAM FITZ-ROBERT (for that was his name) made him many friends at that time. When he became a young man, the King of France, uniting with the French Counts of Anjou and Flanders, supported his cause against the King of England, and took many of the King's towns and castles in Normandy. But, King Henry, artful and cunning always, bribed some of William's friends with money, some with promises, some with power. He bought off the Count of Anjou, by promising to marry his eldest son, also named WILLIAM, to the Count's daughter; and indeed the whole trust of this King's life was in such bargains, and he believed (as many another King has done since, and as one King did in France a very little time ago) that every man's truth and honour can be bought at some price. For all this, he was so afraid of William Fitz-Robert and his friends, that, for a long time, he believed his life to be in danger; and never lay down to sleep, even in his palace surrounded by his guards, without having a sword and buckler at his bedside.

To strengthen his power, the King with great ceremony betrothed his eldest daughter MATILDA, then a child only eight years old, to be the wife of Henry the Fifth, the Emperor of Germany. To raise her marriage-portion, he taxed the English people in a most oppressive manner; then treated them to a great procession, to restore their good humour; and sent Matilda away, in fine state, with the German ambassadors, to be educated in the country of her future husband.

And now his Queen, Maud the Good, unhappily died. It was a sad thought for that gentle lady, that the only hope with which she had married a man whom she had never loved—the hope of reconciling the Norman and English races—had failed. At the very time of her death, Normandy and all France was in arms against England; for, so soon as his last danger was over, King Henry had been false to all the French powers he had promised, bribed, and bought, and they had naturally united against him. After some fighting, however, in which few suffered but the unhappy common people (who always suffered, whatsoever was the matter), he began to promise, bribe, and buy again; and by those means, and by the help of the Pope, who exerted himself to save more bloodshed, and by solemnly declaring, over and over again, that he really was in earnest this time, and would keep his word, the King made peace.

One of the first consequences of this peace was, that the King went over to Normandy with his son Prince William and a great retinue, to have the Prince acknowledged as his successor by the Norman Nobles, and to contract the promised marriage (this was one of the many promises the King had broken) between him and the daughter of the Count of Anjou. Both these things were triumphantly done, with great show and rejoicing; and on the twenty-fifth of November, in the year one thousand one hundred and twenty, the whole retinue prepared to embark at the Port of Barfleur, for the voyage home.

On that day, and at that place, there came to the King, Fitz-Stephen, a sea-captain, and said:

"My liege, my father served your father all his life, upon the sea. He steered the ship with the golden boy upon the prow, in which your father sailed to conquer England. I beseech you to grant me the same office. I have a fair vessel in the harbour here, called The White Ship, manned by fifty sailors of renown. I pray you, Sire, to let your servant have the honour of steering you in The White Ship to England!"

"I am sorry, friend," replied the King, "that my vessel is already chosen, and that I cannot (therefore) sail with the son of the man who served my father. But the Prince and all his company shall go along with you, in the fair White Ship, manned by the fifty sailors of renown."

An hour or two afterwards, the King set sail in the vessel he had chosen, accompanied by other vessels, and, sailing all night with a fair and gentle wind, arrived upon the coast of England in the morning. While it was yet night, the people in some of those ships heard a faint wild cry come over the sea, and wondered what it was.

Now, the Prince was a dissolute, debauched young man of eighteen, who bore no love to the English, and had declared that when he came to the throne he would yoke them to the plough like oxen. He went aboard The White Ship, with one hundred and forty youthful Nobles like himself, among whom were eighteen noble ladies of the highest rank. All this gay company, with their servants and the fifty sailors, made three hundred souls aboard the fair White Ship.

"Give three casks of wine, Fitz-Stephen," said the Prince, "to the fifty sailors of renown! My father the King has sailed out of the harbour. What time is there to make merry here, and yet reach England with the rest?"

"Prince," said Fitz-Stephen, "before morning, my fifty and The White Ship shall overtake the swiftest vessel in attendance on your father the King, if we sail at midnight!"

Then the Prince commanded to make merry; and the sailors drank out the three casks of wine; and the Prince and all the noble company danced in the moonlight on the deck of The White Ship.

When, at last, she shot out of the harbour of Barfleur, there was not a sober seaman on board. But the sails were all set, and the oars all going merrily. Fitz-Stephen had the helm. The gay young nobles and the beautiful ladies, wrapped in mantles of various bright colours to protect them from the cold, talked, laughed, and sang. The Prince encouraged the fifty sailors to row harder yet, for the honour of The White Ship.

Crash! A terrific cry broke from three hundred hearts. It was the cry the people in the distant vessels of the King heard faintly on the water. The White Ship had struck upon a rock—was filling—going down!

Fitz-Stephen hurried the Prince into a boat, with some few Nobles. "Push off," he whispered; "and row to land. It is not far, and the sea is smooth. The rest of us must die."

But, as they rowed away, fast, from the sinking ship, the Prince heard the voice of his sister MARIE, the Countess of Perche, calling for help. He never in his life had been so good as he was then. He cried in an agony, "Row back at any risk! I cannot bear to leave her!"

They rowed back. As the Prince held out his arms to catch his sister, such numbers leaped in, that the boat was overset. And in the same instant The White Ship went down.

Only two men floated. They both clung to the main yard of the ship, which had broken from the mast, and now supported them. One asked the other who he was? He said, "I am a nobleman, GODFREY by name, the son of GILBERT DE L'AIGLE. And you?" said he. "I am BEROLD, a poor butcher of Rouen," was the answer. Then, they said together, "Lord, be merciful to us both!" and tried to encourage one another, as they drifted in the cold benumbing sea on that unfortunate November night.

By-and-by, another man came swimming towards them, whom they knew, when he pushed aside his long wet hair, to be Fitz-Stephen. "Where is the Prince?" said he. "Gone! Gone!" the two cried together. "Neither he, nor his brother, nor his sister, nor the King's niece, nor her brother, nor any one of all the brave three hundred, noble or commoner, except we three, has risen above the water!" Fitz-Stephen, with a ghastly face, cried, "Woe! woe, to me!" and sunk to the bottom.

The other two clung to the yard for some hours. At length the young noble said faintly, "I am exhausted, and chilled with the cold, and can hold no longer. Farewell, good friend! God preserve you!" So, he dropped and sunk; and of all the brilliant crowd, the poor Butcher of Rouen alone was saved. In the morning, some fishermen saw him floating in his sheep-skin coat, and got him into their boat—the sole relater of the dismal tale.

For three days, no one dared to carry the intelligence to the King. At length, they sent into his presence a little boy, who, weeping bitterly, and kneeling at his feet, told him that The White Ship was lost with all on board. The King fell to the ground like a dead man, and never, never afterwards was seen to smile.

But he plotted again, and promised again, and bribed and bought again, in his old deceitful way. Having no son to succeed him, after all his pains ("The Prince will never yoke us to the plough, now!" said the English people), he took a second wife—ADELAIS or ALICE, a duke's daughter, and the Pope's niece. Having no more children, however, he proposed to the Barons to swear that they would recognise as his successor, his daughter Matilda, whom, as she was now a widow, he married to the eldest son of the Count of Anjou, GEOFFREY, surnamed PLANTAGENET, from a custom he had of wearing a sprig of flowering broom (called Genêt in French) in his cap for a feather. As one false man usually makes many, and as a false King, in particular, is pretty certain to make a false Court, the Barons took the oath about the succession of Matilda (and her children after her), twice over, without in the least intending to keep it. The King was now relieved from any remaining fears of William Fitz-Robert, by his death in the Monastery of St. Omer, in France, at twenty-six years old, of a pike-wound in the hand. And as Matilda gave birth to three sons, he thought the succession to the throne secure.

He spent most of the latter part of his life, which was troubled by family quarrels in Normandy, to be near Matilda. When he had reigned upwards of thirty-five years, and was sixty-seven years old, he died of an indigestion and fever, brought on by eating, when he was far from well, of a fish called Lamprey, against which he had often been cautioned by his physicians. His remains were brought over to Reading Abbey to be buried.

You may perhaps hear the cunning and promise-breaking of King

Henry the First, called "policy" by some people, and "diplomacy" by others. Neither of these fine words will in the least mean that it was true; and nothing that is not true can possibly be good.

His greatest merit, that I know of, was his love of learning. I should have given him greater credit even for that, if it had been strong enough to induce him to spare the eyes of a certain poet he once took prisoner, who was a knight besides. But he ordered the poet's eyes to be torn from his head, because he had laughed at him in his verses; and the poet, in the pain of that torture, dashed out his own brains against his prison wall. King Henry the First was avaricious, revengeful, and so false, that I suppose a man never lived whose word was less to be relied upon.

CHAPTER XI

ENGLAND UNDER MATILDA AND STEPHEN

THE King was no sooner dead than all the plans and schemes he had laboured at so long, and lied so much for, crumbled away like a hollow heap of sand. STEPHEN, whom he had never mistrusted or suspected, started up to claim the throne.

Stephen was the son of ADELA, the Conqueror's daughter, married to the Count of Blois. To Stephen, and to his brother HENRY, the late King had been liberal; making Henry Bishop of Winchester, and finding a good marriage for Stephen, and much enriching him. This did not prevent Stephen from hastily producing a false witness, a servant of the late King, to swear that the King had named him for his heir upon his death-bed. On this evidence the Archbishop of Canterbury crowned him. The new King, so suddenly made, lost not a moment in seizing the Royal treasure, and hiring foreign soldiers with some of it to protect his throne.

If the dead King had even done as the false witness said, he would have had small right to will away the English people, like so many sheep or oxen, without their consent. But he had, in fact, bequeathed all his territory to Matilda; who, supported by ROBERT, Earl of Gloucester, soon began to dispute the crown. Some of the powerful barons and priests took her side; some took Stephen's; all fortified their castles; and again the miserable English people were involved in war, from which they could never derive advantage whosoever was victorious, and in which all parties plundered, tortured, starved, and ruined them.

Five years had passed since the death of Henry the First—and during those five years there had been two terrible invasions by the people of Scotland under their King, David, who was at last defeated with all his army—when Matilda, attended by her brother Robert and a large force, appeared in England to maintain her claim. A battle was fought between her troops and King Stephen's at

Lincoln; in which the King himself was taken prisoner, after bravely fighting until his battle-axe and sword were broken, and was carried into strict confinement at Gloucester. Matilda then submitted herself to the Priests, and the Priests crowned her Queen of England.

She did not long enjoy this dignity. The people of London had a great affection for Stephen; many of the Barons considered it degrading to be ruled by a woman; and the Queen's temper was so haughty that she made innumerable enemies. The people of London revolted; and, in alliance with the troops of Stephen, besieged her at Winchester, where they took her brother Robert prisoner, whom, as her best soldier and chief general, she was glad to exchange for Stephen himself, who thus regained his liberty. Then, the long war went on afresh. Once, she was pressed so hard in the Castle of Oxford, in the winter weather when the snow lay thick upon the ground, that her only chance of escape was to dress herself all in white, and, accompanied by no more than three faithful Knights, dressed in like manner that their figures might not be seen from Stephen's camp as they passed over the snow, to steal away on foot, cross the frozen Thames, walk a long distance, and at last gallop away on horseback. All this she did, but to no great purpose then; for her brother dying while the struggle was yet going on, she at last withdrew to Normandy.

In two or three years after her withdrawal her cause appeared in England, afresh, in the person of her son Henry, young Plantagenet, who, at only eighteen years of age, was very powerful: not only on account of his mother having resigned all Normandy to him, but also from his having married ELEANOR, the divorced wife of the French King, a bad woman, who had great possessions in France. Louis, the French King, not relishing this arrangement, helped EUSTACE, King Stephen's son, to invade Normandy: but Henry drove their united forces out of that country, and then returned here, to assist his partisans, whom the King was then besieging at Wallingford upon the Thames. Here, for two days, divided only by the river, the two armies lay encamped opposite to one another—on the eve, as it seemed to all men, of another desperate fight, when the EARL OF ARUNDEL took heart and said "that it was not reasonable to prolong the unspeakable miseries of two kingdoms to minister to the ambition of two princes."

Many other noblemen repeating and supporting this when it was once uttered, Stephen and young Plantagenet went down, each to his own bank of the river, and held a conversation across it, in which they arranged a truce; very much to the dissatisfaction of Eustace, who swaggered away with some followers, and laid violent hands on the Abbey of St. Edmund's-Bury, where he presently died mad. The truce led to a solemn council at Winchester, in which it was agreed that Stephen should retain the crown, on condition of his declaring Henry his successor; that WILLIAM, another son of the King's, should inherit his father's rightful possessions; and that all the Crown lands that Stephen had given away should be recalled, and all the Castles he had permitted to be built demolished. Thus terminated the bitter war, which had now lasted fifteen years, and had again laid England waste. In the next year STEPHEN died, after a troubled reign of nineteen years.

Although King Stephen was, for the time in which he lived, a humane and moderate man, with many excellent qualities; and although nothing worse is known of him than his usurpation of the Crown, which he probably excused to himself by the consideration that King Henry the First was a usurper too—which was no excuse at all; the people of England suffered more in these dread nineteen years, than at any former period even of their suffering history. In the division of the nobility between the two rival claimants of the Crown, and in the growth of what is called the Feudal System (which made the peasants the born vassals and mere slaves of the Barons), every Noble had his strong Castle, where he reigned the cruel king of all the neighbouring people. Accordingly, he perpetrated whatever cruelties he chose. And never were worse cruelties committed upon earth than in wretched England in those nineteen years.

The writers who were living then describe them fearfully. They say that the castles were filled with devils rather than with men; that the peasants, men and women, were put into dungeons for their gold and silver, were tortured with fire and smoke, were hung up by the thumbs, were hung up by the heels with great weights to their heads, were torn with jagged irons, killed with hunger, broken to death in narrow chests filled with sharp-pointed stones, murdered in countless fiendish ways. In England there was no corn, no meat, no cheese, no butter, there were no tilled lands, no harvests. Ashes of burnt towns, and dreary wastes, were all that the traveller, fearful of the robbers who prowled abroad at all hours, would see in a long day's journey; and from sunrise until night, he could not come upon a home.

The clergy sometimes suffered, and heavily too, from pillage, but many of them had castles of their own, and fought in helmet and armour like the barons, and drew lots with other fighting men for their share of booty. The Pope (or Bishop of Rome), on King Stephen's resisting his ambition, laid England under an Interdict at one period of this reign; which means that he allowed no service to be performed in the churches, no couples to be married, no bells to be rung, no dead bodies to be buried. Any man having the power to refuse these things, no matter whether he were called a Pope or a Poulterer, would, of course, have the power of afflicting numbers of innocent people. That nothing might be wanting to the miseries of King Stephen's time, the Pope threw in this contribution to the public store—not very like the widow's contribution, as I think, when Our Saviour sat in Jerusalem over against the Treasury, "and she threw in two mites, which make a farthing."

CHAPTER XII

ENGLAND UNDER HENRY THE SECOND

Part the First

HENRY PLANTAGENET, when he was but twenty-one years old, quietly succeeded to the throne of England, according to his agreement made with the late King at Winchester. Six weeks after Stephen's death, he and his Queen, Eleanor, were crowned in that city; into which they rode on horseback in great state, side by side, amidst much shouting and rejoicing, and clashing of music, and strewing of flowers.

The reign of King Henry the Second began well. The King had great possessions, and (what with his own rights, and what with those of his wife) was lord of one-third part of France. He was a young man of vigour, ability, and resolution, and immediately applied himself to remove some of the evils which had arisen in the last unhappy reign. He revoked all the grants of land that had been hastily made, on either side, during the late struggles; he obliged numbers of disorderly soldiers to depart from England; he reclaimed all the castles belonging to the Crown; and he forced the wicked nobles to pull down their own castles, to the number of eleven hundred, in which such dismal cruelties had been inflicted on the people. The King's brother, GEOFFREY, rose against him in France, while he was so well employed, and rendered it necessary for him to repair to that country; where, after he had subdued and made a friendly arrangement with his brother (who did not live long), his ambition to increase his possessions involved him in a war with the French King, Louis, with whom he had been on such friendly terms just before, that to the French King's infant daughter, then a baby in the cradle, he had promised one of his little sons in marriage, who was a child of five years old. However, the war came to nothing at last, and the Pope made the two Kings friends again.

Now, the clergy, in the troubles of the last reign, had gone on very ill indeed. There were all kinds of criminals among them—murderers, thieves, and vagabonds; and the worst of the matter was, that the good priests would not give up the bad priests to justice, when they committed crimes, but persisted in sheltering and defending them. The King, well knowing that there could be no peace or rest in England while such things lasted, resolved to reduce the power of the clergy; and, when he had reigned seven years, found (as he considered) a good opportunity for doing so, in the death of the Archbishop of Canterbury. "I will have for the new Archbishop," thought the King, "a friend in whom I can trust, who will help me to humble these rebellious priests, and to have them dealt with, when they do wrong, as other men who do wrong are dealt with." So, he resolved to

make his favourite, the new Archbishop; and this favourite was so
extraordinary a man, and his story is so curious, that I must tell you
all about him.

Once upon a time, a worthy merchant of London, named GILBERT
À BECKET, made a pilgrimage to the Holy Land, and was taken
prisoner by a Saracen lord. This lord, who treated him kindly and
not like a slave, had one fair daughter, who fell in love with the merchant; and who told him that she wanted to become a Christian,
and was willing to marry him if they could fly to a Christian country.
The merchant returned her love, until he found an opportunity to
escape, when he did not trouble himself about the Saracen lady, but
escaped with his servant Richard, who had been taken prisoner along
with him, and arrived in England and forgot her. The Saracen lady,
who was more loving than the merchant, left her father's house in disguise to follow him, and made her way, under many hardships, to
the sea-shore. The merchant had taught her only two English words
(for I suppose he must have learnt the Saracen tongue himself, and
made love in that language), of which LONDON was one, and his own
name, GILBERT, the other. She went among the ships, saying,
"London! London!" over and over again, until the sailors understood
that she wanted to find an English vessel that would carry her there;
so they showed her such a ship, and she paid for her passage with
some of her jewels, and sailed away. Well! The merchant was sitting
in his counting-house in London one day, when he heard a great noise
in the street; and presently Richard came running in from the warehouse, with his eyes wide open and his breath almost gone, saying,
"Master, master, here is the Saracen lady!" The merchant thought
Richard was mad; but Richard said, "No, master! As I live, the
Saracen lady is going up and down the city, calling Gilbert! Gilbert!"
Then, he took the merchant by the sleeve, and pointed out of
window; and there they saw her among the gables and water-spouts
of the dark, dirty street, in her foreign dress, so forlorn, surrounded
by a wondering crowd, and passing slowly along, calling Gilbert,
Gilbert! When the merchant saw her, and thought of the tenderness
she had shown him in his captivity, and of her constancy, his heart
was moved, and he ran down into the street; and she saw him coming,
and with a great cry fainted in his arms. They were married without
loss of time, and Richard (who was an excellent man) danced with
joy the whole day of the wedding; and they all lived happy ever
afterwards.

This merchant and this Saracen lady had one son, THOMAS À
BECKET. He it was who became the Favourite of King Henry the
Second.

He had become Chancellor, when the King thought of making him
Archbishop. He was clever, gay, well educated, brave; had fought in
several battles in France; had defeated a French knight in single
combat, and brought his horse away as a token of the victory. He
lived in a noble palace, he was the tutor of the young Prince Henry, he
was served by one hundred and forty knights, his riches were

immense. The King once sent him as his ambassador to France; and the French people, beholding in what state he travelled, cried out in the streets, "How splendid must the King of England be, when this is only the Chancellor!" They had good reason to wonder at the magnificence of Thomas à Becket, for, when he entered a French town, his procession was headed by two hundred and fifty singing boys; then, came his hounds in couples; then, eight waggons, each drawn by five horses driven by five drivers: two of the waggons filled with strong ale to be given away to the people; four, with his gold and silver plate and stately clothes; two, with the dresses of his numerous servants. Then, came twelve horses, each with a monkey on his back; then, a train of people bearing shields and leading fine war-horses splendidly equipped; then, falconers with hawks upon their wrists; then, a host of knights, and gentlemen and priests; then, the Chancellor with his brilliant garments flashing in the sun, and all the people capering and shouting with delight.

The King was well pleased with all this, thinking that it only made himself the more magnificent to have so magnificent a favourite; but he sometimes jested with the Chancellor upon his splendour too. Once, when they were riding together through the streets of London in hard winter weather, they saw a shivering old man in rags. "Look at the poor object!" said the King. "Would it not be a charitable act to give that aged man a comfortable warm cloak?" "Undoubtedly it would," said Thomas à Becket, "and you do well, Sir, to think of such Christian duties." "Come!" cried the King, "then give him your cloak!" It was made of rich crimson trimmed with ermine. The King tried to pull it off, the Chancellor tried to keep it on, both were near rolling from their saddles in the mud, when the Chancellor submitted, and the King gave the cloak to the old beggar: much to the beggar's astonishment, and much to the merriment of all the courtiers in attendance. For, courtiers are not only eager to laugh when the King laughs, but they really do enjoy a laugh against a Favourite.

"I will make," thought King Henry the Second, "this Chancellor of mine, Thomas à Becket, Archbishop of Canterbury. He will then be the head of the Church, and, being devoted to me, will help me to correct the Church. He has always upheld my power against the power of the clergy, and once publicly told some bishops (I remember), that men of the Church were equally bound to me with men of the sword. Thomas à Becket is the man, of all other men in England, to help me in my great design." So the King, regardless of all objection, either that he was a fighting man, or a lavish man, or a courtly man, or a man of pleasure, or anything but a likely man for the office, made him Archbishop accordingly.

Now, Thomas à Becket was proud and loved to be famous. He was already famous for the pomp of his life, for his riches, his gold and silver plate, his waggons, horses, and attendants. He could do no more in that way than he had done; and being tired of that kind of fame (which is a very poor one), he longed to have his name celebrated for something else. Nothing, he knew, would render him so famous in the world, as the setting of his utmost power and ability against the utmost power and ability of the King. He resolved with the whole strength of his mind to do it.

He may have had some secret grudge against the King besides. The King may have offended his proud humour at some time or other, for anything I know. I think it likely, because it is a common thing for Kings, Princes, and other great people, to try the tempers of their favourites rather severely. Even the little affair of the crimson cloak must have been anything but a pleasant one to a haughty man. Thomas à Becket knew better than any one in England what the King expected of him. In all his sumptuous life, he had never yet been in a position to disappoint the King. He could take up that proud stand now, as head of the Church; and he determined that it should be written in history, either that he subdued the King, or that the King subdued him.

So, of a sudden, he completely altered the whole manner of his life. He turned off all his brilliant followers, ate coarse food, drank bitter water, wore next his skin sackcloth covered with dirt and vermin (for it was then thought very religious to be very dirty), flogged his back to punish himself, lived chiefly in a little cell, washed the feet of thirteen poor people every day, and looked as miserable as he possibly could. If he had put twelve hundred monkeys on horseback instead of twelve, and had gone in procession with eight thousand waggons instead of eight, he could not have half astonished the people so much as by this great change. It soon caused him to be more talked about as an Archbishop than he had been as a Chancellor.

The King was very angry; and was made still more so, when the new Archbishop, claiming various estates from the nobles as being rightfully Church property, required the King himself, for the same reason, to give up Rochester Castle, and Rochester City too. Not satisfied with this, he declared that no power but himself should appoint a priest to any church in the part of England over which he was Archbishop; and when a certain gentleman of Kent made such an appointment, as he claimed to have the right to do, Thomas à Becket excommunicated him.

Excommunication was, next to the Interdict I told you of at the close of the last chapter, the great weapon of the clergy. It consisted in declaring the person who was excommunicated, an outcast from the Church and from all religious offices; and in cursing him all over, from the top of his head to the sole of his foot, whether he was standing up, lying down, sitting, kneeling, walking, running, hopping, jumping, gaping, coughing, sneezing, or whatever else he was doing. This unchristian nonsense would of course have made no sort of difference to the person cursed—who could say his prayers at home if he were shut out of church, and whom none but GOD could judge —but for the fears and superstitions of the people, who avoided excommunicated persons, and made their lives unhappy. So, the King said to the new Archbishop, "Take off this Excommunication from this gentleman of Kent." To which the Archbishop replied, "I shall do no such thing."

The quarrel went on. A priest in Worcestershire committed a most dreadful murder, that aroused the horror of the whole nation. The King demanded to have this wretch delivered up, to be tried in the same court and in the same way as any other murderer. The Archbishop refused, and kept him in the Bishop's prison. The King, holding a solemn assembly in Westminster Hall, demanded that in future all priests found guilty before their Bishops of crimes against the law of the land should be considered priests no longer, and should be delivered over to the law of the land for punishment. The Archbishop again refused. The King required to know whether the clergy would obey the ancient customs of the country? Every priest there, but one, said, after Thomas à Becket, "Saving my order." This really meant that they would only obey those customs when they did not interfere with their own claims; and the King went out of the Hall in great wrath.

Some of the clergy began to be afraid, now, that they were going too far. Though Thomas à Becket was otherwise as unmoved as Westminster Hall, they prevailed upon him, for the sake of their fears, to go to the King at Woodstock, and promise to observe the ancient customs of the country, without saying anything about his order. The King received this submission favourably, and summoned a great council of the clergy to meet at the Castle of Clarendon, by Salisbury. But when the council met, the Archbishop again insisted on the words, "saving my order;" and he still insisted, though lords entreated him, and priests wept before him and knelt to him, and an adjoining room was thrown open, filled with armed soldiers of the King, to threaten him. At length he gave way, for that time, and the ancient customs (which included what the King had demanded in vain) were stated in writing, and were signed and sealed by the chief of the clergy, and were called the Constitutions of Clarendon.

The quarrel went on, for all that. The Archbishop tried to see the King. The King would not see him. The Archbishop tried to escape from England. The sailors on the coast would launch no boat to take him away. Then, he again resolved to do his worst in opposition to the King, and began openly to set the ancient customs at defiance.

The King summoned him before a great council at Northampton, where he accused him of high treason, and made a claim against him, which was not a just one, for an enormous sum of money. Thomas à Becket was alone against the whole assembly, and the very Bishops advised him to resign his office and abandon his contest with the King. His great anxiety and agitation stretched him on a sick-bed for two days, but he was still undaunted. He went to the adjourned council, carrying a great cross in his right hand, and sat down holding it erect before him. The King angrily retired into an inner room. The whole assembly angrily retired and left him there. But there he sat. The Bishops came out again in a body and renounced him as a traitor. He only said, "I hear!" and sat there still. They retired again into the inner room, and his trial proceeded without him. By-and-by, the Earl of Leicester, heading the barons, came out to read his sentence. He refused to hear it, denied the power of the court, and said he would refer his cause to the Pope. As he walked out of the hall, with the cross in his hand, some of those present picked up rushes—rushes were strewn upon the floors in those days by way of carpet—and threw them at him. He proudly turned his head, and said that were he not Archbishop, he would chastise those cowards with the sword he had known how to use in bygone days. He then mounted his horse, and rode away, cheered and surrounded by the common people, to whom he threw open his house that night and gave a supper, supping with them himself. That same night he secretly departed from the town; and so, travelling by night and hiding by day, and calling himself "Brother Dearman," got away, not without difficulty, to Flanders.

The struggle still went on. The angry King took possession of the revenues of the archbishopric, and banished all the relations and servants of Thomas à Becket, to the number of four hundred. The Pope and the French King both protected him, and an abbey was assigned for his residence. Stimulated by this support, Thomas à Becket, on a great festival day, formally proceeded to a great church crowded with people, and going up into the pulpit publicly cursed and excommunicated all who had supported the Constitutions of Clarendon: mentioning many English noblemen by name, and not distantly hinting at the King of England himself.

When intelligence of this new affront was carried to the King in his chamber, his passion was so furious that he tore his clothes, and rolled like a madman on his bed of straw and rushes. But he was soon up and doing. He ordered all the ports and coasts of England to be narrowly watched, that no letters of Interdict might be brought into the kingdom; and sent messengers and bribes to the Pope's palace at Rome. Meanwhile, Thomas à Becket, for his part, was not idle at Rome, but constantly employed his utmost arts in his own behalf. Thus the contest stood, until there was peace between France and England (which had been for some time at war), and until the two children of the two Kings were married in celebration of it. Then, the French King brought about a meeting between Henry and his old favourite, so long his enemy.

Even then, though Thomas à Becket knelt before the King, he was obstinate and immovable as to those words about his order. King Louis of France was weak enough in his veneration for Thomas à Becket and such men, but this was a little too much for him. He said that à Becket "wanted to be greater than the saints and better than St. Peter," and rode away from him with the King of England. His poor French Majesty asked à Becket's pardon for so doing, however, soon afterwards, and cut a very pitiful figure.

At last, and after a world of trouble, it came to this. There was another meeting on French ground between King Henry and Thomas à Becket, and it was agreed that Thomas à Becket should be Archbishop of Canterbury, according to the customs of former Archbishops, and that the King should put him in possession of the revenues of that post. And now, indeed, you might suppose the struggle at an end, and Thomas à Becket at rest. No, not even yet. For Thomas à Becket hearing, by some means, that King Henry, when he was in dread of his kingdom being placed under an interdict, had had his eldest son Prince Henry secretly crowned, not only persuaded the Pope to suspend the Archbishop of York who had performed that ceremony, and to excommunicate the Bishops who had assisted at it, but sent a messenger of his own into England, in spite of all the King's precautions along the coast, who delivered the letters of excommunication into the Bishops' own hands. Thomas à Becket then came over to England himself, after an absence of seven years. He was privately warned that it was dangerous to come, and that an ireful knight, named RANULF DE BROC, had threatened that he should not live to eat a loaf of bread in England; but he came.

The common people received him well, and marched about with him in a soldierly way, armed with such rustic weapons as they could get. He tried to see the young prince who had once been his pupil, but was prevented. He hoped for some little support among the nobles and priests, but found none. He made the most of the peasants who attended him, and feasted them, and went from Canterbury to Harrow-on-the-Hill, and from Harrow-on-the-Hill back to Canterbury, and on Christmas Day preached in the Cathedral there, and told the people in his sermon that he had come to die among them, and that it was likely he would be murdered. He had no fear, however —or, if he had any, he had much more obstinacy—for he, then and there, excommunicated three of his enemies, of whom Ranulf de Broc the ireful knight was one.

As men in general had no fancy for being cursed, in their sitting and walking, and gaping and sneezing, and all the rest of it, it was very natural in the persons so freely excommunicated to complain to the King. It was equally natural in the King, who had hoped that this troublesome opponent was at last quieted, to fall into a mighty rage when he heard of these new affronts; and, on the Archbishop of York telling him that he never could hope for rest while Thomas à Becket lived, to cry out hastily before his court, "Have I no one here who will deliver me from this man?" There were four knights present, who, hearing the King's words, looked at one another, and went out.

The names of these knights were REGINALD FITZURSE, WILLIAM TRACY, HUGH DE MORVILLE, and RICHARD BRITO; three of whom had been in the train of Thomas à Becket in the old days of his splendour. They rode away on horseback, in a very secret manner, and on the third day after Christmas Day arrived at Saltwood House, not far from Canterbury, which belonged to the family of Ranulf de Broc. They quietly collected some followers here, in case they should need any; and proceeding to Canterbury, suddenly appeared (the four knights and twelve men) before the Archbishop, in his own house, at two o'clock in the afternoon. They neither bowed nor spoke, but sat down on the floor in silence, staring at the Archbishop.

Thomas à Becket said, at length, "What do you want?"

"We want," said Reginald Fitzurse, "the excommunication taken from the Bishops, and you to answer for your offences to the King."

Thomas à Becket defiantly replied, that the power of the clergy was above the power of the King. That it was not for such men as they were, to threaten him. That if he were threatened by all the swords in England, he would never yield.

"Then we will do more than threaten!" said the knights. And they went out with the twelve men, and put on their armour, and drew their shining swords, and came back.

His servants, in the meantime, had shut up and barred the great gate of the palace. At first, the knights tried to shatter it with their battle-axes; but, being shown a window by which they could enter, they let the gate alone, and climbed in that way. While they were battering at the door, the attendants of Thomas à Becket had implored him to take refuge in the Cathedral; in which, as a sanctuary or sacred place, they thought the knights would dare to do no violent deed. He told them, again and again, that he would not stir. Hearing the distant voices of the monks singing the evening service, however, he said it was now his duty to attend, and therefore, and for no other reason, he would go.

There was a near way between his Palace and the Cathedral, by some beautiful old cloisters which you may yet see. He went into the Cathedral, without any hurry, and having the Cross carried before him as usual. When he was safely there, his servants would have fastened the door, but he said No! it was the house of God and not a fortress.

As he spoke, the shadow of Reginald Fitzurse appeared in the Cathedral doorway, darkening the little light there was outside, on the dark winter evening. This knight said, in a strong voice, "Follow me, loyal servants of the King!" The rattle of the armour of the other knights echoed through the Cathedral, as they came clashing in.

It was so dark, in the lofty aisles and among the stately pillars of the church, and there were so many hiding-places in the crypt below and in the narrow passages above, that Thomas à Becket might even at that pass have saved himself if he would. But he would not. He told the monks resolutely that he would not. And though they all dispersed and left him there with no other follower than EDWARD GRYME, his faithful cross-bearer, he was as firm then, as ever he had been in his life.

The knights came on, through the darkness, making a terrible noise with their armed tread upon the stone pavement of the church. "Where is the traitor?" they cried out. He made no answer. But when they cried, "Where is the Archbishop?" he said proudly, "I am here!" and came out of the shade and stood before them.

The knights had no desire to kill him, if they could rid the King and themselves of him by any other means. They told him he must either fly or go with them. He said he would do neither; and he threw William Tracy off with such force when he took hold of his sleeve, that Tracy reeled again. By his reproaches and his steadiness, he so incensed them, and exasperated their fierce humour, that Reginald Fitzurse, whom he called by an ill name, said, "Then die!" and struck at his head. But the faithful Edward Gryme put out his arm, and there received the main force of the blow, so that it only made his master bleed. Another voice from among the knights again called to Thomas à Becket to fly; but, with his blood running down his face, and his hands clasped, and his head bent, he commended himself to God, and stood firm. Then they cruelly killed him close to the altar of St. Bennet; and his body fell upon the pavement, which was dirtied with his blood and brains.

It is an awful thing to think of the murdered mortal, who had so showered his curses about, lying, all disfigured, in the church, where a few lamps here and there were but red specks on a pall of darkness; and to think of the guilty knights riding away on horseback, looking over their shoulders at the dim Cathedral, and remembering what they had left inside.

PART THE SECOND

WHEN the King heard how Thomas à Becket had lost his life in Canterbury Cathedral, through the ferocity of the four Knights, he was filled with dismay. Some have supposed that when the King spoke those hasty words, "Have I no one here who will deliver me from this man?" he wished, and meant à Becket to be slain. But few things are more unlikely; for, besides that the King was not naturally cruel (though very passionate), he was wise, and must have known full well what any stupid man in his dominions must have known, namely, that such a murder would rouse the Pope and the whole Church against him.

He sent respectful messengers to the Pope, to represent his innocence (except in having uttered the hasty words); and he swore solemnly and publicly to his innocence, and contrived in time to make his peace. As to the four guilty Knights, who fled into Yorkshire, and never again dared to show themselves at Court, the Pope excommunicated them; and they lived miserably for some time, shunned by all their countrymen. At last, they went humbly to Jerusalem as a penance, and there died and were buried.

It happened, fortunately for the pacifying of the Pope, that an opportunity arose very soon after the murder of à Becket, for the King to declare his power in Ireland—which was an acceptable undertaking to the Pope, as the Irish, who had been converted to Christianity by one Patricius (otherwise Saint Patrick) long ago, before any Pope existed, considered that the Pope had nothing at all to do with them, or they with the Pope, and accordingly refused to pay him Peter's Pence, or that tax of a penny a house which I have elsewhere mentioned. The King's opportunity arose in this way.

The Irish were, at that time, as barbarous a people as you can well imagine. They were continually quarrelling and fighting, cutting one another's throats, slicing one another's noses, burning one another's houses, carrying away one another's wives, and committing all sorts of violence. The country was divided into five kingdoms—DESMOND, THOMOND, CONNAUGHT, ULSTER, and LEINSTER—each governed by a separate King, of whom one claimed to be the chief of the rest. Now, one of these Kings, named DERMOND MAC MURROUGH (a wild kind of name, spelt in more than one wild kind of way), had carried off the wife of a friend of his, and concealed her on an island in a bog. The friend resenting this (though it was quite the custom of the country), complained to the chief King, and, with the chief King's help, drove Dermond Mac Murrough out of his dominions. Dermond came over to England for revenge; and offered to hold his realm as a vassal of King Henry, if King Henry would help him to regain it. The King consented to these terms; but only assisted him, then, with what were called Letters Patent, authorising any English subjects who were so disposed, to enter into his service, and aid his cause.

There was, at Bristol, a certain EARL RICHARD DE CLARE, called STRONGBOW; of no very good character; needy and desperate, and ready for anything that offered him a chance of improving his fortunes. There were, in South Wales, two other broken knights of the same good-for-nothing sort, called ROBERT FITZ-STEPHEN and MAURICE FITZ-GERALD. These three, each with a small band of followers, took up Dermond's cause; and it was agreed that if it proved successful, Strongbow should marry Dermond's daughter EVA, and be declared his heir.

The trained English followers of these knights were so superior in all the discipline of battle to the Irish, that they beat them against immense superiority of numbers. In one fight, early in the war, they cut off three hundred heads, and laid them before Mac Murrough; who turned them every one up with his hands, rejoicing, and, coming to one which was the head of a man whom he had much disliked, grasped it by the hair and ears, and tore off the nose and lips with his teeth. You may judge from this, what kind of a gentleman an Irish King in those times was. The captives all through this war were horribly treated; the victorious party making nothing of breaking their limbs, and casting them into the sea from the tops of high rocks. It was in the midst of the miseries and cruelties attendant on the taking of Waterford, where the dead lay piled in the streets, and the filthy gutters ran with blood, that Strongbow married Eva. An odious marriage-company those mounds of corpses must have made, I think, and one quite worthy of the young lady's father.

He died, after Waterford and Dublin had been taken, and various successes achieved; and Strongbow became King of Leinster. Now came King Henry's opportunity. To restrain the growing power of Strongbow, he himself repaired to Dublin, as Strongbow's Royal Master, and deprived him of his kingdom, but confirmed him in the enjoyment of great possessions. The King, then, holding state in

Dublin, received the homage of nearly all the Irish Kings and Chiefs, and so came home again with a great addition to his reputation as Lord of Ireland, and with a new claim on the favour of the Pope. And now, their reconciliation was completed—more easily and mildly by the Pope, than the King might have expected, I think.

At this period of his reign, when his troubles seemed so few and his prospects so bright, those domestic miseries began which gradually made the King the most unhappy of men, reduced his great spirit, wore away his health, and broke his heart.

He had four sons. HENRY, now aged eighteen—his secret crowning of whom had given such offence to Thomas à Becket; RICHARD, aged sixteen; GEOFFREY, fifteen; and JOHN, his favourite, a young boy whom the courtiers named LACKLAND, because he had no inheritance, but to whom the King meant to give the Lordship of Ireland. All these misguided boys, in their turn, were unnatural sons to him, and unnatural brothers to each other. Prince Henry, stimulated by the French King, and by his bad mother, Queen Eleanor, began the undutiful history.

First, he demanded that his young wife, MARGARET, the French King's daughter, should be crowned as well as he. His father, the King, consented, and it was done. It was no sooner done, than he demanded to have a part of his father's dominions, during his father's life. This being refused, he made off from his father in the night, with his bad heart full of bitterness, and took refuge at the French King's Court. Within a day or two, his brothers Richard and Geoffrey followed. Their mother tried to join them—escaping in man's clothes— but she was seized by King Henry's men, and immured in prison, where she lay, deservedly, for sixteen years. Every day, however, some grasping English noblemen, to whom the King's protection of his people from their avarice and oppression had given offence, deserted him and joined the Princes. Every day he heard some fresh intelligence of the Princes levying armies against him; of Prince Henry's wearing a crown before his own ambassadors at the French Court, and being called the Junior King of England; of all the Princes swearing never to make peace with him, their father, without the consent and approval of the Barons of France. But, with his fortitude and energy unshaken, King Henry met the shock of these disasters with a resolved and cheerful face. He called upon all Royal fathers who had sons, to help him, for his cause was theirs; he hired, out of his riches, twenty thousand men to fight the false French King, who stirred his own blood against him; and he carried on the war with such vigour, that Louis soon proposed a conference to treat for peace.

The conference was held beneath an old wide-spreading green elm-tree, upon a plain in France. It led to nothing. The war recommenced. Prince Richard began his fighting career, by leading an army against his father; but his father beat him and his army back; and thousands of his men would have rued the day in which they fought in such a wicked cause, had not the King received news of an invasion of England by the Scots, and promptly come home through a great storm to repress it. And whether he really began to fear that he suffered these troubles because à Becket had been murdered; or whether he wished to rise in the favour of the Pope, who had now declared à Becket to be a saint, or in the favour of his own people, of whom many believed that even à Becket's senseless tomb could work miracles, I don't know: but the King no sooner landed in England than he went straight to Canterbury; and when he came within sight of the distant Cathedral, he dismounted from his horse, took off his shoes, and walked with bare and bleeding feet to à Becket's grave. There, he lay down on the ground, lamenting, in the presence of many people; and by-and-by he went into the Chapter House, and, removing his clothes from his back and shoulders, submitted himself to be beaten with knotted cords (not beaten very hard, I dare say though) by eighty Priests, one after another. It chanced that on the very day when the King made this curious exhibition of himself, a complete victory was obtained over the Scots; which very much delighted the Priests, who said that it was won because of his great example of repentance. For the Priests in general had found out, since à Becket's death, that they admired him of all things—though they had hated him very cordially when he was alive.

The Earl of Flanders, who was at the head of the base conspiracy of the King's undutiful sons and their foreign friends, took the opportunity of the King being thus employed at home, to lay siege to Rouen, the capital of Normandy. But the King, who was extraordinarily quick and active in all his movements, was at Rouen, too, before it was supposed possible that he could have left England; and there he so defeated the said Earl of Flanders, that the conspirators proposed peace, and his bad sons Henry and Geoffrey submitted. Richard resisted for six weeks; but, being beaten out of castle after castle, he at last submitted too, and his father forgave him.

To forgive these unworthy princes was only to afford them breathing-time for new faithlessness. They were so false, disloyal, and dishonourable, that they were no more to be trusted than common thieves. In the very next year, Prince Henry rebelled again, and was again forgiven. In eight years more, Prince Richard rebelled against his elder brother; and Prince Geoffrey infamously said that the brothers could never agree well together, unless they were united against their father. In the very next year after their reconciliation by the King, Prince Henry again rebelled against his father; and again submitted, swearing to be true; and was again forgiven; and again rebelled with Geoffrey.

But the end of this perfidious Prince was come. He fell sick at a French town; and his conscience terribly reproaching him with his baseness, he sent messengers to the King his father, imploring him to come and see him, and to forgive him for the last time on his bed of death. The generous King, who had a royal and forgiving mind towards his children always, would have gone; but this Prince had been so unnatural, that the noblemen about the King suspected treachery, and represented to him that he could not safely trust his life with such a traitor, though his own eldest son. Therefore the King sent him a ring from off his finger as a token of forgiveness; and when the Prince had kissed it, with much grief and many tears, and had confessed to those around him how bad, and wicked, and undutiful a son he had been; he said to the attendant Priests: "O, tie a rope about my body, and draw me out of bed, and lay me down upon a bed of ashes, that I may die with prayers to God in a repentant manner!" And so he died, at twenty-seven years old.

Three years afterwards, Prince Geoffrey, being unhorsed at a tournament, had his brains trampled out by a crowd of horses passing over him. So, there only remained Prince Richard, and Prince John—who had grown to be a young man now, and had solemnly sworn to be faithful to his father. Richard soon rebelled again, encouraged by his friend the French King, PHILIP THE SECOND (son of Louis, who was dead); and soon submitted and was again forgiven, swearing on the New Testament never to rebel again; and in another year or so, rebelled again; and, in the presence of his father, knelt down on his knee before the King of France; and did the French King homage: and declared that with his aid he would possess himself by force, of all his father's French dominions.

And yet this Richard called himself a soldier of Our Saviour! And yet this Richard wore the Cross, which the Kings of France and England had both taken, in the previous year, at a brotherly meeting underneath the old wide-spreading elm-tree on the plain, when they had sworn (like him) to devote themselves to a new Crusade, for the love and honour of the Truth!

Sick at heart, wearied out by the falsehood of his sons, and almost ready to lie down and die, the unhappy King who had so long stood firm, began to fail. But the Pope, to his honour, supported him; and obliged the French King and Richard, though successful in fight, to treat for peace. Richard wanted to be crowned King of England, and pretended that he wanted to be married (which he really did not) to the French King's sister, his promised wife, whom King Henry detained in England. King Henry wanted, on the other hand, that the French King's sister should be married to his favourite son, John: the only one of his sons (he said) who had never rebelled against him. At last King Henry, deserted by his nobles one by one, distressed, exhausted, broken-hearted, consented to establish peace.

One final heavy sorrow was reserved for him, even yet. When they brought him the proposed treaty of peace, in writing, as he lay very ill in bed, they brought him also the list of the deserters from their allegiance, whom he was required to pardon. The first name upon this list was John, his favourite son, in whom he had trusted to the last.

"O John! child of my heart!" exclaimed the King, in a great agony of mind. "O John, whom I have loved the best! O John, for whom I have contended through these many troubles! Have you betrayed me too!" And then he lay down with a heavy groan, and said, "Now let the world go as it will. I care for nothing more!"

After a time, he told his attendants to take him to the French town of Chinon—a town he had been fond of, during many years. But he was fond of no place now; it was too true that he could care for nothing more upon this earth. He wildly cursed the hour when he was born, and cursed the children whom he left behind him; and expired.

As, one hundred years before, the servile followers of the Court had abandoned the Conqueror in the hour of his death, so they now abandoned his descendant. The very body was stripped, in the plunder of the Royal chamber; and it was not easy to find the means of carrying it for burial to the abbey church of Fontevraud.

Richard was said in after years, by way of flattery, to have the heart of a Lion. It would have been far better, I think, to have had the heart of a Man. His heart, whatever it was, had cause to beat remorsefully within his breast, when he came—as he did—into the solemn abbey, and looked on his dead father's uncovered face. His heart, whatever it was, had been a black and perjured heart, in all its dealings with the deceased King, and more deficient in a single touch of tenderness than any wild beast's in the forest.

There is a pretty story told of this Reign, called the story of FAIR ROSAMOND. It relates how the King doted on Fair Rosamond, who was the loveliest girl in all the world; and how he had a beautiful Bower built for her in a Park at Woodstock; and how it was erected in a labyrinth, and could only be found by a clue of silk. How the bad Queen Eleanor, becoming jealous of Fair Rosamond, found out the secret of the clue, and one day, appeared before her, with a dagger and cup of poison, and left her to the choice between those deaths. How Fair Rosamond, after shedding many piteous tears and offering many useless prayers to the cruel Queen, took the poison, and fell dead in the midst of the beautiful bower, while the unconscious birds sang gaily all around her.

Now, there *was* a fair Rosamond, and she was (I dare say) the loveliest girl in all the world, and the King was certainly very fond of her, and the bad Queen Eleanor was certainly made jealous. But I am afraid—I say afraid, because I like the story so much—that there was no bower, no labyrinth, no silken clue, no dagger, no poison. I am afraid fair Rosamond retired to a nunnery near Oxford, and died there, peaceably; her sister-nuns hanging a silken drapery over her tomb, and often dressing it with flowers, in remembrance of the youth and beauty that had enchanted the King when he too was young, and when his life lay fair before him.

It was dark and ended now; faded and gone. Henry Plantagenet lay quiet in the abbey church of Fontevraud, in the fifty-seventh year of his age—never to be completed—after governing England well, for nearly thirty-five years.

CHAPTER XIII

ENGLAND UNDER RICHARD THE FIRST, CALLED THE LION-HEART

In the year of our Lord one thousand one hundred and eighty-nine, Richard of the Lion Heart succeeded to the throne of King Henry the Second, whose paternal heart he had done so much to break. He had been, as we have seen, a rebel from his boyhood; but, the moment he became a king against whom others might rebel, he found out that rebellion was a great wickedness. In the heat of this pious discovery, he punished all the leading people who had befriended him against his father. He could scarcely have done anything that would have been a better instance of his real nature, or a better warning to fawners and parasites not to trust in lion-hearted princes.

He likewise put his late father's treasurer in chains, and locked him up in a dungeon from which he was not set free until he had relinquished, not only all the Crown treasure, but all his own money too. So, Richard certainly got the Lion's share of the wealth of this wretched treasurer, whether he had a Lion's heart or not.

He was crowned King of England, with great pomp, at Westminster: walking to the Cathedral under a silken canopy stretched on the tops of four lances, each carried by a great lord. On the day of his coronation, a dreadful murdering of the Jews took place, which seems to have given great delight to numbers of savage persons calling themselves Christians. The King had issued a proclamation forbidding the Jews (who were generally hated, though they were the most useful merchants in England) to appear at the ceremony; but as they had assembled in London from all parts, bringing presents to show their respect for the new Sovereign, some of them ventured down to Westminster Hall with their gifts; which were very readily accepted. It is supposed, now, that some noisy fellow in the crowd, pretending to be a very delicate Christian, set up a howl at this, and struck a Jew who was trying to get in at the Hall door with his present. A riot arose. The Jews who had got into the Hall, were driven forth; and some of the rabble cried out that the new King had commanded the unbelieving race to be put to death. Thereupon the crowd rushed through the narrow streets of the city, slaughtering all the Jews they met; and when they could find no more out of doors (on account of their having fled to their houses, and fastened themselves in), they ran madly about, breaking open all the houses where the Jews lived, rushing in and stabbing or spearing them, sometimes even flinging old people and children out of window into blazing fires they had lighted up below. This great cruelty lasted four-and-twenty hours, and only three men were punished for it. Even they forfeited their lives not for murdering and robbing the Jews, but for burning the houses of some Christians.

King Richard, who was a strong, restless, burly man, with one idea always in his head, and that the very troublesome idea of breaking the heads of other man, was mightily impatient to go on a Crusade to the Holy Land, with a great army. As great armies could not be raised to go, even to the Holy Land, without a great deal of money, he sold the Crown domains, and even the high offices of State; recklessly appointing noblemen to rule over his English subjects, not because they were fit to govern, but because they could pay high for the privilege. In this way, and by selling pardons at a dear rate, and by varieties of avarice and oppression, he scraped together a large treasure. He then appointed two Bishops to take care of his kingdom in his absence, and gave great powers and possessions to his brother John, to secure his friendship. John would rather have been made Regent of England; but he was a sly man, and friendly to the expedition; saying to himself, no doubt, "The more fighting, the more chance of my brother being killed; and when he *is* killed, then I become King John!"

Before the newly levied army departed from England, the recruits and the general populace distinguished themselves by astonishing cruelties on the unfortunate Jews: whom, in many large towns, they murdered by hundreds in the most horrible manner.

At York, a large body of Jews took refuge in the Castle, in the absence of its Governor, after the wives and children of many of them had been slain before their eyes. Presently came the Governor, and demanded admission. "How can we give it thee, O Governor!" said the Jews upon the walls, "when, if we open the gate by so much as the width of a foot, the roaring crowd behind thee will press in and kill us?"

Upon this, the unjust Governor became angry, and told the people that he approved of their killing those Jews; and a mischievous maniac of a friar, dressed all in white, put himself, at the head of the assault, and they assaulted the Castle for three days.

Then said JOCEN, the head-Jew (who was a Rabbi or Priest), to the rest, "Brethren, there is no hope for us with the Christians who are hammering at the gates and walls, and who must soon break in. As we and our wives and children must die, either by Christian hands, or by our own, let it be by our own. Let us destroy by fire what jewels and other treasure we have here, then fire the castle, and then perish!"

A few could not resolve to do this, but the greater part complied. They made a blazing heap of all their valuables, and, when those were consumed, set the castle in flames. While the flames roared and crackled around them, and shooting up into the sky, turned it blood-red, Jocen cut the throat of his beloved wife, and stabbed himself. All the others who had wives or children, did the like dreadful deed. When the populace broke in, they found (except the trembling few, cowering in corners, whom they soon killed) only heaps of greasy cinders, with here and there something like part of the blackened trunk of a burnt tree, but which had lately been a human creature, formed by the beneficent hand of the Creator as they were.

After this bad beginning, Richard and his troops went on, in no very good manner, with the Holy Crusade. It was undertaken jointly by the King of England and his old friend Philip of France. They commenced the business by reviewing their forces, to the number of one hundred thousand men. Afterwards, they severally embarked their troops for Messina, in Sicily, which was appointed as the next place of meeting.

King Richard's sister had married the King of this place, but he was dead: and his uncle TANCRED had usurped the crown, cast the Royal Widow into prison, and possessed himself of her estates. Richard fiercely demanded his sister's release, the restoration of her lands, and (according to the Royal custom of the Island) that she should have a golden chair, a golden table, four-and-twenty silver cups, and four-and-twenty silver dishes. As he was too powerful to be successfully resisted, Tancred yielded to his demands; and then the French King grew jealous, and complained that the English King wanted to be absolute in the Island of Messina and everywhere else. Richard, however, cared little or nothing for this complaint; and in consideration of a present of twenty thousand pieces of gold, promised his pretty little nephew ARTHUR, then a child of two years old, in marriage to Tancred's daughter. We shall hear again of pretty little Arthur by-and-by.

This Sicilian affair arranged without anybody's brains being knocked out (which must have rather disappointed him), King Richard took his sister away, and also a fair lady named BERENGARIA, with whom he had fallen in love in France, and whom his mother, Queen Eleanor (so long in prison, you remember, but released by Richard on his coming to the Throne), had brought out there to be his wife; and sailed with them for Cyprus.

He soon had the pleasure of fighting the King of the Island of Cyprus, for allowing his subjects to pillage some of the English troops who were shipwrecked on the shore; and easily conquering this poor monarch, he seized his only daughter, to be a companion to the lady Berengaria, and put the King himself into silver fetters. He then sailed away again with his mother, sister, wife, and the captive princess; and soon arrived before the town of Acre, which the French King with his fleet was besieging from the sea. But the French King was in no triumphant condition, for his army had been thinned by the swords of the Saracens, and wasted by the plague; and SALADIN, the brave Sultan of the Turks, at the head of a numerous army, was at that time gallantly defending the place from the hills that rise above it.

Wherever the united army of Crusaders went, they agreed in few points except in gaming, drinking, and quarrelling, in a most unholy manner; in debauching the people among whom they tarried, whether they were friends or foes; and in carrying disturbance and ruin into quiet places. The French King was jealous of the English King, and the English King was jealous of the French King, and the disorderly and violent soldiers of the two nations were jealous of one another; consequently, the two Kings could not at first agree, even upon a joint assault on Acre; but when they did make up their quarrel for that purpose, the Saracens promised to yield the town, to give up to the Christians the wood of the Holy Cross, to set at liberty all their Christian captives, and to pay two hundred thousand pieces of gold. All this was to be done within forty days ; but, not being done, King Richard ordered some three thousand Saracen prisoners to be brought out in the front of his camp, and there, in full view of their own countrymen, to be butchered.

The French King had no part in this crime; for he was by that time travelling homeward with the greater part of his men; being offended by the overbearing conduct of the English King; being anxious to look after his own dominions; and being ill, besides, from the unwholesome air of that hot and sandy country. King Richard carried on the war without him; and remained in the East, meeting with a variety of adventures, nearly a year and a half. Every night when his army was on the march, and came to a halt, the heralds cried out three times, to remind all the soldiers of the cause in which they were engaged, "Save the Holy Sepulchre!" and then all the soldiers knelt and said "Amen!" Marching or encamping, the army had continually to strive with the hot air of the glaring desert, or with the Saracen soldiers animated and directed by the brave Saladin, or with both together. Sickness and death, battle and wounds, were always among them; but through every difficulty King Richard fought like a giant, and worked like a common labourer. Long and long after he was quiet in his grave, his terrible battle-axe, with twenty English pounds of English steel in its mighty head, was a legend among the Saracens; and when all the Saracen and Christian hosts had been dust for many a year, if a Saracen horse started at any object by the wayside, his rider would exclaim, "What dost thou fear, Fool? Dost thou think King Richard is behind it?"

No one admired this King's renown for bravery more than Saladin himself, who was a generous and gallant enemy. When Richard lay ill of a fever, Saladin sent him fresh fruits from Damascus, and snow from the mountain-tops. Courtly messages and compliments were frequently exchanged between them—and then King Richard would mount his horse and kill as many Saracens as he could; and Saladin would mount his, and kill as many Christians as he could. In this way King Richard fought to his heart's content at Arsoof and at Jaffa; and finding himself with nothing exciting to do at Ascalon, except to rebuild, for his own defence, some fortifications there which the Saracens had destroyed, he kicked his ally the Duke of Austria, for being too proud to work at them.

The army at last came within sight of the Holy City of Jerusalem; but, being then a mere nest of jealousy, and quarrelling and fighting, soon retired, and agreed with the Saracens upon a truce for three years, three months, three days, and three hours. Then, the English Christians, protected by the noble Saladin from Saracen revenge, visited Our Saviour's tomb; and then King Richard embarked with a small force at Acre to return home.

But he was shipwrecked in the Adriatic Sea, and was fain to pass through Germany, under an assumed name. Now, there were many people in Germany who had served in the Holy Land under that proud Duke of Austria who had been kicked; and some of them, easily recognising a man so remarkable as King Richard, carried their intelligence to the kicked Duke, who straightway took him prisoner at a little inn near Vienna.

The Duke's master the Emperor of Germany, and the King of France, were equally delighted to have so troublesome a monarch in safe keeping. Friendships which are founded on a partnership in doing wrong, are never true; and the King of France was now quite as heartily King Richard's foe, as he had ever been his friend in his unnatural conduct to his father. He monstrously pretended that King Richard had designed to poison him in the East; he charged him with having murdered, there, a man whom he had in truth befriended; he bribed the Emperor of Germany to keep him close prisoner; and, finally, through the plotting of these two princes, Richard was brought before the German legislature, charged with the foregoing crimes, and many others. But he defended himself so well, that many of the assembly were moved to tears by his eloquence and earnestness. It was decided that he should be treated, during the rest of his captivity, in a manner more becoming his dignity than he had been, and that he should be set free on the payment of a heavy ransom. This ransom the English people willingly raised. When Queen Eleanor took it over to Germany, it was at first evaded and refused. But she appealed to the honour of all the princes of the German Empire in behalf of her son, and appealed so well that it was accepted, and the King released. Thereupon, the King of France wrote to Prince John—"Take care of thyself. The devil is unchained!"

Prince John had reason to fear his brother, for he had been a traitor to him in his captivity. He had secretly joined the French King; had vowed to the English nobles and people that his brother was dead; and had vainly tried to seize the crown. He was now in France, at a place called Evreux. Being the meanest and basest of men, he contrived a mean and base expedient for making himself acceptable to his brother. He invited the French officers of the garrison in that town to dinner, murdered them all, and then took the fortress. With this recommendation to the good will of a lion-hearted monarch, he hastened to King Richard, fell on his knees before him, and obtained the intercession of Queen Eleanor. "I forgive him," said the King, "and I hope I may forget the injury he has done me, as easily as I know he will forget my pardon."

While King Richard was in Sicily, there had been trouble in his dominions at home: one of the bishops whom he had left in charge thereof, arresting the other; and making, in his pride and ambition, as great a show as if he were King himself. But the King hearing of it at Messina, and appointing a new Regency, this LONGCHAMP (for that was his name) had fled to France in a woman's dress, and had there been encouraged and supported by the French King. With all these causes of offence against Philip in his mind, King Richard had no sooner been welcomed home by his enthusiastic subjects with great display and splendour, and had no sooner been crowned afresh at Winchester, than he resolved to show the French King that the Devil was unchained indeed, and made war against him with great fury.

There was fresh trouble at home about this time, arising out of the discontents of the poor people, who complained that they were far more heavily taxed than the rich, and who found a spirited champion in WILLIAM FITZ-OSBERT, called LONGBEARD. He became the leader of a secret society, comprising fifty thousand men; he was seized by surprise; he stabbed the citizen who first laid hands upon him; and retreated, bravely fighting, to a church, which he maintained four days, until he was dislodged by fire, and run through the body as he came out. He was not killed, though; for he was dragged, half dead, at the tail of a horse to Smithfield, and there hanged. Death was long a favourite remedy for silencing the people's advocates; but as we go on with this history, I fancy we shall find them difficult to make an end of, for all that.

The French war, delayed occasionally by a truce, was still in progress when a certain Lord named VIDOMAR, Viscount of Limoges, chanced to find in his ground a treasure of ancient coins. As the King's vassal, he sent the King half of it; but the King claimed the whole. The lord refused to yield the whole. The King besieged the lord in his castle, swore that he would take the castle by storm, and hang every man of its defenders on the battlements.

There was a strange old song in that part of the country, to the effect that in Limoges an arrow would be made by which King Richard would die. It may be that BERTRAND DE GOURDON, a young man who was one of the defenders of the castle, had often sung it or heard it sung of a winter night, and remembering it when he saw, from his post upon the ramparts, the King attended only by his chief officer riding below the walls surveying the place. He drew an arrow to the head, took steady aim, said between his teeth, "Now I pray God speed thee well, arrow!" discharged it, and struck the King in the left shoulder.

Although the wound was not at first considered dangerous, it was severe enough to cause the King to retire to his tent, and direct the assault to be made without him. The castle was taken; and every man of its defenders was hanged, as the King had sworn all should be, except Bertrand de Gourdon, who was reserved until the royal pleasure respecting him should be known.

By that time unskilful treatment had made the wound mortal, and the King knew that he was dying. He directed Bertrand to be brought into his tent. The young man was brought there, heavily chained. King Richard looked at him steadily. He looked, as steadily, at the King.

"Knave!" said King Richard. "What have I done to thee that thou shouldest take my life?"

"What hast thou done to me?" replied the young man. "With thine own hands thou hast killed my father and my two brothers. Myself thou wouldest have hanged. Let me die, now, by any torture that thou wilt. My comfort is, that no torture can save Thee. Thou too must die; and, through me, the world is quit of thee!"

Again the King looked at the young man steadily. Again the young man looked steadily at him. Perhaps some remembrance of his generous enemy Saladin, who was not a Christian, came into the mind of the dying King.

"Youth!" he said, "I forgive thee. Go unhurt!"

Then, turning to the chief officer who had been riding in his company when he received the wound, King Richard said:

"Take off his chains, give him a hundred shillings, and let him depart."

He sunk down on his couch, and a dark mist seemed in his weakened eyes to fill the tent wherein he had so often rested, and he died. His age was forty-two; he had reigned ten years. His last command was not obeyed; for the chief officer flayed Bertrand de Gourdon alive, and hanged him.

There is an old tune yet known—a sorrowful air will sometimes outlive many generations of strong men, and even last longer than battle-axes with twenty pounds of steel in the head—by which this King is said to have been discovered in his captivity. BLONDEL, a favourite Minstrel of King Richard, as the story relates, faithfully seeking his Royal master, went singing it outside the gloomy walls of many foreign fortresses and prisons; until at last he heard it echoed from within a dungeon, and knew the voice, and cried out in ecstasy, "O Richard, O my King!" You may believe it, if you like; it would be easy to believe worse things. Richard was himself a Minstrel and a Poet. If he had not been a Prince too, he might have been a better man perhaps, and might have gone out of the world with less bloodshed and waste of life to answer for.

CHAPTER XIV

ENGLAND UNDER KING JOHN, CALLED LACKLAND

AT two-and-thirty years of age, JOHN became King of England. His pretty little nephew ARTHUR had the best claim to the throne; but John seized the treasure, and made fine promises to the nobility, and got himself crowned at Westminster within a few weeks after his brother Richard's death. I doubt whether the crown could possibly have been put upon the head of a meaner coward, or a more detestable villain, if England had been searched from end to end to find him out.

The French King, Philip, refused to acknowledge the right of John to his new dignity, and declared in favour of Arthur. You must not suppose that he had any generosity of feeling for the fatherless boy; it merely suited his ambitious schemes to oppose the King of England. So John and the French King went to war about Arthur.

He was a handsome boy, at that time only twelve years old. He was not born when his father, Geoffrey, had his brains trampled out at the tournament; and, besides the misfortune of never having known a father's guidance and protection, he had the additional misfortune to have a foolish mother (CONSTANCE by name), lately married to her third husband. She took Arthur, upon John's accession, to the French King, who pretended to be very much his friend, and who made him a Knight, and promised him his daughter in marriage; but, who cared so little about him in reality, that finding it his interest to make peace with King John for a time, he did so without the least consideration for the poor little Prince, and heartlessly sacrificed all his interests.

Young Arthur, for two years afterwards, lived quietly; and in the course of that time his mother died. But, the French King then finding it his interest to quarrel with King John again, again made Arthur his pretence, and invited the orphan boy to court. "You know your rights, Prince," said the French King, "and you would like to be a King. Is it not so?" "Truly," said Prince Arthur, "I should greatly like to be a King!" "Then," said Philip, "you shall have two hundred gentlemen who are Knights of mine, and with them you shall go to win back the provinces belonging to you, of which your uncle, the usurping King of England, has taken possession. I myself, meanwhile, will head a force against him in Normandy." Poor Arthur was so flattered and so grateful that he signed a treaty with the crafty French King, agreeing to consider him his superior Lord, and that the French King should keep for himself whatever he could take from King John.

Now, King John was so bad in all ways, and King Philip was so perfidious, that Arthur, between the two, might as well have been a lamb between a fox and a wolf. But, being so young, he was ardent and flushed with hope; and, when the people of Brittany (which was his inheritance) sent him five hundred more knights and five thousand foot soldiers, he believed his fortune was made. The people of Brittany had been fond of him from his birth, and had requested that he might be called Arthur, in remembrance of that dimly-famous English Arthur, of whom I told you early in this book, whom they believed to have been the brave friend and companion of an old King of their own. They had tales among them about a prophet called MERLIN (of the same old time), who had foretold that their own King should be restored to them after hundreds of years; and they believed that the prophecy would be fulfilled in Arthur; that the time would come when he would rule them with a crown of Brittany upon his head; and when neither King of France nor King of England would have any power over them. When Arthur found himself riding in a glittering suit of armour on a richly caparisoned horse, at the head of his train of knights and soldiers, he began to believe this too, and to consider old Merlin a very superior prophet.

He did not know—how could he, being so innocent and inexperienced?—that his little army was a mere nothing against the power of the King of England. The French King knew it; but the poor boy's fate was little to him, so that the King of England was worried and distressed. Therefore, King Philip went his way into Normandy, and Prince Arthur went his way towards Mirebeau, a French town near Poictiers, both very well pleased.

Prince Arthur went to attack the town of Mirebeau, because his grandmother Eleanor, who has so often made her appearance in this history (and who had always been his mother's enemy), was living there, and because his Knights said, "Prince, if you can take her prisoner, you will be able to bring the King your uncle to terms!" But she was not to be easily taken. She was old enough by this time —eighty—but she was as full of stratagem as she was full of years and wickedness. Receiving intelligence of young Arthur's approach, she shut herself up in a high tower, and encouraged her soldiers to defend it like men. Prince Arthur with his little army besieged the high tower. King John, hearing how matters stood, came up to the rescue, with *his* army. So here was a strange family-party! The boy-Prince besieging his grandmother, and his uncle besieging him!

This position of affairs did not last long. One summer night King John, by treachery, got his men into the town, surprised Prince Arthur's force, took two hundred of his knights, and seized the Prince himself in his bed. The Knights were put in heavy irons, and driven away in open carts drawn by bullocks, to various dungeons where they were most inhumanly treated, and where some of them were starved to death. Prince Arthur was sent to the castle of Falaise.

One day, while he was in prison at that castle, mournfully thinking it strange that one so young should be in so much trouble, and looking out of the small window in the deep dark wall, at the summer sky and the birds, the door was softly opened, and he saw his uncle the King standing in the shadow of the archway, looking very grim.

"Arthur," said the King, with his wicked eyes more on the stone floor than on his nephew, "will you not trust to the gentleness, the friendship, and the truthfulness of your loving uncle?"

"I will tell my loving uncle that," replied the boy, "when he does me right. Let him restore to me my kingdom of England, and then come to me and ask the question."

The King looked at him and went out. "Keep that boy close prisoner," said he to the warden of the castle.

Then, the King took secret counsel with the worst of his nobles how the Prince was to be got rid of. Some said, "Put out his eyes and keep him in prison, as Robert of Normandy was kept." Others said, "Have him stabbed." Others, "Have him hanged." Others, "Have him poisoned."

King John, feeling that in any case, whatever was done afterwards, it would be a satisfaction to his mind to have those handsome eyes burnt out that had looked at him so proudly while his own royal eyes were blinking at the stone floor, sent certain ruffians to Falaise to blind the boy with red-hot irons. But Arthur so pathetically entreated them, and shed such piteous tears, and so appealed to HUBERT DE BOURG (or BURGH), the warden of the castle, who had a love for him, and was an honourable, tender man, that Hubert could not bear it. To his eternal honour he prevented the torture from being performed, and, at his own risk, sent the savages away.

The chafed and disappointed King bethought himself of the stabbing suggestion next, and, with his shuffling manner and his cruel face, proposed it to one William de Bray. "I am a gentleman and not an executioner," said William de Bray, and left the presence with disdain.

But it was not difficult for a King to hire a murderer in those days. King John found one for his money, and sent him down to the castle of Falaise. "On what errand dost thou come?" said Hubert to this fellow. "To despatch young Arthur," he returned. "Go back to him who sent thee," answered Hubert, "and say that I will do it!"

King John very well knowing that Hubert would never do it, but that he courageously sent this reply to save the Prince or gain time, despatched messengers to convey the young prisoner to the castle of Rouen.

Arthur was soon forced from the good Hubert—of whom he had never stood in greater need than then—carried away by night, and lodged in his new prison: where, through his grated window, he could hear the deep waters of the river Seine rippling against the stone wall below.

One dark night, as he lay sleeping, dreaming perhaps of rescue by those unfortunate gentlemen who were obscurely suffering and dying in his cause, he was roused, and bidden by his jailer to come down the staircase to the foot of the tower. He hurriedly dressed himself and obeyed. When they came to the bottom of the winding stairs, and the night air from the river blew upon their faces, the jailer trod upon his torch and put it out. Then, Arthur, in the darkness, was hurriedly drawn into a solitary boat. And in that boat, he found his uncle and one other man.

He knelt to them, and prayed them not to murder him. Deaf to his entreaties, they stabbed him, and sunk his body in the river with heavy stones. When the spring-morning broke, the tower-door was closed, the boat was gone, the river sparkled on its way, and never more was any trace of the poor boy beheld by mortal eyes.

The news of this atrocious murder being spread in England, awakened a hatred of the King (already odious for his many vices, and for his having stolen away and married a noble lady while his own wife was living) that never slept again through his whole reign. In Brittany, the indignation was intense. Arthur's own sister ELEANOR was in the power of John and shut up in a convent at Bristol, but his half-sister ALICE was in Brittany. The people chose her, and the murdered prince's father-in-law, the last husband of Constance, to represent them; and carried their fiery complaints to King

Philip. King Philip summoned King John (as the holder of territory in France) to come before him and defend himself. King John refusing to appear, King Philip declared him false, perjured, and guilty; and again made war. In a little time, by conquering the greater part of his French territory, King Philip deprived him of one-third of his dominions. And, through all the fighting that took place, King John was always found, either to be eating and drinking, like a gluttonous fool, when the danger was at a distance, or to be running away, like a beaten cur, when it was near.

You might suppose that when he was losing his dominions at this rate, and when his own nobles cared so little for him or his cause that they plainly refused to follow his banner out of England, he had enemies enough. But he made another enemy of the Pope, which he did in this way.

The Archbishop of Canterbury dying, and the junior monks of that place wishing to get the start of the senior monks in the appointment of his successor, met together at midnight, secretly elected a certain REGINALD, and sent him off to Rome to get the Pope's approval. The senior monks and the King soon finding this out, and being very angry about it, the junior monks gave way, and all the monks together elected the Bishop of Norwich, who was the King's favourite. The Pope, hearing the whole story, declared that neither election would do for him, and that *he* elected STEPHEN LANGTON. The monks submitting to the Pope, the King turned them all out bodily, and banished them as traitors. The Pope sent three bishops to the King, to threaten him with an Interdict. The King told the bishops that if any Interdict were laid upon his kingdom, he would tear out the eyes and cut off the noses of all the monks he could lay hold of, and send them over to Rome in that undecorated state as a present for their master. The bishops, nevertheless, soon published the Interdict, and fled.

After it had lasted a year, the Pope proceeded to his next step; which was Excommunication. King John was declared excommunicated, with all the usual ceremonies. The King was so incensed at this, and was made so desperate by the disaffection of his Barons and the hatred of his people, that it is said he even privately sent ambassadors to the Turks in Spain, offering to renounce his religion and hold his kingdom of them if they would help him. It is related that the ambassadors were admitted to the presence of the Turkish Emir through long lines of Moorish guards, and that they found the Emir with his eyes seriously fixed on the pages of a large book, from which he never once looked up. That they gave him a letter from the King containing his proposals, and were gravely dismissed. That presently the Emir sent for one of them, and conjured him, by his faith in his religion, to say what kind of man the King of England truly was? That the ambassador, thus pressed, replied that the King of England was a false tyrant, against whom his own subjects would soon rise. And that this was quite enough for the Emir.

Money being, in his position, the next best thing to men, King

John spared no means of getting it. He set on foot another oppressing and torturing of the unhappy Jews (which was quite in his way), and invented a new punishment for one wealthy Jew of Bristol. Until such time as that Jew should produce a certain large sum of money, the King sentenced him to be imprisoned, and, every day, to have one tooth violently wrenched from his head—beginning with the double teeth. For seven days, the oppressed man bore the daily pain and lost the daily tooth; but, on the eighth, he paid the money. With the treasure raised in such ways, the King made an expedition into Ireland, where some English nobles had revolted. It was one of the very few places from which he did not run away; because no resistance was shown. He made another expedition into Wales—whence he *did* run away in the end: but not before he had got from the Welsh people, as hostages, twenty-seven young men of the best families; every one of whom he caused to be slain in the following year.

To Interdict and Excommunication, the Pope now added his last sentence; Deposition. He proclaimed John no longer King, absolved all his subjects from their allegiance, and sent Stephen Langton and others to the King of France to tell him that, if he would invade England, he should be forgiven all his sins—at least, should be forgiven them by the Pope, if that would do.

As there was nothing that King Philip desired more than to invade England, he collected a great army at Rouen, and a fleet of seventeen hundred ships to bring them over. But the English people, however bitterly they hated the King, were not a people to suffer invasion quietly. They flocked to Dover, where the English standard was, in such great numbers to enrol themselves as defenders of their native land, that there were not provisions for them, and the King could only select and retain sixty thousand. But, at this crisis, the Pope, who had his own reasons for objecting to either King John or King Philip being too powerful, interfered. He entrusted a legate, whose name was PANDOLF, with the easy task of frightening King John. He sent him to the English Camp, from France, to terrify him with exaggerations of King Philip's power, and his own weakness in the discontent of the English Barons and people. Pandolf discharged his commission so well, that King John, in a wretched panic, consented to acknowledge Stephen Langton; to resign his kingdom "to God, Saint Peter, and Saint Paul"—which meant the Pope; and to hold it, ever afterwards, by the Pope's leave, on payment of an annual sum of money. To this shameful contract he publicly bound himself in the church of the Knights Templars at Dover: where he laid at the legate's feet a part of the tribute, which the legate haughtily trampled upon. But they *do* say, that this was merely a genteel flourish, and that he was afterwards seen to pick it up and pocket it.

There was an unfortunate prophet, of the name of Peter, who had greatly increased King John's terrors by predicting that he would be unknighted (which the King supposed to signify that he would die) before the Feast of the Ascension should be past. That was the day after his humiliation. When the next morning came, and the King, who had been trembling all night, found himself alive and safe, he ordered the prophet—and his son too—to be dragged through the streets at the tails of horses, and then hanged, for having frightened him.

As King John had now submitted, the Pope, to King Philip's great astonishment, took him under his protection, and informed King Philip that he found he could not give him leave to invade England. The angry Philip resolved to do it without his leave; but he gained nothing and lost much; for, the English, commanded by the Earl of Salisbury, went over, in five hundred ships, to the French coast, before the French fleet had sailed away from it, and utterly defeated the whole.

The Pope then took off his three sentences, one after another, and empowered Stephen Langton publicly to receive King John into the favour of the Church again, and to ask him to dinner. The King, who hated Langton with all his might and main—and with reason too, for he was a great and a good man, with whom such a King could have no sympathy—pretended to cry and to be very grateful. There was a little difficulty about settling how much the King should pay as a recompense to the clergy for the losses he had caused them; but, the end of it was, that the superior clergy got a good deal, and the inferior clergy got little or nothing—which has also happened since King John's time, I believe.

When all these matters were arranged, the King in his triumph became more fierce, and false, and insolent to all around him than he had ever been. An alliance of sovereigns against King Philip, gave him an opportunity of landing an army in France; with which he even took a town! But, on the French King's gaining a great victory, he ran away, of course, and made a truce for five years.

And now the time approached when he was to be still further humbled, and made to feel, if he could feel anything, what a wretched creature he was. Of all men in the world, Stephen Langton seemed raised up by Heaven to oppose and subdue him. When he ruthlessly burnt and destroyed the property of his own subjects, because their Lords, the Barons, would not serve him abroad, Stephen Langton fearlessly reproved and threatened him. When he swore to restore the laws of King Edward, or the laws of King Henry the First, Stephen Langton knew his falsehood, and pursued him through all his evasions. When the Barons met at the abbey of Saint Edmund's-Bury, to consider their wrongs and the King's oppressions, Stephen Langton roused them by his fervid words to demand a solemn charter of rights and liberties from their perjured master, and to swear, one by one, on the High Altar, that they would have it, or would wage war against him to the death. When the King hid himself in London from the Barons, and was at last obliged to receive them, they told him roundly they would not believe him unless Stephen Langton became a surety that he would keep his word. When he took the Cross to invest himself with some interest, and belong to something that was received with favour, Stephen Langton was still immovable. When he appealed to the Pope, and the Pope wrote to Stephen Langton in behalf of his new favourite, Stephen Langton was deaf, even to the Pope himself, and saw before him nothing but the welfare of England and the crimes of the English King.

At Easter-time, the Barons assembled at Stamford, in Lincolnshire, in proud array, and, marching near to Oxford where the King was, delivered into the hands of Stephen Langton and two others, a list of grievances. "And these," they said, "he must redress, or we will do it for ourselves!" When Stephen Langton told the King as much, and read the list to him, he went half mad with rage. But that did him no more good than his afterwards trying to pacify the Barons with lies. They called themselves and their followers, "The army of God and the Holy Church." Marching through the country, with the people thronging to them everywhere (except at Northampton, where they failed in an attack upon the castle), they at last triumphantly set up their banner in London itself, whither the whole land, tired of the tyrant, seemed to flock to join them. Seven knights alone, of all the knights in England, remained with the King; who, reduced to this strait, at last sent the Earl of Pembroke to the Barons to say that he approved of everything, and would meet them to sign their charter when they would. "Then," said the Barons, "let the day be the fifteenth of June, and the place, Runny-Mead."

On Monday, the fifteenth of June, one thousand two hundred and fourteen, the King came from Windsor Castle, and the Barons came from the town of Staines, and they met on Runny-Mead, which is still a pleasant meadow by the Thames, where rushes grow in the clear water of the winding river, and its banks are green with grass and trees. On the side of the Barons, came the General of their army, ROBERT FITZ-WALTER, and a great concourse of the nobility of England. With the King, came, in all, some four-and-twenty persons of any note, most of whom despised him, and were merely his advisers in form. On that great day, and in that great company, the King signed MAGNA CHARTA—the great charter of England—by which he pledged himself to maintain the Church in its rights; to relieve the Barons of oppressive obligations as vassals of the Crown—of which the Barons, in their turn, pledged themselves to relieve *their* vassals, the people; to respect the liberties of London and all other cities and boroughs; to protect foreign merchants who came to England; to imprison no man without a fair trial; and to sell, delay, or deny justice to none. As the Barons knew his falsehood well, they further required, as their securities, that he should send out of his kingdom all his foreign troops; that for two months they should hold possession of the city of London, and Stephen Langton of the Tower; and that five-and-twenty of their body, chosen by themselves, should be a lawful committee to watch the keeping of the charter, and to make war upon him if he broke it.

All this he was obliged to yield. He signed the charter with a smile, and, if he could have looked agreeable, would have done so, as he departed from the splendid assembly. When he got home to Windsor Castle, he was quite a madman in his helpless fury. And he broke the charter immediately afterwards.

He sent abroad for foreign soldiers, and sent to the Pope for help, and plotted to take London by surprise, while the Barons should be holding a great tournament at Stamford, which they had agreed to hold there as a celebration of the charter. The Barons, however, found him out and put it off. Then, when the Barons desired to see him and tax him with his treachery, he made numbers of appointments with them, and kept none, and shifted from place to place, and was constantly sneaking and skulking about. At last he appeared at Dover, to join his foreign soldiers, of whom numbers came into his pay; and with them he besieged and took Rochester Castle, which was occupied by knights and soldiers of the Barons. He would have hanged them every one; but the leader of the foreign soldiers, fearful of what the English people might afterwards do to him, interfered to save the knights; therefore the King was fain to satisfy his vengeance with the death of all the common men. Then, he sent the Earl of Salisbury, with one portion of his army, to ravage the eastern part of his own dominions, while he carried fire and slaughter into the northern part; torturing, plundering, killing, and inflicting every possible cruelty upon the people; and, every morning, setting a worthy example to his men by setting fire, with his own monster-hands, to the house where he had slept last night. Nor was this all; for the Pope, coming to the aid of his precious friend, laid the kingdom under an Interdict again, because the people took part with the Barons. It did not much matter, for the people had grown so used to it now, that they had begun to think nothing about it. It occurred to them—perhaps to Stephen Langton too—that they could keep their churches open, and ring their bells, without the Pope's permission as well as with it. So, they tried the experiment—and found that it succeeded perfectly.

It being now impossible to bear the country, as a wilderness of cruelty, or longer to hold any terms with such a forsworn outlaw of a King, the Barons sent to Louis, son of the French monarch, to offer him the English crown. Caring as little for the Pope's excommunication of him if he accepted the offer, as it is possible his father may have cared for the Pope's forgiveness of his sins, he landed at Sandwich (King John immediately running away from Dover, where he happened to be), and went on to London. The Scottish King, with whom many of the Northern English Lords had taken refuge; numbers of the foreign soldiers, numbers of the Barons, and numbers of the people went over to him every day;—King John, the while, continually running away in all directions. The career of Louis was checked, however, by the suspicions of the Barons, founded on the dying declaration of a French Lord, that when the kingdom was conquered he was sworn to banish them as traitors, and to give their estates to some of his own Nobles. Rather than suffer this, some of the Barons hesitated: others even went over to King John.

It seemed to be the turning-point of King John's fortunes, for, in his savage and murderous course, he had now taken some towns and met with some successes. But, happily for England and humanity, his death was near. Crossing a dangerous quicksand, called the Wash, not very far from Wisbeach, the tide came up and nearly drowned his army. He and his soldiers escaped; but, looking back from the shore when he was safe, he saw the roaring water sweep down in a torrent, overturn the waggons, horses, and men, that carried his treasure, and engulf them in a raging whirlpool from which nothing could be delivered.

Cursing, and swearing, and gnawing his fingers, he went on to Swinstead Abbey, where the monks set before him quantities of pears, and peaches, and new cider—some say poison too, but there is very little reason to suppose so—of which he ate and drank in an immoderate and beastly way. All night he lay ill of a burning fever, and haunted with horrible fears. Next day, they put him in a horse-litter, and carried him to Sleaford Castle, where he passed another night of pain and horror. Next day, they carried him, with greater difficulty than on the day before, to the castle of Newark upon Trent; and there, on the eighteenth of October, in the forty-ninth year of his age, and the seventeenth of his vile reign, was an end of this miserable brute.

CHAPTER XV

ENGLAND UNDER HENRY THE THIRD, CALLED, OF WINCHESTER

IF any of the English Barons remembered the murdered Arthur's sister, Eleanor the fair maid of Brittany, shut up in her convent at Bristol, none among them spoke of her now, or maintained her right to the Crown. The dead Usurper's eldest boy, HENRY by name, was taken by the Earl of Pembroke, the Marshal of England, to the city of Gloucester, and there crowned in great haste when he was only ten years old. As the Crown itself had been lost with the King's treasure, in the raging water, and as there was no time to make another, they put a circle of plain gold upon his head instead. "We have been the enemies of this child's father," said Lord Pembroke, a good and true gentleman, to the few Lords who were present, "and he merited our ill-will; but the child himself is innocent, and his youth demands our friendship and protection." Those Lords felt tenderly towards the little boy, remembering their own young children; and they bowed their heads, and said, "Long live King Henry the Third!"

Next, a great council met at Bristol, revised Magna Charta, and made Lord Pembroke Regent or Protector of England, as the King was too young to reign alone. The next thing to be done, was to get rid of Prince Louis of France, and to win over those English Barons who were still ranged under his banner. He was strong in many parts of England, and in London itself; and he held, among other places, a certain Castle called the Castle of Mount Sorel, in Leicestershire. To this fortress, after some skirmishing and truce-making, Lord Pembroke laid siege. Louis despatched an army of six hundred knights and twenty thousand soldiers to relieve it. Lord Pembroke, who was not strong enough for such a force, retired with all his men. The army of the French Prince, which had marched there with fire and plunder, marched away with fire and plunder, and came, in a boastful swaggering manner, to Lincoln. The town submitted; but the Castle in the town, held by a brave widow lady, named NICHOLA DE CAMVILLE (whose property it was), made such a sturdy resistance, that the French Count in command of the army of the French Prince found it necessary to besiege this Castle. While he was thus engaged, word was brought to him that Lord Pembroke, with four hundred knights, two hundred and fifty men with cross-bows, and a stout force both of horse and foot, was marching towards him. "What care I?" said the French Count. "The Englishman is not so mad as to attack me and my great army in a walled town!" But the Englishman did it for all that, and did it—not so madly but so wisely, that he decoyed the great army into the narrow, ill-paved lanes and byways of Lincoln, where its horse-soldiers could not ride in any strong body; and there he made such havoc with them, that the whole force surrendered themselves prisoners, except the Count; who said that he would never yield to any English traitor alive, and accordingly got killed. The end of this victory, which the English called, for a joke, the Fair of Lincoln, was the usual one in those times—the common men were slain without any mercy, and the knights and gentlemen paid ransom and went home.

The wife of Louis, the fair BLANCHE OF CASTILLE, dutifully equipped a fleet of eighty good ships, and sent it over from France to her husband's aid. An English fleet of forty ships, some good and some bad, gallantly met them near the mouth of the Thames, and took or sunk sixty-five in one fight. This great loss put an end to the French Prince's hopes. A treaty was made at Lambeth, in virtue of which the English Barons who had remained attached to his cause returned to their allegiance, and it was engaged on both sides that the Prince and all his troops should retire peacefully to France. It was time to go; for war had made him so poor that he was obliged to borrow money from the citizens of London to pay his expenses home.

Lord Pembroke afterwards applied himself to governing the country justly, and to healing the quarrels and disturbances that had arisen among men in the days of the bad King John. He caused Magna Charta to be still more improved, and so amended the Forest Laws that a Peasant was no longer put to death for killing a stag in a Royal Forest, but was only imprisoned. It would have been well for England if it could have had so good a Protector many years longer, but that was not to be. Within three years after the young King's

Coronation, Lord Pembroke died; and you may see his tomb, at this day, in the old Temple Church in London.

The Protectorship was now divided. PETER DE ROCHES, whom King John had made Bishop of Winchester, was entrusted with the care of the person of the young sovereign; and the exercise of the Royal authority was confided to EARL HUBERT DE BURGH. These two personages had from the first no liking for each other, and soon became enemies. When the young King was declared of age, Peter de Roches, finding that Hubert increased in power and favour, retired discontentedly, and went abroad. For nearly ten years afterwards Hubert had full sway alone.

But ten years is a long time to hold the favour of a King. This King, too, as he grew up, showed a strong resemblance to his father, in feebleness, inconsistency, and irresolution. The best that can be said of him is that he was not cruel. De Roches coming home again, after ten years, and being a novelty, the King began to favour him and to look coldly on Hubert. Wanting money besides, and having made Hubert rich, he began to dislike Hubert. At last he was made to believe, or pretended to believe, that Hubert had misappropriated some of the Royal treasure; and ordered him to furnish an account of all he had done in his administration. Besides which, the foolish charge was brought against Hubert that he had made himself the King's favourite by magic. Hubert very well knowing that he could never defend himself against such nonsense, and that his old enemy must be determined on his ruin, instead of answering the charges fled to Merton Abbey. Then the King, in a violent passion, sent for the Mayor of London, and said to the Mayor, "Take twenty thousand citizens, and drag me Hubert de Burgh out of that abbey, and bring him here." The Mayor posted off to do it, but the Archbishop of Dublin (who was a friend of Hubert's) warning the King that an abbey was a sacred place, and that if he committed any violence there, he must answer for it to the Church, the King changed his mind and called the Mayor back, and declared that Hubert should have four months to prepare his defence, and should be safe and free during that time.

Hubert, who relied upon the King's word, though I think he was old enough to have known better, came out of Merton Abbey upon these conditions, and journeyed away to see his wife: a Scottish Princess who was then at St. Edmund's-Bury.

Almost as soon as he had departed from the Sanctuary, his enemies persuaded the weak King to send out one SIR GODFREY DE CRANCUMB, who commanded three hundred vagabonds called the Black Band, with orders to seize him. They came up with him at a little town in Essex, called Brentwood, when he was in bed. He leaped out of bed, got out of the house, fled to the church, ran up to the altar, and laid his hand upon the cross. Sir Godfrey and the Black Band, caring neither for church, altar, nor cross, dragged him forth to the church door, with their drawn swords flashing round his head, and sent for a Smith to rivet a set of chains upon him. When the Smith (I wish I knew his name!) was brought, all dark and swarthy with the smoke of his forge, and panting with the speed he had made; and the Black Band, falling aside to show him the Prisoner, cried with a loud uproar, "Make the fetters heavy! make them strong!" the Smith dropped upon his knee—but not to the Black Band —and said, "This is the brave Earl Hubert de Burgh, who fought at Dover Castle, and destroyed the French fleet, and has done his country much good service. You may kill me, if you like, but I will never make a chain for Earl Hubert de Burgh!"

The Black Band never blushed, or they might have blushed at this. They knocked the Smith about from one to another, and swore at him, and tied the Earl on horseback, undressed as he was, and carried him off to the Tower of London. The Bishops, however, were so indignant at the violation of the Sanctuary of the Church, that the frightened King soon ordered the Black Band to take him back again; at the same time commanding the Sheriff of Essex to prevent his escaping out of Brentwood Church. Well! the Sheriff dug a deep trench all round the church, and erected a high fence, and watched the church night and day; the Black Band and their Captain watched it too, like three hundred and one black wolves. For thirty-nine days, Hubert de Burgh remained within. At length, upon the fortieth day, cold and hunger were too much for him, and he gave himself up to the Black Band, who carried him off, for the second time, to the Tower. When his trial came on, he refused to plead; but at last it was arranged that he should give up all the royal lands which had been bestowed upon him, and should be kept at the Castle of Devizes, in what was called "free prison," in charge of four knights appointed by four lords. There, he remained almost a year, until, learning that a follower of his old enemy the Bishop was made Keeper of the Castle, and fearing that he might be killed by treachery, he climbed the ramparts one dark night, dropped from the top of the high Castle wall into the moat, and coming safely to the ground, took refuge in another church. From this place he was delivered by a party of horse despatched to his help by some nobles, who were by this time in revolt against the King, and assembled in Wales. He was finally pardoned and restored to his estates, but he lived privately, and never more aspired to a high post in the realm, or to a high place in the King's favour. And thus end—more happily than the stories of many favourites of Kings—the adventures of Earl Hubert de Burgh.

The nobles, who had risen in revolt, were stirred up to rebellion by the overbearing conduct of the Bishop of Winchester, who, finding that the King secretly hated the Great Charter which had been forced from his father, did his utmost to confirm him in that dislike, and in the preference he showed to foreigners over the English. Of this, and of his even publicly declaring that the Barons of England were inferior to those of France, the English lords complained with such bitterness, that the King, finding them well supported by the clergy, became frightened for his throne, and sent away the Bishop and all his foreign associates. On his marriage, however, with ELEANOR, a French lady, the daughter of the Count of Provence, he openly favoured the foreigners again; and so many of his wife's relations came over, and made such an immense family-party at court, and got so many good things, and pocketed so much money, and were so high with the English whose money they pocketed, that the bolder English Barons murmured openly about a clause there was in the Great Charter, which provided for the banishment of unreasonable favourites. But, the foreigners only laughed disdainfully, and said, "What are your English laws to us?"

King Philip of France had died, and had been succeeded by Prince Louis, who had also died after a short reign of three years, and had been succeeded by his son of the same name—so moderate and just a man that he was not the least in the world like a King, as Kings went. ISABELLA, King Henry's mother, wished very much (for a certain spite she had) that England should make war against this King; and, as King Henry was a mere puppet in anybody's hands who knew how to manage his feebleness, she easily carried her point with him. But, the Parliament were determined to give him no money for such a war. So, to defy the Parliament, he packed up thirty large casks of silver—I don't know how he got so much; I dare say he screwed it out of the miserable Jews—and put them aboard ship, and went away himself to carry war into France: accompanied by his mother and his brother Richard, Earl of Cornwall, who was rich and clever. But he only got well beaten, and came home.

The good-humour of the Parliament was not restored by this. They reproached the King with wasting the public money to make greedy foreigners rich, and were so stern with him, and so determined not to let him have more of it to waste if they could help it, that he was at his wit's end for some, and tried so shamelessly to get all he could from his subjects, by excuses or by force, that the people used to say the King was the sturdiest beggar in England. He took the Cross, thinking to get some money by that means; but, as it was very well known that he never meant to go on a crusade, he got none. In all this contention, the Londoners were particularly keen against the King, and the King hated them warmly in return. Hating or loving, however, made no difference; he continued in the same condition for nine or ten years, when at last the Barons said that if he would solemnly confirm their liberties afresh, the Parliament would vote him a large sum.

As he readily consented, there was a great meeting held in Westminster Hall, one pleasant day in May, when all the clergy, dressed in their robes and holding every one of them a burning candle in his hand, stood up (the Barons being also there) while the Archbishop of Canterbury read the sentence of excommunication against any man, and all men, who should henceforth, in any way, infringe the Great Charter of the Kingdom. When he had done, they all put out their burning candles with a curse upon the soul of any one, and every one, who should merit that sentence. The King concluded with an oath to keep the Charter, "As I am a man, as I am a Christian, as I am a Knight, as I am a King!"

It was easy to make oaths, and easy to break them; and the King did both, as his father had done before him. He took to his old courses again when he was supplied with money, and soon cured of their weakness the few who had ever really trusted him. When his money was gone, and he was once more borrowing and begging everywhere with a meanness worthy of his nature, he got into a difficulty with the Pope respecting the Crown of Sicily, which the Pope said he had a right to give away, and which he offered to King Henry for his second son, PRINCE EDMUND. But, if you or I give away what we have not got, and what belongs to somebody else, it is likely that the person to whom we give it, will have some trouble in taking it. It was exactly so in this case. It was necessary to conquer the Sicilian Crown before it could be put upon young Edmund's head. It could not be conquered without money. The Pope ordered the clergy to raise money. The clergy, however, were not so obedient to him as usual; they had been disputing with him for some time about his unjust preference of Italian Priests in England; and they had begun to doubt whether the King's chaplain, whom he allowed to be paid for preaching in seven hundred churches, could possibly be, even by the Pope's favour, in seven hundred places at once. "The Pope and the King together," said the Bishop of London, "may take the mitre off my head; but, if they do, they will find that I shall put on a soldier's helmet. I pay nothing." The Bishop of Worcester was as bold as the Bishop of London, and would pay nothing either. Such sums as the more timid or more helpless of the clergy did raise were squandered away, without doing any good to the King, or bringing the Sicilian Crown an inch nearer to Prince Edmund's head. The end of the business was, that the Pope gave the Crown to the brother of the King of France (who conquered it for himself), and sent the King of England in, a bill of one hundred thousand pounds for the expenses of not having won it.

The King was now so much distressed that we might almost pity him, if it were possible to pity a King so shabby and ridiculous. His clever brother, Richard, had bought the title of King of the Romans from the German people, and was no longer near him, to help him with advice. The clergy, resisting the very Pope, were in alliance with the Barons. The Barons were headed by SIMON DE MONTFORT, Earl of Leicester, married to King Henry's sister, and, though a foreigner himself, the most popular man in England against the foreign favourites. When the King next met his Parliament, the Barons, led by this Earl, came before him, armed from head to foot, and cased in armour. When the Parliament again assembled, in a month's time, at Oxford, this Earl was at their head, and the King was obliged to consent, on oath, to what was called a Committee of Government: consisting of twenty-four members: twelve chosen by the Barons, and twelve chosen by himself.

But, at a good time for him, his brother Richard came back. Richard's first act (the Barons would not admit him into England on other terms) was to swear to be faithful to the Committee of Government—which he immediately began to oppose with all his might. Then, the Barons began to quarrel among themselves; especially the proud Earl of Gloucester with the Earl of Leicester, who went abroad in disgust. Then, the people began to be dissatisfied with the Barons, because they did not do enough for them. The King's chances seemed so good again at length, that he took heart enough—or caught it from his brother—to tell the Committee of Government that he abolished them—as to his oath, never mind that, the Pope said!—and to seize all the money in the Mint, and to shut himself up in the Tower of London. Here he was joined by his eldest son, Prince Edward; and, from the Tower, he made public a letter of the Pope's to the world in general, informing all men that he had been an excellent and just King for five-and-forty years.

As everybody knew he had been nothing of the sort, nobody cared much for this document. It so chanced that the proud Earl of Gloucester dying, was succeeded by his son; and that his son, instead of being the enemy of the Earl of Leicester, was (for the time) his friend. It fell out, therefore, that these two Earls joined their forces, took several of the Royal Castles in the country, and advanced as hard as they could on London. The London people, always opposed to the King, declared for them with great joy. The King himself remained shut up, not at all gloriously, in the Tower. Prince Edward made the best of his way to Windsor Castle. His mother, the Queen, attempted to follow him by water; but, the people seeing her barge rowing up the river, and hating her with all their hearts, ran to London Bridge, got together a quantity of stones and mud, and pelted the barge as it came through, crying furiously, "Drown the Witch! Drown her!" They were so near doing it, that the Mayor took the old lady under his protection, and shut her up in St. Paul's until the danger was past.

It would require a great deal of writing on my part, and a great deal of reading on yours, to follow the King through his disputes with the Barons, and to follow the Barons through their disputes with one another—so I will make short work of it for both of us, and only relate the chief events that arose out of these quarrels. The good King of France was asked to decide between them. He gave it as his opinion that the King must maintain the Great Charter, and that the Barons must give up the Committee of Government, and all the rest that had been done by the Parliament at Oxford: which the Royalists, or King's Party, scornfully called the Mad Parliament. The Barons declared that these were not fair terms, and they would not accept them. Then they caused the great bell of St. Paul's to be tolled, for the purpose of rousing up the London people, who armed themselves at the dismal sound and formed quite an army in the streets. I am sorry to say, however, that instead of falling upon the King's party with whom their quarrel was, they fell upon the miserable Jews, and killed at least five hundred of them. They pretended that some of these Jews were on the King's side, and that they kept hidden in their houses, for the destruction of the people, a certain terrible composition called Greek Fire, which could not be put out with water, but only burnt the fiercer for it. What they really did keep in their houses was money; and this their cruel enemies wanted, and this their cruel enemies took, like robbers and murderers.

The Earl of Leicester put himself at the head of these Londoners and other forces, and followed the King to Lewes in Sussex, where he lay encamped with his army. Before giving the King's forces battle here, the Earl addressed his soldiers, and said that King Henry the Third had broken so many oaths, that he had become the enemy of God, and therefore they would wear white crosses on their breasts, as if they were arrayed, not against a fellow-Christian, but against a Turk. White-crossed accordingly, they rushed into the fight. They would have lost the day—the King having on his side all the foreigners in England: and, from Scotland, JOHN COMYN, JOHN BALIOL, and ROBERT BRUCE, with all their men—but for the impatience of PRINCE EDWARD, who, in his hot desire to have vengeance on the people of London, threw the whole of his father's army into confusion. He was taken Prisoner; so was the King; so was the King's brother the King of the Romans; and five thousand Englishmen were left dead upon the bloody grass.

For this success, the Pope excommunicated the Earl of Leicester: which neither the Earl nor the people cared at all about. The people loved him and supported him, and he became the real King; having all the power of the government in his own hands, though he was outwardly respectful to King Henry the Third, whom he took with him wherever he went, like a poor old limp court-card. He summoned a Parliament (in the year one thousand two hundred and sixty-five) which was the first Parliament in England that the people had any real share in electing; and he grew more and more in favour with the people every day, and they stood by him in whatever he did.

Many of the other Barons, and particularly the Earl of Gloucester, who had become by this time as proud as his father, grew jealous of this powerful and popular Earl, who was proud too, and began to conspire against him. Since the battle of Lewes, Prince Edward had been kept as a hostage, and, though he was otherwise treated like a Prince, had never been allowed to go out without attendants appointed by the Earl of Leicester, who watched him. The conspiring Lords found means to propose to him, in secret, that they should assist him to escape, and should make him their leader; to which he very heartily consented.

So, on a day that was agreed upon, he said to his attendants after dinner (being then at Hereford), "I should like to ride on horseback, this fine afternoon, a little way into the country." As they, too, thought it would be very pleasant to have a canter in the sunshine, they all rode out of the town together in a gay little troop. When they came to a fine level piece of turf, the Prince fell to comparing their horses one with another, and offering bets that one was faster than another; and the attendants, suspecting no harm, rode galloping

matches until their horses were quite tired. The Prince rode no
matches himself, but looked on from his saddle, and staked his
money. Thus they passed the whole merry afternoon. Now, the sun
was setting, and they were all going slowly up a hill, the Prince's
horse very fresh and all the other horses very weary, when a strange
rider mounted on a grey steed appeared at the top of the hill, and
waved his hat. "What does the fellow mean?" said the attendants
one to another. The Prince answered on the instant by setting spurs
to his horse, dashing away at his utmost speed, joining the man,
riding into the midst of a little crowd of horsemen who were then seen
waiting under some trees, and who closed around him; and so he
departed in a cloud of dust, leaving the road empty of all but the
baffled attendants, who sat looking at one another, while their horses
drooped their ears and panted.

The Prince joined the Earl of Gloucester at Ludlow. The Earl of
Leicester, with a part of the army and the stupid old King, was at
Hereford. One of the Earl of Leicester's sons, Simon de Montfort,
with another part of the army, was in Sussex. To prevent these two
parts from uniting was the Prince's first object. He attacked Simon
de Montfort by night, defeated him, seized his banners and treasure,
and forced him into Kenilworth Castle in Warwickshire, which
belonged to his family.

His father, the Earl of Leicester, in the meanwhile, not knowing
what had happened, marched out of Hereford, with his part of the
army and the King, to meet him. He came, on a bright morning in
August, to Evesham, which is watered by the pleasant river Avon.
Looking rather anxiously across the prospect towards Kenilworth, he
saw his own banners advancing; and his face brightened with joy.
But, it clouded darkly when he presently perceived that the banners
were captured, and in the enemy's hands; and he said, "It is over.
The Lord have mercy on our souls, for our bodies are Prince
Edward's!"

He fought like a true Knight, nevertheless. When his horse was
killed under him, he fought on foot. It was a fierce battle, and the
dead lay in heaps everywhere. The old King, stuck up in a suit of
armour on a big war-horse, which didn't mind him at all, and which
carried him into all sorts of places where he didn't want to go, got
into everybody's way, and very nearly got knocked on the head by
one of his son's men. But he managed to pipe out, "I am Harry of
Winchester!" and the Prince, who heard him, seized his bridle, and
took him out of peril. The Earl of Leicester still fought bravely, until
his best son Henry was killed, and the bodies of his best friends
choked his path; and then he fell, still fighting, sword in hand. They
mangled his body, and sent it as a present to a noble lady—but a
very unpleasant lady, I should think—who was the wife of his worst
enemy. They could not mangle his memory in the minds of the faithful people, though. Many years afterwards, they loved him more
than ever, and regarded him as a Saint, and always spoke of him as
"Sir Simon the Righteous."

And even though he was dead, the cause for which he had fought still lived, and was strong, and forced itself upon the King in the very hour of victory. Henry found himself obliged to respect the Great Charter, however much he hated it, and to make laws similar to the laws of the Great Earl of Leicester, and to be moderate and forgiving towards the people at last—even towards the people of London, who had so long opposed him. There were more risings before all this was done, but they were set at rest by these means, and Prince Edward did his best in all things to restore peace. One Sir Adam de Gourdon was the last dissatisfied knight in arms; but, the Prince vanquished him in single combat, in a wood, and nobly gave him his life, and became his friend, instead of slaying him. Sir Adam was not ungrateful. He ever afterwards remained devoted to his generous conqueror.

When the troubles of the Kingdom were thus calmed, Prince Edward and his cousin Henry took the Cross, and went away to the Holy Land, with many English Lords and Knights. Four years afterwards the King of the Romans died, and, next year (one thousand two hundred and seventy-two), his brother the weak King of England died. He was sixty-eight years old then, and had reigned fifty-six years. He was as much of a King in death, as he had ever been in life. He was the mere pale shadow of a King at all times.

CHAPTER XVI

ENGLAND UNDER EDWARD THE FIRST, CALLED LONGSHANKS

It was now the year of our Lord one thousand two hundred and seventy-two; and Prince Edward, the heir to the throne, being away in the Holy Land, knew nothing of his father's death. The Barons, however, proclaimed him King, immediately after the Royal funeral; and the people very willingly consented, since most men knew too well by this time what the horrors of a contest for the crown were. So King Edward the First, called, in a not very complimentary manner, LONGSHANKS, because of the slenderness of his legs, was peacefully accepted by the English Nation.

His legs had need to be strong, however long and thin they were; for they had to support him through many difficulties on the fiery sands of Asia, where his small force of soldiers fainted, died, deserted, and seemed to melt away. But his prowess made light of it, and he said, "I will go on, if I go on with no other follower than my groom!"

A Prince of this spirit gave the Turks a deal of trouble. He stormed Nazareth, at which place, of all places on earth, I am sorry to relate, he made a frightful slaughter of innocent people; and then he went to Acre, where he got a truce of ten years from the Sultan. He had very nearly lost his life in Acre, through the treachery of a Saracen Noble, called the Emir of Jaffa, who, making the pretence that he had some idea of turning Christian and wanted to know all about that religion, sent a trusty messenger to Edward very often—with a dagger in his sleeve. At last, one Friday in Whitsun week, when it was very hot, and all the sandy prospect lay beneath the blazing sun, burnt up like a great overdone biscuit, and Edward was lying on a couch, dressed for coolness in only a loose robe, the messenger, with his chocolate-coloured face and his bright dark eyes and white teeth, came creeping in with a letter, and kneeled down like a tame tiger. But, the moment Edward stretched out his hand to take the letter, the tiger made a spring at his heart. He was quick, but Edward was quick too. He seized the traitor by his chocolate throat, threw him to the ground, and slew him with the very dagger he had drawn. The weapon had struck Edward in the arm, and although the wound itself was slight, it threatened to be mortal, for the blade of the dagger had been smeared with poison. Thanks, however, to a better surgeon than was often to be found in those times, and to some wholesome herbs, and above all, to his faithful wife, ELEANOR, who devotedly nursed him, and is said by some to have sucked the poison from the wound with her own red lips (which I am very willing to believe), Edward soon recovered and was sound again.

As the King his father had sent entreaties to him to return home, he now began the journey. He had got as far as Italy, when he met messengers who brought him intelligence of the King's death. Hearing that all was quiet at home, he made no haste to return to his own dominions, but paid a visit to the Pope, and went in state through various Italian Towns, where he was welcomed with acclamations as a mighty champion of the Cross from the Holy Land, and where he received presents of purple mantles and prancing horses, and went along in great triumph. The shouting people little knew that he was the last English monarch who would ever embark in a crusade, or that within twenty years every conquest which the Christians had made in the Holy Land at the cost of so much blood, would be won back by the Turks. But all this came to pass.

There was, and there is, an old town standing in a plain in France, called Châlons. When the King was coming towards this place on his way to England, a wily French Lord, called the Count of Châlons, sent him a polite challenge to come with his knights and hold a fair tournament with the Count and *his* knights, and make a day of it with sword and lance. It was represented to the King that the Count of Châlons was not to be trusted, and that, instead of a holiday fight for mere show and in good humour, he secretly meant a real battle, in which the English should be defeated by superior force.

The King, however, nothing afraid, went to the appointed place on the appointed day with a thousand followers. When the Count came with two thousand and attacked the English in earnest, the English rushed at them with such valour that the Count's men and the Count's horses soon began to be tumbled down all over the field. The Count himself seized the King round the neck, but the King tumbled *him* out of his saddle in return for the compliment, and, jumping from his own horse, and standing over him, beat away at his iron armour like a blacksmith hammering on his anvil. Even when the Count owned himself defeated and offered his sword, the King would not do him the honour to take it, but made him yield it up to a common soldier. There had been such fury shown in this fight, that it was afterwards called the little Battle of Châlons.

The English were very well disposed to be proud of their King after these adventures; so, when he landed at Dover in the year one thousand two hundred and seventy-four (being then thirty-six years old), and went on to Westminster where he and his good Queen were crowned with great magnificence, splendid rejoicings took place. For the coronation-feast there were provided, among other eatables, four hundred oxen, four hundred sheep, four hundred and fifty pigs, eighteen wild boars, three hundred flitches of bacon, and twenty thousand fowls. The fountains and conduits in the street flowed with red and white wine instead of water; the rich citizens hung silks and cloths of the brightest colours out of their windows to increase the beauty of the show, and threw out gold and silver by whole handfuls to make scrambles for the crowd. In short, there was such eating and drinking, such music and capering, such a ringing of bells and tossing of caps, such a shouting, and singing, and revelling, as the narrow overhanging streets of old London City had not witnessed for many a long day. All the people were merry—except the poor Jews, who, trembling within their houses, and scarcely daring to peep out, began to foresee that they would have to find the money for this joviality sooner or later.

To dismiss this sad subject of the Jews for the present, I am sorry to add that in this reign they were most unmercifully pillaged. They were hanged in great numbers, on accusations of having clipped the King's coin—which all kinds of people had done. They were heavily taxed; they were disgracefully badged; they were, on one day, thirteen years after the coronation, taken up with their wives and children and thrown into beastly prisons, until they purchased their release by paying to the King twelve thousand pounds. Finally, every kind of property belonging to them was seized by the King, except so little as would defray the charge of their taking themselves away into foreign countries. Many years elapsed before the hope of gain induced any of their race to return to England, where they had been treated so heartlessly and had suffered so much.

If King Edward the First had been as bad a king to Christians as he was to Jews, he would have been bad indeed. But he was, in general, a wise and great monarch, under whom the country much improved. He had no love for the Great Charter—few Kings had, through many, many years—but he had high qualities. The first bold object which he conceived when he came home, was, to unite under one Sovereign England, Scotland, and Wales; the two last of which countries had each a little king of its own, about whom the people were always quarrelling and fighting, and making a prodigious disturbance—a great deal more than he was worth. In the course of

King Edward's reign he was engaged, besides, in a war with France. To make these quarrels clearer, we will separate their histories and take them thus. Wales, first. France, second. Scotland, third.

LLEWELLYN was the Prince of Wales. He had been on the side of the Barons in the reign of the stupid old King, but had afterwards sworn allegiance to him. When King Edward came to the throne, Llewellyn was required to swear allegiance to him also; which he refused to do. The King, being crowned and in his own dominions, three times more required Llewellyn to come and do homage; and three times more Llewellyn said he would rather not. He was going to be married to ELEANOR DE MONTFORT, a young lady of the family mentioned in the last reign; and it chanced that this young lady, coming from France with her youngest brother, EMERIC, was taken by an English ship, and was ordered by the English King to be detained. Upon this, the quarrel came to a head. The King went, with his fleet, to the coast of Wales, where, so encompassing Llewellyn, that he could only take refuge in the bleak mountain region of Snowdon in which no provisions could reach him, he was soon starved into an apology, and into a treaty of peace, and into paying the expenses of the war. The King, however, forgave him some of the hardest conditions of the treaty, and consented to his marriage. And he now thought he had reduced Wales to obedience.

But, the Welsh, although they were naturally a gentle, quiet, pleasant people, who liked to receive strangers in their cottages among the mountains, and to set before them with free hospitality whatever they had to eat and drink, and to play to them on their harps, and sing their native ballads to them, were a people of great spirit when their blood was up. Englishmen, after this affair, began to be insolent in Wales, and to assume the air of masters; and the Welsh pride could not bear it. Moreover, they believed in that unlucky old Merlin, some of whose unlucky old prophecies somebody always seemed doomed to remember when there was a chance of its doing harm; and just at this time some blind old gentleman with a harp and a long white beard, who was an excellent person, but had become of an unknown age and tedious, burst out with a declaration that Merlin had predicted that when English money had become round, a Prince of Wales would be crowned in London. Now, King Edward had recently forbidden the English penny to be cut into halves and quarters for halfpence and farthings, and had actually introduced a round coin; therefore, the Welsh people said this was the time Merlin meant, and rose accordingly.

King Edward had bought over PRINCE DAVID, Llewellyn's brother, by heaping favours upon him; but he was the first to revolt, being perhaps troubled in his conscience. One stormy night, he surprised the Castle of Hawarden, in possession of which an English nobleman had been left; killed the whole garrison, and carried off the nobleman a prisoner to Snowdon. Upon this, the Welsh people rose like one man. King Edward, with his army, marching from Worcester

to the Menai Strait, crossed it—near to where the wonderful tubular
iron bridge now, in days so different, makes a passage for railway
trains—by a bridge of boats that enabled forty men to march abreast.
He subdued the Island of Anglesea, and sent his men forward to
observe the enemy. The sudden appearance of the Welsh created a
panic among them, and they fell back to the bridge. The tide had in
the meantime risen and separated the boats; the Welsh pursuing
them, they were driven into the sea, and there they sunk, in their
heavy iron armour, by thousands. After this victory Llewellyn,
helped by the severe winter-weather of Wales, gained another battle;
but the King ordering a portion of his English army to advance
through South Wales, and catch him between two foes, and Llewellyn
bravely turning to meet this new enemy, he was surprised and killed
—very meanly, for he was unarmed and defenceless. His head was
struck off and sent to London, where it was fixed upon the Tower,
encircled with a wreath, some say of ivy, some say of willow, some
say of silver, to make it look like a ghastly coin in ridicule of the
prediction.

David, however, still held out for six months, though eagerly
sought after by the King, and hunted by his own countrymen. One
of them finally betrayed him with his wife and children. He was
sentenced to be hanged, drawn, and quartered; and from that time
this became the established punishment of Traitors in England—a
punishment wholly without excuse, as being revolting, vile, and cruel,
after its object is dead; and which has no sense in it, as its only real
degradation (and that nothing can blot out) is to the country that
permits on any consideration such abominable barbarity.

Wales was now subdued. The Queen giving birth to a young prince
in the Castle of Carnarvon, the King showed him to the Welsh people
as their countryman, and called him Prince of Wales; a title that has
ever since been borne by the heir-apparent to the English throne—
which that little Prince soon became, by the death of his elder
brother. The King did better things for the Welsh than that, by improving their laws and encouraging their trade. Disturbances still
took place, chiefly occasioned by the avarice and pride of the English
Lords, on whom Welsh lands and castles had been bestowed; but
they were subdued, and the country never rose again. There is a
legend that to prevent the people from being incited to rebellion by
the songs of their bards and harpers, Edward had them all put to
death. Some of them may have fallen among other men who held out
against the King; but this general slaughter is, I think, a fancy of the
harpers themselves, who, I dare say, made a song about it many
years afterwards, and sang it by the Welsh firesides until it came to
be believed.

The foreign war of the reign of Edward the First arose in this way.
The crews of two vessels, one a Norman ship, and the other an English
ship, happened to go to the same place in their boats to fill their casks
with fresh water. Being rough angry fellows, they began to quarrel,
and then to fight—the English with their fists; the Normans with

their knives—and, in the fight, a Norman was killed. The Norman crew, instead of revenging themselves upon those English sailors with whom they had quarrelled (who were too strong for them, I suspect), took to their ship again in a great rage, attacked the first English ship they met, laid hold of an unoffending merchant who happened to be on board, and brutally hanged him in the rigging of their own vessel with a dog at his feet. This so enraged the English sailors that there was no restraining them; and whenever, and where-ever, English sailors met Norman sailors, they fell upon each other tooth and nail. The Irish and Dutch sailors took part with the English; the French and Genoese sailors helped the Normans; and thus the greater part of the mariners sailing over the sea became, in their way, as violent and raging as the sea itself when it is disturbed.

King Edward's fame had been so high abroad that he had been chosen to decide a difference between France and another foreign power, and had lived upon the Continent three years. At first, neither he nor the French King PHILIP (the good Louis had been dead some time) interfered in these quarrels; but when a fleet of eighty English ships engaged and utterly defeated a Norman fleet of two hundred, in a pitched battle fought round a ship at anchor, in which no quarter was given, the matter became too serious to be passed over. King Edward, as Duke of Guienne, was summoned to present himself before the King of France, at Paris, and answer for the damage done by his sailor subjects. At first, he sent the Bishop of London as his representative, and then his brother EDMUND, who was married to the French Queen's mother. I am afraid Edmund was an easy man, and allowed himself to be talked over by his charming relations, the French court ladies; at all events, he was induced to give up his brother's dukedom for forty days—as a mere form, the French King said, to satisfy his honour—and he was so very much astonished, when the time was out, to find that the French King had no idea of giving it up again, that I should not wonder if it hastened his death; which soon took place.

King Edward was a King to win his foreign dukedom back again, if it could be won by energy and valour. He raised a large army, renounced his allegiance as Duke of Guienne, and crossed the sea to carry war into France. Before any important battle was fought, however, a truce was agreed upon for two years; and in the course of that time, the Pope effected a reconciliation. King Edward, who was now a widower, having lost his affectionate and good wife, Eleanor, married the French King's sister, MARGARET; and the Prince of Wales was contracted to the French King's daughter ISABELLA.

Out of bad things, good things sometimes arise. Out of this hang-ing of the innocent merchant, and the bloodshed and strife it caused, there came to be established one of the greatest powers that the English people now possess. The preparations for the war being very expensive, and King Edward greatly wanting money, and being very arbitrary in his ways of raising it, some of the Barons began firmly to oppose him. Two of them, in particular, HUMPHREY BOHUN, Earl of Hereford, and ROGER BIGOD, Earl of Norfolk, were so stout against him, that they maintained he had no right to command them to head his forces in Guienne, and flatly refused to go there. "By Heaven, Sir Earl," said the King to the Earl of Hereford, in a great passion, "you shall either go or be hanged!" "By Heaven, Sir King," replied the Earl, "I will neither go nor yet will I be hanged!" and both he and the other Earl sturdily left the court, attended by many Lords. The King tried every means of raising money. He taxed the clergy, in spite of all the Pope said to the contrary; and when they refused to pay, reduced them to submission, by saying Very well, then they had no claim upon the government for protection, and any man might plunder them who would—which a good many men were very ready to do, and very readily did, and which the clergy found too losing a game to be played at long. He seized all the wool and leather in the hands of the merchants, promising to pay for it some fine day; and he set a tax upon the exportation of wool, which was so unpopular among the traders that it was called "The evil toll." But all would not do. The Barons, led by those two great Earls, declared any taxes imposed without the consent of Parliament, unlawful; and the Parliament refused to impose taxes, until the King should confirm afresh the two Great Charters, and should solemnly declare in writing, that there was no power in the country to raise money from the people, evermore, but the power of Parliament representing all ranks of the people. The King was very unwilling to diminish his own power by allowing this great privilege in the Parliament; but there was no help for it, and he at last complied. We shall come to another King by-and-by, who might have saved his head from rolling off, if he had profited by this example.

The people gained other benefits in Parliament from the good sense and wisdom of this King. Many of the laws were much improved; provision was made for the greater safety of travellers, and the apprehension of thieves and murderers; the priests were prevented from holding too much land, and so becoming too powerful; and Justices of the Peace were first appointed (though not at first under that name) in various parts of the country.

And now we come to Scotland, which was the great and lasting trouble of the reign of King Edward the First.

About thirteen years after King Edward's coronation, Alexander the Third, the King of Scotland, died of a fall from his horse. He had been married to Margaret, King Edward's sister. All their children being dead, the Scottish crown became the right of a young Princess only eight years old, the daughter of ERIC, King of Norway, who had married a daughter of the deceased sovereign. King Edward proposed, that the Maiden of Norway, as this Princess was called, should be engaged to be married to his eldest son; but, unfortunately, as she was coming over to England she fell sick, and landing on one of the Orkney Islands, died there. A great commotion immediately began in Scotland, where as many as thirteen noisy claimants to the vacant throne started up and made a general confusion.

King Edward being much renowned for his sagacity and justice, it seems to have been agreed to refer the dispute to him. He accepted the trust, and went, with an army, to the Border-land where England and Scotland joined. There, he called upon the Scottish gentlemen to meet him at the Castle of Norham, on the English side of the river Tweed; and to that Castle they came. But, before he would take any step in the business, he required those Scottish gentlemen, one and all, to do homage to him as their superior Lord; and when they hesitated, he said, "By holy Edward, whose crown I wear, I will have my rights, or I will die in maintaining them!" The Scottish gentlemen, who had not expected this, were disconcerted, and asked for three weeks to think about it.

At the end of the three weeks, another meeting took place, on a green plain on the Scottish side of the river. Of all the competitors for the Scottish throne, there were only two who had any real claim, in right of their near kindred to the Royal Family. These were JOHN BALIOL and ROBERT BRUCE: and the right was, I have no doubt, on the side of John Baliol. At this particular meeting John Baliol was not present, but Robert Bruce was; and on Robert Bruce being formally asked whether he acknowledged the King of England for his superior lord, he answered, plainly and distinctly, Yes, he did. Next day, John Baliol appeared, and said the same. This point settled, some arrangements were made for inquiring into their titles.

The inquiry occupied a pretty long time—more than a year. While it was going on, King Edward took the opportunity of making a journey through Scotland, and calling upon the Scottish people of all degrees to acknowledge themselves his vassals, or be imprisoned until they did. In the meanwhile, Commissioners were appointed to conduct the inquiry, a Parliament was held at Berwick about it, the two claimants were heard at full length, and there was a vast amount of talking. At last, in the great hall of the Castle of Berwick, the King gave judgment in favour of John Baliol: who, consenting to receive his crown by the King of England's favour and permission, was crowned at Scone, in an old stone chair which had been used for ages in the abbey there, at the coronations of Scottish Kings. Then, King Edward caused the great seal of Scotland, used since the late King's death, to be broken in four pieces, and placed in the English Treasury; and considered that he now had Scotland (according to the common saying) under his thumb.

Scotland had a strong will of its own yet, however. King Edward, determined that the Scottish King should not forget he was his vassal, summoned him repeatedly to come and defend himself and his Judges before the English Parliament when appeals from the decisions of Scottish courts of justice were being heard. At length, John Baliol, who had no great heart of his own, had so much heart put into him by the brave spirit of the Scottish people, who took this as a national insult, that he refused to come any more. Thereupon, the King further required him to help him in his war abroad (which was then in progress), and to give up, as security for his good behaviour in future, the three strong Scottish Castles of Jedburgh, Roxburgh, and Berwick. Nothing of this being done; on the contrary, the Scottish people concealing their King among their mountains in the Highlands and showing a determination to resist; Edward marched to Berwick with an army of thirty thousand foot, and four thousand horse; took the Castle, and slew its whole garrison, and the inhabitants of the town as well—men, women, and, children. LORD WARRENNE, Earl of Surrey, then went on to the Castle of Dunbar, before which a battle was fought, and the whole Scottish army defeated with great slaughter. The victory being complete, the Earl of Surrey was left as guardian of Scotland; the principal offices in that kingdom were given to Englishmen; the more powerful Scottish Nobles were obliged to come and live in England; the Scottish crown and sceptre were brought away; and even the old stone chair was carried off and placed in Westminster Abbey, where you may see it now. Baliol had the Tower of London lent him for a residence, with permission to range about within a circle of twenty miles. Three years afterwards he was allowed to go to Normandy, where he had estates, and where he passed the remaining six years of his life: far more happily, I dare say, than he had lived for a long while in angry Scotland.

Now, there was, in the West of Scotland, a gentleman of small fortune, named WILLIAM WALLACE, the second son of a Scottish knight. He was a man of great size and great strength; he was very brave and daring; when he spoke to a body of his countrymen, he could rouse them in a wonderful manner by the power of his burning words; he loved Scotland dearly, and he hated England with his utmost might. The domineering conduct of the English who now held the places of trust in Scotland made them as intolerable to the proud Scottish people as they had been, under similar circumstances, to the Welsh; and no man in all Scotland regarded them with so much smothered rage as William Wallace. One day, an Englishman in office, little knowing what he was, affronted *him*. Wallace instantly struck him dead, and taking refuge among the rocks and hills, and there joining with his countryman, SIR WILLIAM DOUGLAS, who was also in arms against King Edward, became the most resolute and undaunted champion of a people struggling for their independence that ever lived upon the earth.

The English Guardian of the Kingdom fled before him, and, thus encouraged, the Scottish people revolted everywhere, and fell upon the English without mercy. The Earl of Surrey, by the King's commands, raised all the power of the Border-counties, and two English armies poured into Scotland. Only one Chief, in the face of those armies, stood by Wallace, who, with a force of forty thousand men, awaited the invaders at a place on the river Forth, within two miles of Stirling. Across the river there was only one poor wooden bridge, called the bridge of Kildean—so narrow, that but two men could cross it abreast. With his eyes upon this bridge, Wallace posted the greater part of his men among some rising grounds, and waited calmly. When the English army came up on the opposite bank of the river, messengers were sent forward to offer terms. Wallace sent them back with a defiance, in the name of the freedom of Scotland. Some of the officers of the Earl of Surrey in command of the English, with *their* eyes also on the bridge, advised him to be discreet and not hasty. He, however, urged to immediate battle by some other officers, and particularly by CRESSINGHAM, King Edward's treasurer, and a rash man, gave the word of command to advance. One thousand English crossed the bridge, two abreast; the Scottish troops were as motionless as stone images. Two thousand English crossed; three thousand, four thousand, five. Not a feather, all this time, had been seen to stir among the Scottish bonnets. Now, they all fluttered. "Forward, one party, to the foot of the Bridge!" cried Wallace, "and let no more English cross! The rest, down with me on the five thousand who have come over, and cut them all to pieces." It was done, in the sight of the whole remainder of the English army, who could give no help. Cressingham himself was killed, and the Scotch made whips for their horses of his skin.

King Edward was abroad at this time, and during the successes on the Scottish side which followed, and which enabled bold Wallace to win the whole country back again, and even to ravage the English borders. But, after a few winter months, the King returned, and took the field with more than his usual energy. One night, when a kick from his horse as they both lay on the ground together broke two of his ribs, and a cry arose that he was killed, he leaped into his saddle, regardless of the pain he suffered, and rode through the camp. Day then appearing, he gave the word (still, of course, in that bruised and aching state) Forward! and led his army on to near Falkirk, where the Scottish forces were seen drawn up on some stony ground, behind a morass. Here, he defeated Wallace and killed fifteen thousand of his men. With the shattered remainder, Wallace drew back to Stirling; but, being pursued, set fire to the town that it might give no help to the English, and escaped. The inhabitants of Perth afterwards set fire to their houses for the same reason, and the King, unable to find provisions, was forced to withdraw his army.

Another ROBERT BRUCE, the grandson of him who had disputed the Scottish crown with Baliol, was now in arms against the King (that elder Bruce being dead), and also JOHN COMYN, Baliol's nephew. These two young men might agree in opposing Edward, but could agree in nothing else, as they were rivals for the throne of Scotland. Probably it was because they knew this, and knew what troubles must arise even if they could hope to get the better of the great English King, that the principal Scottish people applied to the Pope for his interference. The Pope, on the principle of losing nothing for want of trying to get it, very coolly claimed that Scotland belonged to him; but this was a little too much, and the Parliament in a friendly manner told him so.

In the spring time of the year one thousand three hundred and

three, the King sent SIR JOHN SEGRAVE, whom he made Governor of
Scotland, with twenty thousand men, to reduce the rebels. Sir John
was not as careful as he should have been, but encamped at Rosslyn,
near Edinburgh, with his army divided into three parts. The Scottish forces saw their advantage; fell on each part separately; defeated
each; and killed all the prisoners. Then, came the King himself once
more, as soon as a great army could be raised; he passed through the
whole north of Scotland, laying waste whatsoever came in his way;
and he took up his winter quarters at Dunfermline. The Scottish cause
now looked so hopeless, that Comyn and the other nobles made submission and received their pardons. Wallace alone stood out. He was
invited to surrender, though on no distinct pledge that his life should
be spared; but he still defied the ireful King, and lived among the steep
crags of the Highland glens, where the eagles made their nests and
where the mountain torrents roared, and the white snow was deep,
and the bitter winds blew round his unsheltered head, as he lay
through many a pitch-dark night wrapped up in his plaid. Nothing
could break his spirit; nothing could lower his courage; nothing could
induce him to forget or to forgive his country's wrongs. Even when
the Castle of Stirling, which had long held out, was besieged by the
King with every kind of military engine then in use; even when the
lead upon cathedral roofs was taken down to help to make them;
even when the King, though an old man, commanded in the siege as
if he were a youth, being so resolved to conquer; even when the brave
garrison (then found with amazement to be not two hundred people,
including several ladies) were starved and beaten out and were made
to submit on their knees, and with every form of disgrace that could
aggravate their sufferings; even then, when there was not a ray of
hope in Scotland, William Wallace was as proud and firm as if he had
beheld the powerful and relentless Edward lying dead at his feet.

Who betrayed William Wallace in the end, is not quite certain.
That he was betrayed—probably by an attendant—is too true. He
was taken to the Castle of Dumbarton, under SIR JOHN MENTEITH,
and thence to London, where the great fame of his bravery and
resolution attracted immense concourses of people to behold him.
He was tried in Westminster Hall, with a crown of laurel on his head
—it is supposed because he was reported to have said that he ought
to wear, or that he would wear, a crown there—and was found guilty
as a robber, a murderer, and a traitor. What they called a robber (he
said to those who tried him) he was, because he had taken spoil from
the King's men. What they called a murderer, he was, because he
had slain an insolent Englishman. What they called a traitor, he was
not, for he had never sworn allegiance to the King, and had ever
scorned to do it. He was dragged at the tails of horses to West Smithfield, and there hanged on a high gallows, torn open before he was
dead, beheaded and quartered. His head was set upon a pole on
London Bridge, his right arm was sent to Newcastle, his left arm to
Berwick, his legs to Perth and Aberdeen. But, if King Edward had
had his body cut into inches, and had sent every separate inch into

a separate town, he could not have dispersed it half so far and wide as his fame. Wallace will be remembered in songs and stories, while there are songs and stories in the English tongue, and Scotland will hold him dear while her lakes and mountains last.

Released from this dreaded enemy, the King made a fairer plan of Government for Scotland, divided the offices of honour among Scottish gentlemen and English gentlemen, forgave past offences, and thought, in his old age, that his work was done.

But he deceived himself. Comyn and Bruce conspired, and made an appointment to meet at Dumfries, in the church of the Minorites. There is a story that Comyn was false to Bruce, and had informed against him to the King; that Bruce was warned of his danger and the necessity of flight, by receiving, one night as he sat at supper, from his friend the Earl of Gloucester, twelve pennies and a pair of spurs; that as he was riding angrily to keep his appointment (through a snow-storm, with his horse's shoes reversed that he might not be tracked), he met an evil-looking serving man, a messenger of Comyn, whom he killed, and concealed in whose dress he found letters that proved Comyn's treachery. However this may be, they were likely enough to quarrel in any case, being hot-headed rivals; and, whatever they quarrelled about, they certainly did quarrel in the church where they met, and Bruce drew his dagger and stabbed Comyn, who fell upon the pavement. When Bruce came out, pale and disturbed, the friends who were waiting for him asked what was the matter? "I think I have killed Comyn," said he. "You only think so?" returned one of them; "I will make sure!" and going into the church, and finding him alive, stabbed him again and again. Knowing that the King would never forgive this new deed of violence, the party then declared Bruce King of Scotland: got him crowned at Scone—without the chair; and set up the rebellious standard once again.

When the King heard of it he kindled with fiercer anger than he had ever shown yet. He caused the Prince of Wales and two hundred and seventy of the young nobility to be knighted—the trees in the Temple Gardens were cut down to make room for their tents, and they watched their armour all night, according to the old usage: some in the Temple Church: some in Westminster Abbey—and at the public Feast which then took place, he swore, by Heaven, and by two swans covered with gold network which his minstrels placed upon the table, that he would avenge the death of Comyn, and would punish the false Bruce. And before all the company, he charged the Prince his son, in case that he should die before accomplishing his vow, not to bury him until it was fulfilled. Next morning the Prince and the rest of the young Knights rode away to the Border-country to join the English army; and the King, now weak and sick, followed in a horse-litter.

Bruce, after losing a battle and undergoing many dangers and much misery, fled to Ireland, where he lay concealed through the winter. That winter, Edward passed in hunting down and executing

Bruce's relations and adherents, sparing neither youth nor age, and showing no touch of pity or sign of mercy. In the following spring, Bruce reappeared and gained some victories. In these frays, both sides were grievously cruel. For instance—Bruce's two brothers, being taken captives desperately wounded, were ordered by the King to instant execution. Bruce's friend Sir John Douglas, taking his own Castle of Douglas out of the hands of an English Lord, roasted the dead bodies of the slaughtered garrison in a great fire made of every movable within it; which dreadful cookery his men called the Douglas Larder. Bruce, still successful, however, drove the Earl of Pembroke and the Earl of Gloucester into the Castle of Ayr and laid siege to it.

The King, who had been laid up all the winter, but had directed the army from his sick-bed, now advanced to Carlisle, and there, causing the litter in which he had travelled to be placed in the Cathedral as an offering to Heaven, mounted his horse once more, and for the last time. He was now sixty-nine years old, and had reigned thirty-five years. He was so ill, that in four days he could go no more than six miles; still, even at that pace, he went on and resolutely kept his face towards the Border. At length, he lay down at the village of Burgh-upon-Sands; and there, telling those around him to impress upon the Prince that he was to remember his father's vow, and was never to rest until he had thoroughly subdued Scotland, he yielded up his last breath.

CHAPTER XVII

ENGLAND UNDER EDWARD THE SECOND

KING Edward the Second, the first Prince of Wales, was twenty-three years old when his father died. There was a certain favourite of his, a young man from Gascony, named PIERS GAVESTON, of whom his father had so much disapproved that he had ordered him out of England, and had made his son swear by the side of his sick-bed, never to bring him back. But, the Prince no sooner found himself King, than he broke his oath, as so many other Princes and Kings did (they were far too ready to take oaths), and sent for his dear friend immediately.

Now, this same Gaveston was handsome enough, but was a reckless, insolent, audacious fellow. He was detested by the proud English Lords: not only because he had such power over the King, and made the Court such a dissipated place, but, also, because he could ride better than they at tournaments, and was used, in his impudence, to cut very bad jokes on them; calling one, the old hog; another, the stage-player; another, the Jew; another, the black dog of Ardenne. This was as poor wit as need be, but it made those Lords very wroth; and the surly Earl of Warwick, who was the black dog, swore that the time should come when Piers Gaveston should feel the black dog's teeth.

It was not come yet, however, nor did it seem to be coming. The King made him Earl of Cornwall, and gave him vast riches; and, when the King went over to France to marry the French Princess, ISABELLA, daughter of PHILIP LE BEL: who was said to be the most beautiful woman in the world: he made Gaveston, Regent of the Kingdom. His splendid marriage-ceremony in the Church of Our Lady at Boulogne, where there were four Kings and three Queens present (quite a pack of Court Cards, for I dare say the Knaves were not wanting), being over, he seemed to care little or nothing for his beautiful wife; but was wild with impatience to meet Gaveston again.

When he landed at home, he paid no attention to anybody else, but ran into the favourite's arms before a great concourse of people, and hugged him, and kissed him, and called him his brother. At the coronation which soon followed, Gaveston was the richest and brightest of all the glittering company there, and had the honour of carrying the crown. This made the proud Lords fiercer than ever; the people, too, despised the favourite, and would never call him Earl of Cornwall, however much he complained to the King and asked him to punish them for not doing so, but persisted in styling him plain Piers Gaveston.

The Barons were so unceremonious with the King in giving him to understand that they would not bear this favourite, that the King was obliged to send him out of the country. The favourite himself was made to take an oath (more oaths!) that he would never come back, and the Barons supposed him to be banished in disgrace, until they heard that he was appointed Governor of Ireland. Even this was not enough for the besotted King, who brought him home again in a year's time, and not only disgusted the Court and the people by his doting folly, but offended his beautiful wife too, who never liked him afterwards.

He had now the old Royal want—of money—and the Barons had the new power of positively refusing to let him raise any. He summoned a Parliament at York; the Barons refused to make one, while the favourite was near him. He summoned another Parliament at Westminster, and sent Gaveston away. Then, the Barons came, completely armed, and appointed a committee of themselves to correct abuses in the state and in the King's household. He got some money on these conditions, and directly set off with Gaveston to the Border-country, where they spent it in idling away the time, and feasting, while Bruce made ready to drive the English out of Scotland. For, though the old King had even made this poor weak son of his swear (as some say) that he would not bury his bones, but would have them boiled clean in a caldron, and carried before the English army until Scotland was entirely subdued, the second Edward was so unlike the first that Bruce gained strength and power every day.

The committee of Nobles, after some months of deliberation,

ordained that the King should henceforth call a Parliament together, once every year, and even twice if necessary, instead of summoning it only when he chose. Further, that Gaveston should once more be banished, and, this time, on pain of death if he ever came back. The King's tears were of no avail; he was obliged to send his favourite to Flanders. As soon as he had done so, however, he dissolved the Parliament, with the low cunning of a mere fool, and set off to the North of England, thinking to get an army about him to oppose the Nobles. And once again he brought Gaveston home, and heaped upon him all the riches and titles of which the Barons had deprived him.

The Lords saw, now, that there was nothing for it but to put the favourite to death. They could have done so, legally, according to the terms of his banishment; but they did so, I am sorry to say, in a shabby manner. Led by the Earl of Lancaster, the King's cousin, they first of all attacked the King and Gaveston at Newcastle. They had time to escape by sea, and the mean King, having his precious Gaveston with him, was quite content to leave his lovely wife behind. When they were comparatively safe, they separated; the King went to York to collect a force of soldiers; and the favourite shut himself up, in the meantime, in Scarborough Castle, overlooking the sea. This was what the Barons wanted. They knew that the Castle could not hold out; they attacked it, and made Gaveston surrender. He delivered himself up to the Earl of Pembroke—that Lord whom he had called the Jew—on the Earl's pledging his faith and knightly word, that no harm should happen to him and no violence be done him.

Now, it was agreed with Gaveston that he should be taken to the Castle of Wallingford, and there kept in honourable custody. They travelled as far as Dedington, near Banbury, where, in the Castle of that place, they stopped for a night to rest. Whether the Earl of Pembroke left his prisoner there, knowing what would happen, or really left him thinking no harm, and only going (as he pretended) to visit his wife, the Countess, who was in the neighbourhood, is no great matter now; in any case, he was bound as an honourable gentleman to protect his prisoner, and he did not do it. In the morning, while the favourite was yet in bed, he was required to dress himself and come down into the court-yard. He did so without any mistrust, but started and turned pale when he found it full of strange armed men. "I think you know me?" said their leader, also armed from head to foot. "I am the black dog of Ardenne!"

The time was come when Piers Gaveston was to feel the black dog's teeth indeed. They set him on a mule, and carried him, in mock state and with military music, to the black dog's kennel—Warwick Castle —where a hasty council, composed of some great noblemen, considered what should be done with him. Some were for sparing him, but one loud voice—it was the black dog's bark, I dare say—sounded through the Castle Hall, uttering these words: "You have the fox in your power. Let him go now, and you must hunt him again."

They sentenced him to death. He threw himself at the feet of the

Earl of Lancaster—the old hog—but the old hog was as savage as the dog. He was taken out upon the pleasant road, leading from Warwick to Coventry, where the beautiful river Avon, by which, long afterwards, WILLIAM SHAKESPEARE was born and now lies buried, sparkled in the bright landscape of the beautiful May-day; and there they struck off his wretched head, and stained the dust with his blood.

When the King heard of this black deed, in his grief and rage he denounced relentless war against his Barons, and both sides were in arms for half a year. But, it then became necessary for them to join their forces against Bruce, who had used the time well while they were divided, and had now a great power in Scotland.

Intelligence was brought that Bruce was then besieging Stirling Castle, and that the Governor had been obliged to pledge himself to surrender it, unless he should be relieved before a certain day. Hereupon the King ordered the nobles and their fighting-men to meet him at Berwick; but, the nobles cared so little for the King, and so neglected the summons, and lost time, that only on the day before that appointed for the surrender, did the King find himself at Stirling, and even then with a smaller force than he had expected. However, he had, altogether, a hundred thousand men, and Bruce had not more than forty thousand; but, Bruce's army was strongly posted in three square columns, on the ground lying between the Burn or Brook of Bannock and the walls of Stirling Castle.

On the very evening, when the King came up, Bruce did a brave act that encouraged his men. He was seen by a certain HENRY DE BOHUN, an English Knight, riding about before his army on a little horse, with a light battle-axe in his hand, and a crown of gold on his head. This English Knight, who was mounted on a strong war-horse, cased in steel, strongly armed, and able (as he thought) to overthrow Bruce by crushing him with his mere weight, set spurs to his great charger, rode on him, and made a thrust at him with his heavy spear. Bruce parried the thrust, and with one blow of his battle-axe split his skull.

The Scottish men did not forget this, next day when the battle raged. RANDOLPH, Bruce's valiant Nephew, rode, with the small body of men he commanded, into such a host of the English, all shining in polished armour in the sunlight, that they seemed to be swallowed up and lost, as if they had plunged into the sea. But, they fought so well, and did such dreadful execution, that the English staggered. Then came Bruce himself upon them, with all the rest of his army. While they were thus hard pressed and amazed, there appeared upon the hills what they supposed to be a new Scottish army, but what were really only the camp followers, in number fifteen thousand: whom Bruce had taught to show themselves at that place and time. The Earl of Gloucester, commanding the English horse, made a last rush to change the fortune of the day; but Bruce (like Jack the Giant-killer in the story) had had pits dug in the ground, and covered over with turfs and stakes. Into these, as they gave way beneath the weight of the horses, riders and horses rolled by hundreds. The English were completely routed; all their treasure, stores, and engines, were taken by the Scottish men; so many waggons and other wheeled vehicles were seized, that it is related that they would have reached, if they had been drawn out in a line, one hundred and eighty miles. The fortunes of Scotland were, for the time, completely changed; and never was a battle won, more famous upon Scottish ground, than this great battle of BANNOCKBURN.

Plague and famine succeeded in England; and still the powerless King and his disdainful Lords were always in contention. Some of the turbulent chiefs of Ireland made proposals to Bruce, to accept the rule of that country. He sent his brother Edward to them, who was crowned King of Ireland. He afterwards went himself to help his brother in his Irish wars, but his brother was defeated in the end and killed. Robert Bruce, returning to Scotland, still increased his strength there.

As the King's ruin had begun in a favourite, so it seemed likely to end in one. He was too poor a creature to rely at all upon himself; and his new favourite was one HUGH LE DESPENSER, the son of a gentleman of ancient family. Hugh was handsome and brave, but he was the favourite of a weak King, whom no man cared a rush for, and that was a dangerous place to hold. The Nobles leagued against him, because the King liked him; and they lay in wait, both for his ruin and his father's. Now, the King had married him to the daughter of the late Earl of Gloucester, and had given both him and his father great possessions in Wales. In their endeavours to extend these, they gave violent offence to an angry Welsh gentleman, named JOHN DE MOWBRAY, and to divers other angry Welsh gentlemen, who resorted to arms, took their castles, and seized their estates. The Earl of Lancaster had first placed the favourite (who was a poor relation of his own) at Court, and he considered his own dignity offended by the preference he received and the honours he acquired; so he, and the Barons who were his friends, joined the Welshmen, marched on London, and sent a message to the King demanding to have the favourite and his father banished. At first, the King unaccountably took it into his head to be spirited, and to send them a bold reply; but when they quartered themselves around Holborn and Clerkenwell, and went down, armed, to the Parliament at Westminster, he gave way, and complied with their demands.

His turn of triumph came sooner than he expected. It arose out of an accidental circumstance. The beautiful Queen, happening to be travelling, came one night to one of the royal castles, and demanded to be lodged and entertained there until morning. The governor of this castle, who was one of the enraged lords, was away, and in his absence, his wife refused admission to the Queen; a scuffle took place among the common men on either side, and some of the royal attendants were killed. The people, who cared nothing for the King, were very angry that their beautiful Queen should be thus rudely treated in her own dominions; and the King, taking advantage of this feeling, besieged the castle, took it, and then called the two Despensers home. Upon this, the confederate lords and the Welshmen went over to Bruce. The King encountered them at Boroughbridge, gained the victory, and took a number of distinguished prisoners; among them, the Earl of Lancaster, now an old man, upon whose destruction he was resolved. This Earl was taken to his own castle of Pontefract, and there tried and found guilty by an unfair court appointed for the purpose; he was not even allowed to speak in his own defence. He was insulted, pelted, mounted on a starved pony without saddle or bridle, carried out, and beheaded. Eight-and-twenty knights were hanged, drawn, and quartered. When the King had despatched this bloody work, and had made a fresh and a long truce with Bruce, he took the Despensers into greater favour than ever, and made the father Earl of Winchester.

One prisoner, and an important one, who was taken at Boroughbridge, made his escape, however, and turned the tide against the King. This was ROGER MORTIMER, always resolutely opposed to him, who was sentenced to death, and placed for safe custody in the Tower of London. He treated his guards to a quantity of wine into which he had put a sleeping potion; and, when they were insensible, broke out of his dungeon, got into a kitchen, climbed up the chimney, let himself down from the roof of the building with a rope-ladder, passed the sentries, got down to the river, and made away in a boat to where servants and horses were waiting for him. He finally escaped to France, where CHARLES LE BEL, the brother of the beautiful Queen, was King. Charles sought to quarrel with the King of England, on pretence of his not having come to do him homage at his coronation. It was proposed that the beautiful Queen should go over to arrange the dispute; she went, and wrote home to the King, that as he was sick and could not come to France himself, perhaps it would be better to send over the young Prince, their son, who was only twelve years old, who could do homage to her brother in his stead, and in whose company she would immediately return. The King sent him: but, both he and the Queen remained at the French Court, and Roger Mortimer became the Queen's lover.

When the King wrote, again and again, to the Queen to come home, she did not reply that she despised him too much to live with him any more (which was the truth), but said she was afraid of the two Despensers. In short, her design was to overthrow the favourites' power, and the King's power, such as it was, and invade England. Having obtained a French force of two thousand men, and being joined by all the English exiles then in France, she landed, within a year, at Orewell, in Suffolk, where she was immediately joined by the Earls of Kent and Norfolk, the King's two brothers; by other powerful noblemen; and lastly, by the first English general who was despatched to check her : who went over to her with all his men. The people of London, receiving these tidings, would do nothing for the King, but broke open the Tower, let out all his prisoners, and threw up their caps and hurrahed for the beautiful Queen.

The King, with his two favourites, fled to Bristol, where he left old Despenser in charge of the town and castle, while he went on with the son to Wales. The Bristol men being opposed to the King, and it being impossible to hold the town with enemies everywhere within the walls, Despenser yielded it up on the third day, and was instantly brought to trial for having traitorously influenced what was called "the King's mind"—though I doubt if the King ever had any. He was a venerable old man, upwards of ninety years of age, but his age gained no respect or mercy. He was hanged, torn open while he was yet alive, cut up into pieces, and thrown to the dogs. His son was soon taken, tried at Hereford before the same judge on a long series of foolish charges, found guilty, and hanged upon a gallows fifty feet high, with a chaplet of nettles round his head. His poor old father and he were innocent enough of any worse crimes than the crime of having been friends of a King, on whom, as a mere man, they would never have deigned to cast a favourable look. It is a bad crime, I know, and leads to worse; but, many lords and gentlemen—I even think some ladies, too, if I recollect right—have committed it in England, who have neither been given to the dogs, nor hanged up fifty feet high.

The wretched King was running here and there, all this time, and never getting anywhere in particular, until he gave himself up, and was taken off to Kenilworth Castle. When he was safely lodged there, the Queen went to London and met the Parliament. And the Bishop of Hereford, who was the most skilful of her friends, said, What was to be done now? Here was an imbecile, indolent, miserable King upon the throne; wouldn't it be better to take him off, and put his son there instead? I don't know whether the Queen really pitied him at this pass, but she began to cry; so, the Bishop said, Well, my Lords and Gentlemen, what do you think, upon the whole, of sending down to Kenilworth, and seeing if His Majesty (God bless him, and forbid we should depose him!) won't resign?

My Lords and Gentlemen thought it a good notion, so a deputation of them went down to Kenilworth; and there the King came into the great hall of the Castle, commonly dressed in a poor black gown; and when he saw a certain bishop among them, fell down, poor feeble-headed man, and made a wretched spectacle of himself. Somebody lifted him up, and then Sir William Trussel, the Speaker of the House of Commons, almost frightened him to death by making him a tremendous speech to the effect that he was no longer a King, and that everybody renounced allegiance to him. After which, Sir Thomas Blount, the Steward of the Household, nearly finished him, by coming forward and breaking his white wand—which was a ceremony only performed at a King's death. Being asked in this pressing manner what he thought of resigning, the King said he thought it was the best thing he could do. So, he did it, and they proclaimed his son next day.

I wish I could close his history by saying that he lived a harmless life in the Castle and the Castle gardens at Kenilworth, many years—-

that he had a favourite, and plenty to eat and drink—and, having that, wanted nothing. But he was shamefully humiliated. He was outraged, and slighted, and had dirty water from ditches given him to shave with, and wept and said he would have clean warm water, and was altogether very miserable. He was moved from this castle to that castle, and from that castle to the other castle, because this lord or that lord, or the other lord, was too kind to him: until at last he came to Berkeley Castle, near the River Severn, where (the Lord Berkeley being then ill and absent) he fell into the hands of two black ruffians, called THOMAS GOURNAY and WILLIAM OGLE.

One night—it was the night of September the twenty-first, one thousand three hundred and twenty-seven—dreadful screams were heard, by the startled people in the neighbouring town, ringing through the thick walls of the Castle, and the dark deep night; and they said, as they were thus horribly awakened from their sleep, "May Heaven be merciful to the King; for those cries forbode that no good is being done to him in his dismal prison!" Next morning he was dead—not bruised, or stabbed, or marked upon the body, but much distorted in the face; and it was whispered afterwards, that those two villains, Gournay and Ogle, had burnt up his inside with a red-hot iron.

If you ever come near Gloucester, and see the centre tower of its beautiful Cathedral, with its four rich pinnacles, rising lightly in the air; you may remember that the wretched Edward the Second was buried in the old abbey of that ancient city, at forty-three years old, after being for nineteen years and a half a perfectly incapable King.

CHAPTER XVIII

ENGLAND UNDER EDWARD THE THIRD

ROGER MORTIMER, the Queen's lover (who escaped to France in the last chapter), was far from profiting by the examples he had had of the fate of favourites. Having, through the Queen's influence, come into possession of the estates of the two Despensers, he became extremely proud and ambitious, and sought to be the real ruler of England. The young King, who was crowned at fourteen years of age with all the usual solemnities, resolved not to bear this, and soon pursued Mortimer to his ruin.

The people themselves were not fond of Mortimer—first, because he was a Royal favourite; secondly, because he was supposed to have helped to make a peace with Scotland which now took place, and in virtue of which the young King's sister, Joan, only seven years old, was promised in marriage to David, the son and heir of Robert Bruce, who was only five years old. The nobles hated Mortimer because of his pride, riches, and power. They went so far as to take up arms against him; but were obliged to submit. The Earl of Kent, one of those who did so, but who afterwards went over to Mortimer and the Queen, was made an example of in the following cruel manner:

He seems to have been anything but a wise old earl; and he was persuaded by the agents of the favourite and the Queen, that poor King Edward the Second was not really dead; and thus was betrayed into writing letters favouring his rightful claim to the throne. This was made out to be high treason, and he was tried, found guilty, and sentenced to be executed. They took the poor old lord outside the town of Winchester, and there kept him waiting some three or four hours until they could find somebody to cut off his head. At last, a convict said he would do it, if the government would pardon him in return; and they gave him the pardon; and at one blow he put the Earl of Kent out of his last suspense.

While the Queen was in France, she had found a lovely and good young lady, named Philippa, who she thought would make an excellent wife for her son. The young King married this lady, soon after he came to the throne; and her first child, Edward, Prince of Wales, afterwards became celebrated, as we shall presently see, under the famous title of EDWARD THE BLACK PRINCE.

The young King, thinking the time ripe for the downfall of Mortimer, took counsel with Lord Montacute how he should proceed A Parliament was going to be held at Nottingham, and that lord recommended that the favourite should be seized by night in Nottingham Castle, where he was sure to be. Now, this, like many other things, was more easily said than done; because, to guard against treachery, the great gates of the Castle were locked every night, and the great keys were carried up-stairs to the Queen, who laid them under her own pillow. But the Castle had a governor, and the governor being Lord Montacute's friend, confided to him how he knew of a secret passage underground, hidden from observation by the weeds and brambles with which it was overgrown; and how, through that passage, the conspirators might enter in the dead of night, and go straight to Mortimer's room. Accordingly, upon a certain dark night, at midnight, they made their way through this dismal place: startling the rats, and frightening the owls and bats: and came safely to the bottom of the main tower of the Castle, where the King met them, and took them up a profoundly-dark staircase in a deep silence. They soon heard the voice of Mortimer in council with some friends; and bursting into the room with a sudden noise, took him prisoner. The Queen cried out from her bed-chamber, "Oh, my sweet son, my dear son, spare my gentle Mortimer!" They carried him off, however; and, before the next Parliament, accused him of having made differences between the young King and his mother, and of having brought about the death of the Earl of Kent, and even of the late King; for, as you know by this time, when they wanted to get rid of a man in those old days, they were not very particular of what they accused him. Mortimer was found guilty of all this, and was sentenced to he hanged at Tyburn. The King shut his mother up in genteel confinement, where she passed the rest of her life; and now he became King in earnest.

The first effort he made was to conquer Scotland. The English lords who had lands in Scotland, finding that their rights were not respected under the late peace, made war on their own account: choosing for their general, Edward, the son of John Baliol, who made such a vigorous fight, that in less than two months he won the whole Scottish Kingdom. He was joined, when thus triumphant, by the King and Parliament; and he and the King in person besieged the Scottish forces in Berwick. The whole Scottish army coming to the assistance of their countrymen, such a furious battle ensued, that thirty thousand men are said to have been killed in it. Baliol was then crowned King of Scotland, doing homage to the King of England; but little came of his successes after all, for the Scottish men rose against him, within no very long time, and David Bruce came back within ten years and took his kingdom.

France was a far richer country than Scotland, and the King had a much greater mind to conquer it. So, he let Scotland alone, and pretended that he had a claim to the French throne in right of his mother. He had, in reality, no claim at all; but that mattered little in those times. He brought over to his cause many little princes and sovereigns, and even courted the alliance of the people of Flanders— a busy, working community, who had very small respect for kings, and whose head man was a brewer. With such forces as he raised by these means, Edward invaded France; but he did little by that except run into debt in carrying on the war to the extent of three hundred thousand pounds. The next year he did better; gaining a great sea-fight in the harbour of Sluys. This success, however, was very short-lived, for the Flemings took fright at the siege of Saint Omer and ran away, leaving their weapons and baggage behind them. Philip, the French King, coming up with his army, and Edward being very anxious to decide the war, proposed to settle the difference by single combat with him, or by a fight of one hundred knights on each side. The French King said, he thanked him; but being very well as he was, he would rather not. So, after some skirmishing and talking, a short peace was made.

It was soon broken by King Edward's favouring the cause of John, Earl of Montford; a French nobleman, who asserted a claim of his own against the French King, and offered to do homage to England for the Crown of France, if he could obtain it though England's help. This French lord, himself, was soon defeated by the French King's son, and shut up in a tower in Paris; but his wife, a courageous and beautiful woman, who is said to have had the courage of a man, and the heart of a lion, assembled the people of Brittany, where she then was; and, showing them her infant son, made many pathetic entreaties to them not to desert her and their young Lord. They took fire at this appeal, and rallied round her in the strong castle of Hennebon. Here she was not only besieged without by the French under Charles de Blois, but was endangered within by a dreary old bishop, who was always representing to the people what horrors they must undergo if they were faithful—first from famine, and afterwards from fire and sword. But this noble lady, whose heart never failed her, encouraged her soldiers by her own example; went from post to post like a great general; even mounted on horseback fully armed, and, issuing from the castle by a by-path, fell upon the French camp, set fire to the tents, and threw the whole force into disorder. This done, she got safely back to Hennebon again, and was received with loud shouts of joy by the defenders of the castle, who had given her up for lost. As they were now very short of provisions, however, and as they could not dine off enthusiasm, and as the old bishop was always saying, "I told you what it would come to!" they began to lose heart, and to talk of yielding the castle up. The brave Countess retiring to an upper room and looking with great grief out to sea, where she expected relief from England, saw, at this very time, the English ships in the distance, and was relieved and rescued! Sir Walter Manning, the English commander, so admired her courage, that, being come into the castle with the English knights, and having made a feast there, he assaulted the French by way of dessert, and beat them off triumphantly. Then he and the knights came back to the castle with great joy; and the Countess who had watched them from a high tower, thanked them with all her heart, and kissed them every one.

This noble lady distinguished herself afterwards in a sea-fight with the French off Guernsey, when she was on her way to England to ask for more troops. Her great spirit roused another lady, the wife of another French lord (whom the French King very barbarously murdered), to distinguish herself scarcely less. The time was fast coming, however, when Edward, Prince of Wales, was to be the great star of this French and English war.

It was in the month of July, in the year one thousand three hundred and forty-six, when the King embarked at Southampton for France, with an army of about thirty thousand men in all, attended by the Prince of Wales and by several of the chief nobles. He landed at La Hogue in Normandy; and, burning and destroying as he went, according to custom, advanced up the left bank of the River Seine, and fired the small towns even close to Paris ; but, being watched from the right bank of the river by the French King and all his army, it came to this at last, that Edward found himself, on Saturday the twenty-sixth of August, one thousand three hundred and forty-six, on a rising ground behind the little French village of Crecy, face to face with the French King's force. And, although the French King had an enormous army—in number more than eight times his—he there resolved to beat him or be beaten.

The young Prince, assisted by the Earl of Oxford and the Earl of Warwick, led the first division of the English army; two other great Earls led the second; and the King, the third. When the morning dawned, the King received the sacrament, and heard prayers, and then, mounted on horseback with a white wand in his hand, rode rom company to company, and rank to rank, cheering and encouraging both officers and men. Then the whole army breakfasted, each man sitting on the ground where he had stood; and then they remained quietly on the ground with their weapons ready.

Up came the French King with all his great force. It was dark and angry weather; there was an eclipse of the sun; there was a thunderstorm, accompanied with tremendous rain; the frightened birds flew screaming above the soldiers' heads. A certain captain in the French army advised the French King, who was by no means cheerful, not to begin the battle until the morrow. The King, taking this advice, gave the word to halt. But, those behind not understanding it, or desiring to be foremost with the rest, came pressing on. The roads for a great distance were covered with this immense army, and with the common people from the villages, who were flourishing their rude weapons, and making a great noise. Owing to these circumstances, the French army advanced in the greatest confusion; every French lord doing what he liked with his own men, and putting out the men of every other French lord.

Now, their King relied strongly upon a great body of cross-bowmen from Genoa; and these he ordered to the front to begin the battle, on finding that he could not stop it. They shouted once, they shouted twice, they shouted three times, to alarm the English archers; but, the English would have heard them shout three thousand times and would have never moved. At last the crossbowmen went forward a little, and began to discharge their bolts; upon which, the English let fly such a hail of arrows, that the Genoese speedily made off—for their cross-bows, besides being heavy to carry, required to be wound up with a handle, and consequently took time to re-load; the English, on the other hand, could discharge their arrows almost as fast as the arrows could fly.

When the French King saw the Genoese turning, he cried out to his men to kill those scoundrels, who were doing harm instead of service. This increased the confusion. Meanwhile the English archers, continuing to shoot as fast as ever, shot down great numbers of the French soldiers and knights; whom certain sly Cornish-men and Welsh-men, from the English army, creeping along the ground, despatched with great knives.

The Prince and his division were at this time so hard-pressed, that the Earl of Warwick sent a message to the King, who was overlooking the battle from a windmill, beseeching him to send more aid.

"Is my son killed?" said the King.

"No, sire, please God," returned the messenger.

"Is he wounded?" said the King.

"No, sire."

"Is he thrown to the ground?" said the King.

"No, sire, not so; but, he is very hard-pressed."

"Then," said the King, "go back to those who sent you, and tell them I shall send no aid; because I set my heart upon my son proving himself this day a brave knight, and because I am resolved, please

God, that the honour of a great victory shall be his!"

These bold words, being reported to the Prince and his division, so raised their spirits, that they fought better than ever. The King of France charged gallantly with his men many times; but it was of no use. Night closing in, his horse was killed under him by an English arrow, and the knights and nobles who had clustered thick about him early in the day, were now completely scattered. At last, some of his few remaining followers led him off the field by force, since he would not retire of himself, and they journeyed away to Amiens. The victorious English, lighting their watch-fires, made merry on the field, and the King, riding to meet his gallant son, took him in his arms, kissed him, and told him that he had acted nobly, and proved himself worthy of the day and of the crown. While it was yet night, King Edward was hardly aware of the great victory he had gained; but, next day, it was discovered that eleven princes, twelve hundred knights, and thirty thousand common men lay dead upon the French side. Among these was the King of Bohemia, an old blind man; who, having been told that his son was wounded in the battle, and that no force could stand against the Black Prince, called to him two knights, put himself on horseback between them, fastened the three bridles together, and dashed in among the English, where he was presently slain. He bore as his crest three white ostrich feathers, with the motto *Ich dien*, signifying in English "I serve." This crest and motto were taken by the Prince of Wales in remembrance of that famous day, and have been borne by the Prince of Wales ever since.

Five days after this great battle, the King laid siege to Calais. This siege—ever afterwards memorable—lasted nearly a year. In order to starve the inhabitants out, King Edward built so many wooden houses for the lodgings of his troops, that it is said their quarters looked like a second Calais suddenly sprung around the first. Early in the siege, the governor of the town drove out what he called the useless mouths, to the number of seventeen hundred persons, men and women, young and old. King Edward allowed them to pass through his lines, and even fed them, and dismissed them with money; but, later in the siege, he was not so merciful—five hundred more, who were afterwards driven out, dying of starvation and misery. The garrison were so hard-pressed at last, that they sent a letter to King Philip, telling him that they had eaten all the horses, all the dogs, and all the rats and mice that could be found in the place; and, that if he did not relieve them, they must either surrender to the English, or eat one another. Philip made one effort to give them relief; but they were so hemmed in by the English power, that he could not succeed, and was fain to leave the place. Upon this they hoisted the English flag, and surrendered to King Edward. "Tell your general," said he to the humble messengers who came out of the town, "that I require to have sent here, six of the most distinguished citizens, bare-legged, and in their shirts, with ropes about their necks; and let those six men bring with them the keys of the castle and the town."

When the Governor of Calais related this to the people in the Market-place, there was great weeping and distress; in the midst of which, one worthy citizen, named Eustace de Saint Pierre, rose up and said, that if the six men required were not sacrificed, the whole population would be; therefore, he offered himself as the first. Encouraged by this bright example, five other worthy citizens rose up one after another, and offered themselves to save the rest. The Governor, who was too badly wounded to be able to walk, mounted a poor old horse that had not been eaten, and conducted these good men to the gate, while all the people cried and mourned.

Edward received them wrathfully, and ordered the heads of the whole six to be struck off. However, the good Queen fell upon her knees, and besought the King to give them up to her. The King replied, "I wish you had been somewhere else; but I cannot refuse you." So she had them properly dressed, made a feast for them, and sent them back with a handsome present, to the great rejoicing of the whole camp. I hope the people of Calais loved the daughter to whom she gave birth soon afterwards, for her gentle mother's sake.

Now came that terrible disease, the Plague, into Europe, hurrying from the heart of China; and killed the wretched people—especially the poor—in such enormous numbers, that one-half of the inhabitants of England are related to have died of it. It killed the cattle, in great numbers, too; and so few working men remained alive, that there were not enough left to till the ground.

After eight years of differing and quarrelling, the Prince of Wales again invaded France with an army of sixty thousand men. He went through the south of the country, burning and plundering wheresoever he went; while his father, who had still the Scottish war upon his hands, did the like in Scotland, but was harassed and worried in his retreat from that country by the Scottish men, who repaid his cruelties with interest.

The French King, Philip, was now dead, and was succeeded by his son John. The Black Prince, called by that name from the colour of the armour he wore to set off his fair complexion, continuing to burn and destroy in France, roused John into determined opposition; and so cruel had the Black Prince been in his campaign, and so severely had the French peasants suffered, that he could not find one who, for love, or money, or the fear of death, would tell him what the French King was doing, or where he was. Thus it happened that he came upon the French King's forces, all of a sudden, near the town of Poitiers, and found that the whole neighbouring country was occupied by a vast French army. "God help us!" said the Black Prince, "we must make the best of it."

So, on a Sunday morning, the eighteenth of September, the Prince —whose army was now reduced to ten thousand men in all—prepared to give battle to the French King, who had sixty thousand horse alone. While he was so engaged, there came riding from the French camp, a Cardinal, who had persuaded John to let him offer terms, and try to save the shedding of Christian blood. "Save my honour," said the Prince to this good priest, "and save the honour of my army, and I will make any reasonable terms." He offered to give up all the towns, castles, and prisoners, he had taken, and to swear to make no war in France for seven years; but, as John would hear of nothing but his surrender, with a hundred of his chief knights, the treaty was broken off, and the Prince said quietly—"God defend the right; we shall fight to-morrow."

Therefore, on the Monday morning, at break of day, the two armies prepared for battle. The English were posted in a strong place, which could only be approached by one narrow lane, skirted by hedges on both sides. The French attacked them by this lane; but were so galled and slain by English arrows from behind the hedges, that they were forced to retreat. Then went six hundred English bowmen round about, and, coming upon the rear of the French army, rained arrows on them thick and fast. The French knights, thrown into confusion, quitted their banners and dispersed in all directions. Said Sir John Chandos to the Prince, "Ride forward, noble Prince, and the day is yours. The King of France is so valiant a gentleman, that I know he will never fly, and may be taken prisoner." Said the Prince to this, "Advance, English banners, in the name of God and St. George!" and on they pressed until they came up with the French King, fighting fiercely with his battle-axe, and, when all his nobles had forsaken him, attended faithfully to the last by his youngest son Philip, only sixteen years of age. Father and son fought well, and the King had already two wounds in his face, and had been beaten down, when he at last delivered himself to a banished French knight, and gave him his right-hand glove in token that he had done so.

The Black Prince was generous as well as brave, and he invited his royal prisoner to supper in his tent, and waited upon him at table, and, when they afterwards rode into London in a gorgeous procession, mounted the French King on a fine cream-coloured horse, and rode at his side on a little pony. This was all very kind, but I think it was, perhaps, a little theatrical too, and has been made more meritorious than it deserved to be; especially as I am inclined to think that the greatest kindness to the King of France would have been not to have shown him to the people at all. However, it must be said, for these acts of politeness, that in course of time, they did much to soften the horrors of war and the passions of conquerors. It was a long, long time before the common soldiers began to have the benefit of such courtly deeds; but they did at last; and thus it is possible that a poor soldier who asked for quarter at the battle of Waterloo, or any other such great fight, may have owed his life indirectly to Edward the Black Prince.

At this time there stood in the Strand, in London, a palace called the Savoy, which was given up to the captive King of France and his son for their residence. As the King of Scotland had now been King Edward's captive for eleven years too, his success was, at this time, tolerably complete. The Scottish business was settled by the prisoner being released under the title of Sir David, King of Scotland, and by his engaging to pay a large ransom. The state of France encouraged England to propose harder terms to that country, where the people rose against the unspeakable cruelty and barbarity of its nobles; where the nobles rose in turn against the people; where the most frightful outrages were committed on all sides; and where the insurrection of the peasants, called the insurrection of the Jacquerie, from Jacques, a common Christian name among the country people of France, awakened terrors and hatreds that have scarcely yet passed away. A treaty called the Great Peace, was at last signed, under which King Edward agreed to give up the greater part of his conquests, and King John to pay, within six years, a ransom of three million crowns of gold. He was so beset by his own nobles and courtiers for having yielded to these conditions—though they could help him to no better—that he came back of his own will to his old palace-prison of the Savoy, and there died.

There was a Sovereign of Castile at that time, called PEDRO THE CRUEL, who deserved the name remarkably well; having committed, among other cruelties, a variety of murders. This amiable monarch being driven from his throne for his crimes, went to the province of Bordeaux, where the Black Prince—now married to his cousin JOAN, a pretty widow—was residing, and besought his help. The Prince, who took to him much more kindly than a prince of such fame ought to have taken to such a ruffian, readily listened to his fair promises, and agreeing to help him, sent secret orders to some troublesome disbanded soldiers of his and his father's, who called themselves the Free Companions, and who had been a pest to the French people, for some time, to aid this Pedro. The Prince, himself, going into Spain, to head the army of relief, soon set Pedro on his throne again—where he no sooner found himself, than, of course, he behaved like the villain he was, broke his word without the least shame, and abandoned all the promises he had made to the Black Prince.

Now, it had cost the Prince a good deal of money to pay soldiers to support this murderous King; and finding himself, when he came back disgusted to Bordeaux, not only in bad health, but deeply in debt, he began to tax his French subjects to pay his creditors. They appealed to the French King, CHARLES; war again broke out; and the French town of Limoges, which the Prince had greatly benefited, went over to the French King. Upon this he ravaged the province of which it was the capital; burnt, and plundered, and killed in the old sickening way; and refused mercy to the prisoners, men, women, and children taken in the offending town, though he was so ill and so much in need of pity himself from Heaven, that he was carried in a litter. He lived to come home and make himself popular with the people and Parliament, and he died on Trinity Sunday, the eighth of June, one thousand three hundred and seventy-six, at forty-six years old.

The whole nation mourned for him as one of the most renowned and beloved princes it had ever had; and he was buried with great lamentations in Canterbury Cathedral. Near to the tomb of Edward the Confessor, his monument, with his figure, carved in stone, and represented in the old black armour, lying on its back, may be seen at this day, with an ancient coat of mail, a helmet, and a pair of gauntlets hanging from a beam above it, which most people like to believe were once worn by the Black Prince.

King Edward did not outlive his renowned son, long. He was old, and one Alice Perrers, a beautiful lady, had contrived to make him so fond of her in his old age, that he could refuse her nothing, and made himself ridiculous. She little deserved his love, or—what I dare say she valued a great deal more—the jewels of the late Queen, which he gave her among other rich presents. She took the very ring from his finger on the morning of the day when he died, and left him to be pillaged by his faithless servants. Only one good priest was true to him, and attended him to the last.

Besides being famous for the great victories I have related, the reign of King Edward the Third was rendered memorable in better ways, by the growth of architecture and the erection of Windsor Castle. In better ways still, by the rising up of WICKLIFFE, originally a poor parish priest: who devoted himself to exposing, with wonderful power and success, the ambition and corruption of the Pope, and of the whole church of which he was the head.

Some of those Flemings were induced to come to England in this reign too, and to settle in Norfolk, where they made better woollen cloths than the English had ever had before. The Order of the Garter (a very fine thing in its way, but hardly so important as good clothes for the nation) also dates from this period. The King is said to have picked up a lady's garter at a ball, and to have said, *Honi soit qui mal y pense*—in English, "Evil be to him who evil thinks of it." The courtiers were usually glad to imitate what the King said or did, and hence from a slight incident the Order of the Garter was instituted, and became a great dignity. So the story goes.

CHAPTER XIX

ENGLAND UNDER RICHARD THE SECOND

RICHARD, son of the Black Prince, a boy eleven years of age, succeeded to the Crown under the title of King Richard the Second. The whole English nation were ready to admire him for the sake of his brave father. As to the lords and ladies about the Court, they declared him to be the most beautiful, the wisest, and the best—even of princes—whom the lords and ladies about the Court, generally declare to be the most beautiful, the wisest, and the best of mankind. To flatter a poor boy in this base manner was not a very likely way to develop whatever good was in him; and it brought him to anything but a good or happy end.

The Duke of Lancaster, the young King's uncle—commonly called

John of Gaunt, from having been born at Ghent, which the common people so pronounced—was supposed to have some thoughts of the throne himself; but, as he was not popular, and the memory of the Black Prince was, he submitted to his nephew.

The war with France being still unsettled, the Government of England wanted money to provide for the expenses that might arise out of it; accordingly a certain tax, called the Poll-tax, which had originated in the last reign, was ordered to be levied on the people. This was a tax on every person in the kingdom, male and female, above the age of fourteen, of three groats (or three fourpenny pieces) a year; clergymen were charged more, and only beggars were exempt.

I have no need to repeat that the common people of England had long been suffering under great oppression. They were still the mere slaves of the lords of the land on which they lived, and were on most occasions harshly and unjustly treated. But, they had begun by this time to think very seriously of not bearing quite so much; and, probably, were emboldened by that French insurrection I mentioned in the last chapter.

The people of Essex rose against the Poll-tax, and being severely handled by the government officers, killed some of them. At this very time one of the tax-collectors, going his rounds from house to house, at Dartford in Kent came to the cottage of one WAT, a tiler by trade, and claimed the tax upon his daughter. Her mother, who was at home, declared that she was under the age of fourteen; upon that, the collector (as other collectors had already done in different parts of England) behaved in a savage way, and brutally insulted Wat Tyler's daughter. The daughter screamed, the mother screamed. Wat the Tiler, who was at work not far off, ran to the spot, and did what any honest father under such provocation might have done—struck the collector dead at a blow.

Instantly the people of that town uprose as one man. They made Wat Tyler their leader; they joined with the people of Essex, who were in arms under a priest called JACK STRAW; they took out of prison another priest named JOHN BALL; and gathering in numbers as they went along, advanced, in a great confused army of poor men, to Blackheath. It is said that they wanted to abolish all property, and to declare all men equal. I do not think this very likely; because they stopped the travellers on the roads and made them swear to be true to King Richard and the people. Nor were they at all disposed to injure those who had done them no harm, merely because they were of high station; for, the King's mother, who had to pass through their camp at Blackheath, on her way to her young son, lying for safety in the Tower of London, had merely to kiss a few dirty-faced rough-bearded men who were noisily fond of royalty, and so got away in perfect safety. Next day the whole mass marched on to London Bridge.

There was a drawbridge in the middle, which WILLIAM WALWORTH the Mayor caused to be raised to prevent their coming into the city; but they soon terrified the citizens into lowering it again, and spread themselves, with great uproar, over the streets. They broke open the prisons; they burned the papers in Lambeth Palace; they destroyed the DUKE OF LANCASTER'S Palace, the Savoy, in the Strand, said to be the most beautiful and splendid in England; they set fire to the books and documents in the Temple; and made a great riot. Many of these outrages were committed in drunkenness; since those citizens, who had well-filled cellars, were only too glad to throw them open to save the rest of their property; but even the drunken rioters were very careful to steal nothing. They were so angry with one man, who was seen to take a silver cup at the Savoy Palace, and put it in his breast, that they drowned him in the river, cup and all.

The young King had been taken out to treat with them before they committed these excesses; but, he and the people about him were so frightened by the riotous shouts, that they got back to the Tower in the best way they could. This made the insurgents bolder; so they went on rioting away, striking off the heads of those who did not, at a moment's notice, declare for King Richard and the people; and killing as many of the unpopular persons whom they supposed to be their enemies as they could by any means lay hold of. In this manner they passed one very violent day, and then proclamation was made that the King would meet them at Mile-end, and grant their requests.

The rioters went to Mile-end to the number of sixty thousand, and the King met them there, and to the King the rioters peaceably proposed four conditions. First, that neither they, nor their children, nor any coming after them, should be made slaves any more. Secondly, that the rent of land should be fixed at a certain price in money, instead of being paid in service. Thirdly, that they should have liberty to buy and sell in all markets and public places, like other free men. Fourthly, that they should be pardoned for past offences. Heaven knows, there was nothing very unreasonable in these proposals! The young King deceitfully pretended to think so, and kept thirty clerks up, all night, writing out a charter accordingly.

Now, Wat Tyler himself wanted more than this. He wanted the entire abolition of the forest laws. He was not at Mile-end with the rest, but, while that meeting was being held, broke into the Tower of London and slew the archbishop and the treasurer, for whose heads the people had cried out loudly the day before. He and his men even thrust their swords into the bed of the Princess of Wales while the Princess was in it, to make certain that none of their enemies were concealed there.

So, Wat and his men still continued armed, and rode about the city. Next morning, the King with a small train of some sixty gentlemen—among whom was WALWORTH the Mayor—rode into Smithfield, and saw Wat and his people at a little distance. Says Wat to his men, "There is the King. I will go speak with him, and tell him what we want."

Straightway Wat rode up to him, and began to talk. "King," says Wat, "dost thou see all my men there?"

"Ah," says the King. "Why?"

"Because," says Wat, "they are all at my command, and have sworn to do whatever I bid them."

Some declared afterwards that as Wat said this, he laid his hand on the King's bridle. Others declared that he was seen to play with his own dagger. I think, myself, that he just spoke to the King like a rough, angry man as he was, and did nothing more. At any rate he was expecting no attack, and preparing for no resistance, when Walworth the Mayor did the not very valiant deed of drawing a short sword and stabbing him in the throat. He dropped from his horse, and one of the King's people speedily finished him. So fell Wat Tyler. Fawners and flatterers made a mighty triumph of it, and set up a cry which will occasionally find an echo to this day. But Wat was a hard-working man, who had suffered much, and had been foully outraged; and it is probable that he was a man of a much higher nature and a much braver spirit than any of the parasites who exulted then, or have exulted since, over his defeat.

Seeing Wat down, his men immediately bent their bows to avenge his fall. If the young King had not had presence of mind at that dangerous moment, both he and the Mayor to boot, might have followed Tyler pretty fast. But the King riding up to the crowd, cried out that Tyler was a traitor, and that he would be their leader. They were so taken by surprise, that they set up a great shouting, and followed the boy until he was met at Islington by a large body of soldiers.

The end of this rising was the then usual end. As soon as the King found himself safe, he unsaid all he had said, and undid all he had done; some fifteen hundred of the rioters were tried (mostly in Essex) with great rigour, and executed with great cruelty. Many of them were hanged on gibbets, and left there as a terror to the country people; and, because their miserable friends took some of the bodies down to bury, the King ordered the rest to be chained up—which was the beginning of the barbarous custom of hanging in chains. The King's falsehood in this business makes such a pitiful figure, that I think Wat Tyler appears in history as beyond comparison the truer and more respectable man of the two.

Richard was now sixteen years of age, and married Anne of Bohemia, an excellent princess, who was called "the good Queen Anne." She deserved a better husband; for the King had been fawned and flattered into a treacherous, wasteful, dissolute, bad young man.

There were two Popes at this time (as if one were not enough!), and their quarrels involved Europe in a great deal of trouble. Scotland was still troublesome too; and at home there was much jealousy and distrust, and plotting and counter-plotting, because the King feared the ambition of his relations, and particularly of his uncle, the Duke of Lancaster, and the duke had his party against the King, and the King had his party against the duke. Nor were these home troubles lessened when the duke went to Castile to urge his claim to the crown of that kingdom; for then the Duke of Gloucester, another of Richard's uncles, opposed him, and influenced the Parliament to demand the dismissal of the King's favourite ministers. The King said in reply, that he would not for such men dismiss the meanest servant in his kitchen. But, it had begun to signify little what a King said when a Parliament was determined; so Richard was at last obliged to give way, and to agree to another Government of the kingdom, under a commission of fourteen nobles, for a year. His uncle of Gloucester was at the head of this commission, and, in fact, appointed everybody composing it.

Having done all this, the King declared as soon as he saw an opportunity that he had never meant to do it, and that it was all illegal; and he got the judges secretly to sign a declaration to that effect. The secret oozed out directly, and was carried to the Duke of Gloucester. The Duke of Gloucester, at the head of forty thousand men, met the King on his entering into London to enforce his authority; the King was helpless against him; his favourites and ministers were impeached and were mercilessly executed. Among them were two men whom the people regarded with very different feelings; one, Robert Tresilian, Chief Justice, who was hated for having made what was called "the bloody circuit" to try the rioters; the other, Sir Simon Burley, an honourable knight, who had been the dear friend of the Black Prince, and the governor and guardian of the King. For this gentleman's life the good Queen even begged of Gloucester on her knees; but Gloucester (with or without reason) feared and hated him, and replied, that if she valued her husband's crown, she had better beg no more. All this was done under what was called by some the wonderful—and by others, with better reason, the merciless—Parliament.

But Gloucester's power was not to last for ever. He held it for only a year longer; in which year the famous battle of Otterbourne, sung in the old ballad of Chevy Chase, was fought. When the year was out, the King, turning suddenly to Gloucester, in the midst of a great council said, "Uncle, how old am I?" "Your highness," returned the Duke, "is in your twenty-second year." "Am I so much?" said the King; "then I will manage my own affairs! I am much obliged to you, my good lords, for your past services, but I need them no more." He followed this up, by appointing a new Chancellor and a new Treasurer, and announced to the people that he had resumed the Government. He held it for eight years without opposition. Through all that time, he kept his determination to revenge himself some day upon his uncle Gloucester, in his own breast.

At last the good Queen died, and then the King, desiring to take a second wife, proposed to his council that he should marry Isabella, of France, the daughter of Charles the Sixth; who, the French courtiers said (as the English courtiers had said of Richard), was a marvel of beauty and wit, and quite a phenomenon—of seven years old. The council were divided about this marriage, but it took place. It secured peace between England and France for a quarter of a century; but it was strongly opposed to the prejudices of the English people. The Duke of Gloucester, who was anxious to take the occasion of making himself popular, declaimed against it loudly, and this at length decided the King to execute the vengeance he had been nursing so long.

He went with a gay company to the Duke of Gloucester's house, Pleshey Castle, in Essex, where the Duke, suspecting nothing, came out into the court-yard to receive his royal visitor. While the King conversed in a friendly manner with the Duchess, the Duke was quietly seized, hurried away, shipped for Calais, and lodged in the castle there. His friends, the Earls of Arundel and Warwick, were taken in the same treacherous manner, and confined to their castles. A few days after, at Nottingham, they were impeached of high treason. The Earl of Arundel was condemned and beheaded, and the Earl of Warwick was banished. Then, a writ was sent by a messenger to the Governor of Calais, requiring him to send the Duke of Gloucester over to be tried. In three days he returned an answer that he could not do that, because the Duke of Gloucester, had died in prison. The Duke was declared a traitor, his property was confiscated to the King, a real or pretended confession he had made in prison to one of the Justices of the Common Pleas was produced against him, and there was an end of the matter. How the unfortunate duke died, very few cared to know. Whether he really died naturally; whether he killed himself; whether, by the King's order, he was strangled, or smothered between two beds (as a serving-man of the Governor's named Hall, did afterwards declare), cannot be discovered. There is not much doubt that he was killed, somehow or other, by his nephew's orders. Among the most active nobles in these proceedings were the King's cousin, Henry Bolingbroke, whom the King had made Duke of Hereford, to smooth down the old family quarrels, and some others who had in the family-plotting times done just such acts themselves as they now condemned in the duke. They seem to have been a corrupt set of men; but such men were easily found about the court in such days.

The people murmured at all this, and were still very sore about the French marriage. The nobles saw how little the King cared for law, and how crafty he was, and began to be somewhat afraid for themselves. The King's life was a life of continued feasting and excess; his retinue, down to the meanest servants, were dressed in the most costly manner, and caroused at his tables, it is related, to the number of ten thousand persons every day. He himself, surrounded by a body of ten thousand archers, and enriched by a duty on wool which the Commons had granted him for life, saw no danger of ever being otherwise than powerful and absolute, and was as fierce and haughty as a King could be.

He had two of his old enemies left, in the persons of the Dukes of Hereford and Norfolk. Sparing these no more than the others, he tampered with the Duke of Hereford until he got him to declare before the Council that the Duke of Norfolk had lately held some treasonable talk with him, as he was riding near Brentford; and that he had told him, among other things, that he could not believe the King's oath—which nobody could, I should think. For this treachery he obtained a pardon, and the Duke of Norfolk was summoned to appear and defend himself. As he denied the charge and said his accuser was a liar and a traitor, both noblemen, according to the manner of those times, were held in custody, and the truth was ordered to be decided by wager of battle at Coventry. This wager of battle meant that whosoever won the combat was to be considered in the right; which nonsense meant in effect, that no strong man could ever be wrong. A great holiday was made; a great crowd assembled, with much parade and show; and the two combatants were about to rush at each other with their lances, when the King, sitting in a pavilion to see fair, threw down the truncheon he carried in his hand, and forbade the battle. The Duke of Hereford was to be banished for ten years, and the Duke of Norfolk was to be banished for life. So said the King. The Duke of Hereford went to France, and went no farther. The Duke of Norfolk made a pilgrimage to the Holy Land, and afterwards died at Venice of a broken heart.

Faster and fiercer, after this, the King went on in his career. The Duke of Lancaster, who was the father of the Duke of Hereford, died soon after the departure of his son; and, the King, although he had solemnly granted to that son leave to inherit his father's property, if it should come to him during his banishment, immediately seized it all, like a robber. The judges were so afraid of him, that they disgraced themselves by declaring this theft to be just and lawful. His avarice knew no bounds. He outlawed seventeen counties at once, on a frivolous pretence, merely to raise money by way of fines for misconduct. In short, he did as many dishonest things as he could; and cared so little for the discontent of his subjects—though even the spaniel favourites began to whisper to him that there was such a thing as discontent afloat—that he took that time, of all others, for leaving England and making an expedition against the Irish.

He was scarcely gone, leaving the DUKE OF YORK Regent in his absence, when his cousin, Henry of Hereford, came over from France to claim the rights of which he had been so monstrously deprived. He was immediately joined by the two great Earls of Northumberland and Westmoreland; and his uncle, the Regent, finding the King's cause unpopular, and the disinclination of the army to act against Henry, very strong, withdrew with the Royal forces towards Bristol. Henry, at the head of an army, came from Yorkshire (where he had landed) to London and followed him. They joined their forces—how they brought that about, is not distinctly understood—and proceeded to Bristol Castle, whither three noblemen had taken the young Queen. The castle surrendering, they presently put those three noblemen to death. The Regent then remained there, and Henry went on to Chester.

All this time, the boisterous weather had prevented the King from receiving intelligence of what had occurred. At length it was conveyed to him in Ireland, and he sent over the EARL OF SALISBURY, who, landing at Conway, rallied the Welshmen, and waited for the King a whole fortnight; at the end of that time the Welshmen, who were perhaps not very warm for him in the beginning, quite cooled down and went home. When the King did land on the coast at last, he came with a pretty good power, but his men cared nothing for him, and quickly deserted. Supposing the Welshmen to be still at Conway, he disguised himself as a priest, and made for that place in company with his two brothers and some few of their adherents. But, there were no Welshmen left—only Salisbury and a hundred soldiers. In this distress, the King's two brothers, Exeter and Surrey, offered to go to Henry to learn what his intentions were. Surrey, who was true to Richard, was put into prison. Exeter, who was false, took the royal badge, which was a hart, off his shield, and assumed the rose, the badge of Henry. After this, it was pretty plain to the King what Henry's intentions were, without sending any more messengers to ask.

The fallen King, thus deserted—hemmed in on all sides, and pressed with hunger—rode here and rode there, and went to this castle, and went to that castle, endeavouring to obtain some provisions, but could find none. He rode wretchedly back to Conway, and there surrendered himself to the Earl of Northumberland, who came from Henry, in reality to take him prisoner, but in appearance to offer terms; and whose men were hidden not far off. By this earl he was conducted to the castle of Flint, where his cousin Henry met him, and dropped on his knee as if he were still respectful to his sovereign.

"Fair cousin of Lancaster," said the King, "you are very welcome" (very welcome, no doubt; but he would have been more so, in chains or without a head).

"My lord," replied Henry, "I am come a little before my time; but, with your good pleasure, I will show you the reason. Your people complain with some bitterness, that you have ruled them rigorously for two-and-twenty years. Now, if it please God, I will help you to govern them better in future."

"Fair cousin," replied the abject King, "since it pleaseth you, it pleaseth me mightily."

After this, the trumpets sounded, and the King was stuck on a wretched horse, and carried prisoner to Chester, where he was made to issue a proclamation, calling a Parliament. From Chester he was taken on towards London. At Lichfield he tried to escape by getting out of a window and letting himself down into a garden; it was all in vain, however, and he was carried on and shut up in the Tower, where no one pitied him, and where the whole people, whose patience he had quite tired out, reproached him without mercy. Before he got there, it is related, that his very dog left him and departed from his side to lick the hand of Henry.

The day before the Parliament met, a deputation went to this wrecked King, and told him that he had promised the Earl of Northumberland at Conway Castle to resign the crown. He said he was quite ready to do it, and signed a paper in which he renounced his authority and absolved his people from their allegiance to him. He had so little spirit left that he gave his royal ring to his triumphant cousin Henry with his own hand, and said, that if he could have had leave to appoint a successor, that same Henry was the man of all others whom he would have named. Next day, the Parliament assembled in Westminster Hall, where Henry sat at the side of the throne, which was empty and covered with a cloth of gold. The paper just signed by the King was read to the multitude amid shouts of joy, which were echoed through all the streets; when some of the noise had died away, the King was formally deposed. Then Henry arose, and, making the sign of the cross on his forehead and breast, challenged the realm of England as his right; the archbishops of Canterbury and York seated him on the throne.

The multitude shouted again, and the shouts re-echoed throughout all the streets. No one remembered, now, that Richard the Second had ever been the most beautiful, the wisest, and the best of princes; and he now made living (to my thinking) a far more sorry spectacle in the Tower of London, than Wat Tyler had made, lying dead, among the hoofs of the royal horses in Smithfield.

The Poll-tax died with Wat. The Smiths to the King and Royal Family, could make no chains in which the King could hang the people's recollection of him; so the Poll-tax was never collected.

CHAPTER XX

ENGLAND UNDER HENRY THE FOURTH, CALLED BOLINGBROKE

During the last reign, the preaching of Wickliffe against the pride and cunning of the Pope and all his men, had made a great noise in England. Whether the new King wished to be in favour with the priests, or whether he hoped, by pretending to be very religious, to cheat Heaven itself into the belief that he was not a usurper, I don't know. Both suppositions are likely enough. It is certain that he began his reign by making a strong show against the followers of Wickliffe, who were called Lollards, or heretics—although his father, John of Gaunt, had been of that way of thinking, as he himself had been more than suspected of being. It is no less certain that he first established in England the detestable and atrocious custom, brought from abroad, of burning those people as a punishment for their opinions. It was the importation into England of one of the practices of what was called the Holy Inquisition: which was the most unholy and the most infamous tribunal that ever disgraced mankind, and made men more like demons than followers of Our Saviour.

No real right to the crown, as you know, was in this King. Edward Mortimer, the young Earl of March—who was only eight or nine years old, and who was descended from the Duke of Clarence, the elder brother of Henry's father—was, by succession, the real heir to the throne. However, the King got his son declared Prince of Wales; and, obtaining possession of the young Earl of March and his little brother, kept them in confinement (but not severely) in Windsor Castle. He then required the Parliament to decide what was to be done with the deposed King, who was quiet enough, and who only said that he hoped his cousin Henry would be "a good lord" to him. The Parliament replied that they would recommend his being kept in some secret place where the people could not resort, and where his friends could not be admitted to see him. Henry accordingly passed this sentence upon him, and it now began to be pretty clear to the nation that Richard the Second would not live very long.

It was a noisy Parliament, as it was an unprincipled one, and the Lords quarrelled so violently among themselves as to which of them had been loyal and which disloyal, and which consistent and which inconsistent, that forty gauntlets are said to have been thrown upon the floor at one time as challenges to as many battles: the truth being that they were all false and base together, and had been, at one time with the old King, and at another time with the new one, and seldom true for any length of time to any one. They soon began to plot again. A conspiracy was formed to invite the King to a tournament at Oxford, and then to take him by surprise and kill him. This murderous enterprise, which was agreed upon at secret meetings in the house of the Abbot of Westminster, was betrayed by the Earl of Rutland—one of the conspirators. The King, instead of going to the tournament or staying at Windsor (where the conspirators suddenly went, on finding themselves discovered, with the hope of seizing him), retired to London, proclaimed them all traitors, and advanced upon them with a great force. They retired into the west of England, proclaiming Richard King; but, the people rose against them, and they were all slain. Their treason hastened the death of the deposed monarch. Whether he was killed by hired assassins, or whether he was starved to death, or whether he refused food on hearing of his brothers being killed (who were in that plot), is very doubtful. He met his death somehow; and his body was publicly shown at St. Paul's Cathedral with only the lower part of the face uncovered. I can scarcely doubt that he was killed by the King's orders.

The French wife of the miserable Richard was now only ten years old; and, when her father, Charles of France, heard of her misfortunes and of her lonely condition in England, he went mad: as he had several times done before, during the last five or six years. The French Dukes of Burgundy and Bourbon took up the poor girl's cause, without caring much about it, but on the chance of getting something out of England. The people of Bordeaux, who had a sort of superstitious attachment to the memory of Richard, because he was born there, swore by the Lord that he had been the best man in all his kingdom—which was going rather far—and promised to do great things against the English. Nevertheless, when they came to consider that they, and the whole people of France were ruined by their own nobles, and that the English rule was much the better of the two, they cooled down again; and the two dukes, although they were very great men, could do nothing without them. Then, began negotiations between France and England for the sending home to Paris of the poor little Queen with all her jewels and her fortune of two hundred thousand francs in gold. The King was quite willing to restore the young lady, and even the jewels; but he said he really could not part with the money. So, at last she was safely deposited at Paris without her fortune, and then the Duke of Burgundy (who was cousin to the French King) began to quarrel with the Duke of Orleans (who was brother to the French King) about the whole matter; and those two dukes made France even more wretched than ever.

As the idea of conquering Scotland was still popular at home, the King marched to the river Tyne and demanded homage of the King of that country. This being refused, he advanced to Edinburgh, but did little there; for, his army being in want of provisions, and the Scotch being very careful to hold him in check without giving battle, he was obliged to retire. It is to his immortal honour that in this sally he burnt no villages and slaughtered no people, but was particularly careful that his army should be merciful and harmless. It was a great example in those ruthless times.

A war among the border people of England and Scotland went on for twelve months, and then the Earl of Northumberland, the noble-man who had helped Henry to the crown, began to rebel against him —probably because nothing that Henry could do for him would satisfy his extravagant expectations. There was a certain Welsh gentleman, named OWEN GLENDOWER, who had been a student in one of the Inns of Court, and had afterwards been in the service of the late King, whose Welsh property was taken from him by a power-ful lord related to the present King, who was his neighbour. Appeal-ing for redress, and getting none, he took up arms, was made an out-law, and declared himself sovereign of Wales. He pretended to be a magician; and not only were the Welsh people stupid enough to believe him, but, even Henry believed him too; for, making three expeditions into Wales, and being three times driven back by the wildness of the country, the bad weather, and the skill of Glendower, he thought he was defeated by the Welshman's magic arts. However, he took Lord Grey and Sir Edmund Mortimer, prisoners, and allowed the relatives of Lord Grey to ransom him, but would not extend such favour to Sir Edmund Mortimer. Now, Henry Percy, called HOTSPUR, son of the Earl of Northumberland, who was married to Mortimer's sister, is supposed to have taken offence at this; and, therefore, in conjunc-tion with his father and some others, to have joined Owen Glen-dower, and risen against Henry. It is by no means clear that this was the real cause of the conspiracy; but perhaps it was made the pretext. It was formed, and was very powerful; including SCROOP, Arch-bishop of York, and the EARL OF DOUGLAS, a powerful and brave Scottish nobleman. The King was prompt and active, and the two armies met at Shrewsbury.

There were about fourteen thousand men in each. The old Earl of Northumberland being sick, the rebel forces were led by his son. The King wore plain armour to deceive the enemy; and four noblemen, with the same object, wore the royal arms. The rebel charge was so furious, that every one of those gentlemen was killed, the royal standard was beaten down, and the young Prince of Wales was severely wounded in the face. But he was one of the bravest and best soldiers that ever lived, and he fought so well, and the King's troops were so encouraged by his bold example, that they rallied immediately, and cut the enemy's forces all to pieces. Hotspur was killed by an arrow in the brain, and the rout was so complete that the whole rebellion was struck down by this one blow. The Earl of Northumberland surrendered himself soon after hearing of the death of his son, and received a pardon for all his offences.

There were some lingerings of rebellion yet: Owen Glendower being retired to Wales, and a preposterous story being spread among the ignorant people that King Richard was still alive. How they could have believed such nonsense it is difficult to imagine; but they certainly did suppose that the Court fool of the late King, who was something like him, was he, himself; so that it seemed as if, after giving so much trouble to the country in his life, he was still to trouble it after his death. This was not the worst. The young Earl of March and his brother were stolen out of Windsor Castle. Being retaken, and being found to have been spirited away by one Lady Spencer, she accused her own brother, that Earl of Rutland who was in the former conspiracy and was now Duke of York, of being in the plot. For this he was ruined in fortune, though not put to death; and then another plot arose among the old Earl of Northumberland, some other lords, and that same Scroop, Archbishop of York, who was with the rebels before. These conspirators caused a writing to be posted on the church doors, accusing the King of a variety of crimes; but, the King being eager and vigilant to oppose them, they were all taken, and the Archbishop was executed. This was the first time that a great churchman had been slain by the law in England; but the King was resolved that it should be done, and done it was.

The next most remarkable event of this time was the seizure, by Henry, of the heir to the Scottish throne— James, a boy of nine years old. He had been put aboard-ship by his father, the Scottish King Robert, to save him from the designs of his uncle, when, on his way to France, he was accidentally taken by some English cruisers. He remained a prisoner in England for nineteen years, and became in his prison a student and a famous poet.

With the exception of occasional troubles with the Welsh and with the French, the rest of King Henry's reign was quiet enough. But, the King was far from happy, and probably was troubled in his conscience by knowing that he had usurped the crown, and had occasioned the death of his miserable cousin. The Prince of Wales, though brave and generous, is said to have been wild and dissipated, and even to have drawn his sword on GASCOIGNE, the Chief Justice of the King's Bench, because he was firm in dealing impartially with one of his dissolute companions. Upon this the Chief Justice is said to have ordered him immediately to prison; the Prince of Wales is said to have submitted with a good grace; and the King is said to have exclaimed, "Happy is the monarch who has so just a judge, and a son so willing to obey the laws." This is all very doubtful, and so is another story (of which Shakespeare has made beautiful use), that the Prince once took the crown out of his father's chamber as he was sleeping, and tried it on his own head.

The King's health sank more and more, and he became subject to violent eruptions on the face and to bad epileptic fits, and his spirits sank every day. At last, as he was praying before the shrine of St. Edward at Westminster Abbey, he was seized with a terrible fit, and was carried into the Abbot's chamber, where he presently died. It had been foretold that he would die at Jerusalem, which certainly is not, and never was, Westminster. But, as the Abbot's room had long been called the Jerusalem chamber, people said it was all the same thing, and were quite satisfied with the prediction.

The King died on the 20th of March, 1413, in the forty-seventh year of his age, and the fourteenth of his reign. He was buried in Canterbury Cathedral. He had been twice married, and had, by his first wife, a family of four sons and two daughters. Considering his duplicity before he came to the throne, his unjust seizure of it, and above all, his making that monstrous law for the burning of what the priests call heretics, he was a reasonably good king, as kings went.

CHAPTER XXI

ENGLAND UNDER HENRY THE FIFTH

First Part

THE Prince of Wales began his reign like a generous and honest man. He set the young Earl of March free; he restored their estates and their honours to the Percy family, who had lost them by their rebellion against his father; he ordered the imbecile and unfortunate Richard to be honourably buried among the Kings of England; and he dismissed all his wild companions, with assurances that they should not want, if they would resolve to be steady, faithful, and true.

It is much easier to burn men than to burn their opinions; and those of the Lollards were spreading every day. The Lollards were represented by the priests—probably falsely for the most part—to entertain treasonable designs against the new King; and Henry, suffering himself to be worked upon by these representations, sacrificed his friend Sir John Oldcastle, the Lord Cobham, to them, after trying in vain to convert him by arguments. He was declared guilty, as the head of the sect, and sentenced to the flames; but he escaped from the Tower before the day of execution (postponed for fifty days by the King himself), and summoned the Lollards to meet him near London on a certain day. So the priests told the King, at least. I doubt whether there was any conspiracy beyond such as was got up by their agents. On the day appointed, instead of five-and-twenty thousand men, under the command of Sir John Oldcastle, in the meadows of St. Giles, the King found only eighty men, and no Sir John at all. There was, in another place, an addle-headed brewer, who had gold trappings to his horses, and a pair of gilt spurs in his breast—expecting to be made a knight next day by Sir John, and so to gain the right to wear them—but there was no Sir John, nor did anybody give information respecting him, though the King offered great rewards for such intelligence. Thirty of these unfortunate Lollards were hanged and drawn immediately, and were then burnt, gallows and all; and the various prisons in and around London were crammed full of others. Some of these unfortunate men made various confessions of treasonable designs; but, such confessions were easily got, under torture and the fear of fire, and are very little to be trusted. To finish the sad story of Sir John Oldcastle at once, I may mention that he escaped into Wales, and remained there safely, for four years. When discovered by Lord Powis, it is very doubtful if he would have been taken alive—so great was the old soldier's bravery—if a miserable old woman had not come behind him and broken his legs with a stool. He was carried to London in a horse-litter, was fastened by an iron chain to a gibbet, and so roasted to death.

To make the state of France as plain as I can in a few words, I should tell you that the Duke of Orleans, and the Duke of Burgundy, commonly called "John without fear," had had a grand reconciliation of their quarrel in the last reign, and had appeared to be quite in a heavenly state of mind. Immediately after which, on a Sunday, in the public streets of Paris, the Duke of Orleans was murdered by a party of twenty men, set on by the Duke of Burgundy—according to his own deliberate confession. The widow of King Richard had been married in France to the eldest son of the Duke of Orleans. The poor mad King was quite powerless to help her, and the Duke of Burgundy became the real master of France. Isabella dying, her husband (Duke of Orleans since the death of his father) married the daughter of the Count of Armagnac, who, being a much abler man than his young son-in-law, headed his party; thence called after him Armagnacs. Thus, France was now in this terrible condition, that it had in it the party of the King's son, the Dauphin Louis; the party of the Duke of Burgundy, who was the father of the Dauphin's ill-used wife; and the party of the Armagnacs; all hating each other; all fighting together; all composed of the most depraved nobles that the earth has ever known; and all tearing unhappy France to pieces.

The late King had watched these dissensions from England, sensible (like the French people) that no enemy of France could injure her more than her own nobility. The present King now advanced a claim to the French throne. His demand being, of course, refused, he reduced his proposal to a certain large amount of French territory, and to demanding the French princess, Catherine, in marriage, with a fortune of two millions of golden crowns. He was offered less territory and fewer crowns, and no princess; but he called his ambassadors home and prepared for war. Then, he proposed to take the princess with one million of crowns. The French Court replied that he should have the princess with two hundred thousand crowns less; he said this would not do (he had never seen the princess in his life), and assembled his army at Southampton. There was a short plot at home just at that time, for deposing him, and making the Earl of March king; but the conspirators were all speedily condemned and executed, and the King embarked for France.

It is dreadful to observe how long a bad example will be followed; but, it is encouraging to know that a good example is never thrown away. The King's first act on disembarking at the mouth of the river Seine, three miles from Harfleur, was to imitate his father, and to proclaim his solemn orders that the lives and property of the peaceable inhabitants should be respected on pain of death. It is agreed by French writers, to his lasting renown, that even while his soldiers were suffering the greatest distress from want of food, these commands were rigidly obeyed.

With an army in all of thirty thousand men, he besieged the town of Harfleur both by sea and land for five weeks; at the end of which time the town surrendered, and the inhabitants were allowed to depart with only fivepence each, and a part of their clothes. All the rest of their possessions was divided amongst the English army. But, that army suffered so much, in spite of its successes, from disease and privation, that it was already reduced one half. Still, the King was determined not to retire until he had struck a greater blow. Therefore, against the advice of all his counsellors, he moved on with his little force towards Calais. When he came up to the river Somme he was unable to cross, in consequence of the fort being fortified; and, as the English moved up the left bank of the river looking for a crossing, the French, who had broken all the bridges, moved up the right bank, watching them, and waiting to attack them when they should try to pass it. At last the English found a crossing and got safely over. The French held a council of war at Rouen, resolved to give the English battle, and sent heralds to King Henry to know by which road he was going. "By the road that will take me straight to Calais!" said the King, and sent them away with a present of a hundred crowns.

The English moved on, until they beheld the French, and then the King gave orders to form in line of battle. The French not coming on, the army broke up after remaining in battle array till night, and got good rest and refreshment at a neighbouring village. The French were now all lying in another village, through which they knew the English must pass. They were resolved that the English should begin the battle. The English had no means of retreat, if their King had any such intention; and so the two armies passed the night, close together.

To understand these armies well, you must bear in mind that the immense French army had, among its notable persons, almost the whole of that wicked nobility, whose debauchery had made France a desert; and so besotted were they by pride, and by contempt for the common people, that they had scarcely any bowmen (if indeed they had any at all) in their whole enormous number: which, compared with the English army, was at least as six to one. For these proud fools had said that the bow was not a fit weapon for knightly hands, and that France must be defended by gentlemen only. We shall see, presently, what hand the gentlemen made of it.

Now, on the English side, among the little force, there was a good proportion of men who were not gentlemen by any means, but who were good stout archers for all that. Among them, in the morning—having slept little at night, while the French were carousing and making sure of victory—the King rode, on a grey horse; wearing on his head a helmet of shining steel, surmounted by a crown of gold, sparkling with precious stones; and bearing over his armour, embroidered together, the arms of England and the arms of France. The archers looked at the shining helmet and the crown of gold and the sparkling jewels, and admired them all; but, what they admired most was the King's cheerful face, and his bright blue eye, as he told them that, for himself, he had made up his mind to conquer there or to die there, and that England should never have a ransom to pay for *him*. There was one brave knight who chanced to say that he wished some of the many gallant gentlemen and good soldiers, who were then idle at home in England, were there to increase their numbers. But the King told him that, for his part, he did not wish for one more man. "The fewer we have," said he, "the greater will be the honour we shall win!" His men, being now all in good heart, were refreshed with bread and wine, and heard prayers, and waited quietly for the French. The King waited for the French, because they were drawn up thirty deep (the little English force was only three deep), on very difficult and heavy ground; and he knew that when they moved, there must be confusion among them.

As they did not move, he sent off two parties:—one to lie concealed in a wood on the left of the French: the other, to set fire to some houses behind the French after the battle should be begun. This was scarcely done, when three of the proud French gentlemen, who were to defend their country without any help from the base peasants, came riding out, calling upon the English to surrender. The King warned those gentlemen himself to retire with all speed if they cared for their lives, and ordered the English banners to advance. Upon that, Sir Thomas Erpingham, a great English general, who commanded the archers, threw his truncheon into the air, joyfully, and all the English men, kneeling down upon the ground and biting it as if they took possession of the country, rose up with a great shout and fell upon the French.

Every archer was furnished with a great stake tipped with iron; and his orders were, to thrust this stake into the ground, to discharge his arrow, and then to fall back, when the French horsemen came on. As the haughty French gentlemen, who were to break the English archers and utterly destroy them with their knightly lances, came riding up, they were received with such a blinding storm of arrows, that they broke and turned. Horses and men rolled over one another, and the confusion was terrific. Those who rallied and charged the archers got among the stakes on slippery and boggy ground, and were so bewildered that the English archers—who wore no armour, and even took off their leathern coats to be more active—cut them to pieces, root and branch. Only three French horsemen got within the stakes, and these were instantly despatched. All this time the dense French army, being in armour, were sinking knee-deep into the mire; while the light English archers, half-naked, were as fresh and active as if they were fighting on a marble floor.

But now, the second division of the French coming to the relief of the first, closed up in a firm mass; the English, headed by the King, attacked them; and the deadliest part of the battle began. The King's brother, the Duke of Clarence, was struck down, and numbers of the French surrounded him; but, King Henry, standing over the body, fought like a lion until they were beaten off.

Presently, came up a band of eighteen French knights, bearing the banner of a certain French lord, who had sworn to kill or take the English King. One of them struck him such a blow with a battle-axe that he reeled and fell upon his knees; but, his faithful men, immediately closing round him, killed every one of those eighteen knights, and so that French lord never kept his oath.

The French Duke of Alençon, seeing this, made a desperate charge, and cut his way close up to the Royal Standard of England. He beat down the Duke of York, who was standing near it; and, when the King came to his rescue, struck off a piece of the crown he wore. But, he never struck another blow in this world; for, even as he was in the act of saying who he was, and that he surrendered to the King; and even as the King stretched out his hand to give him a safe and honourable acceptance of the offer; he fell dead, pierced by innumerable wounds.

The death of this nobleman decided the battle. The third division of the French army, which had never struck a blow yet, and which was, in itself, more than double the whole English power, broke and fled. At this time of the fight, the English, who as yet had made no prisoners, began to take them in immense numbers, and were still occupied in doing so, or in killing those who would not surrender, when a great noise arose in the rear of the French—their flying banners were seen to stop—and King Henry, supposing a great reinforcement to have arrived, gave orders that all the prisoners should be put to death. As soon, however, as it was found that the noise was only occasioned by a body of plundering peasants, the terrible massacre was stopped.

Then King Henry called to him the French herald, and asked him to whom the victory belonged.

The herald replied, "To the King of England."

"*We* have not made this havoc and slaughter," said the King. "It is the wrath of Heaven on the sins of France. What is the name of that castle yonder?"

The herald answered him, "My lord, it is the castle of Azincourt."

Said the King, "From henceforth this battle shall be known to posterity, by the name of the battle of Azincourt."

Our English historians have made it Agincourt; but, under that name, it will ever be famous in English annals.

The loss upon the French side was enormous. Three Dukes were killed, two more were taken prisoners, seven Counts were killed, three more were taken prisoners, and ten thousand knights and gentlemen were slain upon the field. The English loss amounted to sixteen hundred men, among whom were the Duke of York and the Earl of Suffolk.

War is a dreadful thing; and it is appalling to know how the English were obliged, next morning, to kill those prisoners mortally wounded, who yet writhed in agony upon the ground; how the dead upon the French side were stripped by their own countrymen and countrywomen, and afterwards buried in great pits; how the dead upon the English side were piled up in a great barn, and how their bodies and the barn were all burned together. It is in such things, and in many more much too horrible to relate, that the real desolation and wickedness of war consist. Nothing can make war otherwise than horrible. But the dark side of it was little thought of and soon forgotten; and it cast no shade of trouble on the English people, except on those who had lost friends or relations in the fight. They welcomed their King home with shouts of rejoicing, and plunged into the water to bear him ashore on their shoulders, and flocked out in crowds to welcome him in every town through which he passed, and hung rich carpets and tapestries out of the windows, and strewed the streets with flowers, and made the fountains run with wine, as the great field of Agincourt had run with blood.

SECOND PART

THAT proud and wicked French nobility who dragged their country to destruction, and who were every day and every year regarded with deeper hatred and detestation in the hearts of the French people, learnt nothing, even from the defeat of Agincourt. So far from uniting against the common enemy, they became, among themselves, more violent, more bloody, and more false—if that were possible —than they had been before. The Count of Armagnac persuaded the French King to plunder of her treasures Queen Isabella of Bavaria, and to make her a prisoner. She, who had hitherto been the bitter enemy of the Duke of Burgundy, proposed to join him, in revenge. He carried her off to Troyes, where she proclaimed herself Regent of

France, and made him her lieutenant. The Armagnac party were at that time possessed of Paris; but, one of the gates of the city being secretly opened on a certain night to a party of the duke's men, they got into Paris, threw into the prisons all the Armagnacs upon whom they could lay their hands, and, a few nights afterwards, with the aid of a furious mob of sixty thousand people, broke the prisons open, and killed them all. The former Dauphin was now dead, and the King's third son bore the title. Him, in the height of this murderous scene, a French knight hurried out of bed, wrapped in a sheet, and bore away to Poitiers. So, when the revengeful Isabella and the Duke of Burgundy entered Paris in triumph after the slaughter of their enemies, the Dauphin was proclaimed at Poitiers as the real Regent.

King Henry had not been idle since his victory of Agincourt, but had repulsed a brave attempt of the French to recover Harfleur; had gradually conquered a great part of Normandy; and, at this crisis of affairs, took the important town of Rouen, after a siege of half a year. This great loss so alarmed the French, that the Duke of Burgundy proposed that a meeting to treat of peace should be held between the French and the English kings in a plain by the river Seine. On the appointed day King Henry appeared there, with his two brothers, Clarence and Gloucester, and a thousand men. The unfortunate French King, being more mad than usual that day, could not come; but the Queen came, and with her the Princess Catherine: who was a very lovely creature, and who made a real impression on King Henry, now that he saw her for the first time. This was the most important circumstance that arose out of the meeting.

As if it were impossible for a French nobleman of that time to be true to his word of honour in anything, Henry discovered that the Duke of Burgundy was, at that very moment, in secret treaty with the Dauphin; and he therefore abandoned the negotiation.

The Duke of Burgundy and the Dauphin, each of whom with the best reason distrusted the other as a noble ruffian surrounded by a party of noble ruffians, were rather at a loss how to proceed after this; but, at length they agreed to meet, on a bridge over the river Yonne, where it was arranged that there should be two strong gates put up, with an empty space between them; and that the Duke of Burgundy should come into that space by one gate, with ten men only; and that the Dauphin should come into that space by the other gate, also with ten men, and no more.

So far the Dauphin kept his word, but no farther. When the Duke of Burgundy was on his knee before him in the act of speaking, one of the Dauphin's noble ruffians cut the said duke down with a small axe, and others speedily finished him.

It was in vain for the Dauphin to pretend that this base murder was not done with his consent; it was too bad, even for France, and caused a general horror. The duke's heir hastened to make a treaty with King Henry, and the French Queen engaged that her husband should consent to it, whatever it was. Henry made peace, on condition of receiving the Princess Catherine in marriage, and being made Regent of France during the rest of the King's lifetime, and succeeding to the French crown at his death. He was soon married to the beautiful Princess, and took her proudly home to England, where she was crowned with great honour and glory.

This peace was called the Perpetual Peace; we shall soon see how long it lasted. It gave great satisfaction to the French people, although they were so poor and miserable, that, at the time of the celebration of the Royal marriage, numbers of them were dying with starvation, on the dunghills in the streets of Paris. There was some resistance on the part of the Dauphin in some few parts of France, but King Henry beat it all down.

And now, with his great possessions in France secured, and his beautiful wife to cheer him, and a son born to give him greater happiness, all appeared bright before him. But, in the fulness of his triumph and the height of his power, Death came upon him, and his day was done. When he fell ill at Vincennes, and found that he could not recover, he was very calm and quiet, and spoke serenely to those who wept around his bed. His wife and child, he said, he left to the loving care of his brother the Duke of Bedford, and his other faithful nobles. He gave them his advice that England should establish a friendship with the new Duke of Burgundy, and offer him the regency of France; that it should not set free the royal princes who had been taken at Agincourt; and that, whatever quarrel might arise with France, England should never make peace without holding Normandy. Then, he laid down his head, and asked the attendant priests to chant the penitential psalms. Amid which solemn sounds, on the thirty-first of August, one thousand four hundred and twenty-two, in only the thirty-fourth year of his age and the tenth of his reign, King Henry the Fifth passed away.

Slowly and mournfully they carried his embalmed body in a procession of great state to Paris, and thence to Rouen where his Queen was: from whom the sad intelligence of his death was concealed until he had been dead some days. Thence, lying on a bed of crimson and gold, with a golden crown upon the head, and a golden ball and sceptre lying in the nerveless hands, they carried it to Calais, with such a great retinue as seemed to dye the road black. The King of Scotland acted as chief mourner, all the Royal Household followed, the knights wore black armour and black plumes of feathers, crowds of men bore torches, making the night as light as day; and the widowed Princess followed last of all. At Calais there was a fleet of ships to bring the funeral host to Dover. And so, by way of London Bridge, where the service for the dead was chanted as it passed along, they brought the body to Westminster Abbey, and there buried it with great respect.

CHAPTER XXII

ENGLAND UNDER HENRY THE SIXTH

Part the First

It had been the wish of the late King, that while his infant son King Henry the Sixth, at this time only nine months old, was under age, the Duke of Gloucester should be appointed Regent. The English Parliament, however, preferred to appoint a Council of Regency, with the Duke of Bedford at its head: to be represented, in his absence only, by the Duke of Gloucester. The Parliament would seem to have been wise in this, for Gloucester soon showed himself to be ambitious and troublesome, and, in the gratification of his own personal schemes, gave dangerous offence to the Duke of Burgundy, which was with difficulty adjusted.

As that duke declined the Regency of France, it was bestowed by the poor French King upon the Duke of Bedford. But, the French King dying within two months, the Dauphin instantly asserted his claim to the French throne, and was actually crowned under the title of Charles the Seventh. The Duke of Bedford, to be a match for him, entered into a friendly league with the Dukes of Burgundy and Brittany, and gave them his two sisters in marriage. War with France was immediately renewed, and the Perpetual Peace came to an untimely end.

In the first campaign, the English, aided by this alliance, were speedily successful. As Scotland, however, had sent the French five thousand men, and might send more, or attack the North of England while England was busy with France, it was considered that it would be a good thing to offer the Scottish King, James, who had been so long imprisoned, his liberty, on his paying forty thousand pounds for his board and lodging during nineteen years, and engaging to forbid his subjects from serving under the flag of France. It is pleasant to know, not only that the amiable captive at last regained his freedom upon these terms, but, that he married a noble English lady, with whom he had been long in love, and became an excellent King. I am afraid we have met with some Kings in this history, and shall meet with some more, who would have been very much the better, and would have left the world much happier, if they had been imprisoned nineteen years too.

In the second campaign, the English gained a considerable victory at Verneuil, in a battle which was chiefly remarkable, otherwise, for their resorting to the odd expedient of tying their baggage-horses together by the heads and tails, and jumbling them up with the baggage, so as to convert them into a sort of live fortification—which was found useful to the troops, but which I should think was not agreeable to the horses. For three years afterwards very little was done, owing to both sides being too poor for war, which is a very expensive entertainment; but, a council was then held in Paris, in which it was decided to lay siege to the town of Orleans, which was a place of great importance to the Dauphin's cause. An English army of ten thousand men was despatched on this service, under the command of the Earl of Salisbury, a general of fame. He being unfortunately killed early in the siege, the Earl of Suffolk took his place; under whom (reinforced by SIR JOHN FALSTAFF, who brought up four hundred waggons laden with salt herrings and other provisions for the troops, and, beating off the French who tried to intercept him, came victorious out of a hot skirmish, which was afterwards called in jest the Battle of the Herrings) the town of Orleans was so completely hemmed in, that the besieged proposed to yield it up to their countryman the Duke of Burgundy. The English general, however, replied that his English men had won it, so far, by their blood and valour, and that his English men must have it. There seemed to be no hope for the town, or for the Dauphin, who was so dismayed that he even thought of flying to Scotland or to Spain—when a peasant girl rose up and changed the whole state of affairs.

The story of this peasant girl I have now to tell.

PART THE SECOND

THE STORY OF JOAN OF ARC

IN a remote village among some wild hills in the province of Lorraine, there lived a countryman whose name was JACQUES D'ARC. He had a daughter, JOAN OF ARC, who was at this time in her twentieth year. She had been a solitary girl from her childhood; she had often tended sheep and cattle for whole days where no human figure was seen or human voice heard; and she had often knelt, for hours together, in the gloomy, empty, little village chapel, looking up at the altar and at the dim lamp burning before it, until she fancied that she saw shadowy figures standing there, and even that she heard them speak to her. The people in that part of France were very ignorant and superstitious, and they had many ghostly tales to tell about what they had dreamed, and what they saw among the lonely hills when the clouds and the mists were resting on them. So, they easily believed that Joan saw strange sights, and they whispered among themselves that angels and spirits talked to her.

At last, Joan told her father that she had one day been surprised by a great unearthly light, and had afterwards heard a solemn voice, which said it was Saint Michael's voice, telling her that she was to go and help the Dauphin. Soon after this (she said), Saint Catherine and Saint Margaret had appeared to her with sparkling crowns upon their heads, and had encouraged her to be virtuous and resolute. These visions had returned sometimes; but the Voices very often; and the voices always said, "Joan, thou art appointed by Heaven to go and help the Dauphin!" She almost always heard them while the chapel bells were ringing.

There is no doubt, now, that Joan believed she saw and heard these things. It is very well known that such delusions are a disease which is not by any means uncommon. It is probable enough that there were figures of Saint Michael, and Saint Catherine, and Saint Margaret, in the little chapel (where they would be very likely to have shining crowns upon their heads), and that they first gave Joan the idea of those three personages. She had long been a moping, fanciful girl, and, though she was a very good girl, I dare say she was a little vain, and wishful for notoriety.

Her father, something wiser than his neighbours, said, "I tell thee, Joan, it is thy fancy. Thou hadst better have a kind husband to take care of thee, girl, and work to employ thy mind!" But Joan told him in reply, that she had taken a vow never to have a husband, and that she must go as Heaven directed her, to help the Dauphin.

It happened, unfortunately for her father's persuasions, and most unfortunately for the poor girl, too, that a party of the Dauphin's enemies found their way into the village while Joan's disorder was at this point, and burnt the chapel, and drove out the inhabitants. The cruelties she saw committed, touched Joan's heart and made her worse. She said that the voices and the figures were now continually with her; that they told her she was the girl who, according to an old prophecy, was to deliver France; and she must go and help the Dauphin, and must remain with him until he should be crowned at Rheims: and that she must travel a long way to a certain lord named BAUDRICOURT, who could and would, bring her into the Dauphin's presence.

As her father still said, "I tell thee, Joan, it is thy fancy," she set off to find out this lord, accompanied by an uncle, a poor village wheelwright and cart-maker, who believed in the reality of her visions. They travelled a long way and went on and on, over a rough country, full of the Duke of Burgundy's men, and of all kinds of robbers and marauders, until they came to where this lord was.

When his servants told him that there was a poor peasant girl named Joan of Arc, accompanied by nobody but an old village wheelwright and cart-maker, who wished to see him because she was commanded to help the Dauphin and save France, Baudricourt burst out a-laughing, and bade them send the girl away. But, he soon heard so much about her, lingering in the town, and praying in the churches, and seeing visions, and doing harm to no one, that he sent for her, and questioned her. As she said the same things after she had been well sprinkled with holy water as she had said before the sprinkling, Baudricourt began to think there might be something in it. At all events, he thought it worth while to send her on to the town of Chinon, where the Dauphin was. So, he bought her a horse, and a sword, and gave her two squires to conduct her. As the Voices had told Joan that she was to wear a man's dress, now, she put one on, and girded her sword to her side, and bound spurs to her heels, and mounted her horse and rode away with her two squires. As to her uncle the wheelwright, he stood staring at his niece in wonder until she was out of sight—as well he might—and then went home again. The best place, too.

Joan and her two squires rode on and on, until they came to Chinon, where she was, after some doubt, admitted into the Dauphin's presence. Picking him out immediately from all his court, she told him that she came commanded by Heaven to subdue his enemies and conduct him to his coronation at Rheims. She also told him (or he pretended so afterwards, to make the greater impression upon his soldiers) a number of his secrets known only to himself, and, furthermore, she said there was an old, old sword in the cathedral of Saint Catherine at Fierbois, marked with five old crosses on the blade, which Saint Catherine had ordered her to wear.

Now, nobody knew anything about this old, old sword, but when the cathedral came to be examined—which was immediately done—there, sure enough, the sword was found! The Dauphin then required a number of grave priests and bishops to give him their opinion whether the girl derived her power from good spirits or from evil spirits, which they held prodigiously long debates about, in the course of which several learned men fell fast asleep and snored loudly. At last, when one gruff old gentleman had said to Joan, "What language do your Voices speak?" and when Joan had replied to the gruff old gentleman, "A pleasanter language than yours," they agreed that it was all correct, and that Joan of Arc was inspired from Heaven. This wonderful circumstance put new heart into the Dauphin's soldiers when they heard of it, and dispirited the English army, who took Joan for a witch.

So Joan mounted horse again, and again rode on and on, until she came to Orleans. But she rode now, as never peasant girl had ridden yet. She rode upon a white war-horse, in a suit of glittering armour; with the old, old sword from the cathedral, newly burnished, in her belt; with a white flag carried before her, upon which were a picture of God, and the words JESUS MARIA. In this splendid state, at the head of a great body of troops escorting provisions of all kinds for the starving inhabitants of Orleans, she appeared before that beleaguered city.

When the people on the walls beheld her, they cried out "The Maid is come! The Maid of the Prophecy is come to deliver us!" And this, and the sight of the Maid fighting at the head of their men, made the French so bold, and made the English so fearful, that the English line of forts was soon broken, the troops and provisions were got into the town, and Orleans was saved.

Joan, henceforth called THE MAID OF ORLEANS, remained within the walls for a few days, and caused letters to be thrown over, ordering Lord Suffolk and his Englishmen to depart from before the town according to the will of Heaven. As the English general very positively declined to believe that Joan knew anything about the will of Heaven (which did not mend the matter with his soldiers, for they stupidly said if she were not inspired she was a witch, and it was of no use to fight against a witch), she mounted her white war-horse again, and ordered her white banner to advance.

The besiegers held the bridge, and some strong towers upon the bridge; and here the Maid of Orleans attacked them. The fight was fourteen hours long. She planted a scaling ladder with her own hands, and mounted a tower wall, but was struck by an English arrow in the neck, and fell into the trench. She was carried away and the arrow was taken out, during which operation she screamed and cried with the pain, as any other girl might have done; but presently she said that the Voices were speaking to her and soothing her to rest. After a while, she got up, and was again foremost in the fight. When the English who had seen her fall and supposed her dead, saw this, they were troubled with the strangest fears, and some of them cried out that they beheld Saint Michael on a white horse (probably Joan herself) fighting for the French. They lost the bridge, and lost the towers, and next day set their chain of forts on fire, and left the place.

But as Lord Suffolk himself retired no farther than the town of Jargeau, which was only a few miles off, the Maid of Orleans besieged him there, and he was taken prisoner. As the white banner scaled the walls, she was struck upon the head with a stone, and was again tumbled down into the ditch; but, she only cried all the more, as she lay there, "On, on, my countrymen! And fear nothing, for the Lord hath delivered them into our hands!" After this new success of the Maid's, several other fortresses and places which had previously held out against the Dauphin were delivered up without a battle; and at Patay she defeated the remainder of the English army, and set up her victorious white banner on a field where twelve hundred Englishmen lay dead.

She now urged the Dauphin (who always kept out of the way when there was any fighting) to proceed to Rheims, as the first part of her mission was accomplished; and to complete the whole by being crowned there. The Dauphin was in no particular hurry to do this, as Rheims was a long way off, and the English and the Duke of Burgundy were still strong in the country through which the road lay. However, they set forth, with ten thousand men, and again the Maid of Orleans rode on and on, upon her white war-horse, and in her shining armour. Whenever they came to a town which yielded readily, the soldiers believed in her; but, whenever they came to a town which gave them any trouble, they began to murmur that she was an impostor. The latter was particularly the case at Troyes, which finally yielded, however, through the persuasion of one Richard, a friar of the place. Friar Richard was in the old doubt about the Maid of Orleans, until he had sprinkled her well with holy water, and had also well sprinkled the threshold of the gate by which she came into the city. Finding that it made no change in her or the gate, he said, as the other grave old gentlemen had said, that it was all right, and became her great ally.

So, at last, by dint of riding on and on, the Maid of Orleans, and the Dauphin, and the ten thousand sometimes believing and sometimes unbelieving men, came to Rheims. And in the great cathedral of Rheims, the Dauphin actually was crowned Charles the Seventh in a great assembly of the people. Then, the Maid, who with her white banner stood beside the King in that hour of his triumph, kneeled down upon the pavement at his feet, and said, with tears, that what she had been inspired to do, was done, and that the only recompense she asked for, was, that she should now have leave to go back to her distant home, and her sturdily incredulous father, and her first simple escort the village wheelwright and cart-maker. But the King said "No!" and made her and her family as noble as a King could, and settled upon her the income of a Count.

Ah! happy had it been for the Maid of Orleans, if she had resumed her rustic dress that day, and had gone home to the little chapel and the wild hills, and had forgotten all these things, and had been a good man's wife, and had heard no stranger voices than the voices of little children!

It was not to be, and she continued helping the King (she did a world for him, in alliance with Friar Richard), and trying to improve the lives of the coarse soldiers, and leading a religious, an unselfish, and a modest life, herself, beyond any doubt. Still, many times she prayed the King to let her go home; and once she even took off her bright armour and hung it up in a church, meaning never to wear it more. But, the King always won her back again—while she was of any use to him—and so she went on and on and on, to her doom.

When the Duke of Bedford, who was a very able man, began to be active for England, and, by bringing the war back into France and by holding the Duke of Burgundy to his faith, to distress and disturb Charles very much, Charles sometimes asked the Maid of Orleans what the Voices said about it? But, the Voices had become (very like ordinary voices in perplexed times) contradictory and confused, so that now they said one thing, and now said another, and the Maid lost credit every day. Charles marched on Paris, which was opposed to him, and attacked the suburb of Saint Honoré. In this fight, being again struck down into the ditch, she was abandoned by the whole army. She lay unaided among a heap of dead, and crawled out how she could. Then, some of her believers went over to an opposition Maid, Catherine of La Rochelle, who said she was inspired to tell where there were treasures of buried money—though she never did—and then Joan accidentally broke the old, old sword, and others said that her power was broken with it. Finally, at the siege of Compiègne, held by the Duke of Burgundy, where she did valiant service, she was basely left alone in a retreat, though facing about and fighting to the last; and an archer pulled her off her horse.

O the uproar that was made, and the thanksgivings that were sung, about the capture of this one poor country-girl! O the way in which she was demanded to be tried for sorcery and heresy, and anything else you like, by the Inquisitor-General of France, and by this great man, and by that great man, until it is wearisome to think of! She was bought at last by the Bishop of Beauvais for ten thousand francs, and was shut up in her narrow prison: plain Joan of Arc again, and Maid of Orleans no more.

I should never have done if I were to tell you how they had Joan out to examine her, and cross-examine her, and re-examine her, and worry her into saying anything and everything; and how all sorts of scholars and doctors bestowed their utmost tediousness upon her. Sixteen times she was brought out and shut up again, and worried, and entrapped, and argued with, until she was heart-sick of the dreary business. On the last occasion of this kind she was brought into a burial-place at Rouen, dismally decorated with a scaffold, and a stake and faggots, and the executioner, and a pulpit with a friar therein, and an awful sermon ready. It is very affecting to know that even at that pass the poor girl honoured the mean vermin of a King, who had so used her for his purposes and so abandoned her; and, that while she had been regardless of reproaches heaped upon herself, she spoke out courageously for him.

It was natural in one so young to hold to life. To save her life, she signed a declaration prepared for her—signed it with a cross, for she couldn't write—that all her visions and Voices had come from the Devil. Upon her recanting the past, and protesting that she would never wear a man's dress in future, she was condemned to imprisonment for life, "on the bread of sorrow and the water of affliction."

But, on the bread of sorrow and the water of affliction, the visions and the Voices soon returned. It was quite natural that they should do so, for that kind of disease is much aggravated by fasting, loneliness, and anxiety of mind. It was not only got out of Joan that she considered herself inspired again, but, she was taken in a man's dress, which had been left—to entrap her—in her prison, and which she put on, in her solitude; perhaps, in remembrance of her past glories, perhaps, because the imaginary Voices told her. For this relapse into the sorcery and heresy and anything else you like, she was sentenced to be burnt to death. And, in the market-place of Rouen, in the hideous dress which the monks had invented for such spectacles; with priests and bishops sitting in a gallery looking on, though some had the Christian grace to go away, unable to endure the infamous scene; this shrieking girl—last seen amidst the smoke and fire, holding a crucifix between her hands; last heard, calling upon Christ—was burnt to ashes. They threw her ashes into the river Seine; but they will rise against her murderers on the last day.

From the moment of her capture, neither the French King nor one single man in all his court raised a finger to save her. It is no defence of them that they may have never really believed in her, or that they may have won her victories by their skill and bravery. The more they pretended to believe in her, the more they had caused her to believe in herself; and she had ever been true to them, ever brave, ever nobly devoted. But, it is no wonder, that they, who were in all things false to themselves, false to one another, false to their country, false to Heaven, false to Earth, should be monsters of ingratitude and treachery to a helpless peasant girl.

In the picturesque old town of Rouen, where weeds and grass grow high on the cathedral towers, and the venerable Norman streets are still warm in the blessed sunlight through the monkish fires that once gleamed horribly upon them have long grown cold, there is a statue of Joan of Arc, in the scene of her last agony, the square to which she has given its present name. I know some statues of modern times—even in the World's metropolis, I think—which commemorate less constancy, less earnestness, smaller claims upon the world's attention, and much greater impostors.

Part the Third

Bad deeds seldom prosper, happily for mankind; and the English cause gained no advantage from the cruel death of Joan of Arc. For a long time, the war went heavily on. The Duke of Bedford died; the alliance with the Duke of Burgundy was broken; and Lord Talbot became a great general on the English side in France. But, two of the consequences of wars are, Famine—because the people cannot peacefully cultivate the ground—and Pestilence, which comes of want, misery, and suffering. Both these horrors broke out in both countries, and lasted for two wretched years. Then, the war went on again, and came by slow degrees to be so badly conducted by the English government, that, within twenty years from the execution of the Maid of Orleans, of all the great French conquests, the town of Calais alone remained in English hands.

While these victories and defeats were taking place in the course of time, many strange things happened at home. The young King, as he grew up, proved to be very unlike his great father, and showed himself a miserable puny creature. There was no harm in him—he had a great aversion to shedding blood: which was something—but, he was a weak, silly, helpless young man, and a mere shuttlecock to the great lordly battledores about the Court.

Of these battledores, Cardinal Beaufort, a relation of the King, and the Duke of Gloucester, were at first the most powerful. The Duke of Gloucester had a wife, who was nonsensically accused of practising witchcraft to cause the King's death and lead to her husband's coming to the throne, he being the next heir. She was charged with having, by the help of a ridiculous old woman named Margery (who was called a witch), made a little waxen doll in the King's likeness, and put it before a slow fire that it might gradually melt away. It was supposed, in such cases, that the death of the person whom the doll was made to represent, was sure to happen. Whether the duchess was as ignorant as the rest of them, and really did make such a doll with such an intention, I don't know; but, you and I know very well that she might have made a thousand dolls, if she had been stupid enough, and might have melted them all, without hurting the King or anybody else. However, she was tried for it, and so was old Margery, and so was one of the duke's chaplains, who was charged with having assisted them. Both he and Margery were put to death, and the duchess, after being taken on foot and bearing a lighted candle, three times round the City, as a penance, was imprisoned for life. The duke, himself, took all this pretty quietly, and made as little stir about the matter as if he were rather glad to be rid of the duchess.

But, he was not destined to keep himself out of trouble long. The royal shuttlecock being three-and-twenty, the battledores were very anxious to get him married. The Duke of Gloucester wanted him to marry a daughter of the Count of Armagnac; but, the Cardinal and the Earl of Suffolk were all for MARGARET, the daughter of the King of Sicily, who they knew was a resolute, ambitious woman and would govern the King as she chose. To make friends with this lady, the Earl of Suffolk, who went over to arrange the match, consented to accept her for the King's wife without any fortune, and even to give up the two most valuable possessions England then had in France. So, the marriage was arranged, on terms very advantageous to the lady; and Lord Suffolk brought her to England, and she was married at Westminster. On what pretence this queen and her party charged the Duke of Gloucester with high treason within a couple of years, it is impossible to make out, the matter is so confused; but, they pretended that the King's life was in danger, and they took the duke prisoner. A fortnight afterwards, he was found dead in bed (they said), and his body was shown to the people, and Lord Suffolk came in for the best part of his estates. You know by this time how strangely liable state prisoners were to sudden death.

If Cardinal Beaufort had any hand in this matter, it did him no good, for he died within six weeks; thinking it very hard and curious —at eighty years old!—that he could not live to be Pope.

This was the time when England had completed her loss of all her great French conquests. The people charged the loss principally upon the Earl of Suffolk, now a duke, who had made those easy terms about the Royal Marriage, and who, they believed, had even been bought by France. So he was impeached as a traitor, on a great number of charges, but chiefly on accusations of having aided the French King, and of designing to make his own son King of England. The Commons and the people being violent against him, the King was made (by his friends) to interpose to save him, by banishing him for five years, and proroguing the Parliament. The duke had much ado to escape from a London mob, two thousand strong, who lay in wait for him in St. Giles's fields; but, he got down to his own estates in Suffolk, and sailed away from Ipswich. Sailing across the Channel, he sent into Calais to know if he might land there; but, they kept his boat and men in the harbour, until an English ship, carrying a hundred and fifty men and called the Nicholas of the Tower, came alongside his little vessel, and ordered him on board. "Welcome, traitor, as men say," was the captain's grim and not very respectful salutation. He was kept on board, a prisoner, for eight-and-forty hours, and then a small boat appeared rowing toward the ship. As this boat came nearer, it was seen to have in it a block, a rusty sword, and an executioner in a black mask. The duke was handed down into it, and there his head was cut off with six strokes of the rusty sword. Then, the little boat rowed away to Dover beach, where the body was cast out, and left until the duchess claimed it. By whom, high in authority, this murder was committed, has never appeared. No one was ever punished for it.

There now arose in Kent an Irishman, who gave himself the name of Mortimer, but whose real name was JACK CADE. Jack, in imitation of Wat Tyler, though he was a very different and inferior sort of man, addressed the Kentish men upon their wrongs, occasioned by the bad government of England, among so many battledores and such a poor shuttlecock; and the Kentish men rose up to the number of twenty thousand. Their place of assembly was Blackheath, where, headed by Jack, they put forth two papers, which they called "The Complaint of the Commons of Kent," and "The Requests of the Captain of the Great Assembly in Kent." They then retired to Sevenoaks. The royal army coming up with them here, they beat it and killed their general. Then, Jack dressed himself in the dead general's armour, and led his men to London.

Jack passed into the City from Southwark, over the bridge, and entered it in triumph, giving the strictest orders to his men not to plunder. Having made a show of his forces there, while the citizens looked on quietly, he went back into Southwark in good order, and passed the night. Next day, he came back again, having got hold in the meantime of Lord Say, an unpopular nobleman. Says Jack to the Lord Mayor and judges: "Will you be so good as to make a tribunal in Guildhall, and try me this nobleman?" The court being hastily made, he was found guilty, and Jack and his men cut his head off on Cornhill. They also cut off the head of his son-in-law, and then went back in good order to Southwark again.

But, although the citizens could bear the beheading of an unpopular lord, they could not bear to have their houses pillaged. And it did so happen that Jack, after dinner—perhaps he had drunk a little too much—began to plunder the house where he lodged; upon which, of course, his men began to imitate him. Wherefore, the Londoners took counsel with Lord Scales, who had a thousand soldiers in the Tower; and defended London Bridge, and kept Jack and his people out. This advantage gained, it was resolved by divers great men to divide Jack's army in the old way, by making a great many promises on behalf of the state, that were never intended to be performed. This *did* divide them; some of Jack's men saying that they ought to take the conditions which were offered, and others saying that they ought not, for they were only a snare; some going home at once; others staying where they were; and all doubting and quarrelling among themselves.

Jack, who was in two minds about fighting or accepting a pardon, and who indeed did both, saw at last that there was nothing to expect from his men, and that it was very likely some of them would deliver him up and get a reward of a thousand marks, which was offered for his apprehension. So, after they had travelled and quarrelled all the way from Southwark to Blackheath, and from Blackheath to Rochester, he mounted a good horse and galloped away into Sussex. But, there galloped after him, on a better horse, one Alexander Iden, who came up with him, had a hard fight with him, and killed him. Jack's head was set aloft on London Bridge, with the face looking towards Blackheath, where he had raised his flag; and Alexander Iden got the thousand marks.

It is supposed by some, that the Duke of York, who had been removed from a high post abroad through the Queen's influence, and sent out of the way, to govern Ireland, was at the bottom of this rising of Jack and his men, because he wanted to trouble the government. He claimed (though not yet publicly) to have a better right to the throne than Henry of Lancaster, as one of the family of the Earl of March, whom Henry the Fourth had set aside. Touching this claim, which, being through female relationship, was not according to the usual descent, it is enough to say that Henry the Fourth was the free choice of the people and the Parliament, and that his family had now reigned undisputed for sixty years. The memory of Henry the Fifth was so famous, and the English people loved it so much, that the Duke of York's claim would, perhaps, never have been thought of (it would have been so hopeless) but for the unfortunate circumstance of the present King's being by this time quite an idiot, and the country very ill governed. These two circumstances gave the Duke of York a power he could not otherwise have had.

Whether the Duke knew anything of Jack Cade, or not, he came over from Ireland while Jack's head was on London Bridge; being secretly advised that the Queen was setting up his enemy, the Duke of Somerset, against him. He went to Westminster, at the head of four thousand men, and on his knees before the King, represented to him the bad state of the country, and petitioned him to summon a Parliament to consider it. This the King promised. When the Parliament was summoned, the Duke of York accused the Duke of Somerset, and the Duke of Somerset accused the Duke of York; and, both in and out of Parliament, the followers of each party were full of violence and hatred towards the other. At length the Duke of York put himself at the head of a large force of his tenants, and, in arms, demanded the reformation of the Government. Being shut out of London, he encamped at Dartford, and the royal army encamped at Blackheath. According as either side triumphed, the Duke of York was arrested, or the Duke of Somerset was arrested. The trouble ended, for the moment, in the Duke of York renewing his oath of allegiance, and going in peace to one of his own castles.

Half a year afterwards the Queen gave birth to a son, who was very ill received by the people, and not believed to be the son of the King. It shows the Duke of York to have been a moderate man, unwilling to involve England in new troubles, that he did not take advantage of the general discontent at this time, but really acted for the public good. He was made a member of the cabinet, and the King being now so much worse that he could not be carried about and shown to the people with any decency, the duke was made Lord Protector of the kingdom, until the King should recover, or the Prince should come of age. At the same time the Duke of Somerset was committed to the Tower. So, now the Duke of Somerset was down, and the Duke of York was up. By the end of the year, however, the King recovered his memory and some spark of sense; upon which the Queen used her power—which recovered with him—to get the Protector disgraced, and her favourite released. So now the Duke of York was down, and the Duke of Somerset was up.

These ducal ups and downs gradually separated the whole nation into the two parties of York and Lancaster, and led to those terrible civil wars long known as the Wars of the Red and White Roses, because the red rose was the badge of the House of Lancaster, and the white rose was the badge of the House of York.

The Duke of York, joined by some other powerful noblemen of the White Rose party, and leading a small army, met the King with another small army at St. Alban's, and demanded that the Duke of Somerset should be given up. The poor King, being made to say in answer that he would sooner die, was instantly attacked. The Duke of Somerset was killed, and the King himself was wounded in the neck, and took refuge in the house of a poor tanner. Whereupon, the Duke of York went to him, led him with great submission to the Abbey, and said he was very sorry for what had happened. Having now the King in his possession, he got a Parliament summoned and himself once more made Protector, but, only for a few months; for, on the King getting a little better again, the Queen and her party got him into their possession, and disgraced the Duke once more. So, now the Duke of York was down again.

Some of the best men in power, seeing the danger of these constant changes, tried even then to prevent the Red and the White Rose Wars. They brought about a great council in London between the two parties. The White Roses assembled in Blackfriars, the Red Roses in Whitefriars; and some good priests communicated between them, and made the proceedings known at evening to the King and the judges. They ended in a peaceful agreement that there should be no more quarrelling; and there was a great royal procession to St. Paul's, in which the Queen walked arm-in-arm with her old enemy, the Duke of York, to show the people how comfortable they all were. This state of peace lasted half a year, when a dispute between the Earl of Warwick (one of the Duke's powerful friends) and some of the King's servants at Court, led to an attack upon that Earl—who was a White Rose—and to a sudden breaking out of all old animosities. So, here were greater ups and downs than ever.

There were even greater ups and downs than these, soon after. After various battles, the Duke of York fled to Ireland, and his son the Earl of March to Calais, with their friends the Earls of Salisbury and Warwick; and a Parliament was held declaring them all traitors. Little the worse for this, the Earl of Warwick presently came back, landed in Kent, was joined by the Archbishop of Canterbury and other powerful noblemen and gentlemen, engaged the King's forces at Northampton, signally defeated them, and took the King himself prisoner, who was found in his tent. Warwick would have been glad, I dare say, to have taken the Queen and Prince too, but they escaped into Wales and thence into Scotland.

The King was carried by the victorious force straight to London, and made to call a new Parliament, which immediately declared that the Duke of York and those other noblemen were not traitors, but excellent subjects. Then, back comes the Duke from Ireland at the head of five hundred horsemen, rides from London to Westminster, and enters the House of Lords. There, he laid his hand upon the cloth of gold which covered the empty throne, as if he had half a mind to sit down in it—but he did not. On the Archbishop of Canterbury asking him if he would visit the King, who was in his palace close by, he replied, "I know no one in this country, my lord, who ought not to visit *me*." None of the lords present spoke a single word; so, the duke went out as he had come in, established himself royally in the King's palace, and, six days afterwards, sent in to the Lords a formal statement of his claim to the throne. The lords went to the King on this momentous subject, and after a great deal of discussion, in which the judges and the other law officers were afraid to give an opinion on either side, the question was compromised. It was agreed that the present King should retain the crown for his life, and that it should then pass to the Duke of York and his heirs.

But, the resolute Queen, determined on asserting her son's right, would hear of no such thing. She came from Scotland to the north of England, where several powerful lords armed in her cause. The Duke of York, for his part, set off with some five thousand men, a little time before Christmas Day, one thousand four hundred and sixty, to give her battle. He lodged at Sandal Castle, near Wakefield, and the Red Roses defied him to come out on Wakefield Green, and fight them then and there. His generals said, he had best wait until his gallant son, the Earl of March, came up with his power; but, he was determined to accept the challenge. He did so, in an evil hour. He was hotly pressed on all sides, two thousand of his men lay dead on Wakefield Green, and he himself was taken prisoner. They set him down in mock state on an ant-hill, and twisted grass about his head, and pretended to pay court to him on their knees, saying, "O King, without a kingdom, and Prince without a people, we hope your gracious Majesty is very well and happy!" They did worse than this; they cut his head off, and handed it on a pole to the Queen, who laughed with delight when she saw it (you recollect their walking so religiously and comfortably to St. Paul's!), and had it fixed, with a paper crown upon its head, on the walls of York. The Earl of Salisbury lost his head, too; and the Duke of York's second son, a handsome boy who was flying with his tutor over Wakefield Bridge, was stabbed in the heart by a murderous lord—Lord Clifford by name—whose father had been killed by the White Roses in the fight at St. Alban's.

There was awful sacrifice of life in this battle, for no quarter was given, and the Queen was wild for revenge. When men unnaturally fight against their own countrymen, they are always observed to be more unnaturally cruel and filled with rage than they are against any other enemy.

But, Lord Clifford had stabbed the second son of the Duke of York—not the first. The eldest son, Edward Earl of March, was at Gloucester; and, vowing vengeance for the death of his father, his brother, and their faithful friends, he began to march against the Queen. He had to turn and fight a great body of Welsh and Irish first, who worried his advance. These he defeated in a great fight at Mortimer's Cross, near Hereford, where he beheaded a number of the Red Roses taken in battle, in retaliation for the beheading of the White Roses at Wakefield. The Queen had the next turn of beheading. Having moved towards London, and falling in, between St. Alban's and Barnet, with the Earl of Warwick and the Duke of Norfolk, White Roses both, who were there with an army to oppose her, and had got the King with them; she defeated them with great loss, and struck off the heads of two prisoners of note, who were in the King's tent with him, and to whom the King had promised his protection. Her triumph, however, was very short. She had no treasure, and her army subsisted by plunder. This caused them to be hated and dreaded by the people, and particularly by the London people, who were wealthy. As soon as the Londoners heard that Edward, Earl of March, united with the Earl of Warwick, was advancing towards the city, they refused to send the Queen supplies, and made a great rejoicing.

The Queen and her men retreated with all speed, and Edward and Warwick came on, greeted with loud acclamations on every side. The courage, beauty, and virtues of young Edward could not be sufficiently praised by the whole people. He rode into London like a conqueror, and met with an enthusiastic welcome. A few days afterwards, Lord Falconbridge and the Bishop of Exeter assembled the citizens in St. John's Field, Clerkenwell, and asked them if they would have Henry of Lancaster for their King? To this they all roared, "No, no, no!" and "King Edward! King Edward!" Then, said those noblemen, would they love and serve young Edward? To this they all cried, "Yes, yes!" and threw up their caps and clapped their hands, and cheered tremendously.

Therefore, it was declared that by joining the Queen and not protecting those two prisoners of note, Henry of Lancaster had forfeited the crown; and Edward of York was proclaimed King. He made a great speech to the applauding people at Westminster, and sat down as sovereign of England on that throne, on the golden covering of which his father—worthy of a better fate than the bloody axe which cut the thread of so many lives in England, through so many years—had laid his hand.

CHAPTER XXIII

ENGLAND UNDER EDWARD THE FOURTH

KING EDWARD THE FOURTH was not quite twenty-one years of age when he took that unquiet seat upon the throne of England. The Lancaster party, the Red Roses, were then assembling in great numbers near York, and it was necessary to give them battle instantly. But, the stout Earl of Warwick leading for the young King, and the young King himself closely following him, and the English people crowding round the Royal standard, the White and the Red Roses met, on a wild March day when the snow was falling heavily, at Towton; and there such a furious battle raged between them, that the total loss amounted to forty thousand men—all Englishmen, fighting upon English ground, against one another. The young King gained the day, took down the heads of his father and brother from the walls of York, and put up the heads of some of the most famous noblemen engaged in the battle on the other side. Then, he went to London and was crowned with great splendour.

A new Parliament met. No fewer than one hundred and fifty of the principal noblemen and gentlemen on the Lancaster side were declared traitors, and the King—who had very little humanity, though he was handsome in person and agreeable in manners—resolved to do all he could, to pluck up the Red Rose root and branch.

Queen Margaret, however, was still active for her young son. She obtained help from Scotland and from Normandy, and took several important English castles. But, Warwick soon retook them; the Queen lost all her treasure on board ship in a great storm; and both she and her son suffered great misfortunes. Once, in the winter weather, as they were riding through a forest, they were attacked and plundered by a party of robbers; and, when they had escaped from these men and were passing alone and on foot through a thick dark part of the wood, they came, all at once, upon another robber. So the Queen, with a stout heart, took the little Prince by the hand, and going straight up to that robber, said to him, "My friend, this is the young son of your lawful King! I confide him to your care." The robber was surprised, but took the boy in his arms, and faithfully restored him and his mother to their friends. In the end, the Queen's soldiers being beaten and dispersed, she went abroad again, and kept quiet for the present.

Now, all this time, the deposed King Henry was concealed by a Welsh knight, who kept him close in his castle. But, next year, the Lancaster party recovering their spirits, raised a large body of men, and called him out of his retirement, to put him at their head. They were joined by some powerful noblemen who had sworn fidelity to the new King, but who were ready, as usual, to break their oaths, whenever they thought there was anything to be got by it. One of the worst things in the history of the war of the Red and White Roses, is the ease with which these noblemen, who should have set an example of honour to the people, left either side as they took slight offence, or were disappointed in their greedy expectations, and joined the other. Well! Warwick's brother soon beat the Lancastrians, and the false noblemen, being taken, were beheaded without a moment's loss of time. The deposed King had a narrow escape; three of his servants were taken, and one of them bore his cap of estate, which was set with pearls and embroidered with two golden crowns. However, the head to which the cap belonged, got safely into Lancashire, and lay pretty quietly there (the people in the secret being very true) for more than a year. At length, an old monk gave such intelligence as led to Henry's being taken while he was sitting at dinner in a place called Waddington Hall. He was immediately sent to London, and met at Islington by the Earl of Warwick, by whose directions he was put upon a horse, with his legs tied under it, and paraded three times round the pillory. Then, he was carried off to the Tower, where they treated him well enough.

The White Rose being so triumphant, the young King abandoned himself entirely to pleasure, and led a jovial life. But, thorns were springing up under his bed of roses, as he soon found out. For, having been privately married to ELIZABETH WOODVILLE, a young widow lady, very beautiful and very captivating; and at last resolving to make his secret known, and to declare her his Queen; he gave some offence to the Earl of Warwick, who was usually called the King-Maker, because of his power and influence, and because of his having lent such great help to placing Edward on the throne. This offence was not lessened by the jealousy with which the Nevil family (the Earl of Warwick's) regarded the promotion of the Woodville family. For, the young Queen was so bent on providing for her relations, that she made her father an earl and a great officer of state; married her five sisters to young noblemen of the highest rank; and provided for her younger brother, a young man of twenty, by marrying him to an immensely rich old duchess of eighty. The Earl of Warwick took all this pretty graciously for a man of his proud temper, until the question arose to whom the King's sister, MARGARET, should be married. The Earl of Warwick said, "To one of the French King's sons," and was allowed to go over to the French King to make friendly proposals for that purpose, and to hold all manner of friendly interviews with him. But, while he was so engaged, the Woodville party married the young lady to the Duke of Burgundy! Upon this he came back in great rage and scorn, and shut himself up discontented, in his Castle of Middleham.

A reconciliation, though not a very sincere one, was patched up between the Earl of Warwick and the King, and lasted until the Earl married his daughter, against the King's wishes, to the Duke of Clarence. While the marriage was being celebrated at Calais, the people in the north of England, where the influence of the Nevil family was strongest, broke out into rebellion; their complaint was, that England was oppressed and plundered by the Woodville family, whom they demanded to have removed from power. As they were joined by great numbers of people, and as they openly declared that they were supported by the Earl of Warwick, the King did not know what to do. At last, as he wrote to the earl beseeching his aid, he and his new son-in-law came over to England, and began to arrange the business by shutting the King up in Middleham Castle in the safe keeping of the Archbishop of York; so England was not only in the strange position of having two kings at once, but they were both prisoners at the same time.

Even as yet, however, the King-Maker was so far true to the King, that he dispersed a new rising of the Lancastrians, took their leader prisoner, and brought him to the King, who ordered him to be immediately executed. He presently allowed the King to return to London, and there innumerable pledges of forgiveness and friendship were exchanged between them, and between the Nevils and the Woodvilles; the King's eldest daughter was promised in marriage to the heir of the Nevil family; and more friendly oaths were sworn, and more friendly promises made, than this book would hold.

They lasted about three months. At the end of that time, the Archbishop of York made a feast for the King, the Earl of Warwick, and the Duke of Clarence, at his house, the Moor, in Hertfordshire. The King was washing his hands before supper, when some one whispered him that a body of a hundred men were lying in ambush outside the house. Whether this were true or untrue, the King took fright, mounted his horse, and rode through the dark night to Windsor Castle. Another reconciliation was patched up between him and the King-Maker, but it was a short one, and it was the last. A new rising took place in Lincolnshire, and the King marched to repress it. Having done so, he proclaimed that both the Earl of Warwick and the Duke of Clarence were traitors, who had secretly assisted it, and who had been prepared publicly to join it on the following day. In these dangerous circumstances they both took ship and sailed away to the French court.

And here a meeting took place between the Earl of Warwick and his old enemy, the Dowager Queen Margaret, through whom his father had had his head struck off, and to whom he had been a bitter foe. But, now, when he said that he had done with the ungrateful and perfidious Edward of York, and that henceforth he devoted himself to the restoration of the House of Lancaster, either in the person of her husband or of her little son, she embraced him as if he had ever been her dearest friend. She did more than that; she married her son to his second daughter, the Lady Anne. However agreeable this marriage was to the new friends, it was very disagreeable to the Duke of Clarence, who perceived that his father-in-law, the King-Maker, would never make *him* King, now. So, being but a weak-minded young traitor, possessed of very little worth or sense, he readily listened to an artful court lady sent over for the purpose, and promised to turn traitor once more, and go over to his brother, King

Edward, when a fitting opportunity should come.

The Earl of Warwick, knowing nothing of this, soon redeemed his promise to the Dowager Queen Margaret, by invading England and landing at Plymouth, where he instantly proclaimed King Henry, and summoned all Englishmen between the ages of sixteen and sixty, to join his banner. Then, with his army increasing as he marched along, he went northward, and came so near King Edward, who was in that part of the country, that Edward had to ride hard for it to the coast of Norfolk, and thence to get away in such ships as he could find, to Holland. Thereupon, the triumphant King-Maker and his false son-in-law, the Duke of Clarence, went to London, took the old King out of the Tower, and walked him in a great procession to Saint Paul's Cathedral with the crown upon his head. This did not improve the temper of the Duke of Clarence, who saw himself farther off from being King than ever; but he kept his secret, and said nothing. The Nevil family were restored to all their honours and glories, and the Woodvilles and the rest were disgraced. The King-Maker, less sanguinary than the King, shed no blood except that of the Earl of Worcester, who had been so cruel to the people as to have gained the title of the Butcher. Him they caught hidden in a tree, and him they tried and executed. No other death stained the King-Maker's triumph.

To dispute this triumph, back came King Edward again, next year, landing at Ravenspur, coming on to York, causing all his men to cry "Long live King Henry!" and swearing on the altar, without a blush, that he came to lay no claim to the crown. Now was the time for the Duke of Clarence, who ordered his men to assume the White Rose, and declare for his brother. The Marquis of Montague, though the Earl of Warwick's brother, also declining to fight against King Edward, he went on successfully to London, where the Archbishop of York let him into the City, and where the people made great demonstrations in his favour. For this they had four reasons. Firstly, there were great numbers of the King's adherents hiding in the City, and ready to break out; secondly, the King owed them a great deal of money, which they could never hope to get if he were unsuccessful; thirdly, there was a young prince to inherit the crown; and fourthly, the King was gay and handsome, and more popular than a better man might have been with the City ladies. After a stay of only two days with these worthy supporters, the King marched out to Barnet Common, to give the Earl of Warwick battle. And now it was to be seen, for the last time, whether the King or the King-Maker was to carry the day.

While the battle was yet pending, the faint-hearted Duke of Clarence began to repent, and sent over secret messages to his father-in-law, offering his services in mediation with the King. But, the Earl of Warwick disdainfully rejected them, and replied that Clarence was false and perjured, and that he would settle the quarrel by the sword. The battle began at four o'clock in the morning and lasted until ten, and during the greater part of the time it was fought in a thick mist—

absurdly supposed to be raised by a magician. The loss of life was very great, for the hatred was strong on both sides. The King-Maker was defeated, and the King triumphed. Both the Earl of Warwick and his brother were slain, and their bodies lay in St. Paul's, for some days, as a spectacle to the people.

Margaret's spirit was not broken even by this great blow. Within five days she was in arms again, and raised her standard in Bath, whence she set off with her army, to try and join Lord Pembroke, who had a force in Wales. But the King, coming up with her outside the town of Tewkesbury, and ordering his brother, the DUKE OF GLOUCESTER, who was a brave soldier, to attack her men, she sustained an entire defeat, and was taken prisoner, together with her son, now only eighteen years of age. The conduct of the King to this poor youth was worthy of his cruel character. He ordered him to be led into his tent. "And what," said he, "brought *you* to England?" "I came to England," replied the prisoner, with a spirit which a man of spirit might have admired in a captive, "to recover my father's kingdom, which descended to him as his right, and from him descends to me, as mine." The King, drawing off his iron gauntlet, struck him with it in the face; and the Duke of Clarence and some other lords, who were there, drew their noble swords, and killed him.

His mother survived him, a prisoner, for five years; after her ransom by the King of France, she survived for six years more. Within three weeks of this murder, Henry died one of those convenient sudden deaths which were so common in the Tower; in plainer words, he was murdered by the King's order.

Having no particular excitement on his hands after this great defeat of the Lancaster party, and being perhaps desirous to get rid of some of his fat (for he was now getting too corpulent to be handsome), the King thought of making war on France. As he wanted more money for this purpose than the Parliament could give him, though they were usually ready enough for war, he invented a new way of raising it, by sending for the principal citizens of London, and telling them, with a grave face, that he was very much in want of cash, and would take it very kind in them if they would lend him some. It being impossible for them safely to refuse, they complied, and the moneys thus forced from them were called—no doubt to the great amusement of the King and the Court—as if they were free gifts, "Benevolences." What with grants from Parliament, and what with Benevolences, the King raised an army and passed over to Calais. As nobody wanted war, however, the French King made proposals of peace, which were accepted, and a truce was concluded for seven long years. The proceedings between the Kings of France and England on this occasion, were very friendly, very splendid, and very distrustful. They finished with a meeting between the two Kings, on a temporary bridge over the river Somme, where they embraced through two holes in a strong wooden grating like a lion's cage, and made several bows and fine speeches to one another.

It was time, now, that the Duke of Clarence should be punished for his treacheries; and Fate had his punishment in store. He was, probably, not trusted by the King—for who could trust him who knew him!—and he had certainly a powerful opponent in his brother Richard, Duke of Gloucester, who, being avaricious and ambitious, wanted to marry that widowed daughter of the Earl of Warwick's who had been espoused to the deceased young Prince, at Calais. Clarence, who wanted all the family wealth for himself, secreted this lady, whom Richard found disguised as a servant in the City of London, and whom he married; arbitrators appointed by the King, then divided the property between the brothers. This led to ill-will and mistrust between them. Clarence's wife dying, and he wishing to make another marriage, which was obnoxious to the King, his ruin was hurried by that means, too. At first, the Court struck at his retainers and dependents, and accused some of them of magic and witchcraft, and similar nonsense. Successful against this small game, it then mounted to the Duke himself, who was impeached by his brother the King, in person, on a variety of such charges. He was found guilty, and sentenced to be publicly executed. He never was publicly executed, but he met his death somehow, in the Tower, and, no doubt, through some agency of the King or his brother Gloucester, or both. It was supposed at the time that he was told to choose the manner of his death, and that he chose to be drowned in a butt of Malmsey wine. I hope the story may be true, for it would have been a becoming death for such a miserable creature.

The King survived him some five years. He died in the forty-second year of his life, and the twenty-third of his reign. He had a very good capacity and some good points, but he was selfish, careless, sensual, and cruel. He was a favourite with the people for his showy manners; and the people were a good example to him in the constancy of their attachment. He was penitent on his death-bed for his "benevolences," and other extortions, and ordered restitution to be made to the people who had suffered from them. He also called about his bed the enriched members of the Woodville family, and the proud lords whose honours were of older date, and endeavoured to reconcile them, for the sake of the peaceful succession of his son and the tranquillity of England.

CHAPTER XXIV

ENGLAND UNDER EDWARD THE FIFTH

THE late King's eldest son, the Prince of Wales, called EDWARD after him, was only thirteen years of age at his father's death. He was at Ludlow Castle with his uncle, the Earl of Rivers. The prince's brother, the Duke of York, only eleven years of age, was in London with his mother. The boldest, most crafty, and most dreaded nobleman in England at that time was their uncle RICHARD, Duke of Gloucester,

185*

and everybody wondered how the two poor boys would fare with such an uncle for a friend or a foe.

The Queen, their mother, being exceedingly uneasy about this, was anxious that instructions should be sent to Lord Rivers to raise an army to escort the young King safely to London. But, Lord Hastings, who was of the Court party opposed to the Woodvilles, and who disliked the thought of giving them that power, argued against the proposal, and obliged the Queen to be satisfied with an escort of two thousand horse. The Duke of Gloucester did nothing, at first, to justify suspicion. He came from Scotland (where he was commanding an army) to York, and was there the first to swear allegiance to his nephew. He then wrote a condoling letter to the Queen-Mother, and set off to be present at the coronation in London.

Now, the young King, journeying towards London too, with Lord Rivers and Lord Gray, came to Stony Stratford, as his uncle came to Northampton, about ten miles distant; and when those two lords heard that the Duke of Gloucester was so near, they proposed to the young King that they should go back and greet him in his name. The boy being very willing that they should do so, they rode off and were received with great friendliness, and asked by the Duke of Gloucester to stay and dine with him. In the evening, while they were merry together, up came the Duke of Buckingham with three hundred horsemen; and next morning the two lords and the two dukes, and the three hundred horsemen, rode away together to rejoin the King. Just as they were entering Stony Stratford, the Duke of Gloucester, checking his horse, turned suddenly on the two lords, charged them with alienating from him the affections of his sweet nephew, and caused them to be arrested by the three hundred horsemen and taken back. Then, he and the Duke of Buckingham went straight to the King (whom they had now in their power), to whom they made a show of kneeling down, and offering great love and submission; and then they ordered his attendants to disperse, and took him, alone with them, to Northampton.

A few days afterwards they conducted him to London, and lodged him in the Bishop's Palace. But, he did not remain there long; for, the Duke of Buckingham with a tender face made a speech expressing how anxious he was for the Royal boy's safety, and how much safer he would be in the Tower until his coronation, than he could be anywhere else. So, to the Tower he was taken, very carefully, and the Duke of Gloucester was named Protector of the State.

Although Gloucester had proceeded thus far with a very smooth countenance—and although he was a clever man, fair of speech, and not ill-looking, in spite of one of his shoulders being something higher than the other—and although he had come into the City riding bare-headed at the King's side, and looking very fond of him—he had made the King's mother more uneasy yet; and when the Royal boy was taken to the Tower, she became so alarmed that she took sanctuary in Westminster with her five daughters.

Nor did she do this without reason, for, the Duke of Gloucester, finding that the lords who were opposed to the Woodville family were faithful to the young King nevertheless, quickly resolved to strike a blow for himself. Accordingly, while those lords met in council at the Tower, he and those who were in his interest met in separate council at his own residence, Crosby Palace, in Bishopsgate Street. Being at last quite prepared, he one day appeared unexpectedly at the council in the Tower, and appeared to be very jocular and merry. He was particularly gay with the Bishop of Ely, praising the strawberries that grew in his garden on Holborn Hill, and asking him to have some gathered that he might eat them at dinner. The Bishop, quite proud of the honour, sent one of his men to fetch some; and the Duke, still very jocular and gay, went out; and the council all said what a very agreeable duke he was! In a little time, however, he came back quite altered—not at all jocular—frowning and fierce—and suddenly said,—

"What do those persons deserve who have compassed my destruction; I being the King's lawful, as well as natural, protector?"

To this strange question, Lord Hastings replied, that they deserved death, whosoever they were.

"Then," said the Duke, "I tell you that they are that sorceress my brother's wife;" meaning the Queen: "and that other sorceress, Jane Shore. Who, by witchcraft, have withered my body, and caused my arm to shrink as I now show you."

He then pulled up his sleeve and showed them his arm, which was shrunken, it is true, but which had been so, as they all very well knew, from the hour of his birth.

Jane Shore, being then the lover of Lord Hastings, as she had formerly been of the late King, that lord knew that he himself was attacked. So, he said, in some confusion, "Certainly, my Lord, if they have done this, they be worthy of punishment."

"If?" said the Duke of Gloucester; "do you talk to me of ifs? I tell you that they *have* so done, and I will make it good upon thy body, thou traitor!"

With that, he struck the table a great blow with his fist. This was a signal to some of his people outside to cry "Treason!" They immediately did so, and there was a rush into the chamber of so many armed men that it was filled in a moment.

"First," said the Duke of Gloucester to Lord Hastings, "I arrest thee, traitor! And let him," he added to the armed men who took him, "have a priest at once, for by St. Paul I will not dine until I have seen his head off!"

Lord Hastings was hurried to the green by the Tower chapel, and there beheaded on a log of wood that happened to be lying on the ground. Then, the Duke dined with a good appetite, and after dinner summoning the principal citizens to attend him, told them that Lord Hastings and the rest had designed to murder both himself and the Duke of Buckingham, who stood by his side, if he had not providentially discovered their design. He requested them to be so obliging as to inform their fellow-citizens of the truth of what he said, and issued a proclamation (prepared and neatly copied out beforehand) to the same effect.

On the same day that the Duke did these things in the Tower, Sir Richard Ratcliffe, the boldest and most undaunted of his men, went down to Pontefract; arrested Lord Rivers, Lord Gray, and two other gentlemen; and publicly executed them on the scaffold, without any trial, for having intended the Duke's death. Three days afterwards the Duke, not to lose time, went down the river to Westminster in his barge, attended by divers bishops, lords, and soldiers, and demanded that the Queen should deliver her second son, the Duke of York, into his safe keeping. The Queen, being obliged to comply, resigned the child after she had wept over him; and Richard of Gloucester placed him with his brother in the Tower. Then, he seized Jane Shore, and, because she had been the lover of the late King, confiscated her property, and got her sentenced to do public penance in the streets by walking in a scanty dress, with bare feet, and carrying a lighted candle, to St. Paul's Cathedral, through the most crowded part of the City.

Having now all things ready for his own advancement, he caused a friar to preach a sermon at the cross which stood in front of St. Paul's Cathedral, in which he dwelt upon the profligate manners of the late King, and upon the late shame of Jane Shore, and hinted that the princes were not his children, "Whereas, good people," said the friar, whose name was SHAW, "my Lord the Protector, the noble Duke of Gloucester, that sweet prince, the pattern of all the noblest virtues, is the perfect image and express likeness of his father." There had been a little plot between the Duke and the friar, that the Duke should appear in the crowd at this moment, when it was expected that the people would cry "Long live King Richard!" But, either through the friar saying the words too soon, or through the Duke's coming too late, the Duke and the words did not come together, and the people only laughed, and the friar sneaked off ashamed.

The Duke of Buckingham was a better hand at such business than the friar, so he went to the Guildhall the next day, and addressed the citizens in the Lord Protector's behalf. A few dirty men, who had been hired and stationed there for the purpose, crying when he had done, "God save King Richard!" he made them a great bow, and thanked them with all his heart. Next day, to make an end of it, he went with the mayor and some lords and citizens to Bayard Castle, by the river, where Richard then was, and read an address, humbly entreating him to accept the Crown of England. Richard, who looked down upon them out of a window and pretended to be in great uneasiness and alarm, assured them there was nothing he desired less, and that his deep affection for his nephews forbade him to think of it. To this the Duke of Buckingham replied, with pretended warmth, that the free people of England would never submit to his nephew's rule, and that if Richard, who was the lawful heir, refused the Crown, why then they must find some one else to wear it. The

Duke of Gloucester returned, that since he used that strong language, it became his painful duty to think no more of himself, and to accept the Crown.

Upon that, the people cheered and dispersed; and the Duke of Gloucester and the Duke of Buckingham passed a pleasant evening, talking over the play they had just acted with so much success, and every word of which they had prepared together.

CHAPTER XXV

ENGLAND UNDER RICHARD THE THIRD

KING RICHARD THE THIRD was up betimes in the morning, and went to Westminster Hall. In the Hall was a marble seat, upon which he sat himself down between two great noblemen, and told the people that he began the new reign in that place, because the first duty of a sovereign was to administer the laws equally to all, and to maintain justice. He then mounted his horse and rode back to the City, where he was received by the clergy and the crowd as if he really had a right to the throne, and really were a just man. The clergy and the crowd must have been rather ashamed of themselves in secret, I think, for being such poor-spirited knaves.

The new King and his Queen were soon crowned with a great deal of show and noise, which the people liked very much; and then the King set forth on a royal progress through his dominions. He was crowned a second time at York, in order that the people might have show and noise enough; and wherever he went was received with shouts of rejoicing—from a good many people of strong lungs, who were paid to strain their throats in crying, "God save King Richard!" The plan was so successful that I am told it has been imitated since, by other usurpers, in other progresses through other dominions.

While he was on this journey, King Richard stayed a week at Warwick. And from Warwick he sent instructions home for one of the wickedest murders that ever was done—the murder of the two young princes, his nephews, who were shut up in the Tower of London.

Sir Robert Brackenbury was at that time Governor of the Tower. To him, by the hands of a messenger named JOHN GREEN, did King Richard send a letter, ordering him by some means to put the two young princes to death. But Sir Robert—I hope because he had children of his own, and loved them—sent John Green back again, riding and spurring along the dusty roads, with the answer that he could not do so horrible a piece of work. The King, having frowningly considered a little, called to him SIR JAMES TYRREL, his master of the horse, and to him gave authority to take command of the Tower, whenever he would, for twenty-four hours, and to keep all the keys of the Tower during that space of time. Tyrrel, well knowing what was wanted, looked about him for two hardened ruffians, and chose JOHN DIGHTON, one of his own grooms, and MILES FOREST, who was a murderer by trade. Having secured these two assistants, he went, upon a day in August, to the Tower, showed his authority from the King, took the command for four-and-twenty-hours, and obtained possession of the keys. And when the black night came, he went creeping, creeping, like a guilty villain as he was, up the dark stone winding stairs, and along the dark stone passages, until he came to the door of the room where the two young princes, having said their prayers, lay fast asleep, clasped in each other's arms. And while he watched and listened at the door, he sent in those evil demons, John Dighton and Miles Forest, who smothered the two princes with the bed and pillows, and carried their bodies down the stairs, and buried them under a great heap of stones at the staircase foot. And when the day came, he gave up the command of the Tower, and restored the keys, and hurried away without once looking behind him; and Sir Robert Brackenbury went with fear and sadness to the princes' room, and found the princes gone for ever.

You know, through all this history, how true it is that traitors are never true, and you will not be surprised to learn that the Duke of Buckingham soon turned against King Richard, and joined a great conspiracy that was formed to dethrone him, and to place the crown upon its rightful owner's head. Richard had meant to keep the murder secret; but when he heard through his spies that this conspiracy existed, and that many lords and gentlemen drank in secret to the healths of the two young princes in the Tower, he made it known that they were dead. The conspirators, though thwarted for a moment, soon resolved to set up for the crown against the murderous Richard, HENRY Earl of Richmond, grandson of Catherine: that widow of Henry the Fifth who married Owen Tudor. And as Henry was of the house of Lancaster, they proposed that he should marry the Princess Elizabeth, the eldest daughter of the late King, now the heiress of the house of York, and thus by uniting the rival families put an end to the fatal wars of the Red and White Roses. All being settled, a time was appointed for Henry to come over from Brittany, and for a great rising against Richard to take place in several parts of England at the same hour. On a certain day, therefore, in October, the revolt took place; but unsuccessfully. Richard was prepared, Henry was driven back at sea by a storm, his followers in England were dispersed, and the Duke of Buckingham was taken, and at once beheaded in the market-place at Salisbury.

The time of his success was a good time, Richard thought, for summoning a Parliament and getting some money. So, a Parliament was called, and it flattered and fawned upon him as much as he could possibly desire, and declared him to be the rightful King of England, and his only son Edward, then eleven years of age, the next heir to the throne.

Richard knew full well that, let the Parliament say what it would, the Princess Elizabeth was remembered by people as the heiress of the house of York; and having accurate information besides, of its being designed by the conspirators to marry her to Henry of Richmond, he felt that it would much strengthen him and weaken them, to be beforehand with them, and marry her to his son. With this view he went to the Sanctuary at Westminster, where the late King's widow and her daughter still were, and besought them to come to Court; where (he swore by anything and everything) they should be safely and honourably entertained. They came, accordingly, but had scarcely been at Court a month when his son died suddenly— or was poisoned—and his plan was crushed to pieces.

In this extremity, King Richard, always active, thought, "I must make another plan." And he made the plan of marrying the Princess Elizabeth himself, although she was his niece. There was one difficulty in the way: his wife, the Queen Anne, was alive. But, he knew (remembering his nephews) how to remove that obstacle, and he made love to the Princess Elizabeth, telling her he felt perfectly confident that the Queen would die in February. The Princess was not a very scrupulous young lady, for, instead of rejecting the murderer of her brothers with scorn and hatred, she openly declared she loved him dearly; and, when February came and the Queen did not die, she expressed her impatient opinion that she was too long about it. However, King Richard was not so far out in his prediction, but that she died in March—he took good care of that— and then this precious pair hoped to be married. But they were disappointed, for the idea of such a marriage was so unpopular in the country, that the King's chief counsellors, RATCLIFFE and CATESBY, would by no means undertake to propose it, and the King was even obliged to declare in public that he had never thought of such a thing.

He was, by this time, dreaded and hated by all classes of his subjects. His nobles deserted every day to Henry's side; he dared not call another Parliament, lest his crimes should be denounced there; and for want of money, he was obliged to get Benevolences from the citizens, which exasperated them all against him. It was said too, that, being stricken by his conscience, he dreamed frightful dreams, and started up in the night-time, wild with terror and remorse. Active to the last, through all this, he issued vigorous proclamations against Henry of Richmond and all his followers, when he heard that they were coming against him with a Fleet from France; and took the field as fierce and savage as a wild boar—the animal represented on his shield.

Henry of Richmond landed with six thousand men at Milford Haven, and came on against King Richard, then encamped at Leicester with an army twice as great, through North Wales. On Bosworth Field the two armies met; and Richard, looking along Henry's ranks, and seeing them crowded with the English nobles who had abandoned him, turned pale when he beheld the powerful Lord Stanley and his son (whom he had tried hard to retain) among them. But, he was as brave as he was wicked, and plunged into the thickest of the fight.

He was riding hither and thither, laying about him in all directions, when he observed the Earl of Northumberland—one of his few great allies—to stand inactive, and the main body of his troops to hesitate. At the same moment, his desperate glance caught Henry of Richmond among a little group of his knights. Riding hard at him, and crying "Treason!" he killed his standard-bearer, fiercely unhorsed another gentleman, and aimed a powerful stroke at Henry himself, to cut him down. But, Sir William Stanley parried it as it fell, and before Richard could raise his arm again, he was borne down in a press of numbers, unhorsed, and killed. Lord Stanley picked up the crown, all bruised and trampled, and stained with blood, and put it upon Richmond's head, amid loud and rejoicing cries of "Long live King Henry!"

That night, a horse was led up to the church of the Grey Friars at Leicester; across whose back was tied, like some worthless sack, a naked body brought there for burial. It was the body of the last of the Plantagenet line, King Richard the Third, usurper and murderer, slain at the battle of Bosworth Field in the thirty-second year of his age, after a reign of two years.

CHAPTER XXVI

ENGLAND UNDER HENRY THE SEVENTH

KING HENRY THE SEVENTH did not turn out to be as fine a fellow as the nobility and people hoped, in the first joy of their deliverance from Richard the Third. He was very cold, crafty, and calculating, and would do almost anything for money. He possessed considerable ability, but his chief merit appears to have been that he was not cruel when there was nothing to be got by it.

The new King had promised the nobles who had espoused his cause that he would marry the Princess Elizabeth. The first thing he did, was, to direct her to be removed from the castle of Sheriff Hutton in Yorkshire, where Richard had placed her, and restored to the care of her mother in London. The young Earl of Warwick, Edward Plantagenet, son and heir of the late Duke of Clarence, had been kept a prisoner in the same old Yorkshire Castle with her. This boy, who was now fifteen, the new King placed in the Tower for safety. Then he came to London in great state, and gratified the people with a fine procession; on which kind of show he often very much relied for keeping them in good humour. The sports and feasts which took place were followed by a terrible fever, called the Sweating Sickness; of which great numbers of people died. Lord Mayors and Aldermen are thought to have suffered most from it; whether, because they were in the habit of over-eating themselves, or because they were very jealous of preserving filth and nuisances in the City (as they have been since), I don't know.

The King's coronation was postponed on account of the general ill-health, and he afterwards deferred his marriage, as if he were not very anxious that it should take place: and, even after that, deferred the Queen's coronation so long that he gave offence to the York party. However, he set these things right in the end, by hanging some men and seizing on the rich possessions of others; by granting more popular pardons to the followers of the late King than could, at first, be got from him; and, by employing about his Court, some not very scrupulous persons who had been employed in the previous reign.

As this reign was principally remarkable for two very curious impostures which have become famous in history, we will make those two stories its principal feature.

There was a priest at Oxford of the name of Simons, who had for a pupil a handsome boy named Lambert Simnel, the son of a baker. Partly to gratify his own ambitious ends, and partly to carry out the designs of a secret party formed against the King, this priest declared that his pupil, the boy, was no other than the young Earl of Warwick; who (as everybody might have known) was safely locked up in the Tower of London. The priest and the boy went over to Ireland; and, at Dublin, enlisted in their cause all ranks of the people: who seem to have been generous enough, but exceedingly irrational. The Earl of Kildare, the governor of Ireland, declared that he believed the boy to be what the priest represented; and the boy, who had been well tutored by the priest, told them such things of his childhood, and gave them so many descriptions of the Royal Family, that they were perpetually shouting and hurrahing, and drinking his health, and making all kinds of noisy and thirsty demonstrations, to express their belief in him. Nor was this feeling confined to Ireland alone, for the Earl of Lincoln—whom the late usurper had named as his successor—went over to the young Pretender; and, after holding a secret correspondence with the Dowager Duchess of Burgundy— the sister of Edward the Fourth, who detested the present King and all his race—sailed to Dublin with two thousand German soldiers of her providing. In this promising state of the boy's fortunes, he was crowned there, with a crown taken off the head of a statue of the Virgin Mary; and was then, according to the Irish custom of those days, carried home on the shoulders of a big chieftain possessing a great deal more strength than sense. Father Simons, you may be sure, was mighty busy at the coronation.

Ten days afterwards, the Germans, and the Irish, and the priest, and the boy, and the Earl of Lincoln, all landed in Lancashire to invade England. The King, who had good intelligence of their movements, set up his standard at Nottingham, where vast numbers resorted to him every day; while the Earl of Lincoln could gain but very few. With his small force he tried to make for the town of Newark; but the King's army getting between him and that place, he had no choice but to risk a battle at Stoke. It soon ended in the complete destruction of the Pretender's forces, one half of whom were killed; among them, the Earl himself. The priest and the baker's boy were taken prisoners. The priest, after confessing the trick, was shut up in prison, where he afterwards died—suddenly perhaps. The boy was taken into the King's kitchen and made a turnspit. He was afterwards raised to the station of one of the King's falconers; and so ended this strange imposition.

There seems reason to suspect that the Dowager Queen—always a restless and busy woman—had had some share in tutoring the baker's son. The King was very angry with her, whether or no. He seized upon her property, and shut her up in a convent at Bermondsey.

One might suppose that the end of this story would have put the Irish people on their guard; but they were quite ready to receive a second impostor, as they had received the first, and that same troublesome Duchess of Burgundy soon gave them the opportunity. All of a sudden there appeared at Cork, in a vessel arriving from Portugal, a young man of excellent abilities, of very handsome appearance and most winning manners, who declared himself to be Richard, Duke of York, the second son of King Edward the Fourth. "O," said some, even of those ready Irish believers, "but surely that young Prince was murdered by his uncle in the Tower!" —"It *is* supposed so," said the engaging young man; "and my brother *was* killed in that gloomy prison; but I escaped—it don't matter how, at present—and have been wandering about the world for seven long years." This explanation being quite satisfactory to numbers of the Irish people, they began again to shout and to hurrah, and to drink his health, and to make the noisy and thirsty demonstrations all over again. And the big chieftain in Dublin began to look out for another coronation, and another young King to be carried home on his back.

Now, King Henry being then on bad terms with France, the French King, Charles the Eighth, saw that, by pretending to believe in the handsome young man, he could trouble his enemy sorely. So, he invited him over to the French Court, and appointed him a body-guard, and treated him in all respects as if he really were the Duke of York. Peace, however, being soon concluded between the two Kings, the pretended Duke was turned adrift, and wandered for protection to the Duchess of Burgundy. She, after feigning to inquire into the reality of his claims, declared him to be the very picture of her dear departed brother; gave him a body-guard at her Court, of thirty halberdiers; and called him by the sounding name of the White Rose of England.

The leading members of the White Rose party in England sent over an agent, named Sir Robert Clifford, to ascertain whether the White Rose's claims were good: the King also sent over his agents to inquire into the Rose's history. The White Roses declared the young man to be really the Duke of York; the King declared him to be PERKIN WARBECK, the son of a merchant of the city of Tournay, who had acquired his knowledge of England, its language and manners, from the English merchants who traded in Flanders; it was also stated by the Royal agents that he had been in the service of Lady Brompton, the wife of an exiled English nobleman, and that the Duchess of Burgundy had caused him to be trained and taught, expressly for this deception. The King then required the Archduke Philip—who was the sovereign of Burgundy—to banish this new Pretender, or to deliver him up; but, as the Archduke replied that he could not control the Duchess in her own land, the King, in revenge, took the market of English cloth away from Antwerp, and prevented all commercial intercourse between the two countries.

He also, by arts and bribes, prevailed on Sir Robert Clifford to betray his employers; and he denouncing several famous English noblemen as being secretly the friends of Perkin Warbeck, the King had three of the foremost executed at once. Whether he pardoned the remainder because they were poor, I do not know; but it is only too probable that he refused to pardon one famous nobleman against whom the same Clifford soon afterwards informed separately, because he was rich. This was no other than Sir William Stanley, who had saved the King's life at the battle of Bosworth Field. It is very doubtful whether his treason amounted to much more than his having said, that if he were sure the young man was the Duke of York, he would not take arms against him. Whatever he had done he admitted, like an honourable spirit; and he lost his head for it, and the covetous King gained all his wealth.

Perkin Warbeck kept quiet for three years; but, as the Flemings began to complain heavily of the loss of their trade by the stoppage of the Antwerp market on his account, and as it was not unlikely that they might even go so far as to take his life, or give him up, he found it necessary to do something. Accordingly, he made a desperate sally, and landed, with only a few hundred men, on the coast of Deal. But he was soon glad to get back to the place from whence he came; for the country people rose against his followers, killed a great many, and took a hundred and fifty prisoners: who were all driven to London, tied together with ropes, like a team of cattle. Every one of them was hanged on some part or other of the sea-shore; in order, that if any more men should come over with Perkin Warbeck, they might see the bodies as a warning before they landed.

Then the wary King, by making a treaty of commerce with the Flemings, drove Perkin Warbeck out of that country; and, by completely gaining over the Irish to his side, deprived him of that asylum too. He wandered away to Scotland, and told his story at that Court. King James the Fourth of Scotland, who was no friend to King Henry, and had no reason to be (for King Henry had bribed his Scotch lords to betray him more than once; but had never succeeded in his plots), gave him a great reception, called him his cousin, and gave him in marriage the Lady Catherine Gordon, a beautiful and charming creature related to the royal house of Stuart.

Alarmed by this successful reappearance of the Pretender, the King still undermined, and bought, and bribed, and kept his doings and Perkin Warbeck's story in the dark, when he might, one would imagine, have rendered the matter clear to all England. But, for all this bribing of the Scotch lords at the Scotch King's Court, he could not procure the Pretender to be delivered up to him. James, though not very particular in many respects, would not betray him; and the ever-busy Duchess of Burgundy so provided him with arms, and good soldiers, and with money besides, that he had soon a little army of fifteen hundred men of various nations. With these, and aided by the Scottish King in person, he crossed the border into England, and made a proclamation to the people, in which he called the King "Henry Tudor;" offered large rewards to any who should take or distress him; and announced himself as King Richard the Fourth come to receive the homage of his faithful subjects. His faithful subjects, however, cared nothing for him, and hated his faithful troops: who, being of different nations, quarrelled also among themselves. Worse than this, if worse were possible, they began to plunder the country; upon which the White Rose said, that he would rather lose his rights, than gain them through the miseries of the English people. The Scottish King made a jest of his scruples; but they and their whole force went back again without fighting a battle.

The worst consequence of this attempt was, that a rising took place among the people of Cornwall, who considered themselves too heavily taxed to meet the charges of the expected war. Stimulated by Flammock, a lawyer, and Joseph, a blacksmith, and joined by Lord Audley and some other country gentlemen, they marched on all the way to Deptford Bridge, where they fought a battle with the King's army. They were defeated—though the Cornish men fought with great bravery—and the lord was beheaded, and the lawyer and the blacksmith were hanged, drawn, and quartered. The rest were pardoned. The King, who believed every man to be as avaricious as himself, and thought that money could settle anything, allowed them to make bargains for their liberty with the soldiers who had taken them.

Perkin Warbeck, doomed to wander up and down, and never to find rest anywhere—a sad fate: almost a sufficient punishment for an imposture, which he seems in time to have half believed himself— lost his Scottish refuge through a truce being made between the two Kings; and found himself, once more, without a country before him in which he could lay his head. But James (always honourable and true to him, alike when he melted down his plate, and even the great gold chain he had been used to wear, to pay soldiers in his cause; and now, when that cause was lost and hopeless) did not conclude the treaty, until he had safely departed out of the Scottish dominions. He, and his beautiful wife, who was faithful to him under all reverses, and left her state and home to follow his poor fortunes, were put aboard ship with everything necessary for their comfort and protection, and sailed for Ireland.

But, the Irish people had had enough of counterfeit Earls of Warwick and Dukes of York, for one while; and would give the White

Rose no aid. So, the White Rose—encircled by thorns indeed—resolved to go with his beautiful wife to Cornwall as a forlorn resource, and see what might be made of the Cornish men, who had risen so valiantly a little while before, and who had fought so bravely at Deptford Bridge.

To Whitsand Bay, in Cornwall, accordingly, came Perkin Warbeck and his wife; and the lovely lady he shut up for safety in the Castle of St. Michael's Mount, and then marched into Devonshire at the head of three thousand Cornish men. These were increased to six thousand by the time of his arrival in Exeter; but, there the people made a stout resistance, and he went on to Taunton, where he came in sight of the King's army. The stout Cornish men, although they were few in number, and badly armed, were so bold, that they never thought of retreating; but bravely looked forward to a battle on the morrow. Unhappily for them, the man who was possessed of so many engaging qualities, and who attracted so many people to his side when he had nothing else with which to tempt them, was not as brave as they. In the night, when the two armies lay opposite to each other, he mounted a swift horse and fled. When morning dawned, the poor confiding Cornish men, discovering that they had no leader, surrendered to the King's power. Some of them were hanged, and the rest were pardoned and went miserably home.

Before the King pursued Perkin Warbeck to the sanctuary of Beaulieu, in the New Forest, where it was soon known that he had taken refuge, he sent a body of horsemen to St. Michael's Mount, to seize his wife. She was soon taken and brought as a captive before the King. But she was so beautiful, and so good, and so devoted to the man in whom she believed, that the King regarded her with compassion, treated her with great respect, and placed her at Court, near the Queen's person. And many years after Perkin Warbeck was no more, and when his strange story had become like a nursery tale, *she* was called the White Rose, by the people, in remembrance of her beauty.

The sanctuary at Beaulieu was soon surrounded by the King's men; and the King, pursuing his usual dark, artful ways, sent pretended friends to Perkin Warbeck to persuade him to come out and surrender himself. This he soon did; the King having taken a good look at the man of whom he had heard so much—from behind a screen—directed him to be well mounted, and to ride behind him at a little distance, guarded, but not bound in any way. So they entered London with the King's favourite show—a procession; and some of the people hooted as the Pretender rode slowly through the streets to the Tower; but the greater part were quiet, and very curious to see him. From the Tower, he was taken to the Palace at Westminster, and there lodged like a gentleman, though closely watched. He was examined every now and then as to his imposture; but the King was so secret in all he did, that even then he gave it a consequence, which it cannot be supposed to have in itself deserved.

At last Perkin Warbeck ran away, and took refuge in another

sanctuary near Richmond in Surrey. From this he was again per-suaded to deliver himself up; and, being conveyed to London, he stood in the stocks for a whole day, outside Westminster Hall, and there read a paper purporting to be his full confession, and relating his history as the King's agents had originally described it. He was then shut up in the Tower again, in the company of the Earl of Warwick, who had now been there for fourteen years: ever since his removal out of Yorkshire, except when the King had had him at Court, and had shown him to the people, to prove the imposture of the Baker's boy. It is but too probable, when we consider the crafty character of Henry the Seventh, that these two were brought together for a cruel purpose. A plot was soon discovered between them and the keepers, to murder the Governor, get possession of the keys, and proclaim Perkin Warbeck as King Richard the Fourth. That there was some such plot is likely; that they were tempted into it, is at least as likely; that the unfortunate Earl of Warwick—last male of the Plantagenet line—was too unused to the world, and too ignorant and simple to know much about it, whatever it was, is perfectly certain; and that it was the King's interest to get rid of him, is no less so. He was beheaded on Tower Hill, and Perkin Warbeck was hanged at Tyburn.

Such was the end of the pretended Duke of York, whose shadowy history was made more shadowy—and ever will be—by the mystery and craft of the King. If he had turned his great natural advantages to a more honest account, he might have lived a happy and respected life, even in those days. But he died upon a gallows at Tyburn, leaving the Scottish lady, who had loved him so well, kindly pro-tected at the Queen's Court. After some time she forgot her old loves and troubles, as many people do with Time's merciful assistance, and married a Welsh gentleman. Her second husband, SIR MATTHEW CRADOC, more honest and more happy than her first, lies beside her in a tomb in the old church of Swansea.

The ill-blood between France and England in this reign, arose out of the continued plotting of the Duchess of Burgundy, and disputes respecting the affairs of Brittany. The King feigned to be very patriotic, indignant, and warlike; but he always contrived so as never to make war in reality, and always to make money. His taxation of the people, on pretence of war with France, involved, at one time, a very dangerous insurrection, headed by Sir John Egremont, and a common man called John à Chambre. But it was subdued by the royal forces, under the command of the Earl of Surrey. The knighted John escaped to the Duchess of Burgundy, who was ever ready to receive any one who gave the King trouble; and the plain John was hanged at York, in the midst of a number of his men, but on a much higher gibbet, as being a greater traitor. Hung high or hung low, however, hanging is much the same to the person hung.

Within a year after her marriage, the Queen had given birth to a son, who was called Prince Arthur, in remembrance of the old British prince of romance and story; and who, when all these events had

a claim King Henry made to certain lands in France, war was declared between the two countries. Not to perplex this story with an account of the tricks and designs of all the sovereigns who were engaged in it, it is enough to say that England made a blundering alliance with Spain, and got stupidly taken in by that country; which made its own terms with France when it could, and left England in the lurch. SIR EDWARD HOWARD, a bold admiral, son of the Earl of Surrey, distinguished himself by his bravery against the French in this business; but, unfortunately, he was more brave than wise, for, skimming into the French harbour of Brest with only a few row-boats, he attempted (in revenge for the defeat and death of SIR THOMAS KNYVETT, another bold English admiral) to take some strong French ships, well defended with batteries of cannon. The upshot was, that he was left on board of one of them (in consequence of its shooting away from his own boat), with not more than about a dozen men, and was thrown into the sea and drowned: though not until he had taken from his breast his gold chain and gold whistle, which were the signs of his office, and had cast them into the sea to prevent their being made a boast of by the enemy. After this defeat— which was a great one, for Sir Edward Howard was a man of valoui and fame—the King took it into his head to invade France in person; first executing that dangerous Earl of Suffolk whom his father had left in the Tower, and appointing Queen Catherine to the charge of his kingdom in his absence. He sailed to Calais, where he was joined by MAXIMILIAN, Emperor of Germany, who pretended to be his soldier, and who took pay in his service; with a good deal of non-sense of that sort, flattering enough to the vanity of a vain blusterer. The King might be successful enough in sham fights; but his idea of real battles chiefly consisted in pitching silken tents of bright colours that were ignominiously blown down by the wind, and in making a a vast display of gaudy flags and golden curtains. Fortune, however, favoured him better than he deserved; for, after much waste of time in tent pitching, flag flying, gold curtaining, and other such masquer-ading, he gave the French battle at a place called Guinegate: where they took such an unaccountable panic, and fled with such swiftness, that it was ever afterwards called by the English the Battle of Spurs. Instead of following up his advantage, the King, finding that he had had enough of real fighting, came home again.

The Scottish King, though nearly related to Henry by marriage, had taken part against him in this war. The Earl of Surrey, as the English general, advanced to meet him when he came out of his own dominions and crossed the river Tweed. The two armies came up with one another when the Scottish King had also crossed the river Till, and was encamped upon the last of the Cheviot Hills, called the Hill of Flodden. Along the plain below it, the English, when the hour of battle came, advanced. The Scottish army, which had been drawn up in five great bodies, then came steadily down in perfect silence. So they, in their turn, advanced to meet the English army, which came on in one long line; and they attacked it with a body of spearmen, under LORD HOME. At first they had the best of it; but the English recovered themselves so bravely, and fought with such valour, that, when the Scottish King had almost made his way up to the Royal standard, he was slain, and the whole Scottish power routed. Ten thousand Scottish men lay dead that day on Flodden Field; and among them, numbers of the nobility and gentry. For a long time afterwards, the Scottish peasantry used to believe that their King had not been really killed in this battle, because no Englishman had found an iron belt he wore about his body as a penance for having been an unnatural and undutiful son. But, whatever became of his belt, the English had his sword and dagger, and the ring from his finger, and his body too, covered with wounds. There is no doubt of it; for it was seen and recognised by English gentlemen who had known the Scottish King well.

When King Henry was making ready to renew the war in France, the French King was contemplating peace. His queen, dying at this time, he proposed, though he was upwards of fifty years old, to marry King Henry's sister, the Princess Mary, who, besides being only sixteen, was betrothed to the Duke of Suffolk. As the inclinations of young Princesses were not much considered in such matters, the marriage was concluded, and the poor girl was escorted to France, where she was immediately left as the French King's bride, with only one of all her English attendants. That one was a pretty young girl named ANNE BOLEYN, niece of the Earl of Surrey, who had been made Duke of Norfolk, after the victory of Flodden Field. Anne Boleyn's is a name to be remembered, as you will presently find.

And now the French King, who was very proud of his young wife, was preparing for many years of happiness, and she was looking forward, I dare say, to many years of misery, when he died within three months, and left her a young widow. The new French monarch, FRANCIS THE FIRST, seeing how important it was to his interests that she should take for her second husband no one but an Englishman, advised her first lover, the Duke of Suffolk, when King Henry sent him over to France to fetch her home, to marry her. The Princess being herself so fond of that Duke, as to tell him that he must either do so then, or for ever lose her, they were wedded; and Henry afterwards forgave them. In making interest with the King, the Duke of Suffolk had addressed his most powerful favourite and adviser, THOMAS WOLSEY—a name very famous in history for its rise and downfall.

Wolsey was the son of a respectable butcher at Ipswich, in Suffolk, and received so excellent an education that he became a tutor to the family of the Marquis of Dorset, who afterwards got him appointed one of the late King's chaplains. On the accession of Henry the Eighth, he was promoted and taken into great favour. He was now Archbishop of York; the Pope had made him a Cardinal besides; and whoever wanted influence in England or favour with the King— whether he were a foreign monarch or an English nobleman—was obliged to make a friend of the great Cardinal Wolsey.

He was a gay man, who could dance and jest, and sing and drink; and those were the roads to so much, or rather so little, of a heart as King Henry had. He was wonderfully fond of pomp and glitter, and so was the King. He knew a good deal of the Church learning of that time; much of which consisted in finding artful excuses and pretences for almost any wrong thing, and in arguing that black was white, or any other colour. This kind of learning pleased the King too. For many such reasons, the Cardinal was high in estimation with the King; and, being a man of far greater ability, knew as well how to manage him, as a clever keeper may know how to manage a wolf or a tiger, or any other cruel and uncertain beast, that may turn upon him and tear him any day. Never had there been seen in England such state as my Lord Cardinal kept. His wealth was enormous; equal, it was reckoned, to the riches of the Crown. His palaces were as splendid as the King's, and his retinue was eight hundred strong. He held his Court, dressed out from top to toe in flaming scarlet; and his very shoes were golden, set with precious stones. His followers rode on blood horses; while he, with a wonderful affectation of humility in the midst of his great splendour, ambled on a mule with a red velvet saddle and bridle and golden stirrups.

Through the influence of this stately priest, a grand meeting was arranged to take place between the French and English Kings in France; but on ground belonging to England. A prodigious show of friendship and rejoicing was to be made on the occasion; and heralds were sent to proclaim with brazen trumpets through all the principal cities of Europe, that, on a certain day, the Kings of France and England, as companions and brothers in arms, each attended by eighteen followers, would hold a tournament against all knights who might choose to come.

CHARLES, the new Emperor of Germany (the old one being dead), wanted to prevent too cordial an alliance between these sovereigns, and came over to England before the King could repair to the place of meeting; and, besides making an agreeable impression upon him, secured Wolsey's interest by promising that his influence should make him Pope when the next vacancy occurred. On the day when the Emperor left England, the King and all the Court went over to Calais, and thence to the place of meeting, between Ardres and Guisnes, commonly called the Field of the Cloth of Gold. Here, all manner of expense and prodigality was lavished on the decorations of the show; many of the knights and gentlemen being so superbly dressed that it was said they carried their whole estates upon their shoulders.

There were sham castles, temporary chapels, fountains running wine, great cellars full of wine free as water to all comers, silk tents, gold lace and foil, gilt lions, and such things without end; and, in the midst of all, the rich Cardinal out-shone and out-glittered all the noblemen and gentlemen assembled. After a treaty made between the two Kings with as much solemnity as if they had intended to keep it, the lists—nine hundred feet long, and three hundred and twenty broad—were opened for the tournament; the Queens of France and

England looking on with great array of lords and ladies. Then, for ten days, the two sovereigns fought five combats every day, and always beat their polite adversaries; though they *do* write that the King of England, being thrown in a wrestle one day by the King of France, lost his kingly temper with his brother-in-arms, and wanted to make a quarrel of it. Then, there is a great story belonging to this Field of the Cloth of Gold, showing how the English were distrustful of the French, and the French of the English, until Francis rode alone one morning to Henry's tent; and, going in before he was out of bed, told him in joke that he was his prisoner; and how Henry jumped out of bed and embraced Francis; and how Francis helped Henry to dress, and warmed his linen for him; and how Henry gave Francis a splendid jewelled collar, and how Francis gave Henry, in return, a costly bracelet. All this and a great deal more was so written about, and sung about, and talked about at that time (and, indeed, since that time too), that the world has had good cause to be sick of it, for ever.

Of course, nothing came of all these fine doings but a speedy renewal of the war between England and France, in which the two Royal companions and brothers in arms longed very earnestly to damage one another. But, before it broke out again, the Duke of Buckingham was shamefully executed on Tower Hill, on the evidence of a discharged servant—really for nothing, except the folly of having believed in a friar of the name of HOPKINS, who had pretended to be a prophet, and who had mumbled and jumbled out some nonsense about the Duke's son being destined to be very great in the land. It was believed that the unfortunate Duke had given offence to the great Cardinal by expressing his mind freely about the expense and absurdity of the whole business of the Field of the Cloth of Gold. At any rate, he was beheaded, as I have said, for nothing. And the people who saw it done were very angry, and cried out that it was the work of " the butcher's son!"

The new war was a short one, though the Earl of Surrey invaded France again, and did some injury to that country. It ended in another treaty of peace between the two kingdoms, and in the discovery that the Emperor of Germany was not such a good friend to England in reality, as he pretended to be. Neither did he keep his promise to Wolsey to make him Pope, though the King urged him. Two Popes died in pretty quick succession; but the foreign priests were too much for the Cardinal, and kept him out of the post. So the Cardinal and King together found out that the Emperor of Germany was not a man to keep faith with; broke off a projected marriage between the King's daughter MARY, Princess of Wales, and that sovereign, and began to consider whether it might not be well to marry the young lady, either to Francis himself, or to his eldest son.

There now arose at Wittemberg, in Germany, the great leader of the mighty change in England which is called The Reformation, and which set the people free from their slavery to the priests. This was a learned Doctor, named MARTIN LUTHER, who knew all about them, for he had been a priest, and even a monk himself. The preaching and writing of Wickliffe had set a number of men thinking on this subject; and Luther, finding one day to his great surprise, that there really was a book called the New Testament which the priests did not allow to be read, and which contained truths that they suppressed, began to be very vigorous against the whole body, from the Pope downward. It happened, while he was yet only beginning his vast work of awakening the nation, that an impudent fellow named TETZEL, a friar of very bad character, came into his neighbourhood selling what were called Indulgences, by wholesale, to raise money for beautifying the great Cathedral of St. Peter's, at Rome. Whoever bought an Indulgence of the Pope was supposed to buy himself off from the punishment of Heaven for his offences. Luther told the people that these Indulgences were worthless bits of paper, before God, and that Tetzel and his masters were a crew of impostors in selling them.

The King and the Cardinal were mightily indignant at this presumption; and the King (with the help of SIR THOMAS MORE, a wise man, whom he afterwards repaid by striking off his head) even wrote a book about it, with which the Pope was so well pleased that he gave the King the title of Defender of the Faith. The King and the Cardinal also issued flaming warnings to the people not to read Luther's books, on pain of excommunication. But they did read them for all that; and the rumour of what was in them spread far and wide.

When this great change was thus going on, the King began to show himself in his truest and worst colours. Anne Boleyn, the pretty little girl who had gone abroad to France with his sister, was by this time grown up to be very beautiful, and was one of the ladies in attendance on Queen Catherine. Now, Queen Catherine was no longer young or handsome, and it is likely that she was not particularly good-tempered; having been always rather melancholy, and having been made more so by the deaths of four of her children when they were very young. So, the King fell in love with the fair Anne Boleyn, and said to himself, "How can I be best rid of my own troublesome wife whom I am tired of, and marry Anne?"

You recollect that Queen Catherine had been the wife of Henry's brother. What does the King do, after thinking it over, but calls his favourite priests about him, and says, O! his mind is in such a dreadful state, and he is so frightfully uneasy, because he is afraid it was not lawful for him to marry the Queen! Not one of those priests had the courage to hint that it was rather curious he had never thought of that before, and that his mind seemed to have been in a tolerably jolly condition during a great many years, in which he certainly had not fretted himself thin; but, they all said, Ah! that was very true, and it was a serious business; and perhaps the best way to make it right, would be for his Majesty to be divorced! The King replied, Yes, he thought that would be the best way, certainly; so they all went to work.

If I were to relate to you the intrigues and plots that took place in the endeavour to get this divorce, you would think the History of

England the most tiresome book in the world. So I shall say no more, than that after a vast deal of negotiation and evasion, the Pope issued a commission to Cardinal Wolsey and CARDINAL CAMPEGGIO (whom he sent over from Italy for the purpose), to try the whole case in England. It is supposed—and I think with reason—that Wolsey was the Queen's enemy, because she had reproved him for his proud and gorgeous manner of life. But, he did not at first know that the King wanted to marry Anne Boleyn; and when he did know it, he even went down on his knees, in the endeavour to dissuade him.

The Cardinals opened their court in the Convent of the Black Friars, near to where the bridge of that name in London now stands; and the King and Queen, that they might be near it, took up their lodgings at the adjoining palace of Bridewell, of which nothing now remains but a bad prison. On the opening of the court, when the King and Queen were called on to appear, that poor ill-used lady, with a dignity and firmness and yet with a womanly affection worthy to be always admired, went and kneeled at the King's feet, and said that she had come, a stranger, to his dominions; that she had been a good and true wife to him for twenty years; and that she could acknowledge no power in those Cardinals to try whether she should be considered his wife after all that time, or should be put away. With that, she got up and left the court, and would never afterwards come back to it.

The King pretended to be very much overcome, and said, O! my lords and gentlemen, what a good woman she was to be sure, and how delighted he would be to live with her unto death, but for that terrible uneasiness in his mind which was quite wearing him away! So, the case went on, and there was nothing but talk for two months. Then Cardinal Campeggio, who, on behalf of the Pope, wanted nothing so much as delay, adjourned it for two more months; and before that time was elapsed, the Pope himself adourned it indefinitely, by re-quiring the King and Queen to come to Rome and have it tried there. But by good luck for the King, word was brought to him by some of his people, that they had happened to meet at supper, THOMAS CRANMER, a learned Doctor of Cambridge, who had proposed to urge the Pope on, by referring the case to all the learned doctors and bishops, here and there and everywhere, and getting their opinions that the King's marriage was unlawful. The King, who was now in a hurry to marry Anne Boleyn, thought this such a good idea, that he sent for Cranmer, post haste, and said to LORD ROCHFORT, Anne Boleyn's father, "Take this learned Doctor down to your country-house, and there let him have a good room for a study, and no end of books out of which to prove that I may marry your daughter." Lord Rochfort, not at all reluctant, made the learned Doctor as comfort-able as he could; and the learned Doctor went to work to prove his case. All this time, the King and Anne Boleyn were writing letters to one another almost daily, full of impatience to have the case settled; and Anne Boleyn was showing herself (as I think) very worthy of the fate which afterwards befel her.

It was bad for Cardinal Wolsey that he had left Cranmer to render this help. It was worse for him that he had tried to dissuade the King from marrying Anne Boleyn. Such a servant as he, to such a master as Henry, would probably have fallen in any case; but, between the hatred of the party of the Queen that was, and the hatred of the party of the Queen that was to be, he fell suddenly and heavily. Going down one day to the Court of Chancery, where he now presided, he was waited upon by the Dukes of Norfolk and Suffolk, who told him that they brought an order to him to resign that office, and to withdraw quietly to a house he had at Esher, in Surrey. The Cardinal refusing, they rode off to the King; and next day came back with a letter from him, on reading which, the Cardinal submitted. An inventory was made out of all the riches in his palace at York Place (now Whitehall), and he went sorrowfully up the river, in his barge, to Putney. An abject man he was, in spite of his pride; for being overtaken, riding out of that place towards Esher, by one of the King's chamberlains who brought him a kind message and a ring, he alighted from his mule, took off his cap, and kneeled down in the dirt. His poor Fool, whom in his prosperous days he had always kept in his palace to entertain him, cut a far better figure than he; for, when the Cardinal said to the chamberlain that he had nothing to send to his lord the King as a present, but that jester who was a most excellent one, it took six strong yeomen to remove the faithful fool from his master.

The once proud Cardinal was soon further disgraced, and wrote the most abject letters to his vile sovereign; who humbled him one day and encouraged him the next, according to his humour, until he was at last ordered to go and reside in his diocese of York. He said he was too poor; but I don't know how he made that out, for he took a hundred and sixty servants with him, and seventy-two cart-loads of furniture, food, and wine. He remained in that part of the country for the best part of a year, and showed himself so improved by his misfortunes, and was so mild and so conciliating, that he won all hearts. And indeed, even in his proud days, he had done some magnificent things for learning and education. At last, he was arrested for high treason; and, coming slowly on his journey towards London, got as far as Leicester. Arriving at Leicester Abbey after dark, and very ill, he said—when the monks came out at the gate with lighted torches to receive him—that he had come to lay his bones among them. He had indeed; for he was taken to a bed, from which he never rose again. His last words were, "Had I but served God as diligently as I have served the King, He would not have given me over, in my grey hairs. Howbeit, this is my just reward for my pains and diligence, not regarding my service to God, but only my duty to my prince." The news of his death was quickly carried to the King, who was amusing himself with archery in the garden of the magnificent Palace at Hampton Court, which that very Wolsey had presented to him. The greatest emotion his royal mind displayed at the loss of a servant so faithful and so ruined, was a particular desire to lay hold of fifteen hundred pounds which the Cardinal was reported to have hidden somewhere.

The opinions concerning the divorce, of the learned doctors and bishops and others, being at last collected, and being generally in the King's favour, were forwarded to the Pope, with an entreaty that he would now grant it. The unfortunate Pope, who was a timid man, was half distracted between his fear of his authority being set aside in England if he did not do as he was asked, and his dread of offending the Emperor of Germany, who was Queen Catherine's nephew. In this state of mind he still evaded and did nothing. Then, THOMAS CROMWELL, who had been one of Wolsey's faithful attendants, and had remained so even in his decline, advised the King to take the matter into his own hands, and make himself the head of the whole Church. This, the King by various artful means, began to do; but he recompensed the clergy by allowing them to burn as many people as they pleased, for holding Luther's opinions. You must understand that Sir Thomas More, the wise man who had helped the King with his book, had been made Chancellor in Wolsey's place. But, as he was truly attached to the Church as it was even in its abuses, he, in this state of things, resigned.

Being now quite resolved to get rid of Queen Catherine, and to marry Anne Boleyn without more ado, the King made Cranmer Archbishop of Canterbury, and directed Queen Catherine to leave the Court. She obeyed; but replied that wherever she went, she was Queen of England still, and would remain so, to the last. The King then married Anne Boleyn privately; and the new Archbishop of Canterbury, within half a year, declared his marriage with Queen Catherine void, and crowned Anne Boleyn Queen.

She might have known that no good could ever come from such wrong, and that the corpulent brute who had been so faithless and so cruel to his first wife, could be more faithless and more cruel to his second. She might have known that, even when he was in love with her, he had been a mean and selfish coward, running away, like a frightened cur, from her society and her house, when a dangerous sickness broke out in it, and when she might easily have taken it and died, as several of the household did. But, Anne Boleyn arrived at all this knowledge too late, and bought it at a dear price. Her bad marriage with a worse man came to its natural end.   Its natural end was not, as we shall too soon see, a natural death for her.

CHAPTER XXVIII

ENGLAND UNDER HENRY THE EIGHTH

PART THE SECOND

THE Pope was thrown into a very angry state of mind when he heard of the King's marriage, and fumed exceedingly. Many of the English monks and friars, seeing that their order was in danger, did the same; some even declaimed against the King in church before his face, and were not to be stopped until he himself roared out "Silence!" The King, not much the worse for this, took it pretty quietly; and was very glad when his Queen gave birth to a daughter, who was christened ELIZABETH, and declared Princess of Wales as her sister Mary had already been.

One of the most atrocious features of this reign was that Henry the Eighth was always trimming between the reformed religion and the unreformed one; so that the more he quarrelled with the Pope, the more of his own subjects he roasted alive for not holding the Pope's opinions. Thus, an unfortunate student named John Frith, and a poor simple tailor named Andrew Hewet who loved him very much, and said that whatever John Frith believed *he* believed, were burnt in Smithfield—to show what a capital Christian the King was.

But, these were speedily followed by two much greater victims, Sir Thomas More, and John Fisher, the Bishop of Rochester. The latter, who was a good and amiable old man, had committed no greater offence than believing in Elizabeth Barton, called the Maid of Kent—another of those ridiculous women who pretended to be inspired, and to make all sorts of heavenly revelations, though they indeed uttered nothing but evil nonsense. For this offence—as it was pretended, but really for denying the King to be the supreme Head of the Church—he got into trouble, and was put in prison; but, even then, he might have been suffered to die naturally (short work having been made of executing the Kentish Maid and her principal followers), but that the Pope, to spite the King, resolved to make him a cardinal. Upon that the King made a ferocious joke to the effect that the Pope might send Fisher a red hat—which is the way they make a cardinal—but he should have no head on which to wear it; and he was tried with all unfairness and injustice, and sentenced to death. He died like a noble and virtuous old man, and left a worthy name behind him. The King supposed, I dare say, that Sir Thomas More would be frightened by this example; but, as he was not to be easily terrified, and, thoroughly believing in the Pope, had made up his mind that the King was not the rightful Head of the Church, he positively refused to say that he was. For this crime he too was tried and sentenced, after having been in prison a whole year. When he was doomed to death, and came away from his trial with the edge of the executioner's axe turned towards him—as was always done in those times when a state prisoner came to that hopeless pass—he bore it quite serenely, and gave his blessing to his son, who pressed through the crowd in Westminster Hall and kneeled down to receive it. But, when he got to the Tower Wharf on his way back to his prison, and his favourite daughter, MARGARET ROPER, a very good woman, rushed through the guards again and again, to kiss him and to weep upon his neck, he was overcome at last. He soon recovered, and never more showed any feeling but cheerfulness and courage. When he was going up the steps of the scaffold to his death, he said jokingly to the Lieutenant of the

Tower, observing that they were weak and shook beneath his tread, "I pray you, master Lieutenant, see me safe up; and, for my coming down, I can shift for myself." Also he said to the executioner, after he had laid his head upon the block, "Let me put my beard out of the way; for that, at least, has never committed any treason." Then his head was struck off at a blow. These two executions were worthy of King Henry the Eighth. Sir Thomas More was one of the most virtuous men in his dominions, and the Bishop was one of his oldest and truest friends. But to be a friend of that fellow was almost as dangerous as to be his wife.

When the news of these two murders got to Rome, the Pope raged against the murderer more than ever Pope raged since the world began, and prepared a Bull, ordering his subjects to take arms against him and dethrone him. The King took all possible precautions to keep that document out of his dominions, and set to work in return to suppress a great number of the English monasteries and abbeys.

This destruction was begun by a body of commissioners, of whom Cromwell (whom the King had taken into great favour) was the head; and was carried on through some few years to its entire completion. There is no doubt that many of these religious establishments were religious in nothing but in name, and were crammed with lazy, indolent, and sensual monks. There is no doubt that they imposed upon the people in every possible way; that they had images moved by wires, which they pretended were miraculously moved by Heaven; that they had among them a whole tun measure full of teeth, all purporting to have come out of the head of one saint, who must indeed have been a very extraordinary person with that enormous allowance of grinders; that they had bits of coal which they said had fried Saint Lawrence, and bits of toe-nails which they said belonged to other famous saints; penknives, and boots, and girdles, which they said belonged to others; and that all these bits of rubbish were called Relics, and adored by the ignorant people. But, on the other hand, there is no doubt either, that the King's officers and men punished the good monks with the bad; did great injustice; demolished many beautiful things and many valuable libraries; destroyed numbers of paintings, stained glass windows, fine pavements, and carvings; and that the whole court were ravenously greedy and rapacious for the division of this great spoil among them. The King seems to have grown almost mad in the ardour of this pursuit; for he declared Thomas à Becket a traitor, though he had been dead so many years, and had his body dug up out of his grave. He must have been as miraculous as the monks pretended, if they had told the truth, for he was found with one head on his shoulders, and they had shown another as his undoubted and genuine head ever since his death; it had brought them vast sums of money, too. The gold and jewels on his shrine filled two great chests, and eight men tottered as they carried them away. How rich the monasteries were you may infer from the fact that, when they were all suppressed, one hundred and thirty thousand pounds a year—in those days an immense sum—came to the Crown.

These things were not done without causing great discontent among the people. The monks had been good landlords and hospitable entertainers of all travellers, and had been accustomed to give away a great deal of corn, and fruit, and meat, and other things. In those days it was difficult to change goods into money, in consequence of the roads being very few and very bad, and the carts and waggons of the worst description; and they must either have given away some of the good things they possessed in enormous quantities, or have suffered them to spoil and moulder. So, many of the people missed what it was more agreeable to get idly than to work for; and the monks who were driven out of their homes and wandered about encouraged their discontent; and there were, consequently, great risings in Lincolnshire and Yorkshire. These were put down by terrific executions from which the monks themselves did not escape, and the King went on grunting and growling in his own fat way, like a Royal pig.

I have told all this story of the religious houses at one time, to make it plainer, and to get back to the King's domestic affairs.

The unfortunate Queen Catherine was by this time dead; and the King was by this time as tired of his second Queen as he had been of his first. As he had fallen in love with Anne when she was in the service of Catherine, so he now fell in love with another lady in the service of Anne. See how wicked deeds are punished, and how bitterly and self-reproachfully the Queen must now have thought of her own rise to the throne! The new fancy was a LADY JANE SEYMOUR; and the King no sooner set his mind on her, than he resolved to have Anne Boleyn's head. So, he brought a number of charges against Anne, accusing her of dreadful crimes which she had never committed, and implicating in them her own brother and certain gentlemen in her service: among whom one Norris, and Mark Smeaton a musician, are best remembered. As the lords and councillors were as afraid of the King and as subservient to him as the meanest peasant in England was, they brought in Anne Boleyn guilty, and the other unfortunate persons accused with her, guilty too. Those gentlemen died like men, with the exception of Smeaton, who had been tempted by the King into telling lies, which he called confessions, and who had expected to be pardoned; but who, I am very glad to say, was not. There was then only the Queen to dispose of. She had been surrounded in the Tower with women spies; had been monstrously persecuted and foully slandered; and had received no justice. But her spirit rose with her afflictions; and, after having in vain tried to soften the King by writing an affecting letter to him which still exists, "from her doleful prison in the Tower," she resigned herself to death. She said to those about her, very cheerfully, that she had heard say the executioner was a good one, and that she had a little neck (she laughed and clasped it with her hands as she said that), and would soon be out of her pain. And she *was* soon out of her pain, poor creature, on the Green inside the Tower, and her body was flung into an old box and put away in the ground under the chapel.

There is a story that the King sat in his palace listening very anxiously for the sound of the cannon which was to announce this new murder; and that, when he heard it come booming on the air, he rose up in great spirits and ordered out his dogs to go a-hunting. He was bad enough to do it; but whether he did it or not, it is certain that he married Jane Seymour the very next day.

I have not much pleasure in recording that she lived just long enough to give birth to a son who was christened EDWARD, and then to die of a fever: for, I cannot but think that any woman who married such a ruffian, and knew what innocent blood was on his hands, deserved the axe that would assuredly have fallen on the neck of Jane Seymour, if she had lived much longer.

Cranmer had done what he could to save some of the Church property for purposes of religion and education; but, the great families had been so hungry to get hold of it, that very little could be rescued for such objects. Even MILES COVERDALE, who did the people the inestimable service of translating the Bible into English (which the unreformed religion never permitted to be done), was left in poverty while the great families clutched the Church lands and money. The people had been told that when the Crown came into possession of these funds, it would not be necessary to tax them; but they were taxed afresh directly afterwards. It was fortunate for them, indeed, that so many nobles were so greedy for this wealth; since, if it had remained with the Crown, there might have been no end to tyranny for hundreds of years. One of the most active writers on the Church's side against the King was a member of his own family —a sort of distant cousin, REGINALD POLE by name—who attacked him in the most violent manner (though he received a pension from him all the time), and fought for the Church with his pen, day and night. As he was beyond the King's reach—being in Italy—the King politely invited him over to discuss the subject; but he, knowing better than to come, and wisely staying where he was, the King's rage fell upon his brother Lord Montague, the Marquis of Exeter, and some other gentlemen: who were tried for high treason in corresponding with him and aiding him—which they probably did—and were all executed. The Pope made Reginald Pole a cardinal; but, so much against his will, that it is thought he even aspired in his own mind to the vacant throne of England, and had hopes of marrying the Princess Mary. His being made a high priest, however, put an end to all that. His mother, the venerable Countess of Salisbury— who was, unfortunately for herself, within the tyrant's reach—was the last of his relatives on whom his wrath fell. When she was told to lay her grey head upon the block, she answered the executioner, "No! My head never committed treason, and if you want it, you shall seize it." So, she ran round and round the scaffold with the executioner striking at her, and her grey hair bedabbled with blood; and even when they held her down upon the block she moved her head about to the last, resolved to be no party to her own barbarous murder. All this the people bore, as they had borne everything else.

Indeed they bore much more; for the slow fires of Smithfield were continually burning, and people were constantly being roasted to death—still to show what a good Christian the King was. He defied the Pope and his Bull, which was now issued, and had come into England; but he burned innumerable people whose only offence was that they differed from the Pope's religious opinions. There was a wretched man named LAMBERT, among others, who was tried for this before the King, and with whom six bishops argued one after another. When he was quite exhausted (as well he might be, after six bishops), he threw himself on the King's mercy; but the King blustered out that he had no mercy for heretics. So, *he* too fed the fire.

All this the people bore, and more than all this yet. The national spirit seems to have been banished from the kingdom at this time. The very people who were executed for treason, the very wives and friends of the "bluff" King, spoke of him on the scaffold as a good prince, and a gentle prince—just as serfs in similar circumstances have been known to do, under the Sultan and Bashaws of the East, or under the fierce old tyrants of Russia, who poured boiling and freezing water on them alternately, until they died. The Parliament were as bad as the rest, and gave the King whatever he wanted; among other vile accommodations, they gave him new powers of murdering, at his will and pleasure, any one whom he might choose to call a traitor. But the worst measure they passed was an Act of Six Articles, commonly called at the time "the whip with six strings;" which punished offences against the Pope's opinions, without mercy, and enforced the very worst parts of the monkish religion. Cranmer would have modified it, if he could; but, being overborne by the Romish party, had not the power. As one of the articles declared that priests should not marry, and as he was married himself, he sent his wife and children into Germany, and began to tremble at his danger; none the less because he was, and had long been, the King's friend. This whip of six strings was made under the King's own eye. It should never be forgotten of him how cruelly he supported the worst of the Popish doctrines when there was nothing to be got by opposing them.

This amiable monarch now thought of taking another wife. He proposed to the French King to have some of the ladies of the French Court exhibited before him, that he might make his Royal choice; but the French King answered that he would rather not have his ladies trotted out to be shown like horses at a fair. He proposed to the Dowager Duchess of Milan, who replied that she might have thought of such a match if she had had two heads; but, that only owning one, she must beg to keep it safe. At last Cromwell represented that there was a Protestant Princess in Germany—those who held the reformed religion were called Protestants, because their leaders had Protested

against the abuses and impositions of the unreformed Church—
named ANNE OF CLEVES, who was beautiful, and would answer the
purpose admirably. The King said was she a large woman, because
he must have a fat wife? "O yes," said Cromwell; "she was very
large, just the thing." On hearing this the King sent over his famous
painter, Hans Holbein, to take her portrait. Hans made her out to
be so good-looking that the King was satisfied, and the marriage was
arranged. But, whether anybody had paid Hans to touch up the
picture; or whether Hans, like one or two other painters, flattered a
princess in the ordinary way of business, I cannot say: all I know is,
that when Anne came over and the King went to Rochester to meet
her, and first saw her without her seeing him, he swore she was "a
great Flanders mare," and said he would never marry her. Being
obliged to do it now matters had gone so far, he would not give her
the presents he had prepared, and would never notice her. He never
forgave Cromwell his part in the affair. His downfall dates from that
time.

It was quickened by his enemies, in the interests of the unreformed
religion, putting in the King's way, at a state dinner, a niece of the
Duke of Norfolk, CATHERINE HOWARD, a young lady of fascinating
manners, though small in stature and not particularly beautiful.
Falling in love with her on the spot, the King soon divorced Anne of
Cleves after making her the subject of much brutal talk, on pretence
that she had been previously betrothed to some one else—which
would never do for one of his dignity—and married Catherine. It is
probable that on his wedding day, of all days in the year, he sent his
faithful Cromwell to the scaffold, and had his head struck off. He
further celebrated the occasion by burning at one time, and causing
to be drawn to the fire on the same hurdles, some Protestant prisoners
for denying the Pope's doctrines, and some Roman Catholic prisoners
for denying his own supremacy. Still the people bore it, and not a
gentleman in England raised his hand.

But, by a just retribution, it soon came out that Catherine Howard,
before her marriage, had been really guilty of such crimes as the
King had falsely attributed to his second wife Anne Boleyn; so, again
the dreadful axe made the King a widower, and this Queen passed
away as so many in that reign had passed away before her. As an
appropriate pursuit under the circumstances, Henry then applied
himself to superintending the composition of a religious book called
"A necessary doctrine for any Christian Man." He must have been
a little confused in his mind, I think, at about this period; for he was
so false to himself as to be true to some one: that some one being
Cranmer, whom the Duke of Norfolk and others of his enemies tried
to ruin; but to whom the King was steadfast, and to whom he one
night gave his ring, charging him when he should find himself, next
day, accused of treason, to show it to the council board. This Cranmer did to the confusion of his enemies. I suppose the King thought
he might want him a little longer.

He married yet once more. Yes, strange to say, he found in England another woman who would become his wife, and she was CATHERINE PARR, widow of Lord Latimer. She leaned towards the reformed religion; and it is some comfort to know, that she tormented the King considerably by arguing a variety of doctrinal points with him on all possible occasions. She had very nearly done this to her own destruction. After one of these conversations the King in a very black mood actually instructed GARDINER, one of his Bishops who favoured the Popish opinions, to draw a bill of accusation against her, which would have inevitably brought her to the scaffold where her predecessors had died, but that one of her friends picked up the paper of instructions which had been dropped in the palace, and gave her timely notice. She fell ill with terror; but managed the King so well when he came to entrap her into further statements—by saying that she had only spoken on such points to divert his mind and to get some information from his extraordinary wisdom—that he gave her a kiss and called her his sweetheart. And, when the Chancellor came next day actually to take her to the Tower, the King sent him about his business, and honoured him with the epithets of a beast, a knave, and a fool. So near was Catherine Parr to the block, and so narrow was her escape!

There was war with Scotland in this reign, and a short clumsy war with France for favouring Scotland; but, the events at home were so dreadful, and leave such an enduring stain on the country, that I need say no more of what happened abroad.

A few more horrors, and this reign is over. There was a lady, ANNE ASKEW, in Lincolnshire, who inclined to the Protestant opinions, and whose husband being a fierce Catholic, turned her out of his house. She came to London, and was considered as offending against the six articles, and was taken to the Tower, and put upon the rack—probably because it was hoped that she might, in her agony, criminate some obnoxious persons; if falsely, so much the better. She was tortured without uttering a cry, until the Lieutenant of the Tower would suffer his men to torture her no more; and then two priests who were present actually pulled off their robes, and turned the wheels of the rack with their own hands, so rending and twisting and breaking her that she was afterwards carried to the fire in a chair. She was burned with three others, a gentleman, a clergyman, and a tailor; and so the world went on.

Either the King became afraid of the power of the Duke of Norfolk, and his son the Earl of Surrey, or they gave him some offence, but he resolved to pull *them* down, to follow all the rest who were gone. The son was tried first—of course for nothing—and defended himself bravely; but of course he was found guilty, and of course he was executed. Then his father was laid hold of, and left for death too.

But the King himself was left for death by a Greater King, and the earth was to be rid of him at last. He was now a swollen, hideous spectacle, with a great hole in his leg, and so odious to every sense that it was dreadful to approach him. When he was found to be dying, Cranmer was sent for from his palace at Croydon, and came with all speed, but found him speechless. Happily, in that hour he perished. He was in the fifty-sixth year of his age, and the thirty-eighth of his reign.

Henry the Eighth has been favoured by some Protestant writers, because the Reformation was achieved in his time. But the mighty merit of it lies with other men and not with him; and it can be rendered none the worse by this monster's crimes, and none the better by any defence of them. The plain truth is, that he was a most intolerable ruffian, a disgrace to human nature, and a blot of blood and grease upon the History of England.

CHAPTER XXIX

ENGLAND UNDER EDWARD THE SIXTH

HENRY THE EIGHTH had made a will, appointing a council of sixteen to govern the kingdom for his son while he was under age (he was now only ten years old), and another council of twelve to help them. The most powerful of the first council was the EARL OF HERTFORD, the young King's uncle, who lost no time in bringing his nephew with great state up to Enfield, and thence to the Tower. It was considered at the time a striking proof of virtue in the young King that he was sorry for his father's death; but, as common subjects have that virtue too, sometimes, we will say no more about it.

There was a curious part of the late King's will, requiring his executors to fulfil whatever promises he had made. Some of the court wondering what these might be, the Earl of Hertford and the other noblemen interested, said that they were promises to advance and enrich *them*. So, the Earl of Hertford made himself DUKE OF SOMERSET, and made his brother EDWARD SEYMOUR a baron; and there were various similar promotions, all very agreeable to the parties concerned, and very dutiful, no doubt, to the late King's memory. To be more dutiful still, they made themselves rich out of the Church lands, and were very comfortable. The new Duke of Somerset caused himself to be declared PROTECTOR of the kingdom, and was, indeed, the King.

As young Edward the Sixth had been brought up in the principles of the Protestant religion, everybody knew that they would be maintained. But Cranmer, to whom they were chiefly entrusted, advanced them steadily and temperately. Many superstitious and ridiculous practices were stopped; but practices which were harmless were not interfered with.

The Duke of Somerset, the Protector, was anxious to have the young King engaged in marriage to the young Queen of Scotland, in order to prevent that princess from making an alliance with any foreign power; but, as a large party in Scotland were unfavourable to this plan, he invaded that country. His excuse for doing so was, that the Border men—that is, the Scotch who lived in that part of the country where England and Scotland joined—troubled the English very much. But there were two sides to this question; for the English Border men troubled the Scotch too; and, through many long years, there were perpetual border quarrels which gave rise to numbers of old tales and songs. However, the Protector invaded Scotland; and ARRAN, the Scottish Regent, with an army twice as large as his, advanced to meet him. They encountered on the banks of the river Esk, within a few miles of Edinburgh; and there, after a little skirmish, the Protector made such moderate proposals, in offering to retire if the Scotch would only engage not to marry their princess to any foreign prince, that the Regent thought the English were afraid. But in this he made a horrible mistake; for the English soldiers on land, and the English sailors on the water, so set upon the Scotch, that they broke and fled, and more than ten thousand of them were killed. It was a dreadful battle, for the fugitives were slain without mercy. The ground for four miles, all the way to Edinburgh, was strewn with dead men, and with arms, and legs, and heads. Some hid themselves in streams and were drowned; some threw away their armour and were killed running, almost naked; but in this battle of Pinkey the English lost only two or three hundred men. They were much better clothed than the Scotch; at the poverty of whose appearance and country they were exceedingly astonished.

A Parliament was called when Somerset came back, and it repealed the whip with six strings, and did one or two other good things; though it unhappily retained the punishment of burning for those people who did not make believe to believe, in all religious matters, what the Government had declared that they must and should believe. It also made a foolish law (meant to put down beggars), that any man who lived idly and loitered about for three days together, should be burned with a hot iron, made a slave, and wear an iron fetter. But this savage absurdity soon came to an end, and went the way of a great many other foolish laws.

The Protector was now so proud that he sat in Parliament before all the nobles, on the right hand of the throne. Many other noblemen, who only wanted to be as proud if they could get a chance, became his enemies of course; and it is supposed that he came back suddenly from Scotland because he had received news that his brother, LORD SEYMOUR, was becoming dangerous to him. This lord was now High Admiral of England; a very handsome man, and a great favourite with the Court ladies—even with the young Princess Elizabeth, who romped with him a little more than young princesses in these times do with any one. He had married Catherine Parr, the late King's widow, who was now dead; and, to strengthen his power, he secretly supplied the young King with money. He may even have engaged with some of his brother's enemies in a plot to carry the boy off. On these and other accusations, at any rate, he was confined in the Tower, impeached, and found guilty; his own brother's name being—unnatural and sad to tell—the first signed to the warrant for his execution. He was executed on Tower Hill, and died denying his treason. One of his last proceedings in this world was to write two letters, one to the Princess Elizabeth, and one to the Princess Mary, which a servant of his took charge of, and concealed in his shoe. These letters are supposed to have urged them against his brother, and to revenge his death. What they truly contained is not known; but there is no doubt that he had, at one time, obtained great influence over the Princess Elizabeth.

All this while, the Protestant religion was making progress. The images which the people had gradually come to worship, were removed from the churches; the people were informed that they need not confess themselves to priests unless they chose; a common prayer-book was drawn up in the English language, which all could understand; and many other improvements were made; still moderately. For Cranmer was a very moderate man, and even restrained the Protestant clergy from violently abusing the unreformed religion —as they very often did, and which was not a good example. But the people were at this time in great distress. The rapacious nobility who had come into possession of the Church lands, were very bad landlords. They enclosed great quantities of ground for the feeding of sheep, which was then more profitable than the growing of crops; and this increased the general distress. So the people, who still understood little of what was going on about them, and still readily believed what the homeless monks told them—many of whom had been their good friends in their better days—took it into their heads that all this was owing to the reformed religion, and therefore rose in many parts of the country.

The most powerful risings were in Devonshire and Norfolk. In Devonshire, the rebellion was so strong that ten thousand men united within a few days, and even laid siege to Exeter. But LORD RUSSELL, coming to the assistance of the citizens who defended that town, defeated the rebels; and, not only hanged the Mayor of one place, but hanged the vicar of another from his own church steeple. What with hanging and killing by the sword, four thousand of the rebels are supposed to have fallen in that one county. In Norfolk (where the rising was more against the enclosure of open lands than against the reformed religion), the popular leader was a man named ROBERT KET, a tanner of Wymondham. The mob were, in the first instance, excited against the tanner by one JOHN FLOWERDEW, a gentleman who owed him a grudge: but the tanner was more than a match for the gentleman, since he soon got the people on his side, and established himself near Norwich with quite an army. There was a large oak-tree in that place, on a spot called Moushold Hill, which Ket named the Tree of Reformation; and under its green boughs, he and his men sat, in the midsummer weather, holding courts of justice, and debating affairs of state. They were even impartial enough to allow some rather tiresome public speakers to get up into this Tree of Reformation, and point out their errors to them, in long discourses, while they lay listening (not always without some grumbling and growling) in the shade below. At last, one sunny July day, a herald appeared below the tree, and proclaimed Ket and all his men traitors, unless from that moment they dispersed and went home: in which case they were to receive a pardon. But, Ket and his men made light of the herald and became stronger than ever, until the Earl of Warwick went after them with a sufficient force, and cut them all to pieces. A few were hanged, drawn, and quartered, as traitors, and their limbs were sent into various country places to be a terror to the people. Nine of them were hanged upon nine green branches of the Oak of Reformation; and so, for the time, that tree may be said to have withered away.

The Protector, though a haughty man, had compassion for the real distresses of the common people, and a sincere desire to help them. But he was too proud and too high in degree to hold even their favour steadily; and many of the nobles always envied and hated him, because they were as proud and not as high as he. He was at this time building a great Palace in the Strand: to get the stone for which he blew up church steeples with gunpowder, and pulled down bishops' houses: thus making himself still more disliked. At length, his principal enemy, the Earl of Warwick—Dudley by name, and the son of that Dudley who had made himself so odious with Empson, in the reign of Henry the Seventh—joined with seven other members of the Council against him, formed a separate Council; and, becoming stronger in a few days, sent him to the Tower under twenty-nine articles of accusation. After being sentenced by the Council to the forfeiture of all his offices and lands, he was liberated and pardoned, on making a very humble submission. He was even taken back into the Council again, after having suffered this fall, and married his daughter, LADY ANNE SEYMOUR, to Warwick's eldest son. But such a reconciliation was little likely to last, and did not outlive a year. Warwick, having got himself made Duke of Northumberland, and having advanced the more important of his friends, then finished the history by causing the Duke of Somerset and his friend LORD GREY, and others, to be arrested for treason, in having conspired to seize and dethrone the King. They were also accused of having intended to seize the new Duke of Northumberland, with his friends LORD NORTHAMPTON and LORD PEMBROKE; to murder them if they found need; and to raise the City to revolt. All this the fallen Protector positively denied; except that he confessed to having spoken of the murder of those three noblemen, but having never designed it. He was acquitted of the charge of treason, and found guilty of the other charges; so when the people—who remembered his having been their friend, now that he was disgraced and in danger, saw him come out from his trial with the axe turned from him—they thought he was altogether acquitted, and set up a loud shout of joy.

But the Duke of Somerset was ordered to be beheaded on Tower Hill, at eight o'clock in the morning, and proclamations were issued bidding the citizens keep at home until after ten. They filled the streets, however, and crowded the place of execution as soon as it was light; and, with sad faces and sad hearts, saw the once powerful Protector ascend the scaffold to lay his head upon the dreadful block. While he was yet saying his last words to them with manly courage, and telling them, in particular, how it comforted him, at that pass, to have assisted in reforming the national religion, a member of the Council was seen riding up on horseback. They again thought that the Duke was saved by his bringing a reprieve, and again shouted for joy. But the Duke himself told them they were mistaken, and laid down his head and had it struck off at a blow.

Many of the bystanders rushed forward and steeped their hand-kerchiefs in his blood, as a mark of their affection. He had, indeed, been capable of many good acts, and one of them was discovered after he was no more. The Bishop of Durham, a very good man, had been informed against to the Council, when the Duke was in power, as having answered a treacherous letter proposing a rebellion against the reformed religion. As the answer could not be found, he could not be declared guilty; but it was now discovered, hidden by the Duke himself among some private papers, in his regard for that good man. The Bishop lost his office, and was deprived of his possessions.

It is not very pleasant to know that while his uncle lay in prison under sentence of death, the young King was being vastly entertained by plays, and dances, and sham fights: but there is no doubt of it, for he kept a journal himself. It is pleasanter to know that not a single Roman Catholic was burnt in this reign for holding that religion; though two wretched victims suffered for heresy. One, a woman named JOAN BOCHER, for professing some opinions that even she could only explain in unintelligible jargon. The other, a Dutch-man, named VON PARIS, who practised as a surgeon in London. Edward was, to his credit, exceedingly unwilling to sign the warrant for the woman's execution: shedding tears before he did so, and tell-ing Cranmer, who urged him to do it (though Cranmer really would have spared the woman at first, but for her own determined obstin-acy), that the guilt was not his, but that of the man who so strongly urged the dreadful act. We shall see, too soon, whether the time ever came when Cranmer is likely to have remembered this with sorrow and remorse.

Cranmer and RIDLEY (at first Bishop of Rochester, and afterwards Bishop of London) were the most powerful of the clergy of this reign. Others were imprisoned and deprived of their property for still adhering to the unreformed religion; the most important among whom were GARDINER Bishop of Winchester, HEATH Bishop of Worcester, DAY Bishop of Chichester, and BONNER that Bishop of London who was superseded by Ridley. The Princess Mary, who inherited her mother's gloomy temper, and hated the reformed religion as connected with her mother's wrongs and sorrows—she knew nothing else about it, always refusing to read a single book in which it was truly described—held by the unreformed religion too, and was the only person in the kingdom for whom the old Mass was allowed to be performed; nor would the young King have made that exception even in her favour, but for the strong persuasions of Cranmer and Ridley. He always viewed it with horror; and when he fell into a sickly condition, after having been very ill, first of the measles and then of the small-pox, he was greatly troubled in mind to think that if he died, and she, the next heir to the throne, succeeded, the Roman Catholic religion would be set up again.

This uneasiness, the Duke of Northumberland was not slow to encourage: for, if the Princess Mary came to the throne, he, who had taken part with the Protestants, was sure to be disgraced. Now, the Duchess of Suffolk was descended from King Henry the Seventh; and, if she resigned what little or no right she had, in favour of her daughter LADY JANE GREY, that would be the succession to promote the Duke's greatness; because LORD GUILDFORD DUDLEY, one of his sons, was, at this very time, newly married to her. So, he worked upon the King's fears, and persuaded him to set aside both the Princess Mary and the Princess Elizabeth, and assert his right to appoint his successor. Accordingly the young King handed to the Crown lawyers a writing signed half a dozen times over by himself, appointing Lady Jane Grey to succeed to the Crown, and requiring them to have his will made out according to law. They were much against it at first, and told the King so; but the Duke of Northumberland—being so violent about it that the lawyers even expected him to beat them, and hotly declaring that, stripped to his shirt, he would fight any man in such a quarrel—they yielded. Cranmer, also, at first hesitated; pleading that he had sworn to maintain the succession of the Crown to the Princess Mary; but, he was a weak man in his resolutions, and afterwards signed the document with the rest of the council.

It was completed none too soon; for Edward was now sinking in a rapid decline; and, by way of making him better, they handed him over to a woman-doctor who pretended to be able to cure it. He speedily got worse. On the sixth of July, in the year one thousand five hundred and fifty-three, he died, very peaceably and piously, praying God, with his last breath, to protect the reformed religion.

This King died in the sixteenth year of his age, and in the seventh of his reign. It is difficult to judge what the character of one so young might afterwards have become among so many bad, ambitious, quarrelling nobles. But, he was an amiable boy, of very good abilities, and had nothing coarse or cruel or brutal in his disposition—which in the son of such a father is rather surprising.

CHAPTER XXX

ENGLAND UNDER MARY

THE Duke of Northumberland was very anxious to keep the young King's death a secret, in order that he might get the two Princesses into his power. But, the Princess Mary, being informed of that event as she was on her way to London to see her sick brother, turned her horse's head, and rode away into Norfolk. The Earl of Arundel was her friend, and it was he who sent her warning of what had happened.

As the secret could not be kept, the Duke of Northumberland and the council sent for the Lord Mayor of London and some of the aldermen, and made a merit of telling it to them. Then, they made it known to the people, and set off to inform Lady Jane Grey that she was to be Queen.

She was a pretty girl of only sixteen, and was amiable, learned, and clever. When the lords who came to her, fell on their knees before her, and told her what tidings they brought, she was so astonished that she fainted. On recovering, she expressed her sorrow for the young King's death, and said that she knew she was unfit to govern the kingdom; but that if she must be Queen, she prayed God to direct her. She was then at Sion House, near Brentford; and the lords took her down the river in state to the Tower, that she might remain there (as the custom was) until she was crowned. But the people were not at all favourable to Lady Jane, considering that the right to be Queen was Mary's, and greatly disliking the Duke of Northumberland. They were not put into a better humour by the Duke's causing a vintner's servant, one Gabriel Pot, to be taken up for expressing his dissatisfaction among the crowd, and to have his ears nailed to the pillory, and cut off. Some powerful men among the nobility declared on Mary's side. They raised troops to support her cause, had her proclaimed Queen at Norwich, and gathered around her at the castle of Framlingham, which belonged to the Duke of Norfolk. For, she was not considered so safe as yet, but that it was best to keep her in a castle on the sea-coast, from whence she might be sent abroad, if necessary.

The Council would have despatched Lady Jane's father, the Duke of Suffolk, as the general of the army against this force; but, as Lady Jane implored that her father might remain with her, and as he was known to be but a weak man, they told the Duke of Northumberland that he must take the command himself. He was not very ready to do so, as he mistrusted the Council much; but there was no help for it, and he set forth with a heavy heart, observing to a lord who rode beside him through Shoreditch at the head of the troops, that, although the people pressed in great numbers to look at them, they were terribly silent.

And his fears for himself turned out to be well founded. While he was waiting at Cambridge for further help from the Council, the Council took it into their heads to turn their backs on Lady Jane's cause, and to take up the Princess Mary's. This was chiefly owing to the before-mentioned Earl of Arundel, who represented to the Lord Mayor and aldermen, in a second interview with those sagacious persons, that, as for himself, he did not perceive the Reformed religion to be in much danger—which Lord Pembroke backed by flourishing his sword as another kind of persuasion. The Lord Mayor and aldermen, thus enlightened, said there could be no doubt that the Princess Mary ought to be Queen. So, she was proclaimed at the Cross by St. Paul's, and barrels of wine were given to the people, and they got very drunk, and danced round blazing bonfires—little thinking, poor wretches, what other bonfires would soon be blazing in Queen Mary's name.

After a ten days' dream of royalty, Lady Jane Grey resigned the Crown with great willingness, saying that she had only accepted it in obedience to her father and mother; and went gladly back to her pleasant house by the river, and her books. Mary then came on towards London; and at Wanstead in Essex, was joined by her half-sister, the Princess Elizabeth. They passed through the streets of London to the Tower, and there the new Queen met some eminent prisoners then confined in it, kissed them, and gave them their liberty. Among these was that Gardiner, Bishop of Winchester, who had been imprisoned in the last reign for holding to the unreformed religion. Him she soon made chancellor.

The Duke of Northumberland had been taken prisoner, and, together with his son and five others, was quickly brought before the Council. He, not unnaturally, asked that Council, in his defence, whether it was treason to obey orders that had been issued under the great seal; and, if it were, whether they, who had obeyed them too, ought to be his judges? But they made light of these points; and, being resolved to have him out of the way, soon sentenced him to death. He had risen into power upon the death of another man, and made but a poor show (as might be expected) when he himself lay low. He entreated Gardiner to let him live, if it were only in a mouse's hole; and, when he ascended the scaffold to be beheaded on Tower Hill, addressed the people in a miserable way, saying that he had been incited by others, and exhorting them to return to the unreformed religion, which he told them was his faith. There seems reason to suppose that he expected a pardon even then, in return for this confession; but it matters little whether he did or not. His head was struck off.

Mary was now crowned Queen. She was thirty-seven years of age, short and thin, wrinkled in the face, and very unhealthy. But she had a great liking for show and for bright colours, and all the ladies of her Court were magnificently dressed. She had a great liking too for old customs, without much sense in them; and she was oiled in the oldest way, and blessed in the oldest way, and done all manner of things to in the oldest way, at her coronation. I hope they did her good.

She soon began to show her desire to put down the Reformed religion, and put up the unreformed one: though it was dangerous work as yet, the people being something wiser than they used to be. They even cast a shower of stones—and among them a dagger—at one of the royal chaplains who attacked the Reformed religion in a public sermon. But the Queen and her priests went steadily on. Ridley, the powerful bishop of the last reign, was seized and sent to the Tower. LATIMER, also celebrated among the Clergy of the last reign, was likewise sent to the Tower, and Cranmer speedily followed. Latimer was an aged man; and, as his guards took him through Smithfield, he looked round it, and said, "This is a place that hath long groaned for me." For he knew well, what kind of bonfires would soon be burning. Nor was the knowledge confined to him. The prisons were fast filled with the chief Protestants, who were there left rotting in darkness, hunger, dirt, and separation from their friends; many, who had time left them for escape, fled from the kingdom; and the dullest of the people began, now, to see what was coming.

It came on fast. A Parliament was got together; not without strong suspicion of unfairness; and they annulled the divorce, formerly pronounced by Cranmer between the Queen's mother and King Henry the Eighth, and unmade all the laws on the subject of religion that had been made in the last King Edward's reign. They began their proceedings, in violation of the law, by having the old mass said before them in Latin, and by turning out a bishop who would not kneel down. They also declared guilty of treason, Lady Jane Grey for aspiring to the Crown; her husband, for being her husband; and Cranmer, for not believing in the mass aforesaid. They then prayed the Queen graciously to choose a husband for herself, as soon as might be.

Now, the question who should be the Queen's husband had given rise to a great deal of discussion, and to several contending parties. Some said Cardinal Pole was the man—but the Queen was of opinion that he was *not* the man, he being too old and too much of a student. Others said that the gallant young COURTENAY, whom the Queen had made Earl of Devonshire, was the man—and the Queen thought so too, for a while; but she changed her mind. At last it appeared that PHILIP, PRINCE OF SPAIN, was certainly the man—though certainly not the people's man; for they detested the idea of such a marriage from the beginning to the end, and murmured that the Spaniard would establish in England, by the aid of foreign soldiers, the worst abuses of the Popish religion, and even the terrible Inquisition itself.

These discontents gave rise to a conspiracy for marrying young Courtenay to the Princess Elizabeth, and setting them up, with popular tumults all over the kingdom, against the Queen. This was discovered in time by Gardiner; but in Kent, the old bold county, the people rose in their old bold way. SIR THOMAS WYAT, a man of great daring, was their leader. He raised his standard at Maidstone, marched on to Rochester, established himself in the old castle there, and prepared to hold out against the Duke of Norfolk, who came against him with a party of the Queen's guards, and a body of five hundred London men. The London men, however, were all for Elizabeth, and not at all for Mary. They declared, under the castle walls, for Wyat; the Duke retreated; and Wyat came on to Deptford, at the head of fifteen thousand men.

But these, in their turn, fell away. When he came to Southwark, there were only two thousand left. Not dismayed by finding the London citizens in arms, and the guns at the Tower ready to oppose his crossing the river there, Wyat led them off to Kingston-upon-Thames, intending to cross the bridge that he knew to be in that place, and so to work his way round to Ludgate, one of the old gates of the City. He found the bridge broken down, but mended it, came across, and bravely fought his way up Fleet Street to Ludgate Hill. Finding the gate closed against him, he fought his way back again, sword in hand, to Temple Bar. Here, being overpowered, he surrendered himself, and three or four hundred of his men were taken, besides a hundred killed. Wyat, in a moment of weakness (and perhaps of torture) was afterwards made to accuse the Princess Elizabeth as his accomplice to some very small extent. But his manhood soon returned to him, and he refused to save his life by making any more false confessions. He was quartered and distributed in the usual brutal way, and from fifty to a hundred of his followers were hanged. The rest were led out, with halters round their necks, to be pardoned, and to make a parade of crying out, "God save Queen Mary!"

In the danger of this rebellion, the Queen showed herself to be a woman of courage and spirit. She disdained to retreat to any place of safety, and went down to the Guildhall, sceptre in hand, and made a gallant speech to the Lord Mayor and citizens. But on the day after Wyat's defeat, she did the most cruel act, even of her cruel reign, in signing the warrant for the execution of Lady Jane Grey.

They tried to persuade Lady Jane to accept the unreformed religion; but she steadily refused. On the morning when she was to die, she saw from her window the bleeding and headless body of her husband brought back in a cart from the scaffold on Tower Hill where he had laid down his life. But, as she had declined to see him before his execution, lest she should be overpowered and not make a good end, so, she even now showed a constancy and calmness that will never be forgotten. She came up to the scaffold with a firm step and a quiet face, and addressed the bystanders in a steady voice. They were not numerous; for she was too young, too innocent and fair, to be murdered before the people on Tower Hill, as her husband had just been; so, the place of her execution was within the Tower itself. She said that she had done an unlawful act in taking what was Queen Mary's right; but that she had done so with no bad intent, and that she died a humble Christian. She begged the executioner to despatch her quickly, and she asked him, "Will you take my head off before I lay me down?" He answered, "No, Madam," and then she was very quiet while they bandaged her eyes. Being blinded, and unable to see the block on which she was to lay her young head, she was seen to feel about for it with her hands, and was heard to say, confused, "O what shall I do! Where is it?" Then they guided her to the right place, and the executioner struck off her head. You know too well, now, what dreadful deeds the executioner did in England, through many, many years, and how his axe descended on the hateful block through the necks of some of the bravest, wisest, and best in the land. But it never struck so cruel and so vile a blow as this.

The father of Lady Jane soon followed, but was little pitied. Queen Mary's next object was to lay hold of Elizabeth, and this was pursued with great eagerness. Five hundred men were sent to her retired house at Ashridge, by Berkhampstead, with orders to bring her up, alive or dead. They got there at ten at night, when she was sick in bed. But, their leaders followed her lady into her bed-chamber, whence she was brought out betimes next morning, and put into a litter to be conveyed to London. She was so weak and ill, that she was five days on the road; still, she was so resolved to be seen by the people that she had the curtains of the litter opened; and so, very pale and sickly, passed through the streets. She wrote to her sister, saying she was innocent of any crime, and asking why she was made a prisoner; but she got no answer, and was ordered to the Tower. They took her in by the Traitor's Gate, to which she objected, but in vain. One of the lords who conveyed her offered to cover her with his cloak, as it was raining, but she put it away from her, proudly and scornfully, and passed into the Tower, and sat down in a court-yard on a stone. They besought her to come in out of the wet; but she answered that it was better sitting there, than in a worse place. At length she went to her apartment, where she was kept a prisoner, though not so close a prisoner as at Woodstock, whither she was afterwards removed, and where she is said to have one day envied a milkmaid whom she heard singing in the sunshine as she went through the green fields. Gardiner, than whom there were not many worse men among the fierce and sullen priests, cared little to keep secret his stern desire for her death: being used to say that it was of little service to shake off the leaves, and lop the branches of the tree of heresy, if its root, the hope of heretics, were left. He failed, however, in his benevolent design. Elizabeth was, at length, released; and Hatfield House was assigned to her as a residence, under the care of one SIR THOMAS POPE.

It would seem that Philip, the Prince of Spain, was a main cause of this change in Elizabeth's fortunes. He was not an amiable man, being, on the contrary, proud, overbearing, and gloomy; but he and the Spanish lords who came over with him, assuredly did discountenance the idea of doing any violence to the Princess. It may have been mere prudence, but we will hope it was manhood and honour.

The Queen had been expecting her husband with great impatience, and at length he came, to her great joy, though he never cared much for her. They were married by Gardiner, at Winchester, and there was more holiday-making among the people; but they had their old distrust of this Spanish marriage, in which even the Parliament shared. Though the members of that Parliament were far from honest, and were strongly suspected to have been bought with Spanish money, they would pass no bill to enable the Queen to set aside the Princess Elizabeth and appoint her own successor.

Although Gardiner failed in this object, as well as in the darker one of bringing the Princess to the scaffold, he went on at a great pace in the revival of the unreformed religion. A new Parliament was packed, in which there were no Protestants. Preparations were made to receive Cardinal Pole in England as the Pope's messenger, bringing his holy declaration that all the nobility who had acquired Church property, should keep it—which was done to enlist their selfish interest on the Pope's side. Then a great scene was enacted, which was the triumph of the Queen's plans. Cardinal Pole arrived in great splendour and dignity, and was received with great pomp. The Parliament joined in a petition expressive of their sorrow at the change in the national religion, and praying him to receive the country again into the Popish Church. With the Queen sitting on her throne, and the King on one side of her, and the Cardinal on the other, and the Parliament present, Gardiner read the petition aloud. The Cardinal then made a great speech, and was so obliging as to say that all was forgotten and forgiven, and that the kingdom was solemnly made Roman Catholic again.

Everything was now ready for the lighting of the terrible bonfires. The Queen having declared to the Council, in writing, that she would wish none of her subjects to be burnt without some of the Council being present, and that she would particularly wish there to be good sermons at all burnings, the Council knew pretty well what was to be done next. So, after the Cardinal had blessed all the bishops as a preface to the burnings, the Chancellor Gardiner opened a High Court at Saint Mary Overy, on the Southwark side of London Bridge, for the trial of heretics. Here, two of the late Protestant clergymen, HOOPER, Bishop of Gloucester, and ROGERS, a Prebendary of St. Paul's, were brought to be tried. Hooper was tried first for being married, though a priest, and for not believing in the mass. He admitted both of these accusations, and said that the mass was a wicked imposition. Then they tried Rogers, who said the same. Next morning the two were brought up to be sentenced; and then Rogers said that his poor wife, being a German woman and a stranger in the land, he hoped might be allowed to come to speak to him before he died. To this the inhuman Gardiner replied, that she was not his wife. "Yea, but she is, my lord," said Rogers, "and she hath been my wife these eighteen years." His request was still refused, and they were both sent to Newgate; all those who stood in the streets to sell things, being ordered to put out their lights that the people might not see them. But, the people stood at their doors with candles in their hands, and prayed for them as they went by. Soon afterwards, Rogers was taken out of jail to be burnt in Smithfield; and, in the crowd as he went along, he saw his poor wife and his ten children, of whom the youngest was a little baby. And so he was burnt to death.

The next day, Hooper, who was to be burnt at Gloucester, was brought out to take his last journey, and was made to wear a hood over his face that he might not be known by the people. But, they did know him for all that, down in his own part of the country; and, when he came near Gloucester, they lined the road, making prayers and lamentations. His guards took him to a lodging, where he slept soundly all night. At nine o'clock next morning, he was brought forth leaning on a staff; for he had taken cold in prison, and was infirm. The iron stake, and the iron chain which was to bind him to it, were fixed up near a great elm-tree in a pleasant open place before the cathedral, where, on peaceful Sundays, he had been accustomed to preach and to pray, when he was bishop of Gloucester. This tree, which had no leaves then, it being February, was filled with people; and the priests of Gloucester College were looking complacently on from a window, and there was a great concourse of spectators in every spot from which a glimpse of the dreadful sight could be beheld. When the old man kneeled down on the small platform at the foot of the stake, and prayed aloud, the nearest people were observed to be so attentive to his prayers that they were ordered to stand farther back; for it did not suit the Romish Church to have those Protestant words heard. His prayers concluded, he went up to the stake and was stripped to his shirt, and chained ready for the fire. One of his guards had such compassion on him that, to shorten his agonies, he tied some packets of gunpowder about him. Then they heaped up wood and straw and reeds, and set them all alight. But, unhappily, the wood was green and damp, and there was a wind blowing that blew what flame there was, away. Thus, through three-quarters of an hour, the good old man was scorched and roasted and smoked, as the fire rose and sank; and all that time they saw him, as he burned, moving his lips in prayer, and beating his breast with one hand, even after the other was burnt away and had fallen off.

Cranmer, Ridley, and Latimer, were taken to Oxford to dispute with a commission of priests and doctors about the mass. They were shamefully treated; and it is recorded that the Oxford scholars hissed and howled and groaned, and misconducted themselves in an any-thing but a scholarly way. The prisoners were taken back to jail, and afterwards tried in St. Mary's Church. They were all found guilty. On the sixteenth of the month of October, Ridley and Latimer were brought out, to make another of the dreadful bonfires.

The scene of the suffering of these two good Protestant men was in the City ditch, near Baliol College. On coming to the dreadful spot, they kissed the stakes, and then embraced each other. And then a learned doctor got up into a pulpit which was placed there, and preached a sermon from the text, "Though I give my body to be burned, and have not charity, it profiteth me nothing." When you think of the charity of burning men alive, you may imagine that this learned doctor had a rather brazen face. Ridley would have answered his sermon when it came to an end, but was not allowed. When Latimer was stripped, it appeared that he had dressed himself under his other clothes, in a new shroud; and, as he stood in it before all the people, it was noted of him, and long remembered, that, whereas he had been stooping and feeble but a few minutes before, he now stood upright and handsome, in the knowledge that he was dying for a just and a great cause. Ridley's brother-in-law was there with bags of gunpowder; and when they were both chained up, he tied them round their bodies. Then, a light was thrown upon the pile to fire it. "Be of good comfort, Master Ridley," said Latimer, at that awful moment, "and play the man! We shall this day light such a candle, by God's grace, in England, as I trust shall never be put out." And then he was seen to make motions with his hands as if he were washing them in the flames, and to stroke his aged face with them, and was heard to cry, "Father of Heaven, receive my soul!" He died quickly, but the fire, after having burned the legs of Ridley, sunk. There he lingered, chained to the iron post, and crying, "O! I cannot burn! O! for Christ's sake let the fire come unto me!" And still, when his brother-in-law had heaped on more wood, he was heard through the blinding smoke, still dismally crying, "O! I cannot burn, I cannot burn!" At last, the gunpowder caught fire, and ended his miseries.

Five days after this fearful scene, Gardiner went to his tremendous account before God, for the cruelties he had so much assisted in committing.

Cranmer remained still alive and in prison. He was brought out again in February, for more examining and trying, by Bonner, Bishop of London: another man of blood, who had succeeded to Gardiner's work, even in his lifetime, when Gardiner was tired of it. Cranmer was now degraded as a priest, and left for death; but, if the Queen hated any one on earth, she hated him, and it was resolved that he should be ruined and disgraced to the utmost. There is no doubt that the Queen and her husband personally urged on these deeds, because they wrote to the Council, urging them to be active in the kindling of the fearful fires. As Cranmer was known not to be a firm man, a plan was laid for surrounding him with artful people, and inducing him to recant to the unreformed religion. Deans and friars visited him, played at bowls with him, showed him various attentions, talked persuasively with him, gave him money for his prison comforts, and induced him to sign, I fear, as many as six recantations. But when, after all, he was taken out to be burnt, he was nobly true to his better self, and made a glorious end.

After prayers and a sermon, Dr. Cole, the preacher of the day (who had been one of the artful priests about Cranmer in prison), required him to make a public confession of his faith before the people. This, Cole did, expecting that he would declare himself a Roman Catholic. "I *will* make a profession of my faith," said Cranmer, "and with a good will too."

Then, he arose before them all, and took from the sleeve of his robe a written prayer and read it aloud. That done, he kneeled and said the Lord's Prayer, all the people joining; and then he arose again and told them that he believed in the Bible, and that in what he had lately written, he had written what was not the truth, and that, because his right hand had signed those papers, he would burn his right hand first when he came to the fire. As for the Pope, he did refuse him and denounce him as the enemy of Heaven. Hereupon the pious Dr. Cole cried out to the guards to stop that heretic's mouth and take him away.

So they took him away, and chained him to the stake, where he hastily took off his own clothes to make ready for the flames. And he stood before the people with a bald head and a white and flowing beard. He was so firm now when the worst was come, that he again declared against his recantation, and was so impressive and so undismayed, that a certain lord, who was one of the directors of the execution, called out to the men to make haste! When the fire was lighted, Cranmer, true to his latest word, stretched out his right hand, and crying out, "This hand hath offended!" held it among the flames, until it blazed and burned away. His heart was found entire among his ashes, and he left at last a memorable name in English history. Cardinal Pole celebrated the day by saying his first mass, and next day he was made Archbishop of Canterbury in Cranmer's place.

The Queen's husband, who was now mostly abroad in his own dominions, and generally made a coarse jest of her to his more familiar courtiers, was at war with France, and came over to seek the assistance of England. England was very unwilling to engage in a French war for his sake; but it happened that the King of France, at this very time, aided a descent upon the English coast. Hence, war was declared, greatly to Philip's satisfaction; and the Queen raised a sum of money with which to carry it on, by every unjustifiable means in her power. It met with no profitable return, for the French Duke of Guise surprised Calais, and the English sustained a complete defeat. The losses they met with in France greatly mortified the national pride, and the Queen never recovered the blow.

There was a bad fever raging in England at this time, and I am glad to write that the Queen took it, and the hour of her death came. "When I am dead and my body is opened," she said to those around her, "ye shall find CALAIS written on my heart." I should have thought, if anything were written on it, they would have found the words—JANE GREY, HOOPER, ROGERS, RIDLEY, LATIMER, CRANMER, AND THREE HUNDRED PEOPLE BURNT ALIVE WITHIN FOUR YEARS OF MY WICKED REIGN, INCLUDING SIXTY WOMEN AND FORTY LITTLE CHILDREN. But it is enough that their deaths were written in Heaven.

The Queen died on the seventeenth of November, fifteen hundred and fifty-eight, after reigning not quite five years and a half, and in the forty-fourth year of her age. Cardinal Pole died of the same fever next day.

As BLOODY QUEEN MARY, this woman has become famous, and as BLOODY QUEEN MARY, she will ever be justly remembered with horror and detestation in Great Britain. Her memory has been held in such abhorrence that some writers have arisen in later years to take her part, and to show that she was, upon the whole, quite an amiable and cheerful sovereign! "By their fruits ye shall know them," said OUR SAVIOUR. The stake and the fire were the fruits of this reign, and you will judge this Queen by nothing else.

CHAPTER XXXI

ENGLAND UNDER ELIZABETH

THERE was great rejoicing all over the land when the Lords of the Council went down to Hatfield, to hail the Princess Elizabeth as the new Queen of England. Weary of the barbarities of Mary's reign, the people looked with hope and gladness to the new Sovereign. The nation seemed to wake from a horrible dream; and Heaven, so long hidden by the smoke of the fires that roasted men and women to death, appeared to brighten once more.

Queen Elizabeth was five-and-twenty years of age when she rode through the streets of London, from the Tower to Westminster Abbey, to be crowned. Her countenance was strongly marked, but on the whole, commanding and dignified; her hair was red, and her nose something too long and sharp for a woman's. She was not the beautiful creature her courtiers made out; but she was well enough, and no doubt looked all the better for coming after the dark and gloomy Mary. She was well educated, but a roundabout writer, and rather a hard swearer and coarse talker. She was clever, but cunning and deceitful, and inherited much of her father's violent temper. I mention this now, because she has been so over-praised by one party, and so over-abused by another, that it is hardly possible to understand the greater part of her reign without first understanding what kind of woman she really was.

She began her reign with the great advantage of having a very wise and careful Minister, SIR WILLIAM CECIL, whom she afterwards made LORD BURLEIGH. Altogether, the people had greater reason for rejoicing than they usually had, when there were processions in the streets; and they were happy with some reason. All kinds of shows and images were set up; GOG and MAGOG were hoisted to the top of Temple Bar; and (which was more to the purpose) the Corporation dutifully presented the young Queen with the sum of a thousand marks in gold—so heavy a present, that she was obliged to take it into her carriage with both hands. The coronation was a great success; and, on the next day, one of the courtiers presented a petition to the new Queen, praying that as it was the custom to release some prisoners on such occasions, she would have the goodness to release the four Evangelists, Matthew, Mark, Luke, and John, and also the Apostle Saint Paul, who had been for some time shut up in a strange language so that the people could not get at them.

To this, the Queen replied that it would be better first to inquire of themselves whether they desired to be released or not; and, as a means of finding out, a great public discussion—a sort of religious tournament—was appointed to take place between certain champions of the two religions, in Westminster Abbey. You may suppose that it was soon made pretty clear to common sense, that for people to benefit by what they repeat or read, it is rather necessary they should understand something about it. Accordingly, a Church Service in plain English was settled, and other laws and regulations were made, completely establishing the great work of the Reformation. The Romish bishops and champions were not harshly dealt with, all things considered; and the Queen's ministers were both prudent and merciful.

The one great trouble of this reign, and the unfortunate cause of the greater part of such turmoil and bloodshed as occurred in it, was MARY STUART, QUEEN OF SCOTS. We will try to understand, in as few words as possible, who Mary was, what she was, and how she came to be a thorn in the royal pillow of Elizabeth.

She was the daughter of the Queen Regent of Scotland, MARY OF GUISE. She had been married, when a mere child, to the Dauphin, the son and heir of the King of France. The Pope, who pretended that no one could rightfully wear the crown of England without his gracious permission, was strongly opposed to Elizabeth, who had not asked for the said gracious permission. And as Mary Queen of Scots would have inherited the English crown in right of her birth, supposing the English Parliament not to have altered the succession, the Pope himself, and most of the discontented who were followers of his, maintained that Mary was the rightful Queen of England, and Elizabeth the wrongful Queen. Mary being so closely connected with France, and France being jealous of England, there was far greater danger in this than there would have been if she had had no alliance with that great power. And when her young husband, on the death of his father, became FRANCIS THE SECOND, King of France, the matter grew very serious. For, the young couple styled themselves King and Queen of England, and the Pope was disposed to help them by doing all the mischief he could.

Now, the reformed religion, under the guidance of a stern and powerful preacher, named JOHN KNOX, and other such men, had been making fierce progress in Scotland. It was still a half savage country, where there was a great deal of murdering and rioting continually going on; and the Reformers, instead of reforming those evils as they should have done, went to work in the ferocious old

Scottish spirit, laying churches and chapels waste, pulling down pictures and altars, and knocking about the Grey Friars, and the Black Friars, and the White Friars, and the friars of all sorts of colours, in all directions. This obdurate and harsh spirit of the Scottish reformers (the Scotch have always been rather a sullen and frowning people in religious matters) put up the blood of the Romish French court, and caused France to send troops over to Scotland, with the hope of setting the friars of all sorts of colours on their legs again; of conquering that country first, and England afterwards; and so crushing the Reformation all to pieces. The Scottish Reformers, who had formed a great league which they called The Congregation of the Lord, secretly represented to Elizabeth that, if the reformed religion got the worst of it with them, it would be likely to get the worst of it in England too; and thus, Elizabeth, though she had a high notion of the rights of Kings and Queens to do anything they liked, sent an army to Scotland to support the Reformers, who were in arms against their sovereign. All these proceedings led to a treaty of peace at Edinburgh, under which the French consented to depart from the kingdom. By a separate treaty, Mary and her young husband engaged to renounce their assumed title of King and Queen of England. But this treaty they never fulfilled.

It happened, soon after matters had got to this state, that the young French King died, leaving Mary a young widow. She was then invited by her Scottish subjects to return home and reign over them; and as she was not now happy where she was, she, after a little time, complied.

Elizabeth had been Queen three years, when Mary Queen of Scots embarked at Calais for her own rough, quarrelling country. As she came out of the harbour, a vessel was lost before her eyes, and she said, "O! good God! what an omen this is for such a voyage!" She was very fond of France, and sat on the deck, looking back at it and weeping, until it was quite dark. When she went to bed, she directed to be called at daybreak, if the French coast were still visible, that she might behold it for the last time. As it proved to be a clear morning, this was done, and she again wept for the country she was leaving, and said many times, "Farewell, France! Farewell, France! I shall never see thee again!" All this was long remembered afterwards, as sorrowful and interesting in a fair young princess of nineteen. Indeed, I am afraid it gradually came, together with her other distresses, to surround her with greater sympathy than she deserved.

When she came to Scotland, and took up her abode at the palace of Holyrood in Edinburgh, she found herself among uncouth strangers and wild uncomfortable customs very different from her experiences in the court of France. The very people who were disposed to love her, made her head ache when she was tired out by her voyage, with a serenade of discordant music—a fearful concert of bagpipes, I suppose—and brought her and her train home to her palace on miserable little Scotch horses that appeared to be half starved. Among the people who were not disposed to love her, she found the powerful leaders of the Reformed Church, who were bitter upon her amusements, however innocent, and denounced music and dancing as works of the devil. John Knox himself often lectured her, violently and angrily, and did much to make her life unhappy. All these reasons confirmed her old attachment to the Romish religion, and caused her, there is no doubt, most imprudently and dangerously both for herself and for England too, to give a solemn pledge to the heads of the Romish Church that if she ever succeeded to the English crown, she would set up that religion again. In reading her unhappy history, you must always remember this; and also that during her whole life she was constantly put forward against the Queen, in some form or other, by the Romish party.

That Elizabeth, on the other hand, was not inclined to like her, is pretty certain. Elizabeth was very vain and jealous, and had an extraordinary dislike to people being married. She treated Lady Catherine Grey, sister of the beheaded Lady Jane, with such shameful severity, for no other reason than her being secretly married, that she died and her husband was ruined; so, when a second marriage for Mary began to be talked about, probably Elizabeth disliked her more. Not that Elizabeth wanted suitors of her own, for they started up from Spain, Austria, Sweden, and England. Her English lover at this time, and one whom she much favoured too, was LORD ROBERT DUDLEY, Earl of Leicester—himself secretly married to AMY ROBSART, the daughter of an English gentleman, whom he was strongly suspected of causing to be murdered, down at his country seat, Cumnor Hall in Berkshire, that he might be free to marry the Queen. Upon this story, the great writer, SIR WALTER SCOTT, has founded one of his best romances. But if Elizabeth knew how to lead her handsome favourite on, for her own vanity and pleasure, she knew how to stop him for her own pride; and his love, and all the other proposals, came to nothing. The Queen always declared in good set speeches, that she would never be married at all, but would live and die a Maiden Queen. It was a very pleasant and meritorious declaration, I suppose; but it has been puffed and trumpeted so much, that I am rather tired of it myself.

Divers princes proposed to marry Mary, but the English court had reasons for being jealous of them all, and even proposed as a matter of policy that she should marry that very Earl of Leicester who had aspired to be the husband of Elizabeth. At last, LORD DARNLEY, son of the Earl of Lennox, and himself descended from the Royal Family of Scotland, went over with Elizabeth's consent to try his fortune at Holyrood. He was a tall simpleton; and could dance and play the guitar; but I know of nothing else he could do, unless it were to get very drunk, and eat gluttonously, and make a contemptible spectacle of himself in many mean and vain ways. However, he gained Mary's heart, not disdaining in the pursuit of his object to ally himself with one of her secretaries, DAVID RIZZIO, who had great influence with her. He soon married the Queen.

This marriage does not say much for her, but what followed will presently say less.

Mary's brother, the EARL OF MURRAY, and head of the Protestant party in Scotland, had opposed this marriage, partly on religious grounds, and partly perhaps from personal dislike of the very contemptible bridegroom. When it had taken place, through Mary's gaining over to it the more powerful of the lords about her, she banished Murray for his pains; and, when he and some other nobles rose in arms to support the reformed religion, she herself, within a month of her wedding day, rode against them in armour with loaded pistols in her saddle. Driven out of Scotland, they presented themselves before Elizabeth—who called them traitors in public, and assisted them in private, according to her crafty nature.

Mary had been married but a little while, when she began to hate her husband, who, in his turn, began to hate that David Rizzio, with whom he had leagued to gain her favour, and whom he now believed to be her lover. He hated Rizzio to that extent, that he made a compact with LORD RUTHVEN and three other lords to get rid of him by murder. This wicked agreement they made in solemn secrecy upon the first of March, fifteen hundred and sixty-six, and on the night of Saturday the ninth, the conspirators were brought by Darnley up a private staircase, dark and steep, into a range of rooms where they knew that Mary was sitting at supper with her sister, Lady Argyle, and this doomed man. When they went into the room, Darnley took the Queen round the waist, and Lord Ruthven, who had risen from a bed of sickness to do this murder, came in, gaunt and ghastly, leaning on two men. Rizzio ran behind the Queen for shelter and protection. "Let him come out of the room," said Ruthven. "He shall not leave the room," replied the Queen; "I read his danger in your face, and it is my will that he remain here." They then set upon him, struggled with him, overturned the table, dragged him out, and killed him with fifty-six stabs. When the Queen heard that he was dead, she said, "No more tears. I will think now of revenge!"

Within a day or two, she gained her husband over, and prevailed on the tall idiot to abandon the conspirators and fly with her to Dunbar. There, he issued a proclamation, audaciously and falsely denying that he had any knowledge of the late bloody business; and there they were joined by the EARL BOTHWELL and some other nobles. With their help, they raised eight thousand men, returned to Edinburgh, and drove the assassins into England. Mary soon afterwards gave birth to a son—still thinking of revenge.

That she should have had a greater scorn for her husband after his late cowardice and treachery than she had had before, was natural enough. There is little doubt that she now began to love Bothwell instead, and to plan with him means of getting rid of Darnley. Bothwell had such power over her that he induced her even to pardon the assassins of Rizzio. The arrangements for the christening of the young Prince were entrusted to him, and he was one of the most important people at the ceremony, where the child was named JAMES: Elizabeth being his godmother, though not present on the occasion. A week afterwards, Darnley, who had left Mary and gone to his father's house at Glasgow, being taken ill with the small-pox, she sent her own physician to attend him. But there is reason to apprehend that this was merely a show and a pretence, and that she knew what was doing, when Bothwell within another month proposed to one of the late conspirators against Rizzio, to murder Darnley, "for that it was the Queen's mind that he should be taken away." It is certain that on that very day she wrote to her ambassador in France, complaining of him, and yet went immediately to Glasgow, feigning to be very anxious about him, and to love him very much. If she wanted to get him in her power, she succeeded to her heart's content; for she induced him to go back with her to Edinburgh, and to occupy, instead of the palace, a lone house outside the city called the Kirk of Field. Here, he lived for about a week. One Sunday night, she remained with him until ten o'clock, and then left him, to go to Holyrood to be present at an entertainment given in celebration of the marriage of one of her favourite servants. At two o'clock in the morning the city was shaken by a great explosion, and the Kirk of Field was blown to atoms.

Darnley's body was found next day lying under a tree at some distance. How it came there, undisfigured and unscorched by gunpowder, and how this crime came to be so clumsily and strangely committed, it is impossible to discover. The deceitful character of Mary, and the deceitful character of Elizabeth, have rendered almost every part of their joint history uncertain and obscure. But, I fear that Mary was unquestionably a party to her husband's murder, and that this was the revenge she had threatened. The Scotch people universally believed it. Voices cried out in the streets of Edinburgh in the dead of the night, for justice on the murderess. Placards were posted by unknown hands in the public places denouncing Bothwell as the murderer, and the Queen as his accomplice; and, when he afterwards married her (though himself already married), previously making a show of taking her prisoner by force, the indignation of the people knew no bounds. The women particularly are described as having been quite frantic against the Queen, and to have hooted and cried after her in the streets with terrific vehemence.

Such guilty unions seldom prosper. This husband and wife had lived together but a month, when they were separated for ever by the successes of a band of Scotch nobles who associated against them for the protection of the young Prince: whom Bothwell had vainly endeavoured to lay hold of, and whom he would certainly have murdered, if the EARL OF MAR, in whose hands the boy was, had not been firmly and honourably faithful to his trust. Before this angry power, Bothwell fled abroad, where he died, a prisoner and mad, nine miserable years afterwards. Mary being found by the associated lords to deceive them at every turn, was sent a prisoner to Lochleven Castle; which, as it stood in the midst of a lake, could only be approached by boat. Here, one LORD LINDSAY, who was so much of a brute that the nobles would have done better if they had chosen a mere gentleman for their messenger, made her sign her abdication, and appoint Murray, Regent of Scotland. Here, too, Murray saw her in a sorrowing and humbled state.

She had better have remained in the castle of Lochleven, dull prison as it was, with the rippling of the lake against it, and the moving shadows of the water on the room-walls; but she could not rest there, and more than once tried to escape. The first time she had nearly succeeded, dressed in the clothes of her own washer-woman, but, putting up her hand to prevent one of the boatmen from lifting her veil, the men suspected her, seeing how white it was, and rowed her back again. A short time afterwards, her fascinating manners enlisted in her cause a boy in the Castle, called the little DOUGLAS, who, while the family were at supper, stole the keys of the great gate, went softly out with the Queen, locked the gate on the outside, and rowed her away across the lake, sinking the keys as they went along. On the opposite shore she was met by another Douglas, and some few lords; and, so accompanied, rode away on horseback to Hamilton, where they raised three thousand men. Here, she issued a proclamation declaring that the abdication she had signed in her prison was illegal, and requiring the Regent to yield to his lawful Queen. Being a steady soldier, and in no way discomposed although he was without an army, Murray pretended to treat with her, until he had collected a force about half equal to her own, and then he gave her battle. In one quarter of an hour he cut down all her hopes. She had another weary ride on horseback of sixty long Scotch miles, and took shelter at Dundrennan Abbey, whence she fled for safety to Elizabeth's dominions.

Mary Queen of Scots came to England—to her own ruin, the trouble of the kingdom, and the misery and death of many—in the year one thousand five hundred and sixty-eight. How she left it and the world, nineteen years afterwards, we have now to see.

SECOND PART

WHEN Mary Queen of Scots arrived in England, without money and even without any other clothes than those she wore, she wrote to Elizabeth, representing herself as an innocent and injured piece of Royalty, and entreating her assistance to oblige her Scottish subjects to take her back again and obey her. But, as her character was already known in England to be a very different one from what she made it out to be, she was told in answer that she must first clear herself. Made uneasy by this condition, Mary, rather than stay in England, would have gone to Spain, or to France, or would even have gone back to Scotland. But, as her doing either would have been likely to trouble England afresh, it was decided that she should be detained here. She first came to Carlisle, and, after that, was moved about from castle to castle, as was considered necessary; but

England she never left again.

After trying very hard to get rid of the necessity of clearing herself, Mary, advised by LORD HERRIES, her best friend in England, agreed to answer the charges against her, if the Scottish noblemen who made them would attend to maintain them before such English noblemen as Elizabeth might appoint for that purpose. Accordingly, such an assembly, under the name of a conference, met, first at York, and afterwards at Hampton Court. In its presence Lord Lennox, Darnley's father, openly charged Mary with the murder of his son; and whatever Mary's friends may now say or write in her behalf, there is no doubt that, when her brother Murray produced against her a casket containing certain guilty letters and verses which he stated to have passed between her and Bothwell, she withdrew from the inquiry. Consequently, it is to be supposed that she was then considered guilty by those who had the best opportunities of judging of the truth, and that the feeling which afterwards arose in her behalf was a very generous but not a very reasonable one.

However, the DUKE OF NORFOLK, an honourable but rather weak nobleman, partly because Mary was captivating, partly because he was ambitious, partly because he was over-persuaded by artful plotters against Elizabeth, conceived a strong idea that he would like to marry the Queen of Scots—though he was a little frightened, too, by the letters in the casket. This idea being secretly encouraged by some of the noblemen of Elizabeth's court, and even by the favourite Earl of Leicester (because it was objected to by other favourites who were his rivals), Mary expressed her approval of it, and the King of France and the King of Spain are supposed to have done the same. It was not so quietly planned, though, but that it came to Elizabeth's ears, who warned the Duke "to be careful what sort of pillow he was going to lay his head upon." He made a humble reply at the time; but turned sulky soon afterwards, and, being considered dangerous, was sent to the Tower.

Thus, from the moment of Mary's coming to England she began to be the centre of plots and miseries.

A rise of the Catholics in the north was the next of these, and it was only checked by many executions and much bloodshed. It was followed by a great conspiracy of the Pope and some of the Catholic sovereigns of Europe to depose Elizabeth, place Mary on the throne, and restore the unreformed religion. It is almost impossible to doubt that Mary knew and approved of this; and the Pope himself was so hot in the matter that he issued a bull, in which he openly called Elizabeth the "pretended Queen" of England, excommunicated her, and excommunicated all her subjects who should continue to obey her. A copy of this miserable paper got into London, and was found one morning publicly posted on the Bishop of London's gate. A great hue and cry being raised, another copy was found in the chamber of a student of Lincoln's Inn, who confessed, being put upon the rack, that he had received it from one JOHN FELTON, a rich gentleman who lived across the Thames, near Southwark. This John Felton, being put upon the rack too, confessed that he had posted the placard on the Bishop's gate. For this offence he was, within four days, taken to St. Paul's Churchyard, and there hanged and quartered. As to the Pope's bull, the people by the reformation having thrown off the Pope, did not care much, you may suppose, for the Pope's throwing off them. It was a mere dirty piece of paper, and not half so powerful as a street ballad.

On the very day when Felton was brought to his trial, the poor Duke of Norfolk was released. It would have been well for him if he had kept away from the Tower evermore, and from the snares that had taken him there. But, even while he was in that dismal place he corresponded with Mary, and as soon as he was out of it, he began to plot again. Being discovered in correspondence with the Pope, with a view to a rising in England which should force Elizabeth to consent to his marriage with Mary and to repeal the laws against the Catholics, he was re-committed to the Tower and brought to trial. He was found guilty by the unanimous verdict of the Lords who tried him, and was sentenced to the block.

It is very difficult to make out, at this distance of time, and between opposite accounts, whether Elizabeth really was a humane woman, or desired to appear so, or was fearful of shedding the blood of people of great name who were popular in the country. Twice she commanded and countermanded the execution of this Duke, and it did not take place until five months after his trial. The scaffold was erected on Tower Hill, and there he died like a brave man. He refused to have his eyes bandaged, saying that he was not at all afraid of death; and he admitted the justice of his sentence, and was much regretted by the people.

Although Mary had shrunk at the most important time from disproving her guilt, she was very careful never to do anything that would admit it. All such proposals as were made to her by Elizabeth for her release, required that admission in some form or other, and therefore came to nothing. Moreover, both women being artful and treacherous, and neither ever trusting the other, it was not likely that they could ever make an agreement. So, the Parliament, aggravated by what the Pope had done, made new and strong laws against the spreading of the Catholic religion in England, and declared it treason in any one to say that the Queen and her successors were not the lawful sovereigns of England. It would have done more than this, but for Elizabeth's moderation.

Since the Reformation, there had come to be three great sects of religious people—or people who called themselves so—in England; that is to say, those who belonged to the Reformed Church, those who belonged to the Unreformed Church, and those who were called the Puritans, because they said that they wanted to have everything very pure and plain in all the Church service. These last were for the most part an uncomfortable people, who thought it highly meritorious to dress in a hideous manner, talk through their noses, and oppose all harmless enjoyments. But they were powerful too, and very much in earnest, and they were one and all the determined enemies of the Queen of Scots. The Protestant feeling in England was further strengthened by the tremendous cruelties to which Protestants were exposed in France and in the Netherlands. Scores of thousands of them were put to death in those countries with every cruelty that can be imagined, and at last, in the autumn of the year one thousand five hundred and seventy-two, one of the greatest barbarities ever committed in the world took place at Paris.

It is called in history, THE MASSACRE OF SAINT BARTHOLOMEW, because it took place on Saint Bartholomew's Eve. The day fell on Saturday the twenty-third of August. On that day all the great leaders of the Protestants (who were there called HUGUENOTS) were assembled together, for the purpose, as was represented to them, of doing honour to the marriage of their chief, the young King of Navarre, with the sister of CHARLES THE NINTH: a miserable young King who then occupied the French throne. This dull creature was made to believe by his mother and other fierce Catholics about him that the Huguenots meant to take his life; and he was persuaded to give secret orders that, on the tolling of a great bell, they should be fallen upon by an overpowering force of armed men, and slaughtered wherever they could be found. When the appointed hour was close at hand, the stupid wretch, trembling from head to foot, was taken into a balcony by his mother to see the atrocious work begun. The moment the bell tolled, the murderers broke forth. During all that night and the two next days, they broke into the houses, fired the houses, shot and stabbed the Protestants, men, women, and children, and flung their bodies into the streets. They were shot at in the streets as they passed along, and their blood ran down the gutters. Upwards of ten thousand Protestants were killed in Paris alone; in all France four or five times that number. To return thanks to Heaven for these diabolical murders, the Pope and his train actually went in public procession at Rome, and as if this were not shame enough for them, they had a medal struck to commemorate the event. But, however comfortable the wholesale murders were to these high authorities, they had not that soothing effect upon the doll-King. I am happy to state that he never knew a moment's peace afterwards; that he was continually crying out that he saw the Huguenots covered with blood and wounds falling dead before him; and that he died within a year, shrieking and yelling and raving to that degree, that if all the Popes who had ever lived had been rolled into one, they would not have afforded His guilty Majesty the slightest consolation.

When the terrible news of the massacre arrived in England, it made a powerful impression indeed upon the people. If they began to run a little wild against the Catholics at about this time, this fearful reason for it, coming so soon after the days of bloody Queen Mary, must be remembered in their excuse. The Court was not quite so honest as the people—but perhaps it sometimes is not. It received the French ambassador, with all the lords and ladies dressed in deep mourning, and keeping a profound silence. Nevertheless, a proposal of marriage which he had made to Elizabeth only two days before the eve of Saint Bartholomew, on behalf of the Duke of Alençon, the French King's brother, a boy of seventeen, still went on; while on the other hand, in her usual crafty way, the Queen secretly supplied the Huguenots with money and weapons.

I must say that for a Queen who made all those fine speeches, of which I have confessed myself to be rather tired, about living and dying a Maiden Queen, Elizabeth was "going" to be married pretty often. Besides always having some English favourite or other whom she by turns encouraged and swore at and knocked about—for the Maiden Queen was very free with her fists—she held this French Duke off and on through several years. When he at last came over to England, the marriage articles were actually drawn up, and it was settled that the wedding should take place in six weeks. The Queen was then so bent upon it, that she prosecuted a poor Puritan named STUBBS, and a poor bookseller named PAGE, for writing and publishing a pamphlet against it. Their right hands were chopped off for this crime; and poor Stubbs—more loyal than I should have been myself under the circumstances—immediately pulled off his hat with his left hand, and cried, "God save the Queen!" Stubbs was cruelly treated; for the marriage never took place after all, though the Queen pledged herself to the Duke with a ring from her own finger. He went away, no better than he came, when the courtship had lasted some ten years altogether; and he died a couple of years afterwards, mourned by Elizabeth, who appears to have been really fond of him. It is not much to her credit, for he was a bad enough member of a bad family.

To return to the Catholics. There arose two orders of priests, who were very busy in England, and who were much dreaded. These were the JESUITS (who were everywhere in all sorts of disguises), and the SEMINARY PRIESTS. The people had a great horror of the first, because they were known to have taught that murder was lawful if it were done with an object of which they approved; and they had a great horror of the second, because they came to teach the old religion, and to be the successors of "Queen Mary's priests," as those yet lingering in England were called, when they should die out. The severest laws were made against them, and were most unmercifully executed. Those who sheltered them in their houses often suffered heavily for what was an act of humanity; and the rack, that cruel torture which tore men's limbs asunder, was constantly kept going. What these unhappy men confessed, or what was ever confessed by any one under that agony, must always be received with great doubt, as it is certain that people have frequently owned to the most absurd and impossible crimes to escape such dreadful suffering. But I cannot doubt it to have been proved by papers, that there were many plots, both among the Jesuits, and with France, and with Scotland, and with Spain, for the destruction of Queen Elizabeth, for the placing of Mary on the throne, and for the revival of the old religion.

If the English people were too ready to believe in plots, there were, as I have said, good reasons for it. When the massacre of Saint Bartholomew was yet fresh in their recollection, a great Protestant Dutch hero, the PRINCE OF ORANGE, was shot by an assassin, who confessed that he had been kept and trained for the purpose in a college of Jesuits. The Dutch, in this surprise and distress, offered to make Elizabeth their sovereign, but she declined the honour, and sent them a small army instead, under the command of the Earl of Leicester, who, although a capital Court favourite, was not much of a general. He did so little in Holland, that his campaign there would probably have been forgotten, but for its occasioning the death of one of the best writers, the best knights, and the best gentlemen, of that or any age. This was SIR PHILIP SIDNEY, who was wounded by a musket ball in the thigh as he mounted a fresh horse, after having had his own killed under him. He had to ride back wounded, a long distance, and was very faint with fatigue and loss of blood, when some water, for which he had eagerly asked, was handed to him. But he was so good and gentle even then, that seeing a poor badly wounded common soldier lying on the ground, looking at the water with longing eyes, he said, "Thy necessity is greater than mine," and gave it up to him. This touching action of a noble heart is perhaps as well known as any incident in history—is as famous far and wide as the blood-stained Tower of London, with its axe, and block, and murders out of number. So delightful is an act of true humanity, and so glad are mankind to remember it.

At home, intelligence of plots began to thicken every day. I suppose the people never did live under such continual terrors as those by which they were possessed now, of Catholic risings, and burnings, and poisonings, and I don't know what. Still, we must always remember that they lived near and close to awful realities of that kind, and that with their experience it was not difficult to believe in any enormity. The government had the same fear, and did not take the best means of discovering the truth—for, besides torturing the suspected, it employed paid spies, who will always lie for their own profit. It even made some of the conspiracies it brought to light, by sending false letters to disaffected people, inviting them to join in pretended plots, which they too readily did.

But, one great real plot was at length discovered, and it ended the career of Mary, Queen of Scots. A seminary priest named BALLARD, and a Spanish soldier named SAVAGE, set on and encouraged by certain French priests, imparted a design to one ANTONY BABINGTON —a gentleman of fortune in Derbyshire, who had been for some time a secret agent of Mary's—for murdering the Queen. Babington then confided the scheme to some other Catholic gentlemen who were his friends, and they joined in it heartily. They were vain weak-headed young men, ridiculously confident, and preposterously proud of their plan; for they got a gimcrack painting made, of the six choice spirits who were to murder Elizabeth, with Babington in an attitude for the centre figure. Two of their number, however, one of whom was a priest, kept Elizabeth's wisest minister, SIR FRANCIS WALSING-HAM, acquainted with the whole project from the first. The conspirators were completely deceived to the final point, when Babington gave Savage, because he was shabby, a ring from his finger, and some money from his purse, wherewith to buy himself new clothes in which to kill the Queen. Walsingham, having then full evidence against the whole band, and two letters of Mary's besides, resolved to seize them. Suspecting something wrong, they stole out of the city, one by one, and hid themselves in St. John's Wood, and other places which really were hiding places then; but they were all taken, and all executed. When they were seized, a gentleman was sent from Court to inform Mary of the fact, and of her being involved in the discovery. Her friends have complained that she was kept in very hard and severe custody. It does not appear very likely, for she was going out a hunting that very morning.

Queen Elizabeth had been warned long ago, by one in France who had good information of what was secretly doing, that in holding Mary alive, she held "the wolf who would devour her." The Bishop of London had, more lately, given the Queen's favourite minister the advice in writing, "forthwith to cut off the Scottish Queen's head." The question now was, what to do with her? The Earl of Leicester wrote a little note home from Holland, recommending that she should be quietly poisoned; that noble favourite having accustomed his mind, it is possible, to remedies of that nature. His black advice, however, was disregarded, and she was brought to trial at Fotheringay Castle in Northamptonshire, before a tribunal of forty, composed of both religions. There, and in the Star Chamber at Westminster, the trial lasted a fortnight. She defended herself with great ability, but could only deny the confessions that had been made by Babington and others; could only call her own letters, produced against her by her own secretaries, forgeries; and, in short, could only deny everything. She was found guilty, and declared to have incurred the penalty of death. The Parliament met, approved the sentence, and prayed the Queen to have it executed. The Queen replied that she requested them to consider whether no means could be found of saving Mary's life without endangering her own. The Parliament rejoined, No; and the citizens illuminated their houses and lighted bonfires, in token of their joy that all these plots and troubles were to be ended by the death of the Queen of Scots.

She, feeling sure that her time was now come, wrote a letter to the Queen of England, making three entreaties: first, that she might be buried in France; secondly, that she might not be executed in secret, but before her servants and some others; thirdly, that after her death, her servants should not be molested, but should be suffered to go home with the legacies she left them. It was an affecting letter, and Elizabeth shed tears over it, but sent no answer. Then came a special ambassador from France, and another from Scotland, to intercede for Mary's life; and then the nation began to clamour, more and more, for her death.

What the real feelings or intentions of Elizabeth were, can never be known now; but I strongly suspect her of only wishing one thing more than Mary's death, and that was to keep free of the blame of it. On the first of February, one thousand five hundred and eighty-seven, Lord Burleigh having drawn out the warrant for the execution, the Queen sent to the secretary DAVISON to bring it to her, that she might sign it: which she did. Next day, when Davison told her it was sealed, she angrily asked him why such haste was necessary? Next day but one, she joked about it, and swore a little. Again, next day but one, she seemed to complain that it was not yet done, but still she would not be plain with those about her. So, on the seventh, the Earls of Kent and Shrewsbury, with the Sheriff of Northampton-shire, came with the warrant to Fotheringay, to tell the Queen of Scots to prepare for death.

When those messengers of ill omen were gone, Mary made a frugal supper, drank to her servants, read over her will, went to bed, slept for some hours, and then arose and passed the remainder of the night saying prayers. In the morning she dressed herself in her best clothes; and, at eight o'clock when the sheriff came for her to her chapel, took leave of her servants who were there assembled praying with her, and went down-stairs, carrying a Bible in one hand and a crucifix in the other. Two of her women and four of her men were allowed to be present in the hall; where a low scaffold, only two feet from the ground, was erected and covered with black; and where the execu-tioner from the Tower, and his assistant, stood, dressed in black velvet. The hall was full of people. While the sentence was being read she sat upon a stool; and, when it was finished, she again denied her guilt, as she had done before. The Earl of Kent and the Dean of Peterborough, in their Protestant zeal, made some very unnecessary speeches to her; to which she replied that she died in the Catholic religion, and they need not trouble themselves about that matter. When her head and neck were uncovered by the executioners, she said that she had not been used to be undressed by such hands, or before so much company. Finally, one of her women fastened a cloth over her face, and she laid her neck upon the block, and repeated more than once in Latin, "Into thy hands, O Lord, I commend my spirit!" Some say her head was struck off in two blows, some say in three. However that be, when it was held up streaming with blood, the real hair beneath the false hair she had long worn was seen to be as grey as that of a woman of seventy, though she was at that time only in her forty-sixth year. All her beauty was gone.

But she was beautiful enough to her little dog, who cowered under her dress, frightened, when she went upon the scaffold, and who lay down beside her headless body when all her earthly sorrows were over.

THIRD PART

ON its being formally made known to Elizabeth that the sentence had been executed on the Queen of Scots, she showed the utmost grief and rage, drove her favourites from her with violent indignation, and sent Davison to the Tower; from which place he was only released in the end by paying an immense fine which completely ruined him. Elizabeth not only over-acted her part in making these pretences, but most basely reduced to poverty one of her faithful servants for no other fault than obeying her commands.

James, King of Scotland, Mary's son, made a show likewise of being very angry on the occasion; but he was a pensioner of England to the amount of five thousand pounds a year, and he had known very little of his mother, and he possibly regarded her as the murderer of his father, and he soon took it quietly.

Philip, King of Spain, however, threatened to do greater things than ever had been done yet, to set up the Catholic religion and punish Protestant England. Elizabeth, hearing that he and the Prince of Parma were making great preparations for this purpose, in order to be beforehand with them sent out ADMIRAL DRAKE (a famous navigator, who had sailed about the world, and had already brought great plunder from Spain) to the port of Cadiz, where he burnt a hundred vessels full of stores. This great loss obliged the Spaniards to put off the invasion for a year; but it was none the less formidable for that, amounting to one hundred and thirty ships, nineteen thousand soldiers, eight thousand sailors, two thousand slaves, and between two and three thousand great guns. England was not idle in making ready to resist this great force. All the men between sixteen years old and sixty, were trained and drilled; the national fleet of ships (in number only thirty-four at first) was enlarged by public contributions and by private ships, fitted out by noblemen; the city of London, of its own accord, furnished double the number of ships and men that it was required to provide; and, if ever the national spirit was up in England, it was up all through the country to resist the Spaniards. Some of the Queen's advisers were for seizing the principal English Catholics, and putting them to death; but the Queen—who, to her honour, used to say, that she would never believe any ill of her subjects, which a parent would not believe of her own children—rejected the advice, and only confined a few of those who were the most suspected, in the fens in Lincolnshire. The great body of Catholics deserved this confidence; for they behaved most loyally, nobly, and bravely.

So, with all England firing up like one strong angry man, and with both sides of the Thames fortified, and with the soldiers under arms, and with the sailors in their ships, the country waited for the coming of the proud Spanish fleet, which was called THE INVINCIBLE ARMADA. The Queen herself, riding in armour on a white horse, and the Earl of Essex and the Earl of Leicester holding her bridle rein, made a brave speech to the troops at Tilbury Fort opposite Gravesend, which was received with such enthusiasm as is seldom known. Then came the Spanish Armada into the English Channel, sailing along in the form of a half moon, of such great size that it was seven miles broad. But the English were quickly upon it, and woe then to all the Spanish ships that dropped a little out of the half moon, for the English took them instantly! And it soon appeared that the great Armada was anything but invincible, for on a summer night, bold Drake sent eight blazing fire-ships right into the midst of it. In terrible consternation the Spaniards tried to get out to sea, and so became dispersed; the English pursued them at a great advantage; a storm came on, and drove the Spaniards among rocks and shoals; and the swift end of the Invincible fleet was, that it lost thirty great ships and ten thousand men, and, defeated and disgraced, sailed home again. Being afraid to go by the English Channel, it sailed all round Scotland and Ireland; some of the ships getting cast away on the latter coast in bad weather, the Irish, who were a kind of savages, plundered those vessels and killed their crews. So ended this great attempt to invade and conquer England. And I think it will be a long time before any other invincible fleet coming to England with the same object, will fare much better than the Spanish Armada.

Though the Spanish king had had this bitter taste of English bravery, he was so little the wiser for it, as still to entertain his old designs, and even to conceive the absurd idea of placing his daughter on the English throne. But the Earl of Essex, SIR WALTER RALEIGH, SIR THOMAS HOWARD, and some other distinguished leaders, put to sea from Plymouth, entered the port of Cadiz once more, obtained a complete victory over the shipping assembled there, and got possession of the town. In obedience to the Queen's express instructions, they behaved with great humanity; and the principal loss of the Spaniards was a vast sum of money which they had to pay for ransom. This was one of many gallant achievements on the sea, effected in this reign. Sir Walter Raleigh himself, after marrying a maid of honour and giving offence to the Maiden Queen thereby, had already sailed to South America in search of gold.

The Earl of Leicester was now dead, and so was Sir Thomas Walsingham, whom Lord Burleigh was soon to follow. The principal favourite was the EARL OF ESSEX, a spirited and handsome man, a favourite with the people too as well as with the Queen, and possessed of many admirable qualities. It was much debated at Court whether there should be peace with Spain or no, and he was very urgent for war. He also tried hard to have his own way in the appointment of a deputy to govern in Ireland. One day, while this question was in dispute, he hastily took offence, and turned his back upon the Queen; as a gentle reminder of which impropriety, the Queen gave him a tremendous box on the ear, and told him to go to the devil. He went home instead, and did not reappear at Court for half a year or so, when he and the Queen were reconciled, though never (as some suppose) thoroughly.

From this time the fate of the Earl of Essex and that of the Queen seemed to be blended together. The Irish were still perpetually quarrelling and fighting among themselves, and he went over to Ireland as Lord Lieutenant, to the great joy of his enemies (Sir Walter Raleigh among the rest), who were glad to have so dangerous a rival far off. Not being by any means successful there, and knowing that his enemies would take advantage of that circumstance to injure him with the Queen, he came home again, though against her orders. The Queen being taken by surprise when he appeared before her, gave him her hand to kiss, and he was overjoyed—though it was not a very lovely hand by this time—but in the course of the same day she ordered him to confine himself to his room, and two or three days afterwards had him taken into custody. With the same sort of caprice —and as capricious an old woman she now was, as ever wore a crown or a head either—she sent him broth from her own table on his falling ill from anxiety, and cried about him.

He was a man who could find comfort and occupation in his books, and he did so for a time; not the least happy time, I dare say, of his life. But it happened unfortunately for him, that he held a monopoly in sweet wines: which means that nobody could sell them without purchasing his permission. This right, which was only for a term, expiring, he applied to have it renewed. The Queen refused, with the rather strong observation—but she *did* make strong observations— that an unruly beast must be stinted in his food. Upon this, the angry Earl, who had been already deprived of many offices, thought himself in danger of complete ruin, and turned against the Queen, whom he called a vain old woman who had grown as crooked in her mind as she had in her figure. These uncomplimentary expressions the ladies of the Court immediately snapped up and carried to the Queen, whom they did not put in a better temper, you may believe. The same Court ladies, when they had beautiful dark hair of their own, used to wear false red hair, to be like the Queen. So they were not very high-spirited ladies, however high in rank.

The worst object of the Earl of Essex, and some friends of his who used to meet at LORD SOUTHAMPTON'S house, was to obtain possession of the Queen, and oblige her by force to dismiss her ministers and change her favourites. On Saturday the seventh of February, one thousand six hundred and one, the council suspecting this, summoned the Earl to come before them. He, pretending to be ill, declined; it was then settled among his friends, that as the next day would be Sunday, when many of the citizens usually assembled at the Cross by St. Paul's Cathedral, he should make one bold effort to induce them to rise and follow him to the Palace.

So, on the Sunday morning, he and a small body of adherents started out of his house—Essex House by the Strand, with steps to the river—having first shut up in it, as prisoners, some members of the council who came to examine him—and hurried into the City with the Earl at their head, crying out "For the Queen! For the Queen! A plot is laid for my life!" No one heeded them, however, and when they came to St. Paul's there were no citizens there. In the meantime the prisoners at Essex House had been released by one of the Earl's own friends; he had been promptly proclaimed a traitor in the City itself; and the streets were barricaded with carts and guarded by soldiers. The Earl got back to his house by water, with difficulty, and after an attempt to defend his house against the troops and cannon by which it was soon surrounded, gave himself up that night. He was brought to trial on the nineteenth, and found guilty; on the twenty-fifth, he was executed on Tower Hill, where he died, at thirty-four years old, both courageously and penitently. His step-father suffered with him. His enemy, Sir Walter Raleigh, stood near the scaffold all the time—but not so near as we shall see him stand, before we finish his history.

In this case, as in the cases of the Duke of Norfolk and Mary Queen of Scots, the Queen had commanded, and countermanded, and again commanded, the execution. It is probable that the death of her young and gallant favourite in the prime of his good qualities, was never off her mind afterwards, but she held out, the same vain, obstinate and capricious woman, for another year. Then she danced before her Court on a state occasion—and cut, I should think, a mighty ridiculous figure, doing so in an immense ruff, stomacher and wig, at seventy years old. For another year still, she held out, but, without any more dancing, and as a moody, sorrowful, broken creature. At last, on the tenth of March, one thousand six hundred and three, having been ill of a very bad cold, and made worse by the death of the Countess of Nottingham who was her intimate friend, she fell into a stupor and was supposed to be dead. She recovered her consciousness, however, and then nothing would induce her to go to bed; for she said that she knew that if she did, she should never get up again. There she lay for ten days, on cushions on the floor, without any food, until the Lord Admiral got her into bed at last, partly by persuasions and partly by main force. When they asked her who should succeed her, she replied that her seat had been the seat of Kings, and that she would have for her successor, "No rascal's son, but a King's." Upon this, the lords present stared at one another, and took the liberty of asking whom she meant; to which she replied, "Whom should I mean, but our cousin of Scotland!" This was on the twenty-third of March. They asked her once again that day, after she was speechless, whether she was still in the same mind? She struggled up in bed, and joined her hands over her head in the form of a crown, as the only reply she could make. At three o'clock next morning, she very quietly died, in the forty-fifth year of her reign.

That reign had been a glorious one, and is made for ever memorable by the distinguished men who flourished in it. Apart from the great voyagers, statesmen, and scholars, whom it produced, the names of BACON, SPENSER, and SHAKESPEARE, will always be remembered with pride and veneration by the civilised world, and will always impart (though with no great reason, perhaps) some portion of their lustre to the name of Elizabeth herself. It was a great reign for discovery, for commerce, and for English enterprise and spirit in general. It was a great reign for the Protestant religion and for the Reformation which made England free. The Queen was very popular, and in her progresses, or journeys about her dominions, was everywhere received with the liveliest joy. I think the truth is, that she was not half so good as she has been made out, and not half so bad as she has been made out. She had her fine qualities, but she was coarse, capricious, and treacherous, and had all the faults of an excessively vain young woman long after she was an old one. On the whole, she had a great deal too much of her father in her, to please me.

Many improvements and luxuries were introduced in the course of these five-and-forty years in the general manner of living; but cock-fighting, bull-baiting, and bear-baiting, were still the national amusements; and a coach was so rarely seen, and was such an ugly and cumbersome affair when it was seen, that even the Queen herself, on many high occasions, rode on horseback on a pillion behind the Lord Chancellor.

CHAPTER XXXII

ENGLAND UNDER JAMES THE FIRST

"OUR cousin of Scotland " was ugly, awkward, and shuffling both in mind and person. His tongue was much too large for his mouth, his legs were much too weak for his body, and his dull goggle-eyes stared and rolled like an idiot's. He was cunning, covetous, wasteful, idle, drunken, greedy, dirty, cowardly, a great swearer, and the most conceited man on earth. His figure—what is commonly called rickety from his birth—presented a most ridiculous appearance, dressed in thick padded clothes, as a safeguard against being stabbed (of which he lived in continual fear), of a grass-green colour from head to foot, with a hunting-horn dangling at his side instead of a sword, and his hat and feather sticking over one eye, or hanging on the back of his head, as he happened to toss it on. He used to loll on the necks of his favourite courtiers, and slobber their faces, and kiss and pinch their cheeks; and the greatest favourite he ever had, used to sign himself in his letters to his royal master, His Majesty's "dog and slave," and used to address his majesty as "his Sowship." His majesty was the worst rider ever seen, and thought himself the best. He was one of the most impertinent talkers (in the broadest Scotch) ever heard, and boasted of being unanswerable in all manner of argument. He wrote some of the most wearisome treatises ever read—among others, a book upon witchcraft, in which he was a devout believer—and thought himself a prodigy of authorship. He thought, and wrote, and said, that a king had a right to make and unmake what laws he pleased, and ought to be accountable to nobody on earth. This is the plain, true character of the personage whom the greatest men about the court praised and flattered to that degree, that I doubt if there be anything much more shameful in the annals of human nature.

He came to the English throne with great ease. The miseries of a disputed succession had been felt so long, and so dreadfully, that he was proclaimed within a few hours of Elizabeth's death, and was accepted by the nation, even without being asked to give any pledge that he would govern well, or that he would redress crying grievances. He took a month to come from Edinburgh to London; and, by way of exercising his new power, hanged a pickpocket on the journey without any trial, and knighted everybody he could lay hold of. He made two hundred knights before he got to his palace in London, and seven hundred before he had been in it three months. He also shovelled sixty-two new peers into the House of Lords—and there was a pretty large sprinkling of Scotchmen among them, you may believe.

His Sowship's prime Minister, CECIL (for I cannot do better than call his majesty what his favourite called him), was the enemy of Sir Walter Raleigh, and also of Sir Walter's political friend, LORD COBHAM; and his Sowship's first trouble was a plot originated by these two, and entered into by some others, with the old object of seizing the King and keeping him in imprisonment until he should change his ministers. There were Catholic priests in the plot, and there were Puritan noblemen too; for, although the Catholics and Puritans were strongly opposed to each other, they united at this time against his Sowship, because they knew that he had a design against both, after pretending to be friendly to each; this design being to have only one high and convenient form of the Protestant religion, which everybody should be bound to belong to, whether they liked it or not. This plot was mixed up with another, which may or may not have had some reference to placing on the throne, at some time, the LADY ARABELLA STUART; whose misfortune it was, to be the daughter of the younger brother of his Sowship's father, but who was quite innocent of any part in the scheme. Sir Walter Raleigh was accused on the confession of Lord Cobham—a miserable creature, who said one thing at one time, and another thing at another time, and could be relied upon in nothing. The trial of Sir Walter Raleigh lasted from eight in the morning until nearly midnight; he defended himself with such eloquence, genius, and spirit against all accusations, and against the insults of COKE, the Attorney-General—who, according to the custom of the time, foully abused him—that those who went there to deter the prisoner, came away admiring him, and declaring that any so wonderful and so captivating was never heard. He was guilty, nevertheless, and sentenced to death. Execution was d and he was taken to the Tower. The two Catholic pri fortunate, were executed with the usual atrocity; and Lor and two others were pardoned on the scaffold. His Sowshi wonderfully knowing in him to surprise the people b these three at the very block; but, blundering, and bung he had very nearly overreached himself. For, the mess back who brought the pardon, came so late, that he w outside of the crowd, and was obliged to shout and came for. The miserable Cobham did not gain mu that day. He lived, both as a prisoner and a begg and miserably poor, for thirteen years, and outhouse belonging to one of his former serva

This plot got rid of, and Sir Walter Raleigh safely shut up in the Tower, his Sowship held a great dispute with the Puritans on their presenting a petition to him, and had it all his own way—not so very wonderful, as he would talk continually, and would not hear anybody else—and filled the Bishops with admiration. It was comfortably settled that there was to be only one form of religion, and that all men were to think exactly alike. But, although this was arranged two centuries and a half ago, and although the arrangement was supported by much fining and imprisonment, I do not find that it is quite successful, even yet.

His Sowship, having that uncommonly high opinion of himself as a king, had a very low opinion of Parliament as a power that audaciously wanted to control him. When he called his first Parliament after he had been king a year, he accordingly thought he would take pretty high ground with them, and told them that he commanded them "as an absolute king." The Parliament thought those strong words, and saw the necessity of upholding their authority. His Sowship had three children: Prince Henry, Prince Charles, and the Princess Elizabeth. It would have been well for one of these, and we shall too soon see which, if he had learnt a little wisdom concerning Parliaments from his father's obstinacy.

Now, the people still labouring under their old dread of the Catholic religion, this Parliament revived and strengthened the severe laws against it. And this so angered ROBERT CATESBY, a restless Catholic gentleman of an old family, that he formed one of the most desperate and terrible designs ever conceived in the mind of man; no less a scheme than the Gunpowder Plot.

His object was, when the King, lords, and commons, should be assembled at the next opening of Parliament, to blow them up, one and all, with a great mine of gunpowder. The first person to whom he confided this horrible idea was THOMAS WINTER, a Worcestershire gentleman who had served in the army abroad, and had been secretly employed in Catholic projects. While Winter was yet undecided, and when he had gone over to the Netherlands, to learn from the Spanish Ambassador there whether there was any hope of Catholics being relieved through the intercession of the King of Spain with his Sowship, he found at Ostend a tall dark, daring man, whom he had known when they were both soldiers abroad, and whose name was GUIDO—or GUY—FAWKES. Resolved to join the plot, he proposed it to this man, knowing him to be the man for any desperate deed, and they two came back to England together. Here, they admitted two other conspirators: THOMAS PERCY, related to the Earl of Northumberland, and JOHN WRIGHT, his brother-in-law. All these met together in a solitary house in the open fields which were then near Clement's Inn, now a closely blocked-up part of London; and when they had all taken a great oath of secrecy, Catesby told the rest what his plan was. They then went up-stairs into a garret, and received the Sacrament from FATHER GERARD, a Jesuit, who is said not to have known actually of the Gunpowder Plot, but who, I think, must have had his suspicions that there was something desperate afoot.

Percy was a Gentleman Pensioner, and as he had occasional duties to perform about the Court, then kept at Whitehall, there would be nothing suspicious in his living at Westminster. So, having looked well about him, and having found a house to let, the back of which joined the Parliament House, he hired it of a person named FERRIS, for the purpose of undermining the wall. Having got possession of this house, the conspirators hired another on the Lambeth side of the Thames, which they used as a storehouse for wood, gunpowder, and other combustible matters. These were to be removed at night (and afterwards were removed), bit by bit, to the house at Westminster; and, that there might be some trusty person to keep watch over the Lambeth stores, they admitted another conspirator, by name ROBERT KAY, a very poor Catholic gentleman.

All these arrangements had been made some months, and it was a dark, wintry, December night, when the conspirators, who had been in the meantime dispersed to avoid observation, met in the house at Westminster, and began to dig. They had laid in a good stock of eatables, to avoid going in and out, and they dug and dug with great ardour. But, the wall being tremendously thick, and the work very severe, they took into their plot CHRISTOPHER WRIGHT, a younger brother of John Wright, that they might have a new pair of hands to help. And Christopher Wright fell to like a fresh man, and they dug and dug by night and by day, and Fawkes stood sentinel all the time. And if any man's heart seemed to fail him at all, Fawkes said, "Gentlemen, we have abundance of powder and shot here, and there is no fear of our being taken alive, even if discovered." The same Fawkes, who, in the capacity of sentinel, was always prowling about, soon picked up the intelligence that the King had prorogued the Parliament again, from the seventh of February, the day first fixed upon, until the third of October. When the conspirators knew this, they agreed to separate until after the Christmas holidays, and to take no notice of each other in the meanwhile, and never to write letters to one another on any account. So, the house in Westminster was shut up again, and I suppose the neighbours thought that those strange-looking men who lived there so gloomily, and went out so seldom, were gone away to have a merry Christmas somewhere.

It was the beginning of February, sixteen hundred and five, when Catesby met his fellow-conspirators again at this Westminster house. He had now admitted three more: JOHN GRANT, a Warwickshire gentleman of a melancholy temper, who lived in a doleful house near Stratford-upon-Avon, with a frowning wall all round it, and a deep moat; ROBERT WINTER, eldest brother of Thomas; and Catesby's own servant, THOMAS BATES, who, Catesby thought, had had some suspicion of what his master was about. These three had all suffered more or less for their religion in Elizabeth's time. And now, they all began to dig again, and they dug and dug by night and by day.

They found it dismal work alone there, underground, with such a fearful secret on their minds, and so many murders before them.

They were filled with wild fancies. Sometimes, they thought they heard a great bell tolling, deep down in the earth under the Parliament House; sometimes, they thought they heard low voices muttering about the Gunpowder Plot; once in the morning, they really did hear a great rumbling noise over their heads, as they dug and sweated in their mine. Every man stopped and looked aghast at his neighbour, wondering what had happened, when that bold prowler, Fawkes, who had been out to look, came in and told them that it was only a dealer in coals who had occupied a cellar under the Parliament House, removing his stock in trade to some other place. Upon this, the conspirators, who with all their digging and digging had not yet dug through the tremendously thick wall, changed their plan; hired that cellar, which was directly under the House of Lords; put six-and-thirty barrels of gunpowder in it, and covered them over with fagots and coals. Then they all dispersed again till September, when the following new conspirators were admitted; Sir EDWARD BAYNHAM, of Gloucestershire; Sir EVERARD DIGBY, of Rutlandshire; AMBROSE ROOKWOOD, of Suffolk; FRANCIS TRESHAM, of Northamptonshire. Most of these were rich, and were to assist the plot, some with money and some with horses on which the conspirators were to ride through the country and rouse the Catholics after the Parliament should be blown into air.

Parliament being again prorogued from the third of October to the fifth of November, and the conspirators being uneasy lest their design should have been found out, Thomas Winter said he would go up into the House of Lords on the day of the prorogation, and see how matters looked. Nothing could be better. The unconscious Commissioners were walking about and talking to one another, just over the six-and-thirty barrels of gunpowder. He came back and told the rest so, and they went on with their preparations. They hired a ship, and kept it ready in the Thames, in which Fawkes was to sail for Flanders after firing with a slow match the train that was to explode the powder. A number of Catholic gentlemen not in the secret, were invited, on pretence of a hunting party, to meet Sir Everard Digby at Dunchurch on the fatal day, that they might be ready to act together. And now all was ready.

But, now, the great wickedness and danger which had been all along at the bottom of this wicked plot, began to show itself. As the fifth of November drew near, most of the conspirators, remembering that they had friends and relations who would be in the House of Lords that day, felt some natural relenting, and a wish to warn them to keep away. They were not much comforted by Catesby's declaring that in such a cause he would blow up his own son. LORD MOUNTEAGLE, Tresham's brother-in-law, was certain to be in the House; and when Tresham found that he could not prevail upon the rest to devise any means of sparing their friends, he wrote a mysterious letter to this lord and left it at his lodging in the dusk, urging him to keep away from the opening of Parliament, "since God and man had concurred to punish the wickedness of the times." It contained the words "that the Parliament should receive a terrible blow, and yet should not see who hurt them." And it added, "the danger is past, as soon as you have burnt the letter."

The ministers and courtiers made out that his Sowship, by a direct miracle from Heaven, found out what this letter meant. The truth is, that they were not long (as few men would be) in finding out for themselves; and it was decided to let the conspirators alone, until the very day before the opening of Parliament. That the conspirators had their fears, is certain; for, Tresham himself said before them all, that they were every one dead men; and although even he did not take flight, there is reason to suppose that he had warned other persons besides Lord Mounteagle. However, they were all firm; and Fawkes, who was a man of iron, went down every day and night to keep watch in the cellar as usual. He was there about two in the afternoon of the fourth, when the Lord Chamberlain and Lord Mounteagle threw open the door and looked in. "Who are you, friend?" said they. "Why," said Fawkes, "I am Mr. Percy's servant, and am looking after his store of fuel here." "Your master has laid in a pretty good store," they returned, and shut the door, and went away. Fawkes, upon this, posted off to the other conspirators to tell them all was quiet, and went back and shut himself up in the dark black cellar again, where he heard the bell go twelve o'clock and usher in the fifth of November. About two hours afterwards, he slowly opened the door, and came out to look about him, in his old prowling way. He was instantly seized and bound, by a party of soldiers under SIR THOMAS KNEVETT. He had a watch upon him, some touchwood, some tinder, some slow matches; and there was a dark lantern with a candle in it, lighted, behind the door. He had his boots and spurs on—to ride to the ship, I suppose—and it was well for the soldiers that they took him so suddenly. If they had left him but a moment's time to light a match, he certainly would have tossed it in among the powder, and blown up himself and them.

They took him to the King's bed-chamber first of all, and there the King (causing him to be held very tight, and keeping a good way off), asked him how he could have the heart to intend to destroy so many innocent people? "Because," said Guy Fawkes, "desperate diseases need desperate remedies." To a little Scotch favourite, with a face like a terrier, who asked him (with no particular wisdom) why he had collected so much gunpowder, he replied, because he had meant to blow Scotchmen back to Scotland, and it would take a deal of powder to do that. Next day he was carried to the Tower, but would make no confession. Even after being horribly tortured, he confessed nothing that the Government did not already know; though he must have been in a fearful state—as his signature, still preserved, in contrast with his natural handwriting before he was put upon the dreadful rack, most frightfully shows. Bates, a very different man, soon said the Jesuits had had to do with the plot, and probably, under the torture, would as readily have said anything. Tresham, taken and put in the Tower too, made confessions and unmade them, and died of an illness that was heavy upon him. Rookwood, who had stationed relays of his own horses all the way to Dunchurch, did not mount to escape until the middle of the day, when the news of the plot was all over London. On the road, he came up with the two Wrights, Catesby, and Percy; and they all galloped together into Northamptonshire. Thence to Dunchurch, where they found the proposed party assembled. Finding, however, that there had been a plot, and that it had been discovered, the party disappeared in the course of the night, and left them alone with Sir Everard Digby. Away they all rode again, through Warwickshire and Worcestershire, to a house called Holbeach, on the borders of Staffordshire. They tried to raise the Catholics on their way, but were indignantly driven off by them. All this time they were hotly pursued by the sheriff of Worcester, and a fast increasing concourse of riders. At last, resolving to defend themselves at Holbeach, they shut themselves up in the house, and put some wet powder before the fire to dry. But it blew up, and Catesby was singed and blackened, and almost killed, and some of the others were sadly hurt. Still, knowing that they must die, they resolved to die there, and with only their swords in their hands appeared at the windows to be shot at by the sheriff and his assistants. Catesby said to Thomas Winter, after Thomas had been hit in the right arm which dropped powerless by his side, "Stand by me, Tom, and we will die together!"—which they did, being shot through the body by two bullets from one gun. John Wright, and Christopher Wright, and Percy, were also shot. Rookwood and Digby were taken: the former with a broken arm and a wound in his body too.

It was the fifteenth of January, before the trial of Guy Fawkes, and such of the other conspirators as were left alive, came on. They were all found guilty, all hanged, drawn, and quartered: some, in St. Paul's Churchyard, on the top of Ludgate-hill; some, before the Parliament House. A Jesuit priest, named HENRY GARNET, to whom the dreadful design was said to have been communicated, was taken and tried; and two of his servants, as well as a poor priest who was taken with him, were tortured without mercy. He himself was not tortured, but was surrounded in the Tower by tamperers and traitors, and so was made unfairly to convict himself out of his own mouth. He said, upon his trial, that he had done all he could to prevent the deed, and that he could not make public what had been told him in confession—though I am afraid he knew of the plot in other ways. He was found guilty and executed, after a manful defence, and the Catholic Church made a saint of him; some rich and powerful persons, who had had nothing to do with the project, were fined and imprisoned for it by the Star Chamber; the Catholics, in general, who had recoiled with horror from the idea of the infernal contrivance, were unjustly put under more severe laws than before; and this was the end of the Gunpowder Plot.

SECOND PART

His Sowship would pretty willingly, I think, have blown the House
of Commons into the air himself; for, his dread and jealousy of it knew
no bounds all through his reign. When he was hard pressed for money
he was obliged to order it to meet, as he could get no money without
it; and when it asked him first to abolish some of the monopolies in
necessaries of life which were a great grievance to the people, and to
redress other public wrongs, he flew into a rage and got rid of it again.
At one time he wanted it to consent to the Union of England with
Scotland, and quarrelled about that. At another time it wanted him
to put down a most infamous Church abuse, called the High Commission Court, and he quarrelled with it about that. At another time
it entreated him not to be quite so fond of his archbishops and bishops
who made speeches in his praise too awful to be related, but to have
some little consideration for the poor Puritan clergy who were persecuted for preaching in their own way, and not according to the archbishops and bishops; and they quarrelled about that. In short, what
with hating the House of Commons, and pretending not to hate it;
and what with now sending some of its members who opposed him,
to Newgate or to the Tower, and now telling the rest that they must
not presume to make speeches about the public affairs which could
not possibly concern them; and what with cajoling, and bullying, and
fighting, and being frightened; the House of Commons was the plague
of his Sowship's existence. It was pretty firm, however, in maintaining its rights, and insisting that the Parliament should make the
laws, and not the King by his own single proclamations (which he
tried hard to do); and his Sowship was so often distressed for money,
in consequence, that he sold every sort of title and public office as if
they were merchandise, and even invented a new dignity called a
Baronetcy, which anybody could buy for a thousand pounds.

These disputes with his Parliaments, and his hunting, and his
drinking, and his lying in bed—for he was a great sluggard—occupied
his Sowship pretty well. The rest of his time he chiefly passed in
hugging and slobbering his favourites. The first of these was SIR
PHILIP HERBERT, who had no knowledge whatever, except of dogs,
and horses, and hunting, but whom he soon made EARL OF MONT-
GOMERY. The next, and a much more famous one, was ROBERT CARR,
or KER (for it is not certain which was his right name), who came
from the Border country, and whom he soon made VISCOUNT
ROCHESTER, and afterwards, EARL OF SOMERSET. The way in which
his Sowship doted on this handsome young man, is even more odious
to think of, than the way in which the really great men of England
condescended to bow down before him. The favourite's great friend
was a certain SIR THOMAS OVERBURY, who wrote his love-letters for
him, and assisted him in the duties of his many high places, which his
own ignorance prevented him from discharging. But this same Sir
Thomas having just manhood enough to dissuade the favourite from
a wicked marriage with the beautiful Countess of Essex, who was to

get a divorce from her husband for the purpose, the said Countess, in her rage, got Sir Thomas put into the Tower, and there poisoned him. Then the favourite and this bad woman were publicly married by the King's pet bishop, with as much to-do and rejoicing, as if he had been the best man, and she the best woman, upon the face of the earth.

But, after a longer sunshine than might have been expected—of seven years or so, that is to say—another handsome young man started up and eclipsed the EARL OF SOMERSET. This was GEORGE VILLIERS, the youngest son of a Leicestershire gentleman: who came to Court with all the Paris fashions on him, and could dance as well as the best mountebank that ever was seen. He soon danced himself into the good graces of his Sowship, and danced the other favourite out of favour. Then, it was all at once discovered that the Earl and Countess of Somerset had not deserved all those great promotions and mighty rejoicings, and they were separately tried for the murder of Sir Thomas Overbury, and for other crimes. But, the King was so afraid of his late favourite's publicly telling some disgraceful things he knew of him—which he darkly threatened to do—that he was even examined with two men standing, one on either side of him, each with a cloak in his hand, ready to throw it over his head and stop his mouth if he should break out with what he had it in his power to tell. So, a very lame affair was purposely made of the trial, and his punishment was an allowance of four thousand pounds a year in retirement, while the Countess was pardoned, and allowed to pass into retirement too. They hated one another by this time, and lived to revile and torment each other some years.

While these events were in progress, and while his Sowship was making such an exhibition of himself, from day to day and from year to year, as is not often seen in any sty, three remarkable deaths took place in England. The first was that of the Minister, Robert Cecil, Earl of Salisbury, who was past sixty, and had never been strong, being deformed from his birth. He said at last that he had no wish to live; and no Minister need have had, with his experience of the meanness and wickedness of those disgraceful times. The second was that of the Lady Arabella Stuart, who alarmed his Sowship mightily, by privately marrying WILLIAM SEYMOUR, son of LORD BEAUCHAMP, who was a descendant of King Henry the Seventh and who, his Sowship thought, might consequently increase and strengthen any claim she might one day set up to the throne. She was separated from her husband (who was put in the Tower) and thrust into a boat to be confined at Durham. She escaped in a man's dress to get away in a French ship from Gravesend to France, but unhappily missed her husband, who had escaped too, and was soon taken. She went raving mad in the miserable Tower, and died there after four years. The last, and the most important of these three deaths, was that of Prince Henry, the heir to the throne, in the nineteenth year of his age. He was a promising young prince, and greatly liked; a quiet, well-conducted youth, of whom two very good things are known: first, that

dly, that he was the friend of Sir
ugh all those years in the Tower,
iis father would keep such a bird in
i the preparations for the marriage
abeth with a foreign prince (and an
ut), he came from Richmond, where he
ais new brother-in-law, at the palace at
d a great game at tennis, in his shirt,
veather, and was seized with an alarming
. fortnight of a putrid fever. For this young
gh wrote, in his prison in the Tower, the be-
the World: a wonderful instance how little his
confine a great man's mind, however long he
ody.

ι of Sir Walter Raleigh, who had many faults, but
ι so many merits as in trouble and adversity, may
. to the end of his sad story. After an imprisonment
. twelve long years, he proposed to resume those old
his, and to go to South America in search of gold. His
ided between his wish to be on good terms with the
irough whose territory Sir Walter must pass (he had long
ι of marrying Prince Henry to a Spanish Princess), and his
ι eagerness to get hold of the gold, did not know what to do.
ne end, he set Sir Walter free, taking securities for his return;
Walter fitted out an expedition at his own cost, and, on the
y-eighth of March, one thousand six hundred and seventeen,
ι away in command of one of its ships, which he ominously
ed the Destiny. The expedition failed; the common men, not find-
ι the gold they had expected, mutinied; a quarrel broke out be-
ween Sir Walter and the Spaniards, who hated him for old successes
of his against them; and he took and burnt a little town called SAINT
THOMAS. For this he was denounced to his Sowship by the Spanish
Ambassador as a pirate; and returning almost broken-hearted, with
his hopes and fortunes shattered, his company of friends dispersed,
and his brave son (who had been one of them) killed, he was taken—
through the treachery of SIR LEWIS STUKELY, his near relation, a
scoundrel and a Vice-Admiral—and was once again immured in his
prison-home of so many years.

His Sowship being mightily disappointed in not getting any gold,
Sir Walter Raleigh was tried as unfairly, and with as many lies and
evasions as the judges and law officers and every other authority in
Church and State habitually practised under such a King. After a
great deal of prevarication on all parts but his own, it was declared
that he must die under his former sentence, now fifteen years old.
So, on the twenty-eighth of October, one thousand six hundred and
eighteen, he was shut up in the Gate House at Westminster to pass
his last night on earth, and there he took leave of his good and faithful lady, who was worthy to have lived in better days. At eight o'clock
next morning, after a cheerful breakfast, and a pipe, and a cup of

good wine, he was taken to Old Palace Yard in Westminster, where the scaffold was set up, and where so many people of high degree were assembled to see him die, that it was a matter of some difficulty to get him through the crowd. He behaved most nobly, but if anything lay heavy on his mind, it was that Earl of Essex, whose head he had seen roll off; and he solemnly said that he had had no hand in bringing him to the block, and that he had shed tears for him when he died. As the morning was very cold, the Sheriff said, would he come down to a fire for a little space, and warm himself? But Sir Walter thanked him, and said no, he would rather it were done at once, for he was ill of fever and ague, and in another quarter of an hour his shaking fit would come upon him if he were still alive, and his enemies might then suppose that he trembled for fear. With that, he kneeled and made a very beautiful and Christian prayer. Before he laid his head upon the block he felt the edge of the axe, and said, with a smile upon his face, that it was a sharp medicine, but would cure the worst disease. When he was bent down ready for death, he said to the executioner, finding that he hesitated, "What dost thou fear? Strike, man!" So, the axe came down and struck his head off, in the sixty-sixth year of his age.

The new favourite got on fast. He was made a viscount, he was made Duke of Buckingham, he was made a marquis, he was made Master of the Horse, he was made Lord High Admiral—and the Chief Commander of the gallant English forces that had dispersed the Spanish Armada, was displaced to make room for him. He had the whole kingdom at his disposal, and his mother sold all the profits and honours of the State, as if she had kept a shop. He blazed all over with diamonds and other precious stones, from his hatband and his ear-rings to his shoes. Yet he was an ignorant, presumptuous, swaggering compound of knave and fool, with nothing but his beauty and his dancing to recommend him. This is the gentleman who called himself his Majesty's dog and slave, and called his Majesty Your Sowship. His Sowship called him STEENIE; it is supposed, because that was a nickname for Stephen, and because St. Stephen was generally represented in pictures as a handsome saint.

His Sowship was driven sometimes to his wits'-end by his trimming between the general dislike of the Catholic religion at home, and his desire to wheedle and flatter it abroad, as his only means of getting a rich princess for his son's wife: a part of whose fortune he might cram into his greasy pockets. Prince Charles—or as his Sowship called him, Baby Charles—being now PRINCE OF WALES, the old project of a marriage with the Spanish King's daughter had been revived for him; and as she could not marry a Protestant without leave from the Pope, his Sowship himself secretly and meanly wrote to his Infallibility, asking for it. The negotiation for this Spanish marriage takes up a larger space in great books, than you can imagine, but the upshot of it all is, that when it had been held off by the Spanish Court for a long time, Baby Charles and Steenie set off in disguise as Mr. Thomas Smith and Mr. John Smith, to see the

Spanish Princess; that Baby Charles pretended to be desperately in love with her, and jumped off walls to look at her, and made a considerable fool of himself in a good many ways; that she was called Princess of Wales, and that the whole Spanish Court believed Baby Charles to be all but dying for her sake, as he expressly told them he was; that Baby Charles and Steenie came back to England, and were received with as much rapture as if they had been a blessing to it; that Baby Charles had actually fallen in love with HENRIETTA MARIA, the French King's sister, whom he had seen in Paris; that he thought it a wonderfully fine and princely thing to have deceived the Spaniards, all through; and that he openly said, with a chuckle, as soon as he was safe and sound at home again, that the Spaniards were great fools to have believed him.

Like most dishonest men, the Prince and the favourite complained that the people whom they had deluded were dishonest. They made such misrepresentations of the treachery of the Spaniards in this business of the Spanish match, that the English nation became eager for a war with them. Although the gravest Spaniards laughed at the idea of his Sowship in a warlike attitude, the Parliament granted money for the beginning of hostilities, and the treaties with Spain were publicly declared to be at an end. The Spanish ambassador in London—probably with the help of the fallen favourite, the Earl of Somerset—being unable to obtain speech with his Sowship, slipped a paper into his hand, declaring that he was a prisoner in his own house, and was entirely governed by Buckingham and his creatures. The first effect of this letter was that his Sowship began to cry and whine, and took Baby Charles away from Steenie, and went down to Windsor, gabbling all sorts of nonsense. The end of it was that his Sowship hugged his dog and slave, and said he was quite satisfied.

He had given the Prince and the favourite almost unlimited power to settle anything with the Pope as to the Spanish marriage; and he now, with a view to the French one, signed a treaty that all Roman Catholics in England should exercise their religion freely, and should never be required to take any oath contrary thereto. In return for this, and for other concessions much less to be defended, Henrietta Maria was to become the Prince's wife, and was to bring him a fortune of eight hundred thousand crowns.

His Sowship's eyes were getting red with eagerly looking for the money, when the end of a gluttonous life came upon him; and, after a fortnight's illness, on Sunday the twenty-seventh of March, one thousand six hundred and twenty-five, he died. He had reigned twenty-two years, and was fifty-nine years old. I know of nothing more abominable in history than the adulation that was lavished on this King, and the vice and corruption that such a barefaced habit of lying produced in his court. It is much to be doubted whether one man of honour, and not utterly self-disgraced, kept his place near James the First. Lord Bacon, that able and wise philosopher, as the First Judge in the Kingdom in this reign, became a public spectacle of dishonesty and corruption; and in his base flattery of his Sowship, and in his crawling servility to his dog and slave, disgraced himself even more. But, a creature like his Sowship set upon a throne is like the Plague, and everybody receives infection from him.

CHAPTER XXXIII

ENGLAND UNDER CHARLES THE FIRST

BABY CHARLES became KING CHARLES THE FIRST, in the twenty-fifth year of his age. Unlike his father, he was usually amiable in his private character, and grave and dignified in his bearing; but, like his father, he had monstrously exaggerated notions of the rights of a king, and was evasive, and not to be trusted. If his word could have been relied upon, his history might have had a different end.

His first care was to send over that insolent upstart, Buckingham, to bring Henrietta Maria from Paris to be his Queen; upon which occasion Buckingham—with his usual audacity—made love to the young Queen of Austria, and was very indignant indeed with CARDINAL RICHELIEU, the French Minister, for thwarting his intentions. The English people were very well disposed to like their new Queen, and to receive her with great favour when she came among them as a stranger. But, she held the Protestant religion in great dislike, and brought over a crowd of unpleasant priests, who made her do some very ridiculous things, and forced themselves upon the public notice in many disagreeable ways. Hence, the people soon came to dislike her, and she soon came to dislike them; and she did so much all through this reign in setting the King (who was dotingly fond of her) against his subjects, that it would have been better for him if she had never been born.

Now, you are to understand that King Charles the First—of his own determination to be a high and mighty King not to be called to account by anybody, and urged on by his Queen besides—deliberately set himself to put his Parliament down and to put himself up. You are also to understand, that even in pursuit of this wrong idea (enough in itself to have ruined any king) he never took a straight course, but always took a crooked one.

He was bent upon war with Spain, though neither the House of Commons nor the people were quite clear as to the justice of that war, now that they began to think a little more about the story of the Spanish match. But the King rushed into it hotly, raised money by illegal means to meet its expenses, and encountered a miserable failure at Cadiz, in the very first year of his reign. An expedition to Cadiz had been made in the hope of plunder, but as it was not successful, it was necessary to get a grant of money from the Parliament; and when they met, in no very complying humour, the King told them, "to make haste to let him have it, or it would be the worse for themselves." Not put in a more complying humour by this, they impeached the King's favourite, the Duke of Buckingham, as the cause (which he undoubtedly was) of many great public grievances and wrongs. The King, to save him, dissolved the Parliament without getting the money he wanted; and when the Lords implored him to consider and grant a little delay, he replied, "No, not one minute." He then began to raise money for himself by the following means among others.

He levied certain duties called tonnage and poundage which had not been granted by the Parliament, and could lawfully be levied by no other power; he called upon the seaport towns to furnish, and to pay all the cost for three months of, a fleet of armed ships; and he required the people to unite in lending him large sums of money, the repayment of which was very doubtful. If the poor people refused, they were pressed as soldiers or sailors; if the gentry refused, they were sent to prison. Five gentlemen, named SIR THOMAS DARNEL, JOHN CORBET, WALTER EARL, JOHN HEVENINGHAM, and EVERARD HAMPDEN, for refusing were taken up by a warrant of the King's privy council, and were sent to prison without any cause but the King's pleasure being stated for their imprisonment. Then the question came to be solemnly tried, whether this was not a violation of Magna Charta, and an encroachment by the King on the highest rights of the English people. His lawyers contended No, because to encroach upon the rights of the English people would be to do wrong, and the King could do no wrong. The accommodating judges decided in favour of this wicked nonsense; and here was a fatal division between the King and the people.

For all this, it became necessary to call another Parliament. The people, sensible of the danger in which their liberties were, chose for it those who were best known for their determined opposition to the King; but still the King, quite blinded by his determination to carry everything before him, addressed them when they met, in a contemptuous manner, and just told them in so many words that he had only called them together because he wanted money. The Parliament, strong enough and resolute enough to know that they would lower his tone, cared little for what he said, and laid before him one of the great documents of history, which is called the PETITION OF RIGHT, requiring that the free men of England should no longer be called upon to lend the King money, and should no longer be pressed or imprisoned for refusing to do so; further, that the free men of England should no longer be seized by the King's special mandate or warrant, it being contrary to their rights and liberties and the laws of their country. At first the King returned an answer to this petition, in which he tried to shirk it altogether; but, the House of Commons then showing their determination to go on with the impeachment of Buckingham, the King in alarm returned an answer, giving his consent to all that was required of him. He not only afterwards departed from his word and honour on these points, over and over again, but, at this very time, he did the mean and dissembling act of publishing his first answer and not his second—merely that the people might suppose that the F...

That pestilent...
had by this tim...
with Spain. F...
are wars som...
chief in this...
his carriag...
with him;...
derer lef'...
angry v...
were i...
from...
mu...
aw...

J

obliged it to adjourn without doing anything more—when two members, named Mr. HOLLIS and Mr. VALENTINE, held him down. A scene of great confusion arose among the members; and while many swords were drawn and flashing about, the King, who was kept informed of all that was going on, told the captain of his guard to go down to the House and force the doors. The resolutions were by that time, however, voted, and the House adjourned. Sir John Eliot and those two members who had held the Speaker down, were quickly summoned before the council. As they claimed it to be their privilege not to answer out of Parliament for anything they had said in it, they were committed to the Tower. The King then went down and dissolved the Parliament, in a speech wherein he made mention of these gentlemen as "Vipers"—which did not do him much good that ever I have heard of.

As they refused to gain their liberty by saying they were sorry for what they had done, the King, always remarkably unforgiving, never overlooked their offence. When they demanded to be brought up before the court of King's Bench, he even resorted to the meanness of having them moved about from prison to prison, so that the writs issued for that purpose should not legally find them. At last they came before the court and were sentenced to heavy fines, and to be imprisoned during the King's pleasure. When Sir John Eliot's health had quite given way, and he so longed for change of air and scene as to petition for his release, the King sent back the answer (worthy of his Sowship himself) that the petition was not humble enough. When he sent another petition by his young son, in which he pathetically offered to go back to prison when his health was restored, if he might be released for its recovery, the King still disregarded it. When he died in the Tower, and his children petitioned to be allowed to take his body down to Cornwall, there to lay it among the ashes of his forefathers, the King returned for answer, "Let Sir John Eliot's body be buried in the church of that parish where he died." All this was like a very little King indeed, I think.

And now, for twelve long years, steadily pursuing his design of setting himself up and putting the people down, the King called no Parliament; but ruled without one. If twelve thousand volumes were written in his praise (as a good many have been) it would still remain a fact, impossible to be denied, that for twelve years King Charles the First reigned in England unlawfully and despotically, seized upon his subjects' goods and money at his pleasure, and punished according to his unbridled will all who ventured to oppose him. It is a fashion with some people to think that this King's career was cut short; but I must say myself that I think he ran a pretty long one.

WILLIAM LAUD, Archbishop of Canterbury, was the King's right-hand man in the religious part of the putting down of the people's liberties. Laud, who was a sincere man, of large learning but small sense—for the two things sometimes go together in very different quantities—though a Protestant, held opinions so near those of the Catholics, that the Pope wanted to make a Cardinal of him, if he would have accepted that favour. He looked upon vows, robes, lighted candles, images, and so forth, as amazingly important in religious ceremonies; and he brought in an immensity of bowing and candle-snuffing. He also regarded archbishops and bishops as a sort of miraculous persons, and was inveterate in the last degree against any who thought otherwise. Accordingly, he offered up thanks to Heaven, and was in a state of much pious pleasure, when a Scotch clergyman, named LEIGHTON, was pilloried, whipped, branded in the cheek, and had one of his ears cut off and one of his nostrils slit, for calling bishops trumpery and the inventions of men. He originated on a Sunday morning the prosecution of WILLIAM PRYNNE, a barrister who was of similar opinions, and who was fined a thousand pounds; who was pilloried; who had his ears cut off on two occasions —one ear at a time—and who was imprisoned for life. He highly approved of the punishment of DOCTOR BASTWICK, a physician; who was also fined a thousand pounds; and who afterwards had *his* ears cut off, and was imprisoned for life. These were gentle methods of persuasion, some will tell you: I think, they were rather calculated to be alarming to the people.

In the money part of the putting down of the people's liberties, the King was equally gentle, as some will tell you: as I think, equally alarming. He levied those duties of tonnage and poundage, and increased them as he thought fit. He granted monopolies to companies of merchants on their paying him for them, notwithstanding the great complaints that had, for years and years, been made on the subject of monopolies. He fined the people for disobeying proclamations issued by his Sowship in direct violation of law. He revived the detested Forest laws, and took private property to himself as his forest right. Above all, he determined to have what was called Ship Money; that is to say, money for the support of the fleet—not only from the seaports, but from all the counties of England: having found out that, in some ancient time or other, all the counties paid it. The grievance of this ship money being somewhat too strong, JOHN CHAMBERS, a citizen of London, refused to pay his part of it. For this the Lord Mayor ordered John Chambers to prison, and for that John Chambers brought a suit against the Lord Mayor. LORD SAY, also, behaved like a real nobleman, and declared he would not pay. But, the sturdiest and best opponent of the ship money was JOHN HAMPDEN, a gentleman of Buckinghamshire, who had sat among the "vipers" in the House of Commons when there was such a thing, and who had been the bosom friend of Sir John Eliot. This case was tried before the twelve judges in the Court of Exchequer, and again the King's lawyers said it was impossible that ship money could be wrong, because the King could do no wrong, however hard he tried— and he really did try very hard during these twelve years. Seven of the judges said that was quite true, and Mr. Hampden was bound to pay: five of the judges said that was quite false, and Mr. Hampden was not bound to pay. So, the King triumphed (as he thought), by making Hampden the most popular man in England; where matters were getting to that height now, that many honest Englishmen could not endure their country, and sailed away across the seas to found a colony in Massachusetts Bay in America. It is said that Hampden himself and his relation OLIVER CROMWELL were going with a company of such voyagers, and were actually on board ship, when they were stopped by a proclamation, prohibiting sea captains to carry out such passengers without the royal license. But O! it would have been well for the King if he had let them go!

This was the state of England. If Laud had been a madman just broke loose, he could not have done more mischief than he did in Scotland. In his endeavours (in which he was seconded by the King, then in person in that part of his dominions) to force his own ideas of bishops, and his own religious forms and ceremonies upon the Scotch, he roused that nation to a perfect frenzy. They formed a solemn league, which they called The Covenant, for the preservation of their own religious forms; they rose in arms throughout the whole country; they summoned all their men to prayers and sermons twice a day by beat of drum; they sang psalms, in which they compared their enemies to all the evil spirits that ever were heard of; and they solemnly vowed to smite them with the sword. At first the King tried force, then treaty, then a Scottish Parliament which did not answer at all. Then he tried the EARL OF STRAFFORD, formerly Sir Thomas Wentworth; who, as LORD WENTWORTH, had been governing Ireland. He, too, had carried it with a very high hand there, though to the benefit and prosperity of that country.

Strafford and Laud were for conquering the Scottish people by force of arms. Other lords who were taken into council, recommended that a Parliament should at last be called; to which the King unwillingly consented. So, on the thirteenth of April, one thousand six hundred and forty, that then strange sight, a Parliament, was seen at Westminster. It is called the Short Parliament, for it lasted a very little while. While the members were all looking at one another, doubtful who would dare to speak, Mr. PYM arose and set forth all that the King had done unlawfully during the past twelve years, and what was the position to which England was reduced. This great example set, other members took courage and spoke the truth freely, though with great patience and moderation. The King, a little frightened, sent to say that if they would grant him a certain sum on certain terms, no more ship money should be raised. They debated the matter for two days; and then, as they would not give him all he asked without promise or inquiry, he dissolved them.

But they knew very well that he must have a Parliament now; and he began to make that discovery too, though rather late in the day. Wherefore, on the twenty-fourth of September, being then at York with an army collected against the Scottish people, but his own men sullen and discontented like the rest of the nation, the King told the great council of the Lords, whom he had called to meet him there, that he would summon another Parliament to assemble on the third of November. The soldiers of the Covenant had now forced their way

into England and had taken possession of the northern counties,
where the coals are got. As it would never do to be without coals, and
as the King's troops could make no head against the Covenanters so
full of gloomy zeal, a truce was made, and a treaty with Scotland was
taken into consideration. Meanwhile the northern counties paid the
Covenanters to leave the coals alone, and keep quiet.

We have now disposed of the Short Parliament. We have next to
see what memorable things were done by the Long one.

SECOND PART

THE Long Parliament assembled on the third of November, one
thousand six hundred and forty-one. That day week the Earl of
Strafford arrived from York, very sensible that the spirited and determined men who formed that Parliament were no friends towards him,
who had not only deserted the cause of the people, but who had on all
occasions opposed himself to their liberties. The King told him, for
his comfort, that the Parliament "should not hurt one hair of his
head." But, on the very next day Mr. Pym, in the House of Commons, and with great solemnity, impeached the Earl of Strafford as a
traitor. He was immediately taken into custody and fell from his
proud height.

It was the twenty-second of March before he was brought to trial
in Westminster Hall; where, although he was very ill and suffered
great pain, he defended himself with such ability and majesty, that
it was doubtful whether he would not get the best of it. But on the
thirteenth day of the trial, Pym produced in the House of Commons a
copy of some notes of a council, found by young SIR HARRY VANE in
a red velvet cabinet belonging to his father (Secretary Vane, who sat
at the council-table with the Earl), in which Strafford had distinctly
told the King that he was free from all rules and obligations of government, and might do with his people whatever he liked; and in which
he had added—"You have an army in Ireland that you may employ
to reduce this kingdom to obedience." It was not clear whether by the
words "this kingdom," he had really meant England or Scotland; but
the Parliament contended that he meant England, and this was
treason. At the same sitting of the House of Commons it was resolved
to bring in a bill of attainder declaring the treason to have been committed: in preference to proceeding with the trial by impeachment,
which would have required the treason to be proved.

So, a bill was brought in at once, was carried through the House of
Commons by a large majority, and was sent up to the House of Lords.
While it was still uncertain whether the House of Lords would pass
it and the King consent to it, Pym disclosed to the House of Commons that the King and Queen had both been plotting with the officers
of the army to bring up the soldiers and control the Parliament, and
also to introduce two hundred soldiers into the Tower of London to
effect the Earl's escape. The plotting with the army was revealed by
one GEORGE GORING, the son of a lord of that name: a bad fellow who

was one of the original plotters, and turned traitor. The King had actually given his warrant for the admission of the two hundred men into the Tower, and they would have got in too, but for the refusal of the governor—a sturdy Scotchman of the name of BALFOUR—to admit them. These matters being made public, great numbers of people began to riot outside the Houses of Parliament, and to cry out for the execution of the Earl of Strafford, as one of the King's chief instruments against them. The bill passed the House of Lords while the people were in this state of agitation, and was laid before the King for his assent, together with another bill declaring that the Parliament then assembled should not be dissolved or adjourned without their own consent. The King—not unwilling to save a faithful servant, though he had no great attachment for him—was in some doubt what to do; but he gave his consent to both bills, although he in his heart believed that the bill against the Earl of Strafford was unlawful and unjust. The Earl had written to him, telling him that he was willing to die for his sake. But he had not expected that his royal master would take him at his word quite so readily; for, when he heard his doom, he laid his hand upon his heart, and said, "Put not your trust in Princes!"

The King, who never could be straightforward and plain, through one single day or through one single sheet of paper, wrote a letter to the Lords, and sent it by the young Prince of Wales, entreating them to prevail with the Commons that "that unfortunate man should fulfil the natural course of his life in a close imprisonment." In a postscript to the very same letter, he added, "If he must die, it were charity to reprieve him till Saturday." If there had been any doubt of his fate, this weakness and meanness would have settled it. The very next day, which was the twelfth of May, he was brought out to be beheaded on Tower Hill.

Archbishop Laud, who had been so fond of having people's ears cropped off and their noses slit, was now confined in the Tower too; and when the Earl went by his window to his death, he was there, at his request, to give him his blessing. They had been great friends in the King's cause, and the Earl had written to him in the days of their power that he thought it would be an admirable thing to have Mr. Hampden publicly whipped for refusing to pay the ship money. However, those high and mighty doings were over now, and the Earl went his way to death with dignity and heroism. The governor wished him to get into a coach at the Tower gate, for fear the people should tear him to pieces; but he said it was all one to him whether he died by the axe or by the people's hands. So, he walked, with a firm tread and a stately look, and sometimes pulled off his hat to them as he passed along. They were profoundly quiet. He made a speech on the scaffold from some notes he had prepared (the paper was found lying there after his head was struck off), and one blow of the axe killed him, in the forty-ninth year of his age.

This bold and daring act, the Parliament accompanied by other famous measures, all originating (as even this did) in the King's hav-

ing so grossly and so long abused his power. The name of DELIN-
QUENTS was applied to all sheriffs and other officers who had been
concerned in raising the ship money, or any other money, from the
people, in an unlawful manner; the Hampden judgment was reversed;
the judges who had decided against Hampden were called upon to
give large securities that they would take such consequences as Parliament might impose upon them; and one was arrested as he sat in
High Court, and carried off to prison. Laud was impeached; the unfortunate victims whose ears had been cropped and whose noses had
been slit, were brought out of prison in triumph; and a bill was passed
declaring that a Parliament should be called every third year, and
that if the King and the King's officers did not call it, the people
should assemble of themselves and summon it, as of their own right
and power. Great illuminations and rejoicings took place over all
these things, and the country was wildly excited. That the Parliament took advantage of this excitement and stirred them up by every
means, there is no doubt; but you are always to remember those
twelve long years, during which the King had tried so hard whether
he really could do any wrong or not.

All this time there was a great religious outcry against the right of
the Bishops to sit in Parliament; to which the Scottish people particularly objected. The English were divided on this subject, and,
partly on this account and partly because they had had foolish
expectations that the Parliament would be able to take off nearly all
the taxes, numbers of them sometimes wavered and inclined towards
the King.

I believe myself, that if, at this or almost any other period of his
life, the King could have been trusted by any man not out of his senses,
he might have saved himself and kept his throne. But, on the English
army being disbanded, he plotted with the officers again, as he had
done before, and established the fact beyond all doubt by putting his
signature of approval to a petition against the Parliamentary leaders,
which was drawn up by certain officers. When the Scottish army was
disbanded, he went to Edinburgh in four days—which was going very
fast at that time—to plot again, and so darkly too, that it is difficult
to decide what his whole object was. Some suppose that he wanted
to gain over the Scottish Parliament, as he did in fact gain over, by
presents and favours, many Scottish lords and men of power. Some
think that he went to get proofs against the Parliamentary leaders in
England of their having treasonably invited the Scottish people to
come and help them. With whatever object he went to Scotland, he did
little good by going. At the instigation of the EARL OF MONTROSE, a
desperate man who was then in prison for plotting, he tried to kidnap
three Scottish lords who escaped. A committee of the Parliament at
home, who had followed to watch him, writing an account of this
INCIDENT, as it was called, to the Parliament, the Parliament made a
fresh stir about it; were, or feigned to be, much alarmed for themselves; and wrote to the EARL OF ESSEX, the commander-in-chief, for
a guard to protect them.

It is not absolutely proved that the King plotted in Ireland besides, but it is very probable that he did, and that the Queen did, and that he had some wild hope of gaining the Irish people over to his side by favouring a rise among them. Whether or no, they did rise in a most brutal and savage rebellion; in which, encouraged by their priests, they committed such atrocities upon numbers of the English, of both sexes and of all ages, as nobody could believe, but for their being related on oath by eye-witnesses. Whether one hundred thousand or two hundred thousand Protestants were murdered in this outbreak, is uncertain; but, that it was as ruthless and barbarous an outbreak as ever was known among any savage people, is certain.

The King came home from Scotland, determined to make a great struggle for his lost power. He believed that, through his presents and favours, Scotland would take no part against him; and the Lord Mayor of London received him with such a magnificent dinner that he thought he must have become popular again in England. It would take a good many Lord Mayors, however, to make a people, and the King soon found himself mistaken.

Not so soon, though, but that there was a great opposition in the Parliament to a celebrated paper put forth by Pym and Hampden and the rest, called "THE REMONSTRANCE," which set forth all the illegal acts that the King had ever done, but politely laid the blame of them on his bad advisers. Even when it was passed and presented to him, the King still thought himself strong enough to discharge Balfour from his command in the Tower, and to put in his place a man of bad character; to whom the Commons instantly objected, and whom he was obliged to abandon. At this time, the old outcry about the Bishops became louder than ever, and the old Archbishop of York was so near being murdered as he went down to the House of Lords—being laid hold of by the mob and violently knocked about, in return for very foolishly scolding a shrill boy who was yelping out "No Bishops!"—that he sent for all the Bishops who were in town, and proposed to them to sign a declaration that, as they could no longer without danger to their lives attend their duty in Parliament, they protested against the lawfulness of everything done in their absence. This they asked the King to send to the House of Lords, which he did. Then the House of Commons impeached the whole party of Bishops and sent them off to the Tower.

Taking no warning from this; but encouraged by there being a moderate party in the Parliament who objected to these strong measures, the King, on the third of January, one thousand six hundred and forty-two, took the rashest step that ever was taken by mortal man.

Of his own accord and without advice, he sent the Attorney-General to the House of Lords, to accuse of treason certain members of Parliament who as popular leaders were the most obnoxious to him; LORD KIMBOLTON, SIR ARTHUR HASELRIG, DENZIL HOLLIS, JOHN PYM (they used to call him King Pym, he possessed such power and looked so big), JOHN HAMPDEN, and WILLIAM STRODE. The houses of those members he caused to be entered, and their papers to be sealed up. At the same time, he sent a messenger to the House of Commons demanding to have the five gentlemen who were members of that House immediately produced. To this the house replied that they should appear as soon as there was any legal charge against them, and immediately adjourned.

Next day, the House of Commons sent into the City to let the Lord Mayor know that their privileges are invaded by the King, and that there is no safety for anybody or anything. Then, when the five members are gone out of the way, down comes the King himself, with all his guard and from two to three hundred gentlemen and soldiers, of whom the greater part were armed. These he leaves in the hall; and then, with his nephew at his side, goes into the House, takes off his hat, and walks up to the Speaker's chair. The Speaker leaves it, the King stands in front of it, looks about him steadily for a little while, and says he has come for those five members. No one speaks, and then he calls John Pym by name. No one speaks, and then he calls Denzil Hollis by name. No one speaks, and then he asks the Speaker of the House where those five members are? The Speaker, answering on his knee, nobly replies that he is the servant of that House, and that he has neither eyes to see, nor tongue to speak, anything but what the House commands him. Upon this, the King, beaten from that time evermore, replies that he will seek them himself, for they have committed treason; and goes out, with his hat in his hand, amid some audible murmurs from the members.

No words can describe the hurry that arose out of doors when all this was known. The five members had gone for safety to a house in Coleman-street, in the City, where they were guarded all night; and indeed the whole city watched in arms like an army. At ten o'clock in the morning, the King, already frightened at what he had done, came to the Guildhall, with only half a dozen lords, and made a speech to the people, hoping they would not shelter those whom he accused of treason. Next day, he issued a proclamation for the apprehension of the five members; but the Parliament minded it so little that they made great arrangements for having them brought down to Westminster in great state, five days afterwards. The King was so alarmed now at his own imprudence, if not for his own safety, that he left his palace at Whitehall, and went away with his Queen and children to Hampton Court.

It was the eleventh of May, when the five members were carried in state and triumph to Westminster. They were taken by water. The river could not be seen for the boats on it; and the five members were hemmed in by barges full of men and great guns, ready to protect them, at any cost. Along the Strand a large body of the train-bands of London, under their commander, SKIPPON, marched to be ready to assist the little fleet. Beyond them, came a crowd who choked the streets, roaring incessantly about the Bishops and the Papists, and crying out contemptuously as they passed Whitehall, "What has become of the King?" With this great noise outside the House of

Commons, and with great silence within, Mr. Pym rose and informed the House of the great kindness with which they had been received in the City. Upon that, the House called the sheriffs in and thanked them, and requested the train-bands, under their commander Skippon, to guard the House of Commons every day. Then, came four thousand men on horseback out of Buckinghamshire, offering their services as a guard too, and bearing a petition to the King, complaining of the injury that had been done to Mr. Hampden, who was their county man and much beloved and honoured.

When the King set off for Hampton Court, the gentlemen and soldiers who had been with him followed him out of town as far as Kingston-upon-Thames; next day, Lord Digby came to them from the King at Hampton Court, in his coach and six, to inform them that the King accepted their protection. This, the Parliament said, was making war against the kingdom, and Lord Digby fled abroad. The Parliament then immediately applied themselves to getting hold of the military power of the country, well knowing that the King was already trying hard to use it against them, and that he had secretly sent the Earl of Newcastle to Hull, to secure a valuable magazine of arms and gunpowder that was there. In those times, every county had its own magazines of arms and powder, for its own train-bands or militia; so, the Parliament brought in a bill claiming the right (which up to this time had belonged to the King) of appointing the Lord Lieutenants of counties, who commanded these train-bands; also, of having all the forts, castles, and garrisons in the kingdom, put into the hands of such governors as they, the Parliament, could confide in. It also passed a law depriving the Bishops of their votes. The King gave his assent to that bill, but would not abandon the right of appointing the Lord Lieutenants, though he said he was willing to appoint such as might be suggested to him by the Parliament. When the Earl of Pembroke asked him whether he would not give way on that question for a time, he said, "By God! not for one hour!" and upon this he and the Parliament went to war.

His young daughter was betrothed to the Prince of Orange. On pretence of taking her to the country of her future husband, the Queen was already got safely away to Holland, there to pawn the Crown jewels for money to raise an army on the King's side. The Lord Admiral being sick, the House of Commons now named the Earl of Warwick to hold his place for a year. The King named another gentleman; the House of Commons took its own way, and the Earl of Warwick became Lord Admiral without the King's consent. The Parliament sent orders down to Hull to have that magazine removed to London; the King went down to Hull to take it himself. The citizens would not admit him into the town, and the governor would not admit him into the castle. The Parliament resolved that whatever the two Houses passed, and the King would not consent to, should be called an ORDINANCE, and should be as much a law as if he did consent to it. The King protested against this, and gave notice that these ordinances were not to be obeyed. The King, attended by the majority of the House of Peers, and by many members of the House of Commons, established himself at York. The Chancellor went to him with the Great Seal, and the Parliament made a new Great Seal. The Queen sent over a ship full of arms and ammunition, and the King issued letters to borrow money at high interest. The Parliament raised twenty regiments of foot and seventy-five troops of horse; and the people willingly aided them with their money, plate, jewellery, and trinkets—the married women even with their wedding-rings. Every member of Parliament who could raise a troop or a regiment in his own part of the country, dressed it according to his taste and in his own colours, and commanded it. Foremost among them all, OLIVER CROMWELL raised a troop of horse—thoroughly in earnest and thoroughly well armed—who were, perhaps, the best soldiers that ever were seen.

In some of their proceedings, this famous Parliament passed the bounds of previous law and custom, yielded to and favoured riotous assemblages of the people, and acted tyrannically in imprisoning some who differed from the popular leaders. But again, you are always to remember that the twelve years during which the King had had his own wilful way, had gone before; and that nothing could make the times what they might, could, would, or should have been, if those twelve years had never rolled away.

THIRD PART

I SHALL not try to relate the particulars of the great civil war between King Charles the First and the Long Parliament, which lasted nearly four years, and a full account of which would fill many large books. It was a sad thing that Englishmen should once more be fighting against Englishmen on English ground; but, it is some consolation to know that on both sides there was great humanity, forbearance, and honour. The soldiers of the Parliament were far more remarkable for these good qualities than the soldiers of the King (many of whom fought for mere pay without much caring for the cause); but those of the nobility and gentry who were on the King's side were so brave, and so faithful to him, that their conduct cannot but command our highest admiration. Among them were great numbers of Catholics, who took the royal side because the Queen was so strongly of their persuasion.

The King might have distinguished some of these gallant spirits, if he had been as generous a spirit himself, by giving them the command of his army. Instead of that, however, true to his old high notions of royalty, he entrusted it to his two nephews, PRINCE RUPERT and PRINCE MAURICE, who were of royal blood and came over from abroad to help him. It might have been better for him if they had stayed away; since Prince Rupert was an impetuous, hot-headed fellow, whose only idea was to dash into battle at all times and seasons, and lay about him.

The general-in-chief of the Parliamentary army was the Earl of Essex, a gentleman of honour and an excellent soldier. A little while before the war broke out, there had been some rioting at Westminster between certain officious law students and noisy soldiers, and the shopkeepers and their apprentices, and the general people in the streets. At that time the King's friends called the crowd, Roundheads, because the apprentices wore short hair; the crowd, in return, called their opponents Cavaliers, meaning that they were a blustering set, who pretended to be very military. These two words now began to be used to distinguish the two sides in the civil war. The Royalists also called the Parliamentary men Rebels and Rogues, while the Parliamentary men called *them* Malignants, and spoke of themselves as the Godly, the Honest, and so forth.

The war broke out at Portsmouth, where that double traitor Goring had again gone over to the King and was besieged by the Parliamentary troops. Upon this, the King proclaimed the Earl of Essex and the officers serving under him, traitors, and called upon his loyal subjects to meet him in arms at Nottingham on the twenty-fifth of August. But his loyal subjects came about him in scanty numbers, and it was a windy, gloomy day, and the Royal Standard got blown down, and the whole affair was very melancholy. The chief engagements after this, took place in the vale of the Red Horse near Banbury, at Brentford, at Devizes, at Chalgrove Field (where Mr. Hampden was so sorely wounded while fighting at the head of his men, that he died within a week), at Newbury (in which battle LORD FALKLAND, one of the best noblemen on the King's side, was killed), at Leicester, at Naseby, at Winchester, at Marston Moor near York, at Newcastle, and in many other parts of England and Scotland. These battles were attended with various successes. At one time, the King was victorious; at another time, the Parliament. But almost all the great and busy towns were against the King; and when it was considered necessary to fortify London, all ranks of people, from labouring men and women, up to lords and ladies, worked hard together with heartiness and good will. The most distinguished leaders on the Parliamentary side were HAMPDEN, SIR THOMAS FAIRFAX, and, above all, OLIVER CROMWELL, and his son-in-law IRETON.

During the whole of this war, the people, to whom it was very expensive and irksome, and to whom it was made the more distressing by almost every family being divided—some of its members attaching themselves to one side and some to the other—were over and over again most anxious for peace. So were some of the best men in each cause. Accordingly, treaties of peace were discussed between commissioners from the Parliament and the King; at York, at Oxford (where the King held a little Parliament of his own), and at Uxbridge. But they came to nothing. In all these negotiations, and in all his difficulties, the King showed himself at his best. He was courageous, cool, self-possessed, and clever; but, the old taint of his character was always in him, and he was never for one single moment to be trusted. Lord Clarendon, the historian, one of his highest admirers, supposes that he had unhappily promised the Queen never to make peace without her consent, and that this must often be taken as his excuse. He never kept his word from night to morning. He signed a cessation of hostilities with the blood-stained Irish rebels for a sum of money, and invited the Irish regiments over, to help him against the Parliament. In the battle of Naseby, his cabinet was seized and was found to contain a correspondence with the Queen, in which he expressly told her that he had deceived the Parliament—a mongrel Parliament, he called it now, as an improvement on his old term of vipers— in pretending to recognise it and to treat with it; and from which it further appeared that he had long been in secret treaty with the Duke of Lorraine for a foreign army of ten thousand men. Disappointed in this, he sent a most devoted friend of his, the EARL OF GLAMORGAN, to Ireland, to conclude a secret treaty with the Catholic powers, to send him an Irish army of ten thousand men; in return for which he was to bestow great favours on the Catholic religion. And, when this treaty was discovered in the carriage of a fighting Irish Archbishop who was killed in one of the many skirmishes of those days, he basely denied and deserted his attached friend, the Earl, on his being charged with high treason; and—even worse than this—had left blanks in the secret instructions he gave him with his own kingly hand, expressly that he might thus save himself.

At last, on the twenty-seventh of April, one thousand six hundred and forty-six, the King found himself in the city of Oxford, so surrounded by the Parliamentary army who were closing in upon him on all sides that he felt that if he would escape he must delay no longer. So, that night, having altered the cut of his hair and beard, he was dressed up as a servant and put upon a horse with a cloak strapped behind him, and rode out of the town behind one of his own faithful followers, with a clergyman of that country who knew the road well, for a guide. He rode towards London as far as Harrow, and then altered his plans and resolved, it would seem, to go to the Scottish camp. The Scottish men had been invited over to help the Parliamentary army, and had a large force then in England. The King was so desperately intriguing in everything he did, that it is doubtful what he exactly meant by this step. He took it, anyhow, and delivered himself up to the EARL OF LEVEN, the Scottish general-in-chief, who treated him as an honourable prisoner. Negotiations between the Parliament on the one hand and the Scottish authorities on the other, as to what should be done with him, lasted until the following February. Then, when the King had refused to the Parliament the concession of that old militia point for twenty years, and had refused to Scotland the recognition of its Solemn League and Covenant, Scotland got a handsome sum for its army and its help, and the King into the bargain. He was taken, by certain Parliamentary commissioners appointed to receive him, to one of his own houses, called Holmby House, near Althorpe, in Northamptonshire.

While the Civil War was still in progress, John Pym died, and was buried with great honour in Westminster Abbey—not with greater honour than he deserved, for the liberties of Englishmen owe a mighty debt to Pym and Hampden. The war was but newly over when the Earl of Essex died, of an illness brought on by his having overheated himself in a stag hunt in Windsor Forest. He, too, was buried in Westminster Abbey, with great state. I wish it were not necessary to add that Archbishop Laud died upon the scaffold when the war was not yet done. His trial lasted in all nearly a year, and, it being doubtful even then whether the charges brought against him amounted to treason, the odious old contrivance of the worst kings was resorted to, and a bill of attainder was brought in against him. He was a violently prejudiced and mischievous person; had had strong ear-cropping and nose-splitting propensities, as you know; and had done a world of harm. But he died peacefully, and like a brave old man.

FOURTH PART

WHEN the Parliament had got the King into their hands, they became very anxious to get rid of their army, in which Oliver Cromwell had begun to acquire great power; not only because of his courage and high abilities, but because he professed to be very sincere in the Scottish sort of Puritan religion that was then exceedingly popular among the soldiers. They were as much opposed to the Bishops as to the Pope himself; and the very privates, drummers, and trumpeters, had such an inconvenient habit of starting up and preaching long-winded discourses, that I would not have belonged to that army on any account.

So, the Parliament, being far from sure but that the army might begin to preach and fight against them now it had nothing else to do, proposed to disband the greater part of it, to send another part to serve in Ireland against the rebels, and to keep only a small force in England. But, the army would not consent to be broken up, except upon its own conditions; and, when the Parliament showed an intention of compelling it, it acted for itself in an unexpected manner. A certain cornet, of the name of JOICE, arrived at Holmby House one night, attended by four hundred horsemen, went into the King's room with his hat in one hand and a pistol in the other, and told the King that he had come to take him away. The King was willing enough to go, and only stipulated that he should be publicly required to do so next morning. Next morning, accordingly, he appeared on the top of the steps of the house, and asked Cornet Joice before his men and the guard set there by the Parliament, what authority he had for taking him away? To this Cornet Joice replied, "The authority of the army." "Have you a written commission?" said the King. Joice, pointing to his four hundred men on horseback, replied, "That is my commission." "Well," said the King, smiling, as if he were pleased, "I never before read such a commission; but it is written in fair and legible characters. This is a company of as handsome proper gentlemen as I have seen a long while." He was asked where he would like to live, and he said at Newmarket. So, to Newmarket he and

Cornet Joice and the four hundred horsemen rode; the King remarking, in the same smiling way, that he could ride as far at a spell as Cornet Joice, or any man there.

The King quite believed, I think, that the army were his friends. He said as much to Fairfax when that general, Oliver Cromwell, and Ireton, went to persuade him to return to the custody of the Parliament. He preferred to remain as he was, and resolved to remain as he was. And when the army moved nearer and nearer London to frighten the Parliament into yielding to their demands, they took the King with them. It was a deplorable thing that England should be at the mercy of a great body of soldiers with arms in their hands; but the King certainly favoured them at this important time of his life, as compared with the more lawful power that tried to control him. It must be added, however, that they treated him, as yet, more respectfully and kindly than the Parliament had done. They allowed him to be attended by his own servants, to be splendidly entertained at various houses, and to see his children—at Cavesham House, near Reading—for two days. Whereas, the Parliament had been rather hard with him, and had only allowed him to ride out and play at bowls.

It is much to be believed that if the King could have been trusted, even at this time, he might have been saved. Even Oliver Cromwell expressly said that he did believe that no man could enjoy his possessions in peace, unless the King had his rights. He was not unfriendly towards the King; he had been present when he received his children, and had been much affected by the pitiable nature of the scene; he saw the King often; he frequently walked and talked with him in the long galleries and pleasant gardens of the Palace at Hampton Court, whither he was now removed; and in all this risked something of his influence with the army. But, the King was in secret hopes of help from the Scottish people; and the moment he was encouraged to join them he began to be cool to his new friends, the army, and to tell the officers that they could not possibly do without him. At the very time, too, when he was promising to make Cromwell and Ireton noblemen, if they would help him up to his old height, he was writing to the Queen that he meant to hang them. They both afterwards declared that they had been privately informed that such a letter would be found, on a certain evening, sewed up in a saddle which would be taken to the Blue Boar in Holborn to be sent to Dover; and that they went there, disguised as common soldiers, and sat drinking in the inn-yard until a man came with the saddle, which they ripped up with their knives, and therein found the letter. I see little reason to doubt the story. It is certain that Oliver Cromwell told one of the King's most faithful followers that the King could not be trusted, and that he would not be answerable if anything amiss were to happen to him. Still, even after that, he kept a promise he had made to the King, by letting him know that there was a plot with a certain portion of the army to seize him. I believe that, in fact, he sincerely wanted the King to escape abroad, and so to be got rid of without more trouble or danger. That Oliver himself had work enough with the army is pretty plain; for some of the troops were so mutinous against him, and against those who acted with him at this time, that he found it necessary to have one man shot at the head of his regiment to overawe the rest.

The King, when he received Oliver's warning, made his escape from Hampton Court; after some indecision and uncertainty, he went to Carisbrooke Castle in the Isle of Wight. At first, he was pretty free there; but, even there, he carried on a pretended treaty with the Parliament, while he was really treating with commissioners from Scotland to send an army into England to take his part. When he broke off this treaty with the Parliament (having settled with Scotland) and was treated as a prisoner, his treatment was not changed too soon, for he had plotted to escape that very night to a ship sent by the Queen, which was lying off the island.

He was doomed to be disappointed in his hopes from Scotland. The agreement he had made with the Scottish Commissioners was not favourable enough to the religion of that country to please the Scottish clergy; and they preached against it. The consequence was, that the army raised in Scotland and sent over, was too small to do much; and that, although it was helped by a rising of the Royalists in England and by good soldiers from Ireland, it could make no head against the Parliamentary army under such men as Cromwell and Fairfax. The King's eldest son, the Prince of Wales, came over from Holland with nineteen ships (a part of the English fleet having gone over to him) to help his father; but nothing came of his voyage, and he was fain to return. The most remarkable event of this second civil war was the cruel execution by the Parliamentary General, of SIR CHARLES LUCAS and SIR GEORGE LISLE, two grand Royalist generals, who had bravely defended Colchester under every disadvantage of famine and distress for nearly three months. When Sir Charles Lucas was shot, Sir George Lisle kissed his body, and said to the soldiers who were to shoot him, "Come nearer, and make sure of me." "I warrant you, Sir George," said one of the soldiers, "we shall hit you." "Ay?" he returned with a smile, "but I have been nearer to you, my friends, many a time, and you have missed me."

The Parliament, after being fearfully bullied by the army—who demanded to have seven members whom they disliked given up to them—had voted that they would have nothing more to do with the King. On the conclusion, however, of this second civil war (which did not last more than six months), they appointed commissioners to treat with him. The King, then so far released again as to be allowed to live in a private house at Newport in the Isle of Wight, managed his own part of the negotiation with a sense that was admired by all who saw him, and gave up, in the end, all that was asked of him— even yielding (which he had steadily refused, so far) to the temporary abolition of the bishops, and the transfer of their church land to the Crown. Still, with his old fatal vice upon him, when his best friends joined the commissioners in beseeching him to yield all those points

as the only means of saving himself from the army, he was plotting
to escape from the island; he was holding correspondence with his
friends and the Catholics in Ireland, though declaring that he was
not; and he was writing, with his own hand, that in what he yielded
he meant nothing but to get time to escape.

Matters were at this pass when the army, resolved to defy the
Parliament, marched up to London. The Parliament, not afraid of
them now, and boldly led by Hollis, voted that the King's concessions
were sufficient ground for settling the peace of the kingdom. Upon
that, COLONEL RICH and COLONEL PRIDE went down to the House of
Commons with a regiment of horse soldiers and a regiment of foot;
and Colonel Pride, standing in the lobby with a list of the members
who were obnoxious to the army in his hand, had them pointed out
to him as they came through, and took them all into custody. This
proceeding was afterwards called by the people, for a joke, PRIDE'S
PURGE. Cromwell was in the North, at the head of his men, at the
time, but when he came home, approved of what had been done.

What with imprisoning some members and causing others to stay
away, the army had now reduced the House of Commons to some
fifty or so. These soon voted that it was treason in a king to make war
against his parliament and his people, and sent an ordinance up to
the House of Lords for the King's being tried as a traitor. The House
of Lords, then sixteen in number, to a man rejected it. Thereupon,
the Commons made an ordinance of their own, that they were the
supreme government of the country, and would bring the King to
trial.

The King had been taken for security to a place called Hurst
Castle: a lonely house on a rock in the sea, connected with the coast
of Hampshire by a rough road two miles long at low water. Thence,
he was ordered to be removed to Windsor; thence, after being but
rudely used there, and having none but soldiers to wait upon him at
table, he was brought up to St. James's Palace in London, and told
that his trial was appointed for next day.

On Saturday, the twentieth of January, one thousand six hundred
and forty-nine, this memorable trial began. The House of Commons
had settled that one hundred and thirty-five persons should form the
Court, and these were taken from the House itself, from among the
officers of the army, and from among the lawyers and citizens. JOHN
BRADSHAW, serjeant-at-law, was appointed president. The place was
Westminster Hall. At the upper end, in a red velvet chair, sat the
president, with his hat (lined with plates of iron for his protection)
on his head. The rest of the Court sat on side benches, also wearing
their hats. The King's seat was covered with velvet, like that of the
president, and was opposite to it. He was brought from St. James's
to Whitehall, and from Whitehall he came by water to his trial.

When he came in, he looked round very steadily on the Court, and
on the great number of spectators, and then sat down: presently he
got up, and looked round again. On the indictment "against Charles
Stuart, for high treason," being read, he smiled several times, and he

denied the authority of the Court, saying that there could be no parliament without a House of Lords, and that he saw no House of Lords there. Also, that the King ought to be there, and that he saw no King in the King's right place. Bradshaw replied, that the Court was satisfied with its authority, and that its authority was God's authority and the kingdom's. He then adjourned the Court to the following Monday. On that day, the trial was resumed, and went on all the week. When the Saturday came, as the King passed forward to his place in the Hall, some soldiers and others cried for "justice!" and execution on him. That day, too, Bradshaw, like an angry Sultan, wore a red robe, instead of the black robe he had worn before. The King was sentenced to death that day. As he went out, one solitary soldier said, "God bless you, Sir!" For this, his officer struck him. The King said he thought the punishment exceeded the offence. The silver head of his walking-stick had fallen off while he leaned upon it, at one time of the trial. The accident seemed to disturb him, as if he thought it ominous of the falling of his own head; and he admitted as much, now it was all over.

Being taken back to Whitehall, he sent to the House of Commons, saying that as the time of his execution might be nigh, he wished he might be allowed to see his darling children. It was granted. On the Monday he was taken back to St. James's; and his two children then in England, the PRINCESS ELIZABETH thirteen years old, and the DUKE OF GLOUCESTER nine years old, were brought to take leave of him, from Sion House, near Brentford. It was a sad and touching scene, when he kissed and fondled those poor children, and made a little present of two diamond seals to the Princess, and gave them tender messages to their mother (who little deserved them, for she had a lover of her own whom she married soon afterwards), and told them that he died "for the laws and liberties of the land." I am bound to say that I don't think he did, but I dare say he believed so.

There were ambassadors from Holland that day, to intercede for the unhappy King, whom you and I both wish the Parliament had spared; but they got no answer. The Scottish Commissioners interceded too; so did the Prince of Wales, by a letter in which he offered as the next heir to the throne, to accept any conditions from the Parliament; so did the Queen, by letter likewise. Notwithstanding all, the warrant for the execution was this day signed. There is a story that as Oliver Cromwell went to the table with the pen in his hand to put his signature to it, he drew his pen across the face of one of the commissioners, who was standing near, and marked it with ink. That commissioner had not signed his own name yet, and the story adds that when he came to do it he marked Cromwell's face with ink in the same way.

The King slept well, untroubled by the knowledge that it was his last night on earth, and rose on the thirtieth of January, two hours before day, and dressed himself carefully. He put on two shirts lest he should tremble with the cold, and had his hair very carefully combed. The warrant had been directed to three officers of the army,

COLONEL HACKER, COLONEL HUNKS, and COLONEL PHAYER. At ten o'clock, the first of these came to the door and said it was time to go to Whitehall. The King, who had always been a quick walker, walked at his usual speed through the Park, and called out to the guard, with his accustomed voice of command, "March on apace!" When he came to Whitehall, he was taken to his own bedroom, where a breakfast was set forth. As he had taken the Sacrament, he would eat nothing more; but, at about the time when the church bells struck twelve at noon (for he had to wait, through the scaffold not being ready), he took the advice of the good BISHOP JUXON who was with him, and ate a little bread and drank a glass of claret. Soon after he had taken this refreshment, Colonel Hacker came to the chamber with the warrant in his hand, and called for Charles Stuart.

And then, through the long gallery of Whitehall Palace, which he had often seen light and gay and merry and crowded, in very different times, the fallen King passed along, until he came to the centre window of the Banqueting House, through which he emerged upon the scaffold, which was hung with black. He looked at the two executioners, who were dressed in black and masked; he looked at the troops of soldiers on horseback and on foot, and all looked up at him in silence; he looked at the vast array of spectators, filling up the view beyond, and turning all their faces upon him; he looked at his old Palace of St. James's; and he looked at the block. He seemed a little troubled to find that it was so low, and asked, "if there were no place higher?" Then, to those upon the scaffold, he said "that it was the Parliament who had begun the war, and not he; but he hoped they might be guiltless too, as ill instruments had gone between them. In one respect," he said, "he suffered justly; and that was because he had permitted an unjust sentence to be executed on another." In this he referred to the Earl of Strafford.

He was not at all afraid to die; but he was anxious to die easily. When some one touched the axe while he was speaking, he broke off and called out, "Take heed of the axe! take heed of the axe!" He also said to Colonel Hacker, "Take care that they do not put me to pain." He told the executioner, "I shall say but very short prayers, and then thrust out my hands"—as the sign to strike.

He put his hair up, under a white satin cap which the bishop had carried, and said, "I have a good cause and a gracious God on my side." The bishop told him that he had but one stage more to travel in this weary world, and that, though it was a turbulent and troublesome stage, it was a short one, and would carry him a great way—all the way from earth to Heaven. The King's last word, as he gave his cloak and the George—the decoration from his breast—to the bishop, was, "Remember!" He then kneeled down, laid his head on the block, spread out his hands, and was instantly killed. One universal groan broke from the crowd; and the soldiers, who had sat on their horses and stood in their ranks immovable as statues, were of a sudden all in motion, clearing the streets.

Thus, in the forty-ninth year of his age, falling at the same time of his career as Strafford had fallen in his, perished Charles the First. With all my sorrow for him, I cannot agree with him that he died "the martyr of the people;" for the people had been martyrs to him, and to his ideas of a King's rights, long before. Indeed, I am afraid that he was but a bad judge of martyrs; for he had called that infamous Duke of Buckingham "the Martyr of his Sovereign."

CHAPTER XXXIV

ENGLAND UNDER OLIVER CROMWELL

BEFORE sunset on the memorable day on which King Charles the First was executed, the House of Commons passed an act declaring it treason in any one to proclaim the Prince of Wales—or anybody else—King of England. Soon afterwards, it declared that the House of Lords was useless and dangerous, and ought to be abolished; and directed that the late King's statue should be taken down from the Royal Exchange in the City and other public places. Having laid hold of some famous Royalists who had escaped from prison, and having beheaded the DUKE OF HAMILTON, LORD HOLLAND, and LORD CAPEL, in Palace Yard (all of whom died very courageously), they then appointed a Council of State to govern the country. It consisted of forty-one members, of whom five were peers. Bradshaw was made president. The House of Commons also re-admitted members who had opposed the King's death, and made up its numbers to about a hundred and fifty.

But, it still had an army of more than forty thousand men to deal with, and a very hard task it was to manage them. Before the King's execution, the army had appointed some of its officers to remonstrate between them and the Parliament; and now the common soldiers began to take that office upon themselves. The regiments under orders for Ireland mutinied; one troop of horse in the city of London seized their own flag, and refused to obey orders. For this, the ring-leader was shot: which did not mend the matter, for, both his comrades and the people made a public funeral for him, and accompanied the body to the grave with sound of trumpets and with a gloomy procession of persons carrying bundles of rosemary steeped in blood. Oliver was the only man to deal with such difficulties as these, and he soon cut them short by bursting at midnight into the town of Burford, near Salisbury, where the mutineers were sheltered, taking four hundred of them prisoners, and shooting a number of them by sentence of court-martial. The soldiers soon found, as all men did, that Oliver was not a man to be trifled with. And there was an end of the mutiny.

The Scottish Parliament did not know Oliver yet; so, on hearing of the King's execution, it proclaimed the Prince of Wales King Charles the Second, on condition of his respecting the Solemn League and Covenant. Charles was abroad at that time, and so was Montrose, from whose help he had hopes enough to keep him holding on and off with commissioners from Scotland, just as his father might have done. These hopes were soon at an end; for, Montrose, having raised a few hundred exiles in Germany, and landed with them in Scotland, found that the people there, instead of joining him, deserted the country at his approach. He was soon taken prisoner and carried to Edinburgh. There he was received with every possible insult, and carried to prison in a cart, his officers going two and two before him. He was sentenced by the Parliament to be hanged on a gallows thirty feet high, to have his head set on a spike in Edinburgh, and his limbs distributed in other places, according to the old barbarous manner. He said he had always acted under the Royal orders, and only wished he had limbs enough to be distributed through Christendom, that it might be the more widely known how loyal he had been. He went to the scaffold in a bright and brilliant dress, and made a bold end at thirty-eight years of age. The breath was scarcely out of his body when Charles abandoned his memory, and denied that he had ever given him orders to rise in his behalf. O the family failing was strong in that Charles then!

Oliver had been appointed by the Parliament to command the army in Ireland, where he took a terrible vengeance for the sanguinary rebellion, and made tremendous havoc, particularly in the siege of Drogheda, where no quarter was given, and where he found at least a thousand of the inhabitants shut up together in the great church: every one of whom was killed by his soldiers, usually known as OLIVER'S IRONSIDES. There were numbers of friars and priests among them, and Oliver gruffly wrote home in his despatch that these were "knocked on the head" like the rest.

But, Charles having got over to Scotland where the men of the Solemn League and Covenant led him a prodigiously dull life and made him very weary with long sermons and grim Sundays, the Parliament called the redoubtable Oliver home to knock the Scottish men on the head for setting up that Prince. Oliver left his son-in-law, Ireton, as general in Ireland in his stead (he died there afterwards), and he imitated the example of his father-in-law with such good will that he brought the country to subjection, and laid it at the feet of the Parliament. In the end, they passed an act for the settlement of Ireland, generally pardoning all the common people, but exempting from this grace such of the wealthier sort as had been concerned in the rebellion, or in any killing of Protestants, or who refused to lay down their arms. Great numbers of Irish were got out of the country to serve under Catholic powers abroad, and a quantity of land was declared to have been forfeited by past offences, and was given to people who had lent money to the Parliament early in the war. These were sweeping measures; but, if Oliver Cromwell had had his own way fully, and had stayed in Ireland, he would have done more yet.

However, as I have said, the Parliament wanted Oliver for Scotland; so, home Oliver came, and was made Commander of all the Forces of the Commonwealth of England, and in three days away he went with sixteen thousand soldiers to fight the Scottish men. Now, the Scottish men, being then—as you will generally find them now—mighty cautious, reflected that the troops they had were not used to war like the Ironsides, and would be beaten in an open fight. Therefore they said, "If we live quiet in our trenches in Edinburgh here, and if all the farmers come into the town and desert the country, the Ironsides will be driven out by iron hunger and be forced to go away." This was, no doubt, the wisest plan; but as the Scottish clergy *would* interfere with what they knew nothing about, and would perpetually preach long sermons exhorting the soldiers to come out and fight, the soldiers got it in their heads that they absolutely must come out and fight. Accordingly, in an evil hour for themselves, they came out of their safe position. Oliver fell upon them instantly, and killed three thousand, and took ten thousand prisoners.

To gratify the Scottish Parliament, and preserve their favour, Charles had signed a declaration they laid before him, reproaching the memory of his father and mother, and representing himself as a most religious Prince, to whom the Solemn League and Covenant was as dear as life. He meant no sort of truth in this, and soon afterwards galloped away on horseback to join some tiresome Highland friends, who were always flourishing dirks and broadswords. He was overtaken and induced to return; but this attempt, which was called "The Start," did him just so much service, that they did not preach quite such long sermons at him afterwards as they had done before.

On the first of January, one thousand six hundred and fifty-one, the Scottish people crowned him at Scone. He immediately took the chief command of an army of twenty thousand men, and marched to Stirling. His hopes were heightened, I dare say, by the redoubtable Oliver being ill of an ague; but Oliver scrambled out of bed in no time, and went to work with such energy that he got behind the Royalist army and cut it off from all communication with Scotland. There was nothing for it then, but to go on to England; so it went on as far as Worcester, where the mayor and some of the gentry proclaimed King Charles the Second straightway. His proclamation, however, was of little use to him, for very few Royalists appeared; and, on the very same day, two people were publicly beheaded on Tower Hill for espousing his cause. Up came Oliver to Worcester too, at double quick speed, and he and his Ironsides so laid about them in the great battle which was fought there, that they completely beat the Scottish men, and destroyed the Royalist army; though the Scottish men fought so gallantly that it took five hours to do.

The escape of Charles after this battle of Worcester did him good service long afterwards, for it induced many of the generous English people to take a romantic interest in him, and to think much better of him than he ever deserved. He fled in the night, with not more than sixty followers, to the house of a Catholic lady in Staffordshire.

There, for his greater safety, the whole sixty left him. He cropped his hair, stained his face and hands brown as if they were sunburnt, put on the clothes of a labouring countryman, and went out in the morning with his axe in his hand, accompanied by four wood-cutters who were brothers, and another man who was their brother-in-law. These good fellows made a bed for him under a tree, as the weather was very bad; and the wife of one of them brought him food to eat; and the old mother of the four brothers came and fell down on her knees before him in the wood, and thanked God that her sons were engaged in saving his life. At night, he came out of the forest and went on to another house which was near the river Severn, with the intention of passing into Wales; but the place swarmed with soldiers, and the bridges were guarded, and all the boats were made fast. So, after lying in a hayloft covered over with hay, for some time, he came out of his place, attended by COLONEL CARELESS, a Catholic gentleman who had met him there, and with whom he lay hid, all next day, up in the shady branches of a fine old oak. It was lucky for the King that it was September time, and that the leaves had not begun to fall, since he and the Colonel, perched up in this tree, could catch glimpses of the soldiers riding about below, and could hear the crash in the wood as they went about beating the boughs.

After this, he walked and walked until his feet were all blistered; and, having been concealed all one day in a house which was searched by the troopers while he was there, went with LORD WILMOT, another of his good friends, to a place called Bentley, where one MISS LANE, a Protestant lady, had obtained a pass to be allowed to ride through the guards to see a relation of hers near Bristol. Disguised as a servant, he rode in the saddle before this young lady to the house of SIR JOHN WINTER, while Lord Wilmot rode there boldly, like a plain country gentleman, with dogs at his heels. It happened that Sir John Winter's butler had been servant in Rich-mond Palace, and knew Charles the moment he set eyes upon him; but, the butler was faithful and kept the secret. As no ship could be found to carry him abroad, it was planned that he should go—still travelling with Miss Lane as her servant—to another house, at Trent near Sherborne in Dorsetshire; and then Miss Lane and her cousin, MR. LASCELLES, who had gone on horseback beside her all the way, went home. I hope Miss Lane was going to marry that cousin, for I am sure she must have been a brave, kind girl. If I had been that cousin, I should certainly have loved Miss Lane.

When Charles, lonely for the loss of Miss Lane, was safe at Trent, a ship was hired at Lyme, the master of which engaged to take two gentlemen to France. In the evening of the same day, the King—now riding as servant before another young lady—set off for a public-house at a place called Charmouth, where the captain of the vessel was to take him on board. But, the captain's wife, being afraid of her husband getting into trouble, locked him up and would not let him sail. Then they went away to Bridport; and, coming to the inn there, found the stable-yard full of soldiers who were on the look-out for Charles, and who talked about him while they drank. He had such presence of mind, that he led the horses of his party through the yard as any other servant might have done, and said, "Come out of the way, you soldiers; let us have room to pass here!" As he went along, he met a half-tipsy ostler, who rubbed his eyes and said to him, "Why, I was formerly servant to Mr. Potter at Exeter, and surely I have sometimes seen you there, young man?" He certainly had, for Charles had lodged there. His ready answer was, "Ah, I did live with him once; but I have no time to talk now. We'll have a pot of beer together when I come back."

From this dangerous place he returned to Trent, and lay there concealed several days. Then he escaped to Heale, near Salisbury; where, in the house of a widow lady, he was hidden five days, until the master of a collier lying off Shoreham in Sussex, undertook to convey a "gentleman" to France. On the night of the fifteenth of October, accompanied by two colonels and a merchant, the King rode to Brighton, then a little fishing village, to give the captain of the ship a supper before going on board; but, so many people knew him, that this captain knew him too, and not only he, but the landlord and landlady also. Before he went away, the landlord came behind his chair, kissed his hand, and said he hoped to live to be a lord and to see his wife a lady; at which Charles laughed. They had had a good supper by this time, and plenty of smoking and drinking, at which the King was a first-rate hand; so, the captain assured him that he would stand by him, and he did. It was agreed that the captain should pretend to sail to Deal, and that Charles should address the sailors and say he was a gentleman in debt who was running away from his creditors, and that he hoped they would join him in persuading the captain to put him ashore in France. As the King acted his part very well indeed, and gave the sailors twenty shillings to drink, they begged the captain to do what such a worthy gentleman asked. He pretended to yield to their entreaties, and the King got safe to Normandy.

Ireland being now subdued, and Scotland kept quiet by plenty of forts and soldiers put there by Oliver, the Parliament would have gone on quietly enough, as far as fighting with any foreign enemy went, but for getting into trouble with the Dutch, who in the spring of the year one thousand six hundred and fifty-one sent a fleet into the Downs under their ADMIRAL VAN TROMP, to call upon the bold English ADMIRAL BLAKE (who was there with half as many ships as the Dutch) to strike his flag. Blake fired a raging broadside instead, and beat off Van Tromp; who, in the autumn, came back again with seventy ships, and challenged the bold Blake—who still was only half as strong—to fight him. Blake fought him all day; but, finding that the Dutch were too many for him, got quietly off at night. What does Van Tromp upon this, but goes cruising and boasting about the Channel, between the North Foreland and the Isle of Wight, with a great Dutch broom tied to his masthead, as a sign that he could and would sweep the English off the sea! Within three months, Blake lowered his tone though, and his broom too; for, he and two other bold commanders, DEAN and MONK, fought him three whole days, took twenty-three of his ships, shivered his broom to pieces, and settled his business.

Things were no sooner quiet again, than the army began to complain to the Parliament that they were not governing the nation properly, and to hint that they thought they could do it better themselves. Oliver, who had now made up his mind to be the head of the state, or nothing at all, supported them in this, and called a meeting of officers and his own Parliamentary friends, at his lodgings in Whitehall, to consider the best way of getting rid of the Parliament. It had now lasted just as many years as the King's unbridled power had lasted, before it came into existence. The end of the deliberation was, that Oliver went down to the House in his usual plain black dress, with his usual grey worsted stockings, but with an unusual party of soldiers behind him. These last he left in the lobby, and then went in and sat down. Presently he got up, made the Parliament a speech, told them that the Lord had done with them, stamped his foot and said, "You are no Parliament. Bring them in! Bring them in!" At this signal the door flew open, and the soldiers appeared. "This is not honest," said Sir Harry Vane, one of the members. "Sir Harry Vane!" cried Cromwell; "O, Sir Harry Vane! The Lord deliver me from Sir Harry Vane!" Then he pointed out members one by one, and said this man was a drunkard, and that man a dissipated fellow, and that man a liar, and so on. Then he caused the Speaker to be walked out of his chair, told the guard to clear the House, called the mace upon the table—which is a sign that the House is sitting—"a fool's bauble," and said, "here, carry it away!" Being obeyed in all these orders, he quietly locked the door, put the key in his pocket, walked back to Whitehall again, and told his friends, who were still assembled there, what he had done.

They formed a new Council of State after this extraordinary proceeding, and got a new Parliament together in their own way: which Oliver himself opened in a sort of sermon, and which he said was the beginning of a perfect heaven upon earth. In this Parliament there sat a well-known leather-seller, who had taken the singular name of Praise God Barebones, and from whom it was called, for a joke, Barebones's Parliament, though its general name was the Little Parliament. As it soon appeared that it was not going to put Oliver in the first place, it turned out to be not at all like the beginning of heaven upon earth, and Oliver said it really was not to be borne with. So he cleared off that Parliament in much the same way as he had disposed of the other; and then the council of officers decided that he must be made the supreme authority of the kingdom, under the title of Lord Protector of the Commonwealth.

So, on the sixteenth of December, one thousand six hundred and fifty-three, a great procession was formed at Oliver's door, and he came out in a black velvet suit and a big pair of boots, and got into his coach and went down to Westminster, attended by the judges, and the lord mayor, and the aldermen, and all the other great and wonderful personages of the country. There, in the Court of Chancery, he publicly accepted the office of Lord Protector. Then he was sworn, and the City sword was handed to him, and the seal was handed to him, and all the other things were handed to him which are usually handed to Kings and Queens on state occasions. When Oliver had handed them all back, he was quite made and completely finished off as Lord Protector; and several of the Ironsides preached about it at great length, all the evening.

SECOND PART

OLIVER CROMWELL—whom the people long called OLD NOLL—in accepting the office of Protector, had bound himself by a certain paper which was handed to him, called "the Instrument," to summon a Parliament, consisting of between four and five hundred members, in the election of which neither the Royalists nor the Catholics were to have any share. He had also pledged himself that this Parliament should not be dissolved without its own consent until it had sat five months.

When this Parliament met, Oliver made a speech to them of three hours long, very wisely advising them what to do for the credit and happiness of the country. To keep down the more violent members, he required them to sign a recognition of what they were forbidden by "the Instrument" to do; which was, chiefly, to take the power from one single person at the head of the state or to command the army. Then he dismissed them to go to work. With his usual vigour and resolution he went to work himself with some frantic preachers —who were rather overdoing their sermons in calling him a villain and a tyrant—by shutting up their chapels, and sending a few of them off to prison.

There was not at that time, in England or anywhere else, a man so able to govern the country as Oliver Cromwell. Although he ruled with a strong hand, and levied a very heavy tax on the Royalists (but not until they had plotted against his life), he ruled wisely, and as the times required. He caused England to be so respected abroad, that I wish some lords and gentlemen who have governed it under kings and queens in later days would have taken a leaf out of Oliver Cromwell's book. He sent bold Admiral Blake to the Mediterranean Sea, to make the Duke of Tuscany pay sixty thousand pounds for injuries he had done to British subjects, and spoliation he had committed on English merchants. He further despatched him and his fleet to Algiers, Tunis, and Tripoli, to have every English ship and every English man delivered up to him that had been taken by pirates in those parts. All this was gloriously done; and it began to be thoroughly well known, all over the world, that England was governed by a man in earnest, who would not allow the English name to be insulted or slighted anywhere.

These were not all his foreign triumphs. He sent a fleet to sea against the Dutch; and the two powers, each with one hundred ships upon its side, met in the English Channel off the North Foreland, where the fight lasted all day long. Dean was killed in this fight; but Monk, who commanded in the same ship with him, threw his cloak over his body, that the sailors might not know of his death, and be disheartened. Nor were they. The English broadsides so exceedingly astonished the Dutch that they sheered off at last, though the redoubtable Van Tromp fired upon them with his own guns for deserting their flag. Soon afterwards, the two fleets engaged again, off the coast of Holland. There, the valiant Van Tromp was shot through the heart, and the Dutch gave in, and peace was made.

Further than this, Oliver resolved not to bear the domineering and bigoted conduct of Spain, which country not only claimed a right to all the gold and silver that could be found in South America, and treated the ships of all other countries who visited those regions, as pirates, but put English subjects into the horrible Spanish prisons of the Inquisition. So Oliver told the Spanish ambassador that English ships must be free to go wherever they would, and that English merchants must not be thrown into those same dungeons, no, not for the pleasure of all the priests in Spain. To this, the Spanish ambassador replied that the gold and silver country, and the Holy Inquisition, were his King's two eyes, neither of which he could submit to have put out. Very well, said Oliver, then he was afraid he (Oliver) must damage those two eyes directly.

So, another fleet was despatched under two commanders, PENN and VENABLES, for Hispaniola; where, however, the Spaniards got the better of the fight. Consequently, the fleet came home again, after taking Jamaica on the way. Oliver, indignant with the two commanders who had not done what bold Admiral Blake would have done, clapped them both into prison, declared war against Spain, and made a treaty with France, in virtue of which it was to shelter the King and his brother the Duke of York no longer. Then, he sent a fleet abroad under bold Admiral Blake, which brought the King of Portugal to his senses—just to keep its hand in—and then engaged a Spanish fleet, sunk four great ships, and took two more, laden with silver to the value of two millions of pounds: which dazzling prize was brought from Portsmouth to London in waggons, with the populace of all the towns and villages through which the waggons passed, shouting with all their might. After this victory, bold Admiral Blake sailed away to the port of Santa Cruz to cut off the Spanish treasure-ships coming from Mexico. There, he found them, ten in number, with seven others to take care of them, and a big castle, and seven batteries, all roaring and blazing away at him with great guns. Blake cared no more for great guns than for pop-guns—no more for their hot iron balls than for snow-balls. He dashed into the harbour, captured and burnt every one of the ships, and came sailing out again triumphantly, with the victorious English flag flying at his masthead. This was the last triumph of this great commander, who had sailed and fought until he was quite worn out. He died, as his successful ship was coming into Plymouth Harbour amidst the joyful acclamations of the people, and was buried in state in Westminster Abbey. Not to lie there, long.

Over and above all this, Oliver found that the VAUDOIS, or Protestant people of the valleys of Lucerne, were insolently treated by the Catholic powers, and were even put to death for their religion, in an audacious and bloody manner. Instantly, he informed those powers that this was a thing which Protestant England would not allow; and he speedily carried his point, through the might of his great name, and established their right to worship God in peace after their own harmless manner.

Lastly, his English army won such admiration in fighting with the French against the Spaniards, that, after they had assaulted the town of Dunkirk together, the French King in person gave it up to the English, that it might be a token to them of their might and valour.

There were plots enough against Oliver among the frantic religionists (who called themselves Fifth Monarchy Men), and among the disappointed Republicans. He had a difficult game to play, for the Royalists were always ready to side with either party against him. The "King over the water," too, as Charles was called, had no scruples about plotting with any one against his life; although there is reason to suppose that he would willingly have married one of his daughters, if Oliver would have had such a son-in-law. There was a certain COLONEL SAXBY of the army, once a great supporter of Oliver's but now turned against him, who was a grievous trouble to him through all this part of his career; and who came and went between the discontented in England and Spain, and Charles who put himself in alliance with Spain on being thrown off by France. This man died in prison at last; but not until there had been very serious plots between the Royalists and Republicans, and an actual rising of them in England, when they burst into the city of Salisbury, on a Sunday night, seized the judges who were going to hold the assizes there next day, and would have hanged them but for the merciful objections of the more temperate of their number. Oliver was so vigorous and shrewd that he soon put this revolt down, as he did most other conspiracies; and it was well for one of its chief managers—that same Lord Wilmot who had assisted in Charles's flight, and was now EARL OF ROCHESTER—that he made his escape. Oliver seemed to have eyes and ears everywhere, and secured such sources of information as his enemies little dreamed of. There was a chosen body of six persons, called the Sealed Knot, who were in the closest and most secret confidence of Charles. One of the foremost of these very men, a SIR RICHARD WILLIS, reported to Oliver everything that passed among them, and had two hundred a year for it.

MILES SYNDARCOMB, also of the old army, was another conspirator against the Protector. He and a man named CECIL, bribed one of his

Life Guards to let them have good notice when he was going out—intending to shoot him from a window. But, owing either to his caution or his good fortune, they could never get an aim at him. Disappointed in this design, they got into the chapel in Whitehall, with a basketful of combustibles, which were to explode by means of a slow match in six hours; then, in the noise and confusion of the fire, they hoped to kill Oliver. But, the Life Guardsman himself disclosed this plot; and they were seized, and Miles died (or killed himself in prison) a little while before he was ordered for execution. A few such plotters Oliver caused to be beheaded, a few more to be hanged, and many more, including those who rose in arms against him, to be sent as slaves to the West Indies. If he were rigid, he was impartial too, in asserting the laws of England. When a Portuguese nobleman, the brother of the Portuguese ambassador, killed a London citizen in mistake for another man with whom he had had a quarrel, Oliver caused him to be tried before a jury of Englishmen and foreigners, and had him executed in spite of the entreaties of all the ambassadors in London.

One of Oliver's own friends, the DUKE OF OLDENBURGH, in sending him a present of six fine coach-horses, was very near doing more to please the Royalists than all the plotters put together. One day, Oliver went with his coach, drawn by these six horses, into Hyde Park, to dine with his secretary and some of his other gentlemen under the trees there. After dinner, being merry, he took it into his head to put his friends inside and to drive them home: a postillion riding one of the foremost horses, as the custom was. On account of Oliver's being too free with the whip, the six fine horses went off at a gallop, the postillion got thrown, and Oliver fell upon the coach-pole and narrowly escaped being shot by his own pistol, which got entangled with his clothes in the harness, and went off. He was dragged some distance by the foot, until his foot came out of the shoe, and then he came safely to the ground under the broad body of the coach, and was very little the worse. The gentlemen inside were only bruised, and the discontented people of all parties were much disappointed.

The rest of the history of the Protectorate of Oliver Cromwell is a history of his Parliaments. His first one not pleasing him at all, he waited until the five months were out, and then dissolved it. The next was better suited to his views; and from that he desired to get—if he could with safety to himself—the title of King. He had had this in his mind some time: whether because he thought that the English people, being more used to the title, were more likely to obey it; or whether because he really wished to be a king himself, and to leave the succession to that title in his family, is far from clear. He was already as high, in England and in all the world, as he would ever be, and I doubt if he cared for the mere name. However, a paper, called the "Humble Petition and Advice," was presented to him by the House of Commons, praying him to take a high title and to appoint his successor. That he would have taken the title of King there is no doubt, but for the strong opposition of the army. This induced him to forbear, and to assent only to the other points of the petition. Upon which occasion there was another grand show in Westminster Hall, when the Speaker of the House of Commons formally invested him with a purple robe lined with ermine, and presented him with a splendidly-bound Bible, and put a golden sceptre in his hand. The next time the Parliament met, he called a House of Lords of sixty members, as the petition gave him power to do; but as that Parliament did not please him either, and would not proceed to the business of the country, he jumped into a coach one morning, took six Guards with him, and sent them to the right-about. I wish this had been a warning to Parliaments to avoid long speeches, and do more work.

It was the month of August, one thousand six hundred and fifty-eight, when Oliver Cromwell's favourite daughter, ELIZABETH CLAYPOLE (who had lately lost her youngest son), lay very ill, and his mind was greatly troubled, because he loved her dearly. Another of his daughters was married to LORD FALCONBERG, another to the grandson of the Earl of Warwick, and he had made his son RICHARD one of the Members of the Upper House. He was very kind and loving to them all, being a good father and a good husband; but he loved his daughter the best of the family, and went down to Hampton Court to see her, and could hardly be induced to stir from her sick room until she died. Although his religion had been of a gloomy kind, his disposition had been always cheerful. He had been fond of music in his home, and had kept open table once a week for all officers of the army not below the rank of captain, and had always preserved in his house a quiet, sensible dignity. He encouraged men of genius and learning, and loved to have them about him. MILTON was one of his great friends. He was good humoured too, with the nobility, whose dresses and manners were very different from his; and to show them what good information he had, he would sometimes jokingly tell them when they were his guests, where they had last drunk the health of the "King over the water," and would recommend them to be more private (if they could) another time. But he had lived in busy times, had borne the weight of heavy State affairs, and had often gone in fear of his life. He was ill of the gout and ague; and when the death of his beloved child came upon him in addition, he sank, never to raise his head again. He told his physicians on the twenty-fourth of August that the Lord had assured him that he was not to die in that illness, and that he would certainly get better. This was only his sick fancy, for on the third of September, which was the anniversary of the great battle of Worcester, and the day of the year which he called his fortunate day, he died, in the sixtieth year of his age. He had been delirious, and had lain insensible some hours, but he had been overheard to murmur a very good prayer the day before. The whole country lamented his death. If you want to know the real worth of Oliver Cromwell, and his real services to his country, you can hardly do better than compare England under him, with England under CHARLES THE SECOND.

He had appointed his son Richard to succeed him, and after there had been, at Somerset House in the Strand, a lying in state more splendid than sensible—as all such vanities after death are, I think— Richard became Lord Protector. He was an amiable country gentleman, but had none of his father's great genius, and was quite unfit for such a post in such a storm of parties. Richard's Protectorate, which only lasted a year and a half, is a history of quarrels between the officers of the army and the Parliament, and between the officers among themselves; and of a growing discontent among the people, who had far too many long sermons and far too few amusements, and wanted a change. At last, General Monk got the army well into his own hands, and then in pursuance of a secret plan he seems to have entertained from the time of Oliver's death, declared for the King's cause. He did not do this openly; but, in his place in the House of Commons, as one of the members for Devonshire, strongly advocated the proposals of one SIR JOHN GREENVILLE, who came to the House with a letter from Charles, dated from Breda, and with whom he had previously been in secret communication. There had been plots and counterplots, and a recall of the last members of the Long Parliament, and an end of the Long Parliament, and risings of the Royalists that were made too soon; and most men being tired out, and there being no one to head the country now great Oliver was dead, it was readily agreed to welcome Charles Stuart. Some of the wiser and better members said—what was most true—that in the letter from Breda, he gave no real promise to govern well, and that it would be best to make him pledge himself beforehand as to what he should be bound to do for the benefit of the kingdom. Monk said, however, it would be all right when he came, and he could not come too soon.

So, everybody found out all in a moment that the country *must* be prosperous and happy, having another Stuart to condescend to reign over it; and there was a prodigious firing off of guns, lighting of bonfires, ringing of bells, and throwing up of caps. The people drank the King's health by thousands in the open streets, and everybody rejoiced. Down came the Arms of the Commonwealth, up went the Royal Arms instead, and out came the public money. Fifty thousand pounds for the King, ten thousand pounds for his brother the Duke of York, five thousand pounds for his brother the Duke of Gloucester. Prayers for these gracious Stuarts were put up in all the churches; commissioners were sent to Holland (which suddenly found out that Charles was a great man, and that it loved him) to invite the King home; Monk and the Kentish grandees went to Dover, to kneel down before him as he landed. He kissed and embraced Monk, made him ride in the coach with himself and his brothers, came on to London amid wonderful shoutings, and passed through the army at Blackheath on the twenty-ninth of May (his birthday), in the year one thousand six hundred and sixty. Greeted by splendid dinners under tents, by flags and tapestry streaming from all the houses, by delighted crowds in all the streets, by troops of noblemen and gentlemen in rich dresses, by City companies, train-bands, drummers, trumpeters, the great Lord Mayor, and the majestic Aldermen, the King went on to Whitehall. On entering it, he commemorated his Restoration with the joke that it really would seem to have been his own fault that he had not come long ago, since everybody told him that he had always wished for him with all his heart.

CHAPTER XXXV

ENGLAND UNDER CHARLES THE SECOND, CALLED THE MERRY MONARCH

THERE never were such profligate times in England as under Charles the Second. Whenever you see his portrait, with his swarthy, ill-looking face and great nose, you may fancy him in his Court at Whitehall, surrounded by some of the very worst vagabonds in the kingdom (though they were lords and ladies), drinking, gambling, indulging in vicious conversation, and committing every kind of profligate excess. It has been a fashion to call Charles the Second "The Merry Monarch." Let me try to give you a general idea of some of the merry things that were done, in the merry days when this merry gentleman sat upon his merry throne, in merry England.

The first merry proceeding was—of course—to declare that he was one of the greatest, the wisest, and the noblest kings that ever shone, like the blessed sun itself, on this benighted earth. The next merry and pleasant piece of business was, for the Parliament, in the humblest manner, to give him one million two hundred thousand pounds a year, and to settle upon him for life that old disputed tonnage and poundage which had been so bravely fought for. Then, General Monk being made EARL OF ALBEMARLE, and a few other Royalists similarly rewarded, the law went to work to see what was to be done to those persons (they were called Regicides) who had been concerned in making a martyr of the late King. Ten of these were merrily executed; that is to say, six of the judges, one of the council, Colonel Hacker and another officer who had commanded the Guards, and HUGH PETERS, a preacher who had preached against the martyr with all his heart. These executions were so extremely merry, that every horrible circumstance which Cromwell had abandoned was revived with appalling cruelty. The hearts of the sufferers were torn out of their living bodies; their bowels were burned before their faces; the executioner cut jokes to the next victim, as he rubbed his filthy hands together, that were reeking with the blood of the last; and the heads of the dead were drawn on sledges with the living to the place of suffering. Still, even so merry a monarch could not force one of these dying men to say that he was sorry for what he had done. Nay, the most memorable thing said among them was, that if the thing were to do again they would do it.

Sir Harry Vane, who had furnished the evidence against Strafford, and was one of the most staunch of the Republicans, was also tried, found guilty, and ordered for execution. When he came upon the scaffold on Tower Hill, after conducting his own defence with great power, his notes of what he had meant to say to the people were torn away from him, and the drums and trumpets were ordered to sound lustily and drown his voice; for, the people had been so much impressed by what the Regicides had calmly said with their last breath, that it was the custom now, to have the drums and trumpets always under the scaffold, ready to strike up. Vane said no more than this: "It is a bad cause which cannot bear the words of a dying man:" and bravely died.

These merry scenes were succeeded by another, perhaps even merrier. On the anniversary of the late King's death, the bodies of Oliver Cromwell, Ireton, and Bradshaw, were torn out of their graves in Westminster Abbey, dragged to Tyburn, hanged there on a gallows all day long, and then beheaded. Imagine the head of Oliver Cromwell set upon a pole to be stared at by a brutal crowd, not one of whom would have dared to look the living Oliver in the face for half a moment! Think, after you have read this reign, what England was under Oliver Cromwell who was torn out of his grave and what it was under this merry monarch who sold it, like a merry Judas, over and over again.

Of course, the remains of Oliver's wife and daughter were not to be spared either, though they had been most excellent women. The base clergy of that time gave up their bodies, which had been buried in the Abbey, and—to the eternal disgrace of England—they were thrown into a pit, together with the mouldering bones of Pym and of the brave and bold old Admiral Blake.

The clergy acted this disgraceful part because they hoped to get the nonconformists, or dissenters, thoroughly put down in this reign, and to have but one prayer-book and one service for all kinds of people, no matter what their private opinions were. This was pretty well, I think, for a Protestant Church, which had displaced the Romish Church because people had a right to their own opinions in religious matters. However, they carried it with a high hand, and a prayer-book was agreed upon, in which the extremest opinions of Archbishop Laud were not forgotten. An Act was passed, too, preventing any dissenter from holding any office under any corporation. So, the regular clergy in their triumph were soon as merry as the King. The army being by this time disbanded, and the King crowned, everything was to go on easily for evermore.

I must say a word here about the King's family. He had not been long upon the throne when his brother the Duke of Gloucester, and his sister the PRINCESS OF ORANGE, died within a few months of each other, of small-pox. His remaining sister, the PRINCESS HENRIETTA, married the DUKE OF ORLEANS, the brother of LOUIS THE FOURTEENTH, King of France. His brother JAMES, DUKE OF YORK, was made High Admiral, and by-and-by became a Catholic. He was a gloomy, sullen, bilious sort of man, with a remarkable partiality for the ugliest women in the country. He married, under very discreditable circumstances, ANNE HYDE, the daughter of LORD CLARENDON, then the King's principal Minister—not at all a delicate minister either, but doing much of the dirty work of a very dirty palace. It became important now that the King himself should be married; and divers foreign Monarchs, not very particular about the character of their son-in-law, proposed their daughters to him. The KING OF PORTUGAL offered his daughter, CATHERINE OF BRAGANZA, and fifty thousand pounds: in addition to which, the French King, who was favourable to that match, offered a loan of another fifty thousand. The King of Spain, on the other hand, offered any one out of a dozen of Princesses, and other hopes of gain. But the ready money carried the day, and Catherine came over in state to her marriage.

The whole Court was a great flaunting crowd of debauched men and shameless women; and Catherine's merry husband insulted and outraged her in every possible way, until she consented to receive those worthless creatures as her very good friends, and to degrade herself by their companionship. A MRS. PALMER, whom the King made LADY CASTLEMAINE, and afterwards DUCHESS OF CLEVELAND, was one of the most powerful of the bad women about the Court, and had great influence with the King nearly all though his reign. Another merry lady named MOLL DAVIES, a dancer at the theatre, was afterwards her rival. So was NELL GWYN, first an orange girl and then an actress, who really had good in her, and of whom one of the worst things I know is, that actually she does seem to have been fond of the King. The first DUKE OF ST. ALBANS was this orange girl's child. In like manner the son of a merry waiting-lady, whom the King created DUCHESS OF PORTSMOUTH, became the DUKE OF RICHMOND. Upon the whole it is not so bad a thing to be a commoner.

The Merry Monarch was so exceedingly merry among these merry ladies, and some equally merry (and equally infamous) lords and gentlemen, that he soon got through his hundred thousand pounds, and then, by way of raising a little pocket-money, made a merry bargain. He sold Dunkirk to the French King for five millions of livres. When I think of the dignity to which Oliver Cromwell raised England in the eyes of foreign powers, and when I think of the manner in which he gained for England this very Dunkirk, I am much inclined to consider that if the Merry Monarch had been made to follow his father for this action, he would have received his just deserts.

Though he was like his father in none of that father's greater qualities, he was like him in being worthy of no trust. When he sent that letter to the Parliament, from Breda, he did expressly promise that all sincere religious opinions should be respected. Yet he was no sooner firm in his power than he consented to one of the worst Acts of Parliament ever passed. Under this law, every minister who should not give his solemn assent to the Prayer-Book by a certain day, was declared to be a minister no longer, and to be deprived of his church. The consequence of this was that some two thousand honest men were taken from their congregations, and reduced to dire poverty and distress. It was followed by another outrageous law, called the Conventicle Act, by which any person above the age of sixteen who was present at any religious service not according to the Prayer-Book, was to be imprisoned three months for the first offence, six for the second, and to be transported for the third. This Act alone filled the prisons, which were then most dreadful dungeons, to overflowing.

The Covenanters in Scotland had already fared no better. A base Parliament, usually known as the Drunken Parliament, in consequence of its principal members being seldom sober, had been got together to make laws against the Covenanters, and to force all men to be of one mind in religious matters. The MARQUIS OF ARGYLE, relying on the King's honour, had given himself up to him; but, he was wealthy, and his enemies wanted his wealth. He was tried for treason, on the evidence of some private letters in which he had expressed opinions—as well he might—more favourable to the government of the late Lord Protector than of the present merry and religious King. He was executed, as were two men of mark among the Covenanters; and SHARP, a traitor who had once been the friend of the Presbyterians and betrayed them, was made Archbishop of St. Andrew's, to teach the Scotch how to like bishops.

Things being in this merry state at home, the Merry Monarch undertook a war with the Dutch; principally because they interfered with an African company, established with the two objects of buying gold-dust and slaves, of which the Duke of York was a leading member. After some preliminary hostilities, the said Duke sailed to the coast of Holland with a fleet of ninety-eight vessels of war, and four fire-ships. This engaged with the Dutch fleet, of no fewer than one hundred and thirteen ships. In the great battle between the two forces, the Dutch lost eighteen ships, four admirals, and seven thousand men. But, the English on shore were in no mood of exultation when they heard the news.

For, this was the year and the time of the Great Plague in London. During the winter of one thousand six hundred and sixty-four it had been whispered about, that some few people had died here and there of the disease called the Plague, in some of the unwholesome suburbs around London. News was not published at that time as it is now, and some people believed these rumours, and some disbelieved them, and they were soon forgotten. But, in the month of May, one thousand six hundred and sixty-five, it began to be said all over the town that the disease had burst out with great violence in St. Giles's, and that the people were dying in great numbers. This soon turned out to be awfully true. The roads out of London were choked up by people endeavouring to escape from the infected city, and large sums were paid for any kind of conveyance. The disease soon spread so fast, that it was necessary to shut up the houses in which sick people were, and to cut them off from communication with the living. Every one of these houses was marked on the outside of the door with a red cross, and the words, Lord, have mercy upon us! The streets were all deserted, grass grew in the public ways, and there was a dreadful silence in the air. When night came on, dismal rumblings used to be heard, and these were the wheels of the death-carts, attended by men with veiled faces and holding cloths to their mouths, who rang doleful bells and cried in a loud and solemn voice, "Bring out your dead!" The corpses put into these carts were buried by torchlight in great pits; no service being performed over them; all men being afraid to stay for a moment on the brink of the ghastly graves. In the general fear, children ran away from their parents, and parents from their children. Some who were taken ill, died alone, and without any help. Some were stabbed or strangled by hired nurses who robbed them of all their money, and stole the very beds on which they lay. Some went mad, dropped from the windows, ran through the streets, and in their pain and frenzy flung themselves into the river.

These were not all the horrors of the time. The wicked and dissolute, in wild desperation, sat in the taverns singing roaring songs, and were stricken as they drank, and went out and died. The fearful and superstitious persuaded themselves that they saw supernatural sights—burning swords in the sky, gigantic arms and darts. Others pretended that at nights vast crowds of ghosts walked round and round the dismal pits. One madman, naked, and carrying a brazier full of burning coals upon his head, stalked through the streets, crying out that he was a Prophet, commissioned to denounce the vengeance of the Lord on wicked London. Another always went to and fro, exclaiming, "Yet forty days, and London shall be destroyed!" A third awoke the echoes in the dismal streets, by night and by day, and made the blood of the sick run cold, by calling out incessantly, in a deep hoarse voice, "O, the great and dreadful God!"

Through the months of July and August and September, the Great Plague raged more and more. Great fires were lighted in the streets, in the hope of stopping the infection; but there was a plague of rain too, and it beat the fires out. At last, the winds which usually arise at that time of the year which is called the equinox, when day and night are of equal length all over the world, began to blow, and to purify the wretched town. The deaths began to decrease, the red crosses slowly to disappear, the fugitives to return, the shops to open, pale frightened faces to be seen in the streets. The Plague had been in every part of England, but in close and unwholesome London it had killed one hundred thousand people.

All this time, the Merry Monarch was as merry as ever, and as worthless as ever. All this time, the debauched lords and gentlemen and the shameless ladies danced and gamed and drank, and loved and hated one another, according to their merry ways. So little humanity did the government learn from the late affliction, that one of the first things the Parliament did when it met at Oxford (being as yet afraid to come to London), was to make a law, called the Five Mile Act, expressly directed against those poor ministers who, in the time of the Plague, had manfully come back to comfort the unhappy people. This infamous law, by forbidding them to teach in any school, or to come within five miles of any city, town, or village, doomed them to starvation and death.

The fleet had been at sea, and healthy. The King of France was now in alliance with the Dutch, though his navy was chiefly employed in looking on while the English and Dutch fought. The Dutch gained one victory; and the English gained another and a greater; and Prince Rupert, one of the English admirals, was out in the Channel one windy night, looking for the French Admiral, with the intention of giving him something more to do than he had had yet, when the gale increased to a storm, and blew him into Saint Helen's. That night was the third of September, one thousand six hundred and sixty-six, and that wind fanned the Great Fire of London.

It broke out at a baker's shop near London Bridge, on the spot on which the Monument now stands as a remembrance of those raging flames. It spread and spread, and burned and burned, for three days. The nights were lighter than the days; in the day-time there was an immense cloud of smoke, and in the night-time there was a great tower of fire mounting up into the sky, which lighted the whole country landscape for ten miles round. Showers of hot ashes rose into the air and fell on distant places; flying sparks carried the conflagration to great distances, and kindled it in twenty new spots at a time; church steeples fell down with tremendous crashes; houses crumbled into cinders by the hundred and the thousand. The summer had been intensely hot and dry, the streets were very narrow, and the houses mostly built of wood and plaster. Nothing could stop the tremendous fire, but the want of more houses to burn; nor did it stop until the whole way from the Tower to Temple Bar was a desert, composed of the ashes of thirteen thousand houses and eighty-nine churches.

This was a terrible visitation at the time, and occasioned great loss and suffering to the two hundred thousand burnt-out people, who were obliged to lie in the fields under the open night sky, or in hastily-made huts of mud and straw, while the lanes and roads were rendered impassable by carts which had broken down as they tried to save their goods. But the Fire was a great blessing to the City afterwards, for it arose from its ruins very much improved—built more regularly, more widely, more cleanly and carefully, and therefore much more healthily. It might be far more healthy than it is, but there are some people in it still—even now, at this time, nearly two hundred years later—so selfish, so pig-headed, and so ignorant, that I doubt if even another Great Fire would warm them up to do their duty.

The Catholics were accused of having wilfully set London in flames; one poor Frenchman, who had been mad for years, even accused himself of having with his own hand fired the first house. There is no reasonable doubt, however, that the fire was accidental. An inscription on the Monument long attributed it to the Catholics; but it is removed now, and was always a malicious and stupid untruth.

SECOND PART

THAT the Merry Monarch might be very merry indeed, in the merry times when his people were suffering under pestilence and fire, he drank and gambled and flung away among his favourites the money which the Parliament had voted for the war. The consequence of this was that the stout-hearted English sailors were merrily starving of want, and dying in the streets; while the Dutch, under their admirals DE WITT and DE RUYTER, came into the River Thames, and up the River Medway as far as Upnor, burned the guard-ships, silenced the weak batteries, and did what they would to the English coast for six whole weeks. Most of the English ships that could have prevented them had neither powder nor shot on board; in this merry reign, public officers made themselves as merry as the King did with the public money; and when it was entrusted to them to spend in national defences or preparations, they put it into their own pockets with the merriest grace in the world.

Lord Clarendon had, by this time, run as long a course as is usually allotted to the unscrupulous ministers of bad kings. He was impeached by his political opponents, but unsuccessfully. The King then commanded him to withdraw from England and retire to France, which he did, after defending himself in writing. He was no great loss at home, and died abroad some seven years afterwards.

There then came into power a ministry called the Cabal Ministry, because it was composed of LORD CLIFFORD, the EARL OF ARLINGTON, the DUKE OF BUCKINGHAM (a great rascal, and the King's most powerful favourite), LORD ASHLEY, and the DUKE OF LAUDERDALE, C. A. B. A. L. As the French were making conquests in Flanders, the first Cabal proceeding was to make a treaty with the Dutch, for uniting with Spain to oppose the French. It was no sooner made than the Merry Monarch, who always wanted to get money without being accountable to a Parliament for his expenditure, apologised to the King of France for having had anything to do with it, and concluded a secret treaty with him, making himself his infamous pensioner to the amount of two millions of livres down, and three millions more a year; and engaging to desert that very Spain, to make war against those very Dutch, and to declare himself a Catholic when a convenient time should arrive. This religious king had lately been crying to his Catholic brother on the subject of his strong desire to be a Catholic; and now he merrily concluded this treasonable conspiracy against the country he governed, by undertaking to become one as soon as he safely could. For all of which, though he had had ten merry heads instead of one, he richly deserved to lose them by the headsman's axe.

As his one merry head might have been far from safe, if these things had been known, they were kept very quiet, and war was declared by France and England against the Dutch. But, a very uncommon man, afterwards most important to English history and to the religion and liberty of this land, arose among them, and for many long years defeated the whole projects of France. This was WILLIAM OF NASSAU, PRINCE OF ORANGE, son of the last Prince of Orange of the same name, who married the daughter of Charles the First of England. He was a young man at this time, only just of age; but he was brave, cool, intrepid, and wise. His father had been so detested that, upon his death, the Dutch had abolished the authority to which this son would have otherwise succeeded (Stadtholder it was called), and placed the chief power in the hands of JOHN DE WITT, who educated this young prince. Now, the Prince became very popular, and John de Witt's brother CORNELIUS was sentenced to banishment on a false accusation of conspiring to kill him. John went to the prison where he was, to take him away to exile, in his coach; and a great mob who collected on the occasion, then and there cruelly murdered both the brothers. This left the government in the hands of the Prince, who was really the choice of the nation; and from this time he exercised it with the greatest vigour, against the whole power of France, under its famous generals CONDÉ and TURENNE, and in support of the Protestant religion. It was full seven years before this war ended in a treaty of peace made at Nimeguen, and its details would occupy a very considerable space. It is enough to say that William of Orange established a famous character with the whole world; and that the Merry Monarch, adding to and improving on his former baseness, bound himself to do everything the King of France liked, and nothing the King of France did not like, for a pension of one hundred thousand pounds a year, which was afterwards doubled. Besides this, the King of France, by means of his corrupt ambassador—who wrote accounts of his proceedings in England, which are not always to be believed, I think—bought our English members of Parliament, as he wanted them. So, in point of fact, during a considerable portion of this merry reign, the King of France was the real King of this country.

But there was a better time to come, and it was to come (though his royal uncle little thought so) through that very William, Prince of Orange. He came over to England, saw Mary, the elder daughter of the Duke of York, and married her. We shall see by-and-by what came of that marriage, and why it is never to be forgotten.

This daughter was a Protestant, but her mother died a Catholic. She and her sister ANNE, also a Protestant, were the only survivors of eight children. Anne afterwards married GEORGE, PRINCE OF DENMARK, brother to the King of that country.

Lest you should do the Merry Monarch the injustice of supposing that he was even good humoured (except when he had everything his own way), or that he was high spirited and honourable, I will mention here what was done to a member of the House of Commons, SIR JOHN COVENTRY. He made a remark in a debate about taxing the theatres, which gave the King offence. The King agreed with his illegitimate son, who had been born abroad, and whom he had made DUKE OF MONMOUTH, to take the following merry vengeance. To waylay him at night, fifteen armed men to one, and to slit his nose with a penknife. Like master, like man. The King's favourite, the Duke of Buckingham, was strongly suspected of setting on an assassin to murder the DUKE OF ORMOND as he was returning home from a dinner; and that Duke's spirited son, LORD OSSORY, was so persuaded of his guilt, that he said to him at Court, even as he stood beside the King, "My lord, I know very well that you are at the bottom of this late attempt upon my father. But I give you warning, if he ever come to a violent end, his blood shall be upon you, and wherever I meet you I will pistol you! I will do so, though I find you standing behind the King's chair; and I tell you this in his Majesty's presence, that you may be quite sure of my doing what I threaten." Those were merry times indeed.

There was a fellow named BLOOD, who was seized for making, with two companions, an audacious attempt to steal the crown, the globe, and sceptre, from the place where the jewels were kept in the Tower. This robber, who was a swaggering ruffian, being taken, declared that he was the man who had endeavoured to kill the Duke of Ormond, and that he had meant to kill the King too, but was overawed by the majesty of his appearance, when he might otherwise have done it, as he was bathing at Battersea. The King being but an ill-looking fellow, I don't believe a word of this. Whether he was flattered, or whether he knew that Buckingham had really set Blood on to murder the Duke, is uncertain. But it is quite certain that he pardoned this thief, gave him an estate of five hundred a year in Ireland (which had had the honour of giving him birth), and presented him at Court to the debauched lords and the shameless ladies, who made a great deal of him—as I have no doubt they would have made of the Devil himself, if the King had introduced him.

Infamously pensioned as he was, the King still wanted money, and consequently was obliged to call Parliaments. In these, the great object of the Protestants was to thwart the Catholic Duke of York, who married a second time; his new wife being a young lady only fifteen years old, the Catholic sister of the DUKE OF MODENA. In this they were seconded by the Protestant Dissenters, though to their own disadvantage: since, to exclude Catholics from power, they were even willing to exclude themselves. The King's object was to pretend to be a Protestant, while he was really a Catholic; to swear to the bishops that he was devoutly attached to the English Church, while he knew he had bargained it away to the King of France; and by cheating and deceiving them, and all who were attached to royalty, to become despotic and be powerful enough to confess what a rascal he was. Meantime, the King of France, knowing his merry pensioner well, intrigued with the King's opponents in Parliament, as well as with the King and his friends.

The fears that the country had of the Catholic religion being restored, if the Duke of York should come to the throne, and the low cunning of the King in pretending to share their alarms, led to some very terrible results. A certain DR. TONGE, a dull clergyman in the

City, fell into the hands of a certain TITUS OATES, a most infamous character, who pretended to have acquired among the Jesuits abroad a knowledge of a great plot for the murder of the King, and the re-establishment of the Catholic religion. Titus Oates, being produced by this unlucky Dr. Tonge and solemnly examined before the council, contradicted himself in a thousand ways, told the most ridiculous and improbable stories, and implicated COLEMAN, the Secretary of the Duchess of York. Now, although what he charged against Coleman was not true, and although you and I know very well that the real dangerous Catholic plot was that one with the King of France of which the Merry Monarch was himself the head, there happened to be found among Coleman's papers, some letters, in which he did praise the days of Bloody Queen Mary, and abuse the Protestant religion. This was great good fortune for Titus, as it seemed to confirm him; but better still was in store. SIR EDMUNDBURY GODFREY, the magistrate who had first examined him, being unexpectedly found dead near Primrose Hill, was confidently believed to have been killed by the Catholics. I think there is no doubt that he had been melancholy mad, and that he killed himself; but he had a great Protestant funeral, and Titus was called the Saver of the Nation, and received a pension of twelve hundred pounds a year.

As soon as Oates's wickedness had met with this success, up started another villain, named WILLIAM BEDLOE, who, attracted by a reward of five hundred pounds offered for the apprehension of the murderers of Godfrey, came forward and charged two Jesuits and some other persons with having committed it at the Queen's desire. Oates, going into partnership with this new informer, had the audacity to accuse the poor Queen herself of high treason. Then appeared a third informer, as bad as either of the two, and accused a Catholic banker named STAYLEY of having said that the King was the greatest rogue in the world (which would not have been far from the truth), and that he would kill him with his own hand. This banker, being at once tried and executed, Coleman and two others were tried and executed. Then a miserable wretch named PRANCE, a Catholic silversmith, being accused by Bedloe, was tortured into confessing that he had taken part in Godfrey's murder, and into accusing three other men of having committed it. Then, five Jesuits were accused by Oates, Bedloe, and Prance together, and were all found guilty, and executed on the same kind of contradictory and absurd evidence. The Queen's physician and three monks were next put on their trial; but Oates and Bedloe had for the time gone far enough, and these four were acquitted. The public mind, however, was so full of a Catholic plot, and so strong against the Duke of York, that James consented to obey a written order from his brother, and to go with his family to Brussels, provided that his rights should never be sacrificed in his absence to the Duke of Monmouth. The House of Commons, not satisfied with this as the King hoped, passed a bill to exclude the Duke from ever succeeding to the throne. In return, the

King dissolved the Parliament. He had deserted his old favourite, the Duke of Buckingham, who was now in the opposition.

To give any sufficient idea of the miseries of Scotland in this merry reign, would occupy a hundred pages. Because the people would not have bishops, and were resolved to stand by their solemn League and Covenant, such cruelties were inflicted upon them as make the blood run cold. Ferocious dragoons galloped through the country to punish the peasants for deserting the churches; sons were hanged up at their fathers' doors for refusing to disclose where their fathers were concealed; wives were tortured to death for not betraying their husbands; people were taken out of their fields and gardens, and shot on the public roads without trial; lighted matches were tied to the fingers of prisoners, and a most horrible torment called the Boot was invented, and constantly applied, which ground and mashed the victims' legs with iron wedges. Witnesses were tortured as well as prisoners. All the prisons were full; all the gibbets were heavy with bodies; murder and plunder devastated the whole country. In spite of all, the Covenanters were by no means to be dragged into the churches, and persisted in worshipping God as they thought right. A body of ferocious Highlanders, turned upon them from the mountains of their own country, had no greater effect than the English dragoons under GRAHAME OF CLAVERHOUSE, the most cruel and rapacious of all their enemies, whose name will ever be cursed through the length and breadth of Scotland. Archbishop Sharp had ever aided and abetted all these outrages. But he fell at last; for, when the injuries of the Scottish people were at their height, he was seen, in his coach-and-six coming across a moor, by a body of men, headed by one JOHN BALFOUR, who were waiting for another of their oppressors. Upon this they cried out that Heaven had delivered him into their hands, and killed him with many wounds. If ever a man deserved such a death, I think Archbishop Sharp did.

It made a great noise directly, and the Merry Monarch—strongly suspected of having goaded the Scottish people on, that he might have an excuse for a greater army than the Parliament were willing to give him—sent down his son, the Duke of Monmouth, as commander-in-chief, with instructions to attack the Scottish rebels, or Whigs as they were called, whenever he came up with them. Marching with ten thousand men from Edinburgh, he found them, in number four or five thousand, drawn up at Bothwell Bridge, by the Clyde. They were soon dispersed; and Monmouth showed a more humane character towards them, than he had shown towards that Member of Parliament whose nose he had caused to be slit with a penknife. But the Duke of Lauderdale was their bitter foe, and sent Claverhouse to finish them.

As the Duke of York became more and more unpopular, the Duke of Monmouth became more and more popular. It would have been decent in the latter not to have voted in favour of the renewed bill for the exclusion of James from the throne; but he did so, much to the King's amusement, who used to sit in the House of Lords by the fire, hearing the debates, which he said were as good as a play. The House of Commons passed the bill by a large majority, and it was carried up to the House of Lords by LORD RUSSELL, one of the best of the leaders on the Protestant side. It was rejected there, chiefly because the bishops helped the King to get rid of it; and the fear of Catholic plots revived again. There had been another got up, by a fellow out of Newgate, named DANGERFIELD, which is more famous than it deserves to be, under the name of the MEAL-TUB PLOT. This jail-bird having been got out of Newgate by a MRS. CELLIER, a Catholic nurse, had turned Catholic himself, and pretended that he knew of a plot among the Presbyterians against the King's life. This was very pleasant to the Duke of York, who hated the Presbyterians, who returned the compliment. He gave Dangerfield twenty guineas, and sent him to the King his brother. But Dangerfield, breaking down altogether in his charge, and being sent back to Newgate, almost astonished the Duke out of his five senses by suddenly swearing that the Catholic nurse had put that false design into his head, and that what he really knew about, was, a Catholic plot against the King; the evidence of which would be found in some papers, concealed in a meal-tub in Mrs. Cellier's house. There they were, of course—for he had put them there himself—and so the tub gave the name to the plot. But, the nurse was acquitted on her trial, and it came to nothing.

Lord Ashley, of the Cabal, was now Lord Shaftesbury, and was strong against the succession of the Duke of York. The House of Commons, aggravated to the utmost extent, as we may well suppose, by suspicions of the King's conspiracy with the King of France, made a desperate point of the exclusion still, and were bitter against the Catholics generally. So unjustly bitter were they, I grieve to say, that they impeached the venerable Lord Stafford, a Catholic nobleman seventy years old, of a design to kill the King. The witnesses were that atrocious Oates and two other birds of the same feather. He was found guilty, on evidence quite as foolish as it was false, and was beheaded on Tower Hill. The people were opposed to him when he first appeared upon the scaffold; but, when he had addressed them and shown them how innocent he was and how wickedly he was sent there, their better nature was aroused, and they said, "We believe you, my Lord. God bless you, my Lord!"

The House of Commons refused to let the King have any money until he should consent to the Exclusion Bill; but, as he could get it and did get it from his master the King of France, he could afford to hold them very cheap. He called a Parliament at Oxford, to which he went down with a great show of being armed and protected as if he were in danger of his life, and to which the opposition members also went armed and protected, alleging that they were in fear of the Papists, who were numerous among the King's guards. However, they went on with the Exclusion Bill, and were so earnest upon it that they would have carried it again, if the King had not popped his crown and state robes into a sedan-chair, bundled himself into it along with them, hurried down to the chamber where the House of Lords met, and dissolved the Parliament. After which he scampered home, and the members of Parliament scampered home too, as fast as their legs could carry them.

The Duke of York, then residing in Scotland, had, under the law which excluded Catholics from public trusts, no right whatever to public employment. Nevertheless, he was openly employed as the King's representative in Scotland, and there gratified his sullen and cruel nature to his heart's content by directing the dreadful cruelties against the Covenanters. There were two ministers named GARGILL and CAMERON who had escaped from the battle of Bothwell Bridge, and who returned to Scotland, and raised the miserable but still brave and unsubdued Covenanters afresh, under the name of Cameronians. As Cameron publicly posted a declaration that the King was a forsworn tyrant, no mercy was shown to his unhappy followers after he was slain in battle. The Duke of York, who was particularly fond of the Boot and derived great pleasure from having it applied, offered their lives to some of these people, if they would cry on the scaffold "God save the King." But their relations, friends, and countrymen, had been so barbarously tortured and murdered in this merry reign, that they preferred to die, and did die. The Duke then obtained his merry brother's permission to hold a Parliament in Scotland, which first, with most shameless deceit, confirmed the laws for securing the Protestant religion against Popery, and then declared that nothing must or should prevent the succession of the Popish Duke. After this double-faced beginning, it established an oath which no human being could understand, but which everybody was to take, as a proof that his religion was the lawful religion. The Earl of Argyle, taking it with the explanation that he did not consider it to prevent him from favouring any alteration either in the Church or State which was not inconsistent with the Protestant religion or with his loyalty, was tried for high treason before a Scottish jury of which the MARQUIS OF MONTROSE was foreman, and was found guilty. He escaped the scaffold, for that time, by getting away, in the disguise of a page in the train of his daughter, LADY SOPHIA LINDSAY. It was absolutely proposed, by certain members of the Scottish Council, that this lady should be whipped through the streets of Edinburgh. But this was too much even for the Duke, who had the manliness then (he had very little at most times) to remark that Englishmen were not accustomed to treat ladies in that manner. In those merry times nothing could equal the brutal servility of the Scottish fawners, but the conduct of similar degraded beings in England.

After the settlement of these little affairs, the Duke returned to England, and soon resumed his place at the Council, and his office of High Admiral—all this by his brother's favour, and in open defiance of the law. It would have been no loss to the country, if he had been drowned when his ship, in going to Scotland to fetch his family, struck on a sand-bank, and was lost with two hundred souls on board. But he escaped in a boat with some friends; and the sailors were so brave and unselfish, that, when they saw him rowing away, they gave three cheers, while they themselves were going down for ever.

The Merry Monarch, having got rid of his Parliament, went to work to make himself despotic, with all speed. Having had the villainy to order the execution of OLIVER PLUNKET, BISHOP OF ARMAGH, falsely accused of a plot to establish Popery in that country by means of a French army—the very thing this royal traitor was himself trying to do at home—and having tried to ruin Lord Shaftesbury, and failed—he turned his hand to controlling the corporations all over the country; because, if he could only do that, he could get what juries he chose, to bring in perjured verdicts, and could get what members he chose returned to Parliament. These merry times produced, and made Chief Justice of the Court of King's Bench, a drunken ruffian of the name of JEFFREYS; a red-faced, swollen, bloated, horrible creature, with a bullying, roaring voice, and a more savage nature perhaps than was ever lodged in any human breast. This monster was the Merry Monarch's especial favourite, and he testified his admiration of him by giving him a ring from his own finger, which the people used to call Judge Jeffreys's Bloodstone. Him the King employed to go about and bully the corporations, beginning with London; or, as Jeffreys himself elegantly called it, "to give them a lick with the rough side of his tongue." And he did it so thoroughly, that they soon became the basest and most sycophantic bodies in the kingdom—except the University of Oxford, which, in that respect, was quite pre-eminent and unapproachable.

Lord Shaftesbury (who died soon after the King's failure against him), LORD WILLIAM RUSSELL, the Duke of Monmouth, LORD HOWARD, LORD JERSEY, ALGERNON SIDNEY, JOHN HAMPDEN (grandson of the great Hampden), and some others, used to hold a council together after the dissolution of the Parliament, arranging what it might be necessary to do, if the King carried his Popish plot to the utmost height. Lord Shaftesbury having been much the most violent of this party, brought two violent men into their secrets— RUMSEY, who had been a soldier in the Republican army; and WEST, a lawyer. These two knew an old officer of Cromwell's, called RUMBOLD, who had married a maltster's widow, and so had come into possession of a solitary dwelling called the Rye House, near Hoddesdon, in Hertfordshire. Rumbold said to them what a capital place this house of his would be from which to shoot at the King, who often passed there going to and fro from Newmarket. They liked the idea, and entertained it. But, one of their body gave information; and they, together with SHEPHERD a wine merchant, Lord Russell, Algernon Sidney, LORD ESSEX, LORD HOWARD, and Hampden, were all arrested.

Lord Russell might have easily escaped, but scorned to do so, being innocent of any wrong; Lord Essex might have easily escaped, but scorned to do so, lest his flight should prejudice Lord Russell. But it weighed upon his mind that he had brought into their council,

Lord Howard—who now turned a miserable traitor—against a great dislike Lord Russell had always had of him. He could not bear the reflection, and destroyed himself before Lord Russell was brought to trial at the Old Bailey.

He knew very well that he had nothing to hope, having always been manful in the Protestant cause against the two false brothers, the one on the throne, and the other standing next to it. He had a wife, one of the noblest and best of women, who acted as his secretary on his trial, who comforted him in his prison, who supped with him on the night before he died, and whose love and virtue and devotion have made her name imperishable. Of course, he was found guilty, and was sentenced to be beheaded in Lincoln's Inn-fields, not many yards from his own house. When he had parted from his children on the evening before his death, his wife still stayed with him until ten o'clock at night; and when their final separation in this world was over, and he had kissed her many times, he still sat for a long while in his prison, talking of her goodness. Hearing the rain fall fast at that time, he calmly said, "Such a rain to-morrow will spoil a great show, which is a dull thing on a rainy day." At midnight he went to bed, and slept till four; even when his servant called him, he fell asleep again while his clothes were being made ready. He rode to the scaffold in his own carriage, attended by two famous clergymen, TILLOTSON and BURNET, and sang a psalm to himself very softly, as he went along. He was as quiet and as steady as if he had been going out for an ordinary ride. After saying that he was surprised to see so great a crowd, he laid down his head upon the block, as if upon the pillow of his bed, and had it struck off at the second blow. His noble wife was busy for him even then; for that true-hearted lady printed and widely circulated his last words, of which he had given her a copy. They made the blood of all the honest men in England boil.

The University of Oxford distinguished itself on the very same day by pretending to believe that the accusation against Lord Russell was true, and by calling the King, in a written paper, the Breath of their Nostrils and the Anointed of the Lord. This paper the Parliament afterwards caused to be burned by the common hangman; which I am sorry for, as I wish it had been framed and glazed and hung up in some public place, as a monument of baseness for the scorn of mankind.

Next, came the trial of Algernon Sidney, at which Jeffreys presided, like a great crimson toad, sweltering and swelling with rage. "I pray God, Mr. Sidney," said this Chief Justice of a merry reign, after passing sentence, "to work in you a temper fit to go to the other world, for I see you are not fit for this." "My lord," said the prisoner, composedly holding out his arm, "feel my pulse, and see if I be disordered. I thank Heaven I never was in better temper than I am now." Algernon Sidney was executed on Tower Hill, on the seventh of December, one thousand six hundred and eighty-three. He died a hero, and died, in his own words, "For that good old cause in which he had been engaged from his youth, and for which God had so often and so wonderfully declared himself."

The Duke of Monmouth had been making his uncle, the Duke of York, very jealous, by going about the country in a royal sort of way, playing at the people's games, becoming godfather to their children, and even touching for the King's evil, or stroking the faces of the sick to cure them—though, for the matter of that, I should say he did them about as much good as any crowned king could have done. His father had got him to write a letter, confessing his having had a part in the conspiracy, for which Lord Russell had been beheaded; but he was ever a weak man, and as soon as he had written it, he was ashamed of it and got it back again. For this, he was banished to the Netherlands; but he soon returned and had an interview with his father, unknown to his uncle. It would seem that he was coming into the Merry Monarch's favour again, and that the Duke of York was sliding out of it, when Death appeared to the merry galleries at Whitehall, and astonished the debauched lords and gentlemen, and the shameless ladies, very considerably.

On Monday, the second of February, one thousand six hundred and eighty-five, the merry pensioner and servant of the King of France fell down in a fit of apoplexy. By the Wednesday his case was hopeless, and on the Thursday he was told so. As he made a difficulty about taking the sacrament from the Protestant Bishop of Bath, the Duke of York got all who were present away from the bed, and asked his brother, in a whisper, if he should send for a Catholic priest? The King replied, "For God's sake, brother, do!" The Duke smuggled in, up the back stairs, disguised in a wig and gown, a priest named HUDDLESTON, who had saved the King's life after the battle of Worcester: telling him that this worthy man in the wig had once saved his body, and was now come to save his soul.

The Merry Monarch lived through that night, and died before noon on the next day, which was Friday, the sixth. Two of the last things he said were of a human sort, and your remembrance will give him the full benefit of them. When the Queen sent to say she was too unwell to attend him and to ask his pardon, he said, "Alas! poor woman, *she* beg *my* pardon! I beg hers with all my heart. Take back that answer to her." And he also said, in reference to Nell Gwyn, "Do not let poor Nelly starve."

He died in the fifty-fifth year of his age, and the twenty-fifth of his reign.

CHAPTER XXXVI

ENGLAND UNDER JAMES THE SECOND

KING JAMES THE SECOND was a man so very disagreeable, that even the best of historians has favoured his brother Charles, as becoming, by comparison, quite a pleasant character. The one object of his short reign was to re-establish the Catholic religion in England; and this he doggedly pursued with such a stupid obstinacy, that his career very soon came to a close.

The first thing he did, was, to assure his council that he would make it his endeavour to preserve the Government, both in Church and State, as it was by law established; and that he would always take care to defend and support the Church. Great public acclamations were raised over this fair speech, and a great deal was said, from the pulpits and elsewhere, about the word of a King which was never broken, by credulous people who little supposed that he had formed a secret council for Catholic affairs, of which a mischievous Jesuit, called FATHER PETRE, was one of the chief members. With tears of joy in his eyes, he received, as the beginning of *his* pension from the King of France, five hundred thousand livres; yet, with a mixture of meanness and arrogance that belonged to his contemptible character, he was always jealous of making some show of being independent of the King of France, while he pocketed his money. As —notwithstanding his publishing two papers in favour of Popery (and not likely to do it much service, I should think) written by the King, his brother, and found in his strong-box; and his open display of himself attending mass—the Parliament was very obsequious, and granted him a large sum of money, he began his reign with a belief that he could do what he pleased, and with a determination to do it.

Before we proceed to its principal events, let us dispose of Titus Oates. He was tried for perjury, a fortnight after the coronation, and besides being very heavily fined, was sentenced to stand twice in the pillory, to be whipped from Aldgate to Newgate one day, and from Newgate to Tyburn two days afterwards, and to stand in the pillory five times a year as long as he lived. This fearful sentence was actually inflicted on the rascal. Being unable to stand after his first flogging, he was dragged on a sledge from Newgate to Tyburn, and flogged as he was drawn along. He was so strong a villain that he did not die under the torture, but lived to be afterwards pardoned and rewarded, though not to be ever believed in any more. Dangerfield, the only other one of that crew left alive, was not so fortunate. He was almost killed by a whipping from Newgate to Tyburn, and, as if that were not punishment enough, a ferocious barrister of Gray's Inn gave him a poke in the eye with his cane, which caused his death; for which the ferocious barrister was deservedly tried and executed.

As soon as James was on the throne, Argyle and Monmouth went from Brussels to Rotterdam, and attended a meeting of Scottish exiles held there, to concert measures for a rising in England. It was agreed that Argyle should effect a landing in Scotland, and Monmouth in England; and that two Englishmen should be sent with Argyle to be in his confidence, and two Scotchmen with the Duke of Monmouth.

Argyle was the first to act upon this contract. But, two of his men being taken prisoners at the Orkney Islands, the Government became aware of his intention, and was able to act against him with such vigour as to prevent his raising more than two or three thousand Highlanders, although he sent a fiery cross, by trusty messengers, from clan to clan and from glen to glen, as the custom then was when those wild people were to be excited by their chiefs. As he was moving towards Glasgow with his small force, he was betrayed by some of his followers, taken, and carried, with his hands tied behind his back, to his old prison in Edinburgh Castle. James ordered him to be executed, on his old shamefully unjust sentence, within three days; and he appears to have been anxious that his legs should have been pounded with his old favourite the boot. However, the boot was not applied; he was simply beheaded, and his head was set upon the top of Edinburgh Jail. One of those Englishmen who had been assigned to him was that old soldier Rumbold, the master of the Rye House. He was sorely wounded, and within a week after Argyle had suffered with great courage, was brought up for trial, lest he should die and disappoint the King. He, too, was executed, after defending himself with great spirit, and saying that he did not believe that God had made the greater part of mankind to carry saddles on their backs and bridles in their mouths, and to be ridden by a few, booted and spurred for the purpose—in which I thoroughly agree with Rumbold.

The Duke of Monmouth, partly through being detained and partly through idling his time away, was five or six weeks behind his friend when he landed at Lyme, in Dorset: having at his right hand an unlucky nobleman called LORD GREY OF WERK, who of himself would have ruined a far more promising expedition. He immediately set up his standard in the market-place, and proclaimed the King a tyrant, and a Popish usurper, and I know not what else; charging him, not only with what he had done, which was bad enough, but with what neither he nor anybody else had done, such as setting fire to London, and poisoning the late King. Raising some four thousand men by these means, he marched on to Taunton, where there were many Protestant dissenters who were strongly opposed to the Catholics. Here, both the rich and poor turned out to receive him, ladies waved a welcome to him from all the windows as he passed along the streets, flowers were strewn in his way, and every compliment and honour that could be devised was showered upon him. Among the rest, twenty young ladies came forward, in their best clothes, and in their brightest beauty, and gave him a Bible ornamented with their own fair hands, together with other presents.

Encouraged by this homage, he proclaimed himself King, and went on to Bridgwater. But, here the Government troops, under the EARL OF FEVERSHAM, were close at hand; and he was so dispirited at finding that he made but few powerful friends after all, that it was a question whether he should disband his army and endeavour to escape. It was resolved, at the instance of that unlucky Lord Grey, to make a night attack on the King's army, as it lay encamped on the edge of a morass called Sedgemoor. The horsemen were commanded by the same unlucky lord, who was not a brave man. He gave up the battle almost at the first obstacle—which was a deep drain; and although the poor countrymen, who had turned out for Monmouth, fought bravely with scythes, poles, pitchforks, and such poor weapons as they had, they were soon dispersed by the trained soldiers, and fled in all directions. When the Duke of Monmouth himself fled, was not known in the confusion; but the unlucky Lord Grey was taken early next day, and then another of the party was taken, who had confessed that he had parted from the Duke only four hours before. Strict search being made, he was found disguised as a peasant, hidden in a ditch under fern and nettles, with a few peas in his pocket which he had gathered in the fields to eat. The only other articles he had upon him were a few papers and little books: one of the latter being a strange jumble, in his own writing, of charms, songs, recipes, and prayers. He was completely broken. He wrote a miserable letter to the King, beseeching and entreating to be allowed to see him. When he was taken to London, and conveyed bound into the King's presence, he crawled to him on his knees, and made a most degrading exhibition. As James never forgave or relented towards anybody, he was not likely to soften towards the issuer of the Lyme proclamation, so he told the suppliant to prepare for death.

On the fifteenth of July, one thousand six hundred and eighty-five, this unfortunate favourite of the people was brought out to die on Tower Hill. The crowd was immense, and the tops of all the houses were covered with gazers. He had seen his wife, the daughter of the Duke of Buccleuch, in the Tower, and had talked much of a lady whom he loved far better—the Lady Harriet Wentworth—who was one of the last persons he remembered in this life. Before laying down his head upon the block he felt the edge of the axe, and told the executioner that he feared it was not sharp enough, and that the axe was not heavy enough. On the executioner replying that it was of the proper kind, the Duke said, "I pray you have a care, and do not use me so awkwardly as you used my Lord Russell." The executioner, made nervous by this, and trembling, struck once and merely gashed him in the neck. Upon this, the Duke of Monmouth raised his head and looked the man reproachfully in the face. Then he struck twice, and then thrice, and then threw down the axe, and cried out in a voice of horror that he could not finish that work. The sheriffs, however, threatening him with what should be done to himself if he did not, he took it up again and struck a fourth time and a fifth time. Then the wretched head at last fell off, and James, Duke of Monmouth, was dead, in the thirty-sixth year of his age. He was a showy, graceful man, with many popular qualities, and had found much favour in the open hearts of the English.

The atrocities, committed by the Government, which followed this Monmouth rebellion, form the blackest and most lamentable page in English history. The poor peasants, having been dispersed with great loss, and their leaders having been taken, one would think that the implacable King might have been satisfied. But no; he let loose upon them, among other intolerable monsters, a Colonel Kirk, who had served against the Moors, and whose soldiers—called by the people Kirk's lambs, because they bore a lamb upon their flag, as the emblem of Christianity—were worthy of their leader.

The atrocities committed by these demons in human shape are far too horrible to be related here. It is enough to say, that besides most ruthlessly murdering and robbing them, and ruining them by making them buy their pardons at the price of all they possessed, it was one of Kirk's favourite amusements, as he and his officers sat drinking after dinner, and toasting the King, to have batches of prisoners hanged outside the windows for the company's diversion; and that when their feet quivered in the convulsions of death, he used to swear that they should have music to their dancing, and would order the drums to beat and the trumpets to play. The detestable King informed him, as an acknowledgment of these services, that he was "very well satisfied with his proceedings." But the King's great delight was in the proceedings of Jeffreys, now a peer, who went down into the west, with four other judges, to try persons accused of having had any share in the rebellion. The King pleasantly called this "Jeffreys's campaign." The people down in that part of the country remember it to this day as The Bloody Assize.

It began at Winchester, where a poor deaf old lady, MRS. ALICIA LISLE, the widow of one of the judges of Charles the First (who had been murdered abroad by some Royalist assassins), was charged with having given shelter in her house to two fugitives from Sedgemoor. Three times the jury refused to find her guilty, until Jeffreys bullied and frightened them into that false verdict. When he had extorted it from them, he said, "Gentlemen, if I had been one of you, and she had been my own mother, I would have found her guilty;"— as I dare say he would. He sentenced her to be burned alive, that very afternoon. The clergy of the cathedral and some others interfered in her favour, and she was beheaded within a week. As a high mark of his approbation, the King made Jeffreys Lord Chancellor; and he then went on to Dorchester, to Exeter, to Taunton, and to Wells. It is astonishing, when we read of the enormous injustice and barbarity of this beast, to know that no one struck him dead on the judgment-seat. It was enough for any man or woman to be accused by an enemy, before Jeffreys, to be found guilty of high treason. One man who pleaded not guilty, he ordered to be taken out of court upon the instant, and hanged; and this so terrified the prisoners in general that they mostly pleaded guilty at once. At Dorchester alone, in the course of a few days, Jeffreys hanged eighty people; besides whipping, transporting, imprisoning, and selling as slaves, great numbers. He executed, in all, two hundred and fifty, or three hundred.

These executions took place, among the neighbours and friends of the sentenced, in thirty-six towns and villages. Their bodies were mangled, steeped in caldrons of boiling pitch and tar, and hung up by the roadsides, in the streets, over the very churches. The sight and smell of heads and limbs, the hissing and bubbling of the infernal caldrons, and the tears and terrors of the people, were dreadful beyond all description. One rustic, who was forced to steep the remains in the black pot, was ever afterwards called "Tom Boilman."

The hangman has ever since been called Jack Ketch, because a man of that name went hanging and hanging, all day long, in the train of Jeffreys. You will hear much of the horrors of the great French Revolution. Many and terrible they were, there is no doubt; but I know of nothing worse, done by the maddened people of France in that awful time, than was done by the highest judge in England, with the express approval of the King of England, in The Bloody Assize.

Nor was even this all. Jeffreys was as fond of money for himself as of misery for others, and he sold pardons wholesale to fill his pockets. The King ordered, at one time, a thousand prisoners to be given to certain of his favourites, in order that they might bargain with them for their pardons. The young ladies of Taunton who had presented the Bible, were bestowed upon the maids of honour at court; and those precious ladies made very hard bargains with them indeed. When The Bloody Assize was at its most dismal height, the King was diverting himself with horse-races in the very place where Mrs. Lisle had been executed. When Jeffreys had done his worst, and came home again, he was particularly complimented in the Royal Gazette; and when the King heard that through drunkenness and raging he was very ill, his odious Majesty remarked that such another man could not easily be found in England. Besides all this, a former sheriff of London, named CORNISH, was hanged within sight of his own house, after an abominably conducted trial, for having had a share in the Rye House Plot, on evidence given by Rumsey, which that villain was obliged to confess was directly opposed to the evidence he had given on the trial of Lord Russell. And on the very same day, a worthy widow, named ELIZABETH GAUNT, was burned alive at Tyburn, for having sheltered a wretch who himself gave evidence against her. She settled the fuel about herself with her own hands, so that the flames should reach her quickly: and nobly said, with her last breath, that she had obeyed the sacred command of God, to give refuge to the outcast, and not to betray the wanderer.

After all this hanging, beheading, burning, boiling, mutilating, exposing, robbing, transporting, and selling into slavery, of his unhappy subjects, the King not unnaturally thought that he could do whatever he would. So he went to work to change the religion of the country with all possible speed; and what he did was this.

He first of all tried to get rid of what was called the Test Act—which prevented the Catholics from holding public employments—by his own power of dispensing with the penalties. He tried it in one case, and, eleven of the twelve judges deciding in his favour, he exercised it in three others, being those of three dignitaries of University College, Oxford, who had become Papists, and whom he kept in their places and sanctioned. He revived the hated Ecclesiastical Commission, to get rid of COMPTON, Bishop of London, who manfully opposed him. He solicited the Pope to favour England with an ambassador, which the Pope (who was a sensible man then) rather unwillingly did. He flourished Father Petre before the eyes of the people on all possible occasions. He favoured the establishment of convents in several parts of London. He was delighted to have the streets, and even the court itself, filled with Monks and Friars in the habits of their orders. He constantly endeavoured to make Catholics of the Protestants about him. He held private interviews, which he called "closetings," with those Members of Parliament who held offices, to persuade them to consent to the design he had in view. When they did not consent, they were removed, or resigned of themselves, and their places were given to Catholics. He displaced Protestant officers from the army, by every means in his power, and got Catholics into their places too. He tried the same thing with the corporations, and also (though not so successfully) with the Lord Lieutenants of counties. To terrify the people into the endurance of all these measures, he kept an army of fifteen thousand men encamped on Hounslow Heath, where mass was openly performed in the General's tent, and where priests went among the soldiers endeavouring to persuade them to become Catholics. For circulating a paper among those men advising them to be true to their religion, a Protestant clergyman, named JOHNSON, the chaplain of the late Lord Russell, was actually sentenced to stand three times in the pillory, and was actually whipped from Newgate to Tyburn. He dismissed his own brother-in-law from his Council because he was a Protestant, and made a Privy Councillor of the before-mentioned Father Petre. He handed Ireland over to RICHARD TALBOT, EARL OF TYRCONNELL, a worthless, dissolute knave, who played the same game there for his master, and who played the deeper game for himself of one day putting it under the protection of the French King. In going to these extremities, every man of sense and judgment among the Catholics, from the Pope to a porter, knew that the King was a mere bigoted fool, who would undo himself and the cause he sought to advance; but he was deaf to all reason, and, happily for England ever afterwards, went tumbling off his throne in his own blind way.

A spirit began to arise in the country, which the besotted blunderer little expected. He first found it out in the University of Cambridge. Having made a Catholic a dean at Oxford without any opposition, he tried to make a monk a master of arts at Cambridge: which attempt the University resisted, and defeated him. He then went back to his favourite Oxford. On the death of the President of Magdalen College, he commanded that there should be elected to succeed him, one MR. ANTHONY FARMER, whose only recommendation was, that he was of the King's religion. The University plucked up courage at last, and refused. The King substituted another man, and it still refused, resolving to stand by its own election of a MR. HOUGH. The dull tyrant, upon this, punished Mr. Hough, and five-and-twenty more, by causing them to be expelled and declared incapable of holding any church preferment; then he proceeded to what he supposed to be his highest step, but to what was, in fact, his last plunge head-foremost in his tumble off his throne.

He had issued a declaration that there should be no religious tests or penal laws, in order to let in the Catholics more easily; but the Protestant dissenters, unmindful of themselves, had gallantly joined the regular church in opposing it tooth and nail. The King and Father Petre now resolved to have this read, on a certain Sunday, in all the churches, and to order it to be circulated for that purpose by the bishops. The latter took counsel with the Archbishop of Canterbury, who was in disgrace; and they resolved that the declaration should not be read, and that they would petition the King against it. The Archbishop himself wrote out the petition, and six bishops went into the King's bedchamber the same night to present it, to his infinite astonishment. Next day was the Sunday fixed for the reading, and it was only read by two hundred clergymen out of ten thousand. The King resolved against all advice to prosecute the bishops in the Court of King's Bench, and within three weeks they were summoned before the Privy Council, and committed to the Tower. As the six bishops were taken to that dismal place, by water, the people who were assembled in immense numbers fell upon their knees, and wept for them, and prayed for them. When they got to the Tower, the officers and soldiers on guard besought them for their blessing. While they were confined there, the soldiers every day drank to their release with loud shouts. When they were brought up to the Court of King's Bench for their trial, which the Attorney-General said was for the high offence of censuring the Government, and giving their opinion about affairs of state, they were attended by similar multitudes, and surrounded by a throng of noblemen and gentlemen. When the jury went out at seven o'clock at night to consider of their verdict, everybody (except the King) knew that they would rather starve than yield to the King's brewer, who was one of them, and wanted a verdict for his customer. When they came into court next morning, after resisting the brewer all night, and gave a verdict of not guilty, such a shout rose up in Westminster Hall as it had never heard before; and it was passed on among the people away to Temple Bar, and away again to the Tower. It did not pass only to the east, but passed to the west too, until it reached the camp at Hounslow, where the fifteen thousand soldiers took it up and echoed it. And still, when the dull King, who was then with Lord Feversham, heard the mighty roar, asked in alarm what it was, and was told that it was "nothing but the acquittal of the bishops," he said, in his dogged way, "Call you that nothing? It is so much the worse for them."

Between the petition and the trial, the Queen had given birth to a son, which Father Petre rather thought was owing to Saint Winifred. But I doubt if Saint Winifred had much to do with it as the King's friend, inasmuch as the entirely new prospect of a Catholic successor (for both the King's daughters were Protestants) determined the EARLS OF SHREWSBURY, DANBY, and DEVONSHIRE, LORD LUMLEY, the BISHOP OF LONDON, ADMIRAL RUSSELL, and COLONEL SIDNEY, to invite the Prince of Orange over to England. The Royal Mole, seeing his danger at last, made, in his fright, many great concessions, besides raising an army of forty thousand men; but the Prince of Orange was not a man for James the Second to cope with. His preparations were extraordinarily vigorous, and his mind was resolved.

For a fortnight after the Prince was ready to sail for England, a great wind from the west prevented the departure of his fleet. Even when the wind lulled, and it did sail, it was dispersed by a storm, and was obliged to put back to refit. At last, on the first of November, one thousand six hundred and eighty-eight, the Protestant east wind, as it was long called, began to blow; and on the third, the people of Dover and the people of Calais saw a fleet twenty miles long sailing gallantly by, between the two places. On Monday, the fifth, it anchored at Torbay in Devonshire, and the Prince, with a splendid retinue of officers and men, marched into Exeter. But the people in that western part of the country had suffered so much in The Bloody Assize, that they had lost heart. Few people joined him; and he began to think of returning, and publishing the invitation he had received from those lords, as his justification for having come at all. At this crisis, some of the gentry joined him; the Royal army began to falter; an engagement was signed, by which all who set their hand to it declared that they would support one another in defence of the laws and liberties of the three Kingdoms, of the Protestant religion, and of the Prince of Orange. From that time, the cause received no check; the greatest towns in England began, one after another, to declare for the Prince; and he knew that it was all safe with him when the University of Oxford offered to melt down its plate, if he wanted any money.

By this time the King was running about in a pitiable way, touching people for the King's evil in one place, reviewing his troops in another, and bleeding from the nose in a third. The young Prince was sent to Portsmouth, Father Petre went off like a shot to France, and there was a general and swift dispersal of all the priests and friars. One after another, the King's most important officers and friends deserted him and went over to the Prince. In the night, his daughter Anne fled from Whitehall Palace; and the Bishop of London, who had once been a soldier, rode before her with a drawn sword in his hand, and pistols at his saddle. "God help me," cried the miserable King: "my very children have forsaken me!" In his wildness, after debating with such lords as were in London, whether he should or should not call a Parliament, and after naming three of them to negotiate with the Prince, he resolved to fly to France. He had the little Prince of Wales brought back from Portsmouth; and the child and the Queen crossed the river to Lambeth in an open boat, on a miserable wet night, and got safely away. This was on the night of the ninth of December.

At one o'clock on the morning of the eleventh, the King, who had, in the meantime, received a letter from the Prince of Orange, stating his objects, got out of bed, told LORD NORTHUMBERLAND who lay in his room not to open the door until the usual hour in the morning, and went down the back stairs (the same, I suppose, by which the priest in the wig and gown had come up to his brother) and crossed the river in a small boat: sinking the great seal of England by the way. Horses having been provided, he rode, accompanied by SIR EDWARD HALES, to Feversham, where he embarked in a Custom House Hoy. The master of this Hoy, wanting more ballast, ran into the Isle of Sheppy to get it, where the fishermen and smugglers crowded about the boat, and informed the King of their suspicions that he was a "hatchet-faced Jesuit." As they took his money and would not let him go, he told them who he was, and that the Prince of Orange wanted to take his life; and he began to scream for a boat —and then to cry, because he had lost a piece of wood on his ride which he called a fragment of Our Saviour's cross. He put himself into the hands of the Lord Lieutenant of the county, and his detention was made known to the Prince of Orange at Windsor—who, only wanting to get rid of him, and not caring where he went, so that he went away, was very much disconcerted that they did not let him go. However, there was nothing for it but to have him brought back, with some state in the way of Life Guards, to Whitehall. And as soon as he got there, in his infatuation, he heard mass, and set a Jesuit to say grace at his public dinner.

The people had been thrown into the strangest state of confusion by his flight, and had taken it into their heads that the Irish part of the army were going to murder the Protestants. Therefore, they set the bells a ringing, and lighted watch-fires, and burned Catholic Chapels, and looked about in all directions for Father Petre and the Jesuits, while the Pope's ambassador was running away in the dress of a footman. They found no Jesuits; but a man, who had once been a frightened witness before Jeffreys in court, saw a swollen, drunken face looking through a window down at Wapping, which he well remembered. The face was in a sailor's dress, but he knew it to be the face of that accursed Judge, and he seized him. The people, to their lasting honour, did not tear him to pieces. After knocking him about a little, they took him, in the basest agonies of terror, to the Lord Mayor, who sent him, at his own shrieking petition, to the Tower for safety. There, he died.

Their bewilderment continuing, the people now lighted bonfires and made rejoicings, as if they had any reason to be glad to have the King back again. But, his stay was very short, for the English guards were removed from Whitehall, Dutch guards were marched up to it, and he was told by one of his late ministers that the Prince would enter London, next day, and he had better go to Ham. He said, Ham was a cold, damp place, and he would rather go to Rochester. He thought himself very cunning in this, as he meant to escape from Rochester to France. The Prince of Orange and his friends knew that, perfectly well, and desired nothing more. So, he went to Gravesend, in his royal barge, attended by certain lords, and watched by Dutch troops, and pitied by the generous people, who were far more forgiving than he had ever been, when they saw him in his humiliation. On the night of the twenty-third of December, not even then understanding that everybody wanted to get rid of him, he went out, absurdly, through his Rochester garden, down to the Medway, and got away to France, where he rejoined the Queen.

There had been a council in his absence, of the lords, and the authorities of London. When the Prince came, on the day after the King's departure, he summoned the Lords to meet him, and soon afterwards, all those who had served in any of the Parliaments of King Charles the Second. It was finally resolved by these authorities that the throne was vacant by the conduct of King James the Second; that it was inconsistent with the safety and welfare of this Protestant kingdom, to be governed by a Popish prince; that the Prince and Princess of Orange should be King and Queen during their lives and the life of the survivor of them; and that their children should succeed them, if they had any. That if they had none, the Princess Anne and her children should succeed; that if she had none, the heirs of the Prince of Orange should succeed.

On the thirteenth of January, one thousand six hundred and eighty-nine, the Prince and Princess, sitting on a throne in Whitehall, bound themselves to these conditions. The Protestant religion was established in England, and England's great and glorious Revolution was complete.

CHAPTER XXXVII

I HAVE now arrived at the close of my little history. The events which succeeded the famous Revolution of one thousand six hundred and eighty-eight, would neither be easily related nor easily understood in such a book as this.

William and Mary reigned together, five years. After the death of his good wife, William occupied the throne, alone, for seven years longer. During his reign, on the sixteenth of September, one thousand seven hundred and one, the poor weak creature who had once been James the Second of England, died in France. In the meantime he had done his utmost (which was not much) to cause William to be assassinated, and to regain his lost dominions. James's son was declared, by the French King, the rightful King of England; and was called in France THE CHEVALIER SAINT GEORGE, and in England THE PRETENDER. Some infatuated people in England, and particularly in Scotland, took up the Pretender's cause from time to time—as if the country had not had Stuarts enough!—and many lives were sacrificed, and much misery was occasioned. King William died on Sunday, the seventh of March, one thousand seven hundred and two, of the consequences of an accident occasioned by his horse stumbling with him. He was always a brave, patriotic Prince, and a man of remarkable abilities. His manner was cold, and he made but few friends; but he had truly loved his queen. When he was dead, a lock of her hair, in a ring, was found tied with a black ribbon round his left arm.

He was succeeded by the PRINCESS ANNE, a popular Queen, who reigned twelve years. In her reign, in the month of May, one thousand seven hundred and seven, the Union between England and Scotland was effected, and the two countries were incorporated under the name of GREAT BRITAIN. Then, from the year one thousand seven hundred and fourteen to the year one thousand eight hundred and thirty, reigned the four GEORGES.

It was in the reign of George the Second, one thousand seven hundred and forty-five, that the Pretender did his last mischief, and made his last appearance. Being an old man by that time, he and the Jacobites—as his friends were called—put forward his son, CHARLES EDWARD, known as the Young Chevalier. The Highlanders of Scotland, an extremely troublesome and wrong-headed race on the subject of the Stuarts, espoused his cause, and he joined them, and there was a Scottish rebellion to make him king, in which many gallant and devoted gentlemen lost their lives. It was a hard matter for Charles Edward to escape abroad again, with a high price on his head; but the Scottish people were extraordinarily faithful to him, and, after undergoing many romantic adventures, not unlike those of Charles the Second, he escaped to France. A number of charming stories and delightful songs arose out of the Jacobite feelings, and belong to the Jacobite times. Otherwise I think the Stuarts were a public nuisance altogether.

It was in the reign of George the Third that England lost North America, by persisting in taxing her without her own consent. That immense country, made independent under WASHINGTON, and left to itself, became the United States; one of the greatest nations of the earth. In these times in which I write, it is honourably remarkable for protecting its subjects, wherever they may travel, with a dignity and a determination which is a model for England. Between you and me, England has rather lost ground in this respect since the days of Oliver Cromwell.

The Union of Great Britain with Ireland—which had been getting on very ill by itself—took place in the reign of George the Third, on the second of July, one thousand seven hundred and ninety-eight.

WILLIAM THE FOURTH succeeded George the Fourth, in the year one thousand eight hundred and thirty, and reigned seven years. QUEEN VICTORIA, his niece, the only child of the Duke of Kent, the fourth son of George the Third, came to the throne on the twentieth of June, one thousand eight hundred and thirty-seven. She was married to PRINCE ALBERT of Saxe Gotha on the tenth of February, one thousand eight hundred and forty. She is very good, and much beloved. So I end, like the crier, with

GOD SAVE THE QUEEN!

THE END

Made and Printed in Great Britain by
Hazell, Watson & Viney Ltd. London and Aylesbury